PRAISE FOR

GEORGE R. R. MARTIN

AND

A SONG OF ICE AND FIRE

"'A Song of Ice and Fire' is firmly at the top of the bestseller lists, probably because it's the best fantasy series out there." —*Detroit Free Press*

"For a succinct summation of Martin's medieval fantasy series, imagine a mix of the literary quality of T. H. White's *The Once and Future King,* the in-your-face, you-are-there grittiness of a movie like *Braveheart* and the sort of intricate character development found in a quality television show like *Lost.* . . . Vast, complex and undeniably entertaining . . . Once in a while, there are books and writers that manage to elevate an entire genre. Stephen King did so with horror. George R. R. Martin's 'A Song of Ice and Fire' series has taken fantasy out of the two-dimensional, black and white realm where it once happily existed and dragged it kicking and screaming into a land of believable characters, ambiguous situations, and bloody, sometimes uncertain denouements." —*The Denver Post*

"Grabs hold and won't let go. It's brilliant." —ROBERT JORDAN

"George R. R. Martin has created the unlikely genre of the realpolitik fantasy novel. Complete with warring kings, noble heroes and backroom dealings, it's addictive reading and reflects our current world a lot better than *The Lord of the Rings.*" —*Rolling Stone*

"Such a splendid tale and such a fantistorical! I read my eyes out."
—ANNE MCCAFFREY

By George R. R. Martin

A Song of Ice and Fire

Book One: *A Game of Thrones*
Book Two: *A Clash of Kings*
Book Three: *A Storm of Swords*
Book Four: *A Feast for Crows*
Book Five: *A Dance with Dragons*
*The World of Ice & Fire: The Untold History of
Westeros and the Game of Thrones*

Dying of the Light
Windhaven (with Lisa Tuttle)
Fevre Dream
The Armageddon Rag
Dead Man's Hand (with John J. Miller)

Short Story Collections

Dreamsongs: Volume I
Dreamsongs: Volume II
A Song for Lya and Other Stories
Songs of Stars and Shadows
Sandkings
Songs the Dead Men Sing
Nightflyers
Tuf Voyaging
Portraits of His Children
Quartet

Edited by George R. R. Martin

New Voices in Science Fiction, Volumes 1–4
The Science Fiction Weight Loss Book (with Isaac Asimov and
Martin Harry Greenberg)
The John W. Campbell Awards, Volume 5
Night Visions 3
Wild Cards I–XXII

Co-edited with Gardner Dozois

Warriors I–III
Songs of the Dying Earth
Songs of Love and Death
Down These Strange Streets
Old Mars
Dangerous Women
Rogues
Old Venus

A DANCE WITH DRAGONS

A Dance
with
Dragons

Book Five of
A Song of Ice and Fire

George R. R. Martin

Bantam Books Trade Paperbacks
New York

2015 Bantam Books Movie Tie-in Trade Paperback Edition

Published in the United States by Bantam Books,
an imprint of Random House, a division of
Penguin Random House LLC, New York.

BANTAM BOOKS and the HOUSE colophon are registered trademarks
of Penguin Random House LLC.

Originally published in hardcover in the United States by
Bantam Books, an imprint of Random House,
a division of Penguin Random House LLC, in 2011.

This book contains an excerpt from the forthcoming book
The Winds of Winter by George R. R. Martin.
This excerpt has been set for this edition only and
may not reflect the final content of the forthcoming edition.

ISBN 978-1-101-88604-5
eBook ISBN 978-0-553-90565-6

Printed in the United States of America on acid-free paper

www.bantamdell.com

9 8 7 6 5 4

Book design by Virginia Norey

this one is for my fans

for Lodey, Trebla, Stego, Pod,
Caress, Yags, X-Ray and Mr. X,
Kate, Chataya, Mormont, Mich,
Jamie, Vanessa, Ro,
for Stubby, Louise, Agravaine,
Wert, Malt, Jo,
Mouse, Telisiane, Blackfyre,
Bronn Stone, Coyote's Daughter,
and the rest of the madmen and wild women of
the Brotherhood Without Banners

for my website wizards
Elio and Linda, lords of Westeros,
Winter and Fabio of WIC,
and Gibbs of Dragonstone, who started it all

for men and women of Asshai in Spain
who sang to us of a bear and a maiden fair
and the fabulous fans of Italy
who gave me so much wine
for my readers in Finland, Germany,
Brazil, Portugal, France, and the Netherlands
and all the other distant lands
where you've been waiting for this dance

and for all the friends and fans
I have yet to meet

thanks for your patience

A CAVIL ON CHRONOLOGY

It has been a while between books, I know. So a reminder may be in order.

The book you hold in your hands is the fifth volume of A *Song of Ice and Fire*. The fourth volume was A *Feast for Crows*. However, this volume does not follow that one in the traditional sense, so much as run in tandem with it.

Both *Dance* and *Feast* take up the story immediately after the events of the third volume in the series, A *Storm of Swords*. Whereas *Feast* focused on events in and around King's Landing, on the Iron Islands, and down in Dorne, *Dance* takes us north to Castle Black and the Wall (and beyond), and across the narrow sea to Pentos and Slaver's Bay, to pick up the tales of Tyrion Lannister, Jon Snow, Daenerys Targaryen, and all the other characters you did not see in the preceding volume. Rather than being sequential, the two books are parallel . . . divided geographically, rather than chronologically.

But only up to a point.

A *Dance with Dragons* is a longer book than A *Feast for Crows*, and covers a longer time period. In the latter half of this volume, you will notice certain of the viewpoint characters from A *Feast for Crows* popping up again. And that means just what you think it means: the narrative has moved past the time frame of *Feast*, and the two streams have once again rejoined each other.

Next up, *The Winds of Winter*. Wherein, I hope, everybody will be shivering together once again. . . .

—George R. R. Martin
April 2011

Beyond The Wall

The Land of always Winter
(unmapped)

KEY
- Towns ◆ Castles
- ⬦ Ruined Castles

Thenn

The Land of always Winter (unmapped)

The Shivering Sea

Milkwater

The Skirling Pass

The Frostfangs

Antler River

Fist of the First Men

The Haunted Forest

Craster's Keep

Whitetree

The Wall

Brandon's Gift

Queenscrown

Bay of Ice

The New Gift

Hardhome

Storrold's Point

Skane

Skagos

Bay of Seals

Area of detail below

KINGSROAD

The Wall

Whitetree

Westwatch by-the-Bridge

The Gorge

The Shadow Tower

Sentinel Stand

Greyguard

Stonedoor

Hoarfrost Hill

Icemark

The Nightfort

Deep Lake

Queensgate

Castle Black

Oakenshield

Woodswatch by-the-Pool

Sable Hall

Rimegate

The Long Barrow

The Torches

Greenguard

Eastwatch by-the-Sea

KINGSROAD

Queenscrown

A DANCE WITH DRAGONS

PROLOGUE

T he night was rank with the smell of man.

The warg stopped beneath a tree and sniffed, his grey-brown fur dappled by shadow. A sigh of piney wind brought the man-scent to him, over fainter smells that spoke of fox and hare, seal and stag, even wolf. Those were man-smells too, the warg knew; the stink of old skins, dead and sour, near drowned beneath the stronger scents of smoke and blood and rot. Only man stripped the skins from other beasts and wore their hides and hair.

Wargs have no fear of man, as wolves do. Hate and hunger coiled in his belly, and he gave a low growl, calling to his one-eyed brother, to his small sly sister. As he raced through the trees, his packmates followed hard on his heels. They had caught the scent as well. As he ran, he saw through their eyes too and glimpsed himself ahead. The breath of the pack puffed warm and white from long grey jaws. Ice had frozen between their paws, hard as stone, but the hunt was on now, the prey ahead. *Flesh*, the warg thought, *meat*.

A man alone was a feeble thing. Big and strong, with good sharp eyes, but dull of ear and deaf to smells. Deer and elk and even hares were faster, bears and boars fiercer in a fight. But men in packs were dangerous. As the wolves closed on the prey, the warg heard the wailing of a pup, the crust of last night's snow breaking under clumsy man-paws, the rattle of hardskins and the long grey claws men carried.

Swords, a voice inside him whispered, *spears*.

The trees had grown icy teeth, snarling down from the bare brown branches. One Eye ripped through the undergrowth, spraying snow. His packmates followed. Up a hill and down the slope beyond, until the wood opened before them and the men were there. One was female. The fur-wrapped bundle she clutched was her pup. *Leave her for last*, the voice whispered, *the males are the danger.* They were roaring at each other as men did, but the warg could smell their terror. One had a wooden tooth as tall as he was. He flung it, but his hand was shaking and the tooth sailed high.

Then the pack was on them.

His one-eyed brother knocked the tooth-thrower back into a snowdrift and tore his throat out as he struggled. His sister slipped behind the other male and took him from the rear. That left the female and her pup for him.

She had a tooth too, a little one made of bone, but she dropped it when the warg's jaws closed around her leg. As she fell, she wrapped both arms around her noisy pup. Underneath her furs the female was just skin and bones, but her dugs were full of milk. The sweetest meat was on the pup. The wolf saved the choicest parts for his brother. All around the carcasses, the frozen snow turned pink and red as the pack filled its bellies.

Leagues away, in a one-room hut of mud and straw with a thatched roof and a smoke hole and a floor of hard-packed earth, Varamyr shivered and coughed and licked his lips. His eyes were red, his lips cracked, his throat dry and parched, but the taste of blood and fat filled his mouth, even as his swollen belly cried for nourishment. A *child's flesh,* he thought, remembering Bump. *Human meat.* Had he sunk so low as to hunger after human meat? He could almost hear Haggon growling at him. "Men may eat the flesh of beasts and beasts the flesh of men, but the man who eats the flesh of man is an abomination."

Abomination. That had always been Haggon's favorite word. *Abomination, abomination, abomination.* To eat of human meat was abomination, to mate as wolf with wolf was abomination, and to seize the body of another man was the worst abomination of all. *Haggon was weak, afraid of his own power. He died weeping and alone when I ripped his second life from him.* Varamyr had devoured his heart himself. *He taught me much and more, and the last thing I learned from him was the taste of human flesh.*

That was as a wolf, though. He had never eaten the meat of men with human teeth. He would not grudge his pack their feast, however. The wolves were as famished as he was, gaunt and cold and hungry, and the prey . . . *two men and a woman, a babe in arms, fleeing from defeat to death. They would have perished soon in any case, from exposure or starvation. This way was better, quicker. A mercy.*

"A mercy," he said aloud. His throat was raw, but it felt good to hear a human voice, even his own. The air smelled of mold and damp, the ground was cold and hard, and his fire was giving off more smoke than heat. He moved as close to the flames as he dared, coughing and shivering by turns, his side throbbing where his wound had opened. Blood had soaked his breeches to the knee and dried into a hard brown crust.

Thistle had warned him that might happen. "I sewed it up the best I could," she'd said, "but you need to rest and let it mend, or the flesh will tear open again."

Thistle had been the last of his companions, a spearwife tough as an old root, warty, windburnt, and wrinkled. The others had deserted them along the way. One by one they fell behind or forged ahead, making for their old villages, or the Milkwater, or Hardhome, or a lonely death in the woods. Varamyr did not know, and could not care. *I should have taken one of them when I had the chance. One of the twins, or the big man with the scarred face, or the youth with the red hair.* He had been afraid, though. One of the others might have realized what was happening. Then they would have turned on him and killed him. And Haggon's words had haunted him, and so the chance had passed.

After the battle there had been thousands of them struggling through the forest, hungry, frightened, fleeing the carnage that had descended on them at the Wall. Some had talked of returning to the homes that they'd abandoned, others of mounting a second assault upon the gate, but most were lost, with no notion of where to go or what to do. They had escaped the black-cloaked crows and the knights in their grey steel, but more relentless enemies stalked them now. Every day left more corpses by the trails. Some died of hunger, some of cold, some of sickness. Others were slain by those who had been their brothers-in-arms when they marched south with Mance Rayder, the King-Beyond-the-Wall.

Mance is fallen, the survivors told each other in despairing voices, *Mance is taken, Mance is dead.* "Harma's dead and Mance is captured, the rest run off and left us," Thistle had claimed, as she was sewing up his wound. "Tormund, the Weeper, Sixskins, all them brave raiders. Where are they now?"

She does not know me, Varamyr realized then, *and why should she?* Without his beasts he did not look like a great man. *I was Varamyr Sixskins, who broke bread with Mance Rayder.* He had named himself Varamyr when he was ten. *A name fit for a lord, a name for songs, a mighty name, and fearsome.* Yet he had run from the crows like a frightened rabbit. The terrible Lord Varamyr had gone craven, but he could not bear that she should know that, so he told the spearwife that his name was Haggon. Afterward he wondered why *that* name had come to his lips, of all those he might have chosen. *I ate his heart and drank his blood, and still he haunts me.*

One day, as they fled, a rider came galloping through the woods on a gaunt white horse, shouting that they all should make for the Milkwater, that the Weeper was gathering warriors to cross the Bridge of Skulls and take the Shadow Tower. Many followed him; more did not. Later, a dour warrior in fur and amber went from cookfire to cookfire, urging all the survivors to head north and take refuge in the valley of the Thenns. Why he thought they would be safe there when the Thenns themselves had fled the place Varamyr never learned, but hundreds followed him. Hundreds more went off with the woods witch who'd had a vision of a fleet of ships coming to carry the free folk south. "We must seek the sea," cried Mother Mole, and her followers turned east.

Varamyr might have been amongst them if only he'd been stronger. The sea was grey and cold and far away, though, and he knew that he would never live to see it. He was nine times dead and dying, and this would be his true death. *A squirrel-skin cloak*, he remembered, *he knifed me for a squirrel-skin cloak.*

Its owner had been dead, the back of her head smashed into red pulp flecked with bits of bone, but her cloak looked warm and thick. It was snowing, and Varamyr had lost his own cloaks at the Wall. His sleeping pelts and woolen smallclothes, his sheepskin boots and fur-lined gloves, his store of mead and hoarded food, the hanks of hair he took from the women he bedded, even the golden arm rings Mance had given him, all lost and left behind. *I burned and I died and then I ran, half-mad with pain and terror.* The memory still shamed him, but he had not been alone. Others had run as well, hundreds of them, thousands. *The battle was lost. The knights had come, invincible in their steel, killing everyone who stayed to fight. It was run or die.*

Death was not so easily outrun, however. So when Varamyr came upon the dead woman in the wood, he knelt to strip the cloak from her, and never saw the boy until he burst from hiding to drive the long bone knife into his side and rip the cloak out of his clutching fingers. "His mother," Thistle told him later, after the boy had run off. "It were his mother's cloak, and when he saw you robbing her . . ."

"She was dead," Varamyr said, wincing as her bone needle pierced his flesh. "Someone smashed her head. Some crow."

"No crow. Hornfoot men. I saw it." Her needle pulled the gash in his side closed. "Savages, and who's left to tame them?" *No one. If Mance is dead, the free folk are doomed.* The Thenns, giants, and the Hornfoot men, the cave-dwellers with their filed teeth, and the men of the western shore with their chariots of bone . . . all of them were doomed as well. Even the crows. They might not know it yet, but those black-cloaked bastards would perish with the rest. The enemy was coming.

Haggon's rough voice echoed in his head. "You will die a dozen deaths, boy, and every one will hurt . . . but when your true death comes, you will live again. The second life is simpler and sweeter, they say."

Varamyr Sixskins would know the truth of that soon enough. He could taste his true death in the smoke that hung acrid in the air, feel it in the heat beneath his fingers when he slipped a hand under his clothes to touch his wound. The chill was in him too, though, deep down in his bones. This time it would be cold that killed him.

His last death had been by fire. *I burned.* At first, in his confusion, he thought some archer on the Wall had pierced him with a flaming arrow . . . but the fire had been *inside* him, consuming him. And the pain . . .

Varamyr had died nine times before. He had died once from a spear thrust, once with a bear's teeth in his throat, and once in a wash of blood as he brought forth a stillborn cub. He died his first death when he was only six, as his father's axe crashed through his skull. Even that had not been so agonizing as the fire in his guts, crackling along his wings, *devouring* him. When he tried to fly from it, his terror fanned the flames and made them burn hotter. One moment he had been soaring above the Wall, his eagle's eyes marking the movements of the men below. Then the flames had turned his heart into a blackened cinder and sent his spirit screaming back into his own skin, and for a little while he'd gone mad. Even the memory was enough to make him shudder.

That was when he noticed that his fire had gone out.

Only a grey-and-black tangle of charred wood remained, with a few embers glowing in the ashes. *There's still smoke, it just needs wood.* Gritting his teeth against the pain, Varamyr crept to the pile of broken branches Thistle had gathered before she went off hunting, and tossed a few sticks onto the ashes. "Catch," he croaked. "*Burn.*" He blew upon the embers and said a wordless prayer to the nameless gods of wood and hill and field.

The gods gave no answer. After a while, the smoke ceased to rise as well. Already the little hut was growing colder. Varamyr had no flint, no tinder, no dry kindling. He would never get the fire burning again, not by himself. "Thistle," he called out, his voice hoarse and edged with pain. "*Thistle!*"

Her chin was pointed and her nose flat, and she had a mole on one cheek with four dark hairs growing from it. An ugly face, and hard, yet he would have given much to glimpse it in the door of the hut. *I should have taken her before she left.* How long had she been gone? Two days? Three? Varamyr was uncertain. It was dark inside the hut, and he had been drifting in and out of sleep, never quite sure if it was day or night outside. "Wait," she'd said. "I will be back with food." So like a fool he'd waited, dreaming of Haggon and Bump and all the wrongs he had done in his long life, but days and nights had passed and Thistle had not returned. *She won't be coming back.* Varamyr wondered if he had given himself away. Could she tell what he was thinking just from looking at him, or had he muttered in his fever dream?

Abomination, he heard Haggon saying. It was almost as if he were here, in this very room. "She is just some ugly spearwife," Varamyr told him. "I am a great man. I am Varamyr, the warg, the skinchanger, it is not right that she should live and I should die." No one answered. There was no one there. Thistle was gone. She had abandoned him, the same as all the rest.

His own mother had abandoned him as well. *She cried for Bump, but she never cried for me.* The morning his father pulled him out of bed to deliver him to Haggon, she would not even look at him. He had shrieked and kicked as he was dragged into the woods, until his father slapped him and told him to be quiet. "You belong with your own kind," was all he said when he flung him down at Haggon's feet.

He was not wrong, Varamyr thought, shivering. *Haggon taught me much and more. He taught me how to hunt and fish, how to butcher a carcass and bone a fish, how to find my way through the woods. And he taught me the way of the warg and the secrets of the skinchanger, though my gift was stronger than his own.*

Years later he had tried to find his parents, to tell them that their Lump had become the great Varamyr Sixskins, but both of them were dead and burned. *Gone into the trees and streams, gone into the rocks and earth. Gone to dirt and ashes.* That was what the woods witch told his mother, the day Bump died. Lump did not want to be a clod of earth. The boy had dreamed of a day when bards would sing of his deeds and pretty girls would kiss him. *When I am grown I will be the King-Beyond-the-Wall,* Lump had promised himself. He never had, but he had come close. Varamyr Sixskins was a name men feared. He rode to battle on the back of a snow bear thirteen feet tall, kept three wolves and a shadowcat in thrall, and sat at the right hand of Mance Rayder. *It was Mance who brought me*

*to this place. I should not have listened. I should have slipped inside my
bear and torn him to pieces.*

Before Mance, Varamyr Sixskins had been a lord of sorts. He lived
alone in a hall of moss and mud and hewn logs that had once been Haggon's, attended by his beasts. A dozen villages did him homage in bread
and salt and cider, offering him fruit from their orchards and vegetables
from their gardens. His meat he got himself. Whenever he desired a
woman he sent his shadowcat to stalk her, and whatever girl he'd cast his
eye upon would follow meekly to his bed. Some came weeping, aye, but
still they came. Varamyr gave them his seed, took a hank of their hair to
remember them by, and sent them back. From time to time, some village
hero would come with spear in hand to slay the beastling and save a sister
or a lover or a daughter. Those he killed, but he never harmed the women.
Some he even blessed with children. *Runts. Small, puny things, like
Lump, and not one with the gift.*

Fear drove him to his feet, reeling. Holding his side to staunch the seep
of blood from his wound, Varamyr lurched to the door and swept aside
the ragged skin that covered it to face a wall of white. *Snow.* No wonder it
had grown so dark and smoky inside. The falling snow had buried the hut.

When Varamyr pushed at it, the snow crumbled and gave way, still soft
and wet. Outside, the night was white as death; pale thin clouds danced
attendance on a silver moon, while a thousand stars watched coldly. He
could see the humped shapes of other huts buried beneath drifts of snow,
and beyond them the pale shadow of a weirwood armored in ice. To the
south and west the hills were a vast white wilderness where nothing moved
except the blowing snow. "Thistle," Varamyr called feebly, wondering
how far she could have gone. *"Thistle. Woman. Where are you?"*

Far away, a wolf gave howl.

A shiver went through Varamyr. He knew that howl as well as Lump
had once known his mother's voice. *One Eye.* He was the oldest of his
three, the biggest, the fiercest. Stalker was leaner, quicker, younger, Sly
more cunning, but both went in fear of One Eye. The old wolf was fearless, relentless, savage.

Varamyr had lost control of his other beasts in the agony of the eagle's
death. His shadowcat had raced into the woods, whilst his snow bear
turned her claws on those around her, ripping apart four men before falling to a spear. She would have slain Varamyr had he come within her
reach. The bear hated him, had raged each time he wore her skin or
climbed upon her back.

His wolves, though . . .

My brothers. My pack. Many a cold night he had slept with his wolves, their shaggy bodies piled up around him to help keep him warm. *When I die they will feast upon my flesh and leave only bones to greet the thaw come spring.* The thought was queerly comforting. His wolves had often foraged for him as they roamed; it seemed only fitting that he should feed them in the end. He might well begin his second life tearing at the warm dead flesh of his own corpse.

Dogs were the easiest beasts to bond with; they lived so close to men that they were almost human. Slipping into a dog's skin was like putting on an old boot, its leather softened by wear. As a boot was shaped to accept a foot, a dog was shaped to accept a collar, even a collar no human eye could see. Wolves were harder. A man might befriend a wolf, even break a wolf, but no man could truly *tame* a wolf. "Wolves and women wed for life," Haggon often said. "You take one, that's a marriage. The wolf is part of you from that day on, and you're part of him. Both of you will change."

Other beasts were best left alone, the hunter had declared. Cats were vain and cruel, always ready to turn on you. Elk and deer were prey; wear their skins too long, and even the bravest man became a coward. Bears, boars, badgers, weasels . . . Haggon did not hold with such. "Some skins you never want to wear, boy. You won't like what you'd become." Birds were the worst, to hear him tell it. "Men were not meant to leave the earth. Spend too much time in the clouds and you never want to come back down again. I know skinchangers who've tried hawks, owls, ravens. Even in their own skins, they sit moony, staring up at the bloody blue."

Not all skinchangers felt the same, however. Once, when Lump was ten, Haggon had taken him to a gathering of such. The wargs were the most numerous in that company, the wolf-brothers, but the boy had found the others stranger and more fascinating. Borroq looked so much like his boar that all he lacked was tusks, Orell had his eagle, Briar her shadowcat (the moment he saw them, Lump wanted a shadowcat of his own), the goat woman Grisella . . .

None of them had been as strong as Varamyr Sixskins, though, not even Haggon, tall and grim with his hands as hard as stone. The hunter died weeping after Varamyr took Greyskin from him, driving him out to claim the beast for his own. *No second life for you, old man.* Varamyr Threeskins, he'd called himself back then. Greyskin made four, though the old wolf was frail and almost toothless and soon followed Haggon into death.

Varamyr could take any beast he wanted, bend them to his will, make their flesh his own. Dog or wolf, bear or badger . . .

Thistle, he thought.

Haggon would call it an abomination, the blackest sin of all, but Haggon was dead, devoured, and burned. Mance would have cursed him as well, but Mance was slain or captured. *No one will ever know. I will be Thistle the spearwife, and Varamyr Sixskins will be dead.* His gift would perish with his body, he expected. He would lose his wolves, and live out the rest of his days as some scrawny, warty woman . . . but he would live. *If she comes back. If I am still strong enough to take her.*

A wave of dizziness washed over Varamyr. He found himself upon his knees, his hands buried in a snowdrift. He scooped up a fistful of snow and filled his mouth with it, rubbing it through his beard and against his cracked lips, sucking down the moisture. The water was so cold that he could barely bring himself to swallow, and he realized once again how hot he was.

The snowmelt only made him hungrier. It was food his belly craved, not water. The snow had stopped falling, but the wind was rising, filling the air with crystal, slashing at his face as he struggled through the drifts, the wound in his side opening and closing again. His breath made a ragged white cloud. When he reached the weirwood tree, he found a fallen branch just long enough to use as a crutch. Leaning heavily upon it, he staggered toward the nearest hut. Perhaps the villagers had forgotten something when they fled . . . a sack of apples, some dried meat, anything to keep him alive until Thistle returned.

He was almost there when his crutch snapped beneath his weight, and his legs went out from under him.

How long he sprawled there with his blood reddening the snow Varamyr could not have said. *The snow will bury me.* It would be a peaceful death. *They say you feel warm near the end, warm and sleepy.* It would be good to feel warm again, though it made him sad to think that he would never see the green lands, the warm lands beyond the Wall that Mance used to sing about. "The world beyond the Wall is not for our kind," Haggon used to say. "The free folk fear skinchangers, but they honor us as well. South of the Wall, the kneelers hunt us down and butcher us like pigs."

You warned me, Varamyr thought, *but it was you who showed me Eastwatch too.* He could not have been more than ten. Haggon traded a dozen strings of amber and a sled piled high with pelts for six skins of wine, a block of salt, and a copper kettle. Eastwatch was a better place to trade than Castle Black; that was where the ships came, laden with goods from the fabled lands beyond the sea. The crows knew Haggon as a hunter and a friend to the Night's Watch, and welcomed the news he brought of life beyond their Wall. Some knew him for a skinchanger too, but no one spoke of that. It was there at Eastwatch-by-the-Sea that the boy he'd been first began to dream of the warm south.

Varamyr could feel the snowflakes melting on his brow. *This is not so bad as burning. Let me sleep and never wake, let me begin my second life.* His wolves were close now. He could feel them. He would leave this feeble flesh behind, become one with them, hunting the night and howling at the moon. The warg would become a true wolf. *Which, though?*

Not Sly. Haggon would have called it abomination, but Varamyr had often slipped inside her skin as she was being mounted by One Eye. He did not want to spend his new life as a bitch, though, not unless he had no other choice. Stalker might suit him better, the younger male . . . though One Eye was larger and fiercer, and it was One Eye who took Sly whenever she went into heat.

"They say you forget," Haggon had told him, a few weeks before his own death. "When the man's flesh dies, his spirit lives on inside the beast, but every day his memory fades, and the beast becomes a little less a warg, a little more a wolf, until nothing of the man is left and only the beast remains."

Varamyr knew the truth of that. When he claimed the eagle that had been Orell's, he could feel the other skinchanger raging at his presence. Orell had been slain by the turncloak crow Jon Snow, and his hate for his killer had been so strong that Varamyr found himself hating the beastling boy as well. He had known what Snow was the moment he saw that great white direwolf stalking silent at his side. One skinchanger can always sense another. *Mance should have let me take the direwolf. There would be a second life worthy of a king.* He could have done it, he did not doubt. The gift was strong in Snow, but the youth was untaught, still fighting his nature when he should have gloried in it.

Varamyr could see the weirwood's red eyes staring down at him from the white trunk. *The gods are weighing me.* A shiver went through him. He had done bad things, terrible things. He had stolen, killed, raped. He had gorged on human flesh and lapped the blood of dying men as it gushed red and hot from their torn throats. He had stalked foes through the woods, fallen on them as they slept, clawed their entrails from their bellies and scattered them across the muddy earth. *How sweet their meat had tasted.* "That was the beast, not me," he said in a hoarse whisper. "That was the gift you gave me."

The gods made no reply. His breath hung pale and misty in the air. He could feel ice forming in his beard. Varamyr Sixskins closed his eyes.

He dreamt an old dream of a hovel by the sea, three dogs whimpering, a woman's tears.

Bump. She weeps for Bump, but she never wept for me.

Lump had been born a month before his proper time, and he was sick so often that no one expected him to live. His mother waited until he was almost four to give him a proper name, and by then it was too late. The whole village had taken to calling him Lump, the name his sister Meha had given him when he was still in their mother's belly. Meha had given Bump his name as well, but Lump's little brother had been born in his proper time, big and red and robust, sucking greedily at Mother's teats. She was going to name him after Father. *Bump died, though. He died when he was two and I was six, three days before his nameday.*

"Your little one is with the gods now," the woods witch told his mother, as she wept. "He'll never hurt again, never hunger, never cry. The gods have taken him down into the earth, into the trees. The gods are all around us, in the rocks and streams, in the birds and beasts. Your Bump has gone to join them. He'll be the world and all that's in it."

The old woman's words had gone through Lump like a knife. *Bump sees. He is watching me. He knows.* Lump could not hide from him, could not slip behind his mother's skirts or run off with the dogs to escape his father's fury. *The dogs.* Loptail, Sniff, the Growler. *They were good dogs. They were my friends.*

When his father found the dogs sniffing round Bump's body, he had no way of knowing which had done it, so he took his axe to all three. His hands shook so badly that it took two blows to silence Sniff and four to put the Growler down. The smell of blood hung heavy in the air, and the sounds the dying dogs had made were terrible to hear, yet Loptail still came when father called him. He was the oldest dog, and his training overcame his terror. By the time Lump slipped inside his skin it was too late.

No, Father, please, he tried to say, but dogs cannot speak the tongues of men, so all that emerged was a piteous whine. The axe crashed into the middle of the old dog's skull, and inside the hovel the boy let out a scream. *That was how they knew.* Two days later, his father dragged him into the woods. He brought his axe, so Lump thought he meant to put him down the same way he had done the dogs. Instead he'd given him to Haggon.

Varamyr woke suddenly, violently, his whole body shaking. "Get up," a voice was screaming, "get up, we have to go. There are hundreds of them." The snow had covered him with a stiff white blanket. *So cold.* When he tried to move, he found that his hand was frozen to the ground. He left some skin behind when he tore it loose. "Get up," she screamed again, "they're *coming.*"

Thistle had returned to him. She had him by the shoulders and was shaking him, shouting in his face. Varamyr could smell her breath and feel the warmth of it upon cheeks gone numb with cold. *Now,* he thought, *do it now, or die.*

He summoned all the strength still in him, leapt out of his own skin, and forced himself inside her.

Thistle arched her back and screamed.

Abomination. Was that her, or him, or Haggon? He never knew. His old flesh fell back into the snowdrift as her fingers loosened. The spear-wife twisted violently, shrieking. His shadowcat used to fight him wildly, and the snow bear had gone half-mad for a time, snapping at trees and rocks and empty air, but this was worse. "Get out, *get out!*" he heard her own mouth shouting. Her body staggered, fell, and rose again, her hands flailed, her legs jerked this way and that in some grotesque dance as his spirit and her own fought for the flesh. She sucked down a mouthful of the frigid air, and Varamyr had half a heartbeat to glory in the taste of it and the strength of this young body before her teeth snapped together and filled his mouth with blood. She raised her hands to his face. He tried to push them down again, but the hands would not obey, and she was claw-ing at his eyes. *Abomination,* he remembered, drowning in blood and pain and madness. When he tried to scream, she spat their tongue out.

The white world turned and fell away. For a moment it was as if he were inside the weirwood, gazing out through carved red eyes as a dying man twitched feebly on the ground and a madwoman danced blind and bloody underneath the moon, weeping red tears and ripping at her clothes. Then both were gone and he was rising, melting, his spirit borne on some cold wind. He was in the snow and in the clouds, he was a spar-row, a squirrel, an oak. A horned owl flew silently between his trees, hunt-ing a hare; Varamyr was inside the owl, inside the hare, inside the trees. Deep below the frozen ground, earthworms burrowed blindly in the dark, and he was them as well. *I am the wood, and everything that's in it,* he thought, exulting. A hundred ravens took to the air, cawing as they felt him pass. A great elk trumpeted, unsettling the children clinging to his back. A sleeping direwolf raised his head to snarl at empty air. Before their hearts could beat again he had passed on, searching for his own, for One Eye, Sly, and Stalker, for his pack. His wolves would save him, he told himself.

That was his last thought as a man.

True death came suddenly; he felt a shock of cold, as if he had been plunged into the icy waters of a frozen lake. Then he found himself rushing over moonlit snows with his packmates close behind him. Half the world was dark. *One Eye*, he knew. He bayed, and Sly and Stalker gave echo.

When they reached the crest the wolves paused. *Thistle,* he remembered, and a part of him grieved for what he had lost and another part for what he'd done. Below, the world had turned to ice. Fingers of frost crept slowly up the weirwood, reaching out for each other. The empty village was no longer empty. Blue-eyed shadows walked amongst the mounds of snow. Some wore brown and some wore black and some were naked, their flesh gone white as snow. A wind was sighing through the hills, heavy with their scents: dead flesh, dry blood, skins that stank of mold and rot and urine. Sly gave a growl and bared her teeth, her ruff bristling. *Not men. Not prey. Not these.*

The things below moved, but did not live. One by one, they raised their heads toward the three wolves on the hill. The last to look was the thing that had been Thistle. She wore wool and fur and leather, and over that she wore a coat of hoarfrost that crackled when she moved and glistened in the moonlight. Pale pink icicles hung from her fingertips, ten long knives of frozen blood. And in the pits where her eyes had been, a pale blue light was flickering, lending her coarse features an eerie beauty they had never known in life.

She sees me.

TYRION

He drank his way across the narrow sea.

The ship was small, his cabin smaller, but the captain would not allow him abovedecks. The rocking of the deck beneath his feet made his stomach heave, and the wretched food tasted even worse when retched back up. But why did he need salt beef, hard cheese, and bread crawling with worms when he had wine to nourish him? It was red and sour, very strong. Sometimes he heaved the wine up too, but there was always more.

"The world is full of wine," he muttered in the dankness of his cabin. His father never had any use for drunkards, but what did that matter? His father was dead. He'd killed him. *A bolt in the belly, my lord, and all for you. If only I was better with a crossbow, I would have put it through that cock you made me with, you bloody bastard.*

Belowdecks, there was neither night nor day. Tyrion marked time by the comings and goings of the cabin boy who brought the meals he did not eat. The boy always brought a brush and bucket too, to clean up. "Is this Dornish wine?" Tyrion asked him once, as he pulled a stopper from a skin. "It reminds me of a certain snake I knew. A droll fellow, till a mountain fell on him."

The cabin boy did not answer. He was an ugly boy, though admittedly more comely than a certain dwarf with half a nose and a scar from eye to chin. "Have I offended you?" Tyrion asked, as the boy was scrubbing. "Were you commanded not to talk to me? Or did some dwarf diddle your mother?" That went unanswered too. "Where are we sailing? Tell me that." Jaime had made mention of the Free Cities, but had never said which one. "Is it Braavos? Tyrosh? Myr?" Tyrion would sooner have gone to Dorne. *Myrcella is older than Tommen, by Dornish law the Iron Throne is hers. I will help her claim her rights, as Prince Oberyn suggested.*

Oberyn was dead, though, his head smashed to bloody ruin by the armored fist of Ser Gregor Clegane. And without the Red Viper to urge him on, would Doran Martell even consider such a chancy scheme? *He might clap me in chains instead and hand me back to my sweet sister.* The Wall might be safer. Old Bear Mormont said the Night's Watch had need of men like Tyrion. *Mormont might be dead, though. By now Slynt may be the lord commander.* That butcher's son was not like to have forgotten who sent him to the Wall. *Do I really want to spend the rest of my life eating salt beef and porridge with murderers and thieves?* Not that the rest of his life would last very long. Janos Slynt would see to that.

The cabin boy wet his brush and scrubbed on manfully. "Have you ever visited the pleasure houses of Lys?" the dwarf inquired. "Might that be where whores go?" Tyrion could not seem to recall the Valyrian word for whore, and in any case it was too late. The boy tossed his brush back in his bucket and took his leave.

The wine has blurred my wits. He had learned to read High Valyrian at his maester's knee, though what they spoke in the Nine Free Cities . . . well, it was not so much a dialect as nine dialects on the way to becoming separate tongues. Tyrion had some Braavosi and a smattering of Myrish. In Tyrosh he should be able to curse the gods, call a man a cheat, and order up an ale, thanks to a sellsword he had once known at the Rock. *At least in Dorne they speak the Common Tongue.* Like Dornish food and Dornish law, Dornish speech was spiced with the flavors of the Rhoyne, but a man could comprehend it. *Dorne, yes, Dorne for me.* He crawled into his bunk, clutching that thought like a child with a doll.

Sleep had never come easily to Tyrion Lannister. Aboard that ship it seldom came at all, though from time to time he managed to drink sufficient wine to pass out for a while. At least he did not dream. He had dreamed enough for one small life. *And of such follies: love, justice, friendship, glory. As well dream of being tall.* It was all beyond his reach, Tyrion knew now. But he did not know where whores go.

"Wherever whores go," his father had said. *His last words, and what words they were.* The crossbow *thrumm*ed, Lord Tywin sat back down, and Tyrion Lannister found himself waddling through the darkness with Varys at his side. He must have clambered back down the shaft, two hundred and thirty rungs to where orange embers glowed in the mouth of an iron dragon. He remembered none of it. Only the sound the crossbow made, and the stink of his father's bowels opening. *Even in his dying, he found a way to shit on me.*

Varys had escorted him through the tunnels, but they never spoke until they emerged beside the Blackwater, where Tyrion had won a famous victory and lost a nose. That was when the dwarf turned to the eunuch and said, "I've killed my father," in the same tone a man might use to say, "I've stubbed my toe."

The master of whisperers had been dressed as a begging brother, in a moth-eaten robe of brown roughspun with a cowl that shadowed his smooth fat cheeks and bald round head. "You should not have climbed that ladder," he said reproachfully.

"Wherever whores go." Tyrion had warned his father not to say that word. *If I had not loosed, he would have seen my threats were empty. He would have taken the crossbow from my hands, as once he took Tysha from my arms. He was rising when I killed him.*

"I killed Shae too," he confessed to Varys.

"You knew what she was."

"I did. But I never knew what he was."

Varys tittered. "And now you do."

I should have killed the eunuch as well. A little more blood on his hands, what would it matter? He could not say what had stayed his dagger. Not gratitude. Varys had saved him from a headsman's sword, but only because Jaime had compelled him. *Jaime . . . no, better not to think of Jaime.*

He found a fresh skin of wine instead and sucked at it as if it were a woman's breast. The sour red ran down his chin and soaked through his soiled tunic, the same one he had been wearing in his cell. The deck was swaying beneath his feet, and when he tried to rise it lifted sideways and smashed him hard against a bulkhead. A *storm,* he realized, *or else I am even drunker than I knew.* He retched the wine up and lay in it a while, wondering if the ship would sink. *Is this your vengeance, Father? Has the Father Above made you his Hand?* "Such are the wages of the kinslayer," he said as the wind howled outside. It did not seem fair to drown the cabin boy and the captain and all the rest for something he had done, but when had the gods ever been fair? And around about then, the darkness gulped him down.

When he stirred again, his head felt like to burst and the ship was spinning round in dizzy circles, though the captain was insisting that they'd come to port. Tyrion told him to be quiet and kicked feebly as a huge bald sailor tucked him under one arm and carried him squirming to the hold, where an empty wine cask awaited him. It was a squat little cask, and a tight fit even for a dwarf. Tyrion pissed himself in his struggles, for all the good it did. He was crammed face-first into the cask with his knees pushed up against his ears. The stub of his nose itched horribly, but his arms were pinned so tightly that he could not reach to scratch it. A *palanquin fit for a man of my stature*, he thought as they hammered shut the lid. He could hear voices shouting as he was hoisted up. Every bounce cracked his head against the bottom of the cask. The world went round and round as the cask rolled downward, then stopped with a crash that made him want to scream. Another cask slammed into his, and Tyrion bit his tongue.

That was the longest journey he had ever taken, though it could not have lasted more than half an hour. He was lifted and lowered, rolled and stacked, upended and righted and rolled again. Through the wooden staves he heard men shouting, and once a horse whickered nearby. His stunted legs began to cramp, and soon hurt so badly that he forgot the hammering in his head.

It ended as it had begun, with another roll that left him dizzy and more jouncing. Outside, strange voices were speaking in a tongue he did not know. Someone started pounding on the top of the cask and the lid cracked open suddenly. Light came flooding in, and cool air as well. Tyrion gasped greedily and tried to stand, but only managed to knock the cask over sideways and spill himself out onto a hard-packed earthen floor.

Above him loomed a grotesque fat man with a forked yellow beard, holding a wooden mallet and an iron chisel. His bedrobe was large enough to serve as a tourney pavilion, but its loosely knotted belt had come undone, exposing a huge white belly and a pair of heavy breasts that sagged like sacks of suet covered with coarse yellow hair. He reminded Tyrion of a dead sea cow that had once washed up in the caverns under Casterly Rock.

The fat man looked down and smiled. "A drunken dwarf," he said, in the Common Tongue of Westeros.

"A rotting sea cow." Tyrion's mouth was full of blood. He spat it at the fat man's feet. They were in a long, dim cellar with barrel-vaulted ceilings, its stone walls spotted with nitre. Casks of wine and ale surrounded them, more than enough drink to see a thirsty dwarf safely through the night. *Or through a life.*

"You are insolent. I like that in a dwarf." When the fat man laughed, his flesh bounced so vigorously that Tyrion was afraid he might fall and crush him. "Are you hungry, my little friend? Weary?"

"Thirsty." Tyrion struggled to his knees. "And filthy."

The fat man sniffed. "A bath first, just so. Then food and a soft bed, yes?

My servants shall see to it." His host put the mallet and chisel aside. "My house is yours. Any friend of my friend across the water is a friend to Illyrio Mopatis, yes."

And any friend of Varys the Spider is someone I will trust just as far as I can throw him.

The fat man made good on the promised bath, though. No sooner did Tyrion lower himself into the hot water and close his eyes than he was fast asleep. He woke naked on a goose-down feather bed so soft it felt as if he had been swallowed by a cloud. His tongue was growing hair and his throat was raw, but his cock was as hard as an iron bar. He rolled from the bed, found a chamber pot, and commenced to filling it, with a groan of pleasure.

The room was dim, but there were bars of yellow sunlight showing between the slats of the shutters. Tyrion shook the last drops off and waddled over patterned Myrish carpets as soft as new spring grass. Awkwardly he climbed the window seat and flung the shutters open to see where Varys and the gods had sent him.

Beneath his window six cherry trees stood sentinel around a marble pool, their slender branches bare and brown. A naked boy stood on the water, poised to duel with a bravo's blade in hand. He was lithe and handsome, no older than sixteen, with straight blond hair that brushed his shoulders. So lifelike did he seem that it took the dwarf a long moment to realize he was made of painted marble, though his sword shimmered like true steel.

Across the pool stood a brick wall twelve feet high, with iron spikes along its top. Beyond that was the city. A sea of tiled rooftops crowded close around a bay. He saw square brick towers, a great red temple, a distant manse upon a hill. In the far distance, sunlight shimmered off deep water. Fishing boats were moving across the bay, their sails rippling in the wind, and he could see the masts of larger ships poking up along the shore. *Surely one is bound for Dorne, or for Eastwatch-by-the-Sea.* He had no means to pay for passage, though, nor was he made to pull an oar. *I suppose I could sign on as a cabin boy and earn my way by letting the crew bugger me up and down the narrow sea.*

He wondered where he was. *Even the air smells different here.* Strange spices scented the chilly autumn wind, and he could hear faint cries drifting over the wall from the streets beyond. It sounded something like Valyrian, but he did not recognize more than one word in five. *Not Braavos,* he concluded, *nor Tyrosh.* Those bare branches and the chill in the air argued against Lys and Myr and Volantis as well.

When he heard the door opening behind him, Tyrion turned to confront his fat host. "This is Pentos, yes?"

"Just so. Where else?"

Pentos. Well, it was not King's Landing, that much could be said for it. "Where do whores go?" he heard himself ask.

"Whores are found in brothels here, as in Westeros. You will have no need of such, my little friend. Choose from amongst my servingwomen. None will dare refuse you."

"Slaves?" the dwarf asked pointedly.

The fat man stroked one of the prongs of his oiled yellow beard, a gesture Tyrion found remarkably obscene. "Slavery is forbidden in Pentos, by the terms of the treaty the Braavosi imposed on us a hundred years ago. Still, they will not refuse you." Illyrio gave a ponderous half bow. "But now my little friend must excuse me. I have the honor to be a magister of this great city, and the prince has summoned us to session." He smiled, showing a mouth full of crooked yellow teeth. "Explore the manse and grounds as you like, but on no account stray beyond the walls. It is best that no man knows that you were here."

"*Were?* Have I gone somewhere?"

"Time enough to speak of that this evening. My little friend and I shall eat and drink and make great plans, yes?"

"Yes, my fat friend," Tyrion replied. *He thinks to use me for his profit.* It was all profit with the merchant princes of the Free Cities. "Spice soldiers and cheese lords," his lord father called them, with contempt. Should a day ever dawn when Illyrio Mopatis saw more profit in a dead dwarf than a live one, Tyrion would find himself packed into another wine cask by dusk. *It would be well if I was gone before that day arrives.* That it would arrive he did not doubt; Cersei was not like to forget him, and even Jaime might be vexed to find a quarrel in Father's belly.

A light wind was riffling the waters of the pool below, all around the naked swordsman. It reminded him of how Tysha would riffle his hair during the false spring of their marriage, before he helped his father's guardsmen rape her. He had been thinking of those guardsmen during his flight, trying to recall how many there had been. You would think he might remember that, but no. A dozen? A score? A hundred? He could not say. They had all been grown men, tall and strong . . . though all men were tall to a dwarf of thirteen years. *Tysha knew their number.* Each of them had given her a silver stag, so she would only need to count the coins. *A silver for each and a gold for me.* His father had insisted that he pay her too. *A Lannister always pays his debts.*

"Wherever whores go," he heard Lord Tywin say once more, and once more the bowstring *thrumm*ed.

The magister had invited him to explore the manse. He found clean clothes in a cedar chest inlaid with lapis and mother-of-pearl. The clothes had been made for a small boy, he realized as he struggled into them. The fabrics were rich enough, if a little musty, but the cut was too long in the legs and too short in the arms, with a collar that would have turned his face as black as Joffrey's had he somehow contrived to get it fastened. Moths had been at them too. *At least they do not stink of vomit.*

Tyrion began his explorations with the kitchen, where two fat women and a potboy watched him warily as he helped himself to cheese, bread, and figs. "Good morrow to you, fair ladies," he said with a bow. "Do you know where whores go?" When they did not respond, he repeated the question in High Valyrian, though he had to say *courtesan* in place of *whore.* The younger, fatter cook gave him a shrug that time.

He wondered what they would do if he took them by the hand and dragged them to his bedchamber. *None will dare refuse you,* Illyrio claimed, but somehow Tyrion did not think he meant these two. The younger woman was old enough to be his mother, and the older was likely *her* mother. Both were near as fat as Illyrio, with teats that were larger than his head. *I could smother myself in flesh.* There were worse ways to die. The way his lord father had died, for one. *I should have made him shit a little gold before expiring.* Lord Tywin might have been niggardly with his approval and affection, but he had always been open-handed when it came to coin. *The only thing more pitiful than a dwarf without a nose is a dwarf without a nose who has no gold.*

Tyrion left the fat women to their loaves and kettles and went in search of the cellar where Illyrio had decanted him the night before. It was not hard to find. There was enough wine there to keep him drunk for a hundred years; sweet reds from the Reach and sour reds from Dorne, pale Pentoshi ambers, the green nectar of Myr, three score casks of Arbor gold, even wines from the fabled east, from Qarth and Yi Ti and Asshai by the Shadow. In the end, Tyrion chose a cask of strongwine marked as the private stock of Lord Runceford Redwyne, the grandfather of the present Lord of the Arbor. The taste of it was languorous and heady on the tongue, the color a purple so dark that it looked almost black in the dim-lit cellar. Tyrion filled a cup, and a flagon for good measure, and carried them up to the gardens to drink beneath those cherry trees he'd seen.

As it happened, he left by the wrong door and never found the pool he had spied from his window, but it made no matter. The gardens behind the manse were just as pleasant, and far more extensive. He wandered through them for a time, drinking. The walls would have shamed any proper castle, and the ornamental iron spikes along the top looked strangely naked without heads to adorn them. Tyrion pictured how his sister's head might look up there, with tar in her golden hair and flies buzzing in and out of her mouth. *Yes, and Jaime must have the spike beside her,* he decided. *No one must ever come between my brother and my sister.*

With a rope and a grapnel he might be able to get over that wall. He had strong arms and he did not weigh much. He should be able to clamber over, if he did not impale himself on a spike. *I will search for a rope on the morrow,* he resolved.

He saw three gates during his wanderings—the main entrance with its gatehouse, a postern by the kennels, and a garden gate hidden behind a tangle of pale ivy. The last was chained, the others guarded. The guards were plump, their faces as smooth as babies' bottoms, and every man of them wore a spiked bronze cap. Tyrion knew eunuchs when he saw them. He knew their sort by reputation. They feared nothing and felt no pain, it was said, and were loyal to their masters unto death. *I could make good use of a few hundred of mine own,* he reflected. *A pity I did not think of that before I became a beggar.*

He walked along a pillared gallery and through a pointed arch, and found himself in a tiled courtyard where a woman was washing clothes at a well. She looked to be his own age, with dull red hair and a broad face dotted by freckles. "Would you like some wine?" he asked her. She looked at him uncertainly. "I have no cup for you, we'll have to share." The washerwoman went back to wringing out tunics and hanging them to dry. Tyrion settled on a stone bench with his flagon. "Tell me, how far should I trust Magister Illyrio?" The name made her look up. "That far?" Chuckling, he crossed his stunted legs and took a drink. "I am loath to play whatever part the cheesemonger has in mind for me, yet how can I refuse him? The gates are guarded. Perhaps you might smuggle me out under your skirts? I'd be so grateful; why, I'll even wed you. I have two wives already, why not three? Ah, but where would we live?" He gave her as pleasant a smile as a man with half a nose could manage. "I have a niece in Sunspear, did I tell you? I could make rather a lot of mischief in Dorne with Myrcella. I could set my niece and nephew at war, wouldn't that be droll?" The washerwoman pinned up one of Illyrio's tunics, large enough to double as a sail. "I should be ashamed to think such evil thoughts, you're quite right. Better if I sought the Wall instead. All crimes are wiped clean when a man joins the Night's Watch, they say. Though I fear they would not let me keep you, sweetling. No women in the Watch, no sweet freckly wives to warm your bed at night, only cold winds, salted cod, and small beer. Do you think I might stand taller in black, my lady?" He filled his cup again. "What do you say? North or south? Shall I atone for old sins or make some new ones?"

The washerwoman gave him one last glance, picked up her basket, and walked away. *I cannot seem to hold a wife for very long,* Tyrion reflected. Somehow his flagon had gone dry. *Perhaps I should stumble back down to the cellars.* The strongwine was making his head spin, though, and the cellar steps were very steep. "Where do whores go?" he asked the wash flapping on the line. Perhaps he should have asked the washerwoman. *Not to imply that you're a whore, my dear, but perhaps you know where they go.* Or better yet, he should have asked his father. "Wherever whores go," Lord Tywin said. *She loved me. She was a crofter's daughter, she loved me and she wed me, she put her trust in me.*

The empty flagon slipped from his hand and rolled across the yard. Tyrion pushed himself off the bench and went to fetch it. As he did, he saw some mushrooms growing up from a cracked paving tile. Pale white they were, with speckles, and red-ribbed undersides dark as blood. The dwarf snapped one off and sniffed it. *Delicious,* he thought, *and deadly.*

There were seven of the mushrooms. Perhaps the Seven were trying to tell him something. He picked them all, snatched a glove down from the line, wrapped them carefully, and stuffed them down his pocket. The effort made him dizzy, so afterward he crawled back onto the bench, curled up, and shut his eyes.

When he woke again, he was back in his bedchamber, drowning in the goose-down feather bed once more while a blond girl shook his shoulder. "My lord," she said, "your bath awaits. Magister Illyrio expects you at table within the hour."

Tyrion propped himself against the pillows, his head in his hands. "Do I dream, or do you speak the Common Tongue?"

"Yes, my lord. I was bought to please the king." She was blue-eyed and fair, young and willowy.

"I am sure you did. I need a cup of wine."

She poured for him. "Magister Illyrio said that I am to scrub your back and warm your bed. My name—"

"—is of no interest to me. Do you know where whores go?"

She flushed. "Whores sell themselves for coin."

"Or jewels, or gowns, or castles. But where do they go?"

The girl could not grasp the question. "Is it a riddle, m'lord? I'm no good at riddles. Will you tell me the answer?"

No, he thought. *I despise riddles, myself.* "I will tell you nothing. Do me the same favor." *The only part of you that interests me is the part between your legs,* he almost said. The words were on his tongue, but somehow never passed his lips. *She is not Shae,* the dwarf told himself, *only some little fool who thinks I play at riddles.* If truth be told, even her cunt did not interest him much. *I must be sick, or dead.* "You mentioned a bath? We must not keep the great cheesemonger waiting."

As he bathed, the girl washed his feet, scrubbed his back, and brushed his hair. Afterward she rubbed sweet-smelling ointment into his calves to ease the aches, and dressed him once again in boy's clothing, a musty pair of burgundy breeches and a blue velvet doublet lined with cloth-of-gold. "Will my lord want me after he has eaten?" she asked as she was lacing up his boots.

"No. I am done with women." *Whores.*

The girl took that disappointment too well for his liking. "If m'lord would prefer a boy, I can have one waiting in his bed."

M'lord would prefer his wife. M'lord would prefer a girl named Tysha. "Only if he knows where whores go."

The girl's mouth tightened. *She despises me,* he realized, *but no more than I despise myself.* That he had fucked many a woman who loathed the very sight of him, Tyrion Lannister had no doubt, but the others had at least the grace to feign affection. *A little honest loathing might be refreshing, like a tart wine after too much sweet.*

"I believe I have changed my mind," he told her. "Wait for me abed. Naked, if you please, I'll be a deal too drunk to fumble at your clothing. Keep your mouth shut and your thighs open and the two of us should get on splendidly." He gave her a leer, hoping for a taste of fear, but all she gave him was revulsion. *No one fears a dwarf.* Even Lord Tywin had not been afraid, though Tyrion had held a crossbow in his hands. "Do you moan when you are being fucked?" he asked the bedwarmer.

"If it please m'lord."

"It might please m'lord to strangle you. That's how I served my last whore. Do you think your master would object? Surely not. He has a hundred more like you, but no one else like me." This time, when he grinned, he got the fear he wanted.

Illyrio was reclining on a padded couch, gobbling hot peppers and pearl onions from a wooden bowl. His brow was dotted with beads of sweat, his pig's eyes shining above his fat cheeks. Jewels danced when he

moved his hands; onyx and opal, tiger's eye and tourmaline, ruby, ame-
thyst, sapphire, emerald, jet and jade, a black diamond, and a green pearl.
I could live for years on his rings, Tyrion mused, *though I'd need a cleaver
to claim them.*

"Come sit, my little friend." Illyrio waved him closer.

The dwarf clambered up onto a chair. It was much too big for him, a
cushioned throne intended to accommodate the magister's massive buttocks, with thick sturdy legs to bear his weight. Tyrion Lannister had lived
all his life in a world that was too big for him, but in the manse of Illyrio
Mopatis the sense of disproportion assumed grotesque dimensions. *I am a
mouse in a mammoth's lair,* he mused, *though at least the mammoth keeps
a good cellar.* The thought made him thirsty. He called for wine.

"Did you enjoy the girl I sent you?" Illyrio asked.

"If I had wanted a girl I would have asked for one."

"If she failed to please . . ."

"She did all that was required of her."

"I would hope so. She was trained in Lys, where they make an art of
love. The king enjoyed her greatly."

"I kill kings, hadn't you heard?" Tyrion smiled evilly over his wine cup.
"I want no royal leavings."

"As you wish. Let us eat." Illyrio clapped his hands together, and serving men came running.

They began with a broth of crab and monkfish, and cold egg lime soup
as well. Then came quails in honey, a saddle of lamb, goose livers drowned
in wine, buttered parsnips, and suckling pig. The sight of it all made
Tyrion feel queasy, but he forced himself to try a spoon of soup for the
sake of politeness, and once he had tasted it he was lost. The cooks might
be old and fat, but they knew their business. He had never eaten so well,
even at court.

As he was sucking the meat off the bones of his quail, he asked Illyrio
about the morning's summons. The fat man shrugged. "There are troubles in the east. Astapor has fallen, and Meereen. Ghiscari slave cities that
were old when the world was young." The suckling pig was carved. Illyrio
reached for a piece of the crackling, dipped it in a plum sauce, and ate it
with his fingers.

"Slaver's Bay is a long way from Pentos." Tyrion speared a goose liver
on the point of his knife. *No man is as cursed as the kinslayer,* he mused,
but I could learn to like this hell.

"This is so," Illyrio agreed, "but the world is one great web, and a man
dare not touch a single strand lest all the others tremble. More wine?"

Illyrio popped a pepper into his mouth. "No, something better." He clapped his hands together.

At the sound a serving man entered with a covered dish. He placed it in front of Tyrion, and Illyrio leaned across the table to remove the lid. "Mushrooms," the magister announced, as the smell wafted up. "Kissed with garlic and bathed in butter. I am told the taste is exquisite. Have one, my friend. Have two."

Tyrion had a fat black mushroom halfway to his mouth, but something in Illyrio's voice made him stop abruptly. "After you, my lord." He pushed the dish toward his host.

"No, no." Magister Illyrio pushed the mushrooms back. For a heartbeat it seemed as if a mischievous boy was peering out from inside the cheese-monger's bloated flesh. "After you. I insist. Cook made them specially for you."

"Did she indeed?" He remembered the cook, the flour on her hands, heavy breasts shot through with dark blue veins. "That was kind of her, but . . . no." Tyrion eased the mushroom back into the lake of butter from which it had emerged.

"You are too suspicious." Illyrio smiled through his forked yellow beard. Oiled every morning to make it gleam like gold, Tyrion suspected. "Are you craven? I had not heard that of you."

"In the Seven Kingdoms it is considered a grave breach of hospitality to poison your guest at supper."

"Here as well." Illyrio Mopatis reached for his wine cup. "Yet when a guest plainly wishes to end his own life, why, his host must oblige him, no?" He took a gulp. "Magister Ordello was poisoned by a mushroom not half a year ago. The pain is not so much, I am told. Some cramping in the gut, a sudden ache behind the eyes, and it is done. Better a mushroom than a sword through your neck, is it not so? Why die with the taste of blood in your mouth when it could be butter and garlic?"

The dwarf studied the dish before him. The smell of garlic and butter had his mouth watering. Some part of him wanted those mushrooms, even knowing what they were. He was not brave enough to take cold steel to his own belly, but a bite of mushroom would not be so hard. That frightened him more than he could say. "You mistake me," he heard him-self say.

"Is it so? I wonder. If you would sooner drown in wine, say the word and it shall be done, and quickly. Drowning cup by cup wastes time and wine both."

"You mistake me," Tyrion said again, more loudly. The buttered mushrooms glistened in the lamplight, dark and inviting. "I have no wish to die, I promise you. I have . . ." His voice trailed off into uncertainty. *What do I have? A life to live? Work to do? Children to raise, lands to rule, a woman to love?*

"You have nothing," finished Magister Illyrio, "but we can change that." He plucked a mushroom from the butter, and chewed it lustily. "Delicious."

"The mushrooms are not poisoned." Tyrion was irritated.

"No. Why should I wish you ill?" Magister Illyrio ate another. "We must show a little trust, you and I. Come, eat." He clapped his hands again. "We have work to do. My little friend must keep his strength up."

The serving men brought out a heron stuffed with figs, veal cutlets blanched with almond milk, creamed herring, candied onions, foul-smelling cheeses, plates of snails and sweetbreads, and a black swan in her plumage. Tyrion refused the swan, which reminded him of a supper with his sister. He helped himself to heron and herring, though, and a few of the sweet onions. And the serving men filled his wine cup anew each time he emptied it.

"You drink a deal of wine for such a little man."

"Kinslaying is dry work. It gives a man a thirst."

The fat man's eyes glittered like the gemstones on his fingers. "There are those in Westeros who would say that killing Lord Lannister was merely a good beginning."

"They had best not say it in my sister's hearing, or they will find themselves short a tongue." The dwarf tore a loaf of bread in half. "And you had best be careful what you say of my family, magister. Kinslayer or no, I am a lion still."

That seemed to amuse the lord of cheese no end. He slapped a meaty thigh and said, "You Westerosi are all the same. You sew some beast upon a scrap of silk, and suddenly you are all lions or dragons or eagles. I can take you to a real lion, my little friend. The prince keeps a pride in his menagerie. Would you like to share a cage with them?"

The lords of the Seven Kingdoms did make rather much of their sigils, Tyrion had to admit. "Very well," he conceded. "A Lannister is not a lion. Yet I am still my father's son, and Jaime and Cersei are mine to kill."

"How odd that you should mention your fair sister," said Illyrio, between snails. "The queen has offered a lordship to the man who brings her your head, no matter how humble his birth."

It was no more than Tyrion had expected. "If you mean to take her up on it, make her spread her legs for you as well. The best part of me for the best part of her, that's a fair trade."

"I would sooner have mine own weight in gold." The cheesemonger laughed so hard that Tyrion feared he was about to rupture. "All the gold in Casterly Rock, why not?"

"The gold I grant you," the dwarf said, relieved that he was not about to drown in a gout of half-digested eels and sweetmeats, "but the Rock is mine."

"Just so." The magister covered his mouth and belched a mighty belch. "Do you think King Stannis will give it to you? I am told he is a great one for the law. Your brother wears the white cloak, so you are heir by all the laws of Westeros."

"Stannis might well grant me Casterly Rock," said Tyrion, "but for the small matter of regicide and kinslaying. For those he would shorten me by a head, and I am short enough as I stand. But why would you think I mean to join Lord Stannis?"

"Why else would you go the Wall?"

"Stannis is at the Wall?" Tyrion rubbed at his nose. "What in seven bloody hells is Stannis doing at the Wall?"

"Shivering, I would think. It is warmer down in Dorne. Perhaps he should have sailed that way."

Tyrion was beginning to suspect that a certain freckled washerwoman knew more of the Common Speech than she pretended. "My niece Myrcella is in Dorne, as it happens. And I have half a mind to make her a queen."

Illyrio smiled as his serving men spooned out bowls of black cherries in sweet cream for them both. "What has this poor child done to you that you would wish her dead?"

"Even a kinslayer is not required to slay *all* his kin," said Tyrion, wounded. "Queen her, I said. Not kill her."

The cheesemonger spooned up cherries. "In Volantis they use a coin with a crown on one face and a death's-head on the other. Yet it is the same coin. To queen her is to kill her. Dorne might rise for Myrcella, but Dorne alone is not enough. If you are as clever as our friend insists, you know this."

Tyrion looked at the fat man with new interest. *He is right on both counts. To queen her is to kill her. And I knew that.* "Futile gestures are all that remain to me. This one would make my sister weep bitter tears, at least."

Magister Illyrio wiped sweet cream from his mouth with the back of a fat hand. "The road to Casterly Rock does not go through Dorne, my little friend. Nor does it run beneath the Wall. Yet there is such a road, I tell you."

"I am an attainted traitor, a regicide, and kinslayer." This talk of roads annoyed him. *Does he think this is a game?*

"What one king does, another may undo. In Pentos we have a prince, my friend. He presides at ball and feast and rides about the city in a palanquin of ivory and gold. Three heralds go before him with the golden scales of trade, the iron sword of war, and the silver scourge of justice. On the first day of each new year he must deflower the maid of the fields and the maid of the seas." Illyrio leaned forward, elbows on the table. "Yet should a crop fail or a war be lost, we cut his throat to appease the gods and choose a new prince from amongst the forty families."

"Remind me never to become the Prince of Pentos."

"Are your Seven Kingdoms so different? There is no peace in Westeros, no justice, no faith . . . and soon enough, no food. When men are starving and sick of fear, they look for a savior."

"They may look, but if all they find is Stannis—"

"Not Stannis. Nor Myrcella." The yellow smile widened. "*Another.* Stronger than Tommen, gentler than Stannis, with a better claim than the girl Myrcella. A savior come from across the sea to bind up the wounds of bleeding Westeros."

"Fine words." Tyrion was unimpressed. "Words are wind. Who is this bloody savior?"

"A dragon." The cheesemonger saw the look on his face at that, and laughed. "A dragon with three heads."

DAENERYS

She could hear the dead man coming up the steps. The slow, measured sound of footsteps went before him, echoing amongst the purple pillars of her hall. Daenerys Targaryen awaited him upon the ebon bench that she had made her throne. Her eyes were soft with sleep, her silver-gold hair all tousled.

"Your Grace," said Ser Barristan Selmy, the lord commander of her Queensguard, "there is no need for you to see this."

"He died for me." Dany clutched her lion pelt to her chest. Underneath, a sheer white linen tunic covered her to midthigh. She had been dreaming of a house with a red door when Missandei woke her. There had been no time to dress.

"*Khaleesi*," whispered Irri, "you must not touch the dead man. It is bad luck to touch the dead."

"Unless you killed them yourself." Jhiqui was bigger-boned than Irri, with wide hips and heavy breasts. "That is known."

"It is known," Irri agreed.

Dothraki were wise where horses were concerned, but could be utter fools about much else. *They are only girls, besides.* Her handmaids were of an age with her—women grown to look at them, with their black hair, copper skin, and almond-shaped eyes, but girls all the same. They had been given to her when she wed Khal Drogo. It was Drogo who had given her the pelt she wore, the head and hide of a *hrakkar*, the white lion of the Dothraki sea. It was too big for her and had a musty smell, but it made her feel as if her sun-and-stars was still near her.

Grey Worm appeared atop the steps first, a torch in hand. His bronze cap was crested with three spikes. Behind him followed four of his Unsullied, bearing the dead man on their shoulders. Their caps had only one spike each, and their faces showed so little they might have been cast of bronze as well. They laid the corpse down at her feet. Ser Barristan pulled back the bloodstained shroud. Grey Worm lowered the torch, so she might see.

The dead man's face was smooth and hairless, though his cheeks had been slashed open ear to ear. He had been a tall man, blue-eyed and fair of face. *Some child of Lys or Old Volantis, snatched off a ship by corsairs and sold into bondage in red Astapor.* Though his eyes were open, it was his wounds that wept. There were more wounds than she could count.

"Your Grace," Ser Barristan said, "there was a harpy drawn on the bricks in the alley where he was found . . ."

" . . . drawn in blood." Daenerys knew the way of it by now. The Sons of the Harpy did their butchery by night, and over each kill they left their mark. "Grey Worm, why was this man alone? Had he no partner?" By her command, when the Unsullied walked the streets of Meereen by night they always walked in pairs.

"My queen," replied the captain, "your servant Stalwart Shield had no duty last night. He had gone to a . . . a certain place . . . to drink, and have companionship."

"A certain place? What do you mean?"

"A house of pleasure, Your Grace."

A brothel. Half of her freedmen were from Yunkai, where the Wise Masters had been famed for training bedslaves. *The way of the seven sighs.* Brothels had sprouted up like mushrooms all over Meereen. *It is all they know. They need to survive.* Food was more costly every day, whilst the price of flesh grew cheaper. In the poorer districts between the stepped pyramids of Meereen's slaver nobility, there were brothels catering to every conceivable erotic taste, she knew. *Even so . . .* "What could a eunuch hope to find in a brothel?"

"Even those who lack a man's parts may still have a man's heart, Your Grace," said Grey Worm. "This one has been told that your servant Stalwart Shield sometimes gave coin to the women of the brothels to lie with him and hold him."

The blood of the dragon does not weep. "Stalwart Shield," she said, dry-eyed. "That was his name?"

"If it please Your Grace."

"It is a fine name." The Good Masters of Astapor had not allowed their slave soldiers even names. Some of her Unsullied reclaimed their birth names after she had freed them; others chose new names for themselves. "Is it known how many attackers fell upon Stalwart Shield?"

"This one does not know. Many."

"Six or more," said Ser Barristan. "From the look of his wounds, they swarmed him from all sides. He was found with an empty scabbard. It may be that he wounded some of his attackers."

Dany said a silent prayer that somewhere one of the Harpy's Sons was dying even now, clutching at his belly and writhing in pain. "Why did they cut open his cheeks like that?"

"Gracious queen," said Grey Worm, "his killers had forced the genitals of a goat down the throat of your servant Stalwart Shield. This one removed them before bringing him here."

They could not feed him his own genitals. The Astapori left him neither root nor stem. "The Sons grow bolder," Dany observed. Until now, they had limited their attacks to unarmed freedmen, cutting them down in the streets or breaking into their homes under the cover of darkness to murder them in their beds. "This is the first of my soldiers they have slain."

"The first," Ser Barristan warned, "but not the last."

I am still at war, Dany realized, *only now I am fighting shadows.* She had hoped for a respite from the killing, for some time to build and heal.

Shrugging off the lion pelt, she knelt beside the corpse and closed the dead man's eyes, ignoring Jhiqui's gasp. "Stalwart Shield shall not be forgotten. Have him washed and dressed for battle and bury him with cap and shield and spears."

"It shall be as Your Grace commands," said Grey Worm.

"Send men to the Temple of the Graces and ask if any man has come to the Blue Graces with a sword wound. And spread the word that we will pay good gold for the short sword of Stalwart Shield. Inquire of the butchers and the herdsmen, and learn who has been gelding goats of late." Perhaps some goatherd would confess. "Henceforth, no man of mine walks alone after dark."

"These ones shall obey."

Daenerys pushed her hair back. "Find these cowards for me. Find them, so that I might teach the Harpy's Sons what it means to wake the dragon."

Grey Worm saluted her. His Unsullied closed the shroud once more, lifted the dead man onto their shoulders, and bore him from the hall. Ser Barristan Selmy remained behind. His hair was white, and there were crow's-feet at the corners of his pale blue eyes. Yet his back was still unbent, and the years had not yet robbed him of his skill at arms. "Your Grace," he said, "I fear your eunuchs are ill suited for the tasks you set them."

Dany settled on her bench and wrapped her pelt about her shoulders once again. "The Unsullied are my finest warriors."

"Soldiers, not warriors, if it please Your Grace. They were made for the battlefield, to stand shoulder to shoulder behind their shields with their spears thrust out before them. Their training teaches them to obey, fearlessly, perfectly, without thought or hesitation . . . not to unravel secrets or ask questions."

"Would knights serve me any better?" Selmy was training knights for her, teaching the sons of slaves to fight with lance and longsword in the Westerosi fashion . . . but what good would lances do against cowards who killed from the shadows?

"Not in this," the old man admitted. "And Your Grace has no knights, save me. It will be years before the boys are ready."

"Then who, if not Unsullied? Dothraki would be even worse." Dothraki fought from horseback. Mounted men were of more use in open fields and hills than in the narrow streets and alleys of the city. Beyond Meereen's walls of many-colored brick, Dany's rule was tenuous at best. Thousands of slaves still toiled on vast estates in the hills, growing wheat and olives, herding sheep and goats, and mining salt and copper. Meereen's storehouses held ample supplies of grain, oil, olives, dried fruit, and salted meat, but the stores were dwindling. So Dany had dispatched her tiny *khalasar* to subdue the hinterlands, under the command of her three bloodriders, whilst Brown Ben Plumm took his Second Sons south to guard against Yunkish incursions.

The most crucial task of all she had entrusted to Daario Naharis, glib-tongued Daario with his gold tooth and trident beard, smiling his wicked smile through purple whiskers. Beyond the eastern hills was a range of rounded sandstone mountains, the Khyzai Pass, and Lhazar. If Daario could convince the Lhazarene to reopen the overland trade routes, grains could be brought down the river or over the hills at need . . . but the Lamb Men had no reason to love Meereen. "When the Stormcrows return from Lhazar, perhaps I can use them in the streets," she told Ser Barristan, "but until then I have only the Unsullied." Dany rose. "You must excuse me, ser. The petitioners will soon be at my gates. I must don my floppy ears and become their queen again. Summon Reznak and the Shavepate, I'll see them when I'm dressed."

"As Your Grace commands." Selmy bowed.

The Great Pyramid shouldered eight hundred feet into the sky, from its huge square base to the lofty apex where the queen kept her private chambers, surrounded by greenery and fragrant pools. As a cool blue dawn

broke over the city, Dany walked out onto the terrace. To the west sunlight blazed off the golden domes of the Temple of the Graces, and etched
deep shadows behind the stepped pyramids of the mighty. *In some of those
pyramids, the Sons of the Harpy are plotting new murders even now, and I
am powerless to stop them.*

Viserion sensed her disquiet. The white dragon lay coiled around a
pear tree, his head resting on his tail. When Dany passed his eyes came
open, two pools of molten gold. His horns were gold as well, and the
scales that ran down his back from head to tail. "You're lazy," she told
him, scratching under his jaw. His scales were hot to the touch, like armor
left too long in the sun. *Dragons are fire made flesh.* She had read that in
one of the books Ser Jorah had given her as a wedding gift. "You should
be hunting with your brothers. Have you and Drogon been fighting
again?" Her dragons were growing wild of late. Rhaegal had snapped at
Irri, and Viserion had set Reznak's *tokar* ablaze the last time the seneschal
had called. *I have left them too much to themselves, but where am I to find
the time for them?*

Viserion's tail lashed sideways, thumping the trunk of the tree so hard
that a pear came tumbling down to land at Dany's feet. His wings unfolded, and he half flew, half hopped onto the parapet. *He grows,* she
thought as he launched himself into the sky. *They are all three growing.
Soon they will be large enough to bear my weight.* Then she would fly as
Aegon the Conqueror had flown, up and up, until Meereen was so small
that she could blot it out with her thumb.

She watched Viserion climb in widening circles until he was lost to
sight beyond the muddy waters of the Skahazadhan. Only then did Dany
go back inside the pyramid, where Irri and Jhiqui were waiting to brush
the tangles from her hair and garb her as befit the Queen of Meereen, in
a Ghiscari *tokar.*

The garment was a clumsy thing, a long loose shapeless sheet that had
to be wound around her hips and under an arm and over a shoulder, its
dangling fringes carefully layered and displayed. Wound too loose, it was
like to fall off; wound too tight, it would tangle, trip, and bind. Even
wound properly, the *tokar* required its wearer to hold it in place with the
left hand. Walking in a *tokar* demanded small, mincing steps and exquisite balance, lest one tread upon those heavy trailing fringes. It was not a
garment meant for any man who had to work. The *tokar* was a *master's*
garment, a sign of wealth and power.

Dany had wanted to ban the *tokar* when she took Meereen, but her
advisors had convinced her otherwise. "The Mother of Dragons must don

the *tokar* or be forever hated," warned the Green Grace, Galazza Galare. "In the wools of Westeros or a gown of Myrish lace, Your Radiance shall forever remain a stranger amongst us, a grotesque outlander, a barbarian conqueror. Meereen's queen must be a lady of Old Ghis." Brown Ben Plumm, the captain of the Second Sons, had put it more succinctly. "Man wants to be the king o' the rabbits, he best wear a pair o' floppy ears."

The floppy ears she chose today were made of sheer white linen, with a fringe of golden tassels. With Jhiqui's help, she wound the *tokar* about herself correctly on her third attempt. Irri fetched her crown, wrought in the shape of the three-headed dragon of her House. Its coils were gold, its wings silver, its three heads ivory, onyx, and jade. Dany's neck and shoulders would be stiff and sore from the weight of it before the day was done. *A crown should not sit easy on the head.* One of her royal forebears had said that, once. *Some Aegon, but which one?* Five Aegons had ruled the Seven Kingdoms of Westeros. There would have been a sixth, but the Usurper's dogs had murdered her brother's son when he was still a babe at the breast. *If he had lived, I might have married him. Aegon would have been closer to my age than Viserys.* Dany had only been conceived when Aegon and his sister were murdered. Their father, her brother Rhaegar, perished even earlier, slain by the Usurper on the Trident. Her brother Viserys had died screaming in Vaes Dothrak with a crown of molten gold upon his head. *They will kill me too if I allow it. The knives that slew my Stalwart Shield were meant for me.*

She had not forgotten the slave children the Great Masters had nailed up along the road from Yunkai. They had numbered one hundred sixty-three, a child every mile, nailed to mileposts with one arm outstretched to point her way. After Meereen had fallen, Dany had nailed up a like number of Great Masters. Swarms of flies had attended their slow dying, and the stench had lingered long in the plaza. Yet some days she feared that she had not gone far enough. These Meereenese were a sly and stubborn people who resisted her at every turn. They had freed their slaves, yes . . . only to hire them back as servants at wages so meagre that most could scarce afford to eat. Those too old or young to be of use had been cast into the streets, along with the infirm and the crippled. And still the Great Masters gathered atop their lofty pyramids to complain of how the dragon queen had filled their noble city with hordes of unwashed beggars, thieves, and whores.

To rule Meereen I must win the Meereenese, however much I may despise them. "I am ready," she told Irri.

Reznak and Skahaz waited atop the marble steps. "Great queen," declared Reznak mo Reznak, "you are so radiant today I fear to look on you." The seneschal wore a *tokar* of maroon silk with a golden fringe. A small, damp man, he smelled as if he had bathed in perfume and spoke a bastard form of High Valyrian, much corrupted and flavored with a thick Ghiscari growl.

"You are kind to say so," Dany answered, in the same tongue.

"My queen," growled Skahaz mo Kandaq, of the shaven head. Ghiscari hair was dense and wiry; it had long been the fashion for the men of the Slaver Cities to tease it into horns and spikes and wings. By shaving, Skahaz had put old Meereen behind him to accept the new, and his kin had done the same after his example. Others followed, though whether from fear, fashion, or ambition, Dany could not say; shavepates, they were called. Skahaz was *the* Shavepate . . . and the vilest of traitors to the Sons of the Harpy and their ilk. "We were told about the eunuch."

"His name was Stalwart Shield."

"More will die unless the murderers are punished." Even with his shaven scalp, Skahaz had an odious face—a beetled brow, small eyes with heavy bags beneath them, a big nose dark with blackheads, oily skin that looked more yellow than the usual amber of Ghiscari. It was a blunt, brutal, angry face. She could only pray it was an honest one as well.

"How can I punish them when I do not know who they are?" Dany demanded of him. "Tell me that, bold Skahaz."

"You have no lack of enemies, Your Grace. You can see their pyramids from your terrace. Zhak, Hazkar, Ghazeen, Merreq, Loraq, all the old slaving families. Pahl. Pahl, most of all. A house of women now. Bitter old women with a taste for blood. Women do not forget. Women do not forgive."

No, Dany thought, *and the Usurper's dogs will learn that, when I return to Westeros.* It was true that there was blood between her and the House of Pahl. Oznak zo Pahl had been cut down by Strong Belwas in single combat. His father, commander of Meereen's city watch, had died defending the gates when Joso's Cock smashed them into splinters. Three uncles had been among the hundred sixty-three on the plaza. "How much gold have we offered for information concerning the Sons of the Harpy?" Dany asked.

"One hundred honors, if it please Your Radiance."

"One thousand honors would please us more. Make it so."

"Your Grace has not asked for my counsel," said Skahaz Shavepate, "but I say that blood must pay for blood. Take one man from each of the families I have named and kill him. The next time one of yours is slain, take two from each great House and kill them both. There will not be a third murder."

Reznak squealed in distress. "Noooo . . . gentle queen, such savagery would bring down the ire of the gods. We will find the murderers, I promise you, and when we do they will prove to be baseborn filth, you shall see."

The seneschal was as bald as Skahaz, though in his case the gods were responsible. "Should any hair be so insolent as to appear, my barber stands with razor ready," he had assured her when she raised him up. There were times when Dany wondered if that razor might not be better saved for Reznak's throat. He was a useful man, but she liked him little and trusted him less. The Undying of Qarth had told her she would be thrice betrayed. Mirri Maz Duur had been the first, Ser Jorah the second. Would Reznak be the third? The Shavepate? Daario? *Or will it be someone I would never suspect, Ser Barristan or Grey Worm or Missandei?*

"Skahaz," she told the Shavepate, "I thank you for your counsel. Reznak, see what one thousand honors may accomplish." Clutching her *tokar*, Daenerys swept past them down the broad marble stair. She took one step at a time, lest she trip over her fringe and go tumbling headfirst into court.

Missandei announced her. The little scribe had a sweet, strong voice. *"All kneel for Daenerys Stormborn, the Unburnt, Queen of Meereen, Queen of the Andals and the Rhoynar and the First Men, Khaleesi of Great Grass Sea, Breaker of Shackles, and Mother of Dragons."*

The hall had filled. Unsullied stood with their backs to the pillars, holding shields and spears, the spikes on their caps jutting upward like a row of knives. The Meereenese had gathered beneath the eastern windows. Her freedmen stood well apart from their former masters. *Until they stand together, Meereen will know no peace.* "Arise." Dany settled onto her bench. The hall rose. *That at least they do as one.*

Reznak mo Reznak had a list. Custom demanded that the queen begin with the Astapori envoy, a former slave who called himself Lord Ghael, though no one seemed to know what he was lord of.

Lord Ghael had a mouth of brown and rotten teeth and the pointed yellow face of a weasel. He also had a gift. "Cleon the Great sends these slippers as a token of his love for Daenerys Stormborn, the Mother of Dragons."

Irri slid the slippers onto Dany's feet. They were gilded leather, decorated with green freshwater pearls. *Does the butcher king believe a pair of pretty slippers will win my hand?* "King Cleon is most generous. You may thank him for his lovely gift." *Lovely, but made for a child.* Dany had small feet, yet the pointed slippers mashed her toes together.

"Great Cleon will be pleased to know they pleased you," said Lord Ghael. "His Magnificence bids me say that he stands ready to defend the Mother of Dragons from all her foes."

If he proposes again that I wed King Cleon, I'll throw a slipper at his head, Dany thought, but for once the Astapori envoy made no mention of a royal marriage. Instead he said, "The time has come for Astapor and Meereen to end the savage reign of the Wise Masters of Yunkai, who are sworn foes to all those who live in freedom. Great Cleon bids me tell you that he and his new Unsullied will soon march."

His new Unsullied are an obscene jape. "King Cleon would be wise to tend his own gardens and let the Yunkai'i tend theirs." It was not that Dany harbored any love for Yunkai. She was coming to regret leaving the Yellow City untaken after defeating its army in the field. The Wise Masters had returned to slaving as soon as she moved on, and were busy raising levies, hiring sellswords, and making alliances against her.

Cleon the self-styled Great was no better, however. The Butcher King had restored slavery to Astapor, the only change being that the former slaves were now the masters and the former masters were now the slaves.

"I am only a young girl and know little of the ways of war," she told Lord Ghael, "but we have heard that Astapor is starving. Let King Cleon feed his people before he leads them out to battle." She made a gesture of dismissal. Ghael withdrew.

"Magnificence," prompted Reznak mo Reznak, "will you hear the noble Hizdahr zo Loraq?"

Again? Dany nodded, and Hizdahr strode forth; a tall man, very slender, with flawless amber skin. He bowed on the same spot where Stalwart Shield had lain in death not long before. *I need this man,* Dany reminded herself. Hizdahr was a wealthy merchant with many friends in Meereen, and more across the seas. He had visited Volantis, Lys, and Qarth, had kin in Tolos and Elyria, and was even said to wield some influence in New Ghis, where the Yunkai'i were trying to stir up enmity against Dany and her rule.

And he was rich. Famously and fabulously rich . . .

And like to grow richer, if I grant his petition. When Dany had closed the city's fighting pits, the value of pit shares had plummeted. Hizdahr zo Loraq had grabbed them up with both hands, and now owned most of the fighting pits in Meereen.

The nobleman had wings of wiry red-black hair sprouting from his temples. They made him look as if his head were about to take flight. His long face was made even longer by a beard bound with rings of gold. His purple *tokar* was fringed with amethysts and pearls. "Your Radiance will know the reason I am here."

"Why, it must be because you have no other purpose but to plague me. How many times have I refused you?"

"Five times, Your Magnificence."

"Six now. I will not have the fighting pits reopened."

"If Your Majesty will hear my arguments . . ."

"I have. Five times. Have you brought new arguments?"

"Old arguments," Hizdahr admitted, "new words. Lovely words, and courteous, more apt to move a queen."

"It is your cause I find wanting, not your courtesies. I have heard your arguments so often I could plead your case myself. Shall I?" Dany leaned forward. "The fighting pits have been a part of Meereen since the city was founded. The combats are profoundly religious in nature, a blood sacrifice to the gods of Ghis. The *mortal art* of Ghis is not mere butchery but a display of courage, skill, and strength most pleasing to your gods. Victorious fighters are pampered and acclaimed, and the slain are honored and remembered. By reopening the pits I would show the people of Meereen that I respect their ways and customs. The pits are far-famed across the world. They draw trade to Meereen, and fill the city's coffers with coin from the ends of the earth. All men share a taste for blood, a taste the pits help slake. In that way they make Meereen more tranquil. For criminals condemned to die upon the sands, the pits represent a judgment by battle, a last chance for a man to prove his innocence." She leaned back again, with a toss of her head. "There. How have I done?"

"Your Radiance has stated the case much better than I could have hoped to do myself. I see that you are eloquent as well as beautiful. I am quite persuaded."

She had to laugh. "Ah, but I am not."

"Your Magnificence," whispered Reznak mo Reznak in her ear, "it is customary for the city to claim one-tenth of all the profits from the fighting pits, after expenses, as a tax. That coin might be put to many noble uses."

"It might . . . though if we *were* to reopen the pits, we should take our tenth *before* expenses. I am only a young girl and know little of such matters, but I dwelt with Xaro Xhoan Daxos long enough to learn that much.

Hizdahr, if you could marshal armies as you marshal arguments, you could conquer the world . . . but my answer is still *no*. For the sixth time."

"The queen has spoken." He bowed again, as deeply as before. His pearls and amethysts clattered softly against the marble floor. A very limber man was Hizdahr zo Loraq.

He might be handsome, but for that silly hair. Reznak and the Green Grace had been urging Dany to take a Meereenese noble for her husband, to reconcile the city to her rule. Hizdahr zo Loraq might be worth a careful look. *Sooner him than Skahaz.* The Shavepate had offered to set aside his wife for her, but the notion made her shudder. Hizdahr at least knew how to smile.

"Magnificence," said Reznak, consulting his list, "the noble Grazdan zo Galare would address you. Will you hear him?"

"It would be my pleasure," said Dany, admiring the glimmer of the gold and the sheen of the green pearls on Cleon's slippers while doing her best to ignore the pinching in her toes. Grazdan, she had been forewarned, was a cousin of the Green Grace, whose support she had found invaluable. The priestess was a voice for peace, acceptance, and obedience to lawful authority. *I can give her cousin a respectful hearing, whatever he desires.*

What he desired turned out to be gold. Dany had refused to compensate any of the Great Masters for the value of their slaves, but the Meereenese kept devising other ways to squeeze coin from her. The noble Grazdan had once owned a slave woman who was a very fine weaver, it seemed; the fruits of her loom were greatly valued, not only in Meereen, but in New Ghis and Astapor and Qarth. When this woman had grown old, Grazdan had purchased half a dozen young girls and commanded the crone to instruct them in the secrets of her craft. The old woman was dead now. The young ones, freed, had opened a shop by the harbor wall to sell their weavings. Grazdan zo Galare asked that he be granted a portion of their earnings. "They owe their skill to me," he insisted. "I plucked them from the auction block and gave them to the loom."

Dany listened quietly, her face still. When he was done, she said, "What was the name of the old weaver?"

"The slave?" Grazdan shifted his weight, frowning. "She was . . . Elza, it might have been. Or Ella. It was six years ago she died. I have owned so many slaves, Your Grace."

"Let us say Elza. Here is our ruling. From the girls, you shall have nothing. It was Elza who taught them weaving, not you. From you, the girls shall have a new loom, the finest coin can buy. That is for forgetting the name of the old woman."

Reznak would have summoned another *tokar* next, but Dany insisted that he call upon a freedman. Thereafter she alternated between the former masters and the former slaves. Many and more of the matters brought before her involved redress. Meereen had been sacked savagely after its fall. The stepped pyramids of the mighty had been spared the worst of the ravages, but the humbler parts of the city had been given over to an orgy of looting and killing as the city's slaves rose up and the starving hordes who had followed her from Yunkai and Astapor poured through the broken gates. Her Unsullied had finally restored order, but the sack left a plague of problems in its wake. And so they came to see the queen.

A rich woman came, whose husband and sons had died defending the city walls. During the sack she had fled to her brother in fear. When she returned, she found her house had been turned into a brothel. The whores had bedecked themselves in her jewels and clothes. She wanted her house back, and her jewels. "They can keep the clothes," she allowed. Dany granted her the jewels but ruled the house was lost when she abandoned it.

A former slave came, to accuse a certain noble of the Zhak. The man had recently taken to wife a freedwoman who had been the noble's bedwarmer before the city fell. The noble had taken her maidenhood, used her for his pleasure, and gotten her with child. Her new husband wanted the noble gelded for the crime of rape, and he wanted a purse of gold as well, to pay him for raising the noble's bastard as his own. Dany granted him the gold, but not the gelding. "When he lay with her, your wife was his property, to do with as he would. By law, there was no rape." Her decision did not please him, she could see, but if she gelded every man who ever forced a bedslave, she would soon rule a city of eunuchs.

A boy came, younger than Dany, slight and scarred, dressed up in a frayed grey *tokar* trailing silver fringe. His voice broke when he told of how two of his father's household slaves had risen up the night the gate broke. One had slain his father, the other his elder brother. Both had raped his mother before killing her as well. The boy had escaped with no more than the scar upon his face, but one of the murderers was still living in his father's house, and the other had joined the queen's soldiers as one of the Mother's Men. He wanted them both hanged.

I am queen over a city built on dust and death. Dany had no choice but to deny him. She had declared a blanket pardon for all crimes committed during the sack. Nor would she punish slaves for rising up against their masters.

When she told him, the boy rushed at her, but his feet tangled in his *tokar* and he went sprawling headlong on the purple marble. Strong Belwas was on him at once. The huge brown eunuch yanked him up one-handed and shook him like a mastiff with a rat. "Enough, Belwas," Dany called. "Release him." To the boy she said, "Treasure that *tokar*, for it saved your life. You are only a boy, so we will forget what happened here. You should do the same." But as he left the boy looked back over his shoulder, and when she saw his eyes Dany thought, *The Harpy has another Son.*

By midday Daenerys was feeling the weight of the crown upon her head, and the hardness of the bench beneath her. With so many still waiting on her pleasure, she did not stop to eat. Instead she dispatched Jhiqui to the kitchens for a platter of flatbread, olives, figs, and cheese. She nibbled whilst she listened, and sipped from a cup of watered wine. The figs were fine, the olives even finer, but the wine left a tart metallic aftertaste in her mouth. The small pale yellow grapes native to these regions produced a notably inferior vintage. *We shall have no trade in wine.* Besides, the Great Masters had burned the best arbors along with the olive trees.

In the afternoon a sculptor came, proposing to replace the head of the great bronze harpy in the Plaza of Purification with one cast in Dany's image. She denied him with as much courtesy as she could muster. A pike of unprecedented size had been caught in the Skahazadhan, and the fisherman wished to give it to the queen. She admired the fish extravagantly, rewarded the fisherman with a purse of silver, and sent the pike to her kitchens. A coppersmith had fashioned her a suit of burnished rings to wear to war. She accepted it with fulsome thanks; it was lovely to behold, and all that burnished copper would flash prettily in the sun, though if actual battle threatened, she would sooner be clad in steel. Even a young girl who knew nothing of the ways of war knew *that.*

The slippers the Butcher King had sent her had grown too uncomfortable. Dany kicked them off and sat with one foot tucked beneath her and the other swinging back and forth. It was not a very regal pose, but she was tired of being regal. The crown had given her a headache, and her buttocks had gone to sleep. "Ser Barristan," she called, "I know what quality a king needs most."

"Courage, Your Grace?"

"Cheeks like iron," she teased. "All I do is sit."

"Your Grace takes too much on herself. You should allow your councillors to shoulder more of your burdens."

"I have too many councillors and too few cushions." Dany turned to Reznak. "How many more?"

"Three-and-twenty, if it please Your Magnificence. With as many claims." The seneschal consulted some papers. "One calf and three goats. The rest will be sheep or lambs, no doubt."

"Three-and-twenty." Dany sighed. "My dragons have developed a prodigious taste for mutton since we began to pay the shepherds for their kills. Have these claims been proven?"

"Some men have brought burnt bones."

"Men make fires. Men cook mutton. Burnt bones prove nothing. Brown Ben says there are red wolves in the hills outside the city, and jackals and wild dogs. Must we pay good silver for every lamb that goes astray between Yunkai and the Skahazadhan?"

"No, Magnificence." Reznak bowed. "Shall I send these rascals away, or will you want them scourged?"

Daenerys shifted on the bench. "No man should ever fear to come to me." Some claims were false, she did not doubt, but more were genuine. Her dragons had grown too large to be content with rats and cats and dogs. *The more they eat, the larger they will grow*, Ser Barristan had warned her, *and the larger they grow, the more they'll eat*. Drogon especially ranged far afield and could easily devour a sheep a day. "Pay them for the value of their animals," she told Reznak, "but henceforth claimants must present themselves at the Temple of the Graces and swear a holy oath before the gods of Ghis."

"It shall be done." Reznak turned to the petitioners. "Her Magnificence the Queen has consented to compensate each of you for the animals you have lost," he told them in the Ghiscari tongue. "Present yourselves to my factors on the morrow, and you shall be paid in coin or kind, as you prefer."

The pronouncement was received in sullen silence. *You would think they might be happier*, Dany thought. *They have what they came for. Is there no way to please these people?*

One man lingered behind as the rest were filing out—a squat man with a windburnt face, shabbily dressed. His hair was a cap of coarse red-black wire cropped about his ears, and in one hand he held a sad cloth sack. He stood with his head down, gazing at the marble floor as if he had quite forgotten where he was. *And what does this one want?* Dany wondered.

"*All kneel for Daenerys Stormborn, the Unburnt, Queen of Meereen,*

Queen of the Andals and the Rhoynar and the First Men, Khaleesi of Great Grass Sea, Breaker of Shackles, and Mother of Dragons," cried Missandei in her high, sweet voice.

As Dany stood, her *tokar* began to slip. She caught it and tugged it back in place. "You with the sack," she called, "did you wish to speak with us? You may approach."

When he raised his head, his eyes were red and raw as open sores. Dany glimpsed Ser Barristan sliding closer, a white shadow at her side. The man approached in a stumbling shuffle, one step and then another, clutching his sack. *Is he drunk, or ill?* she wondered. There was dirt beneath his cracked yellow fingernails.

"What is it?" Dany asked. "Do you have some grievance to lay before us, some petition? What would you have of us?"

His tongue flicked nervously over chapped, cracked lips. "I . . . I brought . . ."

"Bones?" she said, impatiently. "Burnt bones?"

He lifted the sack, and spilled its contents on the marble.

Bones they were, broken bones and blackened. The longer ones had been cracked open for their marrow.

"It were the black one," the man said, in a Ghiscari growl, "the winged shadow. He come down from the sky and . . . and . . ."

No. Dany shivered. *No, no, oh no.*

"Are you deaf, fool?" Reznak mo Reznak demanded of the man. "Did you not hear my pronouncement? See my factors on the morrow, and you shall be paid for your sheep."

"Reznak," Ser Barristan said quietly, "hold your tongue and open your eyes. Those are no sheep bones."

No, Dany thought, *those are the bones of a child.*

JON

The white wolf raced through a black wood, beneath a pale cliff as tall as the sky. The moon ran with him, slipping through a tangle of bare branches overhead, across the starry sky.

"Snow," the moon murmured. The wolf made no answer. Snow crunched beneath his paws. The wind sighed through the trees.

Far off, he could hear his packmates calling to him, like to like. They were hunting too. A wild rain lashed down upon his black brother as he tore at the flesh of an enormous goat, washing the blood from his side where the goat's long horn had raked him. In another place, his little sister lifted her head to sing to the moon, and a hundred small grey cousins broke off their hunt to sing with her. The hills were warmer where they were, and full of food. Many a night his sister's pack gorged on the flesh of sheep and cows and horses, the prey of men, and sometimes even on the flesh of man himself.

"Snow," the moon called down again, cackling. The white wolf padded along the man trail beneath the icy cliff. The taste of blood was on his tongue, and his ears rang to the song of the hundred cousins. Once they had been six, five whimpering blind in the snow beside their dead mother, sucking cool milk from her hard dead nipples whilst he crawled off alone. Four remained . . . and one the white wolf could no longer sense.

"Snow," the moon insisted.

The white wolf ran from it, racing toward the cave of night where the sun had hidden, his breath frosting in the air. On starless nights the great cliff was as black as stone, a darkness towering high above the wide world, but when the moon came out it shimmered pale and icy as a frozen stream. The wolf's pelt was thick and shaggy, but when the wind blew along the ice no fur could keep the chill out. On the other side the wind was colder still, the wolf sensed. That was where his brother was, the grey brother who smelled of summer.

"Snow." An icicle tumbled from a branch. The white wolf turned and bared his teeth. "*Snow!*" His fur rose bristling, as the woods dissolved around him. "*Snow, snow, snow!*" He heard the beat of wings. Through the gloom a raven flew.

It landed on Jon Snow's chest with a *thump* and a scrabbling of claws. "*SNOW!*" it screamed into his face.

"I hear you." The room was dim, his pallet hard. Grey light leaked through the shutters, promising another bleak cold day. "Is this how you woke Mormont? Get your feathers out of my face." Jon wriggled an arm out from under his blankets to shoo the raven off. It was a big bird, old and bold and scruffy, utterly without fear. "*Snow,*" it cried, flapping to his bedpost. "*Snow, snow.*" Jon filled his fist with a pillow and let fly, but the bird took to the air. The pillow struck the wall and burst, scattering stuffing everywhere just as Dolorous Edd Tollett poked his head through the door. "Beg pardon," he said, ignoring the flurry of feathers, "shall I fetch m'lord some breakfast?"

"*Corn,*" cried the raven. "*Corn, corn.*"

"Roast raven," Jon suggested. "And half a pint of ale." Having a steward fetch and serve for him still felt strange; not long ago, it would have been him fetching breakfast for Lord Commander Mormont.

"Three corns and one roast raven," said Dolorous Edd. "Very good, m'lord, only Hobb's made boiled eggs, black sausage, and apples stewed with prunes. The apples stewed with prunes are excellent, except for the prunes. I won't eat prunes myself. Well, there was one time when Hobb chopped them up with chestnuts and carrots and hid them in a hen. Never trust a cook, my lord. They'll prune you when you least expect it."

"Later." Breakfast could wait; Stannis could not. "Any trouble from the stockades last night?"

"Not since you put guards on the guards, m'lord."

"Good." A thousand wildlings had been penned up beyond the Wall, the captives Stannis Baratheon had taken when his knights had smashed Mance Rayder's patchwork host. Many of the prisoners were women, and some of the guards had been sneaking them out to warm their beds. King's men, queen's men, it did not seem to matter; a few black brothers had tried the same thing. Men were men, and these were the only women for a thousand leagues.

"Two more wildlings turned up to surrender," Edd went on. "A mother with a girl clinging to her skirts. She had a boy babe too, all swaddled up in fur, but he was dead."

"*Dead*," said the raven. It was one of the bird's favorite words. "*Dead, dead, dead.*"

They had free folk drifting in most every night, starved half-frozen creatures who had run from the battle beneath the Wall only to crawl back when they realized there was no safe place to run to. "Was the mother questioned?" Jon asked. Stannis Baratheon had smashed Mance Rayder's host and made the King-Beyond-the-Wall his captive . . . but the wildlings were still out there, the Weeper and Tormund Giantsbane and thousands more.

"Aye, m'lord," said Edd, "but all she knows is that she ran off during the battle and hid in the woods after. We filled her full of porridge, sent her to the pens, and burned the babe."

Burning dead children had ceased to trouble Jon Snow; live ones were another matter. *Two kings to wake the dragon. The father first and then the son, so both die kings.* The words had been murmured by one of the queen's men as Maester Aemon had cleaned his wounds. Jon had tried to dismiss them as his fever talking. Aemon had demurred. "There is power in a king's blood," the old maester had warned, "and better men than Stannis have done worse things than this." *The king can be harsh and unforgiving, aye, but a babe still on the breast? Only a monster would give a living child to the flames.*

Jon pissed in darkness, filling his chamber pot as the Old Bear's raven muttered complaints. The wolf dreams had been growing stronger, and he found himself remembering them even when awake. *Ghost knows that Grey Wind is dead.* Robb had died at the Twins, betrayed by men he'd believed his friends, and his wolf had perished with him. Bran and Rickon had been murdered too, beheaded at the behest of Theon Greyjoy, who had once been their lord father's ward . . . but if dreams did not lie, their direwolves had escaped. At Queenscrown, one had come out of the darkness to save Jon's life. *Summer, it had to be. His fur was grey, and Shaggydog is black.* He wondered if some part of his dead brothers lived on inside their wolves.

He filled his basin from the flagon of water beside his bed, washed his face and hands, donned a clean set of black woolens, laced up a black leather jerkin, and pulled on a pair of well-worn boots. Mormont's raven watched with shrewd black eyes, then fluttered to the window. "Do you take me for your thrall?" When Jon folded back the window with its thick diamond-shaped panes of yellow glass, the chill of the morning hit him in the face. He took a breath to clear away the cobwebs of the night as the raven flapped away. *That bird is too clever by half.* It had been the Old Bear's companion for long years, but that had not stopped it from eating Mormont's face once he died.

Outside his bedchamber a flight of steps descended to a larger room furnished with a scarred pinewood table and a dozen oak-and-leather chairs. With Stannis in the King's Tower and the Lord Commander's Tower burned to a shell, Jon had established himself in Donal Noye's modest rooms behind the armory. In time, no doubt, he would need larger quarters, but for the moment these would serve whilst he accustomed himself to command.

The grant that the king had presented him for signature was on the table beneath a silver drinking cup that had once been Donal Noye's. The one-armed smith had left few personal effects: the cup, six pennies and a copper star, a niello brooch with a broken clasp, a musty brocade doublet that bore the stag of Storm's End. *His treasures were his tools, and the swords and knives he made. His life was at the forge.* Jon moved the cup aside and read the parchment once again. *If I put my seal to this, I will forever be remembered as the lord commander who gave away the Wall,* he thought, *but if I should refuse . . .*

Stannis Baratheon was proving to be a prickly guest, and a restless one. He had ridden down the kingsroad almost as far as Queenscrown, prowled through the empty hovels of Mole's Town, inspected the ruined forts at Queensgate and Oakenshield. Each night he walked atop the Wall with Lady Melisandre, and during the days he visited the stockades, picking captives out for the red woman to question. *He does not like to be balked.* This would not be a pleasant morning, Jon feared.

From the armory came a clatter of shields and swords, as the latest lot of boys and raw recruits armed themselves. He could hear the voice of Iron Emmett telling them to be quick about it. Cotter Pyke had not been pleased to lose him, but the young ranger had a gift for training men. *He loves to fight, and he'll teach his boys to love it too.* Or so he hoped.

Jon's cloak hung on a peg by the door, his sword belt on another. He donned them both and made his way to the armory. The rug where Ghost slept was empty, he saw. Two guardsmen stood inside the doors, clad in black cloaks and iron halfhelms, spears in their hands. "Will m'lord be wanting a tail?" asked Garse.

"I think I can find the King's Tower by myself." Jon hated having guards trailing after him everywhere he went. It made him feel like a mother duck leading a procession of ducklings.

Iron Emmett's lads were well at it in the yard, blunted swords slamming into shields and ringing against one another. Jon stopped to watch a moment as Horse pressed Hop-Robin back toward the well. Horse had the makings of a good fighter, he decided. He was strong and getting stronger, and his instincts were sound. Hop-Robin was another tale. His clubfoot was bad enough, but he was afraid of getting hit as well. *Perhaps we can make a steward of him.* The fight ended abruptly, with Hop-Robin on the ground.

"Well fought," Jon said to Horse, "but you drop your shield too low when pressing an attack. You will want to correct that, or it is like to get you killed."

"Yes, m'lord. I'll keep it higher next time." Horse pulled Hop-Robin to his feet, and the smaller boy made a clumsy bow.

A few of Stannis's knights were sparring on the far side of the yard. *King's men in one corner and queen's men in another,* Jon did not fail to note, *but only a few. It's too cold for most of them.* As he strode past them, a booming voice called after him. "BOY! YOU THERE! *BOY!*"

Boy was not the worst of the things that Jon Snow had been called since being chosen lord commander. He ignored it.

"*Snow,*" the voice insisted, "*Lord Commander.*"

This time he stopped. "Ser?"

The knight overtopped him by six inches. "A man who bears Valyrian steel should use it for more than scratching his arse."

Jon had seen this one about the castle—a knight of great renown, to hear him tell it. During the battle beneath the Wall, Ser Godry Farring had slain a fleeing giant, pounding after him on horseback and driving a lance through his back, then dismounting to hack off the creature's pitiful small head. The queen's men had taken to calling him Godry the Giantslayer.

Jon remembered Ygritte, crying. *I am the last of the giants.* "I use Longclaw when I must, ser."

"How well, though?" Ser Godry drew his own blade. "Show us. I promise not to hurt you, lad."

How kind of you. "Some other time, ser. I fear that I have other duties just now."

"You fear. I see that." Ser Godry grinned at his friends. "He fears," he repeated, for the slow ones.

"You will excuse me." Jon showed them his back.

Castle Black seemed a bleak and forlorn place in the pale dawn light. *My command,* Jon Snow reflected ruefully, *as much a ruin as it is a strong-*

hold. The Lord Commander's Tower was a shell, the Common Hall a pile of blackened timbers, and Hardin's Tower looked as if the next gust of wind would knock it over . . . though it had looked that way for years. Behind them rose the Wall: immense, forbidding, frigid, acrawl with builders pushing up a new switchback stair to join the remnants of the old. They worked from dawn to dusk. Without the stair, there was no way to reach the top of the Wall save by winch. That would not serve if the wildlings should attack again.

Above the King's Tower the great golden battle standard of House Baratheon cracked like a whip from the roof where Jon Snow had prowled with bow in hand not long ago, slaying Thenns and free folk beside Satin and Deaf Dick Follard. Two queen's men stood shivering on the steps, their hands tucked up into their armpits and their spears leaning against the door. "Those cloth gloves will never serve," Jon told them. "See Bowen Marsh on the morrow, and he'll give you each a pair of leather gloves lined with fur."

"We will, m'lord, and thank you," said the older guard.

"That's if our bloody hands aren't froze off," the younger added, his breath a pale mist. "I used to think that it got cold up in the Dornish Marches. What did I know?"

Nothing, thought Jon Snow, *the same as me.*

Halfway up the winding steps, he came upon Samwell Tarly, headed down. "Are you coming from the king?" Jon asked him.

"Maester Aemon sent me with a letter."

"I see." Some lords trusted their maesters to read their letters and convey the contents, but Stannis insisted on breaking the seals himself. "How did Stannis take it?"

"Not happily, by his face." Sam dropped his voice to a whisper. "I am not supposed to speak of it."

"Then don't." Jon wondered which of his father's bannermen had refused King Stannis homage this time. *He was quick enough to spread the word when Karhold declared for him.* "How are you and your longbow getting on?"

"I found a good book about archery." Sam frowned. "Doing it is harder than reading about it, though. I get blisters."

"Keep at it. We may need your bow on the Wall if the Others turn up some dark night."

"Oh, I hope not."

More guards stood outside the king's solar. "No arms are allowed in His Grace's presence, my lord," their serjeant said. "I'll need that sword. Your knives as well." It would do no good to protest, Jon knew. He handed them his weaponry.

Within the solar the air was warm. Lady Melisandre was seated near the fire, her ruby glimmering against the pale skin of her throat. Ygritte had been kissed by fire; the red priestess *was* fire, and her hair was blood and flame. Stannis stood behind the rough-hewn table where the Old Bear had once been wont to sit and take his meals. Covering the table was a large map of the north, painted on a ragged piece of hide. A tallow candle weighed down one end of it, a steel gauntlet the other.

The king wore lambswool breeches and a quilted doublet, yet somehow he looked as stiff and uncomfortable as if he had been clad in plate and mail. His skin was pale leather, his beard cropped so short that it might have been painted on. A fringe about his temples was all that remained of his black hair. In his hand was a parchment with a broken seal of dark green wax.

Jon took a knee. The king frowned at him, and rattled the parchment angrily. "Rise. Tell me, who is *Lyanna Mormont?*"

"One of Lady Maege's daughters, Sire. The youngest. She was named for my lord father's sister."

"To curry your lord father's favor, I don't doubt. I know how that game is played. How old is this wretched girl child?"

Jon had to think a moment. "Ten. Or near enough to make no matter. Might I know how she has offended Your Grace?"

Stannis read from the letter. *"Bear Island knows no king but the King in the North, whose name is STARK.* A girl of ten, you say, and she presumes to scold her lawful king." His close-cropped beard lay like a shadow over his hollow cheeks. "See that you keep these tidings to yourself, Lord Snow. Karhold is with me, that is all the men need know. I will not have your brothers trading tales of how this child spat on me."

"As you command, Sire." Maege Mormont had ridden south with Robb, Jon knew. Her eldest daughter had joined the Young Wolf's host as well. Even if both of them had died, however, Lady Maege had other daughters, some with children of their own. Had they gone with Robb as well? Surely Lady Maege would have left at least one of the older girls behind as castellan. He did not understand why Lyanna should be writing Stannis, and could not help but wonder if the girl's answer might have been different if the letter had been sealed with a direwolf instead of a crowned stag, and signed by Jon Stark, Lord of Winterfell. *It is too late for such misgivings. You made your choice.*

"Two score ravens were sent out," the king complained, "yet we get no response but silence and defiance. Homage is the duty every leal subject owes his king. Yet your father's bannermen all turn their back on me, save the Karstarks. Is Arnolf Karstark the only man of honor in the north?"

Arnolf Karstark was the late Lord Rickard's uncle. He had been made the castellan of Karhold when his nephew and his sons went south with Robb, and he had been the first to respond to King Stannis's call for homage, with a raven declaring his allegiance. *The Karstarks have no other choice*, Jon might have said. Rickard Karstark had betrayed the direwolf and spilled the blood of lions. The stag was Karhold's only hope. "In times as confused as these, even men of honor must wonder where their duty lies. Your Grace is not the only king in the realm demanding homage."

Lady Melisandre stirred. "Tell me, Lord Snow . . . where were these other kings when the wild people stormed your Wall?"

"A thousand leagues away and deaf to our need," Jon replied. "I have not forgotten that, my lady. Nor will I. But my father's bannermen have wives and children to protect, and smallfolk who will die should they choose wrongly. His Grace asks much of them. Give them time, and you will have your answers."

"Answers such as this?" Stannis crushed Lyanna's letter in his fist.

"Even in the north men fear the wroth of Tywin Lannister. Boltons make bad enemies as well. It is not happenstance that put a flayed man on their banners. They north rode with Robb, bled with him, died for him. They have supped on grief and death, and now you come to offer them another serving. Do you blame them if they hang back? Forgive me, Your Grace, but some will look at you and see only another doomed pretender."

"If His Grace is doomed, your realm is doomed as well," said Lady Melisandre. "Remember that, Lord Snow. It is the one true king of Westeros who stands before you."

Jon kept his face a mask. "As you say, my lady."

Stannis snorted. "You spend your words as if every one were a golden dragon. I wonder, how much gold do you have laid by?"

"Gold?" *Are those the dragons the red woman means to wake? Dragons made of gold?* "Such taxes as we collect are paid in kind, Your Grace. The Watch is rich in turnips but poor in coin."

"Turnips are not like to appease Salladhor Saan. I require gold or silver."

"For that, you need White Harbor. The city cannot compare to Oldtown or King's Landing, but it is still a thriving port. Lord Manderly is the richest of my lord father's bannermen."

"Lord Too-Fat-to-Sit-a-Horse." The letter that Lord Wyman Manderly had sent back from White Harbor had spoken of his age and infirmity, and little more. Stannis had commanded Jon not to speak of that one either.

"Perhaps his lordship would fancy a wildling wife," said Lady Melisandre. "Is this fat man married, Lord Snow?"

"His lady wife is long dead. Lord Wyman has two grown sons, and grandchildren by the elder. And he *is* too fat to sit a horse, thirty stone at least. Val would never have him."

"Just once you might try to give me an answer that would please me, Lord Snow," the king grumbled.

"I would hope the truth would please you, Sire. Your men call Val a princess, but to the free folk she is only the sister of their king's dead wife. If you force her to marry a man she does not want, she is like to slit his throat on their wedding night. Even if she accepts her husband, that does not mean the wildlings will follow him, or you. The only man who can bind them to your cause is Mance Rayder."

"I know that," Stannis said, unhappily. "I have spent hours speaking with the man. He knows much and more of our true enemy, and there is cunning in him, I'll grant you. Even if he were to renounce his kingship, though, the man remains an oathbreaker. Suffer one deserter to live, and you encourage others to desert. No. Laws should be made of iron, not of pudding. Mance Rayder's life is forfeit by every law of the Seven Kingdoms."

"The law ends at the Wall, Your Grace. You could make good use of Mance."

"I mean to. I'll *burn* him, and the north will see how I deal with turncloaks and traitors. I have other men to lead the wildlings. And I have Rayder's son, do not forget. Once the father dies, his whelp will be the King-Beyond-the-Wall."

"Your Grace is mistaken." *You know nothing, Jon Snow,* Ygritte used to say, but he had learned. "The babe is no more a prince than Val is a princess. You do not become King-Beyond-the-Wall because your father was."

"Good," said Stannis, "for I will suffer no other kings in Westeros. Have you signed the grant?"

"No, Your Grace." *And now it comes.* Jon closed his burned fingers and opened them again. "You ask too much."

"*Ask?* I *asked* you to be Lord of Winterfell and Warden of the North. I *require* these castles."

"We have ceded you the Nightfort."

"Rats and ruins. It is a niggard's gift that costs the giver nothing. Your own man Yarwyck says it will be half a year before the castle can be made fit for habitation."

"The other forts are no better."

"I know that. It makes no matter. They are all we have. There are nineteen forts along the Wall, and you have men in only three of them. I mean to have every one of them garrisoned again before the year is out."

"I have no quarrel with that, Sire, but it is being said that you also mean to grant these castles to your knights and lords, to hold as their own seats as vassals to Your Grace."

"Kings are expected to be open-handed to their followers. Did Lord Eddard teach his bastard nothing? Many of my knights and lords abandoned rich lands and stout castles in the south. Should their loyalty go unrewarded?"

"If Your Grace wishes to lose all of my lord father's bannermen, there is no more certain way than by giving northern halls to southron lords."

"How can I lose men I do not have? I had hoped to bestow Winterfell on a northman, you may recall. A son of Eddard Stark. He threw my offer in my face." Stannis Baratheon with a grievance was like a mastiff with a bone; he gnawed it down to splinters.

"By right Winterfell should go to my sister Sansa."

"Lady Lannister, you mean? Are you so eager to see the Imp perched on your father's seat? I promise you, that will not happen whilst I live, Lord Snow."

Jon knew better than to press the point. "Sire, some claim that you mean to grant lands and castles to Rattleshirt and the Magnar of Thenn."

"Who told you that?"

The talk was all over Castle Black. "If you must know, I had the tale from Gilly."

"Who is *Gilly*?"

"The wet nurse," said Lady Melisandre. "Your Grace gave her freedom of the castle."

"Not for running tales. She's wanted for her teats, not for her tongue. I'll have more milk from her, and fewer *messages*."

"Castle Black needs no useless mouths," Jon agreed. "I am sending Gilly south on the next ship out of Eastwatch."

Melisandre touched the ruby at her neck. "Gilly is giving suck to Dalla's son as well as her own. It seems cruel of you to part our little prince from his milk brother, my lord."

Careful now, careful. "Mother's milk is all they share. Gilly's son is larger and more robust. He kicks the prince and pinches him, and shoves him from the breast. Craster was his father, a cruel man and greedy, and blood tells."

The king was confused. "I thought the wet nurse was this man Craster's *daughter?*"

"Wife and daughter both, Your Grace. Craster married all his daughters. Gilly's boy was the fruit of their union."

"Her own *father* got this child on her?" Stannis sounded shocked. "We are well rid of her, then. I will not suffer such abominations here. This is not King's Landing."

"I can find another wet nurse. If there's none amongst the wildlings, I will send to the mountain clans. Until such time, goat's milk should suffice for the boy, if it please Your Grace."

"Poor fare for a prince . . . but better than whore's milk, aye." Stannis drummed his fingers on the map. "If we may return to the matter of these forts . . ."

"Your Grace," said Jon, with chilly courtesy, "I have housed your men and fed them, at dire cost to our winter stores. I have clothed them so they would not freeze."

Stannis was not appeased. "Aye, you've shared your salt pork and porridge, and you've thrown us some black rags to keep us warm. Rags the wildlings would have taken off your corpses if I had not come north."

Jon ignored that. "I have given you fodder for your horses, and once the stair is done I will lend you builders to restore the Nightfort. I have even agreed to allow you to settle wildlings on the Gift, which was given to the Night's Watch in perpetuity."

"You offer me empty lands and desolations, yet deny me the castles I require to reward my lords and bannermen."

"The Night's Watch built those castles . . ."

"And the Night's Watch abandoned them."

" . . . to defend the Wall," Jon finished stubbornly, "not as seats for southron lords. The stones of those forts are mortared with the blood and bones of my brothers, long dead. I cannot give them to you."

"Cannot or will not?" The cords in the king's neck stood out sharp as swords. "I offered you a name."

"I have a name, Your Grace."

"Snow. Was ever a name more ill-omened?" Stannis touched his sword hilt. "Just who do you imagine that you are?"

"The watcher on the walls. The sword in the darkness."

"Don't prate your words at me." Stannis drew the blade he called Lightbringer. "*Here* is your sword in the darkness." Light rippled up and down the blade, now red, now yellow, now orange, painting the king's face in harsh, bright hues. "Even a green boy should be able to see that. Are you blind?"

"No, Sire. I agree these castles must be garrisoned—"

"The boy commander agrees. How fortunate."

"—by the Night's Watch."

"You do not have the men."

"Then give me men, Sire. I will provide officers for each of the abandoned forts, seasoned commanders who know the Wall and the lands beyond, and how best to survive the coming winter. In return for all we've given you, grant me the men to fill out the garrisons. Men-at-arms, crossbowmen, raw boys. I will even take your wounded and infirm."

Stannis stared at him incredulously, then gave a bark of laughter. "You are bold enough, Snow, I grant you that, but you're mad if you think my men will take the black."

"They can wear any color cloak they choose, so long as they obey my officers as they would your own."

The king was unmoved. "I have knights and lords in my service, scions of noble Houses old in honor. They cannot be expected to serve under poachers, peasants, and murderers."

Or bastards, Sire? "Your own Hand is a smuggler."

"Was a smuggler. I shortened his fingers for that. They tell me that you are the nine-hundred-ninety-eighth man to command the Night's Watch, Lord Snow. What do you think the nine-hundred-ninety-ninth might say about these castles? The sight of your head on a spike might inspire him to be more helpful." The king laid his bright blade down on the map, along the Wall, its steel shimmering like sunlight on water. "You are only lord commander by my sufferance. You would do well to remember that."

"I am lord commander because my brothers chose me." There were mornings when Jon Snow did not quite believe it himself, when he woke up thinking surely this was some mad dream. *It's like putting on new clothes,* Sam had told him. *The fit feels strange at first, but once you've worn them for a while you get to feeling comfortable.*

"Alliser Thorne complains about the manner of your choosing, and I cannot say he does not have a grievance." The map lay between them like a battleground, drenched by the colors of the glowing sword. "The count was done by a *blind man* with your fat friend by his elbow. And Slynt names you a turncloak."

And who would know one better than Slynt? "A turncloak would tell you what you wished to hear and betray you later. Your Grace knows that I was fairly chosen. My father always said you were a just man." *Just but harsh* had been Lord Eddard's exact words, but Jon did not think it would be wise to share that.

"Lord Eddard was no friend to me, but he was not without some sense. He would have given me these castles."

Never. "I cannot speak to what my father might have done. I took an oath, Your Grace. The Wall is mine."

"For now. We will see how well you hold it." Stannis pointed at him. "Keep your ruins, as they mean so much to you. I promise you, though, if any remain empty when the year is out, I will take them with your leave or without it. And if even one should fall to the foe, your head will soon follow. Now get out."

Lady Melisandre rose from her place near the hearth. "With your leave, Sire, I will show Lord Snow back to his chambers."

"Why? He knows the way." Stannis waved them both away. "Do what you will. Devan, food. Boiled eggs and lemon water."

After the warmth of the king's solar, the turnpike stair felt bone-chillingly cold. "Wind's rising, m'lady," the serjeant warned Melisandre as he handed Jon back his weapons. "You might want a warmer cloak."

"I have my faith to warm me." The red woman walked beside Jon down the steps. "His Grace is growing fond of you."

"I can tell. He only threatened to behead me twice."

Melisandre laughed. "It is his silences you should fear, not his words." As they stepped out into the yard, the wind filled Jon's cloak and sent it flapping against her. The red priestess brushed the black wool aside and slipped her arm through his. "It may be that you are not wrong about the wildling king. I shall pray for the Lord of Light to send me guidance. When I gaze into the flames, I can see through stone and earth, and find the truth within men's souls. I can speak to kings long dead and children not yet born, and watch the years and seasons flicker past, until the end of days."

"Are your fires never wrong?"

"Never . . . though we priests are mortal and sometimes err, mistaking *this must come* for *this may come*."

Jon could feel her heat, even through his wool and boiled leather. The sight of them arm in arm was drawing curious looks. *They will be whispering in the barracks tonight.* "If you can truly see the morrow in your flames, tell me when and where the next wildling attack will come." He slipped his arm free.

"R'hllor sends us what visions he will, but I shall seek for this man Tormund in the flames." Melisandre's red lips curled into a smile. "I have seen you in my fires, Jon Snow."

"Is that a threat, my lady? Do you mean to burn me too?"

"You mistake my meaning." She gave him a searching look. "I fear that I make you uneasy, Lord Snow."

Jon did not deny it. "The Wall is no place for a woman."

"You are wrong. I have dreamed of your Wall, Jon Snow. Great was the lore that raised it, and great the spells locked beneath its ice. We walk beneath one of the hinges of the world." Melisandre gazed up at it, her breath a warm moist cloud in the air. "This is my place as it is yours, and soon enough you may have grave need of me. Do not refuse my friendship, Jon. I have seen you in the storm, hard-pressed, with enemies on every side. You have so many enemies. Shall I tell you their names?"

"I know their names."

"Do not be so certain." The ruby at Melisandre's throat gleamed red. "It is not the foes who curse you to your face that you must fear, but those who smile when you are looking and sharpen their knives when you turn your back. You would do well to keep your wolf close beside you. Ice, I see, and daggers in the dark. Blood frozen red and hard, and naked steel. It was very cold."

"It is always cold on the Wall."

"You think so?"

"I *know* so, my lady."

"Then you know nothing, Jon Snow," she whispered.

BRAN

Are we there yet?

Bran never said the words aloud, but they were often on his lips as their ragged company trudged through groves of ancient oaks and towering grey-green sentinels, past gloomy soldier pines and bare brown chestnut trees. *Are we near?* the boy would wonder, as Hodor clambered up a stony slope, or descended into some dark crevice where drifts of dirty snow cracked beneath his feet. *How much farther?* he would think, as the great elk splashed across a half-frozen stream. *How much longer? It's so cold. Where is the three-eyed crow?*

Swaying in his wicker basket on Hodor's back, the boy hunched down, ducking his head as the big stableboy passed beneath the limb of an oak. The snow was falling again, wet and heavy. Hodor walked with one eye frozen shut, his thick brown beard a tangle of hoarfrost, icicles drooping from the ends of his bushy mustache. One gloved hand still clutched the rusty iron longsword he had taken from the crypts below Winterfell, and from time to time he would lash out at a branch, knocking loose a spray of snow. "Hod-d-d-dor," he would mutter, his teeth chattering.

The sound was strangely reassuring. On their journey from Winterfell to the Wall, Bran and his companions had made the miles shorter by talking and telling tales, but it was different here. Even Hodor felt it. His *hodor*s came less often than they had south of the Wall. There was a stillness to this wood like nothing Bran had ever known before. Before the snows began, the north wind would swirl around them and clouds of dead brown leaves would kick up from the ground with a faint small rustling sound that reminded him of roaches scurrying in a cupboard, but now all the leaves were buried under a blanket of white. From time to time a raven would fly overhead, big black wings slapping against the cold air. Elsewise the world was silent.

Just ahead, the elk wove between the snowdrifts with his head down, his huge rack of antlers crusted with ice. The ranger sat astride his broad back, grim and silent. *Coldhands* was the name that the fat boy Sam had given him, for though the ranger's face was pale, his hands were black and hard as iron, and cold as iron too. The rest of him was wrapped in layers of wool and boiled leather and ringmail, his features shadowed by his hooded cloak and a black woolen scarf about the lower half of his face.

Behind the ranger, Meera Reed wrapped her arms around her brother, to shelter him from the wind and cold with the warmth of her own body. A crust of frozen snot had formed below Jojen's nose, and from time to time he shivered violently. *He looks so small,* Bran thought, as he watched him sway. *He looks smaller than me now, and weaker too, and I'm the cripple.*

Summer brought up the rear of their little band. The direwolf's breath frosted the forest air as he padded after them, still limping on the hind leg that had taken the arrow back at Queenscrown. Bran felt the pain of the old wound whenever he slipped inside the big wolf's skin. Of late Bran wore Summer's body more often than his own; the wolf felt the bite of the cold, despite the thickness of his fur, but he could see farther and hear better and smell more than the boy in the basket, bundled up like a babe in swaddling clothes.

Other times, when he was tired of being a wolf, Bran slipped into Hodor's skin instead. The gentle giant would whimper when he felt him, and thrash his shaggy head from side to side, but not as violently as he had the first time, back at Queenscrown. *He knows it's me,* the boy liked to tell himself. *He's used to me by now.* Even so, he never felt comfortable inside Hodor's skin. The big stableboy never understood what was happening, and Bran could taste the fear at the back of his mouth. It was better inside Summer. *I am him, and he is me. He feels what I feel.*

Sometimes Bran could sense the direwolf sniffing after the elk, wondering if he could bring the great beast down. Summer had grown accustomed to horses at Winterfell, but this was an elk and elk were prey. The direwolf could sense the warm blood coursing beneath the elk's shaggy hide. Just the smell was enough to make the slaver run from between his jaws, and when it did Bran's mouth would water at the thought of rich, dark meat.

From a nearby oak a raven *quork*ed, and Bran heard the sound of wings as another of the big black birds flapped down to land beside it. By day only half a dozen ravens stayed with them, flitting from tree to tree or riding on the antlers of the elk. The rest of the murder flew ahead or lingered behind. But when the sun sank low they would return, descending from the sky on night-black wings until every branch of every tree was thick with them for yards around. Some would fly to the ranger and mutter at him, and it seemed to Bran that he understood their *quorks* and *squawks*. *They are his eyes and ears. They scout for him, and whisper to him of dangers ahead and behind.*

As now. The elk stopped suddenly, and the ranger vaulted lightly from his back to land in knee-deep snow. Summer growled at him, his fur bristling. The direwolf did not like the way that Coldhands smelled. *Dead meat, dry blood, a faint whiff of rot. And cold. Cold over all.*

"What is it?" Meera wanted to know.

"Behind us," Coldhands announced, his voice muffled by the black wool scarf across his nose and mouth.

"Wolves?" Bran asked. They had known for days that they were being followed. Every night they heard the mournful howling of the pack, and every night the wolves seemed a little closer. *Hunters, and hungry. They can smell how weak we are.* Often Bran woke shivering hours before the dawn, listening to the sound of them calling to one another in the distance as he waited for the sun to rise. *If there are wolves, there must be prey,* he used to think, until it came to him that *they* were the prey.

The ranger shook his head. "Men. The wolves still keep their distance. These men are not so shy."

Meera Reed pushed back her hood. The wet snow that had covered it tumbled to the ground with a soft *thump.* "How many men? Who are they?"

"Foes. I'll deal with them."

"I'll come with you."

"You'll stay. The boy must be protected. There is a lake ahead, hard frozen. When you come on it, turn north and follow the shoreline. You'll come to a fishing village. Take refuge there until I can catch up with you."

Bran thought that Meera meant to argue until her brother said, "Do as he says. He knows this land." Jojen's eyes were a dark green, the color of moss, but heavy with a weariness that Bran had never seen in them before. *The little grandfather.* South of the Wall, the boy from the crannogs had seemed to be wise beyond his years, but up here he was as lost and frightened as the rest of them. Even so, Meera always listened to him.

That was still true. Coldhands slipped between the trees, back the way they'd come, with four ravens flapping after him. Meera watched him go, her cheeks red with cold, breath puffing from her nostrils. She pulled her hood back up and gave the elk a nudge, and their trek resumed. Before they had gone twenty yards, though, she turned to glance behind them and said, "*Men*, he says. What men? Does he mean wildlings? Why won't he say?"

"He said he'd go and deal with them," said Bran.

"He *said*, aye. He said he would take us to this three-eyed crow too. That river we crossed this morning is the same one we crossed four days ago, I swear. We're going in circles."

"Rivers turn and twist," Bran said uncertainly, "and where there's lakes and hills, you need to go around."

"There's been too much *going around*," Meera insisted, "and too many secrets. I don't like it. I don't like *him*. And I don't trust him. Those hands of his are bad enough. He hides his face, and will not speak a name. Who is he? *What* is he? Anyone can put on a black cloak. Anyone, or any *thing*. He does not eat, he never drinks, he does not seem to feel the cold."

It's true. Bran had been afraid to speak of it, but he had noticed. Whenever they took shelter for the night, while he and Hodor and the Reeds huddled together for warmth, the ranger kept apart. Sometimes Coldhands closed his eyes, but Bran did not think he slept. And there was something else . . .

"The scarf." Bran glanced about uneasily, but there was not a raven to be seen. All the big black birds had left them when the ranger did. No one was listening. Even so, he kept his voice low. "The scarf over his mouth, it never gets all hard with ice, like Hodor's beard. Not even when he talks."

Meera gave him a sharp look. "You're right. We've never seen his breath, have we?"

"No." A puff of white heralded each of Hodor's *hodor*s. When Jojen or his sister spoke, their words could be seen too. Even the elk left a warm fog upon the air when he exhaled.

"If he does not breathe . . ."

Bran found himself remembering the tales Old Nan had told him when he was a babe. *Beyond the Wall the monsters live, the giants and the ghouls, the stalking shadows and the dead that walk*, she would say, tucking him in beneath his scratchy woolen blanket, *but they cannot pass so long as the Wall stands strong and the men of the Night's Watch are true. So go to sleep, my little Brandon, my baby boy, and dream sweet dreams. There are no monsters here.* The ranger wore the black of the Night's Watch, but what if he was not a man at all? What if he was some monster, taking them to the other monsters to be devoured?

"The ranger saved Sam and the girl from the wights," Bran said, hesitantly, "and he's taking me to the three-eyed crow."

"Why won't this three-eyed crow come to us? Why couldn't *he* meet us at the Wall? Crows have wings. My brother grows weaker every day. How long can we go on?"

Jojen coughed. "Until we get there."

They came upon the promised lake not long after, and turned north as the ranger had bid them. That was the easy part.

The water was frozen, and the snow had been falling for so long that Bran had lost count of the days, turning the lake into a vast white wilderness. Where the ice was flat and the ground was bumpy, the going was easy, but where the wind had pushed the snow up into ridges, sometimes it was hard to tell where the lake ended and the shore began. Even the trees were not as infallible a guide as they might have hoped, for there were wooded islands in the lake, and wide areas ashore where no trees grew.

The elk went where he would, regardless of the wishes of Meera and Jojen on his back. Mostly he stayed beneath the trees, but where the shore curved away westward he would take the more direct path across the frozen lake, shouldering through snowdrifts taller than Bran as the ice crackled underneath his hooves. Out there the wind was stronger, a cold north wind that howled across the lake, knifed through their layers of wool and leather, and set them all to shivering. When it blew into their faces, it would drive the snow into their eyes and leave them as good as blind.

Hours passed in silence. Ahead, shadows began to steal between the trees, the long fingers of the dusk. Dark came early this far north. Bran had come to dread that. Each day seemed shorter than the last, and where the days were cold, the nights were bitter cruel.

Meera halted them again. "We should have come on the village by now." Her voice sounded hushed and strange.

"Could we have passed it?" Bran asked.

"I hope not. We need to find shelter before nightfall."

She was not wrong. Jojen's lips were blue, Meera's cheeks dark red. Bran's own face had gone numb. Hodor's beard was solid ice. Snow caked his legs almost to the knee, and Bran had felt him stagger more than once. No one was as strong as Hodor, no one. If even his great strength was failing . . .

"Summer can find the village," Bran said suddenly, his words misting in the air. He did not wait to hear what Meera might say, but closed his eyes and let himself flow from his broken body.

As he slipped inside Summer's skin, the dead woods came to sudden life. Where before there had been silence, now he heard: wind in the trees, Hodor's breathing, the elk pawing at the ground in search of fodder. Familiar scents filled his nostrils: wet leaves and dead grass, the rotted carcass of a squirrel decaying in the brush, the sour stink of man-sweat, the musky odor of the elk. *Food. Meat.* The elk sensed his interest. He turned his head toward the direwolf, wary, and lowered his great antlers.

He is not prey, the boy whispered to the beast who shared his skin. *Leave him. Run.*

Summer ran. Across the lake he raced, his paws kicking up sprays of snow behind him. The trees stood shoulder to shoulder, like men in a battle line, all cloaked in white. Over roots and rocks the direwolf sped, through a drift of old snow, the crust crackling beneath his weight. His paws grew wet and cold. The next hill was covered with pines, and the sharp scent of their needles filled the air. When he reached the top, he turned in a circle, sniffing at the air, then raised his head and howled.

The smells were there. Mansmells.

Ashes, Bran thought, *old and faint, but ashes.* It was the smell of burnt wood, soot, and charcoal. A dead fire.

He shook the snow off his muzzle. The wind was gusting, so the smells were hard to follow. The wolf turned this way and that, sniffing. All around were heaps of snow and tall trees garbed in white. The wolf let his tongue loll out between his teeth, tasting the frigid air, his breath misting as snowflakes melted on his tongue. When he trotted toward the scent, Hodor lumbered after him at once. The elk took longer to decide, so Bran returned reluctantly to his own body and said, "That way. Follow Summer. I smelled it."

As the first sliver of a crescent moon came peeking through the clouds, they finally stumbled into the village by the lake. They had almost walked straight through it. From the ice, the village looked no different than a dozen other spots along the lakeshore. Buried under drifts of snow, the round stone houses could just as easily have been boulders or hillocks or fallen logs, like the deadfall that Jojen had mistaken for a building the day before, until they dug down into it and found only broken branches and rotting logs.

The village was empty, abandoned by the wildlings who had once lived there, like all the other villages they had passed. Some had been burned, as if the inhabitants had wanted to make certain they could not come creeping back, but this one had been spared the torch. Beneath the snow they found a dozen huts and a longhall, with its sod roof and thick walls of rough-hewn logs.

"At least we will be out of the wind," Bran said.

"Ho*dor*," said Hodor.

Meera slid down from the elk's back. She and her brother helped lift Bran out of the wicker basket. "Might be the wildlings left some food behind," she said.

That proved a forlorn hope. Inside the longhall they found the ashes of a fire, floors of hard-packed dirt, a chill that went bone deep. But at least they had a roof above their heads and log walls to keep the wind off. A stream ran nearby, covered with a film of ice. The elk had to crack it with his hoof to drink. Once Bran and Jojen and Hodor were safely settled, Meera fetched back some chunks of broken ice for them to suck on. The melting water was so cold it made Bran shudder.

Summer did not follow them into the longhall. Bran could feel the big wolf's hunger, a shadow of his own. "Go hunt," he told him, "but you leave the elk alone." Part of him was wishing he could go hunting too. Perhaps he would, later.

Supper was a fistful of acorns, crushed and pounded into paste, so bitter that Bran gagged as he tried to keep it down. Jojen Reed did not even make the attempt. Younger and frailer than his sister, he was growing weaker by the day.

"Jojen, you have to eat," Meera told him.

"Later. I just want to rest." Jojen smiled a wan smile. "This is not the day I die, sister. I promise you."

"You almost fell off the elk."

"Almost. I am cold and hungry, that's all."

"Then eat."

"Crushed acorns? My belly hurts, but that will only make it worse. Leave me be, sister. I'm dreaming of roast chicken."

"Dreams will not sustain you. Not even greendreams."

"Dreams are what we have."

All we have. The last of the food that they had brought from the south was ten days gone. Since then hunger walked beside them day and night. Even Summer could find no game in these woods. They lived on crushed acorns and raw fish. The woods were full of frozen streams and cold black lakes, and Meera was as good a fisher with her three-pronged frog spear as most men were with hook and line. Some days her lips were blue with cold by the time she waded back to them with her catch wriggling on her tines. It had been three days since Meera caught a fish, however. Bran's belly felt so hollow it might have been three years.

After they choked down their meagre supper, Meera sat with her back against a wall, sharpening her dagger on a whetstone. Hodor squatted down beside the door, rocking back and forth on his haunches and muttering, "Hodor, hodor, hodor."

Bran closed his eyes. It was too cold to talk, and they dare not light a fire. Coldhands had warned them against that. *These woods are not as empty as you think*, he had said. *You cannot know what the light might summon from the darkness.* The memory made him shiver, despite the warmth of Hodor beside him.

Sleep would not come, could not come. Instead there was wind, the biting cold, moonlight on snow, and fire. He was back inside Summer, long leagues away, and the night was rank with the smell of blood. The scent was strong. *A kill, not far.* The flesh would still be warm. Slaver ran between his teeth as the hunger woke inside him. *Not elk. Not deer. Not this.*

The direwolf moved toward the meat, a gaunt grey shadow sliding from tree to tree, through pools of moonlight and over mounds of snow. The wind gusted around him, shifting. He lost the scent, found it, then lost it again. As he searched for it once more, a distant sound made his ears prick up.

Wolf, he knew at once. Summer stalked toward the sound, wary now. Soon enough the scent of blood was back, but now there were other smells: piss and dead skins, bird shit, feathers, and wolf, wolf, wolf. *A pack.* He would need to fight for his meat.

They smelled him too. As he moved out from amongst the darkness of the trees into the bloody glade, they were watching him. The female was chewing on a leather boot that still had half a leg in it, but she let it fall at his approach. The leader of the pack, an old male with a grizzled white muzzle and a blind eye, moved out to meet him, snarling, his teeth bared. Behind him, a younger male showed his fangs as well.

The direwolf's pale yellow eyes drank in the sights around them. A nest of entrails coiled through a bush, entangled with the branches. Steam rising from an open belly, rich with the smells of blood and meat. A head staring sightlessly up at a horned moon, cheeks ripped and torn down to bloody bone, pits for eyes, neck ending in a ragged stump. A pool of frozen blood, glistening red and black.

Men. The stink of them filled the world. Alive, they had been as many as the fingers on a man's paw, but now they were none. *Dead. Done. Meat.* Cloaked and hooded, once, but the wolves had torn their clothing into pieces in their frenzy to get at the flesh. Those who still had faces wore thick beards crusted with ice and frozen snot. The falling snow had begun to bury what remained of them, so pale against the black of ragged cloaks and breeches. *Black.*

Long leagues away, the boy stirred uneasily.

Black. Night's Watch. They were Night's Watch.

The direwolf did not care. They were meat. He was hungry.

The eyes of the three wolves glowed yellow. The direwolf swung his head from side to side, nostrils flaring, then bared his fangs in a snarl. The younger male backed away. The direwolf could smell the fear in him. *Tail,* he knew. But the one-eyed wolf answered with a growl and moved to block his advance. *Head. And he does not fear me though I am twice his size.*

Their eyes met.

Warg!

Then the two rushed together, wolf and direwolf, and there was no more time for thought. The world shrank down to tooth and claw, snow flying as they rolled and spun and tore at one another, the other wolves snarling and snapping around them. His jaws closed on matted fur slick with hoarfrost, on a limb thin as a dry stick, but the one-eyed wolf clawed at his belly and tore himself free, rolled, lunged for him. Yellow fangs snapped closed on his throat, but he shook off his old grey cousin as he would a rat, then charged after him, knocked him down. Rolling, ripping, kicking, they fought until the both of them were ragged and fresh blood dappled the snows around them. But finally the old one-eyed wolf lay down and showed his belly. The direwolf snapped at him twice more, sniffed at his butt, then lifted a leg over him.

A few snaps and a warning growl, and the female and the tail submitted too. The pack was his.

The prey as well. He went from man to man, sniffing, before settling on the biggest, a faceless thing who clutched black iron in one hand. His other hand was missing, severed at the wrist, the stump bound up in leather. Blood flowed thick and sluggish from the slash across his throat. The wolf lapped at it with his tongue, licked the ragged eyeless ruin of his nose and cheeks, then buried his muzzle in his neck and tore it open, gulping down a gobbet of sweet meat. No flesh had ever tasted half as good.

When he was done with that one, he moved to the next, and devoured the choicest bits of that man too. Ravens watched him from the trees, squatting dark-eyed and silent on the branches as snow drifted down around them. The other wolves made do with his leavings; the old male fed first, then the female, then the tail. They were his now. They were pack.

No, the boy whispered, *we have another pack. Lady's dead and maybe Grey Wind too, but somewhere there's still Shaggydog and Nymeria and Ghost. Remember Ghost?*

Falling snow and feasting wolves began to dim. Warmth beat against his face, comforting as a mother's kisses. *Fire,* he thought, *smoke.* His nose twitched to the smell of roasting meat. And then the forest fell away, and he was back in the longhall again, back in his broken body, staring at a fire. Meera Reed was turning a chunk of raw red flesh above the flames, letting it char and spit. "Just in time," she said. Bran rubbed his eyes with the heel of his hand and wriggled backwards against the wall to sit. "You almost slept through supper. The ranger found a sow."

Behind her, Hodor was tearing eagerly at a chunk of hot charred flesh as blood and grease ran down into his beard. Wisps of smoke rose from between his fingers. "Hodor," he muttered between bites, "hodor, hodor." His sword lay on the earthen floor beside him. Jojen Reed nipped at his own joint with small bites, chewing each chunk of meat a dozen times before swallowing.

The ranger killed a pig. Coldhands stood beside the door, a raven on his arm, both staring at the fire. Reflections from the flames glittered off four black eyes. *He does not eat,* Bran remembered, *and he fears the flames.*

"You said no fire," he reminded the ranger.

"The walls around us hide the light, and dawn is close. We will be on our way soon."

"What happened to the men? The foes behind us?"

"They will not trouble you."

"Who were they? Wildlings?"

Meera turned the meat to cook the other side. Hodor was chewing and swallowing, muttering happily under his breath. Only Jojen seemed aware of what was happening as Coldhands turned his head to stare at Bran. "They were foes."

Men of the Night's Watch. "You killed them. You and the ravens. Their faces were all torn, and their eyes were gone." Coldhands did not deny it. "They were your *brothers.* I saw. The wolves had ripped their clothes up, but I could still tell. Their cloaks were black. Like your hands." Coldhands said nothing. "Who are you? *Why are your hands black?*"

The ranger studied his hands as if he had never noticed them before. "Once the heart has ceased to beat, a man's blood runs down into his extremities, where it thickens and congeals." His voice rattled in his throat, as thin and gaunt as he was. "His hands and feet swell up and turn as black as pudding. The rest of him becomes as white as milk."

Meera Reed rose, her frog spear in her hand, a chunk of smoking meat still impaled upon its tines. "Show us your face."

The ranger made no move to obey.

"He's dead." Bran could taste the bile in his throat. "Meera, he's some dead thing. The monsters cannot pass so long as the Wall stands and the men of the Night's Watch stay true, that's what Old Nan used to say. He came to meet us at the Wall, but he could not pass. He sent Sam instead, with that wildling girl."

Meera's gloved hand tightened around the shaft of her frog spear. "Who sent you? Who is this three-eyed crow?"

"A friend. Dreamer, wizard, call him what you will. The last green-seer." The longhall's wooden door banged open. Outside, the night wind howled, bleak and black. The trees were full of ravens, screaming. Cold-hands did not move.

"A monster," Bran said.

The ranger looked at Bran as if the rest of them did not exist. "Your monster, Brandon Stark."

"*Yours,*" the raven echoed, from his shoulder. Outside the door, the ravens in the trees took up the cry, until the night wood echoed to the murderer's song of "*Yours, yours, yours.*"

"Jojen, did you dream this?" Meera asked her brother. "Who is he? What is he? What do we do now?"

"We go with the ranger," said Jojen. "We have come too far to turn back now, Meera. We would never make it back to the Wall alive. We go with Bran's monster, or we die."

TYRION

They departed Pentos by the Sunrise Gate, though Tyrion Lannister never glimpsed the sunrise. "It will be as if you had never come to Pentos, my little friend," promised Magister Illyrio, as he drew shut the litter's purple velvet drapes. "No man must see you leave the city, as no man saw you enter."

"No man except the sailors who stuffed me in that barrel, the cabin boy who cleaned up after me, the girl you sent to warm my bed, and that treacherous freckled washerwoman. Oh, and your guards. Unless you re-moved their wits along with their balls, they know you're not alone in here." The litter was suspended between eight mammoth draft horses on heavy leather straps. Four eunuchs paced beside the horses, two to either side, and more were trudging along behind to guard the baggage train.

"Unsullied tell no tales," Illyrio assured him. "And the galley that deliv-ered you is on her way to Asshai even now. It will be two years before she returns, if the seas are kind. As for my household, they love me well. None would betray me."

Cherish that thought, my fat friend. One day we will carve those words upon your crypt. "We should be aboard that galley," the dwarf said. "The fastest way to Volantis is by sea."

"The sea is hazardous," replied Illyrio. "Autumn is a season rife with storms, and pirates still make their dens upon the Stepstones and venture forth to prey on honest men. It would never do for my little friend to fall into such hands."

"There are pirates on the Rhoyne as well."

"River pirates." The cheesemonger gave a yawn, covering his mouth with the back of his hand. "Cockroach captains scurrying after crumbs."

"One hears talk of stone men as well."

"They are real enough, poor damned things. But why speak of such things? The day is too fine for such talk. We shall see the Rhoyne soon, and there you shall be rid of Illyrio and his big belly. Till then, let us drink and dream. We have sweet wine and savories to enjoy. Why dwell upon disease and death?"

Why indeed? Tyrion heard the *thrum* of a crossbow once again, and wondered. The litter swayed side to side, a soothing movement that made him feel as if he were a child being rocked to sleep in his mother's arms. *Not that I would know what that was like.* Silk pillows stuffed with goose down cushioned his cheeks. The purple velvet walls curved overhead to form a roof, making it pleasantly warm within despite the autumn chill outside.

A train of mules trailed behind them, carrying chests and casks and barrels, and hampers of delectables to keep the lord of cheese from growing peckish. They nibbled on spiced sausage that morning, washed down with a dark smokeberry brown. Jellied eels and Dornish reds filled their afternoon. Come evening there were sliced hams, boiled eggs, and roasted larks stuffed with garlic and onions, with pale ales and Myrish fire wines to help in their digestion. The litter was as slow as it was comfortable, however, and the dwarf soon found himself itching with impatience.

"How many days until we reach the river?" he asked Illyrio that evening. "At this pace, your queen's dragons will be larger than Aegon's three before I can lay eyes upon them."

"Would it were so. A large dragon is more fearsome than a small one." The magister shrugged. "Much as it would please me to welcome Queen Daenerys to Volantis, I must rely on you and Griff for that. I can serve her best in Pentos, smoothing the way for her return. So long as I am with you, though . . . well, an old fat man must have his comforts, yes? Come, drink a cup of wine."

"Tell me," Tyrion said as he drank, "why should a magister of Pentos give three figs who wears the crown in Westeros? Where is the gain for you in this venture, my lord?"

The fat man dabbed grease from his lips. "I am an old man, grown weary of this world and its treacheries. Is it so strange that I should wish to do some good before my days are done, to help a sweet young girl regain her birthright?"

Next you will be offering me a suit of magic armor and a palace in Valyria. "If Daenerys is no more than a sweet young girl, the Iron Throne will cut her into sweet young pieces."

"Fear not, my little friend. The blood of Aegon the Dragon flows in her veins."

Along with the blood of Aegon the Unworthy, Maegor the Cruel, and Baelor the Befuddled. "Tell me more of her."

The fat man grew pensive. "Daenerys was half a child when she came to me, yet fairer even than my second wife, so lovely I was tempted to claim her for myself. Such a fearful, furtive thing, however, I knew I should get no joy from coupling with her. Instead I summoned a bedwarmer and fucked her vigorously until the madness passed. If truth be told, I did not think Daenerys would survive for long amongst the horselords."

"That did not stop you selling her to Khal Drogo . . ."

"Dothraki neither buy nor sell. Say rather that her brother Viserys gave her to Drogo to win the khal's friendship. A vain young man, and greedy. Viserys lusted for his father's throne, but he lusted for Daenerys too, and was loath to give her up. The night before the princess wed he tried to steal into her bed, insisting that if he could not have her hand, he would claim her maidenhead. Had I not taken the precaution of posting guards upon her door, Viserys might have undone years of planning."

"He sounds an utter fool."

"Viserys was Mad Aerys's son, just so. Daenerys . . . Daenerys is quite different." He popped a roasted lark into his mouth and crunched it noisily, bones and all. "The frightened child who sheltered in my manse died on the Dothraki sea, and was reborn in blood and fire. This dragon queen who wears her name is a true Targaryen. When I sent ships to bring her home, she turned toward Slaver's Bay. In a short span of days she conquered Astapor, made Yunkai bend the knee, and sacked Meereen. Mantarys will be next, if she marches west along the old Valyrian roads. If she comes by sea, well . . . her fleet must take on food and water at Volantis."

"By land or by sea, there are long leagues between Meereen and Volantis," Tyrion observed.

"Five hundred fifty, as the dragon flies, through deserts, mountains, swamps, and demon-haunted ruins. Many and more will perish, but those who survive will be stronger by the time they reach Volantis . . . where they shall find you and Griff awaiting them, with fresh forces and sufficient ships to carry them all across the sea to Westeros."

Tyrion pondered all he knew of Volantis, oldest and proudest of the Nine Free Cities. Something was awry here. Even with half a nose, he could smell it. "It's said there are five slaves for every free man in Volantis. Why would the triarchs assist a queen who smashed the slave trade?" He pointed at Illyrio. "For that matter, why would you? Slavery may be forbidden by the laws of Pentos, yet you have a finger in that trade as well, and maybe a whole hand. And yet you conspire for the dragon queen, and not against her. Why? What do you hope to gain from Queen Daenerys?"

"Are we back to that again? You are a persistent little man." Illyrio gave a laugh and slapped his belly. "As you will. The Beggar King swore that I should be his master of coin, and a lordly lord as well. Once he wore his golden crown, I should have my choice of castles . . . even Casterly Rock, if I desired."

Tyrion snorted wine back up the scarred stump that had been his nose. "My father would have loved to hear that."

"Your lord father had no cause for concern. Why would I want a rock? My manse is large enough for any man, and more comfortable than your drafty Westerosi castles. Master of coin, though . . ." The fat man peeled another egg. "I am fond of coins. Is there any sound as sweet as the clink of gold on gold?"

A sister's screams. "Are you quite certain that Daenerys will make good her brother's promises?"

"She will, or she will not." Illyrio bit the egg in half. "I told you, my little friend, not all that a man does is done for gain. Believe as you wish, but even fat old fools like me have friends, and debts of affection to repay."

Liar, thought Tyrion. *There is something in this venture worth more to you than coin or castles.* "You meet so few men who value friendship over gold these days."

"Too true," the fat man said, deaf to the irony.

"How is it that the Spider became so dear to you?"

"We were young together, two green boys in Pentos."

"Varys came from Myr."

"So he did. I met him not long after he arrived, one step ahead of the slavers. By day he slept in the sewers, by night he prowled the rooftops like a cat. I was near as poor, a bravo in soiled silks, living by my blade. Perhaps you chanced to glimpse the statue by my pool? Pytho Malanon carved that when I was six-and-ten. A lovely thing, though now I weep to see it."

"Age makes ruins of us all. I am still in mourning for my nose. But Varys . . ."

"In Myr he was a prince of thieves, until a rival thief informed on him. In Pentos his accent marked him, and once he was known for a eunuch he was despised and beaten. Why he chose me to protect him I may never know, but we came to an arrangement. Varys spied on lesser thieves and took their takings. I offered my help to their victims, promising to recover their valuables for a fee. Soon every man who had suffered a loss knew to come to me, whilst city's footpads and cutpurses sought out Varys . . . half to slit his throat, the other half to sell him what they'd stolen. We both grew rich, and richer still when Varys trained his mice."

"In King's Landing he kept little birds."

"Mice, we called them then. The older thieves were fools who thought no further than turning a night's plunder into wine. Varys preferred orphan boys and young girls. He chose the smallest, the ones who were quick and quiet, and taught them to climb walls and slip down chimneys. He taught them to read as well. We left the gold and gems for common thieves. Instead our mice stole letters, ledgers, charts . . . later, they would read them and leave them where they lay. *Secrets are worth more than silver or sapphires*, Varys claimed. Just so. I grew so respectable that a cousin of the Prince of Pentos let me wed his maiden daughter, whilst whispers of a certain eunuch's talents crossed the narrow sea and reached the ears of a certain king. A very *anxious* king, who did not wholly trust his son, nor his wife, nor his Hand, a friend of his youth who had grown arrogant and overproud. I do believe that you know the rest of this tale, is that not so?"

"Much of it," Tyrion admitted. "I see that you are somewhat more than a cheesemonger after all."

Illyrio inclined his head. "You are kind to say so, my little friend. And for my part, I see that you are just as quick as Lord Varys claimed." He smiled, showing all his crooked yellow teeth, and shouted for another jar of Myrish fire wine.

When the magister drifted off to sleep with the wine jar at his elbow, Tyrion crept across the pillows to work it loose from its fleshy prison and pour himself a cup. He drained it down, and yawned, and filled it once again. *If I drink enough fire wine*, he told himself, *perhaps I'll dream of dragons.*

When he was still a lonely child in the depths of Casterly Rock, he oft rode dragons through the nights, pretending he was some lost Targaryen princeling, or a Valyrian dragonlord soaring high o'er fields and mountains. Once, when his uncles asked him what gift he wanted for his nameday, he begged them for a dragon. "It wouldn't need to be a big one. It could be little, like I am." His uncle Gerion thought that was the funniest thing he had ever heard, but his uncle Tygett said, "The last dragon died a century ago, lad." That had seemed so monstrously unfair that the boy had cried himself to sleep that night.

Yet if the lord of cheese could be believed, the Mad King's daughter had hatched three living dragons. *Two more than even a Targaryen should require.* Tyrion was almost sorry that he had killed his father. He would have enjoyed seeing Lord Tywin's face when he learned that there was a Targaryen queen on her way to Westeros with three dragons, backed by a scheming eunuch and a cheesemonger half the size of Casterly Rock.

The dwarf was so stuffed that he had to undo his belt and the topmost laces on his breeches. The boy's clothes his host had dressed him in made him feel like ten pounds of sausage in a five-pound skin. *If we eat this way every day I will be the size of Illyrio before I meet this dragon queen.* Outside the litter night had fallen. Inside all was dark. Tyrion listened to Illyrio's snores, the creak of the leather straps, the slow *clop clop* of the team's ironshod hooves on the hard Valyrian road, but his heart was listening for the beat of leathern wings.

When he woke, dawn had come. The horses plodded on, the litter creaking and swaying between them. Tyrion pulled the curtain back an inch to peer outside, but there was little to see but ochre fields, bare brown elms, and the road itself, a broad stone highway that ran straight as a spear to the horizon. He had read about Valyrian roads, but this was the first he had seen. The Freehold's grasp had reached as far as Dragonstone, but never to the mainland of Westeros itself. *Odd, that. Dragonstone is no more than a rock. The wealth was farther west, but they had dragons. Surely they knew that it was there.*

He had drunk too much last night. His head was pounding, and even the gentle swaying of the litter was enough to make his gorge rise in his throat. Though he said no word of complaint, his distress must have been plain to Illyrio Mopatis. "Come, drink with me," the fat man said. "A scale from the dragon that burned you, as they say." He poured for them from a flagon of blackberry wine so sweet that it drew more flies than honey. Tyrion shooed them off with the back of his hand and drank deep. The taste was so cloying that it was all he could do to keep it down. The second cup went down easier, however. Even so, he had no appetite, and when Illyrio offered him a bowl of blackberries in cream he waved it off. "I dreamed about the queen," he said. "I was on my knees before her, swearing my allegiance, but she mistook me for my brother, Jaime, and fed me to her dragons."

"Let us hope this dream was not prophetic. You are a clever imp, just as Varys said, and Daenerys will have need of clever men about her. Ser Barristan is a valiant knight and true; but none, I think, has ever called him cunning."

"Knights know only one way to solve a problem. They couch their lances and charge. A dwarf has a different way of looking at the world. What of you, though? You are a clever man yourself."

"You flatter me." Illyrio waggled his hand. "Alas, I am not made for travel, so I will send you to Daenerys in my stead. You did Her Grace a great service when you slew your father, and it is my hope that you will do her many more. Daenerys is not the fool her brother was. She will make good use of you."

As kindling? Tyrion thought, smiling pleasantly.

They changed out teams only thrice that day but seemed to halt twice an hour at the least so Illyrio could climb down from the litter and have himself a piss. *Our lord of cheese is the size of an elephant, but he has a bladder like a peanut,* the dwarf mused. During one stop, he used the time to have a closer look at the road. Tyrion knew what he would find: not packed earth, nor bricks, nor cobbles, but a ribbon of fused stone raised a half foot above the ground to allow rainfall and snowmelt to run off its shoulders. Unlike the muddy tracks that passed for roads in the Seven Kingdoms, the Valyrian roads were wide enough for three wagons to pass abreast, and neither time nor traffic marred them. They still endured, unchanging, four centuries after Valyria itself had met its Doom. He looked for ruts and cracks but found only a pile of warm dung deposited by one of the horses.

The dung made him think of his lord father. *Are you down in some hell, Father? A nice cold hell where you can look up and see me help restore Mad Aerys's daughter to the Iron Throne?*

As they resumed their journey, Illyrio produced a bag of roasted chestnuts and began to speak once more of the dragon queen. "Our last news of Queen Daenerys is old and stale, I fear. By now she will have left Meereen, we must assume. She has her host at last, a ragged host of sellswords, Dothraki horselords, and Unsullied infantry, and she will no doubt lead them west, to take back her father's throne." Magister Illyrio twisted open a pot of garlic snails, sniffed at them, and smiled. "At Volantis, you will have fresh tidings of Daenerys, we must hope," he said, as he sucked one from its shell. "Dragons and young girls are both capricious, and it may be that you will need to adjust your plans. Griff will know what to do. Will you have a snail? The garlic is from my own gardens."

I could ride a snail and make a better pace than this litter of yours. Tyrion waved the dish away. "You place a deal of trust in this man Griff. Another friend of your childhood?"

"No. A sellsword, you would call him, but Westerosi born. Daenerys needs men worthy of her cause." Illyrio raised a hand. "I know! *'Sellswords put gold before honor,'* you are thinking. *'This man Griff will sell me to my sister.'* Not so. I trust Griff as I would trust a brother."

Another mortal error. "Then I shall do likewise."

"The Golden Company marches toward Volantis as we speak, there to await the coming of our queen out of the east."

Beneath the gold, the bitter steel. "I had heard the Golden Company was under contract with one of the Free Cities."

"Myr." Illyrio smirked. "Contracts can be broken."

"There is more coin in cheese than I knew," said Tyrion. "How did you accomplish that?"

The magister waggled his fat fingers. "Some contracts are writ in ink, and some in blood. I say no more."

The dwarf pondered that. The Golden Company was reputedly the finest of the free companies, founded a century ago by Bittersteel, a bastard son of Aegon the Unworthy. When another of Aegon's Great Bastards tried to seize the Iron Throne from his trueborn half-brother, Bittersteel joined the revolt. Daemon Blackfyre had perished on the Redgrass Field, however, and his rebellion with him. Those followers of the Black Dragon who survived the battle yet refused to bend the knee fled across the narrow sea, among them Daemon's younger sons, Bittersteel, and hundreds of landless lords and knights who soon found themselves forced to sell their swords to eat. Some joined the Ragged Standard, some the Second Sons or Maiden's Men. Bittersteel saw the strength of House Blackfyre scattering to the four winds, so he formed the Golden Company to bind the exiles together.

From that day to this, the men of the Golden Company had lived and died in the Disputed Lands, fighting for Myr or Lys or Tyrosh in their pointless little wars, and dreaming of the land their fathers had lost. They were exiles and sons of exiles, dispossessed and unforgiven . . . yet formidable fighters still.

"I admire your powers of persuasion," Tyrion told Illyrio. "How did you convince the Golden Company to take up the cause of our sweet queen when they have spent so much of their history fighting *against* the Targaryens?"

Illyrio brushed away the objection as if it were a fly. "Black or red, a dragon is still a dragon. When Maelys the Monstrous died upon the Stepstones, it was the end of the male line of House Blackfyre." The cheesemonger smiled through his forked beard. "And Daenerys will give the exiles what Bittersteel and the Blackfyres never could. She will take them home."

With fire and sword. It was the kind of homecoming that Tyrion wished for as well. "Ten thousand swords makes for a princely gift, I grant you. Her Grace should be most pleased."

The magister gave a modest bob of his head, chins jiggling. "I would never presume to say what might please Her Grace."

Prudent of you. Tyrion knew much and more about the gratitude of kings. Why should queens be any different?

Soon enough the magister was fast asleep, leaving Tyrion to brood alone. He wondered what Barristan Selmy would think of riding into battle with the Golden Company. During the War of the Ninepenny Kings, Selmy had cut a bloody path through their ranks to slay the last of the Blackfyre Pretenders. *Rebellion makes for queer bedfellows. And none more queer than this fat man and me.*

The cheesemonger woke when they stopped to change the horses and sent for a fresh hamper. "How far have we come?" the dwarf asked him as they stuffed themselves with cold capon and a relish made of carrots, raisins, and bits of lime and orange.

"This is Andalos, my friend. The land your Andals came from. They took it from the hairy men who were here before them, cousins to the hairy men of Ib. The heart of Hugor's ancient realm lies north of us, but we are passing through its southern marches. In Pentos, these are called the Flatlands. Farther east stand the Velvet Hills, whence we are bound."

Andalos. The Faith taught that the Seven themselves had once walked the hills of Andalos in human form. "The Father reached his hand into the heavens and pulled down seven stars," Tyrion recited from memory, "and one by one he set them on the brow of Hugor of the Hill to make a glowing crown."

Magister Illyrio gave him a curious look. "I did not dream my little friend was so devout."

The dwarf shrugged. "A relic of my boyhood. I knew I would not make a knight, so I decided to be High Septon. That crystal crown adds a foot to a man's height. I studied the holy books and prayed until I had scabs on both my knees, but my quest came to a tragic end. I reached that certain age and fell in love."

"A maiden? I know the way of that." Illyrio thrust his right hand up his left sleeve and drew out a silver locket. Inside was a painted likeness of a woman with big blue eyes and pale golden hair streaked by silver. "Serra. I found her in a Lysene pillow house and brought her home to warm my bed, but in the end I wed her. Me, whose first wife had been a cousin of the Prince of Pentos. The palace gates were closed to me thereafter, but I did not care. The price was small enough, for Serra."

"How did she die?" Tyrion knew that she was dead; no man spoke so fondly of a woman who had abandoned him.

"A Braavosi trading galley called at Pentos on her way back from the Jade Sea. The *Treasure* carried cloves and saffron, jet and jade, scarlet samite, green silk . . . and the grey death. We slew her oarsmen as they came ashore and burned the ship at anchor, but the rats crept down the oars and paddled to the quay on cold stone feet. The plague took two thousand before it ran its course." Magister Illyrio closed the locket. "I keep her hands in my bedchamber. Her hands that were so soft . . ."

Tyrion thought of Tysha. He glanced out at the fields where once the gods had walked. "What sort of gods make rats and plagues and dwarfs?" Another passage from *The Seven-Pointed Star* came back to him. "The Maid brought him forth a girl as supple as a willow with eyes like deep blue pools, and Hugor declared that he would have her for his bride. So the Mother made her fertile, and the Crone foretold that she would bear the king four-and-forty mighty sons. The Warrior gave strength to their arms, whilst the Smith wrought for each a suit of iron plates."

"Your Smith must have been Rhoynish," Illyrio quipped. "The Andals learned the art of working iron from the Rhoynar who dwelt along the river. This is known."

"Not by our septons." Tyrion gestured at the fields. "Who dwells in these Flatlands of yours?"

"Tillers and toilers, bound to the land. There are orchards, farms, mines . . . I own some such myself, though I seldom visit them. Why should I spend my days out here, with the myriad delights of Pentos close at hand?"

"Myriad delights." *And huge thick walls.* Tyrion swirled his wine in his cup. "We have seen no towns since Pentos."

"There are ruins." Illyrio waved a chicken leg toward the curtains. "The horselords come this way, whenever some khal takes it into his head to gaze upon the sea. The Dothraki are not fond of towns, you will know this even in Westeros."

"Fall upon one of these *khalasar*s and destroy it, and you may find that the Dothraki are not so quick to cross the Rhoyne."

"It is cheaper to buy off foes with food and gifts."

If only I had thought to bring a nice cheese to the battle on the Blackwater, I might still have all my nose. Lord Tywin had always held the Free Cities in contempt. *They fight with coins instead of swords,* he used to say. *Gold has its uses, but wars are won with iron.* "Give gold to a foe and he will just come back for more, my father always said."

"Is this the selfsame father that you murdered?" Illyrio tossed his chicken bone from the litter. "Sellswords will not stand against Dothraki screamers. That was proved at Qohor."

"Not even your brave Griff?" mocked Tyrion.

"Griff is different. He has a son he dotes on. Young Griff, the boy is called. There never was a nobler lad."

The wine, the food, the sun, the sway of the litter, the buzzing of the flies, all conspired to make Tyrion sleepy. So he slept, woke, drank. Illyrio matched him cup for cup. And as the sky turned a dusky purple, the fat man began to snore.

That night Tyrion Lannister dreamed of a battle that turned the hills of Westeros as red as blood. He was in the midst of it, dealing death with an axe as big as he was, fighting side by side with Barristan the Bold and Bittersteel as dragons wheeled across the sky above them. In the dream he had two heads, both noseless. His father led the enemy, so he slew him once again. Then he killed his brother, Jaime, hacking at his face until it was a red ruin, laughing every time he struck a blow. Only when the fight was finished did he realize that his second head was weeping.

When he woke his stunted legs were stiff as iron. Illyrio was eating olives. "Where are we?" Tyrion asked him.

"We have not yet left the Flatlands, my hasty friend. Soon our road shall pass into the Velvet Hills. There we begin our climb toward Ghoyan Drohe, upon the Little Rhoyne."

Ghoyan Drohe had been a Rhoynar city, until the dragons of Valyria had reduced it to a smoldering desolation. *I am traveling through years as well as leagues*, Tyrion reflected, *back through history to the days when dragons ruled the earth.*

Tyrion slept and woke and slept again, and day and night seemed not to matter. The Velvet Hills proved a disappointment. "Half the whores in Lannisport have breasts bigger than these hills," he told Illyrio. "You ought to call them the Velvet Teats." They saw a circle of standing stones that Illyrio claimed had been raised by giants, and later a deep lake. "Here lived a den of robbers who preyed on all who passed this way," Illyrio said. "It is said they still dwell beneath the water. Those who fish the lake are pulled under and devoured." The next evening they came upon a huge Valyrian sphinx crouched beside the road. It had a dragon's body and a woman's face.

"A dragon queen," said Tyrion. "A pleasant omen."

"Her king is missing." Illyrio pointed out the smooth stone plinth on which the second sphinx once stood, now grown over with moss and flowering vines. "The horselords built wooden wheels beneath him and dragged him back to Vaes Dothrak."

That is an omen too, thought Tyrion, *but not as hopeful.*

That night, drunker than usual, he broke into sudden song.

> *He rode through the streets of the city,*
> > *down from his hill on high,*
> *O'er the wynds and the steps and the cobbles,*
> > *he rode to a woman's sigh.*
> *For she was his secret treasure,*
> > *she was his shame and his bliss.*
> *And a chain and a keep are nothing,*
> > *compared to a woman's kiss.*

Those were all the words he knew, aside from the refrain. *Hands of gold are always cold, but a woman's hands are warm.* Shae's hands had beat at him as the golden hands dug into her throat. He did not remember if they'd been warm or not. As the strength went out of her, her blows became moths fluttering about his face. Each time he gave the chain another twist the golden hands dug deeper. *A chain and a keep are nothing, compared to a woman's kiss.* Had he kissed her one last time, after she was dead? He could not remember . . . though he still recalled the first time they had kissed, in his tent beside the Green Fork. How sweet her mouth had tasted.

He remembered the first time with Tysha as well. *She did not know how, no more than I did. We kept bumping our noses, but when I touched her tongue with mine she trembled.* Tyrion closed his eyes to bring her face to mind, but instead he saw his father, squatting on a privy with his bedrobe hiked up about his waist. "Wherever whores go," Lord Tywin said, and the crossbow *thrummed.*

The dwarf rolled over, pressing half a nose deep into the silken pillows. Sleep opened beneath him like a well, and he threw himself into it with a will and let the darkness eat him up.

THE MERCHANT'S MAN

*A**dventure* stank.

She boasted sixty oars, a single sail, and a long lean hull that promised speed. *Small, but she might serve,* Quentyn thought when he saw her, but that was before he went aboard and got a good whiff of her. *Pigs,* was his first thought, but after a second sniff he changed his mind. Pigs had a cleaner smell. This stink was piss and rotting meat and night-soil, this was the reek of corpse flesh and weeping sores and wounds gone bad, so strong that it overwhelmed the salt air and fish smell of the harbor.

"I want to retch," he said to Gerris Drinkwater. They were waiting for the ship's master to appear, sweltering in the heat as the stench wafted up from the deck beneath them.

"If the captain smells anything like his ship, he may mistake your vomit for perfume," Gerris replied.

Quentyn was about to suggest that they try another ship when the master finally made his appearance, with two vile-looking crewmen at his side. Gerris greeted him with a smile. Though he did not speak the Volantene tongue as well as Quentyn, their ruse required that he speak for them. Back in the Planky Town Quentyn had played the wineseller, but the mummery had chafed at him, so when the Dornishmen changed ships at Lys they had changed roles as well. Aboard the *Meadowlark,* Cletus Yronwood became the merchant, Quentyn the servant; in Volantis, with Cletus slain, Gerris had assumed the master's role.

Tall and fair, with blue-green eyes, sandy hair streaked by the sun, and a lean and comely body, Gerris Drinkwater had a swagger to him, a confidence bordering on arrogance. He never seemed ill at ease, and even when he did not speak the language, he had ways of making himself understood. Quentyn cut a poor figure by comparison — short-legged and stocky, thickly built, with hair the brown of new-turned earth. His forehead was too high, his jaw too square, his nose too broad. *A good honest face*, a girl had called it once, *but you should smile more.*

Smiles had never come easily for Quentyn Martell, any more than they did for his lord father.

"How swift is your *Adventure?*" Gerris said, in a halting approximation of High Valyrian.

The *Adventure*'s master recognized the accent and responded in the Common Tongue of Westeros. "There is none swifter, honored lord. *Adventure* can run down the wind itself. Tell me where you wish to sail, and swiftly I shall bring you there."

"I seek passage to Meereen for myself and two servants."

That gave the captain pause. "I am no stranger to Meereen. I could find the city again, aye . . . but why? There are no slaves to be had in Meereen, no profit to be found there. The silver queen has put an end to that. She has even closed the fighting pits, so a poor sailor cannot even amuse himself as he waits to fill his holds. Tell me, my Westerosi friend, what is there in Meereen that you should want to go there?"

The most beautiful woman in the world, thought Quentyn. *My bride-to-be, if the gods are good.* Sometimes at night he lay awake imagining her face and form, and wondering why such a woman would ever want to marry him, of all the princes in the world. *I am Dorne,* he told himself. *She will want Dorne.*

Gerris answered with the tale they had concocted. "Wine is our family trade. My father owns extensive vineyards back in Dorne, and wishes me to find new markets. It is hoped that the good folk of Meereen will welcome what I sell."

"Wine? *Dornish* wine?" The captain was not convinced. "The slave cities are at war. Can it be you do not know this?"

"The fighting is between Yunkai and Astapor, we had heard. Meereen is not involved."

"Not as yet. But soon. An envoy from the Yellow City is in Volantis even now, hiring swords. The Long Lances have already taken ship for Yunkai, and the Windblown and the Company of the Cat will follow once they have finished filling out their ranks. The Golden Company marches east as well. All this is known."

"If you say so. I deal in wine, not wars. Ghiscari wine is poor stuff, all agree. The Meereenese will pay a good price for my fine Dornish vintages."

"Dead men do not care what kind of wine they drink." The master of

Adventure fingered his beard. "I am not the first captain you have approached, I think. Nor the tenth."

"No," Gerris admitted.

"How many, then? A hundred?"

Close enough, thought Quentyn. The Volantenes were fond of boasting that the hundred isles of Braavos could be dropped into their deep harbor and drowned. Quentyn had never seen Braavos, but he could believe it. Rich and ripe and rotted, Volantis covered the mouth of the Rhoyne like a warm wet kiss, stretching across hill and marsh on both sides of the river. Ships were everywhere, coming down the river or headed out to sea, crowding the wharves and piers, taking on cargo or off-loading it: warships and whalers and trading galleys, carracks and skiffs, cogs, great cogs, longships, swan ships, ships from Lys and Tyrosh and Pentos, Qartheen spicers big as palaces, ships from Tolos and Yunkai and the Basilisks. So many that Quentyn, seeing the port for the first time from the deck of the *Meadowlark,* had told his friends that they would only linger here three days.

Yet twenty days had passed, and here they remained, still shipless. The captains of the *Melantine,* the *Triarch's Daughter,* and the *Mermaid's Kiss* had all refused them. A mate on the *Bold Voyager* had laughed in their faces. The master of the *Dolphin* berated them for wasting his time, and the owner of the *Seventh Son* accused them of being pirates. All on the first day.

Only the captain of the *Fawn* had given them reasons for his refusal. "It is true that I am sailing east," he told them, over watered wine. "South around Valyria and thence into the sunrise. We will take on water and provisions at New Ghis, then bend all oars toward Qarth and the Jade Gates. Every voyage has perils, long ones more than most. Why should I seek out more danger by turning into Slaver's Bay? The *Fawn* is my livelihood. I will not risk her to take three mad Dornishmen into the middle of a war."

Quentyn had begun to think that they might have done better to buy their own ship in the Planky Town. That would have drawn unwanted attention, however. The Spider had informers everywhere, even in the halls of Sunspear. "Dorne will bleed if your purpose is discovered," his father had warned him, as they watched the children frolic in the pools and fountains of the Water Gardens. "What we do is treason, make no mistake. Trust only your companions, and do your best to avoid attracting notice."

So Gerris Drinkwater gave the captain of *Adventure* his most disarming smile. "Truth be told, I have not kept count of all the cowards who refused us, but at the Merchant's House I heard it said that you were a bolder sort of man, the sort who might risk anything for sufficient gold."

A *smuggler*, Quentyn thought. That was how the other traders styled *Adventure*'s master, back at the Merchant's House. "He is a smuggler and a slaver, half pirate and half pander, but it may be that he is your best hope," the innkeep had told them.

The captain rubbed thumb and forefinger together. "And how much gold would you deem sufficient for such a voyage?"

"Thrice your usual fee for passage to Slaver's Bay."

"For each of you?" The captain showed his teeth in something that might have been intended as a smile though it gave his narrow face a feral look. "Perhaps. It is true, I am a bolder man than most. How soon will you wish to leave?"

"The morrow would not be too soon."

"Done. Return an hour before first light, with your friends and your wines. Best to be under way whilst Volantis sleeps, so no one will ask us inconvenient questions about our destination."

"As you say. An hour before first light."

The captain's smile widened. "I am pleased that I can help you. We will have a happy voyage, yes?"

"I am certain of it," said Gerris. The captain called for ale then, and the two of them drank a toast to their venture.

"A sweet man," Gerris said afterward, as he and Quentyn made their way down to the foot of the pier where their hired *hathay* waited. The air hung hot and heavy, and the sun was so bright that both of them were squinting.

"This is a sweet city," Quentyn agreed. *Sweet enough to rot your teeth.* Sweet beets were grown in profusion hereabouts, and were served with almost every meal. The Volantenes made a cold soup of them, as thick and rich as purple honey. Their wines were sweet as well. "I fear our happy voyage will be short, however. That sweet man does not mean to take us to Meereen. He was too quick to accept your offer. He'll take thrice the usual fee, no doubt, and once he has us aboard and out of sight of land, he'll slit our throats and take the rest of our gold as well."

"Or chain us to an oar, beside those wretches we were smelling. We need to find a better class of smuggler, I think."

Their driver awaited them beside his *hathay*. In Westeros, it might have been called an oxcart, though it was a deal more ornate than any cart that

Quentyn had ever seen in Dorne, and lacked an ox. The *hathay* was pulled by a dwarf elephant, her hide the color of dirty snow. The streets of Old Volantis were full of such.

Quentyn would have preferred to walk, but they were miles from their inn. Besides, the innkeep at the Merchant's House had warned him that traveling afoot would taint them in the eyes of foreign captains and the native-born Volantenes alike. Persons of quality traveled by palanquin, or in the back of a *hathay* . . . and as it happened the innkeep had a cousin who owned several such contrivances and would be pleased to serve them in this matter.

Their driver was one of the cousin's slaves, a small man with a wheel tattooed upon one cheek, naked but for a breechclout and a pair of sandals. His skin was the color of teak, his eyes chips of flint. After he had helped them up onto the cushioned bench between the cart's two huge wooden wheels, he clambered onto the elephant's back. "The Merchant's House," Quentyn told him, "but go along the wharves." Beyond the waterfront and its breezes, the streets and alleys of Volantis were hot enough to drown a man in his own sweat, at least on this side of the river.

The driver shouted something at his elephant in the local tongue. The beast began to move, trunk swaying from side to side. The cart lurched along behind her, the driver hooting at sailors and slaves alike to clear the way. It was easy enough to tell one from the other. The slaves were all tattooed: a mask of blue feathers, a lightning bolt that ran from jaw to brow, a coin upon the cheek, a leopard's spots, a skull, a jug. Maester Kedry said there were five slaves for every free man in Volantis though he had not lived long enough to verify his estimate. He had perished on the morning the corsairs swarmed aboard the *Meadowlark*.

Quentyn lost two other friends that same day—Willam Wells with his freckles and his crooked teeth, fearless with a lance, and Cletus Yronwood, handsome despite his lazy eye, always randy, always laughing. Cletus had been Quentyn's dearest friend for half his life, a brother in all but blood. "Give your bride a kiss for me," Cletus had whispered to him, just before he died.

The corsairs had come aboard in the darkness before the dawn, as the *Meadowlark* was anchored off the coast of the Disputed Lands. The crew had beaten them off, at the cost of twelve lives. Afterward the sailors stripped the dead corsairs of boots and belts and weapons, divvied up their purses, and yanked gemstones from their ears and rings from their fingers. One of the corpses was so fat that the ship's cook had to cut his fingers off with a meat cleaver to claim his rings. It took three Meadowlarks to roll the body into the sea. The other pirates were chucked in after him, without a word of prayer or ceremony.

Their own dead received more tender treatment. The sailors sewed their bodies up in canvas, weighed down with ballast stones so they might sink more quickly. The captain of the *Meadowlark* led his crew in a prayer for the souls of their slain shipmates. Then he turned to his Dornish passengers, the three who still remained of the six who had come aboard at the Planky Town. Even the big man had emerged, pale and greensick and unsteady on his feet, struggling up from the depths of the ship's hold to pay his last respects. "One of you should say some words for your dead, before we give them to the sea," the captain said. Gerris had obliged, lying with every other word, since he dare not tell the truth of who they'd been or why they'd come.

It was not supposed to end like that for them. "This will be a tale to tell our grandchildren," Cletus had declared the day they set out from his father's castle. Will made a face at that, and said, "A tale to tell tavern wenches, you mean, in hopes they'll lift their skirts." Cletus had slapped him on the back. "For grandchildren, you need children. For children, you need to lift some skirts." Later, in the Planky Town, the Dornishmen had toasted Quentyn's future bride, made ribald japes about his wedding night to come, and talked about the things they'd see, the deeds they'd do, the glory they would win. *All they won was a sailcloth sack filled with ballast stones.*

As much as he mourned Will and Cletus, it was the maester's loss that Quentyn felt most keenly. Kedry had been fluent in the tongues of all of the Free Cities, and even the mongrel Ghiscari that men spoke along the shores of Slaver's Bay. "Maester Kedry will accompany you," his father said the night they parted. "Heed his counsel. He has devoted half his life to the study of the Nine Free Cities." Quentyn wondered if things might not have gone a deal easier if only he were here to guide them.

"I would sell my mother for a bit of breeze," said Gerris, as they rolled through the dockside throngs. "It's moist as the Maiden's cunt, and still shy of noon. I hate this city."

Quentyn shared the feeling. The sullen wet heat of Volantis sapped his strength and left him feeling dirty. The worst part was knowing that nightfall would bring no relief. Up in the high meadows north of Lord Yronwood's estates, the air was always crisp and cool after dark, no matter how hot the day had been. Not here. In Volantis, the nights were almost as hot as the days.

"The *Goddess* sails for New Ghis on the morrow," Gerris reminded him. "That at least would bring us closer."

"New Ghis is an island, and a much smaller port than this. We would be closer, yes, but we could find ourselves stranded. And New Ghis has allied with the Yunkai'i." That news had not come as a surprise to Quentyn. New Ghis and Yunkai were both Ghiscari cities. "If Volantis should ally with them as well—"

"We need to find a ship from Westeros," suggested Gerris, "some trader out of Lannisport or Oldtown."

"Few come this far, and those who do fill their holds with silk and spice from the Jade Sea, then bend their oars for home."

"Perhaps a Braavosi ship? One hears of purple sails as far away as Asshai and the islands of the Jade Sea."

"The Braavosi are descended from escaped slaves. They do not trade in Slaver's Bay."

"Do we have enough gold to *buy* a ship?"

"And who will sail her? You? Me?" Dornishmen had never been seafarers, not since Nymeria burned her ten thousand ships. "The seas around Valyria are perilous, and thick with corsairs."

"I have had enough of corsairs. Let's not buy a ship."

This is still just a game to him, Quentyn realized, *no different than the time he led six of us up into the mountains to find the old lair of the Vulture King.* It was not in Gerris Drinkwater's nature to imagine they might fail, let alone that they might die. Even the deaths of three friends had not served to chasten him, it would seem. *He leaves that to me. He knows my nature is as cautious as his is bold.*

"Perhaps the big man is right," Ser Gerris said. "Piss on the sea, we can finish the journey overland."

"You know why he says that," Quentyn said. "He'd rather die than set foot on another ship." The big man had been greensick every day of their voyage. In Lys, it had taken him four days to recover his strength. They'd had to take rooms in an inn so Maester Kedry could tuck him into a feather bed and feed him broths and potions until some pink returned to his cheeks.

It was possible to go overland to Meereen, that much was true. The old Valyrian roads would take them there. *Dragon roads,* men called the great stone roadways of the Freehold, but the one that ran eastward from Volantis to Meereen had earned a more sinister name: *the demon road.*

"The demon road is dangerous, and too *slow,*" Quentyn said. "Tywin Lannister will send his own men after the queen once word of her reaches

King's Landing." His father had been certain of that. "His will come with knives. If they reach her first—"

"Let's hope her dragons will sniff them out and eat them," said Gerris. "Well, if we cannot find a ship, and you will not let us ride, we had as well book passage back to Dorne."

Crawl back to Sunspear defeated, with my tail between my legs? His father's disappointment would be more than Quentyn could bear, and the scorn of the Sand Snakes would be withering. Doran Martell had put the fate of Dorne into his hands, he could not fail him, not whilst life remained.

Heat shimmers rose off the street as the *hathay* rattled and jounced along on its iron-rimmed wheels, giving a dreamlike quality to their surroundings. In amongst the warehouses and the wharves, shops and stalls of many sorts crowded the waterfront. Here fresh oysters could be bought, here iron chains and manacles, here *cyvasse* pieces carved of ivory and jade. Here were temples too, where sailors came to sacrifice to foreign gods, cheek by jowl with pillow houses where women called down from balconies to men below. "Have a look at that one," Gerris urged, as they passed one pillow house. "I think she's in love with you."

And how much does a whore's love cost? Truth be told, girls made Quentyn anxious, especially the pretty ones.

When first he'd come to Yronwood, he had been smitten with Ynys, the eldest of Lord Yronwood's daughters. Though he never said a word about his feelings, he nursed his dreams for years . . . until the day she was dispatched to wed Ser Ryon Allyrion, the heir to Godsgrace. The last time he had seen her, she'd had one boy at her breast and another clinging to her skirts.

After Ynys had come the Drinkwater twins, a pair of tawny young maidens who loved hawking, hunting, climbing rocks, and making Quentyn blush. One of them had given him his first kiss, though he never knew which one. As daughters of a landed knight, the twins were too lowborn to marry, but Cletus did not think that was any reason to stop kissing them. "After you're wed you can take one of them for a paramour. Or both, why not?" But Quentyn thought of several reasons why not, so he had done his best to avoid the twins thereafter, and there had been no second kiss.

More recently, the youngest of Lord Yronwood's daughters had taken to following him about the castle. Gwyneth was but twelve, a small, scrawny girl whose dark eyes and brown hair set her apart in that house of blue-eyed blondes. She was clever, though, as quick with words as with her hands, and fond of telling Quentyn that he had to wait for her to flower, so she could marry him.

That was before Prince Doran had summoned him to the Water Gardens. And now the most beautiful woman in the world was waiting in Meereen, and he meant to do his duty and claim her for his bride. *She will not refuse me. She will honor the agreement.* Daenerys Targaryen would need Dorne to win the Seven Kingdoms, and that meant that she would need him. *It does not mean that she will love me, though. She may not even like me.*

The street curved where the river met the sea, and there along the bend a number of animal sellers were clustered together, offering jeweled lizards, giant banded snakes, and agile little monkeys with striped tails and clever pink hands. "Perhaps your silver queen would like a monkey," said Gerris.

Quentyn had no idea what Daenerys Targaryen might like. He had promised his father that he would bring her back to Dorne, but more and more he wondered if he was equal to the task.

I never asked for this, he thought.

Across the wide blue expanse of the Rhoyne, he could see the Black Wall that had been raised by the Valyrians when Volantis was no more than an outpost of their empire: a great oval of fused stone two hundred feet high and so thick that six four-horse chariots could race around its top abreast, as they did each year to celebrate the founding of the city. Outlanders, foreigners, and freedmen were not allowed inside the Black Wall save at the invitation of those who dwelt within, scions of the Old Blood who could trace their ancestry back to Valyria itself.

The traffic was thicker here. They were near the western end of the Long Bridge, which linked the two halves of the city. Wayns and carts and *hathays* crowded the streets, all of them coming from the bridge or making for it. Slaves were everywhere, as numerous as roaches, scurrying about their masters' business.

Not far from Fishermonger's Square and the Merchant's House, shouts erupted from a cross street, and a dozen Unsullied spearmen in ornate armor and tiger-skin cloaks appeared as if from nowhere, waving everyone aside so the triarch could pass through atop his elephant. The triarch's elephant was a grey-skinned behemoth clad in elaborate enameled armor that clattered softly as he moved, the castle on its back so tall that it scraped the top of the ornamental stone arch he was passing underneath. "The triarchs are considered so elevated that their feet are not allowed to touch the ground during their year of service," Quentyn informed his companion. "They ride everywhere on elephants."

"Blocking up the streets and leaving heaps of dung for the likes of us to contend with," said Gerris. "Why Volantis needs three princes when Dorne makes do with one, I will never know."

"The triarchs are neither kings nor princes. Volantis is a freehold, like Valyria of old. All freeborn landholders share the rule. Even women are allowed to vote, provided they own land. The three triarchs are chosen from amongst those noble families who can prove unbroken descent from old Valyria, to serve until the first day of the new year. And you would know all this if you had troubled to read the book that Maester Kedry gave you."

"It had no pictures."

"There were maps."

"Maps do not count. If he had told me it was about tigers and elephants, I might have given it a try. It looked suspiciously like a history."

When their *hathay* reached the edge of the Fishermonger's Square, their elephant lifted her trunk and made a honking noise like some huge white goose, reluctant to plunge into the tangle of wayns, palanquins, and foot traffic ahead. Their driver prodded her with his heel and kept her moving.

The fishmongers were out in strength, crying the morning catch. Quentyn understood one word in two at best, but he did not need to know the words to know the fish. He saw cod and sailfish and sardines, barrels of mussels and clams. Eels hung along the front of one stall. Another displayed a gigantic turtle, strung up by its legs on iron chains, heavy as a horse. Crabs scrabbled inside casks of brine and seaweed. Several of the vendors were frying chunks of fish with onions and beets, or selling peppery fish stew out of small iron kettles.

In the center of the square, under the cracked and headless statue of a dead triarch, a crowd had begun to gather about some dwarfs putting on a show. The little men were done up in wooden armor, miniature knights preparing for a joust. Quentyn saw one mount a dog, as the other hopped onto a pig . . . only to slide right off again, to a smattering of laughter.

"They look amusing," Gerris said. "Shall we stop and watch them fight? A laugh might serve you well, Quent. You look like an old man who has not moved his bowels in half a year."

I am eight-and-ten, six years younger than you, Quentyn thought. *I am no old man.* Instead he said, "I have no need for comic dwarfs. Unless they have a ship."

"A small one, I would think."

Four stories tall, the Merchant's House dominated the docks and wharves and storehouses that surrounded it. Here traders from Oldtown and King's Landing mingled with their counterparts from Braavos and Pentos and Myr, with hairy Ibbenese, pale-skinned voyagers from Qarth, coal-black Summer Islanders in feathered cloaks, even masked shadowbinders from Asshai by the Shadow.

The paving stones felt warm beneath his feet when Quentyn climbed down from the *hathay*, even through the leather of his boots. Outside the Merchant's House a trestle table had been set up in the shade and decorated with striped blue-and-white pennons that fluttered at every breath of air. Four hard-eyed sellswords lounged around the table, calling out to every passing man and boy. *Windblown*, Quentyn knew. The serjeants were looking for fresh meat to fill their ranks before they sailed for Slaver's Bay. *And every man who signs with them is another sword for Yunkai, another blade meant to drink the blood of my bride-to-be.*

One of the Windblown shouted at them. "I do not speak your tongue," Quentyn answered. Though he could read and write High Valyrian, he had little practice speaking it. And the Volantene apple had rolled a fair distance from the Valyrian tree.

"Westerosi?" the man answered, in the Common Tongue.

"Dornishmen. My master is a wineseller."

"Master? Fuck that. Are you a slave? Come with us and be your own master. Do you want to die abed? We'll teach you sword and spear. You'll ride to battle with the Tattered Prince and come home richer than a lord. Boys, girls, gold, whatever you want, if you're man enough to take it. We're the Windblown, and we fuck the goddess slaughter up her arse."

Two of the sellswords began to sing, bellowing out the words to some marching song. Quentyn understood enough to get the gist. *We are the Windblown*, they sang. *Blow us east to Slaver's Bay, we'll kill the butcher king and fuck the dragon queen.*

"If Cletus and Will were still with us, we could come back with the big man and kill the lot of them," said Gerris.

Cletus and Will are dead. "Pay them no mind," Quentyn said. The sellswords threw taunts at their backs as they pushed through the doors of the Merchant's House, mocking them as bloodless cravens and frightened girls.

The big man was waiting in their rooms on the second floor. Though the inn had come well recommended by the master of the *Meadowlark*, that did not mean Quentyn was willing to leave their goods and gold unguarded. Every port had thieves, rats, and whores, and Volantis had more than most.

"I was about to go out looking for you," Ser Archibald Yronwood said as he slid the bar back to admit them. It was his cousin Cletus who had started calling him *the big man*, but the name was well deserved. Arch was six-and-a-half-feet tall, broad of shoulder, huge of belly, with legs like tree trunks, hands the size of hams, and no neck to speak of. Some childhood malady had made all his hair fall out. His bald head reminded Quentyn of a smooth pink boulder. "So," he demanded, "what did the smuggler say? Do we have a boat?"

"A ship," corrected Quentyn. "Aye, he'll take us, but only as far as the nearest hell."

Gerris sat upon a sagging bed and pulled off his boots. "Dorne is sounding more attractive every moment."

The big man said, "I still say we would do better to ride the demon road. Might be it's not as perilous as men say. And if it is, that only means more glory for those who dare it. Who would dare molest us? Drink with his sword, me with my hammer, that's more than any demon could digest."

"And if Daenerys is dead before we reach her?" Quentyn said. "We must have a ship. Even if it is *Adventure*."

Gerris laughed. "You must be more desperate for Daenerys than I knew if you'd endure that stench for months on end. After three days, I'd be begging them to murder me. No, my prince, I pray you, not *Adventure*."

"Do you have a better way?" Quentyn asked him.

"I do. It's just now come to me. It has its risks, and it is not what you would call honorable, I grant you . . . but it will get you to your queen quicker than the demon road."

"Tell me," said Quentyn Martell.

JON

Jon Snow read the letter over until the words began to blur and run together. *I cannot sign this. I will not sign this.*

He almost burned the parchment then and there. Instead he took a sip of ale, the dregs of the half cup that remained from his solitary supper the night before. *I have to sign it. They chose me to be their lord commander. The Wall is mine, and the Watch as well. The Night's Watch takes no part.*

It was a relief when Dolorous Edd Tollett opened the door to tell him that Gilly was without. Jon set Maester Aemon's letter aside. "I will see her." He dreaded this. "Find Sam for me. I will want to speak with him next."

"He'll be down with the books. My old septon used to say that books are dead men talking. Dead men should keep quiet, is what I say. No one wants to hear a dead man's yabber." Dolorous Edd went off muttering of worms and spiders.

When Gilly entered, she went at once to her knees. Jon came around the table and drew her to her feet. "You don't need to take a knee for me. That's just for kings." Though a wife and mother, Gilly still seemed half a child to him, a slender little thing wrapped up in one of Sam's old cloaks. The cloak was so big on her that she could have hidden several other girls beneath its folds. "The babes are well?" he asked her.

The wildling girl smiled timidly from under her cowl. "Yes, m'lord. I was scared I wouldn't have milk enough for both, but the more they suck, the more I have. They're strong."

"I have something hard to tell you." He almost said *ask*, but caught himself at the last instant.

"Is it Mance? Val begged the king to spare him. She said she'd let some kneeler marry her and never slit his throat if only Mance could live. That

Lord o'Bones, he's to be spared. Craster always swore he'd kill him if he ever showed his face about the keep. Mance never did half the things he done."

All Mance ever did was lead an army down upon the realm he once swore to protect. "Mance said our words, Gilly. Then he turned his cloak, wed Dalla, and crowned himself King-Beyond-the-Wall. His life is in the king's hands now. It's not him we need to talk about. It's his son. Dalla's boy."

"The babe?" Her voice trembled. "He never broke no oath, m'lord. He sleeps and cries and sucks, is all; he's never done no harm to no one. Don't let her burn him. Save him, please."

"Only you can do that, Gilly." Jon told her how.

Another woman would have shrieked at him, cursed him, damned him down to seven hells. Another woman might have flown at him in rage, slapped him, kicked him, raked at his eyes with her nails. Another woman might have thrown her defiance in his teeth.

Gilly shook her head. "No. Please, no."

The raven picked up the word. "No," it screamed.

"Refuse, and the boy will burn. Not on the morrow, nor the day after . . . but soon, whenever Melisandre needs to wake a dragon or raise a wind or work some other spell requiring king's blood. Mance will be ash and bone by then, so she will claim his son for the fire, and Stannis will not deny her. If you do not take the boy away, *she will burn him.*"

"I'll go," said Gilly. "I'll take him, I'll take the both o' them, Dalla's boy *and* mine." Tears rolled down her cheeks. If not for the way the candle made them glisten, Jon might never have known that she was weeping. *Craster's wives would have taught their daughters to shed their tears into a pillow. Perhaps they went outside to weep, well away from Craster's fists.*

Jon closed the fingers of his sword hand. "Take both boys and the queen's men will ride after you and drag you back. The boy will still burn . . . and you with him." *If I comfort her, she may think that tears can move me. She has to realize that I will not yield.* "You'll take one boy, and that one Dalla's."

"A mother can't leave her son, or else she's cursed forever. Not a *son.* We *saved* him, Sam and me. Please. Please, m'lord. We saved him from the cold."

"Men say that freezing to death is almost peaceful. Fire, though . . . do you see the candle, Gilly?"

She looked at the flame. "Yes."

"Touch it. Put your hand over the flame."

Her big brown eyes grew bigger still. She did not move.

"Do it." *Kill the boy.* "Now."

Trembling, the girl reached out her hand, held it well above the flickering candle flame.

"Down. Let it kiss you."

Gilly lowered her hand. An inch. Another. When the flame licked her flesh, she snatched her hand back and began to sob.

"Fire is a cruel way to die. Dalla died to give this child life, but you have nourished him, cherished him. You saved your own boy from the ice. Now save hers from the fire."

"They'll burn my babe, then. The red woman. If she can't have Dalla's, she'll burn mine."

"Your son has no king's blood. Melisandre gains nothing by giving him to the fire. Stannis wants the free folk to fight for him, he will not burn an innocent without good cause. Your boy will be safe. I will find a wet nurse for him and he'll be raised here at Castle Black under my protection. He'll learn to hunt and ride, to fight with sword and axe and bow. I'll even see that he is taught to read and write." Sam would like that. "And when he is old enough, he will learn the truth of who he is. He'll be free to seek you out if that is what he wants."

"You will make a crow of him." She wiped at her tears with the back of a small pale hand. "I won't. I won't."

Kill the boy, thought Jon. "You will. Else I promise you, the day that they burn Dalla's boy, yours will die as well."

"*Die*," shrieked the Old Bear's raven. "*Die, die, die.*"

The girl sat hunched and shrunken, staring at the candle flame, tears glistening in her eyes. Finally Jon said, "You have my leave to go. Do not speak of this, but see that you are ready to depart an hour before first light. My men will come for you."

Gilly got to her feet. Pale and wordless, she departed, with never a look back at him. Jon heard her footsteps as she rushed through the armory. She was almost running.

When he went to close the door, Jon saw that Ghost was stretched out beneath the anvil, gnawing on the bone of an ox. The big white direwolf looked up at his approach. "Past time that you were back." He returned to his chair, to read over Maester Aemon's letter once again.

Samwell Tarly turned up a few moments later, clutching a stack of books. No sooner had he entered than Mormont's raven flew at him demanding corn. Sam did his best to oblige, offering some kernels from the sack beside the door. The raven did its best to peck through his palm. Sam yowled, the bird flapped off, corn scattered. "Did that wretch break the skin?" Jon asked.

Sam gingerly removed his glove. "He did. I'm *bleeding*."

"We all shed our blood for the Watch. Wear thicker gloves." Jon shoved a chair toward him with a foot. "Sit, and have a look at this." He handed Sam the parchment.

"What is it?"

"A paper shield."

Sam read it slowly. "A letter to King Tommen?"

"At Winterfell, Tommen fought my brother Bran with wooden swords," Jon said, remembering. "He wore so much padding he looked like a stuffed goose. Bran knocked him to the ground." He went to the window and threw the shutters open. The air outside was cold and bracing, though the sky was a dull grey. "Yet Bran's dead, and pudgy pink-faced Tommen is sitting on the Iron Throne, with a crown nestled amongst his golden curls."

That got an odd look from Sam, and for a moment he looked as if he wanted to say something. Instead he swallowed and turned back to the parchment. "You haven't signed the letter."

Jon shook his head. "The Old Bear begged the Iron Throne for help a hundred times. They sent him Janos Slynt. No letter will make the Lannisters love us better. Not once they hear that we've been helping Stannis."

"Only to defend the Wall, not in his rebellion. That's what it *says* here."

"The distinction may escape Lord Tywin." Jon snatched the letter back. "Why would he help us now? He never did before."

"Well, he will not want it said that Stannis rode to the defense of the realm whilst King Tommen was playing with his toys. That would bring scorn down upon House Lannister."

"It's death and destruction I want to bring down upon House Lannister, not scorn." Jon read from the letter. "*The Night's Watch takes no part in the wars of the Seven Kingdoms. Our oaths are sworn to the realm, and the realm now stands in dire peril. Stannis Baratheon aids us against our foes from beyond the Wall, though we are not his men . . .*"

Sam squirmed in his seat. "Well, we're *not*. Are we?"

"I gave Stannis food, shelter, and the Nightfort, plus leave to settle some free folk in the Gift. That's all."

"Lord Tywin will say it was too much."

"Stannis says it's not enough. The more you give a king, the more he wants. We are walking on a bridge of ice with an abyss on either side. Pleasing one king is difficult enough. Pleasing two is hardly possible."

"Yes, but . . . if the Lannisters should prevail and Lord Tywin decides that we betrayed the king by aiding Stannis, it could mean the end of the Night's Watch. He has the Tyrells behind him, with all the strength of Highgarden. And he did defeat Lord Stannis on the Blackwater."

"The Blackwater was one battle. Robb won all his battles and still lost his head. If Stannis can raise the north . . ."

Sam hesitated, then said, "The Lannisters have northmen of their own. Lord Bolton and his bastard."

"Stannis has the Karstarks. If he can win White Harbor . . ."

"If," Sam stressed. "If not . . . my lord, even a paper shield is better than none."

"I suppose so." *Him and Aemon both.* Somehow he had hoped that Sam Tarly might see it differently. *It is only ink and parchment.* Resigned, he grabbed the quill and signed. "Get the sealing wax." *Before I change my mind.* Sam hastened to obey. Jon fixed the lord commander's seal and handed him the letter. "Take this to Maester Aemon when you leave, and tell him to dispatch a bird to King's Landing."

"I will." Sam sounded relieved. "My lord, if I might ask . . . I saw Gilly leaving. She was almost crying."

"Val sent her to plead for Mance again," Jon lied, and they talked for a while of Mance and Stannis and Melisandre of Asshai, until the raven ate the last corn kernel and screamed, *"Blood."*

"I am sending Gilly away," Jon said. "Her and the boy. We will need to find another wet nurse for his milk brother."

"Goat's milk might serve, until you do. It's better for a babe than cow's milk." Talking about breasts plainly made Sam uncomfortable, and suddenly he began to speak of history, and boy commanders who had lived and died hundreds of years ago. Jon cut him off with, "Tell me something useful. Tell me of our enemy."

"The Others." Sam licked his lips. "They are mentioned in the annals, though not as often as I would have thought. The annals I've found and looked at, that is. There's more I haven't found, I know. Some of the older books are falling to pieces. The pages crumble when I try and turn them. And the *really* old books . . . either they have crumbled all away or they are buried somewhere that I haven't looked yet or . . . well, it could be that there are no such books and never were. The oldest histories we have were written after the Andals came to Westeros. The First Men only left us runes on rocks, so everything we think we know about the Age of Heroes and the Dawn Age and the Long Night comes from accounts set down by septons thousands of years later. There are archmaesters at the Citadel who question all of it. Those old histories are full of kings who reigned for hundreds of years, and knights riding around a thousand years before there *were* knights. You know the tales, Brandon the Builder, Symeon Star-Eyes, Night's King . . . we say that you're the nine-hundred-and-ninety-eighth Lord Commander of the Night's Watch, but the oldest list I've found shows six hundred seventy-four commanders, which suggests that it was written during—"

"Long ago," Jon broke in. "What about the Others?"

"I found mention of dragonglass. The children of the forest used to give the Night's Watch a hundred obsidian daggers every year, during the Age of Heroes. The Others come when it is cold, most of the tales agree. Or else it gets cold when they come. Sometimes they appear during snow-storms and melt away when the skies clear. They hide from the light of the sun and emerge by night . . . or else night falls when they emerge. Some stories speak of them riding the corpses of dead animals. Bears, direwolves, mammoths, horses, it makes no matter, so long as the beast is dead. The one that killed Small Paul was riding a dead horse, so that part's plainly true. Some accounts speak of giant ice spiders too. I don't know what those are. Men who fall in battle against the Others must be burned, or else the dead will rise again as their thralls."

"We knew all this. The question is, how do we fight them?"

"The armor of the Others is proof against most ordinary blades, if the tales can be believed, and their own swords are so cold they shatter steel. Fire will dismay them, though, and they are vulnerable to obsidian. I found one account of the Long Night that spoke of the last hero slaying Others with a blade of dragonsteel. Supposedly they could not stand against it."

"Dragonsteel?" The term was new to Jon. "*Valyrian* steel?"

"That was my first thought as well."

"So if I can just convince the lords of the Seven Kingdoms to give us their Valyrian blades, all is saved? That won't be hard." *No harder than asking them to give up their coin and castles.* He gave a bitter laugh. "Did you find who the Others are, where they come from, what they want?"

"Not yet, my lord, but it may be that I've just been reading the wrong books. There are hundreds I have not looked at yet. Give me more time and I will find whatever there is to be found."

"There is no more time. You need to get your things together, Sam. You're going with Gilly."

"Going?" Sam gaped at him openmouthed, as if he did not understand the meaning of the word. "I'm going? To Eastwatch, my lord? Or . . . where am I . . ."

"Oldtown."

"*Oldtown?*" Sam repeated, in a high-pitched squeak.

"Aemon as well."

"Aemon? *Maester* Aemon? But . . . he's one hundred and two years old, my lord, he can't . . . you're sending him *and* me? Who will tend the ravens? If there's sick or wounded, who . . ."

"Clydas. He's been with Aemon for years."

"Clydas is only a steward, and his eyes are going bad. You need a *maester*. Maester Aemon is so frail, a sea voyage . . . it might . . . he's old, and . . ."

"His life will be at risk. I am aware of that, Sam, but the risk is greater here. Stannis knows who Aemon is. If the red woman requires king's blood for her spells . . ."

"Oh." Sam's fat cheeks seemed to drain of color.

"Dareon will join you at Eastwatch. My hope is that his songs will win some men for us in the south. The *Blackbird* will deliver you to Braavos. From there, you'll arrange your own passage to Oldtown. If you still mean to claim Gilly's babe as your bastard, send her and the child on to Horn Hill. Elsewise, Aemon will find a servant's place for her at the Citadel."

"My b-b-bastard. Yes, I . . . my mother and my sisters will help Gilly with the child. Dareon could see her to Oldtown just as well as me. I'm . . . I've been working at my archery every afternoon with Ulmer, as you commanded . . . well, except when I'm in the vaults, but you told me to find out about the Others. The longbow makes my shoulders ache and raises blisters on my fingers." He showed Jon his hand. "I still do it, though. I can hit the target more often than not now, but I'm still the worst archer who ever bent a bow. I like Ulmer's stories, though. Someone needs to write them down and put them in a book."

"You do it. They have parchment and ink at the Citadel, as well as longbows. I will expect you to continue with your practice. Sam, the Night's Watch has hundreds of men who can loose an arrow, but only a handful who can read or write. I need you to become my new maester."

"My lord, I . . . my work is here, the books . . ."

". . . will be here when you return to us."

Sam put a hand to his throat. "My lord, the Citadel . . . they make you cut up corpses there. I cannot wear a chain."

"You can. You will. Maester Aemon is old and blind. His strength is leaving him. Who will take his place when he dies? Maester Mullin at the Shadow Tower is more fighter than scholar, and Maester Harmune of Eastwatch is drunk more than he's sober."

"If you ask the Citadel for more maesters . . ."

"I mean to. We'll have need of every one. Aemon Targaryen is not so easily replaced, however." *This is not going as I had hoped.* He had known Gilly would be hard, but he had assumed Sam would be glad to trade the dangers of the Wall for the warmth of Oldtown. "I was certain this would please you," he said, puzzled. "There are so many books at the Citadel that no man can hope to read them all. You would do well there, Sam. I know you would."

"No. I could read the books, but . . . a m-maester must be a healer and b-b-blood makes me faint." His hand shook, to prove the truth of that. "I'm Sam the Scared, not Sam the Slayer."

"Scared? Of what? The chidings of old men? Sam, you saw the wights come swarming up the Fist, a tide of living dead men with black hands and bright blue eyes. You slew an Other."

"It was the d-d-d-dragonglass, not me."

"Be quiet," Jon snapped. After Gilly, he had no patience for the fat boy's fears. "You lied and schemed and plotted to make me lord commander. You *will* obey me. You'll go to the Citadel and forge a chain, and if you have to cut up corpses, so be it. At least in Oldtown the corpses won't object."

"My lord, my f-f-f-father, Lord Randyll, he, he, he, he, he . . . the life of a maester is a life of *servitude*. No son of House Tarly will ever wear a chain. The men of Horn Hill do not bow and scrape to petty lords. Jon, I cannot disobey my *father*."

Kill the boy, Jon thought. *The boy in you, and the one in him. Kill the both of them, you bloody bastard.* "You have no father. Only brothers. Only us. Your life belongs to the Night's Watch, so go and stuff your small-clothes into a sack, along with anything else you care to take to Oldtown. You leave an hour before sunrise. And here's another order. From this day forth, you will *not* call yourself a craven. You've faced more things this past year than most men face in a lifetime. You can face the Citadel, but you'll face it as a Sworn Brother of the Night's Watch. I can't command you to be brave, but I *can* command you to hide your fears. You said the words, Sam. Remember?"

"I . . . I'll try."

"You won't try. You will obey."

"*Obey.*" Mormont's raven flapped its great black wings.

Sam seemed to sag. "As my lord commands. Does . . . does Maester Aemon know?"

"It was as much his idea as mine." Jon opened the door for him. "No farewells. The fewer folk who know of this, the better. An hour before first light, by the lichyard."

Sam fled from him just as Gilly had.

Jon was tired. *I need sleep.* He had been up half the night poring over maps, writing letters, and making plans with Maester Aemon. Even after stumbling into his narrow bed, rest had not come easily. He knew what he would face today, and found himself tossing restlessly as he brooded on Maester Aemon's final words. "Allow me to give my lord one last piece of counsel," the old man had said, "the same counsel that I once gave my brother when we parted for the last time. He was three-and-thirty when the Great Council chose him to mount the Iron Throne. A man grown with sons of his own, yet in some ways still a boy. Egg had an innocence to him, a sweetness we all loved. *Kill the boy within you,* I told him the day I took ship for the Wall. *It takes a man to rule. An Aegon, not an Egg. Kill the boy and let the man be born.*" The old man felt Jon's face. "You are half the age that Egg was, and your own burden is a crueler one, I fear. You will have little joy of your command, but I think you have the strength in you to do the things that must be done. Kill the boy, Jon Snow. Winter is almost upon us. Kill the boy and let the man be born."

Jon donned his cloak and strode outside. He made the rounds of Castle Black each day, visiting the men on watch and hearing their reports first hand, watching Ulmer and his charges at the archery butts, talking with king's men and queen's men alike, walking the ice atop the Wall to have a look at the forest. Ghost padded after him, a white shadow at his side.

Kedge Whiteye had the Wall when Jon made his ascent. Kedge had seen forty-odd namedays, thirty of them on the Wall. His left eye was blind, his right eye mean. In the wild, alone with axe and garron, he was as good a ranger as any in the Watch, but he had never gotten on well with the other men. "A quiet day," he told Jon. "Nothing to report, except the wrong-way rangers."

"The wrong-way rangers?" Jon asked.

Kedge grinned. "A pair of knights. Went riding off an hour ago, south along the kingsroad. When Dywen saw them buggering off, he said the southron fools were riding the wrong way."

"I see," said Jon.

He found out more from Dywen himself, as the old forester sucked down a bowl of barley broth in the barracks. "Aye, m'lord, I saw them. Horpe and Massey, it were. Claimed Stannis sent 'em out, but never said where or what for or when they would be back."

Ser Richard Horpe and Ser Justin Massey were both queen's men, and high in the king's councils. *A pair of common freeriders would have served if all that Stannis had in mind was scouting,* Jon Snow reflected, *but knights are better suited to act as messengers or envoys.* Cotter Pyke had sent word from Eastwatch that the Onion Lord and Salladhor Saan had set sail for White Harbor to treat with Lord Manderly. It made sense that Stannis would send out other envoys. His Grace was not a patient man.

Whether the wrong-way rangers would return was another question. Knights they might be, but they did not know the north. *There will be eyes along the kingsroad, not all of them friendly.* It was none of Jon's concern, though. *Let Stannis have his secrets. The gods know that I have mine.*

Ghost slept at the foot of the bed that night, and for once Jon did not dream he was a wolf. Even so, he slept fitfully, tossing for hours before sliding down into a nightmare. Gilly was in it, weeping, pleading with him to leave her babes alone, but he ripped the children from her arms and hacked their heads off, then swapped the heads around and told her to sew them back in place.

When he woke, he found Edd Tollett looming over him in the darkness of his bedchamber. "M'lord? It is time. The hour of the wolf. You left orders to be woken."

"Bring me something hot." Jon threw off his blankets.

Edd was back by the time that he had dressed, pressing a steaming cup into his hands. Jon expected hot mulled wine, and was surprised to find that it was soup, a thin broth that smelled of leeks and carrots but seemed to have no leeks or carrots in it. *The smells are stronger in my wolf dreams,* he reflected, *and food tastes richer too. Ghost is more alive than I am.* He left the empty cup upon the forge.

Kegs was on his door this morning. "I will want to speak with Bedwyck and with Janos Slynt," Jon told him. "Have them both here at first light."

Outside the world was black and still. *Cold, but not dangerously cold. Not yet. It will be warmer when the sun comes up. If the gods are good, the Wall may weep.* When they reached the lichyard, the column had already formed up. Jon had given Black Jack Bulwer command of the escort, with a dozen mounted rangers under him, and two wayns. One was piled high with chests and crates and sacks, provisions for the journey. The other had a stiff roof of boiled leather to keep the wind off. Maester Aemon was seated in the back of it, huddled in a bearskin that made him look as small as a child. Sam and Gilly stood nearby. Her eyes were red and puffy, but the boy was in her arms, bundled tight. Whether it was her boy or Dalla's he could not be sure. He had only seen the two together a few times. Gilly's boy was older, Dalla's more robust, but they were close enough in age and size so that no one who did not know them well would be able to easily tell one from the other.

"Lord Snow," Maester Aemon called out, "I left a book for you in my chambers. The *Jade Compendium*. It was written by the Volantene adventurer Colloquo Votar, who traveled to the east and visited all the lands of the Jade Sea. There is a passage you may find of interest. I've told Clydas to mark it for you."

"I'll be sure to read it."

Maester Aemon wiped his nose. "Knowledge is a weapon, Jon. Arm yourself well before you ride forth to battle."

"I will." Jon felt something wet and cold upon his face. When he raised his eyes, he saw that it was snowing. *A bad omen.* He turned to Black Jack Bulwer. "Make as good a time as you can, but take no foolish risks. You have an old man and a suckling babe with you. See that you keep them warm and well fed."

"You do the same, m'lord." Gilly did not seem in any haste to climb into the wayn. "You do the same for t'other. Find another wet nurse, like you said. You promised me you would. The boy . . . Dalla's boy . . . the little prince, I mean . . . you find him some good woman, so he grows up big and strong."

"You have my word."

"Don't you name him. Don't you do that, till he's past two years. It's ill luck to name them when they're still on the breast. You crows may not know that, but it's true."

"As you command, my lady."

"Don't you call me that. I'm a mother, not a lady. I'm Craster's wife and Craster's daughter, and a *mother*." She gave the babe to Dolorous Edd as she climbed into the wayn and covered herself with furs. When Edd gave her back the child, Gilly put him to her breast. Sam turned away from the sight, red-faced, and heaved himself up onto his mare. "*Let's do this,*" commanded Black Jack Bulwer, snapping his whip. The wayns rolled forward.

Sam lingered a moment. "Well," he said, "farewell."

"And to you, Sam," said Dolorous Edd. "Your boat's not like to sink, I don't think. Boats only sink when I'm aboard."

Jon was remembering. "The first time I saw Gilly she was pressed back against the wall of Craster's Keep, this skinny dark-haired girl with her big belly, cringing away from Ghost. He had gotten in among her rabbits, and I think she was frightened that he would tear her open and devour the babe . . . but it was not the wolf she should have been afraid of, was it?"

"She has more courage than she knows," said Sam.

"So do you, Sam. Have a swift, safe voyage, and take care of her and Aemon and the child." The cold trickles on his face reminded Jon of the day he'd bid farewell to Robb at Winterfell, never knowing that it was for the last time. "And pull your hood up. The snowflakes are melting in your hair."

By the time the little column had dwindled in the distance, the eastern sky had gone from black to grey and the snow was falling heavily. "Giant will be waiting on the lord commander's pleasure," Dolorous Edd reminded him. "Janos Slynt as well."

"Yes." Jon Snow glanced up at the Wall, towering over them like a cliff of ice. *A hundred leagues from end to end, and seven hundred feet high.* The strength of the Wall was its height; the length of the Wall was its weakness. Jon remembered something his father had said once. *A wall is only as strong as the men who stand behind it.* The men of the Night's Watch were brave enough, but they were far too few for the task that confronted them.

Giant was waiting in the armory. His real name was Bedwyck. At a hair and a half over five feet he was the smallest man in the Night's Watch. Jon came directly to the point. "We need more eyes along the Wall. Waycastles where our patrols can get out of the cold and find hot food and a fresh mount. I am putting a garrison in Icemark and giving you command of it."

Giant put the tip of his little finger in his ear to clean out the wax. "Command? Me? M'lord knows I'm just a crofter's get, on the Wall for poaching?"

"You've been a ranger for a dozen years. You survived the Fist of the First Men and Craster's Keep, and came back to tell the tale. The younger men look up to you."

The small man laughed. "Only dwarfs look up to me. I don't read, my lord. On a good day I can write my name."

"I've sent to Oldtown for more maesters. You'll have two ravens for when your need is urgent. When it's not, send riders. Until we have more maesters and more birds, I mean to establish a line of beacon towers along the top of the Wall."

"And how many poor fools will I be commanding?"

"Twenty, from the Watch," said Jon, "and half as many men from Stannis." *Old, green, or wounded.* "They won't be his best men, and none will take the black, but they'll obey. Make what use of them you can. Four of the brothers I'm sending with you will be Kingslanders who came to the Wall with Lord Slynt. Keep one eye on that lot and watch for climbers with the other."

"We can watch, m'lord, but if enough climbers gain the top o' the Wall, thirty men won't be enough to throw them off."

Three hundred might not be enough. Jon kept that doubt to himself. It was true that climbers were desperately vulnerable whilst on the ascent. Stones and spears and pots of burning pitch could be rained down on them from above, and all they could do was cling desperately to the ice. Sometimes the Wall itself seemed to shake them off, as a dog might shake off fleas. Jon had seen that for himself, when a sheet of ice cracked beneath Val's lover Jarl, sending him to his death.

If the climbers reached the top of the Wall undetected, however, everything changed. Given time, they could carve out a toehold for themselves up there, throwing up ramparts of their own and dropping ropes and ladders for thousands more to clamber over after them. That was how Raymun Redbeard had done it, Raymun who had been King-Beyond-the-Wall in the days of his grandfather's grandfather. Jack Musgood had been the lord commander in those days. Jolly Jack, he was called before Redbeard came down upon the north; Sleepy Jack, forever after. Raymun's host had met a bloody end on the shores of Long Lake, caught between Lord William of Winterfell and the Drunken Giant, Harmond Umber. Redbeard had been slain by Artos the Implacable, Lord Willam's younger brother. The Watch arrived too late to fight the wildlings, but in time to bury them, the task that Artos Stark assigned them in his wroth as he grieved above the headless corpse of his fallen brother.

Jon did not intend to be remembered as Sleepy Jon Snow. "Thirty men will stand a better chance than none," he told Giant.

"True enough," the small man said. "Is it just to be Icemark, then, or will m'lord be opening t'other forts as well?"

"I mean to garrison all of them, in time," said Jon, "but for the moment, it will just be Icemark and Greyguard."

"And has m'lord decided who's to command at Greyguard?"

"Janos Slynt," said Jon. *Gods save us.* "A man does not rise to command of the gold cloaks without ability. Slynt was born a butcher's son. He was captain of the Iron Gate when Manly Stokeworth died, and Jon Arryn raised him up and put the defense of King's Landing into his hands. Lord Janos cannot be as great a fool as he seems." *And I want him well away from Alliser Thorne.*

"Might be that's so," said Giant, "but I'd still send him to the kitchens to help Three-Finger Hobb cut up the turnips."

If I did, I'd never dare to eat another turnip.

Half the morning passed before Lord Janos reported as commanded. Jon was cleaning Longclaw. Some men would have given that task to a steward or a squire, but Lord Eddard had taught his sons to care for their own weapons. When Kegs and Dolorous Edd arrived with Slynt, Jon thanked them and bid Lord Janos sit.

That he did, albeit with poor grace, crossing his arms, scowling, and ignoring the naked steel in his lord commander's hands. Jon slid the oil-cloth down his bastard sword, watching the play of morning light across the ripples, thinking how easily the blade would slide through skin and fat and sinew to part Slynt's ugly head from his body. All of a man's crimes were wiped away when he took the black, and all of his allegiances as well, yet he found it hard to think of Janos Slynt as a brother. *There is blood between us. This man helped slay my father and did his best to have me killed as well.*

"Lord Janos." Jon sheathed his sword. "I am giving you command of Greyguard."

That took Slynt aback. "Greyguard . . . Greyguard was where you climbed the Wall with your wildling friends . . ."

"It was. The fort is in a sorry state, admittedly. You will restore it as best you can. Start by clearing back the forest. Steal stones from the structures that have collapsed to repair those still standing." *The work will be hard and brutal,* he might have added. *You'll sleep on stone, too exhausted to complain or plot, and soon you'll forget what it was like to be warm, but you might remember what it was to be a man.* "You will have thirty men. Ten from here, ten from the Shadow Tower, and ten lent to us by King Stannis."

Slynt's face had turned the color of a prune. His meaty jowls began to quiver. "Do you think I cannot see what you are doing? Janos Slynt is not a man to be gulled so easily. I was charged with the defense of King's Landing when you were soiling your swaddling clothes. Keep your ruin, bastard."

I am giving you a chance, my lord. It is more than you ever gave my father. "You mistake me, my lord," Jon said. "That was a command, not an offer. It is forty leagues to Greyguard. Pack up your arms and armor, say your farewells, and be ready to depart at first light on the morrow."

"No." Lord Janos lurched to his feet, sending his chair crashing over backwards. "I will *not* go meekly off to freeze and die. No traitor's bastard gives commands to Janos Slynt! I am not without friends, I warn you. Here, and in King's Landing too. I was the Lord of Harrenhal! Give your ruin to one of the blind fools who cast a stone for you, I will not have it. Do you hear me, boy? *I will not have it!*"

"You will."

Slynt did not deign to answer that, but he kicked the chair aside as he departed.

He still sees me as a boy, Jon thought, *a green boy, to be cowed by angry words.* He could only hope that a night's sleep would bring Lord Janos to his senses.

The next morning proved that hope was vain.

Jon found Slynt breaking his fast in the common room. Ser Alliser Thorne was with him, and several of their cronies. They were laughing about something when Jon came down the steps with Iron Emmett and Dolorous Edd, and behind them Mully, Horse, Red Jack Crabb, Rusty Flowers, and Owen the Oaf. Three-Finger Hobb was ladling out porridge from his kettle. Queen's men, king's men, and black brothers sat at their separate tables, some bent over bowls of porridge, others filling their bellies with fried bread and bacon. Jon saw Pyp and Grenn at one table, Bowen Marsh at another. The air smelled of smoke and grease, and the clatter of knives and spoons echoed off the vaulted ceiling.

All the voices died at once.

"Lord Janos," Jon said, "I will give you one last chance. Put down that spoon and get to the stables. I have had your horse saddled and bridled. It is a long, hard road to Greyguard."

"Then you had best be on your way, boy." Slynt laughed, dribbling porridge down his chest. "Greyguard's a good place for the likes of you, I'm thinking. Well away from decent godly folk. The mark of the beast is on you, bastard."

"You are refusing to obey my order?"

"You can stick your order up your bastard's arse," said Slynt, his jowls quivering.

Alliser Thorne smiled a thin smile, his black eyes fixed on Jon. At another table, Godry the Giantslayer began to laugh.

"As you will." Jon nodded to Iron Emmett. "Please take Lord Janos to the Wall—"

—and confine him to an ice cell, he might have said. A day or ten cramped up inside the ice would leave him shivering and feverish and begging for release, Jon did not doubt. *And the moment he is out, he and Thorne will begin to plot again.*

—and tie him to his horse, he might have said. If Slynt did not wish to go to Greyguard as its commander, he could go as its cook. *It will only be a matter of time until he deserts, then. And how many others will he take with him?*

"—and hang him," Jon finished.

Janos Slynt's face went as white as milk. The spoon slipped from his fingers. Edd and Emmett crossed the room, their footsteps ringing on the stone floor. Bowen Marsh's mouth opened and closed though no words came out. Ser Alliser Thorne reached for his sword hilt. *Go on,* Jon thought. Longclaw was slung across his back. *Show your steel. Give me cause to do the same.*

Half the men in the hall were on their feet. Southron knights and men-at-arms, loyal to King Stannis or the red woman or both, and Sworn Brothers of the Night's Watch. Some had chosen Jon to be their lord commander. Others had cast their stones for Bowen Marsh, Ser Denys Mallister, Cotter Pyke . . . and some for Janos Slynt. *Hundreds of them, as I recall.* Jon wondered how many of those men were in the cellar right now. For a moment the world balanced on a sword's edge.

Alliser Thorne took his hand from his sword and stepped aside to let Edd Tollett pass.

Dolorous Edd took hold of Slynt by one arm, Iron Emmett by the other. Together they hauled him from the bench. "No," Lord Janos protested, flecks of porridge spraying from his lips. "No, unhand me. He's just a boy, a *bastard*. His father was a traitor. The mark of the beast is on him, that wolf of his . . . *Let go of me!* You will rue the day you laid hands on Janos Slynt. I have friends in King's Landing. I warn you—" He was still protesting as they half-marched, half-dragged him up the steps.

Jon followed them outside. Behind him, the cellar emptied. At the cage, Slynt wrenched loose for a moment and tried to make a fight of it, but Iron Emmett caught him by the throat and slammed him back against the iron bars until he desisted. By then all of Castle Black had come outside to watch. Even Val was at her window, her long golden braid across one shoulder. Stannis stood on the steps of the King's Tower, surrounded by his knights.

"If the boy thinks that he can frighten me, he is mistaken," they heard Lord Janos said. "He would not dare to hang me. Janos Slynt has friends, *important* friends, you'll see . . ." The wind whipped away the rest of his words.

This is wrong, Jon thought. "Stop."

Emmett turned back, frowning. "My lord?"

"I will not hang him," said Jon. "Bring him here."

"Oh, Seven save us," he heard Bowen Marsh cry out.

The smile that Lord Janos Slynt smiled then had all the sweetness of rancid butter. Until Jon said, "Edd, fetch me a block," and unsheathed Longclaw.

By the time a suitable chopping block was found, Lord Janos had re-treated into the winch cage, but Iron Emmett went in after him and dragged him out. "No," Slynt cried, as Emmett half-shoved and half-pulled him across the yard. "Unhand me . . . you cannot . . . when Tywin Lannister hears of this, you will all rue—"

Emmett kicked his legs out from under him. Dolorous Edd planted a foot on his back to keep him on his knees as Emmett shoved the block beneath his head. "This will go easier if you stay still," Jon Snow promised him. "Move to avoid the cut, and you will still die, but your dying will be uglier. Stretch out your neck, my lord." The pale morning sunlight ran up and down his blade as Jon clasped the hilt of the bastard sword with both hands and raised it high. "If you have any last words, now is the time to speak them," he said, expecting one last curse.

Janos Slynt twisted his neck around to stare up at him. "Please, my lord. Mercy. I'll . . . I'll go, I will, I . . ."

No, thought Jon. *You closed that door.* Longclaw descended.

"Can I have his boots?" asked Owen the Oaf, as Janos Slynt's head went rolling across the muddy ground. "They're almost new, those boots. Lined with fur."

Jon glanced back at Stannis. For an instant their eyes met. Then the king nodded and went back inside his tower.

TYRION

He woke alone, and found the litter halted.

A pile of crushed cushions remained to show where Illyrio had sprawled. The dwarf's throat felt dry and raspy. He had dreamed . . . what had he dreamed? He did not remember.

Outside, voices were speaking in a tongue he did not know. Tyrion swung his legs through the curtains and hopped to the ground, to find Magister Illyrio standing by the horses with two riders looming over him. Both wore shirts of worn leather beneath cloaks of dark brown wool, but their swords were sheathed and the fat man did not look to be in danger.

"I need a piss," the dwarf announced. He waddled off the road, undid his breeches, and relieved himself into a tangle of thorns. It took quite a long time.

"He pisses well, at least," a voice observed.

Tyrion flicked the last drops off and tucked himself away. "Pissing is the least of my talents. You ought to see me shit." He turned to Magister Illyrio. "Are these two known to you, magister? They look like outlaws. Should I find my axe?"

"Your *axe*?" exclaimed the larger of the riders, a brawny man with a shaggy beard and a shock of orange hair. "Did you hear that, Haldon? The little man wants to fight with us!"

His companion was older, clean-shaved, with a lined ascetic face. His hair had been pulled back and tied in a knot behind his head. "Small men oft feel a need to prove their courage with unseemly boasts," he declared. "I doubt if he could kill a duck."

Tyrion shrugged. "Fetch the duck."

"If you insist." The rider glanced at his companion.

The brawny man unsheathed a bastard sword. "I'm Duck, you mouthy little pisspot."

Oh, gods be good. "I had a smaller duck in mind."

The big man roared with laughter. "Did you hear, Haldon? He wants a *smaller* Duck!"

"I should gladly settle for a quieter one." The man called Haldon studied Tyrion with cool grey eyes before turning back to Illyrio. "You have some chests for us?"

"And mules to carry them."

"Mules are too slow. We have pack horses, we'll shift the chests to them. Duck, attend to that."

"Why is it always Duck who attends to things?" The big man slipped his sword back in its sheath. "What do *you* attend to, Haldon? Who is the knight here, you or me?" Yet he stomped off toward the baggage mules all the same.

"How fares our lad?" asked Illyrio as the chests were being secured. Tyrion counted six, oaken chests with iron hasps. Duck shifted them easily enough, hoisting them on one shoulder.

"He is as tall as Griff now. Three days ago he knocked Duck into a horse trough."

"I wasn't *knocked*. I fell in just to make him laugh."

"Your ploy was a success," said Haldon. "I laughed myself."

"There is a gift for the boy in one of the chests. Some candied ginger. He was always fond of it." Illyrio sounded oddly sad. "I thought I might continue on to Ghoyan Drohe with you. A farewell feast before you start downriver . . ."

"We have no time for feasts, my lord," said Haldon. "Griff means to strike downriver the instant we are back. News has been coming upriver, none of it good. Dothraki have been seen north of Dagger Lake, outriders from old Motho's *khalasar,* and Khal Zekko is not far behind him, moving through the Forest of Qohor."

The fat man made a rude noise. "Zekko visits Qohor every three or four years. The Qohorik give him a sack of gold and he turns east again. As for Motho, his men are near as old as he is, and there are fewer every year. The threat is—"

"—Khal Pono," Haldon finished. "Motho and Zekko flee from him, if the tales are true. The last reports had Pono near the headwaters of the Selhoru with a *khalasar* of thirty thousand. Griff does not want to risk being caught up in the crossing if Pono should decide to risk the

Rhoyne." Haldon glanced at Tyrion. "Does your dwarf ride as well as he pisses?"

"He rides," Tyrion broke in, before the lord of cheese could answer for him, "though he rides best with a special saddle and a horse that he knows well. He talks as well."

"So he does. I am Haldon, the healer in our little band of brothers. Some call me Halfmaester. My companion is Ser Duck."

"Ser *Rolly*," said the big man. "Rolly Duckfield. Any knight can make a knight, and Griff made me. And you, dwarf?"

Illyrio spoke up quickly. "Yollo, he is called."

Yollo? Yollo sounds like something you might name a monkey. Worse, it was a Pentoshi name, and any fool could see that Tyrion was no Pentoshi. "In Pentos I am Yollo," he said quickly, to make what amends he could, "but my mother named me Hugor Hill."

"Are you a little king or a little bastard?" asked Haldon.

Tyrion realized he would do well to be careful around Haldon Half-maester. "Every dwarf is a bastard in his father's eyes."

"No doubt. Well, Hugor Hill, answer me this. How did Serwyn of the Mirror Shield slay the dragon Urrax?"

"He approached behind his shield. Urrax saw only his own reflection until Serwyn had plunged his spear through his eye."

Haldon was unimpressed. "Even Duck knows that tale. Can you tell me the name of the knight who tried the same ploy with Vhagar during the Dance of the Dragons?"

Tyrion grinned. "Ser Byron Swann. He was roasted for his trouble . . . only the dragon was Syrax, not Vhagar."

"I fear that you're mistaken. In *The Dance of the Dragons, A True Telling*, Maester Munkun writes—"

"—that it was Vhagar. *Grand* Maester Munkun errs. Ser Byron's squire saw his master die, and wrote his daughter of the manner of it. His account says it was Syrax, Rhaenyra's she-dragon, which makes more sense than Munken's version. Swann was the son of a marcher lord, and Storm's End was for Aegon. Vhagar was ridden by Prince Aemond, Aegon's brother. Why should Swann want to slay her?"

Haldon pursed his lips. "Try not to tumble off the horse. If you do, best waddle back to Pentos. Our shy maid will not wait for man nor dwarf."

"Shy maids are my favorite sort. Aside from wanton ones. Tell me, where do whores go?"

"Do I look like a man who frequents whores?"

Duck laughed derisively. "He don't dare. Lemore would make him pray for pardon, the lad would want to come along, and Griff might cut his cock off and stuff it down his throat."

"Well," said Tyrion, "a maester does not need a cock."

"Haldon's only half a maester, though."

"You seem to find the dwarf amusing, Duck," said Haldon. "He can ride with you." He wheeled his mount about.

It took another few moments for Duck to finish securing Illyrio's chests to the three pack horses. By that time Haldon had vanished. Duck seemed unconcerned. He swung into the saddle, grabbed Tyrion by the collar, and hoisted the little man up in front of him. "Hold tight to the pommel and you'll do fine. The mare's got a nice sweet gait, and the dragon road's smooth as a maiden's arse." Gathering the reins in his right hand and the leads in his left, Ser Rolly set off at a brisk trot.

"Good fortune," Illyrio called after them. "Tell the boy I am sorry that I will not be with him for his wedding. I will rejoin you in Westeros. That I swear, by my sweet Serra's hands."

The last that Tyrion Lannister saw of Illyrio Mopatis, the magister was standing by his litter in his brocade robes, his massive shoulders slumped. As his figure dwindled in their dust, the lord of cheese looked almost small.

Duck caught up with Haldon Halfmaester a quarter mile on. Thereafter the riders continued side by side. Tyrion clung to the high pommel with his short legs splayed out awkwardly, knowing he could look forward to blisters, cramps, and saddle sores.

"I wonder what the pirates of Dagger Lake will make of our dwarf?" Haldon said as they rode on.

"Dwarf stew?" suggested Duck.

"Urho the Unwashed is the worst of them," Haldon confided. "His stench alone is enough to kill a man."

Tyrion shrugged. "Fortunately, I have no nose."

Haldon gave him a thin smile. "If we should encounter the Lady Korra on *Hag's Teeth*, you may soon be lacking other parts as well. Korra the Cruel, they call her. Her ship is crewed by beautiful young maids who geld every male they capture."

"Terrifying. I may well piss my breeches."

"Best not," Duck warned darkly.

"As you say. If we encounter this Lady Korra, I will just slip into a skirt and say that I am Cersei, the famous bearded beauty of King's Landing."

This time Duck laughed, and Haldon said, "What a droll little fellow you are, Yollo. They say that the Shrouded Lord will grant a boon to any

man who can make him laugh. Perhaps His Grey Grace will choose you
to ornament his stony court."

Duck glanced at his companion uneasily. "It's not good to jape of that
one, not when we're so near the Rhoyne. He hears."

"Wisdom from a duck," said Haldon. "I beg your pardon, Yollo. You
need not look so pale, I was only playing with you. The Prince of Sorrows
does not bestow his grey kiss lightly."

His grey kiss. The thought made his flesh crawl. Death had lost its terror for Tyrion Lannister, but greyscale was another matter. *The Shrouded
Lord is just a legend,* he told himself, *no more real than the ghost of Lann
the Clever that some claim haunts Casterly Rock.* Even so, he held his
tongue.

The dwarf's sudden silence went unnoticed, as Duck had begun to
regale him with his own life story. His father had been an armorer at Bitterbridge, he said, so he had been born with the sound of steel ringing in
his ears and had taken to swordplay at an early age. Such a large and likely
lad drew the eye of old Lord Caswell, who offered him a place in his garrison, but the boy had wanted more. He watched Caswell's weakling son
named a page, a squire, and finally a knight. "A weedy pinch-faced sneak,
he was, but the old lord had four daughters and only the one son, so no
one was allowed to say a word against him. T'other squires hardly dared to
lay a finger on him in the yard."

"You were not so timid, though." Tyrion could see where this tale was
going easily enough.

"My father made a longsword for me to mark my sixteenth nameday,"
said Duck, "but Lorent liked the look of it so much he took it for himself,
and my bloody father never dared to tell him no. When I complained,
Lorent told me to my face that my hand was made to hold a hammer, not
a sword. So I went and got a hammer and beat him with it, till both his
arms and half his ribs were broken. After that I had to leave the Reach,
quick as it were. I made it across the water to the Golden Company. I did
some smithing for a few years as a 'prentice, then Ser Harry Strickland
took me on as squire. When Griff sent word downriver that he needed
someone to help train his son to arms, Harry sent him me."

"And Griff knighted you?"

"A year later."

Haldon Halfmaester smiled a thin smile. "Tell our little friend how you
came by your name, why don't you?"

"A knight needs more than just the one name," the big man insisted, "and, well, we were in a field when he dubbed me, and I looked up and saw these ducks, so . . . don't laugh, now."

Just after sunset, they left the road to rest in an overgrown yard beside an old stone well. Tyrion hopped down to work the cramps out of his calves whilst Duck and Haldon were watering the horses. Tough brown grass and weed trees sprouted from the gaps between the cobbles, and the mossy walls of what once might have been a huge stone manse. After the animals had been tended to, the riders shared a simple supper of salt pork and cold white beans, washed down with ale. Tyrion found the plain fare a pleasant change from all the rich food he had eaten with Illyrio. "Those chests we brought you," he said as they were chewing. "Gold for the Golden Company, I thought at first, until I saw Ser Rolly hoist a chest onto one shoulder. If it were full of coin, he could never have lifted it so easily."

"It's just armor," said Duck, with a shrug.

"Clothing as well," Haldon broke in. "Court clothes, for all our party. Fine woolens, velvets, silken cloaks. One does not come before a queen looking shabby . . . nor empty-handed. The magister has been kind enough to provide us with suitable gifts."

Come moonrise, they were back in their saddles, trotting eastward under a mantle of stars. The old Valyrian road glimmered ahead of them like a long silver ribbon winding through wood and dale. For a little while Tyrion Lannister felt almost at peace. "Lomas Longstrider told it true. The road's a wonder."

"Lomas Longstrider?" asked Duck.

"A scribe, long dead," said Haldon. "He spent his life traveling the world and writing about the lands he visited in two books he called *Wonders* and *Wonders Made by Man*."

"An uncle of mine gave them to me when I was just a boy," said Tyrion. "I read them until they fell to pieces."

"The gods made seven wonders, and mortal man made nine," quoted the Halfmaester. "Rather impious of mortal man to do the gods two better, but there you are. The stone roads of Valyria were one of Longstrider's nine. The fifth, I believe."

"The fourth," said Tyrion, who had committed all sixteen of the wonders to memory as a boy. His uncle Gerion liked to set him on the table during feasts and make him recite them. *I liked that well enough, didn't I? Standing there amongst the trenchers with every eye upon me, proving what a clever little imp I was.* For years afterward, he had cherished a dream that one day he would travel the world and see Longstrider's wonders for himself.

Lord Tywin had put an end to that hope ten days before his dwarf son's sixteenth nameday, when Tyrion asked to tour the Nine Free Cities, as his uncles had done at that same age. "My brothers could be relied upon to bring no shame upon House Lannister," his father had replied. "Neither ever wed a whore." And when Tyrion had reminded him that in ten days he would be a man grown, free to travel where he wished, Lord Tywin had said, "No man is free. Only children and fools think elsewise. Go, by all means. Wear motley and stand upon your head to amuse the spice lords and the cheese kings. Just see that you pay your own way and put aside any thoughts of returning." At that the boy's defiance had crumbled. "If it is useful occupation you require, useful occupation you shall have," his father then said. So to mark his manhood, Tyrion was given charge of all the drains and cisterns within Casterly Rock. *Perhaps he hoped I'd fall into one.* But Tywin had been disappointed in that. The drains never drained half so well as when he had charge of them.

I need a cup of wine, to wash the taste of Tywin from my mouth. A skin of wine would serve me even better.

They rode all night, with Tyrion sleeping fitfully, dozing against the pommel and waking suddenly. From time to time he would begin to slip sideways from the saddle, but Ser Rolly would get a hand on him and yank him upright once again. By dawn the dwarf's legs were aching and his cheeks were chafed and raw.

It was the next day before they reached the site of Ghoyan Drohe, hard beside the river. "The fabled Rhoyne," said Tyrion when he glimpsed the slow green waterway from atop a rise.

"The Little Rhoyne," said Duck.

"It is that." *A pleasant enough river, I suppose, but the smallest fork of the Trident is twice as wide, and all three of them run swifter.* The city was no more impressive. Ghoyan Drohe had never been large, Tyrion recalled from his histories, but it had been a fair place, green and flowering, a city of canals and fountains. *Until the war. Until the dragons came.* A thousand years later, the canals were choked with reeds and mud, and pools of stagnant water gave birth to swarms of flies. The broken stones of temples and palaces were sinking back into the earth, and gnarled old willows grew thick along the riverbanks.

A few people still remained amidst the squalor, tending little gardens in amongst the weeds. The sound of iron hooves ringing on the old Valyrian road sent most of them darting back into the holes they'd crawled from, but the bolder ones lingered in the sun long enough to stare at the passing riders with dull, incurious eyes. One naked girl with mud up to her knees could not seem to take her eyes off Tyrion. *She has never seen a dwarf before*, he realized, *much less a dwarf without a nose.* He made a face and stuck his tongue out, and the girl began to cry.

"What did you do to her?" Duck asked.

"I blew her a kiss. All the girls cry when I kiss them."

Beyond the tangled willows the road ended abruptly and they turned north for a short ways and rode beside the water, until the brush gave way and they found themselves beside an old stone quay, half-submerged and surrounded by tall brown weeds. *"Duck!"* came a shout. *"Haldon!"* Tyrion craned his head to one side, and saw a boy standing on the roof of a low wooden building, waving a wide-brimmed straw hat. He was a lithe and well-made youth, with a lanky build and a shock of dark blue hair. The dwarf put his age at fifteen, sixteen, or near enough to make no matter.

The roof the boy was standing on turned out to be the cabin of the *Shy Maid*, an old ramshackle single-masted poleboat. She had a broad beam and a shallow draft, ideal for making her way up the smallest of streams and crabwalking over sandbars. *A homely maid*, thought Tyrion, *but sometimes the ugliest ones are the hungriest once abed.* The poleboats that plied the rivers of Dorne were often brightly painted and exquisitely carved, but not this maid. Her paintwork was a muddy greyish brown, mottled and flaking; her big curved tiller, plain and unadorned. *She looks like dirt*, he thought, *but no doubt that's the point.*

Duck was hallooing back by then. The mare splashed through the shallows, trampling down the reeds. The boy leapt down off the cabin roof to the poleboat's deck, and the rest of the *Shy Maid*'s crew made their appearance. An older couple with a Rhoynish cast to their features stood close beside the tiller, whilst a handsome septa in a soft white robe stepped through the cabin door and pushed a lock of dark brown hair from her eyes.

But there was no mistaking Griff. "That will be enough shouting," he said. A sudden silence fell upon the river.

This one will be trouble, Tyrion knew at once.

Griff's cloak was made from the hide and head of a red wolf of the Rhoyne. Under the pelt he wore brown leather stiffened with iron rings. His clean-shaved face was leathery too, with wrinkles at the corners of his eyes. Though his hair was as blue as his son's, he had red roots and redder eyebrows. At his hip hung a sword and dagger. If he was happy to have Duck and Haldon back again, he hid it well, but he did not trouble to conceal his displeasure at the sight of Tyrion. "A dwarf? What's this?"

"I know, you were hoping for a wheel of cheese." Tyrion turned to Young Griff and gave the lad his most disarming smile. "Blue hair may serve you well in Tyrosh, but in Westeros children will throw stones at you and girls will laugh in your face."

The lad was taken aback. "My mother was a lady of Tyrosh. I dye my hair in memory of her."

"What is this creature?" Griff demanded.

Haldon answered. "Illyrio sent a letter to explain."

"I will have it, then. Take the dwarf to my cabin."

I do not like his eyes, Tyrion reflected, when the sellsword sat down across from him in the dimness of the boat's interior, with a scarred plank table and a tallow candle between them. They were ice blue, pale, cold. The dwarf misliked pale eyes. Lord Tywin's eyes had been pale green and flecked with gold.

He watched the sellsword read. That he *could* read said something all by itself. How many sellswords could boast of that? *He hardly moves his lips at all,* Tyrion reflected.

Finally Griff looked up from the parchment, and those pale eyes narrowed. "Tywin Lannister dead? At *your* hand?"

"At my finger. This one." Tyrion held it up for Griff to admire. "Lord Tywin was sitting on a privy, so I put a crossbow bolt through his bowels to see if he really did shit gold. He didn't. A pity, I could have used some gold. I also slew my mother, somewhat earlier. Oh, and my nephew Joffrey, I poisoned him at his wedding feast and watched him choke to death. Did the cheesemonger leave that part out? I mean to add my brother and sister to the list before I'm done, if it please your queen."

"*Please* her? Has Illyrio taken leave of his senses? Why does he imagine that Her Grace would welcome the service of a self-confessed kingslayer and betrayer?"

A *fair question,* thought Tyrion, but what he said was, "The king I slew was sitting on her throne, and all those I betrayed were lions, so it seems to me that I have already done the queen good service." He scratched the stump of his nose. "Have no fear, I won't kill you, you are no kin of mine. Might I see what the cheesemonger wrote? I do love to read about myself."

Griff ignored the request. Instead he touched the letter to the candle flame and watched the parchment blacken, curl, and flare up. "There is blood between Targaryen and Lannister. Why would you support the cause of Queen Daenerys?"

"For gold and glory," the dwarf said cheerfully. "Oh, and hate. If you had ever met my sister, you would understand."

"I understand hate well enough." From the way Griff said the word, Tyrion knew that much was true. *He has supped on hate himself, this one. It has warmed him in the night for years.*

"Then we have that in common, ser."

"I am no knight."

Not only a liar, but a bad one. That was clumsy and stupid, my lord. "And yet Ser Duck says you knighted him."

"Duck talks too much."

"Some might wonder that a duck can talk at all. No matter, *Griff.* You are no knight and I am Hugor Hill, a little monster. *Your* little monster, if you like. You have my word, all that I desire is to be leal servant of your dragon queen."

"And how do you propose to serve her?"

"With my tongue." He licked his fingers, one by one. "I can tell Her Grace how my sweet sister thinks, if you call it thinking. I can tell her captains the best way to defeat my brother, Jaime, in battle. I know which lords are brave and which are craven, which are loyal and which are venal. I can deliver allies to her. And I know much and more of dragons, as your halfmaester will tell you. I'm amusing too, and I don't eat much. Consider me your own true imp."

Griff weighed that for a moment. "Understand this, dwarf. You are the last and least of our company. Hold your tongue and do as you are told, or you will soon wish you had."

Yes, Father, Tyrion almost said. "As you say, my lord."

"I am no lord."

Liar. "It was a courtesy, my friend."

"I am not your friend either."

No knight, no lord, no friend. "A pity."

"Spare me your irony. I will take you as far as Volantis. If you show yourself to be obedient and useful, you may remain with us, to serve the queen as best you can. Prove yourself more trouble than you are worth, and you can go your own way."

Aye, and my way will take me to the bottom of the Rhoyne with fish nibbling at what's left of my nose. "Valar dohaeris."

"You may sleep on the deck or in the hold, as you prefer. Ysilla will find bedding for you."

"How kind of her." Tyrion made a waddling bow, but at the cabin door, he turned back. "What if we should find the queen and discover that this talk of dragons was just some sailor's drunken fancy? This wide world is full of such mad tales. Grumkins and snarks, ghosts and ghouls, mermaids, rock goblins, winged horses, winged pigs . . . winged lions."

Griff stared at him, frowning. "I have given you fair warning, Lannister. Guard your tongue or lose it. Kingdoms are at hazard here. Our lives, our names, our honor. This is no game we're playing for your amusement."

Of course it is, thought Tyrion. *The game of thrones.* "As you say, Captain," he murmured, bowing once again.

DAVOS

Lightning split the northern sky, etching the black tower of the Night Lamp against the blue-white sky. Six heartbeats later came the thunder, like a distant drum.

The guards marched Davos Seaworth across a bridge of black basalt and under an iron portcullis showing signs of rust. Beyond lay a deep salt moat and a drawbridge supported by a pair of massive chains. Green waters surged below, sending up plumes of spray to smash against the foundations of the castle. Then came a second gatehouse, larger than the first, its stones bearded with green algae. Davos stumbled across a muddy yard with his hands bound at the wrists. A cold rain stung his eyes. The guards prodded him up the steps, into Breakwater's cavernous stone keep.

Once inside, the captain removed his cloak and hung it from a peg, so as not to leave puddles on the threadbare Myrish carpet. Davos did the same, fumbling at the clasp with his bound hands. He had not forgotten the courtesies he had learned on Dragonstone during his years of service.

They found the lord alone in the gloom of his hall, making a supper of beer and bread and sister's stew. Twenty iron sconces were mounted along his thick stone walls, but only four held torches, and none of them was lit. Two fat tallow candles gave a meagre, flickering light. Davos could hear the rain lashing at the walls, and a steady dripping where the roof had sprung a leak.

"M'lord," said the captain, "we found this man in the Belly o' the Whale, trying to buy his way off island. He had twelve dragons on him, and this thing too." The captain put it on the table by the lord: a wide ribbon of black velvet trimmed with cloth-of-gold, and bearing three seals; a crowned stag stamped in golden beeswax, a flaming heart in red, a hand in white.

Davos waited wet and dripping, his wrists chafing where the wet rope dug into his skin. One word from this lord and he would soon be hanging from the Gallows Gate of Sisterton, but at least he was out of the rain, with solid stone beneath his feet in place of a heaving deck. He was soaked and sore and haggard, worn thin by grief and betrayal, and sick to death of storms.

The lord wiped his mouth with the back of his hand and picked up the ribbon for a closer squint. Lightning flashed outside, making the arrow loops blaze blue and white for half a heartbeat. *One, two, three, four,* Davos counted, before the thunder came. When it quieted, he listened to the dripping, and the duller roar beneath his feet, where the waves were smashing against Breakwater's huge stone arches and swirling through its dungeons. He might well end up down there, fettered to a wet stone floor and left to drown when the tide came rushing in. *No,* he tried to tell himself, *a smuggler might die that way, but not a King's Hand. I'm worth more if he sells me to his queen.*

The lord fingered the ribbon, frowning at the seals. He was an ugly man, big and fleshy, with an oarsman's thick shoulders and no neck. Coarse grey stubble, going white in patches, covered his cheeks and chin. Above a massive shelf of brow he was bald. His nose was lumpy and red with broken veins, his lips thick, and he had a sort of webbing between the three middle fingers of his right hand. Davos had heard that some of the lords of the Three Sisters had webbed hands and feet, but he had always put that down as just another sailor's story.

The lord leaned back. "Cut him free," he said, "and peel those gloves off him. I want to see his hands."

The captain did as he was told. As he jerked up his captive's maimed left hand the lightning flashed again, throwing the shadow of Davos Seaworth's shortened fingers across the blunt and brutal face of Godric Borrell, Lord of Sweetsister. "Any man can steal a ribbon," the lord said, "but those fingers do not lie. You are the onion knight."

"I have been called that, my lord." Davos was a lord himself, and had been a knight for long years now, but deep down he was still what he had always been, a smuggler of common birth who had bought his knighthood with a hold of onions and salt fish. "I have been called worse things too."

"Aye. Traitor. Rebel. Turncloak."

He bristled at the last. "I have never turned my cloak, my lord. I am a king's man."

"Only if Stannis is a king." The lord weighed him with hard black eyes. "Most knights who land upon my shores seek me in my hall, not in the

Belly of the Whale. A vile smuggler's den, that place. Are you returning to your old trade, onion knight?"

"No, my lord. I was looking for passage to White Harbor. The king sent me, with a message for its lord."

"Then you are in the wrong place, with the wrong lord." Lord Godric seemed amused. "This is Sisterton, on Sweetsister."

"I know it is." There was nothing sweet about Sisterton, though. It was a vile town, a sty, small and mean and rank with the odors of pig shit and rotting fish. Davos remembered it well from his smuggling days. The Three Sisters had been a favorite haunt of smugglers for hundreds of years, and a pirate's nest before that. Sisterton's streets were mud and planks, its houses daub-and-wattle hovels roofed with straw, and by the Gallows Gate there were always hanged men with their entrails dangling out.

"You have friends here, I do not doubt," said the lord. "Every smuggler has friends on the Sisters. Some of them are my friends as well. The ones who aren't, them I hang. I let them strangle slowly, with their guts slapping up against their knees." The hall grew bright again, as lightning lit the windows. Two heartbeats later came the thunder. "If it is White Harbor that you want, why are you in Sisterton? What brought you here?"

A king's command and a friend's betrayal, Davos might have said. Instead he answered, "Storms."

Nine-and-twenty ships had set sail from the Wall. If half of them were still afloat, Davos would be shocked. Black skies, bitter winds, and lashing rains had hounded them all the way down the coast. The galleys *Oledo* and *Old Mother's Son* had been driven onto the rocks of Skagos, the isle of unicorns and cannibals where even the Blind Bastard had feared to land; the great cog *Saathos Saan* had foundered off the Grey Cliffs. "Stannis will be paying for them," Salladhor Saan had fumed. "He will be paying for them with good gold, every one." It was as if some angry god was exacting payment for their easy voyage north, when they had ridden a steady southerly from Dragonstone to the Wall. Another gale had ripped away the rigging of the *Bountiful Harvest*, forcing Salla to have her taken under tow. Ten leagues north of Widow's Watch the seas rose again, slamming the *Harvest* into one of the galleys towing her and sinking both. The rest of the Lysene fleet had been scattered across the narrow sea. Some would straggle into one port or another. Others would never be seen again.

"Salladhor the Beggar, that's what your king has made me," Salladhor Saan complained to Davos, as the remnants of his fleet limped across the

Bite. "Salladhor the Smashed. Where are my ships? And my gold, where is all the gold that I was promised?" When Davos had tried to assure him that he would have his payment, Salla had erupted. "When, *when*? On the morrow, on the new moon, when the red comet comes again? He is promising me gold and gems, always promising, but this gold I have not seen. I have his word, he is saying, oh yes, his royal word, he writes it down. Can Salladhor Saan eat the king's word? Can he quench his thirst with parchments and waxy seals? Can he tumble promises into a feather bed and fuck them till they squeal?"

Davos had tried to persuade him to stay true. If Salla abandoned Stannis and his cause, he pointed out, he abandoned all hope of collecting the gold that was due him. A victorious King Tommen was not like to pay his defeated uncle's debts, after all. Salla's only hope was to remain loyal to Stannis Baratheon until he won the Iron Throne. Elsewise he would never see a groat of his money. He had to be patient.

Perhaps some lord with honey on his tongue might have swayed the Lysene pirate prince, but Davos was an onion knight, and his words had only provoked Salla to fresh outrage. "On Dragonstone I was patient," he said, "when the red woman burned wooden gods and screaming men. All the long way to the Wall I was patient. At Eastwatch I was patient . . . and cold, so very cold. Bah, I say. Bah to your patience, and bah to your king. My men are hungry. They are wishing to fuck their wives again, to count their sons, to see the Stepstones and the pleasure gardens of Lys. Ice and storms and empty promises, these they are *not* wanting. This north is much too cold, and getting colder."

I knew the day would come, Davos told himself. *I was fond of the old rogue, but never so great a fool as to trust him.*

"Storms." Lord Godric said the word as fondly as another man might say his lover's name. "Storms were sacred on the Sisters before the Andals came. Our gods of old were the Lady of the Waves and the Lord of the Skies. They made storms every time they mated." He leaned forward. "These kings never bother with the Sisters. Why should they? We are small and poor. And yet you're here. Delivered to me by the storms."

Delivered to you by a friend, Davos thought.

Lord Godric turned to his captain. "Leave this man with me. He was never here."

"No, m'lord. Never." The captain took his leave, his wet boots leaving damp footprints across the carpet. Beneath the floor the sea was rumbling and restless, pounding at the castle's feet. The outer door closed with a sound like distant thunder, and again the lightning came, as if in answer.

"My lord," said Davos, "if you would send me on to White Harbor, His Grace would count it as an act of friendship."

"I could send you to White Harbor," the lord allowed. "Or I could send you to some cold wet hell."

Sisterton is hell enough. Davos feared the worst. The Three Sisters were fickle bitches, loyal only to themselves. Supposedly they were sworn to the Arryns of the Vale, but the Eyrie's grasp upon the islands was tenuous at best.

"Sunderland would require me to hand you over if he knew of you." Borrell did fealty for Sweetsister, as Longthorpe did for Longsister and Torrent for Littlesister; all were sworn to Triston Sunderland, the Lord of the Three Sisters. "He'd sell you to the queen for a pot of that Lannister gold. Poor man needs every dragon, with seven sons all determined to be knights." The lord picked up a wooden spoon and attacked his stew again. "I used to curse the gods who gave me only daughters until I heard Triston bemoaning the cost of destriers. You would be surprised to know how many fish it takes to buy a decent suit of plate and mail."

I had seven sons as well, but four are burned and dead. "Lord Sunderland is sworn to the Eyrie," Davos said. "By rights he should deliver me to Lady Arryn." He would stand a better chance with her than with the Lannisters, he judged. Though she had taken no part in the War of the Five Kings, Lysa Arryn was a daughter of Riverrun, and aunt to the Young Wolf.

"Lysa Arryn's dead," Lord Godric said, "murdered by some singer. Lord Littlefinger rules the Vale now. Where are the pirates?" When Davos did not answer, he rapped his spoon against the table. "The Lyseni. Torrent spied their sails from Littlesister, and before him the Flints from Widow's Watch. Orange sails, and green, and pink. Salladhor Saan. Where is he?"

"At sea." Salla would be sailing around the Fingers and down the narrow sea. He was returning to the Stepstones with what few ships remained him. Perhaps he would acquire a few more along the way, if he came upon some likely merchantmen. *A little piracy to help the leagues go by.* "His Grace has sent him south, to trouble the Lannisters and their friends." The lie was one he had rehearsed as he rowed toward Sisterton through the rain. Soon or late the world would learn that Salladhor Saan had abandoned Stannis Baratheon, leaving him without a fleet, but they would not hear it from the lips of Davos Seaworth.

Lord Godric stirred his stew. "Did that old pirate Saan make you swim to shore?"

"I came ashore in an open boat, my lord." Salla had waited until the beacon of the Night Lamp shone off the *Valyrian*'s port bow before he put him off. Their friendship had been worth that much, at least. The Lyseni would gladly have taken him south with him, he avowed, but Davos had refused. Stannis needed Wyman Manderly, and had trusted Davos to win him. He would not betray that trust, he told Salla. "Bah," the pirate prince replied, "he will kill you with these honors, old friend. He will kill you."

"I have never had a King's Hand beneath my roof before," Lord Godric said. "Would Stannis ransom you, I wonder?"

Would he? Stannis had given Davos lands and titles and offices, but would he pay good gold to buy back his life? *He has no gold. Else he'd still have Salla.* "You will find His Grace at Castle Black if my lord would like to ask that of him."

Borrell grunted. "Is the Imp at Castle Black as well?"

"The Imp?" Davos did not understand the question. "He is at King's Landing, condemned to die for the murder of his nephew."

"The Wall is the last to learn, my father used to say. The dwarf's escaped. He twisted through the bars of his cell and tore his own father apart with his bare hands. A guardsman saw him flee, red from head to heel, as if he'd bathed in blood. The queen will make a lord of any man who kills him."

Davos struggled to believe what he was hearing. "You are telling me that Tywin Lannister is dead?"

"At his son's hand, aye." The lord took a drink of beer. "When there were kings on the Sisters, we did not suffer dwarfs to live. We cast them all into the sea, as an offering to the gods. The septons made us stop that. A pack of pious fools. Why would the gods give a man such a shape but to mark him as a monster?"

Lord Tywin dead. This changes all. "My lord, will you grant me leave to send a raven to the Wall? His Grace will want to know of Lord Tywin's death."

"He'll know. But not from me. Nor you, so long as you are here beneath my leaky roof. I'll not have it said that I gave Stannis aid and counsel. The Sunderlands dragged the Sisters into two of the Blackfyre Rebellions, and we all suffered grievously for that." Lord Godric waved his spoon toward a chair. "Sit. Before you fall, ser. My hall is cold and damp and dark, but not without some courtesy. We'll find dry clothes for you, but first you'll eat." He shouted, and a woman entered the hall. "We have a guest to feed. Bring beer and bread and sister's stew."

The beer was brown, the bread black, the stew a creamy white. She served it in a trencher hollowed out of a stale loaf. It was thick with leeks, carrots, barley, and turnips white and yellow, along with clams and chunks of cod and crabmeat, swimming in a stock of heavy cream and butter. It was the sort of stew that warmed a man right down to his bones, just the thing for a wet, cold night. Davos spooned it up gratefully.

"You have tasted sister's stew before?"

"I have, my lord." The same stew was served all over the Three Sisters, in every inn and tavern.

"This is better than what you've had before. Gella makes it. My daughter's daughter. Are you married, onion knight?"

"I am, my lord."

"A pity. Gella's not. Homely women make the best wives. There's three kinds of crabs in there. Red crabs and spider crabs and conquerors. I won't eat spider crab, except in sister's stew. Makes me feel half a cannibal." His lordship gestured at the banner hanging above the cold black hearth. A spider crab was embroidered there, white on a grey-green field. "We heard tales that Stannis burned his Hand."

The Hand who went before me. Melisandre had given Alester Florent to her god on Dragonstone, to conjure up the wind that bore them north. Lord Florent had been strong and silent as the queen's men bound him to the post, as dignified as any half-naked man could hope to be, but as the flames licked up his legs he had begun to scream, and his screams had blown them all the way to Eastwatch-by-the-Sea, if the red woman could be believed. Davos had misliked that wind. It had seemed to him to smell of burning flesh, and the sound of it was anguished as it played amongst the lines. *It could as easily have been me.* "I did not burn," he assured Lord Godric, "though Eastwatch almost froze me."

"The Wall will do that." The woman brought them a fresh loaf of bread, still hot from the oven. When Davos saw her hand, he stared. Lord Godric did not fail to make note of it. "Aye, she has the mark. Like all Borrells, for five thousand years. My daughter's daughter. Not the one who makes the stew." He tore the bread apart and offered half to Davos. "Eat. It's good."

It was, though any stale crust would have tasted just as fine to Davos; it meant he was a guest here, for this one night at least. The lords of the Three Sisters had a black repute, and none more so than Godric Borrell, Lord of Sweetsister, Shield of Sisterton, Master of Breakwater Castle, and Keeper of the Night Lamp . . . but even robber lords and wreckers were bound by the ancient laws of hospitality. *I will see the dawn, at least,* Davos told himself. *I have eaten of his bread and salt.*

Though there were stranger spices than salt in this sister's stew. "Is it saffron that I'm tasting?" Saffron was worth more than gold. Davos had only tasted it once before, when King Robert had sent a half a fish to him at a feast on Dragonstone.

"Aye. From Qarth. There's pepper too." Lord Godric took a pinch between his thumb and forefinger and sprinkled his own trencher. "Cracked black pepper from Volantis, nothing finer. Take as much as you require if you're feeling peppery. I've got forty chests of it. Not to mention cloves and nutmeg, and a pound of saffron. Took it off a sloe-eyed maid." He laughed. He still had all his teeth, Davos saw, though most of them were yellow and one on the top was black and dead. "She was making for Braavos, but a gale swept her into the Bite and she smashed up against some of my rocks. So you see, you are not the only gift the storms have brought me. The sea's a treacherous cruel thing."

Not as treacherous as men, thought Davos. Lord Godric's forebears had been pirate kings until the Starks came down on them with fire and sword. These days the Sistermen left open piracy to Salladhor Saan and his ilk and confined themselves to wrecking. The beacons that burned along the shores of the Three Sisters were supposed to warn of shoals and reefs and rocks and lead the way to safety, but on stormy nights and foggy ones, some Sistermen would use false lights to draw unwary captains to their doom.

"The storms did you a kindness, blowing you to my door," Lord Godric said. "You'd have found a cold welcome in White Harbor. You come too late, ser. Lord Wyman means to bend his knee, and not to Stannis." He took a swallow of his beer. "The Manderlys are no northmen, not down deep. 'Twas no more than nine hundred years ago when they came north, laden down with all their gold and gods. They'd been great lords on the Mander until they overreached themselves and the green hands slapped them down. The wolf king took their gold, but he gave them land and let them keep their gods." He mopped at his stew with a chunk of bread. "If Stannis thinks the fat man will ride the stag, he's wrong. The *Lionstar* put in at Sisterton twelve days ago to fill her water casks. Do you know her? Crimson sails and a gold lion on her prow. And full of Freys, making for White Harbor."

"Freys?" That was the last thing that Davos would have expected. "The Freys killed Lord Wyman's son, we heard."

"Aye," Lord Godric said, "and the fat man was so wroth that he took a vow to live on bread and wine till he had his vengeance. But before the day was out, he was stuffing clams and cakes into his mouth again. There's ships that go between the Sisters and White Harbor all the time. We sell them crabs and fish and goat cheese, they sell us wood and wool and hides. From all I hear, his lordship's fatter than ever. So much for vows. Words are wind, and the wind from Manderly's mouth means no more than the wind escaping out his bottom." The lord tore off another chunk of bread to swipe out his trencher. "The Freys were bringing the fat fool a bag of bones. Some call that courtesy, to bring a man his dead son's bones. Had it been my son, I would have returned the courtesy and thanked the Freys before I hanged them, but the fat man's too noble for that." He stuffed the bread into his mouth, chewed, swallowed. "I had the Freys to supper. One sat just where you're sitting now. *Rhaegar*, he named himself. I almost laughed right in his face. He'd lost his wife, he said, but he meant to get himself a new one in White Harbor. Ravens have been flying back and forth. Lord Wyman and Lord Walder have made a pact, and mean to seal it with a marriage."

Davos felt as though the lord had punched him in the belly. *If he tells it true, my king is lost.* Stannis Baratheon had desperate need of White Harbor. If Winterfell was the heart of the north, White Harbor was its mouth. Its firth had remained free of ice even in the depths of winter for centuries. With winter coming on, that could mean much and more. So could the city's silver. The Lannisters had all the gold of Casterly Rock, and had wed the wealth of Highgarden. King Stannis's coffers were exhausted. *I must try, at least. There may be some way that I can stop this marriage.* "I have to reach White Harbor," he said. "Your lordship, I beg you, help me."

Lord Godric began to eat his trencher, tearing it apart in his big hands. The stew had softened the stale bread. "I have no love for northmen," he announced. "The maesters say the Rape of the Three Sisters was two thousand years ago, but Sisterton has not forgotten. We were a free people before that, with our kings ruling over us. Afterward, we had to bend our knees to the Eyrie to get the northmen out. The wolf and the falcon fought over us for a thousand years, till between the two of them they had gnawed all the fat and flesh off the bones of these poor islands. As for your King Stannis, when he was Robert's master of ships he sent a fleet into my port without my leave and made me hang a dozen fine friends. Men like you. He went so far as to threaten to hang *me* if it should happen that some ship went aground because the Night Lamp had gone black. I had to eat his arrogance." He ate some of the trencher. "Now he comes north humbled, with his tail between his legs. Why should I give him any aid? Answer me that."

Because he is your rightful king, Davos thought. *Because he is a strong man and a just one, the only man who can restore the realm and defend it against the peril that gathers in the north. Because he has a magic sword that glows with the light of the sun.* The words caught in his throat. None of them would sway the Lord of Sweetsister. None of them would get him a foot closer to White Harbor. *What answer does he want? Must I promise him gold we do not have? A highborn husband for his daughter's daughter? Lands, honors, titles?* Lord Alester Florent had tried to play that game, and the king had burned him for it.

"The Hand has lost his tongue, it seems. He has no taste for sister's stew, or truth." Lord Godric wiped his mouth.

"The lion is dead," said Davos, slowly. "There's your truth, my lord. Tywin Lannister is dead."

"What if he is?"

"Who rules now in King's Landing? Not Tommen, he is just a child. Is it Ser Kevan?"

Candlelight gleamed in Lord Godric's black eyes. "If it were, you'd be in chains. It's the queen who rules."

Davos understood. *He nurses doubts. He does not want to find himself upon the losing side.* "Stannis held Storm's End against the Tyrells and the Redwynes. He took Dragonstone from the last Targaryens. He smashed the Iron Fleet off Fair Isle. This child king will not prevail against him."

"This child king commands the wealth of Casterly Rock and the power of Highgarden. He has the Boltons and the Freys." Lord Godric rubbed his chin. "Still . . . in this world only winter is certain. Ned Stark told my father that, here in this very hall."

"Ned Stark was here?"

"At the dawn of Robert's Rebellion. The Mad King had sent to the Eyrie for Stark's head, but Jon Arryn sent him back defiance. Gulltown stayed loyal to the throne, though. To get home and call his banners, Stark had to cross the mountains to the Fingers and find a fisherman to carry him across the Bite. A storm caught them on the way. The fisherman drowned, but his daughter got Stark to the Sisters before the boat went down. They say he left her with a bag of silver and a bastard in her belly. Jon Snow, she named him, after Arryn.

"Be that as it may. My father sat where I sit now when Lord Eddard came to Sisterton. Our maester urged us to send Stark's head to Aerys, to prove our loyalty. It would have meant a rich reward. The Mad King was open-handed with them as pleased him. By then we knew that Jon Arryn had taken Gulltown, though. Robert was the first man to gain the wall, and slew Marq Grafton with his own hand. 'This Baratheon is fearless,' I said. 'He fights the way a king should fight.' Our maester chuckled at me and told us that Prince Rhaegar was certain to defeat this rebel. That was when Stark said, 'In this world only winter is certain. We may lose our heads, it's true . . . but what if we prevail?' My father sent him on his way with his head still on his shoulders. 'If you lose,' he told Lord Eddard, 'you were never here.' "

"No more than I was," said Davos Seaworth.

JON

They brought forth the King-Beyond-the-Wall with his hands bound by hempen rope and a noose around his neck.

The other end of the rope was looped about the saddle horn of Ser Godry Farring's courser. The Giantslayer and his mount were armored in silvered steel inlaid with niello. Mance Rayder wore only a thin tunic that left his limbs naked to the cold. *They could have let him keep his cloak,* Jon Snow thought, *the one the wildling woman patched with strips of crimson silk.*

Small wonder that the Wall was weeping.

"Mance knows the haunted forest better than any ranger," Jon had told King Stannis, in his final effort to convince His Grace that the King-Beyond-the-Wall would be of more use to them alive than dead. "He knows Tormund Giantsbane. He has fought the Others. And he had the Horn of Joramun and did not blow it. He did not bring down the Wall when he could have."

His words fell on deaf ears. Stannis had remained unmoved. The law was plain; a deserter's life was forfeit.

Beneath the weeping Wall, Lady Melisandre raised her pale white hands. "*We all must choose,*" she proclaimed. "Man or woman, young or old, lord or peasant, our choices are the same." Her voice made Jon Snow think of anise and nutmeg and cloves. She stood at the king's side on a wooden scaffold raised above the pit. "We choose light or we choose darkness. We choose good or we choose evil. We choose the true god or the false."

Mance Rayder's thick grey-brown hair blew about his face as he walked. He pushed it from his eyes with bound hands, smiling. But when he saw the cage, his courage failed him. The queen's men had made it from the trees of the haunted forest, from saplings and supple branches, pine boughs sticky with sap, and the bone-white fingers of the weirwoods. They'd bent them and twisted them around and through each other to weave a wooden lattice, then hung it high above a deep pit filled with logs, leaves, and kindling.

The wildling king recoiled from the sight. "No," he cried, "*mercy*. This is not right, I'm not the king, they—"

Ser Godry gave a pull on the rope. The King-Beyond-the-Wall had no choice but to stumble after him, the rope choking off his words. When he lost his feet, Godry dragged him the rest of the way. Mance was bloody when the queen's men half-shoved, half-carried him to the cage. A dozen men-at-arms heaved together to hoist him into the air.

Lady Melisandre watched him rise. "*FREE FOLK!* Here stands your king of lies. And here is the horn he promised would bring down the Wall." Two queen's men brought forth the Horn of Joramun, black and banded with old gold, eight feet long from end to end. Runes were carved into the golden bands, the writing of the First Men. Joramun had died thousands of years ago, but Mance had found his grave beneath a glacier, high up in the Frostfangs. *And Joramun blew the Horn of Winter, and woke giants from the earth.* Ygritte had told Jon that Mance never found the horn. *She lied, or else Mance kept it secret even from his own.*

A thousand captives watched through the wooden bars of their stockade as the horn was lifted high. All were ragged and half-starved. *Wildlings*, the Seven Kingdoms called them; they named themselves *the free folk*. They looked neither wild nor free—only hungry, frightened, numb.

"The Horn of Joramun?" Melisandre said. "No. Call it the Horn of Darkness. If the Wall falls, night falls as well, the long night that never ends. It must not happen, *will* not happen! The Lord of Light has seen his children in their peril and sent a champion to them, Azor Ahai reborn." She swept a hand toward Stannis, and the great ruby at her throat pulsed with light.

He is stone and she is flame. The king's eyes were blue bruises, sunk deep in a hollow face. He wore grey plate, a fur-trimmed cloak of cloth-of-gold flowing from his broad shoulders. His breastplate had a flaming heart inlaid above his own. Girding his brows was a red-gold crown with points like twisting flames. Val stood beside him, tall and fair. They had crowned her with a simple circlet of dark bronze, yet she looked more regal in bronze than Stannis did in gold. Her eyes were grey and fearless, unflinching. Beneath an ermine cloak, she wore white and gold. Her honey-blond hair had been done up in a thick braid that hung over her right shoulder to her waist. The chill in the air had put color in her cheeks.

Lady Melisandre wore no crown, but every man there knew that she was Stannis Baratheon's real queen, not the homely woman he had left to shiver at Eastwatch-by-the-Sea. Talk was, the king did not mean to send for Queen Selyse and their daughter until the Nightfort was ready for habitation. Jon felt sorry for them. The Wall offered few of the comforts that southron ladies and little highborn girls were used to, and the Nightfort offered none. That was a grim place, even at the best of times.

"*FREE FOLK!*" cried Melisandre. "Behold the fate of those who choose the darkness!"

The Horn of Joramun burst into flame.

It went up with a *whoosh* as swirling tongues of green and yellow fire leapt up crackling all along its length. Jon's garron shied nervously, and up and down the ranks others fought to still their mounts as well. A moan came from the stockade as the free folk saw their hope afire. A few began to shout and curse, but most lapsed into silence. For half a heartbeat the runes graven on the gold bands seemed to shimmer in the air. The queen's men gave a heave and sent the horn tumbling down into the fire pit.

Inside his cage, Mance Rayder clawed at the noose about his neck with bound hands and screamed incoherently of treachery and witchery, denying his kingship, denying his people, denying his name, denying all that he had ever been. He shrieked for mercy and cursed the red woman and began to laugh hysterically.

Jon watched unblinking. He dare not appear squeamish before his brothers. He had ordered out two hundred men, more than half the garrison of Castle Black. Mounted in solemn sable ranks with tall spears in hand, they had drawn up their hoods to shadow their faces . . . and hide the fact that so many were greybeards and green boys. The free folk feared the Watch. Jon wanted them to take that fear with them to their new homes south of the Wall.

The horn crashed amongst the logs and leaves and kindling. Within three heartbeats the whole pit was aflame. Clutching the bars of his cage with bound hands, Mance sobbed and begged. When the fire reached him he did a little dance. His screams became one long, wordless shriek of fear and pain. Within his cage, he fluttered like a burning leaf, a moth caught in a candle flame.

Jon found himself remembering a song.

> *Brothers, oh brothers, my days here are done,*
> *the Dornishman's taken my life,*

But what does it matter, for all men must die,
and I've tasted the Dornishman's wife!

Val stood on the platform as still as if she had been carved of salt. *She will not weep nor look away.* Jon wondered what Ygritte would have done in her place. *The women are the strong ones.* He found himself thinking about Sam and Maester Aemon, about Gilly and the babe. *She will curse me with her dying breath, but I saw no other way.* Eastwatch reported savage storms upon the narrow sea. *I meant to keep them safe. Did I feed them to the crabs instead?* Last night he had dreamed of Sam drowning, of Ygritte dying with his arrow in her (it had not been his arrow, but in his dreams it always was), of Gilly weeping tears of blood.

Jon Snow had seen enough. "Now," he said.

Ulmer of the Kingswood jammed his spear into the ground, unslung his bow, and slipped a black arrow from his quiver. Sweet Donnel Hill threw back his hood to do the same. Garth Greyfeather and Bearded Ben nocked shafts, bent their bows, loosed.

One arrow took Mance Rayder in the chest, one in the gut, one in the throat. The fourth struck one of the cage's wooden bars, and quivered for an instant before catching fire. A woman's sobs echoed off the Wall as the wildling king slid bonelessly to the floor of his cage, wreathed in fire. "And now his Watch is done," Jon murmured softly. Mance Rayder had been a man of the Night's Watch once, before he changed his black cloak for one slashed with bright red silk.

Up on the platform, Stannis was scowling. Jon refused to meet his eyes. The bottom had fallen out of the wooden cage, and its bars were crumbling. Every time the fire licked upward, more branches tumbled free, cherry red and black. "The Lord of Light made the sun and moon and stars to light our way, and gave us fire to keep the night at bay," Melisandre told the wildlings. "None can withstand his flames."

"*None can withstand his flames,*" the queen's men echoed.

The red woman's robes of deep-dyed scarlet swirled about her, and her coppery hair made a halo round her face. Tall yellow flames danced from her fingertips like claws. "*FREE FOLK!* Your false gods cannot help you. Your false horn did not save you. Your false king brought you only death, despair, defeat . . . but here stands the true king. *BEHOLD HIS GLORY!*"

Stannis Baratheon drew Lightbringer.

The sword glowed red and yellow and orange, alive with light. Jon had seen the show before . . . but not like *this*, never before like this. Lightbringer was the sun made steel. When Stannis raised the blade above his head, men had to turn their heads or cover their eyes. Horses shied, and one threw his rider. The blaze in the fire pit seemed to shrink before this storm of light, like a small dog cowering before a larger one. The Wall itself turned red and pink and orange, as waves of color danced across the ice. *Is this the power of king's blood?*

"Westeros has but one king," said Stannis. His voice rang harsh, with none of Melisandre's music. "With this sword I defend my subjects and destroy those who menace them. Bend the knee, and I promise you food, land, and justice. Kneel and live. Or go and die. The choice is yours." He slipped Lightbringer into its scabbard, and the world darkened once again, as if the sun had gone behind a cloud. "Open the gates."

"*OPEN THE GATES,*" bellowed Ser Clayton Suggs, in a voice as deep as a warhorn. "*OPEN THE GATES,*" echoed Ser Corliss Penny, commanding the guards. "*OPEN THE GATES,*" cried the serjeants. Men scrambled to obey. Sharpened stakes were wrenched from the ground, planks were dropped across deep ditches, and the stockade gates were thrown wide. Jon Snow raised his hand and lowered it, and his black ranks parted right and left, clearing a path to the Wall, where Dolorous Edd Tollett pushed open the iron gate.

"Come," urged Melisandre. "Come to the light . . . or run back to the darkness." In the pit below her, the fire was crackling. "If you choose life, come to me."

And they came. Slowly at first, some limping or leaning on their fellows, the captives began to emerge from their rough-hewn pen. *If you would eat, come to me,* Jon thought. *If you would not freeze or starve, submit.* Hesitant, wary of some trap, the first few prisoners edged across the planks and through the ring of the stakes, toward Melisandre and the Wall. More followed, when they saw that no harm had come to those who went before. Then more, until it was a steady stream. Queen's men in studded jacks and halfhelms handed each passing man, woman, or child a piece of white weirwood: a stick, a splintered branch as pale as broken bone, a spray of blood-red leaves. *A piece of the old gods to feed the new.* Jon flexed the fingers of his sword hand.

The heat from the fire pit was palpable even at a distance; for the wildlings, it had to be blistering. He saw men cringing as they neared the flames, heard children cry. A few turned for the forest. He watched a young woman stumble away with a child on either hand. Every few steps she looked back to make certain no one was coming after them, and when she neared the trees she broke into a run. One greybeard took the weirwood branch they handed him and used it as a weapon, laying about with it until the queen's men converged on him with spears. The others had to step around his body, until Ser Corliss had it thrown in the fire. More of the free folk chose the woods after that—one in ten, perhaps.

But most came on. Behind them was only cold and death. Ahead was hope. They came on, clutching their scraps of wood until the time came to feed them to the flames. R'hllor was a jealous deity, ever hungry. So the new god devoured the corpse of the old, and cast gigantic shadows of Stannis and Melisandre upon the Wall, black against the ruddy red reflections on the ice.

Sigorn was the first to kneel before the king. The new Magnar of Thenn was a younger, shorter version of his father—lean, balding, clad in bronze greaves and a leather shirt sewn with bronze scales. Next came Rattleshirt in clattering armor made of bones and boiled leather, his helm a giant's skull. Under the bones lurked a ruined and wretched creature with cracked brown teeth and a yellow tinge to the whites of his eyes. *A small, malicious, treacherous man, as stupid as he is cruel.* Jon did not believe for a moment that he would keep faith. He wondered what Val was feeling as she watched him kneel, forgiven.

Lesser leaders followed. Two clan chiefs of the Hornfoot men, whose feet were black and hard. An old wisewoman revered by the peoples of the Milkwater. A scrawny dark-eyed boy of two-and-ten, the son of Alfyn Crowkiller. Halleck, brother to Harma Dogshead, with her pigs. Each took a knee before the king.

It is too cold for this mummer's show, thought Jon. "The free folk despise kneelers," he had warned Stannis. "Let them keep their pride, and they will love you better." His Grace would not listen. He said, "It is swords I need from them, not kisses."

Having knelt, the wildlings shuffled past the ranks of the black brothers to the gate. Jon had detailed Horse and Satin and half a dozen others to lead them through the Wall with torches. On the far side, bowls of hot onion soup awaited them, and chunks of black bread and sausage. Clothes as well: cloaks, breeches, boots, tunics, good leather gloves. They would sleep on piles of clean straw, with fires blazing to keep the chill of night at bay. This king was nothing if not methodical. Soon or late, however, Tormund Giantsbane would assault the Wall again, and when that hour came Jon wondered whose side Stannis's new-made subjects would choose. *You can give them land and mercy, but the free folk choose their own kings, and it was Mance they chose, not you.*

Bowen Marsh edged his mount up next to Jon's. "This is a day I never thought to see." The Lord Steward had thinned notably since suffering a head wound at the Bridge of Skulls. Part of one ear was gone. *He no longer looks much like a pomegranate,* Jon thought. Marsh said, "We bled to stop the wildlings at the Gorge. Good men were slain there, friends and brothers. For what?"

"The realm will curse us all for this," declared Ser Alliser Thorne in a venomous tone. "Every honest man in Westeros will turn his head and spit at the mention of the Night's Watch."

What would you know of honest men? "Quiet in the ranks." Ser Alliser had grown more circumspect since Lord Janos had lost his head, but the malice was still there. Jon had toyed with the idea of giving him the command Slynt had refused, but he wanted the man close. *He was always the more dangerous of the two.* Instead he had dispatched a grizzled steward from the Shadow Tower to take command at Greyguard.

He hoped the two new garrisons would make a difference. *The Watch can make the free folk bleed, but in the end we cannot hope to stop them.* Giving Mance Rayder to the fire did not change the truth of that. *We are still too few and they are still too many, and without rangers, we're good as blind. I have to send men out. But if I do, will they come back again?*

The tunnel through the Wall was narrow and twisting, and many of the wildlings were old or ill or wounded, so the going was painfully slow. By the time the last of them had bent the knee, night had fallen. The pit fire was burning low, and the king's shadow on the Wall had shrunk to a quarter of its former height. Jon Snow could see his breath in the air. *Cold,* he thought, *and getting colder. This mummer's show has gone on long enough.*

Two score captives lingered by the stockade. Four giants were among them, massive hairy creatures with sloped shoulders, legs as large as tree trunks, and huge splayed feet. Big as they were, they might still have passed through the Wall, but one would not leave his mammoth, and the others would not leave him. The rest of those who remained were all of human stature. Some were dead and some were dying; more were their kin or close companions, unwilling to abandon them even for a bowl of onion soup.

Some shivering, some too numb to shiver, they listened as the king's voice rumbled off the Wall. "You are free to go," Stannis told them. "Tell your people what you witnessed. Tell them that you saw the true king, and that they are welcome in his realm, so long as they keep his peace. Elsewise, they had best flee or hide. I will brook no further attacks upon my Wall."

"*One realm, one god, one king!*" cried Lady Melisandre.

The queen's men took up the cry, beating the butts of their spears against their shields. "*One realm, one god, one king! STANNIS! STAN-NIS! ONE REALM, ONE GOD, ONE KING!*"

Val did not join the chant, he saw. Nor did the brothers of the Night's Watch. During the tumult the few remaining wildlings melted into the trees. The giants were the last to go, two riding on the back of a mammoth, the other two afoot. Only the dead were left behind. Jon watched Stannis descend from the platform, with Melisandre by his side. *His red shadow. She never leaves his side for long.* The king's honor guard fell in around them—Ser Godry, Ser Clayton, and a dozen other knights, queen's men all. Moonlight shimmered on their armor and the wind whipped at their cloaks. "Lord Steward," Jon told Marsh, "break up that stockade for firewood and throw the corpses in the flames."

"As my lord commands." Marsh barked out orders, and a swarm of his stewards broke from ranks to attack the wooden walls. The Lord Steward watched them, frowning. "These wildlings . . . do you think they will keep faith, my lord?"

"Some will. Not all. We have our cowards and our knaves, our weaklings and our fools, as do they."

"Our vows . . . we are sworn to protect the realm . . ."

"Once the free folk are settled in the Gift, they will become part of the realm," Jon pointed out. "These are desperate days, and like to grow more desperate. We have seen the face of our real foe, a dead white face with bright blue eyes. The free folk have seen that face as well. Stannis is not wrong in this. We must make common cause with the wildlings."

"Common cause against a common foe, I could agree with that," said Bowen Marsh, "but that does not mean we should allow tens of thousands of half-starved savages through the Wall. Let them return to their villages and fight the Others there, whilst we seal the gates. It will not be difficult, Othell tells me. We need only fill the tunnels with chunks of stone and pour water through the murder holes. The Wall does the rest. The cold, the weight . . . in a moon's turn, it will be as if no gate had ever been. Any foe would need to hack his way through."

"Or climb."

"Unlikely," said Bowen Marsh. "These are not raiders, out to steal a wife and some plunder. Tormund will have old women with him, children, herds of sheep and goats, even *mammoths*. He needs a *gate*, and only three of those remain. And if he should send climbers up, well, defending against climbers is as simple as spearing fish in a kettle."

Fish never climb out of the kettle and shove a spear through your belly. Jon had climbed the Wall himself.

Marsh went on. "Mance Rayder's bowmen must have loosed ten thousand arrows at us, judging from the number of spent shafts we've gathered up. Fewer than a hundred reached our men atop the Wall, most of those lifted by some errant gust of wind. Red Alyn of the Rosewood was the only man to die up there, and it was his fall that killed him, not the arrow that pricked his leg. Donal Noye died to hold the gate. A gallant act, yes . . . but if the gate had been sealed, our brave armorer might still be with us. Whether we face a hundred foes or a hundred thousand, so long as we're atop the Wall and they're below, they cannot do us harm."

He's not wrong. Mance Rayder's host had broken against the Wall like a wave upon a stony shore, though the defenders were no more than a handful of old men, green boys, and cripples. Yet what Bowen was suggesting went against all of Jon's instincts. "If we seal the gates, we cannot send out rangers," he pointed out. "We will be as good as blind."

"Lord Mormont's last ranging cost the Watch a quarter of its men, my lord. We need to conserve what strength remains us. Every death diminishes us, and we are stretched so thin . . . Take the high ground and win the battle, my uncle used to say. No ground is higher than the Wall, Lord Commander."

"Stannis promises land, food, and justice to any wildlings who bend the knee. He will never permit us to seal the gates."

Marsh hesitated. "Lord Snow, I am not one to bear tales, but there has been talk that you are becoming too . . . too friendly with Lord Stannis. Some even suggest that you are . . . a . . . ."

A rebel and a turncloak, aye, and a bastard and a warg as well. Janos Slynt might be gone, but his lies lingered. "I know what they say." Jon had heard the whispers, had seen men turn away when he crossed the yard. "What would they have me do, take up swords against Stannis and the wildlings both? His Grace has thrice the fighting men we do, and is our guest besides. The laws of hospitality protect him. And we owe him and his a debt."

"Lord Stannis helped us when we needed help," Marsh said doggedly, "but he is still a rebel, and his cause is doomed. As doomed as we'll be if the Iron Throne marks us down as traitors. We must be certain that we do not choose the losing side."

"It is not my intent to choose any side," said Jon, "but I am not as certain of the outcome of this war as you seem to be, my lord. Not with Lord Tywin dead." If the tales coming up the kingsroad could be believed, the

King's Hand had been murdered by his dwarf son whilst sitting on a privy. Jon had known Tyrion Lannister, briefly. *He took my hand and named me friend.* It was hard to believe the little man had it in him to murder his own sire, but the fact of Lord Tywin's demise seemed to be beyond doubt. "The lion in King's Landing is a cub, and the Iron Throne has been known to cut grown men to ribbons."

"A boy he may be, my lord, but . . . King Robert was well loved, and most men still accept that Tommen is his son. The more they see of Lord Stannis the less they love him, and fewer still are fond of Lady Melisandre with her fires and this grim red god of hers. They complain."

"They complained about Lord Commander Mormont too. Men love to complain about their wives and lords, he told me once. Those without wives complain twice as much about their lords." Jon Snow glanced toward the stockade. Two walls were down, a third falling fast. "I will leave you to finish here, Bowen. Make certain every corpse is burned. Thank you for your counsel. I promise you, I will think on all you've said."

Smoke and drifting ash still lingered in the air about the pit as Jon trotted back to the gate. There he dismounted, to walk his garron through the ice to the south side. Dolorous Edd went before him with a torch. Its flames licked the ceiling, so cold tears trickled down upon them with every step.

"It was a relief to see that horn burn, my lord," Edd said. "Just last night I dreamt I was pissing off the Wall when someone decided to give the horn a toot. Not that I'm complaining. It was better than my old dream, where Harma Dogshead was feeding me to her pigs."

"Harma's dead," Jon said.

"But not the pigs. They look at me the way Slayer used to look at ham. Not to say that the wildlings mean us harm. Aye, we hacked their gods apart and made them burn the pieces, but we gave them onion soup. What's a god compared to a nice bowl of onion soup? I could do with one myself."

The odors of smoke and burned flesh still clung to Jon's blacks. He knew he had to eat, but it was company he craved, not food. *A cup of wine with Maester Aemon, some quiet words with Sam, a few laughs with Pyp and Grenn and Toad.* Aemon and Sam were gone, though, and his other friends . . . "I will take supper with the men this evening."

"Boiled beef and beets." Dolorous Edd always seemed to know what was cooking. "Hobb says he's out of horseradish, though. What good is boiled beef without horseradish?"

Since the wildlings had burned the old common hall, the men of the

Night's Watch took their meals in the stone cellar below the armory, a cavernous space divided by two rows of square stone pillars, with barrel-vaulted ceilings and great casks of wine and ale along the walls. When Jon entered, four builders were playing at tiles at the table nearest the steps. Closer to the fire sat a group of rangers and a few king's men, talking quietly.

The younger men were gathered at another table, where Pyp had stabbed a turnip with his knife. "The night is dark and full of turnips," he announced in a solemn voice. "Let us all pray for venison, my children, with some onions and a bit of tasty gravy." His friends laughed—Grenn, Toad, Satin, the whole lot of them.

Jon Snow did not join the laughter. "Making mock of another man's prayer is fool's work, Pyp. And dangerous."

"If the red god's offended, let him strike me down."

All the smiles had died. "It was the priestess we were laughing at," said Satin, a lithe and pretty youth who had once been a whore in Oldtown. "We were only having a jape, my lord."

"You have your gods and she has hers. Leave her be."

"She won't let our gods be," argued Toad. "She calls the Seven false gods, m'lord. The old gods too. She made the wildlings burn weirwood branches. You saw."

"Lady Melisandre is not part of my command. You are. I won't have bad blood between the king's men and my own."

Pyp laid a hand on Toad's arm. "Croak no more, brave Toad, for our Great Lord Snow has spoken." Pyp hopped to his feet and gave Jon a mocking bow. "I beg pardon. Henceforth, I shall not even waggle my ears save by your lordship's lordly leave."

He thinks this is all some game. Jon wanted to shake some sense into him. "Waggle your ears all you like. It's your tongue waggling that makes the trouble."

"I'll see that he's more careful," Grenn promised, "and I'll clout him if he's not." He hesitated. "My lord, will you sup with us? Owen, shove over and make room for Jon."

Jon wanted nothing more. *No,* he had to tell himself, *those days are gone.* The realization twisted in his belly like a knife. They had chosen him to rule. The Wall was his, and their lives were his as well. *A lord may love the men that he commands,* he could hear his lord father saying, *but he cannot be a friend to them. One day he may need to sit in judgment on them, or send them forth to die.* "Another day," the lord commander lied. "Edd, best see to your own supper. I have work to finish."

The outside air seemed even colder than before. Across the castle, he could see candlelight shining from the windows of the King's Tower. Val stood on the tower roof, gazing up at the Wall. Stannis kept her closely penned in rooms above his own, but he did allow her to walk the battlements for exercise. *She looks lonely,* Jon thought. *Lonely, and lovely.* Ygritte had been pretty in her own way, with her red hair kissed by fire, but it was her smile that made her face come alive. Val did not need to smile; she would have turned men's heads in any court in the wide world.

All the same, the wildling princess was not beloved of her gaolers. She scorned them all as "kneelers," and had thrice attempted to escape. When one man-at-arms grew careless in her presence she had snatched his dagger from its sheath and stabbed him in the neck. Another inch to the left and he might have died.

Lonely and lovely and lethal, Jon Snow reflected, *and I might have had her. Her, and Winterfell, and my lord father's name.* Instead he had chosen a black cloak and a wall of ice. Instead he had chosen honor. *A bastard's sort of honor.*

The Wall loomed on his right as he crossed the yard. Its high ice glimmered palely, but down below all was shadow. At the gate a dim orange glow shone through the bars where the guards had taken refuge from the wind. Jon could hear the creak of chains as the winch cage swung and scraped against the ice. Up top, the sentries would be huddling in the warming shed around a brazier, shouting to be heard above the wind. Or else they would have given up the effort, and each man would be sunk in his own pool of silence. *I should be walking the ice. The Wall is mine.*

He was walking beneath the shell of the Lord Commander's Tower, past the spot where Ygritte had died in his arms, when Ghost appeared beside him, his warm breath steaming in the cold. In the moonlight, his red eyes glowed like pools of fire. The taste of hot blood filled Jon's mouth, and he knew that Ghost had killed that night. *No,* he thought. *I am a man, not a wolf.* He rubbed his mouth with the back of a gloved hand and spat.

Clydas still occupied the rooms beneath the rookery. At Jon's knock, he came shuffling, a taper in his hand, to open the door a crack. "Do I intrude?" asked Jon.

"Not at all." Clydas opened the door wider. "I was mulling wine. Will my lord take a cup?"

"With pleasure." His hands were stiff from cold. He pulled off his gloves and flexed his fingers.

Clydas returned to the hearth to stir the wine. *He's sixty if he's a day. An old man. He only seemed young compared with Aemon.* Short and round, he had the dim pink eyes of some nocturnal creature. A few white hairs clung to his scalp. When Clydas poured, Jon held the cup with both hands, sniffed the spices, swallowed. The warmth spread through his chest. He drank again, long and deep, to wash the taste of blood from his mouth.

"The queen's men are saying that the King-Beyond-the-Wall died craven. That he cried for mercy and denied he was a king."

"He did. Lightbringer was brighter than I'd ever seen it. As bright as the sun." Jon raised his cup. "To Stannis Baratheon and his magic sword." The wine was bitter in his mouth.

"His Grace is not an easy man. Few are, who wear a crown. Many good men have been bad kings, Maester Aemon used to say, and some bad men have been good kings."

"He would know." Aemon Targaryen had seen nine kings upon the Iron Throne. He had been a king's son, a king's brother, a king's uncle. "I looked at that book Maester Aemon left me. The *Jade Compendium*. The pages that told of Azor Ahai. Lightbringer was his sword. Tempered with his wife's blood if Votar can be believed. Thereafter Lightbringer was never cold to the touch, but warm as Nissa Nissa had been warm. In battle the blade burned fiery hot. Once Azor Ahai fought a monster. When he thrust the sword through the belly of the beast, its blood began to boil. Smoke and steam poured from its mouth, its eyes melted and dribbled down its cheeks, and its body burst into flame."

Clydas blinked. "A sword that makes its own heat . . ."

". . . would be a fine thing on the Wall." Jon put aside his wine cup and drew on his black moleskin gloves. "A pity that the sword that Stannis wields is cold. I'll be curious to see how *his* Lightbringer behaves in battle. Thank you for the wine. Ghost, with me." Jon Snow raised the hood of his cloak and pulled at the door. The white wolf followed him back into the night.

The armory was dark and silent. Jon nodded to the guards before making his way past the silent racks of spears to his rooms. He hung his sword belt from a peg beside the door and his cloak from another. When he peeled off his gloves, his hands were stiff and cold. It took him a long while to get the candles lit. Ghost curled up on his rug and went to sleep, but Jon could not rest yet. The scarred pinewood table was covered with maps of the Wall and the lands beyond, a roster of rangers, and a letter from the Shadow Tower written in Ser Denys Mallister's flowing hand.

He read the letter from the Shadow Tower again, sharpened a quill, and unstoppered a pot of thick black ink. He wrote two letters, the first to Ser Denys, the second to Cotter Pyke. Both of them had been hounding him for more men. Halder and Toad he dispatched west to the Shadow Tower, Grenn and Pyp to Eastwatch-by-the-Sea. The ink would not flow properly, and all his words seemed curt and crude and clumsy, yet he persisted.

When he finally put the quill down, the room was dim and chilly, and he could feel its walls closing in. Perched above the window, the Old Bear's raven peered down at him with shrewd black eyes. *My last friend,* Jon thought ruefully. *And I had best outlive you, or you'll eat my face as well.* Ghost did not count. Ghost was closer than a friend. Ghost was part of him.

Jon rose and climbed the steps to the narrow bed that had once been Donal Noye's. *This is my lot,* he realized as he undressed, *from now until the end of my days.*

DAENERYS

What is it?" she cried, as Irri shook her gently by the shoulder. It was the black of night outside. *Something is wrong,* she knew at once. "Is it Daario? What's happened?" In her dream they had been man and wife, simple folk who lived a simple life in a tall stone house with a red door. In her dream he had been kissing her all over—her mouth, her neck, her breasts.

"No, *Khaleesi,*" Irri murmured, "it is your eunuch Grey Worm and the bald men. Will you see them?"

"Yes." Her hair was disheveled and her bedclothes all atangle, Dany realized. "Help me dress. I'll have a cup of wine as well. To clear my head." *To drown my dream.* She could hear the soft sounds of sobs. "Who is that weeping?"

"Your slave Missandei." Jhiqui had a taper in her hand.

"My servant. I have no slaves." Dany did not understand. "Why does she weep?"

"For him who was her brother," Irri told her.

The rest she had from Skahaz, Reznak, and Grey Worm, when they were ushered into her presence. Dany knew their tidings were bad before a word was spoken. One glance at the Shavepate's ugly face sufficed to tell her that. "The Sons of the Harpy?"

Skahaz nodded. His mouth was grim.

"How many dead?"

Reznak wrung his hands. "N-nine, Magnificence. Foul work it was, and wicked. A dreadful night, dreadful."

Nine. The word was a dagger in her heart. Every night the shadow war was waged anew beneath the stepped pyramids of Meereen. Every morn the sun rose upon fresh corpses, with harpies drawn in blood on the bricks beside them. Any freedman who became too prosperous or too outspoken was marked for death. *Nine in one night, though . . .* That frightened her. "Tell me."

Grey Worm answered. "Your servants were set upon as they walked the bricks of Meereen to keep Your Grace's peace. All were well armed, with spears and shields and short swords. Two by two they walked, and two by two they died. Your servants Black Fist and Cetherys were slain by crossbow bolts in Mazdhan's Maze. Your servants Mossador and Duran were crushed by falling stones beneath the river wall. Your servants Eladon Goldenhair and Loyal Spear were poisoned at a wineshop where they were accustomed to stop each night upon their rounds."

Mossador. Dany made a fist. Missandei and her brothers had been taken from their home on Naath by raiders from the Basilisk Isles and sold into slavery in Astapor. Young as she was, Missandei had shown such a gift for tongues that the Good Masters had made a scribe of her. Mossador and Marselen had not been so fortunate. They had been gelded and made into Unsullied. "Have any of the murderers been captured?"

"Your servants have arrested the owner of the wineshop and his daughters. They plead their ignorance and beg for mercy."

They all plead ignorance and beg for mercy. "Give them to the Shavepate. Skahaz, keep each apart from the others and put them to the question."

"It will be done, Your Worship. Would you have me question them sweetly, or sharply?"

"Sweetly, to begin. Hear what tales they tell and what names they give you. It may be they had no part in this." She hesitated. "Nine, the noble Reznak said. Who else?"

"Three freedmen, murdered in their homes," the Shavepate said. "A moneylender, a cobbler, and the harpist Rylona Rhee. They cut her fingers off before they killed her."

The queen flinched. Rylona Rhee had played the harp as sweetly as the Maiden. When she had been a slave in Yunkai, she had played for every highborn family in the city. In Meereen she had become a leader amongst the Yunkish freedmen, their voice in Dany's councils. "We have no captives but this wineseller?"

"None, this one grieves to confess. We beg your pardon."

Mercy, thought Dany. *They will have the dragon's mercy.* "Skahaz, I have changed my mind. Question the man sharply."

"I could. Or I could question the daughters sharply whilst the father looks on. That will wring some names from him."

"Do as you think best, but bring me names." Her fury was a fire in her belly. "I will have no more Unsullied slaughtered. Grey Worm, pull your men back to their barracks. Henceforth let them guard my walls and gates and person. From this day, it shall be for Meereenese to keep the peace in Meereen. Skahaz, make me a new watch, made up in equal parts of shavepates and freedmen."

"As you command. How many men?"

"As many as you require."

Reznak mo Reznak gasped. "Magnificence, where is the coin to come from to pay wages for so many men?"

"From the pyramids. Call it a blood tax. I will have a hundred pieces of gold from every pyramid for each freedman that the Harpy's Sons have slain."

That brought a smile to the Shavepate's face. "It will be done," he said, "but Your Radiance should know that the Great Masters of Zhak and Merreq are making preparations to quit their pyramids and leave the city."

Daenerys was sick unto death of Zhak and Merreq; she was sick of all the Mereenese, great and small alike. "Let them go, but see that they take no more than the clothes upon their backs. Make certain that all their gold remains here with us. Their stores of food as well."

"Magnificence," murmured Reznak mo Reznak, "we cannot know that these great nobles mean to join your enemies. More like they are simply making for their estates in the hills."

"They will not mind us keeping their gold safe, then. There is nothing to buy in the hills."

"They are afraid for their children," Reznak said.

Yes, Daenerys thought, *and so am I.* "We must keep them safe as well. I will have two children from each of them. From the other pyramids as well. A boy and a girl."

"Hostages," said Skahaz, happily.

"Pages and cupbearers. If the Great Masters make objection, explain to them that in Westeros it is a great honor for a child to be chosen to serve at court." She left the rest unspoken. "Go and do as I've commanded. I have my dead to mourn."

When she returned to her rooms atop the pyramid, she found Missandei crying softly on her pallet, trying as best she could to muffle the sound of her sobs. "Come sleep with me," she told the little scribe. "Dawn will not come for hours yet."

"Your Grace is kind to this one." Missandei slipped under the sheets. "He was a good brother."

Dany wrapped her arms about the girl. "Tell me of him."

"He taught me how to climb a tree when we were little. He could catch fish with his hands. Once I found him sleeping in our garden with a hundred butterflies crawling over him. He looked so beautiful that morning, this one . . . I mean, I loved him."

"As he loved you." Dany stroked the girl's hair. "Say the word, my sweet, and I will send you from this awful place. I will find a ship somehow and send you home. To Naath."

"I would sooner stay with you. On Naath I'd be afraid. What if the slavers came again? I feel safe when I'm with you."

Safe. The word made Dany's eyes fill up with tears. "I want to keep you safe." Missandei was only a child. With her, she felt as if she could be a child too. "No one ever kept me safe when I was little. Well, Ser Willem did, but then he died, and Viserys . . . I want to protect you but . . . it is so hard. To be strong. I don't always know what I should do. I *must* know, though. I am all they have. I am the queen . . . the . . . the . . ."

" . . . mother," whispered Missandei.

"Mother to dragons." Dany shivered.

"No. Mother to us all." Missandei hugged her tighter. "Your Grace should sleep. Dawn will be here soon, and court."

"We'll both sleep, and dream of sweeter days. Close your eyes." When she did, Dany kissed her eyelids and made her giggle.

Kisses came easier than sleep, however. Dany shut her eyes and tried to think of home, of Dragonstone and King's Landing and all the other places that Viserys had told her of, in a kinder land than this . . . but her thoughts kept turning back to Slaver's Bay, like ships caught in some bitter wind. When Missandei was sound asleep, Dany slipped from her arms and stepped out into the predawn air to lean upon the cool brick parapet and gaze out across the city. A thousand roofs stretched out below her, painted in shades of ivory and silver by the moon.

Somewhere beneath those roofs, the Sons of the Harpy were gathered, plotting ways to kill her and all those who loved her and put her children back in chains. Somewhere down there a hungry child was crying for milk. Somewhere an old woman lay dying. Somewhere a man and a maid embraced, and fumbled at each other's clothes with eager hands. But up here there was only the sheen of moonlight on pyramids and pits, with no hint what lay beneath. Up here there was only her, alone.

She was the blood of the dragon. She could kill the Sons of the Harpy, and the sons of the sons, and the sons of the sons of the sons. But a dragon could not feed a hungry child nor help a dying woman's pain. *And who would ever dare to love a dragon?*

She found herself thinking of Daario Naharis once again, Daario with his gold tooth and trident beard, his strong hands resting on the hilts of his matched *arakh* and stiletto, hilts wrought of gold in the shape of naked women. The day he took his leave of her, as she was bidding him farewell, he had brushed the balls of his thumbs lightly across them, back and forth. *I am jealous of a sword hilt,* she had realized, *of women made of gold.* Sending him to the Lamb Men had been wise. She was a queen, and Daario Naharis was not the stuff of kings.

"It has been so long," she had said to Ser Barristan, just yesterday. "What if Daario has betrayed me and gone over to my enemies?" *Three treasons will you know.* "What if he met another woman, some princess of the Lhazarene?"

The old knight neither liked nor trusted Daario, she knew. Even so, he had answered gallantly. "There is no woman more lovely than Your Grace. Only a blind man could believe otherwise, and Daario Naharis was not blind."

No, she thought. *His eyes are a deep blue, almost purple, and his gold tooth gleams when he smiles for me.*

Ser Barristan was sure he would return, though. Dany could only pray that he was right.

A bath will help soothe me. She padded barefoot through the grass to her terrace pool. The water felt cool on her skin, raising goosebumps. Little fish nibbled at her arms and legs. She closed her eyes and floated.

A soft rustle made her open them again. She sat up with a soft splash. "Missandei?" she called. "Irri? Jhiqui?"

"They sleep," came the answer.

A woman stood under the persimmon tree, clad in a hooded robe that brushed the grass. Beneath the hood, her face seemed hard and shiny. *She is wearing a mask,* Dany knew, *a wooden mask finished in dark red lacquer.* "Quaithe? Am I dreaming?" She pinched her ear and winced at the pain. "I dreamt of you on *Balerion,* when first we came to Astapor."

"You did not dream. Then or now."

"What are you doing here? How did you get past my guards?"

"I came another way. Your guards never saw me."

"If I call out, they will kill you."

"They will swear to you that I am not here."

"*Are* you here?"

"No. Hear me, Daenerys Targaryen. The glass candles are burning.

Soon comes the pale mare, and after her the others. Kraken and dark flame, lion and griffin, the sun's son and the mummer's dragon. Trust none of them. Remember the Undying. Beware the perfumed seneschal."

"Reznak? Why should I fear him?" Dany rose from the pool. Water trickled down her legs, and gooseflesh covered her arms in the cool night air. "If you have some warning for me, speak plainly. What do you want of me, Quaithe?"

Moonlight shone in the woman's eyes. "To show you the way."

"I remember the way. I go north to go south, east to go west, back to go forward. And to touch the light I have to pass beneath the shadow." She squeezed the water from her silvery hair. "I am half-sick of riddling. In Qarth I was a beggar, but here I am a queen. I command you—"

"*Daenerys.* Remember the Undying. Remember who you are."

"The blood of the dragon." *But my dragons are roaring in the darkness.* "I remember the Undying. *Child of three,* they called me. Three mounts they promised me, three fires, and three treasons. One for blood and one for gold and one for . . ."

"Your Grace?" Missandei stood in the door of the queen's bedchamber, a lantern in her hand. "Who are you talking to?"

Dany glanced back toward the persimmon tree. There was no woman there. No hooded robe, no lacquer mask, no Quaithe.

A shadow. A memory. No one. She was the blood of the dragon, but Ser Barristan had warned her that in that blood there was a taint. *Could I be going mad?* They had called her father mad, once. "I was praying," she told the Naathi girl. "It will be light soon. I had best eat something, before court."

"I will bring you food to break your fast."

Alone again, Dany went all the way around the pyramid in hopes of finding Quaithe, past the burned trees and scorched earth where her men had tried to capture Drogon. But the only sound was the wind in the fruit trees, and the only creatures in the gardens were a few pale moths.

Missandei returned with a melon and a bowl of hard-cooked eggs, but Dany found she had no appetite. As the sky lightened and the stars faded one by one, Irri and Jhiqui helped her don a *tokar* of violet silk fringed in gold.

When Reznak and Skahaz appeared, she found herself looking at them askance, mindful of the three treasons. *Beware the perfumed seneschal.* She sniffed suspiciously at Reznak mo Reznak. *I could command the Shavepate to arrest him and put him to the question.* Would that forestall the prophecy? Or would some other betrayer take his place? *Prophecies are treacherous*, she reminded herself, *and Reznak may be no more than he appears.*

In the purple hall, Dany found her ebon bench piled high about with satin pillows. The sight brought a wan smile to her lips. *Ser Barristan's work*, she knew. The old knight was a good man, but sometimes very literal. *It was only a jape, ser*, she thought, but she sat on one of the pillows just the same.

Her sleepless night soon made itself felt. Before long she was fighting off a yawn as Reznak prattled about the craftsmen's guilds. The stonemasons were wroth with her, it seemed. The bricklayers as well. Certain former slaves were carving stone and laying bricks, stealing work from guild journeymen and masters alike. "The freedmen work too cheaply, Magnificence," Reznak said. "Some call themselves journeymen, or even masters, titles that belong by rights only to the craftsmen of the guilds. The masons and the bricklayers do respectfully petition Your Worship to uphold their ancient rights and customs."

"The freedmen work cheaply because they are hungry," Dany pointed out. "If I forbid them to carve stone or lay bricks, the chandlers, the weavers, and the goldsmiths will soon be at my gates asking that they be excluded from those trades as well." She considered a moment. "Let it be written that henceforth only guild members shall be permitted to name themselves journeymen or masters . . . provided the guilds open their rolls to any freedman who can demonstrate the requisite skills."

"So shall it be proclaimed," said Reznak. "Will it please Your Worship to hear the noble Hizdahr zo Loraq?"

Will he never admit defeat? "Let him step forth."

Hizdahr was not in a *tokar* today. Instead he wore a simple robe of grey and blue. He was shorn as well. *He has shaved off his beard and cut his hair*, she realized. The man had not gone shavepate, not quite, but at least those absurd wings of his were gone. "Your barber has served you well, Hizdahr. I hope you have come to show me his work and not to plague me further about the fighting pits."

He made a deep obeisance. "Your Grace, I fear I must."

Dany grimaced. Even her own people would give no rest about the matter. Reznak mo Reznak stressed the coin to be made through taxes. The Green Grace said that reopening the pits would please the gods. The Shavepate felt it would win her support against the Sons of the Harpy. "Let them fight," grunted Strong Belwas, who had once been a champion in the pits. Ser Barristan suggested a tourney instead; his orphans could ride at rings and fight a mêlée with blunted weapons, he said, a suggestion

Dany knew was as hopeless as it was well-intentioned. It was blood the Meereenese yearned to see, not skill. Elsewise the fighting slaves would have worn armor. Only the little scribe Missandei seemed to share the queen's misgivings.

"I have refused you six times," Dany reminded Hizdahr.

"Your Radiance has seven gods, so perhaps she will look upon my seventh plea with favor. Today I do not come alone. Will you hear my friends? There are seven of them as well." He brought them forth one by one. "Here is Khrazz. Here Barsena Blackhair, ever valiant. Here Camarron of the Count and Goghor the Giant. This is the Spotted Cat, this Fearless Ithoke. Last, Belaquo Bonebreaker. They have come to add their voices to mine own, and ask Your Grace to let our fighting pits reopen."

Dany knew his seven, by name if not by sight. All had been amongst the most famed of Meereen's fighting slaves . . . and it had been the fighting slaves, freed from their shackles by her sewer rats, who led the uprising that won the city for her. She owed them a blood debt. "I will hear you," she allowed.

One by one, each of them asked her to let the fighting pits reopen. "Why?" she demanded, when Ithoke had finished. "You are no longer slaves, doomed to die at a master's whim. I freed you. Why should you wish to end your lives upon the scarlet sands?"

"I train since three," said Goghor the Giant. "I kill since six. Mother of Dragons says I am free. Why not free to fight?"

"If it is fighting you want, fight for me. Swear your sword to the Mother's Men or the Free Brothers or the Stalwart Shields. Teach my other freedmen how to fight."

Goghor shook his head. "Before, I fight for master. You say, fight for you. I say, fight for me." The huge man thumped his chest with a fist as big as a ham. "For gold. For glory."

"Goghor speaks for us all." The Spotted Cat wore a leopard skin across one shoulder. "The last time I was sold, the price was three hundred thousand honors. When I was a slave, I slept on furs and ate red meat off the bone. Now that I'm free, I sleep on straw and eat salt fish, when I can get it."

"Hizdahr swears that the winners shall share half of all the coin collected at the gates," said Khrazz. "*Half*, he swears it, and Hizdahr is an honorable man."

No, a cunning man. Daenerys felt trapped. "And the losers? What shall they receive?"

"Their names shall be graven on the Gates of Fate amongst the other valiant fallen," declared Barsena. For eight years she had slain every other woman sent against her, it was said. "All men must die, and women too . . . but not all will be remembered."

Dany had no answer for that. *If this is truly what my people wish, do I have the right to deny it to them? It was their city before it was mine, and it is their own lives they wish to squander.* "I will consider all you've said. Thank you for your counsel." She rose. "We will resume on the morrow."

"*All kneel for Daenerys Stormborn, the Unburnt, Queen of Meereen, Queen of the Andals and the Rhoynar and the First Men,* Khaleesi *of Great Grass Sea, Breaker of Shackles, and Mother of Dragons,*" Missandei called.

Ser Barristan escorted her back up to her chambers. "Tell me a tale, ser," Dany said as they climbed. "Some tale of valor with a happy ending." She felt in need of happy endings. "Tell me how you escaped from the Usurper."

"Your Grace. There is no valor in running for your life."

Dany seated herself on a cushion, crossed her legs, and gazed up at him. "Please. It was the Young Usurper who dismissed you from the Kingsguard . . ."

"Joffrey, aye. They gave my age for a reason, though the truth was elsewise. The boy wanted a white cloak for his dog Sandor Clegane and his mother wanted the Kingslayer to be her lord commander. When they told me, I . . . I took off my cloak as they commanded, threw my sword at Joffrey's feet, and spoke unwisely."

"What did you say?"

"The truth . . . but truth was never welcome at that court. I walked from the throne room with my head high, though I did not know where I was going. I had no home but White Sword Tower. My cousins would find a place for me at Harvest Hall, I knew, but I had no wish to bring Joffrey's displeasure down upon them. I was gathering my things when it came to me that I had brought this on myself by taking Robert's pardon. He was a good knight but a bad king, for he had no right to the throne he sat. That was when I knew that to redeem myself I must find the true king, and serve him loyally with all the strength that still remained me."

"My brother Viserys."

"Such was my intent. When I reached the stables the gold cloaks tried to seize me. Joffrey had offered me a tower to die in, but I had spurned his gift, so now he meant to offer me a dungeon. The commander of the City Watch himself confronted me, emboldened by my empty scabbard, but he had only three men with him and I still had my knife. I slashed one man's face open when he laid his hands upon me, and rode through the others. As I spurred for the gates I heard Janos Slynt shouting for them to go after me. Once outside the Red Keep, the streets were congested, else I might have gotten away clean. Instead they caught me at the River Gate. The gold cloaks who had pursued me from the castle shouted for those at the gate to stop me, so they crossed their spears to bar my way."

"And you without your sword? How did you get past them?"

"A true knight is worth ten guardsmen. The men at the gate were taken by surprise. I rode one down, wrenched away his spear, and drove it through the throat of my closest pursuer. The other broke off once I was through the gate, so I spurred my horse to a gallop and rode hellbent along the river until the city was lost to sight behind me. That night I traded my horse for a handful of pennies and some rags, and the next morning I joined the stream of smallfolk making their way to King's Landing. I'd gone out the Mud Gate, so I returned through the Gate of the Gods, with dirt on my face, stubble on my cheeks, and no weapon but a wooden staff. In roughspun clothes and mud-caked boots, I was just one more old man fleeing the war. The gold cloaks took a stag from me and waved me through. King's Landing was crowded with smallfolk who'd come seeking refuge from the fighting. I lost myself amongst them. I had a little silver, but I needed that to pay my passage across the narrow sea, so I slept in septs and alleys and took my meals in pot shops. I let my beard grow out and cloaked myself in age. The day Lord Stark lost his head, I was there, watching. Afterward I went into the Great Sept and thanked the seven gods that Joffrey had stripped me of my cloak."

"Stark was a traitor who met a traitor's end."

"Your Grace," said Selmy, "Eddard Stark played a part in your father's fall, but he bore you no ill will. When the eunuch Varys told us that you were with child, Robert wanted you killed, but Lord Stark spoke against it. Rather than countenance the murder of children, he told Robert to find himself another Hand."

"Have you forgotten Princess Rhaenys and Prince Aegon?"

"Never. That was Lannister work, Your Grace."

"Lannister or Stark, what difference? Viserys used to call them *the Usurper's dogs*. If a child is set upon by a pack of hounds, does it matter which one tears out his throat? All the dogs are just as guilty. The guilt . . ." The word caught in her throat. *Hazzea*, she thought, and suddenly she heard herself say, "I have to see the pit," in a voice as small as a child's whisper. "Take me down, ser, if you would."

A flicker of disapproval crossed the old man's face, but it was not his way to question his queen. "As you command."

The servants' steps were the quickest way down—not grand, but steep and straight and narrow, hidden in the walls. Ser Barristan brought a lantern, lest she fall. Bricks of twenty different colors pressed close around them, fading to grey and black beyond the lantern light. Thrice they passed Unsullied guards, standing as if they had been carved from stone. The only sound was the soft scruff of their feet upon the steps.

At ground level the Great Pyramid of Meereen was a hushed place, full of dust and shadows. Its outer walls were thirty feet thick. Within them, sounds echoed off arches of many-colored bricks, and amongst the stables, stalls, and storerooms. They passed beneath three massive arches, down a torchlit ramp into the vaults beneath the pyramid, past cisterns, dungeons, and torture chambers where slaves had been scourged and skinned and burned with red-hot irons. Finally they came to a pair of huge iron doors with rusted hinges, guarded by Unsullied.

At her command, one produced an iron key. The door opened, hinges shrieking. Daenerys Targaryen stepped into the hot heart of darkness and stopped at the lip of a deep pit. Forty feet below, her dragons raised their heads. Four eyes burned through the shadows—two of molten gold and two of bronze.

Ser Barristan took her by the arm. "No closer."

"You think they would harm *me*?"

"I do not know, Your Grace, but I would sooner not risk your person to learn the answer."

When Rhaegal roared, a gout of yellow flame turned darkness into day for half a heartbeat. The fire licked along the walls, and Dany felt the heat upon her face, like the blast from an oven. Across the pit, Viserion's wings unfolded, stirring the stale air. He tried to fly to her, but the chains snapped taut as he rose and slammed him down onto his belly. Links as big as a man's fist bound his feet to the floor. The iron collar about his neck was fastened to the wall behind him. Rhaegal wore matching chains. In the light of Selmy's lantern, his scales gleamed like jade. Smoke rose from between his teeth. Bones were scattered on the floor at his feet, cracked and scorched and splintered. The air was uncomfortably hot and smelled of sulfur and charred meat.

"They are larger." Dany's voice echoed off the scorched stone walls. A drop of sweat trickled down her brow and fell onto her breast. "Is it true that dragons never stop growing?"

"If they have food enough, and space to grow. Chained up in here, though . . ."

The Great Masters had used the pit as a prison. It was large enough to hold five hundred men . . . and more than ample for two dragons. *For how long, though? What will happen when they grow too large for the pit? Will they turn on one another with flame and claw? Will they grow wan and weak, with withered flanks and shrunken wings? Will their fires go out before the end?*

What sort of mother lets her children rot in darkness?

If I look back, I am doomed, Dany told herself . . . but how could she not look back? *I should have seen it coming. Was I so blind, or did I close my eyes willfully, so I would not have to see the price of power?*

Viserys had told her all the tales when she was little. He loved to talk of dragons. She knew how Harrenhal had fallen. She knew about the Field of Fire and the Dance of the Dragons. One of her forebears, the third Aegon, had seen his own mother devoured by his uncle's dragon. And there were songs beyond count of villages and kingdoms that lived in dread of dragons till some brave dragonslayer rescued them. At Astapor the slaver's eyes had melted. On the road to Yunkai, when Daario tossed the heads of Sallor the Bald and Prendahl na Ghezn at her feet, her children made a feast of them. Dragons had no fear of men. And a dragon large enough to gorge on sheep could take a child just as easily.

Her name had been Hazzea. She was four years old. *Unless her father lied. He might have lied.* No one had seen the dragon but him. His proof was burned bones, but burned bones proved nothing. He might have killed the little girl himself, and burned her afterward. He would not have been the first father to dispose of an unwanted girl child, the Shavepate claimed. *The Sons of the Harpy might have done it, and made it look like dragon's work to make the city hate me.* Dany wanted to believe that . . . but if that was so, why had Hazzea's father waited until the audience hall was almost empty to come forward? If his purpose had been to inflame the Meereenese against her, he would have told his tale when the hall was full of ears to hear.

The Shavepate had urged her to put the man to death. "At least rip out his tongue. This man's lie could destroy us all, Magnificence." Instead Dany chose to pay the blood price. No one could tell her the worth of a daughter, so she set it at one hundred times the worth of a lamb. "I would give Hazzea back to you if I could," she told the father, "but some things are beyond the power of even a queen. Her bones shall be laid to rest in the Temple of the Graces, and a hundred candles shall burn day and night in her memory. Come back to me each year upon her nameday, and your other children shall not want . . . but this tale must never pass your lips again."

"Men will ask," the grieving father had said. "They will ask me where Hazzea is and how she died."

"She died of a snakebite," Reznak mo Reznak insisted. "A ravening wolf carried her off. A sudden sickness took her. Tell them what you will, but never speak of dragons."

Viserion's claws scrabbled against the stones, and the huge chains rattled as he tried to make his way to her again. When he could not, he gave a roar, twisted his head back as far as he was able, and spat golden flame at the wall behind him. *How soon till his fire burns hot enough to crack stone and melt iron?*

Once, not long ago, he had ridden on her shoulder, his tail coiled round her arm. Once she had fed him morsels of charred meat from her own hand. He had been the first chained up. Daenerys had led him to the pit herself and shut him up inside with several oxen. Once he had gorged himself he grew drowsy. They had chained him whilst he slept.

Rhaegal had been harder. Perhaps he could hear his brother raging in the pit, despite the walls of brick and stone between them. In the end, they had to cover him with a net of heavy iron chain as he basked on her terrace, and he fought so fiercely that it had taken three days to carry him down the servants' steps, twisting and snapping. Six men had been burned in the struggle.

And Drogon . . .

The winged shadow, the grieving father called him. He was the largest of her three, the fiercest, the wildest, with scales as black as night and eyes like pits of fire.

Drogon hunted far afield, but when he was sated he liked to bask in the sun at the apex of the Great Pyramid, where once the harpy of Meereen had stood. Thrice they had tried to take him there, and thrice they had failed. Two score of her bravest had risked themselves trying to capture him. Almost all had suffered burns, and four of them had died. The last she had seen of Drogon had been at sunset on the night of the third attempt. The black dragon had been flying north across the Skahazadhan toward the tall grasses of the Dothraki sea. He had not returned.

Mother of dragons, Daenerys thought. *Mother of monsters. What have I unleashed upon the world? A queen I am, but my throne is made of burned bones, and it rests on quicksand.* Without dragons, how could she hope to hold Meereen, much less win back Westeros? *I am the blood of the dragon,* she thought. *If they are monsters, so am I.*

REEK

The rat squealed as he bit into it, squirming wildly in his hands, frantic to escape. The belly was the softest part. He tore at the sweet meat, the warm blood running over his lips. It was so good that it brought tears to his eyes. His belly rumbled and he swallowed. By the third bite the rat had ceased to struggle, and he was feeling almost content.

Then he heard the sounds of voices outside the dungeon door.

At once he stilled, fearing even to chew. His mouth was full of blood and flesh and hair, but he dare not spit or swallow. He listened in terror, stiff as stone, to the scuff of boots and the clanking of iron keys. *No,* he thought, *no, please gods, not now, not now.* It had taken him so long to catch the rat. *If they catch me with it, they will take it away, and then they'll tell, and Lord Ramsay will hurt me.*

He knew he ought to hide the rat, but he was so *hungry.* It had been two days since he had eaten, or maybe three. Down here in the dark it was hard to tell. Though his arms and legs were thin as reeds, his belly was swollen and hollow, and ached so much that he found he could not sleep. Whenever he closed his eyes, he found himself remembering Lady Hornwood. After their wedding, Lord Ramsay had locked her away in a tower and starved her to death. In the end she had eaten her own fingers.

He crouched down in a corner of his cell, clutching his prize under his chin. Blood ran from the corners of his mouth as he nibbled at the rat with what remained of his teeth, trying to bolt down as much of the warm flesh as he could before the cell was opened. The meat was stringy, but so rich he thought he might be sick. He chewed and swallowed, picking small bones from the holes in his gums where teeth had been yanked out. It hurt to chew, but he was so hungry he could not stop.

The sounds were growing louder. *Please gods, he isn't coming for me,* he prayed, tearing off one of the rat's legs. It had been a long time since anyone had come for him. There were other cells, other prisoners. Sometimes he heard them screaming, even through the thick stone walls. *The women always scream the loudest.* He sucked at the raw meat and tried to spit out the leg bone, but it only dribbled over his lower lip and tangled in his beard. *Go away,* he prayed, *go away, pass me by, please, please.*

But the footsteps stopped just when they were loudest, and the keys clattered right outside the door. The rat fell from his fingers. He wiped his bloody fingers on his breeches. "No," he mumbled, "*noooo.*" His heels scrabbled at the straw as he tried to push himself into the corner, into the cold damp stone walls.

The sound of the lock turning was the most terrible of all. When the light hit him full in the face, he let out a shriek. He had to cover his eyes with his hands. He would have clawed them out if he'd dared, his head was pounding so. "Take it away, do it in the dark, please, oh please."

"That's not him," said a boy's voice. "Look at him. We've got the wrong cell."

"Last cell on the left," another boy replied. "This is the last cell on the left, isn't it?"

"Aye." A pause. "What's he saying?"

"I don't think he likes the light."

"Would you, if you looked like *that*?" The boy hawked and spat. "And the stench of him. I'm like to choke."

"He's been eating rats," said the second boy. "Look."

The first boy laughed. "He has. That's funny."

I had to. The rats bit him when he slept, gnawing at his fingers and his toes, even at his face, so when he got his hands on one he did not hesitate. Eat or be eaten, those were the only choices. "I did it," he mumbled, "I did, I did, I ate him, they do the same to me, please . . ."

The boys moved closer, the straw crunching softly under their feet. "Talk to me," said one of them. He was the smaller of the two, a thin boy, but clever. "Do you remember who you are?"

The fear came bubbling up inside him, and he moaned.

"Talk to me. Tell me your name."

My name. A scream caught in his throat. They had taught him his name, they had, they *had*, but it had been so long that he'd forgotten. *If I say it wrong, he'll take another finger, or worse, he'll . . . he'll . . .* He would not think about that, he could not think about that. There were needles in his jaw, in his eyes. His head was pounding. "Please," he squeaked, his voice thin and weak. He sounded a hundred years old. Perhaps he was. *How long have I been in here?* "Go," he mumbled, through broken teeth and broken fingers, his eyes closed tight against the terrible bright light. "Please, you can have the rat, don't hurt me . . ."

"*Reek*," said the larger of the boys. "Your name is Reek. Remember?" He was the one with the torch. The smaller boy had the ring of iron keys.

Reek? Tears ran down his cheeks. "I remember. I do." His mouth opened and closed. "My name is Reek. It rhymes with leek." In the dark he did not need a name, so it was easy to forget. *Reek, Reek, my name is Reek.* He had not been born with that name. In another life he had been someone else, but here and now, his name was Reek. He remembered.

He remembered the boys as well. They were clad in matching lambswool doublets, silver-grey with dark blue trim. Both were squires, both were eight, and both were Walder Frey. *Big Walder and Little Walder, yes.* Only the big one was Little and the little one was Big, which amused the boys and confused the rest of the world. "I know you," he whispered, through cracked lips. "I know your names."

"You're to come with us," said Little Walder.

"His lordship has need of you," said Big Walder.

Fear went through him like a knife. *They are only children,* he thought. *Two boys of eight.* He could overcome two boys of eight, surely. Even as weak as he was, he could take the torch, take the keys, take the dagger sheathed on Little Walder's hip, escape. *No. No, it is too easy. It is a trap. If I run, he will take another finger from me, he will take more of my teeth.*

He had run before. Years ago, it seemed, when he still had some strength in him, when he had still been defiant. That time it had been Kyra with the keys. She told him she had stolen them, that she knew a postern gate that was never guarded. "Take me back to Winterfell, m'lord," she begged, pale-faced and trembling. "I don't know the way. I can't escape alone. Come with me, please." And so he had. The gaoler was dead drunk in a puddle of wine, with his breeches down around his ankles. The dungeon door was open and the postern gate had been unguarded, just as she had said. They waited for the moon to go behind a cloud, then slipped from the castle and splashed across the Weeping Water, stumbling over stones, half-frozen by the icy stream. On the far side, he had kissed her. "You've saved us," he said. *Fool. Fool.*

It had all been a trap, a game, a jape. Lord Ramsay loved the chase and preferred to hunt two-legged prey. All night they ran through the darkling wood, but as the sun came up the sound of a distant horn came faintly through the trees, and they heard the baying of a pack of hounds. "We should split up," he told Kyra as the dogs drew closer. "They cannot track us both." The girl was crazed with fear, though, and refused to leave his side, even when he swore that he would raise a host of ironborn and come back for her if she should be the one they followed.

Within the hour, they were taken. One dog knocked him to the ground, and a second bit Kyra on the leg as she scrambled up a hillside. The rest surrounded them, baying and snarling, snapping at them every time they moved, holding them there until Ramsay Snow rode up with his huntsmen. He was still a bastard then, not yet a Bolton. "There you are," he said, smiling down at them from the saddle. "You wound me, wandering off like this. Have you grown tired of my hospitality so soon?" That was when Kyra seized a stone and threw it at his head. It missed by a good foot, and Ramsay smiled. "You must be punished."

Reek remembered the desperate, frightened look in Kyra's eyes. She had never looked so young as she did in that moment, still half a girl, but there was nothing he could do. *She brought them down on us,* he thought. *If we had separated as I wanted, one of us might have gotten away.*

The memory made it hard to breathe. Reek turned away from the torch with tears glimmering in his eyes. *What does he want of me this time?* he thought, despairing. *Why won't he just leave me be? I did no wrong, not this time, why won't they just leave me in the dark?* He'd had a rat, a fat one, warm and wriggling . . .

"Should we wash him?" asked Little Walder.

"His lordship likes him stinky," said Big Walder. "That's why he named him Reek."

Reek. My name is Reek, it rhymes with bleak. He had to remember that. *Serve and obey and remember who you are, and no more harm will come to you. He promised, his lordship promised.* Even if he had wanted to resist, he did not have the strength. It had been scourged from him, starved from him, flayed from him. When Little Walder pulled him up and Big Walder waved the torch at him to herd him from the cell, he went along as docile as a dog. If he'd had a tail, he would have tucked it down between his legs.

If I had a tail, the Bastard would have cut it off. The thought came unbidden, a vile thought, dangerous. His lordship was not a bastard anymore. *Bolton, not Snow.* The boy king on the Iron Throne had made Lord Ramsay legitimate, giving him the right to use his lord father's name. Calling him *Snow* reminded him of his bastardy and sent him into a black rage. Reek must remember that. And his name, he must remember his name. For half a heartbeat it eluded him, and that frightened him so badly that he tripped on the steep dungeon steps and tore his breeches open on the stone, drawing blood. Little Walder had to shove the torch at him to get him back on his feet and moving again.

Out in the yard, night was settling over the Dreadfort and a full moon was rising over the castle's eastern walls. Its pale light cast the shadows of the tall triangular merlons across the frozen ground, a line of sharp black teeth. The air was cold and damp and full of half-forgotten smells. *The world,* Reek told himself, *this is what the world smells like.* He did not know how long he had been down there in the dungeons, but it had to have been half a year at least. *That long, or longer. What if it has been five years, or ten, or twenty? Would I even know? What if I went mad down there, and half my life is gone?* But no, that was folly. It could not have been so long. The boys were still boys. If it had been ten years, they would have grown into men. He had to remember that. *I must not let him drive me mad. He can take my fingers and my toes, he can put out my eyes and slice my ears off, but he cannot take my wits unless I let him.*

Little Walder led the way with torch in hand. Reek followed meekly, with Big Walder just behind him. The dogs in the kennels barked as they went by. Wind swirled through the yard, cutting through the thin cloth of the filthy rags he wore and raising gooseprickles on his skin. The night air was cold and damp, but he saw no sign of snow though surely winter was close at hand. Reek wondered if he would be alive to see the snows come. *How many fingers will I have? How many toes?* When he raised a hand, he was shocked to see how white it was, how fleshless. *Skin and bones,* he thought. *I have an old man's hands.* Could he have been wrong about the boys? What if they were not Little Walder and Big Walder after all, but the *sons* of the boys he'd known?

The great hall was dim and smoky. Rows of torches burned to left and right, grasped by skeletal human hands jutting from the walls. High overhead were wooden rafters black from smoke, and a vaulted ceiling lost in shadow. The air was heavy with the smells of wine and ale and roasted meat. Reek's stomach rumbled noisily at the scents, and his mouth began to water.

Little Walder pushed him stumbling past the long tables where the men of the garrison were eating. He could feel their eyes upon him. The best places, up near the dais, were occupied by Ramsay's favorites, the Bastard's Boys. Ben Bones, the old man who kept his lordship's beloved hunting hounds. Damon, called Damon Dance-for-Me, fair-haired and boyish. Grunt, who had lost his tongue for speaking carelessly in Lord Roose's hearing. Sour Alyn. Skinner. Yellow Dick. Farther down, below the salt, were others that Reek knew by sight if not by name: sworn swords and serjeants, soldiers and gaolers and torturers. But there were strangers too, faces he did not know. Some wrinkled their noses as he passed, whilst others laughed at the sight of him. *Guests,* Reek thought, *his lordship's friends, and I am brought up to amuse them.* A shiver of fear went through him.

At the high table the Bastard of Bolton sat in his lord father's seat, drinking from his father's cup. Two old men shared the high table with him, and Reek knew at a glance that both were lords. One was gaunt, with flinty eyes, a long white beard, and a face as hard as a winter frost. His jerkin was a ragged bearskin, worn and greasy. Underneath he wore a ringmail byrnie, even at table. The second lord was thin as well, but twisted where the first was straight. One of his shoulders was much higher than the other, and he stooped over his trencher like a vulture over carrion. His eyes were grey and greedy, his teeth yellow, his forked beard a tangle of snow and silver. Only a few wisps of white hair still clung to his spotted skull, but the cloak he wore was soft and fine, grey wool trimmed with black sable and fastened at the shoulder with a starburst wrought in beaten silver.

Ramsay was clad in black and pink—black boots, black belt and scabbard, black leather jerkin over a pink velvet doublet slashed with dark red satin. In his right ear gleamed a garnet cut in the shape of a drop of blood. Yet for all the splendor of his garb, he remained an ugly man, big-boned and slope-shouldered, with a fleshiness to him that suggested that in later life he would run to fat. His skin was pink and blotchy, his nose broad, his mouth small, his hair long and dark and dry. His lips were wide and meaty, but the thing men noticed first about him were his eyes. He had his lord father's eyes—small, close-set, queerly pale. *Ghost grey,* some men called the shade, but in truth his eyes were all but colorless, like two chips of dirty ice.

At the sight of Reek, he smiled a wet-lipped smile. "There he is. My sour old friend." To the men beside him he said, "Reek has been with me since I was a boy. My lord father gave him to me as a token of his love."

The two lords exchanged a look. "I had heard your serving man was dead," said the one with the stooped shoulder. "Slain by the Starks, they said."

Lord Ramsay chuckled. "The ironmen will tell you that what is dead may never die, but rises again, harder and stronger. Like Reek. He smells of the grave, though, I grant you that."

"He smells of nightsoil and stale vomit." The stoop-shouldered old lord tossed aside the bone that he'd been gnawing on and wiped his fingers on the tablecloth. "Is there some reason you must needs inflict him upon us whilst we're eating?"

The second lord, the straight-backed old man in the mail byrnie, stud-ied Reek with flinty eyes. "Look again," he urged the other lord. "His hair's gone white and he is three stone thinner, aye, but this is no serving man. Have you forgotten?"

The crookback lord looked again and gave a sudden snort. "*Him?* Can it be? Stark's ward. Smiling, always smiling."

"He smiles less often now," Lord Ramsay confessed. "I may have bro-ken some of his pretty white teeth."

"You would have done better to slit his throat," said the lord in mail. "A dog who turns against his master is fit for naught but skinning."

"Oh, he's been skinned, here and there," said Ramsay.

"Yes, my lord. I was bad, my lord. Insolent and . . ." He licked his lip, trying to think of what else he had done. *Serve and obey,* he told himself, *and he'll let you live, and keep the parts that you still have. Serve and obey and remember your name. Reek, Reek, it rhymes with meek.* ". . . bad and . . ."

"There's blood on your mouth," Ramsay observed. "Have you been chewing on your fingers again, Reek?"

"No. No, my lord, I swear." Reek had tried to bite his own ring finger off once, to stop it hurting after they had stripped the skin from it. Lord Ramsay would never simply cut off a man's finger. He preferred to flay it and let the exposed flesh dry and crack and fester. Reek had been whipped and racked and cut, but there was no pain half so excruciating as the pain that followed flaying. It was the sort of pain that drove men mad, and it could not be endured for long. Soon or late the victim would scream, "Please, no more, no more, stop it hurting, *cut it off,*" and Lord Ramsay would oblige. It was a game they played. Reek had learned the rules, as his hands and feet could testify, but that one time he had forgotten and tried to end the pain himself, with his teeth. Ramsay had not been pleased, and the offense had cost Reek another toe. "I ate a rat," he mumbled.

"A rat?" Ramsay's pale eyes glittered in the torchlight. "All the rats in the Dreadfort belong to my lord father. How dare you make a meal of one without my leave."

Reek did not know what to say, so he said nothing. One wrong word could cost him another toe, even a finger. Thus far he had lost two fingers off his left hand and the pinky off his right, but only the little toe off his right foot against three from his left. Sometimes Ramsay would make japes about balancing him out. *My lord was only japing,* he tried to tell himself. *He does not want to hurt me, he told me so, he only does it when I give him cause.* His lord was merciful and kind. He might have flayed his face off for some of the things Reek had said, before he'd learned his true name and proper place.

"This grows tedious," said the lord in the mail byrnie. "Kill him and be done with it."

Lord Ramsay filled his cup with ale. "That would spoil our celebration, my lord. Reek, I have glad tidings for you. I am to be wed. My lord father is bringing me a Stark girl. Lord Eddard's daughter, Arya. You remember little Arya, don't you?"

Arya Underfoot, he almost said. *Arya Horseface*. Robb's younger sister, brown-haired, long-faced, skinny as a stick, always dirty. *Sansa was the pretty one.* He remembered a time when he had thought that Lord Eddard Stark might marry him to Sansa and claim him for a son, but that had only been a child's fancy. Arya, though . . . "I remember her. Arya."

"She shall be the Lady of Winterfell, and me her lord."

She is only a girl. "Yes, my lord. Congratulations."

"Will you attend me at my wedding, Reek?"

He hesitated. "If you wish it, my lord."

"Oh, I do."

He hesitated again, wondering if this was some cruel trap. "Yes, my lord. If it please you. I would be honored."

"We must take you out of that vile dungeon, then. Scrub you pink again, get you some clean clothes, some food to eat. Some nice soft porridge, would you like that? Perhaps a pease pie laced with bacon. I have a little task for you, and you'll need your strength back if you are to serve me. You do want to serve me, I know."

"Yes, my lord. More than anything." A shiver went through him. "I'm your Reek. Please let me serve you. Please."

"Since you ask so nicely, how can I deny you?" Ramsay Bolton smiled. "I ride to war, Reek. And you will be coming with me, to help me fetch home my virgin bride."

BRAN

Something about the way the raven screamed sent a shiver running up Bran's spine. *I am almost a man grown*, he had to remind himself. *I have to be brave now.*

But the air was sharp and cold and full of fear. Even Summer was afraid. The fur on his neck was bristling. Shadows stretched against the hillside, black and hungry. All the trees were bowed and twisted by the weight of ice they carried. Some hardly looked like trees at all. Buried from root to crown in frozen snow, they huddled on the hill like giants, monstrous and misshapen creatures hunched against the icy wind.

"They are here." The ranger drew his longsword.

"Where?" Meera's voice was hushed.

"Close. I don't know. Somewhere."

The raven shrieked again. "Hodor," whispered Hodor. He had his hands tucked up beneath his armpits. Icicles hung from the brown briar of his beard, and his mustache was a lump of frozen snot, glittering redly in the light of sunset.

"Those wolves are close as well," Bran warned them. "The ones that have been following us. Summer can smell them whenever we're downwind."

"Wolves are the least of our woes," said Coldhands. "We have to climb. It will be dark soon. You would do well to be inside before night comes. Your warmth will draw them." He glanced to the west, where the light of the setting sun could be seen dimly through the trees, like the glow of a distant fire.

"Is this the only way in?" asked Meera.

"The back door is three leagues north, down a sinkhole."

That was all he had to say. Not even Hodor could climb down into a sinkhole with Bran heavy on his back, and Jojen could no more walk three leagues than run a thousand.

Meera eyed the hill above. "The way looks clear."

"*Looks*," the ranger muttered darkly. "Can you feel the cold? There's something here. *Where are they?*"

"Inside the cave?" suggested Meera.

"The cave is warded. They cannot pass." The ranger used his sword to point. "You can see the entrance there. Halfway up, between the weirwoods, that cleft in the rock."

"I see it," said Bran. Ravens were flying in and out.

Hodor shifted his weight. "Hodor."

"A fold in the rock, that's all I see," said Meera.

"There's a passage there. Steep and twisty at first, a runnel through the rock. If you can reach it, you'll be safe."

"What about you?"

"The cave is warded."

Meera studied the cleft in the hillside. "It can't be more than a thousand yards from here to there."

No, thought Bran, *but all those yards are upward.* The hill was steep and thickly wooded. The snow had stopped three days ago, but none of it had melted. Beneath the trees, the ground was blanketed in white, still pristine and unbroken. "No one's here," said Bran, bravely. "Look at the snow. There are no footprints."

"The white walkers go lightly on the snow," the ranger said. "You'll find no prints to mark their passage." A raven descended from above to settle on his shoulder. Only a dozen of the big black birds remained with them. The rest had vanished along the way; every dawn when they arose, there had been fewer of them. "*Come*," the bird squawked. "*Come, come.*"

The three-eyed crow, thought Bran. *The greenseer.* "It's not so far," he said. "A little climb, and we'll be safe. Maybe we can have a fire." All of them were cold and wet and hungry, except the ranger, and Jojen Reed was too weak to walk unaided.

"You go." Meera Reed bent down beside her brother. He was settled in the bole of an oak, eyes closed, shivering violently. What little of his face could be seen beneath his hood and scarf was as colorless as the surrounding snow, but breath still puffed faintly from his nostrils whenever he exhaled. Meera had been carrying him all day. *Food and fire will set him right again*, Bran tried to tell himself, though he wasn't sure it would. "I can't fight and carry Jojen both, the climb's too steep," Meera was saying. "Hodor, you take Bran up to that cave."

"Hodor." Hodor clapped his hands together.

"Jojen just needs to eat," Bran said, miserably. It had been twelve days since the elk had collapsed for the third and final time, since Coldhands had knelt beside it in the snowbank and murmured a blessing in some strange tongue as he slit its throat. Bran wept like a little girl when the bright blood came rushing out. He had never felt more like a cripple than he did then, watching helplessly as Meera Reed and Coldhands butchered the brave beast who had carried them so far. He told himself he would not eat, that it was better to go hungry than to feast upon a friend, but in the end he'd eaten twice, once in his own skin and once in Summer's. As gaunt and starved as the elk had been, the steaks the ranger carved from him had sustained them for seven days, until they finished the last of them huddled over a fire in the ruins of an old hillfort.

"He needs to eat," Meera agreed, smoothing her brother's brow. "We all do, but there's no food here. *Go.*"

Bran blinked back a tear and felt it freeze upon his cheek. Coldhands took Hodor by the arm. "The light is fading. If they're not here now, they will be soon. Come."

Wordless for once, Hodor slapped the snow off his legs, and plowed upward through the snowdrifts with Bran upon his back. Coldhands stalked beside them, his blade in a black hand. Summer came after. In some places the snow was higher than he was, and the big direwolf had to stop and shake it off after plunging through the thin crust. As they climbed, Bran turned awkwardly in his basket to watch as Meera slid an arm beneath her brother to lift him to his feet. *He's too heavy for her. She's half-starved, she's not as strong as she was.* She clutched her frog spear in her other hand, jabbing the tines into the snow for a little more support. Meera had just begun to struggle up the hill, half-dragging and half-carrying her little brother, when Hodor passed between two trees, and Bran lost sight of them.

The hill grew steeper. Drifts of snow cracked under Hodor's boots. Once a rock moved beneath his foot and he slid backwards, and almost went tumbling back down the hill. The ranger caught him by the arm and saved him. "Hodor," said Hodor. Every gust of wind filled the air with fine white powder that shone like glass in the last light of day. Ravens flapped around them. One flew ahead and vanished inside the cave. *Only eighty yards now,* Bran thought, *that's not far at all.*

Summer stopped suddenly, at the bottom of a steep stretch of unbroken white snow. The direwolf turned his head, sniffed the air, then snarled. Fur bristling, he began to back away.

"Hodor, stop," said Bran. "Hodor. *Wait.*" Something was wrong. Summer smelled it, and so did he. *Something bad. Something close.* "Hodor, no, go back."

Coldhands was still climbing, and Hodor wanted to keep up. "Hodor, hodor, hodor," he grumbled loudly, to drown out Bran's complaints. His breathing had grown labored. Pale mist filled the air. He took a step, then another. The snow was almost waist deep and the slope was very steep. Hodor was leaning forward, grasping at rocks and trees with his hands as he climbed. Another step. Another. The snow Hodor disturbed slid downhill, starting a small avalanche behind them.

Sixty yards. Bran craned himself sideways to better see the cave. Then he saw something else. "A fire!" In the little cleft between the weirwood trees was a flickering glow, a ruddy light calling through the gathering gloom. "Look, someone—"

Hodor screamed. He twisted, stumbled, fell.

Bran felt the world slide sideways as the big stableboy spun violently around. A jarring impact drove the breath from him. His mouth was full of blood and Hodor was thrashing and rolling, crushing the crippled boy beneath him.

Something has hold of his leg. For half a heartbeat Bran thought maybe a root had gotten tangled round his ankle . . . until the root moved. A *hand*, he saw, as the rest of the wight came bursting from beneath the snow.

Hodor kicked at it, slamming a snow-covered heel full into the thing's face, but the dead man did not even seem to feel it. Then the two of them were grappling, punching and clawing at each other, sliding down the hill. Snow filled Bran's mouth and nose as they rolled over, but in a half a heartbeat he was rolling up again. Something slammed against his head, a rock or a chunk of ice or a dead man's fist, he could not tell, and he found himself out of his basket, sprawled across the hillside, spitting snow, his gloved hand full of hair that he'd torn from Hodor's head.

All around him, wights were rising from beneath the snow.

Two, three, four. Bran lost count. They surged up violently amidst sudden clouds of snow. Some wore black cloaks, some ragged skins, some nothing. All of them had pale flesh and black hands. Their eyes glowed like pale blue stars.

Three of them descended on the ranger. Bran saw Coldhands slash one across the face. The thing kept right on coming, driving him back into the arms of another. Two more were going after Hodor, lumbering clumsily down the slope. Meera was going to climb right into this, Bran realized, with a sick sense of helpless terror. He smashed the snow and shouted out a warning.

Something grabbed hold of him.

That was when his shout became a scream. Bran filled a fist with snow and threw it, but the wight did not so much as blink. A black hand fumbled at his face, another at his belly. Its fingers felt like iron. *He's going to pull my guts out.*

But suddenly Summer was between them. Bran glimpsed skin tear like cheap cloth, heard the splintering of bone. He saw a hand and wrist rip loose, pale fingers wriggling, the sleeve faded black roughspun. *Black,* he thought, *he's wearing black, he was one of the* Watch. Summer flung the arm aside, twisted, and sank his teeth into the dead man's neck under the chin. When the big grey wolf wrenched free, he took most of the creature's throat out in an explosion of pale rotten meat.

The severed hand was still moving. Bran rolled away from it. On his belly, clawing at the snow, he glimpsed the trees above, pale and snow-cloaked, the orange glow between.

Fifty yards. If he could drag himself fifty yards, they could not get him. Damp seeped through his gloves as he clutched at roots and rocks, crawling toward the light. A *little farther, just a little farther. Then you can rest beside the fire.*

The last light had vanished from amongst the trees by then. Night had fallen. Coldhands was hacking and cutting at the circle of dead men that surrounded him. Summer was tearing at the one that he'd brought down, its face between his teeth. No one was paying any mind to Bran. He crawled a little higher, dragging his useless legs behind him. *If I can reach that cave . . .*

"Hooooodor" came a whimper, from somewhere down below.

And suddenly he was not Bran, the broken boy crawling through the snow, suddenly he was Hodor halfway down the hill, with the wight raking at his eyes. Roaring, he came lurching to his feet, throwing the thing violently aside. It went to one knee, began to rise again. Bran ripped Hodor's longsword from his belt. Deep inside he could hear poor Hodor whimpering still, but outside he was seven feet of fury with old iron in his hand. He raised the sword and brought it down upon the dead man, grunting as the blade sheared through wet wool and rusted mail and rotted leather, biting deep into the bones and flesh beneath. "*HODOR!*" he bellowed, and slashed again. This time he took the wight's head off at the neck, and for half a moment he exulted . . . until a pair of dead hands came groping blindly for his throat.

Bran backed away, bleeding, and Meera Reed was there, driving her frog spear deep into the wight's back. "Hodor," Bran roared again, waving her uphill. *"Hodor, hodor."* Jojen was twisting feebly where she'd laid him down. Bran went to him, dropped the longsword, gathered the boy into Hodor's arm, and lurched back to his feet. *"HODOR!"* he bellowed.

Meera led the way back up the hill, jabbing at the wights when they came near. The things could not be hurt, but they were slow and clumsy. "Hodor," Hodor said with every step. "Hodor, hodor." He wondered what Meera would think if he should suddenly tell her that he loved her.

Up above them, flaming figures were dancing in the snow.

The wights, Bran realized. *Someone set the wights on fire.*

Summer was snarling and snapping as he danced around the closest, a great ruin of a man wreathed in swirling flame. *He shouldn't get so close, what is he doing?* Then he saw himself, sprawled facedown in the snow. Summer was trying to drive the thing away from him. *What will happen if it kills me?* the boy wondered. *Will I be Hodor for good or all? Will I go back into Summer's skin? Or will I just be dead?*

The world moved dizzily around him. White trees, black sky, red flames, everything was whirling, shifting, spinning. He felt himself stumbling. He could hear Hodor screaming, "Hodor hodor hodor hodor. Hodor hodor hodor hodor. Hodor hodor hodor hodor hodor." A cloud of ravens was pouring from the cave, and he saw a little girl with a torch in hand, darting this way and that. For a moment Bran thought it was his sister Arya . . . madly, for he knew his little sister was a thousand leagues away, or dead. And yet there she was, whirling, a scrawny thing, ragged, wild, her hair atangle. Tears filled Hodor's eyes and froze there.

Everything turned inside out and upside down, and Bran found himself back inside his own skin, half-buried in the snow. The burning wight loomed over him, etched tall against the trees in their snowy shrouds. It was one of the naked ones, Bran saw, in the instant before the nearest tree shook off the snow that covered it and dropped it all down upon his head.

The next he knew, he was lying on a bed of pine needles beneath a dark stone roof. *The cave. I'm in the cave.* His mouth still tasted of blood where he'd bitten his tongue, but a fire was burning to his right, the heat washing over his face, and he had never felt anything so good. Summer was there, sniffing round him, and Hodor, soaking wet. Meera cradled Jojen's head in her lap. And the Arya thing stood over them, clutching her torch.

"The snow," Bran said. "It fell on me. Buried me."

"Hid you. I pulled you out." Meera nodded at the girl. "It was her who saved us, though. The torch . . . fire kills them."

"Fire *burns* them. Fire is always hungry."

That was not Arya's voice, nor any child's. It was a woman's voice, high and sweet, with a strange music in it like none that he had ever heard and a sadness that he thought might break his heart. Bran squinted, to see her better. It *was* a girl, but smaller than Arya, her skin dappled like a doe's beneath a cloak of leaves. Her eyes were queer—large and liquid, gold and green, slitted like a cat's eyes. *No one has eyes like that.* Her hair was a tangle of brown and red and gold, autumn colors, with vines and twigs and withered flowers woven through it.

"Who are you?" Meera Reed was asking.

Bran knew. "She's a child. A child of the forest." He shivered, as much from wonderment as cold. They had fallen into one of Old Nan's tales.

"The First Men named us children," the little woman said. "The giants called us *woh dak nag gran*, the squirrel people, because we were small and quick and fond of trees, but we are no squirrels, no children. Our name in the True Tongue means *those who sing the song of earth*. Before your Old Tongue was ever spoken, we had sung our songs ten thousand years."

Meera said, "You speak the Common Tongue now."

"For him. The Bran boy. I was born in the time of the dragon, and for two hundred years I walked the world of men, to watch and listen and learn. I might be walking still, but my legs were sore and my heart was weary, so I turned my feet for home."

"Two hundred years?" said Meera.

The child smiled. "Men, they are the children."

"Do you have a name?" asked Bran.

"When I am needing one." She waved her torch toward the black crack in the back wall of the cave. "Our way is down. You must come with me now."

Bran shivered again. "The ranger . . ."

"He cannot come."

"They'll kill him."

"No. They killed him long ago. Come now. It is warmer down deep, and no one will hurt you there. He is waiting for you."

"The three-eyed crow?" asked Meera.

"The greenseer." And with that she was off, and they had no choice but to follow. Meera helped Bran back up onto Hodor's back, though his basket was half-crushed and wet from melting snow. Then she slipped an arm around her brother and shouldered him back onto his feet once more. His eyes opened. "What?" he said. "Meera? Where are we?" When he saw the fire, he smiled. "I had the strangest dream."

The way was cramped and twisty, and so low that Hodor soon was crouching. Bran hunched down as best he could, but even so, the top of his head was soon scraping and bumping against the ceiling. Loose dirt crumbled at each touch and dribbled down into his eyes and hair, and once he smacked his brow on a thick white root growing from the tunnel wall, with tendrils hanging from it and spiderwebs between its fingers.

The child went in front with the torch in hand, her cloak of leaves whispering behind her, but the passage turned so much that Bran soon lost sight of her. Then the only light was what was reflected off the passage walls. After they had gone down a little, the cave divided, but the left branch was dark as pitch, so even Hodor knew to follow the moving torch to the right.

The way the shadows shifted made it seem as if the walls were moving too. Bran saw great white snakes slithering in and out of the earth around him, and his heart thumped in fear. He wondered if they had blundered into a nest of milk snakes or giant grave worms, soft and pale and squishy. *Grave worms have teeth.*

Hodor saw them too. "Hodor," he whimpered, reluctant to go on. But when the girl child stopped to let them catch her, the torchlight steadied, and Bran realized that the snakes were only white roots like the one he'd hit his head on. "It's weirwood roots," he said. "Remember the heart tree in the godswood, Hodor? The white tree with the red leaves? A tree can't hurt you."

"Hodor." Hodor plunged ahead, hurrying after the child and her torch, deeper into the earth. They passed another branching, and another, then came into an echoing cavern as large as the great hall of Winterfell, with stone teeth hanging from its ceiling and more poking up through its floor. The child in the leafy cloak wove a path through them. From time to time she stopped and waved her torch at them impatiently. *This way*, it seemed to say, *this way, this way, faster.*

There were more side passages after that, more chambers, and Bran heard dripping water somewhere to his right. When he looked off that way, he saw eyes looking back at them, slitted eyes that glowed bright, reflecting back the torchlight. *More children*, he told himself, *the girl is not the only one*, but Old Nan's tale of Gendel's children came back to him as well.

The roots were everywhere, twisting through earth and stone, closing off some passages and holding up the roofs of others. *All the color is gone*, Bran realized suddenly. The world was black soil and white wood. The heart tree at Winterfell had roots as thick around as a giant's legs, but these were even thicker. And Bran had never seen so many of them. *There must be a whole grove of weirwoods growing up above us.*

The light dwindled again. Small as she was, the child-who-was-not-a-child moved quickly when she wanted. As Hodor thumped after her, something crunched beneath his feet. His halt was so sudden that Meera and Jojen almost slammed into his back.

"Bones," said Bran. "It's bones." The floor of the passage was littered with the bones of birds and beasts. But there were other bones as well, big ones that must have come from giants and small ones that could have been from children. On either side of them, in niches carved from the stone, skulls looked down on them. Bran saw a bear skull and a wolf skull, half a dozen human skulls and near as many giants. All the rest were small, queerly formed. *Children of the forest.* The roots had grown in and around and through them, every one. A few had ravens perched atop them, watching them pass with bright black eyes.

The last part of their dark journey was the steepest. Hodor made the final descent on his arse, bumping and sliding downward in a clatter of broken bones, loose dirt, and pebbles. The girl child was waiting for them, standing on one end of a natural bridge above a yawning chasm. Down below in the darkness, Bran heard the sound of rushing water. *An underground river.*

"Do we have to cross?" Bran asked, as the Reeds came sliding down behind him. The prospect frightened him. If Hodor slipped on that narrow bridge, they would fall and fall.

"No, boy," the child said. "Behind you." She lifted her torch higher, and the light seemed to shift and change. One moment the flames burned orange and yellow, filling the cavern with a ruddy glow; then all the colors faded, leaving only black and white. Behind them Meera gasped. Hodor turned.

Before them a pale lord in ebon finery sat dreaming in a tangled nest of roots, a woven weirwood throne that embraced his withered limbs as a mother does a child.

His body was so skeletal and his clothes so rotted that at first Bran took him for another corpse, a dead man propped up so long that the roots had grown over him, under him, and through him. What skin the corpse lord showed was white, save for a bloody blotch that crept up his neck onto his cheek. His white hair was fine and thin as root hair and long enough to brush against the earthen floor. Roots coiled around his legs like wooden serpents. One burrowed through his breeches into the desiccated flesh of his thigh, to emerge again from his shoulder. A spray of dark red leaves sprouted from his skull, and grey mushrooms spotted his brow. A little skin remained, stretched across his face, tight and hard as white leather, but even that was fraying, and here and there the brown and yellow bone beneath was poking through.

"Are you the three-eyed crow?" Bran heard himself say. *A three-eyed crow should have three eyes. He has only one, and that one red.* Bran could feel the eye staring at him, shining like a pool of blood in the torchlight. Where his other eye should have been, a thin white root grew from an empty socket, down his cheek, and into his neck.

"A . . . crow?" The pale lord's voice was dry. His lips moved slowly, as if they had forgotten how to form words. "Once, aye. Black of garb and black of blood." The clothes he wore were rotten and faded, spotted with moss and eaten through with worms, but once they had been black. "I have been many things, Bran. Now I am as you see me, and now you will understand why I could not come to you . . . except in dreams. I have watched you for a long time, watched you with a thousand eyes and one. I saw your birth, and that of your lord father before you. I saw your first step, heard your first word, was part of your first dream. I was watching when you fell. And now you are come to me at last, Brandon Stark, though the hour is late."

"I'm here," Bran said, "only I'm broken. Will you . . . will you fix me . . . my legs, I mean?"

"No," said the pale lord. "That is beyond my powers."

Bran's eyes filled with tears. *We came such a long way.* The chamber echoed to the sound of the black river.

"You will never walk again, Bran," the pale lips promised, "but you will fly."

TYRION

For a long while he did not stir, but lay unmoving upon the heap of old sacks that served him for a bed, listening to the wind in the lines, to the lapping of the river at the hull.

A full moon floated above the mast. *It is following me downriver, watching me like some great eye.* Despite the warmth of the musty skins that covered him, a shiver went through the little man. *I need a cup of wine. A dozen cups of wine.* But the moon would blink before that whoreson Griff let him quench his thirst. Instead he drank water, and was condemned to sleepless nights and days of sweats and shakes.

The dwarf sat up, cradling his head in his hands. *Did I dream?* All memory of it had fled. The nights had never been kind to Tyrion Lannister. He slept badly even on soft feather beds. On the *Shy Maid,* he made his bed atop the roof of the cabin, with a coil of hempen rope for a pillow. He liked it better up here than in the boat's cramped hold. The air was fresher, and the river sounds were sweeter than Duck's snoring. There was a price to be paid for such joys, though; the deck was hard, and he woke stiff and sore, his legs cramped and aching.

They were throbbing now, his calves gone hard as wood. He kneaded them with his fingers, trying to rub the ache away, but when he stood the pain was still enough to make him grimace. *I need to bathe.* His boy's clothes stank, and so did he. The others bathed in the river, but thus far he had not joined them. Some of the turtles he'd seen in the shallows looked big enough to bite him in half. *Bonesnappers,* Duck called them. Besides, he did not want Lemore to see him naked.

A wooden ladder led down from the cabin roof. Tyrion pulled on his boots and descended to the afterdeck, where Griff sat wrapped in a wolf-skin cloak beside an iron brazier. The sellsword kept the night watch by himself, rising as the rest of his band sought their beds and retiring when the sun came up.

Tyrion squatted across from him and warmed his hands over the coals. Across the water nightingales were singing. "Day soon," he said to Griff.

"Not soon enough. We need to be under way." If it had been up to Griff, the *Shy Maid* would continue downstream by night as well as day, but Yandry and Ysilla refused to risk their poleboat in the dark. The Upper Rhoyne was full of snags and sawyers, any one of which could rip out the *Shy Maid*'s hull. Griff did not want to hear it. What he wanted was Volantis.

The sellsword's eyes were always moving, searching the night for . . . what? *Pirates? Stone men? Slave-catchers?* The river had perils, the dwarf knew, but Griff himself struck Tyrion as more dangerous than any of them. He reminded Tyrion of Bronn, though Bronn had a sellsword's black humor and Griff had no humor at all.

"I would kill for a cup of wine," muttered Tyrion.

Griff made no reply. *You will die before you drink*, his pale eyes seemed to say. Tyrion had drunk himself blind his first night on the *Shy Maid*. The next day he awoke with dragons fighting in his skull. Griff took one look at him retching over the side of the poleboat, and said, "You are done with drink."

"Wine helps me sleep," Tyrion had protested. *Wine drowns my dreams*, he might have said.

"Then stay awake," Griff had replied, implacable.

To the east, the first pale light of day suffused the sky above the river. The waters of the Rhoyne slowly went from black to blue, to match the sellsword's hair and beard. Griff got to his feet. "The others should wake soon. The deck is yours." As the nightingales fell silent, the river larks took up their song. Egrets splashed amongst the reeds and left their tracks across the sandbars. The clouds in the sky were aglow: pink and purple, maroon and gold, pearl and saffron. One looked like a dragon. *Once a man has seen a dragon in flight, let him stay at home and tend his garden in content*, someone had written once, *for this wide world has no greater wonder*. Tyrion scratched at his scar and tried to recall the author's name. Dragons had been much in his thoughts of late.

"Good morrow, Hugor." Septa Lemore had emerged in her white robes, cinched at the waist with a woven belt of seven colors. Her hair flowed loose about her shoulders. "How did you sleep?"

"Fitfully, good lady. I dreamed of you again." *A waking dream.* He could not sleep, so he had eased a hand between his legs and imagined the septa atop him, breasts bouncing.

"A wicked dream, no doubt. You are a wicked man. Will you pray with me and ask forgiveness for your sins?"

Only if we pray in the fashion of the Summer Isles. "No, but do give the Maiden a long, sweet kiss for me."

Laughing, the septa walked to the prow of the boat. It was her custom to bathe in the river every morning. "Plainly, this boat was not named for you," Tyrion called as she disrobed.

"The Mother and the Father made us in their image, Hugor. We should glory in our bodies, for they are the work of gods."

The gods must have been drunk when they got to me. The dwarf watched Lemore slip into the water. The sight always made him hard. There was something wonderfully wicked about the thought of peeling the septa out of those chaste white robes and spreading her legs. *Innocence despoiled,* he thought . . . though Lemore was not near as innocent as she appeared. She had stretch marks on her belly that could only have come from child-birth.

Yandry and Ysilla had risen with the sun and were going about their business. Yandry stole a glance at Septa Lemore from time to time as he was checking the lines. His small dark wife, Ysilla, took no notice. She fed some wood chips to the brazier on the afterdeck, stirred the coals with a blackened blade, and began to knead the dough for the morning biscuits.

When Lemore climbed back onto the deck, Tyrion savored the sight of water trickling between her breasts, her smooth skin glowing golden in the morning light. She was past forty, more handsome than pretty, but still easy on the eye. *Being randy is the next best thing to being drunk,* he de-cided. It made him feel as if he was still alive. "Did you see the turtle, Hugor?" the septa asked him, wringing water from her hair. "The big ridgeback?"

The early morning was the best time for seeing turtles. During the day they would swim down deep, or hide in cuts along the banks, but when the sun was newly risen they came to the surface. Some liked to swim beside the boat. Tyrion had glimpsed a dozen different sorts: large turtles and small ones, flatbacks and red-ears, softshells and bonesnappers, brown turtles, green turtles, black turtles, clawed turtles and horned turtles, tur-tles whose ridged and patterned shells were covered with whorls of gold and jade and cream. Some were so large they could have borne a man upon their backs. Yandry swore the Rhoynar princes used to ride them across the river. He and his wife were Greenblood born, a pair of Dornish orphans come home to Mother Rhoyne.

"I missed the ridgeback." *I was watching the naked woman.*

"I am sad for you." Lemore slipped her robe over her head. "I know you only rise so early in hopes of seeing turtles."

"I like to watch the sun come up as well." It was like watching a maiden rising naked from her bath. Some might be prettier than others, but every one was full of promise. "The turtles have their charms, I will allow. Nothing delights me so much as the sight of a nice pair of shapely . . . shells."

Septa Lemore laughed. Like everyone else aboard the *Shy Maid*, she had her secrets. She was welcome to them. *I do not want to know her, I only want to fuck her.* She knew it too. As she hung her septa's crystal about her neck, to nestle in the cleft between her breasts, she teased him with a smile.

Yandry pulled up the anchor, slid one of the long poles off the cabin roof, and pushed them off. Two of the herons raised their heads to watch as the *Shy Maid* drifted away from the bank, out into the current. Slowly the boat began to move downstream. Yandry went to the tiller. Ysilla was turning the biscuits. She laid an iron pan atop the brazier and put the bacon in. Some days she cooked biscuits and bacon; some days bacon and biscuits. Once every fortnight there might be a fish, but not today.

When Ysilla turned her back, Tyrion snatched a biscuit off the brazier, darting away just in time to avoid a smack from her fearsome wooden spoon. They were best when eaten hot, dripping with honey and butter. The smell of the bacon cooking soon fetched Duck up from the hold. He sniffed over the brazier, received a swack from Ysilla's spoon, and went back to have his morning piss off the stern.

Tyrion waddled over to join him. "Now here's a sight to see," he quipped as they were emptying their bladders, "a dwarf and a duck, making the mighty Rhoyne that much mightier."

Yandry snorted in derision. "Mother Rhoyne has no need of your water, Yollo. She is the greatest river in the world."

Tyrion shook off the last few drops. "Big enough to drown a dwarf, I grant you. The Mander is as broad, though. So is the Trident, near its mouth. The Blackwater runs deeper."

"You do not know the river. Wait, and you will see."

The bacon turned crisp, the biscuits golden brown. Young Griff stumbled up onto deck yawning. "Good morrow, all." The lad was shorter than Duck, but his lanky build suggested that he had not yet come into his full growth. *This beardless boy could have any maiden in the Seven Kingdoms, blue hair or no. Those eyes of his would melt them.* Like his sire, Young Griff had blue eyes, but where the father's eyes were pale, the son's were dark. By lamplight they turned black, and in the light of dusk they seemed purple. His eyelashes were as long as any woman's.

"I smell bacon," the lad said, pulling on his boots.

"Good bacon," said Ysilla. "Sit."

She fed them on the afterdeck, pressing honeyed biscuits on Young Griff and hitting Duck's hand with her spoon whenever he made a grab for more bacon. Tyrion pulled apart two biscuits, filled them with bacon, and carried one to Yandry at the tiller. Afterward he helped Duck to raise the *Shy Maid's* big lateen sail. Yandry took them out into the center of the river, where the current was strongest. The *Shy Maid* was a sweet boat. Her draft was so shallow she could work her way up even the smallest of the river's vassal streams, negotiating sandbars that would have stranded larger vessels, yet with her sail raised and a current under her, she could make good speed. That could mean life and death on the upper reaches of the Rhoyne, Yandry claimed. "There is no law above the Sorrows, not for a thousand years."

"And no *people*, so far as I can see." He'd glimpsed some ruins along the banks, piles of masonry overgrown by vines and moss and flowers, but no other signs of human habitation.

"You do not know the river, Yollo. A pirate boat may lurk up any stream, and escaped slaves oft hide amongst the ruins. The slave-catchers seldom come so far north."

"Slave-catchers would be a welcome change from turtles." Not being an escaped slave, Tyrion need not fear being caught. And no pirate was like to bother a poleboat moving downstream. The valuable goods came up the river from Volantis.

When the bacon was gone, Duck punched Young Griff in the shoulder. "Time to raise some bruises. Swords today, I think."

"Swords?" Young Griff grinned. "Swords will be sweet."

Tyrion helped him dress for the bout, in heavy breeches, padded doublet, and a dinted suit of old steel plate. Ser Rolly shrugged into his mail and boiled leather. Both set helms upon their heads and chose blunted longswords from the bundle in the weapons chest. They set to on the afterdeck, having at each other lustily whilst the rest of the morning company looked on.

When they fought with mace or blunted longaxe, Ser Rolly's greater size and strength would quickly overwhelm his charge; with swords the contests were more even. Neither man had taken up a shield this morning, so it was a game of slash and parry, back and forth across the deck. The river rang to the sounds of their combat. Young Griff landed more blows, though Duck's were harder. After a while, the bigger man began to tire. His cuts came a little slower, a little lower. Young Griff turned them all and launched a furious attack that forced Ser Rolly back. When they reached the stern, the lad tied up their blades and slammed a shoulder into Duck, and the big man went into the river.

He came up sputtering and cursing, bellowing for someone to fish him out before a 'snapper ate his privates. Tyrion tossed a line to him. "Ducks should swim better than that," he said as he and Yandry were hauling the knight back aboard the *Shy Maid.*

Ser Rolly grabbed Tyrion by the collar. "Let us see how dwarfs swim," he said, chucking him headlong into the Rhoyne.

The dwarf laughed last; he could paddle passably well, and did . . . until his legs began to cramp. Young Griff extended him a pole. "You are not the first to try and drown me," he told Duck, as he was pouring river water from his boot. "My father threw me down a well the day I was born, but I was so ugly that the water witch who lived down there spat me back." He pulled off the other boot, then did a cartwheel along the deck, spraying all of them.

Young Griff laughed. "Where did you learn that?"

"The mummers taught me," he lied. "My mother loved me best of all her children because I was so small. She nursed me at her breast till I was seven. That made my brothers jealous, so they stuffed me in a sack and sold me to a mummer's troupe. When I tried to run off the master mummer cut off half my nose, so I had no choice but to go with them and learn to be amusing."

The truth was rather different. His uncle had taught him a bit of tumbling when he was six or seven. Tyrion had taken to it eagerly. For half a year he cartwheeled his merry way about Casterly Rock, bringing smiles to the faces of septons, squires, and servants alike. Even Cersei laughed to see him once or twice.

All that ended abruptly the day his father returned from a sojourn in King's Landing. That night at supper Tyrion surprised his sire by walking the length of the high table on his hands. Lord Tywin was not pleased. "The gods made you a dwarf. Must you be a fool as well? You were born a lion, not a monkey."

And you're a corpse, Father, so I'll caper as I please.

"You have a gift for making men smile," Septa Lemore told Tyrion as he was drying off his toes. "You should thank the Father Above. He gives gifts to all his children."

"He does," he agreed pleasantly. *And when I die, please let them bury with me a crossbow, so I can thank the Father Above for his gifts the same way I thanked the father below.*

His clothing was still soaked from his involuntary swim, clinging to his arms and legs uncomfortably. Whilst Young Griff went off with Septa Lemore to be instructed in the mysteries of the Faith, Tyrion stripped off the wet clothes and donned dry ones. Duck had a good guffaw when he emerged on deck again. He could not blame him. Dressed as he was, he made a comic sight. His doublet was divided down the middle; the left side was purple velvet with bronze studs; the right, yellow wool embroidered in green floral patterns. His breeches were similarly split; the right leg was solid green, the left leg striped in red and white. One of Illyrio's chests had been packed with a child's clothing, musty but well made. Septa Lemore had slit each garment apart, then sewn them back together, joining half of this to half of that to fashion a crude motley. Griff had even insisted that Tyrion help with the cutting and sewing. No doubt he meant for it to be humbling, but Tyrion enjoyed the needlework. Lemore was always pleasant company, despite her penchant for scolding him whenever he said something rude about the gods. *If Griff wants to cast me as the fool, I'll play the game.* Somewhere, he knew, Lord Tywin Lannister was horrified, and that took the sting from it.

His other duty was anything but foolish. *Duck has his sword, I my quill and parchment.* Griff had commanded him to set down all he knew of dragonlore. The task was a formidable one, but the dwarf labored at it every day, scratching away as best he could as he sat cross-legged on the cabin roof.

Tyrion had read much and more of dragons through the years. The greater part of those accounts were idle tales and could not be relied on, and the books that Illyrio had provided them were not the ones he might have wished for. What he really wanted was the complete text of *The Fires of the Freehold,* Galendro's history of Valyria. No complete copy was known to Westeros, however; even the Citadel's lacked twenty-seven scrolls. *They must have a library in Old Volantis, surely. I may find a better copy there, if I can find a way inside the Black Walls to the city's heart.*

He was less hopeful concerning Septon Barth's *Dragons, Wyrms, and Wyverns: Their Unnatural History.* Barth had been a blacksmith's son who rose to be King's Hand during the reign of Jaehaerys the Conciliator. His enemies always claimed he was more sorcerer than septon. Baelor the Blessed had ordered all Barth's writings destroyed when he came to the Iron Throne. Ten years ago, Tyrion had read a fragment of *Unnatural History* that had eluded the Blessed Baelor, but he doubted that any of Barth's work had found its way across the narrow sea. And of course there was even less chance of his coming on the fragmentary, anonymous, blood-soaked tome sometimes called *Blood and Fire* and sometimes *The Death of Dragons*, the only surviving copy of which was supposedly hidden away in a locked vault beneath the Citadel.

When the Halfmaester appeared on deck, yawning, the dwarf was writing down what he recalled concerning the mating habits of dragons, on which subject Barth, Munkun, and Thomax held markedly divergent views. Haldon stalked to the stern to piss down at the sun where it shimmered on the water, breaking apart with every puff of wind. "We should reach the junction with the Noyne by evening, Yollo," the Halfmaester called out.

Tyrion glanced up from his writing. "My name is Hugor. Yollo is hiding in my breeches. Shall I let him out to play?"

"Best not. You might frighten the turtles." Haldon's smile was as sharp as the blade of a dagger. "What did you tell me was the name of that street in Lannisport where you were born, Yollo?"

"It was an alley. It had no name." Tyrion took a mordant pleasure in inventing the details of the colorful life of Hugor Hill, also known as Yollo, a bastard out of Lannisport. *The best lies are seasoned with a bit of truth.* The dwarf knew he sounded like a westerman, and a highborn westerman at that, so Hugor must needs be some lordling's by-blow. Born in Lannisport because he knew that city better than Oldtown or King's Landing, and cities were where most dwarfs ended up, even those whelped by Goodwife Bumpkin in the turnip patch. The countryside had no grotesqueries or mummer shows . . . though it did have wells aplenty, to swallow up unwanted kittens, three-headed calves, and babes like him.

"I see you have been defacing more good parchment, Yollo." Haldon laced up his breeches.

"Not all of us can be half a maester." Tyrion's hand was cramping. He put his quill aside and flexed his stubby fingers. "Fancy another game of *cyvasse*?" The Halfmaester always defeated him, but it was a way to pass the time.

"This evening. Will you join us for Young Griff's lesson?"

"Why not? Someone needs to correct your errors."

There were four cabins on the *Shy Maid*. Yandry and Ysilla shared one,

Griff and Young Griff another. Septa Lemore had a cabin to herself, as did Haldon. The Halfmaester's cabin was the largest of the four. One wall was lined with bookshelves and bins stacked with old scrolls and parchments; another held racks of ointments, herbs, and potions. Golden light slanted through the wavy yellow glass of the round window. The furnishings included a bunk, a writing desk, a chair, a stool, and the Halfmaester's *cyvasse* table, strewn with carved wooden pieces.

The lesson began with languages. Young Griff spoke the Common Tongue as if he had been born to it, and was fluent in High Valyrian, the low dialects of Pentos, Tyrosh, Myr, and Lys, and the trade talk of sailors. The Volantene dialect was as new to him as it was to Tyrion, so every day they learned a few more words whilst Haldon corrected their mistakes. Meereenese was harder; its roots were Valyrian as well, but the tree had been grafted onto the harsh, ugly tongue of Old Ghis. "You need a bee up your nose to speak Ghiscari properly," Tyrion complained. Young Griff laughed, but the Halfmaester only said, "Again." The boy obeyed, though he rolled his eyes along with his *zzz*s this time. *He has a better ear than me*, Tyrion was forced to admit, *though I'll wager my tongue is still more nimble.*

Geometry followed languages. There the boy was less adroit, but Haldon was a patient teacher, and Tyrion was able to make himself of use as well. He had learned the mysteries of squares and circles and triangles from his father's maesters at Casterly Rock, and they came back more quickly than he would have thought.

By the time they turned to history, Young Griff was growing restive. "We were discussing the history of Volantis," Haldon said to him. "Can you tell Yollo the difference between a tiger and an elephant?"

"Volantis is the oldest of the Nine Free Cities, first daughter of Valyria," the lad replied, in a bored tone. "After the Doom it pleased the Volantenes to consider themselves the heirs of the Freehold and rightful rulers of the world, but they were divided as to how dominion might best be achieved. The Old Blood favored the sword, while the merchants and moneylenders advocated trade. As they contended for rule of the city, the factions became known as the tigers and elephants, respectively.

"The tigers held sway for almost a century after the Doom of Valyria. For a time they were successful. A Volantene fleet took Lys and a Volantene army captured Myr, and for two generations all three cities were ruled from within the Black Walls. That ended when the tigers tried to swallow Tyrosh. Pentos came into the war on the Tyroshi side, along with the Westerosi Storm King. Braavos provided a Lyseni exile with a hundred warships, Aegon Targaryen flew forth from Dragonstone on the Black Dread, and Myr and Lys rose up in rebellion. The war left the Disputed Lands a waste, and freed Lys and Myr from the yoke. The tigers suffered other defeats as well. The fleet they sent to reclaim Valyria vanished in the Smoking Sea. Qohor and Norvos broke their power on the Rhoyne when the fire galleys fought on Dagger Lake. Out of the east came the Dothraki, driving smallfolk from their hovels and nobles from their estates, until only grass and ruins remained from the forest of Qohor to the headwaters of the Selhoru. After a century of war, Volantis found herself broken, bankrupt, and depopulated. It was then that the elephants rose up. They have held sway ever since. Some years the tigers elect a triarch, and some years they do not, but never more than one, so the elephants have ruled the city for three hundred years."

"Just so," said Haldon. "And the present triarchs?"

"Malaquo is a tiger, Nyessos and Doniphos are elephants."

"And what lesson can we draw from Volantene history?"

"If you want to conquer the world, you best have dragons."

Tyrion could not help but laugh.

Later, when Young Griff went up on deck to help Yandry with the sails and poles, Haldon set up his *cyvasse* table for their game. Tyrion watched with mismatched eyes, and said, "The boy is bright. You have done well by him. Half the lords in Westeros are not so learned, sad to say. Languages, history, songs, sums . . . a heady stew for some sellsword's son."

"A book can be as dangerous as a sword in the right hands," said Haldon. "Try to give me a better battle this time, Yollo. You play *cyvasse* as badly as you tumble."

"I am trying to lull you into a false sense of confidence," said Tyrion, as they arranged their tiles on either side of a carved wooden screen. "You *think* you taught me how to play, but things are not always as they seem. Perhaps I learned the game from the cheesemonger, have you considered that?"

"Illyrio does not play *cyvasse*."

No, thought the dwarf, *he plays the game of thrones, and you and Griff and Duck are only pieces, to be moved where he will and sacrificed at need, just as he sacrificed Viserys.* "The blame must fall on you, then. If I play badly, it is your doing."

The Halfmaester chuckled. "Yollo, I shall miss you when the pirates cut your throat."

"Where are these famous pirates? I am beginning to think that you and Illyrio made them all up."

"They are thickest on the stretch of river between Ar Noy and the Sorrows. Above the ruins of Ar Noy, the Qohorik rule the river, and below the Sorrows the galleys of Volantis hold sway, but neither city claims the waters in between, so the pirates have made it their own. Dagger Lake is full of islands where they lurk in hidden caves and secret strongholds. Are you ready?"

"For you? Beyond a doubt. For the pirates? Less so."

Haldon removed the screen. Each of them contemplated the other's opening array. "You are learning," the Halfmaester said.

Tyrion almost grabbed his dragon but thought better of it. Last game he had brought her out too soon and lost her to a trebuchet. "If we do meet these fabled pirates, I may join up with them. I'll tell them that my name is Hugor Halfmaester." He moved his light horse toward Haldon's mountains.

Haldon answered with an elephant. "Hugor Halfwit would suit you better."

"I only need half my wits to be a match for you." Tyrion moved up his heavy horse to support the light. "Perhaps you would care to wager on the outcome?"

The Halfmaester arched an eyebrow. "How much?"

"I have no coin. We'll play for secrets."

"Griff would cut my tongue out."

"Afraid, are you? I would be if I were you."

"The day you defeat me at *cyvasse* will be the day turtles crawl out my arse." The Halfmaester moved his spears. "You have your wager, little man."

Tyrion stretched a hand out for his dragon.

It was three hours later when the little man finally crept back up on deck to empty his bladder. Duck was helping Yandry wrestle down the sail, while Ysilla took the tiller. The sun hung low above the reed-beds along the western bank, as the wind began to gust and rip. *I need that skin of wine,* the dwarf thought. His legs were cramped from squatting on that stool, and he felt so light-headed that he was lucky not to fall into the river.

"Yollo," Duck called. "Where's Haldon?"

"He's taken to his bed, in some discomfort. There are turtles crawling out his arse." He left the knight to sort that out and crawled up the ladder to the cabin roof. Off to the east, there was darkness gathering behind a rocky island.

Septa Lemore found him there. "Can you feel the storms in the air, Hugor Hill? Dagger Lake is ahead of us, where pirates prowl. And beyond that lie the Sorrows."

Not mine. I carry mine own sorrows with me, everywhere I go. He thought of Tysha and wondered where whores go. *Why not Volantis? Perhaps I'll find her there. A man should cling to hope.* He wondered what he would say to her. *I am sorry that I let them rape you, love. I thought you were a whore. Can you find it in your heart to forgive me? I want to go back to our cottage, to the way it was when we were man and wife.*

The island fell away behind them. Tyrion saw ruins rising along the eastern bank: crooked walls and fallen towers, broken domes and rows of rotted wooden pillars, streets choked by mud and overgrown with purple moss. *Another dead city, ten times as large as Ghoyan Drohe.* Turtles lived there now, big bonesnappers. The dwarf could see them basking in the sun, brown and black hummocks with jagged ridges down the center of their shells. A few saw the *Shy Maid* and slid down into the water, leaving ripples in their wake. This would not be a good place for a swim.

Then, through the twisted half-drowned trees and wide wet streets, he glimpsed the silvery sheen of sunlight upon water. *Another river,* he knew at once, *rushing toward the Rhoyne.* The ruins grew taller as the land grew narrower, until the city ended on a point of land where stood the remains of a colossal palace of pink and green marble, its collapsed domes and broken spires looming large above a row of covered archways. Tyrion saw more 'snappers sleeping in the slips where half a hundred ships might once have docked. He knew where he was then. *That was Nymeria's palace, and this is all that remains of Ny Sar, her city.*

"Yollo," shouted Yandry as the *Shy Maid* passed the point, "tell me again of those Westerosi rivers as big as Mother Rhoyne."

"I did not know," he called back. "No river in the Seven Kingdoms is half so wide as this." The new river that had joined them was a close twin to the one they had been sailing down, and that one alone had almost matched the Mander or the Trident.

"This is Ny Sar, where the Mother gathers in her Wild Daughter, Noyne," said Yandry, "but she will not reach her widest point until she meets her other daughters. At Dagger Lake the Qhoyne comes rushing in, the Darkling Daughter, full of gold and amber from the Axe and pinecones from the Forest of Qohor. South of there the Mother meets Lhorulu, the Smiling Daughter from the Golden Fields. Where they join once stood Chroyane, the festival city, where the streets were made of water and the houses made of gold. Then south and east again for long leagues, until at last comes creeping in Selhoru, the Shy Daughter who hides her course in reeds and writhes. There Mother Rhoyne waxes so

wide that a man upon a boat in the center of the stream cannot see a shore
to either side. You shall see, my little friend."

I shall, the dwarf was thinking, when he spied a rippling ahead not six
yards from the boat. He was about to point it out to Lemore when it came
to the surface with a wash of water that rocked the *Shy Maid* sideways.

It was another turtle, a horned turtle of enormous size, its dark green
shell mottled with brown and overgrown with water moss and crusty black
river molluscs. It raised its head and bellowed, a deep-throated thrum-
ming roar louder than any warhorn that Tyrion had ever heard. "We are
blessed," Ysilla was crying loudly, as tears streamed down her face. "We
are blessed, we are blessed."

Duck was hooting, and Young Griff too. Haldon came out on deck to
learn the cause of the commotion . . . but too late. The giant turtle had
vanished below the water once again. "What was the cause of all that
noise?" the Halfmaester asked.

"A turtle," said Tyrion. "A turtle bigger than this boat."

"It was *him*," cried Yandry. "The Old Man of the River."

And why not? Tyrion grinned. *Gods and wonders always appear, to
attend the birth of kings.*

DAVOS

The *Merry Midwife* stole into White Harbor on the evening tide, her patched sail rippling with every gust of wind.

She was an old cog, and even in her youth no one had ever called her pretty. Her figurehead showed a laughing woman holding an infant by one foot, but the woman's cheeks and the babe's bottom were both pocked by wormholes. Uncounted layers of drab brown paint covered her hull; her sails were grey and tattered. She was not a ship to draw a second glance, unless it was to wonder how she stayed afloat. The *Merry Midwife* was known in White Harbor too. For years she had plied a humble trade between there and Sisterton.

It was not the sort of arrival that Davos Seaworth had anticipated when he'd set sail with Salla and his fleet. All this had seemed simpler then. The ravens had not brought King Stannis the allegiance of White Harbor, so His Grace would send an envoy to treat with Lord Manderly in person. As a show of strength, Davos would arrive aboard Salla's galleas *Valyrian*, with the rest of the Lysene fleet behind her. Every hull was striped: black and yellow, pink and blue, green and white, purple and gold. The Lyseni loved bright hues, and Salladhor Saan was the most colorful of all. *Salladhor the Splendid*, Davos thought, *but the storms wrote an end to all of that*.

Instead he would smuggle himself into the city, as he might have done twenty years before. Until he knew how matters stood here, it was more prudent to play the common sailor, not the lord.

White Harbor's walls of whitewashed stone rose before them, on the eastern shore where the White Knife plunged into the firth. Some of the city's defenses had been strengthened since the last time Davos had been here, half a dozen years before. The jetty that divided the inner and outer harbors had been fortified with a long stone wall, thirty feet tall and al-

most a mile long, with towers every hundred yards. There was smoke rising from Seal Rock as well, where once there had been only ruins. *That
could be good or bad, depending on what side Lord Wyman chooses.*

Davos had always been fond of this city, since first he'd come here as a
cabin boy on *Cobblecat.* Though small compared to Oldtown and King's
Landing, it was clean and well-ordered, with wide straight cobbled streets
that made it easy for a man to find his way. The houses were built of
whitewashed stone, with steeply pitched roofs of dark grey slate. Roro
Uhoris, the *Cobblecat's* cranky old master, used to claim that he could tell
one port from another just by the way they smelled. Cities were like
women, he insisted; each one had its own unique scent. Oldtown was as
flowery as a perfumed dowager. Lannisport was a milkmaid, fresh and
earthy, with woodsmoke in her hair. King's Landing reeked like some
unwashed whore. But White Harbor's scent was sharp and salty, and a
little fishy too. "She smells the way a mermaid ought to smell," Roro said.
"She smells of the sea."

She still does, thought Davos, but he could smell the peat smoke drifting off Seal Rock too. The sea stone dominated the approaches to the
outer harbor, a massive grey-green upthrust looming fifty feet above the
waters. Its top was crowned with a circle of weathered stones, a ringfort of
the First Men that had stood desolate and abandoned for hundreds of
years. It was not abandoned now. Davos could see scorpions and spitfires
behind the standing stones, and crossbowmen peering between them. *It
must be cold up there, and wet.* On all his previous visits, seals could be
seen basking on the broken rocks below. The Blind Bastard always made
him count them whenever the *Cobblecat* set sail from White Harbor; the
more seals there were, Roro said, the more luck they would have on their
voyage. There were no seals now. The smoke and the soldiers had frightened them away. *A wiser man would see a caution in that. If I had a thimble full of sense, I would have gone with Salla.* He could have made his
way back south, to Marya and their sons. *I have lost four sons in the king's
service, and my fifth serves as his squire. I should have the right to cherish
the two boys who still remain. It has been too long since I saw them.*

At Eastwatch, the black brothers told him there was no love between
the Manderlys of White Harbor and the Boltons of the Dreadfort. The
Iron Throne had raised Roose Bolton up to Warden of the North, so it
stood to reason that Wyman Manderly should declare for Stannis. *White
Harbor cannot stand alone. The city needs an ally, a protector. Lord Wyman
needs King Stannis as much as Stannis needs him.* Or so it seemed at Eastwatch.

Sisterton had undermined those hopes. If Lord Borrell told it true, if the Manderlys meant to join their strength to the Boltons and the Freys . . . no, he would not dwell on that. He would know the truth soon enough. He prayed he had not come too late.

That jetty wall conceals the inner harbor, he realized, as the *Merry Midwife* was pulling down her sail. The outer harbor was larger, but the inner harbor offered better anchorage, sheltered by the city wall on one side and the looming mass of the Wolf's Den on another, and now by the jetty wall as well. At Eastwatch-by-the-Sea, Cotter Pyke told Davos that Lord Wyman was building war galleys. There could have been a score of ships concealed behind those walls, waiting only a command to put to sea.

Behind the city's thick white walls, the New Castle rose proud and pale upon its hill. Davos could see the domed roof of the Sept of the Snows as well, surmounted by tall statues of the Seven. The Manderlys had brought the Faith north with them when they were driven from the Reach. White Harbor had its godswood too, a brooding tangle of root and branch and stone locked away behind the crumbling black walls of the Wolf's Den, an ancient fortress that served only as a prison now. But for the most part the septons ruled here.

The merman of House Manderly was everywhere in evidence, flying from the towers of the New Castle, above the Seal Gate, and along the city walls. At Eastwatch, the northmen insisted that White Harbor would never abandon its allegiance to Winterfell, but Davos saw no sign of the direwolf of Stark. *There are no lions either. Lord Wyman cannot have declared for Tommen yet, or he would have raised his standard.*

The dockside wharves were swarming. A clutter of small boats were tied up along the fish market, off-loading their catches. He saw three river runners too, long lean boats built tough to brave the swift currents and rocky shoots of the White Knife. It was the seagoing vessels that interested him most, however; a pair of carracks as drab and tattered as the *Merry Midwife,* the trading galley *Storm Dancer,* the cogs *Brave Magister* and *Horn of Plenty,* a galleas from Braavos marked by her purple hull and sails . . .

. . . and there beyond, the warship.

The sight of her sent a knife through his hopes. Her hull was black and gold, her figurehead a lion with an upraised paw. *Lionstar,* read the letters on her stern, beneath a fluttering banner that bore the arms of the boy king on the Iron Throne. A year ago, he would not have been able to read them, but Maester Pylos had taught him some of the letters back on Dragonstone. For once, the reading gave him little pleasure. Davos had been praying that the galley had been lost in the same storms that had ravaged Salla's fleet, but the gods had not been so kind. The Freys were here, and he would need to face them.

The *Merry Midwife* tied up to the end of a weathered wooden pier in the outer harbor, well away from *Lionstar*. As her crew made her fast to the pilings and lowered a gangplank, her captain sauntered up to Davos. Casso Mogat was a mongrel of the narrow sea, fathered on a Sisterton whore by an Ibbenese whaler. Only five feet tall and very hirsute, he dyed his hair and whiskers a mossy green. It made him look like a tree stump in yellow boots. Despite his appearance, he seemed a good sailor, though a hard master to his crew. "How long will you be gone?"

"A day at least. It may be longer." Davos had found that lords liked to keep you waiting. They did it to make you anxious, he suspected, and to demonstrate their power.

"The *Midwife* will linger here three days. No longer. They will look for me back in Sisterton."

"If things go well, I could be back by the morrow."

"And if these things go badly?"

I may not be back at all. "You need not wait for me."

A pair of customs men were clambering aboard as he went down the gangplank, but neither gave him so much as a glance. They were there to see the captain and inspect the hold; common seamen did not concern them, and few men looked as common as Davos. He was of middling height, his shrewd peasant's face weathered by wind and sun, his grizzled beard and brown hair well salted with grey. His garb was plain as well: old boots, brown breeches and blue tunic, a woolen mantle of undyed wool, fastened with a wooden clasp. He wore a pair of salt-stained leather gloves to hide the stubby fingers of the hand that Stannis had shortened, so many years ago. Davos hardly looked a lord, much less a King's Hand. That was all to the good until he knew how matters stood here.

He made his way along the wharf and through the fish market. The *Brave Magister* was taking on some mead. The casks stood four high along the pier. Behind one stack he glimpsed three sailors throwing dice. Farther on the fishwives were crying the day's catch, and a boy was beating time on a drum as a shabby old bear danced in a circle for a ring of river runners. Two spearmen had been posted at the Seal Gate, with the badge of House Manderly upon their breasts, but they were too intent on flirting with a dockside whore to pay Davos any mind. The gate was open, the portcullis raised. He joined the traffic passing through.

Inside was a cobbled square with a fountain at its center. A stone merman rose from its waters, twenty feet tall from tail to crown. His curly beard was green and white with lichen, and one of the prongs of his trident had broken off before Davos had been born, yet somehow he still managed to impress. *Old Fishfoot* was what the locals called him. The square was named for some dead lord, but no one ever called it anything but Fishfoot Yard.

The Yard was teeming this afternoon. A woman was washing her small-clothes in Fishfoot's fountain and hanging them off his trident to dry. Beneath the arches of the peddler's colonnade the scribes and money changers had set up for business, along with a hedge wizard, an herb woman, and a very bad juggler. A man was selling apples from a barrow, and a woman was offering herring with chopped onions. Chickens and children were everywhere underfoot. The huge oak-and-iron doors of the Old Mint had always been closed when Davos had been in Fishfoot Yard before, but today they stood open. Inside he glimpsed hundreds of women, children, and old men, huddled on the floor on piles of furs. Some had little cookfires going.

Davos stopped beneath the colonnade and traded a halfpenny for an apple. "Are people living in the Old Mint?" he asked the apple seller.

"Them as have no other place to live. Smallfolk from up the White Knife, most o' them. Hornwood's people too. With that Bastard o' Bolton running loose, they all want to be inside the walls. I don't know what his lordship means to do with all o' them. Most turned up with no more'n the rags on their backs."

Davos felt a pang of guilt. *They came here for refuge, to a city untouched by the fighting, and here I turn up to drag them back into the war.* He took a bite of the apple and felt guilty about that as well. "How do they eat?"

The apple seller shrugged. "Some beg. Some steal. Lots o' young girls taking up the trade, the way girls always do when it's all they got to sell. Any boy stands five feet tall can find a place in his lordship's barracks, long as he can hold a spear."

He's raising men, then. That might be good . . . or bad, depending. The apple was dry and mealy, but Davos made himself take another bite. "Does Lord Wyman mean to join the Bastard?"

"Well," said the apple seller, "the next time his lordship comes down here hunkering for an apple, I'll be sure and ask him."

"I heard his daughter was to wed some Frey."

"His granddaughter. I heard that too, but his lordship forgot t' invite me to the wedding. Here, you going to finish that? I'll take the rest back. Them seeds is good."

Davos tossed him back the core. *A bad apple, but it was worth half a penny to learn that Manderly is raising men.* He made his way around Old Fishfoot, past where a young girl was selling cups of fresh milk from her nanny goat. He was remembering more of the city now that he was here. Down past where Old Fishfoot's trident pointed was an alley where they sold fried cod, crisp and golden brown outside and flaky white within. Over there was a brothel, cleaner than most, where a sailor could enjoy a woman without fear of being robbed or killed. Off the other way, in one of those houses that clung to the walls of the Wolf's Den like barnacles to an old hull, there used to be a brewhouse where they made a black beer so thick and tasty that a cask of it could fetch as much as Arbor gold in Braavos and the Port of Ibben, provided the locals left the brewer any to sell.

It was wine he wanted, though—sour, dark, and dismal. He strolled across the yard and down a flight of steps, to a winesink called the Lazy Eel, underneath a warehouse full of sheepskins. Back in his smuggling days, the Eel had been renowned for offering the oldest whores and vilest wine in White Harbor, along with meat pies full of lard and gristle that were inedible on their best days and poisonous on their worst. With fare like that, most locals shunned the place, leaving it for sailors who did not know any better. You never saw a city guardsman down in the Lazy Eel, or a customs officer.

Some things never change. Inside the Eel, time stood still. The barrel-vaulted ceiling was stained black with soot, the floor was hard-packed earth, the air smelled of smoke and spoiled meat and stale vomit. The fat tallow candles on the tables gave off more smoke than light, and the wine that Davos ordered looked more brown than red in the gloom. Four whores were seated near the door, drinking. One gave him a hopeful smile as he entered. When Davos shook his head, the woman said something that made her companions laugh. After that none of them paid him any mind.

Aside from the whores and the proprietor, Davos had the Eel to himself. The cellar was large, full of nooks and shadowed alcoves where a man could be alone. He took his wine to one of them and sat with his back to a wall to wait.

Before long, he found himself staring at the hearth. The red woman could see the future in the fire, but all that Davos Seaworth ever saw were the shadows of the past: the burning ships, the fiery chain, the green shadows flashing across the belly of the clouds, the Red Keep brooding over all. Davos was a simple man, raised up by chance and war and Stannis.

He did not understand why the gods would take four lads as young and strong as his sons, yet spare their weary father. Some nights he thought he had been left to rescue Edric Storm . . . but by now King Robert's bastard boy was safe in the Stepstones, yet Davos still remained. *Do the gods have some other task for me?* he wondered. *If so, White Harbor may be some part of it.* He tried the wine, then poured half his cup onto the floor beside his foot.

As dusk fell outside, the benches at the Eel began to fill with sailors. Davos called to the proprietor for another cup. When he brought it, he brought him a candle too. "You want food?" the man asked. "We got meat pies."

"What kind of meat is in them?"

"The usual kind. It's good."

The whores laughed. "It's grey, he means," one said.

"Shut your bloody yap. You eat them."

"I eat all kinds o' shit. Don't mean I like it."

Davos blew the candle out as soon as the proprietor moved off, and sat back in the shadows. Seamen were the worst gossips in the world when the wine was flowing, even wine as cheap as this. All he need do was listen.

Most of what he heard he'd learned in Sisterton, from Lord Godric or the denizens of the Belly of the Whale. Tywin Lannister was dead, butchered by his dwarf son; his corpse had stunk so badly that no one had been able to enter the Great Sept of Baelor for days afterward; the Lady of the Eyrie had been murdered by a singer; Littlefinger ruled the Vale now, but Bronze Yohn Royce had sworn to bring him down; Balon Greyjoy had died as well, and his brothers were fighting for the Seastone Chair; Sandor Clegane had turned outlaw and was plundering and killing in the lands along the Trident; Myr and Lys and Tyrosh were embroiled in another war; a slave revolt was raging in the east.

Other tidings were of greater interest. Robett Glover was in the city and had been trying to raise men, with little success. Lord Manderly had turned a deaf ear to his pleas. White Harbor was weary of war, he was reported to have said. That was bad. The Ryswells and the Dustins had surprised the ironmen on the Fever River and put their longships to the torch. That was worse. And now the Bastard of Bolton was riding south with Hother Umber to join them for an attack on Moat Cailin. "The Whoresbane his own self," claimed a riverman who'd just brought a load of hides and timber down the White Knife, "with three hundred spearmen and a hundred archers. Some Hornwood men have joined them, and Cerwyns too." That was worst of all.

"Lord Wyman best send some men to fight if he knows what's good for him," said the old fellow at the end of the table. "Lord Roose, he's the Warden now. White Harbor's honor bound to answer his summons."

"What did any Bolton ever know o' honor?" said the Eel's proprietor as he filled their cups with more brown wine.

"Lord Wyman won't go no place. He's too bloody fat."

"I heard how he was ailing. All he does is sleep and weep, they say. He's too sick to get out o' his bed most days."

"Too *fat*, you mean."

"Fat or thin's got naught to do with it," said the Eel's proprietor. "The lions got his son."

No one spoke of King Stannis. No one even seemed to know that His Grace had come north to help defend the Wall. Wildlings and wights and giants had been all the talk at Eastwatch, but here no one seemed to be giving them so much as a thought.

Davos leaned into the firelight. "I thought the Freys killed his son. That's what we heard in Sisterton."

"They killed Ser Wendel," said the proprietor. "His bones are resting in the Snowy Sept with candles all around them, if you want to have a look. Ser Wylis, though, he's still a captive."

Worse and worse. He had known that Lord Wyman had two sons, but he'd thought that both of them were dead. *If the Iron Throne has a hostage . . .* Davos had fathered seven sons himself, and lost four on the Blackwater. He knew he would do whatever gods or men required of him to protect the other three. Steffon and Stannis were thousands of leagues from the fighting and safe from harm, but Devan was at Castle Black, a squire to the king. *The king whose cause may rise or fall with White Harbor.*

His fellow drinkers were talking about dragons now. "You're bloody mad," said an oarsman off *Storm Dancer*. "The Beggar King's been dead for years. Some Dothraki horselord cut his head off."

"So they tell us," said the old fellow. "Might be they're lying, though. He died half a world away, if he died at all. Who's to say? If a king wanted me dead, might be I'd oblige him and pretend to be a corpse. None of us has ever seen his body."

"I never saw Joffrey's corpse, nor Robert's," growled the Eel's proprietor. "Maybe they're all alive as well. Maybe Baelor the Blessed's just been having him a little nap all these years."

The old fellow made a face. "Prince Viserys weren't the only dragon, were he? Are we sure they killed Prince Rhaegar's son? A babe, he was."

"Wasn't there some princess too?" asked a whore. She was the same one who'd said the meat was grey.

"Two," said the old fellow. "One was Rhaegar's daughter, t'other was his sister."

"Daena," said the riverman. "That was the sister. Daena of Dragonstone. Or was it Daera?"

"Daena was old King Baelor's wife," said the oarsman. "I rowed on a ship named for her once. The *Princess Daena.*"

"If she was a king's wife, she'd be a queen."

"Baelor never had a queen. He was holy."

"Don't mean he never wed his sister," said the whore. "He just never bedded her, is all. When they made him king, he locked her up in a tower. His other sisters too. There was three."

"Daenela," the proprietor said loudly. "That was her name. The Mad King's daughter, I mean, not Baelor's bloody wife."

"*Daenerys,*" Davos said. "She was named for the Daenerys who wed the Prince of Dorne during the reign of Daeron the Second. I don't know what became of her."

"I do," said the man who'd started all the talk of dragons, a Braavosi oarsman in a somber woolen jack. "When we were down to Pentos we moored beside a trader called the *Sloe-Eyed Maid*, and I got to drinking with her captain's steward. He told me a pretty tale about some slip of a girl who come aboard in Qarth, to try and book passage back to Westeros for her and three dragons. Silver hair she had, and purple eyes. 'I took her to the captain my own self,' this steward swore to me, 'but he wasn't having none of that. There's more profit in cloves and saffron, he tells me, and spices won't set fire to your sails.' "

Laughter swept the cellar. Davos did not join in. He knew what had befallen the *Sloe-Eyed Maid*. The gods were cruel to let a man sail across half the world, then send him chasing a false light when he was almost home. *That captain was a bolder man than me,* he thought, as he made his way to the door. One voyage to the east, and a man could live as rich as a lord until the end of his days. When he'd been younger, Davos had dreamed of making such voyages himself, but the years went dancing by like moths around a flame, and somehow the time had never been quite right. *One day,* he told himself. *One day when the war is done and King Stannis sits the Iron Throne and has no more need of onion knights. I'll take*

Devan with me. Steff and Stanny too if they're old enough. We'll see these dragons and all the wonders of the world.

Outside the wind was gusting, making the flames shiver in the oil lamps that lit the yard. It had grown colder since the sun went down, but Davos remembered Eastwatch, and how the wind would come screaming off the Wall at night, knifing through even the warmest cloak to freeze a man's blood right in his veins. White Harbor was a warm bath by comparison.

There were other places he might get his ears filled: an inn famous for its lamprey pies, the alehouse where the wool factors and the customs men did their drinking, a mummer's hall where bawdy entertainments could be had for a few pennies. But Davos felt that he had heard enough. *I've come too late.* Old instinct made him reach for his chest, where once he'd kept his fingerbones in a little sack on a leather thong. There was nothing there. He had lost his luck in the fires of the Blackwater, when he'd lost his ship and sons.

What must I do now? He pulled his mantle tighter. *Do I climb the hill and present myself at the gates of the New Castle, to make a futile plea? Return to Sisterton? Make my way back to Marya and my boys? Buy a horse and ride the kingsroad, to tell Stannis that he has no friends in White Harbor, and no hope?*

Queen Selyse had feasted Salla and his captains, the night before the fleet had set sail. Cotter Pyke had joined them, and four other high officers of the Night's Watch. Princess Shireen had been allowed to attend as well. As the salmon was being served, Ser Axell Florent had entertained the table with the tale of a Targaryen princeling who kept an ape as a pet. This prince liked to dress the creature in his dead son's clothes and pretend he was a child, Ser Axell claimed, and from time to time he would propose marriages for him. The lords so honored always declined politely, but of course they did decline. "Even dressed in silk and velvet, an ape remains an ape," Ser Axell said. "A wiser prince would have known that you cannot send an ape to do a man's work." The queen's men laughed, and several grinned at Davos. *I am no ape*, he'd thought. *I am as much a lord as you, and a better man.* But the memory still stung.

The Seal Gate had been closed for the night. Davos would not be able to return to the *Merry Midwife* till dawn. He was here for the night. He gazed up at Old Fishfoot with his broken trident. *I have come through rain and wrack and storm. I will not go back without doing what I came for, no matter how hopeless it may seem.* He might have lost his fingers and his luck, but he was no ape in velvet. He was a King's Hand.

Castle Stair was a street with steps, a broad white stone way that led up from the Wolf's Den by the water to the New Castle on its hill. Marble mermaids lit the way as Davos climbed, bowls of burning whale oil cradled in their arms. When he reached the top, he turned to look behind him. From here he could see down into the harbors. Both of them. Behind the jetty wall, the inner harbor was crowded with war galleys. Davos counted twenty-three. Lord Wyman was a fat man, but not an idle one, it seemed.

The gates of the New Castle had been closed, but a postern opened when he shouted, and a guard emerged to ask his business. Davos showed him the black and gold ribbon that bore the royal seals. "I need to see Lord Manderly at once," he said. "My business is with him, and him alone."

DAENERYS

The dancers shimmered, their sleek shaved bodies covered with a fine sheen of oil. Blazing torches whirled from hand to hand to the beat of drums and the trilling of a flute. Whenever two torches crossed in the air, a naked girl leapt between them, spinning. The torchlight shone off oiled limbs and breasts and buttocks.

The three men were erect. The sight of their arousal was arousing, though Daenerys Targaryen found it comical as well. The men were all of a height, with long legs and flat bellies, every muscle as sharply etched as if it had been chiseled out of stone. Even their faces looked the same, somehow . . . which was passing strange, since one had skin as dark as ebony, while the second was as pale as milk, and the third gleamed like burnished copper.

Are they meant to inflame me? Dany stirred amongst her silken cushions. Against the pillars her Unsullied stood like statues in their spiked caps, their smooth faces expressionless. Not so the whole men. Reznak mo Reznak's mouth was open, and his lips glistened wetly as he watched. Hizdahr zo Loraq was saying something to the man beside him, yet all the time his eyes were on the dancing girls. The Shavepate's ugly, oily face was as stern as ever, but he missed nothing.

It was harder to know what her honored guest was dreaming. The pale, lean, hawk-faced man who shared her high table was resplendent in robes of maroon silk and cloth-of-gold, his bald head shining in the torchlight as he devoured a fig with small, precise, elegant bites. Opals winked along the nose of Xaro Xhoan Daxos as his head turned to follow the dancers.

In his honor Daenerys had donned a Qartheen gown, a sheer confection of violet samite cut so as to leave her left breast bare. Her silver-gold hair brushed lightly over her shoulder, falling almost to her nipple. Half the men in the hall had stolen glances at her, but not Xaro. *It was the same in Qarth.* She could not sway the merchant prince that way. *Sway him I must, however.* He had come from Qarth upon the galleas *Silken Cloud* with thirteen galleys sailing attendance, his fleet an answered prayer. Meereen's trade had dwindled away to nothing since she had ended slavery, but Xaro had the power to restore it.

As the drums reached a crescendo, three of the girls leapt above the flames, spinning in the air. The male dancers caught them about the waists and slid them down onto their members. Dany watched as the women arched their backs and coiled their legs around their partners while the flutes wept and the men thrust in time to the music. She had seen the act of love before; the Dothraki mated as openly as their mares and stallions. This was the first time she had seen lust put to music, though.

Her face was warm. *The wine,* she told herself. Yet somehow she found herself thinking of Daario Naharis. His messenger had come that morning. The Stormcrows were returning from Lhazar. Her captain was riding back to her, bringing her the friendship of the Lamb Men. *Food and trade,* she reminded herself. *He did not fail me, nor will he. Daario will help me save my city.* The queen longed to see his face, to stroke his three-pronged beard, to tell him her troubles . . . but the Stormcrows were still many days away, beyond the Khyzai Pass, and she had a realm to rule.

Smoke hung between the purple pillars. The dancers knelt, heads bowed. "You were splendid," Dany told them. "Seldom have I seen such grace, such beauty." She beckoned to Reznak mo Reznak, and the seneschal scurried to her side. Beads of sweat dotted his bald, wrinkled head. "Escort our guests to the baths, that they may refresh themselves, and bring them food and drink."

"It shall be my great honor, Magnificence."

Daenerys held out her cup for Irri to refill. The wine was sweet and strong, redolent with the smell of eastern spices, much superior to the thin Ghiscari wines that had filled her cup of late. Xaro perused the fruits on the platter Jhiqui offered him and chose a persimmon. Its orange skin matched the color of the coral in his nose. He took a bite and pursed his lips. "Tart."

"Would my lord prefer something sweeter?"

"Sweetness cloys. Tart fruit and tart women give life its savor." Xaro took another bite, chewed, swallowed. "Daenerys, sweet queen, I cannot tell you what pleasure it gives me to bask once more in your presence. A child departed Qarth, as lost as she was lovely. I feared she was sailing to her doom, yet now I find her here enthroned, mistress of an ancient city, surrounded by a mighty host that she raised up out of dreams."

No, she thought, *out of blood and fire.* "I am glad you came to me. It is good to see your face again, my friend." *I will not trust you, but I need you. I need your Thirteen, I need your ships, I need your trade.*

For centuries Meereen and her sister cities Yunkai and Astapor had been the linchpins of the slave trade, the place where Dothraki khals and the corsairs of the Basilisk Isles sold their captives and the rest of the world came to buy. Without slaves, Meereen had little to offer traders. Copper was plentiful in the Ghiscari hills, but the metal was not as valuable as it had been when bronze ruled the world. The cedars that had once grown tall along the coast grew no more, felled by the axes of the Old Empire or consumed by dragonfire when Ghis made war against Valyria. Once the trees had gone, the soil baked beneath the hot sun and blew away in thick red clouds. "It was these calamities that transformed my people into slavers," Galazza Galare had told her, at the Temple of the Graces. *And I am the calamity that will change these slavers back into people,* Dany had sworn to herself.

"I had to come," said Xaro in a languid tone. "Even far away in Qarth, fearful tales had reached my ears. I wept to hear them. It is said that your enemies have promised wealth and glory and a hundred virgin slave girls to any man who slays you."

"The Sons of the Harpy." *How does he know that?* "They scrawl on walls by night and cut the throats of honest freedmen as they sleep. When the sun comes up they hide like roaches. They fear my Brazen Beasts." Skahaz mo Kandaq had given her the new watch she had asked for, made up in equal numbers of freedmen and shavepate Meereenese. They walked the streets both day and night, in dark hoods and brazen masks. The Sons of the Harpy had promised grisly death to any traitor who dared serve the dragon queen, and to their kith and kin as well, so the Shavepate's men went about as jackals, owls, and other beasts, keeping their true faces hidden. "I might have cause to fear the Sons if they saw me wandering alone through the streets, but only if it was night and I was naked and unarmed. They are craven creatures."

"A craven's knife can slay a queen as easily as a hero's. I would sleep more soundly if I knew my heart's delight had kept her fierce horselords close around her. In Qarth, you had three bloodriders who never left your side. Wherever have they gone?"

"Aggo, Jhoqo, and Rakharo still serve me." *He is playing games with me.* Dany could play as well. "I am only a young girl and know little of such things, but older, wiser men tell me that to hold Meereen I must control its hinterlands, all the land west of Lhazar as far south as the Yunk-ish hills."

"Your hinterlands are not precious to me. Your person is. Should any ill befall you, this world would lose its savor."

"My lord is good to care so much, but I am well protected." Dany ges-tured toward where Barristan Selmy stood with one hand resting on his sword hilt. "Barristan the Bold, they call him. Twice he has saved me from assassins."

Xaro gave Selmy a cursory inspection. "Barristan the Old, did you say? Your bear knight was younger, and devoted to you."

"I do not wish to speak of Jorah Mormont."

"To be sure. The man was coarse and hairy." The merchant prince leaned across the table. "Let us speak instead of love, of dreams and desire and Daenerys, the fairest woman in this world. I am drunk with the sight of you."

She was no stranger to the overblown courtesies of Qarth. "If you are drunk, blame the wine."

"No wine is half so intoxicating as your beauty. My manse has seemed as empty as a tomb since Daenerys departed, and all the pleasures of the Queen of Cities have been as ashes in my mouth. Why did you abandon me?"

I was hounded from your city in fear for my life. "It was time. Qarth wished me gone."

"Who? The Pureborn? They have water in their veins. The Spicers? There are curds between their ears. And the Undying are all dead. You should have taken me to husband. I am almost certain that I asked you for your hand. Begged you, even."

"Only half a hundred times," Dany teased. "You gave up too easily, my lord. For I *must* marry, all agree."

"A *khaleesi* must have a khal," said Irri, as she filled the queen's cup once again. "This is known."

"Shall I ask again?" wondered Xaro. "No, I know that smile. It is a cruel queen who dices with men's hearts. Humble merchants like myself are no more than stones beneath your jeweled sandals." A single tear ran slowly down his pale white cheek.

Dany knew him too well to be moved. Qartheen men could weep at will. "Oh, stop that." She took a cherry from the bowl on the table and threw it at his nose. "I may be a young girl, but I am not so foolish as to wed a man who finds a fruit platter more enticing than my breast. I saw which dancers you were watching."

Xaro wiped away his tear. "The same ones Your Grace was following, I believe. You see, we are alike. If you will not take me for your husband, I am content to be your slave."

"I want no slave. I free you." His jeweled nose made a tempting target. This time Dany threw an apricot at him.

Xaro caught it in the air and took a bite. "Whence came this madness? Should I count myself fortunate that you did not free my own slaves when you were my guest in Qarth?"

I was a beggar queen and you were Xaro of the Thirteen, Dany thought, *and all you wanted were my dragons.* "Your slaves seemed well treated and content. It was not till Astapor that my eyes were opened. Do you know how Unsullied are made and trained?"

"Cruelly, I have no doubt. When a smith makes a sword, he thrusts the blade into the fire, beats on it with a hammer, then plunges it into iced water to temper the steel. If you would savor the sweet taste of the fruit, you must water the tree."

"This tree has been watered with blood."

"How else, to grow a soldier? Your Radiance enjoyed my dancers. Would it surprise you to know that they are slaves, bred and trained in Yunkai? They have been dancing since they were old enough to walk. How else to achieve such *perfection*?" He took a swallow of his wine. "They are expert in all the erotic arts as well. I had thought to make Your Grace a gift of them."

"By all means." Dany was unsurprised. "I shall free them."

That made him wince. "And what would they do with freedom? As well give a fish a suit of mail. They were made to dance."

"Made by who? Their masters? Perhaps your dancers would sooner build or bake or farm. Have you asked them?"

"Perhaps your elephants would sooner be nightingales. Instead of sweet song, Meereen's nights would be filled with thunderous trumpetings, and your trees would shatter beneath the weight of great grey birds." Xaro sighed. "Daenerys, my delight, beneath that sweet young breast beats a tender heart . . . but take counsel from an older, wiser head. Things are not always as they seem. Much that may seem evil can be good. Consider rain."

"Rain?" *Does he take me for a fool, or just a child?*

"We curse the rain when it falls upon our heads, yet without it we should starve. The world *needs* rain . . . and slaves. You make a face, but it is true. Consider Qarth. In art, music, magic, trade, all that makes us more than beasts, Qarth sits above the rest of mankind as you sit at the summit of this pyramid . . . but below, in place of bricks, the magnificence that is the Queen of Cities rests upon the backs of *slaves*. Ask yourself, if all men must grub in the dirt for food, how shall any man lift his eyes to contemplate the stars? If each of us must break his back to build a hovel, who shall raise the temples to glorify the gods? For some men to be great, others must be enslaved."

He was too eloquent for her. Dany had no answer for him, only the raw feeling in her belly. "Slavery is not the same as rain," she insisted. "I have been rained on and I have been sold. It is *not the same*. No man wants to be *owned*."

Xaro gave a languid shrug. "As it happens, when I came ashore in your sweet city, I chanced to see upon the riverbank a man who had once been a guest in my manse, a merchant who dealt in rare spices and choice wines. He was naked from the waist up, red and peeling, and seemed to be digging a hole."

"Not a hole. A ditch, to bring water from the river to the fields. We mean to plant beans. The beanfields must have water."

"How kind of my old friend to help with the digging. And how very unlike him. Is it possible he was given no choice in the matter? No, surely not. You have no slaves in Meereen."

Dany flushed. "Your friend is being paid with food and shelter. I cannot give him back his wealth. Meereen needs beans more than it needs rare spices, and beans require water."

"Would you set my dancers to digging ditches as well? Sweet queen, when he saw me, my old friend fell to his knees and begged me to buy him as a slave and take him back to Qarth."

She felt as if he'd slapped her. "Buy him, then."

"If it please you. I know it will please *him*." He put his hand upon her arm. "There are truths only a friend may tell you. I helped you when you came to Qarth a beggar, and I have crossed long leagues and stormy seas to help you once again. Is there some place where we might speak frankly?"

Dany could feel the warmth of his fingers. *He was warm in Qarth as well*, she recalled, *until the day he had no more use for me*. She rose to her feet. "Come," she said, and Xaro followed her through the pillars, to the wide marble steps that led up to her private chambers at the apex of the pyramid.

"Oh most beautiful of women," Xaro said, as they began to climb, "there are footsteps behind us. We are followed."

"My old knight does not frighten you, surely? Ser Barristan is sworn to keep my secrets."

She took him out onto the terrace that overlooked the city. A full moon swam in the black sky above Meereen. "Shall we walk?" Dany slipped her arm through his. The air was heavy with the scent of night-blooming flowers. "You spoke of help. Trade with me, then. Meereen has salt to sell, and wine . . ."

"Ghiscari wine?" Xaro made a sour face. "The sea provides all the salt that Qarth requires, but I would gladly take as many olives as you cared to sell me. Olive oil as well."

"I have none to offer. The slavers burned the trees." Olives had been grown along the shores of Slaver's Bay for centuries; but the Meereenese had put their ancient groves to the torch as Dany's host advanced on them, leaving her to cross a blackened wasteland. "We are replanting, but it takes seven years before an olive tree begins to bear, and thirty years before it can truly be called productive. What of copper?"

"A pretty metal, but fickle as a woman. Gold, now . . . gold is *sincere*. Qarth will gladly give you gold . . . for slaves."

"Meereen is a free city of free men."

"A poor city that once was rich. A hungry city that once was fat. A bloody city that once was peaceful."

His accusations stung. There was too much truth in them. "Meereen will be rich and fat and peaceful once again, and free as well. Go to the Dothraki if you must have slaves."

"Dothraki make slaves, Ghiscari train them. And to reach Qarth, the horselords must needs drive their captives across the red waste. Hundreds would die, if not thousands . . . and many horses too, which is why no khal will risk it. And there is this: Qarth wants no *khalasars* seething round our walls. The stench of all those horses . . . meaning no offense, *Khaleesi*."

"A horse has an honest smell. That is more than can be said of some great lords and merchant princes."

Xaro took no notice of the sally. "Daenerys, let me be honest with you, as befits a friend. You will *not* make Meereen rich and fat and peaceful. You will only bring it to destruction, as you did Astapor. You are aware that there was battle joined at the Horns of Hazzat? The Butcher King has fled back to his palace, his new Unsullied running at his heels."

"This is known." Brown Ben Plumm had sent back word of the battle from the field. "The Yunkai'i have bought themselves new sellswords, and two legions from New Ghis fought beside them."

"Two will soon become four, then ten. And Yunkish envoys have been sent to Myr and Volantis to hire more blades. The Company of the Cat, the Long Lances, the Windblown. Some say that the Wise Masters have bought the Golden Company as well."

Her brother Viserys had once feasted the captains of the Golden Company, in hopes they might take up his cause. *They ate his food and heard his pleas and laughed at him.* Dany had only been a little girl, but she remembered. "I have sellswords too."

"Two companies. The Yunkai'i will send twenty against you if they must. And when they march, they will not march alone. Tolos and Mantarys have agreed to an alliance."

That was ill news, if true. Daenerys had sent missions to Tolos and Mantarys, hoping to find new friends to the west to balance the enmity of Yunkai to the south. Her envoys had not returned. "Meereen has made alliance with Lhazar."

That only made him chuckle. "The Dothraki horselords call the Lhazarene the *Lamb Men.* When you shear them, all they do is bleat. They are not a martial people."

Even a sheepish friend is better than none. "The Wise Masters should follow their example. I spared Yunkai before, but I will not make that mistake again. If they should dare attack me, this time I shall raze their Yellow City to the ground."

"And whilst you are razing Yunkai, my sweet, Meereen shall rise behind you. Do not close your eyes to your peril, Daenerys. Your eunuchs are fine soldiers, but they are too few to match the hosts that Yunkai will send against you, once Astapor has fallen."

"My freedman—" Dany started.

"Bedslaves, barbers, and brickmakers win no battles."

He was wrong in that, she hoped. The freedmen had been a rabble once, but she had organized the men of fighting age into companies and commanded Grey Worm to make them into soldiers. *Let him think what he will.* "Have you forgotten? I have *dragons.*"

"Do you? In Qarth, you were seldom seen without a dragon on your shoulder . . . yet now that shapely shoulder is as fair and bare as your sweet breast, I observe."

"My dragons have grown, my shoulders have not. They range far afield, hunting." *Hazzea, forgive me.* She wondered how much Xaro knew, what whispers he had heard. "Ask the Good Masters of Astapor about my dragons if you doubt them." *I saw a slaver's eyes melt and go running down his cheeks.* "Tell me true, old friend, why did you seek me out if not to trade?"

"To bring a gift, for the queen of my heart."

"Say on." *What trap is this, now?*

"The gift you begged of me in Qarth. Ships. There are thirteen galleys in the bay. Yours, if you will have them. I have brought you a fleet, to carry you home to Westeros."

A *fleet*. It was more than she could hope for, so of course it made her wary. In Qarth, Xaro had offered her thirty ships . . . for a dragon. "And what price do you ask for these ships?"

"None. I no longer lust for dragons. I saw their work at Astapor on my way here, when my *Silken Cloud* put in for water. The ships are yours, sweet queen. Thirteen galleys, and men to pull the oars."

Thirteen. To be sure. Xaro was one of the Thirteen. No doubt he had convinced each of his fellow members to give up one ship. She knew the merchant prince too well to think that he would sacrifice thirteen of his *own* ships. "I must consider this. May I inspect these ships?"

"You have grown suspicious, Daenerys."

Always. "I have grown wise, Xaro."

"Inspect all you wish. When you are satisfied, swear to me that you shall return to Westeros forthwith, and the ships are yours. Swear by your dragons and your seven-faced god and the ashes of your fathers, and *go*."

"And if I should decide to wait a year, or three?"

A mournful look crossed Xaro's face. "That would make me very sad, my sweet delight . . . for young and strong as you now seem, you shall not live so long. Not here."

He offers the honeycomb with one hand and shows the whip with the other. "The Yunkai'i are not so fearsome as all that."

"Not all your enemies are in the Yellow City. Beware men with cold hearts and blue lips. You had not been gone from Qarth a fortnight when Pyat Pree set out with three of his fellow warlocks, to seek for you in Pentos."

Dany was more amused than afraid. "It is good I turned aside, then. Pentos is half a world from Meereen."

"This is so," he allowed, "yet soon or late word must reach them of the dragon queen of Slaver's Bay."

"Is that meant to frighten me? I lived in fear for fourteen years, my lord. I woke afraid each morning and went to sleep afraid each night . . . but my fears were burned away the day I came forth from the fire. Only one thing frightens me now."

"And what is it that you fear, sweet queen?"

"I am only a foolish young girl." Dany rose on her toes and kissed his cheek. "But not so foolish as to tell you that. My men shall look at these ships. Then you shall have my answer."

"As you say." He touched her bare breast lightly, and whispered, "Let me stay and help persuade you."

For a moment she was tempted. Perhaps the dancers had stirred her after all. *I could close my eyes and pretend that he was Daario.* A dream Daario would be safer than the real one. But she pushed the thought aside. "No, my lord. I thank you, but no." Dany slipped from his arms. "Some other night, perhaps."

"Some other night." His mouth was sad, but his eyes seemed more relieved than disappointed.

If I were a dragon, I could fly to Westeros, she thought when he was gone. *I would have no need of Xaro or his ships.* Dany wondered how many men thirteen galleys could hold. It had taken three to carry her and her *khalasar* from Qarth to Astapor, but that was before she had acquired eight thousand Unsullied, a thousand sellswords, and a vast horde of freedmen. *And the dragons, what am I to do with them?* "Drogon," she whispered softly, "where are you?" For a moment she could almost see him sweeping across the sky, his black wings swallowing the stars.

She turned her back upon the night, to where Barristan Selmy stood silent in the shadows. "My brother once told me a Westerosi riddle. Who listens to everything yet hears nothing?"

"A knight of the Kingsguard." Selmy's voice was solemn.

"You heard Xaro make his offer?"

"I did, Your Grace." The old knight took pains not to look at her bare breast as he spoke to her.

Ser Jorah would not turn his eyes away. He loved me as a woman, where Ser Barristan loves me only as his queen. Mormont had been an informer, reporting to her enemies in Westeros, yet he had given her good counsel too. "What do you think of it? Of him?"

"Of him, little and less. These ships, though . . . Your Grace, with these ships we might be home before year's end."

Dany had never known a home. In Braavos, there had been a house with a red door, but that was all. "Beware of Qartheen bearing gifts, especially merchants of the Thirteen. There is some trap here. Perhaps these ships are rotten, or . . ."

"If they were so unseaworthy, they could not have crossed the sea from Qarth," Ser Barristan pointed out, "but Your Grace was wise to insist upon inspection. I will take Admiral Groleo to the galleys at first light with his captains and two score of his sailors. We can crawl over every inch of those ships."

It was good counsel. "Yes, make it so." *Westeros. Home.* But if she left, what would happen to her city? *Meereen was never your city,* her brother's voice seemed to whisper. *Your cities are across the sea. Your Seven Kingdoms, where your enemies await you. You were born to serve them blood and fire.*

Ser Barristan cleared his throat and said, "This warlock that the merchant spoke of . . ."

"Pyat Pree." She tried to recall his face, but all she could see were his lips. The wine of the warlocks had turned them blue. *Shade-of-the-evening,* it was called. "If a warlock's spell could kill me, I would be dead by now. I left their palace all in ashes." *Drogon saved me when they would have drained my life from me. Drogon burned them all.*

"As you say, Your Grace. Still. I will be watchful."

She kissed him on the cheek. "I know you will. Come, walk me back down to the feast."

The next morning Dany woke as full of hope as she had been since first she came to Slaver's Bay. Daario would soon be at her side once more, and together they would sail for Westeros. *For home.* One of her young hostages brought her morning meal, a plump shy girl named Mezzara, whose father ruled the pyramid of Merreq, and Dany gave her a happy hug and thanked her with a kiss.

"Xaro Xhoan Daxos has offered me thirteen galleys," she told Irri and Jhiqui as they were dressing her for court.

"Thirteen is a bad number, *Khaleesi,*" murmured Jhiqui, in the Dothraki tongue. "It is known."

"It is known," Irri agreed.

"Thirty would be better," Daenerys agreed. "Three hundred better still. But thirteen may suffice to carry us to Westeros."

The two Dothraki girls exchanged a look. "The poison water is accursed, *Khaleesi,*" said Irri. "Horses cannot drink it."

"I do not intend to drink it," Dany promised them.

Only four petitioners awaited her that morning. As ever, Lord Ghael was the first to present himself, looking even more wretched than usual. "Your Radiance," he moaned, as he fell to the marble at her feet, "the armies of the Yunkai'i descend on Astapor. I beg you, come south with all your strength!"

"I warned your king that this war of his was folly," Dany reminded him. "He would not listen."

"Great Cleon sought only to strike down the vile slavers of Yunkai."

"Great Cleon is a slaver himself."

"I know that the Mother of Dragons will not abandon us in our hour of peril. Lend us your Unsullied to defend our walls."

And if I do, who will defend my walls? "Many of my freedmen were slaves in Astapor. Perhaps some will wish to help defend your king. That is their choice, as free men. I gave Astapor its freedom. It is up to you to defend it."

"We are all dead, then. You gave us death, not freedom." Ghael leapt to his feet and spat into her face.

Strong Belwas seized him by the shoulder and slammed him down onto the marble so hard that Dany heard Ghael's teeth crack. The Shavepate would have done worse, but she stopped him.

"Enough," she said, dabbing at her cheek with the end of her *tokar.* "No one has ever died from spittle. Take him away."

They dragged him out feet first, leaving several broken teeth and a trail of blood behind. Dany would gladly have sent the rest of the petitioners away . . . but she was still their queen, so she heard them out and did her best to give them justice.

Late that afternoon Admiral Groleo and Ser Barristan returned from their inspection of the galleys. Dany assembled her council to hear them. Grey Worm was there for the Unsullied, Skahaz mo Kandaq for the Brazen Beasts. In the absence of her bloodriders, a wizened *jaqqa rhan* called Rommo, squint-eyed and bowlegged, came to speak for her Dothraki. Her freedmen were represented by the captains of the three companies she had formed—Mollono Yos Dob of the Stalwart Shields, Symon Stripeback of the Free Brothers, Marselen of the Mother's Men. Reznak mo Reznak hovered at the queen's elbow, and Strong Belwas stood behind her with his huge arms crossed. Dany would not lack for counsel.

Groleo had been a most unhappy man since they had broken up his ship to build the siege engines that won Meereen for her. Dany had tried to console him by naming him her lord admiral, but it was a hollow honor; the Meereenese fleet had sailed for Yunkai when Dany's host approached the city, so the old Pentoshi was an admiral without ships. Yet now he was smiling through his ragged salt-streaked beard in a way that the queen could scarce remember.

"The ships are sound, then?" she said, hoping.

"Sound enough, Your Grace. They are old ships, aye, but most are well maintained. The hull of the *Pureborn Princess* is worm-eaten. I'd not want to take her beyond the sight of land. The *Narraqqa* could stand a new rudder and lines, and the *Banded Lizard* has some cracked oars, but they will serve. The rowers are slaves, but if we offer them an honest oarsman's wage, most will stay with us. Rowing's all they know. Those who leave can be replaced from my own crews. It is a long hard voyage to Westeros, but these ships are sound enough to get us there, I'd judge."

Reznak mo Reznak gave a piteous moan. "Then it is true. Your Worship means to abandon us." He wrung his hands. "The Yunkai'i will restore the Great Masters the instant you are gone, and we who have so faithfully served your cause will be put to the sword, our sweet wives and maiden daughters raped and enslaved."

"Not mine," grumbled Skahaz Shavepate. "I will kill them first, with mine own hand." He slapped his sword hilt.

Dany felt as if he had slapped her face instead. "If you fear what may follow when I leave, come with me to Westeros."

"Wherever the Mother of Dragons goes, the Mother's Men will go as well," announced Marselen, Missandei's remaining brother.

"How?" asked Symon Stripeback, named for the tangle of scars that ridged his back and shoulders, a reminder of the whippings he had suffered as a slave in Astapor. "Thirteen ships . . . that's not enough. A hundred ships might not be enough."

"Wooden horses are no good," objected Rommo, the old *jaqqa rhan.* "Dothraki will ride."

"These ones could march overland along the shore," suggested Grey Worm. "The ships could keep pace and resupply the column."

"That might serve until you reached the ruins of Bhorash," said the Shavepate. "Beyond that, your ships would need to turn south past Tolos and the Isle of Cedars and sail around Valyria, whilst the foot continued on to Mantarys by the old dragon road."

"The *demon road,* they call it now," said Mollono Yos Dob. The plump commander of the Stalwart Shields looked more like a scribe than a soldier, with his inky hands and heavy paunch, but he was as clever as they came. "Many and more of us would die."

"Those left behind in Meereen would envy them their easy deaths," moaned Reznak. "They will make *slaves* of us, or throw us in the pits. All will be as it was, or worse."

"Where is your courage?" Ser Barristan lashed out. "Her Grace freed you from your chains. It is for you to sharpen your swords and defend your own freedom when she leaves."

"Brave words, from one who means to sail into the sunset," Symon Stripeback snarled back. "Will you look back at our dying?"

"Your Grace—"

"Magnificence—"

"Your Worship—"

"*Enough.*" Dany slapped the table. "No one will be left to die. You are all my people." Her dreams of home and love had blinded her. "I will not abandon Meereen to the fate of Astapor. It grieves me to say so, but Westeros must wait."

Groleo was aghast. "We *must* accept these ships. If we refuse this gift . . ."

Ser Barristan went to one knee before her. "My queen, your realm has need of you. You are not wanted here, but in Westeros men will flock to your banners by the thousands, great lords and noble knights. 'She is come,' they will shout to one another, in glad voices. 'Prince Rhaegar's sister has come home at last.' "

"If they love me so much, they will wait for me." Dany stood. "Reznak, summon Xaro Xhoan Daxos."

She received the merchant prince alone, seated on her bench of polished ebony, on the cushions Ser Barristan had brought her. Four Qartheen sailors accompanied him, bearing a rolled tapestry upon their shoulders. "I have brought another gift for the queen of my heart," Xaro announced. "It has been in my family vaults since before the Doom that took Valyria."

The sailors unrolled the tapestry across the floor. It was old, dusty, faded . . . and huge. Dany had to move to Xaro's side before the patterns became plain. "A map? It is beautiful." It covered half the floor. The seas were blue, the lands were green, the mountains black and brown. Cities were shown as stars in gold or silver thread. *There is no Smoking Sea*, she realized. *Valyria is not yet an island.*

"There you see Astapor, and Yunkai, and Meereen." Xaro pointed at three silver stars beside the blue of Slaver's Bay. "Westeros is . . . somewhere down there." His hand waved vaguely toward the far end of the hall. "You turned north when you should have continued south and west, across the Summer Sea, but with my gift you shall soon be back where you belong. Accept my galleys with a joyful heart, and bend your oars westward."

Would that I could. "My lord, I will gladly have those ships, but I cannot give you the promise that you ask." She took his hand. "Give me the galleys, and I swear that Qarth will have the friendship of Meereen until the stars go out. Let me trade with them, and you will have a good part of the profits."

Xaro's glad smile died upon his lips. "What are you saying? Are you telling me you will not go?"

"I *cannot* go."

Tears welled from his eyes, creeping down his nose, past emeralds, amethysts, and black diamonds. "I told the Thirteen that you would heed my wisdom. It grieves me to learn that I was wrong. Take these ships and sail away, or you will surely die screaming. You cannot know how many enemies you have made."

I know one stands before me now, weeping mummer's tears. The realization made her sad.

"When I went to the Hall of a Thousand Thrones to beg the Pureborn for your life, I said that you were no more than a child," Xaro went on, "but Egon Emeros the Exquisite rose and said, 'She is a *foolish* child, mad and heedless and too dangerous to live.' When your dragons were small they were a wonder. Grown, they are death and devastation, a flaming sword above the world." He wiped away the tears. "I should have slain you in Qarth."

"I was a guest beneath your roof and ate of your meat and mead," she said. "In memory of all you did for me, I will forgive those words . . . *once* . . . but never presume to threaten me again."

"Xaro Xhoan Daxos does not threaten. He promises."

Her sadness turned to fury. "And I promise you that if you are not gone before the sun comes up, we will learn how well a liar's tears can quench dragonfire. Leave me, Xaro. *Quickly.*"

He went but left his world behind. Dany seated herself upon her bench again to gaze across the blue silk sea, toward distant Westeros. *One day,* she promised herself.

The next morning Xaro's galleas was gone, but the "gift" that he had brought her remained behind in Slaver's Bay. Long red streamers flew from the masts of the thirteen Qartheen galleys, writhing in the wind. And when Daenerys descended to hold court, a messenger from the ships awaited her. He spoke no word but laid at her feet a black satin pillow, upon which rested a single bloodstained glove.

"What is this?" Skahaz demanded. "A bloody glove . . ."

". . . means war," said the queen.

JON

"Careful of the rats, my lord." Dolorous Edd led Jon down the steps, a lantern in one hand. "They make an awful squeal if you step on them. My mother used to make a similar sound when I was a boy. She must have had some rat in her, now that I think of it. Brown hair, beady little eyes, liked cheese. Might be she had a tail too, I never looked to see."

All of Castle Black was connected underground by a maze of tunnels that the brothers called *the wormways*. It was dark and gloomy underneath the earth, so the wormways were little used in summer, but when the winter winds began to blow and the snows began to fall, the tunnels became the quickest way to move about the castle. The stewards were making use of them already. Jon saw candles burning in several wall niches as they made their way along the tunnel, their footsteps echoing ahead of them.

Bowen Marsh was waiting at a junction where four wormways met. With him he had Wick Whittlestick, tall and skinny as a spear. "These are the counts from three turns ago," Marsh told Jon, offering him a thick sheaf of papers, "for comparison with our present stores. Shall we start with the granaries?"

They moved through the grey gloom beneath the earth. Each store-room had a solid oaken door closed with an iron padlock as big as a supper plate. "Is pilferage a problem?" Jon asked.

"Not as yet," said Bowen Marsh. "Once winter comes, though, your lordship might be wise to post guards down here."

Wick Whittlestick wore the keys on a ring about his neck. They all looked alike to Jon, yet somehow Wick found the right one for every door. Once inside, he would take a fist-sized chunk of chalk from his pouch and mark each cask and sack and barrel as he counted them while Marsh compared the new count to the old.

In the granaries were oats and wheat and barley, and barrels of coarse ground flour. In the root cellars strings of onions and garlic dangled from the rafters, and bags of carrots, parsnips, radishes, and white and yellow turnips filled the shelves. One storeroom held wheels of cheese so large it took two men to move them. In the next, casks of salt beef, salt pork, salt mutton, and salt cod were stacked ten feet high. Three hundred hams and three thousand long black sausages hung from ceiling beams below the smokehouse. In the spice locker they found peppercorns, cloves, and cinnamon, mustard seeds, coriander, sage and clary sage and parsley, blocks of salt. Elsewhere were casks of apples and pears, dried peas, dried figs, bags of walnuts, bags of chestnuts, bags of almonds, planks of dry smoked salmon, clay jars packed with olives in oil and sealed with wax. One storeroom offered potted hare, haunch of deer in honey, pickled cabbage, pickled beets, pickled onions, pickled eggs, and pickled herring.

As they moved from one vault to another, the wormways seemed to grow colder. Before long Jon could see their breath frosting in the lantern light. "We're beneath the Wall."

"And soon inside it," said Marsh. "The meat won't spoil in the cold. For long storage, it's better than salting."

The next door was made of rusty iron. Behind it was a flight of wooden steps. Dolorous Edd led the way with his lantern. Up top they found a tunnel as long as Winterfell's great hall though no wider than the wormways. The walls were ice, bristling with iron hooks. From each hook hung a carcass: skinned deer and elk, sides of beef, huge sows swinging from the ceiling, headless sheep and goats, even horse and bear. Hoarfrost covered everything.

As they did their count, Jon peeled the glove off his left hand and touched the nearest haunch of venison. He could feel his fingers sticking, and when he pulled them back he lost a bit of skin. His fingertips were numb. *What did you expect? There's a mountain of ice above your head, more tons than even Bowen Marsh could count.* Even so, the room felt colder than it should.

"It is worse than I feared, my lord," Marsh announced when he was done. He sounded gloomier than Dolorous Edd.

Jon had just been thinking that all the meat in the world surrounded them. *You know nothing, Jon Snow.* "How so? This seems a deal of food to me."

"It was a long summer. The harvests were bountiful, the lords generous. We had enough laid by to see us through three years of winter. Four, with a bit of scrimping. Now, though, if we must go on feeding all these

king's men and queen's men and wildlings . . . Mole's Town alone has a
thousand useless mouths, and still they come. Three more turned up yesterday at the gates, a dozen the day before. It cannot go on. Settling them
on the Gift, that's well and good, but it is too late to plant crops. We'll be
down to turnips and pease porridge before the year is out. After that we'll
be drinking the blood of our own horses."

"Yum," declared Dolorous Edd. "Nothing beats a hot cup of horse
blood on a cold night. I like mine with a pinch of cinnamon sprinkled on
top."

The Lord Steward paid him no mind. "There will be sickness too," he
went on, "bleeding gums and loose teeth. Maester Aemon used to say that
lime juice and fresh meat would remedy that, but our limes were gone a
year ago and we do not have enough fodder to keep herds afoot for fresh
meat. We should butcher all but a few breeding pairs. It's past time. In
winters past, food could be brought up the kingsroad from the south,
but with the war . . . it is still autumn, I know, but I would advise we go
on winter rations nonetheless, if it please my lord."

The men will love that. "If we must. We'll cut each man's portion by a
quarter." *If my brothers are complaining of me now, what will they say
when they're eating snow and acorn paste?*

"That will help, my lord." The Lord Steward's tone made it plain that
he did not think that it would help *enough.*

Dolorous Edd said, "Now I understand why King Stannis let the wildlings through the Wall. He means for us to eat them."

Jon had to smile. "It will not come to that."

"Oh, good," said Edd. "They look a stringy lot, and my teeth are not as
sharp as when I was younger."

"If we had sufficient coin, we could buy food from the south and bring
it in by ship," the Lord Steward said.

We could, thought Jon, *if we had the gold, and someone willing to sell us
food.* Both of those were lacking. *Our best hope may be the Eyrie.* The
Vale of Arryn was famously fertile and had gone untouched during the
fighting. Jon wondered how Lady Catelyn's sister would feel about feeding Ned Stark's bastard. As a boy, he often felt as if the lady grudged him
every bite.

"We can always hunt if need be," Wick Whittlestick put in. "There's
still game in the woods."

"And wildlings, and darker things," said Marsh. "I would not send out
hunters, my lord. I would not."

No. You would close our gates forever and seal them up with stone and ice. Half of Castle Black agreed with the Lord Steward's views, he knew. The other half heaped scorn on them. "Seal our gates and plant your fat black arses on the Wall, aye, and the free folk'll come swarming o'er the Bridge o' Skulls or through some gate you thought you'd sealed five hundred years ago," the old forester Dywen had declared loudly over supper, two nights past. "We don't have the men to watch a hundred leagues o' Wall. Tormund Giantsbutt and the bloody Weeper knows it too. Ever see a duck frozen in a pond, with his feet in the ice? It works the same for crows." Most rangers echoed Dywen, whilst the stewards and builders inclined toward Bowen Marsh.

But that was a quandary for another day. Here and now, the problem was food. "We cannot leave King Stannis and his men to starve, even if we wished to," Jon said. "If need be, he could simply take all this at swordpoint. We do not have the men to stop them. The wildlings must be fed as well."

"How, my lord?" asked Bowen Marsh.

Would that I knew. "We will find a way."

By the time they returned to the surface, the shadows of the afternoon were growing long. Clouds streaked the sky like tattered banners, grey and white and torn. The yard outside the armory was empty, but inside Jon found the king's squire awaiting him. Devan was a skinny lad of some twelve years, brown of hair and eye. They found him frozen by the forge, hardly daring to move as Ghost sniffed him up and down. "He won't hurt you," Jon said, but the boy flinched at the sound of his voice, and that sudden motion made the direwolf bare his teeth. "*No!*" Jon said. "Ghost, leave him be. *Away.*" The wolf slunk back to his ox bone, silence on four feet.

Devan looked as pale as Ghost, his face damp with perspiration. "M-my lord. His Grace c-commands your presence." The boy was clad in Baratheon gold and black, with the flaming heart of a queen's man sewn above his own.

"You mean *requests*," said Dolorous Edd. "His Grace *requests* the presence of the lord commander. That's how I'd say it."

"Leave it be, Edd." Jon was in no mood for such squabbles.

"Sir Richard and Ser Justin have returned," said Devan. "Will you come, my lord?"

The wrong-way rangers. Massey and Horpe had ridden south, not north. Whatever they had learned did not concern the Night's Watch, but Jon was curious all the same. "If it would please His Grace." He followed the young squire back across the yard. Ghost padded after them until Jon said, "No. *Stay!*" Instead the direwolf ran off.

In the King's Tower, Jon was stripped of his weapons and admitted to the royal presence. The solar was hot and crowded. Stannis and his captains were gathered over the map of the north. The wrong-way rangers were amongst them. Sigorn was there as well, the young Magnar of Thenn, clad in a leather hauberk sewn with bronze scales. Rattleshirt sat scratching at the manacle on his wrist with a cracked yellow fingernail. Brown stubble covered his sunken cheeks and receding chin, and strands of dirty hair hung across his eyes. "Here he comes," he said when he saw Jon, "the brave boy who slew Mance Rayder when he was caged and bound." The big square-cut gem that adorned his iron cuff glimmered redly. "Do you like my ruby, Snow? A token o' love from Lady Red."

Jon ignored him and took a knee. "Your Grace," announced the squire Devan, "I've brought Lord Snow."

"I can see that. Lord Commander. You know my knights and captains, I believe."

"I have that honor." He had made it a point to learn all he could of the men around the king. *Queen's men, all.* It struck Jon as odd that there were no king's men about the king, but that seemed to be the way of it. The king's men had incurred Stannis's ire on Dragonstone if the talk Jon heard was true.

"There is wine. Or water boiled with lemons."

"Thank you, but no."

"As you wish. I have a gift for you, Lord Snow." The king waved a hand at Rattleshirt. "Him."

Lady Melisandre smiled. "You did say you wanted men, Lord Snow. I believe our Lord of Bones still qualifies."

Jon was aghast. "Your Grace, this man cannot be trusted. If I keep him here, someone will slit his throat for him. If I send him ranging, he'll just go back over to the wildlings."

"Not me. I'm done with those bloody fools." Rattleshirt tapped the ruby on his wrist. "Ask your red witch, bastard."

Melisandre spoke softly in a strange tongue. The ruby at her throat throbbed slowly, and Jon saw that the smaller stone on Rattleshirt's wrist was brightening and darkening as well. "So long as he wears the gem he is bound to me, blood and soul," the red priestess said. "This man will serve you faithfully. The flames do not lie, Lord Snow."

Perhaps not, Jon thought, *but you do.*

"I'll range for you, bastard," Rattleshirt declared. "I'll give you sage counsel or sing you pretty songs, as you prefer. I'll even fight for you. Just don't ask me to wear your cloak."

You are not worthy of one, Jon thought, but he held his tongue. No good would come of squabbling before the king.

King Stannis said, "Lord Snow, tell me of Mors Umber."

The Night's Watch takes no part, Jon thought, but another voice within him said, *Words are not swords.* "The elder of the Greatjon's uncles. Crowfood, they call him. A crow once took him for dead and pecked out his eye. He caught the bird in his fist and bit its head off. When Mors was young he was a fearsome fighter. His sons died on the Trident, his wife in childbed. His only daughter was carried off by wildlings thirty years ago."

"*That's* why he wants the head," said Harwood Fell.

"Can this man Mors be trusted?" asked Stannis.

Has Mors Umber bent the knee? "Your Grace should have him swear an oath before his heart tree."

Godry the Giantslayer guffawed. "I had forgotten that you northmen worship trees."

"What sort of god lets himself be pissed upon by dogs?" asked Farring's crony Clayton Suggs.

Jon chose to ignore them. "Your Grace, might I know if the Umbers have declared for you?"

"Half of them, and only if I meet this Crowfood's price," said Stannis, in an irritated tone. "He wants Mance Rayder's skull for a drinking cup, and he wants a pardon for his brother, who has ridden south to join Bolton. Whoresbane, he's called."

Ser Godry was amused by that as well. "What names these northmen have! Did this one bite the head off some whore?"

Jon regarded him coolly. "You might say so. A whore who tried to rob him, fifty years ago in Oldtown." Odd as it might seem, old Hoarfrost Umber had once believed his youngest son had the makings of a maester. Mors loved to boast about the crow who took his eye, but Hother's tale was only told in whispers . . . most like because the whore he'd disemboweled had been a man. "Have other lords declared for Bolton too?"

The red priestess slid closer to the king. "I saw a town with wooden walls and wooden streets, filled with men. Banners flew above its walls: a moose, a battle-axe, three pine trees, longaxes crossed beneath a crown, a horse's head with fiery eyes."

"Hornwood, Cerwyn, Tallhart, Ryswell, and Dustin," supplied Ser Clayton Suggs. "Traitors, all. Lapdogs of the Lannisters."

"The Ryswells and Dustins are tied to House Bolton by marriage," Jon informed him. "These others have lost their lords in the fighting. I do not know who leads them now. Crowfood is no lapdog, though. Your Grace would do well to accept his terms."

Stannis ground his teeth. "He informs me that Umber will not fight Umber, for any cause."

Jon was not surprised. "If it comes to swords, see where Hother's banner flies and put Mors on the other end of the line."

The Giantslayer disagreed. "You would make His Grace look weak. I say, show our strength. Burn Last Hearth to the ground and ride to war with Crowfood's head mounted on a spear, as a lesson to the next lord who presumes to offer half his homage."

"A fine plan if what you want is every hand in the north raised against you. Half is more than none. The Umbers have no love for the Boltons. If Whoresbane has joined the Bastard, it can only be because the Lannisters hold the Greatjon captive."

"That is his pretext, not his reason," declared Ser Godry. "If the nephew dies in chains, these uncles can claim his lands and lordship for themselves."

"The Greatjon has sons and daughters both. In the north the children of a man's body still come before his uncles, ser."

"Unless they die. Dead children come last everywhere."

"Suggest that in the hearing of Mors Umber, Ser Godry, and you will learn more of death than you might wish."

"I have slain a giant, boy. Why should I fear some flea-ridden northman who paints one on his shield?"

"The giant was running away. Mors won't be."

The big knight flushed. "You have a bold tongue in the king's solar, boy. In the yard you sang a different song."

"Oh, leave off, Godry," said Ser Justin Massey, a loose-limbed, fleshy knight with a ready smile and a mop of flaxen hair. Massey had been one of the wrong-way rangers. "We all know what a big giant sword you have, I'm sure. No need for you to wave it in our faces yet again."

"The only thing waving here is your tongue, Massey."

"*Be quiet*," Stannis snapped. "Lord Snow, attend me. I have lingered here in the hopes that the wildlings would be fool enough to mount another attack upon the Wall. As they will not oblige me, it is time I dealt with my other foes."

"I see." Jon's tone was wary. *What does he want of me?* "I have no love for Lord Bolton or his son, but the Night's Watch cannot take up arms against them. Our vows prohibit—"

"I know all about your vows. Spare me your rectitude, Lord Snow, I have strength enough without you. I have a mind to march against the Dreadfort." When he saw the shock on Jon's face, he smiled. "Does that surprise you? Good. What surprises one Snow may yet surprise another. The Bastard of Bolton has gone south, taking Hother Umber with him. On that Mors Umber and Arnolf Karstark are agreed. That can only mean a strike at Moat Cailin, to open the way for his lord father to return to the north. The bastard must think I am too busy with the wildlings to trouble him. Well and good. The boy has shown me his throat. I mean to rip it out. Roose Bolton may regain the north, but when he does he will find that his castle, herds, and harvest all belong to me. If I take the Dreadfort unawares—"

"You won't," Jon blurted.

It was as if he whacked a wasps' nest with a stick. One of the queen's men laughed, one spat, one muttered a curse, and the rest all tried to talk at once. "The boy has milkwater in his veins," said Ser Godry the Giant-slayer. And Lord Sweet huffed, "The craven sees an outlaw behind every blade of grass."

Stannis raised a hand for silence. "Explain your meaning."

Where to begin? Jon moved to the map. Candles had been placed at its corners to keep the hide from rolling up. A finger of warm wax was puddling out across the Bay of Seals, slow as a glacier. "To reach the Dreadfort, Your Grace must travel down the kingsroad past the Last River, turn south by east and cross the Lonely Hills." He pointed. "Those are Umber lands, where they know every tree and every rock. The kingsroad runs along their western marches for a hundred leagues. Mors will cut your host to pieces unless you meet his terms and win him to your cause."

"Very well. Let us say I do that."

"That will bring you to the Dreadfort," said Jon, "but unless your host can outmarch a raven or a line of beacon fires, the castle will know of your approach. It will be an easy thing for Ramsay Bolton to cut off your retreat and leave you far from the Wall, without food or refuge, surrounded by your foes."

"Only if he abandons his siege of Moat Cailin."

"Moat Cailin will fall before you ever reach the Dreadfort. Once Lord Roose has joined his strength to Ramsay's, they will have you outnumbered five to one."

"My brother won battles at worse odds."

"You assume Moat Cailin will fall quickly, Snow," objected Justin Massey, "but the ironmen are doughty fighters, and I've heard it said that the Moat has never been taken."

"From the south. A small garrison in Moat Cailin can play havoc with any army coming up the causeway, but the ruins are vulnerable from the north and east." Jon turned back to Stannis. "Sire, this is a bold stroke, but the risk—" *The Night's Watch takes no part. Baratheon or Bolton should be the same to me.* "If Roose Bolton should catch you beneath his walls with his main strength, it will be the end for all of you."

"Risk is part of war," declared Ser Richard Horpe, a lean knight with a ravaged face whose quilted doublet showed three death's-head moths on a field of ash and bone. "Every battle is a gamble, Snow. The man who does nothing also takes a risk."

"There are risks and risks, Ser Richard. This one . . . it is too much, too soon, too far away. I know the Dreadfort. It is a strong castle, all of stone, with thick walls and massive towers. With winter coming you will find it well provisioned. Centuries ago, House Bolton rose up against the King in the North, and Harlon Stark laid siege to the Dreadfort. It took him two years to starve them out. To have any hope of taking the castle, Your Grace would need siege engines, towers, battering rams . . ."

"Siege towers can be raised if need be," Stannis said. "Trees can be felled for rams if rams are required. Arnolf Karstark writes that fewer than fifty men remain at the Dreadfort, half of them servants. A strong castle weakly held is weak."

"Fifty men inside a castle are worth five hundred outside."

"That depends upon the men," said Richard Horpe. "These will be greybeards and green boys, the men this bastard did not deem fit for battle. Our own men were blooded and tested on the Blackwater, and they are led by knights."

"You saw how we went through the wildlings." Ser Justin pushed back a lock of flaxen hair. "The Karstarks have sworn to join us at the Dreadfort, and we will have our wildlings as well. Three hundred men of fighting age. Lord Harwood made a count as they were passing through the gate. Their women fight as well."

Stannis gave him a sour look. "Not for me, ser. I want no widows wailing in my wake. The women will remain here, with the old, the wounded, and the children. They will serve as hostages for the loyalty of their husbands and fathers. The wildling men will form my van. The Magnar will command them, with their own chiefs as serjeants. First, though, we must needs arm them."

He means to plunder our armory, Jon realized. *Food and clothing, land and castles, now weapons. He draws me in deeper every day.* Words might not be swords, but *swords* were swords. "I could find three hundred spears," he said, reluctantly. "Helms as well, if you'll take them old and dinted and red with rust."

"Armor?" asked the Magnar. "Plate? Mail?"

"When Donal Noye died we lost our armorer." The rest Jon left unspoken. *Give the wildlings mail and they'll be twice as great a danger to the realm.*

"Boiled leather will suffice," said Ser Godry. "Once we've tasted battle, the survivors can loot the dead."

The few who live that long. If Stannis placed the free folk in the van, most would perish quickly. "Drinking from Mance Rayder's skull may give Mors Umber pleasure, but seeing wildlings cross his lands will not. The free folk have been raiding the Umbers since the Dawn of Days, crossing the Bay of Seals for gold and sheep and women. One of those carried off was Crowfood's *daughter.* Your Grace, leave the wildlings here. Taking them will only serve to turn my lord father's bannermen against you."

"Your father's bannermen seem to have no liking for my cause in any case. I must assume they see me as . . . what was it that you called me, Lord Snow? *Another doomed pretender?*" Stannis stared at the map. For a long moment the only sound was the king grinding his teeth. "Leave me. All of you. Lord Snow, remain."

The brusque dismissal did not sit well with Justin Massey, but he had no choice but to smile and withdraw. Horpe followed him out, after giving Jon a measured look. Clayton Suggs drained his cup dry and muttered something to Harwood Fell that made the younger man laugh. *Boy* was part of it. Suggs was an upjumped hedge knight, as crude as he was strong. The last man to take his leave was Rattleshirt. At the door, he gave Jon a mocking bow, grinning through a mouthful of brown and broken teeth.

All of you did not seem to include Lady Melisandre. *The king's red shadow.* Stannis called to Devan for more lemon water. When his cup was filled the king drank, and said, "Horpe and Massey aspire to your father's seat. Massey wants the wildling princess too. He once served my brother Robert as squire and acquired his appetite for female flesh. Horpe will take Val to wife if I command it, but it is battle he lusts for. As a squire he dreamed of a white cloak, but Cersei Lannister spoke against him and Robert passed him over. Perhaps rightly. Ser Richard is too fond of killing. Which would you have as Lord of Winterfell, Snow? The smiler or the slayer?"

Jon said, "Winterfell belongs to my sister Sansa."

"I have heard all I need to hear of Lady Lannister and her claim." The king set the cup aside. "*You* could bring the north to me. Your father's bannermen would rally to the son of Eddard Stark. Even Lord Too-Fat-to-Sit-a-Horse. White Harbor would give me a ready source of supply and a secure base to which I could retreat at need. It is not too late to amend your folly, Snow. Take a knee and swear that bastard sword to me, and rise as Jon Stark, Lord of Winterfell and Warden of the North."

How many times will he make me say it? "My sword is sworn to the Night's Watch."

Stannis looked disgusted. "Your father was a stubborn man as well. *Honor*, he called it. Well, honor has its costs, as Lord Eddard learned to his sorrow. If it gives you any solace, Horpe and Massey are doomed to disappointment. I am more inclined to bestow Winterfell upon Arnolf Karstark. A good northman."

"A northman." *Better a Karstark than a Bolton or a Greyjoy*, Jon told himself, but the thought gave him little solace. "The Karstarks abandoned my brother amongst his enemies."

"After your brother took off Lord Rickard's head. Arnolf was a thousand leagues away. He has Stark blood in him. The blood of Winterfell."

"No more than half the other Houses of the north."

"Those other Houses have not declared for me."

"Arnolf Karstark is an old man with a crooked back, and even in his youth he was never the fighter Lord Rickard was. The rigors of the campaign may well kill him."

"He has heirs," Stannis snapped. "Two sons, six grandsons, some daughters. If Robert had fathered trueborn sons, many who are dead might still be living."

"Your Grace would do better with Mors Crowfood."

"The Dreadfort will be the proof of that."

"Then you mean to go ahead with this attack?"

"Despite the counsel of the great Lord Snow? Aye. Horpe and Massey may be ambitious, but they are not wrong. I dare not sit idle whilst Roose Bolton's star waxes and mine wanes. I must strike and show the north that I am still a man to fear."

"The merman of Manderly was not amongst those banners Lady Melisandre saw in her fires," Jon said. "If you had White Harbor and Lord Wyman's knights . . ."

"*If* is a word for fools. We have had no word from Davos. It may be he never reached White Harbor. Arnolf Karstark writes that the storms have been fierce upon the narrow sea. Be that as it may. I have no time to grieve, nor wait upon the whims of Lord Too-Fat. I must consider White Harbor lost to me. Without a son of Winterfell to stand beside me, I can only hope to win the north by battle. That requires stealing a leaf from my brother's book. Not that Robert ever read one. I must deal my foes a mortal blow before they know that I am on them."

Jon realized that his words were wasted. Stannis would take the Dreadfort or die in the attempt. *The Night's Watch takes no part*, a voice said, but another replied, *Stannis fights for the realm, the ironmen for thralls and plunder.* "Your Grace, I know where you might find more men. Give me the wildlings, and I will gladly tell you where and how."

"I gave you Rattleshirt. Be content with him."

"I want them all."

"Some of your own Sworn Brothers would have me believe that you are half a wildling yourself. Is it true?"

"To you they are only arrow fodder. I can make better use of them upon the Wall. Give them to me to do with as I will, and I'll show you where to find your victory . . . and men as well."

Stannis rubbed the back of his neck. "You haggle like a crone with a codfish, Lord Snow. Did Ned Stark father you on some fishwife? How many men?"

"Two thousand. Perhaps three."

"Three *thousand*? What manner of men are these?"

"Proud. Poor. Prickly where their honor is concerned but fierce fighters."

"This had best not be some bastard's trick. Will I trade three hundred fighters for three thousand? Aye, I will. I am not an utter fool. If I leave the girl with you as well, do I have your word that you will keep our princess closely?"

She is not a princess. "As you wish, Your Grace."

"Do I need to make you swear an oath before a tree?"

"No." *Was that a jape?* With Stannis, it was hard to tell.

"Done, then. Now, where are these men?"

"You'll find them here." Jon spread his burned hand across the map, west of the kingsroad and south of the Gift.

"Those mountains?" Stannis grew suspicious. "I see no castles marked there. No roads, no towns, no villages."

"The map is not the land, my father often said. Men have lived in the high valleys and mountain meadows for thousands of years, ruled by their clan chiefs. Petty lords, you would call them, though they do not use such titles amongst themselves. Clan champions fight with huge two-handed greatswords, while the common men sling stones and batter one another with staffs of mountain ash. A quarrelsome folk, it must be said. When they are not fighting one another, they tend their herds, fish the Bay of Ice, and breed the hardiest mounts you'll ever ride."

"And they will fight for me, you believe?"

"If you ask them."

"Why should I beg for what is owed me?"

"*Ask*, I said, not *beg*." Jon pulled back his hand. "It is no good sending messages. Your Grace will need to go to them yourself. Eat their bread and salt, drink their ale, listen to their pipers, praise the beauty of their daughters and the courage of their sons, and you'll have their swords. The clans have not seen a king since Torrhen Stark bent his knee. Your coming does them honor. *Command* them to fight for you, and they will look at one another and say, 'Who is this man? He is no king of mine.'"

"How many clans are you speaking of?"

"Two score, small and large. Flint, Wull, Norrey, Liddle . . . win Old Flint and Big Bucket, the rest will follow."

"Big *Bucket*?"

"The Wull. He has the biggest belly in the mountains, and the most men. The Wulls fish the Bay of Ice and warn their little ones that ironmen will carry them off if they don't behave. To reach them Your Grace must pass through the Norrey's lands, however. They live the nearest to the Gift and have always been good friends to the Watch. I could give you guides."

"Could?" Stannis missed little. "Or will?"

"Will. You'll need them. And some sure-footed garrons too. The paths up there are little more than goat tracks."

"Goat tracks?" The king's eyes narrowed. "I speak of moving swiftly, and you waste my time with *goat tracks*?"

"When the Young Dragon conquered Dorne, he used a goat track to bypass the Dornish watchtowers on the Boneway."

"I know that tale as well, but Daeron made too much of it in that vainglorious book of his. Ships won that war, not goat tracks. Oakenfist broke the Planky Town and swept halfway up the Greenblood whilst the main

Dornish strength was engaged in the Prince's Pass." Stannis drummed his fingers on the map. "These mountain lords will not hinder my passage?"

"Only with feasts. Each will try to outdo the others with his hospitality. My lord father said he never ate half so well as when visiting the clans."

"For three thousand men, I suppose I can endure some pipes and porridge," the king said, though his tone begrudged even that.

Jon turned to Melisandre. "My lady, fair warning. The old gods are strong in those mountains. The clansmen will not suffer insults to their heart trees."

That seemed to amuse her. "Have no fear, Jon Snow, I will not trouble your mountain savages and their dark gods. My place is here with you and your brave brothers."

That was the last thing Jon Snow would have wanted, but before he could object, the king said, "Where would you have me lead these stalwarts if not against the Dreadfort?"

Jon glanced down at the map. "Deepwood Motte." He tapped it with a finger. "If Bolton means to fight the ironmen, so must you. Deepwood is a motte-and-bailey castle in the midst of thick forest, easy to creep up on unawares. A *wooden* castle, defended by an earthen dike and a palisade of logs. The going will be slower through the mountains, admittedly, but up there your host can move unseen, to emerge almost at the gates of Deepwood."

Stannis rubbed his jaw. "When Balon Greyjoy rose the first time, I beat the ironmen at sea, where they are fiercest. On land, taken unawares . . . aye. I have won a victory over the wildlings and their King-Beyond-the-Wall. If I can smash the ironmen as well, the north will know it has a king again."

And I will have a thousand wildlings, thought Jon, *and no way to feed even half that number.*

TYRION

The *Shy Maid* moved through the fog like a blind man groping his way down an unfamiliar hall.

Septa Lemore was praying. The mists muffled the sound of her voice, making it seem small and hushed. Griff paced the deck, mail clinking softly beneath his wolfskin cloak. From time to time he touched his sword, as if to make certain that it still hung at his side. Rolly Duckfield was pushing at the starboard pole, Yandry at the larboard. Ysilla had the tiller.

"I do not like this place," Haldon Halfmaester muttered.

"Frightened of a little fog?" mocked Tyrion, though in truth there was quite a lot of fog. At the prow of the *Shy Maid*, Young Griff stood with the third pole, to push them away from hazards as they loomed up through the mists. The lanterns had been lit fore and aft, but the fog was so thick that all the dwarf could see from amidships was a light floating out ahead of him and another following behind. His own task was to tend the brazier and make certain that the fire did not go out.

"This is no common fog, Hugor Hill," Ysilla insisted. "It stinks of sorcery, as you would know if you had a nose to smell it. Many a voyager has been lost here, poleboats and pirates and great river galleys too. They wander forlorn through the mists, searching for a sun they cannot find until madness or hunger claim their lives. There are restless spirits in the air here and tormented souls below the water."

"There's one now," said Tyrion. Off to starboard a hand large enough to crush the boat was reaching up from the murky depths. Only the tops of two fingers broke the river's surface, but as the *Shy Maid* eased on past he could see the rest of the hand rippling below the water and a pale face looking up. Though his tone was light, he was uneasy. This was a bad place, rank with despair and death. *Ysilla is not wrong. This fog is not natural.* Something foul grew in the waters here, and festered in the air. *Small wonder the stone men go mad.*

"You should not make mock," warned Ysilla. "The whispering dead hate the warm and quick and ever seek for more damned souls to join them."

"I doubt they have a shroud my size." The dwarf stirred the coals with a poker.

"Hatred does not stir the stone men half so much as hunger." Haldon Halfmaester had wrapped a yellow scarf around his mouth and nose, muffling his voice. "Nothing any sane man would want to eat grows in these fogs. Thrice each year the triarchs of Volantis send a galley upriver with provisions, but the mercy ships are oft late and sometimes bring more mouths than food."

Young Griff said, "There must be fish in the river."

"I would not eat any fish taken from these waters," said Ysilla. "I would not."

"We'd do well not to breathe the fog either," said Haldon. "Garin's Curse is all about us."

The only way not to breathe the fog is not to breathe. "Garin's Curse is only greyscale," said Tyrion. The curse was oft seen in children, especially in damp, cold climes. The afflicted flesh stiffened, calcified, and cracked, though the dwarf had read that greyscale's progress could be stayed by limes, mustard poultices, and scalding-hot baths (the maesters said) or by prayer, sacrifice, and fasting (the septons insisted). Then the disease passed, leaving its young victims disfigured but alive. Maesters and septons alike agreed that children marked by greyscale could never be touched by the rarer mortal form of the affliction, nor by its terrible swift cousin, the grey plague. "Damp is said to be the culprit," he said. "Foul humors in the air. Not curses."

"The conquerors did not believe either, Hugor Hill," said Ysilla. "The men of Volantis and Valyria hung Garin in a golden cage and made mock as he called upon his Mother to destroy them. But in the night the waters rose and drowned them, and from that day to this they have not rested. They are down there still beneath the water, they who were once the lords of fire. Their cold breath rises from the murk to make these fogs, and their flesh has turned as stony as their hearts."

The stump of Tyrion's nose was itching fiercely. He gave it a scratch. *The old woman may be right. This place is no good. I feel as if I am back in the privy again, watching my father die.* He would go mad as well if he had to spend his days in this grey soup whilst his flesh and bones turned to stone.

Young Griff did not seem to share his misgivings. "Let them try and trouble us, we'll show them what we're made of."

"We are made of blood and bone, in the image of the Father and the Mother," said Septa Lemore. "Make no vainglorious boasts, I beg you. Pride is a grievous sin. The stone men were proud as well, and the Shrouded Lord was proudest of them all."

The heat from the glowing coals brought a flush to Tyrion's face. "Is there a Shrouded Lord? Or is he just some tale?"

"The Shrouded Lord has ruled these mists since Garin's day," said Yandry. "Some say that he himself is Garin, risen from his watery grave."

"The dead do not rise," insisted Haldon Halfmaester, "and no man lives a thousand years. Yes, there is a Shrouded Lord. There have been a score of them. When one dies another takes his place. This one is a corsair from the Basilisk Islands who believed the Rhoyne would offer richer pickings than the Summer Sea."

"Aye, I've heard that too," said Duck, "but there's another tale I like better. The one that says he's not like t'other stone men, that he started as a statue till a grey woman came out of the fog and kissed him with lips as cold as ice."

"*Enough,*" said Griff. "Be quiet, all of you."

Septa Lemore sucked in her breath. "*What was that?*"

"Where?" Tyrion saw nothing but the fog.

"Something moved. I saw the water rippling."

"A turtle," the prince announced cheerfully. "A big 'snapper, that's all it was." He thrust his pole out ahead of them and pushed them away from a towering green obelisk.

The fog clung to them, damp and chilly. A sunken temple loomed up out of the greyness as Yandry and Duck leaned upon their poles and paced slowly from prow to stern, pushing. They passed a marble stair that spiraled up from the mud and ended jaggedly in air. Beyond, half-seen, were other shapes: shattered spires, headless statues, trees with roots bigger than their boat.

"This was the most beautiful city on the river, and the richest," said Yandry. "Chroyane, the festival city."

Too rich, thought Tyrion, *too beautiful. It is never wise to tempt the dragons.* The drowned city was all around them. A half-seen shape flapped by overhead, pale leathery wings beating at the fog. The dwarf craned his head around to get a better look, but the thing was gone as suddenly as it had appeared.

Not long after, another light floated into view. "Boat," a voice called across the water, faintly. "Who are you?"

"*Shy Maid*," Yandry shouted back.

"*Kingfisher*. Up or down?"

"Down. Hides and honey, ale and tallow."

"Up. Knives and needles, lace and linen, spice wine."

"What word from old Volantis?" Yandry called.

"War," the word came back.

"Where?" Griff shouted. "When?"

"When the year turns," came the answer, "Nyessos and Malaquo go hand in hand, and the elephants show stripes." The voice faded as the other boat moved away from them. They watched its light dwindle and disappear.

"Is it wise to shout through the fog at boats we cannot see?" asked Tyrion. "What if they were pirates?" They had been fortunate where the pirates were concerned, slipping down Dagger Lake by night, unseen and unmolested. Once Duck had caught a glimpse of a hull that he insisted belonged to Urho the Unwashed. The *Shy Maid* had been upwind, however, and Urho—if Urho it had been—had shown no interest in them.

"The pirates will not sail into the Sorrows," said Yandry.

"Elephants with stripes?" Griff muttered. "What is that about? Nyessos and Malaquo? Illyrio has paid Triarch Nyessos enough to own him eight times over."

"In gold or cheese?" quipped Tyrion.

Griff rounded on him. "Unless you can cut this fog with your next witticism, keep it to yourself."

Yes, Father, the dwarf almost said. *I'll be quiet. Thank you.* He did not know these Volantenes, yet it seemed to him that elephants and tigers might have good reason to make common cause when faced with dragons. *Might be the cheesemonger has misjudged the situation. You can buy a man with gold, but only blood and steel will keep him true.*

The little man stirred the coals again and blew on them to make them burn brighter. *I hate this. I hate this fog, I hate this place, and I am less than fond of Griff.* Tyrion still had the poison mushrooms he had plucked from the grounds of Illyrio's manse, and there were days when he was sore tempted to slip them into Griff's supper. The trouble was, Griff scarce seemed to eat.

Duck and Yandry pushed against the poles. Ysilla turned the tiller. Young Griff pushed the *Shy Maid* away from a broken tower whose windows stared down like blind black eyes. Overhead her sail hung limp and heavy. The water deepened under her hull, until their poles could not touch bottom, but still the current pushed them downstream, until . . .

All Tyrion could see was something massive rising from the river, humped and ominous. He took it for a hill looming above a wooded island, or some colossal rock overgrown with moss and ferns and hidden by the fog. As the *Shy Maid* drew nearer, though, the shape of it came clearer. A wooden keep could be seen beside the water, rotted and overgrown. Slender spires took form above it, some of them snapped off like broken spears. Roofless towers appeared and disappeared, thrusting blindly upward. Halls and galleries drifted past: graceful buttresses, delicate arches, fluted columns, terraces and bowers.

All ruined, all desolate, all fallen.

The grey moss grew thickly here, covering the fallen stones in great mounds and bearding all the towers. Black vines crept in and out of windows, through doors and over archways, up the sides of high stone walls. The fog concealed three-quarters of the palace, but what they glimpsed was more than enough for Tyrion to know that this island fastness had been ten times the size of the Red Keep once and a hundred times more beautiful. He knew where he was. "The Palace of Love," he said softly.

"That was the Rhoynar name," said Haldon Halfmaester, "but for a thousand years this has been the Palace of Sorrow."

The ruin was sad enough, but knowing what it had been made it even sadder. *There was laughter here once,* Tyrion thought. *There were gardens bright with flowers and fountains sparkling golden in the sun. These steps once rang to the sound of lovers' footsteps, and beneath that broken dome marriages beyond count were sealed with a kiss.* His thoughts turned to Tysha, who had so briefly been his lady wife. *It was Jaime,* he thought, despairing. *He was my own blood, my big strong brother. When I was small he brought me toys, barrel hoops and blocks and a carved wooden lion. He gave me my first pony and taught me how to ride him. When he said that he had bought you for me, I never doubted him. Why would I? He was Jaime, and you were just some girl who'd played a part. I had feared it from the start, from the moment you first smiled at me and let me touch your hand. My own father could not love me. Why would you if not for gold?*

Through the long grey fingers of the fog, he heard again the deep shuddering *thrum* of a bowstring snapping taut, the grunt Lord Tywin made as the quarrel took him beneath the belly, the slap of cheeks on stone as he sat back down to die. "Wherever whores go," he said. *And where is that?* Tyrion wanted to ask him. *Where did Tysha go, Father?* "How much more of this fog must we endure?"

"Another hour should see us clear of the Sorrows," said Haldon Half-maester. "From there on, this should be a pleasure cruise. There's a village around every bend along the lower Rhoyne. Orchards and vineyards and fields of grain ripening in the sun, fisherfolk on the water, hot baths and sweet wines. Selhorys, Valysar, and Volon Therys are walled towns so large they would be cities in the Seven Kingdoms. I believe I'll—"

"Light ahead," warned Young Griff.

Tyrion saw it too. Kingfisher, *or another poleboat,* he told himself, but somehow he knew that was not right. His nose itched. He scratched at it savagely. The light grew brighter as the *Shy Maid* approached it. A soft star in the distance, it glimmered faintly through the fog, beckoning them on. Shortly it became two lights, then three: a ragged row of beacons rising from the water.

"The Bridge of Dream," Griff named it. "There will be stone men on the span. Some may start to wail at our approach, but they are not like to molest us. Most stone men are feeble creatures, clumsy, lumbering, witless. Near the end they all go mad, but that is when they are most dangerous. If need be, fend them off with the torches. On no account let them touch you."

"They may not even see us," said Haldon Halfmaester. "The fog will hide us from them until we are almost at the bridge, and then we will be past before they know that we are here."

Stone eyes are blind eyes, thought Tyrion. The mortal form of greyscale began in the extremities, he knew: a tingling in a fingertip, a toenail turning black, a loss of feeling. As the numbness crept into the hand, or stole past the foot and up the leg, the flesh stiffened and grew cold and the victim's skin took on a greyish hue, resembling stone. He had heard it said that there were three good cures for greyscale: axe and sword and cleaver. Hacking off afflicted parts did sometimes stop the spread of the disease, Tyrion knew, but not always. Many a man had sacrificed one arm or foot, only to find the other going grey. Once that happened, hope was gone. Blindness was common when the stone reached the face. In the final stages the curse turned inward, to muscles, bones, and inner organs.

Ahead of them, the bridge grew larger. *The Bridge of Dream,* Griff called it, but this dream was smashed and broken. Pale stone arches marched off into the fog, reaching from the Palace of Sorrow to the river's western bank. Half of them had collapsed, pulled down by the weight of the grey moss that draped them and the thick black vines that snaked upward from the water. The broad wooden span of the bridge had rotted through, but some of the lamps that lined the way were still aglow. As the *Shy Maid* drew closer, Tyrion could see the shapes of stone men moving in the light, shuffling aimlessly around the lamps like slow grey moths. Some were naked, others clad in shrouds.

Griff drew his longsword. "Yollo, light the torches. Lad, take Lemore back to her cabin and stay with her."

Young Griff gave his father a stubborn look. "Lemore knows where her cabin is. I want to stay."

"We are sworn to protect you," Lemore said softly.

"I don't need to be protected. I can use a sword as well as Duck. I'm half a knight."

"And half a boy," said Griff. "Do as you are told. Now."

The youth cursed under his breath and flung his pole down onto the deck. The sound echoed queerly in the fog, and for a moment it was as if poles were falling around them. "Why should I run and hide? Haldon is staying, and Ysilla. Even Hugor."

"Aye," said Tyrion, "but I'm small enough to hide behind a duck." He thrust half a dozen torches into the brazier's glowing coals and watched the oiled rags flare up. *Don't stare at the fire,* he told himself. The flames would leave him night blind.

"You're a *dwarf,*" Young Griff said scornfully.

"My secret is revealed," Tyrion agreed. "Aye, I'm less than half of Haldon, and no one gives a mummer's fart whether I live or die." *Least of all me.* "You, though . . . you are everything."

"Dwarf," said Griff, "I warned you—"

A wail came shivering through the fog, faint and high.

Lemore whirled, trembling. "Seven save us all."

The broken bridge was a bare five yards ahead. Around its piers, the water rippled white as the foam from a madman's mouth. Forty feet above, the stone men moaned and muttered beneath a flickering lamp. Most took no more notice of the *Shy Maid* than of a drifting log. Tyrion clutched his torch tighter and found that he was holding his breath. And then they were beneath the bridge, white walls heavy with curtains of grey fungus looming to either side, water foaming angrily around them. For a moment it looked as though they might crash into the right-hand pier, but Duck raised his pole and shoved off, back into the center of the channel, and a few heartbeats later they were clear.

Tyrion had no sooner exhaled than Young Griff grabbed hold of his arm. "What do you mean? I am *everything*? What did you mean by that? Why am I everything?"

"Why," said Tyrion, "if the stone men had taken Yandry or Griff or our lovely Lemore, we would have grieved for them and gone on. Lose *you*, and this whole enterprise is undone, and all those years of feverish plotting by the cheesemonger and the eunuch will have been for naught . . . isn't that so?"

The boy looked to Griff. "He knows who I am."

If I did not know before, I would now. By then the *Shy Maid* was well downstream of the Bridge of Dream. All that remained was a dwindling light astern, and soon enough that would be gone as well. "You're Young Griff, son of Griff the sellsword," said Tyrion. "Or perhaps you are the Warrior in mortal guise. Let me take a closer look." He held up his torch, so that the light washed over Young Griff's face.

"Leave off," Griff commanded, "or you will wish you had."

The dwarf ignored him. "The blue hair makes your eyes seem blue, that's good. And the tale of how you color it in honor of your dead Tyroshi mother was so touching it almost made me cry. Still, a curious man might wonder why some sellsword's whelp would need a soiled septa to instruct him in the Faith, or a chainless maester to tutor him in history and tongues. And a clever man might question why your father would engage a hedge knight to train you in arms instead of simply sending you off to apprentice with one of the free companies. It is almost as if someone wanted to keep you hidden whilst still preparing you for . . . what? Now, there's a puzzlement, but I'm sure that in time it will come to me. I must admit, you have noble features for a dead boy."

The boy flushed. *"I am not dead."*

"How not? My lord father wrapped your corpse in a crimson cloak and laid you down beside your sister at the foot of the Iron Throne, his gift to the new king. Those who had the stomach to lift the cloak said that half your head was gone."

The lad backed off a step, confused. "Your—?"

"—*father*, aye. Tywin of House Lannister. Perhaps you may have heard of him."

Young Griff hesitated. *"Lannister?* Your father—"

"—is dead. At my hand. If it please Your Grace to call me Yollo or Hugor, so be it, but know that I was born Tyrion of House Lannister, true-born son of Tywin and Joanna, both of whom I slew. Men will tell you that I am a kingslayer, a kinslayer, and a liar, and all of that is true . . . but then, we are a company of liars, are we not? Take your feigned father. *Griff*, is it?" The dwarf sniggered. "You should thank the gods that Varys the Spider is a part of this plot of yours. *Griff* would not have fooled the cockless wonder for an instant, no more than it did me. *No lord*, my lordship says, *no knight*. And I'm no dwarf. Just saying a thing does not make it true. Who better to raise Prince Rhaegar's infant son than Prince Rhaegar's dear friend Jon Connington, once Lord of Griffin's Roost and Hand of the King?"

"Be quiet." Griff's voice was uneasy.

On the larboard side of the boat, a huge stone hand was visible just below the water. Two fingers broke the surface. *How many of those are there?* Tyrion wondered. A trickle of moisture ran down his spine and made him shudder. The Sorrows drifted by them. Peering through the mists, he glimpsed a broken spire, a headless hero, an ancient tree torn from the ground and upended, its huge roots twisting through the roof and windows of a broken dome. *Why does all of this seem so familiar?*

Straight on, a tilted stairway of pale marble rose up out of the dark water in a graceful spiral, ending abruptly ten feet above their heads. *No*, thought Tyrion, *that is not possible.*

"Ahead." Lemore's voice was shivery. "A light."

All of them looked. All of them saw it.

"*Kingfisher*," said Griff. "Her, or some other like her." But he drew his sword again.

No one said a word. The *Shy Maid* moved with the current. Her sail had not been raised since she first entered the Sorrows. She had no way to move but with the river. Duck stood squinting, clutching his pole with both hands. After a time even Yandry stopped pushing. Every eye was on the distant light. As they grew closer, it turned into two lights. Then three.

"The Bridge of Dream," said Tyrion.

"Inconceivable," said Haldon Halfmaester. "We've left the bridge behind. Rivers only run one way."

"Mother Rhoyne runs how she will," murmured Yandry.

"Seven save us," said Lemore.

Up ahead, the stone men on the span began to wail. A few were pointing down at them. "Haldon, get the prince below," commanded Griff.

It was too late. The current had them in its teeth. They drifted inexorably toward the bridge. Yandry stabbed out with his pole to keep them from smashing into a pier. The thrust shoved them sideways, through a curtain of pale grey moss. Tyrion felt tendrils brush against his face, soft as a whore's fingers. Then there was a crash behind him, and the deck tilted so suddenly that he almost lost his feet and went pitching over the side.

A stone man crashed down into the boat.

He landed on the cabin roof, so heavily that the *Shy Maid* seemed to rock, and roared a word down at them in a tongue that Tyrion did not know. A second stone man followed, landing back beside the tiller. The weathered planks splintered beneath the impact, and Ysilla let out a shriek.

Duck was closest to her. The big man did not waste time reaching for his sword. Instead he swung his pole, slamming it into the stone man's chest and knocking him off the boat into the river, where he sank at once without a sound.

Griff was on the second man the instant he shambled down off the cabin roof. With a sword in his right hand and a torch in his left, he drove the creature backwards. As the current swept the *Shy Maid* beneath the bridge, their shifting shadows danced upon the mossy walls. When the stone man moved aft, Duck blocked his way, pole in hand. When he went forward, Haldon Halfmaester waved a second torch at him and drove him back. He had no choice but to come straight at Griff. The captain slid aside, his blade flashing. A spark flew where the steel bit into the stone man's calcified grey flesh, but his arm tumbled to the deck all the same. Griff kicked the limb aside. Yandry and Duck had come up with their poles. Together they forced the creature over the side and into the black waters of the Rhoyne.

By then the *Shy Maid* had drifted out from under the broken bridge. "Did we get them all?" asked Duck. "How many jumped?"

"Two," said Tyrion, shivering.

"Three," said Haldon. "Behind you."

The dwarf turned, and there he stood.

The leap had shattered one of his legs, and a jagged piece of pale bone jutted out through the rotted cloth of his breeches and the grey meat beneath. The broken bone was speckled with brown blood, but still he lurched forward, reaching for Young Griff. His hand was grey and stiff, but blood oozed between his knuckles as he tried to close his fingers to grasp. The boy stood staring, as still as if he too were made of stone. His hand was on his sword hilt, but he seemed to have forgotten why.

Tyrion kicked the lad's leg out from under him and leapt over him when he fell, thrusting his torch into the stone man's face to send him stumbling backwards on his shattered leg, flailing at the flames with stiff grey hands. The dwarf waddled after him, slashing with the torch, jabbing it at the stone man's eyes. *A little farther. Back, one more step, another.* They were at the edge of the deck when the creature rushed him, grabbed the torch, and ripped it from his hands. *Bugger me*, thought Tyrion.

The stone man flung the torch away. There was a soft *hiss* as the black waters quenched the flames. The stone man howled. He had been a Summer Islander, before; his jaw and half his cheek had turned to stone, but his skin was black as midnight where it was not grey. Where he had grasped the torch, his skin had cracked and split. Blood was seeping from his knuckles though he did not seem to feel it. That was some small mercy, Tyrion supposed. Though mortal, greyscale was supposedly not painful.

"*Stand aside!*" someone shouted, far away, and another voice said, "The prince! Protect the boy!" The stone man staggered forward, his hands outstretched and grasping.

Tyrion drove a shoulder into him.

It felt like slamming into a castle wall, but this castle stood upon a shattered leg. The stone man went over backwards, grabbing hold of Tyrion as he fell. They hit the river with a towering splash, and Mother Rhoyne swallowed up the two of them.

The sudden cold hit Tyrion like a hammer. As he sank he felt a stone hand fumbling at his face. Another closed around his arm, dragging him down into darkness. Blind, his nose full of river, choking, sinking, he kicked and twisted and fought to pry the clutching fingers off his arm, but the stone fingers were unyielding. Air bubbled from his lips. The world was black and growing blacker. He could not breathe.

There are worse ways to die than drowning. And if truth be told, he had perished long ago, back in King's Landing. It was only his revenant who remained, the small vengeful ghost who throttled Shae and put a crossbow bolt through the great Lord Tywin's bowels. No man would mourn the thing that he'd become. *I'll haunt the Seven Kingdoms*, he thought, sinking deeper. *They would not love me living, so let them dread me dead.*

When he opened his mouth to curse them all, black water filled his lungs, and the dark closed in around him.

DAVOS

His lordship will hear you now, smuggler."

The knight wore silver armor, his greaves and gauntlet inlaid with niello to suggest flowing fronds of seaweed. The helm beneath his arm was the head of the merling king, with a crown of mother-of-pearl and a jutting beard of jet and jade. His own beard was as grey as the winter sea.

Davos rose. "May I know your name, ser?"

"Ser Marlon Manderly." He was a head taller than Davos and three stones heavier, with slate-grey eyes and a haughty way of speaking. "I have the honor to be Lord Wyman's cousin and commander of his garrison. Follow me."

Davos had come to White Harbor as an envoy, but they had made him a captive. His chambers were large, airy, and handsomely furnished, but there were guards outside his doors. From his window he could see the streets of White Harbor beyond the castle walls, but he was not allowed to walk them. He could see the harbor too, and had watched *Merry Midwife* make her way down the firth. Casso Mogat had waited four days instead of three before departing. Another fortnight had passed since then.

Lord Manderly's household guard wore cloaks of blue-green wool and carried silver tridents in place of common spears. One went before him, one behind, and one to either side. They walked past the faded banners, broken shields, and rusted swords of a hundred ancient victories, and a score of wooden figures, cracked and worm-riddled, that could only have adorned the prows of ships.

Two marble mermen flanked his lordship's court, Fishfoot's smaller cousins. As the guards threw open the doors, a herald slammed the butt of his staff against an old plank floor. "*Ser Davos of House Seaworth,*" he called in a ringing voice.

As many times as he had visited White Harbor, Davos had never set foot inside the New Castle, much less the Merman's Court. Its walls and floor and ceiling were made of wooden planks notched cunningly together and decorated with all the creatures of the sea. As they approached the dais, Davos trod on painted crabs and clams and starfish, half-hidden amongst twisting black fronds of seaweed and the bones of drowned sailors. On the walls to either side, pale sharks prowled painted blue-green depths, whilst eels and octopods slithered amongst rocks and sunken ships. Shoals of herring and great codfish swam between the tall arched windows. Higher up, near where the old fishing nets drooped down from the rafters, the surface of the sea had been depicted. To his right a war galley stroked serene against the rising sun; to his left, a battered old cog raced before a storm, her sails in rags. Behind the dais a kraken and grey leviathan were locked in battle beneath the painted waves.

Davos had hoped to speak with Wyman Manderly alone, but he found a crowded court. Along the walls, the women outnumbered the men by five to one; what few males he did see had long grey beards or looked too young to shave. There were septons as well, and holy sisters in white robes and grey. Near the top of the hall stood a dozen men in the blue and silver-grey of House Frey. Their faces had a likeness a blind man could have seen; several wore the badge of the Twins, two towers connected by a bridge.

Davos had learned to read men's faces long before Maester Pylos had taught him to read words on paper. *These Freys would gladly see me dead,* he realized at a glance.

Nor did he find any welcome in the pale blue eyes of Wyman Manderly. His lordship's cushioned throne was wide enough to accommodate three men of common girth, yet Manderly threatened to overflow it. His lordship *sagged* into his seat, his shoulders slumped, his legs splayed, his hands resting on the arms of his throne as if the weight of them were too much to bear. *Gods be good,* thought Davos, when he saw Lord Wyman's face, *this man looks half a corpse.* His skin was pallid, with an undertone of grey.

Kings and corpses always draw attendants, the old saying went. So it was with Manderly. Left of the high seat stood a maester nigh as fat as the lord he served, a rosy-cheeked man with thick lips and a head of golden curls. Ser Marlon claimed the place of honor at his lordship's right hand. On a cushioned stool at his feet perched a plump pink lady. Behind Lord Wyman stood two younger women, sisters by the look of them. The elder wore her brown hair bound in a long braid. The younger, no more than fifteen, had an even longer braid, dyed a garish green.

None chose to honor Davos with a name. The maester was the first to speak. "You stand before Wyman Manderly, Lord of White Harbor and Warden of the White Knife, Shield of the Faith, Defender of the Dispossessed, Lord Marshal of the Mander, a Knight of the Order of the Green Hand," he said. "In the Merman's Court, it is customary for vassals and petitioners to kneel."

The onion knight would have bent his knee, but a King's Hand could not; to do so would suggest that the king he served was less than this fat lord. "I have not come as a petitioner," Davos replied. "I have a string of titles too. Lord of the Rainwood, Admiral of the Narrow Sea, Hand of the King."

The plump woman on the stool rolled her eyes. "An admiral without ships, a hand without fingers, in service to a king without a throne. Is this a knight who comes before us, or the answer to a child's riddle?"

"He is a messenger, good-daughter," Lord Wyman said, "an onion of ill omen. Stannis did not like the answer his ravens brought him, so he has sent this . . . this *smuggler*." He squinted at Davos through eyes half-buried in rolls of fat. "You have visited our city before, I think, taking coin from our pockets and food off our table. How much did you steal from me, I wonder?"

Not enough that you ever missed a meal. "I paid for my smuggling at Storm's End, my lord." Davos pulled off his glove and held up his left hand, with its four shortened fingers.

"Four fingertips, for a lifetime's worth of theft?" said the woman on the stool. Her hair was yellow, her face round and pink and fleshy. "You got off cheaply, Onion Knight."

Davos did not deny it. "If it please my lord, I would request a privy audience."

It did not please the lord. "I keep no secrets from my kin, nor from my leal lords and knights, good friends all."

"My lord," said Davos, "I would not want my words to be heard by His Grace's enemies . . . or by your lordship's."

"Stannis may have enemies in this hall. I do not."

"Not even the men who slew your son?" Davos pointed. "These Freys were amongst his hosts at the Red Wedding."

One of the Freys stepped forward, a knight long and lean of limb, clean-shaved but for a grey mustache as thin as a Myrish stiletto. "The Red Wedding was the Young Wolf's work. He changed into a beast before our eyes and tore out the throat of my cousin Jinglebell, a harmless simpleton. He would have slain my lord father too, if Ser Wendel had not put himself in the way."

Lord Wyman blinked back tears. "Wendel was always a brave boy. I was not surprised to learn he died a hero."

The enormity of the lie made Davos gasp. "Is it your claim that *Robb Stark* killed Wendel Manderly?" he asked the Frey.

"And many more. Mine own son Tytos was amongst them, and my daughter's husband. When Stark changed into a wolf, his northmen did the same. The mark of the beast was on them all. Wargs birth other wargs with a bite, it is well-known. It was all my brothers and I could do to put them down before they slew us all."

The man was *smirking* as he told the tale. Davos wanted to peel his lips off with a knife. "Ser, may I have your name?"

"Ser Jared, of House Frey."

"Jared of House Frey, I name you liar."

Ser Jared seemed amused. "Some men cry when slicing onions, but I have never had that weakness." Steel whispered against leather as he drew his sword. "If you are indeed a knight, ser, defend that slander with your body."

Lord Wyman's eyes fluttered open. "I'll have no bloodshed in the Merman's Court. Put up your steel, Ser Jared, else I must ask you to leave my presence."

Ser Jared sheathed his sword. "Beneath your lordship's roof, your lordship's word is law . . . but I shall want a reckoning with this onion lord before he leaves this city."

"*Blood!*" howled the woman on the stool. "That's what this ill onion wants of us, my lord. See how he stirs up trouble? Send him away, I beg you. He wants the blood of your people, the blood of your brave sons. Send him *away*. Should the queen hear that you gave audience to this traitor, she may question our own loyalty. She might . . . she could . . . she . . ."

"It will not come to that, good-daughter," Lord Wyman said. "The Iron Throne shall have no cause to doubt us."

Davos misliked the sound of that, but he had not come all this way to hold his tongue. "The boy on the Iron Throne is a usurper," he said, "and I am no traitor, but the Hand of Stannis Baratheon, the First of His Name, the trueborn King of Westeros."

The fat maester cleared his throat. "Stannis Baratheon was brother to our late King Robert, may the Father judge him justly. Tommen is the issue of Robert's body. The laws of succession are clear in such a case. A son must come before a brother."

"Maester Theomore speaks truly," said Lord Wyman. "He is wise in all such matters, and has always given me good counsel."

"A *trueborn* son comes before a brother," Davos agreed, "but Tommen-called-Baratheon is bastard-born, as his brother Joffrey was before him. They were sired by the Kingslayer, in defiance of all the laws of gods and men."

Another of the Freys spoke up. "He speaks treason with his own lips, my lord. Stannis took his thieving fingers. You should take his lying tongue."

"Take his head, rather," suggested Ser Jared. "Or let him meet me on the field of honor."

"What would a Frey know of honor?" Davos threw back.

Four of the Freys started forward until Lord Wyman halted them with an upraised hand. "Step back, my friends. I will hear him out before I . . . before I deal with him."

"Can you offer any proof of this incest, ser?" Maester Theomore asked, folding his soft hands atop his belly.

Edric Storm, thought Davos, *but I sent him far away across the narrow sea, to keep him safe from Melisandre's fires.* "You have the word of Stannis Baratheon that all I've said is true."

"Words are wind," said the young woman behind Lord Wyman's high seat, the handsome one with the long brown braid. "And men will lie to get their way, as any maid could tell you."

"Proof requires more than some lord's unsupported word," declared Maester Theomore. "Stannis Baratheon would not be the first man who ever lied to win a throne."

The pink woman pointed a plump finger down at Davos. "We want no part of any treason, you. We are good people in White Harbor, lawful, loyal people. Pour no more poison in our ears, or my good-father will send you to the Wolf's Den."

How have I offended this one? "Might I have the honor of my lady's name?"

The pink woman gave an angry sniff and let the maester answer. "The Lady Leona is wife to Lord Wyman's son Ser Wylis, presently a captive of the Lannisters."

She speaks from fear. If White Harbor should declare for Stannis, her husband would answer with his life. *How can I ask Lord Wyman to condemn his son to death? What would I do in his place if Devan were a hostage?* "My lord," said Davos, "I pray no harm will come to your son, or to any man of White Harbor."

"Another lie," said Lady Leona from her stool.

Davos thought it best to ignore her. "When Robb Stark took up arms against the bastard Joffrey-called-Baratheon, White Harbor marched with him. Lord Stark has fallen, but his war goes on."

"Robb Stark was my liege lord," said Lord Wyman. "Who is this man Stannis? Why does he trouble us? He never felt the need to journey north before, as best I can recall. Yet he turns up now, a beaten cur with his helm in his hand, begging for alms."

"He came to save the realm, my lord," Davos insisted. "To defend your lands against the ironborn and the wildlings."

Next to the high seat, Ser Marlon Manderly gave a snort of disdain. "It has been centuries since White Harbor has seen any wildlings, and the ironmen have never troubled this coast. Does Lord Stannis propose to defend us from snarks and dragons too?"

Laughter swept the Merman's Court, but at Lord Wyman's feet, Lady Leona began to sob. "Ironmen from the isles, wildlings from beyond the Wall . . . and now this traitor lord with his outlaws, rebels, and sorcerers." She pointed a finger at Davos. "We have heard of your red witch, oh yes. She would turn us against the Seven to bow before a fire demon!"

Davos had no love for the red priestess, but he dare not let Lady Leona go unanswered. "Lady Melisandre is a priestess of the red god. Queen Selyse has adopted her faith, along with many others, but more of His Grace's followers still worship the Seven. Myself among them." He prayed no one would ask him to explain about the sept at Dragonstone or the godswood at Storm's End. *If they ask, I must needs tell them. Stannis would not have me lie.*

"The Seven defend White Harbor," Lady Leona declared. "We do not fear your red queen or her god. Let her send what spells she will. The prayers of godly men will shield us against evil."

"Indeed." Lord Wyman gave Lady Leona a pat on the shoulder. "Lord Davos, if you *are* a lord, I know what your so-called king would have of me. Steel and silver and a bended knee." He shifted his weight to lean upon an elbow. "Before he was slain, Lord Tywin offered White Harbor full pardon for our support of the Young Wolf. He promised that my son would be returned to me once I paid a ransom of three thousand dragons and proved my loyalty beyond a doubt. Roose Bolton, who is named our Warden of the North, requires that I give up my claim to Lord Hornwood's lands and castles but swears my other holdings shall remain untouched. Walder Frey, his good-father, offers one of his daughters to be my wife, and husbands for my son's daughters here behind me. These terms seem generous to me, a good basis for a fair and lasting peace. You would have me spurn them. So I ask you, Onion Knight—what does Lord Stannis offer me in return for my allegiance?"

War and woe and the screams of burning men, Davos might have said. "The chance to do your duty," he replied instead. That was the answer Stannis would have given Wyman Manderly. *The Hand should speak with the king's voice.*

Lord Wyman sagged back in his chair. "Duty. I see."

"White Harbor is not strong enough to stand alone. You need His Grace as much as he needs you. Together you can defeat your common enemies."

"My lord," said Ser Marlon, in his ornate silver armor, "will you permit me to ask a few questions of Lord Davos?"

"As you wish, cousin." Lord Wyman closed his eyes.

Ser Marlon turned to Davos. "How many northern lords have declared for Stannis? Tell us that."

"Arnolf Karstark has vowed to join His Grace."

"Arnolf is no true lord, only a castellan. What castles does Lord Stannis hold at present, pray?"

"His Grace has taken the Nightfort for his seat. In the south, he holds Storm's End and Dragonstone."

Maester Theomore cleared his throat. "Only for the nonce. Storm's End and Dragonstone are lightly held and must soon fall. And the Nightfort is a haunted ruin, a drear and dreadful place."

Ser Marlon went on. "How many men can Stannis put into the field, can you tell us that? How many knights ride with him? How many bowmen, how many freeriders, how many men-at-arms?"

Too few, Davos knew. Stannis had come north with no more than fifteen hundred men . . . but if he told them that, his mission here was doomed. He fumbled for words and found none.

"Your silence is all the answer I require, ser. Your king brings us only enemies." Ser Marlon turned to his lord cousin. "Your lordship asked the onion knight what Stannis offers us. Let me answer. He offers us defeat and death. He would have you mount a horse of air and give battle with a sword of wind."

The fat lord opened his eyes slowly, as if the effort were almost too much for him. "My cousin cuts to the bone, as ever. Do you have any more to say to me, Onion Knight, or can we put an end to this mummer's farce? I grow weary of your face."

Davos felt a stab of despair. *His Grace should have sent another man, a*

lord or knight or maester, someone who could speak for him without trip-
ping on his own tongue. "Death," he heard himself say, "there will be
death, aye. Your lordship lost a son at the Red Wedding. I lost four upon
the Blackwater. And why? Because the Lannisters stole the throne. Go to
King's Landing and look on Tommen with your own eyes, if you doubt
me. A blind man could see it. What does Stannis offer you? Vengeance.
Vengeance for my sons and yours, for your husbands and your fathers and
your brothers. Vengeance for your murdered lord, your murdered king,
your butchered princes. *Vengeance!*"

"Yes," piped a girl's voice, thin and high.

It belonged to the half-grown child with the blond eyebrows and the
long green braid. "They killed Lord Eddard and Lady Catelyn and King
Robb," she said. "He was our *king*! He was brave and good, and the Freys
murdered him. If Lord Stannis will avenge him, we should join Lord Stannis."

Manderly pulled her close. "Wylla, every time you open your mouth
you make me want to send you to the silent sisters."

"I only said—"

"We heard what you said," said the older girl, her sister. "A child's foolishness. Speak no ill of our friends of Frey. One of them will be your lord
and husband soon."

"No," the girl declared, shaking her head. "I won't. I won't *ever*. They
killed *the king*."

Lord Wyman flushed. "You will. When the appointed day arrives, you
will speak your wedding vows, else you will join the silent sisters and never
speak again."

The poor girl looked stricken. "Grandfather, *please . . .*"

"Hush, child," said Lady Leona. "You heard your lord grandfather.
Hush! You know nothing."

"I know about the promise," insisted the girl. "Maester Theomore, tell
them! A thousand years before the Conquest, a promise was made, and
oaths were sworn in the Wolf's Den before the old gods and the new.
When we were sore beset and friendless, hounded from our homes and in
peril of our lives, the wolves took us in and nourished us and protected us
against our enemies. The city is built upon the land they gave us. In return we swore that we should always be their men. *Stark* men!"

The maester fingered the chain about his neck. "Solemn oaths were
sworn to the Starks of Winterfell, aye. But Winterfell has fallen and House
Stark has been extinguished."

"That's because they *killed them all*!"

Another Frey spoke up. "Lord Wyman, if I may?"

Wyman Manderly gave him a nod. "Rhaegar. We are always pleased to hear your noble counsel."

Rhaegar Frey acknowledged the compliment with a bow. He was thirty, or nigh unto, round-shouldered and kettle-bellied, but richly dressed in a doublet of soft grey lambswool trimmed in cloth-of-silver. His cloak was cloth-of-silver too, lined with vair and clasped at the collar with a brooch in the shape of the twin towers. "Lady Wylla," he said to the girl with the green braid, "loyalty is a virtue. I hope you will be as loyal to Little Walder when you are joined in wedlock. As to the Starks, that House is extinguished only in the male line. Lord Eddard's sons are dead, but his daughters live, and the younger girl is coming north to wed brave Ramsay Bolton."

"Ramsay *Snow*," Wylla Manderly threw back.

"Have it as you will. By any name, he shall soon be wed to Arya Stark. If you would keep faith with your promise, give *him* your allegiance, for he shall be your Lord of Winterfell."

"He won't ever be *my* lord! He made Lady Hornwood marry him, then shut her in a dungeon and made her eat her *fingers*."

A murmur of assent swept the Merman's Court. "The maid tells it true," declared a stocky man in white and purple, whose cloak was fastened with a pair of crossed bronze keys. "Roose Bolton's cold and cunning, aye, but a man can deal with Roose. We've all known worse. But this bastard son of his . . . they say he's mad and cruel, a monster."

"*They* say?" Rhaegar Frey sported a silky beard and a sardonic smile. "His *enemies* say, aye . . . but it was the Young Wolf who was the monster. More beast than boy, that one, puffed up with pride and bloodlust. And he was faithless, as my lord grandfather learned to his sorrow." He spread his hands. "I do not fault White Harbor for supporting him. My grandsire made the same grievous mistake. In all the Young Wolf's battles, White Harbor and the Twins fought side by side beneath his banners. Robb Stark betrayed us all. He abandoned the north to the cruel mercies of the ironmen to carve out a fairer kingdom for himself along the Trident. Then he abandoned the riverlords who had risked much and more for him, breaking his marriage pact with my grandfather to wed the first western wench who caught his eye. The Young Wolf? He was a vile dog and died like one."

The Merman's Court had grown still. Davos could feel the chill in the air. Lord Wyman was looking down at Rhaegar as if he were a roach in need of a hard heel . . . yet then, abruptly, he gave a ponderous nod that set his chins to wobbling. "A dog, aye. He brought us only grief and death. A vile dog indeed. Say on."

Rhaegar Frey went on. "Grief and death, aye . . . and this onion lord will bring you more with his talk of vengeance. Open your eyes, as my lord grandsire did. The War of the Five Kings is all but done. Tommen is our king, our *only* king. We must help him bind up the wounds of this sad war. As Robert's trueborn son, the heir of stag and lion, the Iron Throne is his by rights."

"Wise words, and true," said Lord Wyman Manderly.

"They *weren't.*" Wylla Manderly stamped her foot.

"Be quiet, wretched child," scolded Lady Leona. "Young girls should be an ornament to the eye, not an ache in the ear." She seized the girl by her braid and pulled her squealing from the hall. *There went my only friend in this hall,* thought Davos.

"Wylla has always been a willful child," her sister said, by way of apology. "I fear that she will make a willful wife."

Rhaegar shrugged. "Marriage will soften her, I have no doubt. A firm hand and a quiet word."

"If not, there are the silent sisters." Lord Wyman shifted in his seat. "As for you, Onion Knight, I have heard sufficient treason for one day. You would have me risk my city for a false king and a false god. You would have me sacrifice my only living son so Stannis Baratheon can plant his puckered arse upon a throne to which he has no right. I will not do it. Not for you. Not for your lord. Not for any man." The Lord of White Harbor pushed himself to his feet. The effort brought a red flush to his neck. "You *are* still a smuggler, ser, come to steal my gold and blood. You would take my son's head. I think I shall take yours instead. *Guards!* Seize this man!"

Before Davos could even think to move, he was surrounded by silver tridents. "My lord," he said, "I am an envoy."

"Are you? You came sneaking into my city like a smuggler. I say you are no lord, no knight, no envoy, only a thief and a spy, a peddler of lies and treasons. I should tear your tongue out with hot pincers and deliver you to the Dreadfort to be flayed. But the Mother is merciful, and so am I." He beckoned to Ser Marlon. "Cousin, take this creature to the Wolf's Den and cut off his head and hands. I want them brought to me before I sup. I shall not be able to eat a bite until I see this smuggler's head upon a spike, with an onion shoved between his lying teeth."

REEK

They gave him a horse and a banner, a soft woolen doublet and a warm fur cloak, and set him loose. For once, he did not stink. "Come back with that castle," said Damon Dance-for-Me as he helped Reek climb shaking into the saddle, "or keep going and see how far you get before we catch you. He'd like that, he would." Grinning, Damon gave the horse a lick across the rump with his whip, and the old stot whinnied and lurched into motion.

Reek did not dare to look back, for fear that Damon and Yellow Dick and Grunt and the rest were coming after him, that all of this was just another of Lord Ramsay's japes, some cruel test to see what he would do if they gave him a horse and set him free. *Do they think that I will run?* The stot they had given him was a wretched thing, knock-kneed and half-starved; he could never hope to outdistance the fine horses Lord Ramsay and his hunters would be riding. And Ramsay loved nothing more than to set his girls baying on the trail of some fresh prey.

Besides, where would he run to? Behind him were the camps, crowded with Dreadfort men and those the Ryswells had brought from the Rills, with the Barrowton host between them. South of Moat Cailin, another army was coming up the causeway, an army of Boltons and Freys marching beneath the banners of the Dreadfort. East of the road lay a bleak and barren shore and a cold salt sea, to the west the swamps and bogs of the Neck, infested with serpents, lizard lions, and bog devils with their poisoned arrows.

He would not run. He could not run.

I will deliver him the castle. I will. I must.

It was a grey day, damp and misty. The wind was from the south, moist as a kiss. The ruins of Moat Cailin were visible in the distance, threaded through with wisps of morning mist. His horse moved toward them at a walk, her hooves making faint wet squelching sounds as they pulled free of the grey-green muck.

I have come this way before. It was a dangerous thought, and he regretted it at once. "No," he said, "no, that was some other man, that was before you knew your name." His name was Reek. He had to remember that. *Reek, Reek, it rhymes with leek.*

When that other man had come this way, an army had followed close behind him, the great host of the north riding to war beneath the grey-and-white banners of House Stark. Reek rode alone, clutching a peace banner on a pinewood staff. When that other man had come this way, he had been mounted on a courser, swift and spirited. Reek rode a broken-down stot, all skin and bone and ribs, and he rode her slowly for fear he might fall off. The other man had been a good rider, but Reek was uneasy on horseback. It had been so long. He was no rider. He was not even a man. He was Lord Ramsay's creature, lower than a dog, a worm in human skin. "You will pretend to be a prince," Lord Ramsay told him last night, as Reek was soaking in a tub of scalding water, "but we know the truth. You're Reek. You'll always be Reek, no matter how sweet you smell. Your nose may lie to you. Remember your name. Remember who you are."

"Reek," he said. "Your Reek."

"Do this little thing for me, and you can be my dog and eat meat every day," Lord Ramsay promised. "You will be tempted to betray me. To run or fight or join our foes. No, quiet, I'll not hear you deny it. Lie to me, and I'll take your tongue. A man *would* turn against me in your place, but we know what you are, don't we? Betray me if you want, it makes no matter . . . but count your fingers first and know the cost."

Reek knew the cost. *Seven,* he thought, *seven fingers. A man can make do with seven fingers. Seven is a sacred number.* He remembered how much it had hurt when Lord Ramsay had commanded Skinner to lay his ring finger bare.

The air was wet and heavy, and shallow pools of water dotted the ground. Reek picked his way between them carefully, following the remnants of the log-and-plank road that Robb Stark's vanguard had laid down across the soft ground to speed the passage of his host. Where once a mighty curtain wall had stood, only scattered stones remained, blocks of black basalt so large it must once have taken a hundred men to hoist them into place. Some had sunk so deep into the bog that only a corner showed; others lay strewn about like some god's abandoned toys, cracked and crumbling, spotted with lichen. Last night's rain had left the huge stones wet and glistening, and the morning sunlight made them look as if they were coated in some fine black oil.

Beyond stood the towers.

The Drunkard's Tower leaned as if it were about to collapse, just as it had for half a thousand years. The Children's Tower thrust into the sky as straight as a spear, but its shattered top was open to the wind and rain. The Gatehouse Tower, squat and wide, was the largest of the three, slimy with moss, a gnarled tree growing sideways from the stones of its north side, fragments of broken wall still standing to the east and west. *The Karstarks took the Drunkard's Tower and the Umbers the Children's Tower,* he recalled. *Robb claimed the Gatehouse Tower for his own.*

If he closed his eyes, he could see the banners in his mind's eye, snapping bravely in a brisk north wind. *All gone now, all fallen.* The wind on his cheeks was blowing from the south, and the only banners flying above the remains of Moat Cailin displayed a golden kraken on a field of black.

He was being watched. He could feel the eyes. When he looked up, he caught a glimpse of pale faces peering from behind the battlements of the Gatehouse Tower and through the broken masonry that crowned the Children's Tower, where legend said the children of the forest had once called down the hammer of the waters to break the lands of Westeros in two.

The only dry road through the Neck was the causeway, and the towers of Moat Cailin plugged its northern end like a cork in a bottle. The road was narrow, the ruins so positioned that any enemy coming up from the south must pass beneath and between them. To assault any of the three towers, an attacker must expose his back to arrows from the other two, whilst climbing damp stone walls festooned with streamers of slimy white ghostskin. The swampy ground beyond the causeway was impassable, an endless morass of suckholes, quicksands, and glistening green swards that looked solid to the unwary eye but turned to water the instant you trod upon them, the whole of it infested with venomous serpents and poisonous flowers and monstrous lizard lions with teeth like daggers. Just as dangerous were its people, seldom seen but always lurking, the swamp-dwellers, the frog-eaters, the mud-men. Fenn and Reed, Peat and Boggs, Cray and Quagg, Greengood and Blackmyre, those were the sorts of names they gave themselves. The ironborn called them all *bog devils.*

Reek passed the rotted carcass of a horse, an arrow jutting from its neck. A long white snake slithered into its empty eye socket at his approach. Behind the horse he spied the rider, or what remained of him. The crows had stripped the flesh from the man's face, and a feral dog had burrowed beneath his mail to get at his entrails. Farther on, another corpse had sunk so deep into the muck that only his face and fingers showed.

Closer to the towers, corpses littered the ground on every side. Blood-blooms had sprouted from their gaping wounds, pale flowers with petals plump and moist as a woman's lips.

The garrison will never know me. Some might recall the boy he'd been before he learned his name, but Reek would be a stranger to them. It had been a long while since he last looked into a glass, but he knew how old he must appear. His hair had turned white; much of it had fallen out, and what was left was stiff and dry as straw. The dungeons had left him weak as an old woman and so thin a strong wind could knock him down.

And his hands . . . Ramsay had given him gloves, fine gloves of black leather, soft and supple, stuffed with wool to conceal his missing fingers, but if anyone looked closely, he would see that three of his fingers did not bend.

"*No closer!*" a voice rang out. "What do you want?"

"Words." He spurred the stot onward, waving the peace banner so they could not fail to see it. "I come unarmed."

There was no reply. Inside the walls, he knew, the ironmen were discussing whether to admit him or fill his chest with arrows. *It makes no matter.* A quick death here would be a hundred times better than returning to Lord Ramsay as a failure.

Then the gatehouse doors flung open. "*Quickly.*" Reek was turning toward the sound when the arrow struck. It came from somewhere to his right, where broken chunks of the curtain wall lay half-submerged beneath the bog. The shaft tore through the folds of his banner and hung spent, the point a bare foot from his face. It startled him so badly that he dropped the peace banner and tumbled from his saddle.

"Inside," the voice shouted, "hurry, fool, *hurry!*"

Reek scrambled up the steps on hands and knees as another arrow fluttered over his head. Someone seized him and dragged him inside, and he heard the door crash shut behind him. He was pulled to his feet and shoved against a wall. Then a knife was at his throat, a bearded face so close to his that he could count the man's nose hairs. "Who are you? What's your purpose here? Quick now, or I'll do you the same as him." The guard jerked his head toward a body rotting on the floor beside the door, its flesh green and crawling with maggots.

"I am ironborn," Reek answered, lying. The boy he'd been before had been ironborn, true enough, but Reek had come into this world in the dungeons of the Dreadfort. "Look at my face. I am Lord Balon's son. Your prince." He would have said the name, but somehow the words caught in his throat. *Reek, I'm Reek, it rhymes with squeak.* He had to forget that for a little while, though. No man would ever yield to a creature such as Reek, no matter how desperate his situation. He must pretend to be a prince again.

His captor stared at his face, squinting, his mouth twisted in suspicion. His teeth were brown, and his breath stank of ale and onion. "Lord Balon's sons were killed."

"My brothers. Not me. Lord Ramsay took me captive after Winterfell. He's sent me here to treat with you. Do you command here?"

"Me?" The man lowered his knife and took a step backwards, almost stumbling over the corpse. "Not me, m'lord." His mail was rusted, his leathers rotting. On the back of one hand an open sore wept blood. "Ralf Kenning has the command. The captain said. I'm on the door, is all."

"And who is this?" Reek gave the corpse a kick.

The guard stared at the dead man as if seeing him for the first time. "Him . . . he drank the water. I had to cut his throat for him, to stop his screaming. Bad belly. You can't drink the water. That's why we got the ale." The guard rubbed his face, his eyes red and inflamed. "We used to drag the dead down into the cellars. All the vaults are flooded down there. No one wants to take the trouble now, so we just leave them where they fall."

"The cellar is a better place for them. Give them to the water. To the Drowned God."

The man laughed. "No gods down there, m'lord. Only rats and water snakes. White things, thick as your leg. Sometimes they slither up the steps and bite you in your sleep."

Reek remembered the dungeons underneath the Dreadfort, the rat squirming between his teeth, the taste of warm blood on his lips. *If I fail, Ramsay will send me back to that, but first he'll flay the skin from another finger.* "How many of the garrison are left?"

"Some," said the ironman. "I don't know. Fewer than we was before. Some in the Drunkard's Tower too, I think. Not the Children's Tower. Dagon Codd went over there a few days back. Only two men left alive, he said, and they was eating on the dead ones. He killed them both, if you can believe that."

Moat Cailin has fallen, Reek realized then, *only no one has seen fit to tell them.* He rubbed his mouth to hide his broken teeth, and said, "I need to speak with your commander."

"Kenning?" The guard seemed confused. "He don't have much to say these days. He's dying. Might be he's dead. I haven't seen him since . . . I don't remember when . . ."

"Where is he? Take me to him."

"Who will keep the door, then?"

"Him." Reek gave the corpse a kick.

That made the man laugh. "Aye. Why not? Come with me, then." He pulled a torch down from a wall sconce and waved it till it blazed up bright and hot. "This way." The guard led him through a door and up a spiral stair, the torchlight glimmering off black stone walls as they climbed.

The chamber at the top of the steps was dark, smoky, and oppressively hot. A ragged skin had been hung across the narrow window to keep the damp out, and a slab of peat smoldered in a brazier. The smell in the room was foul, a miasma of mold and piss and nightsoil, of smoke and sickness. Soiled rushes covered the floor, whilst a heap of straw in the corner passed for a bed.

Ralf Kenning lay shivering beneath a mountain of furs. His arms were stacked beside him—sword and axe, mail hauberk, iron warhelm. His shield bore the storm god's cloudy hand, lightning crackling from his fingers down to a raging sea, but the paint was discolored and peeling, the wood beneath starting to rot.

Ralf was rotting too. Beneath the furs he was naked and feverish, his pale puffy flesh covered with weeping sores and scabs. His head was misshapen, one cheek grotesquely swollen, his neck so engorged with blood that it threatened to swallow his face. The arm on that same side was big as a log and crawling with white worms. No one had bathed him or shaved him for many days, from the look of him. One eye wept pus, and his beard was crusty with dried vomit. "What happened to him?" asked Reek.

"He was on the parapets and some bog devil loosed an arrow at him. It was only a graze, but . . . they poison their shafts, smear the points with shit and worse things. We poured boiling wine into the wound, but it made no difference."

I cannot treat with this thing. "Kill him," Reek told the guard. "His wits are gone. He's full of blood and worms."

The man gaped at him. "The captain put him in command."

"You'd put a dying horse down."

"What horse? I never had no horse."

I did. The memory came back in a rush. Smiler's screams had sounded almost human. His mane afire, he had reared up on his hind legs, blind with pain, lashing out with his hooves. *No, no. Not mine, he was not mine, Reek never had a horse.* "I will kill him for you." Reek snatched up Ralf

Kenning's sword where it leaned against his shield. He still had fingers enough to clasp the hilt. When he laid the edge of the blade against the swollen throat of the creature on the straw, the skin split open in a gout of black blood and yellow pus. Kenning jerked violently, then lay still. An awful stench filled the room. Reek bolted for the steps. The air was damp and cold there, but much cleaner by comparison. The ironman stumbled out after him, white-faced and struggling not to retch. Reek grasped him by the arm. "Who was second-in-command? Where are the rest of the men?"

"Up on the battlements, or in the hall. Sleeping, drinking. I'll take you if you like."

"Do it now." Ramsay had only given him a day.

The hall was dark stone, high ceilinged and drafty, full of drifting smoke, its stone walls spotted by huge patches of pale lichen. A peat fire burned low in a hearth blackened by the hotter blazes of years past. A massive table of carved stone filled the chamber, as it had for centuries. *There was where I sat, the last time I was here,* he remembered. *Robb was at the head of the table, with the Greatjon to his right and Roose Bolton on his left. The Glovers sat next to Helman Tallhart. Karstark and his sons were across from them.*

Two dozen ironborn sat drinking at the table. A few looked at him with dull, flat eyes when he entered. The rest ignored him. All the men were strangers to him. Several wore cloaks fastened by brooches in the shape of silver codfish. The Codds were not well regarded in the Iron Islands; the men were said to be thieves and cowards, the women wantons who bedded with their own fathers and brothers. It did not surprise him that his uncle had chosen to leave these men behind when the Iron Fleet went home. *This will make my task that much easier.* "Ralf Kenning is dead," he said. "Who commands here?"

The drinkers stared at him blankly. One laughed. Another spat. Finally one of the Codds said, "Who asks?"

"Lord Balon's son." *Reek, my name is Reek, it rhymes with cheek.* "I am here at the command of Ramsay Bolton, Lord of the Hornwood and heir to the Dreadfort, who captured me at Winterfell. His host is north of you, his father's to the south, but Lord Ramsay is prepared to be merciful if you yield Moat Cailin to him before the sun goes down." He drew out the letter that they'd given him and tossed it on the table before the drinkers.

One of them picked it up and turned it over in his hands, picking at the pink wax that sealed it. After a moment he said, "Parchment. What good is that? It's cheese we need, and meat."

"Steel, you mean," said the man beside him, a greybeard whose left arm ended in a stump. "Swords. Axes. Aye, and bows, a hundred more bows, and men to loose the arrows."

"Ironborn do not surrender," said a third voice.

"Tell that to my father. Lord Balon bent the knee when Robert broke his wall. Elsewise he would have died. As you will if you do not yield." He gestured at the parchment. "Break the seal. Read the words. That is a safe conduct, written in Lord Ramsay's own hand. Give up your swords and come with me, and his lordship will feed you and give you leave to march unmolested to the Stony Shore and find a ship for home. Elsewise you die."

"Is that a threat?" One of the Codds pushed to his feet. A big man, but pop-eyed and wide of mouth, with dead white flesh. He looked as if his father had sired him on a fish, but he still wore a longsword. "Dagon Codd yields to no man."

No, please, you have to listen. The thought of what Ramsay would do to him if he crept back to camp without the garrison's surrender was almost enough to make him piss his breeches. *Reek, Reek, it rhymes with leak.* "Is that your answer?" The words rang feebly in his ears. "Does this codfish speak for all of you?"

The guard who had met him at the door seemed less certain. "Victarion commanded us to hold, he did. I heard him with my own ears. *Hold here till I return*, he told Kenning."

"Aye," said the one-armed man. "That's what he said. The kingsmoot called, but he swore that he'd be back, with a driftwood crown upon his head and a thousand men behind him."

"My uncle is never coming back," Reek told them. "The kingswood crowned his brother Euron, and the Crow's Eye has other wars to fight. You think my uncle values you? He doesn't. You are the ones he left behind to die. He scraped you off the same way he scrapes mud off his boots when he wades ashore."

Those words struck home. He could see it in their eyes, in the way they looked at one another or frowned above their cups. *They all feared they'd been abandoned, but it took me to turn fear into certainty.* These were not the kin of famous captains nor the blood of the great Houses of the Iron Islands. These were the sons of thralls and salt wives.

"If we yield, we walk away?" said the one-armed man. "Is that what it says on this here writing?" He nudged the roll of parchment, its wax seal still unbroken.

"Read it for yourself," he answered, though he was almost certain that none of them could read. "Lord Ramsay treats his captives honorably so long as they keep faith with him." *He has only taken toes and fingers and that other thing, when he might have had my tongue, or peeled the skin off my legs from heel to thigh.* "Yield up your swords to him, and you will live."

"Liar." Dagon Codd drew his longsword. "You're the one they call Turncloak. Why should we believe your promises?"

He is drunk, Reek realized. *The ale is speaking.* "Believe what you want. I have brought Lord Ramsay's message. Now I must return to him. We'll sup on wild boar and neeps, washed down with strong red wine. Those who come with me will be welcome at the feast. The rest of you will die within a day. The Lord of the Dreadfort will bring his knights up the causeway, whilst his son leads his own men down on you from the north. No quarter will be granted. The ones that die fighting will be the lucky ones. Those who live will be given to the bog devils."

"Enough," snarled Dagon Codd. "You think you can frighten ironborn with *words*? Begone. Run back to your master before I open your belly, pull your entrails out, and make you eat them."

He might have said more, but suddenly his eyes gaped wide. A throwing axe sprouted from the center of his forehead with a solid *thunk*. Codd's sword fell from his fingers. He jerked like a fish on a hook, then crashed face-first onto the table.

It was the one-armed man who'd flung the axe. As he rose to his feet he had another in his hand. "Who else wants to die?" he asked the other drinkers. "Speak up, I'll see you do." Thin red streams were spreading out across the stone from the pool of blood where Dagon Codd's head had come to rest. "Me, I mean to live, and that don't mean staying here to rot."

One man took a swallow of ale. Another turned his cup over to wash away a finger of blood before it reached the place where he was seated. No one spoke. When the one-armed man slid the throwing axe back through his belt, Reek knew he had won. He almost felt a man again. *Lord Ramsay will be pleased with me.*

He pulled down the kraken banner with his own two hands, fumbling some because of his missing fingers but thankful for the fingers that Lord Ramsay had allowed him to keep. It took the better part of the afternoon before the ironborn were ready to depart. There were more of them than he would have guessed—forty-seven in the Gatehouse Tower and another eighteen in the Drunkard's Tower. Two of those were so close to dead there was no hope for them, another five too weak to walk. That still left fifty-eight who were fit enough to fight. Weak as they were, they would have taken three times their own number with them if Lord Ramsay had stormed the ruins. *He did well to send me,* Reek told himself as he climbed back onto his stot to lead his ragged column back across the boggy ground to where the northmen were encamped. "Leave your weapons here," he told the prisoners. "Swords, bows, daggers. Armed men will be slain on sight."

It took them thrice as long to cover the distance as it had taken Reek alone. Crude litters had been patched together for four of the men who could not walk; the fifth was carried by his son, upon his back. It made for slow going, and all the ironborn were well aware of how exposed they were, well within bowshot of the bog devils and their poisoned arrows. *If I die, I die.* Reek only prayed the archer knew his business, so death would be quick and clean. *A man's death, not the end Ralf Kenning suffered.*

The one-armed man walked at the head of the procession, limping heavily. His name, he said, was Adrack Humble, and he had a rock wife and three salt wives back on Great Wyk. "Three of the four had big bellies when we sailed," he boasted, "and Humbles run to twins. First thing I'll need to do when I get back is count up my new sons. Might be I'll even name one after you, m'lord."

Aye, name him Reek, he thought, *and when he's bad you can cut his toes off and give him rats to eat.* He turned his head and spat, and wondered if Ralf Kenning hadn't been the lucky one.

A light rain had begun to piss down out of the slate-grey sky by the time Lord Ramsay's camp appeared in front of them. A sentry watched them pass in silence. The air was full of drifting smoke from the cookfires drowning in the rain. A column of riders came wheeling up behind them, led by a lordling with a horsehead on his shield. *One of Lord Ryswell's sons,* Reek knew. *Roger, or maybe Rickard.* He could not tell the two of them apart. "Is this all of them?" the rider asked from atop a chestnut stallion.

"All who weren't dead, my lord."

"I thought there would be more. We came at them three times, and three times they threw us back."

We are ironborn, he thought, with a sudden flash of pride, and for half a heartbeat he was a prince again, Lord Balon's son, the blood of Pyke. Even thinking was dangerous, though. He had to remember his name. *Reek, my name is Reek, it rhymes with weak.*

They were just outside the camp when the baying of a pack of hounds told of Lord Ramsay's approach. Whoresbane was with him, along with half a dozen of his favorites, Skinner and Sour Alyn and Damon Dance-for-Me, and the Walders Big and Little too. The dogs swarmed

around them, snapping and snarling at the strangers. *The Bastard's girls,*
Reek thought, before he remembered that one must never, never, *never*
use that word in Ramsay's presence.

Reek swung down from his saddle and took a knee. "My lord, Moat
Cailin is yours. Here are its last defenders."

"So few. I had hoped for more. They were such stubborn foes." Lord
Ramsay's pale eyes shone. "You must be starved. Damon, Alyn, see to
them. Wine and ale, and all the food that they can eat. Skinner, show
their wounded to our maesters."

"Aye, my lord."

A few of the ironborn muttered thanks before they shambled off toward
the cookfires in the center of the camp. One of the Codds even tried to
kiss Lord Ramsay's ring, but the hounds drove him back before he could
get close, and Alison took a chunk of his ear. Even as the blood streamed
down his neck, the man bobbed and bowed and praised his lordship's
mercy.

When the last of them were gone, Ramsay Bolton turned his smile on
Reek. He clasped him by the back of the head, pulled his face close,
kissed him on his cheek, and whispered, "My old friend Reek. Did they
really take you for their prince? What bloody fools, these ironmen. The
gods are laughing."

"All they want is to go home, my lord."

"And what do *you* want, my sweet Reek?" Ramsay murmured, as softly
as a lover. His breath smelled of mulled wine and cloves, so sweet. "Such
valiant service deserves a reward. I cannot give you back your fingers or
your toes, but surely there is something you would have of me. Shall I free
you instead? Release you from my service? Do you want to go with them,
return to your bleak isles in the cold grey sea, be a prince again? Or would
you sooner stay my leal serving man?"

A cold knife scraped along his spine. *Be careful,* he told himself, *be
very, very careful.* He did not like his lordship's smile, the way his eyes
were shining, the spittle glistening at the corner of his mouth. He had
seen such signs before. *You are no prince. You're Reek, just Reek, it rhymes
with freak. Give him the answer that he wants.*

"My lord," he said, "my place is here, with you. I'm your Reek. I only
want to serve you. All I ask . . . a skin of wine, that would be reward enough
for me . . . red wine, the strongest that you have, all the wine a man can
drink . . ."

Lord Ramsay laughed. "You're not a man, Reek. You're just my creature. You'll have your wine, though. Walder, see to it. And fear not, I

won't return you to the dungeons, you have my word as a Bolton. We'll make a dog of you instead. Meat every day, and I'll even leave you teeth enough to eat it. You can sleep beside my girls. Ben, do you have a collar for him?"

"I'll have one made, m'lord," said old Ben Bones.

The old man did better than that. That night, besides the collar, there was a ragged blanket too, and half a chicken. Reek had to fight the dogs for the meat, but it was the best meal he'd had since Winterfell.

And the wine . . . the wine was dark and sour, but *strong*. Squatting amongst the hounds, Reek drank until his head swam, retched, wiped his mouth, and drank some more. Afterward he lay back and closed his eyes. When he woke a dog was licking vomit from his beard, and dark clouds were scuttling across the face of a sickle moon. Somewhere in the night, men were screaming. He shoved the dog aside, rolled over, and went back to sleep.

The next morning Lord Ramsay dispatched three riders down the causeway to take word to his lord father that the way was clear. The flayed man of House Bolton was hoisted above the Gatehouse Tower, where Reek had hauled down the golden kraken of Pyke. Along the rotting-plank road, wooden stakes were driven deep into the boggy ground; there the corpses festered, red and dripping. *Sixty-three*, he knew, *there are sixty-three of them*. One was short half an arm. Another had a parchment shoved between its teeth, its wax seal still unbroken.

Three days later, the vanguard of Roose Bolton's host threaded its way through the ruins and past the row of grisly sentinels—four hundred mounted Freys clad in blue and grey, their spearpoints glittering whenever the sun broke through the clouds. Two of old Lord Walder's sons led the van. One was brawny, with a massive jut of jaw and arms thick with muscle. The other had hungry eyes close-set above a pointed nose, a thin brown beard that did not quite conceal the weak chin beneath it, a bald head. *Hosteen and Aenys*. He remembered them from before he knew his name. Hosteen was a bull, slow to anger but implacable once roused, and by repute the fiercest fighter of Lord Walder's get. Aenys was older, crueler, and more clever—a commander, not a swordsman. Both were seasoned soldiers.

The northmen followed hard behind the van, their tattered banners streaming in the wind. Reek watched them pass. Most were afoot, and there were so few of them. He remembered the great host that marched south with Young Wolf, beneath the direwolf of Winterfell. Twenty thousand swords and spears had gone off to war with Robb, or near enough to make no matter, but only two in ten were coming back, and most of those were Dreadfort men.

Back where the press was thickest at the center of the column rode a man armored in dark grey plate over a quilted tunic of blood-red leather. His rondels were wrought in the shape of human heads, with open mouths that shrieked in agony. From his shoulders streamed a pink woolen cloak embroidered with droplets of blood. Long streamers of red silk fluttered from the top of his closed helm. *No crannogman will slay Roose Bolton with a poisoned arrow,* Reek thought when he first saw him. An enclosed wagon groaned along behind him, drawn by six heavy draft horses and defended by crossbowmen, front and rear. Curtains of dark blue velvet concealed the wagon's occupants from watching eyes.

Farther back came the baggage train—lumbering wayns laden with provisions and loot taken in the war, and carts crowded with wounded men and cripples. And at the rear, more Freys. At least a thousand, maybe more: bowmen, spearmen, peasants armed with scythes and sharpened sticks, freeriders and mounted archers, and another hundred knights to stiffen them.

Collared and chained and back in rags again, Reek followed with the other dogs at Lord Ramsay's heels when his lordship strode forth to greet his father. When the rider in the dark armor removed his helm, however, the face beneath was not one that Reek knew. Ramsay's smile curdled at the sight, and anger flashed across his face. "What is this, some mockery?"

"Just caution," whispered Roose Bolton, as he emerged from behind the curtains of the enclosed wagon.

The Lord of the Dreadfort did not have a strong likeness to his bastard son. His face was clean-shaved, smooth-skinned, ordinary, not handsome but not quite plain. Though Roose had been in battles, he bore no scars. Though well past forty, he was as yet unwrinkled, with scarce a line to tell of the passage of time. His lips were so thin that when he pressed them together they seemed to vanish altogether. There was an agelessness about him, a stillness; on Roose Bolton's face, rage and joy looked much the same. All he and Ramsay had in common were their eyes. *His eyes are ice.* Reek wondered if Roose Bolton ever cried. *If so, do the tears feel cold upon his cheeks?*

Once, a boy called Theon Greyjoy had enjoyed tweaking Bolton as they sat at council with Robb Stark, mocking his soft voice and making japes about leeches. *He must have been mad. This is no man to jape with.* You had only to look at Bolton to know that he had more cruelty in his pinky toe than all the Freys combined.

"Father." Lord Ramsay knelt before his sire.

Lord Roose studied him for a moment. "You may rise." He turned to help two young women down from inside the wagon.

The first was short and very fat, with a round red face and three chins wobbling beneath a sable hood. "My new wife," Roose Bolton said. "Lady Walda, this is my natural son. Kiss your stepmother's hand, Ramsay." He did. "And I am sure you will recall the Lady Arya. Your betrothed."

The girl was slim, and taller than he remembered, but that was only to be expected. *Girls grow fast at that age.* Her dress was grey wool bordered with white satin; over it she wore an ermine cloak clasped with a silver wolf's head. Dark brown hair fell halfway down her back. And her eyes . . .

That is not Lord Eddard's daughter.

Arya had her father's eyes, the grey eyes of the Starks. A girl her age might let her hair grow long, add inches to her height, see her chest fill out, but she could not change the color of her eyes. *That's Sansa's little friend, the steward's girl. Jeyne, that was her name. Jeyne Poole.*

"Lord Ramsay." The girl dipped down before him. That was wrong as well. *The real Arya Stark would have spat into his face.* "I pray that I will make you a good wife and give you strong sons to follow after you."

"That you will," promised Ramsay, "and soon."

JON

His candle had guttered out in a pool of wax, but morning light was shining through the shutters of his window. Jon had fallen asleep over his work again. Books covered his table, tall stacks of them. He'd fetched them up himself, after spending half the night searching through dusty vaults by lantern light. Sam was right, the books desperately needed to be sorted, listed, and put in order, but that was no task for stewards who could neither read nor write. It would need to wait for Sam's return.

If he does return. Jon feared for Sam and Maester Aemon. Cotter Pyke had written from Eastwatch to report that the *Storm Crow* had sighted the wreckage of a galley along the coast of Skagos. Whether the broken ship was *Blackbird*, one of Stannis Baratheon's sellsails, or some passing trader, the crew of the *Storm Crow* had not been able to discern. *I meant to send Gilly and the babe to safety. Did I send them to their graves instead?*

Last night's supper had congealed beside his elbow, scarce touched. Dolorous Edd had filled his trencher almost to overflowing to allow Three-Finger Hobb's infamous three-meat stew to soften the stale bread. The jest among the brothers was that the three meats were mutton, mutton, and mutton, but carrot, onion, and turnip would have been closer to the mark. A film of cold grease glistened atop the remains of the stew.

Bowen Marsh had urged him to move into the Old Bear's former chambers in the King's Tower after Stannis vacated them, but Jon had declined. Moving into the king's chambers could too easily be taken to mean he did not expect the king to return.

A strange listlessness had settled over Castle Black since Stannis had marched south, as if the free folk and the black brothers alike were holding their breath, waiting to see what would come. The yards and dining hall were empty more oft than not, the Lord Commander's Tower was a shell, the old common hall a pile of blackened timbers, and Hardin's

Tower looked as if the next gust of wind would knock it over. The only sound of life that Jon could hear was the faint clash of swords coming from the yard outside the armory. Iron Emmett was shouting at Hop-Robin to keep his shield up. *We had all best keep our shields up.*

Jon washed and dressed and left the armory, stopping in the yard outside just long enough to say a few words of encouragement to Hop-Robin and Emmett's other charges. He declined Ty's offer of a tail, as usual. He would have men enough about him; if it came to blood, two more would hardly matter. He did take Longclaw, though, and Ghost followed at his heels.

By the time he reached the stable, Dolorous Edd had the lord commander's palfrey saddled and bridled and waiting for him. The wayns were forming up beneath Bowen Marsh's watchful eye. The Lord Steward was trotting down the column, pointing and fussing, his cheeks red from the cold. When he spied Jon, they reddened even more. "Lord Commander. Are you still intent on this . . ."

". . . folly?" finished Jon. "Please tell me you were not about to say *folly*, my lord. Yes, I am. We have been over this. Eastwatch wants more men. The Shadow Tower wants more men. Greyguard and Icemark as well, I have no doubt, and we have fourteen other castles still sitting empty, long leagues of Wall that remain unwatched and undefended."

Marsh pursed his lips. "Lord Commander Mormont—"

"—is dead. And not at wildling hands, but at the hands of his own Sworn Brothers, men he trusted. Neither you nor I can know what he would or would not have done in my place." Jon wheeled his horse around. "Enough talk. Away."

Dolorous Edd had heard the entire exchange. As Bowen Marsh trotted off, he nodded toward his back and said, "Pomegranates. All those seeds. A man could choke to death. I'd sooner have a turnip. Never knew a turnip to do a man any harm."

It was at times like this that Jon missed Maester Aemon the most. Clydas tended to the ravens well enough, but he had not a tenth of Aemon Targaryen's knowledge or experience, and even less of his wisdom. Bowen was a good man in his way, but the wound he had taken at the Bridge of Skulls had hardened his attitudes, and the only song he ever sang now was his familiar refrain about sealing the gates. Othell Yarwyck was as stolid and unimaginative as he was taciturn, and the First Rangers seemed to die as quick as they were named. *The Night's Watch has lost too many of its best men,* Jon reflected, as the wagons began to move. *The Old Bear, Qhorin Halfhand, Donal Noye, Jarmen Buckwell, my uncle . . .*

A light snow began to fall as the column made its way south along the kingsroad, the long line of wagons wending past fields and streams and wooded hillsides, with a dozen spearmen and a dozen archers riding escort. The last few trips had seen some ugliness at Mole's Town, a little pushing and shoving, some muttered curses, a lot of sullen looks. Bowen Marsh felt it best not to take chances, and for once he and Jon were agreed.

The Lord Steward led the way. Jon rode a few yards back, Dolorous Edd Tollett at his side. Half a mile south of Castle Black, Edd urged his garron close to Jon's and said, "M'lord? Look up there. The big drunkard on the hill."

The drunkard was an ash tree, twisted sideways by centuries of wind. And now it had a face. A solemn mouth, a broken branch for a nose, two eyes carved deep into the trunk, gazing north up the kingsroad, toward the castle and the Wall.

The wildlings brought their gods with them after all. Jon was not surprised. Men do not give up their gods so easily. The whole pageant that Lady Melisandre had orchestrated beyond the Wall suddenly seemed as empty as a mummer's farce. "Looks a bit like you, Edd," he said, trying to make light of it.

"Aye, m'lord. I don't have leaves growing out my nose, but elsewise . . . Lady Melisandre won't be happy."

"She's not like to see it. See that no one tells her."

"She sees things in those fires, though."

"Smoke and cinders."

"And people burning. Me, most like. With leaves up my nose. I always feared I'd burn, but I was hoping to die first."

Jon glanced back at the face, wondering who had carved it. He had posted guards around Mole's Town, both to keep his crows away from the wildling women and to keep the free folk from slipping off southward to raid. Whoever had carved up the ash had eluded his sentries, plainly. And if one man could slip through the cordon, others could as well. *I could double the guard again,* he thought sourly. *Waste twice as many men, men who might otherwise be walking the Wall.*

The wagons continued on their slow way south through frozen mud and blowing snow. A mile farther on, they came upon a second face, carved into a chestnut tree that grew beside an icy stream, where its eyes could watch the old plank bridge that spanned its flow. "Twice as much trouble," announced Dolorous Edd.

The chestnut was leafless and skeletal, but its bare brown limbs were not empty. On a low branch overhanging the stream a raven sat hunched, its feathers ruffled up against the cold. When it spied Jon it spread its wings and gave a scream. When he raised his fist and whistled, the big black bird came flapping down, crying, "*Corn, corn, corn.*"

"Corn for the free folk," Jon told him. "None for you." He wondered if they would all be reduced to eating ravens before the coming winter had run its course.

The brothers on the wagons had seen this face as well, Jon did not doubt. No one spoke of it, but the message was plain to read for any man with eyes. Jon had once heard Mance Rayder say that most kneelers were sheep. "Now, a dog can herd a flock of sheep," the King-Beyond-the-Wall had said, "but free folk, well, some are shadowcats and some are stones. One kind prowls where they please and will tear your dogs to pieces. The other will not move at all unless you kick them." Neither shadowcats nor stones were like to give up the gods they had worshiped all their lives to bow down before one they hardly knew.

Just north of Mole's Town they came upon the third watcher, carved into the huge oak that marked the village perimeter, its deep eyes fixed upon the kingsroad. *That is not a friendly face,* Jon Snow reflected. The faces that the First Men and the children of the forest had carved into the weirwoods in eons past had stern or savage visages more oft than not, but the great oak looked especially angry, as if it were about to tear its roots from the earth and come roaring after them. *Its wounds are as fresh as the wounds of the men who carved it.*

Mole's Town had always been larger than it seemed; most of it was underground, sheltered from the cold and snow. That was more true than ever now. The Magnar of Thenn had put the empty village to the torch when he passed through on his way to attack Castle Black, and only heaps of blackened beams and old scorched stones remained above-ground . . . but down beneath the frozen earth, the vaults and tunnels and deep cellars still endured, and that was where the free folk had taken refuge, huddled together in the dark like the moles from which the village took its name.

The wagons drew up in a crescent in front of what had once been the village smithy. Nearby a swarm of red-faced children were building a snow fort, but they scattered at the sight of the black-cloaked brothers, vanishing down one hole or another. A few moments later the adults began to emerge from the earth. A stench came with them, the smell of unwashed bodies and soiled clothing, of nightsoil and urine. Jon saw one of his men wrinkle his nose and say something to the man beside him.

Some jape about the smell of freedom, he guessed. Too many of his brothers were making japes about the stench of the savages in Mole's Town.

Pig ignorance, Jon thought. The free folk were no different than the men of the Night's Watch; some were clean, some dirty, but most were clean at times and dirty at other times. This stink was just the smell of a thousand people jammed into cellars and tunnels that had been dug to shelter no more than a hundred.

The wildlings had done this dance before. Wordless, they formed up in lines behind the wagons. There were three women for every man, many with children—pale skinny things clutching at their skirts. Jon saw very few babes in arms. *The babes in arms died during the march,* he realized, *and those who survived the battle died in the king's stockade.*

The fighters had fared better. Three hundred men of fighting age, Justin Massey had claimed in council. Lord Harwood Fell had counted them. *There will be spearwives too. Fifty, sixty, maybe as many as a hundred.* Fell's count had included men who had suffered wounds, Jon knew. He saw a score of those—men on crude crutches, men with empty sleeves and missing hands, men with one eye or half a face, a legless man carried between two friends. And every one grey-faced and gaunt. *Broken men,* he thought. *The wights are not the only sort of living dead.*

Not all the fighting men were broken, though. Half a dozen Thenns in bronze scale armor stood clustered round one cellar stair, watching sullenly and making no attempt to join the others. In the ruins of the old village smithy Jon spied a big bald slab of a man he recognized as Halleck, the brother of Harma Dogshead. Harma's pigs were gone, though. *Eaten, no doubt.* Those two in furs were Hornfoot men, as savage as they were scrawny, barefoot even in the snow. *There are wolves amongst these sheep, still.*

Val had reminded him of that, on his last visit with her. "Free folk and kneelers are more alike than not, Jon Snow. Men are men and women women, no matter which side of the Wall we were born on. Good men and bad, heroes and villains, men of honor, liars, cravens, brutes . . . we have plenty, as do you."

She was not wrong. The trick was telling one from the other, parting the sheep from the goats.

The black brothers began to pass out food. They'd brought slabs of hard salt beef, dried cod, dried beans, turnips, carrots, sacks of barley meal and wheaten flour, pickled eggs, barrels of onions and apples. "You can have an onion or an apple," Jon heard Hairy Hal tell one woman, "but not both. You got to pick."

The woman did not seem to understand. "I need two of each. One o' each for me, t'others for my boy. He's sick, but an apple will set him right."

Hal shook his head. "He has to come get his own apple. Or his onion. Not both. Same as you. Now, is it an apple or an onion? Be quick about it, now, there's more behind you."

"An apple," she said, and he gave her one, an old dried thing, small and withered.

"Move along, woman," shouted a man three places back. "It's cold out here."

The woman paid the shout no mind. "Another apple," she said to Hairy Hal. "For my son. Please. This one is so little."

Hal looked to Jon. Jon shook his head. They would be out of apples soon enough. If they started giving two to everyone who wanted two, the latecomers would get none.

"Out of the way," a girl behind the woman said. Then she shoved her in the back. The woman staggered, lost her apple, and fell. The other foodstuffs in her arms went flying. Beans scattered, a turnip rolled into a mud puddle, a sack of flour split and spilled its precious contents in the snow.

Angry voices rose, in the Old Tongue and the Common. More shoving broke out at another wagon. "It's not *enough*," an old man snarled. "You bloody crows are starving us to death." The woman who'd been knocked down was scrabbling on her knees after her food. Jon saw the flash of naked steel a few yards away. His own bowmen nocked arrows to their strings.

He turned in his saddle. "Rory. Quiet them."

Rory lifted his great horn to his lips and blew.

AAAAhoooooooooooooooooooooooooooooooooooooooooooooo.

The tumult and the shoving died. Heads turned. A child began to cry. Mormont's raven walked from Jon's left shoulder to his right, bobbing its head and muttering, "*Snow, snow, snow.*"

Jon waited until the last echoes had faded, then spurred his palfrey forward where everyone could see him. "We're feeding you as best we can, as much as we can spare. Apples, onions, neeps, carrots . . . there's a long winter ahead for all of us, and our stores are not inexhaustible."

"You crows eat good enough." Halleck shoved forward.

For now. "We hold the Wall. The Wall protects the realm . . . and you now. You know the foe we face. You know what's coming down on us. Some of you have faced them before. Wights and white walkers, dead things with blue eyes and black hands. I've seen them too, fought them, sent one to hell. They kill, then they send your dead against you. The giants were not able to stand against them, nor you Thenns, the ice-river clans, the Hornfoots, the free folk . . . and as the days grow shorter and the nights colder, they are growing stronger. You left your homes and came south in your hundreds and your thousands . . . why, but to escape them? To be safe. Well, it's the Wall that keeps you safe. It's *us* that keeps you safe, the black crows you despise."

"Safe and starved," said a squat woman with a windburned face, a spearwife by the look of her.

"You want more food?" asked Jon. "The food's for fighters. Help us hold the Wall, and you'll eat as well as any crow." *Or as poorly, when the food runs short.*

A silence fell. The wildlings exchanged wary looks. "*Eat,*" the raven muttered. "*Corn, corn.*"

"Fight for you?" This voice was thickly accented. Sigorn, the young Magnar of Thenn, spoke the Common Tongue haltingly at best. "Not fight for you. Kill you better. Kill all you."

The raven flapped its wings. "*Kill, kill.*"

Sigorn's father, the old Magnar, had been crushed beneath the falling stair during his attack on Castle Black. *I would feel the same if someone asked me to make common cause with the Lannisters,* Jon told himself. "Your father tried to kill us all," he reminded Sigorn. "The Magnar was a brave man, yet he failed. And if he had succeeded . . . who would hold the Wall?" He turned away from the Thenns. "Winterfell's walls were strong as well, but Winterfell stands in ruins today, burned and broken. A wall is only as good as the men defending it."

An old man with a turnip cradled against his chest said, "You kill us, you starve us, now you want t' make us slaves."

A chunky red-faced man shouted assent. "I'd sooner go naked than wear one o' them black rags on my back."

One of the spearwives laughed. "Even your wife don't want to see *you* naked, Butts."

A dozen voices all began to speak at once. The Thenns were shouting in the Old Tongue. A little boy began to cry. Jon Snow waited until all of it had died down, then turned to Hairy Hal and said, "Hal, what was it that you told this woman?"

Hal looked confused. "About the food, you mean? An apple or an onion? That's all I said. They got to pick."

"*You have to pick,*" Jon Snow repeated. "All of you. No one is asking you to take our vows, and I do not care what gods you worship. My own gods are the old gods, the gods of the North, but you can keep the red god, or the Seven, or any other god who hears your prayers. It's spears we need. Bows. Eyes along the Wall.

"I will take any boy above the age of twelve who knows how to hold a spear or string a bow. I will take your old men, your wounded, and your cripples, even those who can no longer fight. There are other tasks they may be able to perform. Fletching arrows, milking goats, gathering fire-wood, mucking out our stables . . . the work is endless. And yes, I will take your women too. I have no need of blushing maidens looking to be pro-tected, but I will take as many spearwives as will come."

"And girls?" a girl asked. She looked as young as Arya had, the last time Jon had seen her.

"Sixteen and older."

"You're taking boys as young as twelve."

Down in the Seven Kingdoms boys of twelve were often pages or squires; many had been training at arms for years. Girls of twelve were children. *These are wildlings, though.* "As you will. Boys *and* girls as young as twelve. But only those who know how to obey an order. That goes for all of you. I will never ask you to kneel to me, but I will set captains over you, and serjeants who will tell you when to rise and when to sleep, where to eat, when to drink, what to wear, when to draw your swords and loose your arrows. The men of the Night's Watch serve for life. I will not ask that of you, but so long as you are on the Wall you will be under my com-mand. Disobey an order, and I'll have your head off. Ask my brothers if I won't. They've seen me do it."

"*Off,*" screamed the Old Bear's raven. "*Off, off, off.*"

"The choice is yours," Jon Snow told them. "Those who want to help us hold the Wall, return to Castle Black with me and I'll see you armed and fed. The rest of you, get your turnips and your onions and crawl back inside your holes."

The girl was the first to come forward. "I can fight. My mother was a spearwife." Jon nodded. *She may not even be twelve,* he thought, as she squirmed between a pair of old men, but he was not about to turn away his only recruit.

A pair of striplings followed her, boys no older than fourteen. Next a scarred man with a missing eye. "I seen them too, the dead ones. Even crows are better'n that." A tall spearwife, an old man on crutches, a moon-faced boy with a withered arm, a young man whose red hair reminded Jon of Ygritte.

And then Halleck. "I don't like you, crow," he growled, "but I never liked the Mance neither, no more'n my sister did. Still, we fought for him. Why not fight for you?"

The dam broke then. Halleck was a man of note. *Mance was not wrong.* "Free folk don't follow names, or little cloth animals sewn on a tunic," the King-Beyond-the-Wall had told him. "They won't dance for coins, they don't care how you style yourself or what that chain of office means or who your grandsire was. They follow strength. They follow the man."

Halleck's cousins followed Halleck, then one of Harma's banner-bearers, then men who'd fought with her, then others who had heard tales of their prowess. Greybeards and green boys, fighting men in their prime, wounded men and cripples, a good score of spearwives, even three Horn-foot men.

But no Thenns. The Magnar turned and vanished back into the tunnels, and his bronze-clad minions followed hard at his heels.

By the time the last withered apple had been handed out, the wagons were crowded with wildlings, and they were sixty-three stronger than when the column had set out from Castle Black that morning. "What will you do with them?" Bowen Marsh asked Jon on the ride back up the kingsroad.

"Train them, arm them, and split them up. Send them where they're needed. Eastwatch, the Shadow Tower, Icemark, Greyguard. I mean to open three more forts as well."

The Lord Steward glanced back. "Women too? Our brothers are not accustomed to having women amongst them, my lord. Their vows . . . there will be fights, rapes . . ."

"These women have knives and know how to use them."

"And the first time one of these spearwives slits the throat of one of our brothers, what then?"

"We will have lost a man," said Jon, "but we have just gained sixty-three. You're good at counting, my lord. Correct me if I'm wrong, but my reckoning leaves us sixty-two ahead."

Marsh was unconvinced. "You've added sixty-three more mouths, my lord . . . but how many are fighters, and whose side will they fight on? If it's the Others at the gates, most like they'll stand with us, I grant you . . . but if it's Tormund Giantsbane or the Weeping Man come calling with ten thousand howling killers, what then?"

"Then we'll know. So let us hope it never comes to that."

TYRION

He dreamt of his lord father and the Shrouded Lord. He dreamt that they were one and the same, and when his father wrapped stone arms around him and bent to give him his grey kiss, he woke with his mouth dry and rusty with the taste of blood and his heart hammering in his chest.

"Our dead dwarf has returned to us," Haldon said.

Tyrion shook his head to clear away the webs of dream. *The Sorrows. I was lost in the Sorrows.* "I am not dead."

"That remains to be seen." The Halfmaester stood over him. "Duck, be a fine fowl and boil some broth for our little friend here. He must be famished."

He was on the *Shy Maid*, Tyrion saw, under a scratchy blanket that smelled of vinegar. *The Sorrows are behind us. It was just a dream I dreamed as I was drowning.* "Why do I stink of vinegar?"

"Lemore has been washing you with it. Some say it helps prevent the greyscale. I am inclined to doubt that, but there was no harm in trying. It was Lemore who forced the water from your lungs after Griff had pulled you up. You were as cold as ice, and your lips were blue. Yandry said we ought to throw you back, but the lad forbade it."

The prince. Memory came rushing back: the stone man reaching out with cracked grey hands, the blood seeping from his knuckles. *He was heavy as a boulder, pulling me under.* "Griff brought me up?" *He must hate me, or he would have let me die.* "How long have I been sleeping? What place is this?"

"Selhorys." Haldon produced a small knife from his sleeve. "Here," he said, tossing it underhand at Tyrion.

The dwarf flinched. The knife landed between his feet and stood quivering in the deck. He plucked it out. "What's this?"

"Take off your boots. Prick each of your toes and fingers."

"That sounds . . . painful."

"I hope so. Do it."

Tyrion yanked off one boot and then the other, peeled down his hose, squinted at his toes. It seemed to him they looked no better or worse than usual. He poked gingerly at one big toe.

"Harder," urged Haldon Halfmaester.

"Do you want me to draw blood?"

"If need be."

"I'll have a scab on every toe."

"The purpose of the exercise is not to count your toes. I want to see you wince. So long as the pricks hurt, you are safe. It is only when you cannot feel the blade that you will have cause to fear."

Greyscale. Tyrion grimaced. He stabbed another toe, cursed as a bead of blood welled up around the knife's point. "That hurt. Are you happy?"

"Dancing with joy."

"Your feet smell worse than mine, Yollo." Duck had a cup of broth. "Griff warned you not to lay hands upon the stone men."

"Aye, but he forgot to warn the stone men not to lay their hands upon me."

"As you prick, look for patches of dead grey skin, for nails beginning to turn black," said Haldon. "If you see such signs, do not hesitate. Better to lose a toe than a foot. Better to lose an arm than spend your days wailing on the Bridge of Dream. Now the other foot, if you please. Then your fingers."

The dwarf recrossed his stunted legs and began to prick the other set of toes. "Shall I prick my prick as well?"

"It would not hurt."

"It would not hurt *you* is what you mean. Though I had as well slice it off for all the use I make of it."

"Feel free. We will have it tanned and stuffed and sell it for a fortune. A dwarf's cock has magical powers."

"I have been telling all the women that for years." Tyrion drove the dagger's point into the ball of his thumb, watched the blood bead up, sucked it away. "How long must I continue to torture myself? When will we be certain that I'm clean?"

"Truly?" said the Halfmaester. "Never. You swallowed half the river. You may be going grey even now, turning to stone from inside out, starting with your heart and lungs. If so, pricking your toes and bathing in vinegar will not save you. When you're done, come have some broth."

The broth was good, though Tyrion noted that the Halfmaester kept the table between them as he ate. The *Shy Maid* was moored to a weathered pier on the east bank of the Rhoyne. Two piers down, a Volantene river galley was discharging soldiers. Shops and stalls and storehouses huddled beneath a sandstone wall. The towers and domes of the city were visible beyond it, reddened by the light of the setting sun.

No, not a city. Selhorys was still accounted a mere town, and was ruled from Old Volantis. This was not Westeros.

Lemore emerged on deck with the prince in tow. When she saw Tyrion, she rushed across the deck to hug him. "The Mother is merciful. We have prayed for you, Hugor."

You did, at least. "I won't hold that against you."

Young Griff's greeting was less effusive. The princeling was in a sullen mood, angry that he had been forced to remain on the *Shy Maid* instead of going ashore with Yandry and Ysilla. "We only want to keep you safe," Lemore told him. "These are unsettled times."

Haldon Halfmaester explained. "On the way down from the Sorrows to Selhorys, we thrice glimpsed riders moving south along the river's eastern shore. Dothraki. Once they were so close we could hear the bells tinkling in their braids, and sometimes at night their fires could be seen beyond the eastern hills. We passed warships as well, Volantene river galleys crammed with slave soldiers. The triarchs fear an attack upon Selhorys, plainly."

Tyrion understood that quick enough. Alone amongst the major river towns, Selhorys stood upon the eastern bank of the Rhoyne, making it much more vulnerable to the horselords than its sister towns across the river. *Even so, it is a small prize. If I were khal, I would feint at Selhorys, let the Volantenes rush to defend it, then swing south and ride hard for Volantis itself.*

"I know how to use a sword," Young Griff was insisting.

"Even the bravest of your forebears kept his Kingsguard close about him in times of peril." Lemore had changed out of her septa's robes into garb more befitting the wife or daughter of a prosperous merchant. Tyrion watched her closely. He had sniffed out the truth beneath the dyed blue hair of Griff and Young Griff easily enough, and Yandry and Ysilla seemed to be no more than they claimed to be, whilst Duck was somewhat less. Lemore, though . . . *Who is she, really? Why is she here? Not for gold, I'd judge. What is this prince to her? Was she ever a true septa?*

Haldon took note of her change of garb as well. "What are we to make of this sudden loss of faith? I preferred you in your septa's robes, Lemore."

"I preferred her naked," said Tyrion.

Lemore gave him a reproachful look. "That is because you have a wicked soul. Septa's robes scream of Westeros and might draw unwelcome eyes onto us." She turned back to Prince Aegon. "You are not the only one who must needs hide."

The lad did not seem appeased. *The perfect prince but still half a boy for all that, with little and less experience of the world and all its woes.* "Prince Aegon," said Tyrion, "since we're both stuck aboard this boat, perhaps you will honor me with a game of *cyvasse* to while away the hours?"

The prince gave him a wary look. "I am sick of *cyvasse*."

"Sick of losing to a dwarf, you mean?"

That pricked the lad's pride, just as Tyrion had known it would. "Go fetch the board and pieces. This time I mean to smash you."

They played on deck, sitting cross-legged behind the cabin. Young Griff arrayed his army for attack, with dragon, elephants, and heavy horse up front. *A young man's formation, as bold as it is foolish. He risks all for the quick kill.* He let the prince have first move. Haldon stood behind them, watching the play.

When the prince reached for his dragon, Tyrion cleared his throat. "I would not do that if I were you. It is a mistake to bring your dragon out too soon." He smiled innocently. "Your father knew the dangers of being overbold."

"Did you know my true father?"

"Well, I saw him twice or thrice, but I was only ten when Robert killed him, and mine own sire had me hidden underneath a rock. No, I cannot claim I knew Prince Rhaegar. Not as your false father did. Lord Connington was the prince's dearest friend, was he not?"

Young Griff pushed a lock of blue hair out of his eyes. "They were squires together at King's Landing."

"A true friend, our Lord Connington. He must be, to remain so fiercely loyal to the grandson of the king who took his lands and titles and sent him into exile. A pity about that. Elsewise Prince Rhaegar's friend might have been on hand when my father sacked King's Landing, to save Prince Rhaegar's precious little son from getting his royal brains dashed out against a wall."

The lad flushed. "That was not me. I told you. That was some tanner's son from Pisswater Bend whose mother died birthing him. His father sold him to Lord Varys for a jug of Arbor gold. He had other sons but had never tasted Arbor gold. Varys gave the Pisswater boy to my lady mother and carried me away."

"Aye." Tyrion moved his elephants. "And when the pisswater prince was safely dead, the eunuch smuggled you across the narrow sea to his fat friend the cheesemonger, who hid you on a poleboat and found an exile lord willing to call himself your father. It does make for a splendid story, and the singers will make much of your escape once you take the Iron Throne . . . assuming that our fair Daenerys takes you for her consort."

"She will. She must."

"*Must?*" Tyrion made a *tsk*ing sound. "That is not a word queens like to hear. You are her perfect prince, agreed, bright and bold and comely as any maid could wish. Daenerys Targaryen is no maid, however. She is the widow of a Dothraki khal, a mother of dragons and sacker of cities, Aegon the Conqueror with teats. She may not prove as willing as you wish."

"She'll be willing." Prince Aegon sounded shocked. It was plain that he had never before considered the possibility that his bride-to-be might refuse him. "You don't know her." He picked up his heavy horse and put it down with a *thump*.

The dwarf shrugged. "I know that she spent her childhood in exile, impoverished, living on dreams and schemes, running from one city to the next, always fearful, never safe, friendless but for a brother who was by all accounts half-mad . . . a brother who sold her maidenhood to the Dothraki for the promise of an army. I know that somewhere out upon the grass her dragons hatched, and so did she. I know she is proud. How not? What else was left her but pride? I know she is strong. How not? The Dothraki despise weakness. If Daenerys had been weak, she would have perished with Viserys. I know she is fierce. Astapor, Yunkai, and Meereen are proof enough of that. She has crossed the grasslands and the red waste, survived assassins and conspiracies and fell sorceries, grieved for a brother and a husband and a son, trod the cities of the slavers to dust beneath her dainty sandaled feet. Now, how do you suppose this queen will react when you turn up with your begging bowl in hand and say, 'Good morrow to you, Auntie. I am your nephew, Aegon, returned from the dead. I've been hiding on a poleboat all my life, but now I've washed the blue dye from my hair and I'd like a dragon, please . . . and oh, did I mention, my claim to the Iron Throne is stronger than your own?'"

Aegon's mouth twisted in fury. "I will *not* come to my aunt a beggar. I will come to her a kinsman, with an army."

"A small army." *There, that's made him good and angry.* The dwarf could not help but think of Joffrey. *I have a gift for angering princes.* "Queen Daenerys has a large one, and no thanks to you." Tyrion moved his crossbows.

"Say what you want. She will be my bride, Lord Connington will see to it. I trust him as much as if he were my own blood."

"Perhaps you should be the fool instead of me. *Trust no one*, my prince. Not your chainless maester, not your false father, not the gallant Duck nor the lovely Lemore nor these other fine friends who grew you from a bean. Above all, trust not the cheesemonger, nor the Spider, nor this little dragon queen you mean to marry. All that mistrust will sour your stomach and keep you awake by night, 'tis true, but better that than the long sleep that does not end." The dwarf pushed his black dragon across a range of mountains. "But what do I know? Your false father is a great lord, and I am just some twisted little monkey man. Still, I'd do things differently."

That got the boy's attention. "How differently?"

"If I were you? I would go west instead of east. Land in Dorne and raise my banners. The Seven Kingdoms will never be more ripe for conquest than they are right now. A boy king sits the Iron Throne. The north is in chaos, the riverlands a devastation, a rebel holds Storm's End and Dragonstone. When winter comes, the realm will starve. And who remains to deal with all of this, who rules the little king who rules the Seven Kingdoms? Why, my own sweet sister. There is no one else. My brother, Jaime, thirsts for battle, not for power. He's run from every chance he's had to rule. My uncle Kevan would make a passably good regent if someone pressed the duty on him, but he will never reach for it. The gods shaped him to be a follower, not a leader." *Well, the gods and my lord father.* "Mace Tyrell would grasp the sceptre gladly, but mine own kin are not like to step aside and give it to him. And everyone hates Stannis. Who does that leave? Why, only Cersei.

"Westeros is torn and bleeding, and I do not doubt that even now my sweet sister is binding up the wounds . . . with salt. Cersei is as gentle as King Maegor, as selfless as Aegon the Unworthy, as wise as Mad Aerys. She never forgets a slight, real or imagined. She takes caution for cowardice and dissent for defiance. And she is greedy. Greedy for power, for honor, for love. Tommen's rule is bolstered by all of the alliances that my lord father built so carefully, but soon enough she will destroy them, every one. Land and raise your banners, and men will flock to your cause. Lords great and small, and smallfolk too. But do not wait too long, my prince. The moment will not last. The tide that lifts you now will soon recede. Be certain you reach Westeros before my sister falls and someone more competent takes her place."

"But," Prince Aegon said, "without Daenerys and her dragons, how could we hope to win?"

"You do not *need* to win," Tyrion told him. "All you need to do is raise your banners, rally your supporters, and hold, until Daenerys arrives to join her strength to yours."

"You said she might not have me."

"Perhaps I overstated. She may take pity on you when you come begging for her hand." The dwarf shrugged. "Do you want to wager your throne upon a woman's whim? Go to Westeros, though . . . ah, then you are a rebel, not a beggar. Bold, reckless, a true scion of House Targaryen, walking in the footsteps of Aegon the Conqueror. A *dragon*.

"I told you, I know our little queen. Let her hear that her brother Rhaegar's murdered son is still alive, that this brave boy has raised the dragon standard of her forebears in Westeros once more, that he is fighting a desperate war to avenge his father and reclaim the Iron Throne for House Targaryen, hard-pressed on every side . . . and she will fly to your side as fast as wind and water can carry her. You are the last of her line, and this Mother of Dragons, this Breaker of Chains, is above all a *rescuer*. The girl who drowned the slaver cities in blood rather than leave strangers to their chains can scarcely abandon her own brother's son in his hour of peril. And when she reaches Westeros, and meets you for the first time, you will meet as equals, man and woman, not queen and supplicant. How can she help but love you then, I ask you?" Smiling, he seized his dragon, flew it across the board. "I hope Your Grace will pardon me. Your king is trapped. Death in four."

The prince stared at the playing board. "My dragon—"

"—is too far away to save you. You should have moved her to the center of the battle."

"But you said—"

"I lied. *Trust no one*. And keep your dragon close."

Young Griff jerked to his feet and kicked over the board. *Cyvasse* pieces flew in all directions, bouncing and rolling across the deck of the *Shy Maid*. "Pick those up," the boy commanded.

He may well be a Targaryen after all. "If it please Your Grace." Tyrion got down on his hands and knees and began to crawl about the deck, gathering up pieces.

It was close to dusk when Yandry and Ysilla returned to the *Shy Maid*. A porter trotted at their heels, pushing a wheelbarrow heaped high with provisions: salt and flour, fresh-churned butter, slabs of bacon wrapped in linen, sacks of oranges, apples, and pears. Yandry had a wine cask on one shoulder, while Ysilla had slung a pike over hers. The fish was as large as Tyrion.

When she saw the dwarf standing at the end of the gangplank, Ysilla stopped so suddenly that Yandry blundered into her, and the pike almost slid off her back into the river. Duck helped her rescue it. Ysilla glared at Tyrion and made a peculiar stabbing gesture with three of her fingers. A *sign to ward off evil.* "Let me help you with that fish," he said to Duck.

"No," Ysilla snapped. "Stay away. Touch no food besides the food you eat yourself."

The dwarf raised both hands. "As you command."

Yandry thumped the wine cask down onto the deck. "Where's Griff?" he demanded of Haldon.

"Asleep."

"Then rouse him. We have tidings he'd best hear. The queen's name is on every tongue in Selhorys. They say she still sits in Meereen, sore beset. If the talk in the markets can be believed, Old Volantis will soon join the war against her."

Haldon pursed his lips. "The gossip of fishmongers is not to be relied on. Still, I suppose Griff will want to hear. You know how he is." The Halfmaester went below.

The girl never started for the west. No doubt she had good reasons. Between Meereen and Volantis lay five hundred leagues of deserts, mountains, swamps, and ruins, plus Mantarys with its sinister repute. *A city of monsters, they say, but if she marches overland, where else is she to turn for food and water? The sea would be swifter, but if she does not have the ships . . .*

By the time Griff appeared on deck, the pike was spitting and sizzling over the brazier whilst Ysilla hovered over it with a lemon, squeezing. The sellsword wore his mail and wolfskin cloak, soft leather gloves, dark woolen breeches. If he was surprised to see Tyrion awake, he gave no sign beyond his customary scowl. He took Yandry back to the tiller, where they spoke in low voices, too quietly for the dwarf to hear.

Finally Griff beckoned to Haldon. "We need to know the truth of these rumors. Go ashore and learn what you can. Qavo will know, if you can find him. Try the Riverman and the Painted Turtle. You know his other places."

"Aye. I'll take the dwarf as well. Four ears hear more than two. And you know how Qavo is about his *cyvasse.*"

"As you wish. Be back before the sun comes up. If for any reason you're delayed, make your way to the Golden Company."

Spoken like a lord. Tyrion kept the thought to himself.

Haldon donned a hooded cloak, and Tyrion shed his homemade motley for something drab and grey. Griff allowed them each a purse of silver from Illyrio's chests. "To loosen tongues."

Dusk was giving way to darkness as they made their way along the riverfront. Some of the ships they passed appeared deserted, their gangplanks drawn up. Others crawled with armed men who eyed them with suspicion. Under the town walls, parchment lanterns had been lit above the stalls, throwing pools of colored light upon the cobbled path. Tyrion watched as Haldon's face turned green, then red, then purple. Under the cacophony of foreign tongues, he heard queer music playing from somewhere up ahead, a thin high fluting accompanied by drums. A dog was barking too, behind them.

And the whores were out. River or sea, a port was a port, and wherever you found sailors, you'd find whores. *Is that what my father meant? Is that where whores go, to the sea?*

The whores of Lannisport and King's Landing were free women. Their sisters of Selhorys were slaves, their bondage indicated by the tears tattooed beneath their right eyes. *Old as sin and twice as ugly, the lot of them.* It was almost enough to put a man off whoring. Tyrion felt their eyes upon them as he waddled by, and heard them whispering to one another and giggling behind their hands. *You would think they had never seen a dwarf before.*

A squad of Volantene spearmen stood guard at the river gate. Torchlight gleamed off the steel claws that jutted from their gauntlets. Their helms were tiger's masks, the faces beneath marked by green stripes tattooed across both cheeks. The slave soldiers of Volantis were fiercely proud of their tiger stripes, Tyrion knew. *Do they yearn for freedom?* he wondered. *What would they do if this child queen bestowed it on them? What are they, if not tigers? What am I, if not a lion?*

One of the tigers spied the dwarf and said something that made the others laugh. As they reached the gate, he pulled off his clawed gauntlet and the sweaty glove beneath, locked one arm around the dwarf's neck, and roughly rubbed his head. Tyrion was too startled to resist. It was all over in a heartbeat. "Was there some reason for that?" he demanded of the Halfmaester.

"He says that it is good luck to rub the head of a dwarf," Haldon said after an exchange with the guard in his own tongue.

Tyrion forced himself to smile at the man. "Tell him that it is even better luck to suck on a dwarf's cock."

"Best not. Tigers have been known to have sharp teeth."

A different guard motioned them through the gate, waving a torch at them impatiently. Haldon Halfmaester led the way into Selhorys proper, with Tyrion waddling warily at his heels.

A great square opened up before them. Even at this hour, it was crowded and noisy and ablaze with light. Lanterns swung from iron chains above the doors of inns and pleasure houses, but within the gates, they were made of colored glass, not parchment. To their right a nightfire burned outside a temple of red stone. A priest in scarlet robes stood on the temple balcony, haranguing the small crowd that had gathered around the flames. Elsewhere, travelers sat playing *cyvasse* in front of an inn, drunken soldiers wandered in and out of what was obviously a brothel, a woman beat a mule outside a stable. A two-wheeled cart went rumbling past them, pulled by a white dwarf elephant. *This is another world*, thought Tyrion, *but not so different from the world I know.*

The square was dominated by a white marble statue of a headless man in impossibly ornate armor, astride a warhorse similarly arrayed. "Who might that be?" wondered Tyrion.

"Triarch Horonno. A Volantene hero from the Century of Blood. He was returned as triarch every year for forty years, until he wearied of elections and declared himself triarch for life. The Volantenes were not amused. He was put to death soon after. Tied between two elephants and torn in half."

"His statue seems to lack a head."

"He was a tiger. When the elephants came to power, their followers went on a rampage, knocking the heads from the statues of those they blamed for all the wars and deaths." He shrugged. "That was another age. Come, we'd best hear what that priest is going on about. I swear I heard the name Daenerys."

Across the square they joined the growing throng outside the red temple. With the locals towering above him on every hand, the little man found it hard to see much beyond their arses. He could hear most every word the priest was saying, but that was not to say he understood them. "Do you understand what he is saying?" he asked Haldon in the Common Tongue.

"I would if I did not have a dwarf piping in my ear."

"I do not *pipe*." Tyrion crossed his arms and looked behind him, studying the faces of the men and women who had stopped to listen. Everywhere he turned, he saw tattoos. *Slaves. Four of every five of them are slaves.*

"The priest is calling on the Volantenes to go to war," the Halfmaester told him, "but on the side of right, as soldiers of the Lord of Light, R'hllor who made the sun and stars and fights eternally against the darkness. Nyessos and Malaquo have turned away from the light, he says, their hearts darkened by the yellow harpies from the east. He says . . ."

"*Dragons.* I understood that word. He said *dragons.*"

"Aye. The dragons have come to carry her to glory."

"Her. Daenerys?"

Haldon nodded. "Benerro has sent forth the word from Volantis. Her coming is the fulfillment of an ancient prophecy. From smoke and salt was she born to make the world anew. She is Azor Ahai returned . . . and her triumph over darkness will bring a summer that will never end . . . death itself will bend its knee, and all those who die fighting in her cause shall be reborn . . ."

"Do I have to be reborn in this same body?" asked Tyrion. The crowd was growing thicker. He could feel them pressing in around them. "Who is Benerro?"

Haldon raised an eyebrow. "High Priest of the red temple in Volantis. Flame of Truth, Light of Wisdom, First Servant of the Lord of Light, Slave of R'hllor."

The only red priest Tyrion had ever known was Thoros of Myr, the portly, genial, wine-stained roisterer who had loitered about Robert's court swilling the king's finest vintages and setting his sword on fire for mêlées. "Give me priests who are fat and corrupt and cynical," he told Haldon, "the sort who like to sit on soft satin cushions, nibble sweetmeats, and diddle little boys. It's the ones who believe in gods who make the trouble."

"It may be that we can use this trouble to our advantage. I know where we may find answers." Haldon led them past the headless hero to where a big stone inn fronted on the square. The ridged shell of some immense turtle hung above its door, painted in garish colors. Inside a hundred dim red candles burned like distant stars. The air was fragrant with the smell of roasted meat and spices, and a slave girl with a turtle on one cheek was pouring pale green wine.

Haldon paused in the doorway. "There. Those two."

In the alcove two men sat over a carved stone *cyvasse* table, squinting at their pieces by the light of a red candle. One was gaunt and sallow, with thinning black hair and a blade of a nose. The other was wide of shoulder and round of belly, with corkscrew ringlets tumbling past his collar. Neither deigned to look up from their game until Haldon drew up a chair between them and said, "My dwarf plays better *cyvasse* than both of you combined."

The bigger man raised his eyes to gaze at the intruders in distaste and said something in the tongue of Old Volantis, too fast for Tyrion to hope to follow. The thinner one leaned back in his chair. "Is he for sale?" he asked in the Common Tongue of Westeros. "The triarch's grotesquerie is in need of a *cyvasse*-playing dwarf."

"Yollo is no slave."

"What a pity." The thin man shifted an onyx elephant.

Across the *cyvasse* table, the man behind the alabaster army pursed his lips in disapproval. He moved his heavy horse.

"A blunder," said Tyrion. He had as well play his part.

"Just so," the thin man said. He answered with his own heavy horse. A flurry of quick moves followed, until finally the thin man smiled and said, "Death, my friend."

The big man glowered at the board, then rose and growled something in his own tongue. His opponent laughed. "Come now. The dwarf does not stink as bad as that." He beckoned Tyrion toward the empty chair. "Up with you, little man. Put your silver on the table, and we will see how well you play the game."

Which game? Tyrion might have asked. He climbed onto the chair. "I play better with a full belly and a cup of wine to hand." The thin man turned obligingly and called for the slave girl to fetch them food and drink.

Haldon said, "The noble Qavo Nogarys is the customs officer here in Selhorys. I have never once defeated him at *cyvasse*."

Tyrion understood. "Perhaps I will be more fortunate." He opened his purse and stacked silver coins beside the board, one atop another until finally Qavo smiled.

As each of them was setting up his pieces behind the *cyvasse* screen, Haldon said, "What news from downriver? Will it be war?"

Qavo shrugged. "The Yunkai'i would have it so. They style themselves the Wise Masters. Of their wisdom I cannot speak, but they do not lack for cunning. Their envoy came to us with chests of gold and gems and two hundred slaves, nubile girls and smooth-skinned boys trained in the way of the seven sighs. I am told his feasts are memorable and his bribes lavish."

"The Yunkishmen have bought your triarchs?"

"Only Nyessos." Qavo removed the screen and studied the placement of Tyrion's army. "Malaquo may be old and toothless, but he is a tiger still, and Doniphos will not be returned as triarch. The city thirsts for war."

"Why?" wondered Tyrion. "Meereen is long leagues across the sea. How has this sweet child queen offended Old Volantis?"

"Sweet?" Qavo laughed. "If even half the stories coming back from Slaver's Bay are true, this *child* is a monster. They say that she is blood-thirsty, that those who speak against her are impaled on spikes to die lin-gering deaths. They say she is a sorceress who feeds her dragons on the flesh of newborn babes, an oathbreaker who mocks the gods, breaks truces, threatens envoys, and turns on those who have served her loyally. They say her lust cannot be sated, that she mates with men, women, eu-nuchs, even dogs and children, and woe betide the lover who fails to sat-isfy her. She gives her body to men to take their souls in thrall."

Oh, good, thought Tyrion. *If she gives her body to me, she is welcome to my soul, small and stunted though it is.*

"They say," said Haldon. "By *they,* you mean the slavers, the exiles she drove from Astapor and Meereen. Mere calumnies."

"The best calumnies are spiced with truth," suggested Qavo, "but the girl's true sin cannot be denied. This arrogant child has taken it upon herself to smash the slave trade, but that traffic was never confined to Slaver's Bay. It was part of the sea of trade that spanned the world, and the dragon queen has clouded the water. Behind the Black Wall, lords of an-cient blood sleep poorly, listening as their kitchen slaves sharpen their long knives. Slaves grow our food, clean our streets, teach our young. They guard our walls, row our galleys, fight our battles. And now when they look east, they see this young queen shining from afar, this *breaker of chains.* The Old Blood cannot suffer that. Poor men hate her too. Even the vilest beggar stands higher than a slave. This dragon queen would rob him of that consolation."

Tyrion advanced his spearmen. Qavo replied with his light horse. Tyrion moved his crossbowmen up a square and said, "The red priest outside seemed to think Volantis should fight for this silver queen, not against her."

"The red priests would be wise to hold their tongues," said Qavo No-garys. "Already there has been fighting between their followers and those who worship other gods. Benerro's rantings will only serve to bring a sav-age wrath down upon his head."

"What rantings?" the dwarf asked, toying with his rabble.

The Volantene waved a hand. "In Volantis, thousands of slaves and freedmen crowd the temple plaza every night to hear Benerro shriek of bleeding stars and a sword of fire that will cleanse the world. He has been preaching that Volantis will surely burn if the triarchs take up arms against the silver queen."

"That's a prophecy even I could make. Ah, supper."

Supper was a plate of roasted goat served on a bed of sliced onions. The meat was spiced and fragrant, charred outside and red and juicy within. Tyrion plucked at a piece. It was so hot it burned his fingers, but so good he could not help but reach for another chunk. He washed it down with the pale green Volantene liquor, the closest thing he'd had to wine for ages. "Very good," he said, plucking up his dragon. "The most powerful piece in the game," he announced, as he removed one of Qavo's elephants. "And Daenerys Targaryen has three, it's said."

"Three," Qavo allowed, "against thrice three thousand enemies. Grazdan mo Eraz was not the only envoy sent out from the Yellow City. When the Wise Masters move against Meereen, the legions of New Ghis will fight beside them. Tolosi. Elyrians. Even the Dothraki."

"You have Dothraki outside your own gates," Haldon said.

"Khal Pono." Qavo waved a pale hand in dismissal. "The horselords come, we give them gifts, the horselords go." He moved his catapult again, closed his hand around Tyrion's alabaster dragon, removed it from the board.

The rest was slaughter, though the dwarf held on another dozen moves. "The time has come for bitter tears," Qavo said at last, scooping up the pile of silver. "Another game?"

"No need," said Haldon. "My dwarf has had his lesson in humility. I think it is best we get back to our boat."

Outside in the square, the nightfire was still burning, but the priest was gone and the crowd was long dispersed. The glow of candles glimmered from the windows of the brothel. From inside came the sound of women's laughter. "The night is still young," said Tyrion. "Qavo may not have told us everything. And whores hear much and more from the men they service."

"Do you need a woman so badly, Yollo?"

"A man grows weary of having no lovers but his fingers." *Selhorys may be where whores go. Tysha might be in there even now, with tears tattooed upon her cheek.* "I almost drowned. A man needs a woman after that. Besides, I need to make sure my prick hasn't turned to stone."

The Halfmaester laughed. "I will wait for you in the tavern by the gate. Do not be too long about your business."

"Oh, have no fear on that count. Most women prefer to be done with me as quickly as they can."

The brothel was a modest one compared to those the dwarf had been wont to frequent in Lannisport and King's Landing. The proprietor did not seem to speak any tongue but that of Volantis, but he understood the *clank* of silver well enough and led Tyrion through an archway into a long room that smelled of incense, where four bored slave girls were lounging about in various states of undress. Two had seen at least forty namedays come and go, he guessed; the youngest was perhaps fifteen or sixteen. None was as hideous as the whores he'd seen working the docks, though they fell well short of beauty. One was plainly pregnant. Another was just fat, and sported iron rings in both her nipples. All four had tears tattooed beneath one eye.

"Do you have a girl who speaks the tongue of Westeros?" asked Tyrion. The proprietor squinted, uncomprehending, so he repeated the question in High Valyrian. This time the man seemed to grasp a word or three and replied in Volantene. "Sunset girl" was all the dwarf could get out of his answer. He took that to mean a girl from the Sunset Kingdoms.

There was only one such in the house, and she was not Tysha. She had freckled cheeks and tight red curls upon her head, which gave promise of freckled breasts and red hair between her legs. "She'll do," said Tyrion, "and I'll have a flagon too. Red wine with red flesh." The whore was looking at his noseless face with revulsion in her eyes. "Do I offend you, sweet-ling? I am an offensive creature, as my father would be glad to tell you if he were not dead and rotting."

Though she did look Westerosi, the girl spoke not a word of the Common Tongue. *Perhaps she was captured by some slaver as a child.* Her bedchamber was small, but there was a Myrish carpet on the floor and a mattress stuffed with feathers in place of straw. *I have seen worse.* "Will you give me your name?" he asked, as he took a cup of wine from her. "No?" The wine was strong and sour and required no translation. "I suppose I shall settle for your cunt." He wiped his mouth with the back of his hand. "Have you ever bedded a monster before? Now's as good a time as any. Out of your clothes and onto your back, if it please you. Or not."

She looked at him uncomprehending, until he took the flagon from her hands and lifted her skirts up over her head. After that she understood what was required of her, though she did not prove the liveliest of part-ners. Tyrion had been so long without a woman that he spent himself in-side her on the third thrust.

He rolled off feeling more ashamed than sated. *This was a mistake. What a wretched creature I've become.* "Do you know a woman by the name of Tysha?" he asked, as he watched his seed dribble out of her onto the bed. The whore did not respond. "Do you know where whores go?" She did not answer that one either. Her back was crisscrossed by ridges of scar tissue. *This girl is as good as dead. I have just fucked a corpse.* Even her eyes looked dead. *She does not even have the strength to loathe me.*

He needed wine. A lot of wine. He seized the flagon with both hands and raised it to his lips. The wine ran red. Down his throat, down his chin. It dripped from his beard and soaked the feather bed. In the candlelight it looked as dark as the wine that had poisoned Joffrey. When he was done he tossed the empty flagon aside and half-rolled and half-staggered to the floor, groping for a chamber pot. There was none to be found. His stomach heaved, and he found himself on his knees, retching on the carpet, that wonderful thick Myrish carpet, as comforting as lies.

The whore cried out in distress. *They will blame her for this,* he realized, ashamed. "Cut off my head and take it to King's Landing," Tyrion urged her. "My sister will make a lady of you, and no one will ever whip you again." She did not understand that either, so he shoved her legs apart, crawled between them, and took her once more. That much she could comprehend, at least.

Afterward the wine was done and so was he, so he wadded up the girl's clothing and tossed it at the door. She took the hint and fled, leaving him alone in the darkness, sinking deeper into his feather bed. *I am stinking drunk.* He dare not close his eyes, for fear of sleep. Beyond the veil of dream, the Sorrows were waiting for him. Stone steps ascending endlessly, steep and slick and treacherous, and somewhere at the top, the Shrouded Lord. *I do not want to meet the Shrouded Lord.* Tyrion fumbled back into his clothes again and groped his way to the stair. *Griff will flay me. Well, why not? If ever a dwarf deserved a skinning, I'm him.*

Halfway down the steps, he lost his footing. Somehow he managed to break his tumble with his hands and turn it into a clumsy thumping cartwheel. The whores in the room below looked up in astonishment when he landed at the foot of the steps. Tyrion rolled onto his feet and gave them a bow. "I am more agile when I'm drunk." He turned to the proprietor. "I fear I ruined your carpet. The girl's not to blame. Let me pay." He pulled out a fistful of coins and tossed them at the man.

"*Imp,*" a deep voice said, behind him.

In the corner of the room, a man sat in a pool of shadow, with a whore squirming on his lap. *I never saw that girl. If I had, I would have taken her upstairs instead of freckles.* She was younger than the others, slim and pretty, with long silvery hair. Lyseni, at a guess . . . but the man whose lap she filled was from the Seven Kingdoms. Burly and broad-shouldered, forty if he was a day, and maybe older. Half his head was bald, but coarse stubble covered his cheeks and chin, and hair grew thickly down his arms, sprouting even from his knuckles.

Tyrion did not like the look of him. He liked the big black bear on his surcoat even less. *Wool. He's wearing wool, in this heat. Who else but a knight would be so fucking mad?* "How pleasant to hear the Common Tongue so far from home," he made himself say, "but I fear you have mistaken me. My name is Hugor Hill. May I buy you a cup of wine, my friend?"

"I've drunk enough." The knight shoved his whore aside and got to his feet. His sword belt hung on a peg beside him. He took it down and drew his blade. Steel whispered against leather. The whores were watching avidly, candlelight shining in their eyes. The proprietor had vanished. "You're mine, *Hugor.*"

Tyrion could no more outrun him than outfight him. Drunk as he was, he could not even hope to outwit him. He spread his hands. "And what do you mean to do with me?"

"Deliver you," the knight said, "to the queen."

DAENERYS

Galazza Galare arrived at the Great Pyramid attended by a dozen White Graces, girls of noble birth who were still too young to have served their year in the temple's pleasure gardens. They made for a pretty portrait, the proud old woman all in green surrounded by the little girls robed and veiled in white, armored in their innocence.

The queen welcomed them warmly, then summoned Missandei to see that the girls were fed and entertained whilst she shared a private supper with the Green Grace.

Her cooks had prepared them a magnificent meal of honeyed lamb, fragrant with crushed mint and served with the small green figs she liked so much. Two of Dany's favorite hostages served the food and kept the cups filled—a doe-eyed little girl called Qezza and a skinny boy named Grazhar. They were brother and sister, and cousins of the Green Grace, who greeted them with kisses when she swept in, and asked them if they had been good.

"They are very sweet, the both of them," Dany assured her. "Qezza sings for me sometimes. She has a lovely voice. And Ser Barristan has been instructing Grazhar and the other boys in the ways of western chivalry."

"They are of my blood," the Green Grace said, as Qezza filled her cup with a dark red wine. "It is good to know they have pleased Your Radiance. I hope I may do likewise." The old woman's hair was white and her skin was parchment thin, but the years had not dimmed her eyes. They were as green as her robes; sad eyes, full of wisdom. "If you will forgive my saying so, Your Radiance looks . . . weary. Are you sleeping?"

It was all Dany could do not to laugh. "Not well. Last night three Qartheen galleys sailed up the Skahazadhan under the cover of darkness. The Mother's Men loosed flights of fire arrows at their sails and flung pots of burning pitch onto their decks, but the galleys slipped by quickly and suffered no lasting harm. The Qartheen mean to close the river to us, as they have closed the bay. And they are no longer alone. Three galleys from New Ghis have joined them, and a carrack out of Tolos." The Tolosi had replied to her request for an alliance by proclaiming her a whore and demanding that she return Meereen to its Great Masters. Even that was preferable to the answer of Mantarys, which came by way of caravan in a cedar chest. Inside she had found the heads of her three envoys, pickled. "Perhaps your gods can help us. Ask them to send a gale and sweep the galleys from the bay."

"I shall pray and make sacrifice. Mayhaps the gods of Ghis will hear me." Galazza Galare sipped her wine, but her eyes did not leave Dany. "Storms rage within the walls as well as without. More freedmen died last night, or so I have been told."

"Three." Saying it left a bitter taste in her mouth. "The cowards broke in on some weavers, freedwomen who had done no harm to anyone. All they did was make beautiful things. I have a tapestry they gave me hanging over my bed. The Sons of the Harpy broke their loom and raped them before slitting their throats."

"This we have heard. And yet Your Radiance has found the courage to answer butchery with mercy. You have not harmed any of the noble children you hold as hostage."

"Not as yet, no." Dany had grown fond of her young charges. Some were shy and some were bold, some sweet and some sullen, but all were innocent. "If I kill my cupbearers, who will pour my wine and serve my supper?" she said, trying to make light of it.

The priestess did not smile. "The Shavepate would feed them to your dragons, it is said. A life for a life. For every Brazen Beast cut down, he would have a child die."

Dany pushed her food about her plate. She dare not glance over to where Grazhar and Qezza stood, for fear that she might cry. *The Shavepate has a harder heart than mine.* They had fought about the hostages half a dozen times. "The Sons of the Harpy are laughing in their pyramids," Skahaz said, just this morning. "What good are hostages if you will not take their heads?" In his eyes, she was only a weak woman. *Hazzea was enough. What good is peace if it must be purchased with the blood of little children?* "These murders are not their doing," Dany told the Green Grace, feebly. "I am no butcher queen."

"And for that Meereen gives thanks," said Galazza Galare. "We have heard that the Butcher King of Astapor is dead."

"Slain by his own soldiers when he commanded them to march out and attack the Yunkai'i." The words were bitter in her mouth. "He was hardly cold before another took his place, calling himself Cleon the Second. That one lasted eight days before his throat was opened. Then his killer claimed the crown. So did the first Cleon's concubine. King Cutthroat and Queen Whore, the Astapori call them. Their followers are fighting battles in the streets, while the Yunkai'i and their sellswords wait outside the walls."

"These are grievous times. Your Radiance, might I presume to offer you my counsel?"

"You know how much I value your wisdom."

"Then heed me now and marry."

"Ah." Dany had been expecting this.

"Oftimes I have heard you say that you are only a young girl. To look at you, you still seem half a child, too young and frail to face such trials by yourself. You need a king beside you to help you bear these burdens."

Dany speared a chunk of lamb, took a bite from it, chewed slowly. "Tell me, can this king puff his cheeks up and blow Xaro's galleys back to Qarth? Can he clap his hands and break the siege of Astapor? Can he put food in the bellies of my children and bring peace back to my streets?"

"Can you?" the Green Grace asked. "A king is not a god, but there is still much that a strong man might do. When my people look at you, they see a conqueror from across the seas, come to murder us and make slaves of our children. A king could change that. A highborn king of pure Ghiscari blood could reconcile the city to your rule. Elsewise, I fear, your reign must end as it began, in blood and fire."

Dany pushed her food about her plate. "And who would the gods of Ghis have me take as my king and consort?"

"Hizdahr zo Loraq," Galazza Galare said firmly.

Dany did not trouble to feign surprise. "Why Hizdahr? Skahaz is noble born as well."

"Skahaz is Kandaq, Hizdahr Loraq. Your Radiance will forgive me, but only one who is not herself Ghiscari would not understand the difference. Oft have I heard that yours is the blood of Aegon the Conqueror, Jaehaerys the Wise, and Daeron the Dragon. The noble Hizdahr is of the blood of Mazdhan the Magnificent, Hazrak the Handsome, and Zharaq the Liberator."

"His forebears are as dead as mine. Will Hizdahr raise their shades to defend Meereen against its enemies? I need a man with ships and swords. You offer me ancestors."

"We are an old people. Ancestors are important to us. Wed Hizdahr zo

Loraq and make a son with him, a son whose father is the harpy, whose mother is the dragon. In him the prophecies shall be fulfilled, and your enemies will melt away like snow."

He shall be the stallion that mounts the world. Dany knew how it went with prophecies. They were made of words, and words were wind. There would be no son for Loraq, no heir to unite dragon and harpy. *When the sun rises in the west and sets in the east, when the seas go dry and mountains blow in the wind like leaves.* Only then would her womb quicken once again . . .

. . . but Daenerys Targaryen had other children, tens of thousands who had hailed her as their mother when she broke their chains. She thought of Stalwart Shield, of Missandei's brother, of the woman Rylona Rhee, who had played the harp so beautifully. No marriage would ever bring them back to life, but if a husband could help end the slaughter, then she owed it to her dead to marry.

If I wed Hizdahr, will that turn Skahaz against me? She trusted Skahaz more than she trusted Hizdahr, but the Shavepate would be a disaster as a king. He was too quick to anger, too slow to forgive. She saw no gain in wedding a man as hated as herself. Hizdahr was well respected, so far as she could see. "What does my prospective husband think of this?" she asked the Green Grace. *What does he think of me?*

"Your Grace need only ask him. The noble Hizdahr awaits below. Send down to him if that is your pleasure."

You presume too much, priestess, the queen thought, but she swallowed her anger and made herself smile. "Why not?" She sent for Ser Barristan and told the old knight to bring Hizdahr to her. "It is a long climb. Have the Unsullied help him up."

By the time the nobleman had made the ascent, the Green Grace had finished eating. "If it please Your Magnificence, I will take my leave. You and the noble Hizdahr will have many things to discuss, I do not doubt." The old woman dabbed a smear of honey off her lips, gave Qezza and Grazhar each a parting kiss upon the brow, and fastened her silken veil across her face. "I shall return to the Temple of the Graces and pray for the gods to show my queen the course of wisdom."

When she was gone, Dany let Qezza fill her cup again, dismissed the children, and commanded that Hizdahr zo Loraq be admitted to her presence. *And if he dares say one word about his precious fighting pits, I may have him thrown off the terrace.*

Hizdahr wore a plain green robe beneath a quilted vest. He bowed low when he entered, his face solemn. "Have you no smile for me?" Dany asked him. "Am I as fearful as all that?"

"I always grow solemn in the presence of such beauty."

It was a good start. "Drink with me." Dany filled his cup herself. "You know why you are here. The Green Grace seems to feel that if I take you for my husband, all my woes will vanish."

"I would never make so bold a claim. Men are born to strive and suffer. Our woes only vanish when we die. I can be of help to you, however. I have gold and friends and influence, and the blood of Old Ghis flows in my veins. Though I have never wed, I have two natural children, a boy and a girl, so I can give you heirs. I can reconcile the city to your rule and put an end to this nightly slaughter in the streets."

"Can you?" Dany studied his eyes. "Why should the Sons of the Harpy lay down their knives for you? Are you one of them?"

"No."

"Would you tell me if you were?"

He laughed. "No."

"The Shavepate has ways of finding the truth."

"I do not doubt that Skahaz would soon have me confessing. A day with him, and I will be one of the Harpy's Sons. Two days, and I will be the Harpy. Three, and it will turn out I slew your father too, back in the Sunset Kingdoms when I was yet a boy. Then he will impale me on a stake and you can watch me die . . . but afterward the killings will go on." Hizdahr leaned closer. "Or you can marry me and let me try to stop them."

"Why would you *want* to help me? For the crown?"

"A crown would suit me well, I will not deny that. It is more than that, however. Is it so strange that I would want to protect my own people, as you protect your freedmen? Meereen cannot endure another war, Your Radiance."

That was a good answer, and an honest one. "I have never wanted war. I defeated the Yunkai'i once and spared their city when I might have sacked it. I refused to join King Cleon when he marched against them. Even now, with Astapor besieged, I stay my hand. And Qarth . . . I have never done the Qartheen any harm . . ."

"Not by intent, no, but Qarth is a city of merchants, and they love the clink of silver coins, the gleam of yellow gold. When you smashed the slave trade, the blow was felt from Westeros to Asshai. Qarth depends upon its slaves. So too Tolos, New Ghis, Lys, Tyrosh, Volantis . . . the list is long, my queen."

"Let them come. In me they shall find a sterner foe than Cleon. I would sooner perish fighting than return my children to bondage."

"There may be another choice. The Yunkai'i can be persuaded to allow all your freedmen to remain free, I believe, if Your Worship will agree that the Yellow City may trade and train slaves unmolested from this day forth. No more blood need flow."

"Save for the blood of those slaves that the Yunkai'i will *trade* and *train*," Dany said, but she recognized the truth in his words even so. *It may be that is the best end we can hope for.* "You have not said you love me."

"I will, if it would please Your Radiance."

"That is not the answer of a man in love."

"What is love? Desire? No man with all his parts could ever look on you and not desire you, Daenerys. That is not why I would marry you, however. Before you came Meereen was dying. Our rulers were old men with withered cocks and crones whose puckered cunts were dry as dust. They sat atop their pyramids sipping apricot wine and talking of the glories of the Old Empire whilst the centuries slipped by and the very bricks of the city crumbled all around them. Custom and caution had an iron grip upon us till you awakened us with fire and blood. A new time has come, and new things are possible. Marry me."

He is not hard to look at, Dany told herself, *and he has a king's tongue.* "Kiss me," she commanded.

He took her hand again, and kissed her fingers.

"Not that way. Kiss me as if I were your wife."

Hizdahr took her by the shoulders as tenderly as if she were a baby bird. Leaning forward, he pressed his lips to hers. His kiss was light and dry and quick. Dany felt no stirrings.

"Shall I . . . kiss you again?" he asked when it was over.

"No." On her terrace, in her bathing pool, the little fish would nibble at her legs as she soaked. Even they kissed with more fervor than Hizdahr zo Loraq. "I do not love you."

Hizdahr shrugged. "That may come, in time. It has been known to happen that way."

Not with us, she thought. *Not whilst Daario is so close. It's him I want, not you.* "One day I will want to return to Westeros, to claim the Seven Kingdoms that were my father's."

"One day all men must die, but it serves no good to dwell on death. I prefer to take each day as it comes."

Dany folded her hands together. "Words are wind, even words like *love* and *peace*. I put more trust in deeds. In my Seven Kingdoms, knights go on quests to prove themselves worthy of the maiden that they love. They seek for magic swords, for chests of gold, for crowns stolen from a dragon's hoard."

Hizdahr arched an eyebrow. "The only dragons that I know are yours, and magic swords are even scarcer. I will gladly bring you rings and crowns and chests of gold if that is your desire."

"Peace is my desire. You say that you can help me end the nightly slaughter in my streets. I say *do it*. Put an end to this shadow war, my lord. That is your quest. Give me ninety days and ninety nights without a murder, and I will know that you are worthy of a throne. Can you do that?"

Hizdahr looked thoughtful. "Ninety days and ninety nights without a corpse, and on the ninety-first we wed?"

"Perhaps," said Dany, with a coy look. "Though young girls have been known to be fickle. I may still want a magic sword."

Hizdahr laughed. "Then you shall have that too, Radiance. Your wish is my command. Best tell your seneschal to begin making preparations for our wedding."

"Nothing would please the noble Reznak more." If Meereen knew that a wedding was in the offing, that alone might buy her a few nights' respite, even if Hizdahr's efforts came to naught. *The Shavepate will not be happy with me, but Reznak mo Reznak will dance for joy.* Dany did not know which of those concerned her more. She needed Skahaz and the Brazen Beasts, and she had come to mistrust all of Reznak's counsel. *Beware the perfumed seneschal. Has Reznak made common cause with Hizdahr and the Green Grace and set some trap to snare me?*

No sooner had Hizdahr zo Loraq taken his leave of her than Ser Barristan appeared behind her in his long white cloak. Years of service in the Kingsguard had taught the white knight how to remain unobtrusive when she was entertaining, but he was never far. *He knows,* she saw at once, *and he disapproves.* The lines around his mouth had deepened. "So," she said to him, "it seems that I may wed again. Are you happy for me, ser?"

"If that is your command, Your Grace."

"Hizdahr is not the husband you would have chosen for me."

"It is not my place to choose your husband."

"It is not," she agreed, "but it is important to me that you should understand. My people are bleeding. Dying. A queen belongs not to herself, but to the realm. Marriage or carnage, those are my choices. A wedding or a war."

"Your Grace, may I speak frankly?"

"Always."

"There is a third choice."

"Westeros?"

He nodded. "I am sworn to serve Your Grace, and to keep you safe from harm wherever you may go. My place is by your side, whether here or in King's Landing . . . but your place is back in Westeros, upon the Iron Throne that was your father's. The Seven Kingdoms will never accept Hizdahr zo Loraq as king."

"No more than Meereen will accept Daenerys Targaryen as queen. The Green Grace has the right of that. I need a king beside me, a king of old Ghiscari blood. Elsewise they will always see me as the uncouth barbarian who smashed through their gates, impaled their kin on spikes, and stole their wealth."

"In Westeros you will be the lost child who returns to gladden her father's heart. Your people will cheer when you ride by, and all good men will love you."

"Westeros is far away."

"Lingering here will never bring it any closer. The sooner we take our leave of this place—"

"I know. I *do*." Dany did not know how to make him see. She wanted Westeros as much as he did, but first she must heal Meereen. "Ninety days is a long time. Hizdahr may fail. And if he does, the trying buys me time. Time to make alliances, to strengthen my defenses, to—"

"And if he does not fail? What will Your Grace do then?"

"Her duty." The word felt cold upon her tongue. "You saw my brother Rhaegar wed. Tell me, did he wed for love or duty?"

The old knight hesitated. "Princess Elia was a good woman, Your Grace. She was kind and clever, with a gentle heart and a sweet wit. I know the prince was very fond of her."

Fond, thought Dany. The word spoke volumes. *I could become fond of Hizdahr zo Loraq, in time. Perhaps.*

Ser Barristan went on. "I saw your father and your mother wed as well. Forgive me, but there was no fondness there, and the realm paid dearly for that, my queen."

"Why did they wed if they did not love each other?"

"Your grandsire commanded it. A woods witch had told him that the prince was promised would be born of their line."

"A woods witch?" Dany was astonished.

"She came to court with Jenny of Oldstones. A stunted thing, grotesque to look upon. A dwarf, most people said, though dear to Lady Jenny, who always claimed that she was one of the children of the forest."

"What became of her?"

"Summerhall." The word was fraught with doom.

Dany sighed. "Leave me now. I am very weary."

"As you command." Ser Barristan bowed and turned to go. But at the door, he stopped. "Forgive me. Your Grace has a visitor. Shall I tell him to return upon the morrow?"

"Who is it?"

"Naharis. The Stormcrows have returned to the city."

Daario. Her heart gave a flutter in her chest. "How long has . . . when did he . . . ?" She could not seem to get the words out.

Ser Barristan seemed to understand. "Your Grace was with the priestess when he arrived. I knew you would not want to be disturbed. The captain's news can wait until the morrow."

"No." *How could I ever hope to sleep, knowing that my captain so close?* "Send him up at once. And . . . I will have no more need of you this evening. I shall be safe with Daario. Oh, and send Irri and Jhiqui, if you would be so good. And Missandei." *I need to change, to make myself beautiful.*

She said as much to her handmaids when they came. "What does Your Grace wish to wear?" asked Missandei.

Starlight and seafoam, Dany thought, *a wisp of silk that leaves my left breast bare for Daario's delight. Oh, and flowers for my hair.* When first they met, the captain brought her flowers every day, all the way from Yunkai to Meereen. "Bring the grey linen gown with the pearls on the bodice. Oh, and my white lion's pelt." She always felt safer wrapped in Drogo's lionskin.

Daenerys received the captain on her terrace, seated on a carved stone bench beneath a pear tree. A half-moon floated in the sky above the city, attended by a thousand stars. Daario Naharis entered swaggering. *He swaggers even when he is standing still.* The captain wore striped pantaloons tucked into high boots of purple leather, a white silk shirt, a vest of golden rings. His trident beard was purple, his flamboyant mustachios gold, his long curls equal parts of both. On one hip he wore a stiletto, on the other a Dothraki *arakh.* "Bright queen," he said, "you have grown more beautiful in my absence. How is this thing possible?"

The queen was accustomed to such praise, yet somehow the compliment meant more coming from Daario than from the likes of Reznak,

Xaro, or Hizdahr. "Captain. They tell us you did us good service in Lhazar." *I have missed you so much.*

"Your captain lives to serve his cruel queen."

"Cruel?"

Moonlight glimmered in his eyes. "He raced ahead of all his men to see her face the sooner, only to be left languishing whilst she ate lamb and figs with some dried-up old woman."

They never told me you were here, Dany thought, *or I might have played the fool and sent for you at once.* "I was supping with the Green Grace." It seemed best not to mention Hizdahr. "I had urgent need of her wise counsel."

"I have only one urgent need: Daenerys."

"Shall I send for food? You must be hungry."

"I have not eaten in two days, but now that I am here, it is enough for me to feast upon your beauty."

"My beauty will not fill up your belly." She plucked down a pear and tossed it at him. "Eat this."

"If my queen commands it." He took a bite of the pear, his gold tooth gleaming. Juice ran down into his purple beard.

The girl in her wanted to kiss him so much it hurt. *His kisses would be hard and cruel,* she told herself, *and he would not care if I cried out or commanded him to stop.* But the queen in her knew that would be folly. "Tell me of your journey."

He gave a careless shrug. "The Yunkai'i sent some hired swords to close the Khyzai Pass. The Long Lances, they name themselves. We descended on them in the night and sent a few to hell. In Lhazar I slew two of my own serjeants for plotting to steal the gems and gold plate my queen had entrusted to me as gifts for the Lamb Men. Elsewise, all went as I had promised."

"How many men did you lose in the fighting?"

"Nine," said Daario, "but a dozen of the Long Lances decided they would sooner be Stormcrows than corpses, so we came out three ahead. I told them they would live longer fighting with your dragons than against them, and they saw the wisdom in my words."

That made her wary. "They might be spying for Yunkai."

"They are too stupid to be spies. You do not know them."

"Neither do you. Do you trust them?"

"I trust all my men. Just as far as I can spit." He spat out a seed and smiled at her suspicions. "Shall I bring their heads to you? I will, if you command it. One is bald and two have braids and one dyes his beard four different colors. What spy would wear such a beard, I ask you? The slinger can put a stone through a gnat's eye at forty paces, and the ugly one has a way with horses, but if my queen says that they must die . . ."

"I did not say that. I only . . . see that you keep your eye on them, that's all." She felt foolish saying it. She always felt a little foolish when she was with Daario. *Gawky and girlish and slow-witted. What must he think of me?* She changed the subject. "Will the Lamb Men send us food?"

"Grain will come down the Skahazadhan by barge, my queen, and other goods by caravan over the Khyzai."

"Not the Skahazadhan. The river has been closed to us. The seas as well. You will have seen the ships out in the bay. The Qartheen have driven off a third of our fishing fleet and seized another third. The others are too frightened to leave port. What little trade we still had has been cut off."

Daario tossed away the pear stem. "Qartheen have milk in their veins. Let them see your dragons, and they'll run."

Dany did not want to talk about the dragons. Farmers still came to her court with burned bones, complaining of missing sheep, though Drogon had not returned to the city. Some reported seeing him north of the river, above the grass of the Dothraki sea. Down in the pit, Viserion had snapped one of his chains; he and Rhaegal grew more savage every day. Once the iron doors had glowed red-hot, her Unsullied told her, and no one dared to touch them for a day. "Astapor is under siege as well."

"This I knew. One of the Long Lances lived long enough to tell us that men were eating one another in the Red City. He said Meereen's turn would come soon, so I cut his tongue out and fed it to a yellow dog. No dog will eat a liar's tongue. When the yellow dog ate his, I knew he spoke the truth."

"I have war inside the city too." She told him of the Harpy's Sons and the Brazen Beasts, of blood upon the bricks. "My enemies are all around me, within the city and without."

"Attack," he said at once. "A man surrounded by foes cannot defend himself. Try, and the axe will take you in the back whilst you are parrying the sword. No. When faced with many enemies, choose the weakest, kill him, ride over him, and escape."

"Where should I escape to?"

"Into my bed. Into my arms. Into my heart." The hilts of Daario's *arakh* and stiletto were wrought in the shape of golden women, naked and wanton. He brushed his thumbs across them in a way that was remarkably obscene and smiled a wicked smile.

Dany felt blood rushing to her face. It was almost as if he were caressing her. *Would he think me wanton too if I pulled him into bed?* He made her want to be his wanton. *I should never see him alone. He is too dangerous to have near me.* "The Green Grace says that I must take a Ghiscari king," she said, flustered. "She urges me to wed the noble Hizdahr zo Loraq."

"That one?" Daario chuckled. "Why not Grey Worm, if you want a eunuch in your bed? Do you *want* a king?"

I want you. "I want peace. I gave Hizdahr ninety days to end the killings. If he does, I will take him for a husband."

"Take me for your husband. I will do it in nine."

You know I cannot do that, she almost said.

"You are fighting shadows when you should be fighting the men who cast them," Daario went on. "Kill them all and take their treasures, I say. Whisper the command, and your Daario will make you a pile of their heads taller than this pyramid."

"If I knew who they were—"

"Zhak and Pahl and Merreq. Them, and all the rest. The Great Masters. Who else would it be?"

He is as bold as he is bloody. "We have no proof this is their work. Would you have me slaughter my own subjects?"

"Your own subjects would gladly slaughter you."

He had been so long away, Dany had almost forgotten what he was. Sellswords were treacherous by nature, she reminded herself. *Fickle, faithless, brutal. He will never be more than he is. He will never be the stuff of kings.* "The pyramids are strong," she explained to him. "We could take them only at great cost. The moment we attack one the others will rise against us."

"Then winkle them out of their pyramids on some pretext. A wedding might serve. Why not? Promise your hand to Hizdahr and all the Great Masters will come to see you married. When they gather in the Temple of the Graces, turn us loose upon them."

Dany was appalled. *He is a monster. A gallant monster, but a monster still.* "Do you take me for the Butcher King?"

"Better the butcher than the meat. All kings are butchers. Are queens so different?"

"This queen is."

Daario shrugged. "Most queens have no purpose but to warm some king's bed and pop out sons for him. If that's the sort of queen you mean to be, best marry Hizdahr."

Her anger flashed. "Have you forgotten who I am?"

"No. Have you?"

Viserys would have his head off for that insolence. "I am the blood of the dragon. Do not presume to teach me lessons." When Dany stood, the lion pelt slipped from her shoulders and tumbled to the ground. "Leave me."

Daario gave her a sweeping bow. "I live to obey."

When he was gone, Daenerys called Ser Barristan back. "I want the Stormcrows back in the field."

"Your Grace? They have only now returned . . ."

"I want them *gone*. Let them scout the Yunkish hinterlands and give protection to any caravans coming over the Khyzai Pass. Henceforth Daario shall make his reports to you. Give him every honor that is due him and see that his men are well paid, but on no account admit him to my presence."

"As you say, Your Grace."

That night she could not sleep but turned and twisted restlessly in her bed. She even went so far as to summon Irri, hoping her caresses might help ease her way to rest, but after a short while she pushed the Dothraki girl away. Irri was sweet and soft and willing, but she was not Daario.

What have I done? she thought, huddled in her empty bed. *I have waited so long for him to come back, and I send him away.* "He would make a monster of me," she whispered, "a butcher queen." But then she thought of Drogon far away, and the dragons in the pit. *There is blood on my hands too, and on my heart. We are not so different, Daario and I. We are both monsters.*

THE LOST LORD

It should not have taken this long, Griff told himself as he paced the deck of the *Shy Maid*. Had they lost Haldon as they had Tyrion Lannister? Could the Volantenes have taken him? *I should have sent Duckfield with him.* Haldon alone could not be trusted; he had proved that in Selhorys when he let the dwarf escape.

The *Shy Maid* was tied up in one of the meaner sections of the long, chaotic riverfront, between a listing poleboat that had not left the pier in years and the gaily painted mummers' barge. The mummers were a loud and lively lot, always quoting speeches at each other and drunk more oft than not.

The day was hot and sticky, as all the days had been since they left the Sorrows. A ferocious southern sun beat down upon the crowded riverfront of Volon Therys, but heat was the last and least of Griff's concerns. The Golden Company was encamped three miles south of town, well north of where he had expected them, and Triarch Malaquo had come north with five thousand foot and a thousand horse to cut them off from the delta road. Daenerys Targaryen remained a world away, and Tyrion Lannister . . . well, he could be most anywhere. If the gods were good, Lannister's severed head was halfway back to King's Landing by now, but more like the dwarf was hale and whole and somewhere close, stinking drunk and plotting some new infamy.

"Where in the seven hells is Haldon?" Griff complained to Lady Lemore. "How long should it take to buy three horses?"

She shrugged. "My lord, wouldn't it be safer to leave the boy here aboard the boat?"

"Safer, yes. Wiser, no. He is a man grown now, and this is the road that he was born to walk." Griff had no patience for this quibbling. He was sick of hiding, sick of waiting, sick of caution. *I do not have time enough for caution.*

"We have gone to great lengths to keep Prince Aegon hidden all these years," Lemore reminded him. "The time will come for him to wash his hair and declare himself, I know, but that time is not now. Not to a camp of sellswords."

"If Harry Strickland means him ill, hiding him on the *Shy Maid* will not protect him. Strickland has ten thousand swords at his command. We have Duck. Aegon is all that could be wanted in a prince. They need to see that, Strickland and the rest. These are his own men."

"His because they're bought and paid for. Ten thousand armed strangers, plus hangers-on and camp followers. All it takes is one to bring us all to ruin. If Hugor's head was worth a lord's honors, how much will Cersei Lannister pay for the rightful heir to the Iron Throne? You do not know these men, my lord. It has been a dozen years since you last rode with the Golden Company, and your old friend is dead."

Blackheart. Myles Toyne had been so full of life the last time Griff had left him, it was hard to accept that he was gone. *A golden skull atop a pole, and Homeless Harry Strickland in his place.* Lemore was not wrong, he knew. Whatever their sires or their grandsires might have been back in Westeros before their exile, the men of the Golden Company were sellswords now, and no sellsword could be trusted. Even so . . .

Last night he'd dreamt of Stoney Sept again. Alone, with sword in hand, he ran from house to house, smashing down doors, racing up stairs, leaping from roof to roof, as his ears rang to the sound of distant bells. Deep bronze booms and silver chiming pounded through his skull, a maddening cacophony of noise that grew ever louder until it seemed as if his head would explode.

Seventeen years had come and gone since the Battle of the Bells, yet the sound of bells ringing still tied a knot in his guts. Others might claim that the realm was lost when Prince Rhaegar fell to Robert's warhammer on the Trident, but the Battle of the Trident would never have been fought if the griffin had only slain the stag there in Stoney Sept. *The bells tolled for all of us that day. For Aerys and his queen, for Elia of Dorne and her little daughter, for every true man and honest woman in the Seven Kingdoms. And for my silver prince.*

"The plan was to reveal Prince Aegon only when we reached Queen Daenerys," Lemore was saying.

"That was when we believed the girl was coming west. Our dragon queen has burned that plan to ash, and thanks to that fat fool in Pentos, we have grasped the she-dragon by the tail and burned our fingers to the bone."

"Illyrio could not have been expected to know that the girl would choose to remain at Slaver's Bay."

"No more than he knew that the Beggar King would die young, or that Khal Drogo would follow him into the grave. Very little of what the fat man has anticipated has come to pass." Griff slapped the hilt of his long-sword with a gloved hand. "I have danced to the fat man's pipes for years, Lemore. What has it availed us? The prince is a man grown. His time is—"

"*Griff*," Yandry called loudly, above the clanging of the mummers' bell. "It's Haldon."

So it was. The Halfmaester looked hot and bedraggled as he made his way along the waterfront to the foot of the pier. Sweat had left dark rings beneath the arms of his light linen robes, and he had the same sour look on his long face as at Selhorys, when he returned to the *Shy Maid* to con-fess that the dwarf was gone. He was leading three horses, however, and that was all that mattered.

"Bring the boy," Griff told Lemore. "See that he's ready."

"As you say," she answered, unhappily.

So be it. He had grown fond of Lemore, but that did not mean he re-quired her approval. Her task had been to instruct the prince in the doc-trines of the Faith, and she had done that. No amount of prayer would put him on the Iron Throne, however. That was Griff's task. He had failed Prince Rhaegar once. He would not fail his son, not whilst life remained in his body.

Haldon's horses did not please him. "Were these the best that you could find?" he complained to the Halfmaester.

"They were," said Haldon, in an irritated tone, "and you had best not ask what they cost us. With Dothraki across the river, half the populace of Volon Therys has decided they would sooner be elsewhere, so horseflesh grows more expensive every day."

I should have gone myself. After Selhorys, he had found it difficult to put the same trust in Haldon as previously. *He let the dwarf beguile him with that glib tongue of his. Let him wander off into a whorehouse alone while he lingered like a mooncalf in the square*. The brothel keeper had insisted that the little man had been carried off at swordpoint, but Griff was still not sure he believed that. The Imp was clever enough to have conspired in his own escape. This drunken captor that the whores spoke of could have been some henchman in his hire. *I share the blame. After the dwarf put himself between Aegon and the stone man, I let down my guard. I should have slit his throat the first time I laid eyes on him.*

"They will do well enough, I suppose," he told Haldon. "The camp is only three miles south." The *Shy Maid* would have gotten them there more quickly, but he preferred to keep Harry Strickland ignorant of where he and the prince had been. Nor did he relish the prospect of splashing through the shallows to climb some muddy riverbank. That sort of entrance might serve for a sellsword and his son, but not for a great lord and his prince.

When the lad emerged from the cabin with Lemore by his side, Griff looked him over carefully from head to heel. The prince wore sword and dagger, black boots polished to a high sheen, a black cloak lined with blood-red silk. With his hair washed and cut and freshly dyed a deep, dark blue, his eyes looked blue as well. At his throat he wore three huge square-cut rubies on a chain of black iron, a gift from Magister Illyrio. *Red and black. Dragon colors.* That was good. "You look a proper prince," he told the boy. "Your father would be proud if he could see you."

Young Griff ran his fingers through his hair. "I am sick of this blue dye. We should have washed it out."

"Soon enough." Griff would be glad to go back to his own true colors too, though his once red hair had gone to grey. He clapped the lad on the shoulder. "Shall we go? Your army awaits your coming."

"I like the sound of that. My army." A smile flashed across his face, then vanished. "Are they, though? They're sellswords. Yollo warned me to trust no one."

"There is wisdom in that," Griff admitted. It might have been different if Blackheart still commanded, but Myles Toyne was four years dead, and Homeless Harry Strickland was a different sort of man. He would not say that to the boy, however. That dwarf had already planted enough doubts in his young head. "Not every man is what he seems, and a prince especially has good cause to be wary . . . but go too far down that road, and the mistrust can poison you, make you sour and fearful." *King Aerys was one such. By the end, even Rhaegar saw that plain enough.* "You would do best to walk a middle course. Let men earn your trust with leal service . . . but when they do, be generous and openhearted."

The boy nodded. "I will remember."

They gave the prince the best of the three horses, a big grey gelding so pale that he was almost white. Griff and Haldon rode beside him on lesser mounts. The road ran south beneath the high white walls of Volon Therys for a good half mile. Then they left the town behind, following the winding course of the Rhoyne through willow groves and poppy fields and past a tall wooden windmill whose blades creaked like old bones as they turned.

They found the Golden Company beside the river as the sun was lowering in the west. It was a camp that even Arthur Dayne might have approved of—compact, orderly, defensible. A deep ditch had been dug around it, with sharpened stakes inside. The tents stood in rows, with broad avenues between them. The latrines had been placed beside the river, so the current would wash away the wastes. The horse lines were to the north, and beyond them, two dozen elephants grazed beside the water, pulling up reeds with their trunks. Griff glanced at the great grey beasts with approval. *There is not a warhorse in all of Westeros that will stand against them.*

Tall battle standards of cloth-of-gold flapped atop lofty poles along the perimeters of the camp. Beneath them, armed and armored sentries walked their rounds with spears and crossbows, watching every approach. Griff had feared that the company might have grown lax under Harry Strickland, who had always seemed more concerned with making friends than enforcing discipline; but it would seem his worries had been misplaced.

At the gate, Haldon said something to the serjeant of guards, and a runner was sent off to find a captain. When he turned up, he was just as ugly as the last time Griff laid eyes on him. A big-bellied, shambling hulk of a man, the sellsword had a seamed face crisscrossed with old scars. His right ear looked as if a dog had chewed on it and his left was missing. "Have they made *you* a captain, Flowers?" Griff said. "I thought the Golden Company had standards."

"It's worse than that, you bugger," said Franklyn Flowers. "They knighted me as well." He clasped Griff by the forearm, pulled him into a bone-crushing hug. "You look awful, even for a man's been dead a dozen years. Blue hair, is it? When Harry said you'd be turning up, I almost shit myself. And Haldon, you icy cunt, good to see you too. Still have that stick up your arse?" He turned to Young Griff. "And this would be . . ."

"My squire. Lad, this is Franklyn Flowers."

The prince acknowledged him with a nod. "Flowers is a bastard name. You're from the Reach."

"Aye. My mother was a washerwoman at Cider Hall till one of milord's sons raped her. Makes me a sort o' brown apple Fossoway, the way I see it." Flowers waved them through the gate. "Come with me. Strickland's

called all the officers to his tent. War council. The bloody Volantenes are
rattling their spears and demanding to know our intentions."

The men of the Golden Company were outside their tents, dicing,
drinking, and swatting away flies. Griff wondered how many of them
knew who he was. *Few enough. Twelve years is a long time.* Even the men
who'd ridden with him might not recognize the exile lord Jon Connington of the fiery red beard in the lined, clean-shaved face and dyed blue
hair of the sellsword Griff. So far as most of them were concerned, Connington had drunk himself to death in Lys after being driven from the
company in disgrace for stealing from the war chest. The shame of the lie
still stuck in his craw, but Varys had insisted it was necessary. "We want no
songs about the gallant exile," the eunuch had tittered, in that mincing
voice of his. "Those who die heroic deaths are long remembered, thieves
and drunks and cravens soon forgotten."

What does a eunuch know of a man's honor? Griff had gone along with
the Spider's scheme for the boy's sake, but that did not mean he liked it
any better. *Let me live long enough to see the boy sit the Iron Throne, and
Varys will pay for that slight and so much more. Then we'll see who's soon
forgotten.*

The captain-general's tent was made of cloth-of-gold and surrounded
by a ring of pikes topped with gilded skulls. One skull was larger than the
rest, grotesquely malformed. Below it was a second, no larger than a
child's fist. *Maelys the Monstrous and his nameless brother.* The other
skulls had a sameness to them, though several had been cracked and
splintered by the blows that had slain them, and one had filed, pointed
teeth. "Which one is Myles?" Griff found himself asking.

"There. On the end." Flowers pointed. "Wait. I'll go announce you."
He slipped inside the tent, leaving Griff to contemplate the gilded skull of
his old friend. In life, Ser Myles Toyne had been ugly as sin. His famous
forebear, the dark and dashing Terrence Toyne of whom the singers sang,
had been so fair of face that even the king's mistress could not resist him;
but Myles had been possessed of jug ears, a crooked jaw, and the biggest
nose that Jon Connington had ever seen. When he smiled at you, though,
none of that mattered. Blackheart, his men had named him, for the sigil
on his shield. Myles had loved the name and all it hinted at. "A
captain-general should be feared, by friend and foe alike," he had once
confessed. "If men think me cruel, so much the better." The truth was
otherwise. Soldier to the bone, Toyne was fierce but always fair, a father to
his men and always generous to the exile lord Jon Connington.

Death had robbed him of his ears, his nose, and all his warmth. The smile remained, transformed into a glittering golden grin. All the skulls were grinning, even Bittersteel's on the tall pike in the center. *What does he have to grin about? He died defeated and alone, a broken man in an alien land.* On his deathbed, Ser Aegor Rivers had famously commanded his men to boil the flesh from his skull, dip it in gold, and carry it before them when they crossed the sea to retake Westeros. His successors had followed his example.

Jon Connington might have been one of those successors if his exile had gone otherwise. He had spent five years with the company, rising from the ranks to a place of honor at Toyne's right hand. Had he stayed, it might well have been him the men turned to after Myles died, instead of Harry Strickland. But Griff did not regret the path he'd chosen. *When I return to Westeros, it will not be as a skull atop a pole.*

Flowers stepped out of the tent. "Go on in."

The high officers of the Golden Company rose from stools and camp chairs as they entered. Old friends greeted Griff with smiles and embraces, the new men more formally. *Not all of them are as glad to see us as they would have me believe.* He sensed knives behind some of the smiles. Until quite recently, most of them had believed that Lord Jon Connington was safely in his grave, and no doubt many felt that was a fine place for him, a man who would steal from his brothers-in-arms. Griff might have felt the same way in their place.

Ser Franklyn did the introductions. Some of the sellsword captains bore bastard names, as Flowers did: Rivers, Hill, Stone. Others claimed names that had once loomed large in the histories of the Seven Kingdoms; Griff counted two Strongs, three Peakes, a Mudd, a Mandrake, a Lothston, a pair of Coles. Not all were genuine, he knew. In the free companies, a man could call himself whatever he chose. By any name, the sellswords displayed a rude splendor. Like many in their trade, they kept their worldly wealth upon their persons: jeweled swords, inlaid armor, heavy torcs, and fine silks were much in evidence, and every man there wore a lord's ransom in golden arm rings. Each ring signified one year's service with the Golden Company. Marq Mandrake, whose pox-scarred face had a hole in one cheek where a slave's mark had been burned away, wore a chain of golden skulls as well.

Not every captain was of Westerosi blood. Black Balaq, a white-haired Summer Islander with skin dark as soot, commanded the company's archers, as in Blackheart's day. He wore a feathered cloak of green and orange, magnificent to behold. The cadaverous Volantene, Gorys Edoryen, had replaced Strickland as paymaster. A leopard skin was draped across one shoulder, and hair as red as blood tumbled to his shoulders in oiled ringlets though his pointed beard was black. The spymaster was new to Griff, a Lyseni named Lysono Maar, with lilac eyes and white-gold hair and lips that would have been the envy of a whore. At first glance, Griff had almost taken him for a woman. His fingernails were painted purple, and his earlobes dripped with pearls and amethysts.

Ghosts and liars, Griff thought, as he surveyed their faces. *Revenants from forgotten wars, lost causes, failed rebellions, a brotherhood of the failed and the fallen, the disgraced and the disinherited. This is my army. This is our best hope.*

He turned to Harry Strickland.

Homeless Harry looked little like a warrior. Portly, with a big round head, mild grey eyes, and thinning hair that he brushed sideways to conceal a bald spot, Strickland sat in a camp chair soaking his feet in a tub of salt water. "You will pardon me if I do not rise," he said by way of greeting. "Our march was wearisome, and my toes are prone to blisters. It is a curse."

It is a mark of weakness. You sound like an old woman. The Stricklands had been part of the Golden Company since its founding, Harry's great-grandsire having lost his lands when he rose with the Black Dragon during the first Blackfyre Rebellion. "Gold for four generations," Harry would boast, as if four generations of exile and defeat were something to take pride in.

"I can make you an ointment for that," said Haldon, "and there are certain mineral salts that will toughen your skin."

"That is kind of you." Strickland beckoned to his squire. "Watkyn, wine for our friends."

"Thank you, but no," said Griff. "We will drink water."

"As you prefer." The captain-general smiled up at the prince. "And this must be your son."

Does he know? Griff wondered. *How much did Myles tell him?* Varys had been adamant about the need for secrecy. The plans that he and Illyrio had made with Blackheart had been known to them alone. The rest of the company had been left ignorant. What they did not know they could not let slip.

That time was done, though. "No man could have asked for a worthier son," Griff said, "but the lad is not of my blood, and his name is not Griff. My lords, I give you Aegon Targaryen, firstborn son of Rhaegar, Prince of

Dragonstone, by Princess Elia of Dorne . . . soon, with your help, to be Aegon, the Sixth of His Name, King of Andals, the Rhoynar, and the First Men, and Lord of the Seven Kingdoms."

Silence greeted his announcement. Someone cleared his throat. One of the Coles refilled his wine cup from the flagon. Gorys Edoryen played with one of his corkscrew ringlets and murmured something in a tongue Griff did not know. Laswell Peake coughed, Mandrake and Lothston exchanged a glance. *They know*, Griff realized then. *They have known all along.* He turned to look at Harry Strickland. "When did you tell them?"

The captain-general wriggled his blistered toes in his footbath. "When we reached the river. The company was restless, with good reason. We walked away from an easy campaign in the Disputed Lands, and for what? So we could swelter in this god-awful heat watching our coins melt away and our blades go to rust whilst I turn away rich contracts?"

That news made Griff's skin crawl. "Who?"

"The Yunkishmen. The envoy that they sent to woo Volantis has already dispatched three free companies to Slaver's Bay. He wishes us to be the fourth and offers twice what Myr was paying us, plus a slave for every man in the company, ten for every officer, and a hundred choice maidens all for me."

Bloody hell. "That would require thousands of slaves. Where do the Yunkishmen expect to find so many?"

"In Meereen." Strickland beckoned to his squire. "Watkyn, a towel. This water's growing cool, and my toes have wrinkled up like raisins. No, not that towel, the soft one."

"You refused him," said Griff.

"I told him I would think on his proposal." Harry winced as his squire toweled his feet. "Gentle with the toes. Think of them as thin-skinned grapes, lad. You want to dry them without crushing them. *Pat*, do not scrub. Yes, like that." He turned back to Griff. "A blunt refusal would have been unwise. The men might rightly ask if I had taken leave of my wits."

"You will have work for your blades soon enough."

"Will we?" asked Lysono Maar. "I assume you know that the Targaryen girl has not started for the west?"

"We heard that tale in Selhorys."

"No tale. Simple truth. The why of it is harder to grasp. Sack Meereen, aye, why not? I would have done the same in her place. The slaver cities reek of gold, and conquest requires coin. But why linger? Fear? Madness? Sloth?"

"The why of it does not matter." Harry Strickland unrolled a pair of

striped woolen stockings. "She is in Meereen and we are here, where the
Volantenes grow daily more unhappy with our presence. We came to raise
up a king and queen who would lead us home to Westeros, but this Targaryen girl seems more intent on planting olive trees than in reclaiming
her father's throne. Meanwhile, her foes gather. Yunkai, New Ghis, Tolos.
Bloodbeard and the Tattered Prince will both be in the field against
her . . . and soon enough the fleets of Old Volantis will descend on her as
well. What does she have? Bedslaves with sticks?"

"Unsullied," said Griff. "And dragons."

"Dragons, aye," the captain-general said, "but young ones, hardly more
than hatchlings." Strickland eased his sock over his blisters and up his
ankle. "How much will they avail her when all these armies close about
her city like a fist?"

Tristan Rivers drummed his fingers on his knee. "All the more reason
that we must reach her quickly, I say. If Daenerys will not come to us, we
must go to Daenerys."

"Can we walk across the waves, ser?" asked Lysono Maar. "I tell you
again, we cannot reach the silver queen by sea. I slipped into Volantis
myself, posing as a trader, to learn how many ships might be available to
us. The harbor teems with galleys, cogs, and carracks of every sort and
size, yet even so I soon found myself consorting with smugglers and pirates. We have ten thousand men in the company, as I am sure Lord Connington remembers from his years of service with us. Five hundred
knights, each with three horses. Five hundred squires, with one mount
apiece. And elephants, we must not forget the elephants. A pirate ship will
not suffice. We would need a pirate *fleet* . . . and even if we found one, the
word has come back from Slaver's Bay that Meereen has been closed off
by blockade."

"We could feign acceptance of the Yunkish offer," urged Gorys Edoryen. "Allow the Yunkai'i to transport us to the east, then return their gold
beneath the walls of Meereen."

"One broken contract is stain enough upon the honor of the company." Homeless Harry Strickland paused with his blistered foot in hand.
"Let me remind you, it was Myles Toyne who put his seal to this secret
pact, not me. I would honor his agreement if I could, but how? It seems
plain to me that the Targaryen girl is never coming west. Westeros was her
father's kingdom. Meereen is hers. If she can break the Yunkai'i, she'll be
Queen of Slaver's Bay. If not, she'll die long before we could hope to
reach her."

His words came as no surprise to Griff. Harry Strickland had always been a genial man, better at hammering out contracts than at hammering on foes. He had a nose for gold, but whether he had the belly for battle was another question.

"There is the land route," suggested Franklyn Flowers.

"The demon road is death. We will lose half the company to desertion if we attempt that march, and bury half of those who remain beside the road. It grieves me to say it, but Magister Illyrio and his friends may have been unwise to put so much hope on this child queen."

No, thought Griff, *but they were most unwise to put their hopes on you.*

And then Prince Aegon spoke. "Then put your hopes on me," he said. "Daenerys is Prince Rhaegar's sister, but I am Rhaegar's son. I am the only dragon that you need."

Griff put a black-gloved hand upon Prince Aegon's shoulder. "Spoken boldly," he said, "but think what you are saying."

"I have," the lad insisted. "Why should I go running to my aunt as if I were a beggar? My claim is better than her own. Let her come to me . . . in Westeros."

Franklyn Flowers laughed. "I like it. Sail west, not east. Leave the little queen to her olives and seat Prince Aegon upon the Iron Throne. The boy has stones, give him that."

The captain-general looked as if someone had slapped his face. "Has the sun curdled your brains, Flowers? We need the girl. We need the marriage. If Daenerys accepts our princeling and takes him for her consort, the Seven Kingdoms will do the same. Without her, the lords will only mock his claim and brand him a fraud and a pretender. And how do you propose to get to Westeros? You heard Lysono. There are no ships to be had."

This man is afraid to fight, Griff realized. *How could they have chosen him to take the Blackheart's place?* "No ships for Slaver's Bay. Westeros is another matter. The east is closed to us, not the sea. The triarchs would be glad to see the back of us, I do not doubt. They might even help us arrange passage back to the Seven Kingdoms. No city wants an army on its doorstep."

"He's not wrong," said Lysono Maar.

"By now the lion surely has the dragon's scent," said one of the Coles, "but Cersei's attentions will be fixed upon Meereen and this other queen. She knows nothing of our prince. Once we land and raise our banners, many and more will flock to join us."

"Some," allowed Homeless Harry, "not *many*. Rhaegar's sister has *drag-*

ons. Rhaegar's son does not. We do not have the strength to take the realm without Daenerys and her army. Her Unsullied."

"The first Aegon took Westeros without eunuchs," said Lysono Maar. "Why shouldn't the sixth Aegon do the same?"

"The plan—"

"Which plan?" said Tristan Rivers. "The fat man's plan? The one that changes every time the moon turns? First *Viserys* Targaryen was to join us with fifty thousand Dothraki screamers at his back. Then the Beggar King was dead, and it was to be the sister, a pliable young child queen who was on her way to Pentos with three new-hatched dragons. Instead the girl turns up on Slaver's Bay and leaves a string of burning cities in her wake, and the fat man decides we should meet her by Volantis. Now that plan is in ruins as well.

"I have had enough of Illyrio's plans. Robert Baratheon won the Iron Throne without the benefit of dragons. We can do the same. And if I am wrong and the realm does not rise for us, we can always retreat back across the narrow sea, as Bittersteel once did, and others after him."

Strickland shook his head stubbornly. "The risk—"

"—is not what it was, now that Tywin Lannister is dead. The Seven Kingdoms will never be more ripe for conquest. Another boy king sits the Iron Throne, this one even younger than the last, and rebels are thick upon the ground as autumn leaves."

"Even so," said Strickland, "alone, we cannot hope to—"

Griff had heard enough of the captain-general's cowardice. "We will not be alone. Dorne will join us, *must* join us. Prince Aegon is Elia's son as well as Rhaegar's."

"That's so," the boy said, "and who is there left in Westeros to oppose us? A woman."

"A *Lannister* woman," insisted the captain-general. "The bitch will have the Kingslayer at her side, count on that, and they will have all the wealth of Casterly Rock behind them. And Illyrio says this boy king is betrothed to the Tyrell girl, which means we must face the power of Highgarden as well."

Laswell Peake rapped his knuckles on the table. "Even after a century, some of us still have friends in the Reach. The power of Highgarden may not be what Mace Tyrell imagines."

"Prince Aegon," said Tristan Rivers, "we are your men. Is this your wish, that we sail west instead of east?"

"It is," Aegon replied eagerly. "If my aunt wants Meereen, she's welcome to it. I will claim the Iron Throne by myself, with your swords and your allegiance. Move fast and strike hard, and we can win some easy victories before the Lannisters even know that we have landed. That will bring others to our cause."

Rivers was smiling in approval. Others traded thoughtful looks. Then Peake said, "I would sooner die in Westeros than on the demon road," and Marq Mandrake chuckled and responded, "Me, I'd sooner live, win lands and some great castle," and Franklyn Flowers slapped his sword hilt and said, "So long as I can kill some Fossoways, I'm for it."

When all of them began to speak at once, Griff knew the tide had turned. *This is a side of Aegon I never saw before.* It was not the prudent course, but he was tired of prudence, sick of secrets, weary of waiting. Win or lose, he would see Griffin's Roost again before he died, and be buried in the tomb beside his father's.

One by one, the men of the Golden Company rose, knelt, and laid their swords at the feet of his young prince. The last to do so was Homeless Harry Strickland, blistered feet and all.

The sun was reddening the western sky and painting scarlet shadows on the golden skulls atop their spears when they took their leave of the captain-general's tent. Franklyn Flowers offered to take the prince around the camp and introduce him to some of what he called *the lads*. Griff gave his consent. "But remember, so far as the company is concerned, he must remain Young Griff until we cross the narrow sea. In Westeros we'll wash his hair and let him don his armor."

"Aye, understood." Flowers clapped a hand on Young Griff's back. "With me. We'll start with the cooks. Good men to know."

When they were gone, Griff turned to the Halfmaester. "Ride back to the *Shy Maid* and return with Lady Lemore and Ser Rolly. We'll need Illyrio's chests as well. All the coin, and the armor. Give Yandry and Ysilla our thanks. Their part in this is done. They will not be forgotten when His Grace comes into his kingdom."

"As you command, my lord."

Griff left him there, and slipped inside the tent that Homeless Harry had assigned him.

The road ahead was full of perils, he knew, but what of it? All men must die. All he asked was time. He had waited so long, surely the gods would grant him a few more years, enough time to see the boy he'd called a son seated on the Iron Throne. To reclaim his lands, his name, his honor. To still the bells that rang so loudly in his dreams whenever he closed his eyes to sleep.

Alone in the tent, as the gold and scarlet rays of the setting sun shone through the open flap, Jon Connington shrugged off his wolfskin cloak, slipped his mail shirt off over his head, settled on a camp stool, and peeled the glove from his right hand. The nail on his middle finger had turned as black as jet, he saw, and the grey had crept up almost to the first knuckle. The tip of his ring finger had begun to darken too, and when he touched it with the point of his dagger, he felt nothing.

Death, he knew, *but slow. I still have time. A year. Two years. Five. Some stone men live for ten. Time enough to cross the sea, to see Griffin's Roost again. To end the Usurper's line for good and all, and put Rhaegar's son upon the Iron Throne.*

Then Lord Jon Connington could die content.

THE WINDBLOWN

The word passed through the camp like a hot wind. *She is coming. Her host is on the march. She is racing south to Yunkai, to put the city to the torch and its people to the sword, and we are going north to meet her.*

Frog had it from Dick Straw who had it from Old Bill Bone who had it from a Pentoshi named Myrio Myrakis, who had a cousin who served as cupbearer to the Tattered Prince. "Coz heard it in the command tent, from Caggo's own lips," Dick Straw insisted. "We'll march before the day is out, see if we don't."

That much proved true. The command came down from the Tattered Prince through his captains and his serjeants: strike the tents, load the mules, saddle the horses, we march for Yunkai at the break of day. "Not that them Yunkish bastards will be wanting us inside their Yellow City, sniffing round their daughters," predicted Baqq, the squint-eyed Myrish crossbowman whose name meant *Beans*. "We'll get provisions in Yunkai, maybe fresh horses, then it will be on to Meereen to dance with the dragon queen. So hop quick, Frog, and put a nice edge on your master's sword. Might be he'll need it soon."

In Dorne Quentyn Martell had been a prince, in Volantis a merchant's man, but on the shores of Slaver's Bay he was only Frog, squire to the big bald Dornish knight the sellswords called Greenguts. The men of the Windblown used what names they would, and changed them at a whim. They'd fastened *Frog* on him because he hopped so fast when the big man shouted a command.

Even the commander of the Windblown kept his true name to himself. Some free companies had been born during the century of blood and chaos that had followed the Doom of Valyria. Others had been formed yesterday and would be gone upon the morrow. The Windblown went back thirty years, and had known but one commander, the soft-spoken, sad-eyed Pentoshi nobleman called the Tattered Prince. His hair and mail were silver-grey, but his ragged cloak was made of twists of cloth of many colors, blue and grey and purple, red and gold and green, magenta and vermilion and cerulean, all faded by the sun. When the Tattered Prince was three-and-twenty, as Dick Straw told the story, the magisters of Pentos had chosen him to be their new prince, hours after beheading their old prince. Instead he'd buckled on a sword, mounted his favorite horse, and fled to the Disputed Lands, never to return. He had ridden with the Second Sons, the Iron Shields, and the Maiden's Men, then joined with five brothers-in-arms to form the Windblown. Of those six founders, only he survived.

Frog had no notion whether any of that was true. Since signing into the Windblown in Volantis, he had seen the Tattered Prince only at a distance. The Dornishmen were new hands, raw recruits, arrow fodder, three amongst two thousand. Their commander kept more elevated company. "I am not a squire," Quentyn had protested when Gerris Drinkwater—known here as Dornish Gerrold, to distinguish him from Gerrold Redback and Black Gerrold, and sometimes as Drink, since the big man had slipped and called him that—suggested the ruse. "I earned my spurs in Dorne. I am as much a knight as you are."

But Gerris had the right of it; he and Arch were here to protect Quentyn, and that meant keeping him by the big man's side. "Arch is the best fighter of the three of us," Drinkwater had pointed out, "but only you can hope to wed the dragon queen."

Wed her or fight her; either way, I will face her soon. The more Quentyn heard of Daenerys Targaryen, the more he feared that meeting. The Yunkai'i claimed that she fed her dragons on human flesh and bathed in the blood of virgins to keep her skin smooth and supple. Beans laughed at that but relished the tales of the silver queen's promiscuity. "One of her captains comes of a line where the men have foot-long members," he told them, "but even he's not big enough for her. She rode with the Dothraki and grew accustomed to being fucked by stallions, so now no man can fill her." And Books, the clever Volantene swordsman who always seemed to have his nose poked in some crumbly scroll, thought the dragon queen both murderous and mad. "Her khal killed her brother to make her queen. Then she killed her khal to make herself *khaleesi*. She practices blood sacrifice, lies as easily as she breathes, turns against her own on a whim. She's broken truces, tortured envoys . . . her father was mad too. It runs in the blood."

It runs in the blood. King Aerys II *had* been mad, all of Westeros knew that. He had exiled two of his Hands and burned a third. *If Daenerys is as murdeous as her father, must I still marry her?* Prince Doran had never spoken of that possibility.

Frog would be glad to put Astapor behind him. The Red City was the closest thing to hell he ever hoped to know. The Yunkai'i had sealed the broken gates to keep the dead and dying inside the city, but the sights that he had seen riding down those red brick streets would haunt Quentyn Martell forever. A river choked with corpses. The priestess in her torn robes, impaled upon a stake and attended by a cloud of glistening green flies. Dying men staggering through the streets, bloody and befouled. Children fighting over half-cooked puppies. The last free king of Astapor, screaming naked in the pit as he was set on by a score of starving dogs. And fires, fires everywhere. He could close his eyes and see them still: flames whirling from brick pyramids larger than any castle he had ever seen, plumes of greasy smoke coiling upward like great black snakes.

When the wind blew from the south, the air smelled of smoke even here, three miles from the city. Behind its crumbling red brick walls, Astapor was still asmolder, though by now most of the great fires had burned out. Ashes floated lazy on the breeze like fat grey snowflakes. It would be good to go.

The big man agreed. "Past time," he said, when Frog found him dicing with Beans and Books and Old Bill Bone, and losing yet again. The sellswords loved Greenguts, who bet as fearlessly as he fought, but with far less success. "I'll want my armor, Frog. Did you scrub that blood off my mail?"

"Aye, ser." Greenguts's mail was old and heavy, patched and patched again, much worn. The same was true of his helm, his gorget, greaves, and gauntlets, and the rest of his mismatched plate. Frog's kit was only slightly better, and Ser Gerris's was notably worse. *Company steel*, the armorer had called it. Quentyn had not asked how many other men had worn it before him, how many men had died in it. They had abandoned their own fine armor in Volantis, along with their gold and their true names. Wealthy knights from Houses old in honor did not cross the narrow sea to sell their swords, unless exiled for some infamy. "I'd sooner pose as poor than evil," Quentyn had declared, when Gerris had explained his ruse to them.

It took the Windblown less than an hour to strike their camp. "And now we ride," the Tattered Prince proclaimed from his huge grey warhorse, in a classic High Valyrian that was the closest thing they had to a company tongue. His stallion's spotted hindquarters were covered with ragged strips of cloth torn from the surcoats of men his master had slain.

The prince's cloak was sewn together from more of the same. An old man he was, past sixty, yet he still sat straight and tall in the high saddle, and his voice was strong enough to carry to every corner of the field. "Astapor was but a taste," he said, "Meereen will be the feast," and the sellswords sent up a wild cheer. Streamers of pale blue silk fluttered from their lances, whilst fork-tailed blue-and-white banners flew overhead, the standards of the Windblown.

The three Dornishmen cheered with all the rest. Silence would have drawn notice. But as the Windblown rode north along the coast road, close behind Bloodbeard and the Company of the Cat, Frog fell in beside Dornish Gerrold. "Soon," he said, in the Common Tongue of Westeros. There were other Westerosi in the company, but not many, and not near. "We need to do it soon."

"Not here," warned Gerris, with a mummer's empty smile. "We'll speak of this tonight, when we make camp."

It was a hundred leagues from Astapor to Yunkai by the old Ghiscari coast road, and another fifty from Yunkai to Meereen. The free companies, well mounted, could reach Yunkai in six days of hard riding, or eight at a more leisurely pace. The legions from Old Ghis would take half again as long, marching afoot, and the Yunkai'i and their slave soldiers . . . "With their generals, it's a wonder they don't march into the sea," Beans said.

The Yunkai'i did not lack for commanders. An old hero named Yurkhaz zo Yunzak had the supreme command, though the men of the Windblown glimpsed him only at a distance, coming and going in a palanquin so huge it required forty slaves to carry it.

They could not help but see his underlings, however. The Yunkish lordlings scuttled everywhere, like roaches. Half of them seemed to be named Ghazdan, Grazdan, Mazdhan, or Ghaznak; telling one Ghiscari name from another was an art few of the Windblown had mastered, so they gave them mocking styles of their own devising.

Foremost amongst them was the Yellow Whale, an obscenely fat man who always wore yellow silk *tokars* with golden fringes. Too heavy even to stand unassisted, he could not hold his water, so he always smelled of piss, a stench so sharp that even heavy perfumes could not conceal it. But he was said to be the richest man in Yunkai, and he had a passion for grotesques; his slaves included a boy with the legs and hooves of a goat, a bearded woman, a two-headed monster from Mantarys, and a hermaphrodite who warmed his bed at night. "Cock and cunny both," Dick Straw told them. "The Whale used to own a giant too, liked to watch him fuck his slave girls. Then he died. I hear the Whale'd give a sack o' gold for a new one."

Then there was the Girl General, who rode about on a white horse with a red mane and commanded a hundred strapping slave soldiers that she had bred and trained herself, all of them young, lean, rippling with muscle, and naked but for breechclouts, yellow cloaks, and long bronze shields with erotic inlays. Their mistress could not have been more than sixteen and fancied herself Yunkai's own Daenerys Targaryen.

The Little Pigeon was not quite a dwarf, but he might have passed for one in a bad light. Yet he strutted about as if he were a giant, with his plump little legs spread wide and his plump little chest puffed out. His soldiers were the tallest that any of the Windblown had ever seen; the shortest stood seven feet tall, the tallest close to eight. All were long-faced and long-legged, and the stilts built into the legs of their ornate armor made them longer still. Pink-enameled scales covered their torsos; on their heads were perched elongated helms complete with pointed steel beaks and crests of bobbing pink feathers. Each man wore a long curved sword upon his hip, and each clasped a spear as tall as he was, with a leaf-shaped blade at either end.

"The Little Pigeon breeds them," Dick Straw informed them. "He buys tall slaves from all over the world, mates the men to the women, and keeps their tallest offspring for the Herons. One day he hopes to be able to dispense with the stilts."

"A few sessions on the rack might speed along the process," suggested the big man.

Gerris Drinkwater laughed. "A fearsome lot. Nothing scares me worse than stilt-walkers in pink scales and feathers. If one was after me, I'd laugh so hard my bladder might let go."

"Some say that herons are majestic," said Old Bill Bone.

"If your king eats frogs while standing on one leg."

"Herons are craven," the big man put in. "One time me and Drink and Cletus were hunting, and we came on these herons wading in the shallows, feasting on tadpoles and small fish. They made a pretty sight, aye, but then a hawk passed overhead, and they all took to the wing like they'd seen a dragon. Kicked up so much wind it blew me off my horse, but Cletus nocked an arrow to his string and brought one down. Tasted like duck, but not so greasy."

Even the Little Pigeon and his Herons paled beside the folly of the brothers the sellswords called the Clanker Lords. The last time the slave soldiers of Yunkai'i had faced the dragon queen's Unsullied, they broke and ran. The Clanker Lords had devised a stratagem to prevent that; they chained their troops together in groups of ten, wrist to wrist and ankle to ankle. "None of the poor bastards can run unless they all run," Dick Straw explained, laughing. "And if they do all run, they won't run very fast."

"They don't fucking march very fast either," observed Beans. "You can hear them clanking ten leagues off."

There were more, near as mad or worse: Lord Wobblecheeks, the Drunken Conqueror, the Beastmaster, Pudding Face, the Rabbit, the Charioteer, the Perfumed Hero. Some had twenty soldiers, some two hundred or two thousand, all slaves they had trained and equipped themselves. Every one was wealthy, every one was arrogant, and every one was a captain and commander, answerable to no one but Yurkhaz zo Yunzak, disdainful of mere sellswords, and prone to squabbles over precedence that were as endless as they were incomprehensible.

In the time it took the Windblown to ride three miles, the Yunkai'i had fallen two-and-a-half miles behind. "A pack of stinking yellow fools," Beans complained. "They still ain't managed to puzzle out why the Stormcrows and the Second Sons went over to the dragon queen."

"For gold, they believe," said Books. "Why do you think they're paying us so well?"

"Gold is sweet, but life is sweeter," said Beans. "We were dancing with cripples at Astapor. Do you want to face real Unsullied with that lot on your side?"

"We fought the Unsullied at Astapor," the big man said.

"I said *real* Unsullied. Hacking off some boy's stones with a butcher's cleaver and handing him a pointy hat don't make him Unsullied. That dragon queen's got the real item, the kind that don't break and run when you fart in their general direction."

"Them, and dragons too." Dick Straw glanced up at the sky as if he thought the mere mention of dragons might be enough to bring them down upon the company. "Keep your swords sharp, boys, we'll have us a real fight soon."

A *real fight,* thought Frog. The words stuck in his craw. The fight beneath the walls of Astapor had seemed real enough to him, though he knew the sellswords felt otherwise. "That was butchery, not battle," the warrior bard Denzo D'han had been heard to declare afterward. Denzo was a captain, and veteran of a hundred battles. Frog's experience was limited to practice yard and tourney ground, so he did not think it was his place to dispute the verdict of such a seasoned warrior.

It seemed like a battle when it first began, though. He remembered how his gut had clenched when he was kicked awake at dawn with the big man looming over him. "Into your armor, slugabed," he'd boomed. "The Butcher's coming out to give us battle. Up, unless you mean to be his meat."

"The Butcher King is dead," Frog had protested sleepily. That was the story all of them had heard as they scrambled from the ships that had brought them from Old Volantis. A second King Cleon had taken the crown and died in turn, supposedly, and now the Astapori were ruled by a whore and a mad barber whose followers were fighting with each other to control the city.

"Maybe they lied," the big man had replied. "Or else this is some other butcher. Might be the first one come back screaming from his tomb to kill some Yunkishmen. Makes no bloody matter, Frog. *Get your armor on.*" The tent slept ten, and all of them had been on their feet by then, wriggling into breeches and boots, sliding long coats of ringmail down onto their shoulders, buckling breastplates, tightening the straps on greaves or vambraces, grabbing for helms and shields and sword belts. Gerris, quick as ever, was the first one fully clad, Arch close behind him. Together they helped Quentyn don his own harness.

Three hundred yards away, Astapor's new Unsullied had been pouring through their gates and forming up in ranks beneath their city's crumbling red brick walls, dawn light glinting off their spiked bronze helmets and the points of their long spears.

The three Dornishmen spilled from the tent together to join the fighters sprinting for the horse lines. *Battle.* Quentyn had trained with spear and sword and shield since he was old enough to walk, but that meant nothing now. *Warrior, make me brave,* Frog had prayed, as drums beat in the distance, *BOOM boom BOOM boom BOOM boom.* The big man pointed out the Butcher King to him, sitting stiff and tall upon an armored horse in a suit of copper scale that flashed brilliantly in the morning sun. He remembered Gerris sidling up just before the fight began. "Stay close to Arch, whatever happens. Remember, you're the only one of us who can get the girl." By then the Astapori were advancing.

Dead or alive, the Butcher King still took the Wise Masters unawares. The Yunkishmen were still running about in fluttering *tokars* trying to get their half-trained slave soldiers into some semblance of order as Unsullied spears came crashing through their siege lines. If not for their allies and their despised hirelings they might well have been overwhelmed, but the Windblown and the Company of the Cat were ahorse in minutes and came thundering down on the Astapori flanks even as a legion from New Ghis pushed through the Yunkish camp from the other side and met the Unsullied spear to spear and shield to shield.

The rest was butchery, but this time it was the Butcher King on the wrong end of the cleaver. Caggo was the one who finally cut him down, fighting through the king's protectors on his monstrous warhorse and opening Cleon the Great from shoulder to hip with one blow of his curved Valyrian *arakh*. Frog did not see it, but those who did claimed Cleon's copper armor rent like silk, and from within came an awful stench and a hundred wriggling grave worms. Cleon had been dead after all. The desperate Astapori had pulled him from his tomb, clapped him into armor, and tied him onto a horse in hopes of giving heart to their Unsullied.

Dead Cleon's fall wrote an end to that. The new Unsullied threw down their spears and shields and ran, only to find the gates of Astapor shut behind them. Frog had done his part in the slaughter that followed, riding down the frightened eunuchs with the other Windblown. Hard by the big man's hip he rode, slashing right and left as their wedge went through the Unsullied like a spearpoint. When they burst through on the other side, the Tattered Prince had wheeled them round and led them through again. It was only coming back that Frog got a good look at the faces beneath the spiked bronze caps and realized that most were no older than he. *Green boys screaming for their mothers,* he'd thought, but he killed them all the same. By the time he'd left the field, his sword was running red with blood and his arm was so tired he could hardly lift it.

Yet that was no real fight, he thought. *The real fight will be on us soon, and we must be away before it comes, or we'll find ourselves fighting on the wrong side.*

That night the Windblown made camp beside the shore of Slaver's Bay. Frog drew the first watch and was sent to guard the horse lines. Gerris met him there just after sundown, as a half-moon shone upon the waters.

"The big man should be here as well," said Quentyn.

"He's gone to look up Old Bill Bone and lose the rest of his silver," Gerris said. "Leave him out of this. He'll do as we say, though he won't like it much."

"No." There was much and more about this Quentyn did not like himself. Sailing on an overcrowded ship tossed by wind and sea, eating hardbread crawling with weevils and drinking black tar rum to sweet oblivion, sleeping on piles of moldy straw with the stench of strangers in his nostrils . . . all that he had expected when he made his mark on that scrap of parchment in Volantis, pledging the Tattered Prince his sword and service for a year. Those were hardships to be endured, the stuff of all adventures.

But what must come next was plain betrayal. The Yunkai'i had brought them from Old Volantis to fight for the Yellow City, but now the Dornishmen meant to turn their cloaks and go over to the other side. That meant abandoning their new brothers-in-arms as well. The Windblown were not the sort of companions Quentyn would have chosen, but he had crossed the sea with them, shared their meat and mead, fought beside them, traded tales with those few whose talk he understood. And if all his tales were lies, well, that was the cost of passage to Meereen.

It is not what you'd call honorable, Gerris had warned them, back at the Merchant's House.

"Daenerys may be halfway to Yunkai by now, with an army at her back," Quentyn said as they walked amongst the horses.

"She may be," Gerris said, "but she's not. We've heard such talk before. The Astapori were convinced Daenerys was coming south with her dragons to break the siege. She didn't come then, and she's not coming now."

"We can't know that, not for certain. We need to steal away before we end up fighting the woman I was sent to woo."

"Wait till Yunkai." Gerris gestured at the hills. "These lands belong to the Yunkai'i. No one is like to want to feed or shelter three deserters. North of Yunkai, that's no-man's-land."

He was not wrong. Even so, Quentyn felt uneasy. "The big man's made too many friends. He knows the plan was always to steal off and make our way to Daenerys, but he's not going to feel good about abandoning men he's fought with. If we wait too long, it's going to feel as if we're deserting them on the eve of battle. He will never do that. You know him as well as I do."

"It's desertion whenever we do it," argued Gerris, "and the Tattered Prince takes a dim view of deserters. He'll send hunters after us, and Seven save us if they catch us. If we're lucky, they'll just chop off a foot to make sure we never run again. If we're unlucky, they'll give us to Pretty Meris."

That last gave Quentyn pause. Pretty Meris frightened him. A Westerosi woman, but taller than he was, just a thumb under six feet. After twenty years amongst the free companies, there was nothing pretty about her, inside or out.

Gerris took him by the arm. "Wait. A few more days, that's all. We have crossed half the world, be patient for a few more leagues. Somewhere north of Yunkai our chance will come."

"If you say," said Frog doubtfully . . .

. . . but for once the gods were listening, and their chance came much sooner than that.

It was two days later. Hugh Hungerford reined up by their cookfire, and said, "Dornish. You're wanted in the command tent."

"Which one of us?" asked Gerris. "We're all Dornish."

"All of you, then." Sour and saturnine, with a maimed hand, Hungerford had been company paymaster for a time, until the Tattered Prince had caught him stealing from the coffers and removed three of his fingers. Now he was just a serjeant.

What could this be? Up to now, Frog had no notion that their commander knew he was alive. Hungerford had already ridden off, however, so there was no time for questions. All they could do was gather up the big man and report as ordered. "Admit to nothing and be prepared to fight," Quentyn told his friends.

"I am always prepared to fight," said the big man.

The great grey sailcloth pavilion that the Tattered Prince liked to call his canvas castle was crowded when the Dornishmen arrived. It took Quentyn only a moment to realize that most of those assembled were from the Seven Kingdoms, or boasted Westerosi blood. *Exiles or the sons of exiles.* Dick Straw claimed there were three score Westerosi in the company; a good third of those were here, including Dick himself, Hugh Hungerford, Pretty Meris, and golden-haired Lewis Lanster, the company's best archer.

Denzo D'han was there as well, with Caggo huge beside him. *Caggo Corpsekiller* the men were calling him now, though not to his face; he was quick to anger, and that curved black sword of his was as nasty as its owner. There were hundreds of Valyrian longswords in the world, but only a handful of Valyrian *arakhs*. Neither Caggo nor D'han was Westerosi, but both were captains and stood high in the Tattered Prince's regard. *His right arm and his left. Something major is afoot.*

It was the Tattered Prince himself who did the speaking. "Orders have come down from Yurkhaz," he said. "What Astapori still survive have come creeping from their hidey-holes, it seems. There's nothing left in Astapor but corpses, so they're pouring out into the countryside, hundreds of them, maybe thousands, all starved and sick. The Yunkai'i don't want them near their Yellow City. We've been commanded to hunt them down and turn them, drive them back to Astapor or north to Meereen. If the dragon queen wants to take them in, she's welcome to them. Half of them have the bloody flux, and even the healthy ones are mouths to feed."

"Yunkai is closer than Meereen," Hugh Hungerford objected. "What if they won't turn, my lord?"

"That's why you have swords and lances, Hugh. Though bows might serve you better. Stay well away from those who show signs of the flux. I'm sending half our strength into the hills. Fifty patrols, twenty riders each. Bloodbeard's got the same orders, so the Cats will be in the field as well."

A look passed between the men, and a few muttered under their breath. Though the Windblown and the Company of the Cat were both under contract to Yunkai, a year ago in the Disputed Lands they had been on opposite sides of the battle lines, and bad blood still lingered. Bloodbeard, the savage commander of the Cats, was a roaring giant with a ferocious appetite for slaughter who made no secret of his disdain for "old grey-beards in rags."

Dick Straw cleared his throat. "Begging your pardon, but we're all Seven Kingdoms born here. M'lord never broke up the company by blood or tongue before. Why send us lot together?"

"A fair question. You're to ride east, deep into the hills, then swing wide about Yunkai, making for Meereen. Should you come on any Astapori, drive them north or kill them . . . but know that is not the purpose of your mission. Beyond the Yellow City, you're like to come up against the dragon queen's patrols. Second Sons or Stormcrows. Either will serve. Go over to them."

"Go over to them?" said the bastard knight, Ser Orson Stone. "You'd have us turn our cloaks?"

"I would," said the Tattered Prince.

Quentyn Martell almost laughed aloud. *The gods are mad.*

The Westerosi shifted uneasily. Some stared into their wine cups, as if they hoped to find some wisdom there. Hugh Hungerford frowned. "You think Queen Daenerys will take us in . . ."

"I do."

". . . but if she does, what then? Are we spies? Assassins? *Envoys?* Are you thinking to change sides?"

Caggo scowled. "That is for the prince to decide, Hungerford. Your part is to do as you are told."

"Always." Hungerford raised his two-fingered hand.

"Let us be frank," said Denzo D'han, the warrior bard. "The Yunkai'i do not inspire confidence. Whatever the outcome of this war, the Windblown should share in the spoils of victory. Our prince is wise to keep all roads open."

"Meris will command you," said the Tattered Prince. "She knows my mind in this . . . and Daenerys Targaryen may be more accepting of another woman."

Quentyn glanced back to Pretty Meris. When her cold dead eyes met his, he felt a shiver. *I do not like this.*

Dick Straw still had doubts as well. "The girl would be a fool to trust us. Even with Meris. *Especially* with Meris. Hell, *I* don't trust Meris, and I've fucked her a few times." He grinned, but no one laughed. Least of all Pretty Meris.

"I think you are mistaken, Dick," the Tattered Prince said. "You are all Westerosi. Friends from home. You speak her same tongue, worship her same gods. As for motive, all of you have suffered wrongs at my hands. Dick, I've whipped you more than any man in the company, and you have the back to prove it. Hugh lost three fingers to my discipline. Meris was raped half round the company. Not *this* company, true, but we need not mention that. Will of the Woods, well, you're just filth. Ser Orson blames me for dispatching his brother to the Sorrows and Ser Lucifer is still seething about that slave girl Caggo took from him."

"He could have given her back when he'd had her," Lucifer Long complained. "He had no cause to kill her."

"She was ugly," said Caggo. "That's cause enough."

The Tattered Prince went on as if no one had spoken. "Webber, you nurse claims to lands lost in Westeros. Lanster, I killed that boy you were so fond of. You Dornish three, you think we lied to you. The plunder from Astapor was much less than you were promised in Volantis, and I took the lion's share of it."

"The last part's true," Ser Orson said.

"The best ruses always have some seed of truth," said the Tattered Prince. "Every one of you has ample reason for wanting to abandon me. And Daenerys Targaryen knows that sellswords are a fickle lot. Her own Second Sons and Stormcrows took Yunkish gold but did not hesitate to join her when the tide of battle began to flow her way."

"When should we leave?" asked Lewis Lanster.

"At once. Be wary of the Cats and any Long Lances you may encounter. No one will know your defection is a ruse but those of us in this tent. Turn your tiles too soon, and you will be maimed as deserters or disemboweled as turncloaks."

The three Dornishmen were silent as they left the command tent. *Twenty riders, all speaking the Common Tongue,* thought Quentyn. *Whispering has just gotten a deal more dangerous.*

The big man slapped him hard across the back. "So. This is sweet, Frog. A dragon hunt."

THE WAYWARD BRIDE

Asha Greyjoy was seated in Galbart Glover's longhall drinking Galbart Glover's wine when Galbart Glover's maester brought the letter to her.

"My lady." The maester's voice was anxious, as it always was when he spoke to her. "A bird from Barrowton." He thrust the parchment at her as if he could not wait to be rid of it. It was tightly rolled and sealed with a button of hard pink wax.

Barrowton. Asha tried to recall who ruled in Barrowton. *Some northern lord, no friend of mine.* And that seal . . . the Boltons of the Dreadfort went into battle beneath pink banners spattered with little drops of blood. It only stood to reason that they would use pink sealing wax as well.

This is poison that I hold, she thought. *I ought to burn it.* Instead she cracked the seal. A scrap of leather fluttered down into her lap. When she read the dry brown words, her black mood grew blacker still. *Dark wings, dark words.* The ravens never brought glad tidings. The last message sent to Deepwood had been from Stannis Baratheon, demanding homage. This was worse. "The northmen have taken Moat Cailin."

"The Bastard of Bolton?" asked Qarl, beside her.

"*Ramsay Bolton, Lord of Winterfell,* he signs himself. But there are other names as well." Lady Dustin, Lady Cerwyn, and four Ryswells had appended their own signatures beneath his. Beside them was drawn a crude giant, the mark of some Umber.

Those were done in maester's ink, made of soot and coal tar, but the message above was scrawled in brown in a huge, spiky hand. It spoke of the fall of Moat Cailin, of the triumphant return of the Warden of the North to his domains, of a marriage soon to be made. The first words were, "*I write this letter in the blood of ironmen,*" the last, "*I send you each a piece of prince. Linger in my lands, and share his fate.*"

Asha had believed her little brother dead. *Better dead than this.* The scrap of skin had fallen into her lap. She held it to the candle and watched the smoke curl up, until the last of it had been consumed and the flame was licking at her fingers.

Galbart Glover's maester hovered expectantly at her elbow. "There will be no answer," she informed him.

"May I share these tidings with Lady Sybelle?"

"If it please you." Whether Sybelle Glover would find any joy in the fall of Moat Cailin, Asha could not say. Lady Sybelle all but lived in her gods-wood, praying for her children and her husband's safe return. *Another prayer like to go unanswered. Her heart tree is as deaf and blind as our Drowned God.* Robett Glover and his brother Galbart had ridden south with the Young Wolf. If the tales they had heard of the Red Wedding were even half-true, they were not like to ride north again. *Her children are alive, at least, and that is thanks to me.* Asha had left them at Ten Towers in the care of her aunts. Lady Sybelle's infant daughter was still on the breast, and she had judged the girl too delicate to expose to the rigors of another stormy crossing. Asha shoved the letter into the maester's hands. "Here. Let her find some solace here if she can. You have my leave to go."

The maester inclined his head and departed. After he was gone, Tris Botley turned to Asha. "If Moat Cailin has fallen, Torrhen's Square will soon follow. Then it will be our turn."

"Not for a while yet. The Cleftjaw will make them bleed." Torrhen's Square was not a ruin like Moat Cailin, and Dagmer was iron to the bone. He would die before he'd yield.

If my father still lived, Moat Cailin would never have fallen. Balon Greyjoy had known that the Moat was the key to holding the north. Euron knew that as well; he simply did not care. No more than he cared what happened to Deepwood Motte or Torrhen's Square. "Euron has no interest in Balon's conquests. My nuncle's off chasing dragons." The Crow's Eye had summoned all the strength of the Iron Isles to Old Wyk and sailed out into the deepness of the Sunset Sea, with his brother Victarion following behind like a whipped cur. There was no one left on Pyke to appeal to, save for her own lord husband. "We stand alone."

"Dagmer will smash them," insisted Cromm, who had never met a woman he loved half so much as battle. "They are only wolves."

"The wolves are all slain." Asha picked at the pink wax with her thumbnail. "These are the skinners who slew them."

"We should go to Torrhen's Square and join the fight," urged Quenton Greyjoy, a distant cousin and captain of the *Salty Wench*.

"Aye," said Dagon Greyjoy, a cousin still more distant. Dagon the Drunkard, men called him, but drunk or sober he loved to fight. "Why should the Cleftjaw have all the glory for himself?"

Two of Galbart Glover's serving men brought forth the roast, but that strip of skin had taken Asha's appetite. *My men have given up all hope of victory*, she realized glumly. *All they look for now is a good death.* The wolves would give them that, she had no doubt. *Soon or late, they will come to take this castle back.*

The sun was sinking behind the tall pines of the wolfswood as Asha climbed the wooden steps to the bedchamber that had once been Galbart Glover's. She had drunk too much wine and her head was pounding. Asha Greyjoy loved her men, captains and crew alike, but half of them were fools. *Brave fools, but fools nonetheless. Go to the Cleftjaw, yes, as if we could . . .*

Between Deepwood and Dagmer lay long leagues, rugged hills, thick woods, wild rivers, and more northmen than she cared to contemplate. Asha had four longships and not quite two hundred men . . . including Tristifer Botley, who could not be relied on. For all his talk of love, she could not imagine Tris rushing off to Torrhen's Square to die with Dagmer Cleftjaw.

Qarl followed her up to Galbart Glover's bedchamber. "Get out," she told him. "I want to be alone."

"What you want is me." He tried to kiss her.

Asha pushed him away. "Touch me again and I'll—"

"What?" He drew his dagger. "Undress yourself, girl."

"Fuck yourself, you beardless boy."

"I'd sooner fuck you." One quick slash unlaced her jerkin. Asha reached for her axe, but Qarl dropped his knife and caught her wrist, twisting back her arm until the weapon fell from her fingers. He pushed her back onto Glover's bed, kissed her hard, and tore off her tunic to let her breasts spill out. When she tried to knee him in the groin, he twisted away and forced her legs apart with his knees. "I'll have you now."

"Do it," she spat, "and I'll kill you in your sleep."

She was sopping wet when he entered her. "Damn you," she said. "Damn you damn you damn you." He sucked her nipples till she cried out half in pain and half in pleasure. Her cunt became the world. She forgot Moat Cailin and Ramsay Bolton and his little piece of skin, forgot the kingsmoot, forgot her failure, forgot her exile and her enemies and her husband. Only his hands mattered, only his mouth, only his arms around her, his cock inside her. He fucked her till she screamed, and then again until she wept, before he finally spent his seed inside her womb.

"I am a woman wed," she reminded him, afterward. "You've despoiled me, you beardless boy. My lord husband will cut your balls off and put you in a dress."

Qarl rolled off her. "If he can get out of his chair."

The room was cold. Asha rose from Galbart Glover's bed and took off her torn clothes. The jerkin would need fresh laces, but her tunic was ruined. *I never liked it anyway.* She tossed it on the flames. The rest she left in a puddle by the bed. Her breasts were sore, and Qarl's seed was trickling down her thigh. She would need to brew some moon tea or risk bringing another kraken into the world. *What does it matter? My father's dead, my mother's dying, my brother's being flayed, and there's naught that I can do about any of it. And I'm married. Wedded and bedded . . . though not by the same man.*

When she slipped back beneath the furs, Qarl was asleep. "Now your life is mine. Where did I put my dagger?" Asha pressed herself against his back and slid her arms about him. On the isles he was known as Qarl the Maid, in part to distinguish him from Qarl Shepherd, Queer Qarl Kenning, Qarl Quickaxe, and Qarl the Thrall, but more for his smooth cheeks. When Asha had first met him, Qarl had been trying to raise a beard. "Peach fuzz," she had called it, laughing. Qarl confessed that he had never seen a peach, so she told him he must join her on her next voyage south.

It had still been summer then; Robert sat the Iron Throne, Balon brooded on the Seastone Chair, and the Seven Kingdoms were at peace. Asha sailed the *Black Wind* down the coast, trading. They called at Fair Isle and Lannisport and a score of smaller ports before reaching the Arbor, where the peaches were always huge and sweet. "You see," she'd said, the first time she'd held one up against Qarl's cheek. When she made him try a bite, the juice ran down his chin, and she had to kiss it clean.

That night they'd spent devouring peaches and each other, and by the time daylight returned Asha was sated and sticky and as happy as she'd ever been. *Was that six years ago, or seven?* Summer was a fading memory, and it had been three years since Asha last enjoyed a peach. She still enjoyed Qarl, though. The captains and the kings might not have wanted her, but he did.

Asha had known other lovers; some shared her bed for half a year, some for half a night. Qarl pleased her more than all the rest together. He might shave but once a fortnight, but a shaggy beard does not make a man. She liked the feel of his smooth, soft skin beneath her fingers. She liked the way his long, straight hair brushed against his shoulders. She liked the way he kissed. She liked how he grinned when she brushed her thumbs across his nipples. The hair between his legs was a darker shade of sand than the hair on his head, but fine as down compared to the coarse black bush around her own sex. She liked that too. He had a swimmer's body, long and lean, with not a scar upon him.

A shy smile, strong arms, clever fingers, and two sure swords. What more could any woman want? She would have married Qarl, and gladly, but she was Lord Balon's daughter and he was common-born, the grandson of a thrall. *Too lowborn for me to wed, but not too low for me to suck his cock.* Drunk, smiling, she crawled beneath the furs and took him in her mouth. Qarl stirred in his sleep, and after a moment he began to stiffen. By the time she had him hard again, he was awake and she was wet. Asha draped the furs across her bare shoulders and mounted him, drawing him so deep inside her that she could not tell who had the cock and who the cunt. This time the two of them reached their peak together.

"My sweet lady," he murmured after, in a voice still thick with sleep. "My sweet queen."

No, Asha thought, *I am no queen, nor shall I ever be.* "Go back to sleep." She kissed his cheek, padded across Galbart Glover's bedchamber, and threw the shutters open. The moon was almost full, the night so clear that she could see the mountains, their peaks crowned with snow. *Cold and bleak and inhospitable, but beautiful in the moonlight.* Their summits glimmered pale and jagged as a row of sharpened teeth. The foothills and the smaller peaks were lost in shadow.

The sea was closer, only five leagues north, but Asha could not see it. Too many hills stood in the way. *And trees, so many trees.* The wolfswood, the northmen named the forest. Most nights you could hear the wolves, calling to each other through the dark. *An ocean of leaves. Would it were an ocean of water.*

Deepwood might be closer to the sea than Winterfell, but it was still too far for her taste. The air smelled of pines instead of salt. Northeast of those grim grey mountains stood the Wall, where Stannis Baratheon had raised his standards. *The enemy of my enemy is my friend,* men said, but the other side of that coin was, *the enemy of my friend is my enemy.* The ironborn were the enemies of the northern lords this Baratheon pretender needed desperately. *I could offer him my fair young body,* she thought, pushing a strand of hair from her eyes, but Stannis was wed and so was she, and he and the ironborn were old foes. During her father's first rebellion, Stannis had smashed the Iron Fleet off Fair Isle and subdued Great Wyk in his brother's name.

Deepwood's mossy walls enclosed a wide, rounded hill with a flattened top, crowned by a cavernous longhall with a watchtower at one end, rising fifty feet above the hill. Beneath the hill was the bailey, with its stables, paddock, smithy, well, and sheepfold, defended by a deep ditch, a sloping earthen dike, and a palisade of logs. The outer defenses made an oval, following the contours of the land. There were two gates, each protected by a pair of square wooden towers, and wallwalks around the perimeter. On the south side of the castle, moss grew thick upon the palisade and crept halfway up the towers. To east and west were empty fields. Oats and barley had been growing there when Asha took the castle, only to be crushed underfoot during her attack. A series of hard frosts had killed the crops they'd planted afterward, leaving only mud and ash and wilted, rotting stalks.

It was an old castle, but not a strong one. She had taken it from the Glovers, and the Bastard of Bolton would take it from her. He would not flay her, though. Asha Greyjoy did not intend to be taken alive. She would die as she had lived, with an axe in her hand and a laugh upon her lips.

Her lord father had given her thirty longships to capture Deepwood. Four remained, counting her own *Black Wind,* and one of those belonged to Tris Botley, who had joined her when all her other men were fleeing. *No. That is not just. They sailed home to do homage to their king. If anyone fled, it was me.* The memory still shamed her.

"Go," the Reader had urged, as the captains were bearing her uncle Euron down Nagga's hill to don his driftwood crown.

"Said the raven to the crow. Come with me. I need you to raise the men of Harlaw." Back then, she'd meant to fight.

"The men of Harlaw are here. The ones who count. Some were shouting Euron's name. I will not set Harlaw against Harlaw."

"Euron's mad. And dangerous. That hellhorn . . ."

"I heard it. *Go,* Asha. Once Euron has been crowned, he'll look for you. You dare not let his eye fall upon you."

"If I stand with my other uncles . . ."

". . . you will die outcast, with every hand against you. When you put your name before the captains you submitted yourself to their judgment. You cannot go against that judgment now. Only once has the choice of a kingsmoot been overthrown. Read Haereg."

Only Rodrik the Reader would talk of some old book whilst their lives were balanced on a sword's edge. "If you are staying, so am I," she told him stubbornly.

"Don't be a fool. Euron shows the world his smiling eye tonight, but come the morrow . . . Asha, you are Balon's daughter, and your claim is stronger than his own. So long as you draw breath you remain a danger to him. If you stay, you will be killed or wed to the Red Oarsman. I don't know which would be worse. Go. You will not have another chance."

Asha had landed *Black Wind* on the far side of the island for just such an eventuality. Old Wyk was not large. She could be back aboard her ship before the sun came up, on her way to Harlaw before Euron realized she was missing. Yet she hesitated until her uncle said, "Do it for the love you bear me, child. Do not make me watch you die."

So she went. To Ten Towers first, to bid farewell to her mother. "It may be a long while before I come again," Asha warned her. Lady Alannys had not understood. "Where is Theon?" she asked. "Where is my baby boy?" Lady Gwynesse only wanted to know when Lord Rodrik would return. "I am seven years his elder. Ten Towers should be mine."

Asha was still at Ten Towers taking on provisions when the tidings of her marriage reached her. "My wayward niece needs taming," the Crow's Eye was reported to have said, "and I know the man to tame her." He had married her to Erik Ironmaker and named the Anvil-Breaker to rule the Iron Islands whilst he was chasing dragons. Erik had been a great man in his day, a fearless reaver who could boast of having sailed with her grandsire's grandsire, that same Dagon Greyjoy whom Dagon the Drunkard had been named for. Old women on Fair Isle still frightened their grandchildren with tales of Lord Dagon and his men. *I wounded Eric's pride at the kingsmoot,* Asha reflected. *He is not like to forget that.*

She had to pay her nuncle his just due. With one stroke, Euron had turned a rival into a supporter, secured the isles in his absence, and removed Asha as a threat. *And enjoyed a good belly laugh too.* Tris Botley said that the Crow's Eye had used a seal to stand in for her at her wedding. "I hope Erik did not insist on a consummation," she'd said.

I cannot go home, she thought, *but I dare not stay here much longer.* The quiet of the woods unnerved her. Asha had spent her life on islands and on ships. The sea was never silent. The sound of the waves washing against a rocky shore was in her blood, but there were no waves at Deepwood Motte . . . only the trees, the endless trees, soldier pines and sentinels, beech and ash and ancient oaks, chestnut trees and ironwoods and firs. The sound they made was softer than the sea, and she heard it only when the wind was blowing; then the sighing seemed to come from all around her, as if the trees were whispering to one another in some language that she could not understand.

Tonight the whispering seemed louder than before. *A rush of dead brown leaves,* Asha told herself, *bare branches creaking in the wind.* She turned away from the window, away from the woods. *I need a deck beneath my feet again. Or failing that, some food in my belly.* She'd had too much wine tonight, but too little bread and none of that great bloody roast.

The moonlight was bright enough to find her clothes. She donned thick black breeches, a quilted tunic, and a green leather jerkin covered with overlapping plates of steel. Leaving Qarl to his dreams, she padded down the keep's exterior stair, the steps creaking under her bare feet. One of the men walking sentry on the walls spied her making her descent and lifted his spear to her. Asha whistled back at him. As she crossed the inner yard to the kitchens, Galbart Glover's dogs began to bark. *Good,* she thought. *That will drown out the sound of the trees.*

She was cutting a wedge of yellow cheese from a round as big as a cart wheel when Tris Botley stepped into the kitchen, bundled up in a thick fur cloak. "My queen."

"Don't mock me."

"You will always rule my heart. No amount of fools shouting at a kingsmoot can change that."

What am I to do with this boy? Asha could not doubt his devotion. Not only had he stood her champion on Nagga's hill and shouted out her name, but he had even crossed the sea to join her afterward, abandoning his king and kin and home. *Not that he dared defy Euron to his face.* When the Crow's Eye took the fleet to sea Tris had simply lagged behind, changing course only when the other ships were lost to sight. Even that took a certain courage, though; he could never return to the isles. "Cheese?" she asked him. "There's ham as well, and mustard."

"It's not food I want, my lady. You know that." Tris had grown himself a thick brown beard at Deepwood. He claimed it helped to keep his face warm. "I saw you from the watchtower."

"If you have the watch, what are you doing here?"

"Cromm's up there, and Hagen the Horn. How many eyes do we need to watch leaves rustle in the moonlight? We need to talk."

"Again?" She sighed. "You know Hagen's daughter, the one with the red hair. She steers a ship as well as any man and has a pretty face. Seventeen, and I've seen her looking at you."

"I don't want Hagen's daughter." He almost touched her before thinking better of it. "Asha, it is time to go. Moat Cailin was the only thing holding back the tide. If we remain here, the northmen will kill us all, you know that."

"Would you have me run?"

"I would have you live. I love you."

No, she thought, *you love some innocent maiden who lives only in your head, a frightened child in need of your protection.* "I do not love you," she said bluntly, "and I do not run."

"What's here that you should hold so tight to it but pine and mud and foes? We have our ships. Sail away with me, and we'll make new lives upon the sea."

"As pirates?" It was almost tempting. *Let the wolves have back their gloomy woods and retake the open sea.*

"As traders," he insisted. "We'll voyage east as the Crow's Eye did, but we'll come back with silks and spices instead of a dragon's horn. One voyage to the Jade Sea and we'll be as rich as gods. We can have a manse in Oldtown or one of the Free Cities."

"You and me and Qarl?" She saw him flinch at the mention of Qarl's name. "Hagen's girl might like to sail the Jade Sea with you. I am still the kraken's daughter. My place is—"

"—*where?* You cannot return to the isles. Not unless you mean to submit to your lord husband."

Asha tried to picture herself abed with Erik Ironmaker, crushed beneath his bulk, suffering his embraces. *Better him than the Red Oarsman or Left-Hand Lucas Codd.* The Anvil-Breaker had once been a roaring giant, fearsomely strong, fiercely loyal, utterly without fear. *It might not be so bad. He's like to die the first time he tries to do his duty as a husband.* That would make her Erik's widow instead of Erik's wife, which could be better or a good deal worse, depending on his grandsons. *And my nuncle. In the end, all the winds blow me back toward Euron.* "I have hostages, on Harlaw," she reminded him. "And there is still Sea Dragon Point . . . if I cannot have my father's kingdom, why not make one of my own?" Sea Dragon Point had not always been as thinly peopled as it was now. Old ruins could still be found amongst its hills and bogs, the remains of ancient strongholds of the First Men. In the high places, there were weirwood circles left by the children of the forest.

"You are clinging to Sea Dragon Point the way a drowning man clings to a bit of wreckage. What does Sea Dragon have that anyone could ever want? There are no mines, no gold, no silver, not even tin or iron. The land is too wet for wheat or corn."

I do not plan on planting wheat or corn. "What's there? I'll tell you. Two long coastlines, a hundred hidden coves, otters in the lakes, salmon in the rivers, clams along the shore, colonies of seals offshore, tall pines for building ships."

"Who will build these ships, my queen? Where will Your Grace find subjects for her kingdom if the northmen let you have it? Or do you mean to rule over a realm of seals and otters?"

She gave a rueful laugh. "Otters might be easier to rule than men, I grant you. And seals are smarter. No, you may be right. My best course may still be to return to Pyke. There are those on Harlaw who would welcome my return. On Pyke as well. And Euron won no friends on Black-tyde when he slew Lord Baelor. I could find my nuncle Aeron, raise the isles." No one had seen the Damphair since the kingsmoot, but his Drowned Men claimed he was hiding on Great Wyk and would soon come forth to call down the wroth of the Drowned God on the Crow's Eye and his minions.

"The Anvil-Breaker is searching for the Damphair too. He is hunting down the Drowned Men. Blind Beron Blacktyde was taken and put to the question. Even the Old Grey Gull was given shackles. How will you find the priest when all of Euron's men cannot?"

"He is my blood. My father's brother." It was a feeble answer, and Asha knew it.

"Do you know what I think?"

"I am about to, I suspect."

"I think the Damphair's dead. I think the Crow's Eye slit his throat for him. Ironmaker's search is just to make us believe the priest escaped. Euron is afraid to be seen as a kinslayer."

"Never let my nuncle hear you say that. Tell the Crow's Eye he's afraid of kinslaying, and he'll murder one of his own sons just to prove you wrong." Asha was feeling almost sober by then. Tristifer Botley had that effect on her.

"Even if you did find your uncle Damphair, the two of you would fail. You were both *part* of the kingsmoot, so you cannot say it was unlawful called, as Torgon did. You are bound to its decision by all the laws of gods and men. You—"

Asha frowned. "Wait. Torgon? Which Torgon?"

"Torgon the Latecomer."

"He was a king during the Age of Heroes." She recalled that much about him, but little else. "What of him?"

"Torgon Greyiron was the king's eldest son. But the king was old and Torgon restless, so it happened that when his father died he was raiding along the Mander from his stronghold on Greyshield. His brothers sent no word to him but instead quickly called a kingsmoot, thinking that one of them would be chosen to wear the driftwood crown. But the captains and the kings chose Urragon Goodbrother to rule instead. The first thing the new king did was command that all the sons of the old king be put to death, and so they were. After that men called him *Badbrother*, though in truth they'd been no kin of his. He ruled for almost two years."

Asha remembered now. "Torgon came home . . ."

". . . and said the kingsmoot was unlawful since he had not been there to make his claim. Badbrother had proved to be as mean as he was cruel and had few friends left upon the isles. The priests denounced him, the lords rose against him, and his own captains hacked him into pieces. Torgon the Latecomer became the king and ruled for forty years."

Asha took Tris Botley by the ears and kissed him full upon the lips. He was red and breathless by the time she let him go. "What was that?" he said.

"A kiss, it's called. Drown me for a fool, Tris, I should have remembered—" She broke off suddenly. When Tris tried to speak, she shushed him, listening. "That's a warhorn. Hagen." Her first thought was of her husband. Could Erik Ironmaker have come all this way to claim his wayward wife? "The Drowned God loves me after all. Here I was wondering what to do, and he has sent me foes to fight." Asha got to her feet and slammed her knife back into its sheath. "The battle's come to us."

She was trotting by the time she reached the castle bailey, with Tris dogging her heels, but even so she came too late. The fight was done. Asha found two northmen bleeding by the eastern wall not far from the postern gate, with Lorren Longaxe, Six-Toed Harl, and Grimtongue standing over them. "Cromm and Hagen saw them coming over the wall," Grimtongue explained.

"Just these two?" asked Asha.

"Five. We killed two before they could get over, and Harl slew another on the wallwalk. These two made it to the yard."

One man was dead, his blood and brains crusting Lorren's longaxe, but the second was still breathing raggedly, though Grimtongue's spear had pinned him to the ground in a spreading pool of blood. Both were clad in boiled leather and mottled cloaks of brown and green and black, with branches, leaves, and brush sewn about their heads and shoulders.

"Who are you?" Asha asked the wounded man.

"A Flint. Who are you?"

"Asha of House Greyjoy. This is my castle."

"Deepwood be Galbart Glover's seat. No home for squids."

"Are there any more of you?" Asha demanded of him. When he did not answer, she seized Grimtongue's spear and turned it, and the northman cried out in anguish as more blood gushed from his wound. "What was your purpose here?"

"The lady," he said, shuddering. "Gods, stop. We come for the lady. T' rescue her. It was just us five."

Asha looked into his eyes. When she saw the falsehood there, she leaned upon the spear, twisting it. "*How many more?*" she said. "Tell me, or I'll make your dying last until the dawn."

"Many," he finally sobbed, between screams. "*Thousands.* Three thousand, four . . . *aieeee* . . . please . . ."

She ripped the spear out of him and drove it down two-handed through his lying throat. Galbart Glover's maester had claimed the mountain clans were too quarrelsome to ever band together without a Stark to lead them. *He might not have been lying. He might just have been wrong.* She had learned what *that* tasted like at her nuncle's kingsmoot. "These five were sent to open our gates before the main attack," she said. "Lorren, Harl, fetch me Lady Glover and her maester."

"Whole or bloody?" asked Lorren Longaxe.

"Whole and unharmed. Grimtongue, get up that thrice-damned tower and tell Cromm and Hagen to keep a sharp eye out. If they see so much as a hare, I want to know of it."

Deepwood's bailey was soon full of frightened people. Her own men were struggling into armor or climbing up onto the wallwalks. Galbart Glover's folk looked on with fearful faces, whispering to one another. Glover's steward had to be carried up from the cellar, having lost a leg when Asha took the castle. The maester protested noisily until Lorren cracked him hard across the face with a mailed fist. Lady Glover emerged from the godswood on the arm of her bedmaid. "I warned you that this day would come, my lady," she said, when she saw the corpses on the ground.

The maester pushed forward, with blood dripping from a broken nose. "Lady Asha, I beg you, strike your banners and let me bargain for your life. You have used us fairly, and with honor. I will tell them so."

"We will exchange you for the children." Sybelle Glover's eyes were red, from tears and sleepless nights. "Gawen is four now. I missed his nameday. And my sweet girl . . . give me back my children, and no harm need come to you. Nor to your men."

The last part was a lie, Asha knew. *She* might be exchanged, perhaps, shipped back to the Iron Islands to her husband's loving arms. Her cousins would be ransomed too, as would Tris Botley and a few more of her company, those whose kin had coin enough to buy them back. For the rest it would be the axe, the noose, or the Wall. *Still, they have the right to choose.*

Asha climbed on a barrel so all of them could see her. "The wolves are coming down on us with their teeth bared. They will be at our gates before the sun comes up. Shall we throw down our spears and axes and plead with them to spare us?"

"No." Qarl the Maid drew his sword. "No," echoed Lorren Longaxe. "*No*," boomed Rolfe the Dwarf, a bear of a man who stood a head taller than anyone else in her crew. "*Never.*" And Hagen's horn sounded again from on high, ringing out across the bailey.

AHooooooooooooooooooooooo, the warhorn cried, long and low, a sound to curdle blood. Asha had begun to hate the sound of horns. On Old Wyk her uncle's hellhorn had blown a death knell for her dreams, and now Hagen was sounding what might well be her last hour on earth. *If I must die, I will die with an axe in my hand and a curse upon my lips.*

"To the walls," Asha Greyjoy told her men. She turned her own steps for the watchtower, with Tris Botley right behind her.

The wooden watchtower was the tallest thing this side of the mountains, rising twenty feet above the biggest sentinels and soldier pines in the surrounding woods. "There, Captain," said Cromm, when she made the platform. Asha saw only trees and shadows, the moonlit hills and the snowy peaks beyond. Then she realized that trees were creeping closer. "Oho," she laughed, "these mountain goats have cloaked themselves in pine boughs." The woods were on the move, creeping toward the castle like a slow green tide. She thought back to a tale she had heard as a child, about the children of the forest and their battles with the First Men, when the greenseers turned the trees to warriors.

"We cannot fight so many," Tris Botley said.

"We can fight as many as come, pup," insisted Cromm. "The more there are, the more the glory. Men will sing of us."

Aye, but will they sing of your courage or my folly? The sea was five long leagues away. Would they do better to stand and fight behind Deepwood's deep ditches and wooden walls? *Deepwood's wooden walls did the Glovers small good when I took their castle*, she reminded herself. *Why should they serve me any better?*

"Come the morrow we will feast beneath the sea." Cromm stroked his axe as if he could not wait.

Hagen lowered his horn. "If we die with dry feet, how will we find our way to the Drowned God's watery halls?"

"These woods are full of little streams," Cromm assured him. "All of them lead to rivers, and all the rivers to the sea."

Asha was not ready to die, not here, not yet. "A living man can find the sea more easily than a dead one. Let the wolves keep their gloomy woods. We are making for the ships."

She wondered who was in command of her foes. *If it were me, I would take the strand and put our longships to the torch before attacking Deepwood.* The wolves would not find that easy, though, not without longships of their own. Asha never beached more than half her ships. The other half stood safely off to sea, with orders to raise sail and make for Sea Dragon Point if the northmen took the strand. "Hagen, blow your horn and make the forest shake. Tris, don some mail, it's time you tried out that sweet sword of yours." When she saw how pale he was, she pinched his cheek. "Splash some blood upon the moon with me, and I promise you a kiss for every kill."

"My queen," said Tristifer, "here we have the walls, but if we reach the sea and find that the wolves have taken our ships or driven them away . . ."

". . . we die," she finished cheerfully, "but at least we'll die with our feet wet. Ironborn fight better with salt spray in their nostrils and the sound of the waves at their backs."

Hagen blew three short blasts in quick succession, the signal that would send the ironborn back to their ships. From below came shouting, the clatter of spear and sword, the whinnying of horses. *Too few horses and too few riders.* Asha headed for the stair. In the bailey, she found Qarl the Maid waiting with her chestnut mare, her warhelm, and her throwing axes. Ironmen were leading horses from Galbart Glover's stables.

"A *ram!*" a voice shouted down from the walls. "*They have a battering ram!*"

"Which gate?" asked Asha, mounting up.

"The north!" From beyond Deepwood's mossy wooden walls came the sudden sound of trumpets.

Trumpets? Wolves with trumpets? That was wrong, but Asha had no time to ponder it. "Open the south gate," she commanded, even as the north gate shook to the impact of the ram. She pulled a short-hafted throwing axe from the belt across her shoulder. "The hour of the owl has fled, my brothers. Now comes the hour of the spear, the sword, the axe. Form up. We're going home."

From a hundred throats came roars of "*Home!*" and "*Asha!*" Tris Botley galloped up beside her on a tall roan stallion. In the bailey, her men closed about each other, hefting shields and spears. Qarl the Maid, no horse rider, took his place between Grimtongue and Lorren Longaxe. As Hagen came scrambling down the watchtower steps, a wolfling's arrow caught him in the belly and sent him plunging headfirst to the ground. His daughter ran to him, wailing. "Bring her," Asha commanded. This was no time for mourning. Rolfe the Dwarf pulled the girl onto his horse, her red hair flying. Asha could hear the north gate groaning as the ram slammed into it again. *We may need to cut our way through them,* she thought, as the south gate swung wide before them. The way was clear. *For how long?*

"Move out!" Asha drove her heels into her horse's flanks.

Men and mounts alike were trotting by the time they reached the trees on the far side of the sodden field, where dead shoots of winter wheat rotted beneath the moon. Asha held her horsemen back as a rear guard, to keep the stragglers moving and see that no one was left behind. Tall soldier pines and gnarled old oaks closed in around them. Deepwood was aptly named. The trees were huge and dark, somehow threatening. Their limbs wove through one another and creaked with every breath of wind, and their higher branches scratched at the face of the moon. *The sooner we are shut of here, the better I will like it,* Asha thought. *The trees hate us all, deep in their wooden hearts.*

They pressed on south and southwest, until the wooden towers of Deepwood Motte were lost to sight and the sounds of trumpets had been swallowed by the woods. *The wolves have their castle back,* she thought, *perhaps they will be content to let us go.*

Tris Botley trotted up beside her. "We are going the wrong way," he said, gesturing at the moon as it peered down through the canopy of branches. "We need to turn north, for the ships."

"West first," Asha insisted. "West until the sun comes up. Then north." She turned to Rolfe the Dwarf and Roggon Rustbeard, her best riders. "Scout ahead and make sure our way is clear. I want no surprises when we reach the shore. If you come on wolves, ride back to me with word."

"If we must," promised Roggon through his huge red beard.

After the scouts had vanished into the trees, the rest of the ironborn resumed their march, but the going was slow. The trees hid the moon and stars from them, and the forest floor beneath their feet was black and treacherous. Before they had gone half a mile, her cousin Quenton's mare stumbled into a pit and shattered her foreleg. Quenton had to slit her throat to stop her screaming. "We should make torches," urged Tris.

"Fire will bring the northmen down on us." Asha cursed beneath her breath, wondering if it had been a mistake to leave the castle. *No. If we had stayed and fought, we might all be dead by now.* But it was no good blundering on through the dark either. *These trees will kill us if they can.* She took off her helm and pushed back her sweat-soaked hair. "The sun will be up in a few hours. We'll stop here and rest till break of day."

Stopping proved simple; rest came hard. No one slept, not even Droop-eye Dale, an oarsman who had been known to nap between strokes. Some of the men shared a skin of Galbart Glover's apple wine, passing it from hand to hand. Those who had brought food shared it with those who had not. The riders fed and watered their horses. Her cousin Quenton Grey-joy sent three men up trees, to watch for any sign of torches in the woods. Cromm honed his axe, and Qarl the Maid his sword. The horses cropped dead brown grass and weeds. Hagen's red-haired daughter seized Tris Botley by the hand to draw him off into the trees. When he refused her, she went off with Six-Toed Harl instead.

Would that I could do the same. It would be sweet to lose herself in Qarl's arms one last time. Asha had a bad feeling in her belly. Would she ever feel *Black Wind*'s deck beneath her feet again? And if she did, where would she sail her? *The isles are closed to me, unless I mean to bend my knees and spread my legs and suffer Eric Ironmaker's embraces, and no port in Westeros is like to welcome the kraken's daughter.* She could turn merchanter, as Tris seemed to want, or else make for the Stepstones and join the pirates there. *Or . . .*

"I send you each a piece of prince," she muttered.

Qarl grinned. "I would sooner have a piece of you," he whispered, "the sweet piece that's—"

Something flew from the brush to land with a soft *thump* in their midst, bumping and bouncing. It was round and dark and wet, with long hair that whipped about it as it rolled. When it came to rest amongst the roots of an oak, Grimtongue said, "Rolfe the Dwarf's not so tall as he once was." Half her men were on their feet by then, reaching for shields and spears and axes. *They lit no torches either,* Asha had time enough to think, *and they know these woods better than we ever could.* Then the trees erupted all around them, and the northmen poured in howling. *Wolves,* she thought, *they howl like bloody wolves. The war cry of the north.* Her ironborn screamed back at them, and the fight began.

No singer would ever make a song about that battle. No maester would ever write down an account for one of the Reader's beloved books. No banners flew, no warhorns moaned, no great lord called his men about him to hear his final ringing words. They fought in the predawn gloom, shadow against shadow, stumbling over roots and rocks, with mud and rotting leaves beneath their feet. The ironborn were clad in mail and salt-stained leather, the northmen in furs and hides and piney branches. The moon and stars looked down upon their struggle, their pale light filtered through the tangle of bare limbs that twisted overhead.

The first man to come at Asha Greyjoy died at her feet with her throwing axe between his eyes. That gave her respite enough to slip her shield onto her arm. *"To me!"* she called, but whether she was calling to her own men or the foes even Asha could not have said for certain. A northman with an axe loomed up before her, swinging with both hands as he howled in wordless fury. Asha raised her shield to block his blow, then shoved in close to gut him with her dirk. His howling took on a different tone as he fell. She spun and found another wolf behind her, and slashed him across the brow beneath his helm. His own cut caught her below the breast, but her mail turned it, so she drove the point of her dirk into his throat and left him to drown in his own blood. A hand seized her hair, but short as it was he could not get a good enough grip to wrench her head back. Asha slammed her boot heel down onto his instep and wrenched loose when he cried out in pain. By the time she turned the man was down and dying, still clutching a handful of her hair. Qarl stood over him, with his longsword dripping and moonlight shining in his eyes.

Grimtongue was counting the northmen as he killed them, calling out, "Four," as one went down and, "Five," a heartbeat later. The horses screamed and kicked and rolled their eyes in terror, maddened by the butchery and blood . . . all but Tris Botley's big roan stallion. Tris had gained the saddle, and his mount was rearing and wheeling as he laid about with his sword. *I may owe him a kiss or three before the night is done,* thought Asha.

"Seven," shouted Grimtongue, but beside him Lorren Longaxe sprawled with one leg twisted under him, and the shadows kept on coming, shouting and rustling. *We are fighting shrubbery,* Asha thought as she slew a man who had more leaves on him than most of the surrounding trees. That made her laugh. Her laughter drew more wolves to her, and she killed them too, wondering if she should start a count of her own. *I am a woman wed, and here's my suckling babe.* She pushed her dirk into a northman's chest through fur and wool and boiled leather. His face was so close to hers that she could smell the sour stench of his breath, and his hand was at her throat. Asha felt iron scraping against bone as her point slid over a rib. Then the man shuddered and died. When she let go of him, she was so weak she almost fell on top of him.

Later, she stood back-to-back with Qarl, listening to the grunts and curses all around them, to brave men crawling through the shadows weeping for their mothers. A bush drove at her with a spear long enough to punch through her belly and Qarl's back as well, pinning them together as they died. *Better that than die alone*, she thought, but her cousin Quenton killed the spearman before he reached her. A heartbeat later another bush killed Quenton, driving an axe into the base of his skull.

Behind her Grimtongue shouted, "*Nine*, and damn you all." Hagen's daughter burst naked from beneath the trees with two wolves at her heels. Asha wrenched loose a throwing axe and sent it flying end over end to take one of them in the back. When he fell, Hagen's daughter stumbled to her knees, snatched up his sword, stabbed the second man, then rose again, smeared with blood and mud, her long red hair unbound, and plunged into the fight.

Somewhere in the ebb and flow of battle, Asha lost Qarl, lost Tris, lost all of them. Her dirk was gone as well, and all her throwing axes; instead she had a sword in hand, a short sword with a broad thick blade, almost like a butcher's cleaver. For her life she could not have said where she had gotten it. Her arm ached, her mouth tasted of blood, her legs were trembling, and shafts of pale dawn light were slanting through the trees. *Has it been so long? How long have we been fighting?*

Her last foe was a northman with an axe, a big man bald and bearded, clad in a byrnie of patched and rusted mail that could only mean he was a chief or champion. He was not pleased to find himself fighting a woman. "*Cunt!*" he roared each time he struck at her, his spittle dampening her cheeks. "*Cunt! Cunt!*"

Asha wanted to shout back at him, but her throat was so dry she could do no more than grunt. His axe was shivering her shield, cracking the wood on the downswing, tearing off long pale splinters when he wrenched it back. Soon she would have only a tangle of kindling on her arm. She backed away and shook free of the ruined shield, then backed away some more and danced left and right and left again to avoid the downrushing axe.

And then her back came up hard against a tree, and she could dance no more. The wolf raised the axe above his head to split her head in two. Asha tried to slip to her right, but her feet were tangled in some roots, trapping her. She twisted, lost her footing, and the axehead crunched against her temple with a scream of steel on steel. The world went red and black and red again. Pain crackled up her leg like lightning, and far away she heard her northman say, "You bloody cunt," as he lifted up his axe for the blow that would finish her.

A trumpet blew.

That's wrong, she thought. *There are no trumpets in the Drowned God's watery halls. Below the waves the merlings hail their lord by blowing into seashells.*

She dreamt of red hearts burning, and a black stag in a golden wood with flame streaming from his antlers.

TYRION

By the time they reached Volantis, the sky was purple to the west and black to the east, and the stars were coming out. *The same stars as in Westeros*, Tyrion Lannister reflected.

He might have taken some comfort in that if he had not been trussed up like a goose and lashed to a saddle. He had given up squirming. The knots that bound him were too tight. Instead he'd gone as limp as a sack of meal. *Saving my strength*, he told himself, though for what he could not have said.

Volantis closed its gates at dark, and the guardsmen on its northern gate were grumbling impatiently at the stragglers. They joined the queue behind a wagon laden with limes and oranges. The guards motioned the wagon through with their torches but took a harder look at the big Andal on his warhorse, with his longsword and his mail. A captain was summoned. Whilst he and the knight exchanged some words in Volantene, one of the guardsmen pulled off his clawed gauntlet and gave Tyrion's head a rub. "I'm full of good fortune," the dwarf told him. "Cut me loose, friend, and I'll see you're well rewarded."

His captor overheard. "Save your lies for those who speak your tongue, Imp," he said, when the Volantenes waved them on.

They were moving again, through the gate and beneath the city's massive walls. "*You* speak my tongue. Can I sway you with promises, or are you determined to buy a lordship with my head?"

"I *was* a lord, by right of birth. I want no hollow titles."

"That's all you're like to get from my sweet sister."

"And here I'd heard a Lannister always pays his debts."

"Oh, every penny . . . but never a groat more, my lord. You'll get the meal you bargained for, but it won't be sauced with gratitude, and in the end it will not nourish you."

"Might be all I want is to see you pay for crimes. The kinslayer is ac-cursed in the eyes of gods and men."

"The gods are blind. And men see only what they wish."

"I see you plain enough, Imp." Something dark had crept into the knight's tone. "I have done things I am not proud of, things that brought shame onto my House and my father's name . . . but to kill your own sire? How could any man do that?"

"Give me a crossbow and pull down your breeches, and I'll show you." *Gladly.*

"You think this is a jape?"

"I think life is a jape. Yours, mine, everyone's."

Inside the city walls, they rode past guildhalls, markets, and bathhouses. Fountains splashed and sang in the centers of wide squares, where men sat at stone tables, moving *cyvasse* pieces and sipping wine from glass flutes as slaves lit ornate lanterns to hold the dark at bay. Palms and cedars grew along the cobbled road, and monuments stood at every junction. Many of the statues lacked heads, the dwarf noted, yet even headless they still managed to look imposing in the purple dusk.

As the warhorse plodded south along the river, the shops grew smaller and meaner, the trees along the street became a row of stumps. Cobble-stones gave way to devilgrass beneath their horse's hooves, then to soft wet mud the color of a baby's nightsoil. The little bridges that spanned the small streams that fed the Rhoyne creaked alarmingly beneath their weight. Where a fort had once overlooked the river now stood a broken gate, gaping open like an old man's toothless mouth. Goats could be glimpsed peering over the parapets.

Old Volantis, first daughter of Valyria, the dwarf mused. *Proud Volantis, queen of the Rhoyne and mistress of the Summer Sea, home to noble lords and lovely ladies of the most ancient blood.* Never mind the packs of naked children that roamed the alleys screaming in shrill voices, or the bravos standing in the doors of wineshops fingering their sword hilts, or the slaves with their bent backs and tattooed faces who scurried everywhere like cockroaches. *Mighty Volantis, grandest and most populous of the Nine Free Cities.* Ancient wars had depopulated much of the city, however, and large areas of Volantis had begun to sink back into the mud on which it stood. *Beautiful Volantis, city of fountains and flowers.* But half the fountains were dry, half the pools cracked and stagnant. Flowering vines sent up creepers from every crack in the wall or pavement, and young trees had taken root in the walls of abandoned shops and roofless temples.

And then there was the smell. It hung in the hot, humid air, rich, rank, pervasive. *There's fish in it, and flowers, and some elephant dung as well. Something sweet and something earthy and something dead and rotten.* "This city smells like an old whore," Tyrion announced. "Like some sagging slattern who has drenched her privy parts in perfume to drown the stench between her legs. Not that I am complaining. With whores, the young ones smell much better, but the old ones know more tricks."

"You would know more of that than I do."

"Ah, of course. That brothel where we met, did you take it for a sept? Was that your virgin sister squirming in your lap?"

That made him scowl. "Give that tongue of yours a rest unless you'd rather I tied it in a knot."

Tyrion swallowed his retort. His lip was still fat and swollen from the last time he had pushed the big knight too far. *Hard hands and no sense of humor makes for a bad marriage.* That much he'd learned on the road from Selhorys. His thoughts went to his boot, to the mushrooms in the toe. His captor had not searched him quite as thoroughly as he might have. *There is always that escape. Cersei will not have me alive, at least.*

Farther south, signs of prosperity began to reappear. Abandoned buildings were seen less often, the naked children vanished, the bravos in the doorways seemed more sumptuously dressed. A few of the inns they passed actually looked like places where a man might sleep without fear of having his throat slit. Lanterns swung from iron stanchions along the river road, swaying when the wind blew. The streets grew broader, the buildings more imposing. Some were topped with great domes of colored glass. In the gathering dusk, with fires lit beneath them, the domes glowed blue and red and green and purple.

Even so, there was something in the air that made Tyrion uneasy. West of the Rhoyne, he knew, the wharves of Volantis teemed with sailors, slaves, and traders, and the wineshops, inns, and brothels all catered to them. East of the river, strangers from across the seas were seen less seldom. *We are not wanted here,* the dwarf realized.

The first time they passed an elephant, Tyrion could not help but stare. There had been an elephant in the menagerie at Lannisport when he had been a boy, but she had died when he was seven . . . and this great grey behemoth looked to be twice her size.

Farther on, they fell in behind a smaller elephant, white as old bone and pulling an ornate cart. "Is an oxcart an oxcart without an ox?" Tyrion asked his captor. When that sally got no response, he lapsed back into silence, contemplating the rolling rump of the white dwarf elephant ahead of them.

Volantis was overrun with white dwarf elephants. As they drew closer to the Black Wall and the crowded districts near the Long Bridge, they saw a dozen of them. Big grey elephants were not uncommon either—huge beasts with castles on their backs. And in the half-light of evening the dung carts had come out, attended by half-naked slaves whose task it was to shovel up the steaming piles left by elephants both great and small. Swarms of flies followed the carts, so the dung slaves had flies tattooed upon their cheeks, to mark them for what they were. *There's a trade for my sweet sister,* Tyrion mused. *She'd look so pretty with a little shovel and flies tattooed on those sweet pink cheeks.*

By then they had slowed to a crawl. The river road was thick with traffic, almost all of it flowing south. The knight went with it, a log caught in a current. Tyrion eyed the passing throngs. Nine men of every ten bore slave marks on their cheeks. "So many slaves . . . where are they all going?"

"The red priests light their nightfires at sunset. The High Priest will be speaking. I would avoid it if I could, but to reach the Long Bridge we must pass the red temple."

Three blocks later the street opened up before them onto a huge torchlit plaza, and there it stood. *Seven save me, that's got to be three times the size of the Great Sept of Baelor.* An enormity of pillars, steps, buttresses, bridges, domes, and towers flowing into one another as if they had all been chiseled from one collossal rock, the Temple of the Lord of Light loomed like Aegon's High Hill. A hundred hues of red, yellow, gold, and orange met and melded in the temple walls, dissolving one into the other like clouds at sunset. Its slender towers twisted ever upward, frozen flames dancing as they reached for the sky. *Fire turned to stone.* Huge nightfires burned beside the temple steps, and between them the High Priest had begun to speak.

Benerro. The priest stood atop a red stone pillar, joined by a slender stone bridge to a lofty terrace where the lesser priests and acolytes stood. The acolytes were clad in robes of pale yellow and bright orange, priests and priestesses in red.

The great plaza before them was packed almost solid. Many and more of the worshipers were wearing some scrap of red cloth pinned to their sleeves or tied around their brows. Every eye was on the high priest, save theirs. "Make way," the knight growled as his horse pushed through the throng. "Clear a path." The Volantenes gave way resentfully, with mutters and angry looks.

Benerro's high voice carried well. Tall and thin, he had a drawn face and skin white as milk. Flames had been tattooed across his cheeks and chin and shaven head to make a bright red mask that crackled about his eyes and coiled down and around his lipless mouth. "Is that a slave tattoo?" asked Tyrion.

The knight nodded. "The red temple buys them as children and makes them priests or temple prostitutes or warriors. Look there." He pointed at the steps, where a line of men in ornate armor and orange cloaks stood before the temple's doors, clasping spears with points like writhing flames. "The Fiery Hand. The Lord of Light's sacred soldiers, defenders of the temple."

Fire knights. "And how many fingers does this hand have, pray?"

"One thousand. Never more, and never less. A new flame is kindled for every one that gutters out."

Benerro jabbed a finger at the moon, made a fist, spread his hands wide. When his voice rose in a crescendo, flames leapt from his fingers with a sudden *whoosh* and made the crowd gasp. The priest could trace fiery letters in the air as well. *Valyrian glyphs.* Tyrion recognized perhaps two in ten; one was *Doom*, the other *Darkness*.

Shouts erupted from the crowd. Women were weeping and men were shaking their fists. *I have a bad feeling about this.* The dwarf was reminded of the day Myrcella sailed for Dorne and the riot that boiled up as they made their way back to the Red Keep.

Haldon Halfmaester had spoken of using the red priest to Young Griff's advantage, Tyrion recalled. Now that he had seen and heard the man himself, that struck him as a very bad idea. He hoped that Griff had better sense. *Some allies are more dangerous than enemies. But Lord Connington will need to puzzle that one out for himself. I am like to be a head on a spike.*

The priest was pointing at the Black Wall behind the temple, gesturing up at its parapets, where a handful of armored guardsmen stood gazing down. "What is he saying?" Tyrion asked the knight.

"That Daenerys stands in peril. The dark eye has fallen upon her, and the minions of night are plotting her destruction, praying to their false gods in temples of deceit . . . conspiring at betrayal with godless outlanders . . ."

The hairs on the back of Tyrion's neck began to prickle. *Prince Aegon will find no friend here.* The red priest spoke of ancient prophecy, a prophecy that foretold the coming of a hero to deliver the world from darkness. *One hero. Not two. Daenerys has dragons, Aegon does not.* The dwarf did not need to be a prophet himself to foresee how Benerro and his followers might react to a second Targaryen. *Griff will see that too, surely*, he thought, surprised to find how much he cared.

The knight had forced their way through most of the press at the back of the plaza, ignoring the curses that were flung at them as they passed. One man stepped in front of them, but his captor gripped the hilt of his longsword and drew it just far enough to show a foot of naked steel. The man melted away, and all at once an alley opened up before them. The knight urged his mount to a trot, and they left the crowd behind them. For a while Tyrion could still hear Benerro's voice growing fainter at their back and the roars his words provoked, sudden as thunder.

They came upon a stable. The knight dismounted, then hammered on the door until a haggard slave with a horsehead on his cheek came running. The dwarf was pulled down roughly from the saddle and lashed to a post whilst his captor woke the stable's owner and haggled with him over the price of his horse and saddle. *Cheaper to sell a horse than to ship one half across the world.* Tyrion sensed a ship in his immediate future. Perhaps he was a prophet after all.

When the dickering was done, the knight slung his weapons, shield, and saddlebag over his shoulder and asked for directions to the nearest smithy. That proved shuttered too, but opened quick enough at the knight's shout. The smith gave Tyrion a squint, then nodded and accepted a fistful of coins. "Come here," the knight told his prisoner. He drew his dagger and slit Tyrion's bonds apart. "My thanks," said the dwarf as he rubbed his wrists, but the knight only laughed and said, "Save your gratitude for someone who deserves it, Imp. You will not like this next bit."

He was not wrong.

The manacles were black iron, thick and heavy, each weighing a good two pounds, if the dwarf was any judge. The chains added even more weight. "I must be more fearsome than I knew," Tyrion confessed as the last links were hammered closed. Each blow sent a shock up his arm almost to the shoulder. "Or were you afraid that I would dash away on these stunted little legs of mine?"

The ironsmith did not so much as look up from his work, but the knight chuckled darkly. "It's your mouth that concerns me, not your legs. In fetters, you're a slave. No one will listen to a word you say, not even those who speak the tongue of Westeros."

"There's no need for this," Tyrion protested. "I will be a good little prisoner, I will, I will."

"Prove it, then, and shut your mouth."

So he bowed his head and bit his tongue as the chains were fixed, wrist to wrist, wrist to ankle, ankle to ankle. *These bloody things weigh more than I do.* Still, at least he drew breath. His captor could just as easily have cut his head off. That was all Cersei required, after all. Not striking it off straightaway had been his captor's first mistake. *There is half a world between Volantis and King's Landing, and much and more can happen along the way, ser.*

The rest of the way they went by foot, Tyrion clanking and clattering as he struggled to keep up with his captor's long, impatient strides. Whenever he threatened to fall behind, the knight would seize his fetters and yank them roughly, sending the dwarf stumbling and hopping along beside him. *It could be worse. He could be urging me along with a whip.*

Volantis straddled one mouth of the Rhoyne where the river kissed the sea, its two halves joined by the Long Bridge. The oldest, richest part of the city was east of the river, but sellswords, barbarians, and other uncouth outlanders were not welcome there, so they must needs cross over to the west.

The gateway to the Long Bridge was a black stone arch carved with sphinxes, manticores, dragons, and creatures stranger still. Beyond the arch stretched the great span that the Valyrians had built at the height of their glory, its fused stone roadway supported by massive piers. The road was just wide enough for two carts to pass abreast, so whenever a wagon headed west passed one going east, both had to slow to a crawl.

It was well they were afoot. A third of the way out, a wagon laden with melons had gotten its wheels tangled with one piled high with silken carpets and brought all wheeled traffic to a halt. Much of the foot traffic had stopped as well, to watch the drivers curse and scream at one another, but the knight grabbed hold of Tyrion's chain and bulled a path through the throng for both of them. In the middle of the press, a boy tried to reach into his purse, but a hard elbow put an end to that and spread the thief's bloody nose across half his face.

Buildings rose to either side of them: shops and temples, taverns and inns, *cyvasse* parlors and brothels. Most were three or four stories tall, each floor overhanging the one beneath it. Their top floors almost kissed. Crossing the bridge felt like passing through a torchlit tunnel. Along the span were shops and stalls of every sort; weavers and lacemakers displayed their wares cheek by jowl with glassblowers, candlemakers, and fishwives selling eels and oysters. Each goldsmith had a guard at his door, and every spicer had two, for their goods were twice as valuable. Here and there, between the shops, a traveler might catch a glimpse of the river he was crossing. To the north the Rhoyne was a broad black ribbon bright with stars, five times as wide as the Blackwater Rush at King's Landing. South of the bridge the river opened up to embrace the briny sea.

At the bridge's center span, the severed hands of thieves and cutpurses hung like strings of onions from iron stanchions along the roadway. Three heads were on display as well—two men and a woman, their crimes scrawled on tablets underneath them. A pair of spearmen attended them, clad in polished helms and shirts of silver mail. Across their cheeks were tiger stripes as green as jade. From time to time the guards waved their spears to chase away the kestrels, gulls, and carrion crows paying court to the deceased. The birds returned to the heads within moments.

"What did they do?" Tyrion inquired innocently.

The knight glanced at the inscriptions. "The woman was a slave who raised her hand to her mistress. The older man was accused of fomenting rebellion and spying for the dragon queen."

"And the young one?"

"Killed his father."

Tyrion gave the rotting head a second look. *Why, it almost looks as if those lips are smiling.*

Farther on, the knight paused briefly to consider a jeweled tiara displayed upon a bed of purple velvet. He passed that by, but a few steps on he stopped again to haggle over a pair of gloves at a leatherworker's stall. Tyrion was grateful for the respites. The headlong pace had left him puffing, and his wrists were chafed raw from the manacles.

From the far end of the Long Bridge, it was only a short walk through the teeming waterfront districts of the west bank, down torchlit streets crowded with sailors, slaves, and drunken merrymakers. Once an elephant lumbered past with a dozen half-naked slave girls waving from the castle on its back, teasing passersby with glimpses of their breasts and crying, "Malaquo, Malaquo." They made such an entrancing sight that Tyrion almost waddled right into the steaming pile of dung the elephant had left to mark its passage. He was saved at the last instant when the knight snatched him aside, yanking on his chain so hard it made him reel and stumble.

"How much farther?" the dwarf asked.

"Just there. Fishmonger's Square."

Their destination proved to be the Merchant's House, a four-story monstrosity that squatted amongst the warehouses, brothels, and taverns of the waterside like some enormous fat man surrounded by children. Its

common room was larger than the great halls of half the castles in Westeros, a dim-lit maze of a place with a hundred private alcoves and hidden
nooks whose blackened beams and cracked ceilings echoed to the din of
sailors, traders, captains, money changers, shippers, and slavers, lying,
cursing, and cheating each other in half a hundred different tongues.

Tyrion approved the choice of hostelry. Soon or late the *Shy Maid*
must reach Volantis. This was the city's biggest inn, first choice for shippers, captains, and merchantmen. A lot of business was done in that cavernous warren of a common room. He knew enough of Volantis to know
that. Let Griff turn up here with Duck and Haldon, and he would be free
again soon enough.

Meanwhile, he would be patient. His chance would come.

The rooms upstairs proved rather less than grand, however, particularly
the cheap ones up on the fourth floor. Wedged into a corner of the building beneath a sloping roof, the bedchamber his captor had engaged featured a low ceiling, a sagging feather bed with an unpleasant odor, and a
slanting wood-plank floor that reminded Tyrion of his sojourn at the
Eyrie. *At least this room has walls.* It had windows too; those were its chief
amenity, along with the iron ring set in the wall, so useful for chaining up
one's slaves. His captor paused only long enough to light a tallow candle
before securing Tyrion's chains to the ring.

"Must you?" the dwarf protested, rattling feebly. "Where am I going to
go, out the window?"

"You might."

"We are four floors up, and I cannot fly."

"You can fall. I want you alive."

Aye, but why? Cersei is not like to care. Tyrion rattled his chains. "I
know who you are, ser." It had not been hard to puzzle out. The bear on
his surcoat, the arms on his shield, the lost lordship he had mentioned. "I
know *what* you are. And if you know who I am, you also know that I was
the King's Hand and sat in council with the Spider. Would it interest you
to know that it was the eunuch who dispatched me on this journey?" *Him
and Jaime, but I'll leave my brother out of it.* "I am as much his creature as
you are. We ought not be at odds."

That did not please the knight. "I took the Spider's coin, I'll not deny it,
but I was never his creature. And my loyalties lie elsewhere now."

"With Cersei? More fool you. All my sister requires is my head, and
you have a fine sharp sword. Why not end this farce now and spare us
both?"

The knight laughed. "Is this some dwarf's trick? Beg for death in hopes I'll let you live?" He went to the door. "I'll bring you something from the kitchens."

"How kind of you. I'll wait here."

"I know you will." Yet when the knight left, he locked the door behind him with a heavy iron key. The Merchant's House was famous for its locks. *As secure as a gaol*, the dwarf thought bitterly, *but at least there are those windows.*

Tyrion knew that the chances of his escaping his chains were little and less, but even so, he felt obliged to try. His efforts to slip a hand through the manacle served only to scrape off more skin and leave his wrist slick with blood, and all his tugging or twisting could not pull the iron ring from the wall. *Bugger this,* he thought, slumping back as far as his chains would allow. His legs had begun to cramp. This was going to be a hellishly uncomfortable night. *The first of many, I do not doubt.*

The room was stifling, so the knight had opened the shutters to let in a cross breeze. Cramped into a corner of the building under the eaves, the chamber was fortunate in having two windows. One looked toward the Long Bridge and the black-walled heart of Old Volantis across the river. The other opened on the square below. Fishermonger's Square, Mormont called it. As tight as the chains were, Tyrion found he could see out the latter by leaning sideways and letting the iron ring support his weight. *Not as long a fall as the one from Lysa Arryn's sky cells, but it would leave me just as dead. Perhaps if I were drunk . . .*

Even at this hour the square was crowded, with sailors roistering, whores prowling for custom, and merchants going about their business. A red priestess scurried past, attended by a dozen acolytes with torches, their robes whisking about their ankles. Elsewhere a pair of *cyvasse* players waged war outside a tavern. A slave stood beside their table, holding a lantern over the board. Tyrion could hear a woman singing. The words were strange, the tune was soft and sad. *If I knew what she was singing, I might cry.* Closer to hand, a crowd was gathering around a pair of jugglers throwing flaming torches at each other.

His captor returned shortly, carrying two tankards and a roasted duck. He kicked the door shut, ripped the duck in two, and tossed half of it to Tyrion. He would have snatched it from the air, but his chains brought him up short when he tried to lift his arms. Instead the bird struck his temple and slid hot and greasy down his face, and he had to hunker down and stretch for it with fetters clanking. He got it on the third try and tore into it happily with his teeth. "Some ale to wash this down?"

Mormont handed him a tankard. "Most of Volantis is getting drunk, why not you?"

The ale was sweet as well. It tasted of fruit. Tyrion drank a healthy swallow and belched happily. The tankard was pewter, very heavy. *Empty it and fling it at his head,* he thought. *If I am lucky, it might crack his skull. If I'm very lucky, it will miss, and he'll beat me to death with his fists.* He took another gulp. "Is this some holy day?"

"Third day of their elections. They last for ten. Ten days of madness. Torchlight marches, speeches, mummers and minstrels and dancers, bravos fighting death duels for the honor of their candidates, elephants with the names of would-be triarchs painted on their sides. Those jugglers are performing for Methyso."

"Remind me to vote for someone else." Tyrion licked grease from his fingers. Below, the crowd was flinging coins at the jugglers. "Do all these would-be triarchs provide mummer shows?"

"They do whatever they think will win them votes," said Mormont. "Food, drink, spectacle . . . Alios has sent a hundred pretty slave girls out into the streets to lie with voters."

"I'm for him," Tyrion decided. "Bring me a slave girl."

"They're for freeborn Volantenes with enough property to vote. Precious few voters west of the river."

"And this goes on for ten days?" Tyrion laughed. "I might enjoy that, though three kings is two too many. I am trying to imagine ruling the Seven Kingdoms with my sweet sister and brave brother beside me. One of us would kill the other two inside a year. I am surprised these triarchs don't do the same."

"A few have tried. Might be the Volantenes are the clever ones and us Westerosi the fools. Volantis has known her share of follies, but she's never suffered a boy triarch. Whenever a madman's been elected, his colleagues restrain him until his year has run its course. Think of the dead who might still live if Mad Aerys only had two fellow kings to share the rule."

Instead he had my father, Tyrion thought.

"Some in the Free Cities think that we're all savages on our side of the narrow sea," the knight went on. "The ones who don't think that we're children, crying out for a father's strong hand."

"Or a mother's?" *Cersei will love that. Especially when he presents her with my head.* "You seem to know this city well."

"I spent the best part of a year here." The knight sloshed the dregs at the bottom of his tankard. "When Stark drove me into exile, I fled to Lys with my second wife. Braavos would have suited me better, but Lynesse wanted someplace warm. Instead of serving the Braavosi I fought them on the Rhoyne, but for every silver I earned my wife spent ten. By the time I got back to Lys, she had taken a lover, who told me cheerfully that I would be enslaved for debt unless I gave her up and left the city. That was how I came to Volantis . . . one step ahead of slavery, owning nothing but my sword and the clothes upon my back."

"And now you want to run home."

The knight drained the last of his ale. "On the morrow I'll find us a ship. The bed is mine. You can have whatever piece of floor your chains will let you reach. Sleep if you can. If not, count your crimes. That should see you through till the morning."

You have your crimes to answer for, Jorah Mormont, the dwarf thought, but it seemed wiser to keep that thought to himself.

Ser Jorah hung his sword belt on a bedpost, kicked off his boots, pulled his chain mail over his head, and stripped out of his wool and leather and sweat-stained undertunic to reveal a scarred, brawny torso covered with dark hair. *If I could skin him, I could sell that pelt for a fur cloak,* Tyrion thought as Mormont tumbled into the slightly smelly comfort of his sagging feather bed.

In no time at all the knight was snoring, leaving his prize alone with his chains. With both windows open wide, the light of the waning moon spilled across the bedchamber. Sounds drifted up from the square below: snatches of drunken song, the yowling of a cat in heat, the far-off ring of steel on steel. *Someone's about to die,* thought Tyrion.

His wrist was throbbing where he'd torn the skin, and his fetters made it impossible for him to sit, let alone stretch out. The best he could do was twist sideways to lean against the wall, and before long he began to lose all feeling in his hands. When he moved to relieve the strain, sensation came flooding back as pain. He had to grind his teeth to keep from screaming. He wondered how much his father had hurt when the quarrel punched through his groin, what Shae had felt as he twisted the chain around her lying throat, what Tysha had been feeling as they raped her. His sufferings were nothing compared to their own, but that did not make him hurt any less. *Just make it stop.*

Ser Jorah had rolled onto one side, so all that Tyrion could see of him was a broad, hairy, muscular back. *Even if I could slip these chains, I'd need to climb over him to reach his sword belt. Perhaps if I could ease the dagger loose . . .* Or else he could try for the key, unlock the door, creep down the stairs and through the common room . . . *and go where? I have no friends, no coin, I do not even speak the local tongue.*

Exhaustion finally overwhelmed his pains, and Tyrion drifted off into a fitful sleep. But every time another cramp took root inside his calf and twisted, the dwarf would cry out in his sleep, trembling in his chains. He woke with every muscle aching, to find morning streaming through the windows bright and golden as the lion of Lannister. Below he could hear the cries of fishmongers and the rumble of iron-rimmed wheels on cobblestones.

Jorah Mormont was standing over him. "If I take you off the ring, will you do as you're told?"

"Will it involve dancing? I might find dancing difficult. I cannot feel my legs. They may have fallen off. Elsewise, I am your creature. On my honor as a Lannister."

"The Lannisters have no honor." Ser Jorah loosed his chains anyway. Tyrion took two wobbly steps and fell. The blood rushing back into his hands brought tears to his eyes. He bit his lip and said, "Wherever we're going, you will need to roll me there."

Instead the big knight carried him, hoisting him by the chain between his wrists.

The common room of the Merchant's House was a dim labyrinth of alcoves and grottoes built around a central courtyard where a trellis of flowering vines threw intricate patterns across the flagstone floor and green and purple moss grew between the stones. Slave girls scurried through light and shadow, bearing flagons of ale and wine and some iced green drink that smelled of mint. One table in twenty was occupied at this hour of the morning.

One of those was occupied by a dwarf. Clean-shaved and pink-cheeked, with a mop of chestnut hair, a heavy brow, and a squashed nose, he perched on a high stool with a wooden spoon in hand, contemplating a bowl of purplish gruel with red-rimmed eyes. *Ugly little bastard,* Tyrion thought.

The other dwarf felt his stare. When he raised his head and saw Tyrion, the spoon slipped from his hand.

"He saw me," Tyrion warned Mormont.

"What of it?"

"He *knows* me. Who I am."

"Should I stuff you in a sack, so no one will see you?" The knight touched the hilt of his longsword. "If he means to try and take you, he is welcome to try."

Welcome to die, you mean, thought Tyrion. *What threat could he pose to a big man like you? He is only a dwarf.*

Ser Jorah claimed a table in a quiet corner and ordered food and drink. They broke their fast with warm soft flatbread, pink fish roe, honey sausage, and fried locusts, washed down with a bittersweet black ale. Tyrion ate like a man half-starved. "You have a healthy appetite this morning," the knight observed.

"I've heard the food in hell is wretched." Tyrion glanced at the door, where a man had just come in: tall and stooped, his pointed beard dyed a splotchy purple. *Some Tyroshi trader.* A gust of sound came with him from outside; the cries of gulls, a woman's laughter, the voices of the fishmongers. For half a heartbeat he thought he glimpsed Illyrio Mopatis, but it was only one of those white dwarf elephants passing the front door.

Mormont spread some fish roe across a slice of flatbread and took a bite. "Are you expecting someone?"

Tyrion shrugged. "You never know who the wind might blow in. My one true love, my father's ghost, a duck." He popped a locust into his mouth and crunched it. "Not bad. For a bug."

"Last night the talk here was all of Westeros. Some exiled lord has hired the Golden Company to win back his lands for him. Half the captains in Volantis are racing upriver to Volon Therys to offer him their ships."

Tyrion had just swallowed another locust. He almost choked on it. *Is he mocking me? How much could he know of Griff and Aegon?* "Bugger," he said. "I meant to hire the Golden Company myself, to win me Casterly Rock." *Could this be some ploy of Griff's, false reports deliberately spread? Unless . . .* Could the pretty princeling have swallowed the bait? Turned them west instead of east, abandoning his hopes of wedding Queen Daenerys? *Abandoning the dragons . . . would Griff allow that?* "I'll gladly hire you as well, ser. My father's seat is mine by rights. Swear me your sword, and once I win it back I'll drown you in gold."

"I saw a man drowned in gold once. It was not a pretty sight. If you ever get my sword, it will be through your bowels."

"A sure cure for constipation," said Tyrion. "Just ask my father." He reached for his tankard and took a slow swallow, to help conceal whatever might be showing on his face. It had to be a stratagem, designed to lull Volantene suspicions. *Get the men aboard with this false pretext and seize the ships when the fleet is out to sea. Is that Griff's plan?* It might work. The Golden Company was ten thousand strong, seasoned and disciplined. *None of them seamen, though. Griff will need to keep a sword at every throat, and should they come on Slaver's Bay and need to fight . . .*

The serving girl returned. "The widow will see you next, noble ser. Have you brought a gift for her?"

"Yes. Thank you." Ser Jorah slipped a coin into the girl's palm and sent her on her way.

Tyrion frowned. "Whose widow is this?"

"The widow of the waterfront. East of the Rhoyne they still call her Vogarro's whore, though never to her face."

The dwarf was not enlightened. "And Vogarro was . . . ?"

"An elephant, seven times a triarch, very rich, a power on the docks. Whilst other men built the ships and sailed them, he built piers and store-houses, brokered cargoes, changed money, insured shipowners against the hazards of the sea. He dealt in slaves as well. When he grew besotted with one of them, a bedslave trained at Yunkai in the way of seven sighs, it was a great scandal . . . and a greater scandal when he freed her and took her for his wife. After he died, she carried on his ventures. No freed-man may dwell within the Black Wall, so she was compelled to sell Vogarro's manse. She took up residence at the Merchant's House. That was thirty-two years ago, and she remains here to this day. That's her be-hind you, back by the courtyard, holding court at her customary table. No, don't look. There's someone with her now. When he's done, it will be our turn."

"And this old harridan will help you how?"

Ser Jorah stood. "Watch and see. He's leaving."

Tyrion hopped down off his chair with a rattle of iron. *This should be enlightening.*

There was something vulpine about the way the woman sat in her cor-ner by the courtyard, something reptilian about her eyes. Her white hair was so thin that the pink of her scalp showed through. Under one eye she still bore faint scars where a knife had cut away her tears. The remnants of her morning meal littered the table — sardine heads, olive pits, chunks of flatbread. Tyrion did not fail to note how well chosen her "customary table" was; solid stone at her back, a leafy alcove to one side for entrances and exits, a perfect view of the inn's front door, yet so steeped in shadow that she herself was nigh invisible.

The sight of him made the old woman smile. "A dwarf," she purred, in a voice as sinister as it was soft. She spoke the Common Tongue with only a trace of accent. "Volantis has been overrun with dwarfs of late, it seems. Does this one do tricks?"

Yes, Tyrion wanted to say. *Give me a crossbow, and I'll show you my favorite.* "No," Ser Jorah answered.

"A pity. I once had a monkey who could perform all sorts of clever tricks. Your dwarf reminds me of him. Is he a gift?"

"No. I brought you these." Ser Jorah produced his pair of gloves, and slapped them down on the table beside the other gifts the widow had received this morning: a silver goblet, an ornate fan carved of jade leaves so thin they were translucent, and an ancient bronze dagger marked with runes. Beside such treasures the gloves looked cheap and tawdry.

"Gloves for my poor old wrinkled hands. How nice." The widow made no move to touch them.

"I bought them on the Long Bridge."

"A man can buy most anything on the Long Bridge. Gloves, slaves, monkeys." The years had bent her spine and put a crone's hump upon her back, but the widow's eyes were bright and black. "Now tell this old widow how she may be of service to you."

"We need swift passage to Meereen."

One word. Tyrion Lannister's world turned upside down.

One word. *Meereen.* Or had he misheard?

One word. *Meereen, he said Meereen, he's taking me to Meereen.* Meereen meant life. Or hope for life, at least.

"Why come to me?" the widow said. "I own no ships."

"You have many captains in your debt."

Deliver me to the queen, he says. Aye, but which queen? He isn't selling me to Cersei. He's giving me to Daenerys Targaryen. That's why he hasn't hacked my head off. We're going east, and Griff and his prince are going west, the bloody fools.

Oh, it was all too much. *Plots within plots, but all roads lead down the dragon's gullet.* A guffaw burst from his lips, and suddenly Tyrion could not stop laughing.

"Your dwarf is having a fit," the widow observed.

"My dwarf will be quiet, or I'll see him gagged."

Tyrion covered his mouth with his hands. *Meereen!*

The widow of the waterfront decided to ignore him. "Shall we have a drink?" she asked. Dust motes floated in the air as a serving girl filled two green glass cups for Ser Jorah and the widow. Tyrion's throat was dry, but no cup was poured for him. The widow took a sip, rolled the wine round her mouth, swallowed. "All the other exiles are sailing west, or so these old ears have heard. And all those captains in my debt are falling over one another to take them there and leach a little gold from the coffers of the Golden Company. Our noble triarchs have pledged a dozen warships to the cause, to see the fleet safely as far as the Stepstones. Even old Doniphos has given his assent. Such a glorious adventure. And yet you would go the other way, ser."

"My business is in the east."

"And what business is that, I wonder? Not slaves, the silver queen has put an end to that. She has closed the fighting pits as well, so it cannot be a taste for blood. What else could Meereen offer to a Westerosi knight? Bricks? Olives? *Dragons?* Ah, there it is." The old woman's smile turned feral. "I have heard it said that the silver queen feeds them with the flesh of infants while she herself bathes in the blood of virgin girls and takes a different lover every night."

Ser Jorah's mouth had hardened. "The Yunkai'i are pouring poison in your ears. My lady should not believe such filth."

"I am no lady, but even Vogarro's whore knows the taste of falsehood. This much is true, though . . . the dragon queen has enemies . . . Yunkai, New Ghis, Tolos, Qarth . . . aye, and Volantis, soon enough. You would travel to Meereen? Just wait a while, ser. Swords will be wanted soon enough, when the warships bend their oars eastward to bring down the silver queen. Tigers love to bare their claws, and even elephants will kill if threatened. Malaquo hungers for a taste of glory, and Nyessos owes much of his wealth to the slave trade. Let Alios or Parquello or Belicho gain the triarchy, and the fleets will sail."

Ser Jorah scowled. "If Doniphos is returned . . ."

"Vogarro will be returned first, and my sweet lord has been dead these thirty years."

Behind them, some sailor was bellowing loudly. "They call this ale? *Fuck.* A monkey could piss better ale."

"And you would drink it," another voice replied.

Tyrion twisted around for a look, hoping against hope that it was Duck and Haldon he was hearing. Instead he saw two strangers . . . and the dwarf, who was standing a few feet away staring at him intently. He seemed somehow familiar.

The widow sipped daintily at her wine. "Some of the first elephants were women," she said, "the ones who brought the tigers down and ended the old wars. Trianna was returned four times. That was three hundred years ago, alas. Volantis has had no female triarch since, though some women have the vote. Women of good birth who dwell in ancient palaces behind the Black Walls, not creatures such as me. The Old Blood will have their dogs and children voting before any freedman. No, it will be Belicho, or perhaps Alios, but either way it will be war. Or so they think."

"And what do you think?" Ser Jorah asked.

Good, thought Tyrion. *The right question.*

"Oh, I think it will be war as well, but not the war they want." The old woman leaned forward, her black eyes gleaming. "I think that red R'hllor has more worshipers in this city than all the other gods together. Have you heard Benerro preach?"

"Last night."

"Benerro can see the morrow in his flames," the widow said. "Triarch Malaquo tried to hire the Golden Company, did you know? He meant to clean out the red temple and put Benerro to the sword. He dare not use tiger cloaks. Half of them worship the Lord of Light as well. Oh, these are dire days in Old Volantis, even for wrinkled old widows. But not half so dire as in Meereen, I think. So tell me, ser . . . why do you seek the silver queen?"

"That is my concern. I can pay for our passage and pay well. I have the silver."

Fool, thought Tyrion. *It's not coin she wants, it's respect. Haven't you heard a word she's said?* He glanced back over his shoulder again. The dwarf had moved closer to their table. And he seemed to have a knife in his hand. The hairs on the back of Tyrion's neck began to prickle.

"Keep your silver. I have gold. And spare me your black looks, ser. I am too old to be frightened of a scowl. You are a hard man, I see, and no doubt skilled with that long sword at your side, but this is my realm. Let me crook a finger and you may find yourself traveling to Meereen chained to an oar in the belly of a galley." She lifted her jade fan and opened it. There was a rustle of leaves, and a man slid from the overgrown archway to her left. His face was a mass of scars, and in one hand he held a sword, short and heavy as a cleaver. *"Seek the widow of the waterfront,* someone told you, but they should have also warned you, *beware the widow's sons.* It is such a sweet morning, though, I shall ask again. Why would you seek Daenerys Targaryen, whom half the world wants dead?"

Jorah Mormont's face was dark with anger, but he answered. "To serve her. Defend her. Die for her, if need be."

That made the widow laugh. "You want to *rescue* her, is that the way of it? From more enemies than I can name, with swords beyond count . . . *this* is what you'd have the poor widow believe? That you are a true and chivalrous Westerosi knight crossing half the world to come to the aid of this . . . well, she is no maiden, though she may still be fair." She laughed again. "Do you think your dwarf will please her? Will she bathe in his blood, do you think, or content herself with striking off his head?"

Ser Jorah hesitated. "The dwarf is—"

"—I know who the dwarf is, and what he is." Her black eyes turned to

Tyrion, hard as stone. "Kinslayer, kingslayer, murderer, turncloak. *Lannister.*" She made the last a curse. "What do *you* plan to offer the dragon queen, little man?"

My hate, Tyrion wanted to say. Instead he spread his hands as far as the fetters would allow. "Whatever she would have of me. Sage counsel, savage wit, a bit of tumbling. My cock, if she desires it. My tongue, if she does not. I will lead her armies or rub her feet, as she desires. And the only reward I ask is I might be allowed to rape and kill my sister."

That brought the smile back to the old woman's face. "This one at least is honest," she announced, "but you, ser . . . I have known a dozen Westerosi knights and a thousand adventurers of the same ilk, but none so pure as you would paint yourself. Men are beasts, selfish and brutal. However gentle the words, there are always darker motives underneath. I do not trust you, ser." She flicked them off with her fan, as if they were no more than flies buzzing about her head. "If you want to get to Meereen, swim. I have no help to give you."

Then seven hells broke out at once.

Ser Jorah started to rise, the widow snapped her fan closed, her scarred man slid out of the shadows . . . and behind them a girl screamed. Tyrion spun just in time to see the dwarf rushing toward him. *She's a girl,* he realized all at once, *a girl dressed up in man's clothes. And she means to gut me with that knife.*

For half a heartbeat Ser Jorah, the widow, and the scarred man stood still as stone. Idlers watched from nearby tables, sipping ale and wine, but no one moved to interfere. Tyrion had to move both hands at once, but his chains had just enough give for him to reach the flagon on the table. He closed his fist around it, spun, dashed its contents into the face of the charging dwarf girl, then threw himself to one side to avoid her knife. The flagon shattered underneath him as the floor came up to smack him in the head. Then the girl was on him once again. Tyrion rolled on one side as she buried the knife blade in the floorboards, yanked it free, raised it again . . .

. . . and suddenly she was rising off the floor, legs kicking wildly as she struggled in Ser Jorah's grasp. "No!" she wailed, in the Common Tongue of Westeros. "Let *go*!" Tyrion heard her tunic rip as she fought to free herself.

Mormont had her by the collar with one hand. With the other he wrenched the dagger from her grasp. "Enough."

The landlord made his appearance then, a cudgel in his hand. When he saw the broken flagon, he uttered a blistering curse and demanded to know what had happened here. "Dwarf fight," replied the Tyroshi with the purple beard, chuckling.

Tyrion blinked up at the dripping girl twisting in the air. "Why?" he demanded. "What did I ever do to you?"

"They killed him." All the fight went out of her at that. She hung limply in Mormont's grasp as her eyes filled with tears. "My brother. They took him and they killed him."

"Who killed him?" asked Mormont.

"Sailors. Sailors from the Seven Kingdoms. There were five of them, drunk. They saw us jousting in the square and followed us. When they realized I was a girl they let me go, but they took my brother and killed him. *They cut his head off.*"

Tyrion felt a sudden shock of recognition. *They saw us jousting in the square.* He knew who the girl was then. "Did you ride the pig?" he asked her. "Or the dog?"

"The dog," she sobbed. "Oppo always rode the pig."

The dwarfs from Joffrey's wedding. It was their show that had started all the trouble that night. *How strange, to encounter them again half a world away.* Though perhaps not so strange as that. *If they had half the wits of their pig, they would have fled King's Landing the night Joff died, before Cersei could assign them some share of blame in her son's death.* "Let her down, ser," he told Ser Jorah Mormont. "She won't do us any harm."

Ser Jorah dumped the dwarf girl on the floor. "I am sorry for your brother . . . but we had no part in his murder."

"He did." The girl pushed herself to her knees, clutching her torn, wine-drenched tunic to small, pale breasts. "It was him they wanted. They thought Oppo was *him.*" The girl was weeping, begging for help from anyone who would listen. "He should die, the way my poor brother died. Please. Someone help me. Someone kill him." The landlord seized her roughly by one arm and wrenched her back to her feet, shouting in Volantene, demanding to know who was going to pay for this damage.

The widow of the waterfront gave Mormont a cool look. "Knights defend the weak and protect the innocent, they say. And I am the fairest maid in all Volantis." Her laugh was full of scorn. "What do they call you, child?"

"Penny."

The old woman called out to the landlord in the tongue of Old Volantis. Tyrion knew enough to understand that she was telling him to take the dwarf girl up to her rooms, give her wine, and find some clothes for her to wear.

When they were gone, the widow studied Tyrion, her black eyes shining. "Monsters should be larger, it seems to me. You are worth a lordship back in Westeros, little man. Here, I fear, your worth is somewhat less. But I think I had best help you after all. Volantis is no safe place for dwarfs, it seems."

"You are too kind." Tyrion gave her his sweetest smile. "Perhaps you would remove these charming iron bracelets as well? This monster has but half a nose, and it itches most abominably. The chains are too short for me to scratch it. I'll make you a gift of them, and gladly."

"How generous. But I have worn iron in my time, and now I find that I prefer gold and silver. And sad to say, this is Volantis, where fetters and chains are cheaper than day-old bread and it is forbidden to help a slave escape."

"I'm no slave."

"Every man ever taken by slavers sings that same sad song. I dare not help you . . . here." She leaned forward again. "Two days from now, the cog *Selaesori Qhoran* will set sail for Qarth by way of New Ghis, carrying tin and iron, bales of wool and lace, fifty Myrish carpets, a corpse pickled in brine, twenty jars of dragon peppers, and a red priest. Be on her when she sails."

"We will," said Tyrion, "and thank you."

Ser Jorah frowned. "Qarth is not our destination."

"She will never reach Qarth. Benerro has seen it in his fires." The crone smiled a vulpine smile.

"As you say." Tyrion grinned. "If I were Volantene, and free, and had the blood, you'd have my vote for triarch, my lady."

"I am no lady," the widow replied, "just Vogarro's whore. You want to be gone from here before the tigers come. Should you reach your queen, give her a message from the slaves of Old Volantis." She touched the faded scar upon her wrinkled cheek, where her tears had been cut away. "Tell her we are waiting. Tell her to come soon."

JON

When he heard the order, Ser Alliser's mouth twisted into a semblance of a smile, but his eyes remained as cold and hard as flint. "So the bastard boy sends me out to die."

"Die," cried Mormont's raven. *"Die, die, die."*

You are not helping. Jon swatted the bird away. "The bastard boy is sending you out to range. To find our foes and kill them if need be. You are skilled with a blade. You were master-at-arms, here and at Eastwatch."

Thorne touched the hilt of his longsword. "Aye. I have squandered a third of my life trying to teach the rudiments of swordplay to churls, muttonheads, and knaves. Small good that will do me in those woods."

"Dywen will be with you, and another seasoned ranger."

"We'll learn you what you need t' know, ser," Dywen told Thorne, cackling. "Teach you how t' wipe your highborn arse with leaves, just like a proper ranger."

Kedge Whiteye laughed at that, and Black Jack Bulwer spat. Ser Alliser only said, "You would like me to refuse. Then you could hack off my head, same as you did for Slynt. I'll not give you that pleasure, bastard. You'd best pray that it's a wildling blade that kills me, though. The ones the Others kill don't stay dead . . . and they *remember.* I'm coming back, Lord Snow."

"I pray you do." Jon would never count Ser Alliser Thorne amongst his friends, but he was still a brother. *No one ever said you had to like your brothers.*

It was no easy thing to send men into the wild, knowing that the chances were good that they might never return. *They are all seasoned men,* Jon told himself . . . but his uncle Benjen and his rangers had been seasoned men as well, and the haunted forest had swallowed them up without a trace. When two of them finally came straggling back to the Wall, it had been as wights. Not for the first time, or the last, Jon Snow found himself wondering what had become of Benjen Stark. *Perhaps the rangers will come upon some sign of them,* he told himself, never truly believing it.

Dywen would lead one ranging, Black Jack Bulwer and Kedge Whiteye the other two. They at least were eager for the duty. "Feels good to have a horse under me again," Dywen said at the gate, sucking on his wooden teeth. "Begging your pardon, m'lord, but we were all o' us getting splinters up our arses from sitting about." No man in Castle Black knew the woods as well as Dywen did, the trees and streams, the plants that could be eaten, the ways of predator and prey. *Thorne is in better hands than he deserves.*

Jon watched the riders go from atop the Wall—three parties, each of three men, each carrying a pair of ravens. From on high their garrons looked no larger than ants, and Jon could not tell one ranger from another. He knew them, though. Every name was graven on his heart. *Eight good men,* he thought, *and one . . . well, we shall see.*

When the last of the riders had disappeared into the trees, Jon Snow rode the winch cage down with Dolorous Edd. A few scattered snowflakes were falling as they made their slow descent, dancing on the gusty wind. One followed the cage down, drifting just beyond the bars. It was falling faster than they were descending and from time to time would vanish beneath them. Then a gust of wind would catch it and push it upward once again. Jon could have reached through the bars and caught it if he had wished.

"I had a frightening dream last night, m'lord," Dolorous Edd confessed. "You were my steward, fetching my food and cleaning up my leavings. I was lord commander, with never a moment's peace."

Jon did not smile. "Your nightmare, my life."

Cotter Pyke's galleys were reporting ever-increasing numbers of free folk along the wooded shores to the north and east of the Wall. Camps had been seen, half-built rafts, even the hull of a broken cog that someone had begun repairing. The wildlings always vanished into the woods when seen, no doubt to reemerge as soon as Pyke's ships had passed. Meanwhile, Ser Denys Mallister was still seeing fires in the night north of the Gorge. Both commanders were asking for more men.

And where am I to get more men? Jon had sent ten of the Mole's Town wildlings to each of them: green boys, old men, some wounded and infirm, but all capable of doing work of one sort or another. Far from being pleased, Pyke and Mallister had both written back to complain. "When I asked for men, I had in mind men of the Night's Watch, trained and disciplined, whose loyalty I should never have reason to doubt," wrote Ser

Denys. Cotter Pyke was blunter. "I could hang them from the Wall as a warning to other wildlings to stay away, but I don't see any other use for them," Maester Harmune wrote for him. "I wouldn't trust such to clean my chamber pot, and *ten is not enough.*"

The iron cage moved downward at the end of its long chain, creaking and rattling, until it finally jerked to a halt a foot above the ground at the base of the Wall. Dolorous Edd pushed open the door and hopped down, his boots breaking the crust of the last snow. Jon followed.

Outside the armory, Iron Emmett was still urging on his charges in the yard. The song of steel on steel woke a hunger in Jon. It reminded him of warmer, simpler days, when he had been a boy at Winterfell matching blades with Robb under the watchful eye of Ser Rodrik Cassel. Ser Rodrik too had fallen, slain by Theon Turncloak and his ironmen as he'd tried to retake Winterfell. The great stronghold of House Stark was a scorched desolation. *All my memories are poisoned.*

When Iron Emmett spied him, he raised a hand and combat ceased. "Lord Commander. How may we serve you?"

"With your three best."

Emmett grinned. "Arron. Emrick. Jace."

Horse and Hop-Robin fetched padding for the lord commander, along with a ringmail hauberk to go over it, and greaves, gorget, and halfhelm. A black shield rimmed with iron for his left arm, a blunted longsword for his right hand. The sword gleamed silvery grey in the dawn light, almost new. *One of the last to come from Donal's forge. A pity he did not live long enough to put an edge on it.* The blade was shorter than Longclaw but made of common steel, which made it heavier. His blows would be a little slower. "It will serve." Jon turned to face his foes. "Come."

"Which one do you want first?" asked Arron.

"All three of you. At once."

"Three on one?" Jace was incredulous. "That wouldn't be fair." He was one of Conwy's latest bunch, a cobbler's son from Fair Isle. Maybe that explained it.

"True. Come here."

When he did, Jon's blade slammed him alongside his head, knocking him off his feet. In the blink of an eye the boy had a boot on his chest and a swordpoint at his throat. "War is never fair," Jon told him. "It's two on one now, and you're dead."

When he heard gravel crunch, he knew the twins were coming. *Those two will make rangers yet.* He spun, blocking Arron's cut with the edge of his shield and meeting Emrick's with his sword. "Those aren't spears," he shouted. "Get in close." He went to the attack to show them how it was done. Emrick first. He slashed at his head and shoulders, right and left and right again. The boy got his shield up and tried a clumsy countercut. Jon slammed his own shield into Emrick's, and brought him down with a blow to the lower leg . . . none too soon, because Arron was on him, with a crunching cut to the back of his thigh that sent him to one knee. *That will leave a bruise.* He caught the next cut on his shield, then lurched back to his feet and drove Arron across the yard. *He's quick,* he thought, as the longswords kissed once and twice and thrice, *but he needs to get stronger.* When he saw relief in Arron's eyes, he knew Emrick was behind him. He came around and dealt him a cut to the back of the shoulders that sent him crashing into his brother. By that time Jace had found his feet, so Jon put him down again. "I hate it when dead men get up. You'll feel the same the day you meet a wight." Stepping back, he lowered his sword.

"The big crow can peck the little crows," growled a voice behind him, "but has he belly enough to fight a man?"

Rattleshirt was leaning against a wall. A coarse stubble covered his sunken cheeks, and thin brown hair was blowing across his little yellow eyes.

"You flatter yourself," Jon said.

"Aye, but I'd flatten you."

"Stannis burned the wrong man."

"No." The wildling grinned at him through a mouth of brown and broken teeth. "He burned the man he had to burn, for all the world to see. We all do what we have to do, Snow. Even kings."

"Emmett, find some armor for him. I want him in steel, not old bones."

Once clad in mail and plate, the Lord of Bones seemed to stand a little straighter. He seemed taller too, his shoulders thicker and more powerful than Jon would have thought. *It's the armor, not the man,* he told himself. *Even Sam could appear almost formidable, clad head to heel in Donal Noye's steel.* The wildling waved away the shield Horse offered him. Instead he asked for a two-handed sword. "There's a sweet sound," he said, slashing at the air. "Flap closer, Snow. I mean to make your feathers fly."

Jon rushed him hard.

Rattleshirt took a step backwards and met the charge with a two-handed slash. If Jon had not interposed his shield, it might have staved his breastplate in and broken half his ribs. The force of the blow staggered him for a moment and sent a solid jolt up his arm. *He hits harder than I would have thought.* His quickness was another unpleasant surprise. They circled round each other, trading blow for blow. The Lord of Bones gave as good as he was getting. By rights the two-handed greatsword should have been a deal more cumbersome than Jon's longsword, but the wildling wielded it with blinding speed.

Iron Emmett's fledglings cheered their lord commander at the start, but the relentless speed of Rattleshirt's attack soon beat them down to silence. *He cannot keep this up for long,* Jon told himself as he stopped another blow. The impact made him grunt. Even dulled, the greatsword cracked his pinewood shield and bent the iron rim. *He will tire soon. He must.* Jon slashed at the wildling's face, and Rattleshirt pulled back his head. He hacked down at Rattleshirt's calf, only to have him deftly leap the blade. The greatsword crashed down onto Jon's shoulder, hard enough to ding his pouldron and numb the arm beneath. Jon backed away. The Lord of Bones came after, chortling. *He has no shield,* Jon reminded himself, *and that monster sword's too cumbersome for parries. I should be landing two blows for every one of his.*

Somehow he wasn't, though, and the blows he did land were having no effect. The wildling always seemed to be moving away or sliding sideways, so Jon's longsword glanced off a shoulder or an arm. Before long he found himself giving more ground, trying to avoid the other's crashing cuts and failing half the time. His shield had been reduced to kindling. He shook it off his arm. Sweat was running down his face and stinging his eyes beneath his helm. *He is too strong and too quick,* he realized, *and with that greatsword he has weight and reach on me.* It would have been a different fight if Jon had been armed with Longclaw, but . . .

His chance came on Rattleshirt's next backswing. Jon threw himself forward, bulling into the other man, and they went down together, legs entangled. Steel slammed on steel. Both men lost their swords as they rolled on the hard ground. The wildling drove a knee between Jon's legs. Jon lashed out with a mailed fist. Somehow Rattleshirt ended up on top, with Jon's head in his hands. He smashed it against the ground, then wrenched his visor open. "If I had me a dagger, you'd be less an eye by now," he snarled, before Horse and Iron Emmett dragged him off the lord commander's chest. "Let go o' me, you bloody crows," he roared.

Jon struggled to one knee. His head was ringing, and his mouth was full of blood. He spat it out and said, "Well fought."

"You flatter yourself, crow. I never broke a sweat."

"Next time you will," said Jon. Dolorous Edd helped him to his feet and unbuckled his helm. It had acquired several deep dents that had not been there when he'd donned it. "Release him." Jon tossed the helm to Hop-Robin, who dropped it.

"My lord," said Iron Emmett, "he threatened your life, we all heard. He said that if he had a dagger—"

"He does have a dagger. Right there on his belt." *There is always some-one quicker and stronger*, Ser Rodrik had once told Jon and Robb. *He's the man you want to face in the yard before you need to face his like upon a battlefield.*

"Lord Snow?" a soft voice said.

He turned to find Clydas standing beneath the broken archway, a parchment in his hand. "From Stannis?" Jon had been hoping for some word from the king. The Night's Watch took no part, he knew, and it should not matter to him which king emerged triumphant. Somehow it did. "Is it Deepwood?"

"No, my lord." Clydas thrust the parchment forward. It was tightly rolled and sealed, with a button of hard pink wax. *Only the Dreadfort uses pink sealing wax.* Jon ripped off his gauntlet, took the letter, cracked the seal. When he saw the signature, he forgot the battering Rattleshirt had given him.

Ramsay Bolton, Lord of the Hornwood, it read, in a huge, spiky hand. The brown ink came away in flakes when Jon brushed it with his thumb. Beneath Bolton's signature, Lord Dustin, Lady Cerwyn, and four Ryswells had appended their own marks and seals. A cruder hand had drawn the giant of House Umber. "Might we know what it says, my lord?" asked Iron Emmett.

Jon saw no reason not to tell him. "Moat Cailin is taken. The flayed corpses of the ironmen have been nailed to posts along the kingsroad. Roose Bolton summons all leal lords to Barrowton, to affirm their loyalty to the Iron Throne and celebrate his son's wedding to . . ." His heart seemed to stop for a moment. *No, that is not possible. She died in King's Landing, with Father.*

"Lord Snow?" Clydas peered at him closely with his dim pink eyes. "Are you . . . unwell? You seem . . ."

"He's to marry Arya Stark. My little sister." Jon could almost see her in that moment, long-faced and gawky, all knobby knees and sharp elbows, with her dirty face and tangled hair. They would wash the one and comb the other, he did not doubt, but he could not imagine Arya in a wedding gown, nor Ramsay Bolton's bed. *No matter how afraid she is, she will not show it. If he tries to lay a hand on her, she'll fight him.*

"Your sister," Iron Emmett said, "how old is . . ."

By now she'd be eleven, Jon thought. *Still a child.* "I have no sister. Only brothers. Only you." Lady Catelyn would have rejoiced to hear those words, he knew. That did not make them easier to say. His fingers closed around the parchment. *Would that they could crush Ramsay Bolton's throat as easily.*

Clydas cleared his throat. "Will there be an answer?"

Jon shook his head and walked away.

By nightfall the bruises that Rattleshirt had given him had turned purple. "They'll go yellow before they fade away," he told Mormont's raven. "I'll look as sallow as the Lord of Bones."

"*Bones,*" the bird agreed. "*Bones, bones.*"

He could hear the faint murmur of voices coming from outside, although the sound was too weak to make out words. *They sound a thousand leagues away.* It was Lady Melisandre and her followers at their nightfire. Every night at dusk the red woman led her followers in their twilight prayer, asking her red god to see them through the dark. *For the night is dark and full of terrors.* With Stannis and most of the queen's men gone, her flock was much diminished; half a hundred of the free folk up from Mole's Town, the handful of guards the king had left her, perhaps a dozen black brothers who had taken her red god for their own.

Jon felt as stiff as a man of sixty years. *Dark dreams,* he thought, *and guilt.* His thoughts kept returning to Arya. *There is no way I can help her. I put all kin aside when I said my words. If one of my men told me his sister was in peril, I would tell him that was no concern of his.* Once a man had said the words his blood was black. *Black as a bastard's heart.* He'd had Mikken make a sword for Arya once, a bravo's blade, made small to fit her hand. *Needle.* He wondered if she still had it. *Stick them with the pointy end,* he'd told her, but if she tried to stick the Bastard, it could mean her life.

"*Snow,*" muttered Lord Mormont's raven. "*Snow, snow.*"

Suddenly he could not suffer it a moment longer.

He found Ghost outside his door, gnawing on the bone of an ox to get at the marrow. "When did you get back?" The direwolf got to his feet, abandoning the bone to come padding after Jon.

Mully and Kegs stood inside the doors, leaning on their spears. "A cruel cold out there, m'lord," warned Mully through his tangled orange beard. "Will you be out long?"

"No. I just need a breath of air." Jon stepped out into the night. The sky was full of stars, and the wind was gusting along the Wall. Even the moon looked cold; there were goosebumps all across its face. Then the first gust caught him, slicing through his layers of wool and leather to set his teeth to chattering. He stalked across the yard, into the teeth of that wind. His cloak flapped loudly from his shoulders. Ghost came after. *Where am I going? What am I doing?* Castle Black was still and silent, its halls and towers dark. *My seat*, Jon Snow reflected. *My hall, my home, my command. A ruin.*

In the shadow of the Wall, the direwolf brushed up against his fingers. For half a heartbeat the night came alive with a thousand smells, and Jon Snow heard the crackle of the crust breaking on a patch of old snow. Someone was behind him, he realized suddenly. Someone who smelled warm as a summer day.

When he turned he saw Ygritte.

She stood beneath the scorched stones of the Lord Commander's Tower, cloaked in darkness and in memory. The light of the moon was in her hair, her red hair kissed by fire. When he saw that, Jon's heart leapt into his mouth. "Ygritte," he said.

"Lord Snow." The voice was Melisandre's.

Surprise made him recoil from her. "Lady Melisandre." He took a step backwards. "I mistook you for someone else." *At night all robes are grey.* Yet suddenly hers were red. He did not understand how he could have taken her for Ygritte. She was taller, thinner, older, though the moonlight washed years from her face. Mist rose from her nostrils, and from pale hands naked to the night. "You will freeze your fingers off," Jon warned.

"If that is the will of R'hllor. Night's powers cannot touch one whose heart is bathed in god's holy fire."

"Your heart does not concern me. Just your hands."

"The heart is all that matters. Do not despair, Lord Snow. Despair is a weapon of the enemy, whose name may not be spoken. Your sister is not lost to you."

"I have no sister." The words were knives. *What do you know of my heart, priestess? What do you know of my sister?*

Melisandre seemed amused. "What is her name, this little sister that you do not have?"

"Arya." His voice was hoarse. "My half-sister, truly . . ."

". . . for you are bastard born. I had not forgotten. I have seen your sister in my fires, fleeing from this marriage they have made for her. Coming here, to you. A girl in grey on a dying horse, I have seen it plain as day. It has not happened yet, but it will." She gazed at Ghost. "May I touch your . . . wolf?"

The thought made Jon uneasy. "Best not."

"He will not harm me. You call him Ghost, yes?"

"Yes, but . . ."

"*Ghost.*" Melisandre made the word a song.

The direwolf padded toward her. Wary, he stalked about her in a circle, sniffing. When she held out her hand he smelled that too, then shoved his nose against her fingers.

Jon let out a white breath. "He is not always so . . ."

". . . warm? Warmth calls to warmth, Jon Snow." Her eyes were two red stars, shining in the dark. At her throat, her ruby gleamed, a third eye glowing brighter than the others. Jon had seen Ghost's eyes blazing red the same way, when they caught the light just right. "*Ghost,*" he called. "To me."

The direwolf looked at him as if he were a stranger.

Jon frowned in disbelief. "That's . . . queer."

"You think so?" She knelt and scratched Ghost behind his ear. "Your Wall is a queer place, but there is power here, if you will use it. Power in you, and in this beast. You resist it, and that is your mistake. Embrace it. Use it."

I am not a wolf, he thought. "And how would I do that?"

"I can show you." Melisandre draped one slender arm over Ghost, and the direwolf licked her face. "The Lord of Light in his wisdom made us male and female, two parts of a greater whole. In our joining there is power. Power to make life. Power to make light. Power to cast shadows."

"Shadows." The world seemed darker when he said it.

"Every man who walks the earth casts a shadow on the world. Some are thin and weak, others long and dark. You should look behind you, Lord Snow. The moon has kissed you and etched your shadow upon the ice twenty feet tall."

Jon glanced over his shoulder. The shadow was there, just as she had said, etched in moonlight against the Wall. *A girl in grey on a dying horse,* he thought. *Coming here, to you. Arya.* He turned back to the red priestess. Jon could feel her warmth. *She has power.* The thought came unbidden, seizing him with iron teeth, but this was not a woman he cared to be indebted to, not even for his little sister. "Dalla told me something once. Val's sister, Mance Rayder's wife. She said that sorcery was a sword without a hilt. There is no safe way to grasp it."

"A wise woman." Melisandre rose, her red robes stirring in the wind. "A sword without a hilt is still a sword, though, and a sword is a fine thing to have when foes are all about. Hear me now, Jon Snow. Nine crows flew into the white wood to find your foes for you. Three of them are dead. They have not died yet, but their death is out there waiting for them, and they ride to meet it. You sent them forth to be your eyes in the darkness, but they will be eyeless when they return to you. I have seen their pale dead faces in my flames. Empty sockets, weeping blood." She pushed her red hair back, and her red eyes shone. "You do not believe me. You will. The cost of that belief will be three lives. A small price to pay for wisdom, some might say . . . but not one you had to pay. Remember that when you behold the blind and ravaged faces of your dead. And come that day, take my hand." The mist rose from her pale flesh, and for a moment it seemed as if pale, sorcerous flames were playing about her fingers. "Take my hand," she said again, "and let me save your sister."

DAVOS

Even in the gloom of the Wolf's Den, Davos Seaworth could sense that something was awry this morning.

He woke to the sound of voices and crept to the door of his cell, but the wood was too thick and he could not make out the words. Dawn had come, but not the porridge Garth brought him every morn to break his fast. That made him anxious. All the days were much the same inside the Wolf's Den, and any change was usually for the worse. *This may be the day I die. Garth may be sitting with a whetstone even now, to put an edge on Lady Lu.*

The onion knight had not forgotten Wyman Manderly's last words to him. *Take this creature to the Wolf's Den and cut off head and hands,* the fat lord had commanded. *I shall not be able to eat a bite until I see this smuggler's head upon a spike, with an onion shoved between his lying teeth.* Every night Davos went to sleep with those words in his head, and every morn he woke to them. And should he forget, Garth was always pleased to remind him. Dead man was his name for Davos. When he came by in the morning, it was always, "Here, porridge for the dead man." At night it was, "Blow out the candle, dead man."

Once Garth brought his ladies by to introduce them to the dead man. "The Whore don't look like much," he said, fondling a rod of cold black iron, "but when I heat her up red-hot and let her touch your cock, you'll cry for mother. And this here's my Lady Lu. It's her who'll take your head and hands, when Lord Wyman sends down word." Davos had never seen a bigger axe than Lady Lu, nor one with a sharper edge. Garth spent his days honing her, the other keepers said. *I will not plead for mercy,* Davos resolved. He would go to his death a knight, asking only that they take his head before his hands. Even Garth would not be so cruel as to deny him that, he hoped.

The sounds coming through the door were faint and muffled. Davos rose and paced his cell. As cells went, it was large and queerly comfortable. He suspected it might once have been some lordling's bedchamber. It was thrice the size of his captain's cabin on *Black Bessa*, and even larger than the cabin Salladhor Saan enjoyed on his *Valyrian*. Though its only window had been bricked in years before, one wall still boasted a hearth big enough to hold a kettle, and there was an actual privy built into a corner nook. The floor was made of warped planks full of splinters, and his sleeping pallet smelled of mildew, but those discomforts were mild compared to what Davos had expected.

The food had come as a surprise as well. In place of gruel and stale bread and rotten meat, the usual dungeon fare, his keepers brought him fresh-caught fish, bread still warm from the oven, spiced mutton, turnips, carrots, even crabs. Garth was none too pleased by that. "The dead should not eat better than the living," he complained, more than once. Davos had furs to keep him warm by night, wood to feed his fire, clean clothing, a greasy tallow candle. When he asked for paper, quill, and ink, Therry brought them the next day. When he asked for a book, so he might keep at his reading, Therry turned up with *The Seven-Pointed Star*.

For all its comforts, though, his cell remained a cell. Its walls were solid stone, so thick that he could hear nothing of the outside world. The door was oak and iron, and his keepers kept it barred. Four sets of heavy iron fetters dangled from the ceiling, waiting for the day Lord Manderly decided to chain him up and give him over to the Whore. *Today may be that day. The next time Garth opens my door, it may not be to bring me porridge.*

His belly was rumbling, a sure sign that the morning was creeping past, and still no sign of food. *The worst part is not the dying, it's not knowing when or how.* He had seen the inside of a few gaols and dungeons in his smuggling days, but those he'd shared with other prisoners, so there was always someone to talk with, to share your fears and hopes. Not here. Aside from his keepers, Davos Seaworth had the Wolf's Den to himself.

He knew there were true dungeons down in the castle cellars—oubliettes and torture chambers and dank pits where huge black rats scrabbled in the darkness. His gaolers claimed all of them were unoccupied at present. "Only us here, Onion," Ser Bartimus had told him. He was the chief gaoler, a cadaverous one-legged knight, with a scarred face and a blind eye. When Ser Bartimus was in his cups (and Ser Bartimus was in his cups most every day), he liked to boast of how he had saved Lord Wyman's life at the Battle of the Trident. The Wolf's Den was his reward.

The rest of "us" consisted of a cook Davos never saw, six guardsmen in the ground-floor barracks, a pair of washerwomen, and the two turnkeys who looked after the prisoner. Therry was the young one, the son of one of the washerwomen, a boy of ten-and-four. The old one was Garth, huge and bald and taciturn, who wore the same greasy leather jerkin every day and always seemed to have a glower on his face.

His years as a smuggler had given Davos Seaworth a sense of when a man was wrong, and Garth was wrong. The onion knight took care to hold his tongue in Garth's presence. With Therry and Ser Bartimus he was less reticent. He thanked them for his food, encouraged them to talk about their hopes and histories, answered their questions politely, and never pressed too hard with queries of his own. When he made requests, they were small ones: a basin of water and a bit of soap, a book to read, more candles. Most such favors were granted, and Davos was duly grateful.

Neither man would speak about Lord Manderly or King Stannis or the Freys, but they would talk of other things. Therry wanted to go off to war when he was old enough, to fight in battles and become a knight. He liked to complain about his mother too. She was bedding two of the guardsmen, he confided. The men were on different watches and neither knew about the other, but one day one man or t'other would puzzle it out, and then there would be blood. Some nights the boy would even bring a skin of wine to the cell and ask Davos about the smuggler's life as they drank.

Ser Bartimus had no interest in the world outside, or indeed anything that had happened since he lost his leg to a riderless horse and a maester's saw. He had come to love the Wolf's Den, however, and liked nothing more than to talk about its long and bloody history. The Den was much older than White Harbor, the knight told Davos. It had been raised by King Jon Stark to defend the mouth of the White Knife against raiders from the sea. Many a younger son of the King in the North had made his seat there, many a brother, many an uncle, many a cousin. Some passed the castle to their own sons and grandsons, and offshoot branches of House Stark had arisen; the Greystarks had lasted the longest, holding the Wolf's Den for five centuries, until they presumed to join the Dreadfort in rebellion against the Starks of Winterfell.

After their fall, the castle had passed through many other hands. House Flint held it for a century, House Locke for almost two. Slates, Longs, Holts, and Ashwoods had held sway here, charged by Winterfell to keep the river safe. Reavers from the Three Sisters took the castle once, making it their toehold in the north. During the wars between Winterfell and the Vale, it was besieged by Osgood Arryn, the Old Falcon, and burned by his son, the one remembered as the Talon. When old King Edrick Stark had grown too feeble to defend his realm, the Wolf's Den was captured by slavers from the Stepstones. They would brand their captives with hot irons and break them to the whip before shipping them off across the sea, and these same black stone walls bore witness.

"Then a long cruel winter fell," said Ser Bartimus. "The White Knife froze hard, and even the firth was icing up. The winds came howling from the north and drove them slavers inside to huddle round their fires, and whilst they warmed themselves the new king come down on them. *Brandon* Stark this was, Edrick Snowbeard's great-grandson, him that men called Ice Eyes. He took the Wolf's Den back, stripped the slavers naked, and gave them to the slaves he'd found chained up in the dungeons. It's said they hung their entrails in the branches of the heart tree, as an offering to the gods. The *old* gods, not these new ones from the south. Your Seven don't know winter, and winter don't know them."

Davos could not argue with the truth of that. From what he had seen at Eastwatch-by-the-Sea, he did not care to know winter either. "What gods do you keep?" he asked the one-legged knight.

"The old ones." When Ser Bartimus grinned, he looked just like a skull. "Me and mine were here before the Manderlys. Like as not, my own forebears strung those entrails through the tree."

"I never knew that northmen made blood sacrifice to their heart trees."

"There's much and more you southrons do not know about the north," Ser Bartimus replied.

He was not wrong. Davos sat beside his candle and looked at the letters he had scratched out word by word during the days of his confinement. *I was a better smuggler than a knight,* he had written to his wife, *a better knight than a King's Hand, a better King's Hand than a husband. I am so sorry. Marya, I have loved you. Please forgive the wrongs I did you. Should Stannis lose his war, our lands will be lost as well. Take the boys across the narrow sea to Braavos and teach them to think kindly of me, if you would. Should Stannis gain the Iron Throne, House Seaworth will survive and Devan will remain at court. He will help you place the other boys with noble lords, where they can serve as pages and squires and win their knighthoods.* It was the best counsel he had for her, though he wished it sounded wiser.

He had written to each of his three surviving sons as well, to help them remember the father who had bought them names with his fingertips. His notes to Steffon and young Stannis were short and stiff and awkward; if truth be told, he did not know them half as well as he had his older boys, the ones who'd burned or drowned upon the Blackwater. To Devan he wrote more, telling him how proud he was to see his own son as a king's squire and reminding him that as the eldest it was his duty to protect his lady mother and his younger brothers. *Tell His Grace I did my best,* he ended. *I am sorry that I failed him. I lost my luck when I lost my finger-bones, the day the river burned below King's Landing.*

Davos shuffled through the letters slowly, reading each one over several times, wondering whether he should change a word here or add one there. A man should have more to say when staring at the end of his life, he thought, but the words came hard. *I did not do so ill,* he tried to tell himself. *I rose up from Flea Bottom to be a King's Hand, and I learned to read and write.*

He was still hunched over the letters when he heard the sound of iron keys rattling on a ring. Half a heartbeat later, the door to his cell came swinging open.

The man who stepped through the door was not one of his gaolers. He was tall and haggard, with a deeply lined face and a shock of grey-brown hair. A longsword hung from his hip, and his deep-dyed scarlet cloak was fastened at the shoulder with a heavy silver brooch in the shape of a mailed fist. "Lord Seaworth," he said, "we do not have much time. Please, come with me."

Davos eyed the stranger warily. The "please" confused him. Men about to lose their heads and hands were not oft accorded such courtesies. "Who are you?"

"Robett Glover, if it please, my lord."

"Glover. Your seat was Deepwood Motte."

"My brother Galbart's seat. It was and is, thanks to your King Stannis. He has taken Deepwood back from the iron bitch who stole it and offers to restore it to its rightful owners. Much and more has happened whilst you have been confined within these walls, Lord Davos. Moat Cailin has fallen, and Roose Bolton has returned to the north with Ned Stark's younger daughter. A host of Freys came with him. Bolton has sent forth ravens, summoning all the lords of the north to Barrowton. He demands homage and hostages . . . and witnesses to the wedding of Arya Stark and his bastard Ramsay Snow, by which match the Boltons mean to lay claim to Winterfell. Now, will you come with me, or no?"

"What choice do I have, my lord? Come with you, or remain with Garth and Lady Lu?"

"Who is Lady Lu? One of the washerwomen?" Glover was growing impatient. "All will be explained if you will come."

Davos rose to his feet. "If I should die, I beseech my lord to see that my letters are delivered."

"You have my word on that . . . though if you die, it will not be at Glover's hands, nor Lord Wyman's. Quickly now, with me."

Glover led him along a darkened hall and down a flight of worn steps. They crossed the castle's godswood, where the heart tree had grown so huge and tangled that it had choked out all the oaks and elms and birch and sent its thick, pale limbs crashing through the walls and windows that looked down on it. Its roots were as thick around as a man's waist, its trunk so wide that the face carved into it looked fat and angry. Beyond the weir-wood, Glover opened a rusted iron gate and paused to light a torch. When it was blazing red and hot, he took Davos down more steps into a barrel-vaulted cellar where the weeping walls were crusted white with salt, and seawater sloshed beneath their feet with every step. They passed through several cellars, and rows of small, damp, foul-smelling cells very different from the room where Davos had been confined. Then there was a blank stone wall that turned when Glover pushed on it. Beyond was a long narrow tunnel and still more steps. These led up.

"Where are we?" asked Davos as they climbed. His words echoed faintly though the darkness.

"The steps beneath the steps. The passage runs beneath the Castle Stair up to the New Castle. A secret way. It would not do for you to be seen, my lord. You are supposed to be dead."

Porridge for the dead man. Davos climbed.

They emerged through another wall, but this one was lath and plaster on the far side. The room beyond was snug and warm and comfortably furnished, with a Myrish carpet on the floor and beeswax candles burning on a table. Davos could hear pipes and fiddles playing, not far away. On the wall hung a sheepskin with a map of the north painted across it in faded colors. Beneath the map sat Wyman Manderly, the colossal Lord of White Harbor.

"Please sit." Lord Manderly was richly garbed. His velvet doublet was a soft blue-green, embroidered with golden thread at hem and sleeves and collar. His mantle was ermine, pinned at the shoulder with a golden tri-dent. "Are you hungry?"

"No, my lord. Your gaolers have fed me well."

"There is wine, if you have a thirst."

"I will treat with you, my lord. My king commanded that of me. I do not have to drink with you."

Lord Wyman sighed. "I have treated you most shamefully, I know. I had my reasons, but . . . please, sit and drink, I beg you. Drink to my boy's safe return. Wylis, my eldest son and heir. He is home. That is the welcoming feast you hear. In the Merman's Court they are eating lamprey pie and venison with roasted chestnuts. Wynafryd is dancing with the Frey she is to marry. The other Freys are raising cups of wine to toast our friendship."

Beneath the music, Davos could hear the murmur of many voices, the clatter of cups and platters. He said nothing.

"I have just come from the high table," Lord Wyman went on. "I have eaten too much, as ever, and all White Harbor knows my bowels are bad. My friends of Frey will not question a lengthy visit to the privy, we hope." He turned his cup over. "There. You will drink and I will not. Sit. Time is short, and there is much we need to say. Robett, wine for the Hand, if you will be so good. Lord Davos, you will not know, but you are dead."

Robett Glover filled a wine cup and offered it to Davos. He took it, sniffed it, drank. "How did I die, if I may ask?"

"By the axe. Your head and hands were mounted above the Seal Gate, with your face turned so your eyes looked out across the harbor. By now you are well rotted, though we dipped your head in tar before we set it upon the spike. Carrion crows and seabirds squabbled over your eyes, they say."

Davos shifted uncomfortably. It was a queer feeling, being dead. "If it please my lord, who died in my place?"

"Does it matter? You have a common face, Lord Davos. I hope my saying so does not offend you. The man had your coloring, a nose of the same shape, two ears that were not dissimilar, a long beard that could be trimmed and shaped like yours. You can be sure we tarred him well, and the onion shoved between his teeth served to twist the features. Ser Bartimus saw that the fingers of his left hand were shortened, the same as yours. The man was a criminal, if that gives you any solace. His dying may accomplish more good than anything he ever did whilst living. My lord, I bear you no ill will. The rancor I showed you in the Merman's Court was a mummer's farce put on to please our friends of Frey."

"My lord should take up a life of mummery," said Davos. "You and yours were most convincing. Your good-daughter seemed to want me dead most earnestly, and the little girl . . ."

"Wylla." Lord Wyman smiled. "Did you see how brave she was? Even when I threatened to have her tongue out, she reminded me of the debt White Harbor owes to the Starks of Winterfell, a debt that can never be repaid. Wylla spoke from the heart, as did Lady Leona. Forgive her if you can, my lord. She is a foolish, frightened woman, and Wylis is her life. Not every man has it in him to be Prince Aemon the Dragonknight or Symeon Star-Eyes, and not every woman can be as brave as my Wylla and her sister Wynafryd . . . who *did* know, yet played her own part fearlessly.

"When treating with liars, even an honest man must lie. I did not dare defy King's Landing so long as my last living son remained a captive. Lord Tywin Lannister wrote me himself to say that he had Wylis. If I would have him freed unharmed, he told me, I must repent my treason, yield my city, declare my loyalty to the boy king on the Iron Throne . . . and bend my knee to Roose Bolton, his Warden of the North. Should I refuse, Wylis would die a traitor's death, White Harbor would be stormed and sacked, and my people would suffer the same fate as the Reynes of Castamere.

"I am fat, and many think that makes me weak and foolish. Mayhaps Tywin Lannister was one such. I sent him back a raven to say that I would bend my knee and open my gates *after* my son was returned, but not before. There the matter stood when Tywin died. Afterward the Freys turned up with Wendel's bones . . . to make a peace and seal it with a marriage pact, they claimed, but I was not about to give them what they wanted until I had Wylis, safe and whole, and they were not about to give me Wylis until I proved my loyalty. Your arrival gave me the means to do that. That was the reason for the discourtesy I showed you in the Merman's Court, and for the head and hands rotting above the Seal Gate."

"You took a great risk, my lord," Davos said. "If the Freys had seen through your deception . . ."

"I took no risk at all. If any of the Freys had taken it upon themselves to climb my gate for a close look at the man with the onion in his mouth, I would have blamed my gaolers for the error and produced you to appease them."

Davos felt a shiver up his spine. "I see."

"I hope so. You have sons of your own, you said."

Three, thought Davos, *though I fathered seven.*

"Soon I must return to the feast to toast my friends of Frey," Manderly continued. "They watch me, ser. Day and night their eyes are on me, noses sniffing for some whiff of treachery. You saw them, the arrogant Ser Jared and his nephew Rhaegar, that smirking worm who wears a dragon's name. Behind them both stands Symond, clinking coins. That one has bought and paid for several of my servants and two of my knights. One of his wife's handmaids has found her way into the bed of my own fool. If Stannis wonders that my letters say so little, it is because I dare not even trust my maester. Theomore is all head and no heart. You heard him in my hall. Maesters are supposed to put aside old loyalties when they don their chains, but I cannot forget that Theomore was born a Lannister of Lannisport and claims some distant kinship to the Lannisters of Casterly Rock. Foes and false friends are all around me, Lord Davos. They infest my city like roaches, and at night I feel them crawling over me." The fat man's fingers coiled into a fist, and all his chins trembled. "My son Wendel came to the Twins a guest. He ate Lord Walder's bread and salt, and hung his sword upon the wall to feast with friends. And they murdered him. *Murdered,* I say, and may the Freys choke upon their fables. I drink with Jared, jape with Symond, promise Rhaegar the hand of my own beloved granddaughter . . . but never think that means I have forgotten. The north remembers, Lord Davos. The north remembers, and the mummer's farce is almost done. My son is home."

Something about the way Lord Wyman said that chilled Davos to the bone. "If it is justice that you want, my lord, look to King Stannis. No man is more just."

Robett Glover broke in to add, "Your loyalty does you honor, my lord, but Stannis Baratheon remains your king, not our own."

"Your own king is dead," Davos reminded them, "murdered at the Red Wedding beside Lord Wyman's son."

"The Young Wolf is dead," Manderly allowed, "but that brave boy was not Lord Eddard's only son. Robett, bring the lad."

"At once, my lord." Glover slipped out the door.

The lad? Was it possible that one of Robb Stark's brothers had survived the ruin of Winterfell? Did Manderly have a Stark heir hidden away in his castle? *A found boy or a feigned boy?* The north would rise for either, he suspected . . . but Stannis Baratheon would never make common cause with an imposter.

The lad who followed Robett Glover through the door was not a Stark, nor could he ever hope to pass for one. He was older than the Young Wolf's murdered brothers, fourteen or fifteen by the look of him, and his eyes were older still. Beneath a tangle of dark brown hair his face was almost feral, with a wide mouth, sharp nose, and pointed chin. "Who are you?" Davos asked.

The boy looked to Robett Glover.

"He is a mute, but we have been teaching him his letters. He learns quickly." Glover drew a dagger from his belt and gave it to the boy. "Write your name for Lord Seaworth."

There was no parchment in the chamber. The boy carved the letters into a wooden beam in the wall. *W . . . E . . . X.* He leaned hard into the

X. When he was done he flipped the dagger in the air, caught it, and stood admiring his handiwork.

"Wex is ironborn. He was Theon Greyjoy's squire. Wex was at Winterfell." Glover sat. "How much does Lord Stannis know of what transpired at Winterfell?"

Davos thought back on the tales they'd heard. "Winterfell was captured by Theon Greyjoy, who had once been Lord Stark's ward. He had Stark's two young sons put to death and mounted their heads above the castle walls. When the northmen came to oust him, he put the entire castle to sword, down to the last child, before he himself was slain by Lord Bolton's bastard."

"Not slain," said Glover. "Captured, and carried back to the Dreadfort. The Bastard has been flaying him."

Lord Wyman nodded. "The tale you tell is one we all have heard, as full of lies as a pudding's full of raisins. It was the Bastard of Bolton who put Winterfell to the sword . . . Ramsay Snow, he was called then, before the boy king made him a Bolton. Snow did not kill them all. He spared the women, roped them together, and marched them to the Dreadfort for his sport."

"His sport?"

"He is a great hunter," said Wyman Manderly, "and women are his favorite prey. He strips them naked and sets them loose in the woods. They have a half day's start before he sets out after them with hounds and horns. From time to time some wench escapes and lives to tell the tale. Most are less fortunate. When Ramsay catches them he rapes them, flays them, feeds their corpses to his dogs, and brings their skins back to the Dreadfort as trophies. If they have given him good sport, he slits their throats before he skins them. Elsewise, t'other way around."

Davos paled. "Gods be good. How could any man—"

"The evil is in his blood," said Robett Glover. "He is a bastard born of rape. A *Snow*, no matter what the boy king says."

"Was ever snow so black?" asked Lord Wyman. "Ramsay took Lord Hornwood's lands by forcibly wedding his widow, then locked her in a tower and forgot her. It is said she ate her own fingers in her extremity . . . and the Lannister notion of king's justice is to reward her killer with Ned Stark's little girl."

"The Boltons have always been as cruel as they were cunning, but this one seems a beast in human skin," said Glover.

The Lord of White Harbor leaned forward. "The Freys are no better. They speak of wargs and skinchangers and assert that it was Robb Stark who slew my Wendel. The arrogance of it! They do not expect the north to believe their lies, not truly, but they think we must pretend to believe or die. Roose Bolton lies about his part in the Red Wedding, and his bastard lies about the fall of Winterfell. And yet so long as they held Wylis I had no choice but to eat all this excrement and praise the taste."

"And now, my lord?" asked Davos.

He had hoped to hear Lord Wyman say, *And now I shall declare for King Stannis*, but instead the fat man smiled an odd, twinkling smile and said, "And now I have a wedding to attend. I am too fat to sit a horse, as any man with eyes can plainly see. As a boy I loved to ride, and as a young man I handled a mount well enough to win some small acclaim in the lists, but those days are done. My body has become a prison more dire than the Wolf's Den. Even so, I must go to Winterfell. Roose Bolton wants me on my knees, and beneath the velvet courtesy he shows the iron mail. I shall go by barge and litter, attended by a hundred knights and my good friends from the Twins. The Freys came here by sea. They have no horses with them, so I shall present each of them with a palfrey as a guest gift. Do hosts still give guest gifts in the south?"

"Some do, my lord. On the day their guest departs."

"Perhaps you understand, then." Wyman Manderly lurched ponderously to his feet. "I have been building warships for more than a year. Some you saw, but there are as many more hidden up the White Knife. Even with the losses I have suffered, I still command more heavy horse than any other lord north of the Neck. My walls are strong, and my vaults are full of silver. Oldcastle and Widow's Watch will take their lead from me. My bannermen include a dozen petty lords and a hundred landed knights. I can deliver King Stannis the allegiance of all the lands east of the White Knife, from Widow's Watch and Ramsgate to the Sheepshead Hills and the headwaters of the Broken Branch. All this I pledge to do if you will meet my price."

"I can bring your terms to the king, but—"

Lord Wyman cut him off. "If *you* will meet my price, I said. Not Stannis. It's not a king I need but a smuggler."

Robett Glover took up the tale. "We may never know all that happened at Winterfell, when Ser Rodrik Cassel tried to take the castle back from Theon Greyjoy's ironmen. The Bastard of Bolton claims that Greyjoy murdered Ser Rodrik during a parley. Wex says no. Until he learns more letters we will never know half the truth . . . but he came to us knowing *yes* and *no*, and those can go a long way once you find the right questions."

"It was the Bastard who murdered Ser Rodrik and the men of Winterfell," said Lord Wyman. "He slew Greyjoy's ironmen as well. Wex saw men cut down trying to yield. When we asked how he escaped, he took a chunk of chalk and drew a tree with a face."

Davos thought about that. "The old gods saved him?"

"After a fashion. He climbed the heart tree and hid himself amongst the leaves. Bolton's men searched the godswood twice and killed the men they found there, but none thought to clamber up into the trees. Is that how it happened, Wex?"

The boy flipped up Glover's dagger, caught it, nodded.

Glover said, "He stayed up in the tree a long time. He slept amongst the branches, not daring to descend. Finally he heard voices down beneath him."

"The voices of the dead," said Wyman Manderly.

Wex held up five fingers, tapped each one with the dagger, then folded four away and tapped the last again.

"Six of them," asked Davos. "There were six."

"Two of them Ned Stark's murdered sons."

"How could a mute tell you that?"

"With chalk. He drew two boys . . . and two wolves."

"The lad is ironborn, so he thought it best not to show himself," said Glover. "He listened. The six did not linger long amongst the ruins of Winterfell. Four went one way, two another. Wex stole after the two, a woman and a boy. He must have stayed downwind, so the wolf would not catch his scent."

"He knows where they went," Lord Wyman said.

Davos understood. "You want the boy."

"Roose Bolton has Lord Eddard's daughter. To thwart him White Harbor must have Ned's son . . . and the direwolf. The wolf will prove the boy is who we say he is, should the Dreadfort attempt to deny him. That is my price, Lord Davos. Smuggle me back my liege lord, and I will take Stannis Baratheon as my king."

Old instinct made Davos Seaworth reach for his throat. His fingerbones had been his luck, and somehow he felt he would have need of luck to do what Wyman Manderly was asking of him. The bones were gone, though, so he said, "You have better men than me in your service. Knights and lords and maesters. Why would you need a smuggler? You have ships."

"Ships," Lord Wyman agreed, "but my crews are rivermen, or fisherfolk who have never sailed beyond the Bite. For this I must have a man who's sailed in darker waters and knows how to slip past dangers, unseen and unmolested."

"Where is the boy?" Somehow Davos knew he would not like the answer. "Where is it you want me to go, my lord?"

Robett Glover said, "Wex. Show him."

The mute flipped the dagger, caught it, then flung it end over end at the sheepskin map that adorned Lord Wyman's wall. It struck quivering. Then he grinned.

For half a heartbeat Davos considered asking Wyman Manderly to send him back to the Wolf's Den, to Ser Bartimus with his tales and Garth with his lethal ladies. In the Den even prisoners ate porridge in the morning. But there were other places in this world where men were known to break their fast on human flesh.

DAENERYS

E ach morning, from her western ramparts, the queen would count the sails on Slaver's Bay.

Today she counted five-and-twenty, though some were far away and moving, so it was hard to be certain. Sometimes she missed one, or counted one twice. *What does it matter? A strangler only needs ten fingers.* All trade had stopped, and her fisherfolk did not dare put out into the bay. The boldest still dropped a few lines into the river, though even that was hazardous; more remained tied up beneath Meereen's walls of many-colored brick.

There were ships from Meereen out in the bay too, warships and trading galleys whose captains had taken them to sea when Dany's host first laid siege to the city, now returned to augment the fleets from Qarth, Tolos, and New Ghis.

Her admiral's counsel had proved worse than useless. "Let them see your dragons," Groleo said. "Let the Yunkishmen have a taste of fire, and the trade will flow again."

"Those ships are strangling us, and all my admiral can do is talk of dragons," Dany said. "You *are* my admiral, are you not?"

"An admiral without ships."

"*Build* ships."

"Warships cannot be made from brick. The slavers burned every stand of timber within twenty leagues of here."

"Then ride out two-and-twenty leagues. I will give you wagons, workers, mules, whatever you require."

"I am a sailor, not a shipwright. I was sent to fetch Your Grace back to Pentos. Instead you brought us here and tore my *Saduleon* to pieces for some nails and scraps of wood. I will never see her like again. I may never see my home again, nor my old wife. It was not me who refused the ships this Daxos offered. I cannot fight the Qartheen with fishing boats."

His bitterness dismayed her, so much so that Dany found herself wondering if the grizzled Pentoshi could be one of her three betrayers. *No, he is only an old man, far from home and sick at heart.* "There must be *something* we can do."

"Aye, and I've told you what. These ships are made of rope and pitch and canvas, of Qohorik pine and teak from Sothoros, old oak from Great Norvos, yew and ash and spruce. Wood, Your Grace. Wood burns. The dragons—"

"I will hear no more about my dragons. Leave me. Go pray to your Pentoshi gods for a storm to sink our foes."

"No sailor prays for storms, Your Grace."

"I am tired of hearing what you will not do. Go."

Ser Barristan remained. "Our stores are ample for the moment," he reminded her, "and Your Grace has planted beans and grapes and wheat. Your Dothraki have harried the slavers from the hills and struck the shackles from their slaves. They are planting too, and will be bringing their crops to Meereen to market. And you will have the friendship of Lhazar."

Daario won that for me, for all that it is worth. "The Lamb Men. Would that lambs had teeth."

"That would make the wolves more cautious, no doubt."

That made her laugh. "How fare your orphans, ser?"

The old knight smiled. "Well, Your Grace. It is good of you to ask." The boys were his pride. "Four or five have the makings of knights. Perhaps as many as a dozen."

"One would be enough if he were as true as you." The day might come soon when she would have need of every knight. "Will they joust for me? I should like that." Viserys had told her stories of the tourneys he had witnessed in the Seven Kingdoms, but Dany had never seen a joust herself.

"They are not ready, Your Grace. When they are, they will be pleased to demonstrate their prowess."

"I hope that day comes quickly." She would have kissed her good knight on the cheek, but just then Missandei appeared beneath the arched doorway. "Missandei?"

"Your Grace. Skahaz awaits your pleasure."

"Send him up."

The Shavepate was accompanied by two of his Brazen Beasts. One wore a hawk mask, the other the likeness of a jackal. Only their eyes could be seen behind the brass. "Your Radiance, Hizdahr was seen to enter the pyramid of Zhak last evening. He did not depart until well after dark."

"How many pyramids has he visited?" asked Dany.

"Eleven."

"And how long since the last murder?"

"Six-and-twenty days." The Shavepate's eyes brimmed with fury. It had been his notion to have the Brazen Beasts follow her betrothed and take note of all his actions.

"So far Hizdahr has made good on his promises."

"*How?* The Sons of the Harpy have put down their knives, but why? Because the noble Hizdahr asked sweetly? He is one of them, I tell you. That's why they obey him. He may well be the Harpy."

"If there is a Harpy." Skahaz was convinced that somewhere in Meereen the Sons of the Harpy had a highborn overlord, a secret general commanding an army of shadows. Dany did not share his belief. The Brazen Beasts had taken dozens of the Harpy's Sons, and those who had survived their capture had yielded names when questioned sharply . . . too many names, it seemed to her. It would have been pleasant to think that all the deaths were the work of a single enemy who might be caught and killed, but Dany suspected that the truth was otherwise. *My enemies are legion.* "Hizdahr zo Loraq is a persuasive man with many friends. And he is wealthy. Perhaps he has bought this peace for us with gold, or convinced the other highborn that our marriage is in their best interests."

"If he is not the Harpy, he knows him. I can find the truth of that easy enough. Give me your leave to put Hizdahr to the question, and I will bring you a confession."

"No," she said. "I do not trust these confessions. You've brought me too many of them, all of them worthless."

"Your Radiance—"

"*No*, I said."

The Shavepate's scowl turned his ugly face even uglier. "A mistake. The Great Master Hizdahr plays Your Worship for a fool. Do you want a serpent in your bed?"

I want Daario in my bed, but I sent him away for the sake of you and yours. "You may continue to watch Hizdahr zo Loraq, but no harm is to come to him. Is that understood?"

"I am not deaf, Magnificence. I will obey." Skahaz drew a parchment scroll from his sleeve. "Your Worship should have a look at this. A list of all the Meereenese ships in the blockade, with their captains. Great Masters all."

Dany studied the scroll. All the ruling families of Meereen were named: Hazkar, Merreq, Quazzar, Zhak, Rhazdar, Ghazeen, Pahl, even Reznak and Loraq. "What am I to do with a list of names?"

"Every man on that list has kin within the city. Sons and brothers, wives and daughters, mothers and fathers. Let my Brazen Beasts seize them. Their lives will win you back those ships."

"If I send the Brazen Beasts into the pyramids, it will mean open war inside the city. I have to trust in Hizdahr. I have to hope for peace." Dany held the parchment above a candle and watched the names go up in flame, while Skahaz glowered at her.

Afterward, Ser Barristan told her that her brother Rhaegar would have been proud of her. Dany remembered the words Ser Jorah had spoken at Astapor: *Rhaegar fought valiantly, Rhaegar fought nobly, Rhaegar fought honorably. And Rhaegar* died.

When she descended to the purple marble hall, she found it almost empty. "Are there no petitioners today?" Dany asked Reznak mo Reznak. "No one who craves justice or silver for a sheep?"

"No, Your Worship. The city is afraid."

"There is nothing to fear."

But there was much and more to fear as she learned that evening. As her young hostages Miklaz and Kezmya were laying out a simple supper of autumn greens and ginger soup for her, Irri came to tell her that Galazza Galare had returned, with three Blue Graces from the temple. "Grey Worm is come as well, *Khaleesi*. They beg words with you, most urgently."

"Bring them to my hall. And summon Reznak and Skahaz. Did the Green Grace say what this was about?"

"Astapor," said Irri.

Grey Worm began the tale. "He came out of the morning mists, a rider on a pale horse, dying. His mare was staggering as she approached the city gates, her sides pink with blood and lather, her eyes rolling with terror. Her rider called out, '*She is burning, she is burning,*' and fell from the saddle. This one was sent for, and gave orders that the rider be brought to the Blue Graces. When your servants carried him inside the gates, he cried out again, '*She is burning.*' Under his *tokar* he was a skeleton, all bones and fevered flesh."

One of the Blue Graces took up the tale from there. "The Unsullied brought this man to the temple, where we stripped him and bathed him in cool water. His clothes were soiled, and my sisters found half an arrow in his thigh. Though he had broken off the shaft, the head remained inside him, and the wound had mortified, filling him with poisons. He died within the hour, still crying out that she was burning."

" 'She is burning,' " Daenerys repeated. "Who is *she*?"

"Astapor, Your Radiance," said another of the Blue Graces. "He said it, once. He said '*Astapor* is burning.'"

"It might have been his fever talking."

"Your Radiance speaks wisely," said Galazza Galare, "but Ezzara saw something else."

The Blue Grace called Ezzara folded her hands. "My queen," she murmured, "his fever was not brought on by the arrow. He had soiled himself, not once but many times. The stains reached to his knees, and there was dried blood amongst his excrement."

"His horse was bleeding, Grey Worm said."

"This thing is true, Your Grace," the eunuch confirmed. "The pale mare was bloody from his spur."

"That may be so, Your Radiance," said Ezzara, "but this blood was mingled with his stool. It stained his smallclothes."

"He was bleeding from the bowels," said Galazza Galare.

"We cannot be certain," said Ezzara, "but it may be that Meereen has more to fear than the spears of the Yunkai'i."

"We must pray," said the Green Grace. "The gods sent this man to us. He comes as a harbinger. He comes as a sign."

"A sign of what?" asked Dany.

"A sign of wroth and ruin."

She did not want to believe that. "He was one man. One sick man with an arrow in his leg. A horse brought him here, not a god." *A pale mare.* Dany rose abruptly. "I thank you for your counsel and for all that you did for this poor man."

The Green Grace kissed Dany's fingers before she took her leave. "We shall pray for Astapor."

And for me. Oh, pray for me, my lady. If Astapor had fallen, nothing remained to prevent Yunkai from turning north.

She turned to Ser Barristan. "Send riders into the hills to find my bloodriders. Recall Brown Ben and the Second Sons as well."

"And the Stormcrows, Your Grace?"

Daario. "Yes. Yes." Just three nights ago she had dreamed of Daario lying dead beside the road, staring sightlessly into the sky as crows quarreled above his corpse. Other nights she tossed in her bed, imagining that he'd betrayed her, as he had once betrayed his fellow captains in the

Stormcrows. *He brought me their heads.* What if he had taken his company back to Yunkai, to sell her for a pot of gold? *He would not do that. Would he?* "The Stormcrows too. Send riders after them at once."

The Second Sons were the first to return, eight days after the queen sent forth her summons. When Ser Barristan told her that her captain desired words with her, she thought for a moment that it was Daario, and her heart leapt. But the captain that he spoke of was Brown Ben Plumm.

Brown Ben had a seamed and weathered face, skin the color of old teak, white hair, and wrinkles at the corners of his eyes. Dany was so pleased to see his leathery brown face that she hugged him. His eyes crinkled in amusement. "I heard talk Your Grace was going to take a husband," he said, "but no one told me it was me." They laughed together as Reznak sputtered, but the laughter ceased when Brown Ben said, "We caught three Astapori. Your Worship had best hear what they say."

"Bring them."

Daenerys received them in the grandeur of her hall as tall candles burned amongst the marble pillars. When she saw that the Astapori were half-starved, she sent for food at once. These three were all that remained of a dozen who had set out together from the Red City: a bricklayer, a weaver, and a cobbler. "What befell the rest of your party?" the queen asked.

"Slain," said the cobbler. "Yunkai's sellswords roam the hills north of Astapor, hunting down those who flee the flames."

"Has the city fallen, then? Its walls were thick."

"This is so," said the bricklayer, a stoop-backed man with rheumy eyes, "but they were old and crumbling as well."

The weaver raised her head. "Every day we told each other that the dragon queen was coming back." The woman had thin lips and dull dead eyes, set in a pinched and narrow face. "Cleon had sent for you, it was said, and you were coming."

He sent for me, thought Dany. *That much is true, at least.*

"Outside our walls, the Yunkai'i devoured our crops and slaughtered our herds," the cobbler went on. "Inside we starved. We ate cats and rats and leather. A horsehide was a feast. King Cutthroat and Queen Whore accused each other of feasting on the flesh of the slain. Men and women gathered in secret to draw lots and gorge upon the flesh of him who drew the black stone. The pyramid of Nakloz was despoiled and set aflame by those who claimed that Kraznys mo Nakloz was to blame for all our woes."

"Others blamed Daenerys," said the weaver, "but more of us still loved you. 'She is on her way,' we said to one another. 'She is coming at the head of a great host, with food for all.' "

I can scarce feed my own folk. If I had marched to Astapor, I would have lost Meereen.

The cobbler told them how the body of the Butcher King had been disinterred and clad in copper armor, after the Green Grace of Astapor had a vision that he would deliver them from the Yunkai'i. Armored and stinking, the corpse of Cleon the Great was strapped onto the back of a starving horse to lead the remnants of his new Unsullied on a sortie, but they rode right into the iron teeth of a legion from New Ghis and were cut down to a man.

"Afterward the Green Grace was impaled upon a stake in the Plaza of Punishment and left until she died. In the pyramid of Ullhor, the survivors had a great feast that lasted half the night, and washed the last of their food down with poison wine so none need wake again come morning. Soon after came the sickness, a bloody flux that killed three men of every four, until a mob of dying men went mad and slew the guards on the main gate."

The old brickmaker broke in to say, "No. That was the work of healthy men, running to escape the flux."

"Does it matter?" asked the cobbler. "The guards were torn apart and the gates thrown open. The legions of New Ghis came pouring into Astapor, followed by the Yunkai'i and the sellswords on their horses. Queen Whore died fighting them with a curse upon her lips. King Cutthroat yielded and was thrown into a fighting pit, to be torn apart by a pack of starving dogs."

"Even then some said that you were coming," said the weaver. "They swore they had seen you mounted on a dragon, flying high above the camps of the Yunkai'i. Every day we looked for you."

I could not come, the queen thought. *I dare not.*

"And when the city fell?" demanded Skahaz. "What then?"

"The butchery began. The Temple of the Graces was full of the sick who had come to ask the gods to heal them. The legions sealed the doors and set the temple ablaze with torches. Within the hour fires were burning in every corner of the city. As they spread they joined with one another. The streets were full of mobs, running this way and that to escape the flames, but there was no way out. The Yunkai'i held the gates."

"Yet *you* escaped," the Shavepate said. "How is that?"

The old man answered. "I am by trade a brickmaker, as my father and his father were before me. My grandfather built our house up against the city walls. It was an easy thing to work loose a few bricks every night. When I told my friends, they helped me shore up the tunnel so it would not collapse. We all agreed that it might be good to have our own way out."

I left you with a council to rule over you, Dany thought, *a healer, a scholar, and a priest.* She could still recall the Red City as she had first seen it, dry and dusty behind its red brick walls, dreaming cruel dreams, yet full of life. *There were islands in the Worm where lovers kissed, but in the Plaza of Punishment they peeled the skin off men in strips and left them hanging naked for the flies.* "It is good that you have come," she told the Astapori. "You will be safe in Meereen."

The cobbler thanked her for that, and the old brickmaker kissed her foot, but the weaver looked at her with eyes as hard as slate. *She knows I lie,* the queen thought. *She knows I cannot keep them safe. Astapor is burning, and Meereen is next.*

"There's more coming," Brown Ben announced when the Astapori had been led away. "These three had horses. Most are afoot."

"How many are they?" asked Reznak.

Brown Ben shrugged. "Hundreds. Thousands. Some sick, some burned, some wounded. The Cats and the Windblown are swarming through the hills with lance and lash, driving them north and cutting down the laggards."

"Mouths on feet. And *sick,* you say?" Reznak wrung his hands. "Your Worship must not allow them in the city."

"I wouldn't," said Brown Ben Plumm. "I'm no maester, mind you, but I know you got to keep the bad apples from the good."

"These are not apples, Ben," said Dany. "These are men and women, sick and hungry and afraid." *My children.* "I should have gone to Astapor."

"Your Grace could not have saved them," said Ser Barristan. "You warned King Cleon against this war with Yunkai. The man was a fool, and his hands were red with blood."

And are my hands any cleaner? She remembered what Daario had said—that all kings must be butchers, or meat. "Cleon was the enemy of our enemy. If I had joined him at the Horns of Hazzat, we might have crushed the Yunkai'i between us."

The Shavepate disagreed. "If you had taken the Unsullied south to Hazzat, the Sons of the Harpy—"

"I know. I *know.* It is Eroeh all over again."

Brown Ben Plumm was puzzled. "Who is Eroeh?"

"A girl I thought I'd saved from rape and torment. All I did was make it worse for her in the end. And all I did in Astapor was make ten thousand Eroehs."

"Your Grace could not have known—"

"I am the queen. It was my place to know."

"What is done is done," said Reznak mo Reznak. "Your Worship, I beg you, take the noble Hizdahr for your king at once. He can speak with the Wise Masters, make a peace for us."

"On what terms?" *Beware the perfumed seneschal,* Quaithe had said. The masked woman had foretold the coming of the pale mare, was she right about the noble Reznak too? "I may be a young girl innocent of war, but I am not a lamb to walk bleating into the harpy's den. I still have my Unsullied. I have the Stormcrows and the Second Sons. I have three companies of freedmen."

"Them, and dragons," said Brown Ben Plumm, with a grin.

"In the pit, in chains," wailed Reznak mo Reznak. "What good are dragons that cannot be controlled? Even the Unsullied grow fearful when they must open the doors to feed them."

"What, o' the queen's little pets?" Brown Ben's eyes crinkled in amusement. The grizzled captain of the Second Sons was a creature of the free companies, a mongrel with the blood of a dozen different peoples flowing through his veins, but he had always been fond of the dragons, and them of him.

"Pets?" screeched Reznak. "Monsters, rather. Monsters that feed on children. We cannot—"

"*Silence,*" said Daenerys. "We will not speak of that."

Reznak shrank away from her, flinching from the fury in her tone. "Forgive me, Magnificence, I did not . . ."

Brown Ben Plumm bulled over him. "Your Grace, the Yunkish got three free companies against our two, and there's talk the Yunkishmen sent to Volantis to fetch back the Golden Company. Those bastards field ten thousand. Yunkai's got four Ghiscari legions too, maybe more, and I heard it said they sent riders across the Dothraki sea to maybe bring some big *khalasar* down on us. We *need* them dragons, the way I see it."

Dany sighed. "I am sorry, Ben. I dare not loose the dragons." She could see that was not the answer that he wanted.

Plumm scratched at his speckled whiskers. "If there's no dragons in the balance, well . . . we should leave before them Yunkish bastards close the trap . . . only first, make the slavers pay to see our backs. They pay the khals to leave their cities be, why not us? Sell Meereen back to them and start west with wagons full o' gold and gems and such."

"You want me to loot Meereen and flee? No, I will not do that. Grey Worm, are my freedmen ready for battle?"

The eunuch crossed his arms against his chest. "They are not Unsullied, but they will not shame you. This one will swear to that by spear and sword, Your Worship."

"Good. That's good." Daenerys looked at the faces of the men around her. The Shavepate, scowling. Ser Barristan, with his lined face and sad blue eyes. Reznak mo Reznak, pale, sweating. Brown Ben, white-haired, grizzled, tough as old leather. Grey Worm, smooth-cheeked, stolid, expressionless. *Daario should be here, and my bloodriders,* she thought. *If there is to be a battle, the blood of my blood should be with me.* She missed Ser Jorah Mormont too. *He lied to me, informed on me, but he loved me too, and he always gave good counsel.* "I defeated the Yunkai'i before. I will defeat them again. Where, though? How?"

"You mean to take the field?" The Shavepate's voice was thick with disbelief. "That would be folly. Our walls are taller and thicker than the walls of Astapor, and our defenders are more valiant. The Yunkai'i will not take this city easily."

Ser Barristan disagreed. "I do not think we should allow them to invest us. Theirs is a patchwork host at best. These slavers are no soldiers. If we take them unawares . . ."

"Small chance of that," the Shavepate said. "The Yunkai'i have many friends inside the city. They will know."

"How large an army can we muster?" Dany asked.

"Not large enough, begging your royal pardon," said Brown Ben Plumm. "What does Naharis have to say? If we're going to make a fight o' this, we need his Stormcrows."

"Daario is still in the field." *Oh, gods, what have I done? Have I sent him to his death?* "Ben, I will need your Second Sons to scout our enemies. Where they are, how fast they are advancing, how many men they have, and how they are disposed."

"We'll need provisions. Fresh horses too."

"Of course. Ser Barristan will see to it."

Brown Ben scratched his chin. "Might be we could get some o' them to come over. If Your Grace could spare a few bags o' gold and gems . . . just to give their captains a good taste, as it were . . . well, who knows?"

"Buy them, why not?" Dany said. That sort of thing went on all the time amongst the free companies of the Disputed Lands, she knew. "Yes, very good. Reznak, see to it. Once the Second Sons ride out, close the gates and double the watch upon the walls."

"It shall be done, Magnificence," said Reznak mo Reznak. "What of these Astapori?"

My children. "They are coming here for help. For succor and protection. We cannot turn our backs on them."

Ser Barristan frowned. "Your Grace, I have known the bloody flux to destroy whole armies when left to spread unchecked. The seneschal is right. We cannot have the Astapori in Meereen."

Dany looked at him helplessly. It was good that dragons did not cry. "As you say, then. We will keep them outside the walls until this . . . this curse has run its course. Set up a camp for them beside the river, west of the city. We will send them what food we can. Perhaps we can separate the healthy from the sick." All of them were looking at her. "Will you make me say it twice? Go and do as I've commanded you." Dany rose, brushed past Brown Ben, and climbed the steps to the sweet solitude of her terrace.

Two hundred leagues divided Meereen from Astapor, yet it seemed to her that the sky was darker to the southwest, smudged and hazy with the smoke of the Red City's passing. *Brick and blood built Astapor, and brick and blood its people.* The old rhyme rang in her head. *Ash and bone is Astapor, and ash and bone its people.* She tried to recall Eroeh's face, but the dead girl's features kept turning into smoke.

When Daenerys finally turned away, Ser Barristan stood near her, wrapped in his white cloak against the chill of evening. "Can we make a fight of this?" she asked him.

"Men can always fight, Your Grace. Ask rather if we can win. Dying is easy, but victory comes hard. Your freedmen are half-trained and un-blooded. Your sellswords once served your foes, and once a man turns his cloak he will not scruple to turn it again. You have two dragons who cannot be controlled, and a third that may be lost to you. Beyond these walls your only friends are the Lhazarene, who have no taste for war."

"My walls are strong, though."

"No stronger than when we sat outside them. And the Sons of the Harpy are inside the walls with us. So are the Great Masters, both those you did not kill and the sons of those you did."

"I know." The queen sighed. "What do you counsel, ser?"

"Battle," said Ser Barristan. "Meereen is overcrowded and full of hungry mouths, and you have too many enemies within. We cannot long withstand a siege, I fear. Let me meet the foe as he comes north, on ground of my own choosing."

"Meet the foe," she echoed, "with the freedmen you've called half-trained and unblooded."

"We were all unblooded once, Your Grace. The Unsullied will help stiffen them. If I had five hundred knights . . ."

"Or five. And if I give you the Unsullied, I will have no one but the Brazen Beasts to hold Meereen." When Ser Barristan did not dispute her, Dany closed her eyes. *Gods,* she prayed, *you took Khal Drogo, who was my sun-and-stars. You took our valiant son before he drew a breath. You have had your blood of me. Help me now, I pray you. Give me the wisdom to see the path ahead and the strength to do what I must to keep my children safe.*

The gods did not respond.

When she opened her eyes again, Daenerys said, "I cannot fight two enemies, one within and one without. If I am to hold Meereen, I must have the city behind me. The *whole* city. I need . . . I need . . ." She could not say it.

"Your Grace?" Ser Barristan prompted, gently.

A queen belongs not to herself but to her people.

"I need Hizdahr zo Loraq."

MELISANDRE

It was never truly dark in Melisandre's chambers.

Three tallow candles burned upon her windowsill to keep the terrors of the night at bay. Four more flickered beside her bed, two to either side. In the hearth a fire was kept burning day and night. The first lesson those who would serve her had to learn was that the fire must never, ever be allowed to go out.

The red priestess closed her eyes and said a prayer, then opened them once more to face the hearthfire. *One more time.* She had to be certain. Many a priest and priestess before her had been brought down by false visions, by seeing what they wished to see instead of what the Lord of Light had sent. Stannis was marching south into peril, the king who carried the fate of the world upon his shoulders, Azor Ahai reborn. Surely R'hllor would vouchsafe her a glimpse of what awaited him. *Show me Stannis, Lord,* she prayed. *Show me your king, your instrument.*

Visions danced before her, gold and scarlet, flickering, forming and melting and dissolving into one another, shapes strange and terrifying and seductive. She saw the eyeless faces again, staring out at her from sockets weeping blood. Then the towers by the sea, crumbling as the dark tide came sweeping over them, rising from the depths. Shadows in the shape of skulls, skulls that turned to mist, bodies locked together in lust, writhing and rolling and clawing. Through curtains of fire great winged shadows wheeled against a hard blue sky.

The girl. I must find the girl again, the grey girl on the dying horse. Jon Snow would expect that of her, and soon. It would not be enough to say the girl was fleeing. He would want more, he would want the when and where, and she did not have that for him. She had seen the girl only once. *A girl as grey as ash, and even as I watched she crumbled and blew away.*

A face took shape within the hearth. *Stannis?* she thought, for just a moment . . . but no, these were not his features. *A wooden face, corpse white.* Was this the enemy? A thousand red eyes floated in the rising flames. *He sees me.* Beside him, a boy with a wolf's face threw back his head and howled.

The red priestess shuddered. Blood trickled down her thigh, black and smoking. The fire was inside her, an agony, an ecstasy, filling her, searing her, transforming her. Shimmers of heat traced patterns on her skin, insistent as a lover's hand. Strange voices called to her from days long past. "Melony," she heard a woman cry. A man's voice called, "Lot Seven." She was weeping, and her tears were flame. And still she drank it in.

Snowflakes swirled from a dark sky and ashes rose to meet them, the grey and the white whirling around each other as flaming arrows arced above a wooden wall and dead things shambled silent through the cold, beneath a great grey cliff where fires burned inside a hundred caves. Then the wind rose and the white mist came sweeping in, impossibly cold, and one by one the fires went out. Afterward only the skulls remained.

Death, thought Melisandre. *The skulls are death.*

The flames crackled softly, and in their crackling she heard the whispered name *Jon Snow.* His long face floated before her, limned in tongues of red and orange, appearing and disappearing again, a shadow half-seen behind a fluttering curtain. Now he was a man, now a wolf, now a man again. But the skulls were here as well, the skulls were all around him. Melisandre had seen his danger before, had tried to warn the boy of it. *Enemies all around him, daggers in the dark.* He would not listen.

Unbelievers never listened until it was too late.

"What do you see, my lady?" the boy asked, softly.

Skulls. A thousand skulls, and the bastard boy again. Jon Snow. Whenever she was asked what she saw within her fires, Melisandre would answer, "Much and more," but seeing was never as simple as those words suggested. It was an art, and like all arts it demanded mastery, discipline, study. *Pain. That too.* R'hllor spoke to his chosen ones through blessed fire, in a language of ash and cinder and twisting flame that only a god could truly grasp. Melisandre had practiced her art for years beyond count, and she had paid the price. There was no one, even in her order, who had her skill at seeing the secrets half-revealed and half-concealed within the sacred flames.

Yet now she could not even seem to find her king. *I pray for a glimpse of Azor Ahai, and R'hllor shows me only Snow.* "Devan," she called, "a drink." Her throat was raw and parched.

"Yes, my lady." The boy poured her a cup of water from the stone jug by the window and brought it to her.

"Thank you." Melisandre took a sip, swallowed, and gave the boy a smile. That made him blush. The boy was half in love with her, she knew. *He fears me, he wants me, and he worships me.*

All the same, Devan was not pleased to be here. The lad had taken great pride in serving as a king's squire, and it had wounded him when Stannis commanded him to remain at Castle Black. Like any boy his age, his head was full of dreams of glory; no doubt he had been picturing the prowess he would display at Deepwood Motte. Other boys his age had gone south, to serve as squires to the king's knights and ride into battle at their side. Devan's exclusion must have seemed a rebuke, a punishment for some failure on his part, or perhaps for some failure of his father.

In truth, he was here because Melisandre had asked for him. The four eldest sons of Davos Seaworth had perished in the battle on the Blackwater, when the king's fleet had been consumed by green fire. Devan was the fifthborn and safer here with her than at the king's side. Lord Davos would not thank her for it, no more than the boy himself, but it seemed to her that Seaworth had suffered enough grief. Misguided as he was, his loyalty to Stannis could not be doubted. She had seen that in her flames.

Devan was quick and smart and able too, which was more than could be said about most of her attendants. Stannis had left a dozen of his men behind to serve her when he marched south, but most of them were useless. His Grace had need of every sword, so all he could spare were greybeards and cripples. One man had been blinded by a blow to his head in the battle by the Wall, another lamed when his falling horse crushed his legs. Her serjeant had lost an arm to a giant's club. Three of her guard were geldings that Stannis had castrated for raping wildling women. She had two drunkards and a craven too. The last should have been hanged, as the king himself admitted, but he came from a noble family, and his father and brothers had been stalwart from the first.

Having guards about her would no doubt help keep the black brothers properly respectful, the red priestess knew, but none of the men that Stannis had given her were like to be much help should she find herself in peril. It made no matter. Melisandre of Asshai did not fear for herself. R'hllor would protect her.

She took another sip of water, laid her cup aside, blinked and stretched and rose from her chair, her muscles sore and stiff. After gazing into the flames so long, it took her a few moments to adjust to the dimness. Her eyes were dry and tired, but if she rubbed them, it would only make them worse.

Her fire had burned low, she saw. "Devan, more wood. What hour is it?"

"Almost dawn, my lady."

Dawn. Another day is given us, R'hllor be praised. The terrors of the night recede. Melisandre had spent the night in her chair by the fire, as she often did. With Stannis gone, her bed saw little use. She had no time for sleep, with the weight of the world upon her shoulders. And she feared to dream. *Sleep is a little death, dreams the whisperings of the Other, who would drag us all into his eternal night.* She would sooner sit bathed in the ruddy glow of her red lord's blessed flames, her cheeks flushed by the wash of heat as if by a lover's kisses. Some nights she drowsed, but never for more than an hour. One day, Melisandre prayed, she would not sleep at all. One day she would be free of dreams. *Melony,* she thought. *Lot Seven.*

Devan fed fresh logs to the fire until the flames leapt up again, fierce and furious, driving the shadows back into the corners of the room, devouring all her unwanted dreams. *The dark recedes again . . . for a little while. But beyond the Wall, the enemy grows stronger, and should he win the dawn will never come again.* She wondered if it had been his face that she had seen, staring out at her from the flames. *No. Surely not. His visage would be more frightening than that, cold and black and too terrible for any man to gaze upon and live.* The wooden man she had glimpsed, though, and the boy with the wolf's face . . . they were his servants, surely . . . his champions, as Stannis was hers.

Melisandre went to her window, pushed open the shutters. Outside the east had just begun to lighten, and the stars of morning still hung in a pitch-black sky. Castle Black was already beginning to stir as men in black cloaks made their way across the yard to break their fast with bowls of porridge before they relieved their brothers atop the Wall. A few snowflakes drifted by the open window, floating on the wind.

"Does my lady wish to break her fast?" asked Devan.

Food. Yes, I should eat. Some days she forgot. R'hllor provided her with all the nourishment her body needed, but that was something best concealed from mortal men.

It was Jon Snow she needed, not fried bread and bacon, but it was no use sending Devan to the lord commander. He would not come to her summons. Snow still chose to dwell behind the armory, in a pair of modest rooms previously occupied by the Watch's late blacksmith. Perhaps he did not think himself worthy of the King's Tower, or perhaps he did not care. That was his mistake, the false humility of youth that is itself a sort of pride. It was never wise for a ruler to eschew the trappings of power, for power itself flows in no small measure from such trappings.

The boy was not entirely naive, however. He knew better than to come to Melisandre's chambers like a supplicant, insisting she come to him instead should she have need of words with him. And oft as not, when she did come, he would keep her waiting or refuse to see her. That much, at least, was shrewd.

"I will have nettle tea, a boiled egg, and bread with butter. Fresh bread, if you please, not fried. You may find the wildling as well. Tell him that I must speak with him."

"Rattleshirt, my lady?"

"And quickly."

While the boy was gone, Melisandre washed herself and changed her robes. Her sleeves were full of hidden pockets, and she checked them carefully as she did every morning to make certain all her powders were in place. Powders to turn fire green or blue or silver, powders to make a flame roar and hiss and leap up higher than a man is tall, powders to make smoke. A smoke for truth, a smoke for lust, a smoke for fear, and the thick black smoke that could kill a man outright. The red priestess armed herself with a pinch of each of them.

The carved chest that she had brought across the narrow sea was more than three-quarters empty now. And while Melisandre had the knowledge to make more powders, she lacked many rare ingredients. *My spells should suffice.* She was stronger at the Wall, stronger even than in Asshai. Her every word and gesture was more potent, and she could do things that she had never done before. *Such shadows as I bring forth here will be terrible, and no creature of the dark will stand before them.* With such sorceries at her command, she should soon have no more need of the feeble tricks of alchemists and pyromancers.

She shut the chest, turned the lock, and hid the key inside her skirts in another secret pocket. Then came a rapping at her door. Her one-armed serjeant, from the tremulous sound of his knock. "Lady Melisandre, the Lord o' Bones is come."

"Send him in." Melisandre settled herself back into the chair beside the hearth.

The wildling wore a sleeveless jerkin of boiled leather dotted with bronze studs beneath a worn cloak mottled in shades of green and brown. *No bones.* He was cloaked in shadows too, in wisps of ragged grey mist, half-seen, sliding across his face and form with every step he took. *Ugly things. As ugly as his bones.* A widow's peak, close-set dark eyes, pinched cheeks, a mustache wriggling like a worm above a mouthful of broken brown teeth.

Melisandre felt the warmth in the hollow of her throat as her ruby stirred at the closeness of its slave. "You have put aside your suit of bones," she observed.

"The clacking was like to drive me mad."

"The bones protect you," she reminded him. "The black brothers do not love you. Devan tells me that only yesterday you had words with some of them over supper."

"A few. I was eating bean-and-bacon soup whilst Bowen Marsh was going on about the high ground. The Old Pomegranate thought that I was spying on him and announced that he would not suffer murderers listening to their councils. I told him that if that was true, maybe they shouldn't have them by the fire. Bowen turned red and made some choking sounds, but that was as far as it went." The wildling sat on the edge of the window, slid his dagger from its sheath. "If some crow wants to slip a knife between my ribs whilst I'm spooning up some supper, he's welcome to try. Hobb's gruel would taste better with a drop of blood to spice it."

Melisandre paid the naked steel no mind. If the wildling had meant her harm, she would have seen it in her flames. Danger to her own person was the first thing she had learned to see, back when she was still half a child, a slave girl bound for life to the great red temple. It was still the first thing she looked for whenever she gazed into a fire. "It is their eyes that should concern you, not their knives," she warned him.

"The glamor, aye." In the black iron fetter about his wrist, the ruby seemed to pulse. He tapped it with the edge of his blade. The steel made a faint *click* against the stone. "I feel it when I sleep. Warm against my skin, even through the iron. Soft as a woman's kiss. *Your* kiss. But sometimes in my dreams it starts to burn, and your lips turn into teeth. Every day I think how easy it would be to pry it out, and every day I don't. Must I wear the bloody bones as well?"

"The spell is made of shadow and suggestion. Men see what they expect to see. The bones are part of that." *Was I wrong to spare this one?* "If the glamor fails, they will kill you."

The wildling began to scrape the dirt out from beneath his nails with the point of his dagger. "I've sung my songs, fought my battles, drunk summer wine, tasted the Dornishman's wife. A man should die the way he's lived. For me that's steel in hand."

Does he dream of death? Could the enemy have touched him? Death is his domain, the dead his soldiers. "You shall have work for your steel soon enough. The enemy is moving, the true enemy. And Lord Snow's rangers will return before the day is done, with their blind and bloody eyes."

The wildling's own eyes narrowed. Grey eyes, brown eyes; Melisandre could see the color change with each pulse of the ruby. "Cutting out the eyes, that's the Weeper's work. The best crow's a blind crow, he likes to say. Sometimes I think he'd like to cut out his own eyes, the way they're always watering and itching. Snow's been assuming the free folk would turn to Tormund to lead them, because that's what he would do. He liked Tormund, and the old fraud liked him too. If it's the Weeper, though . . . that's not good. Not for him, and not for us."

Melisandre nodded solemnly, as if she had taken his words to heart, but this Weeper did not matter. None of his free folk mattered. They were a lost people, a doomed people, destined to vanish from the earth, as the children of the forest had vanished. Those were not words he would wish to hear, though, and she could not risk losing him, not now. "How well do you know the north?"

He slipped his blade away. "As well as any raider. Some parts more than others. There's a lot of north. Why?"

"The girl," she said. "A girl in grey on a dying horse. Jon Snow's sister." Who else could it be? She was racing to him for protection, that much Melisandre had seen clearly. "I have seen her in my flames, but only once. We must win the lord commander's trust, and the only way to do that is to save her."

"Me save her, you mean? The Lord o' Bones?" He laughed. "No one ever trusted Rattleshirt but fools. Snow's not that. If his sister needs saving, he'll send his crows. I would."

"He is not you. He made his vows and means to live by them. The Night's Watch takes no part. But you are not Night's Watch. You can do what he cannot."

"If your stiff-necked lord commander will allow it. Did your fires show you where to find this girl?"

"I saw water. Deep and blue and still, with a thin coat of ice just forming on it. It seemed to go on and on forever."

"Long Lake. What else did you see around this girl?"

"Hills. Fields. Trees. A deer, once. Stones. She is staying well away from villages. When she can she rides along the bed of little streams, to throw hunters off her trail."

He frowned. "That will make it difficult. She was coming north, you said. Was the lake to her east or to her west?"

Melisandre closed her eyes, remembering. "West."

"She is not coming up the kingsroad, then. Clever girl. There are fewer watchers on the other side, and more cover. And some hidey-holes I have used myself from time—" He broke off at the sound of a warhorn and rose swiftly to his feet. All over Castle Black, Melisandre knew, the same sudden hush had fallen, and every man and boy turned toward the Wall, listening, waiting. One long blast of the horn meant rangers returning, but two . . .

The day has come, the red priestess thought. *Lord Snow will have to listen to me now.*

After the long mournful cry of the horn had faded away, the silence seemed to stretch out to an hour. The wildling finally broke the spell. "Only one, then. Rangers."

"Dead rangers." Melisandre rose to her feet as well. "Go put on your bones and wait. I will return."

"I should go with you."

"Do not be foolish. Once they find what they will find, the sight of any wildling will inflame them. Stay here until their blood has time to cool."

Devan was coming up the steps of the King's Tower as Melisandre made her descent, flanked by two of the guards Stannis had left her. The boy was carrying her half-forgotten breakfast on a tray. "I waited for Hobb to pull the fresh loaves from the ovens, my lady. The bread's still hot."

"Leave it in my chambers." The wildling would eat it, like as not. "Lord Snow has need of me, beyond the Wall." *He does not know it yet, but soon . . .*

Outside, a light snow had begun to fall. A crowd of crows had gathered around the gate by the time Melisandre and her escort arrived, but they made way for the red priestess. The lord commander had preceded her through the ice, accompanied by Bowen Marsh and twenty spearmen. Snow had also sent a dozen archers to the top of the Wall, should any foes be hidden in the nearby woods. The guards on the gate were not queen's men, but they passed her all the same.

It was cold and dark beneath the ice, in the narrow tunnel that crooked and slithered through the Wall. Morgan went before her with a torch and Merrel came behind her with an axe. Both men were hopeless drunkards, but they were sober at this hour of the morning. Queen's men, at least in name, both had a healthy fear of her, and Merrel could be formidable when he was not drunk. She would have no need of them today, but

Melisandre made it a point to keep a pair of guards about her everywhere she went. It sent a certain message. *The trappings of power.*

By the time the three of them emerged north of the Wall the snow was falling steadily. A ragged blanket of white covered the torn and tortured earth that stretched from the Wall to the edge of the haunted forest. Jon Snow and his black brothers were gathered around three spears, some twenty yards away.

The spears were eight feet long and made of ash. The one on the left had a slight crook, but the other two were smooth and straight. At the top of each was impaled a severed head. Their beards were full of ice, and the falling snow had given them white hoods. Where their eyes had been, only empty sockets remained, black and bloody holes that stared down in silent accusation.

"Who were they?" Melisandre asked the crows.

"Black Jack Bulwer, Hairy Hal, and Garth Greyfeather," Bowen Marsh said solemnly. "The ground is half-frozen. It must have taken the wildlings half the night to drive the spears so deep. They could still be close. Watching us." The Lord Steward squinted at the line of trees.

"Could be a hundred of them out there," said the black brother with the dour face. "Could be a thousand."

"No," said Jon Snow. "They left their gifts in the black of night, then ran." His huge white direwolf prowled around the shafts, sniffing, then lifted his leg and pissed on the spear that held the head of Black Jack Bulwer. "Ghost would have their scent if they were still out there."

"I hope the Weeper burned the bodies," said the dour man, the one called Dolorous Edd. "Elsewise they might come looking for their heads."

Jon Snow grasped the spear that bore Garth Greyfeather's head and wrenched it violently from the ground. "Pull down the other two," he commanded, and four of the crows hurried to obey.

Bowen Marsh's cheeks were red with cold. "We should never have sent out rangers."

"This is not the time and place to pick at that wound. Not here, my lord. Not now." To the men struggling with the spears Snow said, "Take the heads and burn them. Leave nothing but bare bone." Only then did he seem to notice Melisandre. "My lady. Walk with me, if you would."

At last. "If it please the lord commander."

As they walked beneath the Wall, she slipped her arm through his. Morgan and Merrel went before them, Ghost came prowling at their heels. The priestess did not speak, but she slowed her pace deliberately, and where she walked the ice began to drip. *He will not fail to notice that.*

Beneath the iron grating of a murder hole Snow broke the silence, as she had known he would. "What of the other six?"

"I have not seen them," Melisandre said.

"Will you look?"

"Of course, my lord."

"We've had a raven from Ser Denys Mallister at the Shadow Tower," Jon Snow told her. "His men have seen fires in the mountains on the far side of the Gorge. Wildlings massing, Ser Denys believes. He thinks they are going to try to force the Bridge of Skulls again."

"Some may." Could the skulls in her vision have signified this bridge? Somehow Melisandre did not think so. "If it comes, that attack will be no more than a diversion. I saw towers by the sea, submerged beneath a black and bloody tide. That is where the heaviest blow will fall."

"Eastwatch?"

Was it? Melisandre had seen Eastwatch-by-the-Sea with King Stannis. That was where His Grace left Queen Selyse and their daughter Shireen when he assembled his knights for the march to Castle Black. The towers in her fire had been different, but that was oft the way with visions. "Yes. Eastwatch, my lord."

"When?"

She spread her hands. "On the morrow. In a moon's turn. In a year. And it may be that if you act, you may avert what I have seen entirely." *Else what would be the point of visions?*

"Good," said Snow.

The crowd of crows beyond the gate had swollen to two score by the time they emerged from beneath the Wall. The men pressed close about them. Melisandre knew a few by name: the cook Three-Finger Hobb, Mully with his greasy orange hair, the dim-witted boy called Owen the Oaf, the drunkard Septon Celladar.

"Is it true, m'lord?" said Three-Finger Hobb.

"Who is it?" asked Owen the Oaf. "Not Dywen, is it?"

"Nor Garth," said the queen's man she knew as Alf of Runnymudd, one of the first to exchange his seven false gods for the truth of R'hllor. "Garth's too clever for them wildlings."

"How many?" Mully asked.

"Three," Jon told them. "Black Jack, Hairy Hal, and Garth."

Alf of Runnymudd let out a howl loud enough to wake sleepers in the Shadow Tower. "Put him to bed and get some mulled wine into him," Jon told Three-Finger Hobb.

"Lord Snow," Melisandre said quietly. "Will you come with me to the King's Tower? I have more to share with you."

He looked at her face for a long moment with those cold grey eyes of his. His right hand closed, opened, closed again. "As you wish. Edd, take Ghost back to my chambers."

Melisandre took that as a sign and dismissed her own guard as well. They crossed the yard together, just the two of them. The snow fell all around them. She walked as close to Jon Snow as she dared, close enough to feel the mistrust pouring off him like a black fog. *He does not love me, will never love me, but he will make use of me. Well and good.* Melisandre had danced the same dance with Stannis Baratheon, back in the beginning. In truth, the young lord commander and her king had more in common than either one would ever be willing to admit. Stannis had been a younger son living in the shadow of his elder brother, just as Jon Snow, bastard-born, had always been eclipsed by his trueborn sibling, the fallen hero men had called the Young Wolf. Both men were unbelievers by nature, mistrustful, suspicious. The only gods they truly worshiped were honor and duty.

"You have not asked about your sister," Melisandre said, as they climbed the spiral steps of the King's Tower.

"I told you. I have no sister. We put aside our kin when we say our words. I cannot help Arya, much as I—"

He broke off as they stepped inside her chambers. The wildling was within, seated at her board, spreading butter on a ragged chunk of warm brown bread with his dagger. He had donned the bone armor, she was pleased to see. The broken giant's skull that was his helm rested on the window seat behind him.

Jon Snow tensed. "You."

"Lord Snow." The wildling grinned at them through a mouth of brown and broken teeth. The ruby on his wrist glimmered in the morning light like a dim red star.

"What are you doing here?"

"Breaking my fast. You're welcome to share."

"I'll not break bread with you."

"Your loss. The loaf's still warm. Hobb can do that much, at least." The wildling ripped off a bite. "I could visit you as easily, my lord. Those guards at your door are a bad jape. A man who has climbed the Wall half a hundred times can climb in a window easy enough. But what good would come of killing you? The crows would only choose someone worse." He chewed, swallowed. "I heard about your rangers. You should have sent me with them."

"So you could betray them to the Weeper?"

"Are we talking about betrayals? What was the name of that wildling wife of yours, Snow? Ygritte, wasn't it?" The wildling turned to Melisandre. "I will need horses. Half a dozen good ones. And this is nothing I can do alone. Some of the spearwives penned up at Mole's Town should serve. Women would be best for this. The girl's more like to trust them, and they will help me carry off a certain ploy I have in mind."

"What is he talking about?" Lord Snow asked her.

"Your sister." Melisandre put her hand on his arm. "You cannot help her, but he can."

Snow wrenched his arm away. "I think not. You do not know this creature. Rattleshirt could wash his hands a hundred times a day and he'd still have blood beneath his nails. He'd be more like to rape and murder Arya than to save her. No. If this was what you have seen in your fires, my lady, you must have ashes in your eyes. If he tries to leave Castle Black without my leave, I'll take his head off myself."

He leaves me no choice. So be it. "Devan, leave us," she said, and the squire slipped away and closed the door behind him.

Melisandre touched the ruby at her neck and spoke a word.

The sound echoed queerly from the corners of the room and twisted like a worm inside their ears. The wildling heard one word, the crow another. Neither was the word that left her lips. The ruby on the wildling's wrist darkened, and the wisps of light and shadow around him writhed and faded.

The bones remained—the rattling ribs, the claws and teeth along his arms and shoulders, the great yellowed collarbone across his shoulders. The broken giant's skull remained a broken giant's skull, yellowed and cracked, grinning its stained and savage grin.

But the widow's peak dissolved. The brown mustache, the knobby chin, the sallow yellowed flesh and small dark eyes, all melted. Grey fingers crept through long brown hair. Laugh lines appeared at the corners of his mouth. All at once he was bigger than before, broader in the chest and shoulders, long-legged and lean, his face clean-shaved and windburnt.

Jon Snow's grey eyes grew wider. "Mance?"

"Lord Snow." Mance Rayder did not smile.

"She burned you."

"She burned the Lord of Bones."

Jon Snow turned to Melisandre. "What sorcery is this?"

"Call it what you will. Glamor, seeming, illusion. R'hllor is Lord of Light, Jon Snow, and it is given to his servants to weave with it, as others weave with thread."

Mance Rayder chuckled. "I had my doubts as well, Snow, but why not let her try? It was that, or let Stannis roast me."

"The bones help," said Melisandre. "The bones remember. The strongest glamors are built of such things. A dead man's boots, a hank of hair, a bag of fingerbones. With whispered words and prayer, a man's shadow can be drawn forth from such and draped about another like a cloak. The wearer's essence does not change, only his seeming."

She made it sound a simple thing, and easy. They need never know how difficult it had been, or how much it had cost her. That was a lesson Melisandre had learned long before Asshai; the more effortless the sorcery appears, the more men fear the sorcerer. When the flames had licked at Rattleshirt, the ruby at her throat had grown so hot that she had feared her own flesh might start to smoke and blacken. Thankfully Lord Snow had delivered her from that agony with his arrows. Whilst Stannis had seethed at the defiance, she had shuddered with relief.

"Our false king has a prickly manner," Melisandre told Jon Snow, "but he will not betray you. We hold his son, remember. And he owes you his very life."

"Me?" Snow sounded startled.

"Who else, my lord? Only his life's blood could pay for his crimes, your laws said, and Stannis Baratheon is not a man to go against the law . . . but as you said so sagely, the laws of men end at the Wall. I told you that the Lord of Light would hear your prayers. You wanted a way to save your little sister and still hold fast to the honor that means so much to you, to the vows you swore before your wooden god." She pointed with a pale finger. "There he stands, Lord Snow. Arya's deliverance. A gift from the Lord of Light . . . and me."

REEK

He heard the girls first, barking as they raced for home. The drum of hoofbeats echoing off flagstone jerked him to his feet, chains rattling. The one between his ankles was no more than a foot long, shortening his stride to a shuffle. It was hard to move quickly that way, but he tried as best he could, hopping and clanking from his pallet. Ramsay Bolton had returned and would want his Reek on hand to serve him.

Outside, beneath a cold autumnal sky, the hunters were pouring through the gates. Ben Bones led the way, with the girls baying and barking all around him. Behind came Skinner, Sour Alyn, and Damon Dance-for-Me with his long greased whip, then the Walders riding the grey colts Lady Dustin had given them. His lordship himself rode Blood, a red stallion with a temper to match his own. He was laughing. That could be very good or very bad, Reek knew.

The dogs were on him before he could puzzle out which, drawn to his scent. The dogs were fond of Reek; he slept with them oft as not, and sometimes Ben Bones let him share their supper. The pack raced across the flagstones barking, circling him, jumping up to lick his filthy face, nipping at his legs. Helicent caught his left hand between her teeth and worried it so fiercely Reek feared he might lose two more fingers. Red Jeyne slammed into his chest and knocked him off his feet. She was lean, hard muscle, where Reek was loose, grey skin and brittle bones, a white-haired starveling.

The riders were dismounting by the time he pushed Red Jeyne off and struggled to his knees. Two dozen horsemen had gone out and two dozen had returned, which meant the search had been a failure. That was bad. Ramsay did not like the taste of failure. *He will want to hurt someone.*

Of late, his lord had been forced to restrain himself, for Barrowton was full of men House Bolton needed, and Ramsay knew to be careful around the Dustins and Ryswells and his fellow lordlings. With them he was always courteous and smiling. What he was behind closed doors was something else.

Ramsay Bolton was attired as befit the lord of the Hornwood and heir to the Dreadfort. His mantle was stitched together from wolfskins and clasped against the autumn chill by the yellowed teeth of the wolf's head on his right shoulder. On one hip he wore a falchion, its blade as thick and heavy as a cleaver; on the other a long dagger and a small curved flaying knife with a hooked point and a razor-sharp edge. All three blades had matched hilts of yellow bone. "Reek," his lordship called down from Blood's high saddle, "you stink. I can smell you clear across the yard."

"I know, my lord," Reek had to say. "I beg your pardon."

"I brought you a gift." Ramsay twisted, reached behind him, pulled something from his saddle, and flung it. "Catch!"

Between the chain, the fetters, and his missing fingers, Reek was clumsier than he had been before he learned his name. The head struck his maimed hands, bounced away from the stumps of his fingers, and landed at his feet, raining maggots. It was so crusted with dried blood as to be unrecognizable.

"I told you to catch it," said Ramsay. "Pick it up."

Reek tried to lift the head up by the ear. It was no good. The flesh was green and rotting, and the ear tore off between his fingers. Little Walder laughed, and a moment later all the other men were laughing too. "Oh, leave him be," said Ramsay. "Just see to Blood. I rode the bastard hard."

"Yes, my lord. I will." Reek hurried to the horse, leaving the severed head for the dogs.

"You smell like pigshit today, Reek," said Ramsay.

"On him, that's an improvement," said Damon Dance-for-Me, smiling as he coiled his whip.

Little Walder swung down from the saddle. "You can see to my horse too, Reek. And to my little cousin's."

"I can see to my own horse," said Big Walder. Little Walder had become Lord Ramsay's best boy and grew more like him every day, but the smaller Frey was made of different stuff and seldom took part in his cousin's games and cruelties.

Reek paid the squires no mind. He led Blood off toward the stables, hopping aside when the stallion tried to kick him. The hunters strode into the hall, all but Ben Bones, who was cursing at the dogs to stop them fighting over the severed head.

Big Walder followed him into the stables, leading his own mount. Reek stole a look at him as he removed Blood's bit. "Who was he?" he said softly, so the other stablehands would not hear.

"No one." Big Walder pulled the saddle off his grey. "An old man we met on the road, is all. He was driving an old nanny goat and four kids."

"His lordship slew him for his goats?"

"His lordship slew him for calling him Lord Snow. The goats were good, though. We milked the mother and roasted up the kids."

Lord Snow. Reek nodded, his chains clinking as he wrestled with Blood's saddle straps. *By any name, Ramsay's no man to be around when he is in a rage. Or when he's not.* "Did you find your cousins, my lord?"

"No. I never thought we would. They're dead. Lord Wyman had them killed. That's what I would have done if I was him."

Reek said nothing. Some things were not safe to say, not even in the stables with his lordship in the hall. One wrong word could cost him another toe, even a finger. *Not my tongue, though. He will never take my tongue. He likes to hear me plead with him to spare me from the pain. He likes to make me say it.*

The riders had been sixteen days on the hunt, with only hard bread and salt beef to eat, aside from the occasional stolen kid, so that night Lord Ramsay commanded that a feast be laid to celebrate his return to Barrow-ton. Their host, a grizzled one-armed petty lord by the name of Harwood Stout, knew better than to refuse him, though by now his larders must be well nigh exhausted. Reek had heard Stout's servants muttering at how the Bastard and his men were eating through the winter stores. "He'll bed Lord Eddard's little girl, they say," Stout's cook complained when she did not know that Reek was listening, "but we're the ones who'll be fucked when the snows come, you mark my words."

Yet Lord Ramsay had decreed a feast, so feast they must. Trestle tables were set up in Stout's hall, an ox was slaughtered, and that night as the sun went down the empty-handed hunters ate roasts and ribs, barley bread, a mash of carrots and pease, washing it all down with prodigious quantities of ale.

It fell to Little Walder to keep Lord Ramsay's cup filled, whilst Big Walder poured for the others at the high table. Reek was chained up be-side the doors lest his odor put the feasters off their appetites. He would eat later, off whatever scraps Lord Ramsay thought to send him. The dogs enjoyed the run of the hall, however, and provided the night's best enter-tainment, when Maude and Grey Jeyne tore into one of Lord Stout's hounds over an especially meaty bone that Will Short had tossed them. Reek was the only man in the hall who did not watch the three dogs fight. He kept his eyes on Ramsay Bolton.

The fight did not end until their host's dog was dead. Stout's old hound never stood a mummer's chance. He had been one against two, and Ramsay's bitches were young, strong, and savage. Ben Bones, who liked the dogs better than their master, had told Reek they were all named after peasant girls Ramsay had hunted, raped, and killed back when he'd still been a bastard, running with the first Reek. "The ones who give him good sport, anywise. The ones who weep and beg and won't run don't get to come back as bitches." The next litter to come out of the Dreadfort's kennels would include a Kyra, Reek did not doubt. "He's trained 'em to kill wolves as well," Ben Bones had confided. Reek said nothing. He knew which wolves the girls were meant to kill, but he had no wish to watch the girls fighting over his severed toe.

Two serving men were carrying off the dead dog's carcass and an old woman had fetched out a mop and rake and bucket to deal with the blood-soaked rushes when the doors to the hall flew open in a wash of wind, and a dozen men in grey mail and iron halfhelms stalked through, shouldering past Stout's pasty-faced young guards in their leather brigandines and cloaks of gold and russet. A sudden silence seized the feasters . . . all but Lord Ramsay, who tossed aside the bone he had been gnawing, wiped his mouth on his sleeve, smiled a greasy, wet-lipped smile, and said, "Father."

The Lord of the Dreadfort glanced idly at the remnants of the feast, at the dead dog, at the hangings on the walls, at Reek in his chains and fetters. "Out," he told the feasters, in a voice as soft as a murmur. "Now. The lot of you."

Lord Ramsay's men pushed back from the tables, abandoning cups and trenchers. Ben Bones shouted at the girls, and they trotted after him, some with bones still in their jaws. Harwood Stout bowed stiffly and relinquished his hall without a word. "Unchain Reek and take him with you," Ramsay growled at Sour Alyn, but his father waved a pale hand and said, "No, leave him."

Even Lord Roose's own guards retreated, pulling the doors shut behind them. When the echo died away, Reek found himself alone in the hall with the two Boltons, father and son.

"You did not find our missing Freys." The way Roose Bolton said it, it was more a statement than a question.

"We rode back to where Lord Lamprey claims they parted ways, but the girls could not find a trail."

"You asked after them in villages and holdfasts."

"A waste of words. The peasants might as well be blind for all they ever see." Ramsay shrugged. "Does it matter? The world won't miss a few Freys. There's plenty more down at the Twins should we ever have need of one."

Lord Roose tore a small piece off a heel of bread and ate it. "Hosteen and Aenys are distressed."

"Let them go looking, if they like."

"Lord Wyman blames himself. To hear him tell it, he had become especially fond of Rhaegar."

Lord Ramsay was turning wroth. Reek could see it in his mouth, the curl of those thick lips, the way the cords stood up in his neck. "The fools should have stayed with Manderly."

Roose Bolton shrugged. "Lord Wyman's litter moves at a snail's pace . . . and of course his lordship's health and girth do not permit him to travel more than a few hours a day, with frequent stops for meals. The Freys were anxious to reach Barrowton and be reunited with their kin. Can you blame them for riding on ahead?"

"If that's what they did. Do you believe Manderly?"

His father's pale eyes glittered. "Did I give you that impression? Still. His lordship is most distraught."

"Not so distraught that he can't eat. Lord Pig must have brought half the food in White Harbor with him."

"Forty wayns full of foodstuffs. Casks of wine and hippocras, barrels of fresh-caught lampreys, a herd of goats, a hundred pigs, crates of crabs and oysters, a monstrous codfish . . . Lord Wyman likes to eat. You may have noticed."

"What I noticed was that he brought no hostages."

"I noticed that as well."

"What do you mean to do about it?"

"It is a quandary." Lord Roose found an empty cup, wiped it out on the tablecloth, and filled it from a flagon. "Manderly is not alone in throwing feasts, it would seem."

"It should have been you who threw the feast, to welcome me back," Ramsay complained, "and it should have been in Barrow Hall, not this pisspot of a castle."

"Barrow Hall and its kitchens are not mine to dispose of," his father said mildly. "I am only a guest there. The castle and the town belong to Lady Dustin, and she cannot abide you."

Ramsay's face darkened. "If I cut off her teats and feed them to my girls, will she abide me then? Will she abide me if I strip off her skin to make myself a pair of boots?"

"Unlikely. And those boots would come dear. They would cost us Barrowton, House Dustin, and the Ryswells." Roose Bolton seated himself across the table from his son. "Barbrey Dustin is my second wife's younger sister, Rodrik Ryswell's daughter, sister to Roger, Rickard, and mine own namesake, Roose, cousin to the other Ryswells. She was fond of my late son and suspects you of having some part in his demise. Lady Barbrey is a woman who knows how to nurse a grievance. Be grateful for that. Barrowton is staunch for Bolton largely because she still holds Ned Stark to blame for her husband's death."

"*Staunch?*" Ramsay seethed. "All she does is spit on me. The day will come when I'll set her precious wooden town afire. Let her spit on that, see if it puts out the flames."

Roose made a face, as if the ale he was sipping had suddenly gone sour. "There are times you make me wonder if you truly are my seed. My forebears were many things, but never fools. No, be quiet now, I have heard enough. We appear strong for the moment, yes. We have powerful friends in the Lannisters and Freys, and the grudging support of much of the north . . . but what do you imagine is going to happen when one of Ned Stark's sons turns up?"

Ned Stark's sons are all dead, Reek thought. *Robb was murdered at the Twins, and Bran and Rickon . . . we dipped the heads in tar . . .* His own head was pounding. He did not want to think about anything that had happened before he knew his name. There were things too hurtful to remember, thoughts almost as painful as Ramsay's flaying knife . . .

"Stark's little wolflings are dead," said Ramsay, sloshing some more ale into his cup, "and they'll stay dead. Let them show their ugly faces, and my girls will rip those wolves of theirs to pieces. The sooner they turn up, the sooner I kill them again."

The elder Bolton sighed. "*Again?* Surely you misspeak. You never slew Lord Eddard's sons, those two sweet boys we loved so well. That was Theon Turncloak's work, remember? How many of our grudging friends do you imagine we'd retain if the truth were known? Only Lady Barbrey, whom you would turn into a pair of boots . . . *inferior* boots. Human skin is not as tough as cowhide and will not wear as well. By the king's decree you are now a Bolton. Try and act like one. Tales are told of you, Ramsay. I hear them everywhere. People fear you."

"Good."

"You are mistaken. It is not good. No tales were ever told of me. Do you think I would be sitting here if it were otherwise? Your amusements are your own, I will not chide you on that count, but you must be more discreet. A peaceful land, a quiet people. That has always been my rule. Make it yours."

"Is this why you left Lady Dustin and your fat pig wife? So you could come down here and tell me to be *quiet*?"

"Not at all. There are tidings that you need to hear. Lord Stannis has finally left the Wall."

That got Ramsay halfway to his feet, a smile glistening on his wide, wet lips. "Is he marching on the Dreadfort?"

"He is not, alas. Arnolf does not understand it. He swears that he did all he could to bait the trap."

"I wonder. Scratch a Karstark and you'll find a Stark."

"After the scratch the Young Wolf gave Lord Rickard, that may be somewhat less true than formerly. Be that as it may. Lord Stannis has taken Deepwood Motte from the ironmen and restored it to House Glover. Worse, the mountain clans have joined him, Wull and Norrey and Liddle and the rest. His strength is growing."

"Ours is greater."

"Now it is."

"Now is the time to smash him. Let me march on Deepwood."

"After you are wed."

Ramsay slammed down his cup, and the dregs of his ale erupted across the tablecloth. "I'm sick of waiting. We have a girl, we have a tree, and we have lords enough to witness. I'll wed her on the morrow, plant a son between her legs, and march before her maiden's blood has dried."

She'll pray for you to march, Reek thought, *and she'll pray that you never come back to her bed.*

"You will plant a son in her," Roose Bolton said, "but not here. I've decided you shall wed the girl at Winterfell."

That prospect did not appear to please Lord Ramsay. "I laid waste to Winterfell, or had you forgotten?"

"No, but it appears you have . . . the *ironmen* laid waste to Winterfell, and butchered all its people. Theon Turncloak."

Ramsay gave Reek a suspicious glance. "Aye, so he did, but still . . . a wedding in that ruin?"

"Even ruined and broken, Winterfell remains Lady Arya's home. What better place to wed her, bed her, and stake your claim? That is only half of it, however. We would be fools to march on Stannis. Let Stannis march on us. He is too cautious to come to Barrowton . . . but he *must* come to Winterfell. His clansmen will not abandon the daughter of their precious Ned to such as you. Stannis must march or lose them . . . and being the careful commander that he is, he will summon all his friends and allies when he marches. He will summon Arnolf Karstark."

Ramsay licked his chapped lips. "And we'll have him."

"If the gods will it." Roose rose to his feet. "You'll wed at Winterfell. I shall inform the lords that we march in three days and invite them to accompany us."

"You are the Warden of the North. Command them."

"An invitation will accomplish the same thing. Power tastes best when sweetened by courtesy. You had best learn that if you ever hope to rule." The Lord of the Dreadfort glanced at Reek. "Oh, and unchain your pet. I am taking him."

"Taking him? Where? He's mine. You cannot have him."

Roose seemed amused by that. "All you have I gave you. You would do well to remember that, bastard. As for this . . . Reek . . . if you have not ruined him beyond redemption, he may yet be of some use to us. Get the keys and remove those chains from him, before you make me rue the day I raped your mother."

Reek saw the way Ramsay's mouth twisted, the spittle glistening between his lips. He feared he might leap the table with his dagger in his hand. Instead he flushed red, turned his pale eyes from his father's paler ones, and went to find the keys. But as he knelt to unlock the fetters around Reek's wrists and ankles, he leaned close and whispered, "Tell him nothing and remember every word he says. I'll have you back, no matter what that Dustin bitch may tell you. Who are you?"

"Reek, my lord. Your man. I'm Reek, it rhymes with sneak."

"It does. When my father brings you back, I'm going to take another finger. I'll let you choose which one."

Unbidden, tears began to trickle down his cheeks. "*Why?*" he cried, his voice breaking. "I never asked for him to take me from you. I'll do whatever you want, serve, obey, I . . . please, no . . ."

Ramsay slapped his face. "Take him," he told his father. "He's not even a man. The way he smells disgusts me."

The moon was rising over the wooden walls of Barrowton when they stepped outside. Reek could hear the wind sweeping across the rolling plains beyond the town. It was less than a mile from Barrow Hall to Harwood Stout's modest keep beside the eastern gates. Lord Bolton offered him a horse. "Can you ride?"

"I . . . my lord, I . . . I think so."

"Walton, help him mount."

Even with the fetters gone, Reek moved like an old man. His flesh hung loosely on his bones, and Sour Alyn and Ben Bones said he twitched. And his smell . . . even the mare they'd brought for him shied away when he tried to mount.

She was a gentle horse, though, and she knew the way to Barrow Hall. Lord Bolton fell in beside him as they rode out the gate. The guards fell back to a discreet distance. "What would you have me call you?" the lord asked, as they trotted down the broad straight streets of Barrowton.

Reek, I'm Reek, it rhymes with wreak. "Reek," he said, "if it please my lord."

"*M'lord.*" Bolton's lips parted just enough to show a quarter inch of teeth. It might have been a smile.

He did not understand. "My lord? I said—"

"—*my lord,* when you should have said *m'lord.* Your tongue betrays your birth with every word you say. If you want to sound a proper peasant, say it as if you had mud in your mouth, or were too stupid to realize it was two words, not just one."

"If it please my—m'lord."

"Better. Your stench *is* quite appalling."

"Yes, m'lord. I beg your pardon, m'lord."

"Why? The way you smell is my son's doing, not your own. I am well aware of that." They rode past a stable and a shuttered inn with a wheat sheaf painted on its sign. Reek heard music coming through its windows. "I knew the first Reek. He stank, though not for want of washing. I have never known a cleaner creature, truth be told. He bathed thrice a day and wore flowers in his hair as if he were a maiden. Once, when my second wife was still alive, he was caught stealing scent from her bedchamber. I had him whipped for that, a dozen lashes. Even his blood smelled wrong. The next year he tried it again. This time he drank the perfume and almost died of it. It made no matter. The smell was something he was born with. A curse, the smallfolk said. The gods had made him stink so that men would know his soul was rotting. My old maester insisted it was a sign of sickness, yet the boy was otherwise as strong as a young bull. No one could stand to be near him, so he slept with the pigs . . . until the day that Ramsay's mother appeared at my gates to demand that I provide a servant for my bastard, who was growing up wild and unruly. I gave her Reek. It was meant to be amusing, but he and Ramsay became inseparable. I do wonder, though . . . was it Ramsay who corrupted Reek, or Reek Ramsay?" His lordship glanced at the new Reek with eyes as pale and strange as two white moons. "What was he whispering whilst he unchained you?"

"He . . . he said . . ." *He said to tell you nothing.* The words caught in his throat, and he began to cough and choke.

"Breathe deep. I know what he said. You're to spy on me and keep his secrets." Bolton chuckled. "As if he had secrets. Sour Alyn, Luton, Skinner, and the rest, where does he think they came from? Can he truly believe they are *his* men?"

"His men," Reek echoed. Some comment seemed to be expected of him, but he did not know what to say.

"Has my bastard ever told you how I got him?"

That he *did* know, to his relief. "Yes, my . . . *m'lord.* You met his mother whilst out riding and were smitten by her beauty."

"Smitten?" Bolton laughed. "Did he use that word? Why, the boy has a singer's soul . . . though if you believe that song, you may well be dimmer than the first Reek. Even the riding part is wrong. I was hunting a fox along the Weeping Water when I chanced upon a mill and saw a young woman washing clothes in the stream. The old miller had gotten himself a new young wife, a girl not half his age. She was a tall, willowy creature, very *healthy*-looking. Long legs and small firm breasts, like two ripe plums. Pretty, in a common sort of way. The moment that I set eyes on her I wanted her. Such was my due. The maesters will tell you that King Jaehaerys abolished the lord's right to the first night to appease his shrewish queen, but where the old gods rule, old customs linger. The Umbers keep the first night too, deny it as they may. Certain of the mountain clans as well, and on Skagos . . . well, only heart trees ever see half of what they do on Skagos.

"This miller's marriage had been performed without my leave or knowledge. The man had cheated me. So I had him hanged, and claimed my rights beneath the tree where he was swaying. If truth be told, the wench was hardly worth the rope. The fox escaped as well, and on our way back to the Dreadfort my favorite courser came up lame, so all in all it was a dismal day.

"A year later this same wench had the impudence to turn up at the Dreadfort with a squalling, red-faced monster that she claimed was my own get. I should've had the mother whipped and thrown her child down a well . . . but the babe *did* have my eyes. She told me that when her dead husband's brother saw those eyes, he beat her bloody and drove her from the mill. That annoyed me, so I gave her the mill and had the brother's tongue cut out, to make certain he did not go running to Winterfell with tales that might disturb Lord Rickard. Each year I sent the woman some piglets and chickens and a bag of stars, on the understanding that she was never to tell the boy who had fathered him. A peaceful land, a quiet people, that has always been my rule."

"A fine rule, m'lord."

"The woman disobeyed me, though. You see what Ramsay is. She made him, her and Reek, always whispering in his ear about his rights. He should have been content to grind corn. Does he truly think that he can ever rule the north?"

"He fights for you," Reek blurted out. "He's strong."

"Bulls are strong. Bears. I have seen my bastard fight. He is not entirely to blame. Reek was his tutor, the first Reek, and Reek was never trained at arms. Ramsay is ferocious, I will grant you, but he swings that sword like a butcher hacking meat."

"He's not afraid of anyone, m'lord."

"He should be. Fear is what keeps a man alive in this world of treachery and deceit. Even here in Barrowton the crows are circling, waiting to feast upon our flesh. The Cerwyns and the Tallharts are not to be relied on, my fat friend Lord Wyman plots betrayal, and Whoresbane . . . the Umbers may seem simple, but they are not without a certain low cunning. Ramsay should fear them all, as I do. The next time you see him, tell him that."

"Tell him . . . tell him to be afraid?" Reek felt ill at the very thought of it. "M'lord, I . . . if I did that, he'd . . ."

"I know." Lord Bolton sighed. "His blood is bad. He needs to be leeched. The leeches suck away the bad blood, all the rage and pain. No man can think so full of anger. Ramsay, though . . . his tainted blood would poison even leeches, I fear."

"He is your only son."

"For the moment. I had another, once. Domeric. A quiet boy, but most accomplished. He served four years as Lady Dustin's page, and three in the Vale as a squire to Lord Redfort. He played the high harp, read histories, and rode like the wind. Horses . . . the boy was mad for horses, Lady Dustin will tell you. Not even Lord Rickard's daughter could outrace him, and that one was half a horse herself. Redfort said he showed great promise in the lists. A great jouster must be a great horseman first."

"Yes, m'lord. Domeric. I . . . I have heard his name . . ."

"Ramsay killed him. A sickness of the bowels, Maester Uthor says, but I say poison. In the Vale, Domeric had enjoyed the company of Redfort's sons. He wanted a brother by his side, so he rode up the Weeping Water to seek my bastard out. I forbade it, but Domeric was a man grown and thought that he knew better than his father. Now his bones lie beneath the Dreadfort with the bones of his brothers, who died still in the cradle, and I am left with Ramsay. Tell me, my lord . . . if the kinslayer is accursed, what is a father to do when one son slays another?"

The question frightened him. Once he had heard Skinner say that the Bastard had killed his trueborn brother, but he had never dared to believe it. *He could be wrong. Brothers die sometimes, it does not mean that they were killed. My brothers died, and I never killed them.* "My lord has a new wife to give him sons."

"And won't my bastard love that? Lady Walda *is* a Frey, and she has a fertile feel to her. I have become oddly fond of my fat little wife. The two before her never made a sound in bed, but this one squeals and shudders. I find that quite endearing. If she pops out sons the way she pops in tarts, the Dreadfort will soon be overrun with Boltons. Ramsay will kill them all, of course. That's for the best. I will not live long enough to see new sons to manhood, and boy lords are the bane of any House. Walda will grieve to see them die, though."

Reek's throat was dry. He could hear the wind rattling the bare branches of the elms that lined the street. "My lord, I—"

"*M'lord*, remember?"

"M'lord. If I might ask . . . why did you want me? I'm no use to anyone, I'm not even a man, I'm broken, and . . . the smell . . ."

"A bath and change of clothes will make you smell sweeter."

"A bath?" Reek felt a clenching in his guts. "I . . . I would sooner not, m'lord. Please. I have . . . wounds, I . . . and these clothes, Lord Ramsay gave them to me, he . . . he said that I was never to take them off, save at his command . . ."

"You are wearing rags," Lord Bolton said, quite patiently. "Filthy things, torn and stained and stinking of blood and urine. And thin. You must be cold. We'll put you in lambswool, soft and warm. Perhaps a fur-lined cloak. Would you like that?"

"No." He could not let them take the clothes Lord Ramsay gave him. He could not let them *see* him.

"Would you prefer to dress in silk and velvet? There was a time when you were fond of such, I do recall."

"*No*," he insisted, shrilly. "No, I only want these clothes. Reek's clothes. I'm Reek, it rhymes with peek." His heart was beating like a drum, and his voice rose to a frightened squeak. "I don't want a bath. Please, m'lord, don't take my clothes."

"Will you let us wash them, at least?"

"No. No, m'lord. *Please.*" He clutched his tunic to his chest with both hands and hunched down in the saddle, half-afraid that Roose Bolton might command his guardsmen to tear the clothes off him right there in the street.

"As you wish." Bolton's pale eyes looked empty in the moonlight, as if there were no one behind them at all. "I mean you no harm, you know. I owe you much and more."

"You do?" Some part of him was screaming, *This is a trap, he is playing with you, the son is just the shadow of the father.* Lord Ramsay played with his hopes all the time. "What . . . what do you owe me, m'lord?"

"The north. The Starks were done and doomed the night that you took Winterfell." He waved a pale hand, dismissive. "All this is only squabbling over spoils."

Their short journey reached its end at the wooden walls of Barrow Hall. Banners flew from its square towers, flapping in the wind: the flayed man of the Dreadfort, the battle-axe of Cerwyn, Tallhart's pines, the merman of Manderly, old Lord Locke's crossed keys, the Umber giant and the stony hand of Flint, the Hornwood moose. For the Stouts, chevrony russet and gold, for Slate, a grey field within a double tressure white. Four horseheads proclaimed the four Ryswells of the Rills—one grey, one black, one gold, one brown. The jape was that the Ryswells could not even agree upon the color of their arms. Above them streamed the stag-and-lion of the boy who sat upon the Iron Throne a thousand leagues away.

Reek listened to the vanes turning on the old windmill as they rode beneath the gatehouse into a grassy courtyard where stableboys ran out to take their horses. "This way, if you please." Lord Bolton led him toward the keep, where the banners were those of the late Lord Dustin and his widowed wife. His showed a spiked crown above crossed longaxes; hers quartered those same arms with Rodrik Ryswell's golden horsehead.

As he climbed a wide flight of wooden steps to the hall, Reek's legs began to shake. He had to stop to steady them, staring up at the grassy slopes of the Great Barrow. Some claimed it was the grave of the First King, who had led the First Men to Westeros. Others argued that it must be some King of the Giants who was buried there, to account for its size. A few had even been known to say it was no barrow, just a hill, but if so it was a lonely hill, for most of the barrowlands were flat and windswept.

Inside the hall, a woman stood beside the hearth, warming thin hands above the embers of a dying fire. She was clad all in black, from head to heel, and wore no gold nor gems, but she was highborn, that was plain to see. Though there were wrinkles at the corners of her mouth and more around her eyes, she still stood tall, unbent, and handsome. Her hair was brown and grey in equal parts and she wore it tied behind her head in a widow's knot.

"Who is this?" she said. "Where is the boy? Did your bastard refuse to give him up? Is this old man his . . . oh, gods be good, what is that *smell*? Has this creature soiled himself?"

"He has been with Ramsay. Lady Barbrey, allow me to present the rightful Lord of the Iron Islands, Theon of House Greyjoy."

No, he thought, *no, don't say that name, Ramsay will hear you, he'll know, he'll know, he'll hurt me.*

Her mouth pursed. "He is not what I expected."

"He is what we have."

"What did your bastard do to him?"

"Removed some skin, I would imagine. A few small parts. Nothing too essential."

"Is he mad?"

"He may be. Does it matter?"

Reek could hear no more. "Please, m'lord, m'lady, there's been some mistake." He fell to his knees, trembling like a leaf in a winter storm, tears streaming down his ravaged cheeks. "I'm not him, I'm not the turncloak, he died at Winterfell. My name is Reek." He had to remember his *name.* "It rhymes with freak."

TYRION

The *Selaesori Qhoran* was seven days from Volantis when Penny finally emerged from her cabin, creeping up on deck like some timid woodland creature emerging from a long winter's sleep.

It was dusk and the red priest had lit his nightfire in the great iron brazier amidships as the crew gathered round to pray. Moqorro's voice was a bass drum that seemed to boom from somewhere deep within his massive torso. *"We thank you for your sun that keeps us warm,"* he prayed. *"We thank you for your stars that watch over us as we sail this cold black sea."* A huge man, taller than Ser Jorah and wide enough to make two of him, the priest wore scarlet robes embroidered at sleeve and hem and collar with orange satin flames. His skin was black as pitch, his hair as white as snow; the flames tattooed across his cheeks and brow yellow and orange. His iron staff was as tall as he was and crowned with a dragon's head; when he stamped its butt upon the deck, the dragon's maw spat crackling green flame.

His guardsmen, five slave warriors of the Fiery Hand, led the responses. They chanted in the tongue of Old Volantis, but Tyrion had heard the prayers enough to grasp the essence. *Light our fire and protect us from the dark, blah blah, light our way and keep us toasty warm, the night is dark and full of terrors, save us from the scary things, and blah blah blah some more.*

He knew better than to voice such thoughts aloud. Tyrion Lannister had no use for any god, but on this ship it was wise to show a certain respect for red R'hllor. Jorah Mormont had removed Tyron's chains and fetters once they were safely under way, and the dwarf did not wish to give him cause to clap them on again.

The *Selaesori Qhoran* was a wallowing tub of five hundred tons, with a deep hold, high castles fore and aft, and a single mast between. At her

forecastle stood a grotesque figurehead, some worm-eaten wooden emi-
nence with a constipated look and a scroll tucked up under one arm.
Tyrion had never seen an uglier ship. Her crew was no prettier. Her captain, a mean-mouthed, flinty, kettle-bellied man with close-set, greedy
eyes, was a bad *cyvasse* player and a worse loser. Under him served four
mates, freedmen all, and fifty slaves bound to the ship, each with a crude
version of the cog's figurehead tattooed upon one cheek. *No-Nose*, the
sailors liked to call Tyrion, no matter how many times he told them his
name was Hugor Hill.

Three of the mates and more than three-quarters of the crew were fer-
vent worshipers of the Lord of Light. Tyrion was less certain about the
captain, who always emerged for the evening prayers but took no other
part in them. But Moqorro was the true master of the *Selaesori Qhoran*, at
least for this voyage.

"*Lord of Light, bless your slave Moqorro, and light his way in the dark
places of the world*," the red priest boomed. "*And defend your righteous
slave Benerro. Grant him courage. Grant him wisdom. Fill his heart with
fire.*"

That was when Tyrion noticed Penny, watching the mummery from
the steep wooden stair that led down beneath the sterncastle. She stood
on one of the lower steps, so only the top of her head was visible. Beneath
her hood her eyes shone big and white in the light of the nightfire. She
had her dog with her, the big grey hound she rode in the mock jousts.

"My lady," Tyrion called softly. In truth, she was no lady, but he could
not bring himself to mouth that silly name of hers, and he was not about
to call her *girl* or *dwarf*.

She cringed back. "I . . . I did not see you."

"Well, I am small."

"I . . . I was unwell . . ." Her dog barked.

Sick with grief, you mean. "If I can be of help . . ."

"No." And quick as that she was gone again, retreating back below to
the cabin she shared with her dog and sow. Tyrion could not fault her.
The crew of the *Selaesori Qhoran* had been pleased enough when he first
came on board; a dwarf was good luck, after all. His head had been rubbed
so often and so vigorously that it was a wonder he wasn't bald. But Penny
had met with a more mixed reaction. She might be a dwarf, but she was
also a woman, and women were bad luck aboard ship. For every man who
tried to rub her head, there were three who muttered maledictions under
their breath when she went by.

And the sight of me can only be salt in her wound. They hacked off her brother's head in the hope that it was mine, yet here I sit like some bloody gargoyle, offering empty consolations. If I were her, I'd want nothing more than to shove me into the sea.

He felt nothing but pity for the girl. She did not deserve the horror visited on her in Volantis, any more than her brother had. The last time he had seen her, just before they left port, her eyes had been raw from crying, two ghastly red holes in a wan, pale face. By the time they raised sail she had locked herself in her cabin with her dog and her pig, but at night they could hear her weeping. Only yesterday he had heard one of the mates say that they ought to throw her overboard before her tears could swamp the ship. Tyrion was not entirely sure he had been japing.

When the evening prayers had ended and the ship's crew had once again dispersed, some to their watch and others to food and rum and hammocks, Moqorro remained beside his nightfire, as he did every night. The red priest rested by day but kept vigil through the dark hours, to tend his sacred flames so that the sun might return to them at dawn.

Tyrion squatted across from him and warmed his hands against the night's chill. Moqorro took no notice of him for several moments. He was staring into the flickering flames, lost in some vision. *Does he see days yet to come, as he claims?* If so, that was a fearsome gift. After a time the priest raised his eyes to meet the dwarf's. "Hugor Hill," he said, inclining his head in a solemn nod. "Have you come to pray with me?"

"Someone told me that the night is dark and full of terrors. What do you see in those flames?"

"Dragons," Moqorro said in the Common Tongue of Westeros. He spoke it very well, with hardly a trace of accent. No doubt that was one reason the high priest Benerro had chosen him to bring the faith of R'hllor to Daenerys Targaryen. "Dragons old and young, true and false, bright and dark. And you. A small man with a big shadow, snarling in the midst of all."

"Snarling? An amiable fellow like me?" Tyrion was almost flattered. *And no doubt that is just what he intends. Every fool loves to hear that he's important.* "Perhaps it was Penny you saw. We're almost of a size."

"No, my friend."

My friend? When did that happen, I wonder? "Did you see how long it will take us to reach Meereen?"

"You are eager to behold the world's deliverer?"

Yes and no. The world's deliverer may snick off my head or give me to her dragons as a savory. "Not me," said Tyrion. "For me, it is all about the olives. Though I fear I may grow old and die before I taste one. I could dog-paddle faster than we're sailing. Tell me, was *Selaesori Qhoran* a tri-arch or a turtle?"

The red priest chuckled. "Neither. *Qhoran* is . . . not a ruler, but one who serves and counsels such, and helps conduct his business. You of Westeros might say *steward* or *magister*."

King's Hand? That amused him. "And *selaesori*?"

Moqorro touched his nose. "Imbued with a pleasant aroma. Fragrant, would you say? Flowery?"

"So *Selaesori Qhoran* means *Stinky Steward*, more or less?"

"*Fragrant Steward*, rather."

Tyrion gave a crooked grin. "I believe I will stay with *Stinky*. But I do thank you for the lesson."

"I am pleased to have enlightened you. Perhaps someday you will let me teach you the truth of R'hllor as well."

"Someday." *When I am a head on a spike.*

The quarters he shared with Ser Jorah were a cabin only by courtesy; the dank, dark, foul-smelling closet had barely enough space to hang a pair of sleeping hammocks, one above the other. He found Mormont stretched out in the lower one, swaying slowly with the motion of the ship. "The girl finally poked her nose abovedecks," Tyrion told him. "One look at me and she scurried right back down below."

"You're not a pretty sight."

"Not all of us can be as comely as you. The girl is lost. It would not surprise me if the poor creature wasn't sneaking up to jump over the side and drown herself."

"The poor creature's name is Penny."

"I know her name." He hated her name. Her brother had gone by the name of Groat, though his true name had been Oppo. *Groat and Penny. The smallest coins, worth the least, and what's worse, they chose the names themselves.* It left a bad taste in Tyrion's mouth. "By any name, she needs a friend."

Ser Jorah sat up in his hammock. "Befriend her, then. Marry her, for all I care."

That left a bad taste in his mouth as well. "Like with like, is that your notion? Do you mean to find a she-bear for yourself, ser?"

"You were the one who insisted that we bring her."

"I said we could not abandon her in Volantis. That does not mean I want to fuck her. She wants me dead, have you forgotten? I'm the last person she's like to want as a friend."

"You're both dwarfs."

"Yes, and so was her brother, who was killed because some drunken fools took him for me."

"Feeling guilty, are you?"

"No." Tyrion bristled. "I have sins enough to answer for; I'll have no part of this one. I might have nurtured some ill will toward her and her brother for the part they played the night of Joffrey's wedding, but I never wished them harm."

"You are a harmless creature, to be sure. Innocent as a lamb." Ser Jorah got to his feet. "The dwarf girl is your burden. Kiss her, kill her, or avoid her, as you like. It's naught to me." He shouldered past Tyrion and out of the cabin.

Twice exiled, and small wonder, Tyrion thought. *I'd exile him too if I could. The man is cold, brooding, sullen, deaf to humor. And those are his good points.* Ser Jorah spent most of his waking hours pacing the forecastle or leaning on the rail, gazing out to sea. *Looking for his silver queen. Looking for Daenerys, willing the ship to sail faster. Well, I might do the same if Tysha waited in Meereen.*

Could Slaver's Bay be where whores went? It seemed unlikely. From what he'd read, the slaver cities were the place where whores were made. *Mormont should have bought one for himself.* A pretty slave girl might have done wonders to improve his temper . . . particularly one with silvery hair, like the whore who had been sitting on his cock back in Selhorys.

On the river Tyrion had to endure Griff, but there had at least been the mystery of the captain's true identity to divert him and the more congenial companionship of the rest of the poleboat's little company. On the cog, alas, everyone was just who they appeared to be, no one was particularly congenial, and only the red priest was interesting. *Him, and maybe Penny. But the girl hates me, and she should.*

Life aboard the *Selaesori Qhoran* was nothing if not tedious, Tyrion had found. The most exciting part of his day was pricking his toes and fingers with a knife. On the river there had been wonders to behold: giant turtles, ruined cities, stone men, naked septas. One never knew what might be lurking around the next bend. The days and nights at sea were all the same. Leaving Volantis, the cog had sailed within sight of land at first, so Tyrion could gaze at passing headlands, watch clouds of seabirds rise from stony cliffs and crumbling watchtowers, count bare brown islands as they slipped past. He saw many other ships as well: fishing boats, lumbering merchantmen, proud galleys with their oars lashing the waves into white foam. But once they struck out into deeper waters, there was only sea and sky, air and water. The water looked like water. The sky looked like sky. Sometimes there was a cloud. *Too much blue.*

And the nights were worse. Tyrion slept badly at the best of times, and this was far from that. Sleep meant dreams as like as not, and in his dreams the Sorrows waited, and a stony king with his father's face. That left him with the beggar's choice of climbing up into his hammock and listening to Jorah Mormont snore beneath him, or remaining abovedecks to contemplate the sea. On moonless nights the water was as black as maester's ink, from horizon to horizon. Dark and deep and forbidding, beautiful in a chilly sort of way, but when he looked at it too long Tyrion found himself musing on how easy it would be to slip over the gunwale and drop down into that darkness. One very small splash, and the pathetic little tale that was his life would soon be done. *But what if there is a hell and my father's waiting for me?*

The best part of each evening was supper. The food was not especially good, but it was plentiful, so that was where the dwarf went next. The galley where he took his meals was a cramped and uncomfortable space, with a ceiling so low that the taller passengers were always in danger of cracking their heads, a hazard the strapping slave soldiers of the Fiery Hand seemed particularly prone to. As much as Tyrion enjoyed sniggering at that, he had come to prefer taking his meals alone. Sitting at a crowded table with men who did not share a common language with you, listening to them talk and jape whilst understanding none of it, had quickly grown wearisome. Particularly since he always found himself wondering if the japes and laughter were directed at him.

The galley was also where the ship's books were kept. Her captain being an especially bookish man, she carried three—a collection of nautical poetry that went from bad to worse, a well-thumbed tome about the erotic adventures of a young slave girl in a Lysene pillow house, and the fourth and final volume of *The Life of the Triarch Belicho*, a famous Volantene patriot whose unbroken succession of conquests and triumphs ended rather abruptly when he was eaten by giants. Tyrion had finished them all by their third day at sea. Then, for lack of any other books, he started reading them again. The slave girl's story was the worst written but the most engrossing, and that was the one he took down this evening to see him through a supper of buttered beets, cold fish stew, and biscuits that could have been used to drive nails.

He was reading the girl's account of the day she and her sister were taken by slavers when Penny entered the galley. "Oh," she said, "I thought . . . I did not mean to disturb m'lord, I . . ."

"You are not disturbing me. You're not going to try to kill me again, I hope."

"No." She looked away, her face reddening.

"In that case, I would welcome some company. There's little enough aboard this ship." Tyrion closed the book. "Come. Sit. Eat." The girl had left most of her meals untouched outside her cabin door. By now she must be starving. "The stew is almost edible. The fish is fresh, at least."

"No, I . . . I choked on a fish bone once, I can't eat fish."

"Have some wine, then." He filled a cup and slid it toward her. "Compliments of our captain. Closer to piss than Arbor gold, if truth be told, but even piss tastes better than the black tar rum the sailors drink. It might help you sleep."

The girl made no move to touch the cup. "Thank you, m'lord, but no." She backed away. "I should not be bothering you."

"Do you mean to spend your whole life running away?" Tyrion asked before she could slip back out the door.

That stopped her. Her cheeks turned a bright pink, and he was afraid she was about to start weeping again. Instead she thrust out her lip defiantly and said, "You're running too."

"I am," he confessed, "but I am running *to* and you are running *from*, and there's a world of difference there."

"We would never have had to run at all but for you."

It took some courage to say that to my face. "Are you speaking of King's Landing or Volantis?"

"Both." Tears glistened in her eyes. "Everything. Why couldn't you just come joust with us, the way the king wanted? You wouldn't have gotten hurt. What would that have cost m'lord, to climb up on our dog and ride a tilt to please the boy? It was just a bit of fun. They would have laughed at you, that's all."

"They would have laughed at me," said Tyrion. *I made them laugh at Joff instead. And wasn't that a clever ploy?*

"My brother says that is a good thing, making people laugh. A *noble* thing, and honorable. My brother says . . . he . . ." The tears fell then, rolling down her face.

"I am sorry about your brother." Tyrion had said the same words to her before, back in Volantis, but she was so far gone in grief back there that he doubted she had heard them.

She heard them now. "Sorry. You are sorry." Her lip was trembling, her cheeks were wet, her eyes were red-rimmed holes. "We left King's Landing that very night. My brother said it was for the best, before someone wondered if we'd had some part in the king's death and decided to torture us to find out. We went to Tyrosh first. My brother thought that would be far enough, but it wasn't. We knew a juggler there. For years and years he would juggle every day by the Fountain of the Drunken God. He was old, so his hands were not as deft as they had been, and sometimes he would drop his balls and chase them across the square, but the Tyroshi would laugh and throw him coins all the same. Then one morning we heard that his body had been found at the Temple of Trios. Trios has three heads, and there's a big statue of him beside the temple doors. The old man had been cut into three parts and pushed inside the threefold mouths of Trios. Only when the parts were sewn back together, his head was gone."

"A gift for my sweet sister. He was another dwarf."

"A little man, aye. Like you, and Oppo. Groat. Are you sorry about the juggler too?"

"I never knew your juggler existed until this very moment . . . but yes, I am sorry he is dead."

"He died for you. His blood is on your hands."

The accusation stung, coming so hard on the heels of Jorah Mormont's words. "His blood is on my sister's hands, and the hands of the brutes who killed him. My hands . . ." Tyrion turned them over, inspected them, coiled them into fists. ". . . my hands are crusted with old blood, aye. Call me kinslayer, and you won't be wrong. Kingslayer, I'll answer to that one as well. I have killed mothers, fathers, nephews, lovers, men and women, kings and whores. A singer once annoyed me, so I had the bastard stewed. But I have never killed a juggler, nor a dwarf, and I am not to blame for what happened to your bloody brother."

Penny picked the cup of wine he'd poured for her and threw it in his face. *Just like my sweet sister.* He heard the galley door slam but never saw her leave. His eyes were stinging, and the world was a blur. *So much for befriending her.*

Tyrion Lannister had scant experience with other dwarfs. His lord father had not welcomed any reminders of his son's deformities, and such mummers as featured little folk in their troupes soon learned to stay away from Lannisport and Casterly Rock, at the risk of his displeasure. Growing up, Tyrion heard reports of a dwarf jester at the seat of the Dornish Lord Fowler, a dwarf maester in service on the Fingers, and a female dwarf amongst the silent sisters, but he never felt the least need to seek them out. Less reliable tales also reached his ears, of a dwarf witch who haunted a hill in the riverlands, and a dwarf whore in King's Landing renowned for coupling with dogs. His own sweet sister had told him of the last, even offering to find him a bitch in heat if he cared to try it out. When he asked politely if she were referring to herself, Cersei had thrown a cup of wine in his face. *That was red, as I recall, and this is gold.* Tyrion mopped at his face with a sleeve. His eyes still stung.

He did not see Penny again until the day of the storm.

The salt air lay still and heavy that morning, but the western sky was a fiery red, streaked with lowering clouds that glowed as bright as Lannister crimson. Sailors were dashing about battening hatches, running lines, clearing the decks, lashing down everything that was not already lashed down. "Bad wind coming," one warned him. "No-Nose should get below."

Tyrion remembered the storm he'd suffered crossing the narrow sea, the way the deck had jumped beneath his feet, the hideous creaking sounds the ship had made, the taste of wine and vomit. "No-Nose will stay up here." If the gods wanted him, he would sooner die by drowning than choking on his own vomit. And overhead the cog's canvas sail rippled slowly, like the fur of some great beast stirring from a long sleep, then filled with a sudden *crack* that turned every head on the ship.

The winds drove the cog before them, far off her chosen course. Behind them black clouds piled one atop another against a blood-red sky. By midmorning they could see lightning flickering to the west, followed by the distant crash of thunder. The sea grew rougher, and dark waves rose up to smash against the hull of the *Stinky Steward*. It was about then that the crew started hauling down the canvas. Tyrion was underfoot amidships, so he climbed the forecastle and hunkered down, savoring the lash of cold rain on his cheeks. The cog went up and down, bucking more wildly than any horse he'd ever ridden, lifting with each wave before sliding down into the troughs between, jarring him to the bones. Even so, it was better here where he could see than down below locked in some airless cabin.

By the time the storm broke, evening was upon them and Tyrion Lannister was soaked through to the smallclothes, yet somehow he felt elated . . . and even more so later, when he found a drunken Jorah Mormont in a pool of vomit in their cabin.

The dwarf lingered in the galley after supper, celebrating his survival by sharing a few tots of black tar rum with the ship's cook, a great greasy loutish Volantene who spoke only one word of the Common Tongue (*fuck*), but played a ferocious game of *cyvasse*, particularly when drunk. They played three games that night. Tyrion won the first, then lost the other two. After that he decided that he'd had enough and stumbled back up on deck to clear his head of rum and elephants alike.

He found Penny on the forecastle, where he had so often found Ser Jorah, standing by the rail beside the cog's hideous half-rotted figurehead and gazing out across the inky sea. From behind, she looked as small and vulnerable as a child.

Tyrion thought it best to leave her undisturbed, but it was too late. She had heard him. "Hugor Hill."

"If you like." *We both know better.* "I am sorry to intrude on you. I will retire."

"No." Her face was pale and sad, but she did not look to have been crying. "I'm sorry too. About the wine. It wasn't you who killed my brother or that poor old man in Tyrosh."

"I played a part, though not by choice."

"I miss him so much. My brother. I . . ."

"I understand." He found himself thinking of Jaime. *Count yourself lucky. Your brother died before he could betray you.*

"I thought I wanted to die," she said, "but today when the storm came and I thought the ship would sink, I . . . I . . ."

"You realized that you wanted to live after all." *I have been there too. Something else we have in common.*

Her teeth were crooked, which made her shy with her smiles, but she smiled now. "Did you truly cook a singer in a stew?"

"Who, me? No. I do not cook."

When Penny giggled, she sounded like the sweet young girl she was . . . seventeen, eighteen, no more than nineteen. "What did he do, this singer?"

"He wrote a song about me." *For she was his secret treasure, she was his shame and his bliss. And a chain and a keep are nothing, compared to a woman's kiss.* It was queer how quick the words came back to him. Perhaps they had never left him. *Hands of gold are always cold, but a woman's hands are warm.*

"It must have been a very bad song."

"Not really. It was no 'Rains of Castamere,' mind you, but some parts were . . . well . . ."

"How did it go?"

He laughed. "No. You do *not* want to hear me sing."

"My mother used to sing to us when we were children. My brother and me. She always said that it didn't matter what your voice was like so long as you loved the song."

"Was she . . . ?"

". . . a little person? No, but our father was. His own father sold him to a slaver when he was three, but he grew up to be such a famous mummer that he bought his freedom. He traveled to all the Free Cities, and Westeros as well. In Oldtown they used to call him Hop-Bean."

Of course they did. Tyrion tried not to wince.

"He's dead now," Penny went on. "My mother too. Oppo . . . he was my last family, and now he's gone too." She turned her head away and gazed out across the sea. "What will I do? Where will I go? I have no trade, just the jousting show, and that needs two."

No, thought Tyrion. *That is not a place you want to go, girl. Do not ask that of me. Do not even think it.* "Find yourself some likely orphan boy," he suggested.

Penny did not seem to hear that. "It was Father's idea to do the tilts. He even trained the first pig, but by then he was too sick to ride her, so Oppo took his place. I always rode the dog. We performed for the Sealord of Braavos once, and he laughed so hard that afterward he gave each of us a . . . a grand gift."

"Is that where my sister found you? In Braavos?"

"Your sister?" The girl looked lost.

"Queen Cersei."

Penny shook her head. "She never . . . it was a man who came to us, in Pentos. Osmund. No, Oswald. Something like that. Oppo met with him, not me. Oppo made all of our arrangements. My brother always knew what to do, where we should go next."

"Meereen is where we're going next."

She gave him a puzzled look. "Qarth, you mean. We're bound for Qarth, by way of New Ghis."

"Meereen. You'll ride your dog for the dragon queen and come away with your weight in gold. Best start eating more, so you'll be nice and plump when you joust before Her Grace."

Penny did not return the smile. "By myself, all I can do is ride around in circles. And even if the queen should laugh, where will I go afterward? We never stay in one place long. The first time they see us they laugh and laugh, but by the fourth or fifth time, they know what we're going to do before we do it. Then they stop laughing, so we have to go somewhere new. We make the most coin in the big cities, but I always liked the little towns the best. Places like that, the people have no silver, but they feed us at their own tables, and the children follow us everywhere."

That's because they have never seen a dwarf before, in their wretched pisspot towns, Tyrion thought. *The bloody brats would follow around a two-headed goat if one turned up. Until they got bored with its bleating and slaughtered it for supper.* But he had no wish to make her weep again, so instead he said, "Daenerys has a kind heart and a generous nature." It was what she needed to hear. "She will find a place for you at her court, I don't doubt. A safe place, beyond my sister's reach."

Penny turned back to him. "And you will be there too."

Unless Daenerys decides she needs some Lannister blood, to pay for the Targaryen blood my brother shed. "I will."

After that, the dwarf girl was seen more frequently above deck. The next day Tyrion encountered her and her spotted sow amidships in midafternoon, when the air was warm and the sea calm. "Her name is Pretty," the girl told him, shyly.

Pretty the pig and Penny the girl, he thought. *Someone has a deal to answer for.* Penny gave Tyrion some acorns, and he let Pretty eat them from his hand. *Do not think I don't see what you are doing, girl,* he thought, as the big sow snuffled and squealed.

Soon they began to take their meals together. Some nights it was just the two of them; at other meals they crowded in with Moqorro's guards. *The fingers,* Tyrion called them; they were men of the Fiery Hand, after all, and there were five of them. Penny laughed at that, a sweet sound, though not one that he heard often. Her wound was too fresh, her grief too deep.

He soon had her calling the ship the *Stinky Steward,* though she got somewhat wroth with him whenever he called Pretty *Bacon.* To atone for that Tyrion made an attempt to teach her *cyvasse,* though he soon realized that was a lost cause. "No," he said, a dozen times, "the dragon flies, not the elephants."

That same night, she came right out and asked him if he would like to tilt with her. "No," he answered. Only later did it occur to him that perhaps *tilt* did not mean tilt. His answer would still have been no, but he might not have been so brusque.

Back in the cabin he shared with Jorah Mormont, Tyrion twisted in his hammock for hours, slipping in and out of sleep. His dreams were full of grey, stony hands reaching for him from out of the fog, and a stair that led up to his father.

Finally he gave it up and made his way up top for a breath of night air. The *Selaesori Qhoran* had furled her big striped sail for the night, and her decks were all but deserted. One of the mates was on the sterncastle, and amidships Moqorro sat by his brazier, where a few small flames still danced amongst the embers.

Only the brightest stars were visible, all to the west. A dull red glow lit the sky to the northeast, the color of a blood bruise. Tyrion had never seen a bigger moon. Monstrous, swollen, it looked as if it had swallowed the sun and woken with a fever. Its twin, floating on the sea beyond the ship, shimmered red with every wave. "What hour is this?" he asked Moqorro. "That cannot be sunrise unless the east has moved. Why is the sky red?"

"The sky is always red above Valyria, Hugor Hill."

A cold chill went down his back. "Are we close?"

"Closer than the crew would like," Moqorro said in his deep voice. "Do you know the stories, in your Sunset Kingdoms?"

"I know some sailors say that any man who lays eyes upon that coast is doomed." He did not believe such tales himself, no more than his uncle had. Gerion Lannister had set sail for Valyria when Tyrion was eighteen, intent on recovering the lost ancestral blade of House Lannister and any other treasures that might have survived the Doom. Tyrion had wanted desperately to go with them, but his lord father had dubbed the voyage a "fool's quest," and forbidden him to take part.

And perhaps he was not so wrong. Almost a decade had passed since the *Laughing Lion* headed out from Lannisport, and Gerion had never returned. The men Lord Tywin sent to seek after him had traced his course as far as Volantis, where half his crew had deserted him and he had bought slaves to replace them. No free man would willingly sign aboard a ship whose captain spoke openly of his intent to sail into the Smoking Sea. "So those are fires of the Fourteen Flames we're seeing, reflected on the clouds?"

"Fourteen or fourteen thousand. What man dares count them? It is not wise for mortals to look too deeply at those fires, my friend. Those are the fires of god's own wrath, and no human flame can match them. We are small creatures, men."

"Some smaller than others." *Valyria.* It was written that on the day of Doom every hill for five hundred miles had split asunder to fill the air with ash and smoke and fire, blazes so hot and hungry that even the dragons in the sky were engulfed and consumed. Great rents had opened in the earth, swallowing palaces, temples, entire towns. Lakes boiled or turned to acid, mountains burst, fiery fountains spewed molten rock a thousand feet into the air, red clouds rained down dragonglass and the black blood of demons, and to the north the ground splintered and collapsed and fell in on itself and an angry sea came rushing in. The proudest city in all the world was gone in an instant, its fabled empire vanished in a day, the Lands of the Long Summer scorched and drowned and blighted.

An empire built on blood and fire. The Valyrians reaped the seed they had sown. "Does our captain mean to test the curse?"

"Our captain would prefer to be fifty leagues farther out to sea, well away from that accursed shore, but I have commanded him to steer the shortest course. Others seek Daenerys too."

Griff, with his young prince. Could all that talk of the Golden Company sailing west have been a feint? Tyrion considered saying something, then thought better. It seemed to him that the prophecy that drove the red priests had room for just one hero. A second Targaryen would only serve to confuse them. "Have you seen these others in your fires?" he asked, warily.

"Only their shadows," Moqorro said. "One most of all. A tall and twisted thing with one black eye and ten long arms, sailing on a sea of blood."

BRAN

The moon was a crescent, thin and sharp as the blade of a knife. A pale sun rose and set and rose again. Red leaves whispered in the wind. Dark clouds filled the skies and turned to storms. Lightning flashed and thunder rumbled, and dead men with black hands and bright blue eyes shuffled round a cleft in the hillside but could not enter. Under the hill, the broken boy sat upon a weirwood throne, listening to whispers in the dark as ravens walked up and down his arms.

"You will never walk again," the three-eyed crow had promised, "but you will fly." Sometimes the sound of song would drift up from someplace far below. *The children of the forest,* Old Nan would have called the singers, but *those who sing the song of earth* was their own name for themselves, in the True Tongue that no human man could speak. The ravens could speak it, though. Their small black eyes were full of secrets, and they would *caw* at him and peck his skin when they heard the songs.

The moon was fat and full. Stars wheeled across a black sky. Rain fell and froze, and tree limbs snapped from the weight of the ice. Bran and Meera made up names for those who sang the song of earth: Ash and Leaf and Scales, Black Knife and Snowylocks and Coals. Their true names were too long for human tongues, said Leaf. Only she could speak the Common Tongue, so what the others thought of their new names Bran never learned.

After the bone-grinding cold of the lands beyond the Wall, the caves were blessedly warm, and when the chill crept out of the rock the singers would light fires to drive it off again. Down here there was no wind, no snow, no ice, no dead things reaching out to grab you, only dreams and rushlight and the kisses of the ravens. And the whisperer in darkness.

The last greenseer, the singers called him, but in Bran's dreams he was still a three-eyed crow. When Meera Reed had asked him his true name, he made a ghastly sound that might have been a chuckle. "I wore many names when I was quick, but even I once had a mother, and the name she gave me at her breast was Brynden."

"I have an uncle Brynden," Bran said. "He's my mother's uncle, really. Brynden Blackfish, he's called."

"Your uncle may have been named for me. Some are, still. Not so many as before. Men forget. Only the trees remember." His voice was so soft that Bran had to strain to hear.

"Most of him has gone into the tree," explained the singer Meera called Leaf. "He has lived beyond his mortal span, and yet he lingers. For us, for you, for the realms of men. Only a little strength remains in his flesh. He has a thousand eyes and one, but there is much to watch. One day you will know."

"What will I know?" Bran asked the Reeds afterward, when they came with torches burning brightly in their hand, to carry him back to a small chamber off the big cavern where the singers had made beds for them to sleep. "What do the trees remember?"

"The secrets of the old gods," said Jojen Reed. Food and fire and rest had helped restore him after the ordeals of their journey, but he seemed sadder now, sullen, with a weary, haunted look about the eyes. "Truths the First Men knew, forgotten now in Winterfell . . . but not in the wet wild. We live closer to the green in our bogs and crannogs, and we remember. Earth and water, soil and stone, oaks and elms and willows, they were here before us all and will still remain when we are gone."

"So will you," said Meera. That made Bran sad. *What if I don't want to remain when you are gone?* he almost asked, but he swallowed the words unspoken. He was almost a man grown, and he did not want Meera to think he was some weepy babe. "Maybe you could be greenseers too," he said instead.

"No, Bran." Now Meera sounded sad.

"It is given to a few to drink of that green fountain whilst still in mortal flesh, to hear the whisperings of the leaves and see as the trees see, as the gods see," said Jojen. "Most are not so blessed. The gods gave me only greendreams. My task was to get you here. My part in this is done."

The moon was a black hole in the sky. Wolves howled in the wood, sniffing through the snowdrifts after dead things. A murder of ravens erupted from the hillside, screaming their sharp cries, black wings beating above a white world. A red sun rose and set and rose again, painting the snows in shades of rose and pink. Under the hill, Jojen brooded, Meera fretted, and Hodor wandered through dark tunnels with a sword in his right hand and a torch in his left. Or was it Bran wandering?

No one must ever know.

The great cavern that opened on the abyss was as black as pitch, black as tar, blacker than the feathers of a crow. Light entered as a trespasser, unwanted and unwelcome, and soon was gone again; cookfires, candles, and rushes burned for a little while, then guttered out again, their brief lives at an end.

The singers made Bran a throne of his own, like the one Lord Brynden sat, white weirwood flecked with red, dead branches woven through living roots. They placed it in the great cavern by the abyss, where the black air echoed to the sound of running water far below. Of soft grey moss they made his seat. Once he had been lowered into place, they covered him with warm furs.

There he sat, listening to the hoarse whispers of his teacher. "Never fear the darkness, Bran." The lord's words were accompanied by a faint rustling of wood and leaf, a slight twisting of his head. "The strongest trees are rooted in the dark places of the earth. Darkness will be your cloak, your shield, your mother's milk. Darkness will make you strong."

The moon was a crescent, thin and sharp as the blade of a knife. Snowflakes drifted down soundlessly to cloak the soldier pines and sentinels in white. The drifts grew so deep that they covered the entrance to the caves, leaving a white wall that Summer had to dig through whenever he went outside to join his pack and hunt. Bran did not oft range with them in those days, but some nights he watched them from above.

Flying was even better than climbing.

Slipping into Summer's skin had become as easy for him as slipping on a pair of breeches once had been, before his back was broken. Changing his own skin for a raven's night-black feathers had been harder, but not as hard as he had feared, not with *these* ravens. "A wild stallion will buck and kick when a man tries to mount him, and try to bite the hand that slips the bit between his teeth," Lord Brynden said, "but a horse that has known one rider will accept another. Young or old, these birds have all been ridden. Choose one now, and fly."

He chose one bird, and then another, without success, but the third raven looked at him with shrewd black eyes, tilted its head, and gave a *quork,* and quick as that he was not a boy looking at a raven but a raven looking at a boy. The song of the river suddenly grew louder, the torches burned a little brighter than before, and the air was full of strange smells. When he tried to speak it came out in a scream, and his first flight ended when he crashed into a wall and ended back inside his own broken body. The raven was unhurt. It flew to him and landed on his arm, and Bran stroked its feathers and slipped inside of it again. Before long he was flying around the cavern, weaving through the long stone teeth that hung down from the ceiling, even flapping out over the abyss and swooping down into its cold black depths.

Then he realized he was not alone.

"Someone else was in the raven," he told Lord Brynden, once he had returned to his own skin. "Some girl. I felt her."

"A woman, of those who sing the song of earth," his teacher said. "Long dead, yet a part of her remains, just as a part of you would remain in Summer if your boy's flesh were to die upon the morrow. A shadow on the soul. She will not harm you."

"Do all the birds have singers in them?"

"All," Lord Brynden said. "It was the singers who taught the First Men to send messages by raven . . . but in those days, the birds would speak the words. The trees remember, but men forget, and so now they write the messages on parchment and tie them round the feet of birds who have never shared their skin."

Old Nan had told him the same story once, Bran remembered, but when he asked Robb if it was true, his brother laughed and asked him if he believed in grumkins too. He wished Robb were with them now. *I'd tell him I could fly, but he wouldn't believe, so I'd have to show him. I bet that he could learn to fly too, him and Arya and Sansa, even baby Rickon and Jon Snow. We could all be ravens and live in Maester Luwin's rookery.*

That was just another silly dream, though. Some days Bran wondered if all of this wasn't just some dream. Maybe he had fallen asleep out in the snows and dreamed himself a safe, warm place. *You have to wake,* he would tell himself, *you have to wake right now, or you'll go dreaming into death.* Once or twice he pinched his arm with his fingers, really hard, but the only thing that did was make his arm hurt. In the beginning he had tried to count the days by making note of when he woke and slept, but down here sleeping and waking had a way of melting into one another. Dreams became lessons, lessons became dreams, things happened all at once or not at all. Had he done that or only dreamed it?

"Only one man in a thousand is born a skinchanger," Lord Brynden said one day, after Bran had learned to fly, "and only one skinchanger in a thousand can be a greenseer."

"I thought the greenseers were the wizards of the children," Bran said. "The singers, I mean."

"In a sense. Those you call the children of the forest have eyes as golden as the sun, but once in a great while one is born amongst them with eyes as red as blood, or green as the moss on a tree in the heart of the forest. By these signs do the gods mark those they have chosen to receive the gift. The chosen ones are not robust, and their quick years upon the earth are few, for every song must have its balance. But once inside the wood they linger long indeed. A thousand eyes, a hundred skins, wisdom deep as the roots of ancient trees. *Greenseers*."

Bran did not understand, so he asked the Reeds. "Do you like to read books, Bran?" Jojen asked him.

"Some books. I like the fighting stories. My sister Sansa likes the kissing stories, but those are stupid."

"A reader lives a thousand lives before he dies," said Jojen. "The man who never reads lives only one. The singers of the forest had no books. No ink, no parchment, no written language. Instead they had the trees, and the weirwoods above all. When they died, they went into the wood, into leaf and limb and root, and the trees remembered. All their songs and spells, their histories and prayers, everything they knew about this world. Maesters will tell you that the weirwoods are sacred to the old gods. The singers believe they *are* the old gods. When singers die they become part of that godhood."

Bran's eyes widened. "They're going to *kill* me?"

"No," Meera said. "Jojen, you're scaring him."

"He is not the one who needs to be afraid."

The moon was fat and full. Summer prowled through the silent woods, a long grey shadow that grew more gaunt with every hunt, for living game could not be found. The ward upon the cave mouth still held; the dead men could not enter. The snows had buried most of them again, but they were still there, hidden, frozen, waiting. Other dead things came to join them, things that had once been men and women, even children. Dead ravens sat on bare brown branches, wings crusted with ice. A snow bear crashed through the brush, huge and skeletal, half its head sloughed away to reveal the skull beneath. Summer and his pack fell upon it and tore it into pieces. Afterward they gorged, though the meat was rotted and half-frozen, and moved even as they ate it.

Under the hill they still had food to eat. A hundred kinds of mushrooms grew down here. Blind white fish swam in the black river, but they tasted just as good as fish with eyes once you cooked them up. They had cheese and milk from the goats that shared the caves with the singers, even some oats and barleycorn and dried fruit laid by during the long summer. And almost every day they ate blood stew, thickened with barley and onions and chunks of meat. Jojen thought it might be squirrel meat, and Meera said that it was rat. Bran did not care. It was meat and it was good. The stewing made it tender.

The caves were timeless, vast, silent. They were home to more than three score living singers and the bones of thousands dead, and extended far below the hollow hill. "Men should not go wandering in this place," Leaf warned them. "The river you hear is swift and black, and flows down and down to a sunless sea. And there are passages that go even deeper, bottomless pits and sudden shafts, forgotten ways that lead to the very center of the earth. Even my people have not explored them all, and we have lived here for a thousand thousand of your man-years."

Though the men of the Seven Kingdoms might call them the *children of the forest,* Leaf and her people were far from childlike. *Little wise men of the forest* would have been closer. They were small compared to men, as a wolf is smaller than a direwolf. That does not mean it is a pup. They had nut-brown skin, dappled like a deer's with paler spots, and large ears that could hear things that no man could hear. Their eyes were big too, great golden cat's eyes that could see down passages where a boy's eyes saw only blackness. Their hands had only three fingers and a thumb, with sharp black claws instead of nails.

And they *did* sing. They sang in True Tongue, so Bran could not understand the words, but their voices were as pure as winter air. "Where are the rest of you?" Bran asked Leaf, once.

"Gone down into the earth," she answered. "Into the stones, into the trees. Before the First Men came all this land that you call Westeros was home to us, yet even in those days we were few. The gods gave us long lives but not great numbers, lest we overrun the world as deer will overrun a wood where there are no wolves to hunt them. That was in the dawn of days, when our sun was rising. Now it sinks, and this is our long dwindling. The giants are almost gone as well, they who were our bane and our brothers. The great lions of the western hills have been slain, the unicorns are all but gone, the mammoths down to a few hundred. The direwolves will outlast us all, but their time will come as well. In the world that men have made, there is no room for them, or us."

She seemed sad when she said it, and that made Bran sad as well. It was only later that he thought, *Men would not be sad. Men would be wroth. Men would hate and swear a bloody vengeance. The singers sing sad songs, where men would fight and kill.*

One day Meera and Jojen decided to go see the river, despite Leaf's cautions. "I want to come too," Bran said.

Meera gave him a mournful look. The river was six hundred feet below, down steep slopes and twisty passages, she explained, and the last part required climbing down a rope. "Hodor could never make the climb with you on his back. I'm sorry, Bran."

Bran remembered a time when no one could climb as good as him, not even Robb or Jon. Part of him wanted to shout at them for leaving him, and another part wanted to cry. He was almost a man grown, though, so he said nothing. But after they were gone, he slipped inside Hodor's skin and followed them.

The big stableboy no longer fought him as he had the first time, back in the lake tower during the storm. Like a dog who has had all the fight whipped out of him, Hodor would curl up and hide whenever Bran reached out for him. His hiding place was somewhere deep within him, a pit where not even Bran could touch him. *No one wants to hurt you, Hodor,* he said silently, to the child-man whose flesh he'd taken. *I just want to be strong again for a while. I'll give it back, the way I always do.*

No one ever knew when he was wearing Hodor's skin. Bran only had to smile, do as he was told, and mutter "Hodor" from time to time, and he could follow Meera and Jojen, grinning happily, without anyone suspecting it was really him. He often tagged along, whether he was wanted or not. In the end, the Reeds were glad he came. Jojen made it down the rope easily enough, but after Meera caught a blind white fish with her frog spear and it was time to climb back up, his arms began to tremble and he could not make it to the top, so they had to tie the rope around him and let Hodor haul him up. "Hodor," he grunted every time he gave a pull. "Hodor, hodor, hodor."

The moon was a crescent, thin and sharp as the blade of a knife. Summer dug up a severed arm, black and covered with hoarfrost, its fingers opening and closing as it pulled itself across the frozen snow. There was still enough meat on it to fill his empty belly, and after that was done he cracked the arm bones for the marrow. Only then did the arm remember it was dead.

Bran ate with Summer and his pack, as a wolf. As a raven he flew with the murder, circling the hill at sunset, watching for foes, feeling the icy touch of the air. As Hodor he explored the caves. He found chambers full of bones, shafts that plunged deep into the earth, a place where the skeletons of gigantic bats hung upside down from the ceiling. He even crossed the slender stone bridge that arched over the abyss and discovered more passages and chambers on the far side. One was full of singers, enthroned like Brynden in nests of weirwood roots that wove under and through and around their bodies. Most of them looked dead to him, but as he crossed in front of them their eyes would open and follow the light of his torch, and one of them opened and closed a wrinkled mouth as if he were trying to speak. "Hodor," Bran said to him, and he felt the real Hodor stir down in his pit.

Seated on his throne of roots in the great cavern, half-corpse and half-tree, Lord Brynden seemed less a man than some ghastly statue made of twisted wood, old bone, and rotted wool. The only thing that looked alive in the pale ruin that was his face was his one red eye, burning like the last coal in a dead fire, surrounded by twisted roots and tatters of leathery white skin hanging off a yellowed skull.

The sight of him still frightened Bran—the weirwood roots snaking in and out of his withered flesh, the mushrooms sprouting from his cheeks, the white wooden worm that grew from the socket where one eye had been. He liked it better when the torches were put out. In the dark he could pretend that it was the three-eyed crow who whispered to him and not some grisly talking corpse.

One day I will be like him. The thought filled Bran with dread. Bad enough that he was broken, with his useless legs. Was he doomed to lose the rest too, to spend all of his years with a weirwood growing in him and through him? Lord Brynden drew his life from the tree, Leaf told them. He did not eat, he did not drink. He slept, he dreamed, he watched. *I was going to be a knight,* Bran remembered. *I used to run and climb and fight.* It seemed a thousand years ago.

What was he now? Only Bran the broken boy, Brandon of House Stark, prince of a lost kingdom, lord of a burned castle, heir to ruins. He had thought the three-eyed crow would be a sorcerer, a wise old wizard who could fix his legs, but that was some stupid child's dream, he realized now. *I am too old for such fancies,* he told himself. A *thousand eyes, a hundred skins, wisdom deep as the roots of ancient trees.* That was as good as being a knight. *Almost as good, anyway.*

The moon was a black hole in the sky. Outside the cave the world went on. Outside the cave the sun rose and set, the moon turned, the cold winds howled. Under the hill, Jojen Reed grew ever more sullen and solitary, to his sister's distress. She would often sit with Bran beside their little fire, talking of everything and nothing, petting Summer where he slept between them, whilst her brother wandered the caverns by himself. Jojen had even taken to climbing up to the cave's mouth when the day was bright. He would stand there for hours, looking out over the forest, wrapped in furs yet shivering all the same.

"He wants to go home," Meera told Bran. "He will not even try and fight his fate. He says the greendreams do not lie."

"He's being brave," said Bran. *The only time a man can be brave is when he is afraid,* his father had told him once, long ago, on the day they found the direwolf pups in the summer snows. He still remembered.

"He's being stupid," Meera said. "I'd hoped that when we found your three-eyed crow . . . now I wonder why we ever came."

For me, Bran thought. "His greendreams," he said.

"His greendreams." Meera's voice was bitter.

"Hodor," said Hodor.

Meera began to cry.

Bran hated being crippled then. "Don't cry," he said. He wanted to put his arms around her, hold her tight the way his mother used to hold him back at Winterfell when he'd hurt himself. She was right there, only a few feet from him, but so far out of reach it might have been a hundred leagues. To touch her he would need to pull himself along the ground with his hands, dragging his legs behind him. The floor was rough and uneven, and it would be slow going, full of scrapes and bumps. *I could put on Hodor's skin,* he thought. *Hodor could hold her and pat her on the back.* The thought made Bran feel strange, but he was still thinking it when Meera bolted from the fire, back out into the darkness of the tunnels. He heard her steps recede until there was nothing but the voices of the singers.

The moon was a crescent, thin and sharp as the blade of a knife. The days marched past, one after the other, each shorter than the one before. The nights grew longer. No sunlight ever reached the caves beneath the hill. No moonlight ever touched those stony halls. Even the stars were strangers there. Those things belonged to the world above, where time ran in its iron circles, day to night to day to night to day.

"It is time," Lord Brynden said.

Something in his voice sent icy fingers running up Bran's back. "Time for what?"

"For the next step. For you to go beyond skinchanging and learn what it means to be a greenseer."

"The trees will teach him," said Leaf. She beckoned, and another of the singers padded forward, the white-haired one that Meera had named Snowylocks. She had a weirwood bowl in her hands, carved with a dozen faces, like the ones the heart trees wore. Inside was a white paste, thick and heavy, with dark red veins running through it. "You must eat of this," said Leaf. She handed Bran a wooden spoon.

The boy looked at the bowl uncertainly. "What is it?"

"A paste of weirwood seeds."

Something about the look of it made Bran feel ill. The red veins were only weirwood sap, he supposed, but in the torchlight they looked remarkably like blood. He dipped the spoon into the paste, then hesitated. "Will this make me a greenseer?"

"Your blood makes you a greenseer," said Lord Brynden. "This will help awaken your gifts and wed you to the trees."

Bran did want to be married to a tree . . . but who else would wed a broken boy like him? *A thousand eyes, a hundred skins, wisdom deep as the roots of ancient trees. A greenseer.*

He ate.

It had a bitter taste, though not so bitter as acorn paste. The first spoonful was the hardest to get down. He almost retched it right back up. The second tasted better. The third was almost sweet. The rest he spooned up eagerly. Why had he thought that it was bitter? It tasted of honey, of new-fallen snow, of pepper and cinnamon and the last kiss his mother ever gave him. The empty bowl slipped from his fingers and clattered on the cavern floor. "I don't feel any different. What happens next?"

Leaf touched his hand. "The trees will teach you. The trees remember." He raised a hand, and the other singers began to move about the cavern, extinguishing the torches one by one. The darkness thickened and crept toward them.

"Close your eyes," said the three-eyed crow. "Slip your skin, as you do when you join with Summer. But this time, go into the roots instead. Follow them up through the earth, to the trees upon the hill, and tell me what you see."

Bran closed his eyes and slipped free of his skin. *Into the roots,* he thought. *Into the weirwood. Become the tree.* For an instant he could see the cavern in its black mantle, could hear the river rushing by below.

Then all at once he was back home again.

Lord Eddard Stark sat upon a rock beside the deep black pool in the godswood, the pale roots of the heart tree twisting around him like an old man's gnarled arms. The greatsword Ice lay across Lord Eddard's lap, and he was cleaning the blade with an oilcloth.

"*Winterfell,*" Bran whispered.

His father looked up. "Who's there?" he asked, turning . . .

. . . and Bran, frightened, pulled away. His father and the black pool and the godswood faded and were gone and he was back in the cavern, the pale thick roots of his weirwood throne cradling his limbs as a mother does a child. A torch flared to life before him.

"Tell us what you saw." From far away Leaf looked almost a girl, no older than Bran or one of his sisters, but close at hand she seemed far older. She claimed to have seen two hundred years.

Bran's throat was very dry. He swallowed. "Winterfell. I was back in Winterfell. I saw my father. He's not dead, he's *not*, I saw him, he's back at Winterfell, he's still alive."

"No," said Leaf. "He is gone, boy. Do not seek to call him back from death."

"I *saw* him." Bran could feel rough wood pressing against one cheek. "He was cleaning Ice."

"You saw what you wished to see. Your heart yearns for your father and your home, so that is what you saw."

"A man must know how to look before he can hope to see," said Lord Brynden. "Those were shadows of days past that you saw, Bran. You were looking through the eyes of the heart tree in your godswood. Time is different for a tree than for a man. Sun and soil and water, these are the things a weirwood understands, not days and years and centuries. For men, time is a river. We are trapped in its flow, hurtling from past to present, always in the same direction. The lives of trees are different. They root and grow and die in one place, and that river does not move them. The oak is the acorn, the acorn is the oak. And the weirwood . . . a thousand human years are a moment to a weirwood, and through such gates you and I may gaze into the past."

"But," said Bran, "he *heard* me."

"He heard a whisper on the wind, a rustling amongst the leaves. You cannot speak to him, try as you might. I know. I have my own ghosts, Bran. A brother that I loved, a brother that I hated, a woman I desired. Through the trees, I see them still, but no word of mine has ever reached them. The past remains the past. We can learn from it, but we cannot change it."

"Will I see my father again?"

"Once you have mastered your gifts, you may look where you will and see what the trees have seen, be it yesterday or last year or a thousand ages past. Men live their lives trapped in an eternal present, between the mists of memory and the sea of shadow that is all we know of the days to come. Certain moths live their whole lives in a day, yet to them that little span of time must seem as long as years and decades do to us. An oak may live three hundred years, a redwood tree three thousand. A weirwood will live forever if left undisturbed. To them seasons pass in the flutter of a moth's wing, and past, present, and future are one. Nor will your sight be limited to your godswood. The singers carved eyes into their heart trees to awaken them, and those are the first eyes a new greenseer learns to use . . . but in time you will see well beyond the trees themselves."

"When?" Bran wanted to know.

"In a year, or three, or ten. That I have not glimpsed. It will come in time, I promise you. But I am tired now, and the trees are calling me. We will resume on the morrow."

Hodor carried Bran back to his chamber, muttering "Hodor" in a low voice as Leaf went before them with a torch. He had hoped that Meera and Jojen would be there, so he could tell them what he had seen, but their snug alcove in the rock was cold and empty. Hodor eased Bran down onto his bed, covered him with furs, and made a fire for them. *A thousand eyes, a hundred skins, wisdom deep as the roots of ancient trees.*

Watching the flames, Bran decided he would stay awake till Meera came back. Jojen would be unhappy, he knew, but Meera would be glad for him. He did not remember closing his eyes.

. . . but then somehow he was back at Winterfell again, in the godswood looking down upon his father. Lord Eddard seemed much younger this time. His hair was brown, with no hint of grey in it, his head bowed. ". . . let them grow up close as brothers, with only love between them," he prayed, "and let my lady wife find it in her heart to forgive . . ."

"Father." Bran's voice was a whisper in the wind, a rustle in the leaves. "Father, it's me. It's Bran. Brandon."

Eddard Stark lifted his head and looked long at the weirwood, frowning, but he did not speak. *He cannot see me*, Bran realized, despairing. He wanted to reach out and touch him, but all that he could do was watch and listen. *I am in the tree. I am inside the heart tree, looking out of its red eyes, but the weirwood cannot talk, so I can't.*

Eddard Stark resumed his prayer. Bran felt his eyes fill up with tears. But were they his own tears, or the weirwood's? *If I cry, will the tree begin to weep?*

The rest of his father's words were drowned out by a sudden clatter of wood on wood. Eddard Stark dissolved, like mist in a morning sun. Now two children danced across the godswood, hooting at one another as they dueled with broken branches. The girl was the older and taller of the two. *Arya!* Bran thought eagerly, as he watched her leap up onto a rock and cut at the boy. But that couldn't be right. If the girl was Arya, the boy was Bran himself, and he had never worn his hair so long. *And Arya never beat me playing swords, the way that girl is beating him.* She slashed the boy across his thigh, so hard that his leg went out from under him and he fell into the pool and began to splash and shout. "You be quiet, stupid," the girl said, tossing her own branch aside. "It's just *water*. Do you want Old Nan to hear and run tell Father?" She knelt and pulled her brother from the pool, but before she got him out again, the two of them were gone.

After that the glimpses came faster and faster, till Bran was feeling lost and dizzy. He saw no more of his father, nor the girl who looked like Arya, but a woman heavy with child emerged naked and dripping from the black pool, knelt before the tree, and begged the old gods for a son who would avenge her. Then there came a brown-haired girl slender as a spear who stood on the tips of her toes to kiss the lips of a young knight as tall as Hodor. A dark-eyed youth, pale and fierce, sliced three branches off the weirwood and shaped them into arrows. The tree itself was shrinking, growing smaller with each vision, whilst the lesser trees dwindled into saplings and vanished, only to be replaced by other trees that would dwindle and vanish in their turn. And now the lords Bran glimpsed were tall and hard, stern men in fur and chain mail. Some wore faces he remembered from the statues in the crypts, but they were gone before he could put a name to them.

Then, as he watched, a bearded man forced a captive down onto his knees before the heart tree. A white-haired woman stepped toward them through a drift of dark red leaves, a bronze sickle in her hand.

"No," said Bran, "*no, don't*," but they could not hear him, no more than his father had. The woman grabbed the captive by the hair, hooked the sickle round his throat, and slashed. And through the mist of centuries the broken boy could only watch as the man's feet drummed against the earth . . . but as his life flowed out of him in a red tide, Brandon Stark could taste the blood.

JON

The sun had broken through near midday, after seven days of dark skies and snow flurries. Some of the drifts were higher than a man, but the stewards had been shoveling all day and the paths were as clean as they were like to get. Reflections glimmered off the Wall, every crack and crevice glittering pale blue.

Seven hundred feet up, Jon Snow stood looking down upon the haunted forest. A north wind swirled through the trees below, sending thin white plumes of snow crystals flying from the highest branches, like icy banners. Elsewise nothing moved. *Not a sign of life.* That was not entirely reassuring. It was not the living that he feared. Even so . . .

The sun is out. The snow has stopped. It may be a moon's turn before we have another chance as good. It may be a season. "Have Emmett assemble his recruits," he told Dolorous Edd. "We'll want an escort. Ten rangers, armed with dragonglass. I want them ready to leave within the hour."

"Aye, m'lord. And to command?"

"That would be me."

Edd's mouth turned down even more than usual. "Some might think it better if the lord commander stayed safe and warm south of the Wall. Not that I'd say such myself, but some might."

Jon smiled. "Some had best not say so in my presence."

A sudden gust of wind set Edd's cloak to flapping noisily. "Best go down, m'lord. This wind's like to push us off the Wall, and I never did learn the knack of flying."

They rode the winch lift back to the ground. The wind was gusting, cold as the breath of the ice dragon in the tales Old Nan had told when Jon was a boy. The heavy cage was swaying. From time to time it scraped against the Wall, starting small crystalline showers of ice that sparkled in the sunlight as they fell, like shards of broken glass.

Glass, Jon mused, *might be of use here. Castle Black needs its own glass gardens, like the ones at Winterfell. We could grow vegetables even in the deep of winter.* The best glass came from Myr, but a good clear pane was worth its weight in spice, and green and yellow glass would not work as well. *What we need is gold. With enough coin, we could buy 'prentice glass-blowers and glaziers in Myr, bring them north, offer them their freedom for teaching their art to some of our recruits.* That would be the way to go about it. *If we had the gold. Which we do not.*

At the base of the Wall he found Ghost rolling in a snowbank. The big white direwolf seemed to love fresh snow. When he saw Jon he bounded back onto his feet and shook himself off. Dolorous Edd said, "He's going with you?"

"He is."

"A clever wolf, him. And me?"

"You're not."

"A clever lord, you. Ghost's the better choice. I don't have the teeth for biting wildlings anymore."

"If the gods are good, we won't encounter any wildlings. I'll want the grey gelding."

Word spread fast at Castle Black. Edd was still saddling the grey when Bowen Marsh stomped across the yard to confront Jon at the stables. "My lord, I wish you would reconsider. The new men can take their vows in the sept as easily."

"The sept is home to the new gods. The old gods live in the wood, and those who honor them say their words amongst the weirwoods. You know that as well as I."

"Satin comes from Oldtown, and Arron and Emrick from the wester-lands. The old gods are not their gods."

"I do not tell men which god to worship. They were free to choose the Seven or the red woman's Lord of Light. They chose the trees instead, with all the peril that entails."

"The Weeping Man may still be out there, watching."

"The grove is no more than two hours' ride, even with the snow. We should be back by midnight."

"Too long. This is not wise."

"Unwise," said Jon, "but necessary. These men are about to pledge their lives to the Night's Watch, joining a brotherhood that stretches back in an unbroken line for thousands of years. The words matter, and so do these traditions. They bind us all together, highborn and low, young and old, base and noble. They make us brothers." He clapped Marsh on his shoulder. "I promise you, we shall return."

"Aye, my lord," said the Lord Steward, "but will it be as living men or heads on spears with your eyes scooped out? You will be returning through the black of night. The snowdrifts are waist deep in places. I see that you are taking seasoned men with you, that is good, but Black Jack Bulwer knew these woods as well. Even Benjen Stark, your own uncle, he—"

"I have something they did not." Jon turned his head and whistled. "*Ghost. To me.*" The direwolf shook the snow from his back and trotted to Jon's side. The rangers parted to let him through, though one mare whinnied and shied away till Rory gave her reins a sharp tug. "The Wall is yours, Lord Bowen." He took his horse by the bridle and walked him to the gate and the icy tunnel that snaked beneath the Wall.

Beyond the ice, the trees stood tall and silent, huddled in the thick white cloaks. Ghost stalked beside Jon's horse as the rangers and recruits formed up, then stopped and sniffed, his breath frosting in the air. "What is it?" Jon asked. "Is someone there?" The woods were empty as far as he could see, but that was not very far.

Ghost bounded toward the trees, slipped between two white-cloaked pines, and vanished in a cloud of snow. *He wants to hunt, but what?* Jon did not fear for the direwolf so much as for any wildlings he might encounter. *A white wolf in a white wood, silent as a shadow. They will never know he's coming.* He knew better than to go chasing him. Ghost would return when he wanted to and not before. Jon put his heels into his horse. His men fell in around them, the hooves of their garrons breaking through the icy crust to the softer snow beneath. Into the woods they went, at a steady walking pace, as the Wall dwindled behind them.

The soldier pines and sentinels wore thick white coats, and icicles draped the bare brown limbs of the broadleafs. Jon sent Tom Barleycorn ahead to scout for them, though the way to the white grove was oft trod and familiar. Big Liddle and Luke of Longtown slipped into the brush to east and west. They would flank the column to give warning of any approach. All were seasoned rangers, armed with obsidian as well as steel, warhorns slung across their saddles should they need to summon help.

The others were good men too. *Good men in a fight, at least, and loyal to their brothers.* Jon could not speak for what they might have been before they reached the Wall, but he did not doubt that most had pasts as black as their cloaks. Up here, they were the sort of men he wanted at his back. Their hoods were raised against the biting wind, and some had scarves wrapped about their faces, hiding their features. Jon knew them, though. Every name was graven on his heart. They were his men, his brothers.

Six more rode with them—a mix of young and old, large and small, seasoned and raw. *Six to say the words.* Horse had been born and raised in Mole's Town, Arron and Emrick came from Fair Isle, Satin from the brothels of Oldtown at the other end of Westeros. All of them were boys. Leathers and Jax were older men, well past forty, sons of the haunted forest, with sons and grandsons of their own. They had been two of the sixty-three wildlings who had followed Jon Snow back to the Wall the day he made his appeal, so far the only two to decide they wanted a black cloak. Iron Emmett said they all were ready, or as ready as they were ever going to be. He and Jon and Bowen Marsh had weighed each man in turn and assigned him to an order: Leathers, Jax, and Emrick to the rangers, Horse to the builders, Arron and Satin to the stewards. The time had come for them to take their vows.

Iron Emmett rode at the head of the column, mounted on the ugliest horse Jon had ever seen, a shaggy beast that looked to be all hair and hooves. "Talk is there was some trouble at Harlot's Tower last night," the master-at-arms said.

"Hardin's Tower." Of the sixty-three who had come back with him from Mole's Town, nineteen had been women and girls. Jon had housed them in the same abandoned tower where he had once slept when he had been new to the Wall. Twelve were spearwives, more than capable of defending both themselves and the younger girls from the unwanted attentions of black brothers. It was some of the men they'd turned away who'd given Hardin's Tower its new, inflammatory name. Jon was not about to condone the mockery. "Three drunken fools mistook Hardin's for a brothel, that's all. They are in the ice cells now, contemplating their mistake."

Iron Emmett grimaced. "Men are men, vows are words, and words are wind. You should put guards around the women."

"And who will guard the guards?" *You know nothing, Jon Snow.* He had learned, though, and Ygritte had been his teacher. If he could not hold to his own vows, how could he expect more of his brothers? But there were dangers in trifling with wildling women. *A man can own a woman, and a man can own a knife,* Ygritte had told him once, *but no man can own both.* Bowen Marsh had not been all wrong. Hardin's Tower was tinder waiting for a spark. "I mean to open three more castles," Jon said. "Deep Lake, Sable Hall, and the Long Barrow. All garrisoned with free folk, under the command of our own officers. The Long Barrow will be all women, aside from the commander and chief steward." There would be some mingling, he did not doubt, but the distances were great enough to make that difficult, at least.

"And what poor fool will get that choice command?"

"I am riding beside him."

The look of mingled horror and delight that passed across Iron Emmett's face was worth more than a sack of gold. "What have I done to make you hate me so, my lord?"

Jon laughed. "Have no fear, you won't be alone. I mean to give you Dolorous Edd as your second and your steward."

"The spearwives will be so happy. You might do well to bestow a castle on the Magnar."

Jon's smile died. "I might if I could trust him. Sigorn blames me for his father's death, I fear. Worse, he was bred and trained to give orders, not to take them. Do not confuse the Thenns with free folk. *Magnar* means *lord* in the Old Tongue, I am told, but Styr was closer to a god to his people, and his son is cut from the same skin. I do not require men to kneel, but they do need to obey."

"Aye, m'lord, but you had best do something with the Magnar. You'll have trouble with the Thenns if you ignore them."

Trouble is the lord commander's lot, Jon might have said. His visit to Mole's Town was giving him plenty, as it happened, and the women were the least of it. Halleck was proving to be just as truculent as he had feared, and there were some amongst the black brothers whose hatred of the free folk was bone deep. One of Halleck's followers had already cut off a builder's ear in the yard, and like as not that was just a taste of the bloodshed to come. He had to get the old forts open soon, so Harma's brother could be sent off to garrison Deep Lake or Sable Hall. Just now, though, neither of those was fit for human habitation, and Othell Yarwyck and his builders were still off trying to restore the Nightfort. There were nights when Jon Snow wondered if he had not made a grievous mistake by preventing Stannis from marching all the wildlings off to be slaughtered. *I know nothing, Ygritte*, he thought, *and perhaps I never will.*

Half a mile from the grove, long red shafts of autumn sunlight were slanting down between the branches of the leafless trees, staining the snowdrifts pink. The riders crossed a frozen stream, between two jagged rocks armored in ice, then followed a twisting game trail to the northeast. Whenever the wind kicked up, sprays of loose snow filled the air and stung their eyes. Jon pulled his scarf up over his mouth and nose and raised the hood on his cloak. "Not far now," he told the men. No one replied.

Jon smelled Tom Barleycorn before he saw him. Or was it Ghost who smelled him? Of late, Jon Snow sometimes felt as if he and the direwolf were one, even awake. The great white wolf appeared first, shaking off the snow. A few moments later Tom was there. "Wildlings," he told Jon, softly. "In the grove."

Jon brought the riders to a halt. "How many?"

"I counted nine. No guards. Some dead, might be, or sleeping. Most look to be women. One child, but there's a giant too. Just the one that I saw. They got a fire burning, smoke drifting through the trees. Fools."

Nine, and I have seven-and-ten. Four of his were green boys, though, and none were giants.

Jon was not of a mind to fall back to the Wall, however. *If the wildlings are still alive, it may be we can bring them in. And if they are dead, well . . . a corpse or two could be of use.* "We'll continue on foot," he said, dropping lightly to the frozen ground. The snow was ankle deep. "Rory, Pate, stay with the horses." He might have given that duty to the recruits, but they would need to be blooded soon enough. This was as good a time as any. "Spread out and form a crescent. I want to close in on the grove from three sides. Keep the men to your right and left in sight, so the gaps do not widen. The snow should muffle our steps. Less chance of blood if we take them unawares."

Night was falling fast. The shafts of sunlight had vanished when the last thin slice of the sun was swallowed beneath the western woods. The pink snow drifts were going white again, the color leaching out of them as the world darkened. The evening sky had turned the faded grey of an old cloak that had been washed too many times, and the first shy stars were coming out.

Ahead he glimpsed a pale white trunk that could only be a weirwood, crowned with a head of dark red leaves. Jon Snow reached back and pulled Longclaw from his sheath. He looked to right and left, gave Satin and Horse a nod, watched them pass it on to the men beyond. They rushed the grove together, kicking through drifts of old snow with no sound but their breathing. Ghost ran with them, a white shadow at Jon's side.

The weirwoods rose in a circle around the edges of the clearing. There were nine, all roughly of the same age and size. Each one had a face carved into it, and no two faces were alike. Some were smiling, some were screaming, some were shouting at him. In the deepening glow their eyes looked black, but in daylight they would be blood-red, Jon knew. *Eyes like Ghost's.*

The fire in the center of the grove was a small sad thing, ashes and embers and a few broken branches burning slow and smoky. Even then, it had more life than the wildlings huddled near it. Only one of them reacted when Jon stepped from the brush. That was the child, who began to wail, clutching at his mother's ragged cloak. The woman raised her eyes and gasped. By then the grove was ringed by rangers, sliding past the bone-white trees, steel glinting in black-gloved hands, poised for slaughter.

The giant was the last to notice them. He had been asleep, curled up by the fire, but something woke him—the child's cry, the sound of snow crunching beneath black boots, a sudden indrawn breath. When he stirred it was as if a boulder had come to life. He heaved himself into a sitting position with a snort, pawing at his eyes with hands as big as hams to rub the sleep away . . . until he saw Iron Emmett, his sword shining in his hand. Roaring, he came leaping to his feet, and one of those huge hands closed around a maul and jerked it up.

Ghost showed his teeth in answer. Jon grabbed the wolf by the scruff of the neck. "We want no battle here." His men could bring the giant down, he knew, but not without cost. Once blood was shed, the wildlings would join the fray. Most or all would die here, and some of his own brothers too. "This is a holy place. Yield, and we—"

The giant bellowed again, a sound that shook the leaves in the trees, and slammed his maul against the ground. The shaft of it was six feet of gnarled oak, the head a stone as big as a loaf of bread. The impact made the ground shake. Some of the other wildlings went scrambling for their own weapons.

Jon Snow was about to reach for Longclaw when Leathers spoke, from the far side of the grove. His words sounded gruff and guttural, but Jon heard the music in it and recognized the Old Tongue. Leathers spoke for a long while. When he was done, the giant answered. It sounded like growling, interspersed with grunts, and Jon could not understand a word of it. But Leathers pointed at the trees and said something else, and the giant pointed at the trees, ground his teeth, and dropped his maul.

"It's done," said Leathers. "They want no fight."

"Well done. What did you tell him?"

"That they were our gods too. That we came to pray."

"We shall. Put away your steel, all of you. We will have no blood shed here tonight."

Nine, Tom Barleycorn had said, and nine there were, but two were dead and one so weak he might have died by morning. The six who remained included a mother and child, two old men, a wounded Thenn in battered bronze, and one of the Hornfoot folk, his bare feet so badly frostbitten that Jon knew at a glance he would never walk again. Most had been strangers to one another when they came to the grove, he learned subsequently; when Stannis broke Mance Rayder's host, they had fled into the woods to escape the carnage, wandered for a time, lost friends and kin to cold and starvation, and finally washed up here, too weak and weary to go on. "The gods are here," one of the old men said. "This was as good a place to die as any."

"The Wall is only a few hours south of here," said Jon. "Why not seek shelter there? Others yielded. Even Mance."

The wildlings exchanged looks. Finally one said, "We heard stories. The crows burned all them that yielded."

"Even Mance hisself," the woman added.

Melisandre, Jon thought, *you and your red god have much and more to answer for.* "All those who wish are welcome to return with us. There is food and shelter at Castle Black, and the Wall to keep you safe from the things that haunt these woods. You have my word, no one will burn."

"A crow's word," the woman said, hugging her child close, "but who's to say that you can keep it? Who are you?"

"Lord Commander of the Night's Watch, and a son of Eddard Stark of Winterfell." Jon turned to Tom Barleycorn. "Have Rory and Pate bring up the horses. I do not mean to stay here one moment longer than we must."

"As you say, m'lord."

One last thing remained before they could depart: the thing that they had come for. Iron Emmett called forth his charges, and as the rest of the company watched from a respectful distance, they knelt before the weirwoods. The last light of day was gone by then; the only light came from the stars above and the faint red glow of the dying fire in the center of the grove.

With their black hoods and thick black cowls, the six might have been carved from shadow. Their voices rose together, small against the vastness of the night. "Night gathers, and now my watch begins," they said, as thousands had said before them. Satin's voice was sweet as song, Horse's hoarse and halting, Arron's a nervous squeak. "It shall not end until my death."

May those deaths be long in coming. Jon Snow sank to one knee in the snow. *Gods of my fathers, protect these men. And Arya too, my little sister, wherever she might be. I pray you, let Mance find her and bring her safe to me.*

"I shall take no wife, hold no lands, father no children," the recruits promised, in voices that echoed back through years and centuries. "I shall wear no crowns and win no glory. I shall live and die at my post."

Gods of the wood, grant me the strength to do the same, Jon Snow prayed silently. *Give me the wisdom to know what must be done and the courage to do it.*

"I am the sword in the darkness," said the six, and it seemed to Jon as though their voices were changing, growing stronger, more certain. "I am the watcher on the walls. I am the fire that burns against the cold, the light that brings the dawn, the horn that wakes the sleepers, the shield that guards the realms of men."

The shield that guards the realms of men. Ghost nuzzled up against his shoulder, and Jon draped an arm around him. He could smell Horse's unwashed breeches, the sweet scent Satin combed into his beard, the rank sharp smell of fear, the giant's overpowering musk. He could hear the beating of his own heart. When he looked across the grove at the woman with her child, the two greybeards, the Hornfoot man with his maimed feet, all he saw was men.

"I pledge my life and honor to the Night's Watch, for this night and all the nights to come."

Jon Snow was the first onto his feet. "Rise now as men of the Night's Watch." He gave Horse a hand to pull him up.

The wind was rising. It was time to go.

The journey back took much longer than the journey to the grove. The giant's pace was a ponderous one, despite the length and girth of those legs, and he was forever stopping to knock snow off low-hanging limbs with his maul. The woman rode double with Rory, her son with Tom Barleycorn, the old men with Horse and Satin. The Thenn was frightened of the horses, however, and preferred to limp along despite his wounds. The Hornfoot man could not sit a saddle and had to be tied over the back of a garron like a sack of grain; so too the pale-faced crone with the stick-thin limbs, whom they had not been able to rouse.

They did the same with the two corpses, to the puzzlement of Iron Emmett. "They will only slow us, my lord," he said to Jon. "We should chop them up and burn them."

"No," said Jon. "Bring them. I have a use for them."

They had no moon to guide them home, and only now and then a patch of stars. The world was black and white and still. It was a long, slow, endless trek. The snow clung to their boots and breeches, and the wind rattled the pines and made their cloaks snap and swirl. Jon glimpsed the red wanderer above, watching them through the leafless branches of great trees as they made their way beneath. *The Thief*, the free folk called it. The best time to steal a woman was when the Thief was in the Moonmaid, Ygritte had always claimed. She never mentioned the best time to steal a giant. *Or two dead men.*

It was almost dawn before they saw the Wall again.

A sentry's horn greeted them as they approached, sounding from on high like the cry of some huge, deep-throated bird, a single long blast that meant *rangers returning*. Big Liddle unslung his own warhorn and gave answer. At the gate, they had to wait a few moments before Dolorous Edd Tollett appeared to slide back the bolts and swing open the iron bars. When Edd caught sight of the ragged band of wildlings, he pursed his lips and gave the giant a long look. "Might need some butter to slide that one through the tunnel, m'lord. Shall I send someone to the larder?"

"Oh, I think he'll fit. Unbuttered."

So he did . . . on hands and knees, crawling. *A big boy, this one. Fourteen feet, at least. Even bigger than Mag the Mighty.* Mag had died beneath this very ice, locked in mortal struggle with Donal Noye. *A good man. The Watch has lost too many good men.* Jon took Leathers aside. "Take charge of him. You speak his tongue. See that he is fed and find him a warm place by the fire. Stay with him. See that no one provokes him."

"Aye." Leathers hesitated. "M'lord."

The living wildlings Jon sent off to have their wounds and frostbites tended. Some hot food and warm clothes would restore most of them, he hoped, though the Hornfoot man was like to lose both feet. The corpses he consigned to the ice cells.

Clydas had come and gone, Jon noted as he was hanging his cloak on the peg beside the door. A letter had been left on the table in his solar. *Eastwatch or the Shadow Tower*, he assumed at first glance. But the wax was gold, not black. The seal showed a stag's head within a flaming heart. *Stannis.* Jon cracked the hardened wax, flattened the roll of parchment, read. *A maester's hand, but the king's words.*

Stannis had taken Deepwood Motte, and the mountain clans had joined him. Flint, Norrey, Wull, Liddle, all.

And we had other help, unexpected but most welcome, from a daughter of Bear Island. Alysane Mormont, whose men name her the She-Bear, hid fighters inside a gaggle of fishing sloops and took the ironmen unawares where they lay off the strand.

Greyjoy's longships are burned or taken, her crews slain or
surrendered. The captains, knights, notable warriors, and others
of high birth we shall ransom or make other use of, the rest I
mean to hang . . .

The Night's Watch was sworn to take no side in the quarrels and con-
flicts of the realm. Nonetheless, Jon Snow could not help but feel a certain satisfaction. He read on.

. . . more northmen coming in as word spreads of our victory.
Fisherfolk, freeriders, hillmen, crofters from the deep of the
wolfswood and villagers who fled their homes along the stony
shore to escape the ironmen, survivors from the battle outside
the gates of Winterfell, men once sworn to the Hornwoods, the
Cerwyns, and the Tallharts. We are five thousand strong as
I write, our numbers swelling every day. And word has come
to us that Roose Bolton moves toward Winterfell with all his
power, there to wed his bastard to your half sister. He must not
be allowed to restore the castle to its former strength. We march
against him. Arnolf Karstark and Mors Umber will join us.
I will save your sister if I can, and find a better match for her
than Ramsay Snow. You and your brothers must hold the Wall
until I can return.

It was signed, in a different hand,

Done in the Light of Lord, under the sign and seal of Stannis of House
Baratheon, the First of His Name, King of the Andals, the Rhoynar,
and the First Men, Lord of the Seven Kingdoms, and Protector
of the Realm.

The moment Jon set the letter aside, the parchment curled up again,
as if eager to protect its secrets. He was not at all sure how he felt about
what he had just read. Battles had been fought at Winterfell before, but
never one without a Stark on one side or the other. "The castle is a shell,"
he said, "not Winterfell, but the ghost of Winterfell." It was painful just to
think of it, much less say the words aloud. And still . . .

He wondered how many men old Crowfood would bring to the fray,
and how many swords Arnolf Karstark would be able to conjure up. Half
the Umbers would be across the field with Whoresbane, fighting beneath

the flayed man of the Dreadfort, and the greater part of the strength of both houses had gone south with Robb, never to return. Even ruined, Winterfell itself would confer a considerable advantage on whoever held it. Robert Baratheon would have seen that at once and moved swiftly to secure the castle, with the forced marches and midnight rides for which he had been famous. Would his brother be as bold?

Not likely. Stannis was a deliberate commander, and his host was a half-digested stew of clansmen, southron knights, king's men and queen's men, salted with a few northern lords. *He should move on Winterfell swiftly, or not at all,* Jon thought. It was not his place to advise the king, but . . .

He glanced at the letter again. *I will save your sister if I can.* A surprisingly tender sentiment from Stannis, though undercut by that final, brutal *if I can* and the addendum *and find a better match for her than Ramsay Snow.* But what if Arya was not there to be saved? What if Lady Melisandre's flames had told it true? Could his sister truly have escaped such captors? *How would she do that? Arya was always quick and clever, but in the end she's just a little girl, and Roose Bolton is not the sort who would be careless with a prize of such great worth.*

What if Bolton never had his sister? This wedding could well be just some ruse to lure Stannis into a trap. Eddard Stark had never had any reason to complain of the Lord of the Dreadfort, so far as Jon knew, but even so he had never trusted him, with his whispery voice and his pale, pale eyes.

A grey girl on a dying horse, fleeing from her marriage. On the strength of those words he had loosed Mance Rayder and six spearwives on the north. "Young ones, and pretty," Mance had said. The unburnt king supplied some names, and Dolorous Edd had done the rest, smuggling them from Mole's Town. It seemed like madness now. He might have done better to strike down Mance the moment he revealed himself. Jon had a certain grudging admiration for the late King-Beyond-the-Wall, but the man was an oathbreaker and a turncloak. He had even less trust in Melisandre. Yet somehow here he was, pinning his hopes on them. *All to save my sister. But the men of the Night's Watch have no sisters.*

When Jon had been a boy at Winterfell, his hero had been the Young Dragon, the boy king who had conquered Dorne at the age of fourteen. Despite his bastard birth, or perhaps because of it, Jon Snow had dreamed of leading men to glory just as King Daeron had, of growing up to be a conqueror. Now he was a man grown and the Wall was his, yet all he had were doubts. He could not even seem to conquer those.

DAENERYS

The stench of the camp was so appalling it was all that Dany could do not to gag.

Ser Barristan wrinkled up his nose, and said, "Your Grace should not be here, breathing these black humors."

"I am the blood of the dragon," Dany reminded him. "Have you ever seen a dragon with the flux?" Viserys had oft claimed that Targaryens were untroubled by the pestilences that afflicted common men, and so far as she could tell, it was true. She could remember being cold and hungry and afraid, but never sick.

"Even so," the old knight said, "I would feel better if Your Grace would return to the city." The many-colored brick walls of Meereen were half a mile back. "The bloody flux has been the bane of every army since the Dawn Age. Let us distribute the food, Your Grace."

"On the morrow. I am here now. I want to see." She put her heels into her silver. The others trotted after her. Jhogo rode before her, Aggo and Rakharo just behind, long Dothraki whips in hand to keep away the sick and dying. Ser Barristan was at her right, mounted on a dapple grey. To her left was Symon Stripeback of the Free Brothers and Marselen of the Mother's Men. Three score soldiers followed close behind the captains, to protect the food wagons. Mounted men all, Dothraki and Brazen Beasts and freedmen, they were united only by their distaste for this duty.

The Astapori stumbled after them in a ghastly procession that grew longer with every yard they crossed. Some spoke tongues she did not understand. Others were beyond speaking. Many lifted their hands to Dany, or knelt as her silver went by. "Mother," they called to her, in the dialects of Astapor, Lys, and Old Volantis, in guttural Dothraki and the liquid syllables of Qarth, even in the Common Tongue of Westeros. "Mother, please . . . mother, help my sister, she is sick . . . give me food for my little ones . . . please, my old father . . . help him . . . help her . . . help me . . ."

I have no more help to give, Dany thought, despairing. The Astapori had no place to go. Thousands remained outside Meereen's thick walls— men and women and children, old men and little girls and newborn babes. Many were sick, most were starved, and all were doomed to die. Daenerys dare not open her gates to let them in. She had tried to do what she could for them. She had sent them healers, Blue Graces and spell-singers and barber-surgeons, but some of those had sickened as well, and none of their arts had slowed the galloping progression of the flux that had come on the pale mare. Separating the healthy from the sick had proved impractical as well. Her Stalwart Shields had tried, pulling husbands away from wives and children from their mothers, even as the Astapori wept and kicked and pelted them with stones. A few days later, the sick were dead and the healthy ones were sick. Dividing the one from the other had accomplished nothing.

Even feeding them had grown difficult. Every day she sent them what she could, but every day there were more of them and less food to give them. It was growing harder to find drivers willing to deliver the food as well. Too many of the men they had sent into the camp had been stricken by the flux themselves. Others had been attacked on the way back to the city. Yesterday a wagon had been overturned and two of her soldiers killed, so today the queen had determined that she would bring the food herself. Every one of her advisors had argued fervently against it, from Reznak and the Shavepate to Ser Barristan, but Daenerys would not be moved. "I will not turn away from them," she said stubbornly. "A queen must know the sufferings of her people."

Suffering was the only thing they did not lack. "There is scarcely a horse or mule left, though many rode from Astapor," Marselen reported to her. "They've eaten every one, Your Grace, along with every rat and scavenger dog that they could catch. Now some have begun to eat their own dead."

"Man must not eat the flesh of man," said Aggo.

"It is known," agreed Rahkaro. "They will be cursed."

"They're past cursing," said Symon Stripeback.

Little children with swollen stomachs trailed after them, too weak or scared to beg. Gaunt men with sunken eyes squatted amidst sand and stones, shitting out their lives in stinking streams of brown and red. Many shat where they slept now, too feeble to crawl to the ditches she'd commanded them to dig. Two women fought over a charred bone. Nearby a boy of ten stood eating a rat. He ate one-handed, the other clutching a sharpened stick lest anyone try to wrest away his prize. Unburied dead lay everywhere. Dany saw one man sprawled in the dirt under a black cloak, but as she rode past his cloak dissolved into a thousand flies. Skeletal women sat upon the ground clutching dying infants. Their eyes followed her. Those who had the strength called out. "Mother . . . please, Mother . . . bless you, Mother . . ."

Bless me, Dany thought bitterly. *Your city is gone to ash and bone, your people are dying all around you. I have no shelter for you, no medicine, no hope. Only stale bread and wormy meat, hard cheese, a little milk. Bless me, bless me.*

What kind of mother has no milk to feed her children?

"Too many dead," Aggo said. "They should be burned."

"Who will burn them?" asked Ser Barristan. "The bloody flux is everywhere. A hundred die each night."

"It is not good to touch the dead," said Jhogo.

"This is known," Aggo and Rakharo said, together.

"That may be so," said Dany, "but this thing must be done, all the same." She thought a moment. "The Unsullied have no fear of corpses. I shall speak to Grey Worm."

"Your Grace," said Ser Barristan, "the Unsullied are your best fighters. We dare not loose this plague amongst them. Let the Astapori bury their own dead."

"They are too feeble," said Symon Stripeback.

Dany said, "More food might make them stronger."

Symon shook his head. "Food should not be wasted on the dying, Your Worship. We do not have enough to feed the living."

He was not wrong, she knew, but that did not make the words any easier to hear. "This is far enough," the queen decided. "We'll feed them here." She raised a hand. Behind her the wagons bumped to a halt, and her riders spread out around them, to keep the Astapori from rushing at the food. No sooner had they stopped than the press began to thicken around them, as more and more of the afflicted came limping and shambling toward the wagons. The riders cut them off. "Wait your turn," they shouted. "No pushing. Back. Stay back. Bread for everyone. Wait your turn."

Dany could only sit and watch. "Ser," she said to Barristan Selmy, "is there no more we can do? You have provisions."

"Provisions for Your Grace's soldiers. We may well need to withstand a long siege. The Stormcrows and the Second Sons can harry the Yunkish-men, but they cannot hope to turn them. If Your Grace would allow me to assemble an army . . ."

"If there must be a battle, I would sooner fight it from behind the walls of Meereen. Let the Yunkai'i try and storm my battlements." The queen surveyed the scene around her. "If we were to share our food equally . . ."

". . . the Astapori would eat through their portion in days, and we would have that much less for the siege."

Dany gazed across the camp, to the many-colored brick walls of Meer-een. The air was thick with flies and cries. "The gods have sent this pesti-lence to humble me. So many dead . . . I will *not* have them eating corpses." She beckoned Aggo closer. "Ride to the gates and bring me Grey Worm and fifty of his Unsullied."

"*Khaleesi*. The blood of your blood obeys." Aggo touched his horse with his heels and galloped off.

Ser Barristan watched with ill-concealed apprehension. "You should not linger here overlong, Your Grace. The Astapori are being fed, as you commanded. There's no more we can do for the poor wretches. We should repair back to the city."

"Go if you wish, ser. I will not detain you. I will not detain any of you." Dany vaulted down from the horse. "I cannot heal them, but I can show them that their Mother cares."

Jhogo sucked in his breath. "*Khaleesi*, no." The bell in his braid rang softly as he dismounted. "You must not get any closer. Do not let them touch you! Do not!"

Dany walked right past him. There was an old man on the ground a few feet away, moaning and staring up at the grey belly of the clouds. She knelt beside him, wrinkling her nose at the smell, and pushed back his dirty grey hair to feel his brow. "His flesh is on fire. I need water to bathe him. Seawater will serve. Marselen, will you fetch some for me? I need oil as well, for the pyre. Who will help me burn the dead?"

By the time Aggo returned with Grey Worm and fifty of the Unsullied loping behind his horse, Dany had shamed all of them into helping her. Symon Stripeback and his men were pulling the living from the dead and stacking up the corpses, while Jhogo and Rakharo and their Dothraki helped those who could still walk toward the shore to bathe and wash their clothes. Aggo stared at them as if they had all gone mad, but Grey Worm knelt beside the queen and said, "This one would be of help."

Before midday a dozen fires were burning. Columns of greasy black smoke rose up to stain a merciless blue sky. Dany's riding clothes were stained and sooty as she stepped back from the pyres. "Worship," Grey Worm said, "this one and his brothers beg your leave to bathe in the salt sea when our work here is done, that we might be purified according to the laws of our great goddess."

The queen had not known that the eunuchs had a goddess of their own. "Who is this goddess? One of the gods of Ghis?"

Grey Worm looked troubled. "The goddess is called by many names. She is the Lady of Spears, the Bride of Battle, the Mother of Hosts, but her true name belongs only to these poor ones who have burned their manhoods upon her altar. We may not speak of her to others. This one begs your forgiveness."

"As you wish. Yes, you may bathe if that is your desire. Thank you for your help."

"These ones live to serve you."

When Daenerys returned to her pyramid, sore of limb and sick of heart, she found Missandei reading some old scroll whilst Irri and Jhiqui argued about Rakharo. "You are too skinny for him," Jhiqui was saying. "You are almost a boy. Rakharo does not bed with boys. This is known." Irri bristled back. "It is known that you are almost a cow. Rakharo does not bed with cows."

"Rakharo is blood of my blood. His life belongs to me, not you," Dany told the two of them. Rakharo had grown almost half a foot during his time away from Meereen and returned with arms and legs thick with muscle and four bells in his hair. He towered over Aggo and Jhogo now, as her handmaids had both noticed. "Now be quiet. I need to bathe." She had never felt more soiled. "Jhiqui, help me from these clothes, then take them away and burn them. Irri, tell Qezza to find me something light and cool to wear. The day was very hot."

A cool wind was blowing on her terrace. Dany sighed with pleasure as she slipped into the waters of her pool. At her command, Missandei stripped off her clothes and climbed in after her. "This one heard the Astapori scratching at the walls last night," the little scribe said as she was washing Dany's back.

Irri and Jhiqui exchanged a look. "No one was scratching," said Jhiqui. "Scratching . . . how could they scratch?"

"With their hands," said Missandei. "The bricks are old and crumbling. They are trying to claw their way into the city."

"This would take them many years," said Irri. "The walls are very thick. This is known."

"It is known," agreed Jhiqui.

"I dream of them as well." Dany took Missandei's hand. "The camp is a good half-mile from the city, my sweetling. No one was scratching at the walls."

"Your Grace knows best," said Missandei. "Shall I wash your hair? It is almost time. Reznak mo Reznak and the Green Grace are coming to discuss—"

"—the wedding preparations." Dany sat up with a splash. "I had almost forgotten." *Perhaps I wanted to forget.* "And after them, I am to dine with Hizdahr." She sighed. "Irri, bring the green *tokar*, the silk one fringed with Myrish lace."

"That one is being repaired, *Khaleesi*. The lace was torn. The blue *tokar* has been cleaned."

"Blue, then. They will be just as pleased."

She was only half-wrong. The priestess and the seneschal were happy to see her garbed in a *tokar*, a proper Meereenese lady for once, but what they really wanted was to strip her bare. Daenerys heard them out, incredulous. When they were done, she said, "I have no wish to give offense, but I will *not* present myself naked to Hizdahr's mother and sisters."

"But," said Reznak mo Reznak, blinking, "but you must, Your Worship. Before a marriage it is traditional for the women of the man's house to examine the bride's womb and, ah . . . her female parts. To ascertain that they are well formed and, ah . . ."

". . . fertile," finished Galazza Galare. "An ancient ritual, Your Radiance. Three Graces shall be present to witness the examination and say the proper prayers."

"Yes," said Reznak, "and afterward there is a special cake. A women's cake, baked only for betrothals. Men are not allowed to taste it. I am told it is delicious. Magical."

And if my womb is withered and my female parts accursed, is there a special cake for that as well? "Hizdahr zo Loraq may inspect my women's parts after we are wed." *Khal Drogo found no fault with them, why should he?* "Let his mother and his sisters examine one another and share the special cake. I shall not be eating it. Nor shall I wash the noble Hizdahr's noble feet."

"Magnificence, you do not understand," protested Reznak. "The washing of the feet is hallowed by tradition. It signifies that you shall be your husband's handmaid. The wedding garb is fraught with meaning too. The bride is dressed in dark red veils above a *tokar* of white silk, fringed with baby pearls."

The queen of the rabbits must not be wed without her floppy ears. "All those pearls will make me rattle when I walk."

"The pearls symbolize fertility. The more pearls Your Worship wears, the more healthy children she will bear."

"Why would I want a hundred children?" Dany turned to the Green Grace. "If we should wed by Westerosi rites . . ."

"The gods of Ghis would deem it no true union." Galazza Galare's face was hidden behind a veil of green silk. Only her eyes showed, green and wise and sad. "In the eyes of the city you would be the noble Hizdahr's concubine, not his lawful wedded wife. Your children would be bastards. Your Worship must marry Hizdahr in the Temple of the Graces, with all the nobility of Meereen on hand to bear witness to your union."

Get the heads of all the noble houses out of their pyramids on some pretext, Daario had said. *The dragon's words are fire and blood.* Dany pushed the thought aside. It was not worthy of her. "As you wish," she sighed. "I shall marry Hizdahr in the Temple of the Graces wrapped in a white *tokar* fringed with baby pearls. Is there anything else?"

"One more small matter, Your Worship," said Reznak. "To celebrate your nuptials, it would be most fitting if you would allow the fighting pits to open once again. It would be your wedding gift to Hizdahr and to your loving people, a sign that you had embraced the ancient ways and customs of Meereen."

"And most pleasing to the gods as well," the Green Grace added in her soft and kindly voice.

A bride price paid in blood. Daenerys was weary of fighting this battle. Even Ser Barristan did not think she could win. "No ruler can make a people good," Selmy had told her. "Baelor the Blessed prayed and fasted and built the Seven as splendid a temple as any gods could wish for, yet he could not put an end to war and want." *A queen must listen to her people,* Dany reminded herself. "After the wedding Hizdahr will be king. Let him reopen the fighting pits if he wishes. I want no part of it." *Let the blood be on his hands, not mine.* She rose. "If my husband wishes me to wash his feet, he must first wash mine. I will tell him so this evening." She wondered how her betrothed would take that.

She need not have been concerned. Hizdahr zo Loraq arrived an hour after the sun had set. His own *tokar* was burgundy, with a golden stripe and a fringe of golden beads. Dany told him of her meeting with Reznak and the Green Grace as she was pouring wine for him. "These rituals are empty," Hizdahr declared, "just the sort of thing we must sweep aside.

Meereen has been steeped in these foolish old traditions for too long." He kissed her hand and said, "Daenerys, my queen, I will gladly wash you from head to heel if that is what I must do to be your king and consort."

"To be my king and consort, you need only bring me peace. Skahaz tells me you have had messages of late."

"I have." Hizdahr crossed his long legs. He looked pleased with himself. "Yunkai will give us peace, but for a price. The disruption of the slave trade has caused great injury throughout the civilized world. Yunkai and her allies will require an indemnity of us, to be paid in gold and gemstones."

Gold and gems were easy. "What else?"

"The Yunkai'i will resume slaving, as before. Astapor will be rebuilt, as a slave city. You will not interfere."

"The Yunkai'i resumed their slaving before I was two leagues from their city. Did I turn back? King Cleon begged me to join with him against them, and I turned a deaf ear to his pleas. *I want no war with Yunkai.* How many times must I say it? What promises do they require?"

"Ah, there is the thorn in the bower, my queen," said Hizdahr zo Loraq. "Sad to say, Yunkai has no faith in your promises. They keep plucking the same string on the harp, about some envoy that your dragons set on fire."

"Only his *tokar* was burned," said Dany scornfully.

"Be that as it may, they do not trust you. The men of New Ghis feel the same. Words are wind, as you yourself have so oft said. No words of yours will secure this peace for Meereen. Your foes require deeds. They would see us wed, and they would see me crowned as king, to rule beside you."

Dany filled his wine cup again, wanting nothing so much as to pour the flagon over his head and drown his complacent smile. "Marriage or carnage. A wedding or a war. Are those my choices?"

"I see only one choice, Your Radiance. Let us say our vows before the gods of Ghis and make a new Meereen together."

The queen was framing her response when she heard a step behind her. *The food,* she thought. Her cooks had promised her to serve the noble Hizdahr's favorite meal, dog in honey, stuffed with prunes and peppers. But when she turned to look, it was Ser Barristan standing there, freshly bathed and clad in white, his longsword at his side. "Your Grace," he said, bowing, "I am sorry to disturb you, but I thought that you would want to know at once. The Stormcrows have returned to the city, with word of the foe. The Yunkishmen are on the march, just as we had feared."

A flicker of annoyance crossed the noble face of Hizdahr zo Loraq. "The queen is at her supper. These sellswords can wait."

Ser Barristan ignored him. "I asked Lord Daario to make his report to me, as Your Grace had commanded. He laughed and said that he would write it out in his own blood if Your Grace would send your little scribe to show him how to make the letters."

"Blood?" said Dany, horrified. "Is that a jape? No. No, don't tell me, I must see him for myself." She was a young girl, and alone, and young girls can change their minds. "Convene my captains and commanders. Hizdahr, I know you will forgive me."

"Meereen must come first." Hizdahr smiled genially. "We will have other nights. A thousand nights."

"Ser Barristan will show you out." Dany hurried off, calling for her handmaids. She would not welcome her captain home in a *tokar*. In the end she tried a dozen gowns before she found one she liked, but she refused the crown that Jhiqui offered her.

As Daario Naharis took a knee before her, Dany's heart gave a lurch. His hair was matted with dried blood, and on his temple a deep cut glistened red and raw. His right sleeve was bloody almost to the elbow. "You're hurt," she gasped.

"This?" Daario touched his temple. "A crossbowman tried to put a quarrel through my eye, but I outrode it. I was hurrying home to my queen, to bask in the warmth of her smile." He shook his sleeve, spattering red droplets. "This blood is not mine. One of my serjeants said we should go over to the Yunkai'i, so I reached down his throat and pulled his heart out. I meant to bring it to you as a gift for my silver queen, but four of the Cats cut me off and came snarling and spitting after me. One almost caught me, so I threw the heart into his face."

"Very gallant," said Ser Barristan, in a tone that suggested it was anything but, "but do you have tidings for Her Grace?"

"Hard tidings, Ser Grandfather. Astapor is gone, and the slavers are coming north in strength."

"This is old news, and stale," growled the Shavepate.

"Your mother said the same of your father's kisses," Daario replied. "Sweet queen, I would have been here sooner, but the hills are aswarm with Yunkish sellswords. Four free companies. Your Stormcrows had to cut their way through all of them. There is more, and worse. The Yunkai'i are marching their host up the coast road, joined by four legions out of New Ghis. They have elephants, a hundred, armored and towered. Tolosi slingers too, and a corps of Qartheen camelry. Two more Ghiscari legions took ship at Astapor. If our captives told it true, they will be landed beyond the Skahazadhan to cut us off from the Dothraki sea."

As he told his tale, from time to time a drop of bright red blood would patter against the marble floor, and Dany would wince. "How many men were killed?" she asked when he was done.

"Of ours? I did not stop to count. We gained more than we lost, though."

"More turncloaks?"

"More brave men drawn to your noble cause. My queen will like them. One is an axeman from the Basilisk Isles, a brute, bigger than Belwas. You should see him. Some Westerosi too, a score or more. Deserters from the Windblown, unhappy with the Yunkai'i. They'll make good Stormcrows."

"If you say." Dany would not quibble. Meereen might soon have need of every sword.

Ser Barristan frowned at Daario. "Captain, you made mention of *four* free companies. We know of only three. The Windblown, the Long Lances, and the Company of the Cat."

"Ser Grandfather knows how to count. The Second Sons have gone over to the Yunkai'i." Daario turned his head and spat. "That's for Brown Ben Plumm. When next I see his ugly face I will open him from throat to groin and rip out his black heart."

Dany tried to speak and found no words. She remembered Ben's face the last time she had seen it. *It was a warm face, a face I trusted.* Dark skin and white hair, the broken nose, the wrinkles at the corners of his eyes. Even the dragons had been fond of old Brown Ben, who liked to boast that he had a drop of dragon blood himself. *Three treasons will you know. Once for gold and once for blood and once for love.* Was Plumm the third treason, or the second? And what did that make Ser Jorah, her gruff old bear? Would she never have a friend that she could trust? *What good are prophecies if you cannot make sense of them? If I marry Hizdahr before the sun comes up, will all these armies melt away like morning dew and let me rule in peace?*

Daario's announcement had sparked an uproar. Reznak was wailing, the Shavepate was muttering darkly, her bloodriders were swearing vengeance. Strong Belwas thumped his scarred belly with his fist and swore to eat Brown Ben's heart with plums and onions. "Please," Dany said, but only Missandei seemed to hear. The queen got to her feet. "*Be quiet!* I have heard enough."

"Your Grace." Ser Barristan went to one knee. "We are yours to command. What would you have us do?"

"Continue as we planned. Gather food, as much as you can." *If I look back I am lost.* "We must close the gates and put every fighting man upon the walls. No one enters, no one leaves."

The hall was quiet for a moment. The men looked at one another. Then Reznak said, "What of the Astapori?"

She wanted to scream, to gnash her teeth and tear her clothes and beat upon the floor. Instead she said, "*Close the gates*. Will you make me say it thrice?" They were her children, but she could not help them now. "Leave me. Daario, remain. That cut should be washed, and I have more questions for you."

The others bowed and went. Dany took Daario Naharis up the steps to her bedchamber, where Irri washed his cut with vinegar and Jhiqui wrapped it in white linen. When that was done she sent her handmaids off as well. "Your clothes are stained with blood," she told Daario. "Take them off."

"Only if you do the same." He kissed her.

His hair smelled of blood and smoke and horse, and his mouth was hard and hot on hers. Dany trembled in his arms. When they broke apart, she said, "I thought you would be the one to betray me. Once for blood and once for gold and once for love, the warlocks said. I thought . . . I never thought Brown Ben. Even my dragons seemed to trust him." She clutched her captain by the shoulders. "Promise me that you will never turn against me. I could not bear that. Promise me."

"Never, my love."

She believed him. "I swore that I should wed Hizdahr zo Loraq if he gave me ninety days of peace, but now . . . I wanted you from the first time that I saw you, but you were a sellsword, fickle, *treacherous*. You boasted that you'd had a hundred women."

"A hundred?" Daario chuckled through his purple beard. "I lied, sweet queen. It was a thousand. But never once a dragon."

She raised her lips to his. "What are you waiting for?"

THE PRINCE OF WINTERFELL

The hearth was caked with cold black ash, the room unheated but for candles. Every time a door opened their flames would sway and shiver. The bride was shivering too. They had dressed her in white lambs-wool trimmed with lace. Her sleeves and bodice were sewn with freshwater pearls, and on her feet were white doeskin slippers—pretty, but not warm. Her face was pale, bloodless.

A face carved of ice, Theon Greyjoy thought as he draped a fur-trimmed cloak about her shoulders. *A corpse buried in the snow.* "My lady. It is time." Beyond the door, the music called them, lute and pipes and drum.

The bride raised her eyes. Brown eyes, shining in the candlelight. "I will be a good wife to him, and t-true. I . . . I will please him and give him sons. I will be a better wife than the real Arya could have been, he'll see."

Talk like that will get you killed, or worse. That lesson he had learned as Reek. "You are the real Arya, my lady. Arya of House Stark, Lord Eddard's daughter, heir to Winterfell." Her name, she had to know her *name.* "Arya Underfoot. Your sister used to call you Arya Horseface."

"It was me made up that name. Her face was long and horsey. Mine isn't. I was pretty." Tears spilled from her eyes at last. "I was never beautiful like Sansa, but they all said I was pretty. Does Lord Ramsay think I am pretty?"

"Yes," he lied. "He's told me so."

"He knows who I am, though. Who I really am. I see it when he looks at me. He looks so angry, even when he smiles, but it's not my fault. They say he likes to hurt people."

"My lady should not listen to such . . . lies."

"They say that he hurt you. Your hands, and . . ."

His mouth was dry. "I . . . I deserved it. I made him angry. You must not make him angry. Lord Ramsay is a . . . a sweet man, and kindly. Please him, and he will be good to you. Be a good wife."

"Help me." She clutched at him. "Please. I used to watch you in the yard, playing with your swords. You were so handsome." She squeezed his arm. "If we ran away, I could be your wife, or your . . . your whore . . . whatever you wanted. You could be my man."

Theon wrenched his arm away from her. "I'm no . . . I'm no one's man." *A man would help her.* "Just . . . just be Arya, be his wife. Please him, or . . . just please him, and stop this talk about being someone else." *Jeyne, her name is Jeyne, it rhymes with pain.* The music was growing more insistent. "It is time. Wipe those tears from your eyes." *Brown eyes. They should be grey. Someone will see. Someone will remember.* "Good. Now smile."

The girl tried. Her lips, trembling, twitched up and froze, and he could see her teeth. *Pretty white teeth,* he thought, *but if she angers him, they will not be pretty long.* When he pushed the door open, three of the four candles fluttered out. He led the bride into the mist, where the wedding guests were waiting.

"Why me?" he had asked when Lady Dustin told him he must give the bride away.

"Her father is dead and all her brothers. Her mother perished at the Twins. Her uncles are lost or dead or captive."

"She has a brother still." *She has three brothers still,* he might have said. "Jon Snow is with the Night's Watch."

"A half-brother, bastard-born, and bound to the Wall. You were her father's ward, the nearest thing she has to living kin. It is only fitting that you give her hand in marriage."

The nearest thing she has to living kin. Theon Greyjoy had grown up with Arya Stark. Theon would have known an imposter. If he was seen to accept Bolton's feigned girl as Arya, the northern lords who had gathered to bear witness to the match would have no grounds to question her legitimacy. Stout and Slate, Whoresbane Umber, the quarrelsome Ryswells, Hornwood men and Cerwyn cousins, fat Lord Wyman Manderly . . . not one of them had known Ned Stark's daughters half so well as he. And if a few entertained private doubts, surely they would be wise enough to keep those misgivings to themselves.

They are using me to cloak their deception, putting mine own face on their lie. That was why Roose Bolton had clothed him as a lord again, to play his part in this mummer's farce. Once that was done, once their false

Arya had been wedded and bedded, Bolton would have no more use for
Theon Turncloak. "Serve us in this, and when Stannis is defeated we will
discuss how best to restore you to your father's seat," his lordship had said
in that soft voice of his, a voice made for lies and whispers. Theon never
believed a word of it. He would dance this dance for them because he had
no choice, but afterward . . . *He will give me back to Ramsay then,* he
thought, *and Ramsay will take a few more fingers and turn me into Reek
once more.* Unless the gods were good, and Stannis Baratheon descended
on Winterfell and put all of them to the sword, himself included. That
was the best he could hope for.

It was warmer in the godswood, strange to say. Beyond its confines, a
hard white frost gripped Winterfell. The paths were treacherous with
black ice, and hoarfrost sparkled in the moonlight on the broken panes of
the Glass Gardens. Drifts of dirty snow had piled up against the walls, filling every nook and corner. Some were so high they hid the doors behind
them. Under the snow lay grey ash and cinders, and here and there a
blackened beam or a pile of bones adorned with scraps of skin and hair.
Icicles long as lances hung from the battlements and fringed the towers
like an old man's stiff white whiskers. But inside the godswood, the ground
remained unfrozen, and steam rose off the hot pools, as warm as baby's
breath.

The bride was garbed in white and grey, the colors the true Arya would
have worn had she lived long enough to wed. Theon wore black and gold,
his cloak pinned to his shoulder by a crude iron kraken that a smith in
Barrowton had hammered together for him. But under the hood, his hair
was white and thin, and his flesh had an old man's greyish undertone. *A
Stark at last,* he thought. Arm in arm, the bride and he passed through an
arched stone door, as wisps of fog stirred round their legs. The drum was
as tremulous as a maiden's heart, the pipes high and sweet and beckoning.
Up above the treetops, a crescent moon was floating in a dark sky,
half-obscured by mist, like an eye peering through a veil of silk.

Theon Greyjoy was no stranger to this godswood. He had played here as
a boy, skipping stones across the cold black pool beneath the weirwood,
hiding his treasures in the bole of an ancient oak, stalking squirrels with a
bow he made himself. Later, older, he had soaked his bruises in the hot
springs after many a session in the yard with Robb and Jory and Jon Snow.
In amongst these chestnuts and elms and soldier pines he had found secret
places where he could hide when he wanted to be alone. The first time he
had ever kissed a girl had been here. Later, a different girl had made a man
of him upon a ragged quilt in the shade of that tall grey-green sentinel.

He had never seen the godswood like this, though—grey and ghostly, filled with warm mists and floating lights and whispered voices that seemed to come from everywhere and nowhere. Beneath the trees, the hot springs steamed. Warm vapors rose from the earth, shrouding the trees in their moist breath, creeping up the walls to draw grey curtains across the watching windows.

There was a path of sorts, a meandering footpath of cracked stones overgrown with moss, half-buried beneath blown dirt and fallen leaves and made treacherous by thick brown roots pushing up from underneath. He led the bride along it. *Jeyne, her name is Jeyne, it rhymes with pain.* He must not think that, though. Should that name pass his lips, it might cost him a finger or an ear. He walked slowly, watching every step. His missing toes made him hobble when he hurried, and it would not do to stumble. Mar Lord Ramsay's wedding with a misstep, and Lord Ramsay might rectify such clumsiness by flaying the offending foot.

The mists were so thick that only the nearest trees were visible; beyond them stood tall shadows and faint lights. Candles flickered beside the wandering path and back amongst the trees, pale fireflies floating in a warm grey soup. It felt like some strange underworld, some timeless place between the worlds, where the damned wandered mournfully for a time before finding their way down to whatever hell their sins had earned them. *Are we all dead, then? Did Stannis come and kill us in our sleep? Is the battle yet to come, or has it been fought and lost?*

Here and there a torch burned hungrily, casting its ruddy glow over the faces of the wedding guests. The way the mists threw back the shifting light made their features seem bestial, half-human, twisted. Lord Stout became a mastiff, old Lord Locke a vulture, Whoresbane Umber a gargoyle, Big Walder Frey a fox, Little Walder a red bull, lacking only a ring for his nose. Roose Bolton's own face was a pale grey mask, with two chips of dirty ice where his eyes should be.

Above their heads the trees were full of ravens, their feathers fluffed as they hunched on bare brown branches, staring down at the pageantry below. *Maester Luwin's birds.* Luwin was dead, and his maester's tower had been put to the torch, yet the ravens lingered. *This is their home.* Theon wondered what that would be like, to have a home.

Then the mists parted, like the curtain opening at a mummer show to reveal some new tableau. The heart tree appeared in front of them, its bony limbs spread wide. Fallen leaves lay about the wide white trunk in drifts of red and brown. The ravens were the thickest here, muttering to one another in the murderers' secret tongue. Ramsay Bolton stood beneath them, clad in high boots of soft grey leather and a black velvet doublet slashed with pink silk and glittering with garnet teardrops. A smile danced across his face. "Who comes?" His lips were moist, his neck red above his collar. "Who comes before the god?"

Theon answered. "Arya of House Stark comes here to be wed. A woman grown and flowered, trueborn and noble, she comes to beg the blessings of the gods. Who comes to claim her?"

"Me," said Ramsay. "Ramsay of House Bolton, Lord of the Hornwood, heir to the Dreadfort. I claim her. Who gives her?"

"Theon of House Greyjoy, who was her father's ward." He turned to the bride. "Lady Arya, will you take this man?"

She raised her eyes to his. *Brown eyes, not grey. Are all of them so blind?* For a long moment she did not speak, but those eyes were begging. *This is your chance,* he thought. *Tell them. Tell them now. Shout out your name before them all, tell them that you are not Arya Stark, let all the north hear how you were made to play this part.* It would mean her death, of course, and his own as well, but Ramsay in his wroth might kill them quickly. The old gods of the north might grant them that small boon.

"I take this man," the bride said in a whisper.

All around them lights glimmered through the mists, a hundred candles pale as shrouded stars. Theon stepped back, and Ramsay and his bride joined hands and knelt before the heart tree, bowing their heads in token of submission. The weirwood's carved red eyes stared down at them, its great red mouth open as if to laugh. In the branches overhead a raven *quork*ed.

After a moment of silent prayer, the man and woman rose again. Ramsay undid the cloak that Theon had slipped about his bride's shoulders moments before, the heavy white wool cloak bordered in grey fur, emblazoned with the direwolf of House Stark. In its place he fastened a pink cloak, spattered with red garnets like those upon his doublet. On its back was the flayed man of the Dreadfort done in stiff red leather, grim and grisly.

Quick as that, it was done. Weddings went more quickly in the north. It came of not having priests, Theon supposed, but whatever the reason it seemed to him a mercy. Ramsay Bolton scooped his wife up in his arms and strode through the mists with her. Lord Bolton and his Lady Walda followed, then the rest. The musicians began to play again, and the bard Abel began to sing "Two Hearts That Beat as One." Two of his women joined their voices to his own to make a sweet harmony.

Theon found himself wondering if he should say a prayer. *Will the old gods hear me if I do?* They were not his gods, had never been his gods. He was ironborn, a son of Pyke, his god was the Drowned God of the islands . . . but Winterfell was long leagues from the sea. It had been a lifetime since any god had heard him. He did not know who he was, or what he was, why he was still alive, why he had ever been born.

"Theon," a voice seemed to whisper.

His head snapped up. "Who said that?" All he could see were the trees and the fog that covered them. The voice had been as faint as rustling leaves, as cold as hate. *A god's voice, or a ghost's.* How many died the day that he took Winterfell? How many more the day he lost it? *The day that Theon Greyjoy died, to be reborn as Reek. Reek, Reek, it rhymes with shriek.*

Suddenly he did not want to be here.

Once outside the godswood the cold descended on him like a ravening wolf and caught him in its teeth. He lowered his head into the wind and made for the Great Hall, hastening after the long line of candles and torches. Ice crunched beneath his boots, and a sudden gust pushed back his hood, as if a ghost had plucked at him with frozen fingers, hungry to gaze upon his face.

Winterfell was full of ghosts for Theon Greyjoy.

This was not the castle he remembered from the summer of his youth. This place was scarred and broken, more ruin than redoubt, a haunt of crows and corpses. The great double curtain wall still stood, for granite does not yield easily to fire, but most of the towers and keeps within were roofless. A few had collapsed. The thatch and timber had been consumed by fire, in whole or in part, and under the shattered panes of the Glass Garden the fruits and vegetables that would have fed the castle during the winter were dead and black and frozen. Tents filled the yard, half-buried in the snow. Roose Bolton had brought his host inside the walls, along with his friends the Freys; thousands huddled amongst the ruins, crowding every court, sleeping in cellar vaults and under topless towers, and in buildings abandoned for centuries.

Plumes of grey smoke snaked up from the rebuilt kitchens and reroofed barracks keep. The battlements and crenellations were crowned with snow and hung with icicles. All the color had been leached from Winterfell until only grey and white remained. *The Stark colors.* Theon did not know whether he ought to find that ominous or reassuring. Even the sky was grey. *Grey and grey and greyer. The whole world grey, everywhere you look, everything grey except the eyes of the bride.* The eyes of the bride were brown. *Big and brown and full of fear.* It was not right that she should look to him for rescue. What had she been thinking, that he would whistle up a winged horse and fly her out of here, like some hero in the stories she and Sansa used to love? He could not even help himself. *Reek, Reek, it rhymes with meek.*

All about the yard, dead men hung half-frozen at the end of hempen ropes, swollen faces white with hoarfrost. Winterfell had been crawling with squatters when Bolton's van had reached the castle. More than two dozen had been driven at spearpoint from the nests they had made amongst the castle's half-ruined keeps and towers. The boldest and most truculent had been hanged, the rest put to work. Serve well, Lord Bolton told them, and he would be merciful. Stone and timber were plentiful with the wolfswood so close at hand. Stout new gates had gone up first, to replace those that had been burned. Then the collapsed roof of the Great Hall had been cleared away and a new one raised hurriedly in its stead. When the work was done, Lord Bolton hanged the workers. True to his word, he showed them mercy and did not flay a one.

By that time, the rest of Bolton's army had arrived. They raised King Tommen's stag and lion above the walls of Winterfell as the wind came howling from the north, and below it the flayed man of the Dreadfort. Theon arrived in Barbrey Dustin's train, with her ladyship herself, her Barrowton levies, and the bride-to-be. Lady Dustin had insisted that she should have custody of Lady Arya until such time as she was wed, but now that time was done. *She belongs to Ramsay now. She said the words.* By this marriage Ramsay would be Lord of Winterfell. So long as Jeyne took care not to anger him, he should have no cause to harm her. *Arya. Her name is Arya.*

Even inside fur-lined gloves, Theon's hands had begun to throb with pain. It was often his hands that hurt the worst, especially his missing fingers. Had there truly been a time when women yearned for his touch? *I made myself the Prince of Winterfell,* he thought, *and from that came all of this.* He had thought that men would sing of him for a hundred years and tell tales of his daring. But if anyone spoke of him now, it was as Theon Turncloak, and the tales they told were of his treachery. *This was never my home. I was a hostage here.* Lord Stark had not treated him cruelly, but the long steel shadow of his greatsword had always been between them. *He was kind to me, but never warm. He knew that one day he might need to put me to death.*

Theon kept his eyes downcast as he crossed the yard, weaving between the tents. *I learned to fight in this yard,* he thought, remembering warm summer days spent sparring with Robb and Jon Snow under the watchful eyes of old Ser Rodrik. That was back when he was whole, when he could grasp a sword hilt as well as any man. But the yard held darker memories as well. This was where he had assembled Stark's people the night Bran and Rickon fled the castle. Ramsay was Reek then, standing at his side, whispering that he should flay a few of his captives to make them tell him where the boys had gone. *There will be no flaying here whilst I am Prince of Winterfell*, Theon had responded, little dreaming how short his rule would prove. *None of them would help me. I had known them all for half my life, and not one of them would help me.* Even so, he had done his best to protect them, but once Ramsay put Reek's face aside he'd slain all the men, and Theon's ironborn as well. *He set my horse afire.* That was the last sight he had seen the day the castle fell: Smiler burning, the flames leaping from his mane as he reared up, kicking, screaming, his eyes white with terror. *Here in this very yard.*

The doors of the Great Hall loomed up in front of him; new-made, to replace the doors that burned, they seemed crude and ugly to him, raw planks hastily joined. A pair of spearmen guarded them, hunched and shivering under thick fur cloaks, their beards crusty with ice. They eyed Theon resentfully as he hobbled up the steps, pushed against the right-hand door, and slipped inside.

The hall was blessedly warm and bright with torchlight, as crowded as he had ever seen it. Theon let the heat wash over him, then made his way toward the front of the hall. Men sat crammed knee to knee along the benches, so tightly packed that the servers had to squirm between them. Even the knights and lords above the salt enjoyed less space than usual.

Up near the dais, Abel was plucking at his lute and singing "Fair Maids of Summer." *He calls himself a bard. In truth he's more a pander.* Lord Manderly had brought musicians from White Harbor, but none were singers, so when Abel turned up at the gates with a lute and six women, he had been made welcome. "Two sisters, two daughters, one wife, and my old mother," the singer claimed, though not one looked like him. "Some dance, some sing, one plays the pipe and one the drums. Good washerwomen too."

Bard or pander, Abel's voice was passable, his playing fair. Here amongst the ruins, that was as much as anyone might expect.

Along the walls the banners hung: the horseheads of the Ryswells in gold, brown, grey, and black; the roaring giant of House Umber; the stone hand of House Flint of Flint's Finger; the moose of Hornwood and the merman of Manderly; Cerwyn's black battle-axe and the Tallhart pines. Yet their bright colors could not entirely cover the blackened walls behind them, nor the boards that closed the holes where windows once had been. Even the roof was wrong, its raw new timbers light and bright, where the old rafters had been stained almost black by centuries of smoke.

The largest banners were behind the dais, where the direwolf of Winterfell and the flayed man of the Dreadfort hung back of the bride and groom. The sight of the Stark banner hit Theon harder than he had expected. *Wrong, it's wrong, as wrong as her eyes.* The arms of House Poole were a blue plate on white, framed by a grey tressure. Those were the arms they should have hung.

"Theon Turncloak," someone said as he passed. Other men turned away at the sight of him. One spat. *And why not?* He was the traitor who had taken Winterfell by treachery, slain his foster brothers, delivered his own people to be flayed at Moat Cailin, and given his foster sister to Lord Ramsay's bed. Roose Bolton might make use of him, but true northmen must despise him.

The missing toes on his left foot had left him with a crabbed, awkward gait, comical to look upon. Back behind him, he heard a woman laugh. Even here in this half-frozen lichyard of a castle, surrounded by snow and ice and death, there were women. *Washerwomen.* That was the polite way of saying *camp follower,* which was the polite way of saying *whore.*

Where they came from Theon could not say. They just seemed to appear, like maggots on a corpse or ravens after a battle. Every army drew them. Some were hardened whores who could fuck twenty men in a night and drink them all blind. Others looked as innocent as maids, but that was just a trick of their trade. Some were camp brides, bound to the soldiers they followed with words whispered to one god or another but doomed to be forgotten once the war was done. They would warm a man's bed by night, patch the holes in his boots at morning, cook his supper come dusk, and loot his corpse after the battle. Some even did a bit of washing. With them, oft as not, came bastard children, wretched, filthy creatures born in one camp or the other. And even such as these made mock of Theon Turncloak. *Let them laugh.* His pride had perished here in Winterfell; there was no place for such in the dungeons of the Dreadfort. When you have known the kiss of a flaying knife, a laugh loses all its power to hurt you.

Birth and blood accorded him a seat upon the dais at the end of the high table, beside a wall. To his left sat Lady Dustin, clad as ever in black wool, severe in cut and unadorned. To his right sat no one. *They are all afraid the dishonor might rub off on them.* If he had dared, he would have laughed.

The bride had the place of highest honor, between Ramsay and his father. She sat with eyes downcast as Roose Bolton bid them drink to Lady Arya. "In her children our two ancient houses will become as one," he said, "and the long enmity between Stark and Bolton will be ended." His voice was so soft that the hall grew hushed as men strained to hear. "I am sorry that our good friend Stannis has not seen fit to join us yet," he went on, to a ripple of laughter, "as I know Ramsay had hoped to present his head to Lady Arya as a wedding gift." The laughs grew louder. "We shall give him a splendid welcome when he arrives, a welcome worthy of true northmen. Until that day, let us eat and drink and make merry . . . for winter is almost upon us, my friends, and many of us here shall not live to see the spring."

The Lord of White Harbor had furnished the food and drink, black stout and yellow beer and wines red and gold and purple, brought up from the warm south on fat-bottomed ships and aged in his deep cellars. The wedding guests gorged on cod cakes and winter squash, hills of neeps and great round wheels of cheese, on smoking slabs of mutton and beef ribs charred almost black, and lastly on three great wedding pies, as wide across as wagon wheels, their flaky crusts stuffed to bursting with carrots, onions, turnips, parsnips, mushrooms, and chunks of seasoned pork swimming in a savory brown gravy. Ramsay hacked off slices with his falchion and Wyman Manderly himself served, presenting the first steaming portions to Roose Bolton and his fat Frey wife, the next to Ser Hosteen and Ser Aenys, the sons of Walder Frey. "The best pie you have ever tasted, my lords," the fat lord declared. "Wash it down with Arbor gold and savor every bite. I know I shall."

True to his word, Manderly devoured six portions, two from each of the three pies, smacking his lips and slapping his belly and stuffing himself until the front of his tunic was half-brown with gravy stains and his beard was flecked with crumbs of crust. Even Fat Walda Frey could not match his gluttony, though she did manage three slices herself. Ramsay ate heartily as well, though his pale bride did no more than stare at the portion set before her. When she raised her head and looked at Theon, he could see the fear behind her big brown eyes.

No longswords had been allowed within the hall, but every man there wore a dagger, even Theon Greyjoy. How else to cut his meat? Every time he looked at the girl who had been Jeyne Poole, he felt the presence of that steel at his side. *I have no way to save her,* he thought, *but I could kill her easy enough. No one would expect it. I could beg her for the honor of a dance and cut her throat. That would be a kindness, wouldn't it? And if the*

old gods hear my prayer, Ramsay in his wroth might strike me dead as well.
Theon was not afraid to die. Underneath the Dreadfort, he had learned
there were far worse things than death. Ramsay had taught him that lesson, finger by finger and toe by toe, and it was not one that he was ever
like to forget.

"You do not eat," observed Lady Dustin.

"No." Eating was hard for him. Ramsay had left him with so many
broken teeth that chewing was an agony. Drinking was easier, though he
had to grasp the wine cup with both hands to keep from dropping it.

"No taste for pork pie, my lord? The best pork pie we ever tasted, our
fat friend would have us believe." She gestured toward Lord Manderly
with her wine cup. "Have you ever seen a fat man so happy? He is almost
dancing. Serving with his own hands."

It was true. The Lord of White Harbor was the very picture of the jolly
fat man, laughing and smiling, japing with the other lords and slapping
them on the back, calling out to the musicians for this tune or that tune.
"Give us 'The Night That Ended,' singer," he bellowed. "The bride will
like that one, I know. Or sing to us of brave young Danny Flint and make
us weep." To look at him, you would have thought that he was the one
newly wed.

"He's drunk," said Theon.

"Drowning his fears. He is craven to the bone, that one."

Was he? Theon was not certain. His sons had been fat as well, but they
had not shamed themselves in battle. "Ironborn will feast before a battle
too. A last taste of life, should death await. If Stannis comes . . ."

"He will. He must." Lady Dustin chuckled. "And when he does, the fat
man will piss himself. His son died at the Red Wedding, yet he's shared his
bread and salt with Freys, welcomed them beneath his roof, promised one
his granddaughter. He even serves them pie. The Manderlys ran from the
south once, hounded from their lands and keeps by enemies. Blood runs
true. The fat man would like to kill us all, I do not doubt, but he does not
have the belly for it, for all his girth. Under that sweaty flesh beats a heart
as craven and cringing as . . . well . . . yours."

Her last word was a lash, but Theon dared not answer back in kind. Any
insolence would cost him skin. "If my lady believes Lord Manderly wants
to betray us, Lord Bolton is the one to tell."

"You think Roose does not know? Silly boy. Watch him. Watch how he
watches Manderly. No dish so much as touches Roose's lips until he sees
Lord Wyman eat of it first. No cup of wine is sipped until he sees Manderly
drink of the same cask. I think he would be pleased if the fat man at-

tempted some betrayal. It would amuse him. Roose has no feelings, you see. Those leeches that he loves so well sucked all the passions out of him years ago. He does not love, he does not hate, he does not grieve. This is a game to him, mildly diverting. Some men hunt, some hawk, some tumble dice. Roose plays with men. You and me, these Freys, Lord Manderly, his plump new wife, even his bastard, we are but his playthings." A serving man was passing by. Lady Dustin held out her wine cup and let him fill it, then gestured for him to do the same for Theon. "Truth be told," she said, "Lord Bolton aspires to more than mere lordship. Why not King of the North? Tywin Lannister is dead, the Kingslayer is maimed, the Imp is fled. The Lannisters are a spent force, and you were kind enough to rid him of the Starks. Old Walder Frey will not object to his fat little Walda becoming a queen. White Harbor might prove troublesome should Lord Wyman survive this coming battle . . . but I am quite sure that he will not. No more than Stannis. Roose will remove both of them, as he removed the Young Wolf. Who else is there?"

"You," said Theon. "There is you. The Lady of Barrowton, a Dustin by marriage, a Ryswell by birth."

That pleased her. She took a sip of wine, her dark eyes sparkling, and said, "The *widow* of Barrowton . . . and yes, if I so choose, I could be an inconvenience. Of course, Roose sees that too, so he takes care to keep me sweet."

She might have said more, but then she saw the maesters. Three of them had entered together by the lord's door behind the dais—one tall, one plump, one very young, but in their robes and chains they were three grey peas from a black pod. Before the war, Medrick had served Lord Hornwood, Rhodry Lord Cerwyn, and young Henly Lord Slate. Roose Bolton had brought them all to Winterfell to take charge of Luwin's ravens, so messages might be sent and received from here again.

As Maester Medrick went to one knee to whisper in Bolton's ear, Lady Dustin's mouth twisted in distaste. "If I were queen, the first thing I would do would be to kill all those grey rats. They scurry everywhere, living on the leavings of the lords, chittering to one another, whispering in the ears of their masters. But who are the masters and who are the servants, truly? Every great lord has his maester, every lesser lord aspires to one. If you do not have a maester, it is taken to mean that you are of little consequence. The grey rats read and write our letters, even for such lords as cannot read themselves, and who can say for a certainty that they are not twisting the words for their own ends? What good are they, I ask you?"

"They heal," said Theon. It seemed to be expected of him.

"They heal, yes. I never said they were not subtle. They tend to us when we are sick and injured, or distraught over the illness of a parent or a child. Whenever we are weakest and most vulnerable, there they are. Sometimes they heal us, and we are duly grateful. When they fail, they console us in our grief, and we are grateful for that as well. Out of gratitude we give them a place beneath our roof and make them privy to all our shames and secrets, a part of every council. And before too long, the ruler has become the ruled.

"That was how it was with Lord Rickard Stark. Maester Walys was his grey rat's name. And isn't it clever how the maesters go by only one name, even those who had two when they first arrived at the Citadel? That way we cannot know who they truly are or where they come from . . . but if you are dogged enough, you can still find out. Before he forged his chain, Maester Walys had been known as Walys Flowers. Flowers, Hill, Rivers, Snow . . . we give such names to baseborn children to mark them for what they are, but they are always quick to shed them. Walys Flowers had a Hightower girl for a mother . . . and an archmaester of the Citadel for a father, it was rumored. The grey rats are not as chaste as they would have us believe. Oldtown maesters are the worst of all. Once he forged his chain, his secret father and his friends wasted no time dispatching him to Winterfell to fill Lord Rickard's ears with poisoned words as sweet as honey. The Tully marriage was his notion, never doubt it, he—"

She broke off as Roose Bolton rose to his feet, pale eyes shining in the torchlight. "My friends," he began, and a hush swept through the hall, so profound that Theon could hear the wind plucking at the boards over the windows. "Stannis and his knights have left Deepwood Motte, flying the banner of his new red god. The clans of the northern hills come with him on their shaggy runtish horses. If the weather holds, they could be on us in a fortnight. And Crowfood Umber marches down the kingsroad, whilst the Karstarks approach from the east. They mean to join with Lord Stannis here and take this castle from us."

Ser Hosteen Frey pushed to his feet. "We should ride forth to meet them. Why allow them to combine their strength?"

Because Arnolf Karstark awaits only a sign from Lord Bolton before he turns his cloak, thought Theon, as other lords began to shout out counsel. Lord Bolton raised his hands for silence. "The hall is not the place for such discussions, my lords. Let us adjourn to the solar whilst my son consummates his marriage. The rest of you, remain and enjoy the food and drink."

As the Lord of the Dreadfort slipped out, attended by the three maesters, other lords and captains rose to follow. Hother Umber, the gaunt old man called Whoresbane, went grim-faced and scowling. Lord Manderly was so drunk he required four strong men to help him from the hall. "We should have a song about the Rat Cook," he was muttering, as he staggered past Theon, leaning on his knights. "Singer, give us a song about the Rat Cook."

Lady Dustin was amongst the last to bestir herself. When she had gone, all at once the hall seemed stifling. It was not until Theon pushed himself to his feet that he realized how much he'd drunk. When he stumbled from the table, he knocked a flagon from the hands of a serving girl. Wine splashed across his boots and breeches, a dark red tide.

A hand grabbed his shoulder, five fingers hard as iron digging deep into his flesh. "You're wanted, Reek," said Sour Alyn, his breath foul with the smell from his rotten teeth. Yellow Dick and Damon Dance-for-Me were with him. "Ramsay says you're to bring his bride to his bed."

A shiver of fear went through him. *I played my part*, he thought. *Why me?* He knew better than to object, though.

Lord Ramsay had already left the hall. His bride, forlorn and seemingly forgotten, sat hunched and silent beneath the banner of House Stark, clutching a silver goblet in both hands. Judging from the way she looked at him when he approached, she had emptied that goblet more than once. Perhaps she hoped that if she drank enough, the ordeal would pass her by. Theon knew better. "Lady Arya," he said. "Come. It is time you did your duty."

Six of the Bastard's boys accompanied them as Theon led the girl out the back of the hall and across the frigid yard to the Great Keep. It was up three flights of stone steps to Lord Ramsay's bedchamber, one of the rooms the fires had touched but lightly. As they climbed, Damon Dance-for-Me whistled, whilst Skinner boasted that Lord Ramsay had promised him a piece of the bloody sheet as a mark of special favor.

The bedchamber had been well prepared for the consummation. All the furnishings were new, brought up from Barrowton in the baggage train. The canopy bed had a feather mattress and drapes of blood-red velvet. The stone floor was covered with wolfskins. A fire was burning in the hearth, a candle on the bedside table. On the sideboard was a flagon of wine, two cups, and a half wheel of veined white cheese.

There was a chair as well, carved of black oak with a red leather seat. Lord Ramsay was seated in it when they entered. Spittle glistened on his lips. "There's my sweet maid. Good lads. You may leave us now. Not you, Reek. You stay."

Reek, Reek, it rhymes with peek. He could feel his missing fingers cramping: two on his left hand, one on his right. And on his hip his dagger rested, sleeping in its leather sheath, but heavy, oh so heavy. *It is only my pinky gone on my right hand,* Theon reminded himself. *I can still grip a knife.* "My lord. How may I serve you?"

"You gave the wench to me. Who better to unwrap the gift? Let's have a look at Ned Stark's little daughter."

She is no kin to Lord Eddard, Theon almost said. *Ramsay knows, he has to know. What new cruel game is this?* The girl was standing by a bedpost, trembling like a doe. "Lady Arya, if you will turn your back, I must needs unlace your gown."

"No." Lord Ramsay poured himself a cup of wine. "Laces take too long. Cut it off her."

Theon drew the dagger. *All I need do is turn and stab him. The knife is in my hand.* He knew the game by then. *Another trap,* he told himself, remembering Kyra with her keys. *He wants me to try to kill him. And when I fail, he'll flay the skin from the hand I used to hold the blade.* He grabbed a handful of the bride's skirt. "Stand still, my lady." The gown was loose below the waist, so that was where he slid the blade in, slicing upward slowly, so as not to cut her. Steel whispered through wool and silk with a faint, soft sound. The girl was shaking. Theon had to grab her arm to hold her still. *Jeyne, Jeyne, it rhymes with pain.* He tightened his grip, as much as his maimed left hand would allow. "Stay still."

Finally the gown fell away, a pale tangle round her feet. "Her small-clothes too," Ramsay commanded. Reek obeyed.

When it was done the bride stood naked, her bridal finery a heap of white and grey rags about her feet. Her breasts were small and pointed, her hips narrow and girlish, her legs as skinny as a bird's. *A child.* Theon had forgotten how young she was. *Sansa's age. Arya would be even younger.* Despite the fire in the hearth, the bedchamber was chilly. Jeyne's pale skin was pebbled with gooseprickles. There was a moment when her hands rose, as if to cover her breasts, but Theon mouthed a silent *no* and she saw and stopped at once.

"What do you think of her, Reek?" asked Lord Ramsay.

"She . . ." *What answer does he want?* What was it the girl had said, before the godswood? *They all said that I was pretty.* She was not pretty now. He could see a spiderweb of faint thin lines across her back where someone had whipped her. ". . . she is beautiful, so . . . so beautiful."

Ramsay smiled his wet smile. "Does she make your cock hard, Reek? Is it straining against your laces? Would you like to fuck her first?" He laughed. "The Prince of Winterfell should have that right, as all lords did in days of old. The first night. But you're no lord, are you? Only Reek. Not even a man, truth be told." He took another gulp of wine, then threw the cup across the room to shatter off a wall. Red rivers ran down across the stone. "Lady Arya. Get on the bed. Yes, against the pillows, that's a good wife. Now spread your legs. Let us see your cunt."

The girl obeyed, wordless. Theon took a step back toward the door. Lord Ramsay sat beside his bride, slid his hand along her inner thigh, then jammed two fingers up inside her. The girl let out a gasp of pain. "You're dry as an old bone." Ramsay pulled his hand free and slapped her face. "I was told that you'd know how to please a man. Was that a lie?"

"N-no, my lord. I was t-trained."

Ramsay rose, the firelight shining on his face. "Reek, get over here. Get her ready for me."

For a moment he did not understand. "I . . . do you mean . . . m'lord, I have no . . . I . . ."

"With your mouth," Lord Ramsay said. "And be quick about it. If she's not wet by the time I'm done disrobing, I will cut off that tongue of yours and nail it to the wall."

Somewhere in the godswood, a raven screamed. The dagger was still in his hand.

He sheathed it.

Reek, my name is Reek, it rhymes with weak.

Reek bent to his task.

THE WATCHER

L et us look upon this head," his prince commanded.

Areo Hotah ran his hand along the smooth shaft of his longaxe, his ash-and-iron wife, all the while watching. He watched the white knight, Ser Balon Swann, and the others who had come with him. He watched the Sand Snakes, each at a different table. He watched the lords and ladies, the serving men, the old blind seneschal, and the young maester Myles, with his silky beard and servile smile. Standing half in light and half in shadow, he saw all of them. *Serve. Protect. Obey.* That was his task.

All the rest had eyes only for the chest. It was carved of ebony, with silver clasps and hinges. A fine-looking box, no doubt, but many of those assembled here in the Old Palace of Sunspear might soon be dead, depending on what was in that chest.

His slippers whispering against the floor, Maester Caleotte crossed the hall to Ser Balon Swann. The round little man looked splendid in his new robes, with their broad bands of dun and butternut and narrow stripes of red. Bowing, he took the chest from the hands of the white knight and carried it to the dais, where Doran Martell sat in his rolling chair between his daughter Arianne and his dead brother's beloved paramour, Ellaria. A hundred scented candles perfumed the air. Gemstones glittered on the fingers of the lords and the girdles and hairnets of the ladies. Areo Hotah had polished his shirt of copper scales mirror-bright so he would blaze in the candlelight as well.

A hush had fallen across the hall. *Dorne holds its breath.* Maester Caleotte set the box on the floor beside Prince Doran's chair. The maester's fingers, normally so sure and deft, turned clumsy as he worked the latch and opened the lid, to reveal the skull within. Hotah heard someone clear his throat. One of the Fowler twins whispered something to the other. Ellaria Sand had closed her eyes and was murmuring a prayer.

Ser Balon Swann was taut as a drawn bow, the captain of guards observed. This new white knight was not so tall nor comely as the old one, but he was bigger across the chest, burlier, his arms thick with muscle. His snowy cloak was clasped at the throat by two swans on a silver brooch. One was ivory, the other onyx, and it seemed to Areo Hotah as if the two of them were fighting. The man who wore them looked a fighter too. *This one will not die so easy as the other. He will not charge into my axe the way Ser Arys did. He will stand behind his shield and make me come at him.* If it came to that, Hotah would be ready. His longaxe was sharp enough to shave with.

He allowed himself a brief glance at the chest. The skull rested on a bed of black felt, grinning. All skulls grinned, but this one seemed happier than most. *And bigger.* The captain of guards had never seen a larger skull. Its brow shelf was thick and heavy, its jaw massive. The bone shone in the candlelight, white as Ser Balon's cloak. "Place it on the pedestal," the prince commanded. He had tears glistening in his eyes.

The pedestal was a column of black marble three feet taller than Maester Caleotte. The fat little maester hopped up on his toes but still could not quite reach. Areo Hotah was about to go and help him, but Obara Sand moved first. Even without her whip and shield, she had an angry mannish look to her. In place of a gown, she wore men's breeches and a calf-length linen tunic, cinched at the waist with a belt of copper suns. Her brown hair was tied back in a knot. Snatching the skull from the maester's soft pink hands, she placed it up atop the marble column.

"The Mountain rides no more," the prince said, gravely.

"Was his dying long and hard, Ser Balon?" asked Tyene Sand, in the tone a maiden might use to ask if her gown was pretty.

"He screamed for days, my lady," the white knight replied, though it was plain that it pleased him little to say so. "We could hear him all over the Red Keep."

"Does that trouble you, ser?" asked the Lady Nym. She wore a gown of yellow silk so sheer and fine that the candles shone right through it to reveal the spun gold and jewels beneath. So immodest was her garb that the white knight seemed uncomfortable looking at her, but Hotah approved. Nymeria was least dangerous when nearly naked. Elsewise she was sure to have a dozen blades concealed about her person. "Ser Gregor was a bloody brute, all men agree. If ever a man deserved to suffer, it was him."

"That is as it may be, my lady," said Balon Swann, "but Ser Gregor was a knight, and a knight should die with sword in hand. Poison is a foul and filthy way to kill."

Lady Tyene smiled at that. Her gown was cream and green, with long lace sleeves, so modest and so innocent that any man who looked at her might think her the most chaste of maids. Areo Hotah knew better. Her soft, pale hands were as deadly as Obara's callused ones, if not more so. He watched her carefully, alert to every little flutter of her fingers.

Prince Doran frowned. "That is so, Ser Balon, but the Lady Nym is right. If ever a man deserved to die screaming, it was Gregor Clegane. He butchered my good sister, smashed her babe's head against a wall. I only pray that now he is burning in some hell, and that Elia and her children are at peace. This is the justice that Dorne has hungered for. I am glad that I lived long enough to taste it. At long last the Lannisters have proved the truth of their boast and paid this old blood debt."

The prince left it to Ricasso, his blind seneschal, to rise and propose the toast. "Lords and ladies, let us all now drink to Tommen, the First of His Name, King of the Andals, the Rhoynar, and the First Men, and Lord of the Seven Kingdoms."

Serving men had begun to move amongst the guests as the seneschal was speaking, filling cups from the flagons that they bore. The wine was Dornish strongwine, dark as blood and sweet as vengeance. The captain did not drink of it. He never drank at feasts. Nor did the prince himself partake. He had his own wine, prepared by Maester Myles and well laced with poppy juice to ease the agony in his swollen joints.

The white knight did drink, as was only courteous. His companions likewise. So did the Princess Arianne, Lady Jordayne, the Lord of Godsgrace, the Knight of Lemonwood, the Lady of Ghost Hill . . . even Ellaria Sand, Prince Oberyn's beloved paramour, who had been with him in King's Landing when he died. Hotah paid more note to those who did not drink: Ser Daemon Sand, Lord Tremond Gargalen, the Fowler twins, Dagos Manwoody, the Ullers of the Hellholt, the Wyls of the Boneway. *If there is trouble, it could start with one of them.* Dorne was an angry and divided land, and Prince Doran's hold on it was not as firm as it might be. Many of his own lords thought him weak and would have welcomed open war with the Lannisters and the boy king on the Iron Throne.

Chief amongst those were the Sand Snakes, the bastard daughters of the prince's late brother Oberyn, the Red Viper, three of whom were at the feast. Doran Martell was the wisest of princes, and it was not the place of his captain of guards to question his decisions, but Areo Hotah did wonder why he had chosen to release the ladies Obara, Nymeria, and Tyene from their lonely cells in the Spear Tower.

Tyene declined Ricasso's toast with a murmur and Lady Nym with a flick of a hand. Obara let them fill her cup to the brim, then upended it to spill the red wine on the floor. When a serving girl knelt to wipe up the spilled wine, Obara left the hall. After a moment Princess Arianne excused herself and went after her. *Obara would never turn her rage on the little princess*, Hotah knew. *They are cousins, and she loves her well.*

The feast continued late into the night, presided over by the grinning skull on its pillar of black marble. Seven courses were served, in honor of the seven gods and the seven brothers of the Kingsguard. The soup was made with eggs and lemons, the long green peppers stuffed with cheese and onions. There were lamprey pies, capons glazed with honey, a whiskerfish from the bottom of the Greenblood that was so big it took four serving men to carry it to table. After that came a savory snake stew, chunks of seven different sorts of snake slow-simmered with dragon peppers and blood oranges and a dash of venom to give it a good bite. The stew was fiery hot, Hotah knew, though he tasted none of it. Sherbet followed, to cool the tongue. For the sweet, each guest was served a skull of spun sugar. When the crust was broken, they found sweet custard inside and bits of plum and cherry.

Princess Arianne returned in time for the stuffed peppers. *My little princess*, Hotah thought, but Arianne was a woman now. The scarlet silks she wore left no doubt of that. Of late she had changed in other ways as well. Her plot to crown Myrcella had been betrayed and smashed, her white knight had perished bloodily at Hotah's hand, and she herself had been confined to the Spear Tower, condemned to solitude and silence. All of that had chastened her. There was something else as well, though, some secret her father had confided in her before releasing her from her confinement. What that was, the captain did not know.

The prince had placed his daughter between himself and the white knight, a place of high honor. Arianne smiled as she slipped into her seat again, and murmured something in Ser Balon's ear. The knight did not choose to respond. He ate little, Hotah observed: a spoon of soup, a bite of the pepper, the leg off a capon, some fish. He shunned the lamprey pie and tried only one small spoonful of the stew. Even that made his brow break out in sweat. Hotah could sympathize. When first he came to Dorne, the fiery food would tie his bowels in knots and burn his tongue. That was years ago, however; now his hair was white, and he could eat anything a Dornishman could eat.

When the spun-sugar skulls were served, Ser Balon's mouth grew tight, and he gave the prince a lingering look to see if he was being mocked. Doran Martell took no notice, but his daughter did. "It is the cook's little jape, Ser Balon," said Arianne. "Even death is not sacred to a Dornish-men. You won't be cross with us, I pray?" She brushed the back of the white knight's hand with her fingers. "I hope you have enjoyed your time in Dorne."

"Everyone has been most hospitable, my lady."

Arianne touched the pin that clasped his cloak, with its quarreling swans. "I have always been fond of swans. No other bird is half so beauti-ful, this side of the Summer Isles."

"Your peacocks might dispute that," said Ser Balon.

"They might," said Arianne, "but peacocks are vain, proud creatures, strutting about in all those gaudy colors. Give me a swan serene in white or beautiful in black."

Ser Balon gave a nod and sipped his wine. *This one is not so easily se-duced as was his Sworn Brother,* Hotah thought. *Ser Arys was a boy, despite his years. This one is a man, and wary.* The captain had only to look at him to see that the white knight was ill at ease. *This place is strange to him, and little to his liking.* Hotah could understand that. Dorne had seemed a queer place to him as well when first he came here with his own princess, many years ago. The bearded priests had drilled him on the Common Speech of Westeros before they sent him forth, but the Dornishmen all spoke too quickly for him to understand. Dornish women were lewd, Dor-nish wine was sour, and Dornish food was full of queer hot spices. And the Dornish sun was hotter than the pale, wan sun of Norvos, glaring down from a blue sky day after day.

Ser Balon's journey had been shorter but troubling in its own way, the captain knew. Three knights, eight squires, twenty men-at-arms, and sun-dry grooms and servants had accompanied him from King's Landing, but once they crossed the mountains into Dorne their progress had been slowed by a round of feasts, hunts, and celebrations at every castle that they chanced to pass. And now that they had reached Sunspear, neither Princess Myrcella nor Ser Arys Oakheart was on hand to greet them. *The white knight knows that something is amiss,* Hotah could tell, *but it is more than that.* Perhaps the presence of the Sand Snakes unnerved him. If so, Obara's return to the hall must have been vinegar in the wound. She slipped back into her place without a word, and sat there sullen and scowl-ing, neither smiling nor speaking.

Midnight was close at hand when Prince Doran turned to the white knight and said, "Ser Balon, I have read the letter that you brought me from our gracious queen. Might I assume that you are familiar with its contents, ser?"

Hotah saw the knight tense. "I am, my lord. Her Grace informed me that I might be called upon to escort her daughter back to King's Landing. King Tommen has been pining for his sister and would like Princess Myrcella to return to court for a short visit."

Princess Arianne made a sad face. "Oh, but we have all grown so fond of Myrcella, ser. She and my brother Trystane have become inseparable."

"Prince Trystane would be welcome in King's Landing as well," said Balon Swann. "King Tommen would wish to meet him, I am sure. His Grace has so few companions near his own age."

"The bonds formed in boyhood can last a man for life," said Prince Doran. "When Trystane and Myrcella wed, he and Tommen will be as brothers. Queen Cersei has the right of it. The boys should meet, become friends. Dorne will miss him, to be sure, but it is past time Trystane saw something of the world beyond the walls of Sunspear."

"I know King's Landing will welcome him most warmly."

Why is he sweating now? the captain wondered, watching. *The hall is cool enough, and he never touched the stew.*

"As for the other matter that Queen Cersei raises," Prince Doran was saying, "it is true, Dorne's seat upon the small council has been vacant since my brother's death, and it is past time that it was filled again. I am flattered that Her Grace feels my counsel might be of use to her, though I wonder if I have the strength for such a journey. Perhaps if we went by sea?"

"By ship?" Ser Balon seemed taken aback. "That . . . would that be safe, my prince? Autumn is a bad season for storms, or so I've heard, and . . . the pirates in the Stepstones, they . . ."

"The pirates. To be sure. You may be right, ser. Safer to return the way you came." Prince Doran smiled pleasantly. "Let us talk again on the morrow. When we reach the Water Gardens, we can tell Myrcella. I know how excited she will be. She misses her brother too, I do not doubt."

"I am eager to see her once again," said Ser Balon. "And to visit your Water Gardens. I've heard they are very beautiful."

"Beautiful and peaceful," the prince said. "Cool breezes, sparkling water, and the laughter of children. The Water Gardens are my favorite place in this world, ser. One of my ancestors had them built to please his Targaryen bride and free her from the dust and heat of Sunspear. *Daenerys* was her name. She was sister to King Daeron the Good, and it was her marriage that made Dorne part of the Seven Kingdoms. The whole realm knew that the girl loved Daeron's bastard brother Daemon Blackfyre, and was loved by him in turn, but the king was wise enough to see that the good of thousands must come before the desires of two, even if those two were dear to him. It was Daenerys who filled the gardens with laughing children. Her own children at the start, but later the sons and daughters of lords and landed knights were brought in to be companions to the boys and girls of princely blood. And one summer's day when it was scorching hot, she took pity on the children of her grooms and cooks and serving men and invited them to use the pools and fountains too, a tradition that has endured till this day." The prince grasped the wheels of his chair and pushed himself from the table. "But now you must excuse me, ser. All this talk has wearied me, and we should leave at break of day. Obara, would you be so kind as to help me to my bed? Nymeria, Tyene, come as well, and bid your old uncle a fond good night."

So it fell to Obara Sand to roll the prince's chair from Sunspear's feast hall and down a long gallery to his solar. Areo Hotah followed with her sisters, along with Princess Arianne and Ellaria Sand. Maester Caleotte hurried behind on slippered feet, cradling the Mountain's skull as if it were a child.

"You cannot seriously intend to send Trystane and Myrcella to King's Landing," Obara said as she was pushing. Her strides were long and angry, much too fast, and the chair's big wooden wheels *clack*ed noisily across rough-cut stone floors. "Do that, and we will never see the girl again, and your son will spend his life a hostage to the Iron Throne."

"Do you take me for a fool, Obara?" The prince sighed. "There is much you do not know. Things best not discussed here, where anyone can hear. If you hold your tongue, I may enlighten you." He winced. "*Slower*, for the love you bear me. That last jolt sent a knife right through my knee."

Obara slowed her pace by half. "What will you do, then?"

Her sister Tyene gave answer. "What he always does," she purred. "Delay, obscure, prevaricate. Oh, no one does that half so well as our brave uncle."

"You do him wrong," said Princess Arianne.

"Be quiet, all of you," the prince commanded.

Not until the doors of his solar were safely closed behind them did he wheel his chair about to face the women. Even that effort left him breathless, and the Myrish blanket that covered his legs caught between two spokes as he rolled, so he had to clutch it to keep it from being torn away. Beneath the coverlet, his legs were pale, soft, ghastly. Both of his knees were red and swollen, and his toes were almost purple, twice the size they should have been. Areo Hotah had seen them a thousand times and still found them hard to look upon.

Princess Arianne came forward. "Let me help you, Father."

The prince pulled the blanket free. "I can still master mine own blanket. That much at least." It was little enough. His legs had been useless for three years, but there was still some strength in his hands and shoulders.

"Shall I fetch my prince a thimble cup of milk of the poppy?" Maester Caleotte asked.

"I would need a bucket, with this pain. Thank you, but no. I want my wits about me. I'll have no more need of you tonight."

"Very good, my prince." Maester Caleotte bowed, Ser Gregor's head still clutched in his soft pink hands.

"I'll take that." Obara Sand plucked the skull from him and held it at arm's length. "What did the Mountain look like? How do we know that this is him? They could have dipped the head in tar. Why strip it to the bone?"

"Tar would have ruined the box," suggested Lady Nym, as Maester Caleotte scurried off. "No one *saw* the Mountain die, and no one saw his head removed. That troubles me, I confess, but what could the bitch queen hope to accomplish by deceiving us? If Gregor Clegane is alive, soon or late the truth will out. The man was eight feet tall, there is not another like him in all of Westeros. If any such appears again, Cersei Lannister will be exposed as a liar before all the Seven Kingdoms. She would be an utter fool to risk that. What could she hope to gain?"

"The skull is large enough, no doubt," said the prince. "And we know that Oberyn wounded Gregor grievously. Every report we have had since claims that Clegane died slowly, in great pain."

"Just as Father intended," said Tyene. "Sisters, truly, I know the poison Father used. If his spear so much as broke the Mountain's skin, Clegane is dead, I do not care how big he was. Doubt your little sister if you like, but never doubt our sire."

Obara bristled. "I never did and never shall." She gave the skull a mocking kiss. "This is a start, I'll grant."

"A *start*?" said Ellaria Sand, incredulous. "Gods forbid. I would it were a finish. Tywin Lannister is dead. So are Robert Baratheon, Amory Lorch, and now Gregor Clegane, all those who had a hand in murdering Elia and her children. Even Joffrey, who was not yet born when Elia died. I saw the boy perish with mine own eyes, clawing at his throat as he tried to draw a breath. Who else is there to kill? Do Myrcella and Tommen need to die so the shades of Rhaenys and Aegon can be at rest? Where does it end?"

"It ends in blood, as it began," said Lady Nym. "It ends when Casterly Rock is cracked open, so the sun can shine on the maggots and the worms within. It ends with the utter ruin of Tywin Lannister and all his works."

"The man died at the hand of his own son," Ellaria snapped back. "What more could you wish?"

"I could wish that he died at *my* hand." Lady Nym settled in a chair, her long black braid falling across one shoulder to her lap. She had her father's widow's peak. Beneath it her eyes were large and lustrous. Her wine-red lips curled in a silken smile. "If he had, his dying would not have been so easy."

"Ser Gregor does look lonely," said Tyene, in her sweet septa's voice. "He would like some company, I'm certain."

Ellaria's cheeks were wet with tears, her dark eyes shining. *Even weeping, she has a strength in her,* the captain thought.

"Oberyn wanted vengeance for Elia. Now the three of you want vengeance for him. I have four daughters, I remind you. Your sisters. My Elia is fourteen, almost a woman. Obella is twelve, on the brink of maidenhood. They worship you, as Dorea and Loreza worship them. If you should die, must El and Obella seek vengeance for you, then Dorea and Loree for them? Is that how it goes, round and round forever? I ask again, *where does it end?*" Ellaria Sand laid her hand on the Mountain's head. "I saw your father die. Here is his killer. Can I take a skull to bed with me, to give me comfort in the night? Will it make me laugh, write me songs, care for me when I am old and sick?"

"What would you have us do, my lady?" asked the Lady Nym. "Shall we lay down our spears and smile, and forget all the wrongs that have been done to us?"

"War will come, whether we wish it or not," said Obara. "A boy king sits the Iron Throne. Lord Stannis holds the Wall and is gathering northmen to his cause. The two queens are squabbling over Tommen like bitches with a juicy bone. The ironmen have taken the Shields and are raiding up the Mander, deep into the heart of the Reach, which means Highgarden will be preoccupied as well. Our enemies are in disarray. The time is ripe."

"Ripe for what? To make more skulls?" Ellaria Sand turned to the prince. "They will not see. I can hear no more of this."

"Go back to your girls, Ellaria," the prince told her. "I swear to you, no harm will come to them."

"My prince." Ellaria kissed him on the brow and took her leave. Areo Hotah was sad to see her go. *She is a good woman.*

When she had gone, Lady Nym said, "I know she loved our father well, but it is plain she never understood him."

The prince gave her a curious look. "She understood more than you ever will, Nymeria. And she made your father happy. In the end a gentle heart may be worth more than pride or valor. Be that as it may, there are things Ellaria does not know and should not know. This war has already begun."

Obara laughed. "Aye, our sweet Arianne has seen to that."

The princess flushed, and Hotah saw a spasm of anger pass across her father's face. "What she did, she did as much for you as for herself. I would not be so quick to mock."

"That was praise," Obara Sand insisted. "Procrastinate, obscure, prevaricate, dissemble, and delay all you like, Uncle, Ser Balon must still come face-to-face with Myrcella at the Water Gardens, and when he does he's like to see she's short an ear. And when the girl tells him how your captain cut Arys Oakheart from neck to groin with that steel wife of his, well . . ."

"No." Princess Arianne unfolded from the cushion where she sat and put a hand on Hotah's arm. "That wasn't how it happened, Cousin. Ser Arys was slain by Gerold Dayne."

The Sand Snakes looked at one another. "Darkstar?"

"Darkstar did it," his little princess said. "He tried to kill Princess Myrcella too. As she will tell Ser Balon."

Nym smiled. "That part at least is true."

"It is all true," said the prince, with a wince of pain. *Is it his gout that hurts him, or the lie?* "And now Ser Gerold has fled back to High Hermitage, beyond our reach."

"Darkstar," Tyene murmured, with a giggle. "Why not? It is all his doing. But will Ser Balon believe it?"

"He will if he hears it from Myrcella," Arianne insisted.

Obara snorted in disbelief. "She may lie today and lie tomorrow, but soon or late she'll tell the truth. If Ser Balon is allowed to carry tales back to King's Landing, drums will sound and blood will flow. He should not be allowed to leave."

"We could kill him, to be sure," said Tyene, "but then we would need to kill the rest of his party too, even those sweet young squires. That would be . . . oh, so *messy.*"

Prince Doran shut his eyes and opened them again. Hotah could see his leg trembling underneath the blanket. "If you were not my brother's daughters, I would send the three of you back to your cells and keep you there until your bones were grey. Instead I mean to take you with us to the Water Gardens. There are lessons there if you have the wit to see them."

"Lessons?" said Obara. "All I've seen are naked children."

"Aye," the prince said. "I told the story to Ser Balon, but not all of it. As the children splashed in the pools, Daenerys watched from amongst the orange trees, and a realization came to her. She could not tell the high-born from the low. Naked, they were only children. All innocent, all vulnerable, all deserving of long life, love, protection. 'There is your realm,' she told her son and heir, 'remember them, in everything you do.' My own mother said those same words to me when I was old enough to leave the pools. It is an easy thing for a prince to call the spears, but in the end the children pay the price. For their sake, the wise prince will wage no war without good cause, nor any war he cannot hope to win.

"I am not blind, nor deaf. I know that you all believe me weak, frightened, feeble. Your father knew me better. Oberyn was ever the viper. Deadly, dangerous, unpredictable. No man dared tread on him. I was the grass. Pleasant, complaisant, sweet-smelling, swaying with every breeze. Who fears to walk upon the grass? But it is the grass that hides the viper from his enemies and shelters him until he strikes. Your father and I worked more closely than you know . . . but now he is gone. The question is, can I trust his daughters to serve me in his place?"

Hotah studied each of them in turn. Obara, rusted nails and boiled leather, with her angry, close-set eyes and rat-brown hair. Nymeria, languid, elegant, olive-skinned, her long black braid bound up in red-gold wire. Tyene, blue-eyed and blond, a child-woman with her soft hands and little giggles.

Tyene answered for the three of them. "It is doing nothing that is hard, Uncle. Set a task for us, any task, and you shall find us as leal and obedient as any prince could hope for."

"That is good to hear," the prince said, "but words are wind. You are my brother's daughters and I love you, but I have learned I cannot trust you. I want your oath. Will you swear to serve me, to do as I command?"

"If we must," said Lady Nym.

"Then swear it now, upon your father's grave."

Obara's face darkened. "If you were not my uncle—"

"I *am* your uncle. And your prince. Swear, or go."

"I swear," said Tyene. "On my father's grave."

"I swear," said Lady Nym. "By Oberyn Martell, the Red Viper of Dorne, and a better man than you."

"Aye," said Obara. "Me as well. By Father. I swear."

Some of the tension went out of the prince. Hotah saw him sag back into his chair. He held out his hand, and Princess Arianne moved to his side to hold it. "Tell them, Father."

Prince Doran took a jagged breath. "Dorne still has friends at court. Friends who tell us things we were not meant to know. This invitation Cersei sent us is a ruse. Trystane is never meant to reach King's Landing. On the road back, somewhere in the kingswood, Ser Balon's party will be attacked by outlaws, and my son will die. I am asked to court only so that I may witness this attack with my own eyes and thereby absolve the queen of any blame. Oh, and these outlaws? They will be shouting, 'Halfman, Halfman,' as they attack. Ser Balon may even catch a quick glimpse of the Imp, though no one else will."

Areo Hotah would not have believed it possible to shock the Sand Snakes. He would have been wrong.

"Seven save us," whispered Tyene. *"Trystane? Why?"*

"The woman must be mad," Obara said. "He's just a boy."

"This is monstrous," said Lady Nym. "I would not have believed it, not of a Kingsguard knight."

"They are sworn to obey, just as my captain is," the prince said. "I had my doubts as well, but you all saw how Ser Balon balked when I suggested that we go by sea. A ship would have disturbed all the queen's arrangements."

Obara's face was flushed. "Give me back my spear, Uncle. Cersei sent us a head. We should send her back a bag of them."

Prince Doran raised a hand. His knuckles were as dark as cherries and near as big. "Ser Balon is a guest beneath my roof. He has eaten of my bread and salt. I will not do him harm. No. We will travel to the Water Gardens, where he will hear Myrcella's story and send a raven to his queen. The girl will ask him to hunt down the man who hurt her. If he is the man I judge, Swann will not be able to refuse. Obara, you will lead him to High Hermitage to beard Darkstar in his den. The time is not yet come for Dorne to openly defy the Iron Throne, so we must needs return Myrcella to her mother, but I will not be accompanying her. That task will be yours, Nymeria. The Lannisters will not like it, no more than they liked it when I sent them Oberyn, but they dare not refuse. We need a voice in council, an ear at court. Be careful, though. King's Landing is a pit of snakes."

Lady Nym smiled. "Why, Uncle, I love snakes."

"And what of me?" asked Tyene.

"Your mother was a septa. Oberyn once told me that she read to you in the cradle from the *Seven-Pointed Star*. I want you in King's Landing too, but on the other hill. The Swords and the Stars have been re-formed, and this new High Septon is not the puppet that the others were. Try and get close to him."

"Why not? White suits my coloring. I look so . . . pure."

"Good," the prince said, "good." He hesitated. "If . . . if certain things should come to pass, I will send word to each of you. Things can change quickly in the game of thrones."

"I know you will not fail us, cousins." Arianne went to each of them in turn, took their hands, kissed them lightly on the lips. "Obara, so fierce. Nymeria, my sister. Tyene, sweetling. I love you all. The sun of Dorne goes with you."

"*Unbowed, unbent, unbroken,*" the Sand Snakes said, together.

Princess Arianne lingered when her cousins had departed. Areo Hotah remained as well, as was his place.

"They are their father's daughters," the prince said.

The little princess smiled. "Three Oberyns, with teats."

Prince Doran laughed. It had been so long since Hotah last heard him laugh, he had almost forgotten what it sounded like.

"I still say it should be me who goes to King's Landing, not Lady Nym," Arianne said.

"It is too dangerous. You are my heir, the future of Dorne. Your place is by my side. Soon enough, you'll have another task."

"That last part, about the message. Have you had tidings?"

Prince Doran shared his secret smile with her. "From Lys. A great fleet has put in there to take on water. Volantene ships chiefly, carrying an army. No word as to who they are, or where they might be bound. There was talk of elephants."

"No dragons?"

"Elephants. Easy enough to hide a young dragon in a big cog's hold, though. Daenerys is most vulnerable at sea. If I were her, I would keep myself and my intentions hidden as long as I could, so I might take King's Landing unawares."

"Do you think that Quentyn will be with them?"

"He could be. Or not. We will know by where they land if Westeros is indeed their destination. Quentyn will bring her up the Greenblood if he can. But it does no good to speak of it. Kiss me. We leave for the Water Gardens at first light."

We may depart by midday, then, Hotah thought.

Later, when Arianne had gone, he put down his longaxe and lifted Prince Doran into his bed. "Until the Mountain crushed my brother's skull, no Dornishmen had died in this War of the Five Kings," the prince murmured softly, as Hotah pulled a blanket over him. "Tell me, Captain, is that my shame or my glory?"

"That is not for me to say, my prince." *Serve. Protect. Obey. Simple vows for simple men.* That was all he knew.

JON

Val waited by the gate in the predawn cold, wrapped up in a bearskin cloak so large it might well have fit Sam. Beside her was a garron, saddled and bridled, a shaggy grey with one white eye. Mully and Dolorous Edd stood with her, a pair of unlikely guards. Their breath frosted in the cold black air.

"You gave her a blind horse?" Jon said, incredulous.

"He's only half-blind, m'lord," offered Mully. "Elsewise he's sound enough." He patted the garron on the neck.

"The horse may be half-blind, but I am not," said Val. "I know where I must go."

"My lady, you do not have to do this. The risk—"

"—is mine, Lord Snow. And I am no southron lady but a woman of the free folk. I know the forest better than all your black-cloaked rangers. It holds no ghosts for me."

I hope not. Jon was counting on that, trusting that Val could succeed where Black Jack Bulwer and his companions had failed. She need fear no harm from the free folk, he hoped . . . but both of them knew too well that wildlings were not the only ones waiting in the woods. "You have sufficient food?"

"Hard bread, hard cheese, oat cakes, salt cod, salt beef, salt mutton, and a skin of sweet wine to rinse all that salt out of my mouth. I will not die of hunger."

"Then it's time you were away."

"You have my word, Lord Snow. I will return, with Tormund or without him." Val glanced at the sky. The moon was but half-full. "Look for me on the first day of the full moon."

"I will." *Do not fail me,* he thought, *or Stannis will have my head.* "Do I have your word that you will keep our princess closely?" the king had said, and Jon had promised that he would. *Val is no princess, though. I told him that half a hundred times.* It was a feeble sort of evasion, a sad rag wrapped around his wounded word. His father would never have approved. *I am the sword that guards the realm of men,* Jon reminded himself, *and in the end, that must be worth more than one man's honor.*

The road beneath the Wall was as dark and cold as the belly of an ice dragon and as twisty as a serpent. Dolorous Edd led them through with a torch in hand. Mully had the keys for the three gates, where bars of black iron as thick as a man's arm closed off the passage. Spearmen at each gate knuckled their foreheads at Jon Snow but stared openly at Val and her garron.

When they emerged north of the Wall, through a thick door made of freshly hewn green wood, the wildling princess paused for a moment to gaze out across the snow-covered field where King Stannis had won his battle. Beyond, the haunted forest waited, dark and silent. The light of the half-moon turned Val's honey-blond hair a pale silver and left her cheeks as white as snow. She took a deep breath. "The air tastes sweet."

"My tongue is too numb to tell. All I can taste is cold."

"Cold?" Val laughed lightly. "No. When it is cold it will hurt to breathe. When the Others come . . ."

The thought was a disquieting one. Six of the rangers Jon had sent out were still missing. *It is too soon. They may yet be back.* But another part of him insisted, *They are dead, every man of them. You sent them out to die, and you are doing the same to Val.* "Tell Tormund what I've said."

"He may not heed your words, but he will hear them." Val kissed him lightly on the cheek. "You have my thanks, Lord Snow. For the half-blind horse, the salt cod, the free air. For hope."

Their breath mingled, a white mist in the air. Jon Snow drew back and said, "The only thanks I want is—"

"—Tormund Giantsbane. Aye." Val pulled up the hood of her bearskin. The brown pelt was well salted with grey. "Before I go, one question. Did you kill Jarl, my lord?"

"The Wall killed Jarl."

"So I'd heard. But I had to be sure."

"You have my word. I did not kill him." *Though I might have if things had gone otherwise.*

"This is farewell, then," she said, almost playfully.

Jon Snow was in no mood for it. *It is too cold and dark to play, and the hour is too late.* "Only for a time. You will return. For the boy, if for no other reason."

"Craster's son?" Val shrugged. "He is no kin to me."

"I have heard you singing to him."

"I was singing to myself. Am I to blame if he listens?" A faint smile brushed her lips. "It makes him laugh. Oh, very well. He is a sweet little monster."

"Monster?"

"His milk name. I had to call him something. See that he stays safe and warm. For his mother's sake, and mine. And keep him away from the red woman. She knows who he is. She sees things in her fires."

Arya, he thought, hoping it was so. "Ashes and cinders."

"Kings and dragons."

Dragons again. For a moment Jon could almost see them too, coiling in the night, their dark wings outlined against a sea of flame. "If she knew, she would have taken the boy away from us. Dalla's boy, not your monster. A word in the king's ear would have been the end of it." *And of me. Stannis would have taken it for treason.* "Why let it happen if she knew?"

"Because it suited her. Fire is a fickle thing. No one knows which way a flame will go." Val put a foot into a stirrup, swung her leg over her horse's back, and looked down from the saddle. "Do you remember what my sister told you?"

"Yes." *A sword without a hilt, with no safe way to hold it.* But Melisandre had the right of it. Even a sword without a hilt is better than an empty hand when foes are all around you.

"Good." Val wheeled the garron toward the north. "The first night of the full moon, then." Jon watched her ride away wondering if he would ever see her face again. *I am no southron lady,* he could hear her say, *but a woman of the free folk.*

"I don't care what she says," muttered Dolorous Edd, as Val vanished behind a stand of soldier pines. "The air *is* so cold it hurts to breathe. I would stop, but that would hurt worse." He rubbed his hands together. "This is going to end badly."

"You say that of everything."

"Aye, m'lord. Usually I'm right."

Mully cleared his throat. "M'lord? The wildling princess, letting her go, the men may say—"

"—that I am half a wildling myself, a turncloak who means to sell the realm to our raiders, cannibals, and giants." Jon did not need to stare into a fire to know what was being said of him. The worst part was, they were not wrong, not wholly. "Words are wind, and the wind is always blowing at the Wall. Come."

It was still dark when Jon returned to his chambers behind the armory. Ghost was not yet back, he saw. *Still hunting.* The big white direwolf was gone more oft than not of late, ranging farther and farther in search of prey. Between the men of the Watch and the wildlings down in Mole's Town, the hills and fields near Castle Black had been hunted clean, and there had been little enough game to begin with. *Winter is coming,* Jon reflected. *And soon, too soon.* He wondered if they would ever see a spring.

Dolorous Edd made the trek to the kitchens and soon was back with a tankard of brown ale and a covered platter. Under the lid Jon discovered three duck's eggs fried in drippings, a strip of bacon, two sausages, a blood pudding, and half a loaf of bread still warm from the oven. He ate the bread and half an egg. He would have eaten the bacon too, but the raven made off with it before he had the chance. "Thief," Jon said, as the bird flapped up to the lintel above the door to devour its prize.

"*Thief*," the raven agreed.

Jon tried a bite of sausage. He was washing the taste from his mouth with a sip of ale when Edd returned to tell him Bowen Marsh was without. "Othell's with him, and Septon Cellador."

That was quick. He wondered who was telling tales and if there was more than one. "Send them in."

"Aye, m'lord. You'll want to watch your sausages with this lot, though. They have a hungry look about them."

Hungry was not the word Jon would have used. Septon Cellador appeared confused and groggy and in dire need of some scales from the dragon that had flamed him, whilst First Builder Othell Yarwyck looked as if he had swallowed something he could not quite digest. Bowen Marsh was angry. Jon could see it in his eyes, the tightness around his mouth, the flush to those round cheeks. *That red is not from cold.* "Please sit," he said. "May I offer you food or drink?"

"We broke our fast in the commons," said Marsh.

"I could do with more." Yarwyck eased himself down onto a chair. "Good of you to offer."

"Perhaps some wine?" said Septon Cellador.

"*Corn*," screamed the raven from the lintel. "*Corn, corn.*"

"Wine for the septon and a plate for our First Builder," Jon told Dolorous Edd. "Nothing for the bird." He turned back to his visitors. "You're here about Val."

"And other matters," said Bowen Marsh. "The men have concerns, my lord."

And who is it who appointed you to speak for them? "As do I. Othell, how goes the work at the Nightfort? I have had a letter from Ser Axell Florent, who styles himself the Queen's Hand. He tells me that Queen Selyse is not pleased with her quarters at Eastwatch-by-the-Sea and wishes to move into her husband's new seat at once. Will that be possible?"

Yarwyck shrugged. "We've got most of the keep restored and put a roof back on the kitchens. She'd need food and furnishings and firewood, mind you, but it might serve. Not so many comforts as Eastwatch, to be sure. And a long way from the ships, should Her Grace wish to leave us, but . . . aye, she could live there, though it will be years before the place looks a proper castle. Sooner if I had more builders."

"I could offer you a giant."

That gave Othell a start. "The monster in the yard?"

"His name is Wun Weg Wun Dar Wun, Leathers tells me. A lot to wrap a tongue around, I know. Leathers calls him Wun Wun, and that seems to serve." Wun Wun was very little like the giants in Old Nan's tales, those huge savage creatures who mixed blood into their morning porridge and devoured whole bulls, hair and hide and horns. This giant ate no meat at all, though he was a holy terror when served a basket of roots, crunching onions and turnips and even raw hard neeps between his big square teeth. "He's a willing worker, though getting him to understand what you want is not always easy. He speaks the Old Tongue after a fashion, but nothing of the Common. Tireless, though, and his strength is prodigious. He could do the work of a dozen men."

"I . . . my lord, the men would never . . . giants eat human flesh, I think . . . no, my lord, I thank you, but I do not have the men to watch over such a creature, he . . ."

Jon Snow was unsurprised. "As you wish. We will keep the giant here." Truth be told, he would have been loath to part with Wun Wun. *You know nothing, Jon Snow*, Ygritte might say, but Jon spoke with the giant whenever he could, through Leathers or one of the free folk they had brought back from the grove, and was learning much and more about his people and their history. He only wished that Sam were here to write the stories down.

That was not to say that he was blind to the danger Wun Wun represented. The giant would lash out violently when threatened, and those huge hands were strong enough to rip a man apart. He reminded Jon of Hodor. *Hodor twice as big, twice as strong, and half as clever. There's a thought to sober even Septon Cellador. But if Tormund has giants with him, Wun Weg Wun Dar Wun may help us treat with them.*

Mormont's raven muttered his annoyance as the door opened beneath him, heralding the return of Dolorous Edd with a flagon of wine and a plate of eggs and sausages. Bowen Marsh waited with obvious impatience as Edd poured, resuming only when he left again. "Tollett is a good man, and well liked, and Iron Emmett has been a fine master-at-arms," he said then. "Yet the talk is that you mean to send them away."

"We need good men at Long Barrow."

"Whore's Hole, the men have started calling it," said Marsh, "but be that as it may. Is it true that you mean to replace Emmett with this savage Leathers as our master-at-arms? That is an office most oft reserved for knights, or rangers at the least."

"Leathers *is* savage," Jon agreed mildly. "I can attest to that. I've tried him in the practice yard. He's as dangerous with a stone axe as most knights are with castle-forged steel. I grant you, he is not as patient as I'd like, and some of the boys are terrified of him . . . but that's not all for the bad. One day they'll find themselves in a real fight, and a certain familiarity with terror will serve them well."

"He's a *wildling*."

"He was, until he said the words. Now he is our brother. One who can teach the boys more than swordcraft. It would not hurt them to learn a few words of the Old Tongue and something of the ways of the free folk."

"*Free*," the raven muttered. "*Corn. King.*"

"The men do not trust him."

Which men? Jon might have asked. *How many?* But that would lead him down a road he did not mean to ride. "I am sorry to hear that. Is there more?"

Septon Cellador spoke up. "This boy Satin. It's said you mean to make him your steward and squire, in Tollett's place. My lord, the boy's a whore . . . a . . . dare I say . . . a painted *catamite* from the brothels of Oldtown."

And you are a drunk. "What he was in Oldtown is none of our concern. He's quick to learn and very clever. The other recruits started out despising him, but he won them over and made friends of them all. He's fearless in a fight and can even read and write after a fashion. He should be capable of fetching me my meals and saddling my horse, don't you think?"

"Most like," said Bowen Marsh, stony-faced, "but the men do not like it. Traditionally the lord commander's squires are lads of good birth being groomed for command. Does my lord believe the men of the Night's Watch would ever follow a whore into battle?"

Jon's temper flashed. "They have followed worse. The Old Bear left a few cautionary notes about certain of the men, for his successor. We have a cook at the Shadow Tower who was fond of raping septas. He burned a seven-pointed star into his flesh for every one he claimed. His left arm is stars from wrist to elbow, and stars mark his calves as well. At Eastwatch we have a man who set his father's house afire and barred the door. His entire family burned to death, all nine. Whatever Satin may have done in Oldtown, he is our brother now, and he *will* be my squire."

Septon Cellador drank some wine. Othell Yarwyck stabbed a sausage with his dagger. Bower Marsh sat red-faced. The raven flapped its wings and said, "*Corn, corn, kill.*" Finally the Lord Steward cleared his throat. "Your lordship knows best, I am sure. Might I ask about these corpses in the ice cells? They make the men uneasy. And to keep them *under guard*? Surely that is a waste of two good men, unless you fear that they . . ."

". . . will rise? I pray they do."

Septon Cellador paled. "Seven save us." Wine dribbled down his chin in a red line. "Lord Commander, wights are monstrous, unnatural creatures. Abominations before the eyes of the gods. You . . . you cannot mean to try to *talk* with them?"

"*Can* they talk?" asked Jon Snow. "I think not, but I cannot claim to know. Monsters they may be, but they were men before they died. How much remains? The one I slew was intent on killing Lord Commander Mormont. Plainly it remembered who he was and where to find him." Maester Aemon would have grasped his purpose, Jon did not doubt; Sam Tarly would have been terrified, but he would have understood as well. "My lord father used to tell me that a man must know his enemies. We understand little of the wights and less about the Others. We need to learn."

That answer did not please them. Septon Cellador fingered the crystal that hung about his neck and said, "I think this most unwise, Lord Snow. I shall pray to the Crone to lift her shining lamp and lead you down the path of wisdom."

Jon Snow's patience was exhausted. "We could all do with a bit more wisdom, I am sure." *You know nothing, Jon Snow.* "Now, shall we speak of Val?"

"It is true, then?" said Marsh. "You have released her."

"Beyond the Wall."

Septon Cellador sucked in his breath. "The king's prize. His Grace will be most wroth to find her gone."

"Val will return." *Before Stannis, if the gods are good.*

"How can you know that?" demanded Bowen Marsh.

"She said she would."

"And if she lied? If she meets with misadventure?"

"Why, then, you may have a chance to choose a lord commander more to your liking. Until such time, I fear you'll still need to suffer me." Jon took a swallow of ale. "I sent her to find Tormund Giantsbane and bring him my offer."

"If we may know, what offer is this?"

"The same offer I made at Mole's Town. Food and shelter and peace, if he will join his strength to ours, fight our common enemy, help us hold the Wall."

Bowen Marsh did not appear surprised. "You mean to let him pass." His voice suggested he had known all along. "To open the gates for him and his followers. Hundreds, thousands."

"If he has that many left."

Septon Cellador made the sign of the star. Othell Yarwyck grunted. Bowen Marsh said, "Some might call this treason. These are wildlings. Savages, raiders, rapers, more beast than man."

"Tormund is none of those things," said Jon, "no more than Mance Rayder. But even if every word you said was true, they are still men, Bowen. Living men, human as you and me. Winter is coming, my lords, and when it does, we living men will need to stand together against the dead."

"*Snow*," screamed Lord Mormont's raven. "*Snow, Snow.*"

Jon ignored him. "We have been questioning the wildlings we brought back from the grove. Several of them told an interesting tale, of a woods witch called Mother Mole."

"Mother *Mole*?" said Bowen Marsh. "An unlikely name."

"Supposedly she made her home in a burrow beneath a hollow tree. Whatever the truth of that, she had a vision of a fleet of ships arriving to carry the free folk to safety across the narrow sea. Thousands of those who fled the battle were desperate enough to believe her. Mother Mole has led them all to Hardhome, there to pray and await salvation from across the sea."

Othell Yarwyck scowled. "I'm no ranger, but . . . Hardhome is an unholy place, it's said. Cursed. Even your uncle used to say as much, Lord Snow. Why would they go *there*?"

Jon had a map before him on the table. He turned it so they could see. "Hardhome sits on a sheltered bay and has a natural harbor deep enough for the biggest ships afloat. Wood and stone are plentiful near there. The waters teem with fish, and there are colonies of seals and sea cows close at hand."

"All that's true, I don't doubt," said Yarwyck, "but it's not a place I'd want to spend a night. You know the tale."

He did. Hardhome had been halfway toward becoming a town, the only true town north of the Wall, until the night six hundred years ago when hell had swallowed it. Its people had been carried off into slavery or slaughtered for meat, depending on which version of the tale you believed, their homes and halls consumed in a conflagration that burned so hot that watchers on the Wall far to the south had thought the sun was rising in the north. Afterward ashes rained down on haunted forest and Shivering Sea alike for almost half a year. Traders reported finding only nightmarish devastation where Hardhome had stood, a landscape of charred trees and burned bones, waters choked with swollen corpses, blood-chilling shrieks echoing from the cave mouths that pocked the great cliff that loomed above the settlement.

Six centuries had come and gone since that night, but Hardhome was still shunned. The wild had reclaimed the site, Jon had been told, but rangers claimed that the overgrown ruins were haunted by ghouls and demons and burning ghosts with an unhealthy taste for blood. "It is not the sort of refuge I'd choose either," Jon said, "but Mother Mole was heard to preach that the free folk would find salvation where once they found damnation."

Septon Cellador pursed his lips. "Salvation can be found only through the Seven. This witch has doomed them all."

"And saved the Wall, mayhaps," said Bowen Marsh. "These are enemies we speak of. Let them pray amongst the ruins, and if their gods send ships to carry them off to a better world, well and good. In this world I have no food to feed them."

Jon flexed the fingers of his sword hand. "Cotter Pyke's galleys sail past Hardhome from time to time. He tells me there is no shelter there but the caves. *The screaming caves*, his men call them. Mother Mole and those who followed her will perish there, of cold and starvation. Hundreds of them. Thousands."

"Thousands of enemies. Thousands of *wildlings*."

Thousands of people, Jon thought. *Men, women, children*. Anger rose inside him, but when he spoke his voice was quiet and cold. "Are you so blind, or is it that you do not wish to see? What do you think will happen when all these enemies are dead?"

Above the door the raven muttered, "*Dead, dead, dead*."

"Let me tell you what will happen," Jon said. "The dead will rise again, in their hundreds and their thousands. They will rise as wights, with black hands and pale blue eyes, and *they will come for us.*" He pushed himself to his feet, the fingers of his sword hand opening and closing. "You have my leave to go."

Septon Cellador rose grey-faced and sweating, Othell Yarwyck stiffly, Bowen Marsh tight-lipped and pale. "Thank you for your time, Lord Snow." They left without another word.

TYRION

The sow had a sweeter temper than some horses he had ridden. Patient and sure-footed, she accepted Tyrion with hardly a squeal when he clambered onto her back, and remained motionless as he reached for shield and lance. Yet when he gathered up her reins and pressed his feet into her side, she moved at once. Her name was Pretty, short for Pretty Pig, and she had been trained to saddle and bridle since she was a piglet.

The painted wooden armor clattered as Pretty trotted across the deck. Tyrion's armpits were prickly with perspiration, and a bead of sweat was trickling down his scar beneath the oversized, ill-fitting helm, yet for one absurd moment he felt almost like Jaime, riding out onto a tourney field with lance in hand, his golden armor flashing in the sun.

When the laughter began, the dream dissolved. He was no champion, just a dwarf on a pig clutching a stick, capering for the amusement of some restless rum-soaked sailors in hopes of sweetening their mood. Somewhere down in hell his father was seething and Joffrey was chuckling. Tyrion could feel their cold dead eyes watching this mummer's face, as avid as the crew of the *Selaesori Qhoran*.

And now here came his foe. Penny rode her big grey dog, her striped lance waving drunkenly as the beast bounded across the deck. Her shield and armor had been painted red, though the paint was chipped and fading; his own armor was blue. *Not mine. Groat's. Never mine, I pray.*

Tyrion kicked at Pretty's haunches to speed her to a charge as the sailors urged him on with hoots and shouts. Whether they were shouting encouragement or mocking him he could not have said for certain, though he had a fair notion. *Why did I ever allow myself to be talked into this farce?*

He knew the answer, though. For twelve days now the ship had floated

becalmed in the Gulf of Grief. The mood of the crew was ugly, and like
to turn uglier when their daily rum ration went dry. There were only so
many hours a man could devote to mending sails, caulking leaks, and
fishing. Jorah Mormont had heard the muttering about how dwarf luck
had failed them. Whilst the ship's cook still gave Tyrion's head a rub
from time to time, in hopes that it might stir a wind, the rest had taken
to giving him venomous looks whenever he crossed their paths. Penny's
lot was even worse, since the cook had put about the notion that squeezing a dwarf girl's breast might be just the thing to win their luck back.
He had also started referring to Pretty Pig as *Bacon*, a jape that had
seemed much funnier when Tyrion had made it.

"We have to make them laugh," Penny had said, pleading. "We have to
make them like us. If we give them a show, it will help them forget. *Please*,
m'lord." And somehow, somewise, someway he had consented. *It must
have been the rum.* The captain's wine had been the first thing to run out.
You could get drunk much quicker on rum than on wine, Tyrion Lannister had discovered.

So he found himself clad in Groat's painted wooden armor, astride
Groat's sow, whilst Groat's sister instructed him in the finer points of the
mummer's joust that had been their bread and salt. It had a certain delicious irony to it, considering that Tyrion had almost lost his head once by
refusing to mount the dog for his nephew's twisted amusement. Yet somehow he found it difficult to appreciate the humor of it all from sowback.

Penny's lance descended just in time for its blunted point to brush his
shoulder; his own lance wobbled as he brought it down and banged it
noisily off a corner of her shield. She kept her seat. He lost his. But then,
he was supposed to.

Easy as falling off a pig . . . though falling off this particular pig was
harder than it looked. Tyrion curled into a ball as he dropped, remembering his lesson, but even so, he hit the deck with a solid *thump* and bit his
tongue so hard he tasted blood. He felt as if he were twelve again, cart-
wheeling across the supper table in Casterly Rock's great hall. Back then
his uncle Gerion had been on hand to praise his efforts, in place of surly
sailors. Their laughter seemed sparse and strained compared to the great
gales that had greeted Groat's and Penny's antics at Joffrey's wedding feast,
and some hissed at him in anger. "No-Nose, you ride same way you look,
ugly," one man shouted from the sterncastle. "Must have no balls, let girl
beat you." *He wagered coin on me,* Tyrion decided. He let the insult wash
right over him. He had heard worse in his time.

The wooden armor made rising awkward. He found himself flailing like a turtle on its back. That, at least, set a few of the sailors to laughing. *A shame I did not break my leg, that would have left them howling. And if they had been in that privy when I shot my father through the bowels, they might have laughed hard enough to shit their breeches right along with him. But anything to keep the bloody bastards sweet.*

Jorah Mormont finally took pity on Tyrion's struggles and pulled him to his feet. "You looked a fool."

That was the intent. "It is hard to look a hero when mounted on a pig."

"That must be why I stay off pigs."

Tyrion unbuckled his helm, twisted it off, and spat a gobbet of bloody pink phlegm over the side. "It feels as though I bit through half my tongue."

"Next time bite harder." Ser Jorah shrugged. "Truth be told, I've seen worse jousters."

Was that praise? "I fell off the bloody pig and bit my tongue. What could possibly be worse than that?"

"Getting a splinter through your eye and dying."

Penny had vaulted off her dog, a big grey brute called Crunch. "The thing is not to joust well, Hugor." She was always careful to call him Hugor where anyone might hear. "The thing is to make them laugh and throw coins."

Poor payment for the blood and bruises, Tyrion thought, but he kept that to himself as well. "We failed at that as well. No one threw coins." *Not a penny, not a groat.*

"They will when we get better." Penny pulled off her helm. Mouse-brown hair spilled down to her ears. Her eyes were brown too, beneath a heavy shelf of brow, her cheeks smooth and flushed. She pulled some acorns from a leather bag for Pretty Pig. The sow ate them from her hand, squealing happily. "When we perform for Queen Daenerys the silver will rain down, you'll see."

Some of the sailors were shouting at them and slamming their heels against the deck, demanding another tilt. The ship's cook was the loudest, as always. Tyrion had learned to despise that man, even if he was the only half-decent *cyvasse* player on the cog. "You see, they liked us," Penny said, with a hopeful little smile. "Shall we go again, Hugor?"

He was on the point of refusing when a shout from one of the mates spared him the necessity. It was midmorning, and the captain wanted the boats out again. The cog's huge striped sail hung limply from her mast, as it had for days, but he was hopeful that they could find a wind somewhere to the north. That meant rowing. The boats were small, however, and the cog was large; towing it was hot, sweaty, exhausting work that left the hands blistered and the back aching, and accomplished nothing. The crew hated it. Tyrion could not blame them. "The widow should have put us on a galley," he muttered sourly. "If someone could help me out of these bloody planks, I would be grateful. I think I may have a splinter through my crotch."

Mormont did the duty, albeit with poor grace. Penny collected her dog and pig and led them both below. "You might want to tell your lady to keep her door closed and barred when she's inside," Ser Jorah said as he was undoing the buckles on the straps that joined the wooden breastplate to the backplate. "I'm hearing too much talk about ribs and hams and bacon."

"That pig is half her livelihood."

"A Ghiscari crew would eat the dog as well." Mormont pulled the breastplate and backplate apart. "Just tell her."

"As you wish." His tunic was soaked with sweat and clinging to his chest. Tyrion plucked at it, wishing for a bit of breeze. The wooden armor was as hot and heavy as it was uncomfortable. Half of it looked to be old paint, layer on layer on layer of it, from a hundred past repaintings. At Joffrey's wedding feast, he recalled, one rider had displayed the direwolf of Robb Stark, the other the arms and colors of Stannis Baratheon. "We will need both animals if we're to tilt for Queen Daenerys," he said. If the sailors took it in their heads to butcher Pretty Pig, neither he nor Penny could hope to stop them . . . but Ser Jorah's longsword might give them pause, at least.

"Is that how you hope to keep your head, Imp?"

"Ser Imp, if you please. And yes. Once Her Grace knows my true worth, she'll cherish me. I am a lovable little fellow, after all, and I know many useful things about my kin. But until such time I had best keep her amused."

"Caper as you like, it won't wash out your crimes. Daenerys Targaryen is no silly child to be diverted by japes and tumbles. She will deal with you justly."

Oh, I hope not. Tyrion studied Mormont with his mismatched eyes. "And how will she welcome you, this just queen? A warm embrace, a girlish titter, a headsman's axe?" He grinned at the knight's obvious discomfit. "Did you truly expect me to believe you were about the queen's business in that whorehouse? Defending her from half a world away? Or could it be that you were running, that your dragon queen sent you from her side? But why would she . . . oh, wait, you were *spying* on her." Tyrion made a clucking sound. "You hope to buy your way back into her favor by presenting her with me. An ill-considered scheme, I'd say. One might even say an act of drunken desperation. Perhaps if I were Jaime . . . but Jaime killed her father, I only killed my own. You think Daenerys will execute me and pardon you, but the reverse is just as likely. Maybe you *should* hop up on that pig, Ser Jorah. Put on a suit of iron motley, like Florian the—"

The blow the big knight gave him cracked his head around and knocked him sideways, so hard that his head bounced off the deck. Blood filled his mouth as he staggered back onto one knee. He spat out a broken tooth. *Growing prettier every day, but I do believe I poked a wound.* "Did the dwarf say something to offend you, ser?" Tyrion asked innocently, wiping bubbles of blood off his broken lip with the back of his hand.

"I am sick of your mouth, dwarf," said Mormont. "You still have a few teeth left. If you want to keep them, stay away from me for the rest of this voyage."

"That could be difficult. We share a cabin."

"You can find somewhere else to sleep. Down in the hold, up on deck, it makes no matter. Just keep out of my sight."

Tyrion pulled himself back to his feet. "As you wish," he answered, through a mouthful of blood, but the big knight was already gone, his boots pounding on the deckboards.

Below, in the galley, Tyrion was rinsing out his mouth with rum and water and wincing at the sting when Penny found him. "I heard what happened. Oh, are you hurt?"

He shrugged. "A bit of blood and a broken tooth." *But I believe I hurt him more.* "And him a knight. Sad to say, I would not count on Ser Jorah should we need protection."

"What did you do? Oh, your lip is bleeding." She slipped a square from her sleeve and dabbed at it. "What did you say?"

"A few truths Ser Bezoar did not care to hear."

"You mustn't mock him. Don't you know *anything*? You can't talk that way to a big person. They can *hurt* you. Ser Jorah could have tossed you in the sea. The sailors would have laughed to see you drown. You have to be careful around big people. Be jolly and playful with them, keep them smiling, make them laugh, that's what my father always said. Didn't your father ever tell you how to act with big people?"

"My father called them smallfolk," said Tyrion, "and he was not what you'd call a jolly man." He took another sip of watered rum, sloshed it around his mouth, spat it out. "Still, I take your point. I have a deal to learn about being a dwarf. Perhaps you will be good enough to teach me, in between the jousting and the pig-riding."

"I will, m'lord. Gladly. But . . . what were these truths? Why did Ser Jorah hit you so hard?"

"Why, for love. The same reason that I stewed that singer." He thought of Shae and the look in her eyes as he tightened the chain about her throat, twisting it in his fist. A chain of golden hands. *For hands of gold are always cold, but a woman's hands are warm.* "Are you a maid, Penny?"

She blushed. "Yes. Of course. Who would have—"

"Stay that way. Love is madness, and lust is poison. Keep your maidenhead. You'll be happier for it, and you're less like to find yourself in some dingy brothel on the Rhoyne with a whore who looks a bit like your lost love." *Or chasing across half the world, hoping to find wherever whores go.* "Ser Jorah dreams of rescuing his dragon queen and basking in her gratitude, but I know a thing or two about the gratitude of kings, and I'd sooner have a palace in Valyria." He broke off suddenly. "Did you feel that? The ship moved."

"It did." Penny's face lit up with joy. "We're moving again. The wind . . ." She rushed to the door. "I want to see. Come, I'll race you up." Off she went.

She is young, Tyrion had to remind himself, as Penny scrambled from the galley and up the steep wooden steps as fast as her short legs would allow. *Almost a child.* Still, it tickled him to see her excitement. He followed her topside.

The sail had come to life again, billowing, emptying, then billowing again, the red stripes on the canvas wriggling like snakes. Sailors dashed across the decks and hauled on lines as the mates bellowed orders in the tongue of Old Volantis. The rowers in the ship's boats had loosed their tow ropes and turned back toward the cog, stroking hard. The wind was blowing from the west, swirling and gusting, clutching at ropes and cloaks like a mischievous child. The *Selaesori Qhoran* was under way.

Might be we'll make Meereen after all, Tyrion thought.

But when he clambered up the ladder to the sterncastle and looked off from the stern, his smile faltered. *Blue sky and blue sea here, but off west . . . I have never seen a sky that color.* A thick band of clouds ran along the horizon. "A bar sinister," he said to Penny, pointing.

"What does that mean?" she asked.

"It means some big bastard is creeping up behind us."

He was surprised to find that Moqorro and two of his fiery fingers had joined them on the sterncastle. It was only midday, and the red priest and his men did not normally emerge till dusk. The priest gave him a solemn nod. "There you see it, Hugor Hill. God's wroth. The Lord of Light will not be mocked."

Tyrion had a bad feeling about this. "The widow said this ship would never reach her destination. I took that to mean that once we were out to sea beyond the reach of triarchs, the captain would change course for Meereen. Or perhaps that you would seize the ship with your Fiery Hand and take us to Daenerys. But that isn't what your high priest saw at all, is it?"

"No." Moqorro's deep voice tolled as solemnly as a funeral bell. "This is what he saw." The red priest lifted his staff, and inclined its head toward the west.

Penny was lost. "I don't understand. What does it mean?"

"It means we had best get below. Ser Jorah has exiled me from our cabin. Might I hide in yours when the time comes?"

"Yes," she said. "You would be . . . oh . . ."

For the better part of three hours they ran before the wind, as the storm grew closer. The western sky went green, then grey, then black. A wall of dark clouds loomed up behind them, churning like a kettle of milk left on the fire too long. Tyrion and Penny watched from the forecastle, huddled by the figurehead and holding hands, careful to stay out of the way of captain and crew.

The last storm had been thrilling, intoxicating, a sudden squall that had left him feeling cleansed and refreshed. This one felt different right from the first. The captain sensed it too. He changed their course to north by northeast to try and get out of the storm's path.

It was a futile effort. This storm was too big. The seas around them grew rougher. The wind began to howl. The *Stinky Steward* rose and fell as waves smashed against her hull. Behind them lightning stabbed down from the sky, blinding purple bolts that danced across the sea in webs of light. Thunder followed. "The time has come to hide." Tyrion took Penny by the arm and led her belowdecks.

Pretty and Crunch were both half-mad with fear. The dog was barking, barking, barking. He knocked Tyrion right off his feet as they entered. The sow had been shitting everywhere. Tyrion cleaned that up as best he could whilst Penny tried to calm the animals. Then they tied down or put away anything that was still loose. "I'm frightened," Penny confessed. The cabin had begun to tilt and jump, going this way and that as the waves hammered at the hull of the ship.

*There are worse ways to die than drowning. Your brother learned that,
and so did my lord father. And Shae, that lying cunt. Hands of gold are
always cold, but a woman's hands are warm.* "We should play a game,"
Tyrion suggested. "That might help take our thoughts off the storm."

"Not *cyvasse*," she said at once.

"Not *cyvasse*," Tyrion agreed, as the deck rose under him. That would
only lead to pieces flying violently across the cabin and raining down on
sow and dog. "When you were a little girl, did you ever play come-into-
my-castle?"

"No. Can you teach me?"

Could he? Tyrion hesitated. *Fool of a dwarf. Of course she's never played
come-into-my-castle. She never had a castle.* Come-into-my-castle was a
game for highborn children, one meant to teach them courtesy, heraldry,
and a thing or two about their lord father's friends and foes. "That
won't . . ." he started. The deck gave another violent heave, slamming the
two of them together. Penny gave a squeak of fright. "That game won't
do," Tyrion told her, gritting his teeth. "Sorry. I don't know what game—"

"I do." Penny kissed him.

It was an awkward kiss, rushed, clumsy. But it took him utterly by surprise. His hands jerked up and grabbed hold of her shoulders to shove her
away. Instead he hesitated, then pulled her closer, gave her a squeeze.
Her lips were dry, hard, closed up tighter than a miser's purse. *A small
mercy,* thought Tyrion. This was nothing he had wanted. He liked Penny,
he pitied Penny, he even admired Penny in a way, but he did not desire
her. He had no wish to hurt her, though; the gods and his sweet sister had
given her enough pain. So he let the kiss go on, holding her gently by the
shoulders. His own lips stayed firmly shut. The *Selaesori Qhoran* rolled
and shuddered around them.

Finally she pulled back an inch or two. Tyrion could see his own reflection shining in her eyes. *Pretty eyes,* he thought, but he saw other
things as well. *A lot of fear, a little hope . . . but not a bit of lust. She does
not want me, no more than I want her.*

When she lowered her head, he took her under the chin and raised it
up again. "We cannot play that game, my lady." Above the thunder
boomed, close at hand now.

"I never meant . . . I never kissed a boy before, but . . . I only thought,
what if we drown, and I . . . I . . ."

"It was sweet," lied Tyrion, "but I am married. She was with me at the
feast, you may remember her. Lady Sansa."

"Was she your wife? She . . . she was very beautiful . . ."

And false. Sansa, Shae, all my women . . . Tysha was the only one who ever loved me. Where do whores go? "A lovely girl," said Tyrion, "and we were joined beneath the eyes of gods and men. It may be that she is lost to me, but until I know that for a certainty I must be true to her."

"I understand." Penny turned her face away from his.

My perfect woman, Tyrion thought bitterly. *One still young enough to believe such blatant lies.*

The hull was creaking, the deck moving, and Pretty was squealing in distress. Penny crawled across the cabin floor on her hands and knees, wrapped her arms around the sow's head, and murmured reassurance to her. Looking at the two of them, it was hard to know who was comforting whom. The sight was so grotesque it should have been hilarious, but Tyrion could not even find a smile. *The girl deserves better than a pig,* he thought. *An honest kiss, a little kindness, everyone deserves that much, however big or small.* He looked about for his wine cup, but when he found it all the rum had spilled. *Drowning is bad enough,* he reflected sourly, *but drowning sad and sober, that's too cruel.*

In the end, they did not drown . . . though there were times when the prospect of a nice, peaceful drowning had a certain appeal. The storm raged for the rest of that day and well into the night. Wet winds howled around them and waves rose like the fists of drowned giants to smash down on their decks. Above, they learned later, a mate and two sailors were swept overboard, the ship's cook was blinded when a kettle of hot grease flew up into his face, and the captain was thrown from the stern-castle to the main deck so violently he broke both legs. Below, Crunch howled and barked and snapped at Penny, and Pretty Pig began to shit again, turning the cramped, damp cabin into a sty. Tyrion managed to avoid retching his way through all of this, chiefly thanks to the lack of wine. Penny was not so fortunate, but he held her anyway as the ship's hull creaked and groaned alarmingly around them, like a cask about to burst.

Nearby midnight the winds finally died away, and the sea grew calm enough for Tyrion to make his way back up onto deck. What he saw there did not reassure him. The cog was drifting on a sea of dragonglass beneath a bowl of stars, but all around the storm raged on. East, west, north, south, everywhere he looked, the clouds rose up like black mountains, their tumbled slopes and collossal cliffs alive with blue and purple lightning. No rain was falling, but the decks were slick and wet underfoot.

Tyrion could hear someone screaming from below, a thin, high voice hysterical with fear. He could hear Moqorro too. The red priest stood on the forecastle facing the storm, his staff raised above his head as he boomed a prayer. Amidships, a dozen sailors and two of the fiery fingers were struggling with tangled lines and sodden canvas, but whether they were trying to raise the sail again or pull it down he never knew. Whatever they were doing, it seemed to him a very bad idea. And so it was.

The wind returned as a whispered threat, cold and damp, brushing over his cheek, flapping the wet sail, swirling and tugging at Moqorro's scarlet robes. Some instinct made Tyrion grab hold of the nearest rail, just in time. In the space of three heartbeats the little breeze became a howling gale. Moqorro shouted something, and green flames leapt from the dragon's maw atop his staff to vanish in the night. Then the rains came, black and blinding, and forecastle and sterncastle both vanished behind a wall of water. Something huge flapped overhead, and Tyrion glanced up in time to see the sail taking wing, with two men still dangling from the lines. Then he heard a *crack*. *Oh, bloody hell*, he had time to think, *that had to be the mast.*

He found a line and pulled on it, fighting toward the hatch to get himself below out of the storm, but a gust of wind knocked his feet from under him and a second slammed him into the rail and there he clung. Rain lashed at his face, blinding him. His mouth was full of blood again. The ship groaned and growled beneath him like a constipated fat man straining to shit.

Then the mast burst.

Tyrion never saw it, but he heard it. That *crack*ing sound again and then a scream of tortured wood, and suddenly the air was full of shards and splinters. One missed his eye by half an inch, a second found his neck, a third went through his calf, boots and breeches and all. He screamed. But he held on to the line, held on with a desperate strength he did not know he had. *The widow said this ship would never reach her destination*, he remembered. Then he laughed and laughed, wild and hysterical, as thunder boomed and timbers moaned and waves crashed all around him.

By the time the storm abated and the surviving passengers and crew came crawling back on deck, like pale pink worms wriggling to the surface after a rain, the *Selaesori Qhoran* was a broken thing, floating low in the water and listing ten degrees to port, her hull sprung in half a hundred places, her hold awash in seawater, her mast a splintered ruin no taller than a dwarf. Even her figurehead had not escaped; one of his arms had broken off, the one with all his scrolls. Nine men had been lost, including a mate, two of the fiery fingers, and Moqorro himself.

Did Benerro see this in his fires? Tyrion wondered, when he realized the huge red priest was gone. *Did Moqorro?*

"Prophecy is like a half-trained mule," he complained to Jorah Mormont. "It looks as though it might be useful, but the moment you trust in it, it kicks you in the head. That bloody widow knew the ship would never reach her destination, she warned us of that, said Benerro saw it in his fires, only I took that to mean . . . well, what does it matter?" His mouth twisted. "What it really meant was that some bloody big storm would turn our mast to kindling so we could drift aimlessly across the Gulf of Grief until our food ran out and we started eating one another. Who do you suppose they'll carve up first . . . the pig, the dog, or me?"

"The noisiest, I'd say."

The captain died the following day, the ship's cook three nights later. It was all that the remaining crew could do to keep the wreck afloat. The mate who had assumed command reckoned that they were somewhere off the southern end of the Isle of Cedars. When he lowered the ship's boats to tow them toward the nearest land, one sank and the men in the other cut the line and rowed off north, abandoning the cog and all their shipmates.

"Slaves," said Jorah Mormont, contemptuous.

The big knight had slept through the storm, to hear him tell it. Tyrion had his doubts, but he kept them to himself. One day he might want to bite someone in the leg, and for that you needed teeth. Mormont seemed content to ignore their disagreement, so Tyrion decided to pretend it had not happened.

For nineteen days they drifted, as food and water dwindled. The sun beat down on them, relentless. Penny huddled in her cabin with her dog and her pig, and Tyrion brought her food, limping on his bandaged calf and sniffing at the wound by night. When he had nothing else to do, he pricked his toes and fingers too. Ser Jorah made a point of sharpening his sword each day, honing the point until it gleamed. The three remaining fiery fingers lit the nightfire as the sun went down, but they wore their ornate armor as they led the crew in prayer, and their spears were close at hand. And not a single sailor tried to rub the head of either dwarf.

"Should we joust for them again?" Penny asked one night.

"Best not," said Tyrion. "That would only serve to remind them we have a nice plump pig." Though Pretty was growing less plump with every passing day, and Crunch was fur and bones.

That night he dreamed that he was back in King's Landing again, a crossbow in his hand. "Wherever whores go," Lord Tywin said, but when

Tyrion's finger clenched and the bowstring *thrumm*ed, it was Penny with the quarrel buried in her belly.

He woke to the sound of shouting.

The deck was moving under him, and for half a heartbeat he was so confused he thought he was back on the *Shy Maid*. A whiff of pigshit brought him to his senses. The Sorrows were behind him, half a world away, and the joys of that time as well. He remembered how sweet Lemore had looked after her morning swims, with beads of water glistening on her naked skin, but the only maiden here was his poor Penny, the stunted little dwarf girl.

Something was afoot, though. Tyrion slipped from the hammock, yawning, and looked about for his boots. And mad though it was, he looked for the crossbow as well, but of course there was none such to be found. *A pity*, he mused, *it might have been some use when the big folk come to eat me.* He pulled his boots on and climbed on deck to see what the shouting was about. Penny was there before him, her eyes wide with wonder. "A sail," she shouted, "there, there, do you see? A sail, and they've seen us, they have. A *sail*."

This time he kissed her . . . once on each cheek, once on the brow, and one last one on the mouth. She was flushed and laughing by the last kiss, suddenly shy again, but it made no matter. The other ship was closing. A big galley, he saw. Her oars left a long white wake behind her. "What ship is that?" he asked Ser Jorah Mormont. "Can you read her name?"

"I don't need to read her name. We're downwind. I can smell her." Mormont drew his sword. "That's a slaver."

THE TURNCLOAK

The first flakes came drifting down as the sun was setting in the west. By nightfall snow was coming down so heavily that the moon rose behind a white curtain, unseen.

"The gods of the north have unleashed their wroth on Lord Stannis," Roose Bolton announced come morning as men gathered in Winterfell's Great Hall to break their fast. "He is a stranger here, and the old gods will not suffer him to live."

His men roared their approval, banging their fists on the long plank tables. Winterfell might be ruined, but its granite walls would still keep the worst of the wind and weather at bay. They were well stocked with food and drink; they had fires to warm them when off duty, a place to dry their clothes, snug corners to lie down and sleep. Lord Bolton had laid by enough wood to keep the fires fed for half a year, so the Great Hall was always warm and cozy. Stannis had none of that.

Theon Greyjoy did not join the uproar. Neither did the men of House Frey, he did not fail to note. *They are strangers here as well,* he thought, watching Ser Aenys Frey and his half-brother Ser Hosteen. Born and bred in the riverlands, the Freys had never seen a snow like this. *The north has already claimed three of their blood,* Theon thought, recalling the men that Ramsay had searched for fruitlessly, lost between White Harbor and Barrowton.

On the dais, Lord Wyman Manderly sat between a pair of his White Harbor knights, spooning porridge into his fat face. He did not seem to be enjoying it near as much as he had the pork pies at the wedding. Elsewhere one-armed Harwood Stout talked quietly with the cadaverous Whoresbane Umber.

Theon queued up with the other men for porridge, ladled into wooden bowls from a row of copper kettles. The lords and knights had milk and honey and even a bit of butter to sweeten their portions, he saw, but none of that would be offered him. His reign as prince of Winterfell had been a brief one. He had played his part in the mummer's show, giving the feigned Arya to be wed, and now he was of no further use to Roose Bolton.

"First winter I remember, the snows came over my head," said a Horn-wood man in the queue ahead of him.

"Aye, but you were only three foot tall at the time," a rider from the Rills replied.

Last night, unable to sleep, Theon had found himself brooding on escape, of slipping away unseen whilst Ramsay and his lord father had their attention elsewhere. Every gate was closed and barred and heavily guarded, though; no one was allowed to enter or depart the castle without Lord Bolton's leave. Even if he found some secret way out, Theon would not have trusted it. He had not forgotten Kyra and her keys. And if he did get out, where would he go? His father was dead, and his uncles had no use for him. Pyke was lost to him. The nearest thing to a home that remained to him was here, amongst the bones of Winterfell.

A ruined man, a ruined castle. This is my place.

He was still waiting for his porridge when Ramsay swept into the hall with his Bastard's Boys, shouting for music. Abel rubbed the sleep from his eyes, took up his lute, and launched into "The Dornishman's Wife," whilst one of his washerwomen beat time on her drum. The singer changed the words, though. Instead of tasting a Dornishman's wife, he sang of tasting a northman's daughter.

He could lose his tongue for that, Theon thought, as his bowl was being filled. *He is only a singer. Lord Ramsay could flay the skin off both his hands, and no one would say a word.* But Lord Bolton smiled at the lyric and Ramsay laughed aloud. Then others knew that it was safe to laugh as well. Yellow Dick found the song so funny that wine snorted out his nose.

Lady Arya was not there to share the merriment. She had not been seen outside her chambers since her wedding night. Sour Alyn had been saying that Ramsay kept his bride naked and chained to a bedpost, but Theon knew that was only talk. There were no chains, at least none that men could see. Just a pair of guards outside the bedchamber, to keep the girl from wandering. *And she is only naked when she bathes.*

That she did most every night, though. Lord Ramsay wanted his wife clean. "She has no handmaids, poor thing," he had said to Theon. "That leaves you, Reek. Should I put you in a dress?" He laughed. "Perhaps if you beg it of me. Just now, it will suffice for you to be her bath maid. I won't have her smelling like you." So whenever Ramsay had an itch to bed his wife, it fell to Theon to borrow some servingwomen from Lady Walda or Lady Dustin and fetch hot water from the kitchens. Though Arya never spoke to any of them, they could not fail to see her bruises. *It is her own fault. She has not pleased him.* "Just be Arya," he told the girl once, as he helped her into the water. "Lord Ramsay does not want to hurt you. He only hurts us when we . . . when we forget. He never cut me without cause."

"Theon . . ." she whispered, weeping.

"*Reek.*" He grabbed her arm and shook her. "In here I'm Reek. You have to *remember*, Arya." But the girl was no true Stark, only a steward's whelp. *Jeyne, her name is Jeyne. She should not look to me for rescue.* Theon Greyjoy might have tried to help her, once. But Theon had been ironborn, and a braver man than Reek. *Reek, Reek, it rhymes with weak.*

Ramsay had a new plaything to amuse him, one with teats and a cunny . . . but soon Jeyne's tears would lose their savor, and Ramsay would want his Reek again. *He will flay me inch by inch. When my fingers are gone he will take my hands. After my toes, my feet. But only when I beg for it, when the pain grows so bad that I plead for him to give me some relief.* There would be no hot baths for Reek. He would roll in shit again, forbidden to wash. The clothes he wore would turn to rags, foul and stinking, and he would be made to wear them till they rotted. The best he could hope for was to be returned to the kennels with Ramsay's girls for company. *Kyra*, he remembered. *The new bitch he calls Kyra.*

He took his bowl to the back of the hall and found a place on an empty bench, yards away from the nearest torch. Day or night, the benches below the salt were never less than half-full with men drinking, dicing, talking, or sleeping in their clothes in quiet corners. Their serjeants would kick them awake when it came their turn to shrug back into their cloaks and walk the walls. But no man of them would welcome the company of Theon Turncloak, nor did he have much taste for theirs.

The gruel was grey and watery, and he pushed it away after his third spoonful and let it congeal in the bowl. At the next table, men were arguing about the storm and wondering aloud how long the snow would fall. "All day and all night, might be even longer," insisted one big, black-bearded archer with a Cerwyn axe sewn on his breast. A few of the older men spoke of other snowstorms and insisted this was no more than a light dusting compared to what they'd seen in the winters of their youth. The riverlanders were aghast. *They have no love of snow and cold, these southron swords.* Men entering the hall huddled by the fires or clapped their hands together over glowing braziers as their cloaks hung dripping from pegs inside the door.

The air was thick and smoky and a crust had formed atop his porridge when a woman's voice behind him said, "Theon Greyjoy."

My name is Reek, he almost said. "What do you want?"

She sat down next to him, straddling the bench, and pushed a wild mop of red-brown hair out of her eyes. "Why do you eat alone, m'lord? Come, rise, join the dance."

He went back to his porridge. "I don't dance." The Prince of Winterfell had been a graceful dancer, but Reek with his missing toes would be grotesque. "Leave me be. I have no coin."

The woman smiled crookedly. "Do you take me for a whore?" She was one of the singer's washerwomen, the tall skinny one, too lean and leathery to be called pretty . . . though there was a time when Theon would have tumbled her all the same, to see how it felt to have those long legs wrapped around him. "What good would coin do me here? What would I buy with it, some snow?" She laughed. "You could pay me with a smile. I've never seen you smile, not even during your sister's wedding feast."

"Lady Arya is not my sister." *I do not smile either*, he might have told her. *Ramsay hated my smiles, so he took a hammer to my teeth. I can hardly eat.* "She never was my sister."

"A pretty maid, though."

I was never beautiful like Sansa, but they all said I was pretty. Jeyne's words seemed to echo in his head, to the beat of the drums two of Abel's other girls were pounding. Another one had pulled Little Walder Frey up onto the table to teach him how to dance. All the men were laughing. "Leave me be," said Theon.

"Am I not to m'lord's taste? I could send Myrtle to you if you want. Or Holly, might be you'd like her better. All the men like Holly. They're not my sisters neither, but they're sweet." The woman leaned close. Her breath smelled of wine. "If you have no smile for me, tell me how you captured Winterfell. Abel will put it in a song, and you will live forever."

"As a betrayer. As Theon Turncloak."

"Why not Theon the Clever? It was a daring feat, the way we heard it. How many men did you have? A hundred? Fifty?"

Fewer. "It was madness."

"Glorious madness. Stannis has five thousand, they say, but Abel claims ten times as many still could not breach these walls. So how did *you* get in, m'lord? Did you have some secret way?"

I had ropes, Theon thought. *I had grapnels. I had darkness on my side, and surprise. The castle was but lightly held, and I took them unawares.* But he said none of that. If Abel made a song about him, like as not Ramsay would prick his eardrums to make certain that he never heard it.

"You can trust me, m'lord. Abel does." The washerwoman put her hand upon his own. His hands were gloved in wool and leather. Hers were bare, long-fingered, rough, with nails chewed to the quick. "You never asked my name. It's Rowan."

Theon wrenched away. This was a ploy, he knew it. *Ramsay sent her. She's another of his japes, like Kyra with the keys. A jolly jape, that's all. He wants me to run, so he can punish me.*

He wanted to hit her, to smash that mocking smile off her face. He wanted to kiss her, to fuck her right there on the table and make her cry his name. But he knew he dare not touch her, in anger or in lust. *Reek, Reek, my name is Reek. I must not forget my name.* He jerked to his feet and made his way wordlessly to the doors, limping on his maimed feet.

Outside the snow was falling still. Wet, heavy, silent, it had already begun to cover the footsteps left by the men coming and going from the hall. The drifts came almost to the top of his boots. *It will be deeper in the wolfswood . . . and out on the kingsroad, where the wind is blowing, there will be no escape from it.* A battle was being fought in the yard; Ryswells pelting Barrowton boys with snowballs. Above, he could see some squires building snowmen along the battlements. They were arming them with spears and shields, putting iron halfhelms on their heads, and arraying them along the inner wall, a rank of snowy sentinels. "Lord Winter has joined us with his levies," one of the sentries outside the Great Hall japed . . . until he saw Theon's face and realized who he was talking to. Then he turned his head and spat.

Beyond the tents the big destriers of the knights from White Harbor and the Twins were shivering in their horse lines. Ramsay had burned the stables when he sacked Winterfell, so his father had thrown up new ones twice as large as the old, to accommodate the warhorses and palfreys of his lords' bannermen and knights. The rest of the horses were tethered in the wards. Hooded grooms moved amongst them, covering them with blankets to keep them warm.

Theon made his way deeper into the ruined parts of the castle. As he picked through the shattered stone that had once been Maester Luwin's turret, ravens looked down from the gash in the wall above, muttering to one another. From time to time one would let out a raucous scream. He stood in the doorway of a bedchamber that had once been his own (ankle deep in snow that had blown in through a shattered window), visited the ruins of Mikken's forge and Lady Catelyn's sept. Beneath the Burned Tower, he passed Rickard Ryswell nuzzling at the neck of another one of Abel's washerwomen, the plump one with the apple cheeks and pug nose. The girl was barefoot in the snow, bundled up in a fur cloak. He thought she might be naked underneath. When she saw him, she said something to Ryswell that made him laugh aloud.

Theon trudged away from them. There was a stair beyond the mews, seldom used; it was there his feet took him. The steps were steep and treacherous. He climbed carefully and found himself alone on the battlements of the inner wall, well away from the squires and their snowmen. No one had given him freedom of the castle, but no one had denied it to him either. He could go where he would within the walls.

Winterfell's inner wall was the older and taller of the two, its ancient grey crenellations rising one hundred feet high, with square towers at every corner. The outer wall, raised many centuries later, was twenty feet lower, but thicker and in better repair, boasting octagonal towers in place of square ones. Between the two walls was the moat, deep and wide . . . and frozen. Drifts of snow had begun to creep across its icy surface. Snow was building up along the battlements too, filling the gaps between the merlons and putting pale, soft caps on every tower top.

Beyond the walls, as far as he could see, the world was turning white. The woods, the fields, the kingsroad—the snows were covering all of them beneath a pale soft mantle, burying the remnants of the winter town, hiding the blackened walls Ramsay's men had left behind when they put the houses to the torch. *The wounds Snow made, snow conceals,* but that was wrong. Ramsay was a Bolton now, not a Snow, never a Snow.

Farther off, the rutted kingsroad had vanished, lost amidst the fields and rolling hills, all one vast expanse of white. And still the snow was falling, drifting down in silence from a windless sky. *Stannis Baratheon is out there somewhere, freezing.* Would Lord Stannis try to take Winterfell by storm? *If he does, his cause is doomed.* The castle was too strong. Even with the moat frozen over, Winterfell's defenses remained formidable. Theon had captured the castle by stealth, sending his best men to scale the walls and swim the moat under the cover of darkness. The defenders had not even known they were under attack until it was too late. No such subterfuge was possible for Stannis.

He might prefer to cut the castle off from the outside world and starve out its defenders. Winterfell's storerooms and cellar vaults were empty. A long supply train had come with Bolton and his friends of Frey up through the Neck, Lady Dustin had brought food and fodder from Barrowton, and Lord Manderly had arrived well provisioned from White Harbor . . . but the host was large. With so many mouths to feed, their stores could not last for long. *Lord Stannis and his men will be just as hungry, though. And cold and footsore as well, in no condition for a fight . . . but the storm will make them desperate to get inside the castle.*

Snow was falling on the godswood too, melting when it touched the ground. Beneath the white-cloaked trees the earth had turned to mud. Tendrils of mist hung in the air like ghostly ribbons. *Why did I come here? These are not my gods. This is not my place.* The heart tree stood before him, a pale giant with a carved face and leaves like bloody hands.

A thin film of ice covered the surface of the pool beneath the weirwood. Theon sank to his knees beside it. "Please," he murmured through his broken teeth, "I never meant . . ." The words caught in his throat. "Save me," he finally managed. "Give me . . ." *What? Strength? Courage? Mercy?* Snow fell around him, pale and silent, keeping its own counsel. The only sound was a faint soft sobbing. *Jeyne,* he thought. *It is her, sobbing in her bridal bed. Who else could it be?* Gods do not weep. *Or do they?*

The sound was too painful to endure. Theon grabbed hold of a branch and pulled himself back to his feet, knocked the snow off his legs, and limped back toward the lights. *There are ghosts in Winterfell,* he thought, *and I am one of them.*

More snowmen had risen in the yard by the time Theon Greyjoy made his way back. To command the snowy sentinels on the walls, the squires had erected a dozen snowy lords. One was plainly meant to be Lord Manderly; it was the fattest snowman that Theon had ever seen. The one-armed lord could only be Harwood Stout, the snow lady Barbrey Dustin. And the one closest to the door with the beard made of icicles had to be old Whoresbane Umber.

Inside, the cooks were ladling out beef-and-barley stew, thick with carrots and onions, served in trenchers hollowed from loaves of yesterday's bread. Scraps were thrown onto the floor to be gobbled up by Ramsay's girls and the other dogs.

The girls were glad to see him. They knew him by his smell. Red Jeyne loped over to lick at his hand, and Helicent slipped under the table and curled up by his feet, gnawing at a bone. They were good dogs. It was easy to forget that every one was named for a girl that Ramsay had hunted and killed.

Weary as he was, Theon had appetite enough to eat a little stew, washed down with ale. By then the hall had grown raucous. Two of Roose Bolton's scouts had come straggling back through the Hunter's Gate to report that Lord Stannis's advance had slowed to a crawl. His knights rode destriers, and the big warhorses were foundering in the snow. The small, sure-footed garrons of the hill clans were faring better, the scouts said, but the clansmen dared not press too far ahead or the whole host would come apart. Lord Ramsay commanded Abel to give them a marching song in honor of Stannis trudging through the snows, so the bard took up his lute again, whilst one of his washerwomen coaxed a sword from Sour Alyn and mimed Stannis slashing at the snowflakes.

Theon was staring down into the last dregs of his third tankard when Lady Barbrey Dustin swept into the hall and sent two of her sworn swords to bring him to her. When he stood below the dais, she looked him up and down, and sniffed. "Those are the same clothes you wore for the wedding."

"Yes, my lady. They are the clothes I was given." That was one of the lessons he had learned at the Dreadfort: to take what he was given and never ask for more.

Lady Dustin wore black, as ever, though her sleeves were lined with vair. Her gown had a high stiff collar that framed her face. "You know this castle."

"Once."

"Somewhere beneath us are the crypts where the old Stark kings sit in darkness. My men have not been able to find the way down into them. They have been through all the undercrofts and cellars, even the dungeons, but . . ."

"The crypts cannot be accessed from the dungeons, my lady."

"Can you show me the way down?"

"There's nothing down there but—"

"—dead Starks? Aye. And all my favorite Starks are dead, as it happens. Do you know the way or not?"

"I do." He did not like the crypts, had never liked the crypts, but he was no stranger to them.

"Show me. Serjeant, fetch a lantern."

"My lady will want a warm cloak," cautioned Theon. "We will need to go outside."

The snow was coming down heavier than ever when they left the hall, with Lady Dustin wrapped in sable. Huddled in their hooded cloaks, the guards outside were almost indistinguishable from the snowmen. Only their breath fogging the air gave proof that they still lived. Fires burned along the battlements, a vain attempt to drive the gloom away. Their small party found themselves slogging through a smooth, unbroken expanse of white that came halfway up their calves. The tents in the yard were half-buried, sagging under the weight of the accumulation.

The entrance to the crypts was in the oldest section of the castle, near the foot of the First Keep, which had sat unused for hundreds of years. Ramsay had put it to the torch when he sacked Winterfell, and much of what had not burned had collapsed. Only a shell remained, one side open to the elements and filling up with snow. Rubble was strewn all about it: great chunks of shattered masonry, burned beams, broken gargoyles. The falling snow had covered almost all of it, but part of one gargoyle still poked above the drift, its grotesque face snarling sightless at the sky.

This is where they found Bran when he fell. Theon had been out hunting that day, riding with Lord Eddard and King Robert, with no hint of the dire news that awaited them back at the castle. He remembered Robb's face when they told him. No one had expected the broken boy to live. *The gods could not kill Bran, no more than I could.* It was a strange thought, and stranger still to remember that Bran might still be alive.

"There." Theon pointed to where a snowbank had crept up the wall of the keep. "Under there. Watch for broken stones."

It took Lady Dustin's men the better part of half an hour to uncover the entrance, shoveling through the snow and shifting rubble. When they did, the door was frozen shut. Her serjeant had to go find an axe before he could pull it open, hinges screaming, to reveal stone steps spiraling down into darkness.

"It is a long way down, my lady," Theon cautioned.

Lady Dustin was undeterred. "Beron, the light."

The way was narrow and steep, the steps worn in the center by centuries of feet. They went single file—the serjeant with the lantern, then Theon and Lady Dustin, her other man behind them. He had always thought of the crypts as cold, and so they seemed in summer, but now as they descended the air grew warmer. Not *warm*, never warm, but warmer than above. Down there below the earth, it would seem, the chill was constant, unchanging.

"The bride weeps," Lady Dustin said, as they made their way down, step by careful step. "Our little Lady Arya."

Take care now. Take care, take care. He put one hand on the wall. The shifting torchlight made the steps seem to move beneath his feet. "As . . . as you say, m'lady."

"Roose is not pleased. Tell your bastard that."

He is not my bastard, he wanted to say, but another voice inside him said, *He is, he is. Reek belongs to Ramsay, and Ramsay belongs to Reek. You must not forget your name.*

"Dressing her in grey and white serves no good if the girl is left to sob. The Freys may not care, but the northmen . . . they fear the Dreadfort, but they love the Starks."

"Not you," said Theon.

"Not me," the Lady of Barrowton confessed, "but the rest, yes. Old Whoresbane is only here because the Freys hold the Greatjon captive. And do you imagine the Hornwood men have forgotten the Bastard's last marriage, and how his lady wife was left to starve, chewing her own fingers? What do you think passes through their heads when they hear the new bride weeping? Valiant Ned's precious little girl."

No, he thought. *She is not of Lord Eddard's blood, her name is Jeyne, she is only a steward's daughter.* He did not doubt that Lady Dustin suspected, but even so . . .

"Lady Arya's sobs do us more harm than all of Lord Stannis's swords and spears. If the Bastard means to remain Lord of Winterfell, he had best teach his wife to laugh."

"My lady," Theon broke in. "Here we are."

"The steps go farther down," observed Lady Dustin.

"There are lower levels. Older. The lowest level is partly collapsed, I hear. I have never been down there." He pushed the door open and led them out into a long vaulted tunnel, where mighty granite pillars marched two by two into blackness.

Lady Dustin's serjeant raised the lantern. Shadows slid and shifted. A *small light in a great darkness.* Theon had never felt comfortable in the crypts. He could feel the stone kings staring down at him with their stone eyes, stone fingers curled around the hilts of rusted longswords. None had any love for ironborn. A familiar sense of dread filled him.

"So many," Lady Dustin said. "Do you know their names?"

"Once . . . but that was a long time ago." Theon pointed. "The ones on this side were Kings in the North. Torrhen was the last."

"The King Who Knelt."

"Aye, my lady. After him they were only lords."

"Until the Young Wolf. Where is Ned Stark's tomb?"

"At the end. This way, my lady."

Their footsteps echoed through the vault as they made their way between the rows of pillars. The stone eyes of the dead men seemed to follow them, and the eyes of their stone direwolves as well. The faces stirred faint memories. A few names came back to him, unbidden, whispered in the ghostly voice of Maester Luwin. King Edrick Snowbeard, who had ruled the north for a hundred years. Brandon the Shipwright, who had sailed beyond the sunset. Theon Stark, the Hungry Wolf. *My namesake.* Lord Beron Stark, who made common cause with Casterly Rock to war against Dagon Greyjoy, Lord of Pyke, in the days when the Seven Kingdoms were ruled in all but name by the bastard sorcerer men called Bloodraven.

"That king is missing his sword," Lady Dustin observed.

It was true. Theon did not recall which king it was, but the longsword he should have held was gone. Streaks of rust remained to show where it had been. The sight disquieted him. He had always heard that the iron in the sword kept the spirits of the dead locked within their tombs. If a sword was missing . . .

There are ghosts in Winterfell. And I am one of them.

They walked on. Barbrey Dustin's face seemed to harden with every step. *She likes this place no more than I do.* Theon heard himself say, "My lady, why do you hate the Starks?"

She studied him. "For the same reason you love them."

Theon stumbled. "Love them? I never . . . I took this castle from them, my lady. I had . . . had Bran and Rickon put to death, mounted their heads on spikes, I . . ."

". . . rode south with Robb Stark, fought beside him at the Whispering Wood and Riverrun, returned to the Iron Islands as his envoy to treat with your own father. Barrowton sent men with the Young Wolf as well. I gave him as few men as I dared, but I knew that I must needs give him some or risk the wroth of Winterfell. So I had my own eyes and ears in that host. They kept me well informed. I know who you are. I know what you are. Now answer my question. Why do you love the Starks?"

"I . . ." Theon put a gloved hand against a pillar. ". . . I wanted to be one of them . . ."

"And never could. We have more in common than you know, my lord. But come."

Only a little farther on, three tombs were closely grouped together. That was where they halted. "Lord Rickard," Lady Dustin observed, studying the central figure. The statue loomed above them—long-faced, bearded, solemn. He had the same stone eyes as the rest, but his looked sad. "He lacks a sword as well."

It was true. "Someone has been down here stealing swords. Brandon's is gone as well."

"He would hate that." She pulled off her glove and touched his knee, pale flesh against dark stone. "Brandon loved his sword. He loved to hone it. 'I want it sharp enough to shave the hair from a woman's cunt,' he used to say. And how he loved to use it. 'A bloody sword is a beautiful thing,' he told me once."

"You knew him," Theon said.

The lantern light in her eyes made them seem as if they were afire. "Brandon was fostered at Barrowton with old Lord Dustin, the father of the one I'd later wed, but he spent most of his time riding the Rills. He loved to ride. His little sister took after him in that. A pair of centaurs, those two. And my lord father was always pleased to play host to the heir to Winterfell. My father had great ambitions for House Ryswell. He would have served up my maidenhead to any Stark who happened by, but there was no need. Brandon was never shy about taking what he wanted. I am old now, a dried-up thing, too long a widow, but I still remember the look of my maiden's blood on his cock the night he claimed me. I think Brandon liked the sight as well. A bloody sword is a beautiful thing, yes. It hurt, but it was a sweet pain.

"The day I learned that Brandon was to marry Catelyn Tully, though . . . there was nothing sweet about *that* pain. He never wanted her, I promise you that. He told me so, on our last night together . . . but Rickard Stark had great ambitions too. *Southron* ambitions that would not be served by having his heir marry the daughter of one of his own vassals. Afterward my father nursed some hope of wedding me to Brandon's brother Eddard, but Catelyn Tully got that one as well. I was left with young Lord Dustin, until Ned Stark took him from me."

"Robert's Rebellion . . ."

"Lord Dustin and I had not been married half a year when Robert rose and Ned Stark called his banners. I begged my husband not to go. He had kin he might have sent in his stead. An uncle famed for his prowess with an axe, a great-uncle who had fought in the War of the Ninepenny Kings. But he was a man and full of pride, nothing would serve but that he lead the Barrowton levies himself. I gave him a horse the day he set out, a red stallion with a fiery mane, the pride of my lord father's herds. My lord swore that he would ride him home when the war was done.

"Ned Stark returned the horse to me on his way back home to Winterfell. He told me that my lord had died an honorable death, that his body had been laid to rest beneath the red mountains of Dorne. He brought his sister's bones back north, though, and there she rests . . . but I promise you, Lord Eddard's bones will never rest beside hers. I mean to feed them to my dogs."

Theon did not understand. "His . . . his bones . . . ?"

Her lips twisted. It was an ugly smile, a smile that reminded him of Ramsay's. "Catelyn Tully dispatched Lord Eddard's bones north before the Red Wedding, but your iron uncle seized Moat Cailin and closed the way. I have been watching ever since. Should those bones ever emerge from the swamps, they will get no farther than Barrowton." She threw one last lingering look at the likeness of Eddard Stark. "We are done here."

The snowstorm was still raging when they emerged from the crypts. Lady Dustin was silent during their ascent, but when they stood beneath the ruins of the First Keep again she shivered and said, "You would do well not to repeat anything I might have said down there. Is that understood?"

It was. "Hold my tongue or lose it."

"Roose has trained you well." She left him there.

THE KING'S PRIZE

The king's host departed Deepwood Motte by the light of a golden dawn, uncoiling from behind the log palisades like a long, steel serpent emerging from its nest.

The southron knights rode out in plate and mail, dinted and scarred by the battles they had fought, but still bright enough to glitter when they caught the rising sun. Faded and stained, torn and mended, their banners and surcoats still made a riot of colors amidst the winter wood—azure and orange, red and green, purple and blue and gold, glimmering amongst bare brown trunks, grey-green pines and sentinels, drifts of dirty snow.

Each knight had his squires, servants, and men-at-arms. Behind them came armorers, cooks, grooms; ranks of spearmen, axemen, archers; grizzled veterans of a hundred battles and green boys off to fight their first. Before them marched the clansmen from the hills; chiefs and champions astride shaggy garrons, their hirsute fighters trotting beside them, clad in furs and boiled leather and old mail. Some painted their faces brown and green and tied bundles of brush about them, to hide amongst the trees.

Back of the main column the baggage train followed: mules, horses, oxen, a mile of wayns and carts laden with food, fodder, tents, and other provisions. Last the rear guard—more knights in plate and mail, with a screening of outriders following half-hidden to make certain no foe could steal up on them unawares.

Asha Greyjoy rode in the baggage train, in a covered wayn with two huge iron-rimmed wheels, fettered at wrist and ankle and watched over day and night by a She-Bear who snored worse than any man. His Grace King Stannis was taking no chances on his prize escaping captivity. He meant to carry her to Winterfell, to display her there in chains for the lords of the north to see, the kraken's daughter bound and broken, proof of his power.

Trumpets saw the column on its way. Spearpoints shone in the light of the rising sun, and all along the verges the grass glistened with the morning frost. Between Deepwood Motte and Winterfell lay one hundred leagues of forest. Three hundred miles as the raven flies. "Fifteen days," the knights told each other.

"Robert would have done it in ten," Asha heard Lord Fell boasting. His grandsire had been slain by Robert at Summerhall; somehow this had elevated his slayer to godlike prowess in the grandson's eyes. "Robert would have been inside Winterfell a fortnight ago, thumbing his nose at Bolton from the battlements."

"Best not mention that to Stannis," suggested Justin Massey, "or he'll have us marching nights as well as days."

This king lives in his brother's shadow, Asha thought.

Her ankle still gave a stab of pain whenever she tried to put her weight on it. Something was broken down inside, Asha did not doubt. The swelling had gone down at Deepwood, but the pain remained. A sprain would surely have healed by now. Her irons *clack*ed every time she moved. The fetters chafed at her wrists and at her pride. But that was the cost of submission.

"No man has ever died from bending his knee," her father had once told her. "He who kneels may rise again, blade in hand. He who will not kneel stays dead, stiff legs and all." Balon Greyjoy had proved the truth of his own words when his first rebellion failed; the kraken bent the knee to stag and direwolf, only to rise again when Robert Baratheon and Eddard Stark were dead.

And so at Deepwood the kraken's daughter had done the same when she was dumped before the king, bound and limping (though blessedly unraped), her ankle a blaze of pain. "I yield, Your Grace. Do as you wish with me. I ask only that you spare my men." Qarl and Tris and the rest who had survived the wolfswood were all she had to care about. Only nine remained. *We ragged nine,* Cromm named them. He was the worst wounded.

Stannis had given her their lives. Yet she sensed no true mercy in the man. He was determined, beyond a doubt. Nor did he lack for courage. Men said he was just . . . and if his was a harsh, hard-handed sort of justice, well, life on the Iron Islands had accustomed Asha Greyjoy to that. All the same, she could not like this king. Those deep-set blue eyes of his seemed always slitted in suspicion, cold fury boiling just below their surface. Her life meant little and less to him. She was only his hostage, a prize to show the north that he could vanquish the ironborn.

More fool him. Bringing down a woman was not like to awe any north-men, if she knew the breed, and her worth as a hostage was less than naught. Her uncle ruled the Iron Islands now, and the Crow's Eye would not care if she lived or died. It might matter some to the wretched ruin of a husband that Euron had inflicted upon her, but Eric Ironmaker did not have coin enough to ransom her. But there was no explaining such things to Stannis Baratheon. Her very womanhood seemed to offend him. Men from the green lands liked their women soft and sweet in silk, she knew, not clad in mail and leather with a throwing axe in each hand. But her short acquaintance with the king at Deepwood Motte convinced her that he would have been no more fond of her in a gown. Even with Galbart Glover's wife, the pious Lady Sybelle, he had been correct and courteous but plainly uncomfortable. This southron king seemed to be one of those men to whom women are another race, as strange and unfathomable as giants and grumkins and the children of the forest. The She-Bear made him grind his teeth as well.

There was only one woman that Stannis listened to, and he had left her on the Wall. "Though I would sooner she was with us," confessed Ser Justin Massey, the fair-haired knight who commanded the baggage train. "The last time we went into battle without Lady Melisandre was the Blackwater, when Lord Renly's shade came down upon us and drove half our host into the bay."

"The last time?" Asha said. "Was this sorceress at Deepwood Motte? I did not see her."

"Hardly a battle," Ser Justin said, smiling. "Your ironmen fought bravely, my lady, but we had many times your numbers, and we took you unawares. Winterfell will know that we are coming. And Roose Bolton has as many men as we do."

Or more, thought Asha.

Even prisoners have ears, and she had heard all the talk at Deepwood Motte, when King Stannis and his captains were debating this march. Ser Justin had opposed it from the start, along with many of the knights and lords who had come with Stannis from the south. But the wolves insisted; Roose Bolton could not be suffered to hold Winterfell, and the Ned's girl must be rescued from the clutches of his bastard. So said Morgan Liddle, Brandon Norrey, Big Bucket Wull, the Flints, even the She-Bear. "One hundred leagues from Deepwood Motte to Winterfell," said Artos Flint, the night the argument boiled to a head in Galbart Glover's longhall. "Three hundred miles as the raven flies."

"A long march," a knight named Corliss Penny said.

"Not so long as that," insisted Ser Godry, the big knight the others called the Giantslayer. "We have come as far already. The Lord of Light will blaze a path for us."

"And when we arrive before Winterfell?" said Justin Massey. "Two walls with a moat between them, and the inner wall a hundred feet high. Bolton will never march out to face us in the field, and we do not have the provisions to mount a siege."

"Arnolf Karstark will join his strength to ours, never forget," said Harwood Fell. "Mors Umber as well. We will have as many northmen as Lord Bolton. And the woods are thick north of the castle. We will raise siege towers, build rams . . ."

And die by the thousands, Asha thought.

"We might do best to winter here," suggested Lord Peasebury.

"*Winter* here?" Big Bucket roared. "How much food and fodder do you think Galbart Glover has laid by?"

Then Ser Richard Horpe, the knight with the ravaged face and the death's-head moths on his surcoat, turned to Stannis and said, "Your Grace, your brother—"

The king cut him off. "We all know what my brother would do. Robert would gallop up to the gates of Winterfell alone, break them with his warhammer, and ride through the rubble to slay Roose Bolton with his left hand and the Bastard with his right." Stannis rose to his feet. "I am not Robert. But we will march, and we will free Winterfell . . . or die in the attempt."

Whatever doubts his lords might nurse, the common men seemed to have faith in their king. Stannis had smashed Mance Rayder's wildlings at the Wall and cleaned Asha and her ironborn out of Deepwood Motte; he was Robert's brother, victor in a famous sea battle off Fair Isle, the man who had held Storm's End all through Robert's Rebellion. And he bore a hero's sword, the enchanted blade Lightbringer, whose glow lit up the night.

"Our foes are not as formidable as they appear," Ser Justin assured Asha on the first day of the march. "Roose Bolton is feared, but little loved. And his friends the Freys . . . the north has not forgotten the Red Wedding. Every lord at Winterfell lost kinsmen there. Stannis need only bloody Bolton, and the northmen will abandon him."

So you hope, thought Asha, *but first the king must bloody him. Only a fool deserts the winning side.*

Ser Justin called upon her cart half a dozen times that first day, to bring her food and drink and tidings of the march. A man of easy smiles and endless japes, large and well fleshed, with pink cheeks, blue eyes, and a wind-tossed tangle of white-blond hair as pale as flax, he was a considerate gaoler, ever solicitous of his captive's comfort.

"He wants you," said the She-Bear, after his third visit.

Her proper name was Alysane of House Mormont, but she wore the other name as easily as she wore her mail. Short, chunky, muscular, the heir to Bear Island had big thighs, big breasts, and big hands ridged with callus. Even in sleep she wore ringmail under her furs, boiled leather under that, and an old sheepskin under the leather, turned inside out for warmth. All those layers made her look almost as wide as she was tall. *And ferocious.* Sometimes it was hard for Asha Greyjoy to remember that she and the She-Bear were almost of an age.

"He wants my lands," Asha replied. "He wants the Iron Islands." She knew the signs. She had seen the same before in other suitors. Massey's own ancestral holdings, far to the south, were lost to him, so he must needs make an advantageous marriage or resign himself to being no more than a knight of the king's household. Stannis had frustrated Ser Justin's hopes of marrying the wildling princess that Asha had heard so much of, so now he had set his sights on her. No doubt he dreamed of putting her in the Seastone Chair on Pyke and ruling through her, as her lord and master. That would require ridding her of her present lord and master, to be sure . . . not to mention the uncle who had married her to him. *Not likely,* Asha judged. *The Crow's Eye could eat Ser Justin to break his fast and never even belch.*

It made no matter. Her father's lands would never be hers, no matter whom she married. The ironborn were not a forgiving people, and Asha had been defeated twice. Once at the kingsmoot by her uncle Euron, and again at Deepwood Motte by Stannis. More than enough to stamp her as unfit to rule. Wedding Justin Massey, or any of Stannis Baratheon's lordlings, would hurt more than it helped. *The kraken's daughter turned out to be just a woman after all,* the captains and the kings would say. *See how she spreads her legs for this soft green land lord.*

Still, if Ser Justin wished to court her favor with food and wine and words, Asha was not like to discourage him. He made for better company than the taciturn She-Bear, and she was elsewise alone amongst five thousand foes. Tris Botley, Qarl the Maid, Cromm, Roggon, and the rest of her bloodied band had been left behind at Deepwood Motte, in Galbart Glover's dungeons.

The army covered twenty-two miles the first day, by the reckoning of the guides Lady Sybelle had given them, trackers and hunters sworn to

Deepwood with clan names like Forrester and Woods, Branch and Bole. The second day the host made twenty-four, as their vanguard passed beyond the Glover lands into the thick of the wolfswood. *"R'hllor, send your light to lead us through this gloom,"* the faithful prayed that night as they gathered about a roaring blaze outside the king's pavilion. Southron knights and men-at-arms, the lot of them. Asha would have called them king's men, but the other stormlanders and crownlands men named them queen's men . . . though the queen they followed was the red one at Castle Black, not the wife that Stannis Baratheon had left behind at Eastwatch-by-the-Sea. *"Oh, Lord of Light, we beseech you, cast your fiery eye upon us and keep us safe and warm,"* they sang to the flames, *"for the night is dark and full of terrors."*

A big knight named Ser Godry Farring led them. *Godry the Giant-slayer. A big name for a small man.* Farring was broad-chested and well muscled under his plate and mail. He was also arrogant and vain, it seemed to Asha, hungry for glory, deaf to caution, a glutton for praise, and contemptuous of smallfolk, wolves, and women. In the last, he was not unlike his king.

"Let me have a horse," Asha asked Ser Justin, when he rode up to the wayn with half a ham. "I am going mad in these chains. I will not attempt escape. You have my word on that."

"Would that I could, my lady. You are the king's captive, not mine own."

"Your king will not take a woman's word."

The She-Bear growled. "Why should we trust the word of any ironman after what your brother did at Winterfell?"

"I am not Theon," Asha insisted . . . but the chains remained.

As Ser Justin galloped down the column, she found herself remembering the last time she had seen her mother. It had been on Harlaw, at Ten Towers. A candle had been flickering in her mother's chamber, but her great carved bed was empty beneath its dusty canopy. Lady Alannys sat beside a window, staring out across the sea. "Did you bring my baby boy?" she'd asked, mouth trembling. "Theon could not come," Asha had told her, looking down upon the ruin of the woman who had given her birth, a mother who had lost two of her sons. And the third . . .

I send you each a piece of prince.

Whatever befell when battle was joined at Winterfell, Asha Greyjoy did not think her brother likely to survive it. *Theon Turncloak. Even the She-Bear wants his head on a spike.*

"Do you have brothers?" Asha asked her keeper.

"Sisters," Alysane Mormont replied, gruff as ever. "Five, we were. All girls. Lyanna is back on Bear Island. Lyra and Jory are with our mother. Dacey was murdered."

"The Red Wedding."

"Aye." Alysane stared at Asha for a moment. "I have a son. He's only two. My daughter's nine."

"You started young."

"Too young. But better that than wait too late."

A *stab at me*, Asha thought, *but let it be.* "You are wed."

"No. My children were fathered by a bear." Alysane smiled. Her teeth were crooked, but there was something ingratiating about that smile. "Mormont women are skinchangers. We turn into bears and find mates in the woods. Everyone knows."

Asha smiled back. "Mormont women are all fighters too."

The other woman's smile faded. "What we are is what you made us. On Bear Island every child learns to fear krakens rising from the sea."

The Old Way. Asha turned away, chains *clink*ing faintly. On the third day the forest pressed close around them, and the rutted roads dwindled down to game trails that soon proved to be too narrow for their larger wagons. Here and there they wound their way past familiar landmarks: a stony hill that looked a bit like a wolf's head when seen from a certain angle, a half-frozen waterfall, a natural stone arch bearded with grey-green moss. Asha knew them all. She had come this way before, riding to Winterfell to persuade her brother Theon to abandon his conquest and return with her to the safety of Deepwood Motte. *I failed in that as well.*

That day they made fourteen miles, and were glad of it.

When dusk fell, the driver pulled the wayn off under the tree. As he was loosing the horses from the traces, Ser Justin trotted up and undid the fetters around Asha's ankles. He and the She-Bear escorted her through the camp to the king's tent. A captive she might be, but she was still a Greyjoy of Pyke, and it pleased Stannis Baratheon to feed her scraps from his own table, where he supped with his captains and commanders.

The king's pavilion was near as large as the longhall back at Deepwood Motte, but there was little grand about it beyond its size. Its stiff walls of heavy yellow canvas were badly faded, stained by mud and water, with spots of mildew showing. Atop its center pole flew the royal standard, golden, with a stag's head within a burning heart. On three sides the pavilions of the southron lordlings who had come north with Stannis surrounded it. On the fourth side the nightfire roared, lashing at the darkening sky with swirls of flame.

A dozen men were splitting logs to feed the blaze when Asha came limping up with her keepers. *Queen's men.* Their god was Red R'hllor, and a jealous god he was. Her own god, the Drowned God of the Iron Isles, was a demon to their eyes, and if she did not embrace this Lord of Light, she would be damned and doomed. *They would as gladly burn me as those logs and broken branches.* Some had urged that very thing within her hearing after the battle in the woods. Stannis had refused.

The king stood outside his tent, staring into the nightfire. *What does he see there? Victory? Doom? The face of his red and hungry god?* His eyes were sunk in deep pits, his close-cropped beard no more than a shadow across his hollow cheeks and bony jawbone. Yet there was power in his stare, an iron ferocity that told Asha this man would never, ever turn back from his course.

She went to one knee before him. "Sire." *Am I humbled enough for you, Your Grace? Am I beaten, bowed, and broken sufficiently for your liking?* "Strike these chains from my wrists, I beg you. Let me ride. I will attempt no escape."

Stannis looked at her as he might look at a dog who presumed to hump against his leg. "You earned those irons."

"I did. Now I offer you my men, my ships, my wits."

"Your ships are mine, or burnt. Your men . . . how many are left? Ten? Twelve?"

Nine. Six, if you count only those strong enough to fight. "Dagmer Cleftjaw holds Torrhen's Square. A fierce fighter, and a leal servant of House Greyjoy. I can deliver that castle to you, and its garrison as well." *Perhaps,* she might have added, but it would not serve her cause to show doubt before this king.

"Torrhen's Square is not worth the mud beneath my heels. It is Winterfell that matters."

"Strike off these irons and let me help you take it, Sire. Your Grace's royal brother was renowned for turning fallen foes into friends. Make me your man."

"The gods did not make you a man. How can I?" Stannis turned back to the nightfire and whatever he saw dancing there amongst the orange flames.

Ser Justin Massey grasped Asha by the arm and pulled her inside the royal tent. "That was ill judged, my lady," he told her. "Never speak to him of Robert."

I should have known better. Asha knew how it went with little brothers. She remembered Theon as a boy, a shy child who lived in awe, and fear, of Rodrik and Maron. *They never grow out of it,* she decided. *A little brother may live to be a hundred, but he will always be a little brother.* She rattled her iron jewelry and imagined how pleasant it would be to step up behind Stannis and throttle him with the chain that bound her wrists.

They supped that night on a venison stew made from a scrawny hart that a scout called Benjicot Branch had brought down. But only in the royal tent. Beyond those canvas walls, each man got a heel of bread and a chunk of black sausage no longer than a finger, washed down with the last of Galbart Glover's ale.

One hundred leagues from Deepwood Motte to Winterfell. Three hundred miles as the raven flies. "Would that we were ravens," Justin Massey said on the fourth day of the march, the day the snow began to fall. Only a few small flurries at first. Cold and wet, but nothing they could not push through easily.

But it snowed again the next day, and the day after, and the day after that. The thick beards of the wolves were soon caked with ice where their breath had frozen, and every clean-shaved southron boy was letting his whiskers grow out to keep his face warm. Before long the ground ahead of the column was blanketed in white, concealing stones and twisted roots and deadfalls, turning every step into an adventure. The wind picked up as well, driving the snow before it. The king's host became a column of snowmen, staggering through knee-high drifts.

On the third day of snow, the king's host began to come apart. Whilst the southron knights and lordlings struggled, the men of the northern hills fared better. Their garrons were sure-footed beasts that ate less than palfreys, and much less than the big destriers, and the men who rode them were at home in the snow. Many of the wolves donned curious footwear. Bear-paws, they called them, queer elongated things made with bent wood and leather strips. Lashed onto the bottoms of their boots, the things somehow allowed them to walk on top of the snow without breaking through the crust and sinking down to their thighs.

Some had bear-paws for their horses too, and the shaggy little garrons wore them as easily as other mounts wore iron horseshoes . . . but the palfreys and destriers wanted no part of them. When a few of the king's knights strapped them onto their feet nonetheless, the big southern horses balked and refused to move, or tried to shake the things off their feet. One destrier broke an ankle trying to walk in them.

The northmen on their bear-paws soon began to outdistance the rest of the host. They overtook the knights in the main column, then Ser Godry Farring and his vanguard. And meanwhile, the wayns and wagons of the baggage train were falling farther and farther behind, so much so that the men of the rear guard were constantly chivvying them to keep up a faster pace.

On the fifth day of the storm, the baggage train crossed a rippling expanse of waist-high snowdrifts that concealed a frozen pond. When the hidden ice cracked beneath the weight of the wagons, three teamsters and four horses were swallowed up by the freezing water, along with two of the men who tried to rescue them. One was Harwood Fell. His knights pulled him out before he drowned, but not before his lips turned blue and his skin as pale as milk. Nothing they did could seem to warm him afterward. He shivered violently for hours, even when they cut him out of his sodden clothes, wrapped him in warm furs, and sat him by the fire. That same night he slipped into a feverish sleep. He never woke.

That was the night that Asha first heard the queen's men muttering about a sacrifice—an offering to their red god, so he might end the storm. "The gods of the north have unleashed this storm on us," Ser Corliss Penny said.

"False gods," insisted Ser Godry, the Giantslayer.

"R'hllor is with us," said Ser Clayton Suggs.

"Melisandre is not," said Justin Massey.

The king said nothing. But he heard. Asha was certain of that. He sat at the high table as a dish of onion soup cooled before him, hardly tasted, staring at the flame of the nearest candle with those hooded eyes, ignoring the talk around him. The second-in-command, the lean tall knight named Richard Horpe, spoke for him. "The storm must break soon," he declared.

But the storm only worsened. The wind became a lash as cruel as any slaver's whip. Asha thought she had known cold on Pyke, when the wind came howling off the sea, but that was nothing compared to this. *This is a cold that drives men mad.*

Even when the shout came down the line to make camp for the night, it was no easy thing to warm yourself. The tents were damp and heavy, hard to raise, harder to take down, and prone to sudden collapse if too much snow accumulated on top of them. The king's host was creeping through the heart of the largest forest in the Seven Kingdoms, yet dry wood became difficult to find. Every camp saw fewer fires burning, and those that were lit threw off more smoke than heat. Oft as not food was eaten cold, even raw.

Even the nightfire shrank and grew feeble, to the dismay of the queen's men. *"Lord of Light, preserve us from this evil,"* they prayed, led by the deep voice of Ser Godry the Giantslayer. *"Show us your bright sun again, still these winds, and melt these snows, that we may reach your foes and smite them. The night is dark and cold and full of terrors, but yours is the power and glory and the light. R'hllor, fill us with your fire."*

Later, when Ser Corliss Penny wondered aloud whether an entire army had ever frozen to death in a winter storm, the wolves laughed. "This is no winter," declared Big Bucket Wull. "Up in the hills we say that autumn kisses you, but winter fucks you hard. This is only autumn's kiss."

God grant that I never know true winter, then. Asha herself was spared the worst of it; she was the king's prize, after all. Whilst others hungered, she was fed. Whilst others shivered, she was warm. Whilst others struggled through the snows atop weary horses, she rode upon a bed of furs inside a wayn, with a stiff canvas roof to keep the snow off, comfortable in her chains.

The horses and the common men had it hardest. Two squires from the stormlands stabbed a man-at-arms to death in a quarrel over who would sit closest to the fire. The next night some archers desperate for warmth somehow managed to set their tent afire, which had at least the virtue of heating the adjacent tents. Destriers began to perish of exhaustion and exposure. "What is a knight without a horse?" men riddled. "A snowman with a sword." Any horse that went down was butchered on the spot for meat. Their provisions had begun to run low as well.

Peasebury, Cobb, Foxglove, and other southron lords urged the king to make camp until the storm had passed. Stannis would have none of that. Nor would he heed the queen's men when they came to urge him to make an offering to their hungry red god.

That tale she had from Justin Massey, who was less devout than most. "A sacrifice will prove our faith still burns true, Sire," Clayton Suggs had told the king. And Godry the Giantslayer said, "The old gods of the north have sent this storm upon us. Only R'hllor can end it. We must give him an unbeliever."

"Half my army is made up of unbelievers," Stannis had replied. "I will have no burnings. Pray harder."

No burnings today, and none tomorrow . . . but if the snows continue, how long before the king's resolve begins to weaken? Asha had never shared her uncle Aeron's faith in the Drowned God, but that night she prayed as fervently to He Who Dwells Beneath the Waves as ever the Damphair had. The storm did not abate. The march continued, slowing to a stagger, then a crawl. Five miles was a good day. Then three. Then two.

By the ninth day of the storm, every camp saw the captains and commanders entering the king's tent wet and weary, to sink to one knee and report their losses for the day.

"One man dead, three missing."

"Six horses lost, one of them mine own."

"Two dead men, one a knight. Four horses down. We got one up again. The others are lost. Destriers, and one palfrey."

The cold count, Asha heard it named. The baggage train suffered the worst: dead horses, lost men, wayns overturned and broken. "The horses founder in the snow," Justin Massey told the king. "Men wander off or just sit down to die."

"Let them," King Stannis snapped. "We press on."

The northmen fared much better, with their garrons and their bear-paws. Black Donnel Flint and his half-brother Artos only lost one man between them. The Liddles, the Wulls, and the Norreys lost none at all. One of Morgan Liddle's mules had gone astray, but he seemed to think the Flints had stolen him.

One hundred leagues from Deepwood Motte to Winterfell. Three hundred miles as the raven flies. Fifteen days. The fifteenth day of the march came and went, and they had crossed less than half the distance. A trail of broken wayns and frozen corpses stretched back behind them, buried beneath the blowing snow. The sun and moon and stars had been gone so long that Asha was starting to wonder whether she had dreamed them.

It was the twentieth day of the advance when she finally won free of her ankle chains. Late that afternoon, one of the horses drawing her wayn died in the traces. No replacement could be found; what draft horses remained were needed to pull the wagons that held their food and fodder. When Ser Justin Massey rode up, he told them to butcher the dead horse for meat and break up the wagon for firewood. Then he removed the fetters around Asha's ankles, rubbing the stiffness from her calves. "I have no mount to give you, my lady," he said, "and if we tried to ride double, it would be the end of my horse as well. You must walk."

Asha's ankle throbbed beneath her weight with every step. *The cold will numb it soon enough*, she told herself. *In an hour I won't feel my feet at all.* She was only part wrong; it took less time than that. By the time darkness halted the column, she was stumbling and yearning for the comforts of her rolling prison. *The irons made me weak.* Supper found her so exhausted that she fell asleep at the table.

On the twenty-sixth day of the fifteen-day march, the last of the vegetables was consumed. On the thirty-second day, the last of the grain and fodder. Asha wondered how long a man could live on raw, half-frozen horse meat.

"Branch swears we are only three days from Winterfell," Ser Richard Horpe told the king that night after the cold count.

"*If* we leave the weakest men behind," said Corliss Penny.

"The weakest men are beyond saving," insisted Horpe. "Those still strong enough must reach Winterfell or die as well."

"The Lord of Light will deliver us the castle," said Ser Godry Farring. "If Lady Melisandre were with us—"

Finally, after a nightmarish day when the column advanced a bare mile and lost a dozen horses and four men, Lord Peasebury turned against the northmen. "This march was madness. More dying every day, and for what? Some girl?"

"Ned's girl," said Morgan Liddle. He was the second of three sons, so the other wolves called him Middle Liddle, though not often in his hearing. It was Morgan who had almost slain Asha in the fight by Deepwood Motte. He had come to her later, on the march, to beg her pardon . . . for calling her *cunt* in his battle lust, not for trying to split her head open with an axe.

"Ned's girl," echoed Big Bucket Wull. "And we should have had her and the castle both if you prancing southron jackanapes didn't piss your satin breeches at a little snow."

"A *little* snow?" Peasebury's soft girlish mouth twisted in fury. "Your ill counsel forced this march upon us, Wull. I am starting to suspect you have been Bolton's creature all along. Is that the way of it? Did he send you to us to whisper poison in the king's ear?"

Big Bucket laughed in his face. "Lord Pea Pod. If you were a man, I would kill you for that, but my sword is made of too fine a steel to besmirch with craven's blood." He took a drink of ale and wiped his mouth. "Aye, men are dying. More will die before we see Winterfell. What of it? This is war. Men die in war. That is as it should be. As it has always been."

Ser Corliss Penny gave the clan chief an incredulous look. "Do you *want* to die, Wull?"

That seemed to amuse the northman. "I want to live forever in a land where summer lasts a thousand years. I want a castle in the clouds where I can look down over the world. I want to be six-and-twenty again. When I was six-and-twenty I could fight all day and fuck all night. What men want does not matter.

"Winter is almost upon us, boy. And winter is death. I would sooner my men die fighting for Ned's little girl than alone and hungry in the

snow, weeping tears that freeze upon their cheeks. No one sings songs of
men who die like that. As for me, I am old. This will be my last winter. Let
me bathe in Bolton blood before I die. I want to feel it spatter across my
face when my axe bites deep into a Bolton skull. I want to lick it off my
lips and die with the taste of it on my tongue."

"Aye!" shouted Morgan Liddle. "*Blood and battle!*" Then all the hillmen were shouting, banging their cups and drinking horns on the table,
filling the king's tent with the clangor.

Asha Greyjoy would have welcomed a fight herself. *One battle, to put
an end to this misery. Steel on steel, pink snow, broken shields and severed
limbs, and it would all be done.*

The next day the king's scouts chanced upon an abandoned crofters'
village between two lakes—a mean and meagre place, no more than a few
huts, a longhall, and a watchtower. Richard Horpe commanded a halt,
though the army had advanced no more than a half-mile that day and
they were hours shy of dark. It was well past moonrise before the baggage
train and rear guard straggled in. Asha was amongst them.

"There are fish in those lakes," Horpe told the king. "We'll cut holes in
the ice. The northmen know how it's done."

Even in his bulky fur cloak and heavy armor, Stannis looked like a man
with one foot in the grave. What little flesh he'd carried on his tall, spare
frame at Deepwood Motte had melted away during the march. The shape
of his skull could be seen under his skin, and his jaw was clenched so hard
Asha feared his teeth might shatter. "Fish, then," he said, biting off each
word with a snap. "But we march at first light."

Yet when light came, the camp woke to snow and silence. The sky
turned from black to white, and seemed no brighter. Asha Greyjoy awoke
cramped and cold beneath the pile of sleeping furs, listening to the
She-Bear's snores. She had never known a woman to snore so loudly, but
she had grown used to it whilst on the march, and even took some comfort in it now. It was the silence that troubled her. No trumpets blew to
rouse the men to mount up, form column, prepare to march. No warhorns summoned forth the northmen. *Something is wrong.*

Asha crawled out from under her sleeping furs and pushed her way out
of the tent, knocking aside the wall of snow that had sealed them in during
the night. Her irons *clank*ed as she climbed to her feet and took a breath of
the icy morning air. The snow was still falling, even more heavily than
when she'd crawled inside the tent. The lakes had vanished, and the woods
as well. She could see the shapes of other tents and lean-tos and the fuzzy

orange glow of the beacon fire burning atop the watchtower, but not the tower itself. The storm had swallowed the rest.

Somewhere ahead Roose Bolton awaited them behind the walls of Winterfell, but Stannis Baratheon's host sat snowbound and unmoving, walled in by ice and snow, starving.

DAENERYS

The candle was almost gone. Less than an inch remained, jutting from a pool of warm melted wax to cast its light over the queen's bed. The flame had begun to gutter.

It will go out before much longer, Dany realized, *and when it does another night will be at its end.*

Dawn always came too soon.

She had not slept, could not sleep, would not sleep. She had not even dared to close her eyes, for fear it would be morning when she opened them again. If only she had the power, she would have made their nights go on forever, but the best that she could do was stay awake to try and savor every last sweet moment before daybreak turned them into no more than fading memories.

Beside her, Daario Naharis was sleeping as peacefully as a newborn babe. He had a gift for sleeping, he'd boasted, smiling in that cocksure way of his. In the field, he would sleep in the saddle oft as not, he claimed, so as to be well rested should he come upon a battle. Sun or storm, it made no matter. "A warrior who cannot sleep soon has no strength to fight," he said. He was never vexed by nightmares either. When Dany told him how Serwyn of the Mirror Shield was haunted by the ghosts of all the knights he'd killed, Daario only laughed. "If the ones I killed come bother me, I will kill them all again." *He has a sellsword's conscience,* she realized then. *That is to say, none at all.*

Daario lay upon his stomach, the light linen coverlets tangled about his long legs, his face half-buried in the pillows.

Dany ran her hand down his back, tracing the line of his spine. His skin was smooth beneath her touch, almost hairless. *His skin is silk and satin.* She loved the feel of him beneath her fingers. She loved to run her fingers through his hair, to knead the ache from his calves after a long day in the saddle, to cup his cock and feel it harden against her palm.

If she had been some ordinary woman, she would gladly have spent her whole life touching Daario, tracing his scars and making him tell her how he'd come by every one. *I would give up my crown if he asked it of me,* Dany thought . . . but he had not asked it, and never would. Daario might whisper words of love when the two of them were as one, but she knew it was the dragon queen he loved. *If I gave up my crown, he would not want me.* Besides, kings who lost their crowns oft lost their heads as well, and she could see no reason why it would be any different for a queen.

The candle flickered one last time and died, drowned in its own wax. Darkness swallowed the feather bed and its two occupants, and filled every corner of the chamber. Dany wrapped her arms around her captain and pressed herself against his back. She drank in the scent of him, savoring the warmth of his flesh, the feel of his skin against her own. *Remember,* she told herself. *Remember how he felt.* She kissed him on his shoulder.

Daario rolled toward her, his eyes open. "Daenerys." He smiled a lazy smile. That was another of his talents; he woke all at once, like a cat. "Is it dawn?"

"Not yet. We have a while still."

"Liar. I can see your eyes. Could I do that if it were the black of night?" Daario kicked loose of the coverlets and sat up. "The half-light. Day will be here soon."

"I do not want this night to end."

"No? And why is that, my queen?"

"You know."

"The wedding?" He laughed. "Marry me instead."

"You know I cannot do that."

"You are a queen. You can do what you like." He slid a hand along her leg. "How many nights remain to us?"

Two. Only two. "You know as well as I. This night and the next, and we must end this."

"Marry me, and we can have all the nights forever."

If I could, I would. Khal Drogo had been her sun-and-stars, but he had been dead so long that Daenerys had almost forgotten how it felt to love and be loved. Daario had helped her to remember. *I was dead and he brought me back to life. I was asleep and he woke me. My brave captain.* Even so, of late he grew too bold. On the day that he returned from his latest sortie, he had tossed the head of a Yunkish lord at her feet and kissed her in the hall for all the world to see, until Barristan Selmy pulled the two of them apart. Ser Grandfather had been so wroth that Dany feared blood might be shed. "We cannot wed, my love. You know why."

He climbed from her bed. "Marry Hizdahr, then. I will give him a nice set of horns for his wedding gift. Ghiscari men like to prance about in horns. They make them from their own hair, with combs and wax and irons." Daario found his breeches and pulled them on. He did not trouble himself with smallclothes.

"Once I am wed it will be high treason to desire me." Dany pulled the coverlet up over her breasts.

"Then I must be a traitor." He slipped a blue silk tunic over his head and straightened the prongs of his beard with his fingers. He had dyed it afresh for her, taking it from purple back to blue, as it had been when first she met him. "I smell of you," he said, sniffing at his fingers and grinning.

Dany loved the way his gold tooth gleamed when he grinned. She loved the fine hairs on his chest. She loved the strength in his arms, the sound of his laughter, the way he would always look into her eyes and say her name as he slid his cock inside her. "You are beautiful," she blurted as she watched him don his riding boots and lace them up. Some days he let her do that for him, but not today, it seemed. *That's done with too.*

"Not beautiful enough to marry." Daario took his sword belt off the peg where he had hung it.

"Where are you going?"

"Out into your city," he said, "to drink a keg or two and pick a quarrel. It has been too long since I've killed a man. Might be I should seek out your betrothed."

Dany threw a pillow at him. "You will leave Hizdahr be!"

"As my queen commands. Will you hold court today?"

"No. On the morrow I will be a woman wed, and Hizdahr will be king. Let *him* hold court. These are his people."

"Some are his, some are yours. The ones you freed."

"Are you chiding me?"

"The ones you call your children. They want their mother."

"You are. You are *chiding* me."

"Only a little, bright heart. Will you come hold court?"

"After my wedding, perhaps. After the peace."

"This *after* that you speak of never comes. You should hold court. My new men do not believe that you are real. The ones who came over from the Windblown. Bred and born in Westeros, most of them, full of tales about Targaryens. They want to see one with their own eyes. The Frog has a gift for you."

"The Frog?" she said, giggling. "And who is he?"

He shrugged. "Some Dornish boy. He squires for the big knight they call Greenguts. I told him he could give his gift to me and I'd deliver it, but he wouldn't have it."

"Oh, a clever frog. '*Give the gift to me.*' " She threw the other pillow at him. "Would I have ever seen it?"

Daario stroked his gilded mustachio. "Would I steal from my sweet queen? If it were a gift worthy of you, I would have put it into your soft hands myself."

"As a token of your love?"

"As to that I will not say, but I told him that he could give it to you. You would not make a liar of Daario Naharis?"

Dany was helpless to refuse. "As you wish. Bring your frog to court to-morrow. The others too. The Westerosi." It would be nice to hear the Common Tongue from someone besides Ser Barristan.

"As my queen commands." Daario bowed deeply, grinned, and took his leave, his cloak swirling behind him.

Dany sat amongst the rumpled bedclothes with her arms about her knees, so forlorn that she did not hear when Missandei came creeping in with bread and milk and figs. "Your Grace? Are you unwell? In the black of night this one heard you scream."

Dany took a fig. It was black and plump, still moist with dew. *Will Hizdahr ever make me scream?* "It was the wind that you heard screaming." She took a bite, but the fruit had lost its savor now that Daario was gone. Sighing, she rose and called to Irri for a robe, then wandered out onto her terrace.

Her foes were all about her. There were never less than a dozen ships drawn up on the shore. Some days there were as many as a hundred, when the soldiers were disembarking. The Yunkai'i were even bringing in wood by sea. Behind their ditches, they were building catapults, scorpions, tall trebuchets. On still nights she could hear the hammers ringing through the warm, dry air. *No siege towers, though. No battering rams.* They would not try to take Meereen by storm. They would wait behind their siege lines, flinging stones at her until famine and disease had brought her people to their knees.

Hizdahr will bring me peace. He must.

That night her cooks roasted her a kid with dates and carrots, but Dany could only eat a bite of it. The prospect of wrestling with Meereen once more left her feeling weary. Sleep came hard, even when Daario came back, so drunk that he could hardly stand. Beneath her coverlets she tossed and turned, dreaming that Hizdahr was kissing her . . . but his lips were blue and bruised, and when he thrust himself inside her, his manhood was cold as ice. She sat up with her hair disheveled and the bedclothes atangle. Her captain slept beside her, yet she was alone. She wanted to shake him, wake him, make him hold her, fuck her, help her forget, but she knew that if she did, he would only smile and yawn and say, "It was just a dream, my queen. Go back to sleep."

Instead she slipped into a hooded robe and stepped out onto her terrace. She went to the parapet and stood there gazing down upon the city as she had done a hundred times before. *It will never be my city. It will never be my home.*

The pale pink light of dawn found her still out on her terrace, asleep upon the grass beneath a blanket of fine dew. "I promised Daario that I would hold court today," Daenerys told her handmaids when they woke her. "Help me find my crown. Oh, and some clothes to wear, something light and cool."

She made her descent an hour later. "*All kneel for Daenerys Stormborn, the Unburnt, Queen of Meereen, Queen of the Andals and the Rhoynar and the First Men,* Khaleesi *of Great Grass Sea, Breaker of Shackles and Mother of Dragons,*" Missandei called.

Reznak mo Reznak bowed and beamed. "Magnificence, every day you grow more beautiful. I think the prospect of your wedding has given you a glow. Oh, my shining queen!"

Dany sighed. "Summon the first petitioner."

It had been so long since she last held court that the crush of cases was almost overwhelming. The back of the hall was a solid press of people, and scuffles broke out over precedence. Inevitably it was Galazza Galare who stepped forward, her head held high, her face hidden behind a shimmering green veil. "Your Radiance, it might be best were we to speak in private."

"Would that I had the time," said Dany sweetly. "I am to be wed upon the morrow." Her last meeting with the Green Grace had not gone well. "What would you have of me?"

"I would speak to you about the presumption of a certain sellsword captain."

She dares say that in open court? Dany felt a blaze of anger. *She has courage, I grant that, but if she thinks I am about to suffer another scolding, she could not be more wrong.* "The treachery of Brown Ben Plumm has shocked us all," she said, "but your warning comes too late. And now I know you will want to return to your temple to pray for peace."

The Green Grace bowed. "I shall pray for you as well."

Another slap, thought Dany, color rising to her face.

The rest was a tedium the queen knew well. She sat upon her cushions, listening, one foot jiggling with impatience. Jhiqui brought a platter of figs and ham at midday. There seemed to be no end to the petitioners. For every two she sent off smiling, one left red-eyed or muttering.

It was close to sunset before Daario Naharis appeared with his new Stormcrows, the Westerosi who had come over to him from the Wind-blown. Dany found herself glancing at them as yet another petitioner droned on and on. *These are my people. I am their rightful queen.* They seemed a scruffy bunch, but that was only to be expected of sellswords. The youngest could not have been more than a year older than her; the oldest must have seen sixty namedays. A few sported signs of wealth: gold arm rings, silken tunics, silver-studded sword belts. *Plunder.* For the most part, their clothes were plainly made and showed signs of hard wear.

When Daario brought them forward, she saw that one of them was a woman, big and blond and all in mail. "Pretty Meris," her captain named her, though *pretty* was the last thing Dany would have called her. She was six feet tall and earless, with a slit nose, deep scars in both cheeks, and the coldest eyes the queen had ever seen. As for the rest . . .

Hugh Hungerford was slim and saturnine, long-legged, long-faced, clad in faded finery. Webber was short and muscular, with spiders tattooed across his head and chest and arms. Red-faced Orson Stone claimed to be a knight, as did lanky Lucifer Long. Will of the Woods leered at her even as he took a knee. Dick Straw had cornflower-blue eyes, hair as white as flax, and an unsettling smile. Ginger Jack's face was hidden behind a bristly orange beard, and his speech was unintelligible. "He bit off half his tongue in his first battle," Hungerford explained to her.

The Dornishmen seemed different. "If it please Your Grace," said Daario, "these three are Greenguts, Gerrold, and Frog."

Greenguts was huge and bald as a stone, with arms thick enough to rival even Strong Belwas. Gerrold was a lean, tall youth with sun streaks in his hair and laughing blue-green eyes. *That smile has won many a maiden's heart, I'll wager.* His cloak was made of soft brown wool lined with sandsilk, a goodly garment.

Frog, the squire, was the youngest of the three, and the least impressive, a solemn, stocky lad, brown of hair and eye. His face was squarish, with a high forehead, heavy jaw, and broad nose. The stubble on his cheeks and chin made him look like a boy trying to grow his first beard. Dany had no inkling why anyone would call him Frog. *Perhaps he can jump farther than the others.*

"You may rise," she said. "Daario tells me you come to us from Dorne. Dornishmen will always have a welcome at my court. Sunspear stayed loyal to my father when the Usurper stole his throne. You must have faced many perils to reach me."

"Too many," said Gerrold, the handsome one with the sun-streaked hair. "We were six when we left Dorne, Your Grace."

"I am sorry for your losses." The queen turned to his large companion. "Greenguts is a queer sort of name."

"A jape, Your Grace. From the ships. I was greensick the whole way from Volantis. Heaving and . . . well, I shouldn't say."

Dany giggled. "I think that I can guess, ser. It is *ser*, is it not? Daario tells me that you are a knight."

"If it please Your Grace, we are all three knights."

Dany glanced at Daario and saw anger flash across his face. *He did not know.* "I have need of knights," she said.

Ser Barristan's suspicions had awakened. "Knighthood is easily claimed this far from Westeros. Are you prepared to defend that boast with sword or lance?"

"If need be," said Gerrold, "though I will not claim that any of us is the equal of Barristan the Bold. Your Grace, I beg your pardon, but we have come before you under false names."

"I knew someone else who did that once," said Dany, "a man called Arstan Whitebeard. Tell me your true names, then."

"Gladly . . . but if we may beg the queen's indulgence, is there some place with fewer eyes and ears?"

Games within games. "As you wish. Skahaz, clear my court."

The Shavepate roared out orders. His Brazen Beasts did the rest, herding the other Westerosi and the rest of the day's petitioners from the hall. Her counselors remained.

"Now," Dany said, "your names."

Handsome young Gerrold bowed. "Ser Gerris Drinkwater, Your Grace. My sword is yours."

Greenguts crossed his arms against his chest. "And my warhammer. I'm Ser Archibald Yronwood."

"And you, ser?" the queen asked the boy called Frog.

"If it please Your Grace, may I first present my gift?"

"If you wish," Daenerys said, curious, but as Frog started forward Daario Naharis stepped in front of him and held out a gloved hand. "Give this gift to me."

Stone-faced, the stocky lad bent, unlaced his boot, and drew a yellowed parchment from a hidden flap within.

"This is your gift? A scrap of writing?" Daario snatched the parchment out of the Dornishman's hands and unrolled it, squinting at the seals and signatures. "Very pretty, all the gold and ribbons, but I do not read your Westerosi scratchings."

"Bring it to the queen," Ser Barristan commanded. "Now."

Dany could feel the anger in the hall. "I am only a young girl, and young girls must have their gifts," she said lightly. "Daario, please, you must not tease me. Give it here."

The parchment was written in the Common Tongue. The queen unrolled it slowly, studying the seals and signatures. When she saw the name Ser Willem Darry, her heart beat a little faster. She read it over once, and then again.

"May we know what it says, Your Grace?" asked Ser Barristan.

"It is a secret pact," Dany said, "made in Braavos when I was just a little girl. Ser Willem Darry signed for us, the man who spirited my brother and myself away from Dragonstone before the Usurper's men could take us. Prince Oberyn Martell signed for Dorne, with the Sealord of Braavos as witness." She handed the parchment to Ser Barristan, so he might read it for himself. "The alliance is to be sealed by a marriage, it says. In return for Dorne's help overthrowing the Usurper, my brother Viserys is to take Prince Doran's daughter Arianne for his queen."

The old knight read the pact slowly. "If Robert had known of this, he would have smashed Sunspear as he once smashed Pyke, and claimed the heads of Prince Doran and the Red Viper . . . and like as not, the head of this Dornish princess too."

"No doubt that was why Prince Doran chose to keep the pact a secret," suggested Daenerys. "If my brother Viserys had known that he had a Dornish princess waiting for him, he would have crossed to Sunspear as soon as he was old enough to wed."

"And thereby brought Robert's warhammer down upon himself, and Dorne as well," said Frog. "My father was content to wait for the day that Prince Viserys found his army."

"Your father?"

"Prince Doran." He sank back onto one knee. "Your Grace, I have the honor to be Quentyn Martell, a prince of Dorne and your most leal subject."

Dany laughed.

The Dornish prince flushed red, whilst her own court and counselors gave her puzzled looks. "Radiance?" said Skahaz Shavepate, in the Ghiscari tongue. "Why do you laugh?"

"They call him *frog*," she said, "and we have just learned why. In the Seven Kingdoms there are children's tales of frogs who turn into enchanted princes when kissed by their true love." Smiling at the Dornish knights, she switched back to the Common Tongue. "Tell me, Prince Quentyn, are you enchanted?"

"No, Your Grace."

"I feared as much." *Neither enchanted nor enchanting, alas. A pity he's the prince, and not the one with the wide shoulders and the sandy hair.* "You have come for a kiss, however. You mean to marry me. Is that the way of it? The gift you bring me is your own sweet self. Instead of Viserys and your sister, you and I must seal this pact if I want Dorne."

"My father hoped that you might find me acceptable."

Daario Naharis gave a scornful laugh. "I say you are a pup. The queen needs a man beside her, not a mewling boy. You are no fit husband for a woman such as her. When you lick your lips, do you still taste your mother's milk?"

Ser Gerris Drinkwater darkened at his words. "Mind your tongue, sellsword. You are speaking to a prince of Dorne."

"And to his wet nurse, I am thinking." Daario brushed his thumbs across his sword hilts and smiled dangerously.

Skahaz scowled, as only he could scowl. "This boy might serve for Dorne, but Meereen needs a king of Ghiscari blood."

"I know of this Dorne," said Reznak mo Reznak. "Dorne is sand and scorpions, and bleak red mountains baking in the sun."

Prince Quentyn answered him. "Dorne is fifty thousand spears and swords, pledged to our queen's service."

"Fifty thousand?" mocked Daario. "I count three."

"*Enough*," Daenerys said. "Prince Quentyn has crossed half the world to offer me his gift, I will not have him treated with discourtesy." She turned to the Dornishmen. "Would that you had come a year ago. I am pledged to wed the noble Hizdahr zo Loraq."

Ser Gerris said, "It is not too late—"

"I will be the judge of that," Daenerys said. "Reznak, see that the prince and his companions are given quarters suitable to their high birth, and that their wants are attended to."

"As you wish, Your Radiance."

The queen rose. "Then we are done for now."

Daario and Ser Barristan followed her up the steps to her apartments. "This changes everything," the old knight said.

"This changes nothing," Dany said, as Irri removed her crown. "What good are three men?"

"Three knights," said Selmy.

"Three liars," Daario said darkly. "They deceived me."

"And bought you too, I do not doubt." He did not trouble to deny it. Dany unrolled the parchment and examined it again. *Braavos. This was done in Braavos, while we were living in the house with the red door.* Why did that make her feel so strange?

She found herself remembering her nightmare. *Sometimes there is truth in dreams.* Could Hizdahr zo Loraq be working for the warlocks, was that what the dream had meant? Could the dream have been a sending? Were the gods telling her to put Hizdahr aside and wed this Dornish prince instead? Something tickled at her memory. "Ser Barristan, what are the arms of House Martell?"

"A sun in splendor, transfixed by a spear."

The sun's son. A shiver went through her. "Shadows and whispers." What else had Quaithe said? *The pale mare and the sun's son. There was a lion in it too, and a dragon. Or am I the dragon?* "Beware the perfumed seneschal." That she remembered. "Dreams and prophecies. Why must they always be in riddles? I hate this. Oh, leave me, ser. Tomorrow is my wedding day."

That night Daario had her every way a man can have a woman, and she gave herself to him willingly. The last time, as the sun was coming up, she used her mouth to make him hard again, as Doreah had taught her long ago, then rode him so wildly that his wound began to bleed again, and for one sweet heartbeat she could not tell whether he was inside of her, or her inside of him.

But when the sun rose upon her wedding day so did Daario Naharis, donning his clothes and buckling on his sword belt with its gleaming golden wantons. "Where are you going?" Dany asked him. "I forbid you to make a sortie today."

"My queen is cruel," her captain said. "If I cannot slay your foes, how shall I amuse myself whilst you are being wed?"

"By nightfall I shall have no foes."

"It is only dawn, sweet queen. The day is long. Time enough for one last sortie. I will bring you back the head of Brown Ben Plumm for a wedding gift."

"No heads," Dany insisted. "Once you brought me flowers."

"Let Hizdahr bring you flowers. He is not one to stoop and pluck a dandelion, true, but he has servants who will be pleased to do it for him. Do I have your leave to go?"

"No." She wanted him to stay and hold her. *One day he will go and not return,* she thought. *One day some archer will put an arrow through his chest, or ten men will fall on him with spears and swords and axes, ten would-be heroes.* Five of them would die, but that would not make her grief easier to bear. *One day I will lose him, as I lost my sun-and-stars. But please gods, not today.* "Come back to bed and kiss me." No one had ever kissed her like Daario Naharis. "I am your queen, and I command you to fuck me."

She had meant it playfully, but Daario's eyes hardened at her words. "Fucking queens is king's work. Your noble Hizdahr can attend to that, once you're wed. And if he proves to be too highborn for such sweaty work, he has servants who will be pleased to do that for him as well. Or perhaps you can call the Dornish boy into your bed, and his pretty friend as well, why not?" He strode from the bedchamber.

He is going to make a sortie, Dany realized, *and if he takes Ben Plumm's head, he'll walk into the wedding feast and throw it at my feet. Seven save me. Why couldn't he be better born?*

When he was gone, Missandei brought the queen a simple meal of goat cheese and olives, with raisins for a sweet. "Your Grace needs more than wine to break her fast. You are such a tiny thing, and you will surely need your strength today."

That made Daenerys laugh, coming from a girl so small. She relied so much on the little scribe that she oft forgot that Missandei had only turned eleven. They shared the food together on her terrace. As Dany nibbled on an olive, the Naathi girl gazed at her with eyes like molten gold and said, "It is not too late to tell them that you have decided not to wed."

It is, though, the queen thought, sadly. "Hizdahr's blood is ancient and noble. Our joining will join my freedmen to his people. When we become as one, so will our city."

"Your Grace does not love the noble Hizdahr. This one thinks you would sooner have another for your husband."

I must not think of Daario today. "A queen loves where she must, not where she will." Her appetite had left her. "Take this food away," she told Missandei. "It is time I bathed."

Afterward, as Jhiqui was patting Daenerys dry, Irri approached with her *tokar*. Dany envied the Dothraki maids their loose sandsilk trousers and painted vests. They would be much cooler than her in her *tokar*, with its heavy fringe of baby pearls. "Help me wind this round myself, please. I cannot manage all these pearls by myself."

She should be eager with anticipation for her wedding and the night that would follow, she knew. She remembered the night of her first wedding, when Khal Drogo had claimed her maidenhead beneath the stranger stars. She remembered how frightened she had been, and how excited. Would it be the same with Hizdahr? *No. I am not the girl I was, and he is not my sun-and-stars.*

Missandei reemerged from inside the pyramid. "Reznak and Skahaz beg the honor of escorting Your Grace to the Temple of the Graces. Reznak has ordered your palanquin made ready."

Meereenese seldom rode within their city walls. They preferred palanquins, litters, and sedan chairs, borne upon the shoulders of their slaves. "Horses befoul the streets," one man of Zakh had told her, "slaves do not." Dany had freed the slaves, yet palanquins, litters, and sedan chairs still choked the streets as before, and none of them floated magically through the air.

"The day is too hot to be shut up in a palanquin," said Dany. "Have my silver saddled. I would not go to my lord husband upon the backs of bearers."

"Your Grace," said Missandei, "this one is so sorry, but you cannot ride in a *tokar*."

The little scribe was right, as she so often was. The *tokar* was not a garment meant for horseback. Dany made a face. "As you say. Not the palanquin, though. I would suffocate behind those drapes. Have them ready a sedan chair." If she must wear her floppy ears, let all the rabbits see her.

When Dany made her descent, Reznak and Skahaz dropped to their knees. "Your Worship shines so brightly, you will blind every man who dares to look upon you," said Reznak. The seneschal wore a *tokar* of maroon samite with golden fringes. "Hizdahr zo Loraq is most fortunate in you . . . and you in him, if I may be so bold as to say. This match will save our city, you will see."

"So we pray. I want to plant my olive trees and see them fruit." *Does it*

matter that Hizdahr's kisses do not please me? Peace will please me. Am I a
queen or just a woman?

"The crowds will be thick as flies today." The Shavepate was clad in a
pleated black skirt and a muscled breastplate, with a brazen helm shaped
like a serpent's head beneath one arm.

"Should I be afraid of flies? Your Brazen Beasts will keep me safe from
any harm."

It was always dusk inside the base of the Great Pyramid. Walls thirty
feet thick muffled the tumult of the streets and kept the heat outside, so it
was cool and dim within. Her escort was forming up inside the gates.
Horses, mules, and donkeys were stabled in the western walls, elephants
in the eastern. Dany had acquired three of those huge, queer beasts with
her pyramid. They reminded her of hairless grey mammoths, though
their tusks had been bobbed and gilded, and their eyes were sad.

She found Strong Belwas eating grapes, as Barristan Selmy watched a
stableboy cinch the girth on his dapple grey. The three Dornishmen were
with him, talking, but they broke off when the queen appeared. Their
prince went to one knee. "Your Grace, I must entreat you. My father's
strength is failing, but his devotion to your cause is as strong as ever. If my
manner or my person have displeased you, that is my sorrow, but—"

"If you would please me, ser, be happy for me," Daenerys said. "This is
my wedding day. They will be dancing in the Yellow City, I do not doubt."
She sighed. "Rise, my prince, and smile. One day I shall return to Westeros to claim my father's throne, and look to Dorne for help. But on this
day the Yunkai'i have my city ringed in steel. I may die before I see my
Seven Kingdoms. Hizdahr may die. Westeros may be swallowed by the
waves." Dany kissed his cheek. "Come. It's time I wed."

Ser Barristan helped her up onto her sedan chair. Quentyn rejoined
his fellow Dornishmen. Strong Belwas bellowed for the gates to be
opened, and Daenerys Targaryen was carried forth into the sun. Selmy
fell in beside her on his dapple grey.

"Tell me," Dany said, as the procession turned toward the Temple of
the Graces, "if my father and my mother had been free to follow their own
hearts, whom would they have wed?"

"It was long ago. Your Grace would not know them."

"You know, though. Tell me."

The old knight inclined his head. "The queen your mother was always
mindful of her duty." He was handsome in his gold-and-silver armor, his
white cloak streaming from his shoulders, but he sounded like a man in
pain, as if every word were a stone he had to pass. "As a girl, though . . . she

was once smitten with a young knight from the stormlands who wore her favor at a tourney and named her queen of love and beauty. A brief thing."

"What happened to this knight?"

"He put away his lance the day your lady mother wed your father. Afterward he became most pious, and was heard to say that only the Maiden could replace Queen Rhaella in his heart. His passion was impossible, of course. A landed knight is no fit consort for a princess of royal blood."

And Daario Naharis is only a sellsword, not fit to buckle on the golden spurs of even a landed knight. "And my father? Was there some woman he loved better than his queen?"

Ser Barristan shifted in the saddle. "Not . . . not loved. Mayhaps *wanted* is a better word, but . . . it was only kitchen gossip, the whispers of washerwomen and stableboys . . ."

"I want to know. I never knew my father. I want to know everything about him. The good and . . . the rest."

"As you command." The white knight chose his words with care. "Prince Aerys . . . as a youth, he was taken with a certain lady of Casterly Rock, a cousin of Tywin Lannister. When she and Tywin wed, your father drank too much wine at the wedding feast and was heard to say that it was a great pity that the lord's right to the first night had been abolished. A drunken jape, no more, but Tywin Lannister was not a man to forget such words, or the . . . the liberties your father took during the bedding." His face reddened. "I have said too much, Your Grace. I—"

"*Gracious queen, well met!*" Another procession had come up beside her own, and Hizdahr zo Loraq was smiling at her from his own sedan chair. *My king.* Dany wondered where Daario Naharis was, what he was doing. *If this were a story, he would gallop up just as we reached the temple, to challenge Hizdahr for my hand.*

Side by side the queen's procession and Hizdahr zo Loraq's made their slow way across Meereen, until finally the Temple of the Graces loomed up before them, its golden domes flashing in the sun. *How beautiful,* the queen tried to tell herself, but inside her was some foolish little girl who could not help but look about for Daario. *If he loved you, he would come and carry you off at swordpoint, as Rhaegar carried off his northern girl,* the girl in her insisted, but the queen knew that was folly. Even if her captain was mad enough to attempt it, the Brazen Beasts would cut him down before he got within a hundred yards of her.

Galazza Galare awaited them outside the temple doors, surrounded by her sisters in white and pink and red, blue and gold and purple. *There are fewer than there were.* Dany looked for Ezzara and did not see her. *Has the bloody flux taken even her?* Though the queen had let the Astapori starve outside her walls to keep the bloody flux from spreading, it was spreading nonetheless. Many had been stricken: freedmen, sellswords, Brazen Beasts, even Dothraki, though as yet none of the Unsullied had been touched. She prayed the worst was past.

The Graces brought forth an ivory chair and a golden bowl. Holding her *tokar* daintily so as not to tread upon its fringes, Daenerys Targaryen eased herself onto the chair's plush velvet seat, and Hizdahr zo Loraq went to his knees, unlaced her sandals, and washed her feet whilst fifty eunuchs sang and ten thousand eyes looked on. *He has gentle hands*, she mused, as warm fragrant oils ran between her toes. *If he has a gentle heart as well, I may grow fond of him in time.*

When her feet were clean, Hizdahr dried them with a soft towel, laced her sandals on again, and helped her stand. Hand in hand, they followed the Green Grace inside the temple, where the air was thick with incense and the gods of Ghis stood cloaked in shadows in their alcoves.

Four hours later, they emerged again as man and wife, bound together wrist and ankle with chains of yellow gold.

JON

Queen Selyse descended upon Castle Black with her daughter and her daughter's fool, her serving girls and lady companions, and a retinue of knights, sworn swords, and men-at-arms fifty strong. *Queen's men all*, Jon Snow knew. *They may attend Selyse, but it is Melisandre they serve.* The red priestess had warned him of their coming almost a day before the raven arrived from Eastwatch with the same message.

He met the queen's party by the stables, accompanied by Satin, Bowen Marsh, and half a dozen guards in long black cloaks. It would never do to come before this queen without a retinue of his own, if half of what they said of her was true. She might mistake him for a stableboy and hand him the reins of her horse.

The snows had finally moved off to the south and given them a respite. There was even a hint of warmth in the air as Jon Snow took a knee before this southron queen. "Your Grace. Castle Black welcomes you and yours."

Queen Selyse looked down at him. "My thanks. Please escort me to your lord commander."

"My brothers chose me for that honor. I am Jon Snow."

"You? They said you were young, but . . ." Queen Selyse's face was pinched and pale. She wore a crown of red gold with points in the shape of flames, a twin to that worn by Stannis. ". . . you may rise, Lord Snow. This is my daughter, Shireen."

"Princess." Jon inclined his head. Shireen was a homely child, made even uglier by the greyscale that had left her neck and part of her cheek stiff and grey and cracked. "My brothers and I are at your service," he told the girl.

Shireen reddened. "Thank you, my lord."

"I believe you are acquainted with my kinsman, Ser Axell Florent?" the queen went on.

"Only by raven." *And report.* The letters he'd received from Eastwatch-by-the-Sea had a deal to say of Axell Florent, very little of it good. "Ser Axell."

"Lord Snow." A stout man, Florent had short legs and a thick chest. Coarse hair covered his cheeks and jowls and poked from his ears and nostrils.

"My loyal knights," Queen Selyse went on. "Ser Narbert, Ser Benethon, Ser Brus, Ser Patrek, Ser Dorden, Ser Malegorn, Ser Lambert, Ser Perkin." Each worthy bowed in turn. She did not trouble to name her fool, but the cowbells on his antlered hat and the motley tattooed across his puffy cheeks made him hard to overlook. *Patchface.* Cotter Pyke's letters had made mention of him as well. Pyke claimed he was a simpleton.

Then the queen beckoned to another curious member of her entourage: a tall gaunt stick of a man, his height accentuated by an outlandish three-tiered hat of purple felt. "And here we have the honorable Tycho Nestoris, an emissary of the Iron Bank of Braavos, come to treat with His Grace King Stannis."

The banker doffed his hat and made a sweeping bow. "Lord Commander. I thank you and your brothers for your hospitality." He spoke the Common Tongue flawlessly, with only the slightest hint of accent. Half a foot taller than Jon, the Braavosi sported a beard as thin as a rope sprouting from his chin and reaching almost to his waist. His robes were a somber purple, trimmed with ermine. A high stiff collar framed his narrow face. "I hope we shall not inconvenience you too greatly."

"Not at all, my lord. You are most welcome." *More welcome than this queen, if truth be told.* Cotter Pyke had sent a raven ahead to advise them of the banker's coming. Jon Snow had thought of little since.

Jon turned back to the queen. "The royal chambers in the King's Tower have been prepared for Your Grace for so long as you wish to remain with us. This is our Lord Steward, Bowen Marsh. He will find quarters for your men."

"How kind of you to make room for us." The queen's words were courteous enough, though her tone said, *It is no more than your duty, and you had best hope these quarters please me.* "We will not be with you long. A few days at the most. It is our intent to press on to our new seat at the Nightfort as soon as we are rested. The journey from Eastwatch was wearisome."

"As you say, Your Grace," said Jon. "You will be cold and hungry, I am sure. A hot meal awaits you in our common room."

"Very good." The queen glanced about the yard. "First, though, we wish to consult with the Lady Melisandre."

"Of course, Your Grace. Her apartments are in the King's Tower as well. This way, if you will?" Queen Selyse nodded, took her daughter by the hand, and permitted him to lead them from the stables. Ser Axell, the Braavosi banker, and the rest of her party followed, like so many ducklings done up in wool and fur.

"Your Grace," said Jon Snow, "my builders have done all they can to make the Nightfort ready to receive you . . . yet much of it remains in ruins. It is a large castle, the largest on the Wall, and we have only been able to restore a part of it. You might be more comfortable back at Eastwatch-by-the-Sea."

Queen Selyse sniffed. "We are done with Eastwatch. We did not like it there. A queen should be mistress beneath her own roof. We found your Cotter Pyke to be an uncouth and unpleasant man, quarrelsome and niggardly."

You should hear what Cotter says of you. "I am sorry for that, but I fear Your Grace will find conditions at the Nightfort even less to your liking. We speak of a fortress, not a palace. A grim place, and cold. Whereas Eastwatch—"

"Eastwatch *is not safe*." The queen put a hand on her daughter's shoulder. "This is the king's true heir. Shireen will one day sit the Iron Throne and rule the Seven Kingdoms. She must be kept from harm, and Eastwatch is where the attack will come. This Nightfort is the place my husband has chosen for our seat, and there we shall abide. We—*oh!*"

An enormous shadow emerged from behind the shell of the Lord Commander's Tower. Princess Shireen gave a shriek, and three of the queen's knights gasped in harmony. Another swore. "*Seven save us,*" he said, quite forgetting his new red god in his shock.

"Don't be afraid," Jon told them. "There's no harm in him, Your Grace. This is Wun Wun."

"Wun Weg Wun Dar Wun." The giant's voice rumbled like a boulder crashing down a mountainside. He sank to his knees before them. Even kneeling, he loomed over them. "Kneel queen. Little queen." Words that Leathers had taught him, no doubt.

Princess Shireen's eyes went wide as dinner plates. "He's a *giant*! A real true giant, like from the stories. But why does he talk so funny?"

"He only knows a few words of the Common Tongue as yet," said Jon. "In their own land, giants speak the Old Tongue."

"Can I touch him?"

"Best not," her mother warned. "Look at him. A filthy creature." The queen turned her frown on Jon. "Lord Snow, what is this bestial creature doing on our side of the Wall?"

"Wun Wun is a guest of the Night's Watch, as you are."

The queen did not like that answer. Nor did her knights. Ser Axell grimaced in disgust, Ser Brus gave a nervous titter, Ser Narbert said, "I had been told all the giants were dead."

"Almost all." *Ygritte wept for them.*

"In the dark the dead are dancing." Patchface shuffled his feet in a grotesque dance step. "I know, I know, oh oh oh." At Eastwatch someone had sewn him a motley cloak of beaver pelts, sheepskins, and rabbit fur. His hat sported antlers hung with bells and long brown flaps of squirrel fur that hung down over his ears. Every step he took set him to ringing.

Wun Wun gaped at him with fascination, but when the giant reached for him the fool hopped back away, jingling. "Oh no, oh no, oh no." That brought Wun Wun lurching to his feet. The queen grabbed hold of Princess Shireen and pulled her back, her knights reached for their swords, and Patchface reeled away in alarm, lost his footing, and plopped down on his arse in a snowdrift.

Wun Wun began to laugh. A giant's laughter could put to shame a dragon's roar. Patchface covered his ears, Princess Shireen pressed her face into her mother's furs, and the boldest of the queen's knights moved forward, steel in hand. Jon raised an arm to block his path. "You do *not* want to anger him. Sheathe your steel, ser. Leathers, take Wun Wun back to Hardin's."

"Eat now, Wun Wun?" asked the giant.

"Eat now," Jon agreed. To Leathers he said, "I'll send out a bushel of vegetables for him and meat for you. Start a fire."

Leathers grinned. "I will, m'lord, but Hardin's is bone cold. Perhaps m'lord could send out some wine to warm us?"

"For you. Not him." Wun Wun had never tasted wine until he came to Castle Black, but once he had, he had taken a gigantic liking to it. *Too much a liking.* Jon had enough to contend with just now without adding a drunken giant to the mix. He turned back to the queen's knights. "My lord father used to say a man should never draw his sword unless he means to use it."

"Using it was my intent." The knight was clean-shaved and windburnt; beneath a cloak of white fur he wore a cloth-of-silver surcoat emblazoned with a blue five-pointed star. "I had been given to understand that the

Night's Watch defended the realm against such monsters. No one mentioned keeping them as pets."

Another bloody southron fool. "You are . . . ?"

"Ser Patrek of King's Mountain, if it please my lord."

"I do not know how you observe guest right on your mountain, ser. In the north we hold it sacred. Wun Wun is a guest here."

Ser Patrek smiled. "Tell me, Lord Commander, should the Others turn up, do you plan to offer hospitality to them as well?" The knight turned to his queen. "Your Grace, that is the King's Tower there, if I am not mistaken. If I may have the honor?"

"As you wish." The queen took his arm and swept past the men of the Night's Watch with never a second glance.

Those flames on her crown are the warmest thing about her. "Lord Tycho," Jon called. "A moment, please."

The Braavosi halted. "No lord I. Only a simple servant of the Iron Bank of Braavos."

"Cotter Pyke informs me that you came to Eastwatch with three ships. A galleas, a galley, and a cog."

"Just so, my lord. The crossing can be perilous in this season. One ship alone may founder, where three together may aid one another. The Iron Bank is always prudent in such matters."

"Perhaps before you leave we might have a quiet word?"

"I am at your service, Lord Commander. And in Braavos we say there is no time like the present. Will that suit?"

"As good as any. Shall we repair to my solar, or would you like to see the top of the Wall?"

The banker glanced up, to where the ice loomed vast and pale against the sky. "I fear it will be bitter cold up top."

"That, and windy. You learn to walk well away from the edge. Men have been blown off. Still. The Wall is like nothing else on earth. You may never have another chance to see it."

"No doubt I shall rue my caution upon my deathbed, but after a long day in the saddle, a warm room sounds preferable to me."

"My solar, then. Satin, some mulled wine, if you would."

Jon's rooms behind the armory were quiet enough, if not especially warm. His fire had gone out some time ago; Satin was not as diligent in feeding it as Dolorous Edd had been. Mormont's raven greeted them with a shriek of "*Corn!*" Jon hung up his cloak. "You come seeking Stannis, is that correct?"

"It is, my lord. Queen Selyse has suggested that we might send word to

Deepwood Motte by raven, to inform His Grace that I await his pleasure at the Nightfort. The matter that I mean to put to him is too delicate to entrust to letters."

"A debt." *What else could it be?* "His own debt? Or his brother's?"

The banker pressed his fingers together. "It would not be proper for me to discuss Lord Stannis's indebtedness or lack of same. As to King Robert . . . it was indeed our pleasure to assist His Grace in his need. For so long as Robert lived, all was well. Now, however, the Iron Throne has ceased all repayment."

Could the Lannisters truly be so foolish? "You cannot mean to hold Stannis responsible for his brother's debts."

"The debts belong to the Iron Throne," Tycho declared, "and whosoever sits on that chair must pay them. Since young King Tommen and his councillors have become so obdurate, we mean to broach the subject with King Stannis. Should he prove himself more worthy of our trust, it would of course be our great pleasure to lend him whatever help he needs."

"*Help*," the raven screamed. "*Help, help, help.*"

Much of this Jon had surmised the moment he learned that the Iron Bank had sent an envoy to the Wall. "When last we heard, His Grace was marching on Winterfell to confront Lord Bolton and his allies. You may seek him there if you wish, though that carries a risk. You could find yourself caught up in his war."

Tycho bowed his head. "We who serve the Iron Bank face death full as often as you who serve the Iron Throne."

Is that whom I serve? Jon Snow was no longer certain. "I can provide you with horses, provisions, guides, whatever is required to get you as far as Deepwood Motte. From there you will need to make your own way to Stannis." *And you may well find his head upon a spike.* "There will be a price."

"*Price*," screamed Mormont's raven. "*Price, price.*"

"There is always a price, is there not?" The Braavosi smiled. "What does the Watch require?"

"Your ships, for a start. With their crews."

"All three? How will I return to Braavos?"

"I only need them for a single voyage."

"A hazardous voyage, I assume. *For a start*, you said?"

"We need a loan as well. Gold enough to keep us fed till spring. To buy food and hire ships to bring it to us."

"Spring?" Tycho sighed. "It is not possible, my lord."

What was it Stannis had said to him? *You haggle like a crone with a codfish, Lord Snow. Did Lord Eddard father you on a fishwife?* Perhaps he had at that.

It took the better part of an hour before the impossible became possible, and another hour before they could agree on terms. The flagon of mulled wine that Satin delivered helped them settle the more nettlesome points. By the time Jon Snow signed the parchment the Braavosi drew up, both of them were half-drunk and quite unhappy. Jon thought that a good sign.

The three Braavosi ships would bring the fleet at Eastwatch up to eleven, including the Ibbenese whaler that Cotter Pyke had commandeered on Jon's order, a trading galley out of Pentos similarly impressed, and three battered Lysene warships, remnants of Salladhor Saan's former fleet driven back north by the autumn storms. All three of Saan's ships had been in dire need of refitting, but by now the work should be complete.

Eleven ships was not wise enough, but if he waited any longer, the free folk at Hardhome would be dead by the time the rescue fleet arrived. *Sail now or not at all.* Whether Mother Mole and her people would be desperate enough to entrust their lives to the Night's Watch, though . . .

The day had darkened by the time he and Tycho Nestoris left the solar. Snow had begun to fall. "Our respite was a brief one, it would seem." Jon drew his cloak about himself more tightly.

"Winter is nigh upon us. The day I left Braavos, there was ice on the canals."

"Three of my men passed through Braavos not long ago," Jon told him. "An old maester, a singer, and a young steward. They were escorting a wildling girl and her child to Oldtown. I do not suppose you chanced to encounter them?"

"I fear not, my lord. Westerosi pass through Braavos every day, but most come and go from the Ragman's Harbor. The ships of the Iron Bank moor at the Purple Harbor. If you wish, I can make inquiries after them when I return home."

"No need. By now they should be safe in Oldtown."

"Let us hope so. The narrow sea is perilous this time of year, and of late there have been troubling reports of strange ships seen amongst the Stepstones."

"Salladhor Saan?"

"The Lysene pirate? Some say he has returned to his old haunts, this is so. And Lord Redwyne's war fleet creeps through the Broken Arm as well.

On its way home, no doubt. But these men and their ships are well-known to us. No, these other sails . . . from farther east, perhaps . . . one hears queer talk of dragons."

"Would that we had one here. A dragon might warm things up a bit."

"My lord jests. You will forgive me if I do not laugh. We Braavosi are descended from those who fled Valyria and the wroth of its dragonlords. We do not jape of dragons."

No, I suppose not. "My apologies, Lord Tycho."

"None is required, Lord Commander. Now I find that I am hungry. Lending such large sums of gold will give a man an appetite. Will you be so good as to point me to your feast hall?"

"I will take you there myself." Jon gestured. "This way."

Once there, it would have been discourteous not to break bread with the banker, so Jon sent Satin off to fetch them food. The novelty of newcomers had brought out almost all the men who were not on duty or asleep, so the cellar was crowded and warm.

The queen herself was absent, as was her daughter. By now presumably they were settling into the King's Tower. But Ser Brus and Ser Malegorn were on hand, entertaining such brothers as had gathered with the latest tidings from Eastwatch and beyond the sea. Three of the queen's ladies sat together, attended by their serving maids and a dozen admiring men of the Night's Watch.

Nearer the door, the Queen's Hand was attacking a brace of capons, sucking the meat off the bones and washing down each bite with ale. When he espied Jon Snow, Axell Florent tossed a bone aside, wiped his mouth with the back of his hand, and sauntered over. With his bowed legs, barrel chest, and prominent ears, he presented a comical appearance, but Jon knew better than to laugh at him. He was an uncle to Queen Selyse and had been among the first to follow her in accepting Melisandre's red god. *If he is not a kinslayer, he is the next best thing.* Axell Florent's brother had been burned by Melisandre, Maester Aemon had informed him, yet Ser Axell had done little and less to stop it. *What sort of man can stand by idly and watch his own brother being burned alive?*

"Nestoris," said Ser Axell, "and the lord commander. Might I join you?" He lowered himself to the bench before they could reply. "Lord Snow, if I may ask . . . this wildling princess His Grace King Stannis wrote of . . . where might she be, my lord?"

Long leagues from here, Jon thought. *If the gods are good, by now she has found Tormund Giantsbane.* "Val is the younger sister of Dalla, who was Mance Rayder's wife and mother to his son. King Stannis took Val and the child captive after Dalla died in childbed, but she is no princess, not as you mean it."

Ser Axell shrugged. "Whatever she may be, at Eastwatch men claimed the wench was fair. I'd like to see with mine own eyes. Some of these wildling women, well, a man would need to turn them over to do his duty as a husband. If it please the lord commander, bring her out, let us have a look."

"She is not a horse to be paraded for inspection, ser."

"I promise not to count her teeth." Florent grinned. "Oh, never fear, I'll treat her with all the courtesy she is due."

He knows I do not have her. A village has no secrets, and no more did Castle Black. Val's absence was not spoken of openly, but some men knew, and in the common hall at night the brothers talked. *What has he heard?* Jon wondered. *How much does he believe?* "Forgive me, ser, but Val will not be joining us."

"I'll go to her. Where do you keep the wench?"

Away from you. "Somewhere safe. Enough, ser."

The knight's face grew flushed. "My lord, have you forgotten who I am?" His breath smelled of ale and onions. "Must I speak to the queen? A word from Her Grace and I can have this wildling girl delivered naked to the hall for our inspection."

That would be a pretty trick, even for a queen. "The queen would never presume upon our hospitality," Jon said, hoping that was true. "Now I fear I must take my leave, before I forget the duties of a host. Lord Tycho, pray excuse me."

"Yes, of course," the banker said. "A pleasure."

Outside, the snow was coming down more heavily. Across the yard the King's Tower had turned into a hulking shadow, the lights in its windows obscured by falling snow.

Back in his solar, Jon found the Old Bear's raven perched on the back of the oak-and-leather chair behind the trestle table. The bird began to scream for food the moment he entered. Jon took a fistful of dried kernels from the sack by the door and scattered them on the floor, then claimed the chair.

Tycho Nestoris had left behind a copy of their agreement. Jon read it over thrice. *That was simple,* he reflected. *Simpler than I dared hope. Simpler than it should have been.*

It gave him an uneasy feeling. Braavosi coin would allow the Night's Watch to buy food from the south when their own stores ran short, food enough to see them through the winter, however long it might prove to be. *A long hard winter will leave the Watch so deep in debt that we will never climb out,* Jon reminded himself, *but when the choice is debt or death, best borrow.*

He did not have to like it, though. And come spring, when the time came to repay all that gold, he would like it even less. Tycho Nestoris had impressed him as cultured and courteous, but the Iron Bank of Braavos had a fearsome reputation when collecting debts. Each of the Nine Free Cities had its bank, and some had more than one, fighting over every coin like dogs over a bone, but the Iron Bank was richer and more powerful than all the rest combined. When princes defaulted on their debts to lesser banks, ruined bankers sold their wives and children into slavery and opened their own veins. When princes failed to repay the Iron Bank, new princes sprang up from nowhere and took their thrones.

As poor plump Tommen may be about to learn. No doubt the Lannisters had good reason for refusing to honor King Robert's debts, but it was folly all the same. If Stannis was not too stiff-necked to accept their terms, the Braavosi would give him all the gold and silver he required, coin enough to buy a dozen sellsword companies, to bribe a hundred lords, to keep his men paid, fed, clothed, and armed. *Unless Stannis is lying dead beneath the walls of Winterfell, he may just have won the Iron Throne.* He wondered if Melisandre had seen *that* in her fires.

Jon sat back, yawned, stretched. On the morrow he would draft orders for Cotter Pyke. *Eleven ships to Hardhome. Bring back as many as you can, women and children first.* It was time they set sail. *Should I go myself, though, or leave it to Cotter?* The Old Bear had led a ranging. *Aye. And never returned.*

Jon closed his eyes. Just for a moment . . .

. . . and woke, stiff as a board, with the Old Bear's raven muttering, "*Snow, Snow,*" and Mully shaking him. "M'lord, you're wanted. Beg pardon, m'lord. A girl's been found."

"A girl?" Jon sat, rubbing the sleep from his eyes with the back of his hands. "Val? Has Val returned?"

"Not Val, m'lord. This side of the Wall, it were."

Arya. Jon straightened. It had to be her.

"Girl," screamed the raven. "*Girl, girl.*"

"Ty and Dannel came on her two leagues south of Mole's Town. They were chasing down some wildlings who scampered off down the kingsroad. Brought them back as well, but then they come on the girl. She's highborn, m'lord, and she's been asking for you."

"How many with her?" He moved to his basin, splashed water on his face. Gods, but he was tired.

"None, m'lord. She come alone. Her horse was dying under her. All skin and ribs it was, lame and lathered. They cut it loose and took the girl for questioning."

A grey girl on a dying horse. Melisandre's fires had not lied, it would seem. But what had become of Mance Rayder and his spearwives? "Where is the girl now?"

"Maester Aemon's chambers, m'lord." The men of Castle Black still called it that, though by now the old maester should be warm and safe in Oldtown. "Girl was blue from the cold, shivering like all get out, so Ty wanted Clydas to have a look at her."

"That's good." Jon felt fifteen years old again. *Little sister.* He rose and donned his cloak.

The snow was still falling as he crossed the yard with Mully. A golden dawn was breaking in the east, but behind Lady Melisandre's window in the King's Tower a reddish light still flickered. *Does she never sleep? What game are you playing, priestess? Did you have some other task for Mance?*

He wanted to believe it would be Arya. He wanted to see her face again, to smile at her and muss her hair, to tell her she was safe. *She won't be safe, though. Winterfell is burned and broken and there are no more safe places.*

He could not keep her here with him, no matter how much he might want to. The Wall was no place for a woman, much less a girl of noble birth. Nor was he about to turn her over to Stannis or Melisandre. The king would only want to marry her to one of his own men, Horpe or Massey or Godry Giantslayer, and the gods alone knew what use the red woman might want to make of her.

The best solution he could see would mean dispatching her to East-watch and asking Cotter Pyke to put her on a ship to someplace across the sea, beyond the reach of all these quarrelsome kings. It would need to wait until the ships returned from Hardhome, to be sure. *She could return to Braavos with Tycho Nestoris. Perhaps the Iron Bank could help find some noble family to foster her.* Braavos was the nearest of the Free Cities, though . . . which made it both the best and the worst choice. *Lorath or the Port of Ibben might be safer.* Wherever he might send her, though, Arya would need silver to support her, a roof above her head, someone to protect her. She was only a child.

Maester Aemon's old chambers were so warm that the sudden cloud of steam when Mully pulled the door open was enough to blind the both of them. Within, a fresh fire was burning in the hearth, the logs crackling and spitting. Jon stepped over a puddle of damp clothing. "Snow, Snow, Snow," the ravens called down from above. The girl was curled up near the fire, wrapped in a black woolen cloak three times her size and fast asleep.

She looked enough like Arya to give him pause, but only for a moment. A tall, skinny, coltish girl, all legs and elbows, her brown hair was woven in a thick braid and bound about with strips of leather. She had a long face, a pointy chin, small ears.

But she was too old, far too old. *This girl is almost of an age with me.* "Has she eaten?" Jon asked Mully.

"Only bread and broth, my lord." Clydas rose from a chair. "It is best to go slow, Maester Aemon always said. Any more and she might not have been able to digest it."

Mully nodded. "Dannel had one o' Hobb's sausages and offered her a bite, but she wouldn't touch it."

Jon could not blame her for that. Hobb's sausages were made of grease and salt and things that did not bear thinking about. "Perhaps we should just let her rest."

That was when the girl sat up, clutching the cloak to her small, pale breasts. She looked confused. "Where . . . ?"

"Castle Black, my lady."

"The Wall." Her eyes filled up with tears. "I'm here."

Clydas moved closer. "Poor child. How old are you?"

"Sixteen on my next nameday. And no child, but a woman grown and flowered." She yawned, covered her mouth with the cloak. One bare knee peeked through its folds. "You do not wear a chain. Are you a maester?"

"No," said Clydas, "but I have served one."

She does look a bit like Arya, Jon thought. *Starved and skinny, but her hair's the same color, and her eyes.* "I am told you have been asking after me. I am—"

"—Jon Snow." The girl tossed her braid back. "My house and yours are bound in blood and honor. Hear me, kinsman. My uncle Cregan is hard upon my trail. You must not let him take me back to Karhold."

Jon was staring. *I know this girl.* There was something about her eyes, the way she held herself, the way she talked. For a moment the memory eluded him. Then it came. "Alys Karstark."

That brought the ghost of a smile to her lips. "I was not sure you would remember. I was six the last time you saw me."

"You came to Winterfell with your father." *The father Robb beheaded.* "I don't recall what for."

She blushed. "So I could meet your brother. Oh, there was some other pretext, but that was the real reason. I was almost of an age with Robb, and my father thought we might make a match. There was a feast. I danced with you and your brother both. *He* was very courteous and said that I danced beautifully. You were sullen. My father said that was to be expected in a bastard."

"I remember." It was only half a lie.

"You're still a little sullen," the girl said, "but I will forgive you that if you will save me from my uncle."

"Your uncle . . . would that be Lord Arnolf?"

"He is no lord," Alys said scornfully. "My brother Harry is the rightful lord, and by law I am his heir. A daughter comes before an uncle. Uncle Arnolf is only castellan. He's my great-uncle, actually, my *father's* uncle. Cregan is his son. I suppose that makes him a cousin, but we always called him uncle. Now they mean to make me call him husband." She made a fist. "Before the war I was betrothed to Daryn Hornwood. We were only waiting till I flowered to be wed, but the Kingslayer killed Daryn in the Whispering Wood. My father wrote that he would find some southron lord to wed me, but he never did. Your brother Robb cut off his head for killing Lannisters." Her mouth twisted. "I thought the whole reason they marched south was to kill some Lannisters."

"It was . . . not so simple as that. Lord Karstark slew two prisoners, my lady. Unarmed boys, squires in a cell."

The girl did not seem surprised. "My father never bellowed like the Greatjon, but he was no less dangerous in his wroth. He is dead now too, though. So is your brother. But you and I are here, still living. Is there blood feud between us, Lord Snow?"

"When a man takes the black he puts his feuds behind him. The Night's Watch has no quarrel with Karhold, nor with you."

"Good. I was afraid . . . I begged my father to leave one of my brothers as castellan, but none of them wished to miss the glory and ransoms to be won in the south. Now Torr and Edd are dead. Harry was a prisoner at Maidenpool when last we heard, but that was almost a year ago. He may be dead as well. I did not know where else to turn but to the last son of Eddard Stark."

"Why not the king? Karhold declared for Stannis."

"My *uncle* declared for Stannis, in hopes it might provoke the Lannisters to take poor Harry's head. Should my brother die, Karhold should pass to me, but my uncles want my birthright for their own. Once Cregan gets a child by me they won't need me anymore. He's buried two wives already." She rubbed away a tear angrily, the way Arya might have done it. "Will you help me?"

"Marriages and inheritance are matters for the king, my lady. I will write to Stannis on your behalf, but—"

Alys Karstark laughed, but it was the laughter of despair. "Write, but do not look for a reply. Stannis will be dead before he gets your message. My uncle will see to that."

"What do you mean?"

"Arnolf is rushing to Winterfell, 'tis true, but only so he might put his dagger in your king's back. He cast his lot with Roose Bolton long ago . . . for gold, the promise of a pardon, and poor Harry's head. Lord Stannis is marching to a slaughter. So he cannot help me, and would not even if he could." Alys knelt before him, clutching the black cloak. "You are my only hope, Lord Snow. In your father's name, I beg you. Protect me."

THE BLIND GIRL

Her nights were lit by distant stars and the shimmer of moonlight on snow, but every dawn she woke to darkness.

She opened her eyes and stared up blind at the black that shrouded her, her dream already fading. *So beautiful.* She licked her lips, remembering. The bleating of the sheep, the terror in the shepherd's eyes, the sound the dogs had made as she killed them one by one, the snarling of her pack. Game had become scarcer since the snows began to fall, but last night they had feasted. Lamb and dog and mutton and the flesh of man. Some of her little grey cousins were afraid of men, even dead men, but not her. Meat was meat, and men were prey. She was the night wolf.

But only when she dreamed.

The blind girl rolled onto her side, sat up, sprang to her feet, stretched. Her bed was a rag-stuffed mattress on a shelf of cold stone, and she was always stiff and tight when she awakened. She padded to her basin on small, bare, callused feet, silent as a shadow, splashed cool water on her face, patted herself dry. *Ser Gregor,* she thought. *Dunsen, Raff the Sweetling. Ser Ilyn, Ser Meryn, Queen Cersei.* Her morning prayer. Or was it? *No,* she thought, *not mine. I am no one. That is the night wolf's prayer. Someday she will find them, hunt them, smell their fear, taste their blood. Someday.*

She found her smallclothes in a pile, sniffed at them to make sure they were fresh enough to wear, donned them in her darkness. Her servant's garb was where she'd hung it—a long tunic of undyed wool, roughspun and scratchy. She snapped it out and pulled it down over her head with one smooth practiced motion. Socks came last. One black, one white. The black one had stitching round the top, the white none; she could feel which was which, make sure she got each sock on the right leg. Skinny as they were, her legs were strong and springy and growing longer every day.

She was glad of that. A water dancer needs good legs. Blind Beth was no water dancer, but she would not be Beth forever.

She knew the way to the kitchens, but her nose would have led her there even if she hadn't. *Hot peppers and fried fish*, she decided, sniffing down the hall, *and bread fresh from Umma's oven*. The smells made her belly rumble. The night wolf had feasted, but that would not fill the blind girl's belly. Dream meat could not nourish her, she had learned that early on.

She broke her fast on sardines, fried crisp in pepper oil and served so hot they burned her fingers. She mopped up the leftover oil with a chunk of bread torn off the end of Umma's morning loaf and washed it all down with a cup of watered wine, savoring the tastes and the smells, the rough feel of the crust beneath her fingers, the slickness of the oil, the sting of the hot pepper when it got into the half-healed scrape on the back of the hand. *Hear, smell, taste, feel*, she reminded herself. *There are many ways to know the world for those who cannot see.*

Someone had entered the room behind her, moving on soft padded slippers quiet as a mouse. Her nostrils flared. *The kindly man*. Men had a different smell than women, and there was a hint of orange in the air as well. The priest was fond of chewing orange rinds to sweeten his breath, whenever he could get them.

"And who are you this morning?" she heard him ask, as he took his seat at the head of the table. *Tap, tap*, she heard, then a tiny crackling sound. *Breaking his first egg.*

"No one," she replied.

"A lie. I know you. You are that blind beggar girl."

"Beth." She had known a Beth once, back at Winterfell when she was Arya Stark. Maybe that was why she'd picked the name. Or maybe it was just because it went so well with *blind*.

"Poor child," said the kindly man. "Would you like to have your eyes back? Ask, and you shall see."

He asked the same question every morning. "I may want them on the morrow. Not today." Her face was still water, hiding all, revealing nothing.

"As you will." She could hear him peeling the egg, then a faint silvery *clink* as he picked up the salt spoon. He liked his eggs well salted. "Where did my poor blind girl go begging last night?"

"The Inn of the Green Eel."

"And what three new things do you know that you did not know when last you left us?"

"The Sealord is still sick."

"This is no new thing. The Sealord was sick yesterday, and he will still be sick upon the morrow."

"Or dead."

"When he is dead, that will be a new thing."

When he is dead, there will be a choosing, and the knives will come out. That was the way of it in Braavos. In Westeros, a dead king was followed by his eldest son, but the Braavosi had no kings. "Tormo Fregar will be the new sealord."

"Is that what they are saying at the Inn of the Green Eel?"

"Yes."

The kindly man took a bite of his egg. The girl heard him chewing. He never spoke with his mouth full. He swallowed, and said, "Some men say there is wisdom in wine. Such men are fools. At other inns other names are being bruited about, never doubt." He took another bite of egg, chewed, swallowed. "What three new things do you *know*, that you did not know before?"

"I *know* that some men are *saying* that Tormo Fregar will surely be the new sealord," she answered. "Some drunken men."

"Better. And what else do you know?"

It is snowing in the riverlands, in Westeros, she almost said. But he would have asked her how she knew that, and she did not think that he would like her answer. She chewed her lip, thinking back to last night. "The whore S'vrone is with child. She is not certain of the father, but thinks it might have been that Tyroshi sellsword that she killed."

"This is good to know. What else?"

"The Merling Queen has chosen a new Mermaid to take the place of the one that drowned. She is the daughter of a Prestayn serving maid, thirteen and penniless, but lovely."

"So are they all, at the beginning," said the priest, "but you cannot know that she is lovely unless you have seen her with your own eyes, and you have none. Who are you, child?"

"No one."

"Blind Beth the beggar girl is who I see. She is a wretched liar, that one. See to your duties. *Valar morghulis.*"

"*Valar dohaeris.*" She gathered up her bowl and cup, knife and spoon, and pushed to her feet. Last of all she grasped her stick. It was five feet long, slender and supple, thick as her thumb, with leather wrapped around the shaft a foot from the top. *Better than eyes, once you learn how to use it,* the waif had told her.

That was a lie. They often lied to her, to test her. No stick was better than a pair of eyes. It was good to have, though, so she always kept it close. Umma had taken to calling her Stick, but names did not matter. She was her. *No one. I am no one. Just a blind girl, just a servant of Him of Many Faces.*

Each night at supper the waif brought her a cup of milk and told her to drink it down. The drink had a queer, bitter taste that the blind girl soon learned to loathe. Even the faint smell that warned her what it was before it touched her tongue soon made her feel like retching, but she drained the cup all the same.

"How long must I be blind?" she would ask.

"Until darkness is as sweet to you as light," the waif would say, "or until you ask us for your eyes. Ask and you shall see."

And then you will send me away. Better blind than that. They would not make her yield.

On the day she had woken blind, the waif took her by the hand and led her through the vaults and tunnels of the rock on which the House of Black and White was built, up the steep stone steps into the temple proper. "Count the steps as you climb," she had said. "Let your fingers brush the wall. There are markings there, invisible to the eye, plain to the touch."

That was her first lesson. There had been many more.

Poisons and potions were for the afternoons. She had smell and touch and taste to help her, but touch and taste could be perilous when grinding poisons, and with some of the waif's more toxic concoctions even smell was less than safe. Burned pinky tips and blistered lips became familiar to her, and once she made herself so sick she could not keep down any food for days.

Supper was for language lessons. The blind girl understood Braavosi and could speak it passably, she had even lost most of her barbaric accent, but the kindly man was not content. He was insisting that she improve her High Valyrian and learn the tongues of Lys and Pentos too.

In the evening she played the lying game with the waif, but without eyes to see the game was very different. Sometimes all she had to go on was tone and choice of words; other times the waif allowed her to lay hands upon her face. At first the game was much, much harder, the next thing to impossible . . . but just when she was near the point of screaming with frustration, it all became much easier. She learned to *hear* the lies, to feel them in the play of the muscles around the mouth and eyes.

Many of her other duties had remained the same, but as she went about them she stumbled over furnishings, walked into walls, dropped trays, got hopelessly helplessly lost inside the temple. Once she almost fell headlong down the steps, but Syrio Forel had taught her balance in another lifetime, when she was the girl called Arya, and somehow she recovered and caught herself in time.

Some nights she might have cried herself to sleep if she had still been Arry or Weasel or Cat, or even Arya of House Stark . . . but no one had no tears. Without eyes, even the simplest task was perilous. She burned herself a dozen times as she worked with Umma in the kitchens. Once, chopping onions, she cut her finger down to the bone. Twice she could not even find her own room in the cellar and had to sleep on the floor at the base of the steps. All the nooks and alcoves made the temple treacherous, even after the blind girl had learned to use her ears; the way her footsteps bounced off the ceiling and echoed round the legs of the thirty tall stone gods made the walls themselves seem to move, and the pool of still black water did strange things to sound as well.

"You have five senses," the kindly man said. "Learn to use the other four, you will have fewer cuts and scrapes and scabs."

She could feel air currents on her skin now. She could find the kitchens by their smell, tell men from women by their scents. She knew Umma and the servants and the acolytes by the pattern of their footfalls, could tell one from the other before they got close enough to smell (but not the waif or the kindly man, who hardly made a sound at all unless they wanted to). The candles burning in the temple had scents as well; even the unscented ones gave off faint wisps of smoke from their wicks. They had as well been shouting, once she had learned to use her nose.

The dead men had their own smell too. One of her duties was to find them in the temple every morning, wherever they had chosen to lie down and close their eyes after drinking from the pool.

This morning she found two.

One man had died at the feet of the Stranger, a single candle flickering above him. She could feel its heat, and the scent that it gave off tickled her nose. The candle burned with a dark red flame, she knew; for those with eyes, the corpse would have seemed awash in a ruddy glow. Before summoning the serving men to carry him away, she knelt and felt his face, tracing the line of his jaw, brushing her fingers across his cheeks and nose, touching his hair. *Curly hair, and thick. A handsome face, unlined. He was young.* She wondered what had brought him here to seek the gift of death. Dying bravos oft found their way to the House of Black and White, to hasten their ends, but this man had no wounds that she could find.

The second body was that of an old woman. She had gone to sleep upon a dreaming couch, in one of the hidden alcoves where special candles conjured visions of things loved and lost. A sweet death and a gentle one, the kindly man was fond of saying. Her fingers told her that the old woman had died with a smile on her face. She had not been dead long. Her body was still warm to the touch. *Her skin is so soft,* like old thin *leather that's been folded and wrinkled a thousand times.*

When the serving men arrived to bear the corpse away, the blind girl followed them. She let their footsteps be her guide, but when they made their descent she counted. She knew the counts of all the steps by heart. Under the temple was a maze of vaults and tunnels where even men with two good eyes were often lost, but the blind girl had learned every inch of it, and she had her stick to help her find her way should her memory falter.

The corpses were laid out in the vault. The blind girl went to work in the dark, stripping the dead of boots and clothes and other possessions, emptying their purses and counting out their coins. Telling one coin from another by touch alone was one of the first things the waif had taught her, after they took away her eyes. The Braavosi coins were old friends; she need only brush her fingertips across their faces to recognize them. Coins from other lands and cities were harder, especially those from far away. Volantene honors were most common, little coins no bigger than a penny with a crown on one side and a skull on the other. Lysene coins were oval and showed a naked woman. Other coins had ships stamped onto them, or elephants, or goats. The Westerosi coins showed a king's head on the front and a dragon on the back.

The old woman had no purse, no wealth at all but for a ring on one thin finger. On the handsome man she found four golden dragons out of Westeros. She was running the ball of her thumb across the most worn of them, trying to decide which king it showed, when she heard the door opening softly behind her.

"Who is there?" she asked.

"No one." The voice was deep, harsh, cold.

And moving. She stepped to one side, grabbed for her stick, snapped it up to protect her face. Wood *clacked* against wood. The force of the blow almost knocked the stick from her hand. She held on, slashed back . . . and found only empty air where he should have been. "Not there," the voice said. "Are you blind?"

She did not answer. Talking would only muddle any sounds he might be making. He would be moving, she knew. *Left or right?* She jumped left, swung right, hit nothing. A stinging cut from behind her caught her in the back of the legs. "Are you deaf?" She spun, the stick in her left hand, whirling, missing. From the left she heard the sound of laughter. She slashed right.

This time she connected. Her stick smacked off his own. The impact sent a jolt up her arm. "Good," the voice said.

The blind girl did not know whom the voice belonged to. One of the acolytes, she supposed. She did not remember ever hearing his voice before, but what was there to say that the servants of the Many-Faced God could not change their voices as easily as they did their faces? Besides her, the House of Black and White was home to two serving men, three acolytes, Umma the cook, and the two priests that she called the waif and the kindly man. Others came and went, sometimes by secret ways, but those were the only ones who lived here. Her nemesis could be any of them.

The girl darted sideways, her stick spinning, heard a sound behind her, whirled in that direction, struck at air. And all at once his own stick was between her legs, tangling them as she tried to turn again, scraping down her shin. She stumbled and went down to one knee, so hard she bit her tongue.

There she stopped. *Still as stone. Where is he?*

Behind her, he laughed. He rapped her smartly on one ear, then cracked her knuckles as she was scrambling to her feet. Her stick fell clattering to the stone. She hissed in fury.

"Go on. Pick it up. I am done beating you for today."

"No one beat me." The girl crawled on all fours until she found her stick, then sprang back to her feet, bruised and dirty. The vault was still and silent. He was gone. Or was he? He could be standing right beside her, she would never know. *Listen for his breathing,* she told herself, but there was nothing. She gave it another moment, then put her stick aside and resumed her work. *If I had my eyes, I could beat him bloody.* One day the kindly man would give them back, and she would show them all.

The old woman's corpse was cool by now, the bravo's body stiffening. The girl was used to that. Most days, she spent more time with the dead than with the living. She missed the friends she'd had when she was Cat of the Canals; Old Brusco with his bad back, his daughters Talea and Brea, the mummers from the Ship, Merry and her whores at the Happy Port, all the other rogues and wharfside scum. She missed Cat herself the most of all, even more than she missed her eyes. She had liked being Cat, more than she had ever liked being Salty or Squab or Weasel or Arry. *I killed Cat when I killed that singer.* The kindly man had told her that they would have taken her eyes from her anyway, to help her to learn to use her other senses, but not for half a year. Blind acolytes were common in the

House of Black and White, but few as young as she. The girl was not sorry, though. Dareon had been a deserter from the Night's Watch; he had deserved to die.

She had said as much to the kindly man. "And are you a god, to decide who should live and who should die?" he asked her. "We give the gift to those marked by Him of Many Faces, after prayers and sacrifice. So has it always been, from the beginning. I have told you of the founding of our order, of how the first of us answered the prayers of slaves who wished for death. The gift was given only to those who yearned for it, in the beginning . . . but one day, the first of us heard a slave praying not for his own death but for his master's. So fervently did he desire this that he offered all he had, that his prayer might be answered. And it seemed to our first brother that this sacrifice would be pleasing to Him of Many Faces, so that night he granted the prayer. Then he went to the slave and said, 'You offered all you had for this man's death, but slaves have nothing but their lives. That is what the god desires of you. For the rest of your days on earth, you will serve him.' And from that moment, we were two." His hand closed around her arm, gently but firmly. "All men must die. We are but death's instruments, not death himself. When you slew the singer, you took god's powers on yourself. We kill men, but we do not presume to judge them. Do you understand?"

No, she thought. "Yes," she said.

"You lie. And that is why you must now walk in darkness until you see the way. Unless you wish to leave us. You need only ask, and you may have your eyes back."

No, she thought. "No," she said.

That evening, after supper and a short session of the lying game, the blind girl tied a strip of rag around her head to hide her useless eyes, found her begging bowl, and asked the waif to help her don Beth's face. The waif had shaved her head for her when they took her eyes; a mummer's cut, she called it, since many mummers did the same so their wigs might fit them better. But it worked for beggars too and helped to keep their heads free from fleas and lice. More than a wig was needed, though. "I could cover you with weeping sores," the waif said, "but then innkeeps and taverners would chase you from their doors." Instead she gave her pox scars and a mummer's mole on one cheek with a dark hair growing from it. "Is it ugly?" the blind girl asked.

"It is not pretty."

"Good." She had never cared if she was pretty, even when she was stupid Arya Stark. Only her father had ever called her that. *Him, and Jon*

Snow, sometimes. Her mother used to say she *could* be pretty if she would just wash and brush her hair and take more care with her dress, the way her sister did. To her sister and sister's friends and all the rest, she had just been Arya Horseface. But they were all dead now, even Arya, everyone but her half-brother, Jon. Some nights she heard talk of him, in the taverns and brothels of the Ragman's Harbor. The Black Bastard of the Wall, one man had called him. *Even Jon would never know Blind Beth, I bet.* That made her sad.

The clothes she wore were rags, faded and fraying, but warm clean rags for all that. Under them she hid three knives—one in a boot, one up a sleeve, one sheathed at the small of her back. Braavosi were a kindly folk, by and large, more like to help the poor blind beggar girl than try to do her harm, but there were always a few bad ones who might see her as someone they could safely rob or rape. The blades were for them, though so far the blind girl had not been forced to use them. A cracked wooden begging bowl and belt of hempen rope completed her garb.

She set out as the Titan roared the sunset, counting her way down the steps from the temple door, then tapping to the bridge that took her over the canal to the Isle of the Gods. She could tell that the fog was thick from the clammy way her clothes clung to her and the damp feeling of the air on her bare hands. The mists of Braavos did queer things to sounds as well, she had found. *Half the city will be half-blind tonight.*

As she made her way past the temples, she could hear the acolytes of the Cult of Starry Wisdom atop their scrying tower, singing to the evening stars. A wisp of scented smoke hung in the air, drawing her down the winding path to where the red priests had fired the great iron braziers outside the house of the Lord of Light. Soon she could even feel the heat in the air, as red R'hllor's worshipers lifted their voices in prayer. *"For the night is dark and full of terrors,"* they prayed.

Not for me. Her nights were bathed in moonlight and filled with the songs of her pack, with the taste of red meat torn off the bone, with the warm familiar smells of her grey cousins. Only during the days was she alone and blind.

She was no stranger to the waterfront. Cat used to prowl the wharves and alleys of the Ragman's Harbor selling mussels and oysters and clams for Brusco. With her rag and her shaved head and her mummer's mole, she did not look the same as she had then, but just to be safe she stayed away from the Ship and the Happy Port and the other places where Cat had been best known.

She knew each inn and tavern by its scent. The Black Bargeman had a briny smell. Pynto's stank of sour wine, stinky cheese, and Pynto himself, who never changed his clothes or washed his hair. At the Sailmender's the smoky air was always spiced with the scent of roasting meat. The House of Seven Lamps was fragrant with incense, the Satin Palace with the perfumes of pretty young girls who dreamed of being courtesans.

Each place had its own sounds too. Moroggo's and the Inn of the Green Eel had singers performing most nights. At the Outcast Inn the patrons themselves did the singing, in drunken voices and half a hundred tongues. The Foghouse was always crowded with polemen off the serpent boats, arguing about gods and courtesans and whether or not the Sealord was a fool. The Satin Palace was much quieter, a place of whispered endearments, the soft rustle of silk gowns, and the giggling of girls.

Beth did her begging at a different place every night. She had learned early on that innkeeps and taverners were more apt to tolerate her presence if it was not a frequent occurrence. Last night she had spent outside the Inn of the Green Eel, so tonight she turned right instead of left after the Bloody Bridge and made her way to Pynto's at the other end of Ragman's Harbor, right on the edge of the Drowned Town. Loud and smelly he might be, but Pynto had a soft heart under all his unwashed clothes and bluster. Oft as not, he would let her come inside where it was warm if the place was not too crowded, and now and again he might even let her have a mug of ale and a crust of food whilst regaling her with his stories. In his younger days Pynto had been the most notorious pirate in the Stepstones, to hear him tell it; he loved nothing better than to speak at great length about his exploits.

She was in luck tonight. The tavern was near empty, and she was able to claim a quiet corner not far from the fire. No sooner had she settled there and crossed her legs than something brushed up against her thigh. "You again?" said the blind girl. She scratched his head behind one ear, and the cat jumped up into her lap and began to purr. Braavos was full of cats, and no place more than Pynto's. The old pirate believed they brought good luck and kept his tavern free of vermin. "You know me, don't you?" she whispered. Cats were not fooled by a mummer's moles. They remembered Cat of the Canals.

It was a good night for the blind girl. Pynto was in a jolly mood and gave her a cup of watered wine, a chunk of stinky cheese, and half of an eel pie. "Pynto is a very good man," he announced, then settled down to tell her of the time he seized the spice ship, a tale she had heard a dozen times before.

As the hours passed the tavern filled. Pynto was soon too busy to pay her any mind, but several of his regulars dropped coins into her begging bowl. Other tables were occupied by strangers: Ibbenese whalers who reeked of blood and blubber, a pair of bravos with scented oil in their hair, a fat man out of Lorath who complained that Pynto's booths were too small for his belly. And later three Lyseni, sailors off the *Goodheart*, a storm-wracked galley that had limped into Braavos last night and been seized this morning by the Sealord's guards.

The Lyseni took the table nearest to the fire and spoke quietly over cups of black tar rum, keeping their voices low so no one could overhear. But she was no one and she heard most every word. And for a time it seemed that she could see them too, through the slitted yellow eyes of the tomcat purring in her lap. One was old and one was young and one had lost an ear, but all three had the white-blond hair and smooth fair skin of Lys, where the blood of the old Freehold still ran strong.

The next morning, when the kindly man asked her what three things she knew that she had not known before, she was ready.

"I know why the Sealord seized the *Goodheart*. She was carrying slaves. Hundreds of slaves, women and children, roped together in her hold." Braavos had been founded by escaped slaves, and the slave trade was forbidden here.

"I know where the slaves came from. They were wildlings from Westeros, from a place called Hardhome. An old ruined place, accursed." Old Nan had told her tales of Hardhome, back at Winterfell when she had still been Arya Stark. "After the big battle where the King-Beyond-the-Wall was killed, the wildlings ran away, and this woods witch said that if they went to Hardhome, ships would come and carry them away to someplace warm. But no ships came, except these two Lyseni pirates, *Goodheart* and *Elephant*, that had been driven north by a storm. They dropped anchor off Hardhome to make repairs, and saw the wildlings, but there were thousands and they didn't have room for all of them, so they said they'd just take the women and the children. The wildlings had nothing to eat, so the men sent out their wives and daughters, but as soon as the ships were out to sea, the Lyseni drove them below and roped them up. They meant to sell them all in Lys. Only then they ran into another storm and the ships were parted. The *Goodheart* was so damaged her captain had no choice but to put in here, but the *Elephant* may have made it back to Lys. The Lyseni at Pynto's think that she'll return with more ships. The price of slaves is rising, they said, and there are thousands more women and children at Hardhome."

"It is good to know. This is two. Is there a third?"

"Yes. I know that you're the one who has been hitting me." Her stick flashed out, and cracked against his fingers, sending his own stick clattering to the floor.

The priest winced and snatched his hand back. "And how could a blind girl know that?"

I saw you. "I gave you three. I don't need to give you four." Maybe on the morrow she would tell him about the cat that had followed her home last night from Pynto's, the cat that was hiding in the rafters, looking down on them. *Or maybe not.* If he could have secrets, so could she.

That evening Umma served salt-crusted crabs for supper. When her cup was presented to her, the blind girl wrinkled her nose and drank it down in three long gulps. Then she gasped and dropped the cup. Her tongue was on fire, and when she gulped a cup of wine the flames spread down her throat and up her nose.

"Wine will not help, and water will just fan the flames," the waif told her. "Eat this." A heel of bread was pressed into her hand. The girl stuffed it in her mouth, chewed, swallowed. It helped. A second chunk helped more.

And come the morning, when the night wolf left her and she opened her eyes, she saw a tallow candle burning where no candle had been the night before, its uncertain flame swaying back and forth like a whore at the Happy Port. She had never seen anything so beautiful.

A GHOST IN WINTERFELL

The dead man was found at the base of the inner wall, with his neck broken and only his left leg showing above the snow that had buried him during the night.

If Ramsay's bitches had not dug him up, he might have stayed buried till spring. By the time Ben Bones pulled them off, Grey Jeyne had eaten so much of the dead man's face that half the day was gone before they knew for certain who he'd been: a man-at-arms of four-and-forty years who had marched north with Roger Ryswell. "A drunk," Ryswell declared. "Pissing off the wall, I'll wager. He slipped and fell." No one disagreed. But Theon Greyjoy found himself wondering why any man would climb the snow-slick steps to the battlements in the black of night just to take a piss.

As the garrison broke its fast that morning on stale bread fried in bacon grease (the lords and knights ate the bacon), the talk along the benches was of little but the corpse.

"Stannis has friends inside the castle," Theon heard one serjeant mutter. He was an old Tallhart man, three trees sewn on his ragged surcoat. The watch had just changed. Men were coming in from the cold, stomping their feet to knock the snow off their boots and breeches as the midday meal was served—blood sausage, leeks, and brown bread still warm from the ovens.

"Stannis?" laughed one of Roose Ryswell's riders. "Stannis is snowed to death by now. Else he's run back to the Wall with his tail froze between his legs."

"He could be camped five feet from our walls with a hundred thousand men," said an archer wearing Cerwyn colors. "We'd never see a one o' them through this storm."

Endless, ceaseless, merciless, the snow had fallen day and night. Drifts climbed the walls and filled the crenels along the battlements, white blankets covered every roof, tents sagged beneath the weight. Ropes were strung from hall to hall to help men keep from getting lost as they crossed the yards. Sentries crowded into the guard turrets to warm half-frozen hands over glowing braziers, leaving the wallwalks to the snowy sentinels the squires had thrown up, who grew larger and stranger every night as wind and weather worked their will upon them. Ragged beards of ice grew down the spears clasped in their snowy fists. No less a man than Hosteen Frey, who had been heard growling that he did not fear a little snow, lost an ear to frostbite.

The horses in the yards suffered most. The blankets thrown over them to keep them warm soaked through and froze if not changed regularly. When fires were lit to keep the cold at bay, they did more harm than good. The warhorses feared the flames and fought to get away, injuring themselves and other horses as they twisted at their lines. Only the horses in the stables were safe and warm, but the stables were already overcrowded.

"The gods have turned against us," old Lord Locke was heard to say in the Great Hall. "This is their wroth. A wind as cold as hell itself and snows that never end. We are cursed."

"*Stannis* is cursed," a Dreadfort man insisted. "He is the one out there in the storm."

"Lord Stannis might be warmer than we know," one foolish freerider argued. "His sorceress can summon fire. Might be her red god can melt these snows."

That was unwise, Theon knew at once. The man spoke too loudly, and in the hearing of Yellow Dick and Sour Alyn and Ben Bones. When the tale reached Lord Ramsay, he sent his Bastard's Boys to seize the man and drag him out into the snow. "As you seem so fond of Stannis, we will send you to him," he said. Damon Dance-for-Me gave the freerider a few lashes with his long greased whip. Then, whilst Skinner and Yellow Dick made wagers on how fast his blood would freeze, Ramsay had the man dragged up to the Battlements Gate.

Winterfell's great main gates were closed and barred, and so choked with ice and snow that the portcullis would need to be chipped free before it could be raised. Much the same was true of the Hunter's Gate, though there at least ice was not a problem, since the gate had seen recent use. The Kingsroad Gate had not, and ice had frozen those drawbridge chains rock hard. Which left the Battlements Gate, a small arched postern in the inner wall. Only half a gate, in truth, it had a drawbridge that spanned the frozen moat but no corresponding gateway through the outer wall, offering access to the outer ramparts but not the world beyond.

The bleeding freerider was carried across the bridge and up the steps, still protesting. Then Skinner and Sour Alyn seized his arms and legs and tossed him from the wall to the ground eighty feet below. The drifts had climbed so high that they swallowed the man bodily . . . but bowmen on the battlements claimed they glimpsed him sometime later, dragging a broken leg through the snow. One feathered his rump with an arrow as he wriggled away. "He will be dead within the hour," Lord Ramsay promised.

"Or he'll be sucking Lord Stannis's cock before the sun goes down," Whoresbane Umber threw back.

"He best take care it don't break off," laughed Rickard Ryswell. "Any man out there in this, his cock is frozen hard."

"Lord Stannis is lost in the storm," said Lady Dustin. "He's leagues away, dead or dying. Let winter do its worst. A few more days and the snows will bury him and his army both."

And us as well, thought Theon, marveling at her folly. Lady Barbrey was of the north and should have known better. The old gods might be listening.

Supper was pease porridge and yesterday's bread, and that caused muttering amongst the common men as well; above the salt, the lords and knights were seen to be eating ham.

Theon was bent over a wooden bowl finishing the last of his own portion of pease porridge when a light touch on his shoulder made him drop his spoon. "Never touch me," he said, twisting down to snatch the fallen utensil off the floor before one of Ramsay's girls could get hold of it. "*Never* touch me."

She sat down next to him, too close, another of Abel's washerwomen. This one was young, fifteen or maybe sixteen, with shaggy blond hair in need of a good wash and a pair of pouty lips in need of a good kiss. "Some girls like to touch," she said, with a little half-smile. "If it please m'lord, I'm Holly."

Holly the whore, he thought, but she was pretty enough. Once he might have laughed and pulled her into his lap, but that day was done. "What do you want?"

"To see these crypts. Where are they, m'lord? Would you show me?" Holly toyed with a strand of her hair, coiling it around her little finger. "Deep and dark, they say. A good place for touching. All the dead kings watching."

"Did Abel send you to me?"

"Might be. Might be I sent myself. But if it's Abel you're wanting, I could bring him. He'll sing m'lord a sweet song."

Every word she said persuaded Theon that this was all some ploy. *But whose, and to what end?* What could Abel want of him? The man was just a singer, a pander with a lute and a false smile. *He wants to know how I took the castle, but not to make a song of it.* The answer came to him. *He wants to know how we got in so he can get out.* Lord Bolton had Winterfell sewn up tight as a babe's swaddling clothes. No one could come or go without his leave. *He wants to flee, him and his washerwoman.* Theon could not blame him, but even so he said, "I want no part of Abel, or you, or any of your sisters. Just leave me be."

Outside the snow was swirling, dancing. Theon groped his way to the wall, then followed it to the Battlements Gate. He might have taken the guards for a pair of Little Walder's snowmen if he had not seen the white plumes of their breath. "I want to walk the walls," he told them, his own breath frosting in the air.

"Bloody cold up there," one warned.

"Bloody cold down here," the other said, "but you do as you like, turn-cloak." He waved Theon through the gate.

The steps were snow-packed and slippery, treacherous in the dark. Once he reached the wallwalk, it did not take him long to find the place where they'd thrown down the freerider. He knocked aside the wall of fresh-fallen snow filling up the crenel and leaned out between the merlons. *I could jump,* he thought. *He lived, why shouldn't I?* He could jump, and . . . *And what? Break a leg and die beneath the snow? Creep away to freeze to death?*

It was madness. Ramsay would hunt him down, with the girls. Red Jeyne and Jez and Helicent would tear him to pieces if the gods were good. Or worse, he might be taken back alive. "I have to remember my *name*," he whispered.

The next morning Ser Aenys Frey's grizzled squire was found naked and dead of exposure in the old castle lichyard, his face so obscured by hoarfrost that he appeared to be wearing a mask. Ser Aenys put it forth that the man had drunk too much and gotten lost in the storm, though no one could explain why he had taken off his clothes to go outside. *Another drunkard,* Theon thought. Wine could drown a host of suspicions.

Then, before the day was done, a crossbowman sworn to the Flints turned up in the stables with a broken skull. Kicked by a horse, Lord Ramsay declared. *A club, more like,* Theon decided.

It all seemed so familiar, like a mummer show that he had seen before. Only the mummers had changed. Roose Bolton was playing the part that Theon had played the last time round, and the dead men were playing the parts of Aggar, Gynir Rednose, and Gelmarr the Grim. *Reek was there too,* he remembered, *but he was a different Reek, a Reek with bloody hands and lies dripping from his lips, sweet as honey. Reek, Reek, it rhymes with sneak.*

The deaths set Roose Bolton's lords to quarreling openly in the Great Hall. Some were running short of patience. "How long must we sit here waiting for this king who never comes?" Ser Hosteen Frey demanded. "We should take the fight to Stannis and make an end to him."

"Leave the castle?" croaked one-armed Harwood Stout. His tone suggested he would sooner have his remaining arm hacked off. "Would you have us charge blindly into the snow?"

"To fight Lord Stannis we would first need to find him," Roose Ryswell pointed out. "Our scouts go out the Hunter's Gate, but of late, none of them return."

Lord Wyman Manderly slapped his massive belly. "White Harbor does not fear to ride with you, Ser Hosteen. Lead us out, and my knights will ride behind you."

Ser Hosteen turned on the fat man. "Close enough to drive a lance through my back, aye. Where are my kin, Manderly? Tell me that. Your guests, who brought your son back to you."

"His bones, you mean." Manderly speared a chunk of ham with his dagger. "I recall them well. Rhaegar of the round shoulders, with his glib tongue. Bold Ser Jared, so swift to draw his steel. Symond the spymaster, always clinking coins. They brought home Wendel's bones. It was Tywin Lannister who returned Wylis to me, safe and whole, as he had promised. A man of his word, Lord Tywin, Seven save his soul." Lord Wyman popped the meat into his mouth, chewed it noisily, smacked his lips, and said, "The road has many dangers, ser. I gave your brothers guest gifts when we took our leave of White Harbor. We swore we would meet again at the wedding. Many and more bore witness to our parting."

"Many and more?" mocked Aenys Frey. "Or you and yours?"

"What are you suggesting, Frey?" The Lord of White Harbor wiped his mouth with his sleeve. "I do not like your tone, ser. No, not one bloody bit."

"Step out into the yard, you sack of suet, and I'll serve you all the bloody bits that you can stomach," Ser Hosteen said.

Wyman Manderly laughed, but half a dozen of his knights were on their feet at once. It fell to Roger Ryswell and Barbrey Dustin to calm them with quiet words. Roose Bolton said nothing at all. But Theon Greyjoy saw a look in his pale eyes that he had never seen before—an uneasiness, even a hint of fear.

That night the new stable collapsed beneath the weight of the snow that had buried it. Twenty-six horses and two grooms died, crushed beneath the falling roof or smothered under the snows. It took the best part of the morning to dig out the bodies. Lord Bolton appeared briefly in the outer ward to inspect the scene, then ordered the remaining horses brought inside, along with the mounts still tethered in the outer ward. And no sooner had the men finished digging out the dead men and butchering the horses than another corpse was found.

This one could not be waved away as some drunken tumble or the kick of a horse. The dead man was one of Ramsay's favorites, the squat, scrofulous, ill-favored man-at-arms called Yellow Dick. Whether his dick had actually been yellow was hard to determine, as someone had sliced it off and stuffed it into his mouth so forcefully they had broken three of his teeth. When the cooks found him outside the kitchens, buried up to his neck in a snowdrift, both dick and man were blue from cold. "Burn the body," Roose Bolton ordered, "and see that you do not speak of this. I'll not have this tale spread."

The tale spread nonetheless. By midday most of Winterfell had heard, many from the lips of Ramsay Bolton, whose "boy" Yellow Dick had been. "When we find the man who did this," Lord Ramsay promised, "I will flay the skin off him, cook it crisp as crackling, and make him eat it, every bite." Word went out that the killer's name would be worth a golden dragon.

The reek within the Great Hall was palpable by eventide. With hundreds of horses, dogs, and men squeezed underneath one roof, the floors slimy with mud and melting snow, horseshit, dog turds, and even human feces, the air redolent with the smells of wet dog, wet wool, and sodden horse blankets, there was no comfort to be found amongst the crowded benches, but there was food. The cooks served up great slabs of fresh horsemeat, charred outside and bloody red within, with roast onions and neeps . . . and for once, the common soldiers ate as well as the lords and knights.

The horsemeat was too tough for the ruins of Theon's teeth. His attempts to chew gave him excruciating pain. So he mashed the neeps and onions up together with the flat of his dagger and made a meal of that, then cut the horse up very small, sucked on each piece, and spat it out.

That way at least he had the taste, and some nourishment from the grease and blood. The bone was beyond him, though, so he tossed it to the dogs and watched Grey Jeyne make off with it whilst Sara and Willow snapped at her heels.

Lord Bolton commanded Abel to play for them as they ate. The bard sang "Iron Lances," then "The Winter Maid." When Barbrey Dustin asked for something more cheerful, he gave them "The Queen Took Off Her Sandal, the King Took Off His Crown," and "The Bear and the Maiden Fair." The Freys joined the singing, and even a few northmen slammed their fists on the table to the chorus, bellowing, "A *bear! A bear!*" But the noise frightened the horses, so the singers soon let off and the music died away.

The Bastard's Boys gathered beneath a wall sconce where a torch was flaming smokily. Luton and Skinner were throwing dice. Grunt had a woman in his lap, a breast in his hand. Damon Dance-for-Me sat greasing up his whip. "*Reek,*" he called. He tapped the whip against his calf as a man might do to summon his dog. "You are starting to stink again, Reek."

Theon had no reply for that beyond a soft "Yes."

"Lord Ramsay means to cut your lips off when all this is done," said Damon, stroking his whip with a greasy rag.

My lips have been between his lady's legs. That insolence cannot go unpunished. "As you say."

Luton guffawed. "I think he wants it."

"Go away, Reek," Skinner said. "The smell of you turns my stomach." The others laughed.

He fled quickly, before they changed their minds. His tormentors would not follow him outside. Not so long as there was food and drink within, willing women and warm fires. As he left the hall, Abel was singing "The Maids That Bloom in Spring."

Outside the snow was coming down so heavily that Theon could not see more than three feet ahead of him. He found himself alone in a white wilderness, walls of snow looming up to either side of him chest high. When he raised his head, the snowflakes brushed his cheeks like cold soft kisses. He could hear the sound of music from the hall behind him. A soft song now, and sad. For a moment he felt almost at peace.

Farther on, he came upon a man striding in the opposite direction, a hooded cloak flapping behind him. When they found themselves face-to-face their eyes met briefly. The man put a hand on his dagger. "Theon Turncloak. Theon Kinslayer."

"I'm not. I never . . . I was ironborn."

"False is all you were. How is it you still breathe?"

"The gods are not done with me," Theon answered, wondering if this could be the killer, the night walker who had stuffed Yellow Dick's cock into his mouth and pushed Roger Ryswell's groom off the battlements. Oddly, he was not afraid. He pulled the glove from his left hand. "Lord Ramsay is not done with me."

The man looked, and laughed. "I leave you to him, then."

Theon trudged through the storm until his arms and legs were caked with snow and his hands and feet had gone numb from cold, then climbed to the battlements of the inner wall again. Up here, a hundred feet high, a little wind was blowing, stirring the snow. All the crenels had filled up. Theon had to punch through a wall of snow to make a hole . . . only to find that he could not see beyond the moat. Of the outer wall, nothing remained but a vague shadow and a few dim lights floating in the dark.

The world is gone. King's Landing, Riverrun, Pyke, and the Iron Islands, all the Seven Kingdoms, every place that he had ever known, every place that he had ever read about or dreamed of, all gone. Only Winterfell remained.

He was trapped here, with the ghosts. The old ghosts from the crypts and the younger ones that he had made himself, Mikken and Farlen, Gynir Rednose, Aggar, Gelmarr the Grim, the miller's wife from Acorn Water and her two young sons, and all the rest. *My work. My ghosts. They are all here, and they are angry.* He thought of the crypts and those missing swords.

Theon returned to his own chambers. He was stripping off his wet clothes when Steelshanks Walton found him. "Come with me, turncloak. His lordship wants words with you."

He had no clean dry clothes, so he wriggled back into the same damp rags and followed. Steelshanks led him back to the Great Keep and the solar that had once been Eddard Stark's. Lord Bolton was not alone. Lady Dustin sat with him, pale-faced and severe; an iron horsehead brooch clasped Roger Ryswell's cloak; Aenys Frey stood near the fire, pinched cheeks flushed with cold.

"I am told you have been wandering the castle," Lord Bolton began. "Men have reported seeing you in the stables, in the kitchens, in the barracks, on the battlements. You have been observed near the ruins of collapsed keeps, outside Lady Catelyn's old sept, coming and going from the godswood. Do you deny it?"

"No, m'lord." Theon made sure to muddy up the word. He knew that pleased Lord Bolton. "I cannot sleep, m'lord. I walk." He kept his head down, fixed upon the old stale rushes scattered on the floor. It was not wise to look his lordship in the face.

"I was a boy here before the war. A ward of Eddard Stark."

"You were a hostage," Bolton said.

"Yes, m'lord. A hostage." *It was my home, though. Not a true home, but the best I ever knew.*

"Someone has been killing my men."

"Yes, m'lord."

"Not you, I trust?" Bolton's voice grew even softer. "You would not repay all my kindnesses with such treachery."

"No, m'lord, not me. I wouldn't. I . . . only walk, is all."

Lady Dustin spoke up. "Take off your gloves."

Theon glanced up sharply. "Please, no. I . . . I . . ."

"Do as she says," Ser Aenys said. "Show us your hands."

Theon peeled his gloves off and held his hands up for them to see. *It is not as if I stand before them naked. It is not so bad as that.* His left hand had three fingers, his right four. Ramsay had taken only the pinky off the one, the ring finger and forefingers from the other.

"The Bastard did this to you," Lady Dustin said.

"If it please m'lady, I . . . I asked it of him." Ramsay always made him ask. *Ramsay always makes me beg.*

"Why would you do that?"

"I . . . I did not need so many fingers."

"Four is enough." Ser Aenys Frey fingered the wispy brown beard that sprouted from his weak chin like a rat's tail. "Four on his right hand. He could still hold a sword. A dagger."

Lady Dustin laughed. "Are all Freys such fools? Look at him. Hold a dagger? He hardly has the strength to hold a spoon. Do you truly think he could have overcome the Bastard's disgusting creature and shoved his manhood down his throat?"

"These dead were all strong men," said Roger Ryswell, "and none of them were stabbed. The turncloak's not our killer."

Roose Bolton's pale eyes were fixed on Theon, as sharp as Skinner's flaying knife. "I am inclined to agree. Strength aside, he does not have it in him to betray my son."

Roger Ryswell grunted. "If not him, who? Stannis has some man inside the castle, that's plain."

Reek is no man. Not Reek. Not me. He wondered if Lady Dustin had told them about the crypts, the missing swords.

"We must look at Manderly," muttered Ser Aenys Frey. "Lord Wyman loves us not."

Ryswell was not convinced. "He loves his steaks and chops and meat pies, though. Prowling the castle by dark would require him to leave the table. The only time he does that is when he seeks the privy for one of his hourlong squats."

"I do not claim Lord Wyman does the deeds himself. He brought three hundred men with him. A hundred knights. Any of them might have—"

"Night work is not knight's work," Lady Dustin said. "And Lord Wyman is not the only man who lost kin at your Red Wedding, Frey. Do you imagine Whoresbane loves you any better? If you did not hold the Greatjon, he would pull out your entrails and make you eat them, as Lady Hornwood ate her fingers. Flints, Cerwyns, Tallharts, Slates . . . they all had men with the Young Wolf."

"House Ryswell too," said Roger Ryswell.

"Even Dustins out of Barrowton." Lady Dustin parted her lips in a thin, feral smile. "The north remembers, Frey."

Aenys Frey's mouth quivered with outrage. "Stark dishonored us. That is what you northmen had best remember."

Roose Bolton rubbed at his chapped lips. "This squabbling will not serve." He flicked his fingers at Theon. "You are free to go. Take care where you wander. Else it might be you we find upon the morrow, smiling a red smile."

"As you say, m'lord." Theon drew his gloves on over his maimed hands and took his leave, limping on his maimed foot.

The hour of the wolf found him still awake, wrapped in layers of heavy wool and greasy fur, walking yet another circuit of the inner walls, hoping to exhaust himself enough to sleep. His legs were caked with snow to the knee, his head and shoulders shrouded in white. On this stretch of the wall the wind was in his face, and melting snow ran down his cheeks like icy tears.

Then he heard the horn.

A long low moan, it seemed to hang above the battlements, lingering in the black air, soaking deep into the bones of every man who heard it. All along the castle walls, sentries turned toward the sound, their hands tightening around the shafts of their spears. In the ruined halls and keeps of Winterfell, lords hushed other lords, horses nickered, and sleepers stirred in their dark corners. No sooner had the sound of the warhorn died away than a drum began to beat: *BOOM doom BOOM doom BOOM doom.* And a name passed from the lips of each man to the next, written in small white puffs of breath. *Stannis*, they whispered, *Stannis is here, Stannis is come, Stannis, Stannis, Stannis.*

Theon shivered. Baratheon or Bolton, it made no matter to him. Stannis had made common cause with Jon Snow at the Wall, and Jon would take his head off in a heartbeat. *Plucked from the clutches of one bastard to die at the hands of another, what a jape.* Theon would have laughed aloud if he'd remembered how.

The drumming seemed to be coming from the wolfswood beyond the Hunter's Gate. *They are just outside the walls.* Theon made his way along the wallwalk, one more man amongst a score doing the same. But even when they reached the towers that flanked the gate itself, there was nothing to be seen beyond the veil of white.

"Do they mean to try and *blow* our walls down?" japed a Flint when the warhorn sounded once again. "Mayhaps he thinks he's found the Horn of Joramun."

"Is Stannis fool enough to storm the castle?" a sentry asked.

"He's not Robert," declared a Barrowton man. "He'll sit, see if he don't. Try and starve us out."

"He'll freeze his balls off first," another sentry said.

"We should take the fight to him," declared a Frey.

Do that, Theon thought. *Ride out into the snow and die. Leave Winterfell to me and the ghosts.* Roose Bolton would welcome such a fight, he sensed. *He needs an end to this.* The castle was too crowded to withstand a long siege, and too many of the lords here were of uncertain loyalty. Fat Wyman Manderly, Whoresbane Umber, the men of House Hornwood and House Tallhart, the Lockes and Flints and Ryswells, all of them were *northmen*, sworn to House Stark for generations beyond count. It was the girl who held them here, Lord Eddard's blood, but the girl was just a mummer's ploy, a lamb in a direwolf's skin. So why not send the northmen forth to battle Stannis before the farce unraveled? *Slaughter in the snow. And every man who falls is one less foe for the Dreadfort.*

Theon wondered if he might be allowed to fight. Then at least he might die a man's death, sword in hand. That was a gift Ramsay would never give him, but Lord Roose might. *If I beg him. I did all he asked of me, I played my part, I gave the girl away.*

Death was the sweetest deliverance he could hope for.

In the godswood the snow was still dissolving as it touched the earth. Steam rose off the hot pools, fragrant with the smell of moss and mud and decay. A warm fog hung in the air, turning the trees into sentinels, tall soldiers shrouded in cloaks of gloom. During daylight hours, the steamy wood was often full of northmen come to pray to the old gods, but at this hour Theon Greyjoy found he had it all to himself.

And in the heart of the wood the weirwood waited with its knowing red eyes. Theon stopped by the edge of the pool and bowed his head before its carved red face. Even here he could hear the drumming, *boom DOOM boom DOOM boom DOOM boom DOOM*. Like distant thunder, the sound seemed to come from everywhere at once.

The night was windless, the snow drifting straight down out of a cold black sky, yet the leaves of the heart tree were rustling his name. "Theon," they seemed to whisper, "Theon."

The old gods, he thought. *They know me. They know my name. I was Theon of House Greyjoy. I was a ward of Eddard Stark, a friend and brother to his children.* "Please." He fell to his knees. "A sword, that's all I ask. Let me die as Theon, not as Reek." Tears trickled down his cheeks, impossibly warm. "I was ironborn. A son . . . a son of Pyke, of the islands."

A leaf drifted down from above, brushed his brow, and landed in the pool. It floated on the water, red, five-fingered, like a bloody hand. ". . . Bran," the tree murmured.

They know. The gods know. They saw what I did. And for one strange moment it seemed as if it were Bran's face carved into the pale trunk of the weirwood, staring down at him with eyes red and wise and sad. *Bran's ghost*, he thought, but that was madness. Why should Bran want to haunt him? He had been fond of the boy, had never done him any harm. *It was not Bran we killed. It was not Rickon. They were only miller's sons, from the mill by the Acorn Water.* "I had to have two heads, else they would have mocked me . . . laughed at me . . . they . . ."

A voice said, "Who are you talking to?"

Theon spun, terrified that Ramsay had found him, but it was just the washerwomen—Holly, Rowan, and one whose name he did not know. "The ghosts," he blurted. "They whisper to me. They . . . they know my name."

"Theon Turncloak." Rowan grabbed his ear, twisting. "You had to have two heads, did you?"

"Elsewise men would have *laughed* at him," said Holly.

They do not understand. Theon wrenched free. "What do you want?" he asked.

"You," said the third washerwoman, an older woman, deep-voiced, with grey streaks in her hair.

"I told you. I want to touch you, turncloak." Holly smiled. In her hand a blade appeared.

I could scream, Theon thought. *Someone will hear. The castle is full of armed men.* He would be dead before help reached him, to be sure, his blood soaking into the ground to feed the heart tree. *And what would be so wrong with that?* "Touch me," he said. "Kill me." There was more despair than defiance in his voice. "Go on. Do me, the way you did the others. Yellow Dick and the rest. It was you."

Holly laughed. "How could it be us? We're women. Teats and cunnies. Here to be fucked, not feared."

"Did the Bastard hurt you?" Rowan asked. "Chopped off your fingers, did he? Skinned your widdle toes? Knocked your teeth out? Poor lad." She patted his cheek. "There will be no more o' that, I promise. You prayed, and the gods sent us. You want to die as Theon? We'll give you that. A nice quick death, 'twill hardly hurt at all." She smiled. "But not till you've sung for Abel. He's waiting for you."

TYRION

L ot ninety-seven." The auctioneer snapped his whip. "A pair of dwarfs, well trained for your amusement."

The auction block had been thrown up where the broad brown Skahazadhan flowed into Slaver's Bay. Tyrion Lannister could smell the salt in the air, mingled with the stink from the latrine ditches behind the slave pens. He did not mind the heat so much as he did the damp. The very air seemed to weigh him down, like a warm wet blanket across his head and shoulders.

"Dog and pig included in lot," the auctioneer announced. "The dwarfs ride them. Delight the guests at your next feast or use them for a folly."

The bidders sat on wooden benches sipping fruit drinks. A few were being fanned by slaves. Many wore *tokars*, that peculiar garment beloved by the old blood of Slaver's Bay, as elegant as it was impractical. Others dressed more plainly—men in tunics and hooded cloaks, women in colored silks. Whores or priestesses, most like; this far east it was hard to tell the two apart.

Back behind the benches, trading japes and making mock of the proceedings, stood a clot of westerners. *Sellswords*, Tyrion knew. He spied longswords, dirks and daggers, a brace of throwing axes, mail beneath their cloaks. Their hair and beards and faces marked most for men of the Free Cities, but here and there were a few who might have been Westerosi. *Are they buying? Or did they just turn up for the show?*

"Who will open for this pair?"

"Three hundred," bid a matron on an antique palanquin.

"Four," called a monstrously fat Yunkishman from the litter where he sprawled like a leviathan. Covered all in yellow silk fringed with gold, he looked as large as four Illyrios. Tyrion pitied the slaves who had to carry him. *At least we will be spared that duty. What joy to be a dwarf.*

"And one," said a crone in a violet *tokar*. The auctioneer gave her a sour look but did not disallow the bid.

The slave sailors off the *Selaesori Qhoran*, sold singly, had gone for prices ranging from five hundred to nine hundred pieces of silver. Seasoned seamen were a valuable commodity. None had put up any sort of fight when the slavers boarded their crippled cog. For them this was just a change of owner. The ship's mates had been free men, but the widow of the waterfront had written them a binder, promising to stand their ransom in such a case as this. The three surviving fiery fingers had not been sold yet, but they were chattels of the Lord of Light and could count on being bought back by some red temple. The flames tattooed upon their faces were their binders.

Tyrion and Penny had no such reassurance.

"Four-fifty," came the bid.

"Four-eighty."

"Five hundred."

Some bids were called out in High Valyrian, some in the mongrel tongue of Ghis. A few buyers signaled with a finger, the twist of a wrist, or the wave of a painted fan.

"I'm glad they are keeping us together," Penny whispered.

The slave trader shot them a look. "No talk."

Tyrion gave Penny's shoulder a squeeze. Strands of hair, pale blond and black, clung to his brow, the rags of his tunic to his back. Some of that was sweat, some dried blood. He had not been so foolish as to fight the slavers, as Jorah Mormont had, but that did not mean he had escaped punishment. In his case it was his mouth that earned him lashes.

"Eight hundred."

"And fifty."

"And one."

We're worth as much as a sailor, Tyrion mused. Though perhaps it was Pretty Pig the buyers wanted. *A well-trained pig is hard to find.* They certainly were not bidding by the pound.

At nine hundred pieces of silver, the bidding began to slow. At nine hundred fifty-one (from the crone), it stopped. The auctioneer had the scent, though, and nothing would do but that the dwarfs give the crowd a taste of their show. Crunch and Pretty Pig were led up onto the platform. Without saddles or bridles, mounting them proved tricky. The moment the sow began to move Tyrion slid off her rump and landed on his own, provoking gales of laughter from the bidders.

"One thousand," bid the grotesque fat man.

"And one." The crone again.

Penny's mouth was frozen in a rictus of a smile. *Well trained for your amusement.* Her father had a deal to answer for, in whatever small hell was reserved for dwarfs.

"Twelve hundred." The leviathan in yellow. A slave beside him handed him a drink. *Lemon, no doubt.* The way those yellow eyes were fixed upon the block made Tyrion uncomfortable.

"Thirteen hundred."

"And one." The crone.

My father always said a Lannister was worth ten times as much as any common man.

At sixteen hundred the pace began to flag again, so the slave trader invited some of the buyers to come up for a closer look at the dwarfs. "The female's young," he promised. "You could breed the two of them, get good coin for the whelps."

"Half his nose is gone," complained the crone once she'd had a good close look. Her wrinkled face puckered with displeasure. Her flesh was maggot white; wrapped in the violet *tokar*, she looked like a prune gone to mold. "His eyes don't match neither. An ill-favored thing."

"My lady hasn't seen my best part yet." Tyrion grabbed his crotch, in case she missed his meaning.

The hag hissed in outrage, and Tyrion got a lick of the whip across his back, a stinging cut that drove him to his knees. The taste of blood filled his mouth. He grinned and spat.

"Two thousand," called a new voice, back of the benches.

And what would a sellsword want with a dwarf? Tyrion pushed himself back to his feet to get a better look. The new bidder was an older man, white-haired yet tall and fit, with leathery brown skin and a close-cropped salt-and-pepper beard. Half-hidden under a faded purple cloak were a longsword and a brace of daggers.

"Twenty-five hundred." A female voice this time; a girl, short, with a thick waist and heavy bosom, clad in ornate armor. Her sculpted black steel breastplate was inlaid in gold and showed a harpy rising with chains dangling from her claws. A pair of slave soldiers lifted her to shoulder height on a shield.

"Three thousand." The brown-skinned man pushed through the crowd, his fellow sellswords shoving buyers aside to clear a path. *Yes. Come closer.* Tyrion knew how to deal with sellswords. He did not think for a moment that this man wanted him to frolic at feasts. *He knows me. He means to take me back to Westeros and sell me to my sister.* The dwarf rubbed his mouth to hide his smile. Cersei and the Seven Kingdoms were half a world away. Much and more could happen before he got there. *I turned Bronn. Give me half a chance, might be I could turn this one too.*

The crone and the girl on the shield gave up the chase at three thousand, but not the fat man in yellow. He weighed the sellswords with his yellow eyes, flicked his tongue across his yellow teeth, and said, "Five thousand silvers for the lot."

The sellsword frowned, shrugged, turned away.

Seven hells. Tyrion was quite certain that he did not want to become the property of the immense Lord Yellowbelly. Just the sight of him sagging across his litter, a mountain of sallow flesh with piggy yellow eyes and breasts big as Pretty Pig pushing at the silk of his *tokar* was enough to make the dwarf's skin crawl. And the smell wafting off him was palpable even on the block.

"If there are no further bids—"

"Seven thousand," shouted Tyrion.

Laughter rippled across the benches. "The dwarf wants to buy himself," the girl on the shield observed.

Tyrion gave her a lascivious grin. "A clever slave deserves a clever master, and you lot all look like fools."

That provoked more laughter from the bidders, and a scowl from the auctioneer, who was fingering his whip indecisively as he tried to puzzle out whether this would work to his benefit.

"Five thousand is an insult!" Tyrion called out. "I joust, I sing, I say amusing things. I'll fuck your wife and make her scream. Or your enemy's wife if you prefer, what better way to shame him? I'm murder with a crossbow, and men three times my size quail and tremble when we meet across a *cyvasse* table. I have even been known to cook from time to time. I bid *ten* thousand silvers for myself! I'm good for it, I am, I am. My father told me I must always pay my debts."

The sellsword in the purple cloak turned back. His eyes met Tyrion's across the rows of other bidders, and he smiled. *A warm smile, that,* the dwarf reflected. *Friendly. But my, those eyes are cold. Might be I don't want him to buy us after all.*

The yellow enormity was squirming in his litter, a look of annoyance on his huge pie face. He muttered something sour in Ghiscari that Tyrion did not understand, but the tone of it was plain enough. "Was that another bid?" The dwarf cocked his head. "I offer all the gold of Casterly Rock."

He heard the whip before he felt it, a whistle in the air, thin and sharp.

Tyrion grunted under the blow, but this time he managed to stay on his feet. His thoughts flashed back to the beginnings of his journey, when his most pressing problem had been deciding which wine to drink with his midmorning snails. *See what comes of chasing dragons.* A laugh burst from his lips, spattering the first row of buyers with blood and spit.

"You are sold," the auctioneer announced. Then he hit him again, just because he could. This time Tyrion went down.

One of the guards yanked him back to his feet. Another prodded Penny down off the platform with the butt of his spear. The next piece of chattel was already being led up to take their place. A girl, fifteen or sixteen, not off the *Selaesori Qhoran* this time. Tyrion did not know her. *The same age as Daenerys Targaryen, or near enough.* The slaver soon had her naked. *At least we were spared that humiliation.*

Tyrion gazed across the Yunkish camp to the walls of Meereen. Those gates looked so close . . . and if the talk in the slave pens could be believed, Meereen remained a free city for the nonce. Within those crumbling walls, slavery and the slave trade were still forbidden. All he had to do was reach those gates and pass beyond, and he would be a free man again.

But that was hardly possible unless he abandoned Penny. *She'd want to take the dog and the pig along.*

"It won't be so terrible, will it?" Penny whispered. "He paid so much for us. He'll be kind, won't he?"

So long as we amuse him. "We're too valuable to mistreat," he reassured her, with blood still trickling down his back from those last two lashes. *When our show grows stale, however . . . and it does, it does grow stale . . .*

Their master's overseer was waiting to take charge of them, with a mule cart and two soldiers. He had a long narrow face and a chin beard bound about with golden wire, and his stiff red-black hair swept out from his temples to form a pair of taloned hands. "What darling little creatures you are," he said. "You remind me of my own children . . . or would, if my little ones were not dead. I shall take good care of you. Tell me your names."

"Penny." Her voice was a whisper, small and scared.

Tyrion, of House Lannister, rightful lord of Casterly Rock, you sniveling worm. "Yollo."

"Bold Yollo. Bright Penny. You are the property of the noble and valorous Yezzan zo Qaggaz, scholar and warrior, revered amongst the Wise Masters of Yunkai. Count yourselves fortunate, for Yezzan is a kindly and benevolent master. Think of him as you would your father."

Gladly, thought Tyrion, but this time he held his tongue. They would have to perform for their new master soon enough, he did not doubt, and he could not take another lash.

"Your father loves his special treasures best of all, and he will cherish you," the overseer was saying. "And me, think of me as you would the nurse who cared for you when you were small. Nurse is what all my children call me."

"Lot ninety-nine," the auctioneer called. "A warrior."

The girl had sold quickly and was being bundled off to her new owner, clutching her clothing to small, pink-tipped breasts. Two slavers dragged Jorah Mormont onto the block to take her place. The knight was naked but for a breechclout, his back raw from the whip, his face so swollen as to be almost unrecognizable. Chains bound his wrists and ankles. *A little taste of the meal he cooked for me,* Tyrion thought, yet he found that he could take no pleasure from the big knight's miseries.

Even in chains, Mormont looked dangerous, a hulking brute with big, thick arms and sloped shoulders. All that coarse dark hair on his chest made him look more beast than man. Both his eyes were blackened, two dark pits in that grotesquely swollen face. Upon one cheek he bore a brand: a demon's mask.

When the slavers had swarmed aboard the *Selaesori Qhoran,* Ser Jorah had met them with longsword in hand, slaying three before they overwhelmed him. Their shipmates would gladly have killed him, but the captain forbade it; a fighter was always worth good silver. So Mormont had been chained to an oar, beaten within an inch of his life, starved, and branded.

"Big and strong, this one," the auctioneer declared. "Plenty of piss in him. He'll give a good show in the fighting pits. Who will start me out at three hundred?"

No one would.

Mormont paid no mind to the mongrel crowd; his eyes were fixed beyond the siege lines, on the distant city with its ancient walls of many-colored brick. Tyrion could read that look as easy as a book: *so near and yet so distant.* The poor wretch had returned too late. Daenerys Targaryen was wed, the guards on the pens had told them, laughing. She had taken a Meereenese slaver as her king, as wealthy as he was noble, and when the peace was signed and sealed the fighting pits of Meereen would open once again. Other slaves insisted that the guards were lying, that Daenerys Targaryen would never make peace with slavers. *Mhysa,* they called her. Someone told him that meant *Mother.* Soon the silver queen would come forth from her city, smash the Yunkai'i, and break their chains, they whispered to one another.

And then she'll bake us all a lemon pie and kiss our widdle wounds and make them better, the dwarf thought. He had no faith in royal rescues. If need be, he would see to their deliverance himself. The mushrooms jammed into the toe of his boot should be sufficient for both him and Penny. Crunch and Pretty Pig would need to fend for themselves.

Nurse was still lecturing his master's new prizes. "Do all you are told and nothing more, and you shall live like little lords, pampered and adored," he promised. "Disobey . . . but you would never do that, would you? Not my sweetlings." He reached down and pinched Penny on her cheek.

"Two hundred, then," the auctioneer said. "A big brute like this, he's worth three times as much. What a bodyguard he will make! No enemy will dare molest you!"

"Come, my little friends," Nurse said, "I will show you to your new home. In Yunkai you will dwell in the golden pyramid of Qaggaz and dine off silver plates, but here we live simply, in the humble tents of soldiers."

"Who will give me one hundred?" cried the auctioneer.

That drew a bid at last, though it was only fifty silvers. The bidder was a thin man in a leather apron.

"And one," said the crone in the violet *tokar*.

One of the soldiers lifted Penny onto the back of the mule cart. "Who is the old woman?" the dwarf asked him.

"Zahrina," the man said. "Cheap fighters, hers. Meat for heroes. Your friend dead soon."

He was no friend to me. Yet Tyrion Lannister found himself turning to Nurse and saying, "You cannot let her have him."

Nurse squinted at him. "What is this noise you make?"

Tyrion pointed. "That one is part of our show. The bear and the maiden fair. Jorah is the bear, Penny is the maiden, I am the brave knight who rescues her. I dance about and hit him in the balls. Very funny."

The overseer squinted at the auction block. "Him?" The bidding for Jorah Mormont had reached two hundred silvers.

"And one," said the crone in the violet *tokar*.

"Your bear. I see." Nurse went scuttling off through the crowd, bent over the huge yellow Yunkishman in his litter, whispered in his ear. His master nodded, chins wobbling, then raised his fan. "Three hundred," he called out in a wheezy voice.

The crone sniffed and turned away.

"Why did you do that?" Penny asked, in the Common Tongue.

A *fair question*, thought Tyrion. *Why did I?* "Your show was growing dull. Every mummer needs a dancing bear."

She gave him a reproachful look, then retreated to the back of the cart and sat with her arms around Crunch, as if the dog was her last true friend in the world. *Perhaps he is.*

Nurse returned with Jorah Mormont. Two of their master's slave soldiers flung him into the back of the mule cart between the dwarfs. The knight did not struggle. *All the fight went out of him when he heard that his queen had wed,* Tyrion realized. One whispered word had done what fists and whips and clubs could not; it had broken him. *I should have let the crone have him. He's going to be as useful as nipples on a breastplate.*

Nurse climbed onto the front of the mule cart and took up the reins, and they set off through the siege camp to the compound of their new master, the noble Yezzan zo Qaggaz. Four slave soldiers marched beside them, two on either side of the cart.

Penny did not weep, but her eyes were red and miserable, and she never lifted them from Crunch. *Does she think all this might fade away if she does not look at it?* Ser Jorah Mormont looked at no one and nothing. He sat huddled, brooding in his chains.

Tyrion looked at everything and everyone.

The Yunkish encampment was not one camp but a hundred camps raised up cheek by jowl in a crescent around the walls of Meereen, a city of silk and canvas with its own avenues and alleys, taverns and trollops, good districts and bad. Between the siege lines and the bay, tents had sprouted up like yellow mushrooms. Some were small and mean, no more than a flap of old stained canvas to keep off the rain and sun, but beside them stood barracks tents large enough to sleep a hundred men and silken pavilions as big as palaces with harpies gleaming atop their roof poles. Some camps were orderly, with the tents arrayed around a fire pit in concentric circles, weapons and armor stacked around the inner ring, horse lines outside. Elsewhere, pure chaos seemed to reign.

The dry, scorched plains around Meereen were flat and bare and treeless for long leagues, but the Yunkish ships had brought lumber and hides up from the south, enough to raise six huge trebuchets. They were arrayed on three sides of the city, all but the river side, surrounded by piles of broken stone and casks of pitch and resin just waiting for a torch. One of the soldiers walking along beside the cart saw where Tyrion was looking and proudly told him that each of the trebuchets had been given a name:

Dragonbreaker, Harridan, Harpy's Daughter, Wicked Sister, Ghost of Astapor, Mazdhan's Fist. Towering above the tents to a height of forty feet, the trebuchets were the siege camp's chief landmarks. "Just the sight of them drove the dragon queen to her knees," he boasted. "And there she will stay, sucking Hizdahr's noble cock, else we smash her walls to rubble."

Tyrion saw a slave being whipped, blow after blow, until his back was nothing but blood and raw meat. A file of men marched past in irons, clanking with every step; they carried spears and wore short swords, but chains linked them wrist to wrist and ankle to ankle. The air smelled of roasting meat, and he saw one man skinning a dog for his stewpot.

He saw the dead as well, and heard the dying. Under the drifting smoke, the smell of horses, and the sharp salt tang of the bay was a stink of blood and shit. *Some flux,* he realized, as he watched two sellswords carry the corpse of a third from one of the tents. That made his fingers twitch. Disease could wipe out an army quicker than any battle, he had heard his father say once.

All the more reason to escape, and soon.

A quarter mile on, he found good reason to reconsider. A crowd had formed around three slaves taken whilst trying to escape. "I know my little treasures will be sweet and obedient," Nurse said. "See what befalls ones who try to run."

The captives had been tied to a row of crossbeams, and a pair of slingers were using them to test their skills. "Tolosi," one of the guards told them. "The best slingers in the world. They throw soft lead balls in place of stones."

Tyrion had never seen the point of slings, when bows had so much better range . . . but he had never seen Tolosi at work before. Their lead balls did vastly more damage than the smooth stones other slingers used, and more than any bow as well. One struck the knee of one of the captives, and it burst apart in a gout of blood and bone that left the man's lower leg dangling by a rope of dark red tendon. *Well, he won't run again,* Tyrion allowed, as the man began to scream. His shrieks mingled in the morning air with the laughter of camp followers and the curses of those who'd wagered good coin that the slinger would miss. Penny looked away, but Nurse grasped her under the chin and twisted her head back around. "Watch," he commanded. "You too, bear."

Jorah Mormont raised his head and stared at Nurse. Tyrion could see the tightness in his arms. *He's going to throttle him, and that will be the end for all of us.* But the knight only grimaced, then turned to watch the bloody show.

To the east the massive brick walls of Meereen shimmered through the morning heat. That was the refuge these poor fools had hoped to reach. *How long will it remain a refuge, though?*

All three of the would-be escapees were dead before Nurse gathered up the reins again. The mule cart rumbled on.

Their master's camp was south and east of the Harridan, almost in its shadow, and spread over several acres. The humble tent of Yezzan zo Qaggaz proved to be a palace of lemon-colored silk. Gilded harpies stood atop the center poles of each of its nine peaked roofs, shining in the sun. Lesser tents ringed it on all sides. "Those are the dwellings of our noble master's cooks, concubines, and warriors, and a few less-favored kinsmen," Nurse told them, "but you little darlings shall have the rare privilege of sleeping within Yezzan's own pavilion. It pleases him to keep his treasures close." He frowned at Mormont. "Not you, bear. You are big and ugly, you will be chained outside." The knight did not respond. "First, all of you must be fitted for collars."

The collars were made of iron, lightly gilded to make them glitter in the light. Yezzan's name was incised into the metal in Valyrian glyphs, and a pair of tiny bells were affixed below the ears, so the wearer's every step produced a merry little tinkling sound. Jorah Mormont accepted his collar in a sullen silence, but Penny began to cry as the armorer was fastening her own into place. "It's so heavy," she complained.

Tyrion squeezed her hand. "It's solid gold," he lied. "In Westeros, highborn ladies dream of such a necklace." *Better a collar than a brand. A collar can be removed.* He remembered Shae, and the way the golden chain had glimmered as he twisted it tighter and tighter about her throat.

Afterward, Nurse had Ser Jorah's chains fastened to a stake near the cookfire whilst he escorted the two dwarfs inside the master's pavilion and showed them where they would sleep, in a carpeted alcove separated from the main tent by walls of yellow silk. They would share this space with Yezzan's other treasures: a boy with twisted, hairy "goat legs," a two-headed girl out of Mantarys, a bearded woman, and a willowy creature called Sweets who dressed in moonstones and Myrish lace. "You are trying to decide if I'm a man or woman," Sweets said, when she was brought before the dwarfs. Then she lifted her skirts and showed them what was underneath. "I'm both, and master loves me best."

A grotesquerie, Tyrion realized. *Somewhere some god is laughing.*

"Lovely," he said to Sweets, who had purple hair and violet eyes, "but we were hoping to be the pretty ones for once."

Sweets sniggered, but Nurse was not amused. "Save your japes for this evening, when you perform for our noble master. If you please him, you will be well rewarded. If not . . ." He slapped Tyrion across the face.

"You will want to be careful with Nurse," said Sweets when the overseer had departed. "He is the only true monster here." The bearded woman spoke an incomprehensible variety of Ghiscari, the goat boy some guttural sailor's pidgin called the trade talk. The two-headed girl was feebleminded; one head was no bigger than an orange and did not speak at all, the other had filed teeth and was like to growl at anyone who came too close to her cage. But Sweets was fluent in four tongues, one of them High Valyrian.

"What is the master like?" Penny asked, anxiously.

"His eyes are yellow, and he stinks," said Sweets. "Ten years ago he went to Sothoros, and he has been rotting from the inside out ever since. Make him forget that he is dying, even for a little while, and he can be most generous. Deny him nothing."

They had only the afternoon to learn the ways of chattel. Yezzan's body slaves filled a tub with hot water, and the dwarfs were allowed to bathe— Penny first, then Tyrion. Afterward another slave spread a stinging ointment across the cuts on his back to keep them from mortifying, then covered them with a cool poultice. Penny's hair was cut, and Tyrion's beard got a trim. They were given soft slippers and fresh clothing, plain but clean.

As evening fell, Nurse returned to tell them that it was time to don their mummer's plate. Yezzan would be hosting the Yunkish supreme commander, the noble Yurkhaz zo Yunzak, and they would be expected to perform. "Shall we unchain your bear?"

"Not this night," Tyrion said. "Let us joust for our master first and save the bear for some other time."

"Just so. After your capers are concluded, you will help serve and pour. See that you do not spill on the guests, or it will go ill for you."

A juggler began the evening's frolics. Then came a trio of energetic tumblers. After them the goat-legged boy came out and did a grotesque jig whilst one of Yurkhaz's slaves played on a bone flute. Tyrion had half a mind to ask him if he knew "The Rains of Castamere." As they waited their own turn to perform, he watched Yezzan and his guests. The human prune in the place of honor was evidently the Yunkish supreme commander, who looked about as formidable as a loose stool. A dozen other

Yunkish lords attended him. Two sellsword captains were on hand as well, each accompanied by a dozen men of his company. One was an elegant Pentoshi, grey-haired and clad in silk but for his cloak, a ragged thing sewn from dozens of strips of torn, bloodstained cloth. The other captain was the man who'd tried to buy them that morning, the brown-skinned bidder with the salt-and-pepper beard. "Brown Ben Plumm," Sweets named him. "Captain of the Second Sons."

A Westerosi, and a Plumm. Better and better.

"You are next," Nurse informed them. "Be amusing, my little darlings, or you will wish you had."

Tyrion had not mastered half of Groat's old tricks, but he could ride the sow, fall off when he was meant to, roll, and pop back onto his feet. All of that proved well received. The sight of little people running about drunkenly and whacking at one another with wooden weapons appeared to be just as hilarious in a siege camp by Slaver's Bay as at Joffrey's wedding feast in King's Landing. *Contempt*, thought Tyrion, *the universal tongue.*

Their master Yezzan laughed loudest and longest whenever one of his dwarfs suffered a fall or took a blow, his whole vast body shaking like suet in an earthquake; his guests waited to see how Yurkhaz no Yunzak responded before joining in. The supreme commander appeared so frail that Tyrion was afraid laughing might kill him. When Penny's helm was struck off and flew into the lap of a sour-faced Yunkishman in a striped green-and-gold *tokar*, Yurkhaz cackled like a chicken. When said lord reached inside the helm and drew out a large purple melon dribbling pulp, he wheezed until his face turned the same color as the fruit. He turned to his host and whispered something that made their master chortle and lick his lips . . . though there was a hint of anger in those slitted yellow eyes, it seemed to Tyrion.

Afterward the dwarfs stripped off their wooden armor and the sweat-soaked clothing beneath and changed into the fresh yellow tunics that had been provided them for serving. Tyrion was given a flagon of purple wine, Penny a flagon of water. They moved about the tent filling cups, their slippered feet whispering over thick carpets. It was harder work than it appeared. Before long his legs were cramping badly, and one of the cuts on his back had begun to bleed again, the red seeping through the yellow linen of his tunic. Tyrion bit his tongue and kept on pouring.

Most of the guests paid them no more mind than they did the other slaves . . . but one Yunkishman declared drunkenly that Yezzan should make the two dwarfs fuck, and another demanded to know how Tyrion had lost his nose. *I shoved it up your wife's cunt and she bit it off,* he almost replied . . . but the storm had persuaded him that he did not want to die as yet, so instead he said, "It was cut off to punish me for insolence, lord."

Then a lord in a blue *tokar* fringed with tiger's eyes recalled that Tyrion had boasted of his skill at *cyvasse* on the auction block. "Let us put him to the test," he said. A table and set of pieces was duly produced. A scant few moments later, the red-faced lord shoved the table over in fury, scattering the pieces across the carpets to the sound of Yunkish laughter.

"You should have let him win," Penny whispered.

Brown Ben Plumm lifted the fallen table, smiling. "Try me next, dwarf. When I was younger, the Second Sons took contract with Volantis. I learned the game there."

"I am only a slave. My noble master decides when and who I play." Tyrion turned to Yezzan. "Master?"

The yellow lord seemed amused by the notion. "What stakes do you propose, Captain?"

"If I win, give this slave to me," said Plumm.

"No," Yezzan zo Qaggaz said. "But if you can defeat my dwarf, you may have the price I paid for him, in gold."

"Done," the sellsword said. The scattered pieces were picked up off the carpet, and they sat down to play.

Tyrion won the first game. Plumm took the second, for double the stakes. As they set up for their third contest, the dwarf studied his opponent. Brown-skinned, his cheeks and jaw covered by a close-cropped bristly beard of grey and white, his face creased by a thousand wrinkles and a few old scars, Plumm had an amiable look to him, especially when he smiled. *The faithful retainer*, Tyrion decided. *Every man's favorite nuncle, full of chuckles and old sayings and roughspun wisdom.* It was all sham. Those smiles never touched Plumm's eyes, where greed hid behind a veil of caution. *Hungry, but wary, this one.*

The sellsword was nearly as bad a player as the Yunkish lord had been, but his play was stolid and tenacious rather than bold. His opening arrays were different every time, yet all the same—conservative, defensive, passive. *He does not play to win*, Tyrion realized. *He plays so as not to lose.* It worked in their second game, when the little man overreached himself with an unsound assault. It did not work in the third game, nor the fourth, nor the fifth, which proved to be their last.

Near the end of that final contest, with his fortress in ruins, his dragon dead, elephants before him and heavy horse circling round his rear, Plumm looked up smiling and said, "Yollo wins again. Death in four."

"Three." Tyrion tapped his dragon. "I was lucky. Perhaps you should give my head a good rub before our next game, Captain. Some of that luck might rub off on your fingers." *You will still lose, but you might give me a better game.* Grinning, he pushed back from the *cyvasse* table, picked up his wine flagon, and returned to pouring with Yezzan zo Qaggaz considerably richer and Brown Ben Plumm considerably impoverished. His gargantuan master had fallen off into drunken sleep during the third game, his goblet slipping from his yellowed fingers to spill its contents on the carpet, but perhaps he would be pleased when he awakened.

When the supreme commander Yurkhaz zo Yunzak departed, supported by a pair of burly slaves, that seemed to be a general signal for the other guests to take their leaves as well. After the tent had emptied out, Nurse reappeared to tell the servers that they might make their own feast from the leavings. "Eat quickly. All this must be clean again before you sleep."

Tyrion was on his knees, his legs aching and his bloody back screaming with pain, trying to scrub out the stain that the noble Yezzan's spilled wine had left upon the noble Yezzan's carpet, when the overseer tapped his cheek gently with the end of his whip. "Yollo. You have done well. You and your wife."

"She is not my wife."

"Your whore, then. On your feet, both of you."

Tyrion rose unsteadily, one leg trembling beneath him. His thighs were knots, so cramped that Penny had to lend him a hand to pull him to his feet. "What have we done?"

"Much and more," said the overseer. "Nurse said you would be rewarded if you pleased your father, did he not? Though the noble Yezzan is loath to lose his little treasures, as you have seen, Yurkhaz zo Yunzak persuaded him that it would be selfish to keep such droll antics to himself. Rejoice! To celebrate the signing of the peace, you shall have the honor of jousting in the Great Pit of Daznak. Thousands will come see you! Tens of thousands! And, oh, how we shall laugh!"

JAIME

Raventree Hall was old. Moss grew thick between its ancient stones, spiderwebbing up its walls like the veins in a crone's legs. Two huge towers flanked the castle's main gate, and smaller ones defended every angle of its walls. All were square. Drum towers and half-moons held up better against catapults, since thrown stones were more apt to deflect off a curved wall, but Raventree predated that particular bit of builder's wisdom.

The castle dominated the broad fertile valley that maps and men alike called Blackwood Vale. A vale it was, beyond a doubt, but no wood had grown here for several thousand years, be it black or brown or green. Once, yes, but axes had long since cleared the trees away. Homes and mills and holdfasts had risen where once the oaks stood tall. The ground was bare and muddy, and dotted here and there with drifts of melting snow.

Inside the castle walls, however, a bit of the forest still remained. House Blackwood kept the old gods, and worshiped as the First Men had in the days before the Andals came to Westeros. Some of the trees in their godswood were said to be as old as Raventree's square towers, especially the heart tree, a weirwood of colossal size whose upper branches could be seen from leagues away, like bony fingers scratching at the sky.

As Jaime Lannister and his escort wound through the rolling hills into the vale, little remained of the fields and farms and orchards that had once surrounded Raventree—only mud and ashes, and here and there the blackened shells of homes and mills. Weeds and thorns and nettles grew in that wasteland, but nothing that could be called a crop. Everywhere Jaime looked he saw his father's hand, even in the bones they sometimes glimpsed beside the road. Most were sheep bones, but there were horses too, and cattle, and now and again a human skull, or a headless skeleton with weeds poking up through its rib cage.

No great hosts encircled Raventree, as Riverrun had been encircled. This siege was a more intimate affair, the latest step in a dance that went back many centuries. At best Jonos Bracken had five hundred men about the castle. Jaime saw no siege towers, no battering rams, no catapults. Bracken did not mean to break the gates of Raventree nor storm its high, thick walls. With no prospect of relief in sight, he was content to starve his rival out. No doubt there had been sorties and skirmishes at the start of the siege, and arrows flying back and forth; half a year into it, everyone was too tired for such nonsense. Boredom and routine had taken over, the enemies of discipline.

Past time this was ended, thought Jaime Lannister. With Riverrun now safely in Lannister hands, Raventree was the remnant of the Young Wolf's short-lived kingdom. Once it yielded, his work along the Trident would be done, and he would be free to return to King's Landing. *To the king*, he told himself, but another part of him whispered, *to Cersei*.

He would have to face her, he supposed. Assuming the High Septon had not put her to death by the time he got back to the city. *"Come at once,"* she had written, in the letter he'd had Peck burn at Riverrun. *"Help me. Save me. I need you now as I have never needed you before. I love you. I love you. I love you. Come at once."* Her need was real enough, Jaime did not doubt. As for the rest . . . *she's been fucking Lancel and Osmund Kettleblack and Moon Boy for all I know* . . . Even if he had gone back, he could not hope to save her. She was guilty of every treason laid against her, and he was short a sword hand.

When the column came trotting from the fields, the sentries stared at them with more curiosity than fear. No one sounded the alarm, which suited Jaime well enough. Lord Bracken's pavilion did not prove difficult to find. It was the largest in the camp, and the best sited; sitting atop a low rise beside a stream, it commanded a clear view of two of Raventree's gates.

The tent was brown, like the standard flapping from its center pole, where the red stallion of House Bracken reared upon its gold escutcheon. Jaime gave the order to dismount and told his men that they might mingle if they liked. "Not you two," he said to his banner-bearers. "Stay close. This will not keep me long." Jaime vaulted down off Honor and strode to Bracken's tent, his sword rattling in its scabbard.

The guards outside the tent flap exchanged an anxious look at his approach. "My lord," said one. "Shall we announce you?"

"I'll announce myself." Jaime pushed aside the flap with his golden hand and ducked inside.

They were well and truly at it when he entered, so intent on their rutting that neither took any note of his arrival. The woman had her eyes closed. Her hands clutched the coarse brown hair on Bracken's back. She gasped every time he drove into her. His lordship's head was buried in her breasts, his hands locked around her hips. Jaime cleared his throat. "Lord Jonos."

The woman's eyes flew open, and she gave a startled shriek. Jonos Bracken rolled off her, grabbed for his scabbard, and came up with naked steel in hand, cursing. "*Seven bloody hells,*" he started, "*who dares—*" Then he saw Jaime's white cloak and golden breastplate. His swordpoint dropped. "Lannister?"

"I am sorry to disturb you at your pleasure, my lord," said Jaime, with a half-smile, "but I am in some haste. May we talk?"

"Talk. Aye." Lord Jonos sheathed his sword. He was not quite so tall as Jaime, but he was heavier, with thick shoulders and arms that would have made a blacksmith envious. Brown stubble covered his cheeks and chin. His eyes were brown as well, the anger in them poorly hidden. "You took me unawares, my lord. I was not told of your coming."

"And I seem to have prevented yours." Jaime smiled at the woman in the bed. She had one hand over her left breast and the other between her legs, which left her right breast exposed. Her nipples were darker than Cersei's and thrice the size. When she felt Jaime's gaze she covered her right nipple, but that revealed her mound. "Are all camp followers so modest?" he wondered. "If a man wants to sell his turnips, he needs to set them out."

"You been looking at my turnips since you came in, ser." The woman found the blanket and pulled it up high enough to cover herself to the waist, then raised one hand to push her hair back from her eyes. "And they're not for sale, neither."

Jaime gave a shrug. "My apologies if I mistook you for something you're not. My little brother has known a hundred whores, I'm sure, but I've only ever bedded one."

"She's a prize of war." Bracken retrieved his breeches from the floor and shook them out. "She belonged to one of Blackwood's sworn swords till I split his head in two. Put your hands down, woman. My lord of Lannister wants a proper look at those teats."

Jaime ignored that. "You are putting those breeches on backwards, my lord," he told Bracken. As Jonos cursed, the woman slipped off the bed to snatch up her scattered clothing, her fingers fluttering nervously between her breasts and cleft as she bent and turned and reached. Her efforts to conceal herself were oddly provocative, far more so than if she'd simply gone about the business naked. "Do you have a name, woman?" he asked her.

"My mother named me Hildy, ser." She pulled a soiled shift down over her head and shook her hair out. Her face was almost as dirty as her feet and she had enough hair between her legs to pass for Bracken's sister, but there was something appealing about her all the same. That pug nose, her shaggy mane of hair . . . or the way she did a little curtsy after she had stepped into her skirt. "Have you seen my other shoe, m'lord?"

The question seemed to vex Lord Bracken. "Am I a bloody handmaid, to fetch you shoes? Go barefoot if you must. Just go."

"Does that mean m'lord won't be taking me home with him, to pray with his little wife?" Laughing, Hildy gave Jaime a brazen look. "Do you have a little wife, ser?"

No, I have a sister. "What color is my cloak?"

"White," she said, "but your hand is solid gold. I like that in a man. And what is it you like in a woman, m'lord?"

"Innocence."

"In a woman, I said. Not a daughter."

He thought of Myrcella. *I will need to tell her too.* The Dornishmen might not like that. Doran Martell had betrothed her to his son in the belief that she was Robert's blood. *Knots and tangles,* Jaime thought, wishing he could cut through all of it with one swift stroke of his sword. "I have sworn a vow," he told Hildy wearily.

"No turnips for you, then," the girl said, saucily.

"*Get out,*" Lord Jonos roared at her.

She did. But as she slipped past Jaime, clutching one shoe and a pile of her clothes, she reached down and gave his cock a squeeze through his breeches. "*Hildy,*" she reminded him, before she darted half-clothed from the tent.

Hildy, Jaime mused. "And how fares your lady wife?" he asked Lord Jonos when the girl was gone.

"How would I know? Ask her septon. When your father burned our castle, she decided the gods were punishing us. Now all she does is pray." Jonos had finally gotten his breeches turned the right way round and was lacing them up the front. "What brings you here, my lord? The Blackfish? We heard how he escaped."

"Did you?" Jaime settled on a camp stool. "From the man himself, perchance?"

"Ser Brynden knows better than to come running to me. I am fond of the man, I won't deny that. That won't stop me clapping him in chains if he shows his face near me or mine. He knows I've bent the knee. He should have done the same, but he always was a stubborn one. His brother could have told you that."

"Tytos Blackwood has not bent the knee," Jaime pointed out. "Might the Blackfish seek refuge at Raventree?"

"He might seek it, but to find it he'd need to get past my siege lines, and last I heard he hadn't grown wings. Tytos will be needing refuge himself before much longer. They're down to rats and roots in there. He'll yield before the next full moon."

"He'll yield before the sun goes down. I mean to offer him terms and accept him back into the king's peace."

"I see." Lord Jonos shrugged into a brown woolen tunic with the red stallion of Bracken embroidered on the front. "Will my lord take a horn of ale?"

"No, but don't go dry on my account."

Bracken filled a horn for himself, drank half of it, and wiped his mouth. "You spoke of terms. What sort of terms?"

"The usual sort. Lord Blackwood shall be required to confess his treason and abjure his allegiance to the Starks and Tullys. He will swear solemnly before gods and men to henceforth remain a leal vassal of Harrenhal and the Iron Throne, and I will give him pardon in the king's name. We will take a pot or two of gold, of course. The price of rebellion. I'll claim a hostage as well, to ensure that Raventree does not rise again."

"His daughter," suggested Bracken. "Blackwood has six sons, but only the one daughter. He dotes on her. A snot-nosed little creature, couldn't be more than seven."

"Young, but she might serve."

Lord Jonos drained the last of his ale and tossed the horn aside. "What of the lands and castles we were promised?"

"What lands were these?"

"The east bank of the Widow's Wash, from Crossbow Ridge to Rutting Meadow, and all the islands in the stream. Grindcorn Mill and Lord's Mill, the ruins of Muddy Hall, the Ravishment, Battle Valley, Oldforge, the villages of Buckle, Blackbuckle, Cairns, and Claypool, and the market town at Mudgrave. Waspwood, Lorgen's Wood, Greenhill, and Barba's Teats. Missy's Teats, the Blackwoods call them, but they were Barba's first. Honeytree and all the hives. Here, I've marked them out if my lord would like a look." He rooted about on a table and produced a parchment map.

Jaime took it with his good hand, but he had to use the gold to open it and hold it flat. "This is a deal of land," he observed. "You will be increasing your domains by a quarter."

Bracken's mouth set stubbornly. "All these lands belonged to Stone Hedge once. The Blackwoods stole them from us."

"What about this village here, between the Teats?" Jaime tapped the map with a gilded knuckle.

"Pennytree. That was ours once too, but it's been a royal fief for a hundred years. Leave that out. We ask only for the lands stolen by the Blackwoods. Your lord father promised to restore them to us if we would subdue Lord Tytos for him."

"Yet as I was riding up, I saw Tully banners flying from the castle walls, and the direwolf of Stark as well. That would seem to suggest that Lord Tytos has not been subdued."

"We've driven him and his from the field and penned them up inside Raventree. Give me sufficient men to storm his walls, my lord, and I will subdue the whole lot of them to their graves."

"If I gave you sufficient men, they would be doing the subduing, not you. In which case I should reward myself." Jaime let the map roll up again. "I'll keep this if I might."

"The map is yours. The lands are ours. It's said that a Lannister always pays his debts. We fought for you."

"Not half as long as you fought against us."

"The king has pardoned us for that. I lost my nephew to your swords, and my natural son. Your Mountain stole my harvest and burned everything he could not carry off. He put my castle to the torch and raped one of my daughters. I will have recompense."

"The Mountain's dead, as is my father," Jaime told him, "and some might say your head was recompense enough. You *did* declare for Stark, and kept faith with him until Lord Walder killed him."

"Murdered him, and a dozen good men of my own blood." Lord Jonos turned his head and spat. "Aye, I kept faith with the Young Wolf. As I'll keep faith with you, so long as you treat me fair. I bent the knee because I saw no sense in dying for the dead nor shedding Bracken blood in a lost cause."

"A prudent man." *Though some might say that Lord Blackwood has been more honorable.* "You'll get your lands. Some of them, at least. Since you partly subdued the Blackwoods."

That seemed to satisfy Lord Jonos. "We will be content with whatever portion my lord thinks fair. If I may offer you some counsel, though, it does not serve to be too gentle with these Blackwoods. Treachery runs in their blood. Before the Andals came to Westeros, House Bracken ruled this river. We were kings and the Blackwoods were our vassals, but they betrayed us and usurped the crown. Every Blackwood is born a turncloak. You would do well to remember that when you are making terms."

"Oh, I shall," Jaime promised.

When he rode from Bracken's siege camp to the gates of Raventree, Peck went before him with a peace banner. Before they reached the castle, twenty pairs of eyes were watching them from the gatehouse ramparts. He drew Honor to a halt at the edge of the moat, a deep trench lined with stone, its green waters choked by scum. Jaime was about to command Ser Kennos to sound the Horn of Herrock when the drawbridge began to descend.

Lord Tytos Blackwood met him in the outer ward, mounted on a destrier as gaunt as himself. Very tall and very thin, the Lord of Raventree had a hook nose, long hair, and a ragged salt-and-pepper beard that showed more salt than pepper. In silver inlay on the breastplate of his burnished scarlet armor was a white tree bare and dead, surrounded by a flock of onyx ravens taking flight. A cloak of raven feathers fluttered from his shoulders.

"Lord Tytos," Jaime said.

"Ser."

"Thank you for allowing me to enter."

"I will not say that you are welcome. Nor will I deny that I have hoped that you might come. You are here for my sword."

"I am here to make an end of this. Your men have fought valiantly, but your war is lost. Are you prepared to yield?"

"To the king. Not to Jonos Bracken."

"I understand."

Blackwood hesitated a moment. "Is it your wish that I dismount and kneel before you here and now?"

A hundred eyes were looking on. "The wind is cold and the yard is muddy," said Jaime. "You can do your kneeling on the carpet in your solar once we've agreed on terms."

"That is chivalrous of you," said Lord Tytos. "Come, ser. My hall might lack for food, but never for courtesy."

Blackwood's solar was on the second floor of a cavernous timber keep. There was a fire burning in the hearth when they entered. The room was large and airy, with great beams of dark oak supporting the high ceiling. Woolen tapestries covered the walls, and a pair of wide latticework doors looked out upon the godswood. Through their thick, diamond-shaped panes of yellow glass Jaime glimpsed the gnarled limbs of the tree from which the castle took its name. It was a weirwood ancient and colossal, ten times the size of the one in the Stone Garden at Casterly Rock. This tree was bare and dead, though.

"The Brackens poisoned it," said his host. "For a thousand years it has not shown a leaf. In another thousand it will have turned to stone, the maesters say. Weirwoods never rot."

"And the ravens?" asked Jaime. "Where are they?"

"They come at dusk and roost all night. Hundreds of them. They cover the tree like black leaves, every limb and every branch. They have been coming for thousands of years. How or why, no man can say, yet the tree draws them every night." Blackwood settled in a high-backed chair. "For honor's sake I must ask about my liege lord."

"Ser Edmure is on his way to Casterly Rock as my captive. His wife will remain at the Twins until their child is born. Then she and the babe will join him. So long as he does not attempt escape or plot rebellion, Edmure will live a long life."

"Long and bitter. A life without honor. Until his dying day, men will say he was afraid to fight."

Unjustly, Jaime thought. *It was his child he feared for. He knew whose son I am, better than mine own aunt.* "The choice was his. His uncle would have made us bleed."

"We agree on that much." Blackwood's voice gave nothing away. "What have you done with Ser Brynden, if I may ask?"

"I offered to let him take the black. Instead he fled." Jaime smiled. "Do you have him here, perchance?"

"No."

"Would you tell me if you did?"

It was Tytos Blackwood's turn to smile.

Jaime brought his hands together, the gold fingers inside the fleshy ones. "Perhaps it is time we talked of terms."

"Is this where I get down on my knees?"

"If it please you. Or we can say you did."

Lord Blackwood remained seated. They soon reached agreement on the major points: confession, fealty, pardon, a certain sum of gold and silver to be paid. "What lands will you require?" Lord Tytos asked. When Jaime handed him the map, he took one look and chuckled. "To be sure. The turncloak must be given his reward."

"Yes, but a smaller one than he imagines, for a smaller service. Which of these lands will you consent to part with?"

Lord Tytos considered for a moment. "Woodhedge, Crossbow Ridge, and Buckle."

"A ruin, a ridge, and a few hovels? Come, my lord. You must suffer for your treason. He will want one of the mills, at least." Mills were a valuable source of tax. The lord received a tenth of all the grain they ground.

"Lord's Mill, then. Grindcorn is ours."

"And another village. Cairns?"

"I have forebears buried beneath the rocks of Cairns." He looked at the map again. "Give him Honeytree and its hives. All that sweet will make him fat and rot his teeth."

"Done, then. But for one last thing."

"A hostage."

"Yes, my lord. You have a daughter, I believe."

"Bethany." Lord Tytos looked stricken. "I also have two brothers and a sister. A pair of widowed aunts. Nieces, nephews, cousins. I had thought you might consent . . ."

"It must be a child of your blood."

"Bethany is only eight. A gentle girl, full of laughter. She has never been more than a day's ride from my hall."

"Why not let her see King's Landing? His Grace is almost of an age with her. He would be pleased to have another friend."

"One he can hang if the friend's father should displease him?" asked Lord Tytos. "I have four sons. Would you consider one of them instead? Ben is twelve and thirsty for adventure. He could squire for you if it please my lord."

"I have more squires than I know what to do with. Every time I take a piss, they fight for the right to hold my cock. And you have six sons, my lord, not four."

"Once. Robert was my youngest and never strong. He died nine days ago, of a looseness of the bowels. Lucas was murdered at the Red Wedding. Walder Frey's fourth wife was a Blackwood, but kinship counts for no more than guest right at the Twins. I should like to bury Lucas beneath the tree, but the Freys have not yet seen fit to return his bones to me."

"I'll see that they do. Was Lucas your eldest son?"

"My second. Brynden is my eldest, and my heir. Next comes Hoster. A bookish boy, I fear."

"They have books in King's Landing too. I recall my little brother reading them from time to time. Perhaps your son would like a look at them. I will accept Hoster as our hostage."

Blackwood's relief was palpable. "Thank you, my lord." He hesitated a moment. "If I may be so bold, you would do well to require a hostage from Lord Jonos too. One of his daughters. For all his rutting, he has not proved man enough to father sons."

"He had a bastard son killed in the war."

"Did he? Harry was a bastard, true enough, but whether Jonos sired him is a thornier question. A fair-haired boy, he was, and comely. Jonos is neither." Lord Tytos got to his feet. "Will you do me the honor of taking supper with me?"

"Some other time, my lord." The castle was starving; no good would be served by Jaime stealing food from their mouths. "I cannot linger. Riverrun awaits."

"Riverrun? Or King's Landing?"

"Both."

Lord Tytos did not attempt to dissuade him. "Hoster can be ready to depart within the hour."

He was. The boy met Jaime by the stables, with a bedroll slung over one shoulder and a bundle of scrolls beneath his arm. He could not have been any older than sixteen, yet he was even taller than his father, almost seven feet of legs and shins and elbows, a gangling, gawky boy with a cowlick. "Lord Commander. I'm your hostage, Hoster. Hos, they call me." He grinned.

Does he think this is a lark? "Pray, who are *they*?"

"My friends. My brothers."

"I am not your friend and I am not your brother." That cleaned the grin off the boy's face. Jaime turned to Lord Tytos. "My lord, let there be no misunderstanding here. Lord Beric Dondarrion, Thoros of Myr, Sandor Clegane, Brynden Tully, this woman Stoneheart . . . all these are outlaws and rebels, enemies to the king and all his leal subjects. If I should learn that you or yours are hiding them, protecting them, or assisting them in any way, I will not hesitate to send you your son's head. I hope you understand that. Understand this as well: I am not Ryman Frey."

"No." All trace of warmth had left Lord Blackwood's mouth. "I know who I am dealing with. Kingslayer."

"Good." Jaime mounted and wheeled Honor toward the gate. "I wish you a good harvest and the joy of the king's peace."

He did not ride far. Lord Jonos Bracken was waiting for him outside Raventree, just beyond the range of a good crossbow. He was mounted on an armored destrier and had donned his plate and mail, and a grey steel greathelm with a horsehair crest. "I saw them pull the direwolf banner down," he said when Jaime reached him. "Is it done?"

"Done and done. Go home and plant your fields."

Lord Bracken raised his visor. "I trust I have more fields to plant than when you went into that castle."

"Buckle, Woodhedge, Honeytree and all its hives." He was forgetting one. "Oh, and Crossbow Ridge."

"A mill," said Bracken. "I must have a mill."

"Lord's Mill."

Lord Jonos snorted. "Aye, that will serve. For now." He pointed at Hoster Blackwood, riding back with Peck. "Is this what he gave you for a hostage? You were cozened, ser. A weakling, this one. Water for blood. Never mind how tall he is, any one of my girls could snap him like a rotten twig."

"How many daughters do you have, my lord?" Jaime asked him.

"Five. Two by my first wife and three by my third." Too late, he seemed to realize that he might have said too much.

"Send one of them to court. She will have the privilege of attending the Queen Regent."

Bracken's face grew dark as he realized the import of those words. "Is this how you repay the friendship of Stone Hedge?"

"It is a great honor to wait upon the queen," Jaime reminded his lordship. "You might want to impress that on her. We'll look for the girl before the year is out." He did not wait for Lord Bracken to reply but touched Honor lightly with his golden spurs and trotted off. His men formed up and followed, banners streaming. Castle and camp were soon lost behind them, obscured by the dust of their hooves.

Neither outlaws nor wolves had troubled them on their way to Raventree, so Jaime decided to return by a different route. If the gods were good, he might stumble on the Blackfish, or lure Beric Dondarrion into an unwise attack.

They were following the Widow's Wash when they ran out of day. Jaime called his hostage forward and asked him where to find the nearest ford, and the boy led them there. As the column splashed across the shallow waters, the sun was setting behind a pair of grassy hills. "The Teats," said Hoster Blackwood.

Jaime recalled Lord Bracken's map. "There's a village between those hills."

"Pennytree," the lad confirmed.

"We'll camp there for the night." If there were villagers about, they might have knowledge of Ser Brynden or the outlaws. "Lord Jonos made some remark about whose teats they were," he recalled to the Blackwood boy as they rode toward the darkening hills and the last light of the day. "The Brackens call them by one name and the Blackwoods by another."

"Aye, my lord. For a hundred years or so. Before that, they were the Mother's Teats, or just the Teats. There are two of them, and it was thought that they resembled . . ."

"I can see what they resemble." Jaime found himself thinking back on the woman in the tent and the way she'd tried to hide her large, dark nipples. "What changed a hundred years ago?"

"Aegon the Unworthy took Barba Bracken as his mistress," the bookish boy replied. "She was a very buxom wench, they say, and one day when the king was visiting at the Stone Hedge he went out hunting and saw the Teats and . . ."

". . . named them for his mistress." Aegon the Fourth had died long before Jaime had been born, but he recalled enough of the history of his reign to guess what must have happened next. "Only later he put the Bracken girl aside and took up with a Blackwood, was that the way of it?"

"Lady Melissa," Hoster confirmed. "Missy, they called her. There's a statue of her in our godswood. She was *much* more beautiful than Barba Bracken, but slender, and Barba was heard to say that Missy was flat as a boy. When King Aegon heard, he . . ."

". . . gave her Barba's teats." Jaime laughed. "How did all this begin, between Blackwood and Bracken? Is it written down?"

"It is, my lord," the boy said, "but some of the histories were penned by their maesters and some by ours, centuries after the events that they purport to chronicle. It goes back to the Age of Heroes. The Blackwoods were kings in those days. The Brackens were petty lords, renowned for breeding horses. Rather than pay their king his just due, they used the gold their horses brought them to hire swords and cast him down."

"When did all this happen?"

"Five hundred years before the Andals. A thousand, if the *True History* is to be believed. Only no one knows when the Andals crossed the narrow sea. The *True History* says four thousand years have passed since then, but some maesters claim that it was only two. Past a certain point, all the dates grow hazy and confused, and the clarity of history becomes the fog of legend."

Tyrion would like this one. They could talk from dusk to dawn, arguing about books. For a moment his bitterness toward his brother was forgotten, until he remembered what the Imp had done. "So you are fighting over a crown that one of you took from the other back when the Casterlys still held Casterly Rock, is that the root of it? The crown of a kingdom that has not existed for thousands of years?" He chuckled. "So many years, so many wars, so many kings . . . you'd think someone would have made a peace."

"Someone did, my lord. Many someones. We've had a hundred peaces with the Brackens, many sealed with marriages. There's Blackwood blood in every Bracken, and Bracken blood in every Blackwood. The Old King's Peace lasted half a century. But then some fresh quarrel broke out, and the old wounds opened and began to bleed again. That's how it always happens, my father says. So long as men remember the wrongs done to their forebears, no peace will ever last. So we go on century after century, with us hating the Brackens and them hating us. My father says there will never be an end to it."

"There could be."

"How, my lord? The old wounds never heal, my father says."

"My father had a saying too. Never wound a foe when you can kill him. Dead men don't claim vengeance."

"Their sons do," said Hoster, apologetically.

"Not if you kill the sons as well. Ask the Casterlys about that if you doubt me. Ask Lord and Lady Tarbeck, or the Reynes of Castamere. Ask the Prince of Dragonstone." For an instant, the deep red clouds that crowned the western hills reminded him of Rhaegar's children, all wrapped up in crimson cloaks.

"Is that why you killed all the Starks?"

"Not all," said Jaime. "Lord Eddard's daughters live. One has just been wed. The other . . ." *Brienne, where are you? Have you found her?* ". . . if the gods are good, she'll forget she was a Stark. She'll wed some burly blacksmith or fat-faced innkeep, fill his house with children, and never need to fear that some knight might come along to smash their heads against a wall."

"The gods are good," his hostage said, uncertainly.

You go on believing that. Jaime let Honor feel his spurs.

Pennytree proved to be a much larger village than he had anticipated. The war had been here too; blackened orchards and the scorched shells of broken houses testified to that. But for every home in ruins three more had been rebuilt. Through the gathering blue dusk Jaime glimpsed fresh thatch upon a score of roofs, and doors made of raw green wood. Between a duck pond and a blacksmith's forge, he came upon the tree that gave the place its name, an oak ancient and tall. Its gnarled roots twisted in and out of the earth like a nest of slow brown serpents, and hundreds of old copper pennies had been nailed to its huge trunk.

Peck stared at the tree, then at the empty houses. "Where are the people?"

"Hiding," Jaime told him.

Inside the homes all the fires had been put out, but some still smoked, and none of them were cold. The nanny goat that Hot Harry Merrell found rooting through a vegetable garden was the only living creature to be seen . . . but the village had a holdfast as strong as any in the riverlands, with thick stone walls twelve feet high, and Jaime knew that was where he'd find the villagers. *They hid behind those walls when raiders came, that's why there's still a village here. And they are hiding there again, from me.*

He rode Honor up to the holdfast gates. "You in the holdfast. We mean you no harm. We're king's men."

Faces appeared on the wall above the gate. "They was king's men burned our village," one man called down. "Before that, some other king's men took our sheep. They were for a different king, but that didn't matter none to our sheep. King's men killed Harsley and Ser Ormond, and raped Lacey till she died."

"Not my men," Jaime said. "Will you open your gates?"

"When you're gone we will."

Ser Kennos rode close to him. "We could break that gate down easy enough, or put it to the torch."

"While they drop stones on us and feather us with arrows." Jaime shook his head. "It would be a bloody business, and for what? These people have done us no harm. We'll shelter in the houses, but I'll have no stealing. We have our own provisions."

As a half-moon crept up the sky, they staked their horses out in the village commons and supped on salted mutton, dried apples, and hard cheese. Jaime ate sparingly and shared a skin of wine with Peck and Hos the hostage. He tried to count the pennies nailed to the old oak, but there were too many of them and he kept losing count. *What's that all about?* The Blackwood boy would tell him if he asked, but that would spoil the mystery.

He posted sentries to see that no one left the confines of the village. He sent out scouts as well, to make certain no enemy took them unawares. It was near midnight when two came riding back with a woman they had taken captive. "She rode up bold as you please, m'lord, demanding words with you."

Jaime scrambled to his feet. "My lady. I had not thought to see you again so soon." *Gods be good, she looks ten years older than when I saw her last. And what's happened to her face?* "That bandage . . . you've been wounded . . ."

"A bite." She touched the hilt of her sword, the sword that he had given her. *Oathkeeper.* "My lord, you gave me a quest."

"The girl. Have you found her?"

"I have," said Brienne, Maid of Tarth.

"Where is she?"

"A day's ride. I can take you to her, ser . . . but you will need to come alone. Elsewise, the Hound will kill her."

JON

R'hllor," sang Melisandre, her arms upraised against the falling snow, "you are the light in our eyes, the fire in our hearts, the heat in our loins. Yours is the sun that warms our days, yours the stars that guard us in the dark of night."

"All praise R'hllor, the Lord of Light," the wedding guests answered in ragged chorus before a gust of ice-cold wind blew their words away. Jon Snow raised the hood of his cloak.

The snowfall was light today, a thin scattering of flakes dancing in the air, but the wind was blowing from the east along the Wall, cold as the breath of the ice dragon in the tales Old Nan used to tell. Even Melisandre's fire was shivering; the flames huddled down in the ditch, crackling softly as the red priestess sang. Only Ghost seemed not to feel the chill.

Alys Karstark leaned close to Jon. "Snow during a wedding means a cold marriage. My lady mother always said so."

He glanced at Queen Selyse. *There must have been a blizzard the day she and Stannis wed.* Huddled beneath her ermine mantle and surrounded by her ladies, serving girls, and knights, the southron queen seemed a frail, pale, shrunken thing. A strained smile was frozen into place on her thin lips, but her eyes brimmed with reverence. *She hates the cold but loves the flames.* He had only to look at her to see that. *A word from Melisandre, and she would walk into the fire willingly, embrace it like a lover.*

Not all her queen's men seemed to share her fervor. Ser Brus appeared half-drunk, Ser Malegorn's gloved hand was cupped round the arse of the lady beside him, Ser Narbert was yawning, and Ser Patrek of King's Mountain looked angry. Jon Snow had begun to understand why Stannis had left them with his queen.

"The night is dark and filled with terrors," Melisandre sang. "Alone we are born and alone we die, but as we walk through this black vale we draw strength from one another, and from you, our lord." Her scarlet silks and satins swirled with every gust of wind. "Two come forth today to join their lives, so they may face this world's darkness together. Fill their hearts with fire, my lord, so they may walk your shining path hand in hand forever."

"*Lord of Light, protect us,*" cried Queen Selyse. Other voices echoed the response. Melisandre's faithful: pallid ladies, shivering serving girls, Ser Axell and Ser Narbert and Ser Lambert, men-at-arms in iron mail and Thenns in bronze, even a few of Jon's black brothers. "*Lord of Light, bless your children.*"

Melisandre's back was to the Wall, on one side of the deep ditch where her fire burned. The couple to be joined faced her across the ditch. Behind them stood the queen, with her daughter and her tattooed fool. Princess Shireen was wrapped in so many furs that she looked round, breathing in white puffs through the scarf that covered most of her face. Ser Axell Florent and his queen's men surrounded the royal party.

Though only a few men of the Night's Watch had gathered about the ditchfire, more looked down from rooftops and windows and the steps of the great switchback stair. Jon took careful note of who was there and who was not. Some men had the duty; many just off watch were fast asleep. But others had chosen to absent themselves to show their disapproval. Othell Yarwyck and Bowen Marsh were amongst the missing. Septon Chayle had emerged briefly from the sept, fingering the seven-sided crystal on the thong about his neck, only to retreat inside again once the prayers began.

Melisandre raised her hands, and the ditchfire leapt upward toward her fingers, like a great red dog springing for a treat. A swirl of sparks rose to meet the snowflakes coming down. "Oh, Lord of Light, we thank you," she sang to the hungry flames. "We thank you for brave Stannis, by your grace our king. Guide him and defend him, R'hllor. Protect him from the treacheries of evil men and grant him strength to smite the servants of the dark."

"*Grant him strength,*" answered Queen Selyse and her knights and ladies. "*Grant him courage. Grant him wisdom.*"

Alys Karstark slipped her arm through Jon's. "How much longer, Lord Snow? If I'm to be buried beneath this snow, I'd like to die a woman wed."

"Soon, my lady," Jon assured her. "Soon."

"*We thank you for the sun that warms us,*" chanted the queen. "*We thank you for the stars that watch over us in the black of night. We thank you for our hearths and for our torches that keep the savage dark at bay. We thank you for our bright spirits, the fires in our loins and in our hearts."*

And Melisandre said, "Let them come forth, who would be joined." The flames cast her shadow on the Wall behind her, and her ruby gleamed against the paleness of her throat.

Jon turned to Alys Karstark. "My lady. Are you ready?"

"Yes. Oh, yes."

"You're not scared?"

The girl smiled in a way that reminded Jon so much of his little sister that it almost broke his heart. "Let him be scared of me." The snowflakes were melting on her cheeks, but her hair was wrapped in a swirl of lace that Satin had found somewhere, and the snow had begun to collect there, giving her a frosty crown. Her cheeks were flushed and red, and her eyes sparkled.

"Winter's lady." Jon squeezed her hand.

The Magnar of Thenn stood waiting by the fire, clad as if for battle, in fur and leather and bronze scales, a bronze sword at his hip. His receding hair made him look older than his years, but as he turned to watch his bride approach, Jon could see the boy in him. His eyes were big as walnuts, though whether it was the fire, the priestess, or the woman that had put the fear in him Jon could not say. *Alys was more right than she knew.*

"Who brings this woman to be wed?" asked Melisandre.

"I do," said Jon. "Now comes Alys of House Karstark, a woman grown and flowered, of noble blood and birth." He gave her hand one last squeeze and stepped back to join the others.

"Who comes forth to claim this woman?" asked Melisandre.

"Me." Sigorn slapped his chest. "Magnar of Thenn."

"Sigorn," asked Melisandre, "will you share your fire with Alys, and warm her when the night is dark and full of terrors?"

"I swear me." The Magnar's promise was a white cloud in the air. Snow dappled his shoulders. His ears were red. "By the red god's flames, I warm her all her days."

"Alys, do you swear to share your fire with Sigorn, and warm him when the night is dark and full of terrors?"

"Till his blood is boiling." Her maiden's cloak was the black wool of the Night's Watch. The Karstark sunburst sewn on its back was made of the same white fur that lined it.

Melisandre's eyes shone as bright as the ruby at her throat. "Then come to me and be as one." As she beckoned, a wall of flames roared upward,

licking at the snowflakes with hot orange tongues. Alys Karstark took her
Magnar by the hand.

Side by side they leapt the ditch.

"Two went into the flames." A gust of wind lifted the red woman's scarlet skirts till she pressed them down again. "One emerges." Her coppery
hair danced about her head. "What fire joins, none may put asunder."

"*What fire joins, none may put asunder,*" came the echo, from queen's
men and Thenns and even a few of the black brothers.

Except for kings and uncles, thought Jon Snow.

Cregan Karstark had turned up a day behind his niece. With him came
four mounted men-at-arms, a huntsman, and a pack of dogs, sniffing after
Lady Alys as if she were a deer. Jon Snow met them on the kingsroad half
a league south of Mole's Town, before they could turn up at Castle Black,
claim guest right, or call for parley. One of Karstark's men had loosed a
crossbow quarrel at Ty and died for it. That left four, and Cregan himself.

Fortunately they had a dozen ice cells. *Room for all.*

Like so much else, heraldry ended at the Wall. The Thenns had no
family arms as was customary amongst the nobles of the Seven Kingdoms,
so Jon told the stewards to improvise. He thought they had done well. The
bride's cloak Sigorn fastened about Lady Alys's shoulders showed a bronze
disk on a field of white wool, surrounded by flames made with wisps of
crimson silk. The echo of the Karstark sunburst was there for those who
cared to look, but differenced to make the arms appropriate for House
Thenn.

The Magnar all but ripped the maiden's cloak from Alys's shoulders,
but when he fastened her bride's cloak about her he was almost tender. As
he leaned down to kiss her cheek, their breath mingled. The flames roared
once again. The queen's men began to sing a song of praise. "Is it done?"
Jon heard Satin whisper.

"Done and done," muttered Mully, "and a good thing. They're wed
and I'm half-froze." He was muffled up in his best blacks, woolens so new
that they had hardly had a chance to fade yet, but the wind had turned his
cheeks as red as his hair. "Hobb's mulled some wine with cinnamon and
cloves. That'll warm us some."

"What's cloves?" asked Owen the Oaf.

The snow had started to descend more heavily and the fire in the ditch
was guttering out. The crowd began to break apart and stream from the
yard, queen's men, king's men, and free folk alike, all anxious to get out of
the wind and the cold. "Will my lord be feasting with us?" Mully asked
Jon Snow.

"Shortly." Sigorn might take it as a slight if he did not appear. *And this marriage is mine own work, after all.* "I have other matters to attend to first, however."

Jon crossed to Queen Selyse, with Ghost beside him. His boots crunched through piles of old snow. It was growing ever more time-consuming to shovel out the paths from one building to another; more and more, the men were resorting to the underground passages they called wormways.

". . . such a beautiful rite," the queen was saying. "I could feel our lord's fiery gaze upon us. Oh, you cannot know how many times I have begged Stannis to let us be wed again, a true joining of body and spirit blessed by the Lord of Light. I know that I could give His Grace more children if we were bound in fire."

To give him more children you would first need to get him into your bed. Even at the Wall, it was common knowledge that Stannis Baratheon had shunned his wife for years. One could only imagine how His Grace had responded to the notion of a second wedding in the midst of his war.

Jon bowed. "If it please Your Grace, the feast awaits."

The queen glanced at Ghost suspiciously, then raised her head to Jon. "To be sure. Lady Melisandre knows the way."

The red priestess spoke up. "I must attend my fires, Your Grace. Perhaps R'hllor will vouchsafe me a glimpse of His Grace. A glimpse of some great victory, mayhaps."

"Oh." Queen Selyse looked stricken. "To be sure . . . let us pray for a vision from our lord . . ."

"Satin, show Her Grace to her place," said Jon.

Ser Malegorn stepped forward. "I will escort Her Grace to the feast. We shall not require your . . . steward." The way the man drew out the last word told Jon that he had been considering saying something else. *Boy? Pet? Whore?*

Jon bowed again. "As you wish. I shall join you shortly."

Ser Malegorn offered his arm, and Queen Selyse took it stiffly. Her other hand settled on her daughter's shoulder. The royal ducklings fell in behind them as they made their way across the yard, marching to the music of the bells on the fool's hat. "Under the sea the mermen feast on starfish soup, and all the serving men are crabs," Patchface proclaimed as they went. "I know, I know, oh, oh, oh."

Melisandre's face darkened. "That creature is dangerous. Many a time I have glimpsed him in my flames. Sometimes there are skulls about him, and his lips are red with blood."

A wonder you haven't had the poor man burned. All it would take was a word in the queen's ear, and Patchface would feed her fires. "You see fools in your fire, but no hint of Stannis?"

"When I search for him all I see is snow."

The same useless answer. Clydas had dispatched a raven to Deepwood Motte to warn the king of Arnolf Karstark's treachery, but whether the bird had reached His Grace in time Jon did not know. The Braavosi banker was off in search of Stannis as well, accompanied by the guides that Jon had given him, but between the war and weather, it would be a wonder if he found him. "Would you know if the king was dead?" Jon asked the red priestess.

"He is not dead. Stannis is the Lord's chosen, destined to lead the fight against the dark. I have seen it in the flames, read of it in ancient prophecy. When the red star bleeds and the darkness gathers, Azor Ahai shall be born again amidst smoke and salt to wake dragons out of stone. Dragonstone is the place of smoke and salt."

Jon had heard all this before. "Stannis Baratheon was the Lord of Dragonstone, but he was not born there. He was born at Storm's End, like his brothers." He frowned. "And what of Mance? Is he lost as well? What do your fires show?"

"The same, I fear. Only snow."

Snow. It was snowing heavily to the south, Jon knew. Only two days' ride from here, the kingsroad was said to be impassable. *Melisandre knows that too.* And to the east, a savage storm was raging on the Bay of Seals. At last report, the ragtag fleet they had assembled to rescue the free folk from Hardhome still huddled at Eastwatch-by-the-Sea, confined to port by the rough seas. "You are seeing cinders dancing in the updraft."

"I am seeing skulls. And you. I see your face every time I look into the flames. The danger that I warned you of grows very close now."

"Daggers in the dark. I know. You will forgive my doubts, my lady. A *grey girl on a dying horse, fleeing from a marriage,* that was what you said."

"I was not wrong."

"You were not right. Alys is not Arya."

"The vision was a true one. It was my reading that was false. I am as mortal as you, Jon Snow. All mortals err."

"Even lord commanders." Mance Rayder and his spearwives had not returned, and Jon could not help but wonder whether the red woman had lied of a purpose. *Is she playing her own game?*

"You would do well to keep your wolf beside you, my lord."

"Ghost is seldom far." The direwolf raised his head at the sound of his name. Jon scratched him behind the ears. "But now you must excuse me. Ghost, with me."

Carved from the base of the Wall and closed with heavy wooden doors, the ice cells ranged from small to smaller. Some were big enough to allow a man to pace, others so small that prisoners were forced to sit; the smallest were too cramped to allow even that.

Jon had given his chief captive the largest cell, a pail to shit in, enough furs to keep him from freezing, and a skin of wine. It took the guards some time to open his cell, as ice had formed inside the lock. Rusted hinges screamed like damned souls when Wick Whittlestick yanked the door wide enough for Jon to slip through. A faint fecal odor greeted him, though less overpowering than he'd expected. Even shit froze solid in such bitter cold. Jon Snow could see his own reflection dimly inside the icy walls.

In one corner of the cell a heap of furs was piled up almost to the height of a man. "Karstark," said Jon Snow. "Wake up."

The furs stirred. Some had frozen together, and the frost that covered them glittered when they moved. An arm emerged, then a face—brown hair, tangled and matted and streaked with grey, two fierce eyes, a nose, a mouth, a beard. Ice caked the prisoner's mustache, clumps of frozen snot. "Snow." His breath steamed in the air, fogging the ice behind his head. "You have no right to hold me. The laws of hospitality—"

"You are no guest of mine. You came to the Wall without my leave, armed, to carry off your niece against her will. Lady Alys was given bread and salt. She is a guest. You are a prisoner." Jon let that hang for a moment, then said, "Your niece is wed."

Cregan Karstark's lips skinned back from his teeth. "Alys was promised to me." Though past fifty, he had been a strong man when he went into the cell. The cold had robbed him of that strength and left him stiff and weak. "My lord father—"

"Your father is a castellan, not a lord. And a castellan has no right to make marriage pacts."

"My father, Arnolf, is Lord of Karhold."

"A son comes before an uncle by all the laws I know."

Cregan pushed himself to his feet and kicked aside the furs clinging to his ankles. "Harrion is dead."

Or will be soon. "A daughter comes before an uncle too. If her brother is dead, Karhold belongs to Lady Alys. And she has given her hand in marriage to Sigorn, Magnar of Thenn."

"A wildling. A filthy, murdering wildling." Cregan's hands closed into fists. The gloves that covered them were leather, lined with fur to match the cloak that hung matted and stiff from his broad shoulders. His black wool surcoat was emblazoned with the white sunburst of his house. "I see what you are, Snow. Half a wolf and half a wildling, baseborn get of a traitor and a whore. You would deliver a highborn maid to the bed of some stinking savage. Did you sample her yourself first?" He laughed. "If you mean to kill me, do it and be damned for a kinslayer. Stark and Karstark are one blood."

"My name is Snow."

"*Bastard.*"

"Guilty. Of that, at least."

"Let this Magnar come to Karhold. We'll hack off his head and stuff it in a privy, so we can piss into his mouth."

"Sigorn leads two hundred Thenns," Jon pointed out, "and Lady Alys believes Karhold will open its gates to her. Two of your men have already sworn her their service and confirmed all she had to say concerning the plans your father made with Ramsay Snow. You have close kin at Karhold, I am told. A word from you could save their lives. Yield the castle. Lady Alys will pardon the women who betrayed her and allow the men to take the black."

Cregan shook his head. Chunks of ice had formed about the tangles in his hair, and *click*ed together softly when he moved. "Never," he said. "Never, never, never."

I should make his head a wedding gift for Lady Alys and her Magnar, Jon thought, but dare not take the risk. The Night's Watch took no part in the quarrels of the realm; some would say he had already given Stannis too much help. *Behead this fool, and they will claim I am killing northmen to give their lands to wildlings. Release him, and he will do his best to rip apart all I've done with Lady Alys and the Magnar.* Jon wondered what his father would do, how his uncle might deal with this. But Eddard Stark was dead, Benjen Stark lost in the frozen wilds beyond the Wall. *You know nothing, Jon Snow.*

"Never is a long time," Jon said. "You may feel differently on the morrow, or a year from now. Soon or late King Stannis will return to the Wall, however. When he does he will have you put to death . . . unless it happens that you are wearing a black cloak. When a man takes the black, his crimes are wiped away." *Even such a man as you.* "Now pray excuse me. I have a feast to attend."

After the biting cold of the ice cells, the crowded cellar was so hot that Jon felt suffocated from the moment he came down the steps. The air smelled of smoke and roasting meat and mulled wine. Axell Florent was making a toast as Jon took his place upon the dais. "To King Stannis and his wife, Queen Selyse, Light of the North!" Ser Axell bellowed. "To R'hllor, the Lord of Light, may he defend us all! One land, one god, one king!"

"*One land, one god, one king!*" the queen's men echoed.

Jon drank with the rest. Whether Alys Karstark would find any joy in her marriage he could not say, but this one night at least should be one of celebration.

The stewards began to bring out the first dish, an onion broth flavored with bits of goat and carrot. Not precisely royal fare, but nourishing; it tasted good enough and warmed the belly. Owen the Oaf took up his fiddle, and several of the free folk joined in with pipes and drums. *The same pipes and drums they played to sound Mance Rayder's attack upon the Wall.* Jon thought they sounded sweeter now. With the broth came loaves of coarse brown bread, warm from the oven. Salt and butter sat upon the tables. The sight made Jon gloomy. They were well provided with salt, Bowen Marsh had told him, but the last of the butter would be gone within a moon's turn.

Old Flint and The Norrey had been given places of high honor just below the dais. Both men had been too old to march with Stannis; they had sent their sons and grandsons in their stead. But they had been quick enough to descend on Castle Black for the wedding. Each had brought a wet nurse to the Wall as well. The Norrey woman was forty, with the biggest breasts Jon Snow had ever seen. The Flint girl was fourteen and flat-chested as a boy, though she did not lack for milk. Between the two of them, the child Val called Monster seemed to be thriving.

For that much Jon was grateful . . . but he did not believe for a moment that two such hoary old warriors would have hied down from their hills for that alone. Each had brought a tail of fighting men—five for Old Flint, twelve for The Norrey, all clad in ragged skins and studded leathers, fearsome as the face of winter. Some had long beards, some had scars, some had both; all worshiped the old gods of the north, those same gods worshiped by the free folk beyond the Wall. Yet here they sat, drinking to a marriage hallowed by some queer red god from beyond the seas.

Better that than refuse to drink. Neither Flint nor Norrey had turned their cups over to spill their wine upon the floor. That might betoken a certain acceptance. *Or perhaps they just hate to waste good southron wine. They will not have tasted much of it up in those stony hills of theirs.*

Between courses, Ser Axell Florent led Queen Selyse out onto the floor to dance. Others followed—the queen's knights first, partnered with her ladies. Ser Brus gave Princess Shireen her first dance, then took a turn with her mother. Ser Narbert danced with each of Selyse's lady companions in turn.

The queen's men outnumbered the queen's ladies three to one, so even the humblest serving girls were pressed into the dance. After a few songs some black brothers remembered skills learned at the courts and castles of their youth, before their sins had sent them to the Wall, and took the floor as well. That old rogue Ulmer of the Kingswood proved as adept at dancing as he was at archery, no doubt regaling his partners with his tales of the Kingswood Brotherhood, when he rode with Simon Toyne and Big Belly Ben and helped Wenda the White Fawn burn her mark in the buttocks of her highborn captives. Satin was all grace, dancing with three serving girls in turn but never presuming to approach a highborn lady. Jon judged that wise. He did not like the way some of the queen's knights were looking at the steward, particularly Ser Patrek of King's Mountain. *That one wants to shed a bit of blood,* he thought. *He is looking for some provocation.*

When Owen the Oaf began to dance with Patchface the fool, laughter echoed off the vaulted ceiling. The sight made Lady Alys smile. "Do you dance often, here at Castle Black?"

"Every time we have a wedding, my lady."

"You could dance with me, you know. It would be only courteous. You danced with me anon."

"Anon?" teased Jon.

"When we were children." She tore off a bit of bread and threw it at him. "As you know well."

"My lady should dance with her husband."

"My Magnar is not one for dancing, I fear. If you will not dance with me, at least pour me some of the mulled wine."

"As you command." He signaled for a flagon.

"So," said Alys, as Jon poured, "I am now a woman wed. A wildling husband with his own little wildling army."

"Free folk is what they call themselves. Most, at least. The Thenns are a people apart, though. Very old." Ygritte had told him that. *You know nothing, Jon Snow.* "They come from a hidden vale at the north end of the Frostfangs, surrounded by high peaks, and for thousands of years they've had more truck with the giants than with other men. It made them different."

"Different," she said, "but more like us."

"Aye, my lady. The Thenns have lords and laws." *They know how to kneel.* "They mine tin and copper for bronze, forge their own arms and armor instead of stealing it. A proud folk, and brave. Mance Rayder had to best the old Magnar thrice before Styr would accept him as King-Beyond-the-Wall."

"And now they are here, on our side of the Wall. Driven from their mountain fastness and into my bedchamber." She smiled a wry smile. "It is my own fault. My lord father told me I must charm your brother Robb, but I was only six and didn't know how."

Aye, but now you're almost six-and-ten, and we must pray you will know how to charm your new husband. "My lady, how do things stand at Karhold with your food stores?"

"Not well." Alys sighed. "My father took so many of our men south with him that only the women and young boys were left to bring the harvest in. Them, and the men too old or crippled to go off to war. Crops withered in the fields or were pounded into the mud by autumn rains. And now the snows are come. This winter will be hard. Few of the old people will survive it, and many children will perish as well."

It was a tale that any northmen knew well. "My father's grandmother was a Flint of the mountains, on his mother's side," Jon told her. "The First Flints, they call themselves. They say the other Flints are the blood of younger sons, who had to leave the mountains to find food and land and wives. It has always been a harsh life up there. When the snows fall and food grows scarce, their young must travel to the winter town or take service at one castle or the other. The old men gather up what strength remains in them and announce that they are going hunting. Some are found come spring. More are never seen again."

"It is much the same at Karhold."

That did not surprise him. "When your stores begin to dwindle, my lady, remember us. Send your old men to the Wall, let them say our words. Here at least they will not die alone in the snow, with only memories to warm them. Send us boys as well, if you have boys to spare."

"As you say." She touched his hand. "Karhold remembers."

The elk was being carved. It smelled better than Jon had any reason to expect. He dispatched a portion to Leathers out at Hardin's Tower, along with three big platters of roast vegetables for Wun Wun, then ate a healthy slice himself. *Three-Finger Hobb's acquitted himself well.* That had been a concern. Hobb had come to him two nights ago complaining that he'd joined the Night's Watch to kill wildlings, not to cook for them. "Besides, I never done no wedding feast, m'lord. Black brothers don't never take no wifes. It's in the bloody vows, I swear 'tis."

Jon was washing the roast down with a sip of mulled wine when Clydas appeared at his elbow. "A bird," he announced, and slipped a parchment into Jon's hand. The note was sealed with a dot of hard black wax. *Eastwatch,* Jon knew, even before he broke the seal. The letter had been written by Maester Harmune; Cotter Pyke could neither read nor write. But the words were Pyke's, set down as he had spoken them, blunt and to the point.

> *Calm seas today. Eleven ships set sail for Hardhome on the morning tide. Three Braavosi, four Lyseni, four of ours. Two of the Lyseni barely seaworthy. We may drown more wildlings than we save. Your command. Twenty ravens aboard, and Maester Harmune. Will send reports. I command from* Talon, *Tattersalt second on* Blackbird, *Ser Glendon holds Eastwatch.*

"Dark wings, dark words?" asked Alys Karstark.

"No, my lady. This news was long awaited." *Though the last part troubles me.* Glendon Hewett was a seasoned man and a strong one, a sensible choice to command in Cotter Pyke's absence. But he was also as much a friend as Alliser Thorne could boast, and a crony of sorts with Janos Slynt, however briefly. Jon could still recall how Hewett had dragged him from his bed, and the feel of his boot slamming into his ribs. *Not the man I would have chosen.* He rolled the parchment up and slipped it into his belt.

The fish course was next, but as the pike was being boned Lady Alys dragged the Magnar up onto the floor. From the way he moved it was plain that Sigorn had never danced before, but he had drunk enough mulled wine so that it did not seem to matter.

"A northern maid and a wildling warrior, bound together by the Lord of Light." Ser Axell Florent slipped into Lady Alys's vacant seat. "Her Grace approves. I am close to her, my lord, so I know her mind. King Stannis will approve as well."

Unless Roose Bolton has stuck his head on a spear.

"Not all agree, alas." Ser Axell's beard was a ragged brush beneath his sagging chin; coarse hair sprouted from his ears and nostrils. "Ser Patrek feels he would have made a better match for Lady Alys. His lands were lost to him when he came north."

"There are many in this hall who have lost far more than that," said Jon, "and more who have given up their lives in service to the realm. Ser Patrek should count himself fortunate."

Axell Florent smiled. "The king might say the same if he were here. Yet some provision must be made for His Grace's leal knights, surely? They have followed him so far and at such cost. And we must needs bind these wildlings to king and realm. This marriage is a good first step, but I know that it would please the queen to see the wildling princess wed as well."

Jon sighed. He was weary of explaining that Val was no true princess. No matter how often he told them, they never seemed to hear. "You are persistent, Ser Axell, I grant you that."

"Do you blame me, my lord? Such a prize is not easily won. A nubile girl, I hear, and not hard to look upon. Good hips, good breasts, well made for whelping children."

"Who would father these children? Ser Patrek? You?"

"Who better? We Florents have the blood of the old Gardener kings in our veins. Lady Melisandre could perform the rites, as she did for Lady Alys and the Magnar."

"All you are lacking is a bride."

"Easily remedied." Florent's smile was so false that it looked painful. "Where is she, Lord Snow? Have you moved her to one of your other castles? Greyguard or the Shadow Tower? Whore's Burrow, with t'other wenches?" He leaned close. "Some say you have her tucked away for your own pleasure. It makes no matter to me, so long as she is not with child. I'll get my own sons on her. If you've broken her to saddle, well . . . we are both men of the world, are we not?"

Jon had heard enough. "Ser Axell, if you are truly the Queen's Hand, I pity Her Grace."

Florent's face grew flushed with anger. "So it *is* true. You mean to keep her for yourself, I see it now. The bastard wants his father's seat."

The bastard refused his father's seat. If the bastard had wanted Val, all he had to do was ask for her. "You must excuse me, ser," he said. "I need a breath of fresh air." *It stinks in here.* His head turned. "That was a horn."

Others had heard it too. The music and the laughter died at once. Dancers froze in place, listening. Even Ghost pricked up his ears. "Did you hear that?" Queen Selyse asked her knights.

"A warhorn, Your Grace," said Ser Narbert.

The queen's hand went fluttering to her throat. "Are we under attack?"

"No, Your Grace," said Ulmer of the Kingswood. "It's the watchers on the Wall, is all."

One blast, thought Jon Snow. *Rangers returning.*

Then it came again. The sound seemed to fill the cellar.

"Two blasts," said Mully.

Black brothers, northmen, free folk, Thenns, queen's men, all of them fell quiet, listening. Five heartbeats passed. Ten. Twenty. Then Owen the Oaf tittered, and Jon Snow could breathe again. "Two blasts," he announced. "Wildlings." *Val.*

Tormund Giantsbane had come at last.

DAENERYS

The hall rang to Yunkish laughter, Yunkish songs, Yunkish prayers. Dancers danced; musicians played queer tunes with bells and squeaks and bladders; singers sang ancient love songs in the incomprehensible tongue of Old Ghis. Wine flowed—not the thin pale stuff of Slaver's Bay but rich sweet vintages from the Arbor and dreamwine from Qarth, flavored with strange spices. The Yunkai'i had come at King Hizdahr's invitation, to sign the peace and witness the rebirth of Meereen's far-famed fighting pits. Her noble husband had opened the Great Pyramid to fete them.

I hate this, thought Daenerys Targaryen. *How did this happen, that I am drinking and smiling with men I'd sooner flay?*

A dozen different sorts of meat and fish were served: camel, crocodile, singing squid, lacquered ducks and spiny grubs, with goat and ham and horse for those whose tastes were less exotic. Plus dog. No Ghiscari feast was complete without a course of dog. Hizdahr's cooks prepared dog four different ways. "Ghiscari will eat anything that swims or flies or crawls, but for man and dragon," Daario had warned her, "and I'd wager they'd eat dragon too if given half a chance." Meat alone does not make a meal, though, so there were fruits and grains and vegetables as well. The air was redolent with the scents of saffron, cinnamon, cloves, pepper, and other costly spices.

Dany scarce touched a bite. *This is peace,* she told herself. *This is what I wanted, what I worked for, this is why I married Hizdahr. So why does it taste so much like defeat?*

"It is only for a little while more, my love," Hizdahr had assured her. "The Yunkai'i will soon be gone, and their allies and hirelings with them. We shall have all we desired. Peace, food, trade. Our port is open once again, and ships are being permitted to come and go."

"They are *permitting* that, yes," she had replied, "but their warships remain. They can close their fingers around our throat again whenever they wish. *They have opened a slave market within sight of my walls!*"

"*Outside* our walls, sweet queen. That was a condition of the peace, that Yunkai would be free to trade in slaves as before, unmolested."

"In their own city. Not where I have to see it." The Wise Masters had established their slave pens and auction block just south of the Skahaza-dhan, where the wide brown river flowed into Slaver's Bay. "They are mocking me to my face, making a show of how powerless I am to stop them."

"Posing and posturing," said her noble husband. "A show, as you have said. Let them have their mummery. When they are gone, we will make a fruit market of what they leave behind."

"When they are gone," Dany repeated. "And when will they be gone? Riders have been seen beyond the Skahazadhan. Dothraki scouts, Rak-haro says, with a *khalasar* behind them. They will have captives. Men, women, and children, gifts for the slavers." Dothraki did not buy or sell, but they gave gifts and received them. "That is why the Yunkai'i have thrown up this market. They will leave here with thousands of new slaves."

Hizdahr zo Loraq shrugged. "But they will leave. That is the important part, my love. Yunkai will trade in slaves, Meereen will not, this is what we have agreed. Endure this for a little while longer, and it shall pass."

So Daenerys sat silent through the meal, wrapped in a vermilion *tokar* and black thoughts, speaking only when spoken to, brooding on the men and women being bought and sold outside her walls, even as they feasted here within the city. Let her noble husband make the speeches and laugh at the feeble Yunkish japes. That was a king's right and a king's duty.

Much of the talk about the table was of the matches to be fought upon the morrow. Barsena Blackhair was going to face a boar, his tusks against her dagger. Khrazz was fighting, as was the Spotted Cat. And in the day's final pairing, Goghor the Giant would go against Belaquo Bonebreaker. One would be dead before the sun went down. *No queen has clean hands*, Dany told herself. She thought of Doreah, of Quaro, of Eroeh . . . of a little girl she had never met, whose name had been Hazzea. *Better a few should die in the pit than thousands at the gates. This is the price of peace, I pay it willingly. If I look back, I am lost.*

The Yunkish Supreme Commander, Yurkhaz zo Yunzak, might have been alive during Aegon's Conquest, to judge by his appearance. Bent-backed, wrinkled, and toothless, he was carried to the table by two strapping slaves. The other Yunkish lords were hardly more impressive. One was small and stunted, though the slave soldiers who attended him were grotesquely tall and thin. The third was young, fit, and dashing, but so drunk that Dany could scarce understand a word he said. *How could I have been brought to this pass by creatures such as these?*

The sellswords were a different matter. Each of the four free companies serving Yunkai had sent its commander. The Windblown were represented by the Pentoshi nobleman known as the Tattered Prince, the Long Lances by Gylo Rhegan, who looked more shoemaker than soldier and spoke in murmurs. Bloodbeard, from the Company of the Cat, made enough noise for him and a dozen more. A huge man with a great bush of beard and a prodigious appetite for wine and women, he bellowed, belched, farted like a thunderclap, and pinched every serving girl who came within his reach. From time to time he would pull one down into his lap to squeeze her breasts and fondle her between the legs.

The Second Sons were represented too. *If Daario were here, this meal would end in blood.* No promised peace could ever have persuaded her captain to permit Brown Ben Plumm to stroll back into Meereen and leave alive. Dany had sworn that no harm would come to the seven envoys and commanders, though that had not been enough for the Yunkai'i. They had required hostages of her as well. To balance the three Yunkish nobles and four sellsword captains, Meereen sent seven of its own out to the siege camp: Hizdahr's sister, two of his cousins, Dany's bloodrider Jhogo, her admiral Groleo, the Unsullied captain Hero, and Daario Naharis.

"I will leave my girls with you," her captain had said, handing her his sword belt and its gilded wantons. "Keep them safe for me, beloved. We would not want them making bloody mischief amongst the Yunkai'i."

The Shavepate was absent as well. The first thing Hizdahr had done upon being crowned was to remove him from command of the Brazen Beasts, replacing him with his own cousin, the plump and pasty Marghaz zo Loraq. *It is for the best. The Green Grace says there is blood between Loraq and Kandaq, and the Shavepate never made a secret of his disdain for my lord husband. And Daario . . .*

Daario had only grown wilder since her wedding. Her peace did not please him, her marriage pleased him less, and he had been furious at being deceived by the Dornishmen. When Prince Quentyn told them that the other Westerosi had come over to the Stormcrows at the command of the Tattered Prince, only the intercession of Grey Worm and his

Unsullied prevented Daario from killing them all. The false deserters had been imprisoned safely in the bowels of the pyramid . . . but Daario's rage continued to fester.

He will be safer as a hostage. My captain was not made for peace. Dany could not risk his cutting down Brown Ben Plumm, making mock of Hizdahr before the court, provoking the Yunkai'i, or otherwise upsetting the agreement that she had given up so much to win. Daario was war and woe. Henceforth, she must keep him out of her bed, out of her heart, and out of her. If he did not betray her, he would master her. She did not know which of those she feared the most.

When the gluttony was done and all the half-eaten food had been cleared away—to be given to the poor who gathered below, at the queen's insistence—tall glass flutes were filled with a spiced liqueur from Qarth as dark as amber. Then began the entertainments.

A troupe of Yunkish castrati owned by Yurkhaz zo Yunzak sang them songs in the ancient tongue of the Old Empire, their voices high and sweet and impossibly pure. "Have you ever heard such singing, my love?" Hizdahr asked her. "They have the voices of gods, do they not?"

"Yes," she said, "though I wonder if they might not have preferred to have the fruits of men."

All of the entertainers were slaves. That had been part of the peace, that slaveowners be allowed the right to bring their chattels into Meereen without fear of having them freed. In return the Yunkai'i had promised to respect the rights and liberties of the former slaves that Dany had freed. A fair bargain, Hizdahr said, but the taste it left in the queen's mouth was foul. She drank another cup of wine to wash it out.

"If it please you, Yurkhaz will be pleased to give us the singers, I do not doubt," her noble husband said. "A gift to seal our peace, an ornament to our court."

He will give us these castrati, Dany thought, *and then he will march home and make some more. The world is full of boys.*

The tumblers who came next failed to move her either, even when they formed a human pyramid nine levels high, with a naked little girl on top. *Is that meant to represent my pyramid?* the queen wondered. *Is the girl on top meant to be me?*

Afterward her lord husband led his guests onto the lower terrace, so the visitors from the Yellow City might behold Meereen by night. Wine cups in hand, the Yunkai'i wandered the garden in small groups, beneath lemon trees and night-blooming flowers, and Dany found herself face-to-face with Brown Ben Plumm.

He bowed low. "Worship. You look lovely. Well, you always did. None of them Yunkishmen are half so pretty. I thought I might bring a wedding gift for you, but the bidding went too high for old Brown Ben."

"I want no gifts from you."

"This one you might. The head of an old foe."

"Your own?" she said sweetly. "You betrayed me."

"Now that's a harsh way o' putting it, if you don't mind me saying." Brown Ben scratched at his speckled grey-and-white whiskers. "We went over to the winning side, is all. Same as we done before. It weren't all me, neither. I put it to my men."

"So *they* betrayed me, is that what you are saying? Why? Did I mistreat the Second Sons? Did I cheat you on your pay?"

"Never that," said Brown Ben, "but it's not all about the coin, Your High-and-Mightiness. I learned that a long time back, at my first battle. Morning after the fight, I was rooting through the dead, looking for the odd bit o' plunder, as it were. Came upon this one corpse, some axeman had taken his whole arm off at the shoulder. He was covered with flies, all crusty with dried blood, might be why no one else had touched him, but under them he wore this studded jerkin, looked to be good leather. I figured it might fit me well enough, so I chased away the flies and cut it off him. The damn thing was heavier than it had any right to be, though. Under the lining, he'd sewn a fortune in coin. *Gold*, Your Worship, sweet yellow gold. Enough for any man to live like a lord for the rest o' his days. But what good did it do him? There he was with all his coin, lying in the blood and mud with his fucking arm cut off. And that's the lesson, see? Silver's sweet and gold's our mother, but once you're dead they're worth less than that last shit you take as you lie dying. I told you once, there are old sellswords and there are bold sellswords, but there are no old bold sellswords. My boys didn't care to die, that's all, and when I told them that you couldn't unleash them dragons against the Yunkishmen, well . . ."

You saw me as defeated, Dany thought, *and who am I to say that you were wrong?* "I understand." She might have ended it there, but she was curious. "Enough gold to live like a lord, you said. What did you do with all that wealth?"

Brown Ben laughed. "Fool boy that I was, I told a man I took to be my friend, and he told our serjeant, and my brothers-in-arms come and relieved me o' that burden. Serjeant said I was too young, that I'd only waste it all on whores and such. He let me keep the jerkin, though." He spat. "You don't never want to trust a sellsword, m'lady."

"I have learned that much. One day I must be sure to thank you for the lesson."

Brown Ben's eyes crinkled up. "No need. I know the sort o' thanks you have in mind." He bowed again and moved away.

Dany turned to gaze out over her city. Beyond her walls the yellow tents of the Yunkai'i stood in orderly rows beside the sea, protected by the ditches their slaves had dug for them. Two iron legions out of New Ghis, trained and armed in the same fashion as Unsullied, were encamped across the river to the north. Two more Ghiscari legions had made camp to the east, choking off the road to the Khyzai Pass. The horse lines and cookfires of the free companies lay to the south. By day thin plumes of smoke hung against the sky like ragged grey ribbons. By night distant fires could be seen. Hard by the bay was the abomination, the slave market at her door. She could not see it now, with the sun set, but she knew that it was there. That just made her angrier.

"Ser Barristan?" she said softly.

The white knight appeared at once. "Your Grace."

"How much did you hear?"

"Enough. He was not wrong. Never trust a sellsword."

Or a queen, thought Dany. "Is there some man in the Second Sons who might be persuaded to . . . remove . . . Brown Ben?"

"As Daario Naharis once removed the other captains of the Storm-crows?" The old knight looked uncomfortable. "Perhaps. I would not know, Your Grace."

No, she thought, *you are too honest and too honorable.* "If not, the Yunkai'i employ three other companies."

"Rogues and cutthroats, scum of a hundred battlefields," Ser Barristan warned, "with captains full as treacherous as Plumm."

"I am only a young girl and know little of such things, but it seems to me that we *want* them to be treacherous. Once, you'll recall, I convinced the Second Sons and Stormcrows to join us."

"If Your Grace wishes a privy word with Gylo Rhegan or the Tattered Prince, I could bring them up to your apartments."

"This is not the time. Too many eyes, too many ears. Their absence would be noted even if you could separate them discreetly from the Yunkai'i. We must find some quieter way of reaching out to them . . . not tonight, but soon."

"As you command. Though I fear this is not a task for which I am well suited. In King's Landing work of this sort was left to Lord Littlefinger or the Spider. We old knights are simple men, only good for fighting." He patted his sword hilt.

"Our prisoners," suggested Dany. "The Westerosi who came over from the Windblown with the three Dornishmen. We still have them in cells, do we not? Use them."

"Free them, you mean? Is that wise? They were sent here to worm their way into your trust, so they might betray Your Grace at the first chance."

"Then they failed. I do not trust them. I will never trust them." If truth be told, Dany was forgetting how to trust. "We can still use them. One was a woman. Meris. Send her back, as a . . . a gesture of my regard. If their captain is a clever man, he will understand."

"The woman is the worst of all."

"All the better." Dany considered a moment. "We should sound out the Long Lances too. And the Company of the Cat."

"Bloodbeard." Ser Barristan's frown deepened. "If it please Your Grace, we want no part of him. Your Grace is too young to remember the Ninepenny Kings, but this Bloodbeard is cut from the same savage cloth. There is no honor in him, only hunger . . . for gold, for glory, for blood."

"You know more of such men than me, ser." If Bloodbeard might be truly the most dishonorable and greedy of the sellswords, he might be the easiest to sway, but she was loath to go against Ser Barristan's counsel in such matters. "Do as you think best. But do it soon. If Hizdahr's peace should break, I want to be ready. I do not trust the slavers." *I do not trust my husband.* "They will turn on us at the first sign of weakness."

"The Yunkai'i grow weaker as well. The bloody flux has taken hold amongst the Tolosi, it is said, and spread across the river to the third Ghiscari legion."

The pale mare. Daenerys sighed. *Quaithe warned me of the pale mare's coming. She told me of the Dornish prince as well, the sun's son. She told me much and more, but all in riddles.* "I cannot rely on plague to save me from my enemies. Set Pretty Meris free. At once."

"As you command. Though . . . Your Grace, if I may be so bold, there is another road . . ."

"The Dornish road?" Dany sighed. The three Dornishmen had been at the feast, as befit Prince Quentyn's rank, though Reznak had taken care to seat them as far as possible from her husband. Hizdahr did not seem to be of a jealous nature, but no man would be pleased by the presence of a rival suitor near his new bride. "The boy seems pleasant and well spoken, but . . ."

"House Martell is ancient and noble, and has been a leal friend to House Targaryen for more than a century, Your Grace. I had the honor of serving with Prince Quentyn's great-uncle in your father's seven. Prince Lewyn was as valiant a brother-in-arms as any man could wish for. Quentyn Martell is of the same blood, if it please Your Grace."

"It would please me if he had turned up with these fifty thousand swords he speaks of. Instead he brings two knights and a parchment. Will a parchment shield my people from the Yunkai'i? If he had come with a fleet . . ."

"Sunspear has never been a sea power, Your Grace."

"No." Dany knew enough of Westerosi history to know that. Nymeria had landed ten thousand ships upon Dorne's sandy shores, but when she wed her Dornish prince she had burned them all and turned her back upon the sea forever. "Dorne is too far away. To please this prince, I would need to abandon all my people. You should send him home."

"Dornishmen are notoriously stubborn, Your Grace. Prince Quentyn's forebears fought your own for the better part of two hundred years. He will not go without you."

Then he will die here, Daenerys thought, *unless there is more to him than I can see.* "Is he still within?"

"Drinking with his knights."

"Bring him to me. It is time he met my children."

A flicker of doubt passed across the long, solemn face of Barristan Selmy. "As you command."

Her king was laughing with Yurkhaz zo Yunzak and the other Yunkish lords. Dany did not think that he would miss her, but just in case she instructed her handmaids to tell him that she was answering a call of nature, should he inquire after her.

Ser Barristan was waiting by the steps with the Dornish prince. Martell's square face was flushed and ruddy. *Too much wine,* the queen concluded, though he was doing his best to conceal that. Apart from the line of copper suns that ornamented his belt, the Dornishman was plainly dressed. *They call him Frog,* Dany recalled. She could see why. He was not a handsome man.

She smiled. "My prince. It is a long way down. Are you certain that you wish to do this?"

"If it would please Your Grace."

"Then come."

A pair of Unsullied went down the steps before them, bearing torches; behind came two Brazen Beasts, one masked as a fish, the other as a hawk.

Even here in her own pyramid, on this happy night of peace and celebration, Ser Barristan insisted on keeping guards about her everywhere she went. The small company made the long descent in silence, stopping thrice to refresh themselves along the way. "The dragon has three heads," Dany said when they were on the final flight. "My marriage need not be the end of all your hopes. I know why you are here."

"For you," said Quentyn, all awkward gallantry.

"No," said Dany. "For fire and blood."

One of the elephants trumpeted at them from his stall. An answering roar from below made her flush with sudden heat. Prince Quentyn looked up in alarm. "The dragons know when she is near," Ser Barristan told him.

Every child knows its mother, Dany thought. *When the seas go dry and mountains blow in the wind like leaves* . . . "They call to me. Come." She took Prince Quentyn by the hand and led him to the pit where two of her dragons were confined. "Remain outside," Dany told Ser Barristan, as the Unsullied were opening the huge iron doors. "Prince Quentyn will protect me." She drew the Dornish prince inside with her, to stand above the pit.

The dragons craned their necks around, gazing at them with burning eyes. Viserion had shattered one chain and melted the others. He clung to the roof of the pit like some huge white bat, his claws dug deep into the burnt and crumbling bricks. Rhaegal, still chained, was gnawing on the carcass of a bull. The bones on the floor of the pit were deeper than the last time she had been down here, and the walls and floors were black and grey, more ash than brick. They would not hold much longer . . . but behind them was only earth and stone. *Can dragons tunnel through rock, like the firewyrms of old Valyria?* She hoped not.

The Dornish prince had gone as white as milk. "I . . . I had heard that there were three."

"Drogon is hunting." He did not need to hear the rest. "The white one is Viserion, the green is Rhaegal. I named them for my brothers." Her voice echoed off the scorched stone walls. It sounded small—a girl's voice, not the voice of a queen and conqueror, nor the glad voice of a new-made bride.

Rhaegal roared in answer, and fire filled the pit, a spear of red and yellow. Viserion replied, his own flames gold and orange. When he flapped his wings, a cloud of grey ash filled the air. Broken chains clanked and clattered about his legs. Quentyn Martell jumped back a foot.

A crueler woman might have laughed at him, but Dany squeezed his hand and said, "They frighten me as well. There is no shame in that. My children have grown wild and angry in the dark."

"You . . . you mean to ride them?"

"One of them. All I know of dragons is what my brother told me when I was a girl, and some I read in books, but it is said that even Aegon the Conqueror never dared mount Vhagar or Meraxes, nor did his sisters ride Balerion the Black Dread. Dragons live longer than men, some for hundreds of years, so Balerion had other riders after Aegon died . . . but no rider ever flew two dragons."

Viserion hissed again. Smoke rose between his teeth, and deep down in his throat they could see gold fire churning.

"They are . . . they are fearsome creatures."

"They are *dragons*, Quentyn." Dany stood on her toes and kissed him lightly, once on each cheek. "And so am I."

The young prince swallowed. "I . . . I have the blood of the dragon in me as well, Your Grace. I can trace my lineage back to the first Daenerys, the Targaryen princess who was sister to King Daeron the Good and wife to the Prince of Dorne. He built the Water Gardens for her."

"The Water Gardens?" She knew little and less of Dorne or its history, if truth be told.

"My father's favorite palace. It would please me to show them to you one day. They are all of pink marble, with pools and fountains, overlooking the sea."

"They sound lovely." She drew him away from the pit. *He does not belong here. He should never have come.* "You ought to return there. My court is no safe place for you, I fear. You have more enemies than you know. You made Daario look a fool, and he is not a man to forget such a slight."

"I have my knights. My sworn shields."

"Two knights. Daario has five hundred Stormcrows. And you would do well to beware of my lord husband too. He seems a mild and pleasant man, I know, but do not be deceived. Hizdahr's crown derives from mine, and he commands the allegiance of some of the most fearsome fighters in the world. If one of them should think to win his favor by disposing of a rival . . ."

"I am a prince of Dorne, Your Grace. I will not run from slaves and sellswords."

Then you truly are a fool, Prince Frog. Dany gave her wild children one last lingering look. She could hear the dragons screaming as she led the boy back to the door, and see the play of light against the bricks, reflections of their fires. *If I look back, I am lost.* "Ser Barristan will have summoned a pair of sedan chairs to carry us back up to the banquet, but the climb can still be wearisome." Behind them, the great iron doors closed with a resounding *clang.* "Tell me of this other Daenerys. I know less than I should of the history of my father's kingdom. I never had a maester growing up." *Only a brother.*

"It would be my pleasure, Your Grace," said Quentyn.

It was well past midnight before the last of their guests took their leave and Dany retired to her own apartments to join her lord and king. Hizdahr at least was happy, if somewhat drunk. "I keep my promises," he told her, as Irri and Jhiqui were robing them for bed. "You wished for peace, and it is yours."

And you wished for blood, and soon enough I must give it to you, Dany thought, but what she said was, "I am grateful."

The excitement of the day had inflamed her husband's passions. No sooner had her handmaids retired for the night than he tore the robe from her and tumbled her backwards into bed. Dany slid her arms around him and let him have his way. Drunk as he was, she knew he would not be inside her long.

Nor was he. Afterward he nuzzled at her ear and whispered, "Gods grant that we have made a son tonight."

The words of Mirri Maz Duur rang in her head. *When the sun rises in the west and sets in the east. When the seas go dry and mountains blow in the wind like leaves. When your womb quickens again, and you bear a living child. Then he will return, and not before.* The meaning was plain enough; Khal Drogo was as like to return from the dead as she was to bear a living child. But there are some secrets she could not bring herself to share, even with a husband, so she let Hizdahr zo Loraq keep his hopes.

Her noble husband was soon fast asleep. Daenerys could only twist and turn beside him. She wanted to shake him, wake him, make him hold her, kiss her, fuck her again, but even if he did, he would fall back to sleep again afterward, leaving her alone in the darkness. She wondered what Daario was doing. Was he restless as well? Was he thinking about her? Did he love her, truly? Did he hate her for marrying Hizdahr? *I should never have taken him into my bed.* He was only a sellsword, no fit consort for a queen, and yet . . .

I knew that all along, but I did it anyway.

"My queen?" said a soft voice in the darkness.

Dany flinched. "Who is there?"

"Only Missandei." The Naathi scribe moved closer to the bed. "This one heard you crying."

"Crying? I was not crying. Why would I cry? I have my peace, I have my king, I have everything a queen might wish for. You had a bad dream, that was all."

"As you say, Your Grace." She bowed and made to go.

"Stay," said Dany. "I do not wish to be alone."

"His Grace is with you," Missandei pointed out.

"His Grace is dreaming, but I cannot sleep. On the morrow I must bathe in blood. The price of peace." She smiled wanly and patted the bed. "Come. Sit. Talk with me."

"If it please you." Missandei sat down beside her. "What shall we talk of?"

"Home," said Dany. "Naath. Butterflies and brothers. Tell me of the things that make you happy, the things that make you giggle, all your sweetest memories. Remind me that there is still good in the world."

Missandei did her best. She was still talking when Dany finally fell to sleep, to dream queer, half-formed dreams of smoke and fire.

The morning came too soon.

THEON

Day stole upon them just as Stannis had: unseen.
Winterfell had been awake for hours, its battlements and towers crammed with men in wool and mail and leather awaiting an attack that never came. By the time the sky began to lighten the sound of drums had faded away, though warhorns were heard thrice more, each time a little closer. And still the snow fell.

"The storm will end today," one of the surviving stableboys was insisting loudly. "Why, it isn't even winter." Theon would have laughed if he had dared. He remembered tales Old Nan had told them of storms that raged for forty days and forty nights, for a year, for ten years . . . storms that buried castles and cities and whole kingdoms under a hundred feet of snow.

He sat in the back of the Great Hall, not far from the horses, watching Abel, Rowan, and a mousy brown-haired washerwoman called Squirrel attack slabs of stale brown bread fried in bacon grease. Theon broke his own fast with a tankard of dark ale, cloudy with yeast and thick enough to chew on. A few more tankards, and perhaps Abel's plan might not seem quite so mad.

Roose Bolton entered, pale-eyed and yawning, accompanied by his plump and pregnant wife, Fat Walda. Several lords and captains had preceded him, amongst them Whoresbane Umber, Aenys Frey, and Roger Ryswell. Farther down the table Wyman Manderly sat wolfing down sausages and boiled eggs, whilst old Lord Locke beside him spooned gruel into his toothless mouth.

Lord Ramsay soon appeared as well, buckling on his sword belt as he made his way to the front of the hall. *His mood is foul this morning.* Theon could tell. *The drums kept him awake all night,* he guessed, *or someone has displeased him.* One wrong word, an ill-considered look, an ill-timed laugh, any of them could provoke his lordship's wroth and cost a man a strip of skin. *Please, m'lord, don't look this way.* One glance would be all it would take for Ramsay to know everything. *He'll see it written on my face. He'll know. He always knows.*

Theon turned to Abel. "This will not work." His voice was pitched so low that even the horses could not have overheard. "We will be caught before we leave the castle. Even if we do escape, Lord Ramsay will hunt us down, him and Ben Bones and the girls."

"Lord Stannis is outside the walls, and not far by the sound of it. All we need do is reach him." Abel's fingers danced across the strings of his lute. The singer's beard was brown, though his long hair had largely gone to grey. "If the Bastard does come after us, he might live long enough to rue it."

Think that, Theon thought. *Believe that. Tell yourself it's true.* "Ramsay will use your women as his prey," he told the singer. "He'll hunt them down, rape them, and feed their corpses to his dogs. If they lead him a good chase, he may name his next litter of bitches after them. You he'll flay. Him and Skinner and Damon Dance-for-Me, they will make a game of it. You'll be begging them to kill you." He clutched the singer's arm with a maimed hand. "You swore you would not let me fall into his hands again. I have your word on that." He needed to hear it again.

"Abel's word," said Squirrel. "Strong as oak." Abel himself only shrugged. "No matter what, my prince."

Up on the dais, Ramsay was arguing with his father. They were too far away for Theon to make out any of the words, but the fear on Fat Walda's round pink face spoke volumes. He did hear Wyman Manderly calling for more sausages and Roger Ryswell's laughter at some jape from one-armed Harwood Stout.

Theon wondered if he would ever see the Drowned God's watery halls, or if his ghost would linger here at Winterfell. *Dead is dead. Better dead than Reek.* If Abel's scheme went awry, Ramsay would make their dying long and hard. *He will flay me from head to heel this time, and no amount of begging will end the anguish.* No pain Theon had ever known came close to the agony that Skinner could evoke with a little flensing blade. Abel would learn that lesson soon enough. And for what? *Jeyne, her name is Jeyne, and her eyes are the wrong color.* A mummer playing a part. *Lord Bolton knows, and Ramsay, but the rest are blind, even this bloody bard with his sly smiles. The jape is on you, Abel, you and your murdering whores. You'll die for the wrong girl.*

He had come this close to telling them the truth when Rowan had de-

livered him to Abel in the ruins of the Burned Tower, but at the last instant he had held his tongue. The singer seemed intent on making off
with the daughter of Eddard Stark. If he knew that Lord Ramsay's bride
was but a steward's whelp, well . . .

The doors of the Great Hall opened with a crash.

A cold wind came swirling through, and a cloud of ice crystals sparkled
blue-white in the air. Through it strode Ser Hosteen Frey, caked with
snow to the waist, a body in his arms. All along the benches men put down
their cups and spoons to turn and gape at the grisly spectacle. The hall
grew quiet.

Another murder.

Snow slid from Ser Hosteen's cloaks as he stalked toward the high
table, his steps ringing against the floor. A dozen Frey knights and
men-at-arms entered behind him. One was a boy Theon knew—Big
Walder, the little one, fox-faced and skinny as a stick. His chest and arms
and cloak were spattered with blood.

The scent of it set the horses to screaming. Dogs slid out from under
the tables, sniffing. Men rose from the benches. The body in Ser Hosteen's arms sparkled in the torchlight, armored in pink frost. The cold
outside had frozen his blood.

"My brother Merrett's son." Hosteen Frey lowered the body to the
floor before the dais. "Butchered like a hog and shoved beneath a snowbank. A *boy.*"

Little Walder, thought Theon. *The big one.* He glanced at Rowan.
There are six of them, he remembered. *Any of them could have done this.*
But the washerwoman felt his eyes. "This was no work of ours," she said.

"Be quiet," Abel warned her.

Lord Ramsay descended from the dais to the dead boy. His father rose
more slowly, pale-eyed, still-faced, solemn. "This was foul work." For once
Roose Bolton's voice was loud enough to carry. "Where was the body
found?"

"Under that ruined keep, my lord," replied Big Walder. "The one with
the old gargoyles." The boy's gloves were caked with his cousin's blood. "I
told him not to go out alone, but he said he had to find a man who owed
him silver."

"What man?" Ramsay demanded. "Give me his name. Point him out
to me, boy, and I will make you a cloak of his skin."

"He never said, my lord. Only that he won the coin at dice." The Frey
boy hesitated. "It was some White Harbor men who taught dice. I couldn't
say which ones, but it was them."

"My lord," boomed Hosteen Frey. "We know the man who did this. Killed this boy and all the rest. Not by his own hand, no. He is too fat and craven to do his own killing. But by his word." He turned to Wyman Manderly. "Do you deny it?"

The Lord of White Harbor bit a sausage in half. "I confess . . ." He wiped the grease from his lips with his sleeve. ". . . I confess that I know little of this poor boy. Lord Ramsay's squire, was he not? How old was the lad?"

"Nine, on his last nameday."

"So young," said Wyman Manderly. "Though mayhaps this was a blessing. Had he lived, he would have grown up to be a Frey."

Ser Hosteen slammed his foot into the tabletop, knocking it off its trestles, back into Lord Wyman's swollen belly. Cups and platters flew, sausages scattered everywhere, and a dozen Manderly men came cursing to their feet. Some grabbed up knives, platters, flagons, anything that might serve as a weapon.

Ser Hosteen Frey ripped his longsword from its scabbard and leapt toward Wyman Manderly. The Lord of White Harbor tried to jerk away, but the tabletop pinned him to his chair. The blade slashed through three of his four chins in a spray of bright red blood. Lady Walda gave a shriek and clutched at her lord husband's arm. "Stop," Roose Bolton shouted. "*Stop this madness.*" His own men rushed forward as the Manderlys vaulted over the benches to get at the Freys. One lunged at Ser Hosteen with a dagger, but the big knight pivoted and took his arm off at the shoulder. Lord Wyman pushed to his feet, only to collapse. Old Lord Locke was shouting for a maester as Manderly flopped on the floor like a clubbed walrus in a spreading pool of blood. Around him dogs fought over sausages.

It took two score Dreadfort spearmen to part the combatants and put an end to the carnage. By that time six White Harbor men and two Freys lay dead upon the floor. A dozen more were wounded and one of the Bastard's Boys, Luton, was dying noisily, crying for his mother as he tried to shove a fistful of slimy entrails back through a gaping belly wound. Lord Ramsay silenced him, yanking a spear from one of Steelshanks's men and driving it down through Luton's chest. Even then the rafters still rang with shouts and prayers and curses, the shrieks of terrified horses and the growls of Ramsay's bitches. Steelshanks Walton had to slam the butt of his spear against the floor a dozen times before the hall quieted enough for Roose Bolton to be heard.

"I see you all want blood," the Lord of the Dreadfort said. Maester Rhodry stood beside him, a raven on his arm. The bird's black plumage shone like coal oil in the torchlight. *Wet*, Theon realized. *And in his lordship's hand, a parchment. That will be wet as well. Dark wings, dark words.* "Rather than use our swords upon each other, you might try them on Lord Stannis." Lord Bolton unrolled the parchment. "His host lies not three days' ride from here, snowbound and starving, and I for one am tired of waiting on his pleasure. Ser Hosteen, assemble your knights and men-at-arms by the main gates. As you are so eager for battle, you shall strike our first blow. Lord Wyman, gather your White Harbor men by the east gate. They shall go forth as well."

Hosteen Frey's sword was red almost to the hilt. Blood spatters speckled his cheeks like freckles. He lowered his blade and said, "As my lord commands. But after I deliver you the head of Stannis Baratheon, I mean to finish hacking off Lord Lard's."

Four White Harbor knights had formed a ring around Lord Wyman, as Maester Medrick labored over him to staunch his bleeding. "First you must needs come through us, ser," said the eldest of them, a hard-faced greybeard whose bloodstained surcoat showed three silvery mermaids upon a violet field.

"Gladly. One at a time or all at once, it makes no matter."

"*Enough*," roared Lord Ramsay, brandishing his bloody spear. "Another threat, and I'll gut you all myself. My lord father has spoken! Save your wroth for the pretender Stannis."

Roose Bolton gave an approving nod. "As he says. There will be time enough to fight each other once we are done with Stannis." He turned his head, his pale cold eyes searching the hall until they found the bard Abel beside Theon. "Singer," he called, "come sing us something soothing."

Abel bowed. "If it please your lordship." Lute in hand, he sauntered to the dais, hopping nimbly over a corpse or two, and seated himself cross-legged on the high table. As he began to play—a sad, soft song that Theon Greyjoy did not recognize—Ser Hosteen, Ser Aenys, and their fellow Freys turned away to lead their horses from the hall.

Rowan grasped Theon's arm. "The bath. It must be now."

He wrenched free of her touch. "By day? We will be seen."

"The snow will hide us. Are you deaf? Bolton is sending forth his swords. We have to reach King Stannis before they do."

"But . . . Abel . . ."

"Abel can fend for himself," murmured Squirrel.

This is madness. Hopeless, foolish, doomed. Theon drained the last dregs of his ale and rose reluctantly to his feet. "Find your sisters. It takes a deal of water to fill my lady's tub."

Squirrel slipped away, soft-footed as she always was. Rowan walked Theon from the hall. Since she and her sisters had found him in the godswood, one of them had dogged his every step, never letting him out of sight. They did not trust him. *Why should they? I was Reek before and might be Reek again. Reek, Reek, it rhymes with sneak.*

Outside the snow still fell. The snowmen the squires had built had grown into monstrous giants, ten feet tall and hideously misshapen. White walls rose to either side as he and Rowan made their way to the godswood; the paths between keep and tower and hall had turned into a maze of icy trenches, shoveled out hourly to keep them clear. It was easy to get lost in that frozen labyrinth, but Theon Greyjoy knew every twist and turning.

Even the godswood was turning white. A film of ice had formed upon the pool beneath the heart tree, and the face carved into its pale trunk had grown a mustache of little icicles. At this hour they could not hope to have the old gods to themselves. Rowan pulled Theon away from the northmen praying before the tree, to a secluded spot back by the barracks wall, beside a pool of warm mud that stank of rotten eggs. Even the mud was icing up about the edges, Theon saw. "Winter is coming . . ."

Rowan gave him a hard look. "You have no right to mouth Lord Eddard's words. Not you. Not ever. After what you did—"

"You killed a boy as well."

"That was not us. I told you."

"Words are wind." *They are no better than me. We're just the same.* "You killed the others, why not him? Yellow Dick—"

"—stank as bad as you. A pig of a man."

"And Little Walder was a piglet. Killing him brought the Freys and Manderlys to dagger points, that was cunning, you—"

"*Not us.*" Rowan grabbed him by the throat and shoved him back against the barracks wall, her face an inch from his. "Say it again and I will rip your lying tongue out, kinslayer."

He smiled through his broken teeth. "You won't. You need my tongue to get you past the guards. You need my lies."

Rowan spat in his face. Then she let him go and wiped her gloved hands on her legs, as if just touching him had soiled her.

Theon knew he should not goad her. In her own way, this one was as dangerous as Skinner or Damon Dance-for-Me. But he was cold and tired, his head was pounding, he had not slept in days. "I have done terrible things . . . betrayed my own, turned my cloak, ordered the death of men who trusted me . . . but I am no kinslayer."

"Stark's boys were never brothers to you, aye. We know."

That was true, but it was not what Theon had meant. *They were not my blood, but even so, I never harmed them. The two we killed were just some miller's sons.* Theon did not want to think about their mother. He had known the miller's wife for years, had even bedded her. *Big heavy breasts with wide dark nipples, a sweet mouth, a merry laugh. Joys that I will never taste again.*

But there was no use telling Rowan any of that. She would never believe his denials, any more than he believed hers. "There is blood on my hands, but not the blood of brothers," he said wearily. "And I've been punished."

"Not enough." Rowan turned her back on him.

Foolish woman. He might well be a broken thing, but Theon still wore a dagger. It would have been a simple thing to slide it out and drive it down between her shoulder blades. That much he was still capable of, missing teeth and broken teeth and all. It might even be a kindness—a quicker, cleaner end than the one she and her sisters would face when Ramsay caught them.

Reek might have done it. *Would* have done it, in hopes it might please Lord Ramsay. These whores meant to steal Ramsay's bride; Reek could not allow that. But the old gods had known him, had called him Theon. *Ironborn, I was ironborn, Balon Greyjoy's son and rightful heir to Pyke.* The stumps of his fingers itched and twitched, but he kept his dagger in its sheath.

When Squirrel returned, the other four were with her: gaunt grey-haired Myrtle, Willow Witch-Eye with her long black braid, Frenya of the thick waist and enormous breasts, Holly with her knife. Clad as serving girls in layers of drab grey roughspun, they wore brown woolen cloaks lined with white rabbit fur. *No swords,* Theon saw. *No axes, no hammers, no weapons but knives.* Holly's cloak was fastened with a silver clasp, and Frenya had a girdle of hempen rope wound about her middle from her hips to breasts. It made her look even more massive than she was.

Myrtle had servant's garb for Rowan. "The yards are crawling with fools," she warned them. "They mean to ride out."

"Kneelers," said Willow, with a snort of contempt. "Their lordly lord spoke, they must obey."

"They're going to die," chirped Holly, happily.

"Them and us," said Theon. "Even if we do get past the guards, how do you mean to get Lady Arya out?"

Holly smiled. "Six women go in, six come out. Who looks at serving girls? We'll dress the Stark girl up as Squirrel."

Theon glanced at Squirrel. *They are almost of a size. It might work.* "And how does Squirrel get out?"

Squirrel answered for herself. "Out a window, and straight down to the godswood. I was twelve the first time my brother took me raiding south o' your Wall. That's where I got my name. My brother said I looked like a squirrel running up a tree. I've done that Wall six times since, over and back again. I think I can climb down some stone tower."

"Happy, turncloak?" Rowan asked. "Let's be about it."

Winterfell's cavernous kitchen occupied a building all its own, set well apart from the castle's main halls and keeps in case of fire. Inside, the smells changed hour by hour — an ever-changing perfume of roast meats, leeks and onions, fresh-baked bread. Roose Bolton had posted guards at the kitchen door. With so many mouths to feed, every scrap of food was precious. Even the cooks and potboys were watched constantly. But the guards knew Reek. They liked to taunt him when he came to fetch hot water for Lady Arya's bath. None of them dared go further than that, though. Reek was known to be Lord Ramsay's pet.

"The Prince of Stink is come for some hot water," one guard announced when Theon and his serving girls appeared before him. He pushed the door open for them. "Quick now, before all that sweet warm air escapes."

Within, Theon grabbed a passing potboy by the arm. "Hot water for m'lady, boy," he commanded. "Six pails full, and see that it's good and hot. Lord Ramsay wants her pink and clean."

"Aye, m'lord," the boy said. "At once, m'lord."

"At once" took longer than Theon would have liked. None of the big kettles was clean, so the potboy had to scrub one out before filling it with water. Then it seemed to take forever to come to a rolling boil and twice forever to fill six wooden pails. All the while Abel's women waited, their faces shadowed by their cowls. *They are doing it all wrong.* Real serving girls were always teasing the potboys, flirting with the cooks, wheedling a taste of this, a bite of that. Rowan and her scheming sisters did not want to attract notice, but their sullen silence soon had the guards giving them queer looks. "Where's Maisie and Jez and t'other girls?" one asked Theon. "The usual ones."

"Lady Arya was displeased with them," he lied. "Her water was cold before it reached the tub last time."

The hot water filled the air with clouds of steam, melting the snowflakes as they came drifting down. Back through the maze of ice-walled trenches went the procession. With every sloshing step the water cooled. The passages were clogged with troops: armored knights in woolen surcoats and fur cloaks, men-at-arms with spears across their shoulders, archers carrying unstrung bows and sheaves of arrows, freeriders, grooms leading warhorses. The Frey men wore the badge of the two towers, those from White Harbor displayed merman and trident. They shouldered through the storm in opposite directions and eyed each other warily as they passed, but no swords were drawn. Not here. *It may be different out there in the woods.*

Half a dozen seasoned Dreadfort men guarded the doors of the Great Keep. "Another bloody bath?" said their serjeant when he saw the pails of steaming water. He had his hands tucked up into his armpits against the cold. "She had a bath last night. How dirty can one woman get in her own bed?"

Dirtier than you know, when you share that bed with Ramsay, Theon thought, remembering the wedding night and the things that he and Jeyne had been made to do. "Lord Ramsay's command."

"Get in there, then, before the water freezes," the serjeant said. Two of the guards pushed open the double doors.

The entryway was nigh as cold as the air outside. Holly kicked snow from her boots and lowered the hood of her cloak. "I thought that would be harder." Her breath frosted the air.

"There are more guards upstairs at m'lord's bedchamber," Theon warned her. "Ramsay's men." He dare not call them the Bastard's Boys, not here. You never knew who might be listening. "Keep your heads down and your hoods up."

"Do as he says, Holly," Rowan said. "There's some will know your face. We don't need that trouble."

Theon led the way up the stairs. *I have climbed these steps a thousand times before.* As a boy he would run up; descending, he would take the steps three at a time, leaping. Once he leapt right into Old Nan and knocked her to the floor. That earned him the worst thrashing he ever had at Winterfell, though it was almost tender compared to the beatings his brothers used to give him back on Pyke. He and Robb had fought many a heroic battle on these steps, slashing at one another with wooden swords. Good training, that; it brought home how hard it was to fight your way up a spiral stair against determined opposition. Ser Rodrik liked to say that one good man could hold a hundred, fighting down.

That was long ago, though. They were all dead now. Jory, old Ser Rodrik, Lord Eddard, Harwin and Hullen, Cayn and Desmond and Fat Tom, Alyn with his dreams of knighthood, Mikken who had given him his first real sword. Even Old Nan, like as not.

And Robb. Robb who had been more a brother to Theon than any son born of Balon Greyjoy's loins. *Murdered at the Red Wedding, butchered by the Freys. I should have been with him. Where was I? I should have died with him.*

Theon stopped so suddenly that Willow almost plowed into his back. The door to Ramsay's bedchamber was before him. And guarding it were two of the Bastard's Boys, Sour Alyn and Grunt.

The old gods must wish us well. Grunt had no tongue and Sour Alyn had no wits, Lord Ramsay liked to say. One was brutal, the other mean, but both had spent most of their lives in service at the Dreadfort. They did as they were told.

"I have hot water for the Lady Arya," Theon told them.

"Try a wash yourself, Reek," said Sour Alyn. "You smell like horse piss." Grunt grunted in agreement. Or perhaps that noise was meant to be a laugh. But Alyn unlocked the door to the bedchamber, and Theon waved the women through.

No day had dawned inside this room. Shadows covered all. One last log crackled feebly amongst the dying embers in the hearth, and a candle flickered on the table beside a rumpled, empty bed. *The girl is gone,* Theon thought. *She has thrown herself out a window in despair.* But the windows here were shuttered against the storm, sealed up by crusts of blown snow and frost. "Where is she?" Holly asked. Her sisters emptied their pails into the big round wooden tub. Frenya shut the chamber door and put her back against it. "*Where is she?*" Holly said again. Outside a horn was blowing. *A trumpet. The Freys, assembling for battle.* Theon could feel an itching in his missing fingers.

Then he saw her. She was huddled in the darkest corner of the bed-chamber, on the floor, curled up in a ball beneath a pile of wolfskins. Theon might never have spotted her but for the way she trembled. Jeyne had pulled the furs up over herself to hide. *From us? Or was she expecting her lord husband?* The thought that Ramsay might be coming made him want to scream. "My lady." Theon could not bring himself to call her Arya and dare not call her Jeyne. "No need to hide. These are friends."

The furs stirred. An eye peered out, shining with tears. *Dark, too dark. A brown eye.* "Theon?"

"Lady Arya." Rowan moved closer. "You must come with us, and quickly. We've come to take you to your brother."

"Brother?" The girl's face emerged from underneath the wolfskins. "I . . . I have no brothers."

She has forgotten who she is. She has forgotten her name. "That's so," said Theon, "but you had brothers once. Three of them. Robb and Bran and Rickon."

"They're dead. I have no brothers now."

"You have a half-brother," Rowan said. "Lord Crow, he is."

"Jon Snow?"

"We'll take you to him, but you must come at once."

Jeyne pulled her wolfskins up to her chin. "No. This is some trick. It's him, it's my . . . my lord, my sweet lord, he sent you, this is just some test to make sure that I love him. I do, I do, I love him more than anything." A tear ran down her cheek. "Tell him, you tell him. I'll do what he wants . . . whatever he wants . . . with him or . . . or with the dog or . . . please . . . he doesn't need to cut my feet off, I won't try to run away, not ever, I'll give him sons, I swear it, I swear it . . ."

Rowan whistled softly. "Gods curse the man."

"I'm a *good* girl," Jeyne whimpered. "They *trained* me."

Willow scowled. "Someone stop her crying. That guard was mute, not deaf. They're going to hear."

"Get her *up*, turncloak." Holly had her knife in hand. "Get her up or I will. *We have to go.* Get the little cunt up on her feet and shake some courage into her."

"And if she screams?" said Rowan.

We are all dead, Theon thought. *I told them this was folly, but none of them would listen.* Abel had doomed them. All singers were half-mad. In songs, the hero always saved the maiden from the monster's castle, but life was not a song, no more than Jeyne was Arya Stark. *Her eyes are the wrong color. And there are no heroes here, only whores.* Even so, he knelt beside her, pulled down the furs, touched her cheek. "You know me. I'm Theon, you remember. I know you too. I know your name."

"My name?" She shook her head. "My name . . . it's . . ."

He put a finger to her lips. "We can talk about that later. You need to be quiet now. Come with us. With me. We will take you away from here. Away from him."

Her eyes widened. "Please," she whispered. "Oh, please."

Theon slipped his hand through hers. The stumps of his lost fingers tingled as he drew the girl to her feet. The wolfskins fell away from her. Underneath them she was naked, her small pale breasts covered with teeth marks. He heard one of the women suck in her breath. Rowan thrust a bundle of clothes into his hands. "Get her dressed. It's cold outside." Squirrel had stripped down to her smallclothes, and was rooting through a carved cedar chest in search of something warmer. In the end she settled for one of Lord Ramsay's quilted doublets and a well-worn pair of breeches that flapped about her legs like a ship's sails in a storm.

With Rowan's help, Theon got Jeyne Poole into Squirrel's clothes. *If the gods are good and the guards are blind, she may pass.* "Now we are going out and down the steps," Theon told the girl. "Keep your head down and your hood up. Follow Holly. Don't run, don't cry, don't speak, don't look anyone in the eye."

"Stay close to me," Jeyne said. "Don't leave me."

"I will be right beside you," Theon promised as Squirrel slipped into Lady Arya's bed and pulled the blanket up.

Frenya opened the bedchamber door.

"You give her a good wash, Reek?" asked Sour Alyn as they emerged. Grunt gave Willow's breast a squeeze as she went by. They were fortunate in his choice. If the man had touched Jeyne, she might have screamed. Then Holly would have opened his throat for him with the knife hidden up her sleeve. Willow simply twisted away and past him.

For a moment Theon felt almost giddy. *They never looked. They never saw. We walked the girl right by them!*

But on the steps the fear returned. What if they met Skinner or Damon Dance-for-Me or Steelshanks Walton? Or Ramsay himself? *Gods save me, not Ramsay, anyone but him.* What use was it to smuggle the girl out of her bedchamber? They were still inside the castle, with every gate closed and barred and the battlements thick with sentries. Like as not, the guards outside the keep would stop them. Holly and her knife would be of small use against six men in mail with swords and spears.

But the guards outside were huddled by the doors, backs turned against the icy wind and blown snow. Even the serjeant did not spare them more than a quick glance. Theon felt a stab of pity for him and his men. Ramsay would flay them all when he learned his bride was gone, and what he would do to Grunt and Sour Alyn did not bear thinking about.

Not ten yards from the door, Rowan dropped her empty pail, and her sisters did likewise. The Great Keep was already lost to sight behind them. The yard was a white wilderness, full of half-heard sounds that echoed strangely amidst the storm. The icy trenches rose around them, knee high, then waist high, then higher than their heads. They were in the heart of Winterfell with the castle all around them, but no sign of it could be seen. They might have easily been lost amidst the Land of Always Winter, a thousand leagues beyond the Wall. "It's cold," Jeyne Poole whimpered as she stumbled along at Theon's side.

And soon to be colder. Beyond the castle walls, winter was waiting with its icy teeth. *If we get that far.* "This way," he said when they came to a junction where three trenches crossed.

"Frenya, Holly, go with them," Rowan said. "We will be along with Abel. Do not wait for us." And with that, she whirled and plunged into the snow, toward the Great Hall. Willow and Myrtle hurried after her, cloaks snapping in the wind.

Madder and madder, thought Theon Greyjoy. Escape had seemed unlikely with all six of Abel's women; with only two, it seemed impossible. But they had gone too far to return the girl to her bedchamber and pretend none of this had ever happened. Instead he took Jeyne by the arm and drew her down the pathway to the Battlements Gate. *Only a half-gate*, he reminded himself. *Even if the guards let us pass, there is no way through the outer wall.* On other nights, the guards had allowed Theon through, but all those times he'd come alone. He would not pass so easily with three serving girls in tow, and if the guards looked beneath Jeyne's hood and recognized Lord Ramsay's bride . . .

The passage twisted to the left. There before them, behind a veil of falling snow, yawned the Battlements Gate, flanked by a pair of guards. In their wool and fur and leather, they looked as big as bears. The spears they held were eight feet tall. "Who goes there?" one called out. Theon did not recognize the voice. Most of the man's features were covered by the scarf about his face. Only his eyes could be seen. "Reek, is that you?"

Yes, he meant to say. Instead he heard himself reply, "Theon Greyjoy. I . . . I have brought some women for you."

"You poor boys must be freezing," said Holly. "Here, let me warm you up." She slipped past the guard's spearpoint and reached up to his face, pulling loose the half-frozen scarf to plant a kiss upon his mouth. And as their lips touched, her blade slid through the meat of his neck, just below the ear. Theon saw the man's eyes widen. There was blood on Holly's lips as she stepped back, and blood dribbling from his mouth as he fell.

The second guard was still gaping in confusion when Frenya grabbed the shaft of his spear. They struggled for a moment, tugging, till the woman wrenched the weapon from his fingers and clouted him across the temple with its butt. As he stumbled backwards, she spun the spear around and drove its point through his belly with a grunt.

Jeyne Poole let out a shrill, high scream.

"Oh, bloody shit," said Holly. "That will bring the kneelers down on us, and no mistake. *Run!*"

Theon clapped one hand around Jeyne's mouth, grabbed her about the waist with the other, and pulled her past the dead and dying guards, through the gate, and over the frozen moat. And perhaps the old gods were still watching over them; the drawbridge had been left down, to allow Winterfell's defenders to cross to and from the outer battlements more quickly. From behind them came alarums and the sounds of running feet, then the blast of a trumpet from the ramparts of the inner wall.

On the drawbridge, Frenya stopped and turned. "Go on. I will hold the kneelers here." The bloody spear was still clutched in her big hands.

Theon was staggering by the time he reached the foot of the stair. He slung the girl over his shoulder and began to climb. Jeyne had ceased to struggle by then, and she was such a little thing besides . . . but the steps were slick with ice beneath soft powdery snow, and halfway up he lost his footing and went down hard on one knee. The pain was so bad he almost lost the girl, and for half a heartbeat he feared this was as far as he would go. But Holly pulled him back onto his feet, and between the two of them they finally got Jeyne up to the battlements.

As he leaned up against a merlon, breathing hard, Theon could hear the shouting from below, where Frenya was fighting half a dozen guardsmen in the snow. "Which way?" he shouted at Holly. "Where do we go now? *How do we get out?*"

The fury on Holly's face turned to horror. "Oh, fuck me bloody. The rope." She gave a hysterical laugh. *"Frenya has the rope."* Then she grunted and grabbed her stomach. A quarrel had sprouted from her gut. When she wrapped a hand around it, blood leaked through her fingers. "Kneelers on the inner wall . . ." she gasped, before a second shaft appeared between her breasts. Holly grabbed for the nearest merlon and fell. The snow that she'd knocked loose buried her with a soft *thump*.

Shouts rang out from their left. Jeyne Poole was staring down at Holly as the snowy blanket over her turned from white to red. On the inner wall the crossbowman would be reloading, Theon knew. He started right, but there were men coming from that direction too, racing toward them with swords in hand. Far off to the north he heard a warhorn sound. *Stannis,* he thought wildly. *Stannis is our only hope, if we can reach him.* The wind was howling, and he and the girl were trapped.

The crossbow snapped. A bolt passed within a foot of him, shattering the crust of frozen snow that had plugged the closest crenel. Of Abel, Rowan, Squirrel, and the others there was no sign. He and the girl were alone. *If they take us alive, they will deliver us to Ramsay.*

Theon grabbed Jeyne about the waist and jumped.

DAENERYS

The sky was a merciless blue, without a wisp of cloud in sight. *The bricks will soon be baking in the sun*, thought Dany. *Down on the sands, the fighters will feel the heat through the soles of their sandals.*

Jhiqui slipped Dany's silk robe from her shoulders and Irri helped her into her bathing pool. The light of the rising sun shimmered on the water, broken by the shadow of the persimmon tree. "Even if the pits must open, must Your Grace go yourself?" asked Missandei as she was washing the queen's hair.

"Half of Meereen will be there to see me, gentle heart."

"Your Grace," said Missandei, "this one begs leave to say that half of Meereen will be there to watch men bleed and die."

She is not wrong, the queen knew, *but it makes no matter.*

Soon Dany was as clean as she was ever going to be. She pushed herself to her feet, splashing softly. Water ran down her legs and beaded on her breasts. The sun was climbing up the sky, and her people would soon be gathering. She would rather have drifted in the fragrant pool all day, eating iced fruit off silver trays and dreaming of a house with a red door, but a queen belongs to her people, not to herself.

Jhiqui brought a soft towel to pat her dry. "*Khaleesi*, which *tokar* will you want today?" asked Irri.

"The yellow silk." The queen of the rabbits could not be seen without her floppy ears. The yellow silk was light and cool, and it would be blistering down in the pit. *The red sands will burn the soles of those about to die.* "And over it, the long red veils." The veils would keep the wind from blowing sand into her mouth. *And the red will hide any blood spatters.*

As Jhiqui brushed Dany's hair and Irri painted the queen's nails, they chattered happily about the day's matches. Missandei reemerged. "Your Grace. The king bids you join him when you are dressed. And Prince

Quentyn has come with his Dornish Men. They beg a word, if that should please you."

Little about this day shall please me. "Some other day."

At the base of the Great Pyramid, Ser Barristan awaited them beside an ornate open palanquin, surrounded by Brazen Beasts. *Ser Grandfather,* Dany thought. Despite his age, he looked tall and handsome in the armor that she'd given him. "I would be happier if you had Unsullied guards about you today, Your Grace," the old knight said, as Hizdahr went to greet his cousin. "Half of these Brazen Beasts are untried freedmen." *And the other half are Meereenese of doubtful loyalty,* he left unsaid. Selmy mistrusted all the Meereenese, even shavepates.

"And untried they shall remain unless we try them."

"A mask can hide many things, Your Grace. Is the man behind the owl mask the same owl who guarded you yesterday and the day before? How can we know?"

"How should Meereen ever come to trust the Brazen Beasts if I do not? There are good brave men beneath those masks. I put my life into their hands." Dany smiled for him. "You fret too much, ser. I will have you beside me, what other protection do I need?"

"I am one old man, Your Grace."

"Strong Belwas will be with me as well."

"As you say." Ser Barristan lowered his voice. "Your Grace. We set the woman Meris free, as you commanded. Before she went, she asked to speak with you. I met with her instead. She claims this Tattered Prince meant to bring the Windblown over to your cause from the beginning. That he sent her here to treat with you secretly, but the Dornishmen unmasked them and betrayed them before she could make her own approach."

Treachery on treachery, the queen thought wearily. *Is there no end to it?* "How much of this do you believe, ser?"

"Little and less, Your Grace, but those were her words."

"Will they come over to us, if need be?"

"She says they will. But for a price."

"Pay it." Meereen needed iron, not gold.

"The Tattered Prince will want more than coin, Your Grace. Meris says that he wants Pentos."

"Pentos?" Her eyes narrowed. "How can I give him Pentos? It is half a world away."

"He would be willing to wait, the woman Meris suggested. Until we march for Westeros."

And if I never march for Westeros? "Pentos belongs to the Pentoshi. And Magister Illyrio is in Pentos. He who arranged my marriage to Khal Drogo and gave me my dragon eggs. Who sent me you, and Belwas, and Groleo. I owe him much and more. I will *not* repay that debt by giving his city to some sellsword. No."

Ser Barristan inclined his head. "Your Grace is wise."

"Have you ever seen such an auspicious day, my love?" Hizdahr zo Loraq commented when she rejoined him. He helped Dany up onto the palanquin, where two tall thrones stood side by side.

"Auspicious for you, perhaps. Less so for those who must die before the sun goes down."

"All men must die," said Hizdahr, "but not all can die in glory, with the cheers of the city ringing in their ears." He lifted a hand to the soldiers on the doors. "Open."

The plaza that fronted on her pyramid was paved with bricks of many colors, and the heat rose from them in shimmering waves. People swarmed everywhere. Some rode litters or sedan chairs, some forked donkeys, many were afoot. Nine of every ten were moving westward, down the broad brick thoroughfare to Daznak's Pit. When they caught sight of the palanquin emerging from the pyramid, a cheer went up from those nearest and spread across the plaza. *How queer,* the queen thought. *They cheer me on the same plaza where I once impaled one hundred sixty-three Great Masters.*

A great drum led the royal procession to clear their way through the streets. Between each beat, a shavepate herald in a shirt of polished copper disks cried for the crowd to part. *BOMM.* "They come!" *BOMM.* "Make way!" *BOMM.* "The queen!" *BOMM.* "The king!" *BOMM.* Behind the drum marched Brazen Beasts four abreast. Some carried cudgels, others staves; all wore pleated skirts, leathern sandals, and patchwork cloaks sewn from squares of many colors to echo the many-colored bricks of Meereen. Their masks gleamed in the sun: boars and bulls, hawks and herons, lions and tigers and bears, fork-tongued serpents and hideous basilisks.

Strong Belwas, who had no love for horses, walked in front of them in his studded vest, his scarred brown belly jiggling with every step. Irri and Jhiqui followed ahorse, with Aggo and Rakharo, then Reznak in an ornate sedan chair with an awning to keep the sun off his head. Ser Barristan Selmy rode at Dany's side, his armor flashing in the sun. A long cloak flowed from his shoulders, bleached as white as bone. On his left arm was a large white shield. A little farther back was Quentyn Martell, the Dornish prince, with his two companions.

The column crept slowly down the long brick street. *BOMM.* "They come!" *BOMM.* "Our queen. Our king." *BOMM.* "Make way."

Dany could hear her handmaids arguing behind her, debating who was going to win the day's final match. Jhiqui favored the gigantic Goghor, who looked more bull than man, even to the bronze ring in his nose. Irri insisted that Belaquo Bonebreaker's flail would prove the giant's undoing. *My handmaids are Dothraki,* she told herself. *Death rides with every* khalasar. The day she wed Khal Drogo, the *arakhs* had flashed at her wedding feast, and men had died whilst others drank and mated. Life and death went hand in hand amongst the horselords, and a sprinkling of blood was thought to bless a marriage. Her new marriage would soon be drenched in blood. How blessed it would be.

BOMM, BOMM, BOMM, BOMM, BOMM, BOMM, came the drumbeats, faster than before, suddenly angry and impatient. Ser Barristan drew his sword as the column ground to an abrupt halt between the pink-and-white pyramid of Pahl and the green-and-black of Naqqan.

Dany turned. "Why are we stopped?"

Hizdahr stood. "The way is blocked."

A palanquin lay overturned athwart their way. One of its bearers had collapsed to the bricks, overcome by heat. "Help that man," Dany commanded. "Get him off the street before he's stepped on and give him food and water. He looks as though he has not eaten in a fortnight."

Ser Barristan glanced uneasily to left and right. Ghiscari faces were visible on the terraces, looking down with cool and unsympathetic eyes. "Your Grace, I do not like this halt. This may be some trap. The Sons of the Harpy—"

"—have been tamed," declared Hizdahr zo Loraq. "Why should they seek to harm my queen when she has taken me for her king and consort? Now help that man, as my sweet queen has commanded." He took Dany by the hand and smiled.

The Brazen Beasts did as they were bid. Dany watched them at their work. "Those bearers were slaves before I came. I made them free. Yet that palanquin is no lighter."

"True," said Hizdahr, "but those men are paid to bear its weight now. Before you came, that man who fell would have an overseer standing over him, stripping the skin off his back with a whip. Instead he is being given aid."

It was true. A Brazen Beast in a boar mask had offered the litter bearer a skin of water. "I suppose I must be thankful for small victories," the queen said.

"One step, then the next, and soon we shall be running. Together we shall make a new Meereen." The street ahead had finally cleared. "Shall we continue on?"

What could she do but nod? *One step, then the next, but where is it I'm going?*

At the gates of Daznak's Pit two towering bronze warriors stood locked in mortal combat. One wielded a sword, the other an axe; the sculptor had depicted them in the act of killing one another, their blades and bodies forming an archway overhead.

The mortal art, thought Dany.

She had seen the fighting pits many times from her terrace. The small ones dotted the face of Meereen like pockmarks; the larger were weeping sores, red and raw. None compared to this one, though. Strong Belwas and Ser Barristan fell in to either side as she and her lord husband passed beneath the bronzes, to emerge at the top of a great brick bowl ringed by descending tiers of benches, each a different color.

Hizdahr zo Loraq led her down, through black, purple, blue, green, white, yellow, and orange to the red, where the scarlet bricks took the color of the sands below. Around them peddlers were selling dog sausages, roast onions, and unborn puppies on a stick, but Dany had no need of such. Hizdahr had stocked their box with flagons of chilled wine and sweetwater, with figs, dates, melons, and pomegranates, with pecans and peppers and a big bowl of honeyed locusts. Strong Belwas bellowed, "*Locusts!*" as he seized the bowl and began to crunch them by the handful.

"Those are very tasty," advised Hizdahr. "You ought to try a few yourself, my love. They are rolled in spice before the honey, so they are sweet and hot at once."

"That explains the way Belwas is sweating," Dany said. "I believe I will content myself with figs and dates."

Across the pit the Graces sat in flowing robes of many colors, clustered around the austere figure of Galazza Galare, who alone amongst them wore the green. The Great Masters of Meereen occupied the red and orange benches. The women were veiled, and the men had brushed and lacquered their hair into horns and hands and spikes. Hizdahr's kin of the ancient line of Loraq seemed to favor *tokar*s of purple and indigo and lilac, whilst those of Pahl were striped in pink and white. The envoys from Yunkai were all in yellow and filled the box beside the king's, each of them with his slaves and servants. Meereenese of lesser birth crowded the upper tiers, more distant from the carnage. The black and purple benches, highest and most distant from the sand, were crowded with freedmen and other common folk. The sellswords had been placed up there as well, Daenerys saw, their captains seated right amongst the common soldiers. She spied Brown Ben's weathered face and Bloodbeard's fiery red whiskers and long braids.

Her lord husband stood and raised his hands. *"Great Masters!* My queen has come this day, to show her love for you, her people. By her grace and with her leave, I give you now your mortal art. *Meereen!* Let Queen Daenerys hear your love!"

Ten thousand throats roared out their thanks; then twenty thousand; then all. They did not call her name, which few of them could pronounce. *"Mother!"* they cried instead; in the old dead tongue of Ghis, the word was *Mhysa!* They stamped their feet and slapped their bellies and shouted, *"Mhysa, Mhysa, Mhysa,"* until the whole pit seemed to tremble. Dany let the sound wash over her. *I am not your mother,* she might have shouted, back, *I am the mother of your slaves, of every boy who ever died upon these sands whilst you gorged on honeyed locusts.* Behind her, Reznak leaned in to whisper in her ear, "Magnificence, hear how they love you!"

No, she knew, *they love their mortal art.* When the cheers began to ebb, she allowed herself to sit. Their box was in the shade, but her head was pounding. "Jhiqui," she called, "sweet water, if you would. My throat is very dry."

"Khrazz will have the honor of the day's first kill," Hizdahr told her. "There has never been a better fighter."

"Strong Belwas was better," insisted Strong Belwas.

Khrazz was Meereenese, of humble birth—a tall man with a brush of stiff red-black hair running down the center of his head. His foe was an ebon-skinned spearman from the Summer Isles whose thrusts kept Khrazz at bay for a time, but once he slipped inside the spear with his shortsword, only butchery remained. After it was done, Khrazz cut the heart from the black man, raised it above his head red and dripping, and took a bite from it.

"Khrazz believes the hearts of brave men make him stronger," said Hizdahr. Jhiqui murmured her approval. Dany had once eaten a stallion's heart to give strength to her unborn son . . . but that had not saved Rhaego when the *maegi* murdered him in her womb. *Three treasons shall you know. She was the first, Jorah was the second, Brown Ben Plumm the third.* Was she done with betrayals?

"Ah," said Hizdahr, pleased. "Now comes the Spotted Cat. See how he moves, my queen. A poem on two feet."

The foe Hizdahr had found for the walking poem was as tall as Goghor and as broad as Belwas, but slow. They were fighting six feet from Dany's box when the Spotted Cat hamstrung him. As the man stumbled to his knees, the Cat put a foot on his back and a hand around his head and opened his throat from ear to ear. The red sands drank his blood, the wind his final words. The crowd screamed its approval.

"Bad fighting, good dying," said Strong Belwas. "Strong Belwas hates it when they scream." He had finished all the honeyed locusts. He gave a belch and took a swig of wine.

Pale Qartheen, black Summer Islanders, copper-skinned Dothraki, Tyroshi with blue beards, Lamb Men, Jogos Nhai, sullen Braavosi, brindle-skinned half-men from the jungles of Sothoros—from the ends of the world they came to die in Daznak's Pit. "This one shows much promise, my sweet," Hizdahr said of a Lysene youth with long blond hair that fluttered in the wind . . . but his foe grabbed a handful of that hair, pulled the boy off-balance, and gutted him. In death he looked even younger than he had with blade in hand. "A boy," said Dany. "He was only a boy."

"Six-and-ten," Hizdahr insisted. "A man grown, who freely chose to risk his life for gold and glory. No children die today in Daznak's, as my gentle queen in her wisdom has decreed."

Another small victory. Perhaps I cannot make my people good, she told herself, *but I should at least try to make them a little less bad.* Daenerys would have prohibited contests between women as well, but Barsena Blackhair protested that she had as much right to risk her life as any man. The queen had also wished to forbid the follies, comic combats where cripples, dwarfs, and crones had at one another with cleavers, torches, and hammers (the more inept the fighters, the funnier the folly, it was thought), but Hizdahr said his people would love her more if she laughed with them, and argued that without such frolics, the cripples, dwarfs, and crones would starve. So Dany had relented.

It had been the custom to sentence criminals to the pits; that practice she agreed might resume, but only for certain crimes. "Murderers and rapers may be forced to fight, and all those who persist in slaving, but not thieves or debtors."

Beasts were still allowed, though. Dany watched an elephant make short work of a pack of six red wolves. Next a bull was set against a bear in a bloody battle that left both animals torn and dying. "The flesh is not wasted," said Hizdahr. "The butchers use the carcasses to make a health-ful stew for the hungry. Any man who presents himself at the Gates of Fate may have a bowl."

"A good law," Dany said. *You have so few of them.* "We must make certain that this tradition is continued."

After the beast fights came a mock battle, pitting six men on foot against six horsemen, the former armed with shields and longswords, the latter with Dothraki *arakhs.* The mock knights were clad in mail hauberks, whilst the mock Dothraki wore no armor. At first the riders seemed to have the advantage, riding down two of their foes and slashing the ear from a third, but then the surviving knights began to attack the horses, and one by one the riders were unmounted and slain, to Jhiqui's great disgust. "That was no true *khalasar,*" she said.

"These carcasses are not destined for your healthful stew, I would hope," Dany said, as the slain were being removed.

"The horses, yes," said Hizdahr. "The men, no."

"Horsemeat and onions makes you strong," said Belwas.

The battle was followed by the day's first folly, a tilt between a pair of jousting dwarfs, presented by one of the Yunkish lords that Hizdahr had invited to the games. One rode a hound, the other a sow. Their wooden armor had been freshly painted, so one bore the stag of the usurper Robert Baratheon, the other the golden lion of House Lannister. That was for her sake, plainly. Their antics soon had Belwas snorting laughter, though Dany's smile was faint and forced. When the dwarf in red tumbled from the saddle and began to chase his sow across the sands, whilst the dwarf on the dog galloped after him, whapping at his buttocks with a wooden sword, she said, "This is sweet and silly, but . . ."

"Be patient, my sweet," said Hizdahr. "They are about to loose the lions."

Daenerys gave him a quizzical look. "Lions?"

"Three of them. The dwarfs will not expect them."

She frowned. "The dwarfs have wooden swords. Wooden armor. How do you expect them to fight lions?"

"Badly," said Hizdahr, "though perhaps they will surprise us. More like they will shriek and run about and try to climb out of the pit. That is what makes this a folly."

Dany was not pleased. "I forbid it."

"Gentle queen. You do not want to disappoint your people."

"You swore to me that the fighters would be grown men who had freely consented to risk their lives for gold and honor. These dwarfs did not consent to battle lions with wooden swords. You will stop it. Now."

The king's mouth tightened. For a heartbeat Dany thought she saw a flash of anger in those placid eyes. "As you command." Hizdahr beckoned to his pitmaster. "No lions," he said when the man trotted over, whip in hand.

"Not one, Magnificence? Where is the fun in that?"

"My queen has spoken. The dwarfs will not be harmed."

"The crowd will not like it."

"Then bring on Barsena. That should appease them."

"Your Worship knows best." The pitmaster snapped his whip and shouted out commands. The dwarfs were herded off, pig and dog and all, as the spectators hissed their disapproval and pelted them with stones and rotten fruit.

A roar went up as Barsena Blackhair strode onto the sands, naked save for breechclout and sandals. A tall, dark woman of some thirty years, she moved with the feral grace of a panther. "Barsena is much loved," Hizdahr said, as the sound swelled to fill the pit. "The bravest woman I have ever seen."

Strong Belwas said, "Fighting girls is not so brave. Fighting Strong Belwas would be brave."

"Today she fights a boar," said Hizdahr.

Aye, thought Dany, *because you could not find a woman to face her, no matter how plump the purse.* "And not with a wooden sword, it would seem."

The boar was a huge beast, with tusks as long as a man's forearm and small eyes that swam with rage. She wondered whether the boar that had killed Robert Baratheon had looked as fierce. *A terrible creature and a terrible death.* For a heartbeat she felt almost sorry for the Usurper.

"Barsena is very quick," Reznak said. "She will dance with the boar, Magnificence, and slice him when he passes near her. He will be awash in blood before he falls, you shall see."

It began just as he said. The boar charged, Barsena spun aside, her blade flashed silver in the sun. "She needs a spear," Ser Barristan said, as Barsena vaulted over the beast's second charge. "That is no way to fight a boar." He sounded like someone's fussy old grandsire, just as Daario was always saying.

Barsena's blade was running red, but the boar soon stopped. *He is smarter than a bull,* Dany realized. *He will not charge again.* Barsena came to the same realization. Shouting, she edged closer to the boar, tossing her knife from hand to hand. When the beast backed away, she cursed and slashed at his snout, trying to provoke him . . . and succeeding. This time her leap came an instant too late, and a tusk ripped her left leg open from knee to crotch.

A moan went up from thirty thousand throats. Clutching at her torn leg, Barsena dropped her knife and tried to hobble off, but before she had gone two feet the boar was on her once again. Dany turned her face away. "Was that brave enough?" she asked Strong Belwas, as a scream rang out across the sand.

"Fighting pigs is brave, but it is not brave to scream so loud. It hurts Strong Belwas in the ears." The eunuch rubbed his swollen stomach, crisscrossed with old white scars. "It makes Strong Belwas sick in his belly too."

The boar buried his snout in Barsena's belly and began rooting out her entrails. The smell was more than the queen could stand. The heat, the flies, the shouts from the crowd . . . *I cannot breathe.* She lifted her veil and let it flutter away. She took her *tokar* off as well. The pearls rattled softly against one another as she unwound the silk.

"*Khaleesi?*" Irri asked. "What are you doing?"

"Taking off my floppy ears." A dozen men with boar spears came trotting out onto the sand to drive the boar away from the corpse and back to his pen. The pitmaster was with them, a long barbed whip in his hand. As he snapped it at the boar, the queen rose. "Ser Barristan, will you see me safely back to my garden?"

Hizdahr looked confused. "There is more to come. A folly, six old women, and three more matches. Belaquo and Goghor!"

"Belaquo will win," Irri declared. "It is known."

"It is *not* known," Jhiqui said. "Belaquo will die."

"One will die, or the other will," said Dany. "And the one who lives will die some other day. This was a mistake."

"Strong Belwas ate too many locusts." There was a queasy look on Belwas's broad brown face. "Strong Belwas needs milk."

Hizdahr ignored the eunuch. "Magnificence, the people of Meereen have come to celebrate our union. You heard them cheering you. Do not cast away their love."

"It was my floppy ears they cheered, not me. Take me from this abbatoir, husband." She could hear the boar snorting, the shouts of the spearmen, the *crack* of the pitmaster's whip.

"Sweet lady, no. Stay only a while longer. For the folly, and one last match. Close your eyes, no one will see. They will be watching Belaquo and Ghogor. This is no time for—"

A shadow rippled across his face.

The tumult and the shouting died. Ten thousand voices stilled. Every eye turned skyward. A warm wind brushed Dany's cheeks, and above the beating of her heart she heard the sound of wings. Two spearmen dashed for shelter. The pitmaster froze where he stood. The boar went snuffling back to Barsena. Strong Belwas gave a moan, stumbled from his seat, and fell to his knees.

Above them all the dragon turned, dark against the sun. His scales were black, his eyes and horns and spinal plates blood red. Ever the largest of her three, in the wild Drogon had grown larger still. His wings stretched twenty feet from tip to tip, black as jet. He flapped them once as he swept back above the sands, and the sound was like a clap of thunder. The boar raised his head, snorting . . . and flame engulfed him, black fire shot with red. Dany felt the wash of heat thirty feet away. The beast's dying scream sounded almost human. Drogon landed on the carcass and sank his claws into the smoking flesh. As he began to feed, he made no distinction between Barsena and the boar.

"Oh, gods," moaned Reznak, "he's *eating her*!" The seneschal covered his mouth. Strong Belwas was retching noisily. A queer look passed across Hizdahr zo Loraq's long, pale face—part fear, part lust, part rapture. He licked his lips. Dany could see the Pahls streaming up the steps, clutching their *tokar*s and tripping over the fringes in their haste to be away. Others followed. Some ran, shoving at one another. More stayed in their seats.

One man took it on himself to be a hero.

He was one of the spearmen sent out to drive the boar back to his pen. Perhaps he was drunk, or mad. Perhaps he had loved Barsena Blackhair from afar or had heard some whisper of the girl Hazzea. Perhaps he was just some common man who wanted bards to sing of him. He darted forward, his boar spear in his hands. Red sand kicked up beneath his heels, and shouts rang out from the seats. Drogon raised his head, blood dripping from his teeth. The hero leapt onto his back and drove the iron spearpoint down at the base of the dragon's long scaled neck.

Dany and Drogon screamed as one.

The hero leaned into his spear, using his weight to twist the point in deeper. Drogon arched upward with a hiss of pain. His tail lashed sideways. She watched his head crane around at the end of that long serpentine neck, saw his black wings unfold. The dragonslayer lost his footing and went tumbling to the sand. He was trying to struggle back to his feet when the dragon's teeth closed hard around his forearm. "No" was all the man had time to shout. Drogon wrenched his arm from his shoulder and tossed it aside as a dog might toss a rodent in a rat pit.

"Kill it," Hizdahr zo Loraq shouted to the other spearmen. "*Kill the beast!*"

Ser Barristan held her tightly. "Look away, Your Grace."

"Let me *go!*" Dany twisted from his grasp. The world seemed to slow as she cleared the parapet. When she landed in the pit she lost a sandal. Running, she could feel the sand between her toes, hot and rough. Ser Barristan was calling after her. Strong Belwas was still vomiting. She ran faster.

The spearmen were running too. Some were rushing toward the dragon, spears in hand. Others were rushing away, throwing down their weapons as they fled. The hero was jerking on the sand, the bright blood pouring from the ragged stump of his shoulder. His spear remained in Drogon's back, wobbling as the dragon beat his wings. Smoke rose from the wound. As the other spears closed in, the dragon spat fire, bathing two men in black flame. His tail lashed sideways and caught the pitmaster creeping up behind him, breaking him in two. Another attacker stabbed at his eyes until the dragon caught him in his jaws and tore his belly out. The Meereenese were screaming, cursing, howling. Dany could hear someone pounding after her. "Drogon," she screamed. "*Drogon.*"

His head turned. Smoke rose between his teeth. His blood was smoking too, where it dripped upon the ground. He beat his wings again, sending up a choking storm of scarlet sand. Dany stumbled into the hot red cloud, coughing. He snapped.

"No" was all that she had time to say. *No, not me, don't you know me?* The black teeth closed inches from her face. *He meant to tear my head off.* The sand was in her eyes. She stumbled over the pitmaster's corpse and fell on her backside.

Drogon roared. The sound filled the pit. A furnace wind engulfed her. The dragon's long scaled neck stretched toward her. When his mouth opened, she could see bits of broken bone and charred flesh between his black teeth. His eyes were molten. *I am looking into hell, but I dare not look away.* She had never been so certain of anything. *If I run from him, he will burn me and devour me.* In Westeros the septons spoke of seven hells and seven heavens, but the Seven Kingdoms and their gods were far away. If she died here, Dany wondered, would the horse god of the Dothraki part the grass and claim her for his starry *khalasar*, so she might ride the nightlands beside her sun-and-stars? Or would the angry gods of Ghis send their harpies to seize her soul and drag her down to torment? Drogon roared full in her face, his breath hot enough to blister skin. Off to her right Dany heard Barristan Selmy shouting, "*Me!* Try me. Over here. *Me!*"

In the smoldering red pits of Drogon's eyes, Dany saw her own reflection. How small she looked, how weak and frail and scared. *I cannot let him see my fear.* She scrabbled in the sand, pushing against the pitmaster's corpse, and her fingers brushed against the handle of his whip. Touching it made her feel braver. The leather was warm, alive. Drogon roared again, the sound so loud that she almost dropped the whip. His teeth snapped at her.

Dany hit him. "No," she screamed, swinging the lash with all the strength that she had in her. The dragon jerked his head back. "No," she screamed again. "NO!" The barbs raked along his snout. Drogon rose, his wings covering her in shadow. Dany swung the lash at his scaled belly, back and forth until her arm began to ache. His long serpentine neck bent like an archer's bow. With a *hisssssss*, he spat black fire down at her. Dany darted underneath the flames, swinging the whip and shouting, "No, no, no. Get DOWN!" His answering roar was full of fear and fury, full of pain. His wings beat once, twice . . .

. . . and folded. The dragon gave one last *hiss* and stretched out flat upon his belly. Black blood was flowing from the wound where the spear had pierced him, smoking where it dripped onto the scorched sands. *He is fire made flesh,* she thought, *and so am I.*

Daenerys Targaryen vaulted onto the dragon's back, seized the spear, and ripped it out. The point was half-melted, the iron red-hot, glowing. She flung it aside. Drogon twisted under her, his muscles rippling as he gathered his strength. The air was thick with sand. Dany could not see, she could not breathe, she could not think. The black wings cracked like thunder, and suddenly the scarlet sands were falling away beneath her.

Dizzy, Dany closed her eyes. When she opened them again, she glimpsed the Meereenese beneath her through a haze of tears and dust, pouring up the steps and out into the streets.

The lash was still in her hand. She flicked it against Drogon's neck and cried, "*Higher!*" Her other hand clutched at his scales, her fingers scrabbling for purchase. Drogon's wide black wings beat the air. Dany could feel the heat of him between her thighs. Her heart felt as if it were about to burst. *Yes,* she thought, *yes, now, now, do it, do it, take me, take me, FLY!*

JON

He was not a tall man, Tormund Giantsbane, but the gods had given him a broad chest and massive belly. Mance Rayder had named him Tormund Horn-Blower for the power of his lungs, and was wont to say that Tormund could laugh the snow off mountaintops. In his wroth, his bellows reminded Jon of a mammoth trumpeting.

That day Tormund bellowed often and loudly. He roared, he shouted, he slammed his fist against the table so hard that a flagon of water over-turned and spilled. A horn of mead was never far from his hand, so the spittle he sprayed when making threats was sweet with honey. He called Jon Snow a craven, a liar, and a turncloak, cursed him for a black-hearted buggering kneeler, a robber, and a carrion crow, accused him of wanting to fuck the free folk up the arse. Twice he flung his drinking horn at Jon's head, though only after he had emptied it. Tormund was not the sort of man to waste good mead. Jon let it all wash over him. He never raised his own voice nor answered threat with threat, but neither did he give more ground than he had come prepared to give.

Finally, as the shadows of the afternoon grew long outside the tent, Tormund Giantsbane—Tall-Talker, Horn-Blower, and Breaker of Ice, Tormund Thunderfist, Husband to Bears, Mead-King of Ruddy Hall, Speaker to Gods and Father of Hosts—thrust out his hand. "Done then, and may the gods forgive me. There's a hundred mothers never will, I know."

Jon clasped the offered hand. The words of his oath rang through his head. *I am the sword in the darkness. I am the watcher on the walls. I am the fire that burns against the cold, the light that brings the dawn, the horn that wakes the sleepers, the shield that guards the realms of men.* And for him a new refrain: *I am the guard who opened the gates and let the foe march through.* He would have given much and more to know that he was doing the right thing. But he had gone too far to turn back. "Done and done," he said.

Tormund's grip was bone-crushing. That much had not changed about him. The beard was the same as well, though the face under that thicket of white hair had thinned considerably, and there were deep lines graven in those ruddy cheeks. "Mance should have killed you when he had the chance," he said as he did his best to turn Jon's hand to pulp and bone. "Gold for gruel, and boys . . . a cruel price. Whatever happened to that sweet lad I knew?"

They made him lord commander. "A fair bargain leaves both sides unhappy, I've heard it said. Three days?"

"If I live that long. Some o' my own will spit on me when they hear these terms." Tormund released Jon's hand. "Your crows will grumble too, if I know them. And I ought to. I have killed more o' you black buggers than I can count."

"It might be best if you did not mention that so loudly when you come south of the Wall."

"Har!" Tormund laughed. That had not changed either; he still laughed easily and often. "Wise words. I'd not want you crows to peck me to death." He slapped Jon's back. "When all my folk are safe behind your Wall, we'll share a bit o' meat and mead. Till then . . ." The wildling pulled off the band from his left arm and tossed it at Jon, then did the same with its twin upon his right. "Your first payment. Had those from my father and him from his. Now they're yours, you thieving black bastard."

The armbands were old gold, solid and heavy, engraved with the ancient runes of the First Men. Tormund Giantsbane had worn them as long as Jon had known him; they had seemed as much a part of him as his beard. "The Braavosi will melt these down for the gold. That seems a shame. Perhaps you ought to keep them."

"No. I'll not have it said that Tormund Thunderfist made the free folk give up their treasures whilst he kept his own." He grinned. "But I'll keep the ring I wear about me member. Much bigger than those little things. On you it'd be a torque."

Jon had to laugh. "You never change."

"Oh, I do." The grin melted away like snow in summer. "I am not the man I was at Ruddy Hall. Seen too much death, and worse things too. My sons . . ." Grief twisted Tormund's face. "Dormund was cut down in the battle for the Wall, and him still half a boy. One o' your king's knights did for him, some bastard all in grey steel with moths upon his shield. I saw the cut, but my boy was dead before I reached him. And Torwynd . . . it was the cold claimed him. Always sickly, that one. He just up and died one night. The worst o' it, before we ever knew he'd died he rose pale with them blue eyes. Had to see to him m'self. That was hard, Jon." Tears shone in his eyes. "He wasn't much of a man, truth be told, but he'd been me little boy once, and I loved him."

Jon put a hand on his shoulder. "I am so sorry."

"Why? Weren't your doing. There's blood on your hands, aye, same as mine. But not his." Tormund shook his head. "I still have two strong sons."

"Your daughter . . . ?"

"Munda." That brought Tormund's smile back. "Took that Longspear Ryk to husband, if you believe it. Boy's got more cock than sense, you ask me, but he treats her well enough. I told him if he ever hurt her, I'd yank his member off and beat him bloody with it." He gave Jon another hearty slap. "Time you were going back. Keep you any longer, they're like to think we ate you."

"Dawn, then. Three days from now. The boys first."

"I heard you the first ten times, crow. A man'd think there was no trust between us." He spat. "Boys first, aye. Mammoths go the long way round. You make sure Eastwatch expects them. I'll make sure there's no fighting, nor rushing at your bloody gate. Nice and orderly we'll be, ducklings in a row. And me the mother duck. Har!" Tormund led Jon from his tent.

Outside the day was bright and cloudless. The sun had returned to the sky after a fortnight's absence, and to the south the Wall rose blue-white and glittering. There was a saying Jon had heard from the older men at Castle Black: *the Wall has more moods than Mad King Aerys,* they'd say, or sometimes, *the Wall has more moods than a woman.* On cloudy days it looked to be white rock. On moonless nights it was as black as coal. In snowstorms it seemed carved of snow. But on days like this, there was no mistaking it for anything but ice. On days like this the Wall shimmered bright as a septon's crystal, every crack and crevasse limned by sunlight, as frozen rainbows danced and died behind translucent ripples. On days like this the Wall was beautiful.

Tormund's eldest son stood near the horses, talking with Leathers. Tall Toregg, he was called amongst the free folk. Though he barely had an inch on Leathers, he overtopped his father by a foot. Hareth, the strapping Mole's Town boy called Horse, huddled near the fire, his back to the other two. He and Leathers were the only men Jon had brought with him to the parley; any more might have been seen as a sign of fear, and twenty men would have been of no more use than two if Tormund had been intent on blood. Ghost was the only protection Jon needed; the direwolf could sniff out foes, even those who hid their enmity behind smiles.

Ghost was gone, though. Jon peeled off one black glove, put two fingers in his mouth, and whistled. "*Ghost!* To me."

From above came the sudden sound of wings. Mormont's raven flapped from a limb of an old oak to perch upon Jon's saddle. "*Corn,*" it cried. "*Corn, corn, corn.*"

"Did you follow me as well?" Jon reached to shoo the bird away but ended up stroking its feathers. The raven cocked its eye at him. "*Snow,*" it muttered, bobbing its head knowingly. Then Ghost emerged from between two trees, with Val beside him.

They look as though they belong together. Val was clad all in white; white woolen breeches tucked into high boots of bleached white leather, white bearskin cloak pinned at the shoulder with a carved weirwood face, white tunic with bone fastenings. Her breath was white as well . . . but her eyes were blue, her long braid the color of dark honey, her cheeks flushed red from the cold. It had been a long while since Jon Snow had seen a sight so lovely.

"Have you been trying to steal my wolf?" he asked her.

"Why not? If every woman had a direwolf, men would be much sweeter. Even crows."

"Har!" laughed Tormund Giantsbane. "Don't bandy words with this one, Lord Snow, she's too clever for the likes o' you and me. Best steal her quick, before Toregg wakes up and takes her first."

What had that oaf Axell Florent said of Val? "*A nubile girl, not hard to look upon. Good hips, good breasts, well made for whelping children.*" All true enough, but the wildling woman was so much more. She had proved that by finding Tormund where seasoned rangers of the Watch had failed. *She may not be a princess, but she would make a worthy wife for any lord.*

But that bridge had been burned a long time ago, and Jon himself had thrown the torch. "Toregg is welcome to her," he announced. "I took a vow."

"She won't mind. Will you, girl?"

Val patted the long bone knife on her hip. "Lord Crow is welcome to steal into my bed any night he dares. Once he's been gelded, keeping those vows will come much easier for him."

"*Har!*" Tormund snorted again. "You hear that, Toregg? Stay away from this one. I have one daughter, don't need another." Shaking his head, the wildling chief ducked back inside his tent.

As Jon scratched Ghost behind the ear, Toregg brought up Val's horse for her. She still rode the grey garron that Mully had given her the day she left the Wall, a shaggy, stunted thing blind in one eye. As she turned it toward the Wall, she asked, "How fares the little monster?"

"Twice as big as when you left us, and thrice as loud. When he wants the teat, you can hear him wail in Eastwatch." Jon mounted his own horse.

Val fell in beside him. "So . . . I brought you Tormund, as I said I would. What now? Am I to be returned to my old cell?"

"Your old cell is occupied. Queen Selyse has claimed the King's Tower, for her own. Do you remember Hardin's Tower?"

"The one that looks about to collapse?"

"It's looked that way for a hundred years. I've had the top floor made ready for you, my lady. You will have more room than in the King's Tower, though you may not be as comfortable. No one has ever called it Hardin's Palace."

"I would choose freedom over comfort every time."

"Freedom of the castle you shall have, but I regret to say you must remain a captive. I can promise that you will not be troubled by unwanted visitors, however. My own men guard Hardin's Tower, not the queen's. And Wun Wun sleeps in the entry hall."

"A giant as protector? Even Dalla could not boast of that."

Tormund's wildlings watched them pass, peering out from tents and lean-tos beneath leafless trees. For every man of fighting age, Jon saw three women and as many children, gaunt-faced things with hollow cheeks and staring eyes. When Mance Rayder had led the free folk down upon the Wall, his followers drove large herds of sheep and goats and swine before them, but now the only animals to be seen were the mammoths. If not for the ferocity of the giants, those would have been slaughtered too, he did not doubt. There was a lot of meat on a mammoth's bones.

Jon saw signs of sickness too. That disquieted him more than he could say. If Tormund's band were starved and sick, what of the thousands who had followed Mother Mole to Hardhome? *Cotter Pyke should reach them soon. If the winds were kind, his fleet might well be on its way back to Eastwatch even now, with as many of the free folk as he could cram aboard.*

"How did you fare with Tormund?" asked Val.

"Ask me a year from now. The hard part still awaits me. The part where I convince mine own to eat this meal I've cooked for them. None of them are going to like the taste, I fear."

"Let me help."

"You have. You brought me Tormund."

"I can do more."

Why not? thought Jon. *They are all convinced she is a princess.* Val looked the part and rode as if she had been born on horseback. *A warrior princess,* he decided, *not some willowy creature who sits up in a tower, brushing her hair and waiting for some knight to rescue her.* "I must inform the queen of this agreement," he said. "You are welcome to come meet her, if you can find it in yourself to bend a knee." It would never do to offend Her Grace before he even opened his mouth.

"May I laugh when I kneel?"

"You may not. This is no game. A river of blood runs between our peoples, old and deep and red. Stannis Baratheon is one of the few who favors admitting wildlings to the realm. I need his queen's support for what I've done."

Val's playful smile died. "You have my word, Lord Snow. I will be a proper wildling princess for your queen."

She is not my queen, he might have said. *If truth be told, the day of her departure cannot come too fast for me. And if the gods are good, she will take Melisandre with her.*

They rode the rest of the way in silence, Ghost loping at their heels. Mormont's raven followed them as far as the gate, then flapped upward as the rest of them dismounted. Horse went ahead with a brand to light the way through the icy tunnel.

A small crowd of black brothers was waiting by the gate when Jon and his companions emerged south of the Wall. Ulmer of the Kingswood was amongst them, and it was the old archer who came forward to speak for the rest. "If it please m'lord, the lads were wondering. Will it be peace, m'lord? Or blood and iron?"

"Peace," Jon Snow replied. "Three days hence, Tormund Giantsbane will lead his people through the Wall. As friends, not foes. Some may even swell our ranks, as brothers. It will be for us to make them welcome. Now back to your duties." Jon handed the reins of his horse to Satin. "I must see Queen Selyse." Her Grace would take it as a slight if he did not come to her at once. "Afterward I will have letters to write. Bring parchment, quills, and a pot of maester's black to my chambers. Then summon Marsh, Yarwyck, Septon Cellador, Clydas." Cellador would be half-drunk, and Clydas was a poor substitute for a real maester, but they were what he had. *Till Sam returns.* "The northmen too. Flint and Norrey. Leathers, you should be there as well."

"Hobb is baking onion pies," said Satin. "Shall I request that they all join you for supper?"

Jon considered. "No. Ask them to join me atop the Wall at sunset." He turned to Val. "My lady. With me, if you please."

"The crow commands, the captive must obey." Her tone was playful. "This queen of yours must be fierce if the legs of grown men give out beneath them when they meet her. Should I have dressed in mail instead of wool and fur? These clothes were given to me by Dalla, I would sooner not get bloodstains all over them."

"If words drew blood, you might have cause to fear. I think your clothes are safe enough, my lady."

They made their way toward the King's Tower, along fresh-shoveled pathways between mounds of dirty snow. "I have heard it said that your queen has a great dark beard."

Jon knew he should not smile, but he did. "Only a mustache. Very wispy. You can count the hairs."

"How disappointing."

For all her talk about wanting to be mistress of her seat, Selyse Baratheon seemed in no great haste to abandon the comforts of Castle Black for the shadows of the Nightfort. She kept guards, of course—four men posted at the door, two outside on the steps, two inside by the brazier. Commanding them was Ser Patrek of King's Mountain, clad in his knightly raiment of white and blue and silver, his cloak a spatter of five-pointed stars. When presented to Val, the knight sank to one knee to kiss her glove. "You are even lovelier than I was told, princess," he declared. "The queen has told me much and more of your beauty."

"How odd, when she has never seen me." Val patted Ser Patrek on the head. "Up with you now, ser kneeler. Up, up." She sounded as if she were talking to a dog.

It was all that Jon could do not to laugh. Stone-faced, he told the knight that they required audience with the queen. Ser Patrek sent one of the men-at-arms scrambling up the steps to inquire as to whether Her Grace would receive them. "The wolf stays here, though," Ser Patrek insisted.

Jon had expected that. The direwolf made Queen Selyse anxious, almost as much as Wun Weg Wun Dar Wun. "Ghost, stay."

They found Her Grace sewing by the fire, whilst her fool danced about to music only he could hear, the cowbells on his antlers *clanging*. "The crow, the crow," Patchface cried when he saw Jon. "Under the sea the crows are white as snow, I know, I know, oh, oh, oh." Princess Shireen was curled up in a window seat, her hood drawn up to hide the worst of the greyscale that had disfigured her face.

There was no sign of Lady Melisandre. For that much Jon was grateful. Soon or late he would need to face the red priestess, but he would sooner it was not in the queen's presence. "Your Grace." He took a knee. Val did likewise.

Queen Selyse set aside her sewing. "You may rise."

"If it please Your Grace, may I present the Lady Val? Her sister Dalla was—"

"—mother to that squalling babe who keeps us awake at night. I know who she is, Lord Snow." The queen sniffed. "You are fortunate that she returned to us before the king my husband, else it might have gone badly for you. Very badly indeed."

"Are you the wildling princess?" Shireen asked Val.

"Some call me that," said Val. "My sister was wife to Mance Rayder, the King-Beyond-the-Wall. She died giving him a son."

"I'm a princess too," Shireen announced, "but I never had a sister. I used to have a cousin once, before he sailed away. He was just a bastard, but I liked him."

"Honestly, Shireen," her mother said. "I am sure the lord commander did not come to hear about Robert's by-blows. Patchface, be a good fool and take the princess to her room."

The bells on his hat rang. "Away, away," the fool sang. "Come with me beneath the sea, away, away, away." He took the little princess by one hand and drew her from the room, skipping.

Jon said, "Your Grace, the leader of the free folk has agreed to my terms."

Queen Selyse gave the tiniest of nods. "It was ever my lord husband's wish to grant sanctuary to these savage peoples. So long as they keep the king's peace and the king's laws, they are welcome in our realm." She pursed her lips. "I am told they have more giants with them."

Val answered. "Almost two hundred of them, Your Grace. And more than eighty mammoths."

The queen shuddered. "Dreadful creatures." Jon could not tell if she was speaking of the mammoths or the giants. "Though such beasts might be useful to my lord husband in his battles."

"That may be, Your Grace," Jon said, "but the mammoths are too big to pass through our gate."

"Cannot the gate be widened?"

"That . . . that would be unwise, I think."

Selyse sniffed. "If you say so. No doubt you know about such things. Where do you mean to settle these wildlings? Surely Mole's Town is not large enough to contain . . . how many are they?"

"Four thousand, Your Grace. They will help us garrison our abandoned castles, the better to defend the Wall."

"I had been given to understand that those castles were ruins. Dismal places, bleak and cold, hardly more than heaps of rubble. At Eastwatch we heard talk of rats and spiders."

The cold will have killed the spiders by now, thought Jon, *and the rats may be a useful source of meat come winter.* "All true, Your Grace . . . but even ruins offer some shelter. And the Wall will stand between them and the Others."

"I see you have considered all this carefully, Lord Snow. I am sure King Stannis will be pleased when he returns triumphant from his battle."

Assuming he returns at all.

"Of course," the queen went on, "the wildlings must first acknowledge Stannis as their king and R'hllor as their god."

And here we are, face-to-face in the narrow passage. "Your Grace, forgive me. Those were not the terms that we agreed to."

The queen's face hardened. "A grievous oversight." What faint traces of warmth her voice had held vanished all at once.

"Free folk do not kneel," Val told her.

"Then they must be knelt," the queen declared.

"Do that, Your Grace, and we will rise again at the first chance," Val promised. "Rise with blades in hand."

The queen's lips tightened, and her chin gave a small quiver. "You are insolent. I suppose that is only to be expected of a wildling. We must find you a husband who can teach you courtesy." The queen turned her glare on Jon. "I do not approve, Lord Commander. Nor will my lord husband. I cannot prevent you from opening your gate, as we both know full well, but I promise you that you shall answer for it when the king returns from battle. Mayhaps you might want to reconsider."

"Your Grace." Jon knelt again. This time Val did not join him. "I am sorry my actions have displeased you. I did as I thought best. Do I have your leave to go?"

"You do. At once."

Once outside and well away from the queen's men, Val gave vent to her wroth. "You lied about her beard. That one has more hair on her chin than I have between my legs. And the daughter . . . her face . . ."

"Greyscale."

"The grey death is what we call it."

"It is not always mortal in children."

"North of the Wall it is. Hemlock is a sure cure, but a pillow or a blade will work as well. If I had given birth to that poor child, I would have given her the gift of mercy long ago."

This was a Val that Jon had never seen before. "Princess Shireen is the queen's only child."

"I pity both of them. The child is not clean."

"If Stannis wins his war, Shireen will stand as heir to the Iron Throne."

"Then I pity your Seven Kingdoms."

"The maesters say greyscale is not—"

"The maesters may believe what they wish. Ask a woods witch if you would know the truth. The grey death sleeps, only to wake again. *The child is not clean!*"

"She seems a sweet girl. You cannot know—"

"I can. You know nothing, Jon Snow." Val seized his arm. "I want the monster out of there. Him and his wet nurses. You cannot leave them in that same tower as the dead girl."

Jon shook her hand away. "*She is not dead.*"

"She is. Her mother cannot see it. Nor you, it seems. Yet death is there." She walked away from him, stopped, turned back. "I brought you Tormund Giantsbane. Bring me my monster."

"If I can, I will."

"Do. You owe me a debt, Jon Snow."

Jon watched her stride away. *She is wrong. She must be wrong. Greyscale is not so deadly as she claims, not in children.*

Ghost was gone again. The sun was low in the west. *A cup of hot spiced wine would serve me well just now. Two cups would serve me even better.* But that would have to wait. He had foes to face. Foes of the worst sort: brothers.

He found Leathers waiting for him by the winch cage. The two of them rode up together. The higher they went, the stronger the wind. Fifty feet up, the heavy cage began to sway with every gust. From time to time it scraped against the Wall, starting small crystalline showers of ice that sparkled in the sunlight as they fell. They rose above the tallest towers of the castle. At four hundred feet the wind had teeth, and tore at his black cloak so it slapped noisily at the iron bars. At seven hundred it cut right through him. *The Wall is mine,* Jon reminded himself as the winchmen were swinging in the cage, *for two more days, at least.*

Jon hopped down onto the ice, thanked the men on the winch, and nodded to the spearmen standing sentry. Both wore woolen hoods pulled down over their heads, so nothing could be seen of their faces but their eyes, but he knew Ty by the tangled rope of greasy black hair falling down his back and Owen by the sausage stuffed into the scabbard at his hip. He might have known them anyway, just by the way they stood. *A good lord must know his men,* his father had once told him and Robb, back at Winterfell.

Jon walked to the edge of the Wall and gazed down upon the killing ground where Mance Rayder's host had died. He wondered where Mance was now. *Did he ever find you, little sister? Or were you just a ploy he used so I would set him free?*

It had been so long since he had last seen Arya. What would she look like now? Would he even know her? *Arya Underfoot. Her face was always dirty.* Would she still have that little sword he'd had Mikken forge for her? *Stick them with the pointy end,* he'd told her. Wisdom for her wedding night if half of what he heard of Ramsay Snow was true. *Bring her home, Mance. I saved your son from Melisandre, and now I am about to save four thousand of your free folk. You owe me this one little girl.*

In the haunted forest to the north, the shadows of the afternoon crept through the trees. The western sky was a blaze of red, but to the east the first stars were peeking out. Jon Snow flexed the fingers of his sword hand, remembering all he'd lost. *Sam, you sweet fat fool, you played me a cruel jape when you made me lord commander. A lord commander has no friends.*

"Lord Snow?" said Leathers. "The cage is coming up."

"I hear it." Jon moved back from the edge.

First to make the ascent were the clan chiefs Flint and Norrey, clad in fur and iron. The Norrey looked like some old fox—wrinkled and slight of build, but sly-eyed and spry. Torghen Flint was half a head shorter but must weigh twice as much—a stout gruff man with gnarled, red-knuckled hands as big as hams, leaning heavily on a blackthorn cane as he limped across the ice. Bowen Marsh came next, bundled up in a bearskin. After him Othell Yarwyck. Then Septon Cellador, half in his cups.

"Walk with me," Jon told them. They walked west along the Wall, down gravel-strewn paths toward the setting sun. When they had come fifty yards from the warming shed, he said, "You know why I've summoned you. Three days hence at dawn the gate will open, to allow Tormund and his people through the Wall. There is much we need to do in preparation."

Silence greeted his pronouncement. Then Othell Yarwyck said, "Lord Commander, there are *thousands* of—"

"—scrawny wildlings, bone weary, hungry, far from home." Jon pointed at the lights of their campfires. "There they are. Four thousand, Tormund claims."

"Three thousand, I make them, by the fires." Bowen Marsh lived for counts and measures. "More than twice that number at Hardhome with the woods witch, we are told. And Ser Denys writes of great camps in the mountains beyond the Shadow Tower . . ."

Jon did not deny it. "Tormund says the Weeper means to try the Bridge of Skulls again."

The Old Pomegranate touched his scar. He had gotten it defending the Bridge of Skulls the last time the Weeping Man had tried to cut his way across the Gorge. "Surely the lord commander cannot mean to allow that . . . that demon through as well?"

"Not gladly." Jon had not forgotten the heads the Weeping Man had left him, with bloody holes where their eyes had been. *Black Jack Bulwer, Hairy Hal, Garth Greyfeather. I cannot avenge them, but I will not forget their names.* "But yes, my lord, him as well. We cannot pick and choose amongst the free folk, saying this one may pass, this one may not. Peace means peace for all."

The Norrey hawked and spat. "As well make peace with wolves and carrion crows."

"It's peaceful in my dungeons," grumbled Old Flint. "Give the Weeping Man to me."

"How many rangers has the Weeper killed?" asked Othell Yarwyck. "How many women has he raped or killed or stolen?"

"Three of mine own ilk," said Old Flint. "And he blinds the girls he does not take."

"When a man takes the black, his crimes are forgiven," Jon reminded them. "If we want the free folk to fight beside us, we must pardon their past crimes as we would for our own."

"The Weeper will not say the words," insisted Yarwyck. "He will not wear the cloak. Even other raiders do not trust him."

"You need not trust a man to use him." *Else how could I make use of all of you?* "We need the Weeper, and others like him. Who knows the wild better than a wildling? Who knows our foes better than a man who has fought them?"

"All the Weeper knows is rape and murder," said Yarwyck.

"Once past the Wall, the wildlings will have thrice our numbers," said Bowen Marsh. "And that is only Tormund's band. Add the Weeper's men and those at Hardhome, and they will have the strength to end the Night's Watch in a single night."

"Numbers alone do not win a war. You have not seen them. Half of them are dead on their feet."

"I would sooner have them dead in the ground," said Yarwyck. "If it please my lord."

"It does *not* please me." Jon's voice was as cold as the wind snapping at their cloaks. "There are children in that camp, hundreds of them, thousands. Women as well."

"Spearwives."

"Some. Along with mothers and grandmothers, widows and maids . . . would you condemn them all to die, my lord?"

"Brothers should not squabble," Septon Cellador said. "Let us kneel and pray to the Crone to light our way to wisdom."

"Lord Snow," said The Norrey, "where do you mean to put these wildlings o' yours? Not on *my* lands, I hope."

"Aye," declared Old Flint. "You want them in the Gift, that's your folly, but see they don't wander off or I'll send you back their heads. Winter is nigh, I want no more mouths to feed."

"The wildlings will remain upon the Wall," Jon assured them. "Most will be housed in one of our abandoned castles." The Watch now had garrisons at Icemark, Long Barrow, Sable Hall, Greyguard, and Deep Lake, all badly undermanned, but ten castles still stood empty and abandoned. "Men with wives and children, all orphan girls and any orphan boys below the age of ten, old women, widowed mothers, any woman who does not care to fight. The spearwives we'll send to Long Barrow to join their sisters, single men to the other forts we've reopened. Those who take the black will remain here, or be posted to Eastwatch or the Shadow Tower. Tormund will take Oakenshield as his seat, to keep him close at hand."

Bowen Marsh sighed. "If they do not slay us with their swords, they will do so with their mouths. Pray, how does the lord commander propose to feed Tormund and his thousands?"

Jon had anticipated that question. "Through Eastwatch. We will bring in food by ship, as much as might be required. From the riverlands and the stormlands and the Vale of Arryn, from Dorne and the Reach, across the narrow sea from the Free Cities."

"And this food will be paid for . . . how, if I may ask?"

With gold, from the Iron Bank of Braavos, Jon might have replied. Instead he said, "I have agreed that the free folk may keep their furs and
pelts. They will need those for warmth when winter comes. All other
wealth they must surrender. Gold and silver, amber, gemstones, carvings,
anything of value. We will ship it all across the narrow sea to be sold in the
Free Cities."

"All the wealth o' the wildlings," said The Norrey. "That should buy
you a bushel o' barleycorn. Two bushels, might be."

"Lord Commander, why not demand that the wildlings give up their
arms as well?" asked Clydas.

Leathers laughed at that. "You want the free folk to fight beside you
against the common foe. How are we to do that without arms? Would you
have us throw snowballs at the wights? Or will you give us sticks to hit
them with?"

The arms most wildlings carry are little more than sticks, thought Jon.
Wooden clubs, stone axes, mauls, spears with fire-hardened points, knives
of bone and stone and dragonglass, wicker shields, bone armor, boiled
leather. The Thenns worked bronze, and raiders like the Weeper carried
stolen steel and iron swords looted off some corpse . . . but even those
were oft of ancient vintage, dinted from years of hard use and spotted with
rust.

"Tormund Giantsbane will never willingly disarm his people," Jon said.
"He is not the Weeping Man, but he is no craven either. If I had asked that
of him, it would have come to blood."

The Norrey fingered his beard. "You may put your wildlings in these
ruined forts, Lord Snow, but how will you make them stay? What is there
to stop them moving south to fairer, warmer lands?"

"*Our* lands," said Old Flint.

"Tormund has given me his oath. He will serve with us until the spring.
The Weeper and their other captains will swear the same or we will not
let them pass."

Old Flint shook his head. "They will betray us."

"The Weeper's word is worthless," said Othell Yarwyck.

"These are godless savages," said Septon Cellador. "Even in the south
the treachery of wildlings is renowned."

Leathers crossed his arms. "That battle down below? I was on t'other
side, remember? Now I wear your blacks and train your boys to kill. Some
might call me turncloak. Might be so . . . but I am no more savage than
you crows. We have gods too. The same gods they keep in Winterfell."

"The gods of the North, since before this Wall was raised," said Jon.

"Those are the gods that Tormund swore by. He will keep his word. I know him, as I knew Mance Rayder. I marched with them for a time, you may recall."

"I had not forgotten," said the Lord Steward.

No, thought Jon, *I did not think you had.*

"Mance Rayder swore an oath as well," Marsh went on. "He vowed to wear no crowns, take no wife, father no sons. Then he turned his cloak, did all those things, and led a fearsome host against the realm. It is the remnants of that host that waits beyond the Wall."

"Broken remnants."

"A broken sword can be reforged. A broken sword can kill."

"The free folk have neither laws nor lords," Jon said, "but they love their children. Will you admit that much?"

"It is not their children who concern us. We fear the fathers, not the sons."

"As do I. So I insisted upon hostages." *I am not the trusting fool you take me for . . . nor am I half wildling, no matter what you believe.* "One hundred boys between the ages of eight and sixteen. A son from each of their chiefs and captains, the rest chosen by lot. The boys will serve as pages and squires, freeing our own men for other duties. Some may choose to take the black one day. Queerer things have happened. The rest will stand hostage for the loyalty of their sires."

The northmen glanced at one another. "Hostages," mused The Norrey. "Tormund has agreed to this?"

It was that, or watch his people die. "My blood price, he called it," said Jon Snow, "but he will pay."

"Aye, and why not?" Old Flint stomped his cane against the ice. "Wards, we always called them, when Winterfell demanded boys of us, but they were hostages, and none the worse for it."

"None but them whose sires displeased the Kings o' Winter," said The Norrey. "Those came home shorter by a head. So you tell me, boy . . . if these wildling friends o' yours prove false, do you have the belly to do what needs be done?"

Ask Janos Slynt. "Tormund Giantsbane knows better than to try me. I may seem a green boy in your eyes, Lord Norrey, but I am still a son of Eddard Stark."

Yet even that did not appease his Lord Steward. "You say these boys will serve as squires. Surely the lord commander does not mean they will be trained *at arms?*"

Jon's anger flared. "No, my lord, I mean to set them to sewing lacy smallclothes. Of course they shall be trained at arms. They shall also churn butter, hew firewood, muck stables, empty chamber pots, and run messages . . . and in between they will be drilled with spear and sword and longbow."

Marsh flushed a deeper shade of red. "The lord commander must pardon my bluntness, but I have no softer way to say this. What you propose is nothing less than treason. For eight thousand years the men of the Night's Watch have stood upon the Wall and fought these wildlings. Now you mean to let them pass, to shelter them in our castles, to feed them and clothe them and teach them how to fight. Lord Snow, must I remind you? *You swore an oath.*"

"I know what I swore." Jon said the words. "*I am the sword in the darkness. I am the watcher on the walls. I am the fire that burns against the cold, the light that brings the dawn, the horn that wakes the sleepers, the shield that guards the realms of men.* Were those the same words you said when you took your vows?"

"They were. As the lord commander knows."

"Are you certain that I have not forgotten some? The ones about the king and his laws, and how we must defend every foot of his land and cling to each ruined castle? How does that part go?" Jon waited for an answer. None came. "*I am the shield that guards the realms of men.* Those are the words. So tell me, my lord—what are these wildlings, if not men?"

Bowen Marsh opened his mouth. No words came out. A flush crept up his neck.

Jon Snow turned away. The last light of the sun had begun to fade. He watched the cracks along the Wall go from red to grey to black, from streaks of fire to rivers of black ice. Down below, Lady Melisandre would be lighting her nightfire and chanting, *Lord of Light, defend us, for the night is dark and full of terrors.*

"Winter is coming," Jon said at last, breaking the awkward silence, "and with it the white walkers. The Wall is where we stop them. The Wall was *made* to stop them . . . but the Wall must be manned. This discussion is at an end. We have much to do before the gate is opened. Tormund and his people will need to be fed and clothed and housed. Some are sick and will need nursing. Those will fall to you, Clydas. Save as many as you can."

Clydas blinked his dim pink eyes. "I will do my best, Jon. My lord, I mean."

"We will need every cart and wagon made ready to transport the free folk to their new homes. Othell, you shall see to that."

Yarwyck grimaced. "Aye, Lord Commander."

"Lord Bowen, you shall collect the tolls. The gold and silver, the amber, the torques and armbands and necklaces. Sort it all, count it, see that it reaches Eastwatch safely."

"Yes, Lord Snow," said Bowen Marsh.

And Jon thought, *"Ice,"* she said, *"and daggers in the dark. Blood frozen red and hard, and naked steel."* His sword hand flexed. The wind was rising.

CERSEI

Each night seemed colder than the last.

The cell had neither fireplace nor brazier. The only window was too high to allow her a view and too small to squeeze through, but more than large enough to let in the chill. Cersei had torn up the first shift they gave her, demanding the return of her own clothes, but that only left her naked and shivering. When they brought her another shift, she pulled it down over her head and thanked them, choking upon the words.

The window let in sounds as well. That was the only way the queen had to know what might be happening in the city. The septas who brought her food would tell her nothing.

She hated that. Jaime would be coming for her, but how would she know when he arrived? Cersei only hoped he was not so foolish as to go racing ahead of his army. He would need every sword to deal with the ragged horde of Poor Fellows surrounding the Great Sept. She asked about her twin often, but her gaolers gave no answer. She asked about Ser Loras too. At last report the Knight of Flowers had been dying on Dragonstone of wounds received whilst taking the castle. *Let him die,* Cersei thought, *and let him be quick about it.* The boy's death would mean an empty place on the Kingsguard, and that might be her salvation. But the septas were as close-mouthed about Loras Tyrell as they were about Jaime.

Lord Qyburn had been her last and only visitor. Her world had a population of four: herself and her three gaolers, pious and unyielding. Septa Unella was big-boned and mannish, with callused hands and homely, scowling features. Septa Moelle had stiff white hair and small mean eyes perpetually crinkled in suspicion, peering out of a wrinkled face as sharp as the blade of an axe. Septa Scolera was thick-waisted and short, with heavy breasts, olive skin, and a sour smell to her, like milk on the verge of going bad. They brought her food and water, emptied her chamber pot, and took away her shift for washing every few days, leaving her to huddle naked under her blanket until it was returned to her. Sometimes Scolera would read to her from *The Seven-Pointed Star* or *The Book of Holy Prayer*, but elsewise none of them would speak with her or answer any of her questions.

She hated and despised all three of them, almost as much as she hated and despised the men who had betrayed her.

False friends, treacherous servants, men who had professed undying love, even her own blood . . . all of them had deserted her in her hour of need. Osney Kettleblack, that weakling, had broken beneath the lash, filling the High Sparrow's ears with secrets he should have taken to his grave. His brothers, scum of the streets whom she had raised high, did no more than sit upon their hands. Aurane Waters, her admiral, had fled to sea with the dromonds she had built for him. Orton Merryweather had gone running back to Longtable, taking his wife, Taena, who had been the queen's one true friend in these terrible times. Harys Swyft and Grand Maester Pycelle had abandoned her to captivity and offered the realm to the very men who had conspired against her. Meryn Trant and Boros Blount, the king's sworn protectors, were nowhere to be found. Even her cousin Lancel, who once had claimed to love her, was one of her accusers. Her uncle had refused to help her rule when she would have made him the King's Hand.

And Jaime . . .

No, that she could not believe, would not believe. Jaime would be here once he knew of her plight. *"Come at once,"* she had written to him. *"Help me. Save me. I need you now as I have never needed you before. I love you. I love you. I love you. Come at once."* Qyburn had sworn that he would see that her letter reached her twin, off in the riverlands with his army. Qyburn had never returned, however. For all she knew, he might be dead, his head impaled upon a spike above the city Keep's gates. Or perhaps he was languishing in one of the black cells beneath the Red Keep, her letter still unsent. The queen had asked after him a hundred times, but her captors would not speak of him. All she knew for certain was that Jaime had not come.

Not yet, she told herself. *But soon. And once he comes the High Sparrow and his bitches will sing a different song.*

She hated feeling helpless.

She had threatened, but her threats had been received with stony faces and deaf ears. She had commanded, but her commands had been ignored. She had invoked the Mother's mercy, appealing to the natural sympathy of one woman for another, but the three shriveled septas must have put their womanhood aside when they spoke their vows. She had tried charm, speaking to them gently, accepting each new outrage meekly. They were not swayed. She had offered them rewards, promised leniency, honors, gold, positions at court. They treated her promises as they did her threats.

And she had prayed. Oh, how she had prayed. Prayer was what they wanted, so she served it to them, served it on her knees as if she were some common trollop of the streets and not a daughter of the Rock. She had prayed for relief, for deliverance, for Jaime. Loudly she asked the gods to defend her in her innocence; silently she prayed for her accusers to suffer sudden, painful deaths. She prayed until her knees were raw and bloody, until her tongue felt so thick and heavy that she was like to choke on it. All the prayers they had taught her as a girl came back to Cersei in her cell, and she made up new ones as needed, calling on the Mother and the Maiden, on the Father and the Warrior, on the Crone and the Smith. She had even prayed to the Stranger. *Any god in a storm.* The Seven proved as deaf as their earthly servants. Cersei gave them all the words that she had in her, gave them everything but tears. *That they will never have,* she told herself.

She hated feeling weak.

If the gods had given her the strength they gave Jaime and that swaggering oaf Robert, she could have made her own escape. *Oh, for a sword and the skill to wield it.* She had a warrior's heart, but the gods in their blind malice had given her the feeble body of a woman. The queen had tried to fight them early on, but the septas had overwhelmed her. There were too many of them, and they were stronger than they looked. Ugly old women, every one of them, but all that praying and scrubbing and beating novices with sticks had left them tough as roots.

And they would not let her rest. Night or day, whenever the queen closed her eyes to sleep, one of her captors would appear to wake her and demand that she confess her sins. She stood accused of adultery, fornication, high treason, even murder, for Osney Kettleblack had confessed to smothering the last High Septon at her command. "I am come to hear you tell of all your murders and fornications," Septa Unella would growl when she shook the queen awake. Septa Moelle would tell her that it was her sins that kept her sleepless. "Only the innocent know the peace of untroubled sleep. Confess your sins, and you will sleep like a newborn babe."

Wake and sleep and wake again, every night was broken into pieces by the rough hands of her tormentors, and every night was colder and crueler than the night before. The hour of the owl, the hour of the wolf, the hour of the nightingale, moonrise and moonset, dusk and dawn, they staggered past like drunkards. What hour was it? What day was it? Where was she? Was this a dream, or had she woken? The little shards of sleep that they allowed her turned into razors, slicing at her wits. Each day found her duller than the day before, exhausted and feverish. She had lost all sense of how long she had been imprisoned in this cell, high up in one of the seven towers of the Great Sept of Baelor. *I will grow old and die here,* she thought, despairing.

Cersei could not allow that to happen. Her son had need of her. The realm had need of her. She had to free herself, no matter what the risk. Her world had shrunk to a cell six feet square, a chamber pot, a lumpy pallet, and a brown wool blanket thin as hope that made her skin itch, but she was still Lord Tywin's heir, a daughter of the Rock.

Exhausted by her lack of sleep, shivering from the cold that stole into the tower cell each night, feverish and famished by turns, Cersei came at last to know she must confess.

That night, when Septa Unella came to wrench her out of sleep, she found the queen waiting on her knees. "I have sinned," said Cersei. Her tongue was thick in her mouth, her lips raw and chapped. "I have sinned most grievously. I see that now. How could I have been so blind for so long? The Crone came to me with her lamp raised high, and by its holy light I saw the road that I must walk. I want to be clean again. I want only absolution. Please, good septa, I beg of you, take me to the High Septon so that I might confess my crimes and fornications."

"I will tell him, Your Grace," said Septa Unella. "His High Holiness will be most pleased. Only through confession and true repentance may our immortal souls be saved."

And for the rest of that long night they let her sleep. Hours and hours of blessed sleep. The owl and the wolf and the nightingale slipped by for once with their passage unseen and unremarked, whilst Cersei dreamed a long sweet dream where Jaime was her husband and their son was still alive.

Come morning, the queen felt almost like herself again. When her captors came for her, she made pious noises at them again and told them how determined she was to confess her sins and be forgiven for all that she had done.

"We rejoice to hear it," said Septa Moelle.

"It will be a great weight off your soul," said Septa Scolera. "You will feel much better afterward, Your Grace."

Your Grace. Those two simple words thrilled her. During her long captivity, her gaolers had not oft bothered with even that simple courtesy.

"His High Holiness awaits," said Septa Unella.

Cersei lowered her head, humble and obedient. "Might I be allowed to
bathe first? I am in no fit state to attend him."

"You may wash later if His High Holiness allows," said Septa Unella.
"It is the cleanliness of your immortal soul that should concern you now,
not such vanities of the flesh."

The three septas led her down the tower stairs, with Septa Unella going
before her and Septa Moelle and Septa Scolera at her heels, as if they
were afraid that she might try to flee. "It has been so long since I have had
a visitor," Cersei murmured in a quiet voice as they made their descent.
"Is the king well? I ask only as a mother, fearful for her child."

"His Grace is in good health," said Septa Scolera, "and well protected,
day and night. The queen is with him, always."

I am the queen! She swallowed, smiled, and said, "That is good to know.
Tommen loves her so. I never believed those terrible things that were
being said of her." Had Margaery Tyrell somehow wriggled free of the accusations of fornication, adultery, and high treason? "Was there a trial?"

"Soon," said Septa Scolera, "but her brother—"

"*Hush.*" Septa Unella turned to glare back over her shoulder at Scolera. "You chatter too much, you foolish old woman. It is not for us to
speak of such things."

Scolera lowered her head. "Pray forgive me."

They made the rest of the descent in silence.

The High Sparrow received her in his sanctum, an austere seven-sided
chamber where crudely carved faces of the Seven stared out from the
stone walls with expressions almost as sour and disapproving as His High
Holiness himself. When she entered, he was seated behind a rough-hewn
table, writing. The High Septon had not changed since the last time she
had been in his presence, the day he had her seized and imprisoned. He
was still a scrawny grey-haired man with a lean, hard, half-starved look, his
face sharp-featured, lined, his eyes suspicious. In place of the rich robes of
his predecessors, he wore a shapeless tunic of undyed wool that fell down
to his ankles. "Your Grace," he said, by way of greeting. "I understand that
you wish to make confession."

Cersei dropped to her knees. "I do, High Holiness. The Crone came to
me as I slept with her lamp held high—"

"To be sure. Unella, you will stay and make a record of Her Grace's
words. Scolera, Moelle, you have my leave to go." He pressed the fingers

of his hands together, the same gesture she had seen her father use a thousand times.

Septa Unella took a seat behind her, spread out a parchment, dipped a quill in maester's ink. Cersei felt a stab of fright. "Once I have confessed, will I be permitted to—"

"Your Grace shall be dealt with according to your sins."

This man is implacable, she realized once again. She gathered herself for a moment. "Mother have mercy on me, then. I have lain with men outside the bonds of marriage. I confess it."

"Who?" The High Septon's eyes were fixed on hers.

Cersei could hear Unella writing behind her. Her quill made a faint, soft scratching sound. "Lancel Lannister, my cousin. And Osney Kettleblack." Both men had confessed to bedding her, it would do her no good to deny it. "His brothers too. Both of them." She had no way of knowing what Osfryd and Osmund might say. Safer to confess too much than too little. "It does not excuse my sin, High Holiness, but I was lonely and afraid. The gods took King Robert from me, my love and my protector. I was alone, surrounded by schemers, false friends, and traitors who were conspiring at the death of my children. I did not know who to trust, so I . . . I used the only means that I had to bind the Kettleblacks to me."

"By which you mean your female parts?"

"My flesh." She pressed a hand to her face, shuddering. When she lowered it again, her eyes were wet with tears. "Yes. May the Maid forgive me. It was for my children, though, for the realm. I took no pleasure in it. The Kettleblacks . . . they are hard men, and cruel, and they used me roughly, but what else was I to do? Tommen needed men around him I could trust."

"His Grace was protected by the Kingsguard."

"The Kingsguard stood by useless as his brother Joffrey died, murdered at his own wedding feast. I watched one son die, I could not bear to lose another. I have sinned, I have committed wanton fornication, but I did it for Tommen. Forgive me, High Holiness, but I would open my legs for every man in King's Landing if that was what I had to do to keep my children safe."

"Forgiveness comes only from the gods. What of Ser Lancel, who was your cousin and your lord husband's squire? Did you take him into your bed to win his loyalty as well?"

"Lancel." Cersei hesitated. *Careful,* she told herself, *Lancel will have told him everything.* "Lancel loved me. He was half a boy, but I never doubted his devotion to me or my son."

"And yet you still corrupted him."

"I was lonely." She choked back a sob. "I had lost my husband, my son, my lord father. I was regent, but a queen is still a woman, and women are weak vessels, easily tempted . . . Your High Holiness knows the truth of that. Even holy septas have been known to sin. I took comfort with Lancel. He was kind and gentle and I needed someone. It was wrong, I know, but I had no one else . . . a woman *needs* to be loved, she needs a man beside her, she . . . she . . ." She began to sob uncontrollably.

The High Septon made no move to comfort her. He sat there with his hard eyes fixed on her, watching her weep, as stony as the statues of the Seven in the sept above. Long moments passed, but finally her tears were all dried up. By then her eyes were red and raw from crying, and she felt as if she might faint.

The High Sparrow was not done with her, however. "These are common sins," he said. "The wickedness of widows is well-known, and all women are wantons at heart, given to using their wiles and their beauty to work their wills on men. There is no treason here, so long as you did not stray from your marriage bed whilst His Grace King Robert was still alive."

"Never," she whispered, shivering. "*Never*, I swear it."

He paid that no mind. "There are other charges laid against Your Grace, crimes far more grievous than simple fornications. You admit Ser Osney Kettleblack was your lover, and Ser Osney insists that he smothered my predecessor at your behest. He further insists that he bore false witness against Queen Margaery and her cousins, telling tales of fornications, adultery, and high treason, again at your behest."

"No," said Cersei. "It is not true. I love Margaery as I would a daughter. And the other . . . I complained of the High Septon, I admit it. He was Tyrion's creature, weak and corrupt, a stain upon our Holy Faith. Your High Holiness knows that as well as I. It may be that Osney thought that his death would please me. If so, I bear some part of the blame . . . but murder? No. Of that I am innocent. Take me to the sept and I will stand before the Father's judgment seat and swear the truth of that."

"In time," said the High Septon. "You also stand accused of conspiring at the murder of your own lord husband, our late beloved King Robert, First of His Name."

Lancel, Cersei thought. "Robert was killed by a boar. Do they say I am a skinchanger now? A warg? Am I accused of killing Joffrey too, my own sweet son, my firstborn?"

"No. Just your husband. Do you deny it?"

"I deny it. I do. Before gods and men, I deny it."

He nodded. "Last of all, and worst of all, there are some who say your children were not fathered by King Robert, that they are bastards born of incest and adultery."

"Stannis says that," Cersei said at once. "A lie, a lie, a palpable lie. Stannis wants the Iron Throne for himself, but his brother's children stand in his way, so he must needs claim that they are not his brother's. That filthy letter . . . there is no shred of truth to it. I deny it."

The High Septon placed both hands flat upon the table and pushed himself to his feet. "Good. Lord Stannis has turned from the truth of the Seven to worship a red demon, and his false faith has no place in these Seven Kingdoms."

That was almost reassuring. Cersei nodded.

"Even so," His High Holiness went on, "these are terrible charges, and the realm must know the truth of them. If Your Grace has told it true, no doubt a trial will prove your innocence."

A *trial, still.* "I have confessed—"

"—to certain sins, aye. Others you deny. Your trial will separate the truths from the falsehoods. I shall ask the Seven to forgive the sins you have confessed and pray that you be found innocent of these other accusations."

Cersei rose slowly from her knees. "I bow to the wisdom of Your High Holiness," she said, "but if I might beg for just one drop of the Mother's mercy, I . . . it has been so long since I last saw my son, please . . ."

The old man's eyes were chips of flint. "It would not be fitting to allow you near the king until you have been cleansed of all your wickedness. You have taken the first step on your path back to righteousness, however, and in light of that I shall permit you other visitors. One each day."

The queen began to weep again. This time the tears were true. "You are too kind. Thank you."

"The Mother is merciful. It is her that you should thank."

Moelle and Scolera were waiting to lead her back up to her tower cell. Unella followed close behind them. "We have all been praying for Your Grace," Septa Moelle said as they were climbing. "Yes," Septa Scolera echoed, "and you must feel so much lighter now, clean and innocent as a maid on the morning of her wedding."

I fucked Jaime on the morning of my wedding, the queen recalled. "I do," she said, "I feel reborn, as if a festering boil has been lanced and now at last I can begin to heal. I could almost fly." She imagined how sweet it would be to slam an elbow into Septa Scolera's face and send her careening down the spiral steps. If the gods were good, the wrinkled old cunt might crash into Septa Unella and take her down with her.

"It is good to see you smiling again," Scolera said.

"His High Holiness said I might have visitors?"

"He did," said Septa Unella. "If Your Grace will tell us whom you wish to see, we will send word to them."

Jaime, I need Jaime. But if her twin was in the city, why had he not come to her? It might be wiser to wait on Jaime until she had a better notion of what was happening beyond the walls of the Great Sept of Baelor. "My uncle," she said. "Ser Kevan Lannister, my father's brother. Is he in the city?"

"He is," said Septa Unella. "The Lord Regent has taken up residence in the Red Keep. We will send for him at once."

"Thank you," said Cersei, thinking, *Lord Regent, is it?* She could not pretend to be surprised.

A humble and a contrite heart proved to have benefits over and beyond cleansing the soul of sin. That night the queen was moved to a larger cell two floors down, with a window she could actually look out of and warm, soft blankets for her bed. And when time came for supper, instead of stale bread and oaten porridge, she was served a roast capon, a bowl of crisp greens sprinkled with crushed walnuts, and a mound of mashed neeps aswim in butter. That night she crawled into her bed with a full stomach for the first time since she was taken, and slept through the black watches of the night undisturbed.

The next morning, with the dawn, there came her uncle.

Cersei was still at her breakfast when the door swung open and Ser Kevan Lannister stepped through. "Leave us," he told her gaolers. Septa Unella ushered Scolera and Moelle away and closed the door behind them. The queen rose to her feet.

Ser Kevan looked older than when she'd seen him last. He was a big man, broad in the shoulder and thick about the waist, with a close-cropped blond beard that followed the line of his heavy jaw and short blond hair in full retreat from his brow. A heavy woolen cloak, dyed crimson, was clasped at one shoulder with a golden brooch in the shape of a lion's head.

"Thank you for coming," the queen said.

Her uncle frowned. "You should sit. There are things that I must needs tell you—"

She did not want to sit. "You are still angry with me. I hear it in your voice. Forgive me, Uncle. It was wrong of me to throw my wine at you, but—"

"You think I care about a cup of wine? Lancel is my *son*, Cersei. Your own nephew. If I am angry with you, that is the cause. You should have looked after him, guided him, found him a likely girl of good family. Instead you—"

"I know. I know." *Lancel wanted me more than I ever wanted him. He still does, I will wager.* "I was alone, weak. Please. Uncle. Oh, Uncle. It is so good to see your face, your sweet sweet face. I have done wicked things, I know, but I could not bear for you to hate me." She threw her arms around him, kissed his cheek. "Forgive me. Forgive me."

Ser Kevan suffered the embrace for a few heartbeats before he finally raised his own arms to return it. His hug was short and awkward. "Enough," he said, his voice still flat and cold. "You are forgiven. Now sit. I bring some hard tidings, Cersei."

His words frightened her. "Has something happened to Tommen? Please, no. I have been so afraid for my son. No one will tell me anything. Please tell me that Tommen is well."

"His Grace is well. He asks about you often." Ser Kevan laid his hands on her shoulders, held her at arm's length.

"Jaime, then? Is it Jaime?"

"No. Jaime is still in the riverlands, somewhere."

"Somewhere?" She did not like the sound of that.

"He took Raventree and accepted Lord Blackwood's surrender," said her uncle, "but on his way back to Riverrun he left his tail and went off with a woman."

"A woman?" Cersei stared at him, uncomprehending. "What woman? Why? Where did they go?"

"No one knows. We've had no further word of him. The woman may have been the Evenstar's daughter, Lady Brienne."

Her. The queen remembered the Maid of Tarth, a huge, ugly, shambling thing who dressed in man's mail. *Jaime would never abandon me for such a creature. My raven never reached him, elsewise he would have come.*

"We have had reports of sellswords landing all over the south," Ser Kevan was saying. "Tarth, the Stepstones, Cape Wrath . . . where Stannis found the coin to hire a free company I would dearly love to know. I do not have the strength to deal with them, not here. Mace Tyrell does, but he refuses to bestir himself until this matter with his daughter has been settled."

A headsman would settle Margaery quick enough. Cersei did not care a fig for Stannis or his sellswords. *The Others take him and the Tyrells both.*

Let them slaughter each other, the realm will be the better for it. "Please, Uncle, take me out of here."

"How? By force of arms?" Ser Kevan walked to the window and gazed out, frowning. "I would need to make an abbatoir of this holy place. And I do not have the men. The best part of our forces were at Riverrun with your brother. I had no time to raise up a new host." He turned back to face her. "I have spoken with His High Holiness. He will not release you until you have atoned for your sins."

"I have confessed."

"*Atoned*, I said. Before the city. A walk—"

"No." She knew what her uncle was about to say, and she did not want to hear it. "Never. Tell him that, if you speak again. I am a queen, not some dockside whore."

"No harm would come to you. No one will touch—"

"*No*," she said, more sharply. "I would sooner die."

Ser Kevan was unmoved. "If that is your wish, you may soon have it granted. His High Holiness is resolved that you be tried for regicide, deicide, incest, and high treason."

"Deicide?" She almost laughed. "When did I kill a god?"

"The High Septon speaks for the Seven here on earth. Strike at him, and you are striking at the gods themselves." Her uncle raised a hand before she could protest. "It does no good to speak of such things. Not here. The time for all that is at trial." He gazed about her cell. The look on his face spoke volumes.

Someone is listening. Even here, even now, she dare not speak freely. She took a breath. "Who will try me?"

"The Faith," her uncle said, "unless you insist on a trial by battle. In which case you must be championed by a knight of the Kingsguard. Whatever the outcome, your rule is at an end. I will serve as Tommen's regent until he comes of age. Mace Tyrell has been named King's Hand. Grand Maester Pycelle and Ser Harys Swyft will continue as before, but Paxter Redwyne is now lord admiral and Randyll Tarly has assumed the duties of justiciar."

Tyrell bannermen, the both of them. The whole governance of the realm was being handed to her enemies, Queen Margaery's kith and kin. "Margaery stands accused as well. Her and those cousins of hers. How is it that the sparrows freed her and not me?"

"Randyll Tarly insisted. He was the first to reach King's Landing when this storm broke, and he brought his army with him. The Tyrell girls will still be tried, but the case against them is weak, His High Holiness admits. All of the men named as the queen's lovers have denied the accusation or recanted, save for your maimed singer, who appears to be half-mad. So the High Septon handed the girls over to Tarly's custody and Lord Randyll swore a holy oath to deliver them for trial when the time comes."

"And her accusers?" the queen demanded. "Who holds them?"

"Osney Kettleblack and the Blue Bard are here, beneath the sept. The Redwyne twins have been declared innocent, and Hamish the Harper has died. The rest are in the dungeons under the Red Keep, in the charge of your man Qyburn."

Qyburn, thought Cersei. That was good, one straw at least that she could clutch. Lord Qyburn had them, and Lord Qyburn could do wonders. *And horrors. He can do horrors as well.*

"There is more, worse. *Will* you sit down?"

"Sit down?" Cersei shook her head. What could be worse? She was to be tried for high treason whilst the little queen and her cousins flew off as free as birds. "Tell me. What is it?"

"Myrcella. We have had grave news from Dorne."

"*Tyrion*," she said at once. Tyrion had sent her little girl to Dorne, and Cersei had dispatched Ser Balon Swann to bring her home. All Dornishmen were snakes, and the Martells were the worst of them. The Red Viper had even tried to defend the Imp, had come within a hairbreadth of a victory that would have allowed the dwarf to escape the blame for Joffrey's murder. "It's him, he's been in Dorne all this time, and now he's seized my daughter."

Ser Kevan gave her another scowl. "Myrcella was attacked by a Dornish knight named Gerold Dayne. She's alive, but hurt. He slashed her face open, she . . . I'm sorry . . . she lost an ear."

"An ear." Cersei stared at him, aghast. *She was just a child, my precious princess. She was so pretty, too.* "He cut off her ear. And Prince Doran and his Dornish knights, where were they? They could not defend one little girl? Where was Arys Oakheart?"

"Slain, defending her. Dayne cut him down, it's said."

The Sword of the Morning had been a Dayne, the queen recalled, but he was long dead. Who was this Ser Gerold and why would he wish to harm her daughter? She could not make any sense of this, unless . . . "Tyrion lost half his nose in the Battle of the Blackwater. Slashing her face, cutting off an ear . . . the Imp's grubby little fingers are all over this."

"Prince Doran says nothing of your brother. And Balon Swann writes that Myrcella puts it all on this Gerold Dayne. Darkstar, they call him."

She gave a bitter laugh. "Whatever they call him, he is my brother's catspaw. Tyrion has friends amongst the Dornish. The Imp planned this all along. It was Tyrion who betrothed Myrcella to Prince Trystane. Now I see why."

"You see Tyrion in every shadow."

"He is a creature of the shadows. He killed Joffrey. He killed Father. Did you think he would stop there? I feared that the Imp was still in King's Landing plotting harm to Tommen, but he must have gone to Dorne instead to kill Myrcella first." Cersei paced the width of the cell. "I need to be with Tommen. These Kingsguard knights are as useless as nipples on a breastplate." She rounded on her uncle. "Ser Arys was killed, you said."

"At the hands of this man Darkstar, yes."

"Dead, he's *dead*, you are certain of that?"

"That is what we have been told."

"Then there is an empty place amongst the Kingsguard. It must be filled at once. Tommen must be protected."

"Lord Tarly is drawing up a list of worthy knights for your brother to consider, but until Jaime reappears . . ."

"The king can give a man a white cloak. Tommen's a good boy. Tell him who to name and he will name him."

"And who would you have him name?"

She did not have a ready answer. *My champion will need a new name as well as a new face.* "Qyburn will know. Trust him in this. You and I have had our differences, Uncle, but for the blood we share and the love you bore my father, for Tommen's sake and the sake of his poor maimed sister, do as I ask you. Go to Lord Qyburn on my behalf, bring him a white cloak, and tell him that the time has come."

THE QUEENSGUARD

Y ou were the queen's man," said Reznak mo Reznak. "The king desires his own men about him when he holds court."

*I am the queen's man still. Today, tomorrow, always, until my last breath,
or hers.* Barristan Selmy refused to believe that Daenerys Targaryen was
dead.

Perhaps that was why he was being put aside. *One by one, Hizdahr re-
moves us all.* Strong Belwas lingered at the door of death in the temple,
under the care of the Blue Graces . . . though Selmy half suspected they
were finishing the job those honeyed locusts had begun. Skahaz Shavepate had been stripped of his command. The Unsullied had withdrawn to
their barracks. Jhogo, Daario Naharis, Admiral Groleo, and Hero of the
Unsullied remained hostages of the Yunkai'i. Aggo and Rakharo and the
rest of the queen's *khalasar* had been dispatched across the river to search
for their lost queen. Even Missandei had been replaced; the king did not
think it fit to use a child as his herald, and a onetime Naathi slave at that.
And now me.

There was a time when he might have taken this dismissal as a blot
upon his honor. But that was in Westeros. In the viper's pit that was Meereen, honor seemed as silly as a fool's motley. And this mistrust was mutual.
Hizdahr zo Loraq might be his queen's consort, but he would never be his
king. "If His Grace wishes for me to remove myself from court . . ."

"His Radiance," the seneschal corrected. "No, no, no, you misunder-
stand me. His Worship is to receive a delegation from the Yunkai'i, to
discuss the withdrawal of their armies. They may ask for . . . ah . . . recompense for those who lost their lives to the dragon's wroth. A delicate situation. The king feels it will be better if they see a Meereenese king upon
the throne, protected by Meereenese warriors. Surely you can understand
that, ser."

I understand more than you know. "Might I know which men His Grace has chosen to protect him?"

Reznak mo Reznak smiled his slimy smile. "Fearsome fighters, who love His Worship well. Goghor the Giant. Khrazz. The Spotted Cat. Belaquo Bonebreaker. Heroes all."

Pit fighters all. Ser Barristan was unsurprised. Hizdahr zo Loraq sat uneasily on his new throne. It had been a thousand years since Meereen last had a king, and there were some even amongst the old blood who thought they might have made a better choice than him. Outside the city sat the Yunkai'i with their sellswords and their allies; inside were the Sons of the Harpy.

And the king's protectors grew fewer every day. Hizdahr's blunder with Grey Worm had cost him the Unsullied. When His Grace had tried to put them under the command of a cousin, as he had the Brazen Beasts, Grey Worm had informed the king that they were free men who took commands only from their mother. As for the Brazen Beasts, half were freedmen and the rest shavepates, whose true loyalty might still be to Skahaz mo Kandaq. The pit fighters were King Hizdahr's only reliable support, against a sea of enemies.

"May they defend His Grace against all threats." Ser Barristan's tone gave no hint of his true feelings; he had learned to hide such back in King's Landing years ago.

"His *Magnificence*," Reznak mo Reznak stressed. "Your other duties shall remain unchanged, ser. Should this peace fail, His Radiance would still wish for you to command his forces against the enemies of our city."

He has that much sense, at least. Belaquo Bonebreaker and Goghor the Giant might serve as Hizdahr's shields, but the notion of either leading an army into battle was so ludicrous that the old knight almost smiled. "I am His Grace's to command."

"Not *Grace*," the seneschal complained. "That style is Westerosi. His Magnificence, His Radiance, His Worship."

His Vanity would fit better. "As you say."

Reznak licked his lips. "Then we are done." This time his oily smile betokened dismissal. Ser Barristan took his leave, grateful to leave the stench of the seneschal's perfume behind him. *A man should smell of sweat, not flowers.*

The Great Pyramid of Meereen was eight hundred feet high from base to point. The seneschal's chambers were on the second level. The queen's apartments, and his own, occupied the highest step. *A long climb for a man my age,* Ser Barristan thought, as he started up. He had been known to make that climb five or six times a day on the queen's business, as the aches in his knees and the small of his back could attest. *There will come a day when I can no longer face these steps*, he thought, *and that day will be here sooner than I would like.* Before it came, he must make certain that at least a few of his lads were ready to take his place at the queen's side. *I will knight them myself when they are worthy, and give them each a horse and golden spurs.*

The royal apartments were still and silent. Hizdahr had not taken up residence there, preferring to establish his own suite of rooms deep in the heart of the Great Pyramid, where massive brick walls surrounded him on all sides. Mezzara, Miklaz, Qezza, and the rest of the queen's young cupbearers—hostages in truth, but both Selmy and the queen had become so fond of them that it was hard for him to think of them that way—had gone with the king, whilst Irri and Jhiqui departed with the other Dothraki. Only Missandei remained, a forlorn little ghost haunting the queen's chambers at the apex of the pyramid.

Ser Barristan walked out onto the terrace. The sky above Meereen was the color of corpse flesh, dull and white and heavy, a mass of unbroken cloud from horizon to horizon. The sun was hidden behind a wall of cloud. It would set unseen, as it had risen unseen that morning. The night would be hot, a sweaty, suffocating, sticky sort of night without a breath of air. For three days rain had threatened, but not a drop had fallen. *Rain would come as a relief. It might help wash the city clean.*

From here he could see four lesser pyramids, the city's western walls, and the camps of the Yunkishmen by the shores of Slaver's Bay, where a thick column of greasy smoke twisted upward like some monstrous serpent. *The Yunkishmen burning their dead*, he realized. *The pale mare is galloping through their siege camps.* Despite all the queen had done, the sickness had spread, both within the city walls and without. Meereen's markets were closed, its streets empty. King Hizdahr had allowed the fighting pits to remain open, but the crowds were sparse. The Meereenese had even begun to shun the Temple of the Graces, reportedly.

The slavers will find some way to blame Daenerys for that as well, Ser Barristan thought bitterly. He could almost hear them whispering—Great Masters, Sons of the Harpy, Yunkai'i, all telling one another that his queen was dead. Half of the city believed it, though as yet they did not have the courage to say such words aloud. *But soon, I think.*

Ser Barristan felt very tired, very old. *Where have all the years gone?* Of late, whenever he knelt to drink from a still pool, he saw a stranger's face gazing up from the water's depths. When had those crow's-feet first appeared around his pale blue eyes? How long ago had his hair turned from sunlight into snow? *Years ago, old man. Decades.*

Yet it seemed like only yesterday that he had been raised to knighthood, after the tourney at King's Landing. He could still recall the touch of King Aegon's sword upon his shoulder, light as a maiden's kiss. His words had caught in his throat when he spoke his vows. At the feast that night he had eaten ribs of wild boar, prepared the Dornish way with dragon peppers, so hot they burned his mouth. Forty-seven years, and the taste still lingered in his memory, yet he could not have said what he had supped on ten days ago if all seven kingdoms had depended on it. *Boiled dog, most like. Or some other foul dish that tasted no better.*

Not for the first time, Selmy wondered at the strange fates that had brought him here. He was a knight of Westeros, a man of the stormlands and the Dornish marches; his place was in the Seven Kingdoms, not here upon the sweltering shores of Slaver's Bay. *I came to bring Daenerys home.* Yet he had lost her, just as he had lost her father and her brother. *Even Robert. I failed him too.*

Perhaps Hizdahr was wiser than he knew. *Ten years ago I would have sensed what Daenerys meant to do. Ten years ago I would have been quick enough to stop her.* Instead he had stood befuddled as she leapt into the pit, shouting her name, then running uselessly after her across the scarlet sands. *I am become old and slow.* Small wonder Naharis mocked him as Ser Grandfather. *Would Daario have moved more quickly if he had been beside the queen that day?* Selmy thought he knew the answer to that, though it was not one he liked.

He had dreamed of it again last night: Belwas on his knees retching up bile and blood, Hizdahr urging on the dragonslayers, men and women fleeing in terror, fighting on the steps, climbing over one another, screaming and shouting. And Daenerys . . .

Her hair was aflame. She had the whip in her hand and she was shouting, then she was on the dragon's back, flying. The sand that Drogon stirred as he took wing had stung Ser Barristan's eyes, but through a veil of tears he had watched the beast fly from the pit, his great black wings slapping at the shoulders of the bronze warriors at the gates.

The rest he learned later. Beyond the gates had been a solid press of people. Maddened by the smell of dragon, horses below reared in terror, lashing out with iron-shod hooves. Food stalls and palanquins alike were overturned, men knocked down and trampled. Spears were thrown, crossbows were fired. Some struck home. The dragon twisted violently in the air, wounds smoking, the girl clinging to his back. Then he loosed the fire.

It had taken the rest of the day and most of the night for the Brazen Beasts to gather up the corpses. The final count was two hundred fourteen slain, three times as many burned or wounded. Drogon was gone from the city by then, last seen high over the Skahazadhan, flying north. Of Daenerys Targaryen, no trace had been found. Some swore they saw her fall. Others insisted that the dragon had carried her off to devour her. *They are wrong.*

Ser Barristan knew no more of dragons than the tales every child hears, but he knew Targaryens. Daenerys had been *riding* that dragon, as Aegon had once ridden Balerion of old.

"She might be flying home," he told himself, aloud.

"No," murmured a soft voice behind him. "She would not do that, ser. She would not go home without us."

Ser Barristan turned. "Missandei. Child. How long have you been standing there?"

"Not long. This one is sorry if she has disturbed you." She hesitated. "Skahaz mo Kandaq wishes words with you."

"The Shavepate? You spoke with him?" That was rash, rash. The enmity ran deep between Shakaz and the king, and the girl was clever enough to know that. Skahaz had been outspoken in his opposition to the queen's marriage, a fact Hizdahr had not forgotten. "Is he here? In the pyramid?"

"When he wishes. He comes and goes, ser."

Yes. He would. "Who told you he wants words with me?"

"A Brazen Beast. He wore an owl mask."

He wore an owl mask when he spoke to you. By now he could be a jackal, a tiger, a sloth. Ser Barristan had hated the masks from the start and never more than now. Honest men should never need to hide their faces. And the Shavepate . . .

What could he be thinking? After Hizdahr had given command of the Brazen Beasts to his cousin Marghaz zo Loraq, Skahaz had been named Warden of the River, with charge of all the ferries, dredges, and irrigation ditches along the Skahazadhan for fifty leagues, but the Shavepate had refused that ancient and honorable office, as Hizdahr called it, preferring to retire to the modest pyramid of Kandaq. *Without the queen to protect him, he takes a great risk coming here.* And if Ser Barristan were seen speaking with him, suspicion might fall on the knight as well.

He did not like the taste of this. It smelled of deceit, of whispers and lies and plots hatched in the dark, all the things he'd hoped to leave behind with the Spider and Lord Littlefinger and their ilk. Barristan Selmy was not a bookish man, but he had often glanced through the pages of the White Book, where the deeds of his predecessors had been recorded. Some had been heroes, some weaklings, knaves, or cravens. Most were only men—quicker and stronger than most, more skilled with sword and shield, but still prey to pride, ambition, lust, love, anger, jealousy, greed for gold, hunger for power, and all the other failings that afflicted lesser mortals. The best of them overcame their flaws, did their duty, and died with their swords in their hands. The worst . . .

The worst were those who played the game of thrones. "Can you find this owl again?" he asked Missandei.

"This one can try, ser."

"Tell him I will speak with . . . with our friend . . . after dark, by the stables." The pyramid's main doors were closed and barred at sunset. The stables would be quiet at that hour. "Make certain it is the same owl." It would not serve to have the wrong Brazen Beast hear of this.

"This one understands." Missandei turned as if to go, then paused a moment and said, "It is said that the Yunkai'i have ringed the city all about with scorpions, to loose iron bolts into the sky should Drogon return."

Ser Barristan had heard that too. "It is no simple thing to slay a dragon in the sky. In Westeros, many tried to bring down Aegon and his sisters. None succeeded."

Missandei nodded. It was hard to tell if she was reassured. "Do you think that they will find her, ser? The grasslands are so vast, and dragons leave no tracks across the sky."

"Aggo and Rakharo are blood of her blood . . . and who knows the Dothraki sea better than Dothraki?" He squeezed her shoulder. "They will find her if she can be found." *If she still lives.* There were other khals who prowled the grass, horselords with *khalasars* whose riders numbered in the tens of thousands. But the girl did not need to hear that. "You love her well, I know. I swear, I shall keep her safe."

The words seemed to give the girl some comfort. *Words are wind, though,* Ser Barristan thought. *How can I protect the queen when I am not with her?*

Barristan Selmy had known many kings. He had been born during the troubled reign of Aegon the Unlikely, beloved by the common folk, had received his knighthood at his hands. Aegon's son Jaehaerys had bestowed the white cloak on him when he was three-and-twenty, after he slew

Maelys the Monstrous during the War of the Ninepenny Kings. In that same cloak he had stood beside the Iron Throne as madness consumed Jaehaerys's son Aerys. *Stood, and saw, and heard, and yet did nothing.*

But no. That was not fair. He did his duty. Some nights, Ser Barristan wondered if he had not done that duty too well. He had sworn his vows before the eyes of gods and men, he could not in honor go against them . . . but the keeping of those vows had grown hard in the last years of King Aerys's reign. He had seen things that it pained him to recall, and more than once he wondered how much of the blood was on his own hands. If he had not gone into Duskendale to rescue Aerys from Lord Darklyn's dungeons, the king might well have died there as Tywin Lannister sacked the town. Then Prince Rhaegar would have ascended the Iron Throne, mayhaps to heal the realm. Duskendale had been his finest hour, yet the memory tasted bitter on his tongue.

It was his failures that haunted him at night, though. *Jaehaerys, Aerys, Robert. Three dead kings. Rhaegar, who would have been a finer king than any of them. Princess Elia and the children. Aegon just a babe, Rhaenys with her kitten.* Dead, every one, yet he still lived, who had sworn to protect them. And now Daenerys, his bright shining child queen. *She is not dead. I will not believe it.*

Afternoon brought Ser Barristan a brief respite from his doubts. He spent it in the training hall on the pyramid's third level, working with his boys, teaching them the art of sword and shield, horse and lance . . . and chivalry, the code that made a knight more than any pit fighter. Daenerys would need protectors her own age about her after he was gone, and Ser Barristan was determined to give her such.

The lads he was instructing ranged in age from eight to twenty. He had started with more than sixty of them, but the training had proved too rigorous for many. Less than half that number now remained, but some showed great promise. *With no king to guard, I will have more time to train them now,* he realized as he walked from pair to pair, watching them go at one another with blunted swords and spears with rounded heads. *Brave boys. Baseborn, aye, but some will make good knights, and they love the queen. If not for her, all of them would have ended in the pits. King Hizdahr has his pit fighters, but Daenerys will have knights.*

"Keep your shield up," he called. "Show me your strokes. Together now. Low, high, low, low, high, low . . ."

Selmy took his simple supper out onto the queen's terrace that night and ate it as the sun went down. Through the purple twilight he watched fires waken one by one in the great stepped pyramids, as the many-colored bricks of Meereen faded to grey and then to black. Shadows gathered in the streets and alleys below, making pools and rivers. In the dusk, the city seemed a tranquil place, even beautiful. *That is pestilence, not peace,* the old knight told himself with his last sip of wine.

He did not wish to be conspicuous, so when he was finished with his supper he changed out of his court clothes, trading the white cloak of the Queensguard for a hooded brown traveler's cloak such as any common man might wear. He kept his sword and dagger. *This could still be some trap.* He had little trust in Hizdahr and less in Reznak mo Reznak. The perfumed seneschal could well be part of this, trying to lure him into a secret meeting so he could sweep up him and Skahaz both and charge them with conspiring against the king. *If the Shavepate speaks treason, he will leave me no choice but to arrest him. Hizdahr is my queen's consort, however little I may like it. My duty is to him, not Skahaz.*

Or was it?

The first duty of the Kingsguard was to defend the king from harm or threat. The white knights were sworn to obey the king's commands as well, to keep his secrets, counsel him when counsel was requested and keep silent when it was not, serve his pleasure and defend his name and honor. Strictly speaking, it was purely the king's choice whether or not to extend Kingsguard protection to others, even those of royal blood. Some kings thought it right and proper to dispatch Kingsguard to serve and defend their wives and children, siblings, aunts, uncles, and cousins of greater and lesser degree, and occasionally even their lovers, mistresses, and bastards. But others preferred to use household knights and men-at-arms for those purposes, whilst keeping their seven as their own personal guard, never far from their sides.

If the queen had commanded me to protect Hizdahr, I would have had no choice but to obey. But Daenerys Targaryen had never established a proper Queensguard even for herself nor issued any commands in respect to her consort. *The world was simpler when I had a lord commander to decide such matters,* Selmy reflected. *Now I am the lord commander, and it is hard to know which path is right.*

When at last he came to the bottom of the last flight of steps, he found himself all but alone amongst the torchlit corridors inside the pyramid's massive brick walls. The great gates were closed and barred, as he had anticipated. Four Brazen Beasts stood guard outside those doors, four more within. It was those that the old knight encountered—big men, masked as boar, bear, vole, and manticore.

"All quiet, ser," the bear told him.

"Keep it so." It was not unknown for Ser Barristan to walk around at night, to make certain the pyramid was secure.

Deeper inside the pyramid, another four Brazen Beasts had been set to guard the iron doors outside the pit where Viserion and Rhaegal were chained. The light of the torches shimmered off their masks—ape, ram, wolf, crocodile.

"Have they been fed?" Ser Barristan asked.

"Aye, ser," replied the ape. "A sheep apiece."

And how long will that suffice, I wonder? As the dragons grew, so did their appetites.

It was time to find the Shavepate. Ser Barristan made his way past the elephants and the queen's silver mare, to the back of the stables. An ass nickered as he went by, and a few of the horses stirred at the light of his lantern. Elsewise all was dark and silent.

Then a shadow detached itself from inside an empty stall and became another Brazen Beast, clad in pleated black skirt, greaves, and muscled breastplate. "A cat?" said Barristan Selmy when he saw the brass beneath the hood. When the Shavepate had commanded the Brazen Beasts, he had favored a serpent's-head mask, imperious and frightening.

"Cats go everywhere," replied the familiar voice of Skahaz mo Kandaq. "No one ever looks at them."

"If Hizdahr should learn that you are here . . ."

"Who will tell him? Marghaz? Marghaz knows what I want him to know. The Beasts are still mine. Do not forget it." The Shavepate's voice was muffled by his mask, but Selmy could hear the anger in it. "I have the poisoner."

"Who?"

"Hizdahr's confectioner. His name would mean nothing to you. The man was just a catspaw. The Sons of the Harpy took his daughter and swore she would be returned unharmed once the queen was dead. Belwas and the dragon saved Daenerys. No one saved the girl. She was returned to her father in the black of night, in nine pieces. One for every year she lived."

"Why?" Doubts gnawed at him. "The Sons had stopped their killing. Hizdahr's peace—"

"—is a sham. Not at first, no. The Yunkai'i were afraid of our queen, of her Unsullied, of her dragons. This land has known dragons before. Yurkhaz zo Yunzak had read his histories, he knew. Hizdahr as well. Why not a peace? Daenerys wanted it, they could see that. Wanted it too much. She should have marched to Astapor." Skahaz moved closer.

"That was before. The pit changed all. Daenerys gone, Yurkhaz dead. In place of one old lion, a pack of jackals. Bloodbeard . . . that one has no taste for peace. And there is more. Worse. Volantis has launched its fleet against us."

"Volantis." Selmy's sword hand tingled. *We made a peace with Yunkai. Not with Volantis.* "You are certain?"

"Certain. The Wise Masters know. So do their friends. The Harpy, Reznak, Hizdahr. This king will open the city gates to the Volantenes when they arrive. All those Daenerys freed will be enslaved again. Even some who were never slaves will be fitted for chains. You may end your days in a fighting pit, old man. Khrazz will eat your heart."

His head was pounding. "Daenerys must be told."

"Find her first." Skahaz grasped his forearm. His fingers felt like iron. "We cannot wait for her. I have spoken with the Free Brothers, the Mother's Men, the Stalwart Shields. They have no trust in Loraq. We must break the Yunkai'i. But we need the Unsullied. Grey Worm will listen to you. Speak to him."

"To what end?" *He is speaking treason. Conspiracy.*

"Life." The Shavepate's eyes were black pools behind the brazen cat mask. "We must strike before the Volantenes arrive. Break the siege, kill the slaver lords, turn their sellswords. The Yunkai'i do not expect an attack. I have spies in their camps. There's sickness, they say, worse every day. Discipline has gone to rot. The lords are drunk more oft than not, gorging themselves at feasts, telling each other of the riches they'll divide when Meereen falls, squabbling over primacy. Bloodbeard and the Tattered Prince despise each other. No one expects a fight. Not now. Hizdahr's peace has lulled us to sleep, they believe."

"Daenerys signed that peace," Ser Barristan said. "It is not for us to break it without her leave."

"And if she is dead?" demanded Skahaz. "What then, ser? I say she would want us to protect her city. Her children."

Her children were the freedmen. *Mhysa, they called her, all those whose chains she broke.* "Mother." The Shavepate was not wrong. Daenerys would want her children protected. "What of Hizdahr? He is still her consort. Her king. Her husband."

"Her poisoner."

Is he? "Where is your proof?"

"The crown he wears is proof enough. The throne he sits. Open your eyes, old man. That is all he needed from Daenerys, all he ever wanted. Once he had it, why share the rule?"

Why indeed? It had been so hot down in the pit. He could still see the air shimmering above the scarlet sands, smell the blood spilling from the men who'd died for their amusement. And he could still hear Hizdahr, urging his queen to try the honeyed locusts. *Those are very tasty . . . sweet and hot . . . yet he never touched so much as one himself . . .* Selmy rubbed his temple. *I swore no vows to Hizdahr zo Loraq. And if I had, he has cast me aside, just as Joffrey did.* "This . . . this confectioner, I want to question him myself. Alone."

"Is it that way?" The Shavepate crossed his arms against his chest. "Done, then. Question him as you like."

"If . . . if what he has to say convinces me . . . if I join with you in this, this . . . I would require your word that no harm would come to Hizdahr zo Loraq until . . . unless . . . it can be proved that he had some part in this."

"Why do you care so much for Hizdahr, old man? If he is not the Harpy, he is the Harpy's firstborn son."

"All I know for certain is that he is the queen's consort. I want your word on this, or I swear, I shall oppose you."

Skahaz's smile was savage. "My word, then. No harm to Hizdahr till his guilt is proved. But when we have the proof, I mean to kill him with my own hands. I want to pull his entrails out and show them to him before I let him die."

No, the old knight thought. *If Hizdahr conspired at my queen's death, I will see to him myself, but his death will be swift and clean.* The gods of Westeros were far away, yet Ser Barristan Selmy paused for a moment to say a silent prayer, asking the Crone to light his way to wisdom. *For the children,* he told himself. *For the city. For my queen.*

"I will talk to Grey Worm," he said.

THE IRON SUITOR

Grief appeared alone at daybreak, her black sails stark against the pale pink skies of morning.

Fifty-four, Victarion thought sourly when they woke him, *and she sails alone*. Silently he cursed the Storm God for his malice, his rage a black stone in his belly. *Where are my ships?*

He had set sail from the Shields with ninety-three, of the hundred that had once made up the Iron Fleet, a fleet belonging not to a single lord but to the Seastone Chair itself, captained and crewed by men from all the islands. Ships smaller than the great war dromonds of the green lands, aye, but thrice the size of any common longship, with deep hulls and savage rams, fit to meet the king's own fleets in battle.

In the Stepstones they had taken on grain and game and fresh water, after the long voyage along the bleak and barren coast of Dorne with its shoals and whirlpools. There, the *Iron Victory* had captured a fat merchant ship, the great cog *Noble Lady*, on her way to Oldtown by way of Gulltown, Duskendale, and King's Landing, with a cargo of salt cod, whale oil, and pickled herring. The food was a welcome addition to their stores. Five other prizes taken in the Redwyne Straights and along the Dornish coast—three cogs, a galleas, and a galley—had brought their numbers to ninety-nine.

Nine-and-ninety ships had left the Stepstones in three proud fleets, with orders to join up again off the southern tip of the Isle of Cedars. Forty-five had now arrived on the far side of the world. Twenty-two of Victarion's own had straggled in, by threes and fours, sometimes alone; fourteen of Ralf the Limper's; only nine of those that had sailed with Red Ralf Stonehouse. Red Ralf himself was amongst the missing. To their number the fleet had added nine new prizes taken on the seas, so the sum was fifty-four . . . but the captured ships were cogs and fishing boats, merchantmen and slavers, not warships. In battle, they would be poor substitutes for the lost ships of the Iron Fleet.

The last ship to appear had been the *Maiden's Bane*, three days previous. The day before that, three ships had come out of the south together — his captive *Noble Lady*, lumbering along between *Ravenfeeder* and *Iron Kiss*. But the day before and the day before there had been nothing, and only *Headless Jeyne* and *Fear* before that, then two more days of empty seas and cloudless skies after Ralf the Limper appeared with the remnants of his squadron. *Lord Quellon*, *White Widow*, *Lamentation*, *Woe*, *Leviathan*, *Iron Lady*, *Reaper's Wind*, and *Warhammer*, with six more ships behind, two of them storm-wracked and under tow.

"Storms," Ralf the Limper had muttered when he came crawling to Victarion. "Three big storms, and foul winds between. Red winds out of Valyria that smelled of ash and brimstone, and black winds that drove us toward that blighted shore. This voyage was cursed from the first. The Crow's Eye fears you, my lord, why else send you so far away? He does not mean for us to return."

Victarion had thought the same when he met the first storm a day out of Old Volantis. *The gods hate kinslayers*, he brooded, *elsewise Euron Crow's Eye would have died a dozen deaths by my hand*. As the sea crashed around him and the deck rose and fell beneath his feet, he had seen *Dagon's Feast* and *Red Tide* slammed together so violently that both exploded into splinters. *My brother's work*, he'd thought. Those were the first two ships he'd lost from his own third of the fleet. But not the last.

So he had slapped the Limper twice across the face and said, "The first is for the ships you lost, the second for your talk of curses. Speak of that again and I will nail your tongue to the mast. If the Crow's Eye can make mutes, so can I." The throb of pain in his left hand made the words harsher than they might have been elsewise, but he meant what he said. "More ships will come. The storms are done for now. I will have my fleet."

A monkey on the mast above howled derision, almost as if it could taste his frustration. *Filthy, noisy beast*. He could send a man up after it, but the monkeys seemed to like that game and had proved themselves more agile than his crew. The howls rang in his ears, though, and made the throbbing in his hand seem worse.

"Fifty-four," he grumbled. It would have been too much to hope for the full strength of the Iron Fleet after a voyage of such length . . . but seventy ships, even eighty, the Drowned God might have granted him that much. *Would that we had the Damphair with us, or some other priest*. Victarion had made sacrifice before setting sail, and again in the Stepstones when he split the fleet in three, but perhaps he had said the wrong prayers. *That, or the Drowned God has no power here.* More and more, he had come to fear that they had sailed too far, into strange seas where even the gods were queer . . . but such doubts he confided only to his dusky woman, who had no tongue to repeat them.

When *Grief* appeared, Victarion summoned Wulfe One-Ear. "I will want words with the Vole. Send word to Ralf the Limper, Bloodless Tom, and the Black Shepherd. All hunting parties are to be recalled, the shore camps broken up by first light. Load as much fruit as can be gathered and drive the pigs aboard the ships. We can slaughter them at need. *Shark* is to remain here to tell any stragglers where we've gone." She would need that long to make repairs; the storms had left her little more than a hulk. That would bring them down to fifty-three, but there was no help for it. "The fleet departs upon the morrow, on the evening tide."

"As you command," said Wulfe, "but another day might mean another ship, lord Captain."

"Aye. And ten days might mean ten ships, or none at all. We have squandered too many days waiting on the sight of sails. Our victory will be that much the sweeter if we win it with a smaller fleet." *And I must needs reach the dragon queen before the Volantenes.*

In Volantis he had seen the galleys taking on provisions. The whole city had seemed drunk. Sailors and soldiers and tinkers had been observed dancing in the streets with nobles and fat merchants, and in every inn and winesink cups were being raised to the new triarchs. All the talk had been of the gold and gems and slaves that would flood into Volantis once the dragon queen was dead. One day of such reports was all that Victarion Greyjoy could stomach; he paid the gold price for food and water, though it shamed him, and took his ships back out to sea.

The storms would have scattered and delayed the Volantenes, even as they had his own ships. If fortune smiled, many of their warships might have sunk or run aground. But not all. No god was that good, and those green galleys that survived by now could well have sailed around Valyria. *They will be sweeping north toward Meereen and Yunkai, great dromonds of war teeming with slave soldiers. If the Storm God spared them, by now they could be in the Gulf of Grief. Three hundred ships, perhaps as many as five hundred.* Their allies were already off Meereen: Yunkishmen and Astapors, men from New Ghis and Qarth and Tolos and the Storm God knew where else, even Meereen's own warships, the ones that fled the city before its fall. Against all that, Victarion had four-and-fifty. Three-and-fifty, less the *Shark*.

The Crow's Eye had sailed halfway across the world, reaving and plundering from Qarth to Tall Trees Town, calling at unholy ports beyond where only madmen went. Euron had even braved the Smoking Sea and lived to tell of it. *And that with only one ship. If he can mock the gods, so can I.*

"Aye, Captain," said Wulfe One-Ear. He was not half the man that Nute the Barber was, but the Crow's Eye had stolen Nute. By raising him to Lord of Oakenshield, his brother made Victarion's best man his own. "Is it still to be Meereen?"

"Where else? The dragon queen awaits me in Meereen." *The fairest woman in the world if my brother could be believed. Her hair is silver-gold, her eyes are amethysts.*

Was it too much to hope that for once Euron had told it true? *Perhaps.* Like as not, the girl would prove to be some pock-faced slattern with teats slapping against her knees, her "dragons" no more than tattooed lizards from the swamps of Sothoryos. *If she is all that Euron claims, though . . .* They had heard talk of the beauty of Daenerys Targaryen from the lips of pirates in the Stepstones and fat merchants in Old Volantis. It might be true. And Euron had not made Victarion a gift of her; the Crow's Eye meant to take her for himself. *He sends me like a serving man to fetch her. How he will howl when I claim her for myself.* Let the men mutter. They had sailed too far and lost too much for Victarion to turn west without his prize.

The iron captain closed his good hand into a fist. "Go see that my commands are carried out. And find the maester wherever he is hiding and send him to my cabin."

"Aye." Wulfe hobbled off.

Victarion Greyjoy turned back toward the prow, his gaze sweeping across his fleet. Longships filled the sea, sails furled and oars shipped, floating at anchor or run up on the pale sand shore. *The Isle of Cedars.* Where were these cedars? Drowned four hundred years ago, it seemed. Victarion had gone ashore a dozen times, hunting fresh meat, and had yet to see a cedar.

The girlish maester Euron had inflicted upon him back in Westeros claimed this place had once been called 'the Isle of a Hundred Battles,' but the men who had fought those battles had all gone to dust centuries ago. *The Isle of Monkeys, that's what they should call it.* There were pigs as well: the biggest, blackest boars that any of the ironborn had ever seen and plenty of squealing piglets in the brush, bold creatures that had no fear of man. *They were learning, though.* The larders of the Iron Fleet were filling up with smoked hams, salted pork, and bacon.

The monkeys, though . . . the monkeys were a plague. Victarion had forbidden his men to bring any of the demonic creatures aboard ship, yet somehow half his fleet was now infested with them, even his own *Iron Victory.* He could see some now, swinging from spar to spar and ship to ship. *Would that I had a crossbow.*

Victarion did not like this sea, nor these endless cloudless skies, nor the blazing sun that beat down on their heads and baked the decks until the boards were hot enough to scorch bare feet. He did not like these storms, which seemed to come up out of nowhere. The seas around Pyke were often stormy, but there at least a man could smell them coming. These southron storms were as treacherous as women. Even the water was the wrong color—a shimmering turquoise close to shore, and farther out a blue so deep that it was almost black. Victarion missed the grey-green waters of home, with their whitecaps and surges.

He did not like this Isle of Cedars either. The hunting might be good, but the forests were too green and still, full of twisted trees and queer bright flowers like none his men had ever seen before, and there were horrors lurking amongst the broken palaces and shattered statues of drowned Velos, half a league north of the point where the fleet lay at anchor. The last time Victarion had spent a night ashore, his dreams had been dark and disturbing and when he woke his mouth was full of blood. The maester said he had bitten his own tongue in his sleep, but he took it for a sign from the Drowned God, a warning that if he lingered here too long, he would choke on his own blood.

On the day the Doom came to Valyria, it was said, a wall of water three hundred feet high had descended on the island, drowning hundreds of thousands of men, women, and children, leaving none to tell the tale but some fisherfolk who had been at sea and a handful of Velosi spearmen posted in a stout stone tower on the island's highest hill, who had seen the hills and valleys beneath them turn into a raging sea. Fair Velos with its palaces of cedar and pink marble had vanished in a heartbeat. On the north end of the island, the ancient brick walls and stepped pyramids of the slaver port Ghozai had suffered the same fate.

So many drowned men, the Drowned God will be strong there, Victarion had thought when he chose the island for the three parts of his fleet to join up again. He was no priest, though. What if he had gotten it backwards? Perhaps the Drowned God had destroyed the island in his wroth.

His brother Aeron might have known, but the Damphair was back on the Iron Islands, preaching against the Crow's Eye and his rule. *No godless man may sit the Seastone Chair.* Yet the captains and kings had cried for Euron at the kingsmoot, choosing him above Victarion and other godly men.

The morning sun was shining off the water in ripples of light too bright to look upon. Victarion's head had begun to pound, though whether from the sun, his hand, or the doubts that troubled him, he could not say. He made his way below to his cabin, where the air was cool and dim. The dusky woman knew what he wanted without his even asking. As he eased himself into his chair, she took a soft damp cloth from the basin and laid it across his brow. "Good," he said. "Good. And now the hand."

The dusky woman made no reply. Euron had sliced her tongue out before giving her to him. Victarion did not doubt that the Crow's Eye had bedded her as well. That was his brother's way. *Euron's gifts are poisoned,* the captain had reminded himself the day the dusky woman came aboard. *I want none of his leavings.* He had decided then that he would slit her throat and toss her in the sea, a blood sacrifice to the Drowned God. Somehow, though, he had never quite gotten around to it.

They had come a long way since. Victarion could talk to the dusky woman. She never attempted to talk back. "*Grief* is the last," he told her, as she eased his glove off. "The rest are lost or late or sunk." He grimaced as the woman slid the point of her knife beneath the soiled linen wound about his shield hand. "Some will say I should not have split the fleet. Fools. Nine-and-ninety ships we had . . . a cumbersome beast to shepherd across the seas to the far end of the world. If I'd kept them together, the faster ships would have been held hostage to the slowest. And where to find provisions for so many mouths? No port wants so many warships in their waters. The storms would have scattered us, in any case. Like leaves strewn across the Summer Sea."

Instead he had broken the great fleet into squadrons, and sent each by a different route to Slaver's Bay. The swiftest ships he gave to Red Ralf Stonehouse to sail the corsair's road along the northern coast of Sothoryos. The dead cities rotting on that fervid, sweltering shore were best avoided, every seamen knew, but in the mud-and-blood towns of the Basilisks Isles, teeming with escaped slaves, slavers, skinners, whores, hunters, brindled men, and worse, there were always provisions to be had for men who were not afraid to pay the iron price.

The larger, heavier, slower ships made for Lys, to sell the captives taken on the Shields, the women and children of Lord Hewett's Town and other islands, along with such men who decided they would sooner yield than die. Victarion had only contempt for such weaklings. Even so, the selling left a foul taste in his mouth. Taking a man as thrall or a woman as a salt wife, that was right and proper, but men were not goats or fowl to be bought and sold for gold. He was glad to leave the selling to Ralf the Limper, who would use the coin to load his big ships with provisions for the long slow middle passage east.

His own ships crept along the shores of the Disputed Lands to take on food and wine and fresh water at Volantis before swinging south around Valyria. That was the most common way east, and the one most heavily trafficked, with prizes for the taking and small islands where they could shelter during storms, make repairs, and renew their stores if need be.

"Four-and-fifty ships is too few," he told the dusky woman, "but I can wait no longer. The only way"—He grunted as she peeled the bandage off, tearing a crust of scab as well. The flesh beneath was green and black where the sword had sliced him.—"the only way to do this is to take the slavers unawares, as once I did at Lannisport. Sweep in from the sea and smash them, then take the girl and race for home before the Volantenes descend upon us." Victarion was no craven, but no more was he a fool; he could not defeat three hundred ships with fifty-four. "She'll be my wife, and you will be her maid." A maid without a tongue could never let slip any secrets.

He might have said more, but that was when the maester came, rapping at the cabin door as timid as a mouse. "Enter," Victarion called out, "and bar the door. You know why you are here."

"Lord Captain." The maester looked like a mouse as well, with his grey robes and little brown mustachio. *Does he think that makes him look more manly?* Kerwin was his name. He was very young, two-and-twenty maybe. "May I see your hand?" he asked.

A fool's question. Maesters had their uses, but Victarion had nothing but contempt for this Kerwin. With his smooth pink cheeks, soft hands, and brown curls, he looked more girlish than most girls. When first he came aboard the *Iron Victory,* he had a smirky little smile too, but one night off the Stepstones he had smiled at the wrong man, and Burton Humble had knocked out four of his teeth. Not long after that Kerwin had come creeping to the captain to complain that four of the crew had dragged him belowdecks and used him as a woman. "Here is how you put an end to that," Victarion had told him, slamming a dagger down on the table between them. Kerwin took the blade—too afraid to refuse it, the captain judged—but he had never used it.

"My hand is here," Victarion said. "Look all you like."

Maester Kerwin went down to one knee, the better to inspect the wound. He even sniffed at it, like a dog. "I will need to let the pus again. The color . . . lord Captain, the cut is not healing. It may be that I will need to take your hand."

They had talked of this before. "If you take my hand, I will kill you. But first I will tie you over the rail and make the crew a gift of your arse. Get on with it."

"There will be pain."

"Always." *Life is pain, you fool. There is no joy but in the Drowned God's watery halls.* "Do it."

The boy—it was hard to think of one so soft and pink as a man—laid the edge of the dagger across the captain's palm and slashed. The pus that burst forth was thick and yellow as sour milk. The dusky woman wrinkled her nose at the smell, the maester gagged, and even Victarion himself felt his stomach churn. "Cut deeper. Get it all. Show me the blood."

Maester Kerwin pressed the dagger deep. This time it hurt, but blood welled up as well as pus, blood so dark that it looked black in the lantern light.

Blood was good. Victarion grunted in approval. He sat there unflinching as the maester dabbed and squeezed and cleaned the pus away with squares of soft cloth boiled in vinegar. By the time he finished, the clean water in his basin had become a scummy soup. The sight alone would sicken any man. "Take that filth and go." Victarion nodded at the dusky woman. "She can bind me up."

Even after the boy had fled, the stink remained. Of late, there was no escaping it. The maester had suggested that the wound might best be drained up on deck, amidst fresh air and sunlight, but Victarion forbade it. This was not something that his crew could see. They were half a world away from home, too far to let them see that their iron captain had begun to rust.

His left hand still throbbed—a dull pain, but persistent. When he closed his hand into a fist it sharpened, as if a knife were stabbing up his arm. *Not a knife, a longsword. A longsword in the hand of a ghost.* Serry, that had been his name. A knight, and heir to Southshield. *I killed him, but he stabs at me from beyond the grave. From the hot heart of whatever hell I sent him to, he thrusts his steel into my hand and twists.*

Victarion remembered the fight as if it had been yesterday. His shield had been in shards, hanging useless from his arm, so when Serry's longsword came flashing down he had reached up and caught it. The stripling had been stronger than he looked; his blade bit through the lobstered steel of the captain's gauntlet and the padded glove beneath into the meat of his palm. *A scratch from a little kitten*, Victarion told himself afterward. He had washed the cut, poured some boiled vinegar over it, bound it up, and thought little more of it, trusting that the pain would fade and the hand heal itself in time.

Instead the wound had festered, until Victarion began to wonder whether Serry's blade had been poisoned. Why else would the cut refuse to heal? The thought made him rage. No true man killed with poison. At Moat Cailin the bog devils had loosed poisoned arrows at his men, but that was to be expected from such degraded creatures. Serry had been a knight, highborn. Poison was for cravens, women, and Dornishmen.

"If not Serry, who?" he asked the dusky woman. "Could that mouse of a maester be doing this? Maesters know spells and other tricks. He might be using one to poison me, hoping I will let him cut my hand off." The more he thought on it, the more likely it seemed. "The Crow's Eye gave him to me, wretched creature that he is." Euron had taken Kerwin off Greenshield, where he had been in service to Lord Chester, tending his ravens and teaching his children, or perhaps the other away around. And how the mouse had squealed when one of Euron's mutes delivered him aboard the *Iron Victory*, dragging him along by the convenient chain about his neck. "If this is his revenge, he wrongs me. It was Euron who insisted he be taken, to keep him from making mischief with his birds." His brother had given him three cages of ravens too, so Kerwin could send back word of their voyaging, but Victarion had forbidden him to loose them. *Let the Crow's Eye stew and wonder.*

The dusky woman was binding his hand with fresh linen, wrapping it six times around his palm, when Longwater Pyke came pounding at the cabin door to tell him that the captain of *Grief* had come aboard with a prisoner. "Says he's brought us a wizard, Captain. Says he fished him from the sea."

"A wizard?" Could the Drowned God have sent a gift to him, here on the far side of the world? His brother Aeron would have known, but Aeron had seen the majesty of the Drowned God's watery halls below the sea before being returned to life. Victarion had a healthy fear of his god, as all men should, but put his faith in steel. He flexed his wounded hand, grimacing, then pulled his glove on and rose. "Show me this wizard."

Grief's master awaited them on deck. A small man, as hairy as he was homely, he was a Sparr by birth. His men called him the Vole. "Lord Captain," he said when Victarion appeared, "this is Moqorro. A gift to us from the Drowned God."

The wizard was a monster of a man, as tall as Victarion himself and twice as wide, with a belly like a boulder and a tangle of bone-white hair that grew about his face like a lion's mane. His skin was black. Not the nut brown of the Summer Islanders on their swan ships, nor the red-brown of the Dothraki horselords, nor the charcoal-and-earth color of the dusky woman's skin, but *black*. Blacker than coal, blacker than jet, blacker than a raven's wing. *Burned*, Victarion thought, *like a man who has been roasted in the flames until his flesh chars and crisps and falls smoking from his bones*. The fires that had charred him still danced across his cheeks and forehead, where his eyes peered out from amongst a mask of frozen flames. *Slave tattoos*, the captain knew. *Marks of evil*.

"We found him clinging to a broken spar," said the Vole. "He was ten days in the water after his ship went down."

"If he were ten days in the water, he'd be dead, or mad from drinking seawater." Salt water was holy; Aeron Damphair and other priests might bless men with it and swallow a mouthful or two from time to time to strengthen their faith, but no mortal man could drink of the deep sea for days at a time and hope to live. "You claim to be a sorcerer?" Victarion asked the prisoner.

"No, Captain," the black man answered in the Common Tongue. His voice was so deep it seemed to come from the bottom of the sea. "I am but a humble slave of R'hllor, the Lord of Light."

R'hllor. A red priest, then. Victarion had seen such men in foreign cities, tending their sacred fires. Those had worn rich red robes of silk and velvet and lambswool. This one was dressed in faded, salt-stained rags that clung to his thick legs and hung about his torso in tatters . . . but when the captain peered at the rags more closely, it did appear as if they might once have been red. "A pink priest," Victarion announced.

"A demon priest," said Wulfe One-Ear. He spat.

"Might be his robes caught fire, so he jumped overboard to put them out," suggested Longwater Pyke, to general laughter. Even the monkeys were amused. They chattered overhead, and one flung down a handful of his own shit to spatter on the boards.

Victarion Greyjoy mistrusted laughter. The sound of it always left him with the uneasy feeling that he was the butt of some jape he did not understand. Euron Crow's Eye had oft made mock of him when they were boys. So had Aeron, before he had become the Damphair. Their mockery oft came disguised as praise, and sometimes Victarion had not even realized he was being mocked. Not until he heard the laughter. Then came the anger, boiling up in the back of his throat until he was like to choke upon the taste. That was how he felt about the monkeys. Their antics never brought so much as a smile to the captain's face, though his crew would roar and hoot and whistle.

"Send him down to the Drowned God before he brings a curse upon us," urged Burton Humble.

"A ship gone down, and only him clinging to the wreckage," said Wulfe One-Ear. "Where's the crew? Did he call down demons to devour them? What happened to this ship?"

"A storm." Moqorro crossed his arms against his chest. He did not appear frightened, though all around him men were calling for his death. Even the monkeys did not seem to like this wizard. They leapt from line to line overhead, screaming.

Victarion was uncertain. *He came out of the sea. Why would the Drowned God cast him up unless he meant for us to find him?* His brother Euron had his pet wizards. Perhaps the Drowned God meant for Victarion to have one too. "Why do you say this man is a wizard?" he asked the Vole. "I see only a ragged red priest."

"I thought the same, lord Captain . . . but he *knows* things. He knew that we made for Slaver's Bay before any man could tell him, and he knew you would be here, off this island." The small man hesitated. "Lord Captain, he told me . . . he told me you would surely die unless we brought him to you."

"That *I* would die?" Victarion snorted. *Cut his throat and throw him in the sea*, he was about to say, until a throb of pain in his bad hand went stabbing up his arm almost to the elbow, the agony so intense that his words turned to bile in his throat. He stumbled and seized the rail to keep from falling.

"The sorcerer's cursed the captain," a voice said.

Other men took up the cry. *"Cut his throat! Kill him before he calls his demons down on us!"* Longwater Pyke was the first to draw his dirk. *"NO!"* Victarion bellowed. "Stand back! All of you. Pyke, put up your steel. Vole, back to your ship. Humble, take the wizard to my cabin. The rest of you, about your duties." For half a heartbeat he was not certain they would obey. They stood about muttering, half with blades to hand, each looking to the others for resolve. Monkey shit rained down around them all, *splat splat splat*. No one moved until Victarion seized the sorcerer by the arm and pulled him to the hatchway.

As he opened the door to the captain's cabin, the dusky woman turned toward him, silent and smiling . . . but when she saw the red priest at his side her lips drew back from her teeth, and she *hisssssed* in sudden fury, like a snake. Victarion gave her the back of his good hand and knocked her to the deck. "Be quiet, woman. Wine for both of us." He turned to the black man. "Did the Vole speak true? You saw my death?"

"That, and more."

"Where? When? Will I die in battle?" His good hand opened and closed. "If you lie to me, I will split your head open like a melon and let the monkeys eat your brains."

"Your death is with us now, my lord. Give me your hand."

"My hand. What do you know of my hand?"

"I have seen you in the nightfires, Victarion Greyjoy. You come striding through the flames stern and fierce, your great axe dripping blood, blind to the tentacles that grasp you at wrist and neck and ankle, the black strings that make you dance."

"*Dance?*" Victarion bristled. "Your nightfires lie. I was not made for dancing, and I am no man's puppet." He yanked off his glove and shoved his bad hand at the priest's face. "Here. Is this what you wanted?" The new linen was already discolored by blood and pus. "He had a rose on his shield, the man who gave this to me. I scratched my hand on a thorn."

"Even the smallest scratch can prove mortal, lord Captain, but if you will allow me, I will heal this. I will need a blade. Silver would be best, but iron will serve. A brazier as well. I must needs light a fire. There will be pain. Terrible pain, such as you have never known. But when we are done, your hand will be returned to you."

They are all the same, these magic men. The mouse warned me of pain as well. "I am ironborn, priest. I laugh at pain. You will have what you require . . . but if you fail, and my hand is not healed, I will cut your throat myself and give you to the sea."

Moqorro bowed, his dark eyes shining. "So be it."

The iron captain was not seen again that day, but as the hours passed the crew of his *Iron Victory* reported hearing the sound of wild laughter coming from the captain's cabin, laughter deep and dark and mad, and when Longwater Pyke and Wulfe One-Eye tried the cabin door they found it barred. Later singing was heard, a strange high wailing song in a tongue the maester said was High Valyrian. That was when the monkeys left the ship, screeching as they leapt into the water.

Come sunset, as the sea turned black as ink and the swollen sun tinted the sky a deep and bloody red, Victarion came back on deck. He was naked from the waist up, his left arm blood to the elbow. As his crew gathered, whispering and trading glances, he raised a charred and blackened hand. Wisps of dark smoke rose from his fingers as he pointed at the maester. "That one. Cut his throat and throw him in the sea, and the winds will favor us all the way to Meereen." Moqorro had seen that in his fires. He had seen the wench wed too, but what of it? She would not be the first woman Victarion Greyjoy had made a widow.

TYRION

The healer entered the tent murmuring pleasantries, but one sniff of the foul air and a glance at Yezzan zo Qaggaz put an end to that. "The pale mare," the man told Sweets.

What a surprise, Tyrion thought. *Who could have guessed? Aside from any man with a nose and me with half of one.* Yezzan was burning with fever, squirming fitfully in a pool of his own excrement. His shit had turned to brown slime streaked with blood . . . and it fell to Yollo and Penny to wipe his yellow bottom clean. Even with assistance, their master could not lift his own weight; it took all his failing strength to roll onto one side.

"My arts will not avail here," the healer announced. "The noble Yez-zan's life is in the hands of the gods. Keep him cool if you can. Some say that helps. Bring him water." Those afflicted by the pale mare were always thirsty, drinking gallons between their shits. "Clean fresh water, as much as he will drink."

"Not river water," said Sweets.

"By no means." And with that, the healer fled.

We need to flee as well, thought Tyrion. He was a slave in a golden collar, with little bells that tinkled cheerfully with every step he took. *One of Yezzan's special treasures. An honor indistinguishable from a death warrant.* Yezzan zo Qaggaz liked to keep his darlings close, so it had fallen to Yollo and Penny and Sweets and his other treasures to attend him when he grew sick.

Poor old Yezzan. The lord of suet was not so bad as masters went. Sweets had been right about that. Serving at his nightly banquets, Tyrion had soon learned that Yezzan stood foremost amongst those Yunkish lords who favored honoring the peace with Meereen. Most of the others were only biding their time, waiting for the armies of Volantis to arrive. A few wanted to assault the city immediately, lest the Volantenes rob them of their glory and the best part of the plunder. Yezzan would have no part of that. Nor would he consent to returning Meereen's hostages by way of trebuchet, as the sellsword Bloodbeard had proposed.

But much and more can change in two days. Two days ago Nurse had been hale and healthy. Two days ago Yezzan had not heard the pale mare's ghostly hoofbeats. Two days ago the fleets of Old Volantis had been two days farther off. And now . . .

"Is Yezzan going to die?" Penny asked, in that please-say-it-is-not-so voice of hers.

"We are all going to die."

"Of the flux, I meant."

Sweets gave them both a desperate look. "Yezzan *must not* die." The hermaphrodite stroked the brow of their gargantuan master, pushing back his sweat-damp hair. The Yunkishman moaned, and another flood of brown water gushed down his legs. His bedding was stained and stinking, but they had no way to move him.

"Some masters free their slaves when they die," said Penny.

Sweets tittered. It was a ghastly sound. "Only favorites. They free them from the woes of the world, to accompany their beloved master to the grave and serve him in the afterlife."

Sweets should know. His will be the first throat slit.

The goat boy spoke up. "The silver queen—"

"—is dead," insisted Sweets. "Forget her! The dragon took her across the river. She's drowned in that Dothraki sea."

"You can't drown in *grass*," the goat boy said.

"If we were free," said Penny, "we could find the queen. Or go search for her, at least."

You on your dog and me on my sow, chasing a dragon across the Dothraki sea. Tyrion scratched his scar to keep from laughing. "This particular dragon has already evinced a fondness for roast pork. And roast dwarf is twice as tasty."

"It was just a wish," said Penny wistfully. "We could sail away. There are ships again, now that the war is over."

Is it? Tyrion was inclined to doubt that. Parchments had been signed, but wars were not fought on parchments.

"We could sail to Qarth," Penny went on. "The streets are paved with jade there, my brother always said. The city walls are one of the wonders of the world. When we perform in Qarth, gold and silver will rain down on us, you'll see."

"Some of those ships out on the bay are Qartheen," Tyrion reminded her. "Lomas Longstrider saw the walls of Qarth. His books suffice for me. I have gone as far east as I intend to go."

Sweets dabbed at Yezzan's fevered face with a damp cloth. "Yezzan must live. Or we all die with him. The pale mare does not carry off every rider. The master will recover."

That was a bald-faced lie. It would be a wonder if Yezzan lived another day. The lord of suet was already dying from whatever hideous disease he had brought back from Sothoryos, it seemed to Tyrion. This would just hasten his end. *A mercy, really.* But not the sort the dwarf craved for himself. "The healer said he needs fresh water. We will see to that."

"That is good of you." Sweets sounded numb. It was more than just fear of having her throat cut; alone amongst Yezzan's treasures, she actually seemed fond of their immense master.

"Penny, come with me." Tyrion opened the tent flap and ushered her out into the heat of a Meereenese morning. The air was muggy and oppressive, yet still a welcome relief from the miasma of sweat, shit, and sickness that filled the inside of Yezzan's palatial pavilion.

"Water will help the master," Penny said. "That's what the healer said, it must be so. Sweet fresh water."

"Sweet fresh water didn't help Nurse." *Poor old Nurse.* Yezzan's soldiers had tossed him onto the corpse wagon last night at dusk, another victim of the pale mare. When men are dying every hour, no one looks too hard at one more dead man, especially one as well despised as Nurse. Yezzan's other slaves had refused to go near the overseer once the cramps began, so it was left to Tyrion to keep him warm and bring him drinks. *Watered wine and lemonsweet and some nice hot dogtail soup, with slivers of mushroom in the broth. Drink it down, Nursey, that shitwater squirting from your arse needs to be replaced.* The last word Nurse ever said was, "No." The last words he ever heard were, "A Lannister always pays his debts."

Tyrion had kept the truth of that from Penny, but she needed to understand how things stood with their master. "If Yezzan lives to see the sunrise, I'll be stunned."

She clutched his arm. "What will happen to us?"

"He has heirs. Nephews." Four such had come with Yezzan from Yunkai to command his slave soldiers. One was dead, slain by Targaryen sellswords during a sortie. The other three would divide the yellow enormity's slaves amongst them, like as not. Whether any of the nephews shared Yezzan's fondness for cripples, freaks, and grotesques was far less certain. "One of them may inherit us. Or we could end up back on the auction block."

"No." Her eyes got big. "Not that. Please."

"It is not a prospect I relish either."

A few yards away, six of Yezzan's slave soldiers were squatting in the dust, throwing the bones and passing a wineskin from hand to hand. One was the serjeant called Scar, a black-tempered brute with a head as smooth as stone and the shoulders of an ox. *Clever as an ox too,* Tyrion recalled.

He waddled toward them. "Scar," he barked out, "the noble Yezzan has need of fresh, clean water. Take two men and bring back as many pails as you can carry. And be quick about it."

The soldiers broke off their game. Scar rose to his feet, brow beetling. "What did you say, dwarf? Who do you think you are?"

"You know who I am. Yollo. One of our lord's treasures. Now do as I told you."

The soldiers laughed. "Go on, Scar," one mocked, "and be quick about it. Yezzan's monkey gave you a command."

"You do *not* tell soldiers what to do," Scar said.

"Soldiers?" Tyrion affected puzzlement. "Slaves, is what I see. You wear a collar round your neck the same as me."

The savage backhand blow Scar dealt him knocked him to the ground and broke his lip. "Yezzan's collar. Not yours."

Tyrion wiped the blood from his split lip with the back of his hand. When he tried to rise, one leg went out from under him, and he stumbled back onto his knees. He needed Penny's help to regain his feet. "Sweets said the master must have water," he said in his best whine.

"Sweets can go fuck himself. He's made for it. We don't take commands from that freak neither."

No, thought Tyrion. Even amongst slaves there were lords and peasants, as he had been quick to learn. The hermaphrodite had long been their master's special pet, indulged and favored, and the noble Yezzan's other slaves hated him for it.

The soldiers were accustomed to taking their commands from their masters and their overseer. But Nurse was dead and Yezzan too sick to name a successor. As for the three nephews, those brave free men had remembered urgent business elsewhere at the first sound of the pale mare's hooves.

"The w-water," said Tyrion, cringing. "Not river water, the healer said. Clean, fresh well water."

Scar grunted. "*You* go for it. And be quick about it."

"Us?" Tyrion exchanged a hopeless glance with Penny. "Water's heavy. We're not so strong as you. Can we . . . can we take the mule cart?"

"Take your legs."

"We'll need to make a dozen trips."

"Make a hundred trips. It's no shit to me."

"Just the two of us . . . we won't be able to carry all the water that the master needs."

"Take your bear," suggested Scar. "Fetching water is about all that one is good for."

Tyrion backed away. "As you say, master."

Scar grinned. *Master. Oh, he liked that.* "Morgo, bring the keys. You fill the pails and come right back, dwarf. You know what happens to slaves who try to escape."

"Bring the pails," Tyrion told Penny. He went off with the man Morgo to fetch Ser Jorah Mormont from his cage.

The knight had not adapted well to bondage. When called upon to play the bear and carry off the maiden fair, he had been sullen and uncooperative, shuffling lifelessly through his paces when he deigned to take part in their mummery at all. Though he had not attempted escape, nor offered violence to his captors, he would ignore their commands oft as not or reply with muttered curses. None of this had amused Nurse, who made his displeasure clear by confining Mormont in an iron cage and having him beaten every evening as the sun sank into Slaver's Bay. The knight absorbed the beatings silently; the only sounds were the muttered curses of the slaves who beat him and the dull *thuds* of their clubs pounding against Ser Jorah's bruised and battered flesh.

The man is a shell, Tyrion thought, the first time he saw the big knight beaten. *I should have held my tongue and let Zahrina have him. It might have been a kinder fate than this.*

Mormont emerged from the cramped confines of the cage bent and squinting, with both eyes blackened and his back crusty with dried blood. His face was so bruised and swollen that he hardly looked human. He was naked except for a breechclout, a filthy bit of yellow rag. "You're to help them carry water," Morgo told him.

Ser Jorah's only reply was a sullen stare. *Some men would sooner die free than live a slave, I suppose.* Tyrion was not stricken with that affliction himself, thankfully, but if Mormont murdered Morgo, the other slaves might not draw that distinction. "Come," he said, before the knight did something brave and stupid. He waddled off and hoped Mormont would follow.

The gods were good for once. Mormont followed.

Two pails for Penny, two for Tyrion, and four for Ser Jorah, two in either hand. The nearest well was south and west of the Harridan, so they set off in that direction, the bells on their collars ringing merrily with every step. No one paid them any mind. They were just slaves fetching water for their master. Wearing a collar conferred certain advantages, particularly a gilded collar inscribed with the name of Yezzan zo Qaggaz. The chime of those little bells proclaimed their value to anyone with ears. A slave was only as important as his master; Yezzan was the richest man in the Yellow City and had brought six hundred slave soldiers to the war, even if he did look like a monstrous yellow slug and smell of piss. Their collars gave them leave to go anywhere they might wish within the camp.

Until Yezzan dies.

The Clanker Lords had their slave soldiers drilling in the nearest field. The clatter of the chains that bound them made a harsh metallic music as they marched across the sand in lockstep and formed up with their long spears. Elsewhere teams of slaves were raising ramps of stone and sand beneath their mangonels and scorpions, angling them upward at the sky, the better to defend the camp should the black dragon return. It made the dwarf smile to see them sweating and cursing as they wrestled the heavy machines onto the inclines. Crossbows were much in evidence as well. Every other man seemed to be clutching one, with a quiverfull of bolts hanging from his hip.

If anyone had thought to ask him, Tyrion could have told them not to bother. Unless one of those long iron scorpion bolts chanced to find an eye, the queen's pet monster was not like to be brought down by such toys. *Dragons are not so easy to kill as that. Tickle him with these and you'll only make him angry.*

The eyes were where a dragon was most vulnerable. The eyes, and the brain behind them. Not the underbelly, as certain old tales would have it. The scales there were just as tough as those along a dragon's back and flanks. And not down the gullet either. That was madness. These would-be dragonslayers might as well try to quench a fire with a spear thrust. "Death comes out of the dragon's mouth," Septon Barth had written in his *Unnatural History*, "but death does not go in that way."

Farther on, two legions from New Ghis were facing off shield wall to shield wall whilst serjeants in iron halfhelms with horsehair crests screamed commands in their own incomprehensible dialect. To the naked eye the Ghiscari looked more formidable than the Yunkish slave soldiers, but Tyrion nursed doubts. The legionaries might be armed and organized in the same manner as Unsullied . . . but the eunuchs knew no other life, whereas the Ghiscari were free citizens who served for three-year terms.

The line at the well stretched back a quarter mile.

There were only a handful of wells within a day's march of Meereen, so the wait was always long. Most of the Yunkish host drew their drinking water from the Skahazadhan, which Tyrion had known was a very bad idea even before the healer's warning. The clever ones took care to stay upstream of the latrines, but they were still downstream of the city.

The fact that there were any good wells at all within a day's march of the city only went to prove that Daenerys Targaryen was still an innocent where siegecraft was concerned. *She should have poisoned every well. Then all the Yunkishmen would be drinking from the river. See how long their siege lasts then.* That was what his lord father would have done, Tyrion did not doubt.

Every time they shuffled forward another place, the bells on their collars tinkled brightly. *Such a happy sound, it makes me want to scoop out someone's eyeballs with a spoon.* By now Griff and Duck and Haldon Half-maester should be in Westeros with their young prince. *I should be with them . . . but no, I had to have a whore. Kinslaying was not enough, I needed cunt and wine to seal my ruin, and here I am on the wrong side of the world, wearing a slave collar with little golden bells to announce my coming. If I dance just right, maybe I can ring "The Rains of Castamere."*

There was no better place to hear the latest news and rumors than around the well. "I know what I saw," an old slave in a rusted iron collar was saying, as Tyrion and Penny shuffled along in the queue, "and I saw that dragon ripping off arms and legs, tearing men in half, burning them down to ash and bones. People started running, trying to get out of that pit, but I come to see a show, and by all the gods of Ghis, I saw one. I was up in the purple, so I didn't think the dragon was like to trouble me."

"The queen climbed onto the dragon's back and flew away," insisted a tall brown woman.

"She tried," said the old man, "but she couldn't hold on. The crossbows wounded the dragon, and the queen was struck right between her sweet pink teats, I hear. That was when she fell. She died in the gutter, crushed beneath a wagon's wheels. I know a girl who knows a man who saw her die."

In this company, silence was the better part of wisdom, but Tyrion could not help himself. "No corpse was found," he said.

The old man frowned. "What would you know about it?"

"They were there," said the brown woman. "It's them, the jousting dwarfs, the ones who tilted for the queen."

The old man squinted down as if seeing him and Penny for the first time. "You're the ones who rode the pigs."

Our notoriety precedes us. Tyrion sketched a courtly bow, and refrained from pointing out that one of the pigs was really a dog. "The sow I ride is actually my sister. We have the same nose, could you tell? A wizard cast a spell on her, but if you give her a big wet kiss, she will turn into a beautiful woman. The pity is, once you get to know her, you'll want to kiss her again to turn her back."

Laughter erupted all around them. Even the old man joined in. "You saw her, then," said the redheaded boy behind them. "You saw the queen. Is she as beautiful as they say?"

I saw a slender girl with silvery hair wrapped in a tokar, he might have told them. *Her face was veiled, and I never got close enough for a good look. I was riding on a pig.* Daenerys Targaryen had been seated in the owner's box beside her Ghiscari king, but Tyrion's eyes had been drawn to the knight in the white-and-gold armor behind her. Though his features were concealed, the dwarf would have known Barristan Selmy anywhere. *Illyrio was right about that much, at least,* he remembered thinking. *Will Selmy know me, though? And what will he do if he does?*

He had almost revealed himself then and there, but something stopped him—caution, cowardice, instinct, call it what you will. He could not imagine Barristan the Bold greeting him with anything but hostility. Selmy had never approved of Jaime's presence in his precious Kingsguard. Before the rebellion, the old knight thought him too young and untried; afterward, he had been known to say that the Kingslayer should exchange that white cloak for a black one. And his own crimes were worse. Jaime had killed a madman. Tyrion had put a quarrel through the groin of his own sire, a man Ser Barristan had known and served for years. He might have chanced it all the same, but then Penny had landed a blow on his shield and the moment was gone, never to return.

"The queen watched us tilt," Penny was telling the other slaves in line, "but that was the only time we saw her."

"You must have seen the dragon," said the old man.

Would that we had. The gods had not even vouchsafed him that much. As Daenerys Targaryen was taking wing, Nurse had been clapping irons round their ankles to make certain they would not attempt escape on their way back to their master. If the overseer had only taken his leave after delivering them to the abbatoir, or fled with the rest of the slavers when the dragon descended from the sky, the two dwarfs might have strolled away free. *Or run away, more like, our little bells a-jingle.*

"Was there a dragon?" Tyrion said with a shrug. "All I know is that no dead queens were found."

The old man was not convinced. "Ah, they found corpses by the hundred. They dragged them inside the pit and burned them, though half was crisp already. Might be they didn't know her, burned and bloody and crushed. Might be they did but decided to say elsewise, to keep you slaves quiet."

"*Us* slaves?" said the brown woman. "You wear a collar too."

"*Ghazdor's* collar," the old man boasted. "Known him since we was born. I'm almost like a brother to him. Slaves like you, sweepings out of Astapor and Yunkai, you whine about being free, but I wouldn't give the dragon queen my collar if she offered to suck my cock for it. Man has the right master, that's better."

Tyrion did not dispute him. The most insidious thing about bondage was how easy it was to grow accustomed to it. The life of most slaves was not all that different from the life of a serving man at Casterly Rock, it seemed to him. True, some slaveowners and their overseers were brutal and cruel, but the same was true of some Westerosi lords and their stewards and bailiffs. Most of the Yunkai'i treated their chattels decently enough, so long as they did their jobs and caused no trouble . . . and this old man in his rusted collar, with his fierce loyalty to Lord Wobblecheeks, his owner, was not at all atypical.

"Ghazdor the Great-hearted?" Tyrion said, sweetly. "Our master Yezzan has often spoken of his wits." What Yezzan had actually said was on the order of, *I have more wits in the left cheek of my arse than Ghazdor and his brothers have between them.* He thought it prudent to omit the actual words.

Midday had come and gone before he and Penny reached the well, where a scrawny one-legged slave was drawing water. He squinted at them suspiciously. "Nurse always comes for Yezzan's water, with four men and a mule cart." He dropped the bucket down the well once more. There was a soft *splash.* The one-legged man let the bucket fill, then began to draw it upward. His arms were sunburnt and peeling, scrawny to look at but all muscle.

"The mule died," said Tyrion. "So did Nurse, poor man. And now Yezzan himself has mounted the pale mare, and six of his soldiers have the shits. May I have two pails full?"

"As you like." That was the end of idle talk. *Is that hoofbeats you hear?* The lie about the soldiers got old one-leg moving much more quickly.

They started back, each of the dwarfs carrying two brim-full pails of sweet water and Ser Jorah with two pails in each hand. The day was growing hotter, the air as thick and wet as damp wool, and the pails seemed to grow heavier with every step. *A long walk on short legs.* Water sloshed from his pails with every stride, splashing round his legs, whilst his bells played a marching song. *Had I known it would come to this, Father, I might have let you live.* Half a mile east, a dark plume of smoke was rising where a tent had been set afire. *Burning last night's dead.* "This way," Tyrion said, jerking his head to the right.

Penny gave him a puzzled look. "That's not how we came."

"We don't want to breathe that smoke. It's full of malign humors." It was not a lie. *Not entirely.*

Penny was soon puffing, struggling with the weight of her pails. "I need to rest."

"As you wish." Tyrion set the pails of water on the ground, grateful for the halt. His legs were cramping badly, so he found himself a likely rock and sat on it to rub his thighs.

"I could do that for you," offered Penny.

"I know where the knots are." As fond as he had grown of the girl, it still made him uncomfortable when she touched him. He turned to Ser Jorah. "A few more beatings and you'll be uglier than I am, Mormont. Tell me, is there any fight left in you?"

The big knight raised two blackened eyes and looked at him as he might look at a bug. "Enough to crack your neck, Imp."

"Good." Tyrion picked up his pails. "This way, then."

Penny wrinkled her brow. "No. It's to the left." She pointed. "That's the Harridan there."

"And that's the Wicked Sister." Tyrion nodded in the other direction. "Trust me," he said. "My way is quicker." He set off, his bells jingling. Penny would follow, he knew.

Sometimes he envied the girl all her pretty little dreams. She reminded him of Sansa Stark, the child bride he had wed and lost. Despite the horrors Penny had suffered, she remained somehow trusting. *She should know better. She is older than Sansa. And she's a dwarf. She acts as if she has forgotten that, as if she were highborn and fair to look upon, instead of a slave in a grotesquerie.* At night Tyrion would oft hear her praying. *A waste of words. If there are gods to listen, they are monstrous gods who tor-*

ment us for their sport. Who else would make a world like this, so full of bondage, blood, and pain? Who else would shape us as they have? Sometimes he wanted to slap her, shake her, scream at her, anything to wake her from her dreams. *No one is going to save us,* he wanted to scream at her. *The worst is yet to come.* Yet somehow he could never say the words. Instead of giving her a good hard crack across that ugly face of hers to knock the blinders from her eyes, he would find himself squeezing her shoulder or giving her a hug. *Every touch a lie. I have paid her so much false coin that she half thinks she's rich.*

He had even kept the truth of Daznak's Pit from her.

Lions. They were going to set lions on us. It would have been exquisitely ironic, that. Perhaps he would have had time for a short, bitter chortle before being torn apart.

No one ever told him the end that had been planned for them, not in so many words, but it had not been hard to puzzle out, down beneath the bricks of Daznak's Pit, in the hidden world below the seats, the dark domain of the pit fighters and the serving men who tended to them, quick and dead—the cooks who fed them, the ironmongers who armed them, the barber-surgeons who bled them and shaved them and bound up their wounds, the whores who serviced them before and after fights, the corpse handlers who dragged the losers off the sands with chains and iron hooks.

Nurse's face had given Tyrion his first inkling. After their show, he and Penny had returned to the torchlit vault where the fighters gathered before and after their matches. Some sat sharpening their weapons; others sacrificed to queer gods, or dulled their nerves with milk of the poppy before going out to die. Those who'd fought and won were dicing in a corner, laughing as only men who have just faced death and lived can laugh.

Nurse was paying out some silver to a pit man on a lost wager when he spied Penny leading Crunch. The confusion in his eyes was gone in half a heartbeat, but not before Tyrion grasped what it meant. *Nurse did not expect us back.* He had looked around at other faces. *None of them expected us back. We were meant to die out there.* The final piece fell into place when he overheard an animal trainer complaining loudly to the pitmaster. "The lions are hungry. Two days since they ate. I was told not to feed them, and I haven't. The queen should pay for meat."

"You take that up with her the next time she holds court," the pitmaster threw back at him.

Even now, Penny did not suspect. When she spoke about the pit, her chief worry was that more people had not laughed. *They would have pissed themselves laughing if the lions had been loosed,* Tyrion almost told her. Instead he'd squeezed her shoulder.

Penny came to a sudden halt. "We're going the wrong way."

"We're not." Tyrion lowered his pails to the ground. The handles had gouged deep grooves in his fingers. "Those are the tents we want, there."

"The Second Sons?" A queer smile split Ser Jorah's face. "If you think to find help there, you don't know Brown Ben Plumm."

"Oh, I do. Plumm and I have played five games of *cyvasse*. Brown Ben is shrewd, tenacious, not unintelligent . . . but wary. He likes to let his opponent take the risks whilst he sits back and keeps his options open, reacting to the battle as it takes shape."

"Battle? What battle?" Penny backed away from him. "We have to get *back*. The master needs clean water. If we take too long, we'll be whipped. And Pretty Pig and Crunch are there."

"Sweets will see that they are taken care of," Tyrion lied. More like, Scar and his friends would soon be feasting on ham and bacon and a savory dog stew, but Penny did not need to hear that. "Nurse is dead and Yezzan's dying. It could be dark before anyone thinks to miss us. We will never have a better chance than now."

"*No.* You know what they do when they catch slaves trying to escape. You *know.* Please. They'll never let us leave the camp."

"We haven't left the camp." Tyrion picked up his pails. He set off at a brisk waddle, never looking back. Mormont fell in beside him. After a moment he heard the sounds of Penny hurrying after him, down a sandy slope to a circle of ragged tents.

The first guard appeared as they neared the horse lines, a lean spearman whose maroon beard marked him as Tyroshi. "What do we have here? And what have you got in those pails?"

"Water," said Tyrion, "if it please you."

"Beer would please me better." A spearpoint pricked him in the back— a second guard, come up behind them. Tyrion could hear King's Landing in his voice. *Scum from Flea Bottom.* "You lost, dwarf?" the guard demanded.

"We're here to join your company."

A pail slipped from Penny's grasp and overturned. Half the water had spilled before she could right it once again.

"We got fools enough in this company. Why would we want three more?" The Tyroshi flicked at Tyrion's collar with his spearpoint, ringing the little golden bell. "A runaway slave is what I see. Three runaway slaves. Whose collar?"

"The Yellow Whale's." That from a third man, drawn by their voices—a skinny stubble-jawed piece of work with teeth stained red from sourleaf. A *serjeant*, Tyrion knew, from the way the other two deferred to him. He had a hook where his right hand should have been. *Bronn's meaner bastard shadow, or I'm Baelor the Beloved.* "These are the dwarfs Ben tried to buy," the serjeant told the spearmen, squinting, "but the big one . . . best bring him too. All three."

The Tyroshi gestured with his spear. Tyrion moved along. The other sellsword—a stripling, hardly more than a boy, with fuzz on his cheeks and hair the color of dirty straw—scooped up Penny under one arm. "Ooh, mine has teats," he said, laughing. He slipped a hand under Penny's tunic, just to be sure.

"Just bring her," snapped the serjeant.

The stripling slung Penny over one shoulder. Tyrion went ahead as quick as his stunted legs would allow. He knew where they were going: the big tent on the far side of the fire pit, its painted canvas walls cracked and faded by years of sun and rain. A few sellswords turned to watch them pass, and a camp follower sniggered, but no one moved to interfere.

Within the tent, they found camp stools and a trestle table, a rack of spears and halberds, a floor covered with threadbare carpets in half a dozen clashing colors, and three officers. One was slim and elegant, with a pointed beard, a bravo's blade, and a slashed pink doublet. One was plump and balding, with ink stains on his fingers and a quill clutched in one hand.

The third was the man he sought. Tyrion bowed. "Captain."

"We caught them creeping into camp." The stripling dumped Penny onto the carpet.

"Runaways," the Tyroshi declared. "With pails."

"Pails?" said Brown Ben Plumm. When no one ventured to explain, he said, "Back to your posts, boys. And not a word o' this, to anyone." When they were gone, he smiled at Tyrion. "Come for another game of *cyvasse*, Yollo?"

"If you wish. I do enjoy defeating you. I hear you're twice a turncloak, Plumm. A man after mine own heart."

Brown Ben's smile never reached his eyes. He studied Tyrion as a man might study a talking snake. "Why are you here?"

"To make your dreams come true. You tried to buy us at auction. Then you tried to win us at *cyvasse*. Even when I had my nose, I was not so handsome as to provoke such passion . . . save in one who happened to know my true worth. Well, here I am, free for the taking. Now be a friend, send for your smith, and get these collars off us. I'm sick of tinkling when I tinkle."

"I want no trouble with your noble master."

"Yezzan has more urgent matters to concern him than three missing slaves. He's riding the pale mare. And why should they think to look for us here? You have swords enough to discourage anyone who comes nosing round. A small risk for a great gain."

The jackanapes in the slashed pink doublet hissed. "They've brought the sickness amongst us. Into our very tents." He turned to Ben Plumm. "Shall I cut his head off, Captain? We can toss the rest in a latrine pit." He drew a sword, a slender bravo's blade with a jeweled hilt.

"Do be careful with my head," said Tyrion. "You don't want to get any of my blood on you. Blood carries the disease. And you'll want to boil our clothes, or burn them."

"I've a mind to burn them with you still in them, Yollo."

"That is not my name. But you know that. You have known that since you first set eyes on me."

"Might be."

"I know you as well, my lord," said Tyrion. "You're less purple and more brown than the Plumms at home, but unless your name's a lie, you're a westerman, by blood if not by birth. House Plumm is sworn to Casterly Rock, and as it happens I know a bit of its history. Your branch sprouted from a stone spit across the narrow sea, no doubt. A younger son of Viserys Plumm, I'd wager. The queen's dragons were fond of you, were they not?"

That seemed to amuse the sellsword. "Who told you that?"

"No one. Most of the stories you hear about dragons are fodder for fools. Talking dragons, dragons hoarding gold and gems, dragons with four legs and bellies big as elephants, dragons riddling with sphinxes . . . nonsense, all of it. But there are truths in the old books as well. Not only do I know that the queen's dragons took to you, but I know why."

"My mother said my father had a drop of dragon blood."

"Two drops. That, or a cock six feet long. You know that tale? I do. Now, you're a clever Plumm, so you know this head of mine is worth a lordship . . . back in Westeros, half a world away. By the time you get it there, only bone and maggots will remain. My sweet sister will deny the head is mine and cheat you of the promised reward. You know how it is with queens. Fickle cunts, the lot of them, and Cersei is the worst."

Brown Ben scratched at his beard. "Could deliver you alive and wriggling, then. Or pop your head into a jar and pickle it."

"Or throw in with me. That's the wisest move." He grinned. "I was born a second son. This company is my destiny. "

"The Second Sons have no place for mummers," the bravo in pink said scornfully. "It's fighters we need."

"I've brought you one." Tyrion jerked a thumb at Mormont.

"That creature?" The bravo laughed. "An ugly brute, but scars alone don't make a Second Son."

Tyrion rolled his mismatched eyes. "Lord Plumm, who are these two friends of yours? The pink one is annoying."

The bravo curled a lip, whilst the fellow with the quill chuckled at his insolence. But it was Jorah Mormont who supplied their names. "Inkpots is the company paymaster. The peacock calls himself Kasporio the Cunning, though Kasporio the Cunt would be more apt. A nasty piece of work."

Mormont's face might have been unrecognizable in its battered state, but his voice was unchanged. Kasporio gave him a startled look, whilst the wrinkles around Plumm's eyes crinkled in amusement. "Jorah *Mormont*? Is that you? Less proud than when you scampered off, though. Must we still call you *ser*?"

Ser Jorah's swollen lips twisted into a grotesque grin. "Give me a sword and you can call me what you like, Ben."

Kasporio edged backward. "You . . . she sent you away . . ."

"I came back. Call me a fool."

A *fool in love*. Tyrion cleared his throat. "You can talk of old times later . . . after I am done explaining why my head would be of more use to you upon my shoulders. You will find, Lord Plumm, that I can be very generous to my friends. If you doubt me, ask Bronn. Ask Shagga, son of Dolf. Ask Timett, son of Timett."

"And who would they be?" asked the man called Inkpots.

"Good men who pledged me their swords and prospered greatly by that service." He shrugged. "Oh, very well, I lied about the 'good' part. They're bloodthirsty bastards, like you lot."

"Might be," said Brown Ben. "Or might be you just made up some names. *Shagga*, did you say? Is that a woman's name?"

"His teats are big enough. Next time we meet I'll peek beneath his breeches to be sure. Is that a *cyvasse* set over there? Bring it out and we'll have that game. But first, I think, a cup of wine. My throat is dry as an old bone, and I can see that I have a deal of talking to do."

JON

That night he dreamt of wildlings howling from the woods, advancing to the moan of warhorns and the roll of drums. *Boom DOOM boom DOOM boom DOOM* came the sound, a thousand hearts with a single beat. Some had spears and some had bows and some had axes. Others rode on chariots made of bones, drawn by teams of dogs as big as ponies. Giants lumbered amongst them, forty feet tall, with mauls the size of oak trees.

"Stand fast," Jon Snow called. "Throw them back." He stood atop the Wall, alone. "Flame," he cried, "feed them flame," but there was no one to pay heed.

They are all gone. They have abandoned me.

Burning shafts hissed upward, trailing tongues of fire. Scarecrow brothers tumbled down, black cloaks ablaze. "*Snow,*" an eagle cried, as foemen scuttled up the ice like spiders. Jon was armored in black ice, but his blade burned red in his fist. As the dead men reached the top of the Wall he sent them down to die again. He slew a greybeard and a beardless boy, a giant, a gaunt man with filed teeth, a girl with thick red hair. Too late he recognized Ygritte. She was gone as quick as she'd appeared.

The world dissolved into a red mist. Jon stabbed and slashed and cut. He hacked down Donal Noye and gutted Deaf Dick Follard. Qhorin Halfhand stumbled to his knees, trying in vain to staunch the flow of blood from his neck. "I *am* the Lord of Winterfell," Jon screamed. It was Robb before him now, his hair wet with melting snow. Longclaw took his head off. Then a gnarled hand seized Jon roughly by the shoulder. He whirled . . .

. . . and woke with a raven pecking at his chest. "*Snow,*" the bird cried. Jon swatted at it. The raven shrieked its displeasure and flapped up to a bedpost to glare down balefully at him through the predawn gloom.

The day had come. It was the hour of the wolf. Soon enough the sun would rise, and four thousand wildlings would come pouring through the Wall. *Madness.* Jon Snow ran his burned hand through his hair and wondered once again what he was doing. Once the gate was opened there would be no turning back. *It should have been the Old Bear to treat with Tormund. It should have been Jaremy Rykker or Qhorin Halfhand or Denys Mallister or some other seasoned man. It should have been my uncle.* It was too late for such misgivings, though. Every choice had its risks, every choice its consequences. He would play the game to its conclusion.

He rose and dressed in darkness, as Mormont's raven muttered across the room. "*Corn,*" the bird said, and, "*King,*" and, "*Snow, Jon Snow, Jon Snow.*" That was queer. The bird had never said his full name before, as best Jon could recall.

He broke his fast in the cellar with his officers. Fried bread, fried eggs, blood sausages, and barley porridge made up the meal, washed down with thin yellow beer. As they ate they went over the preparations yet again. "All is in readiness," Bowen Marsh assured him. "If the wildlings uphold the terms of the bargain, all will go as you've commanded."

And if not, it may turn to blood and carnage. "Remember," Jon said, "Tormund's people are hungry, cold, and fearful. Some of them hate us as much as some of you hate them. We are dancing on rotten ice here, them and us. One crack, and we all drown. If blood should be shed today, it had best not be one of us who strikes the first blow, or I swear by the old gods and the new that I will have the head of the man who strikes it."

They answered him with ayes and nods and muttered words, with "As you command," and "It will be done," and "Yes, my lord." And one by one they rose and buckled on their swords and donned their warm black cloaks and strode out into the cold.

Last to leave the table was Dolorous Edd Tollett, who had come in during the night with six wagons from the Long Barrow. Whore's Barrow, the black brothers called the fortress now. Edd had been sent to gather up as many spearwives as his wagons would hold and bring them back to join their sisters.

Jon watched him mop up a runny yolk with a chunk of bread. It was strangely comforting to see Edd's dour face again. "How goes the restoration work?" he asked his old steward.

"Ten more years should do it," Tollett replied in his usual gloomy tone. "Place was overrun with rats when we moved in. The spearwives killed the nasty buggers. Now the place is overrun with spearwives. There's days I want the rats back."

"How do you find serving under Iron Emmett?" Jon asked.

"Mostly it's Black Maris serving under him, m'lord. Me, I have the mules. Nettles claims we're kin. It's true we have the same long face, but I'm not near as stubborn. Anyway I never knew their mothers, on my honor." He finished the last of his eggs and sighed. "I do like me a nice runny egg. If it please m'lord, don't let the wildlings eat all our chickens."

Out in the yard, the eastern sky had just begun to lighten. There was not a wisp of cloud in sight. "We have a good day for this, it would seem," Jon said. "A bright day, warm and sunny."

"The Wall will weep. And winter almost on us. It's unnatural, m'lord. A bad sign, you ask me."

Jon smiled. "And if it were to snow?"

"A worse sign."

"What sort of weather would you prefer?"

"The sort they keep indoors," said Dolorous Edd. "If it please m'lord, I should get back to my mules. They miss me when I'm gone. More than I can say for them spearwives."

They parted there, Tollett for the east road, where his wagons waited, Jon Snow for the stables. Satin had his horse saddled and bridled and waiting for him, a fiery grey courser with a mane as black and shiny as maester's ink. He was not the sort of mount that Jon would have chosen for a ranging, but on this morning all that mattered was that he look impressive, and for that the stallion was a perfect choice.

His tail was waiting too. Jon had never liked surrounding himself with guards, but today it seemed prudent to keep a few good men beside him. They made a grim display in their ringmail, iron halfhelms, and black cloaks, with tall spears in their hands and swords and daggers on their belts. For this Jon had passed over all the green boys and greybeards in his command, choosing eight men in their prime: Ty and Mully, Left Hand Lew, Big Liddle, Rory, Fulk the Flea, Garrett Greenspear. And Leathers, Castle Black's new master-at-arms, to show the free folk that even a man who had fought for Mance in the battle beneath the Wall could find a place of honor in the Night's Watch.

A deep red blush had appeared in the east by the time they all assembled at the gate. *The stars are going out,* Jon thought. When next they reappeared, they would be shining down upon a world forever changed. A few queen's men stood watching from beside the embers of Lady Melisandre's nightfire. When Jon glanced at the King's Tower, he glimpsed a flash of red behind a window. Of Queen Selyse he saw no sign.

It was time. "Open the gate," Jon Snow said softly.

"*OPEN THE GATE!*" Big Liddle roared. His voice was thunder.

Seven hundred feet above, the sentries heard and raised their warhorns to their lips. The sound rang out, echoing off the Wall and out across the world. *Ahoooooooooooooooooooooooooooooo.* One long blast. For a thousand years or more, that sound had meant rangers coming home. Today it meant something else. Today it called the free folk to their new homes.

On either end of the long tunnel, gates swung open and iron bars unlocked. Dawn light shimmered on the ice above, pink and gold and purple. Dolorous Edd had not been wrong. The Wall would soon be weeping. *Gods grant it weeps alone.*

Satin led them underneath the ice, lighting the way through the gloom of the tunnel with an iron lantern. Jon followed, leading his horse. Then his guardsmen. After them came Bowen Marsh and his stewards, a score of them, every man assigned a task. Above, Ulmer of the Kingswood had the Wall. Two score of Castle Black's best bowmen stood with him, ready to respond to any trouble down below with a rain of arrows.

North of the Wall, Tormund Giantsbane was waiting, mounted on a runty little garron that looked far too weedy to support his weight. His two remaining sons were with him, tall Toregg and young Dryn, along with three score warriors.

"*Har!*" Tormund called. "Guards, is it? Now where's the trust in that, crow?"

"You brought more men than I did."

"So I did. Come here by me, lad. I want my folk to see you. I got thousands ne'er saw a lord commander, grown men who were told as boys that your rangers would eat them if they didn't behave. They need to see you plain, a long-faced lad in an old black cloak. They need to learn that the Night's Watch is naught t'be feared."

That is a lesson I would sooner they never learned. Jon peeled the glove off his burned hand, put two fingers in his mouth, and whistled. Ghost came racing from the gate. Tormund's horse shied so hard that the wildling almost lost his saddle. "Naught to be feared?" Jon said. "Ghost, stay."

"You are a black-hearted bastard, Lord Crow." Tormund Horn-Blower lifted his own warhorn to his lips. The sound of it echoed off the ice like rolling thunder, and the first of the free folk began to stream toward the gate.

From dawn till dusk Jon watched the wildlings pass.

The hostages went first—one hundred boys between the ages of eight and sixteen. "Your blood price, Lord Crow," Tormund declared. "I hope

the wailing o' their poor mothers don't haunt your dreams at night." Some
of the boys were led to the gate by a mother or a father, others by older
siblings. More came alone. Fourteen- and fifteen-year-old boys were almost men, and did not want to be seen clinging to a woman's skirts.

Two stewards counted the boys as they went by, noting each name on
long sheepskin scrolls. A third collected their valuables for the toll and
wrote that down as well. The boys were going to a place that none had
ever been before, to serve an order that had been the enemy of their kith
and kin for thousands of years, yet Jon saw no tears, heard no wailing
mothers. *These are winter's people,* he reminded himself. *Tears freeze upon
your cheeks where they come from.* Not a single hostage balked or tried to
slink away when his turn came to enter that gloomy tunnel.

Almost all the boys were thin, some past the point of gauntness, with
spindly shanks and arms like twigs. That was no more than Jon expected.
Elsewise they came in every shape and size and color. He saw tall boys
and short boys, brown-haired boys and black-haired boys, honey blonds
and strawberry blonds and redheads kissed by fire, like Ygritte. He saw
boys with scars, boys with limps, boys with pockmarked faces. Many of the
older boys had downy cheeks or wispy little mustachios, but there was one
fellow with a beard as thick as Tormund's. Some dressed in fine soft furs,
some in boiled leather and oddments of armor, more in wool and sealskins, a few in rags. One was naked. Many had weapons: sharpened spears,
stone-headed mauls, knives made of bone or stone or dragonglass, spiked
clubs, tanglenets, even here and there a rust-eaten old sword. The Hornfoot boys walked blithe and barefoot through the snowdrifts. Other lads
had bear-paws on their boots and walked on top of the same drifts, never
sinking through the crust. Six boys arrived on horses, two on mules. A pair
of brothers turned up with a goat. The biggest hostage was six-and-a-half
feet tall but had a baby's face; the smallest was a runty boy who claimed
nine years but looked no more than six.

Of special note were the sons of men of renown. Tormund took care to
point them out as they went by. "The boy there is the son of Soren Shieldbreaker," he said of one tall lad. "Him with the red hair, he's Gerrick
Kingsblood's get. Comes o' the line o' Raymun Redbeard, to hear him tell
it. The line o' Redbeard's little brother, you want it true." Two boys looked
enough alike to be twins, but Tormund insisted they were cousins, born a
year apart. "One was sired by Harle the Huntsman, t'other by Harle the
Handsome, both on the same woman. Fathers hate each other. I was you,
I'd send one to Eastwatch and t'other to your Shadow Tower."

Other hostages were named as sons of Howd Wanderer, of Brogg, of Devyn Sealskinner, Kyleg of the Wooden Ear, Morna White Mask, the Great Walrus . . .

"The Great Walrus? Truly?"

"They have queer names along the Frozen Shore."

Three hostages were sons of Alfyn Crowkiller, an infamous raider slain by Qhorin Halfhand. Or so Tormund insisted. "They do not look like brothers," Jon observed.

"Half-brothers, born o' different mothers. Alfyn's member was a wee thing, even smaller than yours, but he was never shy with where he stuck it. Had a son in every village, that one."

Of a certain runty rat-faced boy, Tormund said, "That one's a whelp of Varamyr Sixskins. You remember Varamyr, Lord Crow?"

He did. "The skinchanger."

"Aye, he was that. A vicious little runt besides. Dead now, like as not. No one's seen him since the battle."

Two of the boys were girls in disguise. When Jon saw them, he dispatched Rory and Big Liddle to bring them to him. One came meekly enough, the other kicking and biting. *This could end badly.* "Do these two have famous fathers?"

"Har! Them skinny things? Not likely. Picked by lot."

"They're girls."

"Are they?" Tormund squinted at the pair of them from his saddle. "Me and Lord Crow made a wager on which o' you has the biggest member. Pull them breeches down, give us a look."

One of the girls turned red. The other glared defiantly. "You leave us alone, Tormund Giantstink. You let us go."

"*Har!* You win, crow. Not a cock between 'em. The little one's got her a set o' balls, though. A spearwife in the making, her." He called to his own men. "Go find them something girly to put on before Lord Snow wets his smallclothes."

"I'll need two boys to take their places."

"How's that?" Tormund scratched his beard. "A hostage is a hostage, seems to me. That big sharp sword o' yours can snick a girl's head off as easy as a boy's. A father loves his daughters too. Well, most fathers."

It is not their fathers who concern me. "Did Mance ever sing of Brave Danny Flint?"

"Not as I recall. Who was he?"

"A girl who dressed up like a boy to take the black. Her song is sad and pretty. What happened to her wasn't." In some versions of the song, her ghost still walked the Nightfort. "I'll send the girls to Long Barrow." The only men there were Iron Emmett and Dolorous Edd, both of whom he trusted. That was not something he could say of all his brothers.

The wildling understood. "Nasty birds, you crows." He spat. "Two more boys, then. You'll have them."

When nine-and-ninety hostages had shuffled by them to pass beneath the Wall, Tormund Giantsbane produced the last one. "My son Dryn. You'll see he's well taken care of, crow, or I'll cook your black liver up and eat it."

Jon gave the boy a close inspection. *Bran's age, or the age he would have been if Theon had not killed him.* Dryn had none of Bran's sweetness, though. He was a chunky boy, with short legs, thick arms, and a wide red face—a miniature version of his father, with a shock of dark brown hair. "He'll serve as my own page," Jon promised Tormund.

"Hear that, Dryn? See that you don't get above yourself." To Jon he said, "He'll need a good beating from time to time. Be careful o' his teeth, though. He bites." He reached down for his horn again, raised it, and blew another blast.

This time it was warriors who came forward. And not just one hundred of them. *Five hundred,* Jon Snow judged, as they moved out from beneath the trees, *perhaps as many as a thousand.* One in every ten of them came mounted but all of them came armed. Across their backs they bore round wicker shields covered with hides and boiled leather, displaying painted images of snakes and spiders, severed heads, bloody hammers, broken skulls, and demons. A few were clad in stolen steel, dinted oddments of armor looted from the corpses of fallen rangers. Others had armored themselves in bones, like Rattleshirt. All wore fur and leather.

There were spearwives with them, long hair streaming. Jon could not look at them without remembering Ygritte: the gleam of fire in her hair, the look on her face when she'd disrobed for him in the grotto, the sound of her voice. "You know nothing, Jon Snow," she'd told him a hundred times.

It is as true now as it was then. "You might have sent the women first," he said to Tormund. "The mothers and the maids."

The wildling gave him a shrewd look. "Aye, I might have. And you crows might decide to close that gate. A few fighters on t'other side, well, that way the gate stays open, don't it?" He grinned. "I bought your bloody horse, Jon Snow. Don't mean that we can't count his teeth. Now don't you go thinking me and mine don't trust you. We trust you just as much as you trust us." He snorted. "You wanted warriors, didn't you? Well, there they are. Every one worth six o' your black crows."

Jon had to smile. "So long as they save those weapons for our common foe, I am content."

"Gave you my word on it, didn't I? The word of Tormund Giantsbane. Strong as iron, 'tis." He turned and spat.

Amongst the stream of warriors were the fathers of many of Jon's hostages. Some stared with cold dead eyes as they went by, fingering their sword hilts. Others smiled at him like long-lost kin, though a few of those smiles discomfited Jon Snow more than any glare. None knelt, but many gave him their oaths. "What Tormund swore, I swear," declared black-haired Brogg, a man of few words. Soren Shieldbreaker bowed his head an inch and growled, "Soren's axe is yours, Jon Snow, if ever you have need of such." Red-bearded Gerrick Kingsblood brought three daughters. "They will make fine wives, and give their husbands strong sons of royal blood," he boasted. "Like their father, they are descended from Raymun Redbeard, who was King-Beyond-the-Wall."

Blood meant little and less amongst the free folk, Jon knew. Ygritte had taught him that. Gerrick's daughters shared her same flame-red hair, though hers had been a tangle of curls and theirs hung long and straight. *Kissed by fire.* "Three princesses, each lovelier than the last," he told their father. "I will see that they are presented to the queen." Selyse Baratheon would take to these three better than she had to Val, he suspected; they were younger and considerably more cowed. *Sweet enough to look at them, though their father seems a fool.*

Howd Wanderer swore his oath upon his sword, as nicked and pitted a piece of iron as Jon had ever seen. Devyn Sealskinner presented him with a sealskin hat, Harle the Huntsman with a bear-claw necklace. The warrior witch Morna removed her weirwood mask just long enough to kiss his gloved hand and swear to be his man or his woman, whichever he preferred. And on and on and on.

As they passed, each warrior stripped off his treasures and tossed them into one of the carts that the stewards had placed before the gate. Amber pendants, golden torques, jeweled daggers, silver brooches set with gemstones, bracelets, rings, niello cups and golden goblets, warhorns and drinking horns, a green jade comb, a necklace of freshwater pearls . . . all yielded up and noted down by Bowen Marsh. One man surrendered a shirt of silver scales that had surely been made for some great lord. Another produced a broken sword with three sapphires in the hilt.

And there were queerer things: a toy mammoth made of actual mammoth hair, an ivory phallus, a helm made from a unicorn's head, complete with horn. How much food such things would buy in the Free Cities, Jon Snow could not begin to say.

After the riders came the men of the Frozen Shore. Jon watched a dozen of their big bone chariots roll past him one by one, clattering like Rattleshirt. Half still rolled as before; others had replaced their wheels with runners. They slid across the snowdrifts smoothly, where the wheeled chariots were foundering and sinking.

The dogs that drew the chariots were fearsome beasts, as big as direwolves. Their women were clad in sealskins, some with infants at their breasts. Older children shuffled along behind their mothers and looked up at Jon with eyes as dark and hard as the stones they clutched. Some of the men wore antlers on their hats, and some wore walrus tusks. The two sorts did not love each other, he soon gathered. A few thin reindeer brought up the rear, with the great dogs snapping at the heels of stragglers.

"Be wary o' that lot, Jon Snow," Tormund warned him. "A savage folk. The men are bad, the women worse." He took a skin off his saddle and offered it up to Jon. "Here. This will make them seem less fearsome, might be. And warm you for the night. No, go on, it's yours to keep. Drink deep."

Within was a mead so potent it made Jon's eyes water and sent tendrils of fire snaking through his chest. He drank deep. "You're a good man, Tormund Giantsbabe. For a wildling."

"Better than most, might be. Not so good as some."

On and on the wildlings came, as the sun crept across the bright blue sky. Just before midday, the movement stopped when an oxcart became jammed at a turn inside the tunnel. Jon Snow went to have a look for himself. The cart was now wedged solid. The men behind were threatening to hack it apart and butcher the ox where he stood, whilst the driver and his kin swore to kill them if they tried. With the help of Tormund and his son Toregg, Jon managed to keep the wildlings from coming to blood, but it took the best part of an hour before the way was opened again.

"You need a bigger gate," Tormund complained to Jon with a sour look up at the sky, where a few clouds had blown in. "Too bloody slow this way. Like sucking the Milkwater through a reed. *Har.* Would that I had the Horn of Joramun. I'd give it a nice toot and we'd climb through the rubble."

"Melisandre burned the Horn of Joramun."

"Did she?" Tormund slapped his thigh and hooted. "She burned that fine big horn, aye. A bloody sin, I call it. A thousand years old, that was. We found it in a giant's grave, and no man o' us had ever seen a horn so big. That must have been why Mance got the notion to tell you it were Joramun's. He wanted you crows to think he had it in his power to blow your bloody Wall down about your knees. But we never found the true horn, not for all our digging. If we had, every kneeler in your Seven Kingdoms would have chunks o' ice to cool his wine all summer."

Jon turned in his saddle, frowning. *And Joramun blew the Horn of Winter and woke giants from the earth.* That huge horn with its bands of old gold, incised with ancient runes . . . had Mance Rayder lied to him, or was Tormund lying now? *If Mance's horn was just a feint, where is the true horn?*

By afternoon the sun had gone, and the day turned grey and gusty. "A snow sky," Tormund announced grimly.

Others had seen the same omen in those flat white clouds. It seemed to spur them on to haste. Tempers began to fray. One man was stabbed when he tried to slip in ahead of others who had been hours in the column. Toregg wrenched the knife away from his attacker, dragged both men from the press, and sent them back to the wildling camp to start again.

"Tormund," Jon said, as they watched four old women pull a cartful of children toward the gate, "tell me of our foe. I would know all there is to know of the Others."

The wildling rubbed his mouth. "Not here," he mumbled, "not this side o' your Wall." The old man glanced uneasily toward the trees in their white mantles. "They're never far, you know. They won't come out by day, not when that old sun's shining, but don't think that means they went away. Shadows never go away. Might be you don't see them, but they're always clinging to your heels."

"Did they trouble you on your way south?"

"They never came in force, if that's your meaning, but they were with us all the same, nibbling at our edges. We lost more outriders than I care to think about, and it was worth your life to fall behind or wander off. Every nightfall we'd ring our camps with fire. They don't like fire much, and no mistake. When the snows came, though . . . snow and sleet and freezing rain, it's bloody hard to find dry wood or get your kindling lit, and the *cold* . . . some nights our fires just seemed to shrivel up and die. Nights like that, you always find some dead come the morning. 'Less they find you first. The night that Torwynd . . . my boy, he . . ." Tormund turned his face away.

"I know," said Jon Snow.

Tormund turned back. "You know nothing. You killed a dead man, aye, I heard. Mance killed a hundred. A man can fight the dead, but when their masters come, when the white mists rise up . . . how do you fight a *mist*, crow? Shadows with teeth . . . air so cold it hurts to breathe, like a knife inside your chest . . . you do not know, you cannot know . . . can your sword cut *cold*?"

We will see, Jon thought, remembering the things that Sam had told him, the things he'd found in his old books. Longclaw had been forged in the fires of old Valyria, forged in dragonflame and set with spells. *Dragonsteel, Sam called it. Stronger than any common steel, lighter, harder, sharper* . . . But words in a book were one thing. The true test came in battle.

"You are not wrong," Jon said. "I do not know. And if the gods are good, I never will."

"The gods are seldom good, Jon Snow." Tormund nodded toward the sky. "The clouds roll in. Already it grows darker, colder. Your Wall no longer weeps. Look." He turned and called out to his son Toregg. "Ride back to the camp and get them moving. The sick ones and the weak ones, the slugabeds and cravens, get them on their bloody feet. Set their bloody tents afire if you must. The gate must close at nightfall. Any man not through the Wall by then had best pray the Others get to him afore I do. You hear?"

"I hear." Toregg put his heels into his horse and galloped back down the column.

On and on the wildlings came. The day grew darker, just as Tormund said. Clouds covered the sky from horizon to horizon, and warmth fled. There was more shoving at the gate, as men and goats and bullocks jostled each other out of the way. *It is more than impatience*, Jon realized. *They are afraid. Warriors, spearwives, raiders, they are frightened of those woods, of shadows moving through the trees. They want to put the Wall between them before the night descends.*

A snowflake danced upon the air. Then another. *Dance with me, Jon Snow*, he thought. *You'll dance with me anon.*

On and on and on the wildlings came. Some were moving faster now, hastening across the battleground. Others—the old, the young, the feeble—could scarce move at all. This morning the field had been covered with a thick blanket of old snow, its white crust shining in the sun. Now the field was brown and black and slimy. The passage of the free folk had turned the ground to mud and muck: wooden wheels and horses' hooves, runners of bone and horn and iron, pig trotters, heavy boots, the cloven feet of cows and bullocks, the bare black feet of the Hornfoot folk, all had left their marks. The soft footing slowed the column even more. "You need a bigger gate," Tormund complained again.

By late afternoon the snow was falling steadily, but the river of wildlings had dwindled to a stream. Columns of smoke rose from the trees where their camp had been. "Toregg," Tormund explained. "Burning the dead. Always some who go to sleep and don't wake up. You find them in their tents, them as have tents, curled up and froze. Toregg knows what to do."

The stream was no more than a trickle by the time Toregg emerged from the wood. With him rode a dozen mounted warriors armed with spears and swords. "My rear guard," Tormund said, with a gap-toothed smile. "You crows have rangers. So do we. Them I left in camp in case we were attacked before we all got out."

"Your best men."

"Or my worst. Every man o' them has killed a crow."

Amongst the riders came one man afoot, with some big beast trotting at his heels. A *boar*, Jon saw. A *monstrous boar*. Twice the size of Ghost, the creature was covered with coarse black hair, with tusks as long as a man's arm. Jon had never seen a boar so huge or ugly. The man beside him was no beauty either; hulking, black-browed, he had a flat nose, heavy jowls dark with stubble, small black close-set eyes.

"Borroq." Tormund turned his head and spat.

"A skinchanger." It was not a question. Somehow he knew.

Ghost turned his head. The falling snow had masked the boar's scent, but now the white wolf had the smell. He padded out in front of Jon, his teeth bared in a silent snarl.

"No!" Jon snapped. "Ghost, down. Stay. *Stay!*"

"Boars and wolves," said Tormund. "Best keep that beast o' yours locked up tonight. I'll see that Borroq does the same with his pig." He glanced up at the darkening sky. "Them's the last, and none too soon. It's going to snow all night, I feel it. Time I had a look at what's on t'other side of all that ice."

"You go ahead," Jon told him. "I mean to be the last one through the ice. I will join you at the feast."

"Feast? *Har!* Now that's a word I like to hear." The wildling turned his garron toward the Wall and slapped her on the rump. Toregg and the riders followed, dismounting by the gate to lead their horses through. Bowen Marsh stayed long enough to supervise as his stewards pulled the last carts into the tunnel. Only Jon Snow and his guards were left.

The skinchanger stopped ten yards away. His monster pawed at the mud, snuffling. A light powdering of snow covered the boar's humped black back. He gave a snort and lowered his head, and for half a heartbeat Jon thought he was about to charge. To either side of him, his men lowered their spears.

"Brother," Borroq said.

"You'd best go on. We are about to close the gate."

"You do that," Borroq said. "You close it good and tight. They're coming, crow." He smiled as ugly a smile as Jon had ever seen and made his way to the gate. The boar stalked after him. The falling snow covered up their tracks behind them.

"That's done, then," Rory said when they were gone.

No, thought Jon Snow, *it has only just begun.*

Bowen Marsh was waiting for him south of the Wall, with a tablet full of numbers. "Three thousand one hundred and nineteen wildlings passed through the gate today," the Lord Steward told him. "Sixty of your hostages were sent off to Eastwatch and the Shadow Tower after they'd been fed. Edd Tollett took six wagons of women back to Long Barrow. The rest remain with us."

"Not for long," Jon promised him. "Tormund means to lead his own folk to Oakenshield within a day or two. The rest will follow, as soon as we sort where to put them."

"As you say, Lord Snow." The words were stiff. The tone suggested that Bowen Marsh knew where *he* would put them.

The castle Jon returned to was far different from the one he'd left that morning. For as long as he had known it, Castle Black had been a place of silence and shadows, where a meagre company of men in black moved like ghosts amongst the ruins of a fortress that had once housed ten times their numbers. All that had changed. Lights now shone through windows where Jon Snow had never seen lights shine before. Strange voices echoed down the yards, and free folk were coming and going along icy paths that had only known the black boots of crows for years. Outside the old Flint Barracks, he came across a dozen men pelting one another with snow. *Playing,* Jon thought in astonishment, *grown men playing like children, throwing snowballs the way Bran and Arya once did, and Robb and me before them.*

Donal Noye's old armory was still dark and silent, however, and Jon's rooms back of the cold forge were darker still. But he had no sooner taken off his cloak than Dannel poked his head through the door to announce that Clydas had brought a message.

"Send him in." Jon lit a taper from an ember in his brazier and three candles from the taper.

Clydas entered pink and blinking, the parchment clutched in one soft hand. "Beg pardon, Lord Commander. I know you must be weary, but I thought you would want to see this at once."

"You did well." Jon read:

> *At Hardhome, with six ships. Wild seas.* Blackbird *lost with all hands, two Lyseni ships driven aground on Skane,* Talon *taking water. Very bad here. Wildlings eating their own dead. Dead things in the woods. Braavosi captains will only take women, children on their ships. Witch women call us slavers. Attempt to take Storm Crow defeated, six crew dead, many wildlings. Eight ravens left. Dead things in the water. Send help by land, seas wracked by storms. From* Talon, *by hand of Maester Harmune.*

Cotter Pyke had made his angry mark below.

"Is it grievous, my lord?" asked Clydas.

"Grievous enough." *Dead things in the wood. Dead things in the water. Six ships left, of the eleven that set sail.* Jon Snow rolled up the parchment, frowning. *Night falls,* he thought, *and now my war begins.*

THE DISCARDED KNIGHT

"All kneel for His Magnificence Hizdahr zo Loraq, Fourteenth of That Noble Name, King of Meereen, Scion of Ghis, Octarch of the Old Empire, Master of the Skahazadhan, Consort to Dragons and Blood of the Harpy," roared the herald. His voice echoed off the marble floor and rang amongst the pillars.

Ser Barristan Selmy slipped a hand beneath the fold of his cloak and loosened his sword in its scabbard. No blades were allowed in the presence of the king save those of his protectors. It seemed as though he still counted amongst that number despite his dismissal. No one had tried to take his sword, at least.

Daenerys Targaryen had preferred to hold court from a bench of polished ebony, smooth and simple, covered with the cushions that Ser Barristan had found to make her more comfortable. King Hizdahr had replaced the bench with two imposing thrones of gilded wood, their tall backs carved into the shape of dragons. The king seated himself in the right-hand throne with a golden crown upon his head and a jeweled sceptre in one pale hand. The second throne remained vacant.

The important throne, thought Ser Barristan. *No dragon chair can replace a dragon no matter how elaborately it's carved.*

To the right of the twin thrones stood Goghor the Giant, a huge hulk of a man with a brutal, scarred face. To the left was the Spotted Cat, a leopard skin flung over one shoulder. Back of them were Belaquo Bonebreaker and the cold-eyed Khrazz. *Seasoned killers all,* thought Selmy, *but it is one thing to face a foe in the pit when his coming is heralded by horns and drums and another to find a hidden killer before he can strike.*

The day was young and fresh, and yet he felt bone-tired, as if he'd fought all night. The older he got, the less sleep Ser Barristan seemed to need. As a squire he could sleep ten hours a night and still be yawning when he stumbled out onto the practice yard. At three-and-sixty he found that five hours a night was more than enough. Last night, he had scarce slept at all. His bedchamber was a small cell off the queen's apartments, originally slave quarters; his furnishings consisted of a bed, a chamber pot, a wardrobe for his clothing, even a chair should he want to sit. On a bedside table he kept a beeswax candle and a small carving of the Warrior. Though he was not a pious man, the carving made him feel less alone here in this queer alien city, and it was to that he had turned in the black watches of night. *Shield me from these doubts that gnaw at me,* he had prayed, *and give me the strength to do what is right.* But neither prayer nor dawn had brought him certainty.

The hall was as crowded as the old knight had ever seen it, but it was the missing faces that Barristan Selmy noted most: Missandei, Belwas, Grey Worm, Aggo and Jhogo and Rakharo, Irri and Jhiqui, Daario Naharis. In the Shavepate's place stood a fat man in a muscled breastplate and lion's mask, his heavy legs poking out beneath a skirt of leather straps: Marghaz zo Loraq, the king's cousin, new commander of the Brazen Beasts. Selmy had already formed a healthy contempt for the man. He had known his sort in King's Landing—fawning to his superiors, harsh to his inferiors, as blind as he was boastful and too proud by half.

Skahaz could be in the hall as well, Selmy realized, *that ugly face of his concealed behind a mask.* Two score Brazen Beasts stood between the pillars, torchlight shining off the polished brass of their masks. The Shavepate could be any one of them.

The hall thrummed to the sound of a hundred low voices, echoing off the pillars and the marble floor. It made an ominous sound, angry. It reminded Selmy of the sound a hornets' nest might make an instant before hornets all came boiling out. And on the faces in the crowd he saw anger, grief, suspicion, fear.

Hardly had the king's new herald called the court to order than the ugliness began. One woman began to wail about a brother who had died at Daznak's Pit, another of the damage to her palanquin. A fat man tore off his bandages to show the court his burned arm, where the flesh was still raw and oozing. And when a man in a blue-and-gold *tokar* began to speak of Harghaz the Hero, a freedman behind him shoved him to the floor. It took six Brazen Beasts to pull them apart and drag them from the hall. *Fox, hawk, seal, locust, lion, toad.* Selmy wondered if the masks had meaning to the men who wore them. Did the same men wear the same masks every day, or did they choose new faces every morning?

"Quiet!" Reznak mo Reznak was pleading. "Please! I will answer if you will only . . ."

"Is it true?" a freedwoman shouted. "Is our mother dead?"

"No, no, no," Reznak screeched. "Queen Daenerys will return to Meereen in her own time in all her might and majesty. Until such time, His Worship King Hizdahr shall—"

"He is no king of mine," a freedman yelled.

Men began to shove at one another. *"The queen is not dead,"* the seneschal proclaimed. "Her bloodriders have been dispatched across the Skahazadhan to find Her Grace and return her to her loving lord and loyal subjects. Each has ten picked riders, and each man has three swift horses, so they may travel fast and far. Queen Daenerys shall be found."

A tall Ghiscari in a brocade robe spoke next, in a voice as sonorous as it was cold. King Hizdahr shifted on his dragon throne, his face stony as he did his best to appear concerned but unperturbed. Once again his seneschal gave answer.

Ser Barristan let Reznak's oily words wash over him. His years in the Kingsguard had taught him the trick of listening without hearing, especially useful when the speaker was intent on proving that words were truly wind. Back at the rear of the hall, he spied the Dornish princeling and his two companions. *They should not have come. Martell does not realize his danger. Daenerys was his only friend at this court, and she is gone.* He wondered how much they understood of what was being said. Even he could not always make sense of the mongrel Ghiscari tongue the slavers spoke, especially when they were speaking fast.

Prince Quentyn was listening intently, at least. *That one is his father's son.* Short and stocky, plain-faced, he seemed a decent lad, sober, sensible, dutiful . . . but not the sort to make a young girl's heart beat faster. And Daenerys Targaryen, whatever else she might be, was still a young girl, as she herself would claim when it pleased her to play the innocent. Like all good queens she put her people first—else she would never have wed Hizdahr zo Loraq—but the girl in her still yearned for poetry, passion, and laughter. *She wants fire, and Dorne sent her mud.*

You could make a poultice out of mud to cool a fever. You could plant seeds in mud and grow a crop to feed your children. Mud would nourish you, where fire would only consume you, but fools and children and young girls would choose fire every time.

Behind the prince, Ser Gerris Drinkwater was whispering something to Yronwood. Ser Gerris was all his prince was not: tall and lean and comely, with a swordsman's grace and a courtier's wit. Selmy did not doubt that many a Dornish maiden had run her fingers through that sun-streaked hair and kissed that teasing smile off his lips. *If this one had been the prince, things might have gone elsewise,* he could not help but think . . . but there was something a bit too pleasant about Drinkwater for his taste. *False coin,* the old knight thought. He had known such men before.

Whatever he was whispering must have been amusing, for his big bald friend gave a sudden snort of laughter, loud enough so that the king himself turned his head toward the Dornishmen. When he saw the prince, Hizdahr zo Loraq frowned.

Ser Barristan did not like that frown. And when the king beckoned his cousin Marghaz closer, leaned down, and whispered in his ear, he liked that even less.

I swore no oath to Dorne, Ser Barristan told himself. But Lewyn Martell had been his Sworn Brother, back in the days when the bonds between the Kingsguard still went deep. *I could not help Prince Lewyn on the Trident, but I can help his nephew now.* Martell was dancing in a vipers' nest, and he did not even see the snakes. His continued presence, even after Daenerys had given herself to another before the eyes of gods and men, would provoke any husband, and Quentyn no longer had the queen to shield him from Hizdahr's wroth. *Although . . .*

The thought hit him like a slap across the face. Quentyn had grown up amongst the courts of Dorne. Plots and poisons were no strangers to him. Nor was Prince Lewyn his only uncle. *He is kin to the Red Viper.* Daenerys had taken another for her consort, but if Hizdahr died, she would be free to wed again. *Could the Shavepate have been wrong? Who can say that the locusts were meant for Daenerys? It was the king's own box. What if he was meant to be the victim all along?* Hizdahr's death would have smashed the fragile peace. The Sons of the Harpy would have resumed their murders, the Yunkishmen their war. Daenerys might have had no better choice than Quentyn and his marriage pact.

Ser Barristan was still wrestling with that suspicion when he heard the sound of heavy boots ascending the steep stone steps at the back of the hall. The Yunkishmen had come. Three Wise Masters led the procession from the Yellow City, each with his own armed retinue. One slaver wore a *tokar* of maroon silk fringed with gold, one a striped *tokar* of teal and orange, the third an ornate breastplate inlaid with erotic scenes done in jet and jade and mother-of-pearl. The sellsword captain Bloodbeard accompanied them with a leathern sack slung across one massive shoulder and a look of mirth and murder on his face.

No Tattered Prince, Selmy noted. *No Brown Ben Plumm.* Ser Barristan eyed Bloodbeard coolly. *Give me half a reason to dance with you, and we will see who is laughing at the end.*

Reznak mo Reznak wormed his way forward. "Wise Masters, you honor us. His Radiance King Hizdahr bids welcome to his friends from Yunkai. We understand—"

"Understand this." Bloodbeard pulled a severed head from his sack and flung it at the seneschal.

Reznak gave a squeak of fright and leapt aside. The head bounced past him, leaving spots of blood on the purple marble floor as it rolled until it fetched up against the foot of King Hizdahr's dragon throne. Up and down the length of the hall, Brazen Beasts lowered their spears. Goghor the Giant lumbered forward to place himself before the king's throne, and the Spotted Cat and Khrazz moved to either side of him to form a wall.

Bloodbeard laughed. "He's dead. He won't bite."

Gingerly, so gingerly, the seneschal approached the head, lifted it delicately by the hair. "Admiral Groleo."

Ser Barristan glanced toward the throne. He had served so many kings, he could not help but imagine how they might have reacted to this provocation. Aerys would have flinched away in horror, likely cutting himself on the barbs of the Iron Throne, then shrieked at his swordsmen to cut the Yunkishmen to pieces. Robert would have shouted for his hammer to repay Bloodbeard in kind. Even Jaehaerys, reckoned weak by many, would have ordered the arrest of Bloodbeard and the Yunkish slavers.

Hizdahr sat frozen, a man transfixed. Reznak set the head on a satin pillow at the king's feet, then scampered away, his mouth twisted up in a moue of distaste. Ser Barristan could smell the seneschal's heavy floral perfume from several yards away.

The dead man stared up reproachfully. His beard was brown with caked blood, but a trickle of red still leaked from his neck. From the look of him, it had taken more than one blow to part his head from his body. In the back of the hall, petitioners began to slip away. One of the Brazen Beasts ripped off his brass hawk's mask and began to spew up his breakfast.

Barristan Selmy was no stranger to severed heads. This one, though . . . he had crossed half the world with the old seafarer, from Pentos to Qarth and back again to Astapor. *Groleo was a good man. He did not deserve this end. All he ever wanted was to go home.* The knight tensed, waiting.

"This," King Hizdahr said at last, "this is not . . . we are not pleased, this . . . what is the meaning of this . . . this . . ."

The slaver in the maroon *tokar* produced a parchment. "I have the honor to bear this message from the council of masters." He unrolled the scroll. "It is here written, '*Seven entered Meereen to sign the peace accords and witness the celebratory games at the Pit of Daznak. As surety for their safety, seven hostages were tendered us. The Yellow City mourns its noble son Yurkhaz zo Yunzak, who perished cruelly whilst a guest of Meereen. Blood must pay for blood.*'"

Groleo had a wife back in Pentos. Children, grandchildren. *Why him, of all the hostages?* Jhogo, Hero, and Daario Naharis all commanded fighting men, but Groleo had been an admiral without a fleet. *Did they draw straws, or did they think Groleo the least valuable to us, the least likely to provoke reprisal?* the knight asked himself . . . but it was easier to pose that question than to answer it. *I have no skill at unraveling such knots.*

"Your Grace," Ser Barristan called out. "If it please you to recall, the noble Yurkhaz died by happenstance. He stumbled on the steps as he tried to flee the dragon and was crushed beneath the feet of his own slaves and companions. That, or his heart burst in terror. He was old."

"Who is this who speaks without the king's leave?" asked the Yunkish lord in the striped *tokar*, a small man with a receding chin and teeth too big for his mouth. He reminded Selmy of a rabbit. "Must the lords of Yunkai attend to the natterings of guards?" He shook the pearls that fringed his *tokar*.

Hizdahr zo Loraq could not seem to look away from the head. Only when Reznak whispered something in his ear did he finally bestir himself. "Yurkhaz zo Yunzak was your supreme commander," he said. "Which of you speaks for Yunkai now?"

"All of us," said the rabbit. "The council of masters."

King Hizdahr found some steel. "Then all of you bear the responsibility for this breach of our peace."

The Yunkishman in the breastplate gave answer. "Our peace has not been breached. Blood pays for blood, a life for a life. To show our good faith, we return three of your hostages." The iron ranks behind him parted. Three Meereenese were ushered forward, clutching at their *tokars*—two women and a man.

"Sister," said Hizdahr zo Loraq, stiffly. "Cousins." He gestured at the bleeding head. "Remove that from our sight."

"The admiral was a man of the sea," Ser Barristan reminded him. "Mayhaps Your Magnificence might ask the Yunkai'i to return his body to us, so we may bury him beneath the waves?"

The rabbit-toothed lord waved a hand. "If it please Your Radiance, this shall be done. A sign of our respect."

Reznak mo Reznak cleared his throat noisily. "Meaning no offense, yet it seems to me that Her Worship Queen Daenerys gave you . . . ah . . . seven hostages. The other three . . ."

"The others shall remain our guests," announced the Yunkish lord in the breastplate, "until the dragons have been destroyed."

A hush fell across the hall. Then came the murmurs and the mutters, whispered curses, whispered prayers, the hornets stirring in their hive. "The dragons . . ." said King Hizdahr.

". . . are monsters, as all men saw in Daznak's Pit. No true peace is possible whilst they live."

Reznak replied. "Her Magnificence Queen Daenerys is Mother of Dragons. Only she can—"

Bloodbeard's scorn cut him off. "She is gone. Burned and devoured. Weeds grow through her broken skull."

A roar greeted those words. Some began to shout and curse. Others stamped their feet and whistled their approval. It took the Brazen Beasts pounding the butts of their spears against the floor before the hall quieted again.

Ser Barristan never once took his eyes off Bloodbeard. *He came to sack a city, and Hizdahr's peace has cheated him of his plunder. He will do whatever he must to start the bloodshed.*

Hizdahr zo Loraq rose slowly from his dragon throne. "I must consult my council. This court is done."

"*All kneel for His Magnificence Hizdahr zo Loraq, Fourteenth of That Ancient Name, King of Meereen, Scion of Ghis, Octarch of the Old Empire, Master of the Skahazadhan, Consort to Dragons and Blood of the Harpy,*" the herald shouted. Brazen Beasts swung out amongst the pillars to form a line, then began a slow advance in lockstep, ushering the petitioners from the hall.

The Dornishmen did not have as far to go as most. As befit his rank and station, Quentyn Martell had been given quarters within the Great Pyramid, two levels down—a handsome suite of rooms with its own privy and walled terrace. Perhaps that was why he and his companions lingered, waiting until the press had lessened before beginning to make their way toward the steps.

Ser Barristan watched them, thoughtful. *What would Daenerys want?* he asked himself. He thought he knew. The old knight strode across the hall, his long white cloak rippling behind him. He caught the Dornish-men at the top of the steps. "Your father's court was never half so lively," he heard Drinkwater japing.

"Prince Quentyn," Selmy called. "Might I beg a word?"

Quentyn Martell turned. "Ser Barristan. Of course. My chambers are one level down."

No. "It is not my place to counsel you, Prince Quentyn . . . but if I were you, I would not return to my chambers. You and your friends should go down the steps and leave."

Prince Quentyn stared. "Leave the pyramid?"

"Leave the city. Return to Dorne."

The Dornishmen exchanged a look. "Our arms and armor are back in our apartments," said Gerris Drinkwater. "Not to mention most of the coin that we have left."

"Swords can be replaced," said Ser Barristan. "I can provide you with coin enough for passage back to Dorne. Prince Quentyn, the king made note of you today. He frowned."

Gerris Drinkwater laughed. "Should we be frightened of Hizdahr zo Loraq? You saw him just now. He quailed before the Yunkishmen. They sent him a *head*, and he did nothing."

Quentyn Martell nodded in agreement. "A prince does well to think before he acts. This king . . . I do not know what to think of him. The queen warned me against him as well, true, but . . ."

"She warned you?" Selmy frowned. "Why are you still here?"

Prince Quentyn flushed. "The marriage pact—"

"—was made by two dead men and contained not a word about the queen or you. It promised your sister's hand to the queen's brother, an-other dead man. It has no force. Until you turned up here, Her Grace was ignorant of its existence. Your father keeps his secrets well, Prince Quen-tyn. Too well, I fear. If the queen had known of this pact in Qarth, she might never have turned aside for Slaver's Bay, but you came too late. I have no wish to salt your wounds, but Her Grace has a new husband and an old paramour, and seems to prefer the both of them to you."

Anger flashed in the prince's dark eyes. "This Ghiscari lordling is no fit consort for the queen of the Seven Kingdoms."

"That is not for you to judge." Ser Barristan paused, wondering if he had said too much already. *No. Tell him the rest of it.* "That day at Daznak's Pit, some of the food in the royal box was poisoned. It was only chance that Strong Belwas ate it all. The Blue Graces say that only his size and freakish strength have saved him, but it was a near thing. He may yet die."

The shock was plain on Prince Quentyn's face. "Poison . . . meant for Daenerys?"

"Her or Hizdahr. Perhaps both. The box was his, though. His Grace made all the arrangements. If the poison was his doing . . . well, he will need a scapegoat. Who better than a rival from a distant land who has no friends at this court? Who better than a suitor the queen spurned?"

Quentyn Martell went pale. "*Me?* I would never . . . you cannot think I had any part in any . . ."

That was the truth, or he is a master mummer. "Others might," said Ser Barristan. "The Red Viper was your uncle. And you have good reason to want King Hizdahr dead."

"So do others," suggested Gerris Drinkwater. "Naharis, for one. The queen's . . ."

". . . paramour," Ser Barristan finished, before the Dornish knight could say anything that might besmirch the queen's honor. "That is what you call them down in Dorne, is it not?" He did not wait for a reply. "Prince Lewyn was my Sworn Brother. In those days there were few secrets amongst the Kingsguard. I know he kept a paramour. He did not feel there was any shame in that."

"No," said Quentyn, red-faced, "but . . ."

"Daario would kill Hizdahr in a heartbeat if he dared," Ser Barristan went on. "But not with poison. Never. And Daario was not there in any case. Hizdahr would be pleased to blame him for the locusts, all the same . . . but the king may yet have need of the Stormcrows, and he will lose them if he appears complicit in the death of their captain. No, my prince. If His Grace needs a poisoner, he will look to you." He had said all that he could safely say. In a few more days, if the gods smiled on them, Hizdahr zo Loraq would no longer rule Meereen . . . but no good would be served by having Prince Quentyn caught up in the bloodbath that was coming. "If you must remain in Meereen, you would do well to stay away from court and hope Hizdahr forgets you," Ser Barristan finished, "but a ship for Volantis would be wiser, my prince. Whatever course you choose, I wish you well."

Before he had gone three steps, Quentyn Martell called out to him. "Barristan the Bold, they call you."

"Some do." Selmy had won that name when he was ten years old, a new-made squire, yet so vain and proud and foolish that he got it in his head that he could joust with tried and proven knights. So he'd borrowed a warhorse and some plate from Lord Dondarrion's armory and entered the lists at Blackhaven as a mystery knight. *Even the herald laughed. My arms were so thin that when I lowered my lance it was all I could do to keep the point from furrowing the ground.* Lord Dondarrion would have been within his rights to pull him off the horse and spank him, but the Prince of Dragonflies had taken pity on the addlepated boy in the ill-fitting armor and accorded him the respect of taking up his challenge. One course was all that it required. Afterward Prince Duncan helped him to his feet and removed his helm. "A boy," he had proclaimed to the crowd. "A bold boy." *Fifty-three years ago. How many men are still alive who were there at Blackhaven?*

"What name do you think they will give me, should I return to Dorne without Daenerys?" Prince Quentyn asked. "Quentyn the Cautious? Quentyn the Craven? Quentyn the Quail?"

The Prince Who Came Too Late, the old knight thought . . . but if a knight of the Kingsguard learns nothing else, he learns to guard his tongue. "Quentyn the Wise," he suggested. And hoped that it was true.

THE SPURNED SUITOR

The hour of ghosts was almost upon them when Ser Gerris Drink-water returned to the pyramid to report that he had found Beans, Books, and Old Bill Bone in one of Meereen's less savory cellars, drinking yellow wine and watching naked slaves kill one another with bare hands and filed teeth.

"Beans pulled a blade and proposed a wager to determine if deserters had bellies full of yellow slime," Ser Gerris reported, "so I tossed him a dragon and asked if yellow gold would do. He bit the coin and asked what I meant to buy. When I told him he slipped the knife away and asked if I was drunk or mad."

"Let him think what he wants, so long as he delivers the message," said Quentyn.

"He'll do that much. I'll wager you get your meeting too, if only so Rags can have Pretty Meris cut your liver out and fry it up with onions. We should be heeding Selmy. When Barristan the Bold tells you to run, a wise man laces up his boots. We should find a ship for Volantis whilst the port is still open."

Just the mention turned Ser Archibald's cheeks green. "No more ships. I'd sooner hop back to Volantis on one foot."

Volantis, Quentyn thought. *Then Lys, then home. Back the way I came, empty-handed. Three brave men dead, for what?*

It would be sweet to see the Greenblood again, to visit Sunspear and the Water Gardens and breathe the clean sweet mountain air of Yronwood in place of the hot, wet, filthy humors of Slaver's Bay. His father would speak no word of rebuke, Quentyn knew, but the disappointment would be there in his eyes. His sister would be scornful, the Sand Snakes would mock him with smiles sharp as swords, and Lord Yronwood, his second father, who had sent his own son along to keep him safe . . .

"I will not keep you here," Quentyn told his friends. "My father laid this task on me, not you. Go home, if that is what you want. By whatever means you like. I am staying."

The big man shrugged. "Then Drink and me are staying too."

The next night, Denzo D'han turned up at Prince Quentyn's door to talk terms. "He will meet with you on the morrow, by the spice market. Look for a door marked with a purple lotus. Knock twice and call for freedom."

"Agreed," said Quentyn. "Arch and Gerris will be with me. He can bring two men as well. No more."

"If it please my prince." The words were polite enough, but Denzo's tone was edged with malice, and the eyes of the warrior poet gleamed bright with mockery. "Come at sunset. And see that you are not followed."

The Dornishmen left the Great Pyramid an hour shy of sunset in case they took a wrong turn or had difficulty finding the purple lotus. Quentyn and Gerris wore their sword belts. The big man had his warhammer slung across his broad back.

"It is still not too late to abandon this folly," Gerris said, as they made their way down a foetid alley toward the old spice market. The smell of piss was in the air, and they could hear the rumble of a corpse cart's iron-rimmed wheels off ahead. "Old Bill Bone used to say that Pretty Maris could stretch out a man's dying for a moon's turn. We *lied* to them, Quent. Used them to get us here, then went over to the Stormcrows."

"As we were commanded."

"Tatters never meant for us to do it for real, though," put in the big man. "His other boys, Ser Orson and Dick Straw, Hungerford, Will of the Woods, that lot, they're still down in some dungeon thanks to us. Old Rags can't have liked that much."

"No," Prince Quentyn said, "but he likes gold."

Gerris laughed. "A pity we have none. Do you trust this peace, Quent? I don't. Half the city is calling the dragonslayer a hero, and the other half spits blood at the mention of his name."

"Harzoo," the big man said.

Quentyn frowned. "His name was Harghaz."

"Hizdahr, Humzum, Hagnag, what does it matter? I call them all Harzoo. He was no dragonslayer. All he did was get his arse roasted black and crispy."

"He was brave." *Would I have the courage to face that monster with nothing but a spear?*

"He died bravely, is what you mean."

"He died screaming," said Arch.

Gerris put a hand on Quentyn's shoulder. "Even if the queen returns, she'll still be married."

"Not if I give King Harzoo a little smack with my hammer," suggested the big man.

"Hizdahr," said Quentyn. "His name is Hizdahr."

"One kiss from my hammer and no one will care what his name was," said Arch.

They do not see. His friends had lost sight of his true purpose here. *The road leads through her, not to her. Daenerys is the means to the prize, not the prize itself.* " 'The dragon has three heads,' she said to me. 'My marriage need not be the end of all your hopes,' she said. 'I know why you are here. For fire and blood.' I have Targaryen blood in me, you know that. I can trace my lineage back—"

"Fuck your lineage," said Gerris. "The dragons won't care about your blood, except maybe how it tastes. You cannot tame a dragon with a history lesson. They're monsters, not maesters. Quent, is this truly what you want to do?"

"This is what I have to do. For Dorne. For my father. For Cletus and Will and Maester Kedry."

"They're dead," said Gerris. "They won't care."

"All dead," Quentyn agreed. "For what? To bring me here, so I might wed the dragon queen. A grand adventure, Cletus called it. Demon roads and stormy seas, and at the end of it the most beautiful woman in the world. A tale to tell our grandchildren. But Cletus will never father a child, unless he left a bastard in the belly of that tavern wench he liked. Will will never have his wedding. Their deaths should have some meaning."

Gerris pointed to where a corpse slumped against a brick wall, attended by a cloud of glistening green flies. "Did his death have meaning?"

Quentyn looked at the body with distaste. "He died of the flux. Stay well away from him." The pale mare was inside the city walls. Small wonder that the streets seemed so empty. "The Unsullied will send a corpse cart for him."

"No doubt. But that was not my question. Men's lives have meaning, not their deaths. I loved Will and Cletus too, but this will not bring them back to us. This is a mistake, Quent. You cannot trust in sellswords."

"They are men like any other men. They want gold, glory, power. That's all I am trusting in." *That, and my own destiny. I am a prince of Dorne, and the blood of dragons is in my veins.*

The sun had sunk below the city wall by the time they found the purple lotus, painted on the weathered wooden door of a low brick hovel squatting amidst a row of similar hovels in the shadow of the great yellow-and-green pyramid of Rhazdar. Quentyn knocked twice, as instructed. A gruff voice answered through the door, growling something unintelligible in the mongrel tongue of Slaver's Bay, an ugly blend of Old Ghiscari and High Valyrian. The prince answered in the same tongue. "Freedom."

The door opened. Gerris entered first, for caution's sake, with Quentyn close behind him and the big man bringing up the rear. Within, the air was hazy with bluish smoke, whose sweet smell could not quite cover up the deeper stinks of piss and sour wine and rotting meat. The space was much larger than it had seemed from without, stretching off to right and left into the adjoining hovels. What had appeared to be a dozen structures from the street turned into one long hall inside.

At this hour the house was less than half full. A few of the patrons favored the Dornishmen with looks bored or hostile or curious. The rest were crowded around the pit at the far end of the room, where a pair of naked men were slashing at each other with knives whilst the watchers cheered them on.

Quentyn saw no sign of the men they had come to meet. Then a door he had not seen before swung open, and an old woman emerged, a shriveled thing in a dark red *tokar* fringed with tiny golden skulls. Her skin was white as mare's milk, her hair so thin that he could see the scalp beneath. "Dorne," she said, "I be Zahrina. Purple Lotus. Go down here, you find them." She held the door and gestured them through.

Beyond was a flight of wooden steps, steep and twisting. This time the big man led the way and Gerris was the rear guard, with the prince between them. *An undercellar.* It was a long way down, and so dark that Quentyn had to feel his way to keep from slipping. Near the bottom Ser Archibald pulled his dagger.

They emerged in a brick vault thrice the size of the winesink above. Huge wooden vats lined the walls as far as the prince could see. A red lantern hung on a hook just inside the door, and a greasy black candle flickered on an overturned barrel serving as a table. That was the only light.

Caggo Corpsekiller was pacing by the wine vats, his black *arakh* hanging at his hip. Pretty Meris stood cradling a crossbow, her eyes as cold and dead as two grey stones. Denzo D'han barred the door once the Dornishmen were inside, then took up a position in front of it, arms crossed against his chest.

One too many, Quentyn thought.

The Tattered Prince himself was seated at the table, nursing a cup of wine. In the yellow candlelight his silver-grey hair seemed almost golden, though the pouches underneath his eyes were etched as large as saddle-bags. He wore a brown wool traveler's cloak, with silvery chain mail glimmering underneath. Did that betoken treachery or simple prudence? *An old sellsword is a cautious sellsword.* Quentyn approached his table. "My lord. You look different without your cloak."

"My ragged raiment?" The Pentoshi gave a shrug. "A poor thing . . . yet those tatters fill my foes with fear, and on the battlefield the sight of my rags blowing in the wind emboldens my men more than any banner. And if I want to move unseen, I need only slip it off to become plain and unremarkable." He gestured at the bench across from him. "Sit. I understand you are a prince. Would that I had known. Will you drink? Zahrina offers food as well. Her bread is stale and her stew is unspeakable. Grease and salt, with a morsel or two of meat. Dog, she says, but I think rat is more likely. It will not kill you, though. I have found that it is only when the food is tempting that one must beware. Poisoners invariably choose the choicest dishes."

"You brought three men," Ser Gerris pointed out, with an edge in his voice. "We agreed on two apiece."

"Meris is no man. Meris, sweet, undo your shirt, show him."

"That will not be necessary," said Quentyn. If the talk he had heard was true, beneath that shirt Pretty Meris had only the scars left by the men who'd cut her breasts off. "Meris is a woman, I agree. You've still twisted the terms."

"Tattered and twisty, what a rogue I am. Three to two is not much of an advantage, it must be admitted, but it counts for something. In this world, a man must learn to seize whatever gifts the gods chose to send him. That was a lesson I learned at some cost. I offer it to you as a sign of my good faith." He gestured at the chair again. "Sit, and say what you came to say. I promise not to have you killed until I have heard you out. That is the least I can do for a fellow prince. Quentyn, is it?"

"Quentyn of House Martell."

"Frog suits you better. It is not my custom to drink with liars and deserters, but you've made me curious."

Quentyn sat. *One wrong word, and this could turn to blood in half a heartbeat.* "I ask your pardon for our deception. The only ships sailing for Slaver's Bay were those that had been hired to bring you to the wars."

The Tattered Prince gave a shrug. "Every turncloak has his tale. You are not the first to swear me your swords, take my coin, and run. All of them have *reasons.* 'My little son is sick,' or 'My wife is putting horns on me,' or 'The other men all make me suck their cocks.' Such a charming boy, the last, but I did not excuse his desertion. Another fellow told me our food was so wretched that he had to flee before it made him sick, so I had his foot cut off, roasted it up, and fed it to him. Then I made him our camp cook. Our meals improved markedly, and when his contract was fulfilled he signed another. You, though . . . several of my best are locked up in the queen's dungeons thanks to that lying tongue of yours, and I doubt that you can even cook."

"I am a prince of Dorne," said Quentyn. "I had a duty to my father and my people. There was a secret marriage pact."

"So I heard. And when the silver queen saw your scrap of parchment she fell into your arms, yes?"

"No," said Pretty Meris.

"No? Oh, I recall. Your bride flew off on a dragon. Well, when she re-turns, do be sure to invite us to your nuptials. The men of the company would love to drink to your happiness, and I do love a Westerosi wedding. The bedding part especially, only . . . oh, wait . . ." He turned to Denzo D'han. "Denzo, I thought you told me that the dragon queen had married some Ghiscari."

"A Meereenese nobleman. Rich."

The Tattered Prince turned back to Quentyn. "Could that be true? Surely not. What of your marriage pact?"

"She laughed at him," said Pretty Meris.

Daenerys never laughed. The rest of Meereen might see him as an amusing curiosity, like the exiled Summer Islander King Robert used to keep at King's Landing, but the queen had always spoken to him gently. "We came too late," said Quentyn.

"A pity you did not desert me sooner." The Tattered Prince sipped at his wine. "So . . . no wedding for Prince Frog. Is that why you've come hopping back to me? Have my three brave Dornish lads decided to honor their contracts?"

"No."

"How vexing."

"Yurkhaz zo Yunzak is dead."

"Ancient tidings. I saw him die. The poor man saw a dragon and stumbled as he tried to flee. Then a thousand of his closest friends stepped on him. No doubt the Yellow City is awash in tears. Did you ask me here to toast his memory?"

"No. Have the Yunkishmen chosen a new commander?"

"The council of masters has been unable to agree. Yezzan zo Qaggaz had the most support, but now he's died as well. The Wise Masters are rotating the supreme command amongst themselves. Today our leader is the one your friends in the ranks dubbed the Drunken Conqueror. On the morrow, it will be Lord Wobblecheeks."

"The Rabbit," said Meris. "Wobblecheeks was yesterday."

"I stand corrected, my sweetling. Our Yunkish friends were kind enough to provide us with a chart. I must strive to be more assiduous about consulting it."

"Yurkhaz zo Yunzak was the man who hired you."

"He signed our contract on behalf of his city. Just so."

"Meereen and Yunkai have made peace. The siege is to be lifted, the armies disbanded. There will be no battle, no slaughter, no city to sack and plunder."

"Life is full of disappointments."

"How long do you think the Yunkishmen will want to continue paying wages to four free companies?"

The Tattered Prince took a sip of wine and said, "A vexing question. But this is the way of life for we men of the free companies. One war ends, another begins. Fortunately there is always someone fighting someone somewhere. Perhaps here. Even as we sit here drinking Bloodbeard is urging our Yunkish friends to present King Hizdahr with another head. Freedmen and slavers eye each other's necks and sharpen their knives, the Sons of the Harpy plot in their pyramids, the pale mare rides down slave and lord alike, our friends from the Yellow City gaze out to sea, and somewhere in the grasslands a dragon nibbles the tender flesh of Daenerys Targaryen. Who rules Meereen tonight? Who will rule it on the morrow?" The Pentoshi gave a shrug. "One thing I am certain of. Someone will have need of our swords."

"I have need of those swords. Dorne will hire you."

The Tattered Prince glanced at Pretty Meris. "He does not lack for gall, this Frog. Must I remind him? My dear prince, the last contract we signed you used to wipe your pretty pink bottom."

"I will double whatever the Yunkishmen are paying you."

"And pay in gold upon the signing of our contract, yes?"

"I will pay you part when we reach Volantis, the rest when I am back in

Sunspear. We brought gold with us when we set sail, but it would have been hard to conceal once we joined the company, so we gave it over to the banks. I can show you papers."

"Ah. Papers. But we will be paid *double*."

"Twice as many papers," said Pretty Meris.

"The rest you'll have in Dorne," Quentyn insisted. "My father is a man of honor. If I put my seal to an agreement, he will fulfill its terms. You have my word on that."

The Tattered Prince finished his wine, turned the cup over, and set it down between them. "So. Let me see if I understand. A proven liar and oathbreaker wishes to contract with us and pay in promises. And for what services? I wonder. Are my Windblown to smash the Yunkai'i and sack the Yellow City? Defeat a Dothraki *khalasar* in the field? Escort you home to your father? Or will you be content if we deliver Queen Daenerys to your bed wet and willing? Tell me true, Prince Frog. What would you have of me and mine?"

"I need you to help me steal a dragon."

Caggo Corpsekiller chuckled. Pretty Meris curled her lip in a half-smile. Denzo D'han whistled.

The Tattered Prince only leaned back on his stool and said, "Double does not pay for dragons, princeling. Even a frog should know that much. Dragons come dear. And men who pay in promises should have at least the sense to promise *more*."

"If you want me to triple—"

"What I want," said the Tattered Prince, "is Pentos."

THE GRIFFIN REBORN

H e sent the archers in first.

Black Balaq commanded one thousand bows. In his youth, Jon Connington had shared the disdain most knights had for bowmen, but he had grown wiser in exile. In its own way, the arrow was as deadly as the sword, so for the long voyage he had insisted that Homeless Harry Strickland break Balaq's command into ten companies of one hundred men and place each company upon a different ship.

Six of those ships had stayed together well enough to deliver their passengers to the shores of Cape Wrath (the other four were lagging but would turn up eventually, the Volantenes assured them, but Griff thought it just as likely they were lost or had landed elsewhere), which left the company with six hundred bows. For this, two hundred proved sufficient. "They will try to send out ravens," he told Black Balaq. "Watch the maester's tower. Here." He pointed to the map he had drawn in the mud of their campsite. "Bring down every bird that leaves the castle."

"This we do," replied the Summer Islander.

A third of Balaq's men used crossbows, another third the double-curved horn-and-sinew bows of the east. Better than these were the big yew longbows borne by the archers of Westerosi blood, and best of all were the great bows of goldenheart treasured by Black Balaq himself and his fifty Summer Islanders. Only a dragonbone bow could outrange one made of goldenheart. Whatever bow they carried, all of Balaq's men were sharp-eyed, seasoned veterans who had proved their worth in a hundred battles, raids, and skirmishes. They proved it again at Griffin's Roost.

The castle rose from the shores of Cape Wrath, on a lofty crag of dark red stone surrounded on three sides by the surging waters of Shipbreaker Bay. Its only approach was defended by a gatehouse, behind which lay the long bare ridge the Conningtons called the griffin's throat. To force the throat could be a bloody business, since the ridge exposed the attackers to the spears, stones, and arrows of defenders in the two round towers that flanked the castle's main gates. And once they reached those gates, the men inside could pour down boiling oil on their heads. Griff expected to lose a hundred men, perhaps more.

They lost four.

The woods had been allowed to encroach on the field beyond the gatehouse, so Franklyn Flowers was able to use the brush for concealment and lead his men within twenty yards of the gates before emerging from the trees with the ram they'd fashioned back at camp. The crash of wood on wood brought two men to the battlements; Black Balaq's archers took down both of them before they could rub the sleep out of their eyes. The gate turned out to be closed but not barred; it gave way at the second blow, and Ser Franklyn's men were halfway up the throat before a warhorn sounded the alarum from the castle proper.

The first raven took flight as their grapnels were arcing above the curtain wall, the second a few moments later. Neither bird had flown a hundred yards before an arrow took it down. A guard inside dumped down a bucket of oil on the first men to reach the gates, but as he'd had no time to heat it, the bucket caused more damage than its contents. Swords were soon ringing in half a dozen places along the battlements. The men of the Golden Company clambered through the merlons and raced along the wallwalks, shouting "*A griffin! A griffin!*," the ancient battle cry of House Connington, which must have left the defenders even more confused.

It was over within minutes. Griff rode up the throat on a white courser beside Homeless Harry Strickland. As they neared the castle, he saw a third raven flap from the maester's tower, only to be feathered by Black Balaq himself. "No more messages," he told Ser Franklyn Flowers in the yard. The next thing to come flying from the maester's tower was the maester. The way his arms were flapping, he might have been mistaken for another bird.

That was the end of all resistance. What guards remained had thrown down their weapons. And quick as that, Griffin's Roost was his again, and Jon Connington was once more a lord.

"Ser Franklyn," he said, "go through the keep and kitchens and roust out everyone you find. Malo, do the same with the maester's tower and the armory. Ser Brendel, the stables, sept, and barracks. Bring them out into the yard, and try not to kill anyone who does not insist on dying. We want to win the stormlands, and we won't do that with slaughter. Be sure you look under the altar of the Mother, there's a hidden stair there that leads down to a secret bolt-hole. And another under the northwest tower that goes straight down to the sea. No one is to escape."

"They won't, m'lord," promised Franklyn Flowers.

Connington watched them dash off, then beckoned to the Halfmaester. "Haldon, take charge of the rookery. I'll have messages to send out to-night."

"Let us hope they left some ravens for us."

Even Homeless Harry was impressed by the swiftness of their victory. "I never thought that it would be so easy," the captain-general said, as they walked into the great hall to have a look at the carved and gilded Griffin Seat where fifty generations of Conningtons had sat and ruled.

"It will get harder. So far we have taken them unawares. That cannot last forever, even if Black Balaq brings down every raven in the realm."

Strickland studied the faded tapestries on the walls, the arched windows with their myriad diamond-shaped panes of red and white glass, the racks of spears and swords and warhammers. "Let them come. This place can stand against twenty times our number, so long as we are well provisioned. And you say there is a way in and out by sea?"

"Below. A hidden cove beneath the crag, which appears only when the tide is out." But Connington had no intention of "letting them come." Griffin's Roost was strong but small, and so long as they sat here they would seem small as well. But there was another castle nearby, vastly larger and impregnable. *Take that, and the realm will shake.* "You must excuse me, Captain-General. My lord father is buried beneath the sept, and it has been too many years since last I prayed for him."

"Of course, my lord."

Yet when they parted, Jon Connington did not go to the sept. Instead his steps led him up to the roof of the east tower, the tallest at Griffin's Roost. As he climbed he remembered past ascents—a hundred with his lord father, who liked to stand and look out over woods and crags and sea and know that all he saw belonged to House Connington, and one (only one!) with Rhaegar Targaryen. Prince Rhaegar was returning from Dorne, and he and his escort had lingered here a fortnight. *He was so young then, and I was younger. Boys, the both of us.* At the welcoming feast, the prince had taken up his silver-stringed harp and played for them. *A song of love and doom,* Jon Connington recalled, *and every woman in the hall was weeping when he put down the harp.* Not the men, of course. Particularly not his own father, whose only love was land. Lord Armond Connington spent the entire evening trying to win the prince to his side in his dispute with Lord Morrigen.

The door to the roof of the tower was stuck so fast that it was plain no one had opened it in years. He had to put his shoulder to it to force it open. But when Jon Connington stepped out onto the high battlements, the view was just as intoxicating as he remembered: the crag with its wind-carved rocks and jagged spires, the sea below growling and worrying at the foot of the castle like some restless beast, endless leagues of sky and cloud, the wood with its autumnal colors. "Your father's lands are beautiful," Prince Rhaegar had said, standing right where Jon was standing now. And the boy he'd been had replied, "One day they will all be mine." *As if that could impress a prince who was heir to the entire realm, from the Arbor to the Wall.*

Griffin's Roost *had* been his, eventually, if only for a few short years. From here, Jon Connington had ruled broad lands extending many leagues to the west, north, and south, just as his father and his father's father had before him. But his father and his father's father had never lost their lands. He had. *I rose too high, loved too hard, dared too much. I tried to grasp a star, overreached, and fell.*

After the Battle of the Bells, when Aerys Targaryen had stripped him of his titles and sent him into exile in a mad fit of ingratitude and suspicion, the lands and lordship had remained within House Connington, passing to his cousin Ser Ronald, the man whom Jon had made his castellan when he went to King's Landing to attend Prince Rhaegar. Robert Baratheon had completed the destruction of the griffins after the war. Cousin Ronald was permitted to retain his castle and his head, but he lost his lordship, thereafter being merely the Knight of Griffin's Roost, and nine-tenths of his lands were taken from him and parceled out to neighbor lords who had supported Robert's claim.

Ronald Connington had died years before. The present Knight of Griffin's Roost, his son Ronnet, was said to be off at war in the riverlands. That was for the best. In Jon Connington's experience, men would fight for things they felt were theirs, even things they'd gained by theft. He did not relish the notion of celebrating his return by killing one of his own kin. Red Ronnet's sire had been quick to take advantage of his lord cousin's downfall, true, but his son had been a child at the time. Jon Connington did not even hate the late Ser Ronald as much as he might have. The fault was his.

He had lost it all at Stoney Sept, in his arrogance.

Robert Baratheon had been hiding somewhere in the town, wounded and alone. Jon Connington had known that, and he had also known that Robert's head upon a spear would have put an end to the rebellion, then and there. He was young and full of pride. How not? King Aerys had named him Hand and given him an army, and he meant to prove himself worthy of that trust, of Rhaegar's love. He would slay the rebel lord himself and carve a place out for himself in all the histories of the Seven Kingdoms.

And so he swept down on Stoney Sept, closed off the town, and began a search. His knights went house to house, smashed in every door, peered into every cellar. He had even sent men crawling through the sewers, yet somehow Robert still eluded him. The townsfolk were *hiding* him. They moved him from one secret bolt-hole to the next, always one step ahead of the king's men. The whole town was a nest of traitors. At the end they had the usurper hidden in a brothel. What sort of king was that, who would hide behind the skirts of women? Yet whilst the search dragged on, Eddard Stark and Hoster Tully came down upon the town with a rebel army. Bells and battle followed, and Robert emerged from his brothel with a blade in hand, and almost slew Jon on the steps of the old sept that gave the town its name.

For years afterward, Jon Connington told himself that he was not to blame, that he had done all that any man could do. His soldiers searched every hole and hovel, he offered pardons and rewards, he took hostages and hung them in crow cages and swore that they would have neither food nor drink until Robert was delivered to him. All to no avail. "Tywin Lannister himself could have done no more," he had insisted one night to Blackheart, during his first year of exile.

"There is where you're wrong," Myles Toyne had replied. "Lord Tywin would not have bothered with a search. He would have burned that town and every living creature in it. Men and boys, babes at the breast, noble knights and holy septons, pigs and whores, rats and rebels, he would have burned them all. When the fires guttered out and only ash and cinders remained, he would have sent his men in to find the bones of Robert Baratheon. Later, when Stark and Tully turned up with their host, he would have offered pardons to the both of them, and they would have accepted and turned for home with their tails between their legs."

He was not wrong, Jon Connington reflected, leaning on the battlements of his forebears. *I wanted the glory of slaying Robert in single combat, and I did not want the name of butcher. So Robert escaped me and cut down Rhaegar on the Trident.* "I failed the father," he said, "but I will not fail the son."

By the time Connington made his descent, his men had gathered the castle garrison and surviving smallfolk together in the yard. Though Ser

Ronnet was indeed off north somewhere with Jaime Lannister, Griffin's Roost was not quite bereft of griffins. Amongst the prisoners were Ronnet's younger brother Raymund, his sister Alynne, and his natural son, a fierce red-haired boy they called Ronald Storm. All would make for useful hostages if and when Red Ronnet should return to try and take back the castle that his father had stolen. Connington ordered them confined to the west tower, under guard. The girl began to cry at that, and the bastard boy tried to bite the spearman closest to him. "Stop it, the both of you," he snapped at them. "No harm will come to any of you unless Red Ronnet proves an utter fool."

Only a few of the captives had been in service here when Jon Connington had last been lord: a grizzled serjeant, blind in one eye; a couple of the washerwomen; a groom who had been a stableboy during Robert's Rebellion; the cook, who had grown enormously fat; the castle armorer. Griff had let his beard grow out during the voyage, for the first time in many years, and to his surprise it had come in mostly red, though here and there ash showed amidst the fire. Clad in a long red-and-white tunic embroidered with the twin griffins of his House, counterchanged and combatant, he looked an older, sterner version of the young lord who had been Prince Rhaegar's friend and companion . . . but the men and women of Griffin's Roost still looked at him with strangers' eyes.

"Some of you will know me," he told them. "The rest will learn. I am your rightful lord, returned from exile. My enemies have told you I am dead. Those tales are false, as you can see. Serve me as faithfully as you have served my cousin, and no harm need come to any of you."

He brought them forward one by one, asked each man his name, then bid them kneel and swear him their allegiance. It all went swiftly. The soldiers of the garrison—only four had survived the attack, the old serjeant and three boys—laid their swords at his feet. No one balked. No one died.

That night in the great hall the victors feasted on roast meats and fresh-caught fish, washed down with rich red wines from the castle cellars. Jon Connington presided from the Griffin's Seat, sharing the high table with Homeless Harry Strickland, Black Balaq, Franklyn Flowers, and the three young griffins they had taken captive. The children were of his blood and he felt that he should know them, but when the bastard boy announced, "My father's going to kill you," he decided that his knowledge was sufficient, ordered them back to their cells, and excused himself.

Haldon Halfmaester had been absent from the feast. Lord Jon found him in the maester's tower, bent over a pile of parchments, with maps spread out all around him. "Hoping to determine where the rest of the company might be?" Connington asked him.

"Would that I could, my lord."

Ten thousand men had sailed from Volon Therys, with all their weapons, horses, elephants. Not quite half that number had turned up thus far on Westeros, at or near their intended landing site, a deserted stretch of coast on the edge of the rainwood . . . lands that Jon Connington knew well, as they had once been his.

Only a few years ago, he would never have dared attempt a landing on Cape Wrath; the storm lords were too fiercely loyal to House Baratheon and to King Robert. But with both Robert and his brother Renly slain, everything was changed. Stannis was too harsh and cold a man to inspire much in the way of loyalty, even if he had not been half a world away, and the stormlands had little reason to love House Lannister. And Jon Connington was not without his own friends here. *Some of the older lords will still remember me, and their sons will have heard the stories. And every man of them will know of Rhaegar, and his young son whose head was smashed against a cold stone wall.*

Fortunately his own ship had been one of the first to reach their destination. Then it had only been a matter of establishing a campsite, assembling his men as they came ashore and moving quickly, before the local lordlings had any inkling of their peril. And there the Golden Company had proved its mettle. The chaos that would inevitably have delayed such a march with a hastily assembled host of household knights and local levies had been nowhere in evidence. These were the heirs of Bittersteel, and discipline was mother's milk to them.

"By this time on the morrow we ought to hold three castles," he said. The force that had taken Griffin's Roost represented a quarter of their available strength; Ser Tristan Rivers had set off simultaneously for the seat of House Morrigen at Crow's Nest, and Laswell Peake for Rain House, the stronghold of the Wyldes, each with a force of comparable size. The rest of their men had remained in camp to guard their landing site and prince, under the command of the company's Volantene paymaster, Gorys Edoryen. Their numbers would continue to swell, one hoped; more ships were straggling in every day. "We still have too few horses."

"And no elephants," the Halfmaester reminded him. Not one of the great cogs carrying the elephants had turned up yet. They had last seen them at Lys, before the storm that had scattered half the fleet. "Horses can be found in Westeros. Elephants—"

"—do not matter." The great beasts would be useful in a pitched battle, no doubt, but it would be some time before they had the strength to face their foes in the field. "Have those parchments told you anything of use?"

"Oh, much and more, my lord." Haldon gave him a thin smile. "The Lannisters make enemies easily but seem to have a harder time keeping friends. Their alliance with the Tyrells is fraying, to judge from what I read here. Queen Cersei and Queen Margaery are fighting over the little king like two bitches with a chicken bone, and both have been accused of treason and debauchery. Mace Tyrell has abandoned his siege of Storm's End to march back to King's Landing and save his daughter, leaving only a token force behind to keep Stannis's men penned up inside the castle."

Connington sat. "Tell me more."

"In the north the Lannisters are relying on the Boltons and in the riverlands upon the Freys, both houses long renowned for treachery and cruelty. Lord Stannis Baratheon remains in open rebellion and the ironborn of the islands have raised up a king as well. No one ever seems to mention the Vale, which suggests to me that the Arryns have taken no part in any of this."

"And Dorne?" The Vale was far away; Dorne was close.

"Prince Doran's younger son has been betrothed to Myrcella Baratheon, which would suggest that the Dornishmen have thrown in with House Lannister, but they have an army in the Boneway and another in the Prince's Pass, just waiting . . ."

"Waiting." He frowned. "For what?" Without Daenerys and her dragons, Dorne was central to their hopes. "Write Sunspear. Doran Martell must know that his sister's son is still alive and has come home to claim his father's throne."

"As you say, my lord." The Halfmaester glanced at another parchment. "We could scarcely have timed our landing better. We have potential friends and allies at every hand."

"But no dragons," said Jon Connington, "so to win these allies to our cause, we must needs have something to offer them."

"Gold and land are the traditional incentives."

"Would that we had either. Promises of land and promises of gold may suffice for some, but Strickland and his men will expect first claim on the choicest fields and castles, those that were taken from their forebears when they fled into exile. No."

"My lord does have one prize to offer," Haldon Halfmaester pointed out. "Prince Aegon's hand. A marriage alliance, to bring some great House to our banners."

A bride for our bright prince. Jon Connington remembered Prince

Rhaegar's wedding all too well. *Elia was never worthy of him. She was frail and sickly from the first, and childbirth only left her weaker.* After the birth of Princess Rhaenys, her mother had been bedridden for half a year, and Prince Aegon's birth had almost been the death of her. She would bear no more children, the maesters told Prince Rhaegar afterward.

"Daenerys Targaryen may yet come home one day," Connington told the Halfmaester. "Aegon must be free to marry her."

"My lord knows best," said Haldon. "In that case, we might consider offering potential friends a lesser prize."

"What would you suggest?"

"You. You are unwed. A great lord, still virile, with no heirs except these cousins we have just now dispossessed, the scion of an ancient House with a fine stout castle and wide, rich lands that will no doubt be restored and perhaps expanded by a grateful king, once we have triumphed. You have a name as a warrior, and as King Aegon's Hand you will speak with his voice and rule this realm in all but name. I would think that many an ambitious lord might be eager to wed his daughter to such a man. Even, perhaps, the prince of Dorne."

Jon Connington's answer was a long cold stare. There were times when the Halfmaester vexed him almost as much as that dwarf had. "I think not." *Death is creeping up my arm. No man must ever know, nor any wife.* He got back to his feet. "Prepare the letter to Prince Doran."

"As my lord commands."

Jon Connington slept that night in the lord's chambers, in the bed that had once been his father's, beneath a dusty canopy of red-and-white velvet. He woke at dawn to the sound of falling rain and the timid knock of a serving man anxious to learn how his new lord would break his fast. "Boiled eggs, fried bread, and beans. And a jug of wine. The worst wine in the cellar."

"The . . . the *worst,* m'lord?"

"You heard me."

When the food and wine had been brought up, he barred the door, emptied the jug into a bowl, and soaked his hand in it. Vinegar soaks and vinegar baths were the treatment Lady Lemore had prescribed for the dwarf, when she feared he might have greyscale, but asking for a jug of vinegar each morning would give the game away. Wine would need to serve, though he saw no sense in wasting a good vintage. The nails on all four fingers were black now, though not yet on his thumb. On the middle finger, the grey had crept up past the second knuckle. *I should hack them off,* he thought, *but how would I explain two missing fingers?* He dare not let the greyscale become known. Queer as it seemed, men who would cheerfully face battle and risk death to rescue a companion would abandon that same companion in a heartbeat if he were known to have greyscale. *I should have let the damned dwarf drown.*

Later that day, garbed and gloved once more, Connington made an inspection of the castle and sent word to Homeless Harry Strickland and his captains to join him for a war council. Nine of them assembled in the solar: Connington and Strickland, Haldon Halfmaester, Black Balaq, Ser Franklyn Flowers, Malo Jayn, Ser Brendel Byrne, Dick Cole, and Lymond Pease. The Halfmaester had good tidings. "Word's reached the camp from Marq Mandrake. The Volantenes put him ashore on what turned out to be Estermont, with close to five hundred men. He's taken Greenstone."

Estermont was an island off Cape Wrath, never one of their objectives. "The damned Volantenes are so eager to be rid of us they are dumping us ashore on any bit of land they see," said Franklyn Flowers. "I'll wager you that we've got lads scattered all over half the bloody Stepstones too."

"With my elephants," Harry Strickland said, in a mournful tone. He missed his elephants, did Homeless Harry.

"Mandrake had no archers with him," said Lymond Pease. "Do we know if Greenstone got off any ravens before it fell?"

"I expect they did," said Jon Connington, "but what messages would they have carried? At best, some garbled account of raiders from the sea." Even before they had sailed from Volon Therys, he had instructed his captains to show no banners during these first attacks—not Prince Aegon's three-headed dragon, nor his own griffins, nor the skulls and golden battle standards of the company. Let the Lannisters suspect Stannis Baratheon, pirates from the Stepstones, outlaws out of the woods, or whoever else they cared to blame. If the reports that reached King's Landing were confused and contradictory, so much the better. The slower the Iron Throne was to react, the longer they would have to gather their strength and bring allies to the cause. "There should be ships on Estermont. It *is* an island. Haldon, send word to Mandrake to leave a garrison behind and bring the rest of his men over to Cape Wrath, along with any noble captives."

"As you command, my lord. House Estermont has blood ties to both kings, as it happens. Good hostages."

"Good ransoms," said Homeless Harry, happily.

"It is time we sent for Prince Aegon as well," Lord Jon announced.

"He will be safer here behind the walls of Griffin's Roost than back at camp."

"I'll send a rider," said Franklyn Flowers, "but the lad won't much like the idea of staying safe, I tell you that. He wants to be in the thick o' things."

So did we all at his age, Lord Jon thought, remembering.

"Has the time come to raise his banner?" asked Pease.

"Not yet. Let King's Landing think this is no more than an exile lord coming home with some hired swords to reclaim his birthright. An old familiar story, that. I will even write King Tommen, stating as much and asking for a pardon and the restoration of my lands and titles. That will give them something to chew over for a while. And whilst they dither, we will send out word secretly to likely friends in the stormlands and the Reach. And Dorne." That was the crucial step. Lesser lords might join their cause for fear of harm or hope of gain, but only the Prince of Dorne had the power to defy House Lannister and its allies. "Above all else, we must have Doran Martell."

"Small chance of that," said Strickland. "The Dornishman is scared of his own shadow. Not what you call daring."

No more than you. "Prince Doran is a cautious man, that's true. He will never join us unless he is convinced that we will win. So to persuade him we must show our strength."

"If Peake and Rivers are successful, we will control the better part of Cape Wrath," argued Strickland. "Four castles in as many days, that's a splendid start, but we are still only at half strength. We need to wait for the rest of my men. We are missing horses as well, and the elephants. Wait, I say. Gather our power, win some small lords to our cause, let Lysono Maar dispatch his spies to learn what we can learn of our foes."

Connington gave the plump captain-general a cool look. *This man is no Blackheart, no Bittersteel, no Maelys. He would wait until all seven hells were frozen if he could rather than risk another bout of blisters.* "We did not cross half the world to wait. Our best chance is to strike hard and fast, before King's Landing knows who we are. I mean to take Storm's End. A nigh-impregnable stronghold, and Stannis Baratheon's last foothold in the south. Once taken, it will give us a secure fastness to which we may retreat at need, and winning it will prove our strength."

The captains of the Golden Company exchanged glances. "If Storm's End is still held by men loyal to Stannis, we will be taking it from him, not the Lannisters," objected Brendel Byrne. "Why not make common cause with him against the Lannisters?"

"Stannis is Robert's brother, of that same ilk that brought down House Targaryen," Jon Connington reminded him. "Moreover, he is a thousand leagues away, with whatever meagre strength he still commands. The whole realm lies between us. It would take half a year just to reach him, and he has little and less to offer us."

"If Storm's End is so impregnable, how do you mean to take it?" asked Malo.

"By guile."

Homeless Harry Strickland disagreed. "We should wait."

"We shall." Jon Connington stood. "Ten days. No longer. It will take that long to prepare. On the morning of the eleventh day, we ride for Storm's End."

The prince arrived to join them four days later, riding at the head of a column of a hundred horse, with three elephants lumbering in his rear. Lady Lemore was with him, garbed once more in the white robes of a septa. Before them went Ser Rolly Duckfield, a snow-white cloak streaming from his shoulders.

A *solid man, and true,* Connington thought as he watched Duck dismount, *but not worthy of the Kingsguard.* He had tried his best to dissuade the prince from giving Duckfield that cloak, pointing out that the honor might best be held in reserve for warriors of greater renown whose fealty would add luster to their cause, and the younger sons of great lords whose support they would need in the coming struggle, but the boy would not be moved. "Duck will die for me if need be," he had said, "and that's all I require in my Kingsguard. The Kingslayer was a warrior of great renown, and the son of a great lord as well."

At least I convinced him to leave the other six slots open, else Duck might have six ducklings trailing after him, each more blindingly adequate than the last. "Escort His Grace to my solar," he commanded. "At once."

Prince Aegon Targaryen was not near as biddable as the boy Young Griff had been, however. The better part of an hour had passed before he finally turned up in the solar, with Duck at his side. "Lord Connington," he said, "I like your castle."

"Your father's lands are beautiful," he said. *His silvery hair was blowing in the wind, and his eyes were a deep purple, darker than this boy's.* "As do I, Your Grace. Please, be seated. Ser Rolly, we'll have no further need of you for now."

"No, I want Duck to stay." The prince sat. "We've been talking with Strickland and Flowers. They told us about this attack on Storm's End that you're planning."

Jon Connington did not let his fury show. "And did Homeless Harry try to persuade you to delay it?"

"He did, actually," the prince said, "but I won't. Harry's an old maid, isn't he? You have the right of it, my lord. I want the attack to go ahead . . . with one change. I mean to lead it."

THE SACRIFICE

On the village green, the queen's men built their pyre.

Or should it be the village white? The snow was knee deep everywhere but where the men had shoveled it away, to hack holes into the frozen ground with axe and spade and pick. The wind was swirling from the west, driving still more snow across the frozen surface of the lakes.

"You do not want to watch this," Aly Mormont said.

"No, but I will." Asha Greyjoy was the kraken's daughter, not some pampered maiden who could not bear to look at ugliness.

It had been a dark, cold, hungry day, like the day before and the day before that. They had spent most of it out on the ice, shivering beside a pair of holes they'd cut in the smaller of the frozen lakes, with fishing lines clutched in mitten-clumsy hands. Not long ago, they could count on hooking one or two fish apiece, and wolfswood men more practiced at ice-fishing were pulling up four or five. Today all that Asha had come back with was a chill that went bone deep. Aly had fared no better. It had been three days since either of them had caught a fish.

The She-Bear tried again. *"I do not need to watch this."*

It is not you the queen's men want to burn. "Then go. You have my word, I will not run. Where would I go? To Winterfell?" Asha laughed. "Only three days' ride, they tell me."

Six queen's men were wrestling two enormous pinewood poles into holes six other queen's men had dug out. Asha did not have to ask their purpose. She knew. *Stakes.* Nightfall would be on them soon, and the red god must be fed. *An offering of blood and fire,* the queen's men called it, *that the Lord of Light may turn his fiery eye upon us and melt these thrice-cursed snows.*

"Even in this place of fear and darkness, the Lord of Light protects us," Ser Godry Farring told the men who gathered to watch as the stakes were hammered down into the holes.

"What has your southron god to do with *snow?*" demanded Artos Flint. His black beard was crusted with ice. "This is the wroth of the old gods come upon us. It is them we should appease."

"Aye," said Big Bucket Wull. "Red Rahloo means nothing here. You will only make the old gods angry. They are watching from their island."

The crofter's village stood between two lakes, the larger dotted with small wooded islands that punched up through the ice like the frozen fists of some drowned giant. From one such island rose a weirwood gnarled and ancient, its bole and branches white as the surrounding snows. Eight days ago Asha had walked out with Aly Mormont to have a closer look at its slitted red eyes and bloody mouth. *It is only sap,* she'd told herself, *the red sap that flows inside these weirwoods.* But her eyes were unconvinced; seeing was believing, and what they saw was frozen blood.

"You northmen brought these snows upon us," insisted Corliss Penny. "You and your demon trees. R'hllor will save us."

"R'hllor will doom us," said Artos Flint.

A pox on both your gods, thought Asha Greyjoy.

Ser Godry the Giantslayer surveyed the stakes, shoving one to make certain it was firmly placed. "Good. Good. They will serve. Ser Clayton, bring forth the sacrifice."

Ser Clayton Suggs was Godry's strong right hand. *Or should it be his withered arm?* Asha did not like Ser Clayton. Where Farring seemed fierce in his devotion to his red god, Suggs was simply cruel. She had seen him at the nightfires, watching, his lips parted and his eyes avid. *It is not the god he loves, it is the flames,* she concluded. When she asked Ser Justin if Suggs had always been that way, he grimaced. "On Dragonstone he would gamble with the torturers and lend them a hand in the questioning of prisoners, especially if the prisoner were a young woman."

Asha was not surprised. Suggs would take a special delight in burning her, she did not doubt. *Unless the storms let up.*

They had been three days from Winterfell for nineteen days. *One hundred leagues from Deepwood Motte to Winterfell. Three hundred miles as the raven flies.* But none of them were ravens, and the storm was unrelenting. Each morning Asha awoke hoping she might see the sun, only to face another day of snow. The storm had buried every hut and hovel beneath a mound of dirty snow, and the drifts would soon be deep enough to engulf the longhall too.

And there was no food, beyond their failing horses, fish taken from the lakes (fewer every day), and whatever meagre sustenance their foragers could find in these cold, dead woods. With the king's knights and lords claiming the lion's share of the horsemeat, little and less remained for the common men. Small wonder then that they had started eating their own dead.

Asha had been as horrified as the rest when the She-Bear told her that four Peasebury men had been found butchering one of the late Lord Fell's, carving chunks of flesh from his thighs and buttocks as one of his forearms turned upon a spit, but she could not pretend to be surprised. The four were not the first to taste human flesh during this grim march, she would wager—only the first to be discovered.

Peasebury's four would pay for their feast with their lives, by the king's decree . . . and by burning end the storm, the queen's men claimed. Asha Greyjoy put no faith in their red god, yet she prayed they had the right of that. If not, there would be other pyres, and Ser Clayton Suggs might get his heart's desire.

The four flesh-eaters were naked when Ser Clayton drove them out, their wrists lashed behind their backs with leathern cords. The youngest of them wept as he stumbled through the snow. Two others walked like men already dead, eyes fixed upon the ground. Asha was surprised to see how ordinary they appeared. *Not monsters,* she realized, *only men.*

The oldest of the four had been their serjeant. He alone remained defiant, spitting venom at the queen's men as they prodded him along with their spears. "Fuck you all, and fuck your red god too," he said. "You hear me, Farring? *Giantslayer?* I laughed when your fucking cousin died, Godry. We should have eaten him too, he smelled so good when they roasted him. I bet the boy was nice and tender. Juicy." A blow from a spear butt drove the man to his knees but did not silence him. When he rose he spat out a mouthful of blood and broken teeth and went right on. "The cock's the choicest part, all crisped up on the spit. A fat little sausage." Even as they wrapped the chains around him, he raved on. "Corliss Penny, come over here. What sort of name is Penny? Is that how much your mother charged? And you, Suggs, you bleeding bastard, you—"

Ser Clayton never said a word. One quick slash opened the serjeant's throat, sending a wash of blood down his chest.

The weeping man wept harder, his body shaking with each sob. He was so thin that Asha could count every rib. "No," he begged, "please, he was dead, he was dead and we was hungry, *please* . . ."

"The serjeant was the clever one," Asha said to Aly Mormont. "He goaded Suggs into killing him." She wondered if the same trick might work twice, should her own turn come.

The four victims were chained up back-to-back, two to a stake. There they hung, three live men and one dead one, as the Lord of Light's devout stacked split logs and broken branches under their feet, then doused the piles with lamp oil. They had to be swift about it. The snow was falling heavily, as ever, and the wood would soon be soaked through.

"Where is the king?" asked Ser Corliss Penny.

Four days ago, one of the king's own squires had succumbed to cold and hunger, a boy named Bryen Farring who'd been kin to Ser Godry. Stannis Baratheon stood grim-faced by the funeral pyre as the lad's body was consigned to the flames. Afterward the king had retreated to his watchtower. He had not emerged since . . . though from time to time His Grace was glimpsed upon the tower roof, outlined against the beacon fire that burned there night and day. *Talking to the red god*, some said. *Calling out for Lady Melisandre*, insisted others. Either way, it seemed to Asha Greyjoy, the king was lost and crying out for help.

"Canty, go find the king and tell him all is ready," Ser Godry said to the nearest man-at-arms.

"The king is here." The voice was Richard Horpe's.

Over his armor of plate and mail Ser Richard wore his quilted doublet, blazoned with three death's-head moths on a field of ash and bone. King Stannis walked beside him. Behind them, struggling to keep pace, Arnolf Karstark came hobbling, leaning on his blackthorn cane. Lord Arnolf had found them eight days past. The northman had brought a son, three grandsons, four hundred spears, two score archers, a dozen mounted lances, a maester, and a cage of ravens . . . but only enough provisions to sustain his own.

Karstark was no lord in truth, Asha had been given to understand, only castellan of Karhold for as long as the true lord remained a captive of the Lannisters. Gaunt and bent and crooked, with a left shoulder half a foot higher than his right, he had a scrawny neck, squinty grey eyes, and yellow teeth. A few white hairs were all that separated him from baldness; his forked beard was equal parts white and grey, but always ragged. Asha thought there was something sour about his smiles. Yet if the talk was true, it was Karstark who would hold Winterfell should they take it. Somewhere in the distant past House Karstark had sprouted from House Stark, and Lord Arnolf had been the first of Eddard Stark's bannermen to declare for Stannis.

So far as Asha knew, the gods of the Karstarks were the old gods of the north, gods they shared with the Wulls, the Norreys, the Flints, and the other hill clans. She wondered if Lord Arnolf had come to view the burning at the king's behest, that he might witness the power of the red god for himself.

At the sight of Stannis, two of the men bound to the stakes began to plead for mercy. The king listened in silence, his jaw clenched. Then he said to Godry Farring, "You may begin."

The Giantslayer raised his arms. *"Lord of Light, hear us."*

"Lord of Light, defend us," the queen's men chanted, *"for the night is dark and full of terrors."*

Ser Godry raised his head toward the darkening sky. *"We thank you for the sun that warms us and pray that you will return it to us, Oh lord, that it might light our path to your enemies."* Snowflakes melted on his face. *"We thank you for the stars that watch over us by night, and pray that you will rip away this veil that hides them, so we might glory in their sight once more."*

"Lord of Light, protect us," the queen's men prayed, *"and keep this savage dark at bay."*

Ser Corliss Penny stepped forward, clutching the torch with both hands. He swung it about his head in a circle, fanning the flames. One of the captives began to whimper.

"R'hllor," Ser Godry sang, *"we give you now four evil men. With glad hearts and true, we give them to your cleansing fires, that the darkness in their souls might be burned away. Let their vile flesh be seared and blackened, that their spirits might rise free and pure to ascend into the light. Accept their blood, Oh lord, and melt the icy chains that bind your servants. Hear their pain, and grant strength to our swords that we might shed the blood of your enemies. Accept this sacrifice, and show us the way to Winterfell, that we might vanquish the unbelievers."*

"Lord of Light, accept this sacrifice," a hundred voices echoed. Ser Corliss lit the first pyre with the torch, then thrust it into the wood at the base of the second. A few wisps of smoke began to rise. The captives began to cough. The first flames appeared, shy as maidens, darting and dancing from log to leg. In moments both the stakes were engulfed in fire.

"He was dead," the weeping boy screamed, as the flames licked up his legs. "We found him dead . . . please . . . we was *hungry* . . ." The fires reached his balls. As the hair around his cock began to burn, his pleading dissolved into one long wordless shriek.

Asha Greyjoy could taste the bile in the back of her throat. On the Iron Islands, she had seen priests of her own people slit the throats of thralls and give their bodies to the sea to honor the Drowned God. Brutal as that was, this was worse.

Close your eyes, she told herself. *Close your ears. Turn away. You do not need to see this.* The queen's men were singing some paean of praise for red R'hllor, but she could not hear the words above the shrieks. The heat of the flames beat against her face, but even so she shivered. The air grew thick with smoke and the stink of burnt flesh, and one of the bodies still twitched against the red-hot chains that bound him to the stake.

After a time the screaming stopped.

Wordless, King Stannis walked away, back to the solitude of his watchtower. *Back to his beacon fire*, Asha knew, *to search the flames for answers.* Arnolf Karstark made to hobble after him, but Ser Richard Horpe took him by the arm and turned him toward the longhall. The watchers began to drift away, each to his own fire and whatever meagre supper he might find.

Clayton Suggs sidled up beside her. "Did the iron cunt enjoy the show?" His breath stank of ale and onions. *He has pig eyes*, Asha thought. That was fitting; his shield and surcoat showed a pig with wings. Suggs pressed his face so close to hers that she could count the blackheads on his nose and said, "The crowd will be even bigger when it's you squirming on a stake."

He was not wrong. The wolves did not love her; she was ironborn and must answer for the crimes of her people, for Moat Cailin and Deepwood Motte and Torrhen's Square, for centuries of reaving along the stony shore, for all Theon did at Winterfell.

"Unhand me, ser." Every time Suggs spoke to her, it left her yearning for her axes. Asha was as good a finger dancer as any man on the isles and had ten fingers to prove it. *If only I could dance with this one.* Some men had faces that cried out for a beard. Ser Clayton's face cried out for an axe between the eyes. But she was axeless here, so the best that she could do was try to wrench away. That just made Ser Clayton grasp her all the tighter, gloved fingers digging into her arm like iron claws.

"My lady asked you to let her go," said Aly Mormont. "You would do well to listen, ser. Lady Asha is not for burning."

"She will be," Suggs insisted. "We have harbored this demon worshiper amongst us too long." He released his grip on Asha's arm all the same. One did not provoke the She-Bear needlessly.

That was the moment Justin Massey chose to appear. "The king has other plans for his prize captive," he said, with his easy smile. His cheeks were red from the cold.

"The king? Or you?" Suggs snorted his contempt. "Scheme all you like, Massey. She'll still be for the fire, her and her king's blood. There's power in king's blood, the red woman used to say. Power to please our lord."

"Let R'hllor be content with the four we just sent him."

"Four baseborn churls. A beggar's offering. Scum like that will never stop the snow. She might."

The She-Bear spoke. "And if you burn her and the snows still fall, what then? Who will you burn next? Me?"

Asha could hold her tongue no longer. "Why not Ser Clayton? Perhaps R'hllor would like one of his own. A faithful man who will sing his praises as the flames lick at his cock."

Ser Justin laughed. Suggs was less amused. "Enjoy your giggle, Massey. If the snow keeps falling, we will see who is laughing then." He glanced at the dead men on their stakes, smiled, and went off to join Ser Godry and the other queen's men.

"My champion," Asha said to Justin Massey. He deserved that much, whatever his motives. "Thank you for the rescue, ser."

"It will not win you friends amongst the queen's men," said the She-Bear. "Have you lost your faith in red R'hllor?"

"I have lost faith in more than that," Massey said, his breath a pale mist in the air, "but I still believe in supper. Will you join me, my ladies?"

Aly Mormont shook her head. "I have no appetite."

"Nor I. But you had best choke down some horsemeat all the same, or you may soon wish you had. We had eight hundred horses when we marched from Deepwood Motte. Last night the count was sixty-four."

That did not shock her. Almost all of their big destriers had failed, including Massey's own. Most of their palfreys were gone as well. Even the garrons of the northmen were faltering for want of fodder. But what did they need horses for? Stannis was no longer marching anywhere. The sun and moon and stars had been gone so long that Asha was starting to wonder whether she had dreamed them. "I will eat."

Aly shook her head. "Not me."

"Let me look after Lady Asha, then," Ser Justin told her. "You have my word, I shall not permit her to escape."

The She-Bear gave her grudging assent, deaf to the japery in his tone. They parted there, Aly to her tent, she and Justin Massey to the longhall. It was not far, but the drifts were deep, the wind was gusty, and Asha's feet were blocks of ice. Her ankle stabbed at her with every step.

Small and mean as it was, the longhall was the largest building in the village, so the lords and captains had taken it for themselves, whilst Stannis settled into the stone watchtower by the lakeshore. A pair of guardsmen flanked its door, leaning on tall spears. One lifted the greased door flap for Massey, and Ser Justin escorted Asha through to the blessed warmth within.

Benches and trestle tables ran along either side of the hall, with room for fifty men . . . though twice that number had squeezed themselves inside. A fire trench had been dug down the middle of the earthen floor, with a row of smokeholes in the roof above. The wolves had taken to sitting on one side of the trench, the knights and southron lords upon the other.

The southerners looked a sorry lot, Asha thought—gaunt and hollow-cheeked, some pale and sick, others with red and wind-scoured faces. By contrast the northmen seemed hale and healthy, big ruddy men with beards as thick as bushes, clad in fur and iron. They might be cold and hungry too, but the marching had gone easier for them, with their garrons and their bear-paws.

Asha peeled off her fur mittens, wincing as she flexed her fingers. Pain shot up her legs as her half-frozen feet began to thaw in the warmth. The crofters had left behind a good supply of peat when they fled, so the air was hazy with smoke and the rich, earthy smell of burning turf. She hung her cloak on a peg inside the door after shaking off the snow that clung to it.

Ser Justin found them places on the bench and fetched supper for the both of them—ale and chunks of horsemeat, charred black outside and red within. Asha took a sip of ale and fell upon the horse flesh. The portion was smaller than the last she'd tasted, but her belly still rumbled at the smell of it. "My thanks, ser," she said, as blood and grease ran down her chin.

"Justin. I insist." Massey cut his own meat into chunks and stabbed one with his dagger.

Down the table, Will Foxglove was telling the men around him that Stannis would resume his march on Winterfell three days hence. He'd had it from the lips of one of the grooms who tended the king's horses. "His Grace has seen victory in his fires," Foxglove said, "a victory that will be sung of for a thousand years in lord's castle and peasant's hut alike."

Justin Massey looked up from his horsemeat. "The cold count last night reached eighty." He pulled a piece of gristle from his teeth and flicked it to the nearest dog. "If we march, we will die by the hundreds."

"We will die by the thousands if we stay here," said Ser Humfrey Clifton. "Press on or die, I say."

"Press on *and* die, I answer. And if we reach Winterfell, what then? How do we take it? Half our men are so weak they can scarce put one foot before another. Will you set them to scaling walls? Building siege towers?"

"We should remain here until the weather breaks," said Ser Ormund

Wylde, a cadaverous old knight whose nature gave the lie to his name. Asha had heard rumors that some of the men-at-arms were wagering on which of the great knights and lords would be the next to die. Ser Ormund had emerged as a clear favorite. *And how much coin was placed on me, I wonder?* Asha thought. *Perhaps there is still time to put down a wager.* "Here at least we have some shelter," Wylde was insisting, "and there are fish in the lakes."

"Too few fish and too many fishermen," Lord Peasebury said gloomily. He had good reason for gloom; it was his men Ser Godry had just burned, and there were some in this very hall who had been heard to say that Peasebury himself surely knew what they were doing and might even have shared in their feasts.

"He's not wrong," grumbled Ned Woods, one of the scouts from Deepwood. Noseless Ned, he was called; frostbite had claimed the tip of his nose two winters past. Woods knew the wolfwood as well as any man alive. Even the king's proudest lords had learned to listen when he spoke. "I know them lakes. You been on them like maggots on a corpse, hundreds o' you. Cut so many holes in the ice it's a bloody wonder more haven't fallen through. Out by the island, there's places look like a cheese the rats been at." He shook his head. "Lakes are done. You fished them out."

"All the more reason to march," insisted Humfrey Clifton. "If death is our fate, let us die with swords in hand."

It was the same argument as last night and the night before. *Press on and die, stay here and die, fall back and die.*

"Feel free to perish as you wish, Humfrey," said Justin Massey. "Myself, I would sooner live to see another spring."

"Some might call that craven," Lord Peasebury replied.

"Better a craven than a cannibal."

Peasebury's face twisted in sudden fury. "You—"

"Death is part of war, Justin." Ser Richard Horpe stood inside the door, his dark hair damp with melting snow. "Those who march with us will have a share in all the plunder we take from Bolton and his bastard, and a greater share of glory undying. Those too weak to march must fend for themselves. But you have my word, we shall send food once we have taken Winterfell."

"*You will not take Winterfell!*"

"Aye, we will," came a cackle from the high table, where Arnolf Karstark sat with his son Arthor and three grandsons. Lord Arnolf shoved himself up, a vulture rising from its prey. One spotted hand clutched at his son's shoulder for support. "We'll take it for the Ned and for his daughter. Aye, and for the Young Wolf too, him who was so cruelly slaughtered. Me and mine will show the way, if need be. I've said as much to His Good Grace the king. *March*, I said, and before the moon can turn, we'll all be bathing in the blood of Freys and Boltons."

Men began to stamp their feet, to pound their fists against the tabletop. Almost all were northmen, Asha noted. Across the fire trench, the southron lords sat silent on the benches.

Justin Massey waited until the uproar had died away. Then he said, "Your courage is admirable, Lord Karstark, but courage will not breach the walls of Winterfell. How do you mean to take the castle, pray? With snowballs?"

One of Lord Arnolf's grandsons gave answer. "We'll cut down trees for rams to break the gates."

"And die."

Another grandson made himself heard. "We'll make ladders, scale the walls."

"And die."

Up spoke Arthor Karstark, Lord Arnolf's younger son. "We'll raise siege towers."

"And die, and die, and die." Ser Justin rolled his eyes. "Gods be good, are all you Karstarks mad?"

"*Gods?*" said Richard Horpe. "You forget yourself, Justin. We have but one god here. Speak not of demons in this company. Only the Lord of Light can save us now. Wouldn't you agree?" He put his hand upon the hilt of his sword, as if for emphasis, but his eyes never left the face of Justin Massey.

Beneath that gaze, Ser Justin wilted. "The Lord of Light, aye. My faith runs as deep as your own, Richard, you know that."

"It is your courage I question, Justin, not your faith. You have preached defeat every step of the way since we rode forth from Deepwood Motte. It makes me wonder whose side you are on."

A flush crept up Massey's neck. "I will not stay here to be insulted." He wrenched his damp cloak down from the wall so hard that Asha heard it tear, then stalked past Horpe and through the door. A blast of cold air blew through the hall, raising ashes from the fire trench and fanning its flames a little brighter.

Broken quick as that, thought Asha. *My champion is made of suet.* Even so, Ser Justin was one of the few who might object should the queen's men try to burn her. So she rose to her feet, donned her own cloak, and followed him out into the blizzard.

She was lost before she had gone ten yards. Asha could see the beacon fire burning atop the watchtower, a faint orange glow floating in the air. Elsewise the village was gone. She was alone in a white world of snow and silence, plowing through snowdrifts as high as her thighs. *"Justin?"* she called. There was no answer. Somewhere to her left she heard a horse whicker. *The poor thing sounds frightened. Perhaps he knows that he's to be tomorrow's supper.* Asha pulled her cloak about her tightly.

She blundered back onto the village green unknowing. The pinewood stakes still stood, charred and scorched but not burned through. The chains about the dead had cooled by now, she saw, but still held the corpses fast in their iron embrace. A raven was perched atop one, pulling at the tatters of burned flesh that clung to its blackened skull. The blowing snow had covered the ashes at the base of the pyre and crept up the dead man's leg as far as his ankle. *The old gods mean to bury him,* Asha thought. *This was no work of theirs.*

"Take a good long gander, cunt," the deep voice of Clayton Suggs said, behind her. "You'll look just as pretty once you're roasted. Tell me, can squids scream?"

God of my fathers, if you can hear me in your watery halls beneath the waves, grant me just one small throwing axe. The Drowned God did not answer. He seldom did. That was the trouble with gods. "Have you seen Ser Justin?"

"That prancing fool? What do you want with him, cunt? If it's a fuck you need, I'm more a man than Massey."

Cunt again? It was odd how men like Suggs used that word to demean women when it was the only part of a woman they valued. And Suggs was worse than Middle Liddle. *When he says the word, he means it.* "Your king gelds men for rape," she reminded him.

Ser Clayton chuckled. "The king's half-blind from staring into fires. But have no fear, cunt, I'll not rape you. I'd need to kill you after, and I'd sooner see you burn."

There's that horse again. "Do you hear that?"

"Hear what?"

"A horse. No, horses. More than one." She turned her head, listening. The snow did queer things to sound. It was hard to know which direction it had come from.

"Is this some squid game? I don't hear—" Suggs scowled. "Bloody hell. Riders." He fumbled at his sword belt, his hands clumsy in their fur-and-leather gloves, and finally succeeded in ripping his longsword from its scabbard.

By then the riders were upon them.

They emerged from the storm like a troop of wraiths, big men on small horses, made even bigger by the bulky furs they wore. Swords rode on their hips, singing their soft steel song as they rattled in their scabbards. Asha saw a battle-axe strapped to one man's saddle, a warhammer on another's back. Shields they bore as well, but so obscured by snow and ice that the arms upon them could not be read. For all her layers of wool and fur and boiled leather, Asha felt naked standing there. *A horn,* she thought, *I need a horn to rouse the camp.*

"Run, you stupid cunt," Ser Clayton shouted. "Run warn the king. Lord Bolton is upon us." A brute he might have been, but Suggs did not want for courage. Sword in hand, he strode through the snow, putting himself between the riders and the king's tower, its beacon glimmering behind him like the orange eye of some strange god. "Who goes there? Halt! *Halt!*"

The lead rider reined up before him. Behind were others, perhaps as many as a score. Asha had no time to count them. Hundreds more might be out there in the storm, coming hard upon their heels. Roose Bolton's entire host might be descending on them, hidden by darkness and swirling snow. These, though . . .

They are too many to be scouts and too few to make a vanguard. And two were all in black. *Night's Watch,* she realized suddenly. "Who are you?" she called.

"Friends," a half-familiar voice replied. "We looked for you at Winterfell, but found only Crowfood Umber beating drums and blowing horns. It took some time to find you." The rider vaulted from his saddle, pulled back his hood, and bowed. So thick was his beard, and so crusted with ice, that for a moment Asha did not know him. Then it came. "*Tris?*" she said.

"My lady." Tristifer Botley took a knee. "The Maid is here as well. Roggon, Grimtongue, Fingers, Rook . . . six of us, all those fit enough to ride. Cromm died of his wounds."

"What is this?" Ser Clayton Suggs demanded. "You're one of hers? How did you get loose of Deepwood's dungeons?"

Tris rose and brushed the snow from his knees. "Sybelle Glover was offered a handsome ransom for our freedom and chose to accept it in the name of the king."

"What ransom? Who would pay good coin for sea scum?"

"I did, ser." The speaker came forward on his garron. He was very tall, very thin, so long-legged that it was a wonder his feet did not drag along the ground. "I had need of a strong escort to see me safely to the king, and

Lady Sybelle had need of fewer mouths to feed." A scarf concealed the tall man's features, but atop his head was perched the queerest hat Asha had seen since the last time she had sailed to Tyrosh, a brimless tower of some soft fabric, like three cylinders stacked one atop the other. "I was given to understand that I might find King Stannis here. It is most urgent that I speak with him at once."

"And who in seven stinking hells are you?"

The tall man slid gracefully from his garron, removed his peculiar hat, and bowed. "I have the honor to be Tycho Nestoris, a humble servant of the Iron Bank of Braavos."

Of all the strange things that might have come riding out of the night, the last one Asha Greyjoy would ever have expected was a Braavosi banker. It was too absurd. She had to laugh. "King Stannis has taken the watchtower for his seat. Ser Clayton will be pleased to show you to him, I'm sure."

"That would be most kind. Time is of the essence." The banker studied her with shrewd dark eyes. "You are the Lady Asha of House Greyjoy, unless I am mistaken."

"I am Asha of House Greyjoy, aye. Opinions differ on whether I'm a lady."

The Braavosi smiled. "We've brought a gift for you." He beckoned to the men behind him. "We had expected to find the king at Winterfell. This same blizzard has engulfed the castle, alas. Beneath its walls we found Mors Umber with a troop of raw green boys, waiting for the king's coming. He gave us this."

A *girl and an old man*, thought Asha, as the two were dumped rudely in the snow before her. The girl was shivering violently, even in her furs. If she had not been so frightened, she might even have been pretty, though the tip of her nose was black with frostbite. The old man . . . no one would ever think him comely. She had seen scarecrows with more flesh. His face was a skull with skin, his hair bone-white and filthy. And he *stank*. Just the sight of him filled Asha with revulsion.

He raised his eyes. "Sister. See. This time I knew you."

Asha's heart skipped a beat. *"Theon?"*

His lips skinned back in what might have been a grin. Half his teeth were gone, and half of those still left him were broken and splintered. "Theon," he repeated. "My name is Theon. You have to know your *name*."

VICTARION

The sea was black and the moon was silver as the Iron Fleet swept down on the prey.

They sighted her in the narrows between the Isle of Cedars and the rugged hills of the Astapori hinterlands, just as the black priest Moqorro had said they would. "Ghiscari," Longwater Pyke shouted down from the crow's nest. Victarion Greyjoy watched her sail grow larger from the forecastle. Soon he could make out her oars rising and falling, and the long white wake behind her shining in the moonlight, like a scar across the sea.

Not a true warship, Victarion realized. *A trading galley, and a big one.* She would make a fine prize. He signaled to his captains to give chase. They would board this ship and take her.

The captain of the galley had realized his peril by then. He changed course for the west, making for the Isle of Cedars, perhaps hoping to shelter in some hidden cove or run his pursuers onto the jagged rocks along the island's northeast coast. His galley was heavy laden, though, and the ironborn had the wind. *Grief* and *Iron Victory* cut across the quarry's course, whilst swift *Sparrowhawk* and agile *Fingerdancer* swept behind her. Even then the Ghiscari captain did not strike his banners. By the time *Lamentation* came alongside the prey, raking her larboard side and splintering her oars, both ships were so close to the haunted ruins of Ghozai that they could hear the monkeys chattering as the first dawn light washed over the city's broken pyramids.

Their prize was named *Ghiscari Dawn,* the galley's captain said when he was delivered to Victarion in chains. She was out of New Ghis and returning there by way of Yunkai after trading at Meereen. The man spoke no decent tongue but only a guttural Ghiscari, full of growls and hisses, as ugly a language as Victarion Greyjoy had ever heard. Moqorro translated the captain's words into the Common Tongue of Westeros. The war for

Meereen was won, the captain claimed; the dragon queen was dead, and a Ghiscari by the name of Hizdak ruled the city now.

Victarion had his tongue torn out for lying. Daenerys Targaryen was *not* dead, Moqorro assured him; his red god R'hllor had shown him the queen's face in his sacred fires. The captain could not abide lies, so he had the Ghiscari captain bound hand and foot and thrown overboard, a sacrifice to the Drowned God. "Your red god will have his due," he promised Moqorro, "but the seas are ruled by the Drowned God."

"There are no gods but R'hllor and the Other, whose name may not be said." The sorcerer priest was garbed in somber black, but for a hint of golden thread at collar, cuffs, and hem. There was no red cloth aboard the *Iron Victory*, but it was not meet that Moqorro go about in the salt-stained rags he had been wearing when the Vole fished him from the sea, so Victarion had commanded Tom Tidewood to sew new robes for him from whatever was at hand, and had even donated some of his own tunics to the purpose. Of black and gold those were, for the arms of House Greyjoy showed a golden kraken on a black field, and the banners and sails of their ships displayed the same. The crimson-and-scarlet robes of the red priests were alien to the ironborn, but Victarion had hoped his men might accept Moqorro more easily once clad in Greyjoy colors.

He hoped in vain. Clad in black from head to heel, with a mask of red-and-orange flames tattooed across his face, the priest appeared more sinister than ever. The crew shunned him when he walked the deck, and men would spit if his shadow chanced to fall upon them. Even the Vole, who had fished the red priest from the sea, had urged Victarion to give him to the Drowned God.

But Moqorro knew these strange shores in ways the ironborn did not, and secrets of the dragonkind as well. *The Crow's Eye keeps wizards, why shouldn't I?* His black sorcerer was more puissant than all of Euron's three, even if you threw them in a pot and boiled them down to one. The Damphair might disapprove, but Aeron and his pieties were far away.

So Victarion closed his burned hand into a mighty fist, and said, "*Ghiscari Dawn* is no fit name for a ship of the Iron Fleet. For you, wizard, I shall rename her *Red God's Wroth*."

His wizard bowed his head. "As the captain says." And the ships of the Iron Fleet numbered four-and-fifty once again.

The next day a sudden squall descended on them. Moqorro had predicted that as well. When the rains moved on, three ships were found to have vanished. Victarion had no way to know whether they had foundered, run aground, or been blown off course. "They know where we are going,"

he told his crew. "If they are still afloat, we will meet again." The iron captain had no time to wait for laggards. Not with his bride encircled by her
enemies. *The most beautiful woman in the world has urgent need of my axe.*

Besides, Moqorro assured him that the three ships were not lost. Each
night, the sorcerer priest would kindle a fire on the forecastle of the *Iron
Victory* and stalk around the flames, chanting prayers. The firelight made
his black skin shine like polished onyx, and sometimes Victarion could
swear that the flames tattooed on his face were dancing too, twisting and
bending, melting into one another, their colors changing with every turn
of the priest's head.

"The black priest is calling demons down on us," one oarsman was
heard to say. When that was reported to Victarion, he had the man
scourged until his back was blood from shoulders to buttocks. So when
Moqorro said, "Your lost lambs will return to the flock off the isle called
Yaros," the captain said, "Pray that they do, priest. Or you may be the next
to taste the whip."

The sea was blue and green and the sun blazing down from an empty
blue sky when the Iron Fleet took its second prize, in the waters north and
west of Astapor.

This time it was a Myrish cog named *Dove*, on her way to Yunkai by
way of New Ghis with a cargo of carpets, sweet green wines, and Myrish
lace. Her captain owned a Myrish eye that made far-off things look
close—two glass lenses in a series of brass tubes, cunningly wrought so
that each section slid into the next, until the eye was no longer than a dirk.
Victarion claimed that treasure for himself. The cog he renamed *Shrike*.
Her crew would be kept for ransom, the captain decreed. They were neither slaves nor slavers, but free Myrmen and seasoned sailors. Such men
were worth good coin. Sailing out of Myr, the *Dove* brought them no
fresh news of Meereen or Daenerys, only stale reports of Dothraki horsemen along the Rhoyne, the Golden Company upon the march, and other
things Victarion already knew.

"What do you see?" the captain asked his black priest that night, as
Moqorro stood before his nightfire. "What awaits us on the morrow? More
rain?" It smelled like rain to him.

"Grey skies and strong winds," Moqorro said. "No rain. Behind come
the tigers. Ahead awaits your dragon."

Your dragon. Victarion liked the sound of that. "Tell me something that
I do not know, priest."

"The captain commands, and I obey," said Moqorro. The crew had
taken to calling him the Black Flame, a name fastened on him by Steffar

Stammerer, who could not say "Moqorro." By any name, the priest had powers. "The coastline here runs west to east," he told Victarion. "Where it turns north, you will come on two more hares. Swift ones, with many legs."

And so it came to pass. This time the prey proved to be a pair of galleys, long and sleek and fast. Ralf the Limper was the first to sight them, but they soon outdistanced *Woe* and *Forlorn Hope,* so Victarion sent *Iron Wing, Sparrowhawk,* and *Kraken's Kiss* to run them down. He had no swifter ships than those three. The pursuit lasted the best part of the day, but in the end both galleys were boarded and taken, after brief but brutal fights. They had been running empty, Victarion learned, making for New Ghis to load supplies and weapons for the Ghiscari legions encamped before Meereen . . . and to bring fresh legionaries to the war, to replace all the men who'd died. "Men slain in battle?" asked Victarion. The crews of the galleys denied it; the deaths were from a bloody flux. The pale mare, they called it. And like the captain of the *Ghiscari Dawn,* the captains of the galleys repeated the lie that Daenerys Targaryen was dead.

"Give her a kiss for me in whatever hell you find her," Victarion said. He called for his axe and took their heads off there and then. Afterward he put their crews to death as well, saving only the slaves chained to the oars. He broke their chains himself and told them they were now free men and would have the privilege of rowing for the Iron Fleet, an honor that every boy in the Iron Islands dreamed of growing up. "The dragon queen frees slaves and so do I," he proclaimed.

The galleys he renamed *Ghost* and *Shade.* "For I mean them to return and haunt these Yunkishmen," he told the dusky woman that night after he had taken his pleasure of her. They were close now, and growing closer every day. "We will fall upon them like a thunderbolt," he said, as he squeezed the woman's breast. He wondered if this was how his brother Aeron felt when the Drowned God spoke to him. He could almost hear the god's voice welling up from the depths of the sea. *You shall serve me well, my captain,* the waves seemed to say. *It was for this I made you.*

But he would feed the red god too, Moqorro's fire god. The arm the priest had healed was hideous to look upon, pork crackling from elbow to fingertips. Sometimes when Victarion closed his hand the skin would split and smoke, yet the arm was stronger than it had ever been. "Two gods are with me now," he told the dusky woman. "No foe can stand before two gods." Then he rolled her on her back and took her once again.

When the cliffs of Yaros appeared off their larboard bows, he found his three lost ships waiting for him, just as Moqorro had promised. Victarion gave the priest a golden torque as a reward.

Now he had a choice to make: should he risk the straits, or take the Iron Fleet around the island? The memory of Fair Isle still rankled in the iron captain's memory. Stannis Baratheon had descended on the Iron Fleet from both north and south whilst they were trapped in the channel between the island and the mainland, dealing Victarion his most crushing defeat. But sailing around Yaros would cost him precious days. With Yunkai so near, shipping in the straits was like to be heavy, but he did not expect to encounter Yunkish warships until they were closer to Meereen.

What would the Crow's Eye do? He brooded on that for a time, then signaled to his captains. "We sail the straits."

Three more prizes were taken before Yaros dwindled off their sterns. A fat galleas fell to the Vole and *Grief*, and a trading galley to Manfryd Merlyn of *Kite*. Their holds were packed with trade goods, wines and silks and spices, rare woods and rarer scents, but the ships themselves were the true prize. Later that same day, a fishing ketch was taken by *Seven Skulls* and *Thrall's Bane*. She was a small, slow, dingy thing, hardly worth the effort of boarding. Victarion was displeased to hear that it had taken two of his own ships to bring the fishermen to heel. Yet it was from their lips that he heard of the black dragon's return. "The silver queen is gone," the ketch's master told him. "She flew away upon her dragon, beyond the Dothraki sea."

"Where is this Dothraki sea?" he demanded. "I will sail the Iron Fleet across it and find the queen wherever she may be."

The fisherman laughed aloud. "That would be a sight worth seeing. The Dothraki sea is made of grass, fool."

He should not have said that. Victarion took him around the throat with his burned hand and lifted him bodily into the air. Slamming him back against the mast, he squeezed till the Yunkishman's face turned as black as the fingers digging into his flesh. The man kicked and writhed for a while, trying fruitlessly to pry loose the captain's grip. "No man calls Victarion Greyjoy a fool and lives to boast of it." When he opened his hand, the man's limp body flopped to the deck. Longwater Pyke and Tom Tidewood chucked it over the rail, another offering to the Drowned God.

"Your Drowned God is a demon," the black priest Moqorro said afterward. "He is no more than a thrall of the Other, the dark god whose name must not be spoken."

"Take care, priest," Victarion warned him. "There are godly men aboard this ship who would tear out your tongue for speaking such blasphemies. Your red god will have his due, I swear it. My word is iron. Ask any of my men."

The black priest bowed his head. "There is no need. The Lord of Light has shown me your worth, lord Captain. Every night in my fires I glimpse the glory that awaits you."

Those words pleased Victarion Greyjoy mightily, as he told the dusky woman that night. "My brother Balon was a great man," he said, "but I shall do what he could not. The Iron Islands shall be free again, and the Old Way will return. Even Dagon could not do that." Almost a hundred years had passed since Dagon Greyjoy sat the Seastone Chair, but the ironborn still told tales of his raids and battles. In Dagon's day a weak king sat the Iron Throne, his rheumy eyes fixed across the narrow sea where bastards and exiles plotted rebellion. So forth from Pyke Lord Dagon sailed, to make the Sunset Sea his own. "He bearded the lion in his den and tied the direwolf's tail in knots, but even Dagon could not defeat the dragons. But I shall make the dragon queen mine own. She will share my bed and bear me many mighty sons."

That night the ships of the Iron Fleet numbered sixty.

Strange sails grew more common north of Yaros. They were very near to Yunkai, and the coast between the Yellow City and Meereen would be teeming with merchantmen and supply ships coming and going, so Victarion took the Iron Fleet out into the deeper waters, beyond the sight of land. Even there they would encounter other vessels. "Let none escape to give warning to our foes," the iron captain commanded. None did.

The sea was green and the sky was grey the morning *Grief* and *Warrior Wench* and Victarion's own *Iron Victory* captured the slaver galley from Yunkai in the waters due north of the Yellow City. In her holds were twenty perfumed boys and four score girls destined for the pleasure houses of Lys. Her crew never thought to find peril so close to their home waters, and the ironborn had little trouble taking her. She was named the *Willing Maiden*.

Victarion put the slavers to the sword, then sent his men below to unchain the rowers. "You row for me now. Row hard, and you shall prosper." The girls he divided amongst his captains. "The Lyseni would have made whores of you," he told them, "but we have saved you. Now you need only serve one man instead of many. Those who please their captains may be taken as salt wives, an honorable station." The perfumed boys he wrapped in chains and threw into the sea. They were unnatural creatures, and the ship smelled better once cleansed of their presence.

For himself, Victarion claimed the seven choicest girls. One had red-gold hair and freckles on her teats. One shaved herself all over. One was brown-haired and brown-eyed, shy as a mouse. One had the biggest breasts he had ever seen. The fifth was a little thing, with straight black hair and golden skin. Her eyes were the color of amber. The sixth was white as milk, with golden rings through her nipples and her nether lips, the seventh black as a squid's ink. The slavers of Yunkai had trained them in the way of the seven sighs, but that was not why Victarion wanted them. His dusky woman was enough to satisfy his appetites until he could reach Meereen and claim his queen. No man had need of candles when the sun awaited him.

The galley he renamed the *Slaver's Scream*. With her, the ships of the Iron Fleet numbered one-and-sixty. "Every ship we capture makes us stronger," Victarion told his ironborn, "but from here it will grow harder. On the morrow or the day after, we are like to meet with warships. We are entering the home waters of Meereen, where the fleets of our foes await us. We will meet with ships from all three Slaver Cities, ships from Tolos and Elyria and New Ghis, even ships from Qarth." He took care not to mention the green galleys of Old Volantis that surely must be sailing up through the Gulf of Grief even as he spoke. "These slavers are feeble things. You have seen how they run before us, heard how they squeal when we put them to the sword. Every man of you is worth twenty of them, for only we are made of iron. Remember this when first we next spy some slaver's sails. Give no quarter and expect none. What need have we of quarter? We are the ironborn, and two gods look over us. We will seize their ships, smash their hopes, and turn their bay to blood."

A great cry went up at his words. The captain answered with a nod, grim-faced, then called for the seven girls he had claimed to be brought on deck, the loveliest of all those found aboard the *Willing Maiden*. He kissed them each upon the cheeks and told them of the honor that awaited them, though they did not understand his words. Then he had them put aboard the fishing ketch that they had captured, cut her loose, and had her set afire.

"With this gift of innocence and beauty, we honor both the gods," he proclaimed, as the warships of the Iron Fleet rowed past the burning ketch. "Let these girls be reborn in light, undefiled by mortal lust, or let them descend to the Drowned God's watery halls, to feast and dance and laugh until the seas dry up."

Near the end, before the smoking ketch was swallowed by the sea, the cries of the seven sweetlings changed to joyous song, it seemed to Victarion Greyjoy. A great wind came up then, a wind that filled their sails and swept them north and east and north again, toward Meereen and its pyramids of many-colored bricks. *On wings of song I fly to you, Daenerys*, the iron captain thought.

That night, for the first time, he brought forth the dragon horn that the Crow's Eye had found amongst the smoking wastes of great Valyria. A twisted thing it was, six feet long from end to end, gleaming black and banded with red gold and dark Valyrian steel. *Euron's hellhorn*. Victarion ran his hand along it. The horn was as warm and smooth as the dusky woman's thighs, and so shiny that he could see a twisted likeness of his own features in its depths. Strange sorcerous writings had been cut into the bands that girded it. "Valyrian glyphs," Moqorro called them.

That much Victarion had known. "What do they say?"

"Much and more." The black priest pointed to one golden band. "Here the horn is named. '*I am Dragonbinder*,' it says. Have you ever heard it sound?"

"Once." One of his brother's mongrels had sounded the hellhorn at the kingsmoot on Old Wyk. A monster of a man he had been, huge and shaven-headed, with rings of gold and jet and jade around arms thick with muscle, and a great hawk tattooed across his chest. "The sound it made . . . it burned, somehow. As if my bones were on fire, searing my flesh from within. Those writings glowed red-hot, then white-hot and painful to look upon. It seemed as if the sound would never end. It was like some long scream. A thousand screams, all melted into one."

"And the man who blew the horn, what of him?"

"He died. There were blisters on his lips, after. His bird was bleeding too." The captain thumped his chest. "The hawk, just here. Every feather dripping blood. I heard the man was all burned up inside, but that might just have been some tale."

"A true tale." Moqorro turned the hellhorn, examining the queer letters that crawled across a second of the golden bands. "Here it says, '*No mortal man shall sound me and live*.' "

Bitterly Victarion brooded on the treachery of brothers. *Euron's gifts are always poisoned*. "The Crow's Eye swore this horn would bind dragons to my will. But how will that serve me if the price is death?"

"Your brother did not sound the horn himself. Nor must you." Moqorro pointed to the band of steel. "Here. '*Blood for fire, fire for blood*.' Who blows the hellhorn matters not. The dragons will come to the horn's master. You must *claim* the horn. With blood."

THE UGLY LITTLE GIRL

Eleven servants of the Many-Faced God gathered that night beneath the temple, more than she had ever seen together at one time. Only the lordling and the fat fellow arrived by the front door; the rest came by secret ways, through tunnels and hidden passages. They wore their robes of black and white, but as they took their seats each man pulled his cowl down to show the face he had chosen to wear that day. Their tall chairs were carved of ebony and weirwood, like the doors of the temple above. The ebon chairs had weirwood faces on their backs, the weirwood chairs faces of carved ebony.

One of the other acolytes stood across the room with a flagon of dark red wine. She had the water. Whenever one of the servants wished to drink, he would raise his eyes or crook a finger, and one or both of them would come and fill his cup. But mostly they stood, waiting on looks that never came. *I am carved of stone*, she reminded herself. *I am a statue, like the Sealords that stand along the Canal of the Heroes.* The water was heavy, but her arms were strong.

The priests used the language of Braavos, though once for several minutes three spoke heatedly in High Valyrian. The girl understood the words, mostly, but they spoke in soft voices, and she could not always hear. "I know this man," she did hear a priest with the face of a plague victim say. "I know this man," the fat fellow echoed, as she was pouring for him. But the handsome man said, "I will give this man the gift, I know him not." Later the squinter said the same thing, of someone else.

After three hours of wine and words, the priests took their leave . . . all but the kindly man, the waif, and the one whose face bore the marks of plague. His cheeks were covered with weeping sores, and his hair had fallen out. Blood dripped from one nostril and crusted at the corners of both eyes. "Our brother would have words with you, child," the kindly

man told her. "Sit, if you wish." She seated herself in a weirwood chair
with a face of ebony. Bloody sores held no terror for her. She had been too
long in the House of Black and White to be afraid of a false face.

"Who are you?" plague face asked when they were alone.

"No one."

"Not so. You are Arya of House Stark, who bites her lip and cannot tell
a lie."

"I was. I'm not now."

"Why are you here, liar?"

"To serve. To learn. To change my face."

"First change your heart. The gift of the Many-Faced God is not a
child's plaything. You would kill for your own purposes, for your own
pleasures. Do you deny it?"

She bit her lip. "I—"

He slapped her.

The blow left her cheek stinging, but she knew that she had earned it.
"Thank you." Enough slaps, and she might stop chewing on her lip. *Arya*
did that, not the night wolf. "I do deny it."

"You lie. I can see the truth in your eyes. You have the eyes of a wolf
and a taste for blood."

Ser Gregor, she could not help but think. *Dunsen, Raff the Sweetling.
Ser Ilyn, Ser Meryn, Queen Cersei.* If she spoke, she would need to lie, and
he would know. She kept silent.

"You were a cat, they tell me. Prowling through the alleys smelling of
fish, selling cockles and mussels for coin. A small life, well suited for a
small creature such as you. Ask, and it can be restored to you. Push your
barrow, cry your cockles, be content. Your heart is too soft to be one of us."

He means to send me away. "I have no heart. I only have a hole. I've
killed lots of people. I could kill you if I wanted."

"Would that taste sweet to you?"

She did not know the right answer. "Maybe."

"Then you do not belong here. Death holds no sweetness in this house.
We are not warriors, nor soldiers, nor swaggering bravos puffed up with
pride. We do not kill to serve some lord, to fatten our purses, to stroke our
vanity. We never give the gift to please ourselves. Nor do we choose the
ones we kill. We are but servants of the God of Many Faces."

"Valar dohaeris." All men must serve.

"You know the words, but you are too proud to serve. A servant must be
humble and obedient."

"I obey. I can be humbler than anyone."

That made him chuckle. "You will be the very goddess of humility, I am sure. But can you pay the price?"

"What price?"

"The price is you. The price is all you have and all you ever hope to have. We took your eyes and gave them back. Next we will take your ears, and you will walk in silence. You will give us your legs and crawl. You will be no one's daughter, no one's wife, no one's mother. Your name will be a lie, and the very face you wear will not be your own."

She almost bit her lip again, but this time she caught herself and stopped. *My face is a dark pool, hiding everything, showing nothing.* She thought of all the names that she had worn: Arry, Weasel, Squab, Cat of the Canals. She thought of that stupid girl from Winterfell called Arya Horseface. Names did not matter. "I can pay the price. Give me a face."

"Faces must be earned."

"Tell me how."

"Give a certain man a certain gift. Can you do that?"

"What man?"

"No one that you know."

"I don't know a lot of people."

"He is one of them. A stranger. No one you love, no one you hate, no one you have ever known. Will you kill him?"

"Yes."

"Then on the morrow, you shall be Cat of the Canals again. Wear that face, watch, obey. And we will see if you are truly worthy to serve Him of Many Faces."

So the next day she returned to Brusco and his daughters in the house on the canal. Brusco's eyes widened when he saw her, and Brea gave a little gasp. "*Valar morghulis,*" Cat said, by way of greeting. "*Valar dohaeris,*" Brusco replied.

After that it was as if she had never been away.

She got her first look at the man she must kill later that morning as she wheeled her barrow through the cobbled streets that fronted on the Purple Harbor. He was an old man, well past fifty. *He has lived too long,* she tried to tell herself. *Why should he have so many years when my father had so few?* But Cat of the Canals had no father, so she kept that thought to herself.

"*Cockles and mussels and clams,*" Cat cried as he went past, "*oysters and prawns and fat green mussels.*" She even smiled at him. Sometimes a smile was all you needed to make them stop and buy. The old man did not smile back. He scowled at her and went on past, sloshing through a puddle. The splash wet her feet.

He has no courtesy, she thought, watching him go. *His face is hard and mean.* The old man's nose was pinched and sharp, his lips thin, his eyes small and close-set. His hair had gone to grey, but the little pointed beard at the end of his chin was still black. Cat thought it must be dyed and wondered why he had not dyed his hair as well. One of his shoulders was higher than the other, giving him a crooked cast.

"He is an evil man," she announced that evening when she returned to the House of Black and White. "His lips are cruel, his eyes are mean, and he has a villain's beard."

The kindly man chuckled. "He is a man like any other, with light in him and darkness. It is not for you to judge him."

That gave her pause. "Have the gods judged him?"

"Some gods, mayhaps. What are gods for if not to sit in judgment over men? The Many-Faced God does not weigh men's souls, however. He gives his gift to the best of men as he gives it to the worst. Elsewise the good would live forever."

The old man's hands were the worst thing about him, Cat decided the next day, as she watched him from behind her barrow. His fingers were long and bony, always moving, scratching at his beard, tugging at an ear, drumming on a table, twitching, twitching, twitching. *He has hands like two white spiders.* The more she watched his hands, the more she came to hate them.

"He moves his hands too much," she told them at the temple. "He must be full of fear. The gift will bring him peace."

"The gift brings all men peace."

"When I kill him he will look in my eyes and thank me."

"If he does, you will have failed. It would be best if he takes no note of you at all."

The old man was some sort of merchant, Cat concluded after watching him for a few days. His trade had to do with the sea, though she never saw him set foot upon a ship. He spent his days sitting in a soup shop near the Purple Harbor, a cup of onion broth cooling at his elbow as he shuffled papers and sealing wax and spoke in sharp tones to a parade of captains, shipowners, and other merchants, none of whom seemed to like him very much.

Yet they brought him money: leather purses plump with gold and silver and the square iron coins of Braavos. The old man would count it out carefully, sorting the coins and stacking them up neatly, like with like. He never looked at the coins. Instead he bit them, always on the left side of his mouth, where he still had all his teeth. From time to time he'd spin one on the table and listen to the sound it made when it came clattering to a stop.

And when all the coins had been counted and tasted, the old man would scrawl upon a parchment, stamp it with his seal, and give it to the captain. Else he'd shake his head and shove the coins back across the table. Whenever he did that, the other man would get red-faced and angry, or pale and scared-looking.

Cat did not understand. "They pay him gold and silver, but he only gives them writing. Are they stupid?"

"A few, mayhaps. Most are simply cautious. Some think to cozen him. He is not a man easily cozened, however."

"But what is he *selling* them?"

"He is writing each a binder. If their ships are lost in a storm or taken by pirates, he promises to pay them for the value of the vessel and all its contents."

"Is it some kind of wager?"

"Of a sort. A wager every captain hopes to lose."

"Yes, but if they win . . ."

". . . they lose their ships, oftimes their very lives. The seas are dangerous, and never more so than in autumn. No doubt many a captain sinking in a storm has taken some small solace in his binder back in Braavos, knowing that his widow and children will not want." A sad smile touched his lips. "It is one thing to write such a binder, though, and another to make good on it."

Cat understood. *One of them must hate him. One of them came to the House of Black and White and prayed for the god to take him.* She wondered who it had been, but the kindly man would not tell her. "It is not for you to pry into such matters," he said. "Who are you?"

"No one."

"No one asks no questions." He took her hands. "If you cannot do this thing, you need only say so. There is no shame in that. Some are made to serve the Many-Faced God and some are not. Say the word, and I shall lift this task from you."

"I will do it. I said I would. I will."

How, though? That was harder.

He had guards. Two of them, a tall thin man and a short thick one. They went with him everywhere, from when he left his house in the

morning till he returned at night. They made certain no one got close
to the old man without his leave. Once a drunk almost staggered into
him as he was coming home from the soup shop, but the tall one stepped
between them and gave the man a sharp shove that knocked him to the
ground. At the soup shop, the short one always tasted the onion broth
first. The old man waited until the broth had cooled before he took a
sip, long enough to be sure his guardsman had suffered no ill effects.

"He's afraid," she realized, "or else he knows that someone wants to kill
him."

"He does not know," said the kindly man, "but he suspects."

"The guards go with him even when he slips out to make water," she
said, "but he doesn't go when they do. The tall one is the quicker. I'll wait
till he is making water, walk into the soup shop, and stab the old man
through the eye."

"And the other guard?"

"He's slow and stupid. I can kill him too."

"Are you some butcher of the battlefield, hacking down every man who
stands in your way?"

"No."

"I would hope not. You are a servant of the Many-Faced God, and we
who serve Him of Many Faces give his gift only to those who have been
marked and chosen."

She understood. *Kill him. Kill only him.*

It took her three more days of watching before she found the way, and
another day of practicing with her finger knife. Red Roggo had taught her
how to use it, but she had not slit a purse since back before they took away
her eyes. She wanted to make certain that she still knew how. *Smooth and
quick, that's the way, no fumbling,* she told herself, and she slipped the
little blade out of her sleeve, again and again and again. When she was
satisfied that she still remembered how to do it, she sharpened the steel on
a whetstone until its edge glimmered silver-blue in the candlelight. The
other part was trickier, but the waif was there to help her. "I will give the
man the gift on the morrow," she announced as she was breaking her fast.

"Him of Many Faces will be pleased." The kindly man rose. "Cat of the
Canals is known to many. If she is seen to have done this deed, it might
bring down trouble on Brusco and his daughters. It is time you had another face."

The girl did not smile, but inside she was pleased. She had lost Cat
once, and mourned her. She did not want to lose her again. "What will I
look like?"

"Ugly. Women will look away when they see you. Children will stare and point. Strong men will pity you, and some may shed a tear. No one who sees you will soon forget you. Come."

The kindly man took the iron lantern off its hook and led her past the still black pool and the rows of dark and silent gods, to the steps at the rear of the temple. The waif fell in behind them as they were making their descent. No one spoke. The soft scuff of slippered feet on the steps was the only sound. Eighteen steps brought them to the vaults, where five arched passageways spread out like the fingers of a man's hand. Down here the steps grew narrower and steeper, but the girl had run up and down them a thousand times and they held no terrors for her. Twenty-two more steps and they were at the subcellar. The tunnels here were cramped and crooked, black wormholes twisting through the heart of the great rock. One passage was closed off by a heavy iron door. The priest hung the lantern from a hook, slipped a hand inside his robe, and produced an ornate key.

Gooseprickles rose along her arms. *The sanctum.* They were going lower still, down to the third level, to the secret chambers where only the priests were permitted.

The key clicked three times, very softly, as the kindly man turned it in a lock. The door swung open on oiled iron hinges, making not a sound. Beyond were still more steps, hewn out of solid rock. The priest took down the lantern once again and led the way. The girl followed the light, counting the steps as she went down. *Four five six seven.* She found herself wishing that she had brought her stick. *Ten eleven twelve.* She knew how many steps there were between the temple and the cellar, between the cellar and the subcellar, she had even counted the steps on the cramped winding stair that spiraled up into the garret and the rungs on the steep wooden ladder that ascended to the rooftop door and the windy perch outside.

This stair was unknown to her, however, and that made it perilous. *One-and-twenty two-and-twenty three-and-twenty.* With every step the air seemed to grow a little colder. When her count reached thirty she knew that they were under even the canals. *Three-and-thirty four-and-thirty.* How deep were they going to go?

She had reached fifty-four when the steps finally ended at another iron door. This one was unlocked. The kindly man pushed it open and stepped through. She followed, with the waif on her heels. Their footsteps echoed through the darkness. The kindly man lifted his lantern and flicked its shutters wide open. Light washed over the walls around them.

A thousand faces were gazing down on her.

They hung upon the walls, before her and behind her, high and low, everywhere she looked, everywhere she turned. She saw old faces and young faces, pale faces and dark faces, smooth faces and wrinkled faces, freckled faces and scarred faces, handsome faces and homely faces, men and women, boys and girls, even babes, smiling faces, frowning faces, faces full of greed and rage and lust, bald faces and faces bristling with hair. *Masks*, she told herself, *it's only masks*, but even as she thought the thought, she knew it wasn't so. They were skins.

"Do they frighten you, child?" asked the kindly man. "It is not too late for you to leave us. Is this truly what you want?"

Arya bit her lip. She did not know what she wanted. *If I leave, where will I go?* She had washed and stripped a hundred corpses, dead things did not frighten her. *They carry them down here and slice their faces off, so what?* She was the night wolf, no scraps of skin could frighten her. *Leather hoods, that's all they are, they cannot hurt me.* "Do it," she blurted out.

He led her across the chamber, past a row of tunnels leading off into side passages. The light of his lantern illuminated each in turn. One tunnel was walled with human bones, its roof supported by columns of skulls. Another opened on winding steps that descended farther still. *How many cellars are there?* she wondered. *Do they just go down forever?*

"Sit," the priest commanded. She sat. "Now close your eyes, child." She closed her eyes. "This will hurt," he warned her, "but pain is the price of power. Do not move."

Still as stone, she thought. She sat unmoving. The cut was quick, the blade sharp. By rights the metal should have been cold against her flesh, but it felt warm instead. She could feel the blood washing down her face, a rippling red curtain falling across her brow and cheeks and chin, and she understood why the priest had made her close her eyes. When it reached her lips the taste was salt and copper. She licked at it and shivered.

"Bring me the face," said the kindly man. The waif made no answer, but she could hear her slippers whispering over the stone floor. To the girl he said, "Drink this," and pressed a cup into her hand. She drank it down at once. It was very tart, like biting into a lemon. A thousand years ago, she had known a girl who loved lemon cakes. *No, that was not me, that was only Arya.*

"Mummers change their faces with artifice," the kindly man was saying, "and sorcerers use glamors, weaving light and shadow and desire to make illusions that trick the eye. These arts you shall learn, but what we do here goes deeper. Wise men can see through artifice, and glamors dissolve before sharp eyes, but the face you are about to don will be as true and solid as that face you were born with. Keep your eyes closed." She felt his fingers brushing back her hair. "Stay still. This will feel queer. You may be dizzy, but you must not move."

Then came a tug and a soft rustling as the new face was pulled down over the old. The leather scraped across her brow, dry and stiff, but as her blood soaked into it, it softened and turned supple. Her cheeks grew warm, flushed. She could feel her heart fluttering beneath her breast, and for one long moment she could not catch her breath. Hands closed around her throat, hard as stone, choking her. Her own hands shot up to claw at the arms of her attacker, but there was no one there. A terrible sense of fear filled her, and she heard a noise, a hideous *crunch*ing noise, accompanied by blinding pain. A face floated in front of her, fat, bearded, brutal, his mouth twisted with rage. She heard the priest say, "Breathe, child. Breathe out the fear. Shake off the shadows. He is dead. She is dead. Her pain is gone. *Breathe*."

The girl took a deep shuddering breath, and realized it was true. No one was choking her, no one was hitting her. Even so, her hand was shaking as she raised it to her face. Flakes of dried blood crumbled at the touch of her fingertips, black in the lantern light. She felt her cheeks, touched her eyes, traced the line of her jaw. "My face is still the same."

"Is it? Are you certain?"

Was she certain? She had not felt any change, but maybe it was not something you could feel. She swept a hand down across her face from top to bottom, as she had once seen Jaqen H'ghar do, back at Harrenhal. When he did it, his whole face had rippled and changed. When she did it, nothing happened. "It feels the same."

"To you," said the priest. "It does not look the same."

"To other eyes, your nose and jaw are broken," said the waif. "One side of your face is caved in where your cheekbone shattered, and half your teeth are missing."

She probed around inside her mouth with her tongue, but found no holes or broken teeth. *Sorcery*, she thought. *I have a new face. An ugly, broken face.*

"You may have bad dreams for a time," warned the kindly man. "Her father beat her so often and so brutally that she was never truly free of pain or fear until she came to us."

"Did you kill him?"

"She asked the gift for herself, not for her father."

You should have killed him.

He must have read her thoughts. "Death came for him in the end, as it comes for all men. As it must come for a certain man upon the morrow." He lifted up the lamp. "We are done here."

For now. As they made their way back to the steps, the empty eyeholes of the skins upon the walls seemed to follow her. For a moment she could almost see their lips moving, whispering dark sweet secrets to one another in words too faint to hear.

Sleep did not come easily that night. Tangled in her blankets, she twisted this way and that in the cold dark room, but whichever way she turned, she saw the faces. *They have no eyes, but they can see me.* She saw her father's face upon the wall. Beside him hung her lady mother, and below them her three brothers all in a row. *No. That was some other girl. I am no one, and my only brothers wear robes of black and white.* Yet there was the black singer, there the stableboy she'd killed with Needle, there the pimply squire from the crossroads inn, and over there the guard whose throat she'd slashed to get them out of Harrenhal. The Tickler hung on the wall as well, the black holes that were his eyes swimming with malice. The sight of him brought back the feel of the dagger in her hand as she had plunged it into his back, again and again and again.

When at last day came to Braavos, it came grey and dark and overcast. The girl had hoped for fog, but the gods ignored her prayers as gods so often did. The air was clear and cold, and the wind had a nasty bite to it. *A good day for a death,* she thought. Unbidden, her prayer came to her lips. *Ser Gregor, Dunsen, Raff the Sweetling. Ser Ilyn, Ser Meryn, Queen Cersei.* She mouthed the names silently. In the House of Black and White, you never knew who might be listening.

The vaults were full of old clothing, garments claimed from those who came to the House of Black and White to drink peace from the temple pool. Everything from beggar's rags to rich silks and velvets could be found there. *An ugly girl should dress in ugly clothing,* she decided, so she chose a stained brown cloak fraying at the hem, a musty green tunic smelling of fish, and a pair of heavy boots. Last of all she palmed her finger knife.

There was no haste, so she decided to take the long way round to the Purple Harbor. Across the bridge she went, to the Isle of the Gods. Cat of the Canals had sold cockles and mussels amongst the temples here, whenever Brusco's daughter Talea had her moon blood flowing and took to her bed. She half-expected to see Talea selling there today, perhaps outside the Warren where all the forgotten godlings had their forlorn little shrines, but that was silly. The day was too cold, and Talea never liked to wake this early. The statue outside the shrine of the Weeping Lady of Lys was crying silver tears as the ugly girl walked by. In the Gardens of Gelenei stood a gilded tree a hundred feet high with leaves of hammered silver. Torchlight glimmered behind windows of leaded glass in the Lord of Harmony's wooden hall, showing half a hundred kinds of butterflies in all their bright colors.

One time, the girl remembered, the Sailor's Wife had walked her rounds with her and told her tales of the city's stranger gods. "That is the house of the Great Shepherd. Three-headed Trios has that tower with three turrets. The first head devours the dying, and the reborn emerge from the third. I don't know what the middle head's supposed to do. Those are the Stones of the Silent God, and there the entrance to the Pattern-maker's Maze. Only those who learn to walk it properly will ever find their way to wisdom, the priests of the Pattern say. Beyond it, by the canal, that's the temple of Aquan the Red Bull. Every thirteenth day, his priests slit the throat of a pure white calf, and offer bowls of blood to beggars."

Today was not the thirteenth day, it seemed; the Red Bull's steps were empty. The brother gods Semosh and Selloso dreamed in twin temples on opposite sides of the Black Canal, linked by a carved stone bridge. The girl crossed there and made her way down to the docks, then through the Ragman's Harbor and past the half-sunken spires and domes of the Drowned Town.

A group of Lysene sailors were staggering from the Happy Port as she went by, but the girl did not see any of the whores. The Ship was closed up and forlorn, its troupe of mummers no doubt still abed. But farther on, on the wharf beside an Ibbenese whaler, she spied Cat's old friend Tagganaro tossing a ball back and forth with Casso, King of Seals, whilst his latest cutpurse worked the crowd of onlookers. When she stopped to watch and listen for a moment, Tagganaro glanced at her without recognition, but Casso barked and clapped his flippers. *He knows me*, the girl thought, *or else he smells the fish.* She hurried on her way.

By the time she reached the Purple Harbor, the old man was ensconced inside the soup shop at his usual table, counting a purse of coins as he haggled with a ship's captain. The tall thin guard was hovering over him. The short thick one was seated near the door, where he would have a good view of anyone who entered. That made no matter. She did not intend to enter. Instead she perched atop a wooden piling twenty yards away as the blustery wind tugged at her cloak with ghostly fingers.

Even on a cold grey day like this, the harbor was a busy place. She saw sailors on the prowl for whores, and whores on the prowl for sailors. A pair of bravos passed in rumpled finery, leaning on each other as they staggered drunkenly past the docks, their blades rattling at their sides. A red priest swept past, his scarlet and crimson robes snapping in the wind.

It was almost noon before she saw the man she wanted, a prosperous shipowner she had seen doing business with the old man three times before. Big and bald and burly, he wore a heavy cloak of plush brown velvet trimmed with fur and a brown leather belt ornamented with silver moons and stars. Some mishap had left one leg stiff. He walked slowly, leaning on a cane.

He would do as well as any and better than most, the ugly girl decided. She hopped off the piling and fell in after him. A dozen strides put her right behind him, her finger knife poised. His purse was on his right side, at his belt, but his cloak was in her way. Her blade flashed out, smooth and quick, one deep slash through the velvet and he never felt a thing. Red Roggo would have smiled to see it. She slipped her hand through the gap, slit the purse open with the finger knife, filled her fist with gold . . .

The big man turned. "What—"

The movement tangled her arm in the folds of his cloak as she was pulling out her hand. Coins rained around their feet. *"Thief!"* The big man raised his stick to strike at her. She kicked his bad leg out from under him, danced away, and bolted as he fell, darting past a mother with a child. More coins fell from between her fingers to bounce along the ground. Shouts of *"thief, thief"* rang out behind her. A potbellied innkeep passing by made a clumsy grab for her arm, but she spun around him, flashed past a laughing whore, raced headlong for the nearest alley.

Cat of the Canals had known these alleys, and the ugly girl remembered. She darted left, vaulted a low wall, leapt across a small canal, and slipped through an unlocked door into some dusty storeroom. All sounds of pursuit had faded by then, but it was best to be sure. She hunkered down behind some crates and waited, arms wrapped around her knees. She waited for the best part of an hour, then decided it was safe to go, climbed straight up the side of the building, and made her way across the rooftops almost as far as the Canal of Heroes. By now the shipowner would have gathered up coins and cane and limped on to the soup shop. He might be drinking a bowl of hot broth and complaining to the old man about the ugly girl who had tried to rob his purse.

The kindly man was waiting for her at the House of Black and White, seated on the edge of the temple pool. The ugly girl sat next to him and put a coin on the lip of the pool between them. It was gold, with a dragon on one face and a king on the other.

"The golden dragon of Westeros," said the kindly man. "And how did you come by this? We are no thieves."

"It wasn't stealing. I took one of his, but I left him one of ours."

The kindly man understood. "And with that coin and the others in his purse, he paid a certain man. Soon after that man's heart gave out. Is that the way of it? Very sad." The priest picked up the coin and tossed it into the pool. "You have much and more to learn, but it may be you are not hopeless."

That night they gave her back the face of Arya Stark.

They brought a robe for her as well, the soft thick robe of an acolyte, black upon one side and white upon the other. "Wear this when you are here," the priest said, "but know that you shall have little need of it for the present. On the morrow you will go to Izembaro to begin your first apprenticeship. Take what clothes you will from the vaults below. The city watch is looking for a certain ugly girl, known to frequent the Purple Harbor, so best you have a new face as well." He cupped her chin, turned her head this way and that, nodded. "A pretty one this time, I think. As pretty as your own. Who are you, child?"

"No one," she replied.

CERSEI

On the last night of her imprisonment, the queen could not sleep. Each time she closed her eyes, her head filled with forebodings and fantasies of the morrow. *I will have guards*, she told herself. *They will keep the crowds away. No one will be allowed to touch me.* The High Sparrow had promised her that much.

Even so, she was afraid. On the day Myrcella sailed for Dorne, the day of the bread riots, gold cloaks had been posted all along the route of the procession, but the mob had broken through their lines to tear the old fat High Septon into pieces and rape Lollys Stokeworth half a hundred times. And if that pale soft stupid creature could incite the animals when fully clothed, how much more lust would a queen inspire?

Cersei paced her cell, restless as the caged lions that had lived in the bowels of Casterly Rock when she was a girl, a legacy of her grandfather's time. She and Jaime used to dare each other to climb into their cage, and once she worked up enough courage to slip her hand between two bars and touch one of the great tawny beasts. She was always bolder than her brother. The lion had turned his head to stare at her with huge golden eyes. Then he licked her fingers. His tongue was as rough as a rasp, but even so she would not pull her hand back, not until Jaime took her by the shoulders and yanked her away from the cage.

"Your turn," she told him afterward. "Pull his mane, I dare you." *He never did. I should have had the sword, not him.*

Barefoot and shivering she paced, a thin blanket draped about her shoulders. She was anxious for the day to come. By evening it would all be done. *A little walk and I'll be home, I'll be back with Tommen, in my own chambers inside Maegor's Holdfast.* Her uncle said it was the only way to save herself. Was it, though? She could not trust her uncle, no more than she trusted this High Septon. *I could still refuse. I could still insist upon my innocence and hazard all upon a trial.*

But she dare not let the Faith sit in judgment on her, as that Margaery Tyrell meant to do. That might serve the little rose well enough, but Cersei had few friends amongst the septas and sparrows around this new High Septon. Her only hope was trial by battle, and for that she must needs have a champion.

If Jaime had not lost his hand . . .

That road led nowhere, though. Jaime's sword hand was gone, and so was he, vanished with the woman Brienne somewhere in the riverlands. The queen had to find another defender or today's ordeal would be the least of her travails. Her enemies were accusing her of treason. She had to reach Tommen, no matter the costs. *He loves me. He will not refuse his own mother. Joff was stubborn and unpredictable, but Tommen is a good little boy, a good little king. He will do as he is told.* If she stayed here, she was doomed, and the only way she would return to the Red Keep was by walking. The High Sparrow had been adamant, and Ser Kevan refused to lift a finger against him.

"No harm will come to me today," Cersei said when the day's first light brushed her window. "Only my pride will suffer." The words rang hollow in her ears. *Jaime may yet come.* She pictured him riding through the morning mists, his golden armor bright in the light of the rising sun. *Jaime, if you ever loved me . . .*

When her gaolers came for her, Septa Unella, Septa Moelle, and Septa Scolera led the procession. With them were four novices and two of the silent sisters. The sight of the silent sisters in their grey robes filled the queen with sudden terrors. *Why are they here? Am I to die?* The silent sisters attended to the dead. "The High Septon promised that no harm would come to me."

"Nor will it." Septa Unella beckoned to the novices. They brought lye soap, a basin of warm water, a pair of shears, and a long straightrazor. The sight of the steel sent a shiver through her. *They mean to shave me. A little more humiliation, a raisin for my porridge.* She would not give them the pleasure of hearing her beg. *I am Cersei of House Lannister, a lion of the Rock, the rightful queen of these Seven Kingdoms, trueborn daughter of Tywin Lannister. And hair grows back.* "Get on with it," she said.

The elder of the two silent sisters took up the shears. A practiced barber, no doubt; her order often cleaned the corpses of the noble slain before returning them to their kin, and trimming beards and cutting hair was part of that. The woman bared the queen's head first. Cersei sat as still as a stone statue as the shears clicked. Drifts of golden hair fell to the floor. She had not been allowed to tend it properly penned up in this cell, but even unwashed and tangled it shone where the sun touched it. *My crown*, the queen thought. *They took the other crown away from me, and now they are stealing this one as well.* When her locks and curls were piled up around her feet, one of the novices soaped her head and the silent sister scraped away the stubble with a razor.

Cersei hoped that would be the end of it, but no. "Remove your shift, Your Grace," Septa Unella commanded.

"Here?" the queen asked. "Why?"

"You must be shorn."

Shorn, she thought, *like a sheep.* She yanked the shift over her head and tossed it to the floor. "Do what you will."

Then it was the soap again, the warm water, and the razor. The hair beneath her arms went next, then her legs, and last of all the fine golden down that covered her mound. When the silent sister crept between her legs with the razor, Cersei found herself remembering all the times that Jaime had knelt where she was kneeling now, planting kisses on the inside of her thighs, making her wet. His kisses were always warm. The razor was ice-cold.

When the deed was done she was as naked and vulnerable as a woman could be. *Not even a hair to hide behind.* A little laugh burst from her lips, bleak and bitter.

"Does Your Grace find this amusing?" said Septa Scolera.

"No, septa," said Cersei. *But one day I will have your tongue ripped out with hot pincers, and that will be hilarious.*

One of the novices had brought a robe for her, a soft white septa's robe to cover her as she made her way down the tower steps and through the sept, so any worshipers they met along the way might be spared the sight of naked flesh. *Seven save us all, what hypocrites they are.* "Will I be permitted a pair of sandals?" she asked. "The streets are filthy."

"Not so filthy as your sins," said Septa Moelle. "His High Holiness has commanded that you present yourself as the gods made you. Did you have sandals on your feet when you came forth from your lady mother's womb?"

"No, septa," the queen was forced to say.

"Then you have your answer."

A bell began to toll. The queen's long imprisonment was at an end. Cersei pulled the robe tighter, grateful for its warmth, and said, "Let us go." Her son awaited her across the city. The sooner she set out, the sooner she would see him.

The rough stone of the steps scraped her soles as Cersei Lannister made her descent. She had come to Baelor's Sept a queen, riding in a litter. She was leaving bald and barefoot. *But I am leaving. That is all that matters.*

The tower bells were singing, summoning the city to bear witness to her shame. The Great Sept of Baelor was crowded with faithful come for the dawn service, the sound of their prayers echoing off the dome overhead, but when the queen's procession made its appearance a sudden silence fell and a thousand eyes turned to follow her as she made her way down the aisle, past the place where her lord father had lain in state after his murder. Cersei swept by them, looking neither right nor left. Her bare feet slapped against the cold marble floor. She could feel the eyes. Behind their altars, the Seven seemed to watch as well.

In the Hall of Lamps, a dozen Warrior's Sons awaited her coming. Rainbow cloaks hung down their backs, and the crystals that crested their greathelms glittered in the lamplight. Their armor was silver plate polished to a mirror sheen, but underneath, she knew, every man of them wore a hair shirt. Their kite shields all bore the same device: a crystal sword shining in the darkness, the ancient badge of those the smallfolk called Swords.

Their captain knelt before her. "Perhaps Your Grace will recall me. I am Ser Theodan the True, and His High Holiness has given me command of your escort. My brothers and I will see you safely through the city."

Cersei's gaze swept across the faces of the men behind him. And there he was: Lancel, her cousin, Ser Kevan's son, who had once professed to love her, before he decided that he loved the gods more. *My blood and my betrayer.* She would not forget him. "You may rise, Ser Theodan. I am ready."

The knight stood, turned, raised a hand. Two of his men stepped to the towering doors and pushed them open, and Cersei walked through them into the open air, blinking at the sunlight like a mole roused from its burrow.

A gusty wind was blowing, and it set the bottom of her robe snapping and flapping at her legs. The morning air was thick with the old familiar stinks of King's Landing. She breathed in the scents of sour wine, bread baking, rotting fish and nightsoil, smoke and sweat and horse piss. No flower had ever smelled so sweet. Huddled in her robe, Cersei paused atop the marble steps as the Warrior's Sons formed up around her.

It came to her suddenly that she had stood in this very spot before, on the day Lord Eddard Stark had lost his head. *That was not supposed to happen. Joff was supposed to spare his life and send him to the Wall.* Stark's eldest son would have followed him as Lord of Winterfell, but Sansa would have stayed at court, a hostage. Varys and Littlefinger had worked out the terms, and Ned Stark had swallowed his precious honor and confessed his treason to save his daughter's empty little head. *I would have made Sansa a good marriage. A Lannister marriage. Not Joff, of course, but Lancel might have suited, or one of his younger brothers.* Petyr Baelish had offered to wed the girl himself, she recalled, but of course that was impossible; he was much too lowborn. *If Joff had only done as he was told, Winterfell would never have gone to war, and Father would have dealt with Robert's brothers.*

Instead Joff had commanded that Stark's head be struck off, and Lord Slynt and Ser Ilyn Payne had hastened to obey. *It was just there,* the queen recalled, gazing at the spot. Janos Slynt had lifted Ned Stark's head by the hair as his life's blood flowed down the steps, and after that there was no turning back.

The memories seemed so distant. Joffrey was dead, and all Stark's sons as well. Even her father had perished. And here she stood on the steps of the Great Sept again, only this time it was her the mob was staring at, not Eddard Stark.

The wide marble plaza below was as crowded as it had been on the day that Stark had died. Everywhere she looked the queen saw eyes. The mob seemed to be equal parts men and women. Some had children on their shoulders. Beggars and thieves, taverners and tradesfolk, tanners and stableboys and mummers, the poorer sort of whore, all the scum had come out to see a queen brought low. And mingled in with them were the Poor Fellows, filthy, unshaven creatures armed with spears and axes and clad in bits of dinted plate, rusted mail, and cracked leather, under roughspun surcoats bleached white and blazoned with the seven-pointed star of the Faith. The High Sparrow's ragged army.

Part of her still yearned for Jaime to appear and rescue her from this humiliation, but her twin was nowhere to be seen. Nor was her uncle present. That did not surprise her. Ser Kevan had made his views plain during his last visit; her shame must not be allowed to tarnish the honor of Casterly Rock. No lions would walk with her today. This ordeal was hers and hers alone.

Septa Unella stood to her right, Septa Moelle to her left, Septa Scolera behind her. If the queen should bolt or balk, the three hags would drag her back inside, and this time they would see to it that she never left her cell.

Cersei raised her head. Beyond the plaza, beyond the sea of hungry eyes and gaping mouths and dirty faces, across the city, Aegon's High Hill rose in the distance, the towers and battlements of the Red Keep blushing pink in the light of the rising sun. *It is not so far.* Once she reached its gates, the worst of her travails would be over. She would have her son again. She would have her champion. Her uncle had promised her. *Tommen is waiting for me. My little king. I can do this. I must.*

Septa Unella stepped forward. "A sinner comes before you," she declared. "She is Cersei of House Lannister, queen dowager, mother to His Grace King Tommen, widow of His Grace King Robert, and she has committed grievous falsehoods and fornications."

Septa Moelle moved up on the queen's right. "This sinner has confessed her sins and begged for absolution and forgiveness. His High Holiness has commanded her to demonstrate her repentance by putting aside all pride and artifice and presenting herself as the gods made her before the good people of the city."

Septa Scolera finished. "So now this sinner comes before you with a humble heart, shorn of secrets and concealments, naked before the eyes of gods and men, to make her walk of atonement."

Cersei had been a year old when her grandfather died. The first thing her father had done on his ascension was to expel his own father's grasping, lowborn mistress from Casterly Rock. The silks and velvets Lord Tytos had lavished on her and the jewelry she had taken for herself had been stripped from her, and she had been sent forth naked to walk through the streets of Lannisport, so the west could see her for what she was.

Though she had been too young to witness the spectacle herself, Cersei had heard the stories growing up from the mouths of washerwomen and guardsmen who had been there. They spoke of how the woman had wept and begged, of the desperate way she clung to her garments when she was commanded to disrobe, of her futile efforts to cover her breasts and her sex with her hands as she hobbled barefoot and naked through the streets to exile. "Vain and proud she was, before," she remembered one guard saying, "so haughty you'd think she'd forgot she come from dirt. Once we got her clothes off her, though, she was just another whore."

If Ser Kevan and the High Sparrow thought that it would be the same with her, they were very much mistaken. Lord Tywin's blood was in her. *I am a lioness. I will not cringe for them.*

The queen shrugged off her robe.

She bared herself in one smooth, unhurried motion, as if she were back in her own chambers disrobing for her bath with no one but her bedmaids looking on. When the cold wind touched her skin, she shivered violently. It took all her strength of will not to try and hide herself with her hands, as her grandfather's whore had done. Her fingers tightened into fists, her nails digging into her palms. They were looking at her, all the hungry eyes. But what were they seeing? *I am beautiful,* she reminded herself. How many times had Jaime told her that? Even Robert had given her that much, when he came to her bed in his cups to pay her drunken homage with his cock.

They looked at Ned Stark the same way, though.

She had to move. Naked, shorn, barefoot, Cersei made a slow descent down the broad marble steps. Gooseprickles rose on her arms and legs. She held her chin high, as a queen should, and her escort fanned out ahead of her. The Poor Fellows shoved men aside to open a way through the crowd whilst the Swords fell in on either side of her. Septa Unella, Septa Scolera, and Septa Moelle followed. Behind them came the novice girls in white.

"Whore!" someone cried out. A woman's voice. Women were always the cruelest where other women were concerned.

Cersei ignored her. *There will be more, and worse. These creatures have no sweeter joy in life than jeering at their betters.* She could not silence them, so she must pretend she did not hear them. She would not see them either. She would keep her eyes on Aegon's High Hill across the city, on the towers of the Red Keep shimmering in the light. That was where she would find her salvation, if her uncle had kept his part of their bargain.

He wanted this. Him and the High Sparrow. And the little rose as well, I do not doubt. I have sinned and must atone, must parade my shame before the eyes of every beggar in the city. They think that this will break my pride, that it will make an end to me, but they are wrong.

Septa Unella and Septa Moelle kept pace with her, with Septa Scolera scurrying behind, ringing a bell. *"Shame,"* the old hag called, *"shame upon the sinner, shame, shame."* Somewhere off to the right, another voice sang counterpoint to hers, some baker's boy shouting, "Meat pies, three pence, hot meat pies here." The marble underfoot was cold and slick, and Cersei had to step carefully for fear of slipping. Their path took them past the statue of Baelor the Blessed, standing tall and serene upon his plinth, his face a study in benevolence. To look at him, you would never guess what a fool he'd been. The Targaryen dynasty had produced kings both bad and good, but none as beloved as Baelor, that pious gentle septon-king who loved the smallfolk and the gods in equal parts, yet imprisoned his own sisters. It was a wonder that his statue did not crumble at the sight of her bare breasts. Tyrion used to say that King Baelor was terrified of his own cock. Once, she recalled, he had expelled all the whores from King's Landing. He prayed for them as they were driven from the city gates, the histories said, but would not look at them.

"Harlot," a voice screamed. Another woman. Something flew out of the crowd. Some rotted vegetable. Brown and oozing, it sailed above her head to splash at the foot of one of the Poor Fellows. *I am not afraid. I am a lioness.* She walked on. "Hot pies," the baker's boy was crying. "Getcha hot pies here." Septa Scolera rang her bell, singing, *"Shame, shame, shame upon the sinner, shame, shame."* The Poor Fellows went before them, forcing men aside with their shields, walling off a narrow path. Cersei followed where they led, her head held stiffly, her eyes on the far distance. Every step brought the Red Keep nearer. Every step brought her closer to her son and her salvation.

It seemed to take a hundred years to cross the plaza, but finally marble gave way to cobblestones beneath her feet, shops and stables and houses closed in all around them, and they began the descent of Visenya's Hill.

The going was slower here. The street was steep and narrow, the crowds jammed together tightly. The Poor Fellows shoved at those who blocked the way, trying to move them aside, but there was nowhere to go, and those in the back of the crowd were shoving back. Cersei tried to keep her head up, only to step in something slick and wet that made her slip. She might have fallen, but Septa Unella caught her arm and kept her on her feet. "Your Grace should watch where she sets her feet."

Cersei wrenched herself free. "Yes, septa," she said in a meek voice, though she was angry enough to spit. The queen walked on, clad only in gooseprickles and pride. She looked for the Red Keep, but it was hidden now, walled off from her gaze by the tall timbered buildings to either side. *"Shame, shame,"* sang Septa Scolera, her bell clanging. Cersei tried to walk faster, but soon came up against the backs of the Stars in front of her and had to slow her steps again. A man just ahead was selling skewers of roast meat from a cart, and the procession halted as the Poor Fellows moved him out of the way. The meat looked suspiciously like rat to Cersei's eyes, but the smell of it filled the air, and half the men around them were gnawing away with sticks in hand by the time the street was clear enough for her to resume her trek. "Want some, Your Grace?" one man called out. He was a big, burly brute with pig eyes, a massive gut, and an unkempt black beard that reminded her of Robert. When she looked away in disgust, he flung the skewer at her. It struck her on the leg and tumbled to the street, and the half-cooked meat left a smear of grease and blood down her thigh.

The shouting seemed louder here than on the plaza, perhaps because the mob was so much closer. "Whore" and "sinner" were most common, but "brotherfucker" and "cunt" and "traitor" were flung at her as well, and now and again she heard someone shout out for Stannis or Margaery. The cobbles underfoot were filthy, and there was so little space that the queen could not even walk around the puddles. *No one has ever died of wet feet,* she told herself. She wanted to believe the puddles were just rainwater, though horse piss was just as likely.

More refuse showered down from windows and balconies: half-rotted fruit, pails of beer, eggs that exploded into sulfurous stink when they cracked open on the ground. Then someone flung a dead cat over the Poor Fellows and Warrior's Sons alike. The carcass hit the cobbles so hard that it burst open, spattering her lower legs with entrails and maggots.

Cersei walked on. *I am blind and deaf, and they are worms,* she told herself. *"Shame, shame,"* the septas sang. "Chestnuts, hot roast chestnuts," a peddler cried. "Queen Cunt," a drunkard pronounced solemnly from a balcony above, lifting his cup to her in a mocking toast. "All hail the royal teats!" *Words are wind,* Cersei thought. *Words cannot harm me.*

Halfway down Visenya's Hill the queen fell for the first time, when her foot slipped in something that might have been nightsoil. When Septa Unella pulled her up, her knee was scraped and bloody. A ragged laugh rippled through the crowd, and some man shouted out an offer to kiss it and make it better. Cersei looked behind her. She could still see the great dome and seven crystal towers of the Great Sept of Baelor atop the hill. *Have I really come such a little way?* Worse, a hundred times worse, she had lost sight of the Red Keep. "Where . . . where . . . ?"

"Your Grace." The captain of her escort stepped up beside her. Cersei had forgotten his name. "You must continue. The crowd is growing unruly."

Yes, she thought. *Unruly.* "I am not afraid—"

"You should be." He yanked at her arm, pulling her along beside him. She staggered down the hill—downward, ever downward—wincing with every step, letting him support her. *It should be Jaime beside me.* He would draw his golden sword and slash a path right through the mob, carving the eyes out of the head of every man who dared to look at her.

The paving stones were cracked and uneven, slippery underfoot, and rough against her soft feet. Her heel came down on something sharp, a stone or piece of broken crockery. Cersei cried out in pain. "I asked for sandals," she spat at Septa Unella. "You could have given me sandals, you could have done that much." The knight wrenched at her arm again, as if she were some common serving wench. *Has he forgotten who I am?* She was the queen of Westeros; he had no right to lay rough hands on her.

Near the bottom of the hill, the slope gentled and the street began to widen. Cersei could see the Red Keep again, shining crimson in the morning sun atop Aegon's High Hill. *I must keep walking.* She wrenched free of Ser Theodan's grasp. "You do not need to drag me, ser." She limped on, leaving a trail of bloody footprints on the stones behind her.

She walked through mud and dung, bleeding, goosefleshed, hobbling. All around her was a babble of sound. "My wife has sweeter teats than those," a man shouted. A teamster cursed as the Poor Fellows ordered his wagon out of the way. "*Shame, shame, shame on the sinner,*" chanted the septas. "Look at this one," a whore called from a brothel window, lifting her skirts to the men below, "it's not had half as many cocks up it as hers." Bells were ringing, ringing, ringing. "That can't be the queen," a boy said, "she's saggy as my mum." *This is my penance,* Cersei told herself. *I have sinned most grievously, this is my atonement. It will be over soon, it will be behind me, then I can forget.*

The queen began to see familiar faces. A bald man with bushy side-whiskers frowned down from a window with her father's frown, and for an instant looked so much like Lord Tywin that she stumbled. A young girl sat beneath a fountain, drenched in spray, and stared at her with Melara Hetherspoon's accusing eyes. She saw Ned Stark, and beside him little Sansa with her auburn hair and a shaggy grey dog that might have been her wolf. Every child squirming through the crowd became her brother Tyrion, jeering at her as he had jeered when Joffrey died. And there was Joff as well, her son, her firstborn, her beautiful bright boy with his golden curls and his sweet smile, he had such lovely lips, he . . .

That was when she fell the second time.

She was shaking like a leaf when they pulled her to her feet. "Please," she said. "Mother have mercy. I confessed."

"You did," said Septa Moelle. "This is your atonement."

"It is not much farther," said Septa Unella. "See?" She pointed. "Up the hill, that's all."

Up the hill. That's all. It was true. They were at the foot of Aegon's High Hill, the castle above them.

"Whore," someone screamed.

"Brotherfucker," another voice added. "Abomination."

"Want a suck on this, Your Grace?" A man in a butcher's apron pulled his cock out of his breeches, grinning. It did not matter. She was almost home.

Cersei began to climb.

If anything, the jeers and shouts were cruder here. Her walk had not taken her through Flea Bottom, so its denizens had packed onto the lower slopes of Aegon's High Hill to see the show. The faces leering out at her from behind the shields and spears of the Poor Fellows seemed twisted, monstrous, hideous. Pigs and naked children were everywhere underfoot, crippled beggars and cutpurses swarmed like roaches through the press. She saw men whose teeth had been filed into points, hags with goiters as big as their heads, a whore with a huge striped snake draped about breasts and shoulders, a man whose cheeks and brow were covered with open sores that wept grey pus. They grinned and licked their lips and hooted at her as she went limping past, her breasts heaving with the effort of the climb. Some shouted obscene proposals, others insults. *Words are wind,* she thought, *words cannot hurt me. I am beautiful, the most beautiful woman in all Westeros, Jaime says so, Jaime would never lie to me. Even Robert, Robert never loved me, but he saw that I was beautiful, he wanted me.*

She did not feel beautiful, though. She felt old, used, filthy, ugly. There were stretch marks on her belly from the children she had borne, and her breasts were not as firm as they had been when she was younger. Without a gown to hold them up, they sagged against her chest. *I should not have done this. I was their queen, but now they've seen, they've seen, they've seen. I should never have let them see.* Gowned and crowned, she was a queen. Naked, bloody, limping, she was only a woman, not so very different from their wives, more like their mothers than their pretty little maiden daughters. *What have I done?*

There was something in her eyes, stinging, blurring her sight. She could not cry, she would not cry, the worms must never see her weep. Cersei rubbed her eyes with the heels of her hands. A gust of cold wind made her shiver violently.

And suddenly the hag was there, standing in the crowd with her pendulous teats and her warty greenish skin, leering with the rest, with malice shining from her crusty yellow eyes. *"Queen you shall be,"* she hissed, *"until there comes another, younger and more beautiful, to cast you down and take all you hold most dear."*

And then there was no stopping the tears. They burned down the queen's cheeks like acid. Cersei gave a sharp cry, covered her nipples with one arm, slid her other hand down to hide her slit, and began to run, shoving her way past the line of Poor Fellows, crouching as she scrambled crab-legged up the hill. Partway up she stumbled and fell, rose, then fell again ten yards farther on. The next thing she knew she was crawling, scrambling uphill on all fours like a dog as the good folks of King's Landing made way for her, laughing and jeering and applauding her.

Then all at once the crowd parted and seemed to dissolve, and there were the castle gates before her, and a line of spearmen in gilded half-helms and crimson cloaks. Cersei heard the gruff, familiar sound of her uncle growling orders and glimpsed a flash of white to either side as Ser Boros Blount and Ser Meryn Trant strode toward her in their pale plate and snowy cloaks. "My son," she cried. "Where is my son? Where is Tommen?"

"Not here. No son should have to bear witness to his mother's shame." Ser Kevan's voice was harsh. "Cover her up."

Then Jocelyn was bending over her, wrapping her in a soft clean blanket of green wool to cover her nakedness. A shadow fell across them both, blotting out the sun. The queen felt cold steel slide beneath her, a pair of great armored arms lifting her off the ground, lifting her up into the air as easily as she had lifted Joffrey when he was still a babe. A *giant*, thought Cersei, dizzy, as he carried her with great strides toward the gatehouse. She had heard that giants could still be found in the godless wild beyond the Wall. *That is just a tale. Am I dreaming?*

No. Her savior was real. Eight feet tall or maybe taller, with legs as thick around as trees, he had a chest worthy of a plow horse and shoulders that would not disgrace an ox. His armor was plate steel, enameled white and bright as a maiden's hopes, and worn over gilded mail. A greathelm hid his face. From its crest streamed seven silken plumes in the rainbow colors of the Faith. A pair of golden seven-pointed stars clasped his billowing cloak at the shoulders.

A white cloak.

Ser Kevan had kept his part of the bargain. Tommen, her precious little boy, had named her champion to the Kingsguard.

Cersei never saw where Qyburn came from, but suddenly he was there beside them, scrambling to keep up with her champion's long strides. "Your Grace," he said, "it is so good to have you back. May I have the honor of presenting our newest member of the Kingsguard? This is Ser Robert Strong."

"Ser Robert," Cersei whispered, as they entered the gates.

"If it please Your Grace, Ser Robert has taken a holy vow of silence," Qyburn said. "He has sworn that he will not speak until all of His Grace's enemies are dead and evil has been driven from the realm."

Yes, thought Cersei Lannister. *Oh, yes.*

TYRION

The pile of parchments was formidably high. Tyrion looked at it and sighed. "I had understood you were a band of brothers. Is this the love a brother bears a brother? Where is the trust? The friendship, the fond regard, the deep affection that only men who have fought and bled together can ever know?"

"All in time," said Brown Ben Plumm.

"After you sign," said Inkpots, sharpening a quill.

Kasporio the Cunning touched his sword hilt. "If you would like to start the bleeding now, I will happ'ly oblige you."

"How kind of you to offer," said Tyrion. "I think not."

Inkpots placed the parchments before Tyrion and handed him the quill. "Here is your ink. From Old Volantis, this. 'Twill last as long as proper maester's black. All you need do is sign and pass the notes to me. I'll do the rest."

Tyrion gave him a crooked grin. "Might I read them first?"

"If you like. They are all the same, by and large. Except for the ones at the bottom, but we'll get to those in due course."

Oh, I am sure we will. For most men, there was no cost to joining a company, but he was not most men. He dipped the quill into the inkpot, leaned over the first parchment, paused, looked up. "Would you prefer me to sign *Yollo* or *Hugor Hill?*"

Brown Ben crinkled up his eyes. "Would you prefer to be returned to Yezzan's heirs or just beheaded?"

The dwarf laughed and signed the parchment, *Tyrion of House Lannister.* As he passed it left to Inkpots, he riffled through the pile underneath. "There are . . . what, fifty? Sixty? I'd thought there were five hundred Second Sons."

"Five hundred thirteen at present," Inkpots said. "When you sign our book, we will be five hundred fourteen."

"So only one in ten receives a note? That hardly seems fair. I thought you were all share-and-share-alike in the free companies." He signed another sheet.

Brown Ben chuckled. "Oh, all share. But not alike. The Second Sons are not unlike a family . . ."

". . . and every family has its drooling cousins." Tyrion signed another note. The parchment crinkled crisply as he slid it toward the paymaster. "There are cells down in the bowels of Casterly Rock where my lord father kept the worst of ours." He dipped his quill in the inkpot. *Tyrion of House Lannister*, he scratched out, promising to pay the bearer of the note one hundred golden dragons. *Every stroke of the quill leaves me a little poorer . . . or would, if I were not a beggar to begin with.* One day he might rue these signatures. *But not this day.* He blew on the wet ink, slid the parchment to the paymaster, and signed the one beneath. And again. And again. And again. "This wounds me deeply, I will have you know," he told them between signatures. "In Westeros, the word of a Lannister is considered good as gold."

Inkpots shrugged. "This is not Westeros. On this side of the narrow sea, we put our promises on paper." As each sheet was passed to him, he scattered fine sand across the signature to drink up excess ink, shook it off, and set the note aside. "Debts written on the wind tend to be . . . forgotten, shall we say?"

"Not by us." Tyrion signed another sheet. And another. He had found a rhythm now. "A Lannister always pays his debts."

Plumm chuckled. "Aye, but a sellsword's word is worthless."

Well, yours is, thought Tyrion, *and thank the gods for that.* "True, but I will not be a sellsword until I've signed your book."

"Soon enough," said Brown Ben. "After the notes."

"I am dancing as fast as I can." He wanted to laugh, but that would have ruined the game. Plumm was enjoying this, and Tyrion had no intention of spoiling his fun. *Let him go on thinking that he's bent me over and fucked me up the arse, and I'll go on buying steel swords with parchment dragons.* If ever he went back to Westeros to claim his birthright, he would have all the gold of Casterly Rock to make good on his promises. If not, well, he'd be dead, and his new brothers could wipe their arses with these parchments. Perhaps some might turn up in King's Landing with their scraps in hand, hoping to convince his sweet sister to make good on them. *And would that I could be a roach in the rushes to witness that.*

The writing on the parchments changed about halfway down the pile. The hundred-dragon notes were all for serjeants. Below them the amounts suddenly grew larger. Now Tyrion was promising to pay the bearer one thousand golden dragons. He shook his head, laughed, signed. And again. And again. "So," he said as he was scrawling, "what will be my duties with the company?"

"You are too ugly to be Bokkoko's butt boy," said Kasporio, "but you might do as arrow fodder."

"Better than you know," said Tyrion, refusing to rise to the bait. "A small man with a big shield will drive the archers mad. A wiser man than you once told me that."

"You will work with Inkpots," said Brown Ben Plumm.

"You will work *for* Inkpots," said Inkpots. "Keeping books, counting coin, writing contracts and letters."

"Gladly," said Tyrion. "I love books."

"What else would you do?" sneered Kasporio. "Look at you. You are not fit to fight."

"I once had charge of all the drains in Casterly Rock," Tyrion said mildly. "Some of them had been stopped up for years, but I soon had them draining merrily away." He dipped the quill in the ink again. Another dozen notes, and he would be done. "Perhaps I could supervise your camp followers. We can't have the men stopped up, now can we?"

That jape did not please Brown Ben. "Stay away from the whores," he warned. "Most o' them are poxy, and they talk. You're not the first escaped slave to join the company, but that don't mean we need to shout your presence. I won't have you parading about where you might be seen. Stay inside as much as you can, and shit into your bucket. Too many eyes at the latrines. And never go beyond our camp without my leave. We can dress you up in squire's steel, pretend you're Jorah's butt boy, but there's some will see right through that. Once Meereen is taken and we're away to Westeros, you can prance about all you like in gold and crimson. Till then, though . . ."

". . . I shall live beneath a rock and never make a sound. You have my word on that." *Tyrion of House Lannister*, he signed once more, with a flourish. That was the last parchment. Three notes remained, different from the rest. Two were written on fine vellum and made out by name. For Kasporio the Cunning, ten thousand dragons. The same for Inkpots, whose true name appeared to be Tybero Istarion. *"Tybero?"* said Tyrion. "That sounds almost Lannister. Are you some long-lost cousin?"

"Perhaps. I always pay my debts as well. It is expected of a paymaster. Sign."

He signed.

Brown Ben's note was the last. That one had been inscribed upon a sheepskin scroll. *One hundred thousand golden dragons, fifty hides of fertile land, a castle, and a lordship. Well and well. This Plumm does not come cheaply.* Tyrion plucked at his scar and wondered if he ought to make a show of indignation. When you bugger a man you expect a squeal or two. He could curse and swear and rant of robbery, refuse to sign for a time, then give in reluctantly, protesting all the while. But he was sick of mummery, so instead he grimaced, signed, and handed the scroll back to Brown Ben. "Your cock is as big as in the stories," he said. "Consider me well and truly fucked, Lord Plumm."

Brown Ben blew on his signature. "My pleasure, Imp. And now, we make you one o' us. Inkpots, fetch the book."

The book was leather-bound with iron hinges, and large enough to eat your supper off. Inside its heavy wooden boards were names and dates going back more than a century. "The Second Sons are amongst the oldest of the free companies," Inkpots said as he was turning pages. "This is the fourth book. The names of every man to serve with us are written here. When they joined, where they fought, how long they served, the manner of their deaths—all in the book. You will find famous names in here, some from your Seven Kingdoms. Aegor Rivers served a year with us, before he left to found the Golden Company. Bittersteel, you call him. The Bright Prince, Aerion Targaryen, he was a Second Son. And Rodrik Stark, the Wandering Wolf, him as well. No, not that ink. Here, use this." He unstoppered a new pot and set it down.

Tyrion cocked his head. "Red ink?"

"A tradition of the company," Inkpots explained. "There was a time when each new man wrote his name in his own blood, but as it happens, blood makes piss-poor ink."

"Lannisters love tradition. Lend me your knife."

Inkpots raised an eyebrow, shrugged, slipped his dagger from its sheath, and handed it across hiltfirst. *It still hurts, Halfmaester, thank you very much,* thought Tyrion, as he pricked the ball of his thumb. He squeezed a fat drop of blood into the inkpot, traded the dagger for a fresh quill, and scrawled, *Tyrion of House Lannister, Lord of Casterly*

Rock, in a big bold hand, just below Jorah Mormont's far more modest signature.

And it's done. The dwarf rocked back on the camp stool. "Is that all that you require of me? Don't I need to swear an oath? Kill a baby? Suck the captain's cock?"

"Suck whatever you like." Inkpots turned the book around and dusted the page with a bit of fine sand. "For most of us, the signature suffices, but I would hate to disappoint a new brother-in-arms. Welcome to the Second Sons, Lord Tyrion."

Lord Tyrion. The dwarf liked the sound of that. The Second Sons might not enjoy the shining reputation of the Golden Company, but they had won some famous victories over the centuries. "Have other lords served with the company?"

"Landless lords," said Brown Ben. "Like you, Imp."

Tyrion hopped down from the stool. "My previous brother was entirely unsatisfactory. I hope for more from my new ones. Now how do I go about securing arms and armor?"

"Will you want a pig to ride as well?" asked Kasporio.

"Why, I did not know your wife was in the company," said Tyrion. "That's kind of you to offer her, but I would prefer a horse."

The bravo reddened, but Inkpots laughed aloud and Brown Ben went so far as to chuckle. "Inkpots, show him to the wagons. He can have his pick from the company steel. The girl too. Put a helm on her, a bit o' mail, might be some will take her for a boy."

"Lord Tyrion, with me." Inkpots held the tent flap to let him waddle through. "I will have Snatch take you to the wagons. Get your woman and meet him by the cook tent."

"She is not my woman. Perhaps you should get her. All she does of late is sleep and glare at me."

"You need to beat her harder and fuck her more often," the paymaster offered helpfully. "Bring her, leave her, do what you will. Snatch will not care. Come find me when you have your armor, and I will start you on the ledgers."

"As you wish."

Tyrion found Penny asleep in a corner of their tent, curled up on a thin straw pallet beneath a heap of soiled bedclothes. When he touched her with the toe of his boot, she rolled over, blinked at him, and yawned. "Hugor? What is it?"

"Talking again, are we?" It was better than her usual sullen silence. *All over an abandoned dog and pig. I saved the two of us from slavery, you would think some gratitude might be in order.* "If you sleep any longer, you're like to miss the war."

"I'm sad." She yawned again. "And tired. So tired."

Tired or sick? Tyrion knelt beside her pallet. "You look pale." He felt her brow. *Is it hot in here, or does she have a touch of fever?* He dared not ask that question aloud. Even hard men like the Second Sons were terrified of mounting the pale mare. If they thought Penny was sick, they would drive her off without a moment's hesitation. *They might even return us to Yezzan's heirs, notes or no notes.* "I have signed their book. The old way, in blood. I am now a Second Son."

Penny sat up, rubbing the sleep from her eyes. "What about me? Can I sign too?"

"I think not. Some free companies have been known to take women, but . . . well, they are not Second Daughters, after all."

"*We,*" she said. "If you're one of them, you should say *we,* not *they.* Has anyone seen Pretty Pig? Inkpots said he'd ask after her. Or Crunch, has there been word of Crunch?"

Only if you trust Kasporio. Plumm's not-so-cunning second-in-command claimed that three Yunkish slave-catchers were prowling through the camps, asking after a pair of escaped dwarfs. One of them was carrying a tall spear with a dog's head impaled upon its point, the way that Kaspo told it. Such tidings were not like to get Penny out of bed, however. "No word as yet," he lied. "Come. We need to find some armor for you."

She gave him a wary look. "Armor? Why?"

"Something my old master-at-arms told me. 'Never go to battle naked, lad,' he said. I take him at his word. Besides, now that I'm a sellsword, I really ought to have a sword to sell." She still showed no signs of moving. Tyrion seized her by the wrist, pulled her to her feet, and threw a fistful of clothing into her face. "Dress. Wear the cloak with the hood and keep your head down. We're supposed to be a pair of likely lads, just in case the slave-catchers are watching."

Snatch was waiting by the cook tent chewing sourleaf when the two dwarfs turned up, cloaked and hooded. "I hear the two o' you are going to fight for us," the serjeant said. "That should have them pissing in Meereen. Either o' you ever killed a man?"

"I have," said Tyrion. "I swat them down like flies."

"What with?"

"An axe, a dagger, a choice remark. Though I'm deadliest with my crossbow."

Snatch scratched at his stubble with the point of his hook. "Nasty thing, a crossbow. How many men you kill with that?"

"Nine." His father counted for at least that many, surely. Lord of Casterly Rock, Warden of the West, Shield of Lannisport, Hand of the King, husband, brother, father, father, father.

"Nine." Snatch snorted and spat out a mouthful of red slime. Aiming for Tyrion's feet, perhaps, but it landed on his knee. Plainly that was what he thought of "nine." The serjeant's fingers were stained a mottled red from the juice of the sourleaf he chewed. He put two of them into his mouth and whistled. "*Kem!* Get over here, you fucking pisspot." Kem came running. "Take Lord and Lady Imp to the wagons, have Hammer fix them up with some company steel."

"Hammer might be passed-out drunk," Kem cautioned.

"Piss in his face. That'll wake him up." Snatch turned back to Tyrion and Penny. "We never had no bloody dwarfs before, but boys we never lacked for. Sons o' this whore or that one, little fools run off from home to have adventures, butt boys, squires, and the like. Some o' their shit might be small enough to fit imps. It's the shit they were wearing when they died, like as not, but I know that won't bother fuckers fierce as you two. Nine, was it?" He shook his head and walked away.

The Second Sons kept their company armor in six big wayns drawn up near the center of their camp. Kem led the way, swinging his spear as if it were a staff. "How does a King's Landing lad end up with a free company?" Tyrion asked him.

The lad gave him a wary squint. "Who told you I was from King's Landing?"

"No one." *Every word out of your mouth reeks of Flea Bottom.* "Your wits gave you away. There's no one clever as a Kingslander, they say."

That seemed to startle him. "Who says that?"

"Everyone." *Me.*

"Since when?"

Since I just made it up. "For ages," he lied. "My father was wont to say it. Did you know Lord Tywin, Kem?"

"The Hand. Once I saw him riding up the hill. His men had red cloaks and little lions on their helms. I liked those helms." His mouth tightened. "I never liked the Hand, though. He sacked the city. And then he smashed us on the Blackwater."

"You were there?"

"With Stannis. Lord Tywin come up with Renly's ghost and took us in the flank. I dropped my spear and ran, but at the ships this bloody knight said, 'Where's your spear, boy? We got no room for cravens,' and they buggered off and left me, and thousands more besides. Later I heard how your father was sending them as fought with Stannis to the Wall, so I made my way across the narrow sea and joined up with the Second Sons."

"Do you miss King's Landing?"

"Some. I miss this boy, he . . . he was a friend of mine. And my brother, Kennet, but he died on the bridge of ships."

"Too many good men died that day." Tyrion's scar was itching fiercely. He picked at it with a fingernail.

"I miss the food too," Kem said wistfully.

"Your mother's cooking?"

"Rats wouldn't eat my mother's cooking. There was this pot shop, though. No one ever made a bowl o' brown like them. So thick you could stand your spoon up in the bowl, with chunks of this and that. You ever have yourself a bowl o' brown, Halfman?"

"A time or two. Singer's stew, I call it."

"Why's that?"

"It tastes so good it makes me want to sing."

Kem liked that. "Singer's stew. I'll ask for that next time I get back to Flea Bottom. What do you miss, Halfman?"

Jaime, thought Tyrion. *Shae. Tysha. My wife, I miss my wife, the wife I hardly knew.* "Wine, whores, and wealth," he answered. "Especially the wealth. Wealth will buy you wine and whores." *It will also buy you swords, and the Kems to wield them.*

"Is it true the chamber pots in Casterly Rock are made of solid gold?" Kem asked him.

"You should not believe everything you hear. Especially where House Lannister is concerned."

"They say all Lannisters are twisty snakes."

"Snakes?" Tyrion laughed. "That sound you hear is my lord father, slithering in his grave. We are *lions*, or so we like to say. But it makes no matter, Kem. Step on a snake or a lion's tail, you'll end up just as dead."

By then they had reached the armory, such as it was. The smith, this fabled Hammer, proved to be a freakish-looking hulk with a left arm that appeared twice as thick as his right. "He's drunk more than not," Kem said. "Brown Ben lets it go, but one day we'll get us a real armorer." Hammer's apprentice was a wiry red-haired youth called Nail. *Of course. What else?* mused Tyrion. Hammer was sleeping off a drunk when they reached the forge, just as Kem had prophesied, but Nail had no objection to the two dwarfs clambering through the wagons. "Crap iron, most of it," he warned them, "but you're welcome to anything you can use."

Under roofs of bent wood and stiffened leather, the wagon beds were heaped high with old weaponry and armor. Tyrion took one look and sighed, remembering the gleaming racks of swords and spears and halberds in the armory of the Lannisters below Casterly Rock. "This may take a while," he declared.

"There's sound steel here if you can find it," a deep voice growled. "None of it is pretty, but it will stop a sword."

A big knight stepped down from the back of a wagon, clad head to heel in company steel. His left greave did not match his right, his gorget was spotted with rust, his vambraces rich and ornate, inlaid with niello flowers. On his right hand was a gauntlet of lobstered steel, on his left a fingerless mitt of rusted mail. The nipples on his muscled breastplate had a pair of iron rings through them. His greathelm sported a ram's horns, one of which was broken.

When he took it off, he revealed the battered face of Jorah Mormont.

He looks every inch a sellsword and not at all like the half-broken thing we took from Yezzan's cage, Tyrion reflected. His bruises had mostly faded by now, and the swelling in his face had largely subsided, so Mormont looked almost human once again . . . though only vaguely like himself. The demon's mask the slavers had burned into his right cheek to mark him for a dangerous and disobedient slave would never leave him. Ser Jorah had never been what one might call a comely man. The brand had transformed his face into something frightening.

Tyrion grinned. "As long as I look prettier than you, I will be happy." He turned to Penny. "You take that wagon. I'll start with this one."

"It will go faster if we look together." She plucked up a rusted iron halfhelm, giggled, and stuck it on her head. "Do I look fearsome?"

You look like a mummer girl with a pot on her head. "That's a halfhelm. You want a greathelm." He found one, and swapped it for the halfhelm.

"It's too big." Penny's voice echoed hollowly inside the steel. "I can't see out." She took the helm off and flung it aside. "What's wrong with the halfhelm?"

"It's open-faced." Tyrion pinched her nose. "I am fond of looking at your nose. I would rather that you kept it."

Her eyes got big. "You like my nose?"

Oh, Seven save me. Tyrion turned away and began rooting amongst some piles of old armor toward the back of the wagon.

"Are there any other parts of me you like?" Penny asked.

Perhaps she meant that to sound playful. It sounded sad instead. "I am fond of all of your parts," Tyrion said, in hopes of ending any further discussion of the subject, "and even fonder of mine own."

"Why should we need armor? We're only mummers. We just *pretend* to fight."

"You pretend very well," said Tyrion, examining a shirt of heavy iron mail so full of holes that it almost looked moth-eaten. *What sort of moths eat chainmail?* "Pretending to be dead is one way to survive a battle. Good armor is another." *Though there is precious little of that here, I fear.* At the Green Fork, he had fought in mismatched scraps of plate from Lord Lefford's wagons, with a spiked bucket helm that made it look as if someone had upended a slops pail over his head. This company steel was worse. Not just old and ill fitting, but dinted, cracked, and brittle. *Is that dried blood, or only rust?* He sniffed at it but still could not be sure.

"Here's a crossbow." Penny showed it to him.

Tyrion glanced at it. "I cannot use a stirrup winch. My legs are not long enough. A crank would serve me better." Though, if truth be told, he did not want a crossbow. They took too long to reload. Even if he lurked by the latrine ditch waiting for some enemy to take a squat, the chances of his losing more than one quarrel would not be good.

Instead he picked up a morningstar, gave it a swing, put it down again. *Too heavy.* He passed over a warhammer (too long), a studded mace (also too heavy), and half a dozen longswords before he found a dirk he liked, a nasty piece of steel with a triangular blade. "This might serve," he said. The blade had a bit of rust on it, but that would only make it nastier. He found a wood-and-leather sheath that fit and slipped the dirk inside.

"A little sword for a little man?" joked Penny.

"It's a dirk and made for a big man." Tyrion showed her an old longsword. "This is a sword. Try it."

Penny took it, swung it, frowned. "Too heavy."

"Steel weighs more than wood. Chop through a man's neck with that thing, though, and his head is not like to turn into a melon." He took the sword back from her and inspected it more closely. "Cheap steel. And notched. Here, see? I take back what I said. You need a better blade to hack off heads."

"I don't *want* to hack off heads."

"Nor should you. Keep your cuts below the knee. Calf, hamstring, ankle . . . even giants fall if you slice their feet off. Once they're down, they're no bigger than you."

Penny looked as though she was about to cry. "Last night I dreamed my brother was alive again. We were jousting before some great lord, riding Crunch and Pretty Pig, and men were throwing roses at us. We were so happy . . ."

Tyrion slapped her.

It was a soft blow, all in all, a little flick of the wrist, with hardly any force behind it. It did not even leave a mark upon her cheek. But her eyes filled with tears all the same.

"If you want to dream, go back to sleep," he told her. "When you wake up, we'll still be escaped slaves in the middle of a siege. Crunch is dead. The pig as well, most like. Now find some armor and put it on, and never mind where it pinches. The mummer show is over. Fight or hide or shit yourself, as you like, but whatever you decide to do, you'll do it clad in steel."

Penny touched the cheek he'd slapped. "We should never have run. We're not sellswords. We're not any kind of swords. It wasn't so bad with Yezzan. It wasn't. Nurse was cruel sometimes but Yezzan never was. We were his favorites, his . . . his . . ."

"*Slaves.* The word you want is *slaves.*"

"Slaves," she said, flushing. "We were his *special* slaves, though. Just like Sweets. His treasures."

His pets, thought Tyrion. *And he loved us so much that he sent us to the pit, to be devoured by lions.*

She was not all wrong. Yezzan's slaves ate better than many peasants back in the Seven Kingdoms and were less like to starve to death come winter. Slaves were chattels, aye. They could be bought and sold, whipped and branded, used for the carnal pleasure of their owners, bred to make more slaves. In that sense they were no more than dogs or horses. But most lords treated their dogs and horses well enough. Proud men might shout that they would sooner die free than live as slaves, but pride was cheap. When the steel struck the flint, such men were rare as dragon's teeth; elsewise the world would not have been so full of slaves. *There has never been a slave who did not choose to be a slave,* the dwarf reflected. *Their choice may be between bondage and death, but the choice is always there.*

Tyrion Lannister did not except himself. His tongue had earned him some stripes on the back in the beginning, but soon enough he had learned the tricks of pleasing Nurse and the noble Yezzan. Jorah Mormont had fought longer and harder, but he would have come to the same place in the end.

And Penny, well . . .

Penny had been searching for a new master since the day her brother Groat had lost his head. *She wants someone to take care of her, someone to tell her what to do.*

It would have been too cruel to say so, however. Instead Tyrion said, "Yezzan's special slaves did not escape the pale mare. They're dead, the lot of them. Sweets was the first to go." Their mammoth master had died on the day of their escape, Brown Ben Plumm had told him. Neither he nor Kasporio nor any of the other sellswords knew the fate of the denizens of Yezzan's grotesquerie . . . but if Pretty Penny needed lies to stop her mooning, lie to her he would. "If you want to be a slave again, I will find you a kind master when this war is done, and sell you for enough gold to get me home," Tyrion promised her. "I'll find you some nice Yunkishman to give you another pretty golden collar, with little bells on it that will tinkle everywhere you go. First, though, you will need to survive what's coming. No one buys dead mummers."

"Or dead dwarfs," said Jorah Mormont. "We are all like to be feeding worms by the time this battle is done. The Yunkai'i have lost this war, though it may take them some time to know it. Meereen has an army of Unsullied infantry, the finest in the world. And Meereen has dragons. Three of them, once the queen returns. She will. She must. Our side consists of two score Yunkish lordlings, each with his own half-trained monkey men. Slaves on stilts, slaves in chains . . . they may have troops of blind men and palsied children too, I would not put it past them."

"Oh, I know," said Tyrion. "The Second Sons are on the losing side. They need to turn their cloaks again and do it now." He grinned. "Leave that to me."

THE KINGBREAKER

A pale shadow and a dark, the two conspirators came together in the quiet of the armory on the Great Pyramid's second level, amongst racks of spears, sheaves of quarrels, and walls hung with trophies from forgotten battles.

"Tonight," said Skahaz mo Kandaq. The brass face of a blood bat peered out from beneath the hood of his patchwork cloak. "All my men will be in place. The word is *Groleo*."

"*Groleo*." *That is fitting, I suppose.* "Yes. What was done to him . . . you were at court?"

"One guardsman amongst forty. All waiting for the empty tabard on the throne to speak the command so we might cut down Bloodbeard and the rest. Do you think the Yunkai'i would ever have dared present *Daenerys* with the head of her hostage?"

No, thought Selmy. "Hizdahr seemed distraught."

"Sham. His own kin of Loraq were returned unharmed. You saw. The Yunkai'i played us a mummer's farce, with noble Hizdahr as chief mummer. The issue was never Yurkhaz zo Yunzak. The other slavers would gladly have trampled that old fool themselves. This was to give Hizdahr a pretext to kill the dragons."

Ser Barristan chewed on that. "Would he dare?"

"He dared to kill his queen. Why not her pets? If we do not act, Hizdahr will hesitate for a time, to give proof of his reluctance and allow the Wise Masters the chance to rid him of the Stormcrow and the bloodrider. *Then* he will act. They want the dragons dead before the Volantene fleet arrives."

Aye, they would. It all fit. That did not mean Barristan Selmy liked it any better. "That will not happen." His queen was the Mother of Dragons; he would not allow her children to come to harm. "The hour of the wolf.

The blackest part of night, when all the world's asleep." He had first heard those words from Tywin Lannister outside the walls of Duskendale. *He gave me a day to bring out Aerys. Unless I returned with the king by dawn of the following day, he would take the town with steel and fire, he told me. It was the hour of the wolf when I went in and the hour of the wolf when we emerged.* "Grey Worm and the Unsullied will close and bar the gates at first light."

"Better to attack at first light," Skahaz said. "Burst from the gates and swarm across the siege lines, smash the Yunkai'i as they come stumbling from their beds."

"No." The two of them had argued this before. "There is a peace, signed and sealed by Her Grace the queen. We will not be the first to break it. Once we have taken Hizdahr, we will form a council to rule in his place and demand that the Yunkai'i return our hostages and withdraw their armies. Should they refuse, then and only then will we inform them that the peace is broken, and go forth to give them battle. Your way is dishonorable."

"Your way is stupid," the Shavepate said. "The hour is ripe. Our freedmen are ready. Hungry."

That much was true, Selmy knew. Symon Stripeback of the Free Brothers and Mollono Yos Dob of the Stalwart Shields were both eager for battle, intent on proving themselves and washing out all the wrongs they had suffered in a tide of Yunkish blood. Only Marselen of the Mother's Men shared Ser Barristan's doubts. "We discussed this. You agreed it would be my way."

"I agreed," the Shavepate grumbled, "but that was before Groleo. The head. The slavers have no honor."

"We do," said Ser Barristan.

The Shavepate muttered something in Ghiscari, then said, "As you wish. Though we will rue your old man's honor before this game is done, I think. What of Hizdahr's guards?"

"His Grace keeps two men by him when he sleeps. One on the door of his bedchamber, a second within, in an adjoining alcove. Tonight it will be Khrazz and Steelskin."

"Khrazz," the Shavepate grumbled. "That I do not like."

"It need not come to blood," Ser Barristan told him. "I mean to talk to Hizdahr. If he understands we do not intend to kill him, he may command his guards to yield."

"And if not? Hizdahr must not escape us."

"He will not escape." Selmy did not fear Khrazz, much less Steelskin.

They were only pit fighters. Hizdahr's fearsome collection of former fighting slaves made indifferent guards at best. Speed and strength and ferocity they had, and some skill at arms as well, but blood games were poor training for protecting kings. In the pits their foes were announced with horns and drums, and after the battle was done and won the victors could have their wounds bound up and quaff some milk of the poppy for the pain, knowing that the threat was past and they were free to drink and feast and whore until the next fight. But the battle was never truly done for a knight of the Kingsguard. Threats came from everywhere and nowhere, at any time of day or night. No trumpets announced the foe: vassals, servants, friends, brothers, sons, even wives, any of them might have knives concealed beneath their cloaks and murder hidden in their hearts. For every hour of fighting, a Kingsguard knight spent ten thousand hours watching, waiting, standing silent in the shadows. King Hizdahr's pit fighters were already growing bored and restive with their new duties, and bored men were lax, slow to react.

"I shall deal with Khrazz," said Ser Barristan. "Just make certain I do not need to deal with any Brazen Beasts as well."

"Have no fear. We will have Marghaz in chains before he can make mischief. I told you, the Brazen Beasts are mine."

"You say you have men amongst the Yunkishmen?"

"Sneaks and spies. Reznak has more."

Reznak cannot be trusted. He smells too sweet and feels too foul. "Someone needs to free our hostages. Unless we get our people back, the Yunkai'i will use them against us."

Skahaz snorted through the noseholes of his mask. "Easy to speak of rescue. Harder to do. Let the slavers threaten."

"And if they do more than threaten?"

"Would you miss them so much, old man? A eunuch, a savage, and a sellsword?"

Hero, Jhogo, and Daario. "Jhogo is the queen's bloodrider, blood of her blood. They came out of the Red Waste together. Hero is Grey Worm's second-in-command. And Daario . . ." *She loves Daario.* He had seen it in her eyes when she looked at him, heard it in her voice when she spoke of him. ". . . Daario is vain and rash, but he is dear to Her Grace. He must be rescued, before his Stormcrows decide to take matters into their own hands. It can be done. I once brought the queen's father safely out of Duskendale, where he was being held captive by a rebel lord, but . . ."

". . . you could never hope to pass unnoticed amongst the Yunkai'i. Every man of them knows your face by now."

I could hide my face, like you, thought Selmy, but he knew the Shavepate was right. Duskendale had been a lifetime ago. He was too old for such heroics. "Then we must needs find some other way. Some other rescuer. Someone known to the Yunkishmen, whose presence in their camp might go unnoticed . . ."

"Daario calls you Ser Grandfather," Skahaz reminded him. "I will not say what he calls me. If you and I were the hostages, would he risk his skin for us?"

Not likely, he thought, but he said, "He might."

"Daario might piss on us if we were burning. Elsewise do not look to him for help. Let the Stormcrows choose another captain, one who knows his place. If the queen does not return, the world will be one sellsword short. Who will grieve?"

"And when she does return?"

"She will weep and tear her hair and curse the Yunkai'i. Not us. No blood on our hands. You can comfort her. Tell her some tale of the old days, she likes those. Poor Daario, her brave captain . . . she will never forget him, no . . . but better for all of us if he is dead, yes? Better for Daenerys too."

Better for Daenerys, and for Westeros. Daenerys Targaryen loved her captain, but that was the girl in her, not the queen. *Prince Rhaegar loved his Lady Lyanna, and thousands died for it. Daemon Blackfyre loved the first Daenerys, and rose in rebellion when denied her. Bittersteel and Bloodraven both loved Shiera Seastar, and the Seven Kingdoms bled. The Prince of Dragonflies loved Jenny of Oldstones so much he cast aside a crown, and Westeros paid the bride price in corpses.* All three of the sons of the fifth Aegon had wed for love, in defiance of their father's wishes. And because that unlikely monarch had himself followed his heart when he chose his queen, he allowed his sons to have their way, making bitter enemies where he might have had fast friends. Treason and turmoil followed, as night follows day, ending at Summerhall in sorcery, fire, and grief.

Her love for Daario is poison. A slower poison than the locusts, but in the end as deadly. "There is still Jhogo," Ser Barristan said. "Him, and Hero. Both precious to Her Grace."

"We have hostages as well," Skahaz Shavepate reminded him. "If the slavers kill one of ours, we kill one of theirs."

For a moment Ser Barristan did not know whom he meant. Then it came to him. "The queen's cupbearers?"

"*Hostages,*" insisted Skahaz mo Kandaq. "Grazdar and Qezza are the blood of the Green Grace. Mezzara is of Merreq, Kezmya is Pahl, Azzak Ghazeen. Bhakaz is Loraq, Hizdahr's own kin. All are sons and daughters of the pyramids. Zhak, Quazzar, Uhlez, Hazkar, Dhazak, Yherizan, all children of Great Masters."

"Innocent girls and sweet-faced boys." Ser Barristan had come to know them all during the time they served the queen, Grazhar with his dreams of glory, shy Mezzara, lazy Miklaz, vain, pretty Kezmya, Qezza with her big soft eyes and angel's voice, Dhazzar the dancer, and the rest. "Children."

"Children of the Harpy. Only blood can pay for blood."

"So said the Yunkishman who brought us Groleo's head."

"He was not wrong."

"I will not permit it."

"What use are hostages if they may not be touched?"

"Mayhaps we might offer three of the children for Daario, Hero, and Jhogo," Ser Barristan allowed. "Her Grace—"

"—is not here. It is for you and me to do what must be done. You know that I am right."

"Prince Rhaegar had two children," Ser Barristan told him. "Rhaenys was a little girl, Aegon a babe in arms. When Tywin Lannister took King's Landing, his men killed both of them. He served the bloody bodies up in crimson cloaks, a gift for the new king." *And what did Robert say when he saw them? Did he smile?* Barristan Selmy had been badly wounded on the Trident, so he had been spared the sight of Lord Tywin's gift, but oft he wondered. *If I had seen him smile over the red ruins of Rhaegar's children, no army on this earth could have stopped me from killing him.* "I will not suffer the murder of children. Accept that, or I'll have no part of this."

Skahaz chuckled. "You are a stubborn old man. Your sweet-faced boys will only grow up to be Sons of the Harpy. Kill them now or kill them then."

"You kill men for the wrongs they have done, not the wrongs that they may do someday."

The Shavepate took an axe down off the wall, inspected it, and grunted. "So be it. No harm to Hizdahr or our hostages. Will that content you, Ser Grandfather?"

Nothing about this will content me. "It will serve. The hour of the wolf. Remember."

"I am not like to forget, ser." Though the bat's brass mouth did not move, Ser Barristan could sense the grin beneath the mask. "Long has Kandaq waited for this night."

That is what I fear. If King Hizdahr was innocent, what they did this day would be treason. But how could he be innocent? Selmy had heard him urging Daenerys to taste the poisoned locusts, shouting at his men to slay the dragon. *If we do not act, Hizdahr will kill the dragons and open the gates to the queen's enemies. We have no choice in this.* Yet no matter how he turned and twisted this, the old knight could find no honor in it.

The rest of that long day raced past as swiftly as a snail.

Elsewhere, he knew, King Hizdahr was consulting with Reznak mo Reznak, Marghaz zo Loraq, Galazza Galare, and his other Meereenese advisors, deciding how best to respond to Yunkai's demands . . . but Barristan Selmy was no longer a part of such councils. Nor did he have a king to guard. Instead he made the rounds of the pyramid from top to bottom, to ascertain that the sentries were all at their posts. That took most of the morning. He spent that afternoon with his orphans, even took up sword and shield himself to provide a sterner test for a few of the older lads.

Some of them had been training for the fighting pits when Daenerys Targaryen took Meereen and freed them from their chains. Those had had a good acquaintance with sword and spear and battle-axe even before Ser Barristan got hold of them. A few might well be ready. *The boy from the Basilisk Isles, for a start. Tumco Lho.* Black as maester's ink he was, but fast and strong, the best natural swordsman Selmy had seen since Jaime Lannister. *Larraq as well. The Lash.* Ser Barristan did not approve of his fighting style, but there was no doubting his skills. Larraq had years of work ahead of him before he mastered proper knightly weapons, sword and lance and mace, but he was deadly with his whip and trident. The old knight had warned him that the whip would be useless against an armored foe . . . until he saw how Larraq used it, snapping it around the legs of his opponents to yank them off their feet. *No knight as yet, but a fierce fighter.*

Larraq and Tumco were his best. After them the Lhazarene, the one the other boys called Red Lamb, though as yet that one was all ferocity and no technique. Perhaps the brothers too, three lowborn Ghiscari enslaved to pay their father's debts.

That made six. *Six out of twenty-seven.* Selmy might have hoped for more, but six was a good beginning. The other boys were younger for the most part, and more familiar with looms and plows and chamber pots than swords and shields, but they worked hard and learned quickly. A few years as squires, and he might have six more knights to give his queen. As for those who would never be ready, well, not every boy was meant to be a knight. *The realm needs candlemakers and innkeeps and armorers as well.* That was as true in Meereen as it was in Westeros.

As he watched them at their drills, Ser Barristan pondered raising Tumco and Larraq to knighthood then and there, and mayhaps the Red Lamb too. It required a knight to make a knight, and if something should go awry tonight, dawn might find him dead or in a dungeon. Who would dub his squires then? On the other hand, a young knight's repute derived at least in part from the honor of the man who conferred knighthood on him. It would do his lads no good at all if it was known that they were given their spurs by a traitor, and might well land them in the dungeon next to him. *They deserve better*, Ser Barristan decided. *Better a long life as a squire than a short one as a soiled knight.*

As the afternoon melted into evening, he bid his charges to lay down their swords and shields and gather round. He spoke to them about what it meant to be a knight. "It is chivalry that makes a true knight, not a sword," he said. "Without honor, a knight is no more than a common killer. It is better to die with honor than to live without it." The boys looked at him strangely, he thought, but one day they would understand.

Afterward, back at the apex of the pyramid, Ser Barristan found Missandei amongst piles of scrolls and books, reading. "Stay here tonight, child," he told her. "Whatever happens, whatever you see or hear, do not leave the queen's chambers."

"This one hears," the girl said. "If she may ask—"

"Best not." Ser Barristan stepped out alone onto the terrace gardens. *I am not made for this*, he reflected as he looked out over the sprawling city. The pyramids were waking, one by one, lanterns and torches flickering to life as shadows gathered in the streets below. *Plots, ploys, whispers, lies, secrets within secrets, and somehow I have become part of them.*

Perhaps by now he should have grown used to such things. The Red Keep had its secrets too. *Even Rhaegar.* The Prince of Dragonstone had never trusted him as he had trusted Arthur Dayne. Harrenhal was proof of that. *The year of the false spring.*

The memory was still bitter. Old Lord Whent had announced the tourney shortly after a visit from his brother, Ser Oswell Whent of the Kingsguard. With Varys whispering in his ear, King Aerys became convinced that his son was conspiring to depose him, that Whent's tourney was but a ploy to give Rhaegar a pretext for meeting with as many great lords as could be brought together. Aerys had not set foot outside the Red Keep since Duskendale, yet suddenly he announced that he would accompany Prince Rhaegar to Harrenhal, and everything had gone awry from there.

If I had been a better knight . . . if I had unhorsed the prince in that last tilt, as I unhorsed so many others, it would have been for me to choose the queen of love and beauty . . .

Rhaegar had chosen Lyanna Stark of Winterfell. Barristan Selmy would have made a different choice. Not the queen, who was not present. Nor Elia of Dorne, though she was good and gentle; had she been chosen, much war and woe might have been avoided. His choice would have been a young maiden not long at court, one of Elia's companions . . . though compared to Ashara Dayne, the Dornish princess was a kitchen drab.

Even after all these years, Ser Barristan could still recall Ashara's smile, the sound of her laughter. He had only to close his eyes to see her, with her long dark hair tumbling about her shoulders and those haunting purple eyes. *Daenerys has the same eyes.* Sometimes when the queen looked at him, he felt as if he were looking at Ashara's daughter . . .

But Ashara's daughter had been stillborn, and his fair lady had thrown herself from a tower soon after, mad with grief for the child she had lost, and perhaps for the man who had dishonored her at Harrenhal as well. She died never knowing that Ser Barristan had loved her. *How could she?* He was a knight of the Kingsguard, sworn to celibacy. No good could have come from telling her his feelings. *No good came from silence either. If I had unhorsed Rhaegar and crowned Ashara queen of love and beauty, might she have looked to me instead of Stark?*

He would never know. But of all his failures, none haunted Barristan Selmy so much as that.

The sky was overcast, the air hot, muggy, oppressive, yet there was something in it that made his spine tingle. *Rain*, he thought. *A storm is coming. If not tonight, upon the morrow.* Ser Barristan wondered if he would live to see it. *If Hizdahr has his own Spider, I am as good as dead.* Should it come to that, he meant to die as he had lived, with his longsword in his hand.

When the last light had faded in the west, behind the sails of the prowling ships on Slaver's Bay, Ser Barristan went back inside, summoned a pair of serving men, and told them to heat some water for a bath. Sparring with his squires in the afternoon heat had left him feeling soiled and sweaty.

The water, when it came, was only lukewarm, but Selmy lingered in the bath until it had grown cold and scrubbed his skin till it was raw. Clean as he had ever been, he rose, dried himself, and clad himself in whites. Stockings, smallclothes, silken tunic, padded jerkin, all fresh-washed and bleached. Over that he donned the armor that the queen had given him as a token of her esteem. The mail was gilded, finely wrought, the links as supple as good leather, the plate enameled, hard as ice and bright as new-fallen snow. His dagger went on one hip, his long-sword on the other, hung from a white leather belt with golden buckles. Last of all he took down his long white cloak and fastened it about his shoulders.

The helm he left upon its hook. The narrow eye slit limited his vision, and he needed to be able to see for what was to come. The halls of the pyramid were dark at night, and foes could come at you from either side. Besides, though the ornate dragon's wings that adorned the helm were splendid to look upon, they could too easily catch a sword or axe. He would leave them for his next tourney if the Seven should grant him one.

Armed and armored, the old knight waited, sitting in the gloom of his small chamber adjoining the queen's apartments. The faces of all the kings that he had served and failed floated before him in the darkness, and the faces of the brothers who had served beside him in the Kingsguard as well. He wondered how many of them would have done what he was about to do. *Some, surely. But not all. Some would not have hesitated to strike down the Shavepate as a traitor.* Outside the pyramid, it began to rain. Ser Barristan sat alone in the dark, listening. *It sounds like tears,* he thought. *It sounds like dead kings, weeping.*

Then it was time to go.

The Great Pyramid of Meereen had been built as an echo to the Great Pyramid of Ghis whose collossal ruins Lomas Longstrider had once visited. Like its ancient predecessor, whose red marble halls were now the haunt of bats and spiders, the Meereenese pyramid boasted three-and-thirty levels, that number being somehow sacred to the gods of Ghis. Ser Barristan began the long descent alone, his white cloak rippling behind him as he started down. He took the servants' steps, not the grand stairways of veined marble, but the narrower, steeper, straighter stairs hidden within the thick brick walls.

Twelve levels down he found the Shavepate waiting, his coarse features still hidden by the mask he had worn that morning, the blood bat. Six Brazen Beasts were with him. All were masked as insects, identical to one another.

Locusts, Selmy realized. "Groleo," he said.

"Groleo," one of the locusts replied.

"I have more locusts if you need them," said Skahaz.

"Six should serve. What of the men on the doors?"

"Mine. You will have no trouble."

Ser Barristan clasped the Shavepate by the arm. "Shed no blood unless you must. Come the morrow we will convene a council and tell the city what we've done and why."

"As you say. Good fortune to you, old man."

They went their separate ways. The Brazen Beasts fell in behind Ser Barristan as he continued his descent.

The king's apartments were buried in the very heart of the pyramid, on the sixteenth and seventeenth levels. When Selmy reached those floors, he found the doors to the interior of the pyramid chained shut, with a pair of Brazen Beasts posted as guards. Beneath the hoods of their patchwork cloaks, one was a rat, the other a bull.

"Groleo," Ser Barristan said.

"Groleo," the bull returned. "Third hall to the right." The rat unlocked the chain. Ser Barristan and his escort stepped through into a narrow, torchlit servants' corridor of red and black brick. Their footsteps echoed on the floors as they strode past two halls and took the third one to the right.

Outside the carved hardwood doors to the king's chambers stood Steelskin, a younger pit fighter, not yet regarded as of the first rank. His cheeks and brow were scarred with intricate tattoos in green and black, ancient Valyrian sorcerer's signs that supposedly made his flesh and skin as hard as steel. Similar markings covered his chest and arms, though whether they would actually stop a sword or axe remained to be seen.

Even without them, Steelskin looked formidable—a lean and wiry youth who overtopped Ser Barristan by half a foot. "Who goes there?" he called out, swinging his longaxe sideways to bar their way. When he saw Ser Barristan, with the brass locusts behind him, he lowered it again. "Old Ser."

"If it please the king, I must needs have words with him."

"The hour is late."

"The hour is late, but the need is urgent."

"I can ask." Steelskin slammed the butt of his longaxe against the door to the king's apartments. A slidehole opened. A child's eye appeared. A child's voice called through the door. Steelskin replied. Ser Barristan heard the sound of a heavy bar being drawn back. The door swung open.

"Only you," said Steelskin. "The beasts wait here."

"As you wish." Ser Barristan nodded to the locusts. One returned his nod. Alone, Selmy slipped through the door.

Dark and windowless, surrounded on all sides by brick walls eight feet thick, the chambers that the king had made his own were large and luxurious within. Great beams of black oak supported the high ceilings. The floors were covered with silk carpets out of Qarth. On the walls were priceless tapestries, ancient and much faded, depicting the glory of the Old Empire of Ghis. The largest of them showed the last survivors of a defeated Valyrian army passing beneath the yoke and being chained. The archway leading to the royal bedchamber was guarded by a pair of sandalwood lovers, shaped and smoothed and oiled. Ser Barristan found them distasteful, though no doubt they were meant to be arousing. *The sooner we are gone from this place, the better.*

An iron brazier gave the only light. Beside it stood two of the queen's cupbearers, Draqaz and Qezza. "Miklaz has gone to wake the king," said Qezza. "May we bring you wine, ser?"

"No. I thank you."

"You may sit," said Draqaz, indicating a bench.

"I prefer to stand." He could hear voices drifting through the archway from the bedchamber. One of them was the king's.

It was still a good few moments before King Hizdahr zo Loraq, Four-teenth of That Noble Name, emerged yawning, knotting the sash that closed his robe. The robe was green satin, richly worked with pearls and silver thread. Under it the king was quite naked. That was good. Naked men felt vulnerable and were less inclined to acts of suicidal heroism.

The woman Ser Barristan glimpsed peering through the archway from behind a gauzy curtain was naked as well, her breasts and hips only par-tially concealed by the blowing silk.

"Ser Barristan." Hizdahr yawned again. "What hour is it? Is there news of my sweet queen?"

"None, Your Grace."

Hizdahr sighed. " 'Your *Magnificence,*' please. Though at this hour, 'Your Sleepiness' would be more apt." The king crossed to the sideboard to pour himself a cup of wine, but only a trickle remained in the bottom of the flagon. A flicker of annoyance crossed his face. "Miklaz, wine. At once."

"Yes, Your Worship."

"Take Draqaz with you. One flagon of Arbor gold, and one of that sweet red. None of our yellow piss, thank you. And the next time I find my flagon dry, I may have to take a switch to those pretty pink cheeks of yours." The boy went running off, and the king turned back to Selmy. "I dreamed you found Daenerys."

"Dreams can lie, Your Grace."

" 'Your Radiance' would serve. What brings you to me at this hour, ser? Some trouble in the city?"

"The city is tranquil."

"Is it so?" Hizdahr looked confused. "Why have you come?"

"To ask a question. Magnificence, are you the Harpy?"

Hizdahr's wine cup slipped through his fingers, bounced off the carpet, rolled. "You come to my bedchamber in the black of night and ask me that? Are you mad?" It was only then that the king seemed to notice that Ser Barristan was wearing his plate and mail. "What . . . why . . . how dare you . . ."

"Was the poison your work, Magnificence?"

King Hizdahr backed away a step. "The locusts? That . . . that was the Dornishman. Quentyn, the so-called prince. Ask Reznak if you doubt me."

"Have you proof of that? Has Reznak?"

"No, else I would have had them seized. Perhaps I should do so in any case. Marghaz will wring a confession out of them, I do not doubt. They're all poisoners, these Dornish. Reznak says they worship snakes."

"They eat snakes," said Ser Barristan. "It was your pit, your box, your seats. Sweet wine and soft cushions, figs and melons and honeyed locusts. You provided all. You urged Her Grace to try the locusts but never tasted one yourself."

"I . . . hot spices do not agree with me. She was my wife. My queen. Why would I want to poison her?"

Was, he says. He believes her dead. "Only you can answer that, Magnificence. It might be that you wished to put another woman in her place." Ser Barristan nodded at the girl peering timidly from the bedchamber. "That one, perhaps?"

The king looked around wildly. "*Her?* She's nothing. A bedslave." He raised his hands. "I misspoke. Not a slave. A free woman. Trained in pleasure. Even a king has needs, she . . . she is none of your concern, ser. I would never harm Daenerys. Never."

"You urged the queen to try the locusts. I heard you."

"I thought she might enjoy them." Hizdahr retreated another step. "Hot and sweet at once."

"Hot and sweet and poisoned. With mine own ears I heard you commanding the men in the pit to kill Drogon. Shouting at them."

Hizdahr licked his lips. "The beast devoured Barsena's flesh. Dragons prey on men. It was killing, burning . . ."

". . . burning men who meant harm to your queen. Harpy's Sons, as like as not. Your friends."

"Not my friends."

"You say that, yet when you told them to stop killing they obeyed. Why would they do that if you were not one of them?"

Hizdahr shook his head. This time he did not answer.

"Tell me true," Ser Barristan said, "did you ever love her, even a little? Or was it just the crown you lusted for?"

"Lust? You dare speak to me of *lust*?" The king's mouth twisted in anger. "I lusted for the crown, aye . . . but not half so much as she lusted for her sellsword. Perhaps it was her precious captain who tried to poison her, for putting him aside. And if I had eaten of his locusts too, well, so much the better."

"Daario is a killer but not a poisoner." Ser Barristan moved closer to the king. "Are you the Harpy?" This time he put his hand on the hilt of his longsword. "Tell me true, and I promise you shall have a swift, clean death."

"You presume too much, ser," said Hizdahr. "I am done with these questions, and with you. You are dismissed from my service. Leave Meer-een at once and I will let you live."

"If you are not the Harpy, give me his name." Ser Barristan pulled his sword from the scabbard. Its sharp edge caught the light from the brazier, became a line of orange fire.

Hizdahr broke. "Khrazz!" he shrieked, stumbling backwards toward his bedchamber. "Khrazz! *Khrazz!*"

Ser Barristan heard a door open, somewhere to his left. He turned in time to see Khrazz emerge from behind a tapestry. He moved slowly, still groggy from sleep, but his weapon of choice was in his hand: a Dothraki *arakh*, long and curved. A slasher's sword, made to deliver deep, slicing cuts from horseback. *A murderous blade against half-naked foes, in the pit or on the battlefield.* But here at close quarters, the *arakh*'s length would tell against it, and Barristan Selmy was clad in plate and mail.

"I am here for Hizdahr," the knight said. "Throw down your steel and stand aside, and no harm need come to you."

Khrazz laughed. "Old man. I will eat your heart." The two men were of a height, but Khrazz was two stone heavier and forty years younger, with pale skin, dead eyes, and a crest of bristly red-black hair that ran from his brow to the base of his neck.

"Then come," said Barristan the Bold.

Khrazz came.

For the first time all day, Selmy felt certain. *This is what I was made for,* he thought. *The dance, the sweet steel song, a sword in my hand and a foe before me.*

The pit fighter was fast, blazing fast, as quick as any man Ser Barristan had ever fought. In those big hands, the *arakh* became a whistling blur, a steel storm that seemed to come at the old knight from three directions at once. Most of the cuts were aimed at his head. Khrazz was no fool. Without a helm, Selmy was most vulnerable above the neck.

He blocked the blows calmly, his longsword meeting each slash and turning it aside. The blades rang and rang again. Ser Barristan retreated. On the edge of his vision, he saw the cupbearers watching with eyes as big and white as chicken eggs. Khrazz cursed and turned a high cut into a low one, slipping past the old knight's blade for once, only to have his blow scrape uselessly off a white steel greave. Selmy's answering slash found the pit fighter's left shoulder, parting the fine linen to bite the flesh beneath. His yellow tunic began to turn pink, then red.

"Only cowards dress in iron," Khrazz declared, circling. No one wore armor in the fighting pits. It was blood the crowds came for: death, dismemberment, and shrieks of agony, the music of the scarlet sands.

Ser Barristan turned with him. "This coward is about to kill you, ser." The man was no knight, but his courage had earned him that much courtesy. Khrazz did not know how to fight a man in armor. Ser Barristan could see it in his eyes: doubt, confusion, the beginnings of fear. The pit fighter came on again, screaming this time, as if sound could slay his foe where steel could not. The *arakh* slashed low, high, low again.

Selmy blocked the cuts at his head and let his armor stop the rest, whilst his own blade opened the pit fighter's cheek from ear to mouth, then traced a raw red gash across his chest. Blood welled from Khrazz's wounds. That only seemed to make him wilder. He seized the brazier with his off hand and flipped it, scattering embers and hot coals at Selmy's feet. Ser Barristan leapt over them. Khrazz slashed at his arm and caught him, but the *arakh* could only chip the hard enamel before it met the steel below.

"In the pit that would have taken your arm off, old man."

"We are not in the pit."

"Take off that armor!"

"It is not too late to throw down your steel. Yield."

"Die," spat Khrazz . . . but as he lifted his *arakh*, its tip grazed one of the wall hangings and hung. That was all the chance Ser Barristan required. He slashed open the pit fighter's belly, parried the *arakh* as it wrenched free, then finished Khrazz with a quick thrust to the heart as the pit fighter's entrails came sliding out like a nest of greasy eels.

Blood and viscera stained the king's silk carpets. Selmy took a step back. The longsword in his hand was red for half its length. Here and there the carpets had begun to smolder where some of the scattered coals had fallen. He could hear poor Qezza sobbing. "Don't be afraid," the old knight said. "I mean you no harm, child. I want only the king."

He wiped his sword clean on a curtain and stalked into the bedchamber, where he found Hizdahr zo Loraq, Fourteenth of His Noble Name, hiding behind a tapestry and whimpering. "Spare me," he begged. "I do not want to die."

"Few do. Yet all men die, regardless." Ser Barristan sheathed his sword and pulled Hizdahr to his feet. "Come. I will escort you to a cell." By now, the Brazen Beasts should have disarmed Steelskin. "You will be kept a prisoner until the queen returns. If nothing can be proved against you, you will not come to harm. You have my word as a knight." He took the king's arm and led him from the bedchamber, feeling strangely light-headed, almost drunk. *I was a Kingsguard. What am I now?*

Miklaz and Draqaz had returned with Hizdahr's wine. They stood in the open door, cradling the flagons against their chests and staring wide-eyed at the corpse of Khrazz. Qezza was still crying, but Jezhene had appeared to comfort her. She hugged the younger girl, stroking her hair. Some of the other cupbearers stood behind them, watching. "Your Worship," Miklaz said, "the noble Reznak mo Reznak says to t-tell you, come at once."

The boy addressed the king as if Ser Barristan were not there, as if there were no dead man sprawled upon the carpet, his life's blood slowly staining the silk red. *Skahaz was supposed to take Reznak into custody until we could be certain of his loyalty. Had something gone awry?* "Come where?" Ser Barristan asked the boy. "Where does the seneschal want His Grace to go?"

"Outside." Miklaz seemed to see him for the first time. "Outside, ser. To the t-terrace. To see."

"To see what?"

"D-d-dragons. The dragons have been loosed, ser."

Seven save us all, the old knight thought.

THE DRAGONTAMER

The night crept past on slow black feet. The hour of the bat gave way to the hour of the eel, the hour of the eel to the hour of ghosts. The prince lay abed, staring at his ceiling, dreaming without sleeping, remembering, imagining, twisting beneath his linen coverlet, his mind feverish with thoughts of fire and blood.

Finally, despairing of rest, Quentyn Martell made his way to his solar, where he poured himself a cup of wine and drank it in the dark. The taste was sweet solace on his tongue, so he lit a candle and poured himself another. *Wine will help me sleep*, he told himself, but he knew that was a lie.

He stared at the candle for a long time, then put down his cup and held his palm above the flame. It took every bit of will he had to lower it until the fire touched his flesh, and when it did he snatched his hand back with a cry of pain.

"Quentyn, are you mad?"

No, just scared. I do not want to burn. "Gerris?"

"I heard you moving about."

"I could not sleep."

"Are burns a cure for that? Some warm milk and a lullaby might serve you well. Or better still, I could take you to the Temple of the Graces and find a girl for you."

"A whore, you mean."

"They call them Graces. They come in different colors. The red ones are the only ones who fuck." Gerris seated himself across the table. "The septas back home should take up the custom, if you ask me. Have you noticed that old septas always look like prunes? That's what a life of chastity will do to you."

Quentyn glanced out at the terrace, where night's shadows lay thick amongst the trees. He could hear the soft sound of falling water. "Is that rain? Your whores will be gone."

"Not all of them. There are little snuggeries in the pleasure gardens, and they wait there every night until a man chooses them. Those who are not chosen must remain until the sun comes up, feeling lonely and neglected. We could console them."

"They could console me, is what you mean."

"That too."

"That is not the sort of consolation I require."

"I disagree. Daenerys Targaryen is not the only woman in the world. Do you want to die a man-maid?"

Quentyn did not want to die at all. *I want to go back to Yronwood and kiss both of your sisters, marry Gwyneth Yronwood, watch her flower into beauty, have a child by her. I want to ride in tourneys, hawk and hunt, visit with my mother in Norvos, read some of those books my father sends me. I want Cletus and Will and Maester Kedry to be alive again.* "Do you think Daenerys would be pleased to hear that I had bedded some whore?"

"She might be. Men may be fond of maidens, but women like a man who knows what he's about in the bedchamber. It's another sort of swordplay. Takes training to be good at it."

The gibe stung. Quentyn had never felt so much a boy as when he'd stood before Daenerys Targaryen, pleading for her hand. The thought of bedding her terrified him almost as much as her dragons had. What if he could not please her? "Daenerys has a paramour," he said defensively. "My father did not send me here to amuse the queen in the bedchamber. You know why we have come."

"You cannot marry her. She has a husband."

"She does not love Hizdahr zo Loraq."

"What has love to do with marriage? A prince should know better. Your father married for love, it's said. How much joy has he had of that?"

Little and less. Doran Martell and his Norvoshi wife had spent half their marriage apart and the other half arguing. It was the only rash thing his father had ever done, to hear some tell it, the only time he had followed his heart instead of his head, and he had lived to rue it. "Not all risks lead to ruin," he insisted. "This is my duty. My destiny." *You are supposed to be my friend, Gerris. Why must you mock my hopes? I have doubts enough without your throwing oil on the fire of my fear.* "This will be my grand adventure."

"Men die on grand adventures."

He was not wrong. That was in the stories too. The hero sets out with his friends and companions, faces dangers, comes home triumphant. Only some of his companions don't return at all. *The hero never dies, though. I must be the hero.* "All I need is courage. Would you have Dorne remember me as a failure?"

"Dorne is not like to remember any of us for long."

Quentyn sucked at the burned spot on his palm. "Dorne remembers Aegon and his sisters. Dragons are not so easily forgotten. They will remember Daenerys as well."

"Not if she's died."

"She lives." *She must.* "She is lost, but I can find her." *And when I do, she will look at me the way she looks at her sellsword. Once I have proven myself worthy of her.*

"From dragonback?"

"I have been riding horses since I was six years old."

"And you've been thrown a time or three."

"That never stopped me from getting back into the saddle."

"You've never been thrown off a thousand feet above the ground," Gerris pointed out. "And horses seldom turn their riders into charred bones and ashes."

I know the dangers. "I'll hear no more of this. You have my leave to go. Find a ship and run home, Gerris." The prince rose, blew the candle out, and crept back to his bed and its sweat-soaked linen sheets. *I should have kissed one of the Drinkwater twins, or maybe both of them. I should have kissed them whilst I could. I should have gone to Norvos to see my mother and the place that gave her birth, so she would know that I had not forgotten her.* He could hear the rain falling outside, drumming against the bricks.

By the time the hour of the wolf crept upon them, the rain was falling steadily, slashing down in a hard, cold torrent that would soon turn the brick streets of Meereen into rivers. The three Dornishmen broke their fast in the predawn chill—a simple meal of fruit and bread and cheese, washed down with goat milk. When Gerris made to pour himself a cup of wine, Quentyn stopped him. "No wine. There will be time enough for drink afterward."

"One hopes," said Gerris.

The big man looked out toward the terrace. "I knew it would rain," he said in a gloomy tone. "My bones were aching last night. They always ache before it rains. The dragons won't like this. Fire and water don't mix, and that's a fact. You get a good cookfire lit, blazing away nice, then it starts to piss down rain and next thing your wood is sodden and your flames are dead."

Gerris chuckled. "Dragons are not made of wood, Arch."

"Some are. That old King Aegon, the randy one, he built wooden dragons to conquer us. That ended bad, though."

So may this, the prince thought. The follies and failures of Aegon the Unworthy did not concern him, but he was full of doubts and misgivings. The labored banter of his friends was only making his head ache. *They do not understand. They may be Dornish, but I am Dorne. Years from now, when I am dead, this will be the song they sing of me*. He rose abruptly. "It's time."

His friends got to their feet. Ser Archibald drained the last of his goat's milk and wiped the milk mustache from his upper lip with the back of a big hand. "I'll get our mummer's garb."

He returned with the bundle that they had collected from the Tattered Prince at their second meeting. Within were three long hooded cloaks made from myriad small squares of cloth sewn together, three cudgels, three shortswords, three masks of polished brass. A bull, a lion, and an ape.

Everything required to be a Brazen Beast.

"They may ask for a word," the Tattered Prince had warned them when he handed over the bundle. "It's *dog*."

"You are certain of that?" Gerris had asked him.

"Certain enough to wager a life upon it."

The prince did not mistake his meaning. "My life."

"That would be the one."

"How did you learn their word?"

"We chanced upon some Brazen Beasts and Meris asked them prettily. But a prince should know better than to pose such questions, Dornish. In Pentos, we have a saying. Never ask the baker what went into the pie. Just eat."

Just eat. There was wisdom in that, Quentyn supposed.

"I'll be the bull," Arch announced.

Quentyn handed him the bull mask. "The lion for me."

"Which makes a monkey out of me." Gerris pressed the ape mask to his face. "How do they breathe in these things?"

"Just put it on." The prince was in no mood for japes.

The bundle contained a whip as well — a nasty piece of old leather with a handle of brass and bone, stout enough to peel the hide off an ox. "What's that for?" Arch asked.

"Daenerys used a whip to cow the black beast." Quentyn coiled the whip and hung it from his belt. "Arch, bring your hammer as well. We may have need of it."

It was no easy thing to enter the Great Pyramid of Meereen by night. The doors were closed and barred each day at sunset and remained closed until first light. Guards were posted at every entrance, and more guards patrolled the lowest terrace, where they could look down on the street. Formerly those guards had been Unsullied. Now they were Brazen Beasts. And that would make all the difference, Quentyn hoped.

The watch changed when the sun came up, but dawn was still half an hour off as the three Dornishmen made their way down the servants' steps. The walls around them were made of bricks of half a hundred colors, but the shadows turned them all to grey until touched by the light of the torch that Gerris carried. They encountered no one on the long descent. The only sound was the scuff of their boots on the worn bricks beneath their feet.

The pyramid's main gates fronted on Meereen's central plaza, but the Dornishmen made their way to a side entrance opening on an alley. These were the gates that slaves had used in former days as they went about their masters' business, where smallfolk and tradesmen came and went and made their deliveries.

The doors were solid bronze, closed with a heavy iron bar. Before them stood two Brazen Beasts, armed with cudgels, spears, and short swords. Torchlight glimmered off the polished brass of their masks—a rat and a fox. Quentyn gestured for the big man to stay back in the shadows. He and Gerris strode forward together.

"You come early," the fox said.

Quentyn shrugged. "We can leave again, if you like. You're welcome to stand our watch." He sounded not at all Ghiscari, he knew; but half the Brazen Beasts were freed slaves, with all manner of native tongues, so his accent went unremarked.

"Bugger that," the rat remarked.

"Give us the day's word," said the fox.

"Dog," said the Dornishman.

The two Brazen Beasts exchanged a look. For three long heartbeats Quentyn was afraid that something had gone amiss, that somehow Pretty Meris and the Tattered Prince had gotten the word wrong. Then the fox grunted. "Dog, then," he said. "The door is yours." As they moved off, the prince began to breathe again.

They did not have long. The real relief would doubtless turn up shortly. "Arch," he called, and the big man appeared, the torchlight shining off his bull's mask. "The bar. Hurry."

The iron bar was thick and heavy, but well oiled. Ser Archibald had no trouble lifting it. As he was standing it on end, Quentyn pulled the doors open and Gerris stepped through, waving the torch. "Bring it in now. Be quick about it."

The butcher's wagon was outside, waiting in the alley. The driver gave the mule a lick and rumbled through, iron-rimmed wheels *clack*ing loudly over bricks. The quartered carcass of an ox filled the wagon bed, along with two dead sheep. Half a dozen men entered afoot. Five wore the cloaks and masks of Brazen Beasts, but Pretty Meris had not troubled to disguise herself. "Where is your lord?" he asked Meris.

"I have no *lord*," she answered. "If you mean your fellow prince, he is near, with fifty men. Bring your dragon out, and he will see you safe away, as promised. Caggo commands here."

Ser Archibald was giving the butcher's wagon the sour eye. "Will that cart be big enough to hold a dragon?" he asked.

"Should. It's held two oxen." The Corpsekiller was garbed as a Brazen Beast, his seamed, scarred face hidden behind a cobra mask, but the familiar black *arakh* slung at his hip gave him away. "We were told these beasts are smaller than the queen's monster."

"The pit has slowed their growth." Quentyn's readings had suggested that the same thing had occurred in the Seven Kingdoms. None of the dragons bred and raised in the Dragonpit of King's Landing had ever approached the size of Vhagar or Meraxes, much less that of the Black Dread, King Aegon's monster. "Have you brought sufficient chains?"

"How many dragons do you have?" said Pretty Meris. "We have chains enough for ten, concealed beneath the meat."

"Very good." Quentyn felt light-headed. None of this seemed quite real. One moment it felt like a game, the next like some nightmare, like a bad dream where he found himself opening a dark door, knowing that horror and death waited on the other side, yet somehow powerless to stop himself. His palms were slick with sweat. He wiped them on his legs and said, "There will be more guards outside the pit."

"We know," said Gerris.

"We need to be ready for them."

"We are," said Arch.

There was a cramp in Quentyn's belly. He felt a sudden need to move his bowels, but knew he dare not beg off now. "This way, then." He had seldom felt more like a boy. Yet they followed; Gerris and the big man, Meris and Caggo and the other Windblown. Two of the sellswords had produced crossbows from some hiding place within the wagon.

Beyond the stables, the ground level of the Great Pyramid became a labyrinth, but Quentyn Martell had been through here with the queen, and he remembered the way. Under three huge brick arches they went, then down a steep stone ramp into the depths, through the dungeons and torture chambers and past a pair of deep stone cisterns. Their footsteps echoed hollowly off the walls, the butcher's cart rumbling behind them. The big man snatched a torch down from a wall sconce to lead the way.

At last a pair of heavy iron doors rose before them, rust-eaten and forbidding, closed with a length of chain whose every link was as thick around as a man's arm. The size and thickness of those doors was enough to make Quentyn Martell question the wisdom of this course. Even worse, both doors were plainly dinted by something inside trying to get out. The thick iron was cracked and splitting in three places, and the upper corner of the left-hand door looked partly melted.

Four Brazen Beasts stood guarding the door. Three held long spears; the fourth, the serjeant, was armed with short sword and dagger. His mask was wrought in the shape of a basilisk's head. The other three were masked as insects.

Locusts, Quentyn realized. "Dog," he said.

The serjeant stiffened.

That was all it took for Quentyn Martell to realize that something had gone awry. "Take them," he croaked, even as the basilisk's hand darted for his shortsword.

He was quick, that serjeant. The big man was quicker. He flung the torch at the nearest locust, reached back, and unslung his warhammer. The basilisk's blade had scarce slipped from its leather sheath when the hammer's spike slammed into his temple, crunching through the thin brass of his mask and the flesh and bone beneath. The serjeant staggered sideways half a step before his knees folded under him and he sank down to the floor, his whole body shaking grotesquely.

Quentyn stared transfixed, his belly roiling. His own blade was still in its sheath. He had not so much as reached for it. His eyes were locked on the serjeant dying before him, jerking. The fallen torch was on the floor, guttering, making every shadow leap and twist in a monstrous mockery of the dead man's shaking. The prince never saw the locust's spear coming toward him until Gerris slammed into him, knocking him aside. The spearpoint grazed the cheek of the lion's head he wore. Even then the blow was so violent it almost tore the mask off. *It would have gone right through my throat,* the prince thought, dazed.

Gerris cursed as the locusts closed around him. Quentyn heard the sound of running feet. Then the sellswords came rushing from the shadows. One of the guards glanced at them just long enough for Gerris to get inside his spear. He drove the point of his sword under the brass mask and up through the wearer's throat, even as the second locust sprouted a crossbow bolt from his chest.

The last locust dropped his spear. "Yield. I yield."

"No. You die." Caggo took the man's head off with one swipe of his *arakh*, the Valyrian steel shearing through flesh and bone and gristle as if they were so much suet. "Too much noise," he complained. "Any man with ears will have heard."

"Dog," Quentyn said. "The day's word was supposed to be dog. Why wouldn't they let us pass? We were told . . ."

"You were told your scheme was madness, have you forgotten?" said Pretty Meris. "Do what you came to do."

The dragons, Prince Quentyn thought. *Yes. We came for the dragons.* He felt as though he might be sick. *What am I doing here? Father, why? Four men dead in as many heartbeats, and for what?* "Fire and blood," he whispered, "blood and fire." The blood was pooling at his feet, soaking into the brick floor. The fire was beyond those doors. "The chains . . . we have no key . . ."

Arch said, "I have the key." He swung his warhammer hard and fast. Sparks flew when the hammmerhead struck the lock. And then again, again, again. On his fifth swing the lock shattered, and the chains fell away in a rattling clatter so loud Quentyn was certain half the pyramid must have heard them. "Bring the cart." The dragons would be more docile once fed. *Let them gorge themselves on charred mutton.*

Archibald Yronwood grasped the iron doors and pulled them apart. Their rusted hinges let out a pair of screams, for all those who might have slept through the breaking of the lock. A wash of sudden heat assaulted them, heavy with the odors of ash, brimstone, and burnt meat.

It was black beyond the doors, a sullen stygian darkness that seemed alive and threatening, hungry. Quentyn could sense that there was something in that darkness, coiled and waiting. *Warrior, grant me courage,* he prayed. He did not want to do this, but he saw no other way. *Why else would Daenerys have shown me the dragons? She wants me to prove myself to her.* Gerris handed him a torch. He stepped through the doors.

The green one is Rhaegal, the white Viserion, he reminded himself. *Use their names, command them, speak to them calmly but sternly. Master them, as Daenerys mastered Drogon in the pit.* The girl had been alone, clad in wisps of silk, but fearless. *I must not be afraid. She did it, so can I.* The main thing was to show no fear. *Animals can smell fear, and dragons . . .* What did he know of dragons? *What does any man know of dragons? They have been gone from the world for more than a century.*

The lip of the pit was just ahead. Quentyn edged forward slowly, moving the torch from side to side. Walls and floor and ceiling drank the light. *Scorched,* he realized. *Bricks burned black, crumbling into ash.* The air grew warmer with every step he took. He began to sweat.

Two eyes rose up before him.

Bronze, they were, brighter than polished shields, glowing with their own heat, burning behind a veil of smoke rising from the dragon's nostrils. The light of Quentyn's torch washed over scales of dark green, the green of moss in the deep woods at dusk, just before the last light fades. Then the dragon opened its mouth, and light and heat washed over them. Behind a fence of sharp black teeth he glimpsed the furnace glow, the shimmer of a sleeping fire a hundred times brighter than his torch. The dragon's head was larger than a horse's, and the neck stretched on and on, uncoiling like some great green serpent as the head rose, until those two glowing bronze eyes were staring down at him.

Green, the prince thought, *his scales are green.* "Rhaegal," he said. His voice caught in his throat, and what came out was a broken croak. *Frog,* he thought, *I am turning into Frog again.* "The food," he croaked, remembering. "Bring the food."

The big man heard him. Arch wrestled one of the sheep off the wagon by two legs, then spun and flung it into the pit.

Rhaegal took it in the air. His head snapped round, and from between his jaws a lance of flame erupted, a swirling storm of orange-and-yellow fire shot through with veins of green. The sheep was burning before it began to fall. Before the smoking carcass could strike the bricks, the dragon's teeth closed round it. A nimbus of flames still flickered about the body. The air stank of burning wool and brimstone. *Dragonstink.*

"I thought there were two," the big man said.

Viserion. Yes. Where is Viserion? The prince lowered his torch to throw some light into the gloom below. He could see the green dragon ripping at the smoking carcass of the sheep, his long tail lashing from side to side as he ate. A thick iron collar was visible about his neck, with three feet of broken chain dangling from it. Shattered links were strewn across the floor of the pit amongst the blackened bones—twists of metal, partly melted. *Rhaegal was chained to the wall and floor the last time I was here,* the prince recalled, *but Viserion hung from the ceiling.* Quentyn stepped back, lifted the torch, craned his head back.

For a moment he saw only the blackened arches of the bricks above, scorched by dragonflame. A trickle of ash caught his eye, betraying movement. Something pale, half-hidden, stirring. *He's made himself a cave,* the prince realized. *A burrow in the brick.* The foundations of the Great Pyramid of Meereen were massive and thick to support the weight of the huge structure overhead; even the interior walls were three times thicker than any castle's curtain walls. But Viserion had dug himself a hole in them with flame and claw, a hole big enough to sleep in.

And we've just woken him. He could see what looked like some huge white serpent uncoiling inside the wall, up where it curved to become the ceiling. More ash went drifting downward, and a bit of crumbling brick fell away. The serpent resolved itself into a neck and tail, and then the dragon's long horned head appeared, his eyes glowing in the dark like golden coals. His wings rattled, stretching.

All of Quentyn's plans had fled his head. He could hear Caggo Corpsekiller shouting to his sellswords. *The chains, he is sending for the chains,* the Dornish prince thought. The plan had been to feed the beasts and chain them in their torpor, just as the queen had done. One dragon, or preferably both.

"More meat," Quentyn said. *Once the beasts were fed they will become sluggish.* He had seen it work with snakes in Dorne, but here, with these monsters . . . "Bring . . . bring . . ."

Viserion launched himself from the ceiling, pale leather wings unfolding, spreading wide. The broken chain dangling from his neck swung wildly. His flame lit the pit, pale gold shot through with red and orange, and the stale air exploded in a cloud of hot ash and sulfur as the white wings beat and beat again.

A hand seized Quentyn by the shoulder. The torch spun from his grip to bounce across the floor, then tumbled into the pit, still burning. He found himself face-to-face with a brass ape. *Gerris.* "Quent, this will not work. They are too wild, they . . ."

The dragon came down between the Dornishmen and the door with a roar that would have sent a hundred lions running. His head moved side to side as he inspected the intruders—Dornishmen, Windblown, Caggo. Last and longest the beast stared at Pretty Meris, sniffing. *The woman,* Quentyn realized. *He knows that she is female. He is looking for Daenerys. He wants his mother and does not understand why she's not here.*

Quentyn wrenched free of Gerris's grip. "Viserion," he called. *The white one is Viserion.* For half a heartbeat he was afraid he'd gotten it wrong. "Viserion," he called again, fumbling for the whip hanging from his belt. *She cowed the black one with a whip. I need to do the same.*

The dragon knew his name. His head turned, and his gaze lingered on the Dornish prince for three long heartbeats. Pale fires burned behind the shining black daggers of his teeth. His eyes were lakes of molten gold, and smoke rose from his nostrils.

"Down," Quentyn said. Then he coughed, and coughed again. The air was thick with smoke and the sulfur stench was choking.

Viserion lost interest. The dragon turned back toward the Windblown and lurched toward the door. Perhaps he could smell the blood of the dead guards or the meat in the butcher's wagon. Or perhaps he had only now seen that the way was open.

Quentyn heard the sellswords shouting. Caggo was calling for the chains, and Pretty Meris was screaming at someone to step aside. The dragon moved awkwardly on the ground, like a man scrabbling on his knees and elbows, but quicker than the Dornish prince would have believed. When the Windblown were too late to get out of his way, Viserion let loose with another roar. Quentyn heard the rattle of chains, the deep *thrum* of a crossbow.

"No," he screamed, "no, don't, *don't*," but it was too late. *The fool* was all that he had time to think as the quarrel caromed off Viserion's neck to vanish in the gloom. A line of fire gleamed in its wake—dragon's blood, glowing gold and red.

The crossbowman was fumbling for another quarrel as the dragon's teeth closed around his neck. The man wore the mask of a Brazen Beast, the fearsome likeness of a tiger. As he dropped his weapon to try and pry apart Viserion's jaws, flame gouted from the tiger's mouth. The man's eyes burst with soft popping sounds, and the brass around them began to run. The dragon tore off a hunk of flesh, most of the sellsword's neck, then gulped it down as the burning corpse collapsed to the floor.

The other Windblown were pulling back. This was more than even Pretty Meris had the stomach for. Viserion's horned head moved back and forth between them and his prey, but after a moment he forgot the sellswords and bent his neck to tear another mouthful from the dead man. A lower leg this time.

Quentyn let his whip uncoil. "Viserion," he called, louder this time. He could do this, he would do this, his father had sent him to the far ends of the earth for this, he would not fail him. "*VISERION!*" He snapped the whip in the air with a *crack* that echoed off the blackened walls.

The pale head rose. The great gold eyes narrowed. Wisps of smoke spiraled upward from the dragon's nostrils.

"Down," the prince commanded. *You must not let him smell your fear.* "Down, down, *down.*" He brought the whip around and laid a lash across the dragon's face. Viserion *hissed.*

And then a hot wind buffeted him and he heard the sound of leathern wings and the air was full of ash and cinders and a monstrous roar went echoing off the scorched and blackened bricks and he could hear his friends shouting wildly. Gerris was calling out his name, over and over, and the big man was bellowing, "Behind you, behind you, *behind you!*"

Quentyn turned and threw his left arm across his face to shield his eyes from the furnace wind. *Rhaegal,* he reminded himself, *the green one is Rhaegal.*

When he raised his whip, he saw that the lash was burning. His hand as well. All of him, all of him was burning.

Oh, he thought. Then he began to scream.

JON

"Let them die," said Queen Selyse.

It was the answer that Jon Snow had expected. *This queen never fails to disappoint.* Somehow that did not soften the blow. "Your Grace," he persisted stubbornly, "they are starving at Hardhome by the thousands. Many are women—"

"—and children, yes. Very sad." The queen pulled her daughter closer to her and kissed her cheek. *The cheek unmarred by greyscale,* Jon did not fail to note. "We are sorry for the little ones, of course, but we must be sensible. We have no food for them, and they are too young to help the king my husband in his wars. Better that they be reborn into the light."

That was just a softer way of saying *let them die.*

The chamber was crowded. Princess Shireen stood beside her mother's seat, with Patchface cross-legged at her feet. Behind the queen loomed Ser Axell Florent. Melisandre of Asshai stood closer to the fire, the ruby at her throat pulsing with every breath she took. The red woman too had her attendants—the squire Devan Seaworth and two of the guardsmen the king had left her.

Queen Selyse's protectors stood along the walls, shining knights all in a row: Ser Malegorn, Ser Benethon, Ser Narbert, Ser Patrek, Ser Dorden, Ser Brus. With so many bloodthirsty wildlings infesting Castle Black, Selyse kept her sworn shields about her night and day. Tormund Giantsbane had roared to hear it. "Afraid of being carried off, is she? I hope you never said how big me member is, Jon Snow, that'd frighten any woman. I always wanted me one with a mustache." Then he laughed and laughed.

He would not be laughing now.

Jon had wasted enough time here. "I'm sorry to have troubled Your Grace. The Night's Watch will attend to this matter."

The queen's nostrils flared. "You still mean to ride to Hardhome. I see it on your face. *Let them die,* I said, yet you will persist in this mad folly. Do not deny it."

"I must do as I think best. With respect, Your Grace, the Wall is mine, and so is this decision."

"It is," Selyse allowed, "and you will answer for it when the king returns. And for other decisions you have made, I fear. But I see that you are deaf to sense. Do what you must."

Up spoke Ser Malegorn. "Lord Snow, who will lead this ranging?"

"Are you offering yourself, ser?"

"Do I look so foolish?"

Patchface jumped up. "I will lead it!" His bells rang merrily. "We will march into the sea and out again. Under the waves we will ride seahorses, and mermaids will blow seashells to announce our coming, oh, oh, oh."

They all laughed. Even Queen Selyse allowed herself a thin smile. Jon was less amused. "I will not ask my men to do what I would not do myself. I mean to lead the ranging."

"How bold of you," said the queen. "We approve. Afterward some bard will make a stirring song about you, no doubt, and we shall have a more prudent lord commander." She took a sip of wine. "Let us speak of other matters. Axell, bring in the wildling king, if you would be so good."

"At once, Your Grace." Ser Axell went through a door and returned a moment later with Gerrick Kingsblood. "Gerrick of House Redbeard," he announced, "King of the Wildlings."

Gerrick Kingsblood was a tall man, long of leg and broad of shoulder. The queen had dressed him in some of the king's old clothes, it appeared. Scrubbed and groomed, clad in green velvets and an ermine half-cape, with his long red hair freshly washed and his fiery beard shaped and trimmed, the wildling looked every inch a southron lord. *He could walk into the throne room at King's Landing, and no one would blink an eye,* Jon thought.

"Gerrick is the true and rightful king of the wildlings," the queen said, "descended in an unbroken male line from their great king Raymun Redbeard, whereas the usurper Mance Rayder was born of some common woman and fathered by one of your black brothers."

No, Jon might have said, *Gerrick is descended from a younger brother of Raymun Redbeard.* To the free folk that counted about as much as being descended from Raymun Redbeard's horse. *They know nothing, Ygritte. And worse, they will not learn.*

"Gerrick has graciously agreed to give the hand of his eldest daughter to my beloved Axell, to be united by the Lord of Light in holy wedlock,"

Queen Selyse said. "His other girls shall wed at the same time—the second daughter with Ser Brus Buckler and the youngest with Ser Malegorn of Redpool."

"Sers." Jon inclined his head to the knights in question. "May you find happiness with your betrothed."

"Under the sea, men marry fishes." Patchface did a little dance step, jingling his bells. "They do, they do, they do."

Queen Selyse sniffed again. "Four marriages can be made as simply as three. It is past time that this woman Val was settled, Lord Snow. I have decided that she shall wed my good and leal knight, Ser Patrek of King's Mountain."

"Has Val been told, Your Grace?" asked Jon. "Amongst the free folk, when a man desires a woman, he steals her, and thus proves his strength, his cunning, and his courage. The suitor risks a savage beating if he is caught by the woman's kin, and worse than that if she herself finds him unworthy."

"A savage custom," Axell Florent said.

Ser Patrek only chuckled. "No man has ever had cause to question my courage. No woman ever will."

Queen Selyse pursed her lips. "Lord Snow, as Lady Val is a stranger to our ways, please send her to me, that I might instruct her in the duties of a noble lady toward her lord husband."

That will go splendidly, I know. Jon wondered if the queen would be so eager to see Val married to one of her own knights if she knew Val's feelings about Princess Shireen. "As you wish," he said, "though if I might speak freely—"

"No, I think not. You may take your leave of us."

Jon Snow bent his knee, bowed his head, withdrew.

He took the steps two at a time, nodding to the queen's guards as he descended. Her Grace had posted men on every landing to keep her safe from murderous wildlings. Halfway down, a voice called out from above him. "Jon Snow."

Jon turned. "Lady Melisandre."

"We must speak."

"Must we?" *I think not.* "My lady, I have duties."

"It is those duties I would speak of." She made her way down, the hem of her scarlet skirts swishing over the steps. It almost seemed as if she floated. "Where is your direwolf?"

"Asleep in my chambers. Her Grace does not allow Ghost in her presence. She claims he scares the princess. And so long as Borroq and his boar are about, I dare not let him loose." The skinchanger was to accompany Soren Shieldbreaker to Stonedoor once the wayns carrying the Sealskinner's clan to Greenguard returned. Until such time, Borroq had taken up residence in one of the ancient tombs beside the castle lichyard. The company of men long dead seemed to suit him better than that of the living, and his boar seemed happy rooting amongst the graves, well away from other animals. "That thing is the size of a bull, with tusks as long as swords. Ghost would go after him if he were loose, and one or both of them would not survive the meeting."

"Borroq is the least of your concerns. This ranging . . ."

"A word from you might have swayed the queen."

"Selyse has the right of this, Lord Snow. *Let them die.* You cannot save them. Your ships are lost—"

"Six remain. More than half the fleet."

"Your ships are lost. *All* of them. Not a man shall return. I have seen that in my fires."

"Your fires have been known to lie."

"I have made mistakes, I have admitted as much, but—"

"A grey girl on a dying horse. Daggers in the dark. A promised prince, born in smoke and salt. It seems to me that you make nothing *but* mistakes, my lady. Where is Stannis? What of Rattleshirt and his spearwives? *Where is my sister?*"

"All your questions shall be answered. Look to the skies, Lord Snow. And when you have your answers, send to me. Winter is almost upon us now. I am your only hope."

"A fool's hope." Jon turned and left her.

Leathers was prowling the yard outside. "Toregg has returned," he reported when Jon emerged. "His father's settled his people at Oakenshield and will be back this afternoon with eighty fighting men. What did the bearded queen have to say?"

"Her Grace can provide no help."

"Too busy plucking out her chin hairs, is she?" Leathers spat. "Makes no matter. Tormund's men and ours will be enough."

Enough to get us there, perhaps. It was the journey back that concerned Jon Snow. Coming home, they would be slowed by thousands of free folk, many sick and starved. *A river of humanity moving slower than a river of ice.* That would leave them vulnerable. *Dead things in the woods. Dead things in the water.* "How many men are enough?" he asked Leathers. "A hundred? Two hundred? Five hundred? A thousand?" *Should I take more men, or fewer?* A smaller ranging would reach Hardhome sooner . . . but what good were swords without food? Mother Mole and her people were already at the point of eating their own dead. To feed them, he would need to bring carts and wagons, and draft animals to haul them—horses, oxen, dogs. Instead of flying through the wood, they would be condemned to crawl. "There is still much to decide. Spread the word. I want all the leading men in the Shieldhall when the evening watch begins. Tormund should be back by then. Where can I find Toregg?"

"With the little monster, like as not. He's taken a liking to one o' them milkmaids, I hear."

He has taken a liking to Val. Her sister was a queen, why not her? Tormund had once thought to make himself the King-Beyond-the-Wall, before Mance had bested him. Toregg the Tall might well be dreaming the same dream. *Better him than Gerrick Kingsblood.* "Let them be," said Jon. "I can speak with Toregg later." He glanced up past the King's Tower. The Wall was a dull white, the sky above it whiter. *A snow sky.* "Just pray we do not get another storm."

Outside the armory, Mully and the Flea stood shivering at guard. "Shouldn't you be inside, out of this wind?" Jon asked.

"That'd be sweet, m'lord," said Fulk the Flea, "but your wolf's in no mood for company today."

Mully agreed. "He tried to take a bite o' me, he did."

"*Ghost?*" Jon was shocked.

"Unless your lordship has some other white wolf, aye. I never seen him like this, m'lord. All wild-like, I mean."

He was not wrong, as Jon discovered for himself when he slipped inside the doors. The big white direwolf would not lie still. He paced from one end of the armory to the other, past the cold forge and back again. "Easy, Ghost," Jon called. "Down. Sit, Ghost. *Down.*" Yet when he made to touch him, the wolf bristled and bared his teeth. *It's that bloody boar. Even in here, Ghost can smell his stink.*

Mormont's raven seemed agitated too. "*Snow,*" the bird kept screaming. "*Snow, snow, snow.*" Jon shooed him off, had Satin start a fire, then sent him out after Bowen Marsh and Othell Yarwyck. "Bring a flagon of mulled wine as well."

"Three cups, m'lord?"

"Six. Mully and the Flea look in need of something warm. So will you."

When Satin left, Jon seated himself and had another look at the maps of the lands north of the Wall. The fastest way to Hardhome was along the coast . . . from Eastwatch. The woods were thinner near the sea, the terrain mostly flatlands, rolling hills, and salt marshes. And when the autumn storms came howling, the coast got sleet and hail and freezing rain rather than snow. *The giants are at Eastwatch, and Leathers says that some will help.* From Castle Black the way was more difficult, right through the heart of the haunted forest. *If the snow is this deep at the Wall, how much worse up there?*

Marsh entered snuffling, Yarwyck dour. "Another storm," the First Builder announced. "How are we to work in this? I need more builders."

"Use the free folk," Jon said.

Yarwyck shook his head. "More trouble than they're worth, that lot. Sloppy, careless, lazy . . . some good woodworkers here and there, I'll not deny it, but hardly a mason amongst them, and nary a smith. Strong backs, might be, but they won't do as they are told. And us with all these ruins to turn back into forts. Can't be done, my lord. I tell you true. It can't be done."

"It will be done," said Jon, "or they will live in ruins."

A lord needed men about him he could rely upon for honest counsel. Marsh and Yarwyck were no lickspittles, and that was to the good . . . but they were seldom any *help* either. More and more, he found he knew what they would say before he asked them.

Especially when it concerned the free folk, where their disapproval went bone deep. When Jon settled Stonedoor on Soren Shieldbreaker, Yarwyck complained that it was too isolated. How could they know what mischief Soren might get up to, off in those hills? When he conferred Oakenshield on Tormund Giantsbane and Queensgate on Morna White Mask, Marsh pointed out that Castle Black would now have foes on either side who could easily cut them off from the rest of the Wall. As for Borroq, Othell Yarwyck claimed the woods north of Stonedoor were full of wild boars. Who was to say the skinchanger would not make his own pig army?

Hoarfrost Hill and Rimegate still lacked garrisons, so Jon had asked their views on which of the remaining wildling chiefs and war lords might be best suited to hold them. "We have Brogg, Gavin the Trader, the Great Walrus . . . Howd Wanderer walks alone, Tormund says, but there's still Harle the Huntsman, Harle the Handsome, Blind Doss . . . Ygon Oldfather commands a following, but most are his owns sons and grandsons. He has eighteen wives, half of them stolen on raids. Which of these . . ."

"None," Bowen Marsh had said. "I know all these men by their deeds. We should be fitting them for nooses, not giving them our castles."

"Aye," Othell Yarwyck had agreed. "Bad and worse and worst makes a beggar's choice. My lord had as well present us with a pack of wolves and ask which we'd like to tear our throats out."

It was the same again with Hardhome. Satin poured whilst Jon told them of his audience with the queen. Marsh listened attentively, ignoring the mulled wine, whilst Yarwyck drank one cup and then another. But no sooner had Jon finished than the Lord Steward said, "Her Grace is wise. Let them die."

Jon sat back. "Is that the only counsel you can offer, my lord? Tormund is bringing eighty men. How many should we send? Shall we call upon the giants? The spearwives at Long Barrow? If we have women with us, it may put Mother Mole's people at ease."

"Send women, then. Send giants. Send suckling babes. Is that what my lord wishes to hear?" Bowen Marsh rubbed at the scar he had won at the Bridge of Skulls. "Send them all. The more we lose, the fewer mouths we'll have to feed."

Yarwyck was no more helpful. "If the wildlings at Hardhome need saving, let the wildlings here go save them. Tormund knows the way to Hardhome. To hear him talk, he can save them all himself with his huge member."

This was pointless, Jon thought. *Pointless, fruitless, hopeless.* "Thank you for your counsel, my lords."

Satin helped them back into their cloaks. As they walked through the armory, Ghost sniffed at them, his tail upraised and bristling. *My brothers.* The Night's Watch needed leaders with the wisdom of Maester Aemon, the learning of Samwell Tarly, the courage of Qhorin Halfhand, the stubborn strength of the Old Bear, the compassion of Donal Noye. What it had instead was them.

The snow was falling heavily outside. "Wind's from the south," Yarwyck observed. "It's blowing the snow right up against the Wall. See?"

He was right. The switchback stair was buried almost to the first landing, Jon saw, and the wooden doors of the ice cells and storerooms had vanished behind a wall of white. "How many men do we have in ice cells?" he asked Bowen Marsh.

"Four living men. Two dead ones."

The corpses. Jon had almost forgotten them. He had hoped to learn something from the bodies they'd brought back from the weirwood grove, but the dead men had stubbornly remained dead. "We need to dig those cells out."

"Ten stewards and ten spades should do it," said Marsh.

"Use Wun Wun too."

"As you command."

Ten stewards and one giant made short work of the drifts, but even when the doors were clear again, Jon was not satisfied. "Those cells will be buried again by morning. We'd best move the prisoners before they smother."

"Karstark too, m'lord?" asked Fulk the Flea. "Can't we just leave that one shivering till spring?"

"Would that we could." Cregan Karstark had taken to howling in the night of late, and throwing frozen feces at whoever came to feed him. That had not made him beloved of his guards. "Take him to the Lord Commander's Tower. The undervault should hold him." Though partly collapsed, the Old Bear's former seat would be warmer than the ice cells. Its subcellars were largely intact.

Cregan kicked at the guards when they came through the door, twisted and shoved when they grabbed him, even tried to bite them. But the cold had weakened him, and Jon's men were bigger, younger, and stronger. They hauled him out, still struggling, and dragged him through thigh-high snow to his new home.

"What would the lord commander like us to do with his corpses?" asked Marsh when the living men had been moved.

"Leave them." If the storm entombed them, well and good. He would need to burn them eventually, no doubt, but for the nonce they were bound with iron chains inside their cells. That, and being dead, should suffice to hold them harmless.

Tormund Giantsbane timed his arrival perfectly, thundering up with his warriors when all the shoveling was done. Only fifty seemed to have turned up, not the eighty Toregg promised Leathers, but Tormund was not called Tall-Talker for naught. The wildling arrived red-faced, shouting for a horn of ale and something hot to eat. He had ice in his beard and more crusting his mustache.

Someone had already told the Thunderfist about Gerrick Kingsblood and his new style. "King o' the Wildlings?" Tormund roared. "Har! King o' My Hairy Butt Crack, more like."

"He has a regal look to him," Jon said.

"He has a little red cock to go with all that red hair, that's what he has. Raymund Redbeard and his sons died at Long Lake, thanks to your bloody Starks and the Drunken Giant. Not the little brother. Ever wonder why they called him the Red Raven?" Tormund's mouth split in a gap-toothed grin. "First to fly the battle, he was. 'Twas a song about it, after. The singer had to find a rhyme for *craven*, so . . ." He wiped his nose. "If your queen's knights want those girls o' his, they're welcome to them."

"*Girls*," squawked Mormont's raven. "*Girls, girls.*"

That set Tormund to laughing all over again. "Now there's a bird with sense. How much do you want for him, Snow? I gave you a son, the least you could do is give me the bloody bird."

"I would," said Jon, "but like as not you'd eat him."

Tormund roared at that as well. "*Eat*," the raven said darkly, flapping its black wings. "*Corn? Corn? Corn?*"

"We need to talk about the ranging," said Jon. "I want us to be of one mind at the Shieldhall, we must—" He broke off when Mully poked his nose inside the door, grim-faced, to announce that Clydas had brought a letter.

"Tell him to leave it with you. I will read it later."

"As you say, m'lord, only . . . Clydas don't look his proper self . . . he's more white than pink, if you get my meaning . . . and he's shaking."

"Dark wings, dark words," muttered Tormund. "Isn't that what you kneelers say?"

"We say, *Bleed a cold but feast a fever* too," Jon told him. "We say, *Never drink with Dornishmen when the moon is full.* We say a lot of things."

Mully added his two groats. "My old grandmother always used to say, *Summer friends will melt away like summer snows, but winter friends are friends forever.*"

"I think that's sufficient wisdom for the moment," said Jon Snow. "Show Clydas in if you would be so good."

Mully had not been wrong; the old steward *was* trembling, his face as pale as the snows outside. "I am being foolish, Lord Commander, but . . . this letter frightens me. See here?"

Bastard, was the only word written outside the scroll. No *Lord Snow* or *Jon Snow* or *Lord Commander*. Simply *Bastard*. And the letter was sealed with a smear of hard pink wax. "You were right to come at once," Jon said. *You were right to be afraid.* He cracked the seal, flattened the parchment, and read.

> *Your false king is dead, bastard. He and all his host were smashed in seven days of battle. I have his magic sword. Tell his red whore.*
>
> *Your false king's friends are dead. Their heads upon the walls of Winterfell. Come see them, bastard. Your false king lied, and*

so did you. You told the world you burned the King-Beyond-the-Wall. Instead you sent him to Winterfell to steal my bride from me.

I will have my bride back. If you want Mance Rayder back, come and get him. I have him in a cage for all the north to see, proof of your lies. The cage is cold, but I have made him a warm cloak from the skins of the six whores who came with him to Winterfell.

I want my bride back. I want the false king's queen. I want his daughter and his red witch. I want his wildling princess. I want his little prince, the wildling babe. And I want my Reek. Send them to me, bastard, and I will not trouble you or your black crows. Keep them from me, and I will cut out your bastard's heart and eat it.

It was signed,

Ramsay Bolton,
Trueborn Lord of Winterfell.

"Snow?" said Tormund Giantsbane. "You look like your father's bloody head just rolled out o' that paper."

Jon Snow did not answer at once. "Mully, help Clydas back to his chambers. The night is dark, and the paths will be slippery with snow. Satin, go with them." He handed Tormund Giantsbane the letter. "Here, see for yourself."

The wildling gave the letter a dubious look and handed it right back. "Feels nasty . . . but Tormund Thunderfist had better things to do than learn to make papers talk at him. They never have any good to say, now do they?"

"Not often," Jon Snow admitted. *Dark wings, dark words.* Perhaps there was more truth to those wise old sayings than he'd known. "It was sent by Ramsay Snow. I'll read you what he wrote."

When he was done, Tormund whistled. "Har. That's buggered, and no mistake. What was that about Mance? Has him in a cage, does he? How, when hundreds saw your red witch burn the man?"

That was Rattleshirt, Jon almost said. *That was sorcery. A glamor, she called it.* "Melisandre . . . *look to the skies,* she said." He set the letter

down. "A raven in a storm. She saw this coming." *When you have your
answers, send to me.*

"Might be all a skin o' lies." Tormund scratched under his beard. "If I
had me a nice goose quill and a pot o' maester's ink, I could write down
that me member was long and thick as me arm, wouldn't make it so."

"He has Lightbringer. He talks of heads upon the walls of Winterfell.
He knows about the spearwives and their number." *He knows about
Mance Rayder.* "No. There is truth in there."

"I won't say you're wrong. What do you mean to do, crow?"

Jon flexed the fingers of his sword hand. *The Night's Watch takes no
part.* He closed his fist and opened it again. *What you propose is nothing
less than treason.* He thought of Robb, with snowflakes melting in his hair.
Kill the boy and let the man be born. He thought of Bran, clambering up
a tower wall, agile as a monkey. Of Rickon's breathless laughter. Of Sansa,
brushing out Lady's coat and singing to herself. *You know nothing, Jon
Snow.* He thought of Arya, her hair as tangled as a bird's nest. *I made him
a warm cloak from the skins of the six whores who came with him to Winterfell . . . I want my bride back . . . I want my bride back . . . I want my bride
back . . .*

"I think we had best change the plan," Jon Snow said.

They talked for the best part of two hours.

Horse and Rory had replaced Fulk and Mully at the armory door with
the change of watch. "With me," Jon told them, when the time came.
Ghost would have followed as well, but as the wolf came padding after
them, Jon grabbed him by the scruff of his neck and wrestled him back
inside. Borroq might be amongst those gathering at the Shieldhall. The
last thing he needed just now was his wolf savaging the skinchanger's
boar.

The Shieldhall was one of the older parts of Castle Black, a long drafty
feast hall of dark stone, its oaken rafters black with the smoke of centuries.
Back when the Night's Watch had been much larger, its walls had been
hung with rows of brightly colored wooden shields. Then as now, when a
knight took the black, tradition decreed that he set aside his former arms
and take up the plain black shield of the brotherhood. The shields thus
discarded would hang in the Shieldhall.

Hundreds of knights meant hundreds of shields. Hawks and eagles,
dragons and griffins, suns and stags, wolves and wyverns, manticores, bulls,
trees and flowers, harps, spears, crabs and krakens, red lions and golden
lions and chequy lions, owls, lambs, maids and mermen, stallions, stars,
buckets and buckles, flayed men and hanged men and burning men, axes,

longswords, turtles, unicorns, bears, quills, spiders and snakes and scorpions, and a hundred other heraldic charges had adorned the Shieldhall
walls, blazoned in more colors than any rainbow ever dreamed of.

But when a knight died, his shield was taken down, that it might go
with him to his pyre or his tomb, and over the years and centuries fewer
and fewer knights had taken the black. A day came when it no longer
made sense for the knights of Castle Black to dine apart. The Shieldhall
was abandoned. In the last hundred years, it had been used only infre-
quently. As a dining hall, it left much to be desired—it was dark, dirty,
drafty, and hard to heat in winter, its cellars infested with rats, its massive
wooden rafters worm-eaten and festooned with cobwebs.

But it was large and long enough to seat two hundred, and half again
that many if they crowded close. When Jon and Tormund entered, a
sound went through the hall, like wasps stirring in a nest. The wildlings
outnumbered the crows by five to one, judging by how little black he saw.
Fewer than a dozen shields remained, sad grey things with faded paint
and long cracks in the wood. But fresh torches burned in the iron sconces
along the walls, and Jon had ordered benches and tables brought in. Men
with comfortable seats were more inclined to listen, Maester Aemon had
once told him; standing men were more inclined to shout.

At the top of the hall a sagging platform stood. Jon mounted it, with
Tormund Giantsbane at his side, and raised his hands for quiet. The wasps
only buzzed the louder. Then Tormund put his warhorn to his lips and
blew a blast. The sound filled the hall, echoing off the rafters overhead.
Silence fell.

"I summoned you to make plans for the relief of Hardhome," Jon Snow
began. "Thousands of the free folk are gathered there, trapped and starving, and we have had reports of dead things in the wood." To his left he
saw Marsh and Yarwyck. Othell was surrounded by his builders, whilst
Bowen had Wick Whittlestick, Left Hand Lew, and Alf of Runnymudd
beside him. To his right, Soren Shieldbreaker sat with his arms crossed
against his chest. Farther back, Jon saw Gavin the Trader and Harle the
Handsome whispering together. Ygon Oldfather sat amongst his wives,
Howd Wanderer alone. Borroq leaned against a wall in a dark corner.
Mercifully, his boar was nowhere in evidence. "The ships I sent to take off
Mother Mole and her people have been wracked by storms. We must
send what help we can by land or let them die." Two of Queen Selyse's
knights had come as well, Jon saw. Ser Narbert and Ser Benethon stood
near the door at the foot of the hall. But the rest of the queen's men were
conspicuous in their absence. "I had hoped to lead the ranging myself

and bring back as many of the free folk as could survive the journey." A flash of red in the back of the hall caught Jon's eye. Lady Melisandre had arrived. "But now I find I cannot go to Hardhome. The ranging will be led by Tormund Giantsbane, known to you all. I have promised him as many men as he requires."

"*And where will you be, crow?*" Borroq thundered. "Hiding here in Castle Black with your white dog?"

"No. I ride south." Then Jon read them the letter Ramsay Snow had written.

The Shieldhall went mad.

Every man began to shout at once. They leapt to their feet, shaking fists. *So much for the calming power of comfortable benches.* Swords were brandished, axes smashed against shields. Jon Snow looked to Tormund. The Giantsbane sounded his horn once more, twice as long and twice as loud as the first time.

"The Night's Watch takes no part in the wars of the Seven Kingdoms," Jon reminded them when some semblance of quiet had returned. "It is not for us to oppose the Bastard of Bolton, to avenge Stannis Baratheon, to defend his widow and his daughter. This *creature* who makes cloaks from the skins of women has sworn to cut my heart out, and I mean to make him answer for those words . . . but I will not ask my brothers to forswear their vows.

"The Night's Watch will make for Hardhome. I ride to Winterfell alone, unless . . ." Jon paused. ". . . is there any man here who will come stand with me?"

The roar was all he could have hoped for, the tumult so loud that the two old shields tumbled from the walls. Soren Shieldbreaker was on his feet, the Wanderer as well. Toregg the Tall, Brogg, Harle the Huntsman and Harle the Handsome both, Ygon Oldfather, Blind Doss, even the Great Walrus. *I have my swords,* thought Jon Snow, *and we are coming for you, Bastard.*

Yarwyck and Marsh were slipping out, he saw, and all their men behind them. It made no matter. He did not need them now. He did not *want* them. *No man can ever say I made my brothers break their vows. If this is oathbreaking, the crime is mine and mine alone.* Then Tormund was pounding him on the back, all gap-toothed grin from ear to ear. "Well spoken, crow. Now bring out the mead! Make them yours and get them drunk, that's how it's done. We'll make a wildling o' you yet, boy. Har!"

"I will send for ale," Jon said, distracted. Melisandre was gone, he realized, and so were the queen's knights. *I should have gone to Selyse first.*

She has the right to know her lord is dead. "You must excuse me. I'll leave you to get them drunk."

"Har! A task I'm well suited for, crow. On your way!"

Horse and Rory fell in beside Jon as he left the Shieldhall. *I should talk with Melisandre after I see the queen,* he thought. *If she could see a raven in a storm, she can find Ramsay Snow for me.* Then he heard the shouting . . . and a roar so loud it seemed to shake the Wall. "That come from Hardin's Tower, m'lord," Horse reported. He might have said more, but the scream cut him off.

Val, was Jon's first thought. But that was no woman's scream. *That is a man in mortal agony.* He broke into a run. Horse and Rory raced after him. "Is it wights?" asked Rory. Jon wondered. Could his corpses have escaped their chains?

The screaming had stopped by the time they came to Hardin's Tower, but Wun Weg Wun Dar Wun was still roaring. The giant was dangling a bloody corpse by one leg, the same way Arya used to dangle her doll when she was small, swinging it like a morningstar when menaced by vegetables. *Arya never tore her dolls to pieces, though.* The dead man's sword arm was yards away, the snow beneath it turning red.

"Let him go," Jon shouted. "Wun Wun, *let him go.*"

Wun Wun did not hear or did not understand. The giant was bleeding himself, with sword cuts on his belly and his arm. He swung the dead knight against the grey stone of the tower, again and again and again, until the man's head was red and pulpy as a summer melon. The knight's cloak flapped in the cold air. Of white wool it had been, bordered in cloth-of-silver and patterned with blue stars. Blood and bone were flying everywhere.

Men poured from the surrounding keeps and towers. Northmen, free folk, queen's men . . . "Form a line," Jon Snow commanded them. "Keep them back. Everyone, but especially the queen's men." The dead man was Ser Patrek of King's Mountain; his head was largely gone, but his heraldry was as distinctive as his face. Jon did not want to risk Ser Malegorn or Ser Brus or any of the queen's other knights trying to avenge him.

Wun Weg Wun Dar Wun howled again and gave Ser Patrek's other arm a twist and pull. It tore loose from his shoulder with a spray of bright red blood. *Like a child pulling petals off a daisy,* thought Jon. "Leathers, talk to him, calm him. The Old Tongue, he understands the Old Tongue. *Keep back,* the rest of you. Put away your steel, we're scaring him." Couldn't they see the giant had been cut? Jon had to put an end to this or more men would die. They had no idea of Wun Wun's strength. *A horn, I need a horn.* He saw the glint of steel, turned toward it. *"No blades!"* he screamed. "Wick, put that knife . . ."

. . . *away*, he meant to say. When Wick Whittlestick slashed at his throat, the word turned into a grunt. Jon twisted from the knife, just enough so it barely grazed his skin. *He cut me.* When he put his hand to the side of his neck, blood welled between his fingers. *"Why?"*

"For the Watch." Wick slashed at him again. This time Jon caught his wrist and bent his arm back until he dropped the dagger. The gangling steward backed away, his hands upraised as if to say, *Not me, it was not me.* Men were screaming. Jon reached for Longclaw, but his fingers had grown stiff and clumsy. Somehow he could not seem to get the sword free of its scabbard.

Then Bowen Marsh stood there before him, tears running down his cheeks. "For the Watch." He punched Jon in the belly. When he pulled his hand away, the dagger stayed where he had buried it.

Jon fell to his knees. He found the dagger's hilt and wrenched it free. In the cold night air the wound was smoking. "Ghost," he whispered. Pain washed over him. *Stick them with the pointy end.* When the third dagger took him between the shoulder blades, he gave a grunt and fell face-first into the snow. He never felt the fourth knife. Only the cold . . .

THE QUEEN'S HAND

The Dornish prince was three days dying.

He took his last shuddering breath in the bleak black dawn, as cold rain hissed from a dark sky to turn the brick streets of the old city into rivers. The rain had drowned the worst of the fires, but wisps of smoke still rose from the smoldering ruin that had been the pyramid of Hazkar, and the great black pyramid of Yherizan where Rhaegal had made his lair hulked in the gloom like a fat woman bedecked with glowing orange jewels.

Perhaps the gods are not deaf after all, Ser Barristan Selmy reflected as he watched those distant embers. *If not for the rain, the fires might have consumed all of Meereen by now.*

He saw no sign of dragons, but he had not expected to. The dragons did not like the rain. A thin red slash marked the eastern horizon where the sun might soon appear. It reminded Selmy of the first blood welling from a wound. Often, even with a deep cut, the blood came before the pain.

He stood beside the parapets of the highest step of the Great Pyramid, searching the sky as he did every morning, knowing that the dawn must come and hoping that his queen would come with it. *She will not have abandoned us, she would never leave her people,* he was telling himself, when he heard the prince's death rattle coming from the queen's apartments.

Ser Barristan went inside. Rainwater ran down the back of his white cloak, and his boots left wet tracks on the floors and carpets. At his command, Quentyn Martell had been laid out in the queen's own bed. He had been a knight, and a prince of Dorne besides. It seemed only kind to let him die in the bed he had crossed half a world to reach. The bedding was ruined—sheets, covers, pillows, mattress, all reeked of blood and smoke, but Ser Barristan thought Daenerys would forgive him.

Missandei sat at the bedside. She had been with the prince night and day, tending to such needs as he could express, giving him water and milk of the poppy when he was strong enough to drink, listening to the few tortured words he gasped out from time to time, reading to him when he fell quiet, sleeping in her chair beside him. Ser Barristan had asked some of the queen's cupbearers to help, but the sight of the burned man was too much for even the boldest of them. And the Blue Graces had never come, though he'd sent for them four times. Perhaps the last of them had been carried off by the pale mare by now.

The tiny Naathi scribe looked up at his approach. "Honored ser. The prince is beyond pain now. His Dornish gods have taken him home. See? He smiles."

How can you tell? He has no lips. It would have been kinder if the dragons had devoured him. That at least would have been quick. This . . . *Fire is a hideous way to die. Small wonder half the hells are made of flame.* "Cover him."

Missandei pulled the coverlet over the prince's face. "What will be done with him, ser? He is so very far from home."

"I'll see that he's returned to Dorne." *But how? As ashes?* That would require more fire, and Ser Barristan could not stomach that. *We'll need to strip the flesh from his bones. Beetles, not boiling.* The silent sisters would have seen to it at home, but this was Slaver's Bay. The nearest silent sister was ten thousand leagues away. "You should go sleep now, child. In your own bed."

"If this one may be so bold, ser, you should do the same. You do not sleep the whole night through."

Not for many years, child. Not since the Trident. Grand Maester Pycelle had once told him that old men do not need as much sleep as the young, but it was more than that. He had reached that age when he was loath to close his eyes, for fear that he might never open them again. Other men might wish to die in bed asleep, but that was no death for a knight of the Kingsguard.

"The nights are too long," he told Missandei, "and there is much and more to do, always. Here, as in the Seven Kingdoms. But you have done enough for now, child. Go and rest." *And if the gods are good, you will not dream of dragons.*

After the girl was gone, the old knight peeled back the coverlet for one last look at Quentyn Martell's face, or what remained of it. So much of the prince's flesh had sloughed away that he could see the skull beneath. His eyes were pools of pus. *He should have stayed in Dorne. He should have stayed a frog. Not all men are meant to dance with dragons.* As he covered the boy once more, he found himself wondering whether there would be anyone to cover his queen, or whether her own corpse would lie unmourned amongst the tall grasses of the Dothraki sea, staring blindly at the sky until her flesh fell from her bones.

"No," he said aloud. "Daenerys is not dead. She was riding that dragon. I saw it with mine own two eyes." He had said the same a hundred times before . . . but every day that passed made it harder to believe. *Her hair was afire. I saw that too. She was burning . . . and if I did not see her fall, hundreds swear they did.*

Day had crept upon the city. Though the rain still fell, a vague light suffused the eastern sky. And with the sun arrived the Shavepate. Skahaz was clad in his familiar garb of pleated black skirt, greaves, and muscled breastplate. The brazen mask beneath his arm was new—a wolf's head with lolling tongue. "So," he said, by way of greeting, "the fool is dead, is he?"

"Prince Quentyn died just before first light." Selmy was not surprised that Skahaz knew. Word traveled quickly within the pyramid. "Is the council assembled?"

"They await the Hand's pleasure below."

I am no Hand, a part of him wanted to cry out. *I am only a simple knight, the queen's protector. I never wanted this.* But with the queen gone and the king in chains, someone had to rule, and Ser Barristan did not trust the Shavepate. "Has there been any word from the Green Grace?"

"She is not yet returned to the city." Skahaz had opposed sending the priestess. Nor had Galazza Galare herself embraced the task. She would go, she allowed, for the sake of peace, but Hizdahr zo Loraq was better suited to treat with the Wise Masters. But Ser Barristan did not yield easily, and finally the Green Grace had bowed her head and sworn to do her best.

"How stands the city?" Selmy asked the Shavepate now.

"All the gates are closed and barred, as you commanded. We are hunting down any sellswords or Yunkai'i left inside the city and expelling or arresting those we catch. Most seem to have gone to ground. Inside the pyramids, beyond a doubt. The Unsullied man the walls and towers, ready for any assault. There are two hundred highborn gathered in the square, standing in the rain in their *tokar*s and howling for audience. They want Hizdahr free and me dead, and they want you to slay these dragons. Someone told them knights were good at that. Men are still pulling corpses from the pyramid of Hazkar. The Great Masters of Yherizan and Uhlez have abandoned their own pyramids to the dragons."

Ser Barristan had known all that. "And the butcher's tally?" he asked, dreading the answer.

"Nine-and-twenty."

"*Nine-and-twenty?*" That was far worse than he could ever have imagined. The Sons of the Harpy had resumed their shadow war two days ago. Three murders the first night, nine the second. But to go from nine to nine-and-twenty in a single night . . .

"The count will pass thirty before midday. Why do you look so grey, old man? What did you expect? The Harpy wants Hizdahr free, so he has sent his sons back into the streets with knives in hand. The dead are all freedmen and shavepates, as before. One was mine, a Brazen Beast. The sign of the Harpy was left beside the bodies, chalked on the pavement or scratched into a wall. There were messages as well. '*Dragons must die,*' they wrote, and '*Harghaz the Hero.*' '*Death to Daenerys*' was seen as well, before the rain washed out the words."

"The blood tax . . ."

"Twenty-nine hundred pieces of gold from each pyramid, aye," Skahaz grumbled. "It will be collected . . . but the loss of a few coins will never stay the Harpy's hand. Only blood can do that."

"So you say." *The hostages again. He would kill them every one if I allowed it.* "I heard you the first hundred times. No."

"Queen's Hand," Skahaz grumbled with disgust. "An old woman's hand, I am thinking, wrinkled and feeble. I pray Daenerys returns to us soon." He pulled his brazen wolf's mask down over his face. "Your council will be growing restless."

"They are the queen's council, not mine." Selmy exchanged his damp cloak for a dry one and buckled on his sword belt, then accompanied the Shavepate down the steps.

The pillared hall was empty of petitioners this morning. Though he had assumed the title of Hand, Ser Barristan would not presume to hold court in the queen's absence, nor would he permit Skahaz mo Kandaq to do such. Hizdahr's grotesque dragon thrones had been removed at Ser Barristan's command, but he had not brought back the simple pillowed bench the queen had favored. Instead a large round table had been set up in the center of the hall, with tall chairs all around it where men might sit and talk as peers.

They rose when Ser Barristan came down the marble steps, Skahaz

Shavepate at his side. Marselen of the Mother's Men was present, with Symon Stripeback, commander of the Free Brothers. The Stalwart Shields had chosen a new commander, a black-skinned Summer Islander called Tal Toraq, their old captain, Mollono Yos Dob, having been carried off by the pale mare. Grey Worm was there for the Unsullied, attended by three eunuch serjeants in spiked bronze caps. The Stormcrows were represented by two seasoned sellswords, an archer named Jokin and the scarred and sour axeman known simply as the Widower. The two of them had assumed joint command of the company in the absence of Daario Naharis. Most of the queen's *khalasar* had gone with Aggo and Rakharo to search for her on the Dothraki sea, but the squinty, bowlegged *jaqqa rhan* Rommo was there to speak for the riders who remained.

And across the table from Ser Barristan sat four of King Hizdahr's erstwhile guardsmen, the pit fighters Goghor the Giant, Belaquo Bonebreaker, Camarron of the Count, and the Spotted Cat. Selmy had insisted on their presence, over the objections of Skahaz Shavepate. They had helped Daenerys Targaryen take this city once, and that should not be forgotten. Blood-soaked brutes and killers they might be, but in their own way they had been loyal . . . to King Hizdahr, yes, but to the queen as well.

Last to come, Strong Belwas lumbered into the hall.

The eunuch had looked death in the face, so near he might have kissed her on the lips. It had marked him. He looked to have lost two stone of weight, and the dark brown skin that had once stretched tight across a massive chest and belly, crossed by a hundred faded scars, now hung on him in loose folds, sagging and wobbling, like a robe cut three sizes too large. His step had slowed as well, and seemed a bit uncertain.

Even so, the sight of him gladdened the old knight's heart. He had once crossed the world with Strong Belwas, and he knew he could rely on him, should all this come to swords. "Belwas. We are pleased that you could join us."

"Whitebeard." Belwas smiled. "Where is liver and onions? Strong Belwas is not so strong as before, he must eat, get big again. They made Strong Belwas sick. Someone must die."

Someone will. Many someones, like as not. "Sit, my friend." When Belwas sat and crossed his arms, Ser Barristan went on. "Quentyn Martell died this morning, just before the dawn."

The Widower laughed. "The dragonrider."

"Fool, I call him," said Symon Stripeback.

No, just a boy. Ser Barristan had not forgotten the follies of his own youth. "Speak no ill of the dead. The prince paid a ghastly price for what he did."

"And the other Dornish?" asked Tal Taraq.

"Prisoners, for the nonce." Neither of the Dornishmen had offered any resistance. Archibald Yronwood had been cradling his prince's scorched and smoking body when the Brazen Beasts had found him, as his burned hands could testify. He had used them to beat out the flames that had engulfed Quentyn Martell. Gerris Drinkwater was standing over them with sword in hand, but he had dropped the blade the moment the locusts had appeared. "They share a cell."

"Let them share a gibbet," said Symon Stripeback. "They unleashed two dragons on the city."

"Open the pits and give them swords," urged the Spotted Cat. "I will kill them both as all Meereen shouts out my name."

"The fighting pits will remain closed," said Selmy. "Blood and noise would only serve to call the dragons."

"All three, perhaps," suggested Marselen. "The black beast came once, why not again? This time with our queen."

Or without her. Should Drogon return to Meereen without Daenerys mounted on his back, the city would erupt in blood and flame, of that Ser Barristan had no doubt. The very men sitting at this table would soon be at dagger points with one another. A young girl she might be, but Daenerys Targaryen was the only thing that held them all together.

"Her Grace will return when she returns," said Ser Barristan. "We have herded a thousand sheep into the Daznak's Pit, filled the Pit of Ghrazz with bullocks, and the Golden Pit with beasts that Hizdahr zo Loraq had gathered for his games." Thus far both dragons seemed to have a taste for mutton, returning to Daznak's whenever they grew hungry. If either one was hunting man, inside or outside the city, Ser Barristan had yet to hear of it. The only Meereenese the dragons had slain since Harghaz the Hero had been the slavers foolish enough to object when Rhaegal attempted to make his lair atop the pyramid of Hazkar. "We have more pressing matters to discuss. I have sent the Green Grace to the Yunkishmen to make arrangements for the release of our hostages. I expect her back by midday with their answer."

"With words," said the Widower. "The Stormcrows know the Yunkai'i. Their tongues are worms that wriggle this way or that. The Green Grace will come back with worm words, not the captain."

"If it pleases the Queen's Hand to recall, the Wise Masters hold our Hero too," said Grey Worm. "Also the horselord Jhogo, the queen's own bloodrider."

"Blood of her blood," agreed the Dothraki Rommo. "He must be freed. The honor of the *khalasar* demands it."

"He shall be freed," said Ser Barristan, "but first we must needs wait and see if the Green Grace can accomplish—"

Skahaz Shavepate slammed his fist upon the table. "The Green Grace will accomplish *nothing*. She may be conspiring with the Yunkai'i even as we sit here. *Arrangements*, did you say? *Make arrangements?* What sort of *arrangements?*"

"Ransom," said Ser Barristan. "Each man's weight in gold."

"The Wise Masters do not need our gold, ser," said Marselen. "They are richer than your Westerosi lords, every one."

"Their sellswords will want the gold, though. What are the hostages to them? If the Yunkishmen refuse, it will drive a blade between them and their hirelings." *Or so I hope.* It had been Missandei who suggested the ploy to him. He would never have thought of such a thing himself. In King's Landing, bribes had been Littlefinger's domain, whilst Lord Varys had the task of fostering division amongst the crown's enemies. His own duties had been more straightforward. *Eleven years of age, yet Missandei is as clever as half the men at this table and wiser than all of them.* "I have instructed the Green Grace to present the offer only when all of the Yunkish commanders have assembled to hear it."

"They will refuse, even so," insisted Symon Stripeback. "They will say they want the dragons dead, the king restored."

"I pray that you are wrong." *And fear that you are right.*

"Your gods are far away, Ser Grandfather," said the Widower. "I do not think they hear your prayers. And when the Yunkai'i send back the old woman to spit in your eye, what then?"

"*Fire and blood,*" said Barristan Selmy, softly, softly.

For a long moment no one spoke. Then Strong Belwas slapped his belly and said, "Better than liver and onions," and Skahaz Shavepate stared through the eyes of his wolf's head mask and said, "You would break King Hizdahr's peace, old man?"

"I would shatter it." Once, long ago, a prince had named him Barristan the Bold. A part of that boy was in him still. "We have built a beacon atop the pyramid where once the Harpy stood. Dry wood soaked with oil, covered to keep the rain off. Should the hour come, and I pray that it does not, we will light that beacon. The flames will be your signal to pour out of our gates and attack. Every man of you will have a part to play, so every man must be in readiness at all times, day or night. We will destroy our foes or be destroyed ourselves." He raised a hand to signal to his waiting squires. "I have had some maps prepared to show the dispositions of our foes, their camps and siege lines and trebuchets. If we can break the slavers, their sellswords will abandon them. I know you will have concerns and questions. Voice them here. By the time we leave this table, all of us must be of a single mind, with a single purpose."

"Best send down for some food and drink, then," suggested Symon Stripeback. "This will take a while."

It took the rest of the morning and most of the afternoon. The captains and commanders argued over the maps like fishwives over a bucket of crabs. Weak points and strong points, how to best employ their small company of archers, whether the elephants should be used to break the Yunkish lines or held in reserve, who should have the honor of leading the first advance, whether their horse cavalry was best deployed on the flanks or in the vanguard.

Ser Barristan let each man speak his mind. Tal Toraq thought that they should march on Yunkai once they had broken through the lines; the Yellow City would be almost undefended, so the Yunkai'i would have no choice but to lift the siege and follow. The Spotted Cat proposed to challenge the enemy to send forth a champion to face him in single combat. Strong Belwas liked that notion but insisted he should fight, not the Cat. Camarron of the Count put forth a scheme to seize the ships tied up along the riverfront and use the Skahazadhan to bring three hundred pit fighters around the Yunkish rear. Every man there agreed that the Unsullied were their best troops, but none agreed on how they should be deployed. The Widower wanted to use the eunuchs as an iron fist to smash through the heart of the Yunkish defenses. Marselen felt they would be better placed at either end of the main battle line, where they could beat back any attempt by the foe to turn their flanks. Symon Stripeback wanted them split into three and divided amongst the three companies of freedmen. His Free Brothers were brave and eager for the fight, he claimed, but without the Unsullied to stiffen them he feared his unblooded troops might not have the discipline to face battle-seasoned sellswords by themselves. Grey Worm said only that the Unsullied would obey, whatever might be asked of them.

And when all that had been discussed, debated, and decided, Symon Stripeback raised one final point. "As a slave in Yunkai I helped my master bargain with the free companies and saw to the payment of their wages.

I know sellswords, and I know that the Yunkai'i cannot pay them near enough to face dragonflame. So I ask you . . . if the peace should fail and this battle should be joined, will the dragons come? Will they join the fight?"

They will come, Ser Barristan might have said. *The noise will bring them, the shouts and screams, the scent of blood. That will draw them to the battlefield, just as the roar from Daznak's Pit drew Drogon to the scarlet sands. But when they come, will they know one side from the other?* Somehow he did not think so. So he said only, "The dragons will do what the dragons will do. If they do come, it may be that just the shadow of their wings will be enough to dishearten the slavers and send them fleeing." Then he thanked them and dismissed them all.

Grey Worm lingered after the others had left. "These ones will be ready when the beacon fire is lit. But the Hand must surely know that when we attack, the Yunkai'i will kill the hostages."

"I will do all I can to prevent that, my friend. I have a . . . notion. But pray excuse me. It is past time the Dornishmen heard that their prince is dead."

Grey Worm inclined his head. "This one obeys."

Ser Barristan took two of his new-made knights with him down into the dungeons. Grief and guilt had been known to drive good men into madness, and Archibald Yronwood and Gerris Drinkwater had both played roles in their friend's demise. But when they reached the cell, he told Tum and the Red Lamb to wait outside whilst he went in to tell the Dornish that the prince's agony was over.

Ser Archibald, the big bald one, had nothing to say. He sat on the edge of his pallet, staring down at his bandaged hands in their linen wrappings. Ser Gerris punched a wall. "I told him it was folly. I begged him to go home. Your bitch of a queen had no use for him, any man could see that. He crossed the world to offer her his love and fealty, and she laughed in his face."

"She never laughed," said Selmy. "If you knew her, you would know that."

"She spurned him. He offered her his heart, and she threw it back at him and went off to fuck her sellsword."

"You had best guard that tongue, ser." Ser Barristan did not like this Gerris Drinkwater, nor would he allow him to vilify Daenerys. "Prince Quentyn's death was his own doing, and yours."

"*Ours?* How are we at fault, ser? Quentyn was our friend, yes. A bit of a fool, you might say, but all dreamers are fools. But first and last he was our prince. We owed him our obedience."

Barristan Selmy could not dispute the truth of that. He had spent the best part of his own life obeying the commands of drunkards and madmen. "He came too late."

"He offered her his heart," Ser Gerris said again.

"She needed swords, not hearts."

"He would have given her the spears of Dorne as well."

"Would that he had." No one had wanted Daenerys to look with favor on the Dornish prince more than Barristan Selmy. "He came too late, though, and this folly . . . buying sellswords, loosing two dragons on the city . . . that was madness and worse than madness. That was treason."

"What he did he did for love of Queen Daenerys," Gerris Drinkwater insisted. "To prove himself worthy of her hand."

The old knight had heard enough. "What Prince Quentyn did he did for Dorne. Do you take me for some doting grandfather? I have spent my life around kings and queens and princes. Sunspear means to take up arms against the Iron Throne. No, do not trouble to deny it. Doran Martell is not a man to call his spears without hope of victory. Duty brought Prince Quentyn here. Duty, honor, thirst for glory . . . never love. Quentyn was here for dragons, not Daenerys."

"You did not know him, ser. He—"

"He's dead, Drink." Yronwood rose to his feet. "Words won't fetch him back. Cletus and Will are dead too. So shut your bloody mouth before I stick my fist in it." The big knight turned to Selmy. "What do you mean to do with us?"

"Skahaz Shavepate wants you hanged. You slew four of his men. Four of the *queen's* men. Two were freedmen who had followed Her Grace since Astapor."

Yronwood did not seem surprised. "The beast men, aye. I only killed the one, the basilisk head. The sellswords did the others. Don't matter, though, I know that."

"We were protecting Quentyn," said Drinkwater. "We—"

"Be *quiet*, Drink. He knows." To Ser Barristan the big knight said, "No need to come and talk if you meant to hang us. So it's not that, is it?"

"No." *This one may not be as slow-witted as he seems.* "I have more use for you alive than dead. Serve me, and afterward I will arrange a ship to take you back to Dorne and give you Prince Quentyn's bones to return to his lord father."

Ser Archibald grimaced. "Why is it always ships? Someone needs to take Quent home, though. What do you ask of us, ser?"

"Your swords."

"You have thousands of swords."

"The queen's freedmen are as yet unblooded. The sellswords I do not trust. Unsullied are brave soldiers . . . but not warriors. Not *knights*." He paused. "What happened when you tried to take the dragons? Tell me."

The Dornishmen exchanged a look. Then Drinkwater said, "Quentyn told the Tattered Prince he could control them. It was in his blood, he said. He had Targaryen blood."

"Blood of the dragon."

"Yes. The sellswords were supposed to help us get the dragons chained up so we could get them to the docks."

"Rags arranged for a ship," said Yronwood. "A big one, in case we got both dragons. And Quent was going to ride one." He looked at his bandaged hands. "The moment we got in, though, you could see none of it was going to work. The dragons were too wild. The chains . . . there were bits of broken chain everywhere, *big* chains, links the size of your head mixed in with all these cracked and splintered bones. And Quent, Seven save him, he looked like he was going to shit his smallclothes. Caggo and Meris weren't blind, they saw it too. Then one of the crossbowmen let fly. Maybe they meant to kill the dragons all along and were only using us to get to them. You never know with Tatters. Any way you hack it off, it weren't clever. The quarrel just made the dragons angry, and they hadn't been in such a good mood to start with. Then . . . then things got bad."

"And the Windblown blew away," said Ser Gerris. "Quent was screaming, covered in flames, and they were gone. Caggo, Pretty Meris, all but the dead one."

"Ah, what did you expect, Drink? A cat will kill a mouse, a pig will wallow in shit, and a sellsword will run off when he's needed most. Can't be blamed. Just the nature of the beast."

"He's not wrong," Ser Barristan said. "What did Prince Quentyn promise the Tattered Prince in return for all this help?"

He got no answer. Ser Gerris looked at Ser Archibald. Ser Archibald looked at his hands, the floor, the door.

"Pentos," said Ser Barristan. "He promised him Pentos. Say it. No words of yours can help or harm Prince Quentyn now."

"Aye," said Ser Archibald unhappily. "It was Pentos. They made marks on a paper, the two of them."

There is a chance here. "We still have Windblown in the dungeons. Those feigned deserters."

"I remember," said Yronwood. "Hungerford, Straw, that lot. Some of them weren't so bad for sellswords. Others, well, might be they could stand a bit of dying. What of them?"

"I mean to send them back to the Tattered Prince. And you with them. You will be two amongst thousands. Your presence in the Yunkish camps should pass unnoticed. I want you to deliver a message to the Tattered Prince. Tell him that I sent you, that I speak with the queen's voice. Tell him that we'll pay his price if he delivers us our hostages, unharmed and whole."

Ser Archibald grimaced. "Rags and Tatters is more like to give the two of us to Pretty Meris. He won't do it."

"Why not? The task is simple enough." *Compared to stealing dragons.* "I once brought the queen's father out of Duskendale."

"That was Westeros," said Gerris Drinkwater.

"This is Meereen."

"Arch cannot even hold a sword with those hands."

"He ought not need to. You will have the sellswords with you, unless I mistake my man."

Gerris Drinkwater pushed back his mop of sun-streaked hair. "Might we have some time to discuss this amongst ourselves?"

"No," said Selmy.

"I'll do it," offered Ser Archibald, "just so long as there's no bloody boats involved. Drink will do it too." He grinned. "He don't know it yet, but he will."

And that was done.

The simple part, at least, thought Barristan Selmy, as he made the long climb back to the summit of the pyramid. The hard part he'd left in Dornish hands. His grandfather would have been aghast. The Dornishmen were knights, at least in name, though only Yronwood impressed him as having the true steel. Drinkwater had a pretty face, a glib tongue, and a fine head of hair.

By the time the old knight returned to the queen's rooms atop the pyramid, Prince Quentyn's corpse had been removed. Six of the young cupbearers were playing some child's game as he entered, sitting in a circle on the floor as they took turns spinning a dagger. When it wobbled to a stop they cut a lock of hair off whichever of them the blade was pointing at. Ser Barristan had played a similar game with his cousins when he was just a boy at Harvest Hall . . . though in Westeros, as he recalled, kissing had been involved as well. "Bhakaz," he called. "A cup of wine, if you would be so good. Grazhar, Azzak, the door is yours. I am expecting the Green Grace. Show her in at once when she arrives. Elsewise, I do not wish to be disturbed."

Azzak scrambled to his feet. "As you command, Lord Hand."

Ser Barristan went out onto the terrace. The rain had stopped, though a wall of slate-grey clouds hid the setting sun as it made its descent into Slaver's Bay. A few wisps of smoke still rose from the blackened stones of Hazdar, twisted like ribbons by the wind. Far off to the east, beyond the city walls, he saw pale wings moving above a distant line of hills. *Viserion.* Hunting, mayhaps, or flying just to fly. He wondered where Rhaegal was. Thus far the green dragon had shown himself to be more dangerous than the white.

When Bhakaz brought his wine, the old knight took one long swallow and sent the boy for water. A few cups of wine might be just the thing to help him sleep, but he would need his wits about him when Galazza Galare returned from treating with the foe. So he drank his wine well watered, as the world grew dark around him. He was very tired, and full of doubts. The Dornishmen, Hizdahr, Reznak, the attack . . . was he doing the right things? Was he doing what Daenerys would have wanted? *I was not made for this.* Other Kingsguard had served as Hand before him. Not many, but a few. He had read of them in the White Book. Now he found himself wondering whether they had felt as lost and confused as he did.

"Lord Hand." Grazhar stood in the door, a taper in his hand. "The Green Grace has come. You asked to be told."

"Show her in. And light some candles."

Galazza Galare was attended by four Pink Graces. An aura of wisdom and dignity seemed to surround her that Ser Barristan could not help but admire. *This is a strong woman, and she has been a faithful friend to Daenerys.* "Lord Hand," she said, her face hidden behind shimmering green veils. "May I sit? These bones are old and weary."

"Grazhar, a chair for the Green Grace." The Pink Graces arrayed themselves behind her, with eyes lowered and hands clasped before them. "May I offer you refreshment?" asked Ser Barristan.

"That would be most welcome, Ser Barristan. My throat is dry from talking. A juice, perhaps?"

"As you wish." He beckoned to Kezmya and had her fetch the priestess a goblet of lemon juice, sweetened with honey. To drink it, the priestess had to remove her veil, and Selmy was reminded of just how old she was.

Twenty years my elder, or more. "If the queen were here, I know she would join me in thanking you for all that you have done for us."

"Her Magnificence has always been most gracious." Galazza Galare finished her drink and fastened up her veil again. "Have there been any further tidings of our sweet queen?"

"None as yet."

"I shall pray for her. And what of King Hizdahr, if I may be so bold? Might I be permitted to see His Radiance?"

"Soon, I hope. He is unharmed, I promise you."

"I am pleased to hear that. The Wise Masters of Yunkai asked after him. You will not be surprised to hear that they wish the noble Hizdahr to be restored at once to his rightful place."

"He shall be, if it can be proved that he did not try to kill our queen. Until such time, Meereen will be ruled by a council of the loyal and just. There is a place for you on that council. I know that you have much to teach us all, Your Benevolence. We need your wisdom."

"I fear you flatter me with empty courtesies, Lord Hand," the Green Grace said. "If you truly think me wise, heed me now. Release the noble Hizdahr and restore him to his throne."

"Only the queen can do that."

Beneath her veils, the Green Grace sighed. "The peace that we worked so hard to forge flutters like a leaf in an autumn wind. These are dire days. Death stalks our streets, riding the pale mare from thrice-cursed Astapor. Dragons haunt the skies, feasting on the flesh of children. Hundreds are taking ship, sailing for Yunkai, for Tolos, for Qarth, for any refuge that will have them. The pyramid of Hazkar has collapsed into a smoking ruin, and many of that ancient line lie dead beneath its blackened stones. The pyramids of Uhlez and Yherizan have become the lairs of monsters, their masters homeless beggars. My people have lost all hope and turned against the gods themselves, giving over their nights to drunkenness and fornication."

"And murder. The Sons of the Harpy slew thirty in the night."

"I grieve to hear this. All the more reason to free the noble Hizdahr zo Loraq, who stopped such killings once."

And how did he accomplish that, unless he is himself the Harpy? "Her Grace gave her hand to Hizdahr zo Loraq, made him her king and consort, restored the mortal art as he beseeched her. In return he gave her poisoned locusts."

"In return he gave her peace. Do not cast it away, ser, I beg you. Peace is the pearl beyond price. Hizdahr is of Loraq. Never would he soil his hands with poison. He is innocent."

"How can you be certain?" *Unless you know the poisoner.*

"The gods of Ghis have told me."

"My gods are the Seven, and the Seven have been silent on this matter. Your Wisdom, did you present my offer?"

"To all the lords and captains of Yunkai, as you commanded me . . . yet I fear you will not like their answer."

"They refused?"

"They did. No amount of gold will buy your people back, I was told. Only the blood of dragons may set them free again."

It was the answer Ser Barristan had expected, if not the one that he had hoped for. His mouth tightened.

"I know these were not the words you wished to hear," said Galazza Galare. "Yet for myself, I understand. These dragons are fell beasts. Yunkai fears them . . . and with good cause, you cannot deny. Our histories speak of the dragonlords of dread Valyria and the devastation that they wrought upon the peoples of Old Ghis. Even your own young queen, fair Daenerys who called herself the Mother of Dragons . . . we saw her burning, that day in the pit . . . even she was not safe from the dragon's wroth."

"Her Grace is not . . . she . . ."

". . . is dead. May the gods grant her sweet sleep." Tears glistened behind her veils. "Let her dragons die as well."

Selmy was groping for an answer when he heard the sound of heavy footsteps. The door burst inward, and Skahaz mo Kandaq stormed in with four Brazen Beasts behind him. When Grazhar tried to block his path, he slammed the boy aside.

Ser Barristan was on his feet at once. "What is it?"

"The trebuchets," the Shavepate growled. "All six."

Galazza Galare rose. "Thus does Yunkai make reply to your offers, ser. I warned you that you would not like their answer."

They choose war, then. So be it. Ser Barristan felt oddly relieved. War he understood. "If they think they will break Meereen by throwing stones—"

"Not stones." The old woman's voice was full of grief, of fear. "Corpses."

DAENERYS

The hill was a stony island in a sea of green.

It took Dany half the morning to climb down. By the time she reached the bottom she was winded. Her muscles ached, and she felt as if she had the beginnings of a fever. The rocks had scraped her hands raw. *They are better than they were, though*, she decided as she picked at a broken blister. Her skin was pink and tender, and a pale milky fluid was leaking from her cracked palms, but her burns were healing.

The hill loomed larger down here. Dany had taken to calling it Dragonstone, after the ancient citadel where she'd been born. She had no memories of that Dragonstone, but she would not soon forget this one. Scrub grass and thorny bushes covered its lower slopes; higher up a jagged tangle of bare rock thrust steep and sudden into the sky. There, amidst broken boulders, razor-sharp ridges, and needle spires, Drogon made his lair inside a shallow cave. He had dwelt there for some time, Dany had realized when she first saw the hill. The air smelled of ash, every rock and tree in sight was scorched and blackened, the ground strewn with burned and broken bones, yet it had been home to him.

Dany knew the lure of home.

Two days ago, climbing on a spire of rock, she had spied water to the south, a slender thread that glittered briefly as the sun was going down. A *stream*, Dany decided. Small, but it would lead her to a larger stream, and that stream would flow into some little river, and all the rivers in this part of the world were vassals of the Skahazadhan. Once she found the Skahazadhan she need only follow it downstream to Slaver's Bay.

She would sooner have returned to Meereen on dragon's wings, to be sure. But that was a desire Drogon did not seem to share.

The dragonlords of old Valyria had controlled their mounts with binding spells and sorcerous horns. Daenerys made do with a word and a whip. Mounted on the dragon's back, she oft felt as if she were learning to ride all over again. When she whipped her silver mare on her right flank the mare went left, for a horse's first instinct is to flee from danger. When she laid the whip across Drogon's right side he veered right, for a dragon's first instinct is always to attack. Sometimes it did not seem to matter where she struck him, though; sometimes he went where he would and took her with him. Neither whip nor words could turn Drogon if he did not wish to be turned. The whip annoyed him more than it hurt him, she had come to see; his scales had grown harder than horn.

And no matter how far the dragon flew each day, come nightfall some instinct drew him home to Dragonstone. *His home, not mine.* Her home was back in Meereen, with her husband and her lover. That was where she belonged, surely.

Keep walking. If I look back I am lost.

Memories walked with her. Clouds seen from above. Horses small as ants thundering through the grass. A silver moon, almost close enough to touch. Rivers running bright and blue below, glimmering in the sun. *Will I ever see such sights again?* On Drogon's back she felt *whole*. Up in the sky the woes of this world could not touch her. How could she abandon that?

It was time, though. A girl might spend her life at play, but she was a woman grown, a queen, a wife, a mother to thousands. Her children had need of her. Drogon had bent before the whip, and so must she. She had to don her crown again and return to her ebon bench and the arms of her noble husband.

Hizdahr, of the tepid kisses.

The sun was hot this morning, the sky blue and cloudless. That was good. Dany's clothes were hardly more than rags, and offered little in the way of warmth. One of her sandals had slipped off during her wild flight from Meereen and she had left the other up by Drogon's cave, preferring to go barefoot rather than half-shod. Her *tokar* and veils she had abandoned in the pit, and her linen undertunic had never been made to withstand the hot days and cold nights of the Dothraki sea. Sweat and grass and dirt had stained it, and Dany had torn a strip off the hem to make a bandage for her shin. *I must look a ragged thing, and starved,* she thought, *but if the days stay warm, I will not freeze.*

Hers had been a lonely sojourn, and for most of it she had been hurt and hungry . . . yet despite it all she had been strangely happy here. *A few aches, an empty belly, chills by night . . . what does it matter when you can fly? I would do it all again.*

Jhiqui and Irri would be waiting atop her pyramid back in Meereen, she told herself. Her sweet scribe Missandei as well, and all her little pages. They would bring her food, and she could bathe in the pool beneath the persimmon tree. It would be good to feel clean again. Dany did not need a glass to know that she was filthy.

She was hungry too. One morning she had found some wild onions growing halfway down the south slope, and later that same day a leafy reddish vegetable that might have been some queer sort of cabbage. Whatever it was, it had not made her sick. Aside from that, and one fish that she had caught in the spring-fed pool outside of Drogon's cave, she had survived as best she could on the dragon's leavings, on burned bones and chunks of smoking meat, half-charred and half-raw. She needed more, she knew. One day she kicked at a cracked sheep's skull with the side of a bare foot and sent it bouncing over the edge of the hill. And as she watched it tumble down the steep slope toward the sea of grass, she realized she must follow.

Dany set off through the tall grass at a brisk pace. The earth felt warm between her toes. The grass was as tall as she was. *It never seemed so high when I was mounted on my silver, riding beside my sun-and-stars at the head of his* khalasar. As she walked, she tapped her thigh with the pitmaster's whip. That, and the rags on her back, were all she had taken from Meereen.

Though she walked through a green kingdom, it was not the deep rich green of summer. Even here autumn made its presence felt, and winter would not be far behind. The grass was paler than she remembered, a wan and sickly green on the verge of going yellow. After that would come brown. The grass was dying.

Daenerys Targaryen was no stranger to the Dothraki sea, the great ocean of grass that stretched from the forest of Qohor to the Mother of Mountains and the Womb of the World. She had seen it first when she was still a girl, newly wed to Khal Drogo and on her way to Vaes Dothrak to be presented to the crones of the *dosh khaleen*. The sight of all that grass stretching out before her had taken her breath away. *The sky was blue, the grass was green, and I was full of hope.* Ser Jorah had been with her then, her gruff old bear. She'd had Irri and Jhiqui and Doreah to care for her, her sun-and-stars to hold her in the night, his child growing inside her. *Rhaego. I was going to name him Rhaego, and the* dosh khaleen *said he would be the Stallion Who Mounts the World.* Not since those half-remembered days in Braavos when she lived in the house with the red door had she been as happy.

But in the Red Waste, all her joy had turned to ashes. Her sun-and-stars had fallen from his horse, the *maegi* Mirri Maz Duur had murdered Rhaego in her womb, and Dany had smothered the empty shell of Khal Drogo with her own two hands. Afterward Drogo's great *khalasar* had shattered. Ko Pono named himself Khal Pono and took many riders with him, and many slaves as well. Ko Jhaqo named himself Khal Jhaqo and rode off with even more. Mago, his bloodrider, raped and murdered Eroeh, a girl Daenerys had once saved from him. Only the birth of her dragons amidst the fire and smoke of Khal Drogo's funeral pyre had spared Dany herself from being dragged back to Vaes Dothrak to live out the remainder of her days amongst the crones of the *dosh khaleen*.

The fire burned away my hair, but elsewise it did not touch me. It had been the same in Daznak's Pit. That much she could recall, though much of what followed was a haze. *So many people, screaming and shoving.* She remembered rearing horses, a food cart spilling melons as it overturned. From below a spear came flying, followed by a flight of crossbow bolts. One passed so close that Dany felt it brush her cheek. Others skittered off Drogon's scales, lodged between them, or tore through the membrane of his wings. She remembered the dragon twisting beneath her, shuddering at the impacts, as she tried desperately to cling to his scaled back. The wounds were smoking. Dany saw one of the bolts burst into sudden flame. Another fell away, shaken loose by the beating of his wings. Below, she saw men whirling, wreathed in flame, hands up in the air as if caught in the throes of some mad dance. A woman in a green *tokar* reached for a weeping child, pulling him down into her arms to shield him from the flames. Dany saw the color vividly, but not the woman's face. People were stepping on her as they lay tangled on the bricks. Some were on fire.

Then all of that had faded, the sounds dwindling, the people shrinking, the spears and arrows falling back beneath them as Drogon clawed his way into the sky. Up and up and up he'd borne her, high above the pyramids and pits, his wings outstretched to catch the warm air rising from the city's sunbaked bricks. *If I fall and die, it will still have been worth it,* she had thought.

North they flew, beyond the river, Drogon gliding on torn and tattered wings through clouds that whipped by like the banners of some ghostly army. Dany glimpsed the shores of Slaver's Bay and the old Valyrian road that ran beside it through sand and desolation until it vanished in the west. *The road home.* Then there was nothing beneath them but grass rippling in the wind.

Was that first flight a thousand years ago? Sometimes it seemed as if it must be.

The sun grew hotter as it rose, and before long her head was pounding. Dany's hair was growing out again, but slowly. "I need a hat," she said aloud. Up on Dragonstone she had tried to make one for herself, weaving stalks of grass together as she had seen Dothraki women do during her time with Drogo, but either she was using the wrong sort of grass or she simply lacked the necessary skill. Her hats all fell to pieces in her hands. *Try again*, she told herself. *You will do better the next time. You are the blood of the dragon, you can make a hat.* She tried and tried, but her last attempt had been no more successful than her first.

It was afternoon by the time Dany found the stream she had glimpsed atop the hill. It was a rill, a rivulet, a trickle, no wider than her arm . . . and her arm had grown thinner every day she spent on Dragonstone. Dany scooped up a handful of water and splashed it on her face. When she cupped her hands, her knuckles squished in the mud at the bottom of the stream. She might have wished for colder, clearer water . . . but no, if she were going to pin her hopes on wishes, she would wish for rescue.

She still clung to the hope that someone would come after her. Ser Barristan might come seeking her; he was the first of her Queensguard, sworn to defend her life with his own. And her bloodriders were no strangers to the Dothraki sea, and their lives were bound to her own. Her husband, the noble Hizdahr zo Loraq, might dispatch searchers. And Daario . . . Dany pictured him riding toward her through the tall grass, smiling, his golden tooth gleaming with the last light of the setting sun.

Only Daario had been given to the Yunkai'i, a hostage to ensure no harm came to the Yunkish captains. *Daario and Hero, Jhogo and Groleo, and three of Hizdahr's kin.* By now, surely, all of her hostages would have been released. But . . .

She wondered if her captain's blades still hung upon the wall beside her bed, waiting for Daario to return and claim them. *"I will leave my girls with you,"* he had said. *"Keep them safe for me, beloved."* And she wondered how much the Yunkai'i knew about what her captain meant to her. She had asked Ser Barristan that question the afternoon the hostages went forth. "They will have heard the talk," he had replied. "Naharis may even have boasted of Your Grace's . . . of your great . . . regard . . . for him. If you will forgive my saying so, modesty is not one of the captain's virtues. He takes great pride in his . . . his swordsmanship."

He boasts of bedding me, you mean. But Daario would not have been so foolish as to make such a boast amongst her enemies. *It makes no matter. By now the Yunkai'i will be marching home.* That was why she had done all that she had done. For peace.

She turned back the way she'd come, to where Dragonstone rose above the grasslands like a clenched fist. *It looks so close. I've been walking for hours, yet it still looks as if I could reach out and touch it.* It was not too late to go back. There were fish in the spring-fed pool by Drogon's cave. She had caught one her first day there, she might catch more. And there would be scraps, charred bones with bits of flesh still on them, the remnants of Drogon's kills.

No, Dany told herself. *If I look back I am lost.* She might live for years amongst the sunbaked rocks of Dragonstone, riding Drogon by day and gnawing at his leavings every evenfall as the great grass sea turned from gold to orange, but that was not the life she had been born to. So once again she turned her back upon the distant hill and closed her ears to the song of flight and freedom that the wind sang as it played amongst the hill's stony ridges. The stream was trickling south by southeast, as near as she could tell. She followed it. *Take me to the river, that is all I ask of you. Take me to the river, and I will do the rest.*

The hours passed slowly. The stream bent this way and that, and Dany followed, beating time upon her leg with the whip, trying not to think about how far she had to go, or the pounding in her head, or her empty belly. *Take one step. Take the next. Another step. Another.* What else could she do?

It was quiet on her sea. When the wind blew the grass would sigh as the stalks brushed against each other, whispering in a tongue that only gods could understand. Now and again the little stream would gurgle where it flowed around a stone. Mud squished between her toes. Insects buzzed around her, lazy dragonflies and glistening green wasps and stinging midges almost too small to see. She swatted at them absently when they landed on her arms. Once she came upon a rat drinking from the stream, but it fled when she appeared, scurrying between the stalks to vanish in the high grass. Sometimes she heard birds singing. The sound made her belly rumble, but she had no nets to snare them with, and so far she had not come on any nests. *Once I dreamed of flying,* she thought, *and now I've flown, and dream of stealing eggs.* That made her laugh. "Men are mad and gods are madder," she told the grass, and the grass murmured its agreement.

Thrice that day she caught sight of Drogon. Once he was so far off that he might have been an eagle, slipping in and out of distant clouds, but Dany knew the look of him by now, even when he was no more than a speck. The second time he passed before the sun, his black wings spread, and the world darkened. The last time he flew right above her, so close she could hear the sound of his wings. For half a heartbeat Dany thought that he was hunting her, but he flew on without taking any notice of her and vanished somewhere in the east. *Just as well*, she thought.

Evening took her almost unawares. As the sun was gilding the distant spires of Dragonstone, Dany stumbled onto a low stone wall, overgrown and broken. Perhaps it had been part of a temple, or the hall of the village lord. More ruins lay beyond it—an old well, and some circles in the grass that marked the sites where hovels had once stood. They had been built of mud and straw, she judged, but long years of wind and rain had worn them away to nothing. Dany found eight before the sun went down, but there might have been more farther out, hidden in the grass.

The stone wall had endured better than the rest. Though it was no-where more than three feet high, the angle where it met another, lower wall still offered some shelter from the elements, and night was coming on fast. Dany wedged herself into that corner, making a nest of sorts by tearing up handfuls of the grass that grew around the ruins. She was very tired, and fresh blisters had appeared on both her feet, including a matched set upon her pinky toes. *It must be from the way I walk*, she thought, giggling.

As the world darkened, Dany settled in and closed her eyes, but sleep refused to come. The night was cold, the ground hard, her belly empty. She found herself thinking of Meereen, of Daario, her love, and Hizdahr, her husband, of Irri and Jhiqui and sweet Missandei, Ser Barristan and Reznak and Skahaz Shavepate. *Do they fear me dead? I flew off on a dragon's back. Will they think he ate me?* She wondered if Hizdahr was still king. His crown had come from her, could he hold it in her absence? *He wanted Drogon dead. I heard him. "Kill it," he screamed, "kill the beast," and the look upon his face was lustful.* And Strong Belwas had been on his knees, heaving and shuddering. *Poison. It had to be poison. The honeyed locusts. Hizdahr urged them on me, but Belwas ate them all.* She had made Hizdahr her king, taken him into her bed, opened the fighting pits for him, he had no reason to want her dead. Yet who else could it have been? Reznak, her perfumed seneschal? The Yunkai'i? The Sons of the Harpy?

Off in the distance, a wolf howled. The sound made her feel sad and lonely, but no less hungry. As the moon rose above the grasslands, Dany slipped at last into a restless sleep.

She dreamed. All her cares fell away from her, and all her pains as well, and she seemed to float upward into the sky. She was flying once again, spinning, laughing, dancing, as the stars wheeled around her and whispered secrets in her ear. "To go north, you must journey south. To reach the west, you must go east. To go forward, you must go back. To touch the light you must pass beneath the shadow."

"Quaithe?" Dany called. "Where are you, Quaithe?"

Then she saw. *Her mask is made of starlight.*

"Remember who you are, Daenerys," the stars whispered in a woman's voice. "The dragons know. Do you?"

The next morning she woke stiff and sore and aching, with ants crawling on her arms and legs and face. When she realized what they were, she kicked aside the stalks of dry brown grass that had served as her bed and blanket and struggled to her feet. She had bites all over her, little red bumps, itchy and inflamed. *Where did all the ants come from?* Dany brushed them from her arms and legs and belly. She ran a hand across her stubbly scalp where her hair had burned away, and felt more ants on her head, and one crawling down the back of her neck. She knocked them off and crushed them under her bare feet. There were so many . . .

It turned out that their anthill was on the other side of her wall. She wondered how the ants had managed to climb over it and find her. To them these tumbledown stones must loom as huge as the Wall of Westeros. *The biggest wall in all the world,* her brother Viserys used to say, as proud as if he'd built it himself.

Viserys told her tales of knights so poor that they had to sleep beneath the ancient hedges that grew along the byways of the Seven Kingdoms. Dany would have given much and more for a nice thick hedge. *Preferably one without an anthill.*

The sun was only just coming up. A few bright stars lingered in the cobalt sky. *Perhaps one of them is Khal Drogo, sitting on his fiery stallion in the night lands and smiling down on me.* Dragonstone was still visible above the grasslands. *It looks so close. I must be leagues away by now, but it looks as if I could be back in an hour.* She wanted to lie back down, close her eyes, and give herself up to sleep. *No. I must keep going. The stream. Just follow the stream.*

Dany took a moment to make certain of her directions. It would not do to walk the wrong way and lose her stream. "My friend," she said aloud. "If I stay close to my friend I won't get lost." She would have slept beside the water if she dared, but there were animals who came down to the stream to drink at night. She had seen their tracks. Dany would make a poor meal for a wolf or lion, but even a poor meal was better than none.

Once she was certain which way was south, she counted off her paces. The stream appeared at eight. Dany cupped her hands to drink. The water made her belly cramp, but cramps were easier to bear than thirst. She had no other drink but the morning dew that glistened on the tall grass, and no food at all unless she cared to eat the grass. *I could try eating ants.* The little yellow ones were too small to provide much in the way of nourishment, but there were red ants in the grass, and those were bigger. "I am lost at sea," she said as she limped along beside her meandering rivulet, "so perhaps I'll find some crabs, or a nice fat fish." Her whip slapped softly against her thigh, *wap wap wap*. One step at a time, and the stream would see her home.

Just past midday she came upon a bush growing by the stream, its twisted limbs covered with hard green berries. Dany squinted at them suspiciously, then plucked one from a branch and nibbled at it. Its flesh was tart and chewy, with a bitter aftertaste that seemed familiar to her. "In the *khalasar*, they used berries like these to flavor roasts," she decided. Saying it aloud made her more certain of it. Her belly rumbled, and Dany found herself picking berries with both hands and tossing them into her mouth.

An hour later, her stomach began to cramp so badly that she could not go on. She spent the rest of that day retching up green slime. *If I stay here, I will die. I may be dying now.* Would the horse god of the Dothraki part the grass and claim her for his starry *khalasar*, so she might ride the night-lands with Khal Drogo? In Westeros the dead of House Targaryen were given to the flames, but who would light her pyre here? *My flesh will feed the wolves and carrion crows,* she thought sadly, *and worms will burrow through my womb.* Her eyes went back to Dragonstone. It looked smaller. She could see smoke rising from its wind-carved summit, miles away. *Drogon has returned from hunting.*

Sunset found her squatting in the grass, groaning. Every stool was looser than the one before, and smelled fouler. By the time the moon came up she was shitting brown water. The more she drank, the more she shat, but the more she shat, the thirstier she grew, and her thirst sent her crawling to the stream to suck up more water. When she closed her eyes at last, Dany did not know whether she would be strong enough to open them again.

She dreamt of her dead brother.

Viserys looked just as he had the last time she'd seen him. His mouth was twisted in anguish, his hair was burnt, and his face was black and smoking where the molten gold had run down across his brow and cheeks and into his eyes.

"You are dead," Dany said.

Murdered. Though his lips never moved, somehow she could hear his voice, whispering in her ear. *You never mourned me, sister. It is hard to die unmourned.*

"I loved you once."

Once, he said, so bitterly it made her shudder. *You were supposed to be my wife, to bear me children with silver hair and purple eyes, to keep the blood of the dragon pure. I took care of you. I taught you who you were. I fed you. I sold our mother's crown to keep you fed.*

"You hurt me. You frightened me."

Only when you woke the dragon. I loved you.

"You sold me. You betrayed me."

No. You were the betrayer. You turned against me, against your own blood. They cheated me. Your horsey husband and his stinking savages. They were cheats and liars. They promised me a golden crown and gave me this. He touched the molten gold that was creeping down his face, and smoke rose from his finger.

"You could have had your crown," Dany told him. "My sun-and-stars would have won it for you if only you had waited."

I waited long enough. I waited my whole life. I was their king, their rightful king. They laughed at me.

"You should have stayed in Pentos with Magister Illyrio. Khal Drogo had to present me to the *dosh khaleen,* but you did not have to ride with us. That was your choice. Your mistake."

Do you want to wake the dragon, you stupid little whore? Drogo's khalasar was mine. I bought them from him, a hundred thousand screamers. I paid for them with your maidenhead.

"You never understood. Dothraki do not buy and sell. They give gifts and receive them. If you had waited . . ."

I did wait. For my crown, for my throne, for you. All those years, and all I ever got was a pot of molten gold. Why did they give the dragon's eggs to you? They should have been mine. If I'd had a dragon, I would have taught the world the meaning of our words. Viserys began to laugh, until his jaw fell away from his face, smoking, and blood and molten gold ran from his mouth.

When she woke, gasping, her thighs were slick with blood.

For a moment she did not realize what it was. The world had just begun to lighten, and the tall grass rustled softly in the wind. *No, please, let me sleep some more. I'm so tired.* She tried to burrow back beneath the pile of grass she had torn up when she went to sleep. Some of the stalks felt wet.

Had it rained again? She sat up, afraid that she had soiled herself as she slept. When she brought her fingers to her face, she could smell the blood on them. *Am I dying?* Then she saw the pale crescent moon, floating high above the grass, and it came to her that this was no more than her moon blood.

If she had not been so sick and scared, that might have come as a relief. Instead she began to shiver violently. She rubbed her fingers through the dirt, and grabbed a handful of grass to wipe between her legs. *The dragon does not weep.* She was bleeding, but it was only woman's blood. *The moon is still a crescent, though. How can that be?* She tried to remember the last time she had bled. The last full moon? The one before? The one before that? *No, it cannot have been so long as that.* "I am the blood of the dragon," she told the grass, aloud.

Once, the grass whispered back, *until you chained your dragons in the dark.*

"Drogon killed a little girl. Her name was . . . her name . . ." Dany could not recall the child's name. That made her so sad that she would have cried if all her tears had not been burned away. "I will never have a little girl. I was the Mother of Dragons."

Aye, the grass said, *but you turned against your children.*

Her belly was empty, her feet sore and blistered, and it seemed to her that the cramping had grown worse. Her guts were full of writhing snakes biting at her bowels. She scooped up a handful of mud and water in trembling hands. By midday the water would be tepid, but in the chill of dawn it was almost cool and helped her keep her eyes open. As she splashed her face, she saw fresh blood on her thighs. The ragged hem of her undertunic was stained with it. The sight of so much red frightened her. *Moon blood, it's only my moon blood,* but she did not remember ever having such a heavy flow. *Could it be the water?* If it was the water, she was doomed. She had to drink or die of thirst.

"Walk," Dany commanded herself. "Follow the stream and it will take you to the Skahazadhan. That's where Daario will find you." But it took all her strength just to get back to her feet, and when she did all she could do was stand there, fevered and bleeding. She raised her eyes to the empty blue sky, squinting at the sun. *Half the morning gone already,* she realized, dismayed. She made herself take a step, and then another, and then she was walking once again, following the little stream.

The day grew warmer, and the sun beat down upon her head and the burnt remnants of her hair. Water splashed against the soles of her feet.

She was walking in the stream. How long had she been doing that? The soft brown mud felt good between her toes and helped to soothe her blisters. *In the stream or out of it, I must keep walking. Water flows downhill. The stream will take me to the river, and the river will take me home.*

Except it wouldn't, not truly.

Meereen was not her home, and never would be. It was a city of strange men with strange gods and stranger hair, of slavers wrapped in fringed *tokars*, where grace was earned through whoring, butchery was art, and dog was a delicacy. Meereen would always be the Harpy's city, and Daenerys could not be a harpy.

Never, said the grass, in the gruff tones of Jorah Mormont. *You were warned, Your Grace. Let this city be, I said. Your war is in Westeros, I told you.*

The voice was no more than a whisper, yet somehow Dany felt that he was walking just behind her. *My bear*, she thought, *my old sweet bear, who loved me and betrayed me.* She had missed him so. She wanted to see his ugly face, to wrap her arms around him and press herself against his chest, but she knew that if she turned around Ser Jorah would be gone. "I am dreaming," she said. "A waking dream, a walking dream. I am alone and lost."

Lost, because you lingered, in a place that you were never meant to be, murmured Ser Jorah, as softly as the wind. *Alone, because you sent me from your side.*

"You betrayed me. You informed on me, for gold."

For home. Home was all I ever wanted.

"And me. You wanted me." Dany had seen it in his eyes.

I did, the grass whispered, sadly.

"You kissed me. I never said you could, but you did. You sold me to my enemies, but you meant it when you kissed me."

I gave you good counsel. Save your spears and swords for the Seven Kingdoms, I told you. Leave Meereen to the Meereenese and go west, I said. You would not listen.

"I had to take Meereen or see my children starve along the march." Dany could still see the trail of corpses she had left behind her crossing the Red Waste. It was not a sight she wished to see again. "I had to take Meereen to feed my people."

You took Meereen, he told her, *yet still you lingered.*

"To be a queen."

You are a queen, her bear said. *In Westeros.*

"It is such a long way," she complained. "I was tired, Jorah. I was weary of war. I wanted to rest, to laugh, to plant trees and see them grow. I am only a young girl."

No. You are the blood of the dragon. The whispering was growing fainter, as if Ser Jorah were falling farther behind. *Dragons plant no trees. Remember that. Remember who you are, what you were made to be. Remember your words.*

"Fire and Blood," Daenerys told the swaying grass.

A stone turned under her foot. She stumbled to one knee and cried out in pain, hoping against hope that her bear would gather her up and help her to her feet. When she turned her head to look for him, all she saw was trickling brown water . . . and the grass, still moving slightly. *The wind,* she told herself, *the wind shakes the stalks and makes them sway.* Only no wind was blowing. The sun was overhead, the world still and hot. Midges swarmed in the air, and a dragonfly floated over the stream, darting here and there. And the grass was moving when it had no cause to move.

She fumbled in the water, found a stone the size of her fist, pulled it from the mud. It was a poor weapon but better than an empty hand. From the corner of her eye Dany saw the grass move again, off to her right. The grass swayed and bowed low, as if before a king, but no king appeared to her. The world was green and empty. The world was green and silent. The world was yellow, dying. *I should get up,* she told herself. *I have to walk. I have to follow the stream.*

Through the grass came a soft silvery tinkling.

Bells, Dany thought, smiling, remembering Khal Drogo, her sun-and-stars, and the bells he braided into his hair. *When the sun rises in the west and sets in the east, when the seas go dry and mountains blow in the wind like leaves, when my womb quickens again and I bear a living child, Khal Drogo will return to me.*

But none of those things had happened. *Bells,* Dany thought again. Her bloodriders had found her. "Aggo," she whispered. "Jhogo. Rakharo." Might Daario have come with them?

The green sea opened. A rider appeared. His braid was black and shiny, his skin as dark as burnished copper, his eyes the shape of bitter almonds. Bells sang in his hair. He wore a medallion belt and painted vest, with an *arakh* on one hip and a whip on the other. A hunting bow and a quiver of arrows were slung from his saddle.

One rider, and alone. A scout. He was one who rode before the *khalasar* to find the game and the good green grass, and sniff out foes wherever they might hide. If he found her there, he would kill her, rape her, or enslave her. At best, he would send her back to the crones of the *dosh khaleen,* where good *khaleesi* were supposed to go when their khals had died.

He did not see her, though. The grass concealed her, and he was looking elsewhere. Dany followed his eyes, and there the shadow flew, with wings spread wide. The dragon was a mile off, and yet the scout stood frozen until his stallion began to whicker in fear. Then he woke as if from a dream, wheeled his mount about, and raced off through the tall grass at a gallop.

Dany watched him go. When the sound of his hooves had faded away to silence, she began to shout. She called until her voice was hoarse . . . and Drogon came, snorting plumes of smoke. The grass bowed down before him. Dany leapt onto his back. She stank of blood and sweat and fear, but none of that mattered. "To go forward I must go back," she said. Her bare legs tightened around the dragon's neck. She kicked him, and Drogon threw himself into the sky. Her whip was gone, so she used her hands and feet and turned him north by east, the way the scout had gone. Drogon went willingly enough; perhaps he smelled the rider's fear.

In a dozen heartbeats they were past the Dothraki, as he galloped far below. To the right and left, Dany glimpsed places where the grass was burned and ashen. *Drogon has come this way before,* she realized. Like a chain of grey islands, the marks of his hunting dotted the green grass sea.

A vast herd of horses appeared below them. There were riders too, a score or more, but they turned and fled at the first sight of the dragon. The horses broke and ran when the shadow fell upon them, racing through the grass until their sides were white with foam, tearing the ground with their hooves . . . but as swift as they were, they could not fly. Soon one horse began to lag behind the others. The dragon descended on him, roaring, and all at once the poor beast was aflame, yet somehow he kept on running, screaming with every step, until Drogon landed on him and broke his back. Dany clutched the dragon's neck with all her strength to keep from sliding off.

The carcass was too heavy for him to bear back to his lair, so Drogon consumed his kill there, tearing at the charred flesh as the grasses burned around them, the air thick with drifting smoke and the smell of burnt horsehair. Dany, starved, slid off his back and ate with him, ripping chunks of smoking meat from the dead horse with bare, burned hands. *In Meereen I was a queen in silk, nibbling on stuffed dates and honeyed lamb,* she remembered. *What would my noble husband think if he could see me now?* Hizdahr would be horrified, no doubt. But Daario . . .

Daario would laugh, carve off a hunk of horsemeat with his *arakh*, and squat down to eat beside her.

As the western sky turned the color of a blood bruise, she heard the sound of approaching horses. Dany rose, wiped her hands on her ragged undertunic, and went to stand beside her dragon.

That was how Khal Jhaqo found her, when half a hundred mounted warriors emerged from the drifting smoke.

EPILOGUE

"I am no traitor," the Knight of Griffin's Roost declared. "I am King Tommen's man, and yours."

A steady *drip-drip-drip* punctuated his words, as snowmelt ran off his cloak to puddle on the floor. The snow had been falling on King's Landing most of the night; outside the drifts were ankle deep. Ser Kevan Lannister pulled his cloak about himself more closely. "So you say, ser. Words are wind."

"Then let me prove the truth of them with my sword." The light of the torches made a fiery blaze of Ronnet Connington's long red hair and beard. "Send me against my uncle, and I will bring you back his head, and the head of this false dragon too."

Lannister spearmen in crimson cloaks and lion-crested halfhelms stood along the west wall of the throne room. Tyrell guards in green cloaks faced them from the opposite wall. The chill in the throne room was palpable. Though neither Queen Cersei nor Queen Margaery was amongst them, their presence could be felt poisoning the air, like ghosts at a feast.

Behind the table where the five members of the king's small council were seated, the Iron Throne crouched like some great black beast, its barbs and claws and blades half-shrouded in shadow. Kevan Lannister could feel it at his back, an itch between the shoulder blades. It was easy to imagine old King Aerys perched up there, bleeding from some fresh cut, glowering down. But today the throne was empty. He had seen no reason for Tommen to join them. Kinder to let the boy remain with his mother. The Seven only knew how long mother and son might have together before Cersei's trial . . . and possibly her execution.

Mace Tyrell was speaking. "We shall deal with your uncle and his feigned boy in due time." The new King's Hand was seated on an oaken throne carved in the shape of a hand, an absurd vanity his lordship had produced the day Ser Kevan agreed to grant him the office he coveted. "You will bide here until we are ready to march. Then you shall have the chance to prove your loyalty."

Ser Kevan took no issue with that. "Escort Ser Ronnet back to his chambers," he said. *And see that he remains there* went unspoken. However loud his protestations, the Knight of Griffin's Roost remained suspect. Supposedly the sellswords who had landed in the south were being led by one of his own blood.

As the echoes of Connington's footsteps faded away, Grand Maester Pycelle gave a ponderous shake of his head. "His uncle once stood just where the boy was standing now and told King Aerys how he would deliver him the head of Robert Baratheon."

That is how it is when a man grows as old as Pycelle. Everything you see or hear reminds you of something you saw or heard when you were young. "How many men-at-arms accompanied Ser Ronnet to the city?" Ser Kevan asked.

"Twenty," said Lord Randyll Tarly, "and most of them Gregor Clegane's old lot. Your nephew Jaime gave them to Connington. To rid himself of them, I'd wager. They had not been in Maidenpool a day before one killed a man and another was accused of rape. I had to hang the one and geld the other. If it were up to me, I would send them all to the Night's Watch, and Connington with them. The Wall is where such scum belong."

"A dog takes after its master," declared Mace Tyrell. "Black cloaks would suit them, I agree. I will not suffer such men in the city watch." A hundred of his own Highgarden men had been added to the gold cloaks, yet plainly his lordship meant to resist any balancing infusion of westermen.

The more I give him, the more he wants. Kevan Lannister was beginning to understand why Cersei had grown so resentful of the Tyrells. But this was not the moment to provoke an open quarrel. Randyll Tarly and Mace Tyrell had both brought armies to King's Landing, whilst the best part of the strength of House Lannister remained in the riverlands, fast melting away. "The Mountain's men were always fighters," he said in a conciliatory tone, "and we may have need of every sword against these sellswords. If this truly is the Golden Company, as Qyburn's whisperers insist —"

"Call them what you will," said Randyll Tarly. "They are still no more than adventurers."

"Perhaps," Ser Kevan said. "But the longer we ignore these adventurers, the stronger they grow. We have had a map prepared, a map of the incursions. Grand Maester?"

The map was beautiful, painted by a master's hand on a sheet of the finest vellum, so large it covered the table. "Here." Pycelle pointed with a spotted hand. Where the sleeve of his robe rode up, a flap of pale flesh could be seen dangling beneath his forearm. "Here and here. All along the coast, and on the islands. Tarth, the Stepstones, even Estermont. And now we have reports that Connington is moving on Storm's End."

"If it is Jon Connington," said Randyll Tarly.

"Storm's End." Lord Mace Tyrell grunted the words. "He cannot take Storm's End. Not if he were Aegon the Conqueror. And if he does, what of it? Stannis holds it now. Let the castle pass from one pretender to another, why should that trouble us? I shall recapture it after my daughter's innocence is proved."

How can you recapture it when you have never captured it to begin with? "I understand, my lord, but—"

Tyrell did not let him finish. "These charges against my daughter are filthy lies. I ask again, *why* must we play out this mummer's farce? Have King Tommen declare my daughter innocent, ser, and put an end to the foolishness here and now."

Do that, and the whispers will follow Margaery the rest of her life. "No man doubts your daughter's innocence, my lord," Ser Kevan lied, "but His High Holiness insists upon a trial."

Lord Randyll snorted. "What have we become, when kings and high lords must dance to the twittering of sparrows?"

"We have foes on every hand, Lord Tarly," Ser Kevan reminded him. "Stannis in the north, ironmen in the west, sellswords in the south. Defy the High Septon, and we will have blood running in the gutters of King's Landing as well. If we are seen to be going against the gods, it will only drive the pious into the arms of one or the other of these would-be usurpers."

Mace Tyrell remained unmoved. "Once Paxter Redwyne sweeps the ironmen from the seas, my sons will retake the Shields. The snows will do for Stannis, or Bolton will. As for Connington . . ."

"If it is him," Lord Randyll said.

". . . as for Connington," Tyrell repeated, "what victories has he ever won that we should fear him? He could have ended Robert's Rebellion at Stoney Sept. He failed. Just as the Golden Company has always failed. Some may rush to join them, aye. The realm is well rid of such fools."

Ser Kevan wished that he could share his certainty. He had known Jon Connington, slightly—a proud youth, the most headstrong of the gaggle of young lordlings who had gathered around Prince Rhaegar Targaryen, competing for his royal favor. *Arrogant, but able and energetic.* That, and his skill at arms, was why Mad King Aerys had named him Hand. Old Lord Merryweather's inaction had allowed the rebellion to take root and spread, and Aerys wanted someone young and vigorous to match Robert's own youth and vigor. "Too soon," Lord Tywin Lannister had declared when word of the king's choice had reached Casterly Rock. "Connington is too young, too bold, too eager for glory."

The Battle of the Bells had proved the truth of that. Ser Kevan had expected that afterward Aerys would have no choice but to summon Tywin once more . . . but the Mad King had turned to the Lords Chelsted and Rossart instead, and paid for it with life and crown. *That was all so long ago, though. If this is indeed Jon Connington, he will be a different man. Older, harder, more seasoned . . . more dangerous.* "Connington may have more than the Golden Company. It is said he has a Targaryen pretender."

"A feigned boy is what he has," said Randyll Tarly.

"That may be. Or not." Kevan Lannister had been here, in this very hall when Tywin had laid the bodies of Prince Rhaegar's children at the foot of the Iron Throne, wrapped up in crimson cloaks. The girl had been recognizably the Princess Rhaenys, but the boy . . . *a faceless horror of bone and brain and gore, a few hanks of fair hair. None of us looked long. Tywin said that it was Prince Aegon, and we took him at his word.* "We have these tales coming from the east as well. A second Targaryen, and one whose blood no man can question. Daenerys Stormborn."

"As mad as her father," declared Lord Mace Tyrell.

That would be the same father that Highgarden and House Tyrell supported to the bitter end and well beyond. "Mad she may be," Ser Kevan said, "but with so much smoke drifting west, surely there must be some fire burning in the east."

Grand Maester Pycelle bobbed his head. "Dragons. These same stories have reached Oldtown. Too many to discount. A silver-haired queen with three dragons."

"At the far end of the world," said Mace Tyrell. "Queen of Slaver's Bay, aye. She is welcome to it."

"On that we can agree," Ser Kevan said, "but the girl is of the blood of Aegon the Conqueror, and I do not think she will be content to remain in Meereen forever. If she should reach these shores and join her strength to Lord Connington and this prince of his, feigned or no . . . we must destroy Connington and his pretender *now*, before Daenerys Stormborn can come west."

Mace Tyrell crossed his arms. "I mean to do just that, ser. *After* the trials."

"Sellswords fight for coin," declared Grand Maester Pycelle. "With enough gold, we might persuade the Golden Company to hand over Lord Connington and the pretender."

"Aye, if we had gold," Ser Harys Swyft said. "Alas, my lords, our vaults contain only rats and roaches. I have written again to the Myrish bankers. If they will agree to make good the crown's debt to the Braavosi and extend us a new loan, mayhaps we will not have to raise the taxes. Elsewise—"

"The magisters of Pentos have been known to lend money as well," said Ser Kevan. "Try them." The Pentoshi were even less like to be of help than the Myrish money changers, but the effort must be made. Unless a new source of coin could be found, or the Iron Bank persuaded to relent, he would have no choice but to pay the crown's debts with Lannister gold. He dare not resort to new taxes, not with the Seven Kingdoms crawling with rebellion. Half the lords in the realm could not tell taxation from tyranny, and would bolt to the nearest usurper in a heartbeat if it would save them a clipped copper. "If that fails, you may well need to go to Braavos, to treat with the Iron Bank yourself."

Ser Harys quailed. "Must I?"

"You *are* the master of coin," Lord Randyll said sharply.

"I am." The puff of white hair at the end of Swyft's chin quivered in outrage. "Must I remind my lord, this trouble is not of my doing? And not all of us have had the opportunity to refill our coffers with the plunder of Maidenpool and Dragonstone."

"I resent your implication, Swyft," Mace Tyrell said, bristling. "No wealth was found on Dragonstone, I promise you. My son's men have searched every inch of that damp and dreary island and turned up not so much as a single gemstone or speck of gold. Nor any sign of this fabled hoard of dragon eggs."

Kevan Lannister had seen Dragonstone with his own eyes. He doubted very much that Loras Tyrell had searched every inch of that ancient stronghold. The Valyrians had raised it, after all, and all their works stank of sorcery. And Ser Loras was young, prone to all the rash judgments of youth, and had been grievously wounded storming the castle besides. But it would not do to remind Tyrell that his favorite son was fallible. "If there was wealth on Dragonstone, Stannis would have found it," he declared.

"Let us move along, my lords. We have two queens to try for high treason, you may recall. My niece has elected trial by battle, she informs me. Ser Robert Strong will champion her."

"The silent giant." Lord Randyll grimaced.

"Tell me, ser, where did this man come from?" demanded Mace Tyrell. "Why have we never heard his name before? He does not speak, he will not show his face, he is never seen without his armor. Do we know for a certainty that he is even a knight?"

We do not even know if he's alive. Meryn Trant claimed that Strong took neither food nor drink, and Boros Blount went so far as to say he had never seen the man use the privy. *Why should he? Dead men do not shit.* Kevan Lannister had a strong suspicion of just who this Ser Robert really was beneath that gleaming white armor. A suspicion that Mace Tyrell and Randyll Tarly no doubt shared. Whatever the face hidden behind Strong's helm, it must remain hidden for now. The silent giant was his niece's only hope. *And pray that he is as formidable as he appears.*

But Mace Tyrell could not seem to see beyond the threat to his own daughter. "His Grace named Ser Robert to the Kingsguard," Ser Kevan reminded him, "and Qyburn vouches for the man as well. Be that as it may, we need Ser Robert to prevail, my lords. If my niece is proved guilty of these treasons, the legitimacy of her children will be called into question. If Tommen ceases to be a king, Margaery will cease to be a queen." He let Tyrell chew on that a moment. "Whatever Cersei may have done, she is still a daughter of the Rock, of mine own blood. I will not let her die a traitor's death, but I have made sure to draw her fangs. All her guards have been dismissed and replaced with my own men. In place of her former ladies-in-waiting, she will henceforth be attended by a septa and three novices selected by the High Septon. She is to have no further voice in the governance of the realm, nor in Tommen's education. I mean to return her to Casterly Rock after the trial and see that she remains there. Let that suffice."

The rest he left unsaid. Cersei was soiled goods now, her power at an end. Every baker's boy and beggar in the city had seen her in her shame and every tart and tanner from Flea Bottom to Pisswater Bend had gazed upon her nakedness, their eager eyes crawling over her breasts and belly and woman's parts. No queen could expect to rule again after that. In gold and silk and emeralds Cersei had been a queen, the next thing to a goddess; naked, she was only human, an aging woman with stretch marks on her belly and teats that had begun to sag . . . as the shrews in the crowds had been glad to point out to their husbands and lovers. *Better to live shamed than die proud,* Ser Kevan told himself. "My niece will make no further mischief," he promised Mace Tyrell. "You have my word on that, my lord."

Tyrell gave a grudging nod. "As you say. My Margaery prefers to be tried by the Faith, so the whole realm can bear witness to her innocence."

If your daughter is as innocent as you'd have us believe, why must you have your army present when she faces her accusers? Ser Kevan might have asked. "Soon, I hope," he said instead, before turning to Grand Maester Pycelle. "Is there aught else?"

The Grand Maester consulted his papers. "We should address the Rosby inheritance. Six claims have been put forth—"

"We can settle Rosby at some later date. What else?"

"Preparations should be made for Princess Myrcella."

"This is what comes of dealing with the Dornish," Mace Tyrell said. "Surely a better match can be found for the girl?"

Such as your own son Willas, perhaps? Her disfigured by one Dornishman, him crippled by another? "No doubt," Ser Kevan said, "but we have enemies enough without offending Dorne. If Doran Martell were to join his strength to Connington's in support of this feigned dragon, things could go very ill for all of us."

"Mayhaps we can persuade our Dornish friends to deal with Lord Connington," Ser Harys Swyft said with an irritating titter. "That would save a deal of blood and trouble."

"It would," Ser Kevan said wearily. *Time to put an end to this.* "Thank you, my lords. Let us convene again five days hence. After Cersei's trial."

"As you say. May the Warrior lend strength to Ser Robert's arms." The words were grudging, the dip of the chin Mace Tyrell gave the Lord Regent the most cursory of bows. But it was something, and for that much Ser Kevan Lannister was grateful.

Randyll Tarly left the hall with his liege lord, their green-cloaked spearmen right behind them. *Tarly is the real danger,* Ser Kevan reflected as he watched their departure. *A narrow man, but iron-willed and shrewd, and as good a soldier as the Reach could boast. But how do I win him to our side?*

"Lord Tyrell loves me not," Grand Maester Pycelle said in gloomy tones when the Hand had departed. "This matter of the moon tea . . . I would never have spoken of such, but the Queen Dowager commanded me! If it please the Lord Regent, I would sleep more soundly if you could lend me some of your guards."

"Lord Tyrell might take that amiss."

Ser Harys Swyft tugged at his chin beard. "I am in need of guards myself. These are perilous times."

Aye, thought Kevan Lannister, *and Pycelle is not the only council member our Hand would like to replace.* Mace Tyrell had his own candidate for lord treasurer: his uncle, Lord Seneschal of Highgarden, whom men called Garth the Gross. *The last thing I need is another Tyrell on the small council.* He was already outnumbered. Ser Harys was his wife's father, and Pycelle could be counted upon as well. But Tarly was sworn to Highgarden, as was Paxter Redwyne, lord admiral and master of ships, presently sailing his fleet around Dorne to deal with Euron Greyjoy's ironmen. Once Redwyne returned to King's Landing, the council would stand at three and three, Lannister and Tyrell.

The seventh voice would be the Dornishwoman now escorting Myrcella home. *The Lady Nym. But no lady, if even half of what Qyburn reports is true.* A bastard daughter of the Red Viper, near as notorious as her father and intent on claiming the council seat that Prince Oberyn himself had occupied so briefly. Ser Kevan had not yet seen fit to inform Mace Tyrell of her coming. The Hand, he knew, would not be pleased. *The man we need is Littlefinger. Petyr Baelish had a gift for conjuring dragons from the air.*

"Hire the Mountain's men," Ser Kevan suggested. "Red Ronnet will have no further use for them." He did not think that Mace Tyrell would be so clumsy as to try to murder either Pycelle or Swyft, but if guards made them feel safer, let them have guards.

The three men walked together from the throne room. Outside the snow was swirling round the outer ward, a caged beast howling to be free. "Have you ever felt such cold?" asked Ser Harys.

"The time to speak of the cold," said Grand Maester Pycelle, "is not when we are standing out in it." He made his slow way across the outer ward, back to his chambers.

The others lingered for a moment on the throne room steps. "I put no faith in these Myrish bankers," Ser Kevan told his good-father. "You had best prepare to go to Braavos."

Ser Harys did not look happy at the prospect. "If I must. But I say again, this trouble is not of my doing."

"No. It was Cersei who decided that the Iron Bank would wait for their due. Should I send her to Braavos?"

Ser Harys blinked. "Her Grace . . . that . . . that . . ."

Ser Kevan rescued him. "That was a jape. A bad one. Go and find a warm fire. I mean to do the same." He yanked his gloves on and set off across the yard, leaning hard into the wind as his cloak snapped and swirled behind him.

The dry moat surrounding Maegor's Holdfast was three feet deep in snow, the iron spikes that lined it glistening with frost. The only way in or out of Maegor's was across the drawbridge that spanned that moat. A knight of the Kingsguard was always posted at its far end. Tonight the duty had fallen to Ser Meryn Trant. With Balon Swann hunting the rogue knight Darkstar down in Dorne, Loras Tyrell gravely wounded on Dragonstone, and Jaime vanished in the riverlands, only four of the White Swords remained in King's Landing, and Ser Kevan had thrown Osmund Kettleblack (and his brother Osfryd) into the dungeon within hours of Cersei's confessing that she had taken both men as lovers. That left only Trant, the feeble Boros Blount, and Qyburn's mute monster Robert Strong to protect the young king and royal family.

I will need to find some new swords for the Kingsguard. Tommen should have seven good knights about him. In the past the Kingsguard had served for life, but that had not stopped Joffrey from dismissing Ser Barristan Selmy to make a place for his dog, Sandor Clegane. Kevan could make use of that precedent. *I could put Lancel in a white cloak,* he reflected. *There is more honor in that than he will ever find in the Warrior's Sons.*

Kevan Lannister hung his snow-sodden cloak inside his solar, pulled off his boots, and commanded his serving man to fetch some fresh wood for his fire. "A cup of mulled wine would go down well," he said as he settled by the hearth. "See to it."

The fire soon thawed him, and the wine warmed his insides nicely. It also made him sleepy, so he dare not drink another cup. His day was far from done. He had reports to read, letters to write. *And supper with Cersei and the king.* His niece had been subdued and submissive since her walk of atonement, thank the gods. The novices who attended her reported that she spent a third of her waking hours with her son, another third in prayer, and the rest in her tub. She was bathing four or five times a day, scrubbing herself with horsehair brushes and strong lye soap, as if she meant to scrape her skin off.

She will never wash the stain away, no matter how hard she scrubs. Ser Kevan remembered the girl she once had been, so full of life and mischief. And when she'd flowered, ahhhh . . . had there ever been a maid so sweet to look upon? *If Aerys had agreed to marry her to Rhaegar, how many deaths might have been avoided?* Cersei could have given the prince the sons he wanted, lions with purple eyes and silver manes . . . and with such a wife, Rhaegar might never have looked twice at Lyanna Stark. The northern girl had a wild beauty, as he recalled, though however bright a torch might burn it could never match the rising sun.

But it did no good to brood on lost battles and roads not taken. That was a vice of old done men. Rhaegar had wed Elia of Dorne, Lyanna Stark had died, Robert Baratheon had taken Cersei to bride, and here they were. And tonight his own road would take him to his niece's chambers and face-to-face with Cersei.

I have no reason to feel guilty, Ser Kevan told himself. *Tywin would understand that, surely. It was his daughter who brought shame down on our name, not I. What I did I did for the good of House Lannister.*

It was not as if his brother had never done the same. In their father's final years, after their mother's passing, their sire had taken the comely daughter of a candlemaker as mistress. It was not unknown for a widowed lord to keep a common girl as bedwarmer . . . but Lord Tytos soon began seating the woman beside him in the hall, showering her with gifts and honors, even asking her views on matters of state. Within a year she was dismissing servants, ordering about his household knights, even speaking for his lordship when he was indisposed. She grew so influential that it was said about Lannisport that any man who wished for his petition to be heard should kneel before her and speak loudly to her lap . . . for Tytos Lannister's ear was between his lady's legs. She had even taken to wearing their mother's jewels.

Until the day their lord father's heart had burst in his chest as he was ascending a steep flight of steps to her bed, that is. All the self-seekers who had named themselves her friends and cultivated her favor had abandoned her quickly enough when Tywin had her stripped naked and paraded through Lannisport to the docks, like a common whore. Though no man laid a hand on her, that walk spelled the end of her power. Surely Tywin would never have dreamed that same fate awaited his own golden daughter.

"It had to be," Ser Kevan muttered over the last of his wine. His High Holiness had to be appeased. Tommen needed the Faith behind him in the battles to come. And Cersei . . . the golden child had grown into a vain, foolish, greedy woman. Left to rule, she would have ruined Tommen as she had Joffrey.

Outside the wind was rising, clawing at the shutters of his chamber. Ser Kevan pushed himself to his feet. Time to face the lioness in her den. *We have pulled her claws. Jaime, though* . . . But no, he would not brood on that.

He donned an old, well-worn doublet, in case his niece had a mind to throw another cup of wine in his face, but he left his sword belt hanging on the back of his chair. Only the knights of the Kingsguard were permitted swords in Tommen's presence.

Ser Boros Blount was in attendance on the boy king and his mother when Ser Kevan entered the royal chambers. Blount wore enameled scale, white cloak, and halfhelm. He did not look well. Of late Boros had grown notably heavier about the face and belly, and his color was not good. And he was leaning against the wall behind him, as if standing had become too great an effort for him.

The meal was served by three novices, well-scrubbed girls of good birth between the ages of twelve and sixteen. In their soft white woolens, each seemed more innocent and unworldly than the last, yet the High Septon had insisted that no girl spend more than seven days in the queen's service, lest Cersei corrupt her. They tended the queen's wardrobe, drew her bath, poured her wine, changed her bedclothes of a morning. One shared the queen's bed every night, to ascertain she had no other company; the other two slept in an adjoining chamber with the septa who looked over them.

A tall stork of a girl with a pockmarked face escorted him into the royal presence. Cersei rose when he entered and kissed him lightly on the cheek. "Dear uncle. It is so good of you to sup with us." The queen was dressed as modestly as any matron, in a dark brown gown that buttoned up to her throat and a hooded green mantle that covered her shaved head. *Before her walk she would have flaunted her baldness beneath a golden crown.* "Come, sit," she said. "Will you have wine?"

"A cup." He sat, still wary.

A freckled novice filled their cups with hot spiced wine. "Tommen tells me that Lord Tyrell intends to rebuild the Tower of the Hand," Cersei said.

Ser Kevan nodded. "The new tower will be twice as tall as the one you burned, he says."

Cersei gave a throaty laugh. "Long lances, tall towers . . . is Lord Tyrell hinting at something?"

That made him smile. *It is good that she still remembers how to laugh.* When he asked if she had all that she required, the queen said, "I am well served. The girls are sweet, and the good septas make certain that I say my prayers. But once my innocence is proved, it would please me if Taena Merryweather might attend me once again. She could bring her son to court. Tommen needs other boys about him, friends of noble birth."

It was a modest request. Ser Kevan saw no reason why it should not be granted. He could foster the Merryweather boy himself, whilst Lady Taena accompanied Cersei back to Casterly Rock. "I will send for her after the trial," he promised.

Supper began with beef-and-barley soup, followed by a brace of quail and a roast pike near three feet long, with turnips, mushrooms, and plenty of hot bread and butter. Ser Boros tasted every dish that was set before the king. A humiliating duty for a knight of the Kingsguard, but perhaps all Blount was capable of these days . . . and wise, after the way Tommen's brother had died.

The king seemed happier than Kevan Lannister had seen him in a long time. From soup to sweet Tommen burbled about the exploits of his kittens, whilst feeding them morsels of pike off his own royal plate. "The bad cat was outside my window last night," he informed Kevan at one point, "but Ser Pounce hissed at him and he ran off across the roofs."

"The bad cat?" Ser Kevan said, amused. *He is a sweet boy.*

"An old black tomcat with a torn ear," Cersei told him. "A filthy thing, and foul-tempered. He clawed Joff's hand once." She made a face. "The cats keep the rats down, I know, but that one . . . he's been known to attack ravens in the rookery."

"I will ask the ratters to set a trap for him." Ser Kevan could not remember ever seeing his niece so quiet, so subdued, so demure. All for the good, he supposed. But it made him sad as well. *Her fire is quenched, she who used to burn so bright.* "You have not asked about your brother," he said, as they were waiting for the cream cakes. Cream cakes were the king's favorite.

Cersei lifted her chin, her green eyes shining in the candlelight. "Jaime? Have you had word?"

"None. Cersei, you may need to prepare yourself for—"

"If he were dead, I would know it. We came into this world together, Uncle. He would not go without me." She took a drink of wine. "Tyrion can leave whenever he wishes. You have had no word of him either, I suppose."

"No one has tried to sell us a dwarf's head of late, no."

She nodded. "Uncle, may I ask you a question?"

"Whatever you wish."

"Your wife . . . do you mean to bring her to court?"

"No." Dorna was a gentle soul, never comfortable but at home with friends and kin around her. She had done well by their children, dreamed of having grandchildren, prayed seven times a day, loved needlework and flowers. In King's Landing she would be as happy as one of Tommen's kittens in a pit of vipers. "My lady wife mislikes travel. Lannisport is her place."

"It is a wise woman who knows her place."

He did not like the sound of that. "Say what you mean."

"I thought I did." Cersei held out her cup. The freckled girl filled it once again. The cream cakes appeared then, and the conversation took a lighter turn. Only after Tommen and his kittens were escorted off to the royal bedchamber by Ser Boros did their talk turn to the queen's trial.

"Osney's brothers will not stand by idly and watch him die," Cersei warned him.

"I did not expect that they would. I've had the both of them arrested."

That seemed to take her aback. "For what crime?"

"Fornication with a queen. His High Holiness says that you confessed to bedding both of them—had you forgotten?"

Her face reddened. "No. What will you do with them?"

"The Wall, if they admit their guilt. If they deny it, they can face Ser Robert. Such men should never have been raised so high."

Cersei lowered her head. "I . . . I misjudged them."

"You misjudged a good many men, it seems."

He might have said more, but the dark-haired novice with the round cheeks returned to say, "My lord, my lady, I am sorry to intrude, but there is a boy below. Grand Maester Pycelle begs the favor of the Lord Regent's presence at once."

Dark wings, dark words, Ser Kevan thought. *Could Storm's End have fallen? Or might this be word from Bolton in the north?*

"It might be news of Jaime," the queen said.

There was only one way to know. Ser Kevan rose. "Pray excuse me." Before he took his leave, he dropped to one knee and kissed his niece upon the hand. If her silent giant failed her, it might be the last kiss she would ever know.

The messenger was a boy of eight or nine, so bundled up in fur he seemed a bear cub. Trant had kept him waiting out on the drawbridge rather than admit him into Maegor's. "Go find a fire, lad," Ser Kevan told him, pressing a penny into his hand. "I know the way to the rookery well enough."

The snow had finally stopped falling. Behind a veil of ragged clouds, a full moon floated fat and white as a snowball. The stars shone cold and distant. As Ser Kevan made his way across the inner ward, the castle seemed an alien place, where every keep and tower had grown icy teeth, and all familiar paths had vanished beneath a white blanket. Once an icicle long as a spear fell to shatter by his feet. *Autumn in King's Landing,* he brooded. *What must it be like up on the Wall?*

The door was opened by a serving girl, a skinny thing in a fur-lined robe much too big for her. Ser Kevan stamped the snow off his boots, removed his cloak, tossed it to her. "The Grand Maester is expecting me," he announced. The girl nodded, solemn and silent, and pointed to the steps.

Pycelle's chambers were beneath the rookery, a spacious suite of rooms cluttered with racks of herbs and salves and potions and shelves jammed full of books and scrolls. Ser Kevan had always found them uncomfortably hot. Not tonight. Once past the chamber door, the chill was palpable. Black ash and dying embers were all that remained of the hearthfire. A few flickering candles cast pools of dim light here and there.

The rest was shrouded in shadow . . . except beneath the open window, where a spray of ice crystals glittered in the moonlight, swirling in the wind. On the window seat a raven loitered, pale, huge, its feathers ruffled. It was the largest raven that Kevan Lannister had ever seen. Larger than any hunting hawk at Casterly Rock, larger than the largest owl. Blowing snow danced around it, and the moon painted it silver.

Not silver. White. The bird is white.

The white ravens of the Citadel did not carry messages, as their dark cousins did. When they went forth from Oldtown, it was for one purpose only: to herald a change of seasons.

"Winter," said Ser Kevan. The word made a white mist in the air. He turned away from the window.

Then something slammed him in the chest between the ribs, hard as a giant's fist. It drove the breath from him and sent him lurching backwards. The white raven took to the air, its pale wings slapping him about the head. Ser Kevan half-sat and half-fell onto the window seat. *What . . . who . . .* A quarrel was sunk almost to the fletching in his chest. *No. No, that was how my brother died.* Blood was seeping out around the shaft. "Pycelle," he muttered, confused. "Help me . . . I . . ."

Then he saw. Grand Maester Pycelle was seated at his table, his head pillowed on the great leather-bound tome before him. *Sleeping,* Kevan thought . . . until he blinked and saw the deep red gash in the old man's spotted skull and the blood pooled beneath his head, staining the pages of his book. All around his candle were bits of bone and brain, islands in a lake of melted wax.

He wanted guards, Ser Kevan thought. *I should have sent him guards.* Could Cersei have been right all along? Was this his nephew's work? "Tyrion?" he called. "Where . . . ?"

"Far away," a half-familiar voice replied.

He stood in a pool of shadow by a bookcase, plump, pale-faced, round-shouldered, clutching a crossbow in soft powdered hands. Silk slippers swaddled his feet.

"Varys?"

The eunuch set the crossbow down. "Ser Kevan. Forgive me if you can. I bear you no ill will. This was not done from malice. It was for the realm. For the children."

I have children. I have a wife. Oh, Dorna. Pain washed over him. He closed his eyes, opened them again. "There are . . . there are hundreds of Lannister guardsmen in this castle."

"But none in this room, thankfully. This pains me, my lord. You do not deserve to die alone on such a cold dark night. There are many like you, good men in service to bad causes . . . but you were threatening to undo all the queen's good work, to reconcile Highgarden and Casterly Rock, bind the Faith to your little king, unite the Seven Kingdoms under Tommen's rule. So . . ."

A gust of wind blew up. Ser Kevan shivered violently.

"Are you cold, my lord?" asked Varys. "Do forgive me. The Grand Maester befouled himself in dying, and the stink was so abominable that I thought I might choke."

Ser Kevan tried to rise, but the strength had left him. He could not feel his legs.

"I thought the crossbow fitting. You shared so much with Lord Tywin, why not that? Your niece will think the Tyrells had you murdered, mayhaps with the connivance of the Imp. The Tyrells will suspect her. Someone somewhere will find a way to blame the Dornishmen. Doubt, division, and mistrust will eat the very ground beneath your boy king, whilst Aegon raises his banner above Storm's End and the lords of the realm gather round him."

"Aegon?" For a moment he did not understand. Then he remembered. A babe swaddled in a crimson cloak, the cloth stained with his blood and brains. "Dead. He's dead."

"No." The eunuch's voice seemed deeper. "He is here. Aegon has been shaped for rule since before he could walk. He has been trained in arms, as befits a knight to be, but that was not the end of his education. He reads and writes, he speaks several tongues, he has studied history and law and poetry. A septa has instructed him in the mysteries of the Faith since he was old enough to understand them. He has lived with fisherfolk, worked with his hands, swum in rivers and mended nets and learned to wash his own clothes at need. He can fish and cook and bind up a wound, he knows what it is like to be hungry, to be hunted, to be afraid. Tommen has been taught that kingship is his right. Aegon knows that kingship is his duty, that a king must put his people first, and live and rule for them."

Kevan Lannister tried to cry out . . . to his guards, his wife, his brother . . . but the words would not come. Blood dribbled from his mouth. He shuddered violently.

"I am sorry." Varys wrung his hands. "You are suffering, I know, yet here I stand going on like some silly old woman. Time to make an end to it." The eunuch pursed his lips and gave a little whistle.

Ser Kevan was cold as ice, and every labored breath sent a fresh stab of pain through him. He glimpsed movement, heard the soft scuffling sound of slippered feet on stone. A child emerged from a pool of darkness, a pale boy in a ragged robe, no more than nine or ten. Another rose up behind the Grand Maester's chair. The girl who had opened the door for him was there as well. They were all around him, half a dozen of them, white-faced children with dark eyes, boys and girls together.

And in their hands, the daggers.

WESTEROS

THE BOY KING

TOMMEN BARATHEON, the First of His Name, King of the Andals, the Rhoynar, and the First Men, Lord of the Seven Kingdoms, a boy of eight years,

— his wife, QUEEN MARGAERY of House Tyrell, thrice wed, twice widowed, accused of high treason, held captive in the Great Sept of Baelor,
 — her lady companions and cousins, MEGGA, ALLA, and ELINOR TYRELL, accused of fornications,
  — Elinor's betrothed, ALYN AMBROSE, squire,
— his mother, CERSEI of House Lannister, Queen Dowager, Lady of Casterly Rock, accused of high treason, captive in the Great Sept of Baelor,
— his siblings:
 — his elder brother, {KING JOFFREY I BARATHEON}, poisoned during his wedding feast,
 — his elder sister, PRINCESS MYRCELLA BARATHEON, a girl of nine, a ward of Prince Doran Martell at Sunspear, betrothed to his son Trystane,
— his kittens, SER POUNCE, LADY WHISKERS, BOOTS,
— his uncles:
 — SER JAIME LANNISTER, called THE KINGSLAYER, twin to Queen Cersei, Lord Commander of the Kingsguard,
 — TYRION LANNISTER, called THE IMP, a dwarf, accused and condemned for regicide and kinslaying,
— his other kin:
 — his grandfather, {TYWIN LANNISTER}, Lord of Casterly Rock,

Warden of the West, and Hand of the King, murdered in the privy by his son Tyrion,

—his great-uncle, SER KEVAN LANNISTER, Lord Regent and Protector of the Realm, m. Dorna Swyft,
   —their children:
   —SER LANCEL LANNISTER, a knight of the Holy Order of the Warrior's Sons,
   —{WILLEM}, twin to Martyn, murdered at Riverrun,
   —MARTYN, twin to Willem, a squire,
   —JANEI, a girl of three,
—his great-aunt, GENNA LANNISTER, m. Ser Emmon Frey,
   —their children:
   —{SER CLEOS FREY}, killed by outlaws,
      —his son, SER TYWIN FREY, called TY,
      —his son, WILLEM FREY, a squire,
   —SER LYONEL FREY, Lady Genna's second son,
   —{TION FREY}, a squire, murdered at Riverrun,
   —WALDER FREY, called RED WALDER, a page at Casterly Rock,
—his great-uncle, {SER TYGETT LANNISTER}, m. Darlessa Marbrand
   —their children:
   —TYREK LANNISTER, a squire, vanished during the food riots in King's Landing,
      —LADY ERMESANDE HAYFORD, Tyrek's child wife,
—his great uncle, GERION LANNISTER, lost at sea,
   —JOY HILL, his bastard daughter,

—King Tommen's small council:
   —SER KEVAN LANNISTER, Lord Regent,
   —LORD MACE TYRELL, Hand of the King,
   —GRAND MAESTER PYCELLE, counselor and healer,
   —SER JAIME LANNISTER, Lord Commander of the Kingsguard,
   —LORD PAXTER REDWYNE, grand admiral and master of ships,
   —QYBURN, a disgraced maester and reputed necromancer, master of whisperers,

—Queen Cersei's former small council,
   —{LORD GYLES ROSBY}, lord treasurer and master of coin, dead of a cough,
   —LORD ORTON MERRYWEATHER, justiciar and master of laws, fled to Longtable upon Queen Cersei's arrest,

—AURANE WATERS, the Bastard of Driftmark, grand admiral and master of ships, fled to sea with the royal fleet upon Queen Cersei's arrest,

—King Tommen's Kingsguard:
  —SER JAIME LANNISTER, Lord Commander,
  —SER MERYN TRANT,
  —SER BOROS BLOUNT, removed and thence restored,
  —SER BALON SWANN, in Dorne with Princess Myrcella,
  —SER OSMUND KETTLEBLACK,
  —SER LORAS TYRELL, the Knight of Flowers,
  —{SER ARYS OAKHEART}, dead in Dorne,

—Tommen's court at King's Landing:
  —MOON BOY, the royal jester and fool,
  —PATE, a lad of eight, King Tommen's whipping boy,
  —ORMOND OF OLDTOWN, the royal harper and bard,
  —SER OSFRYD KETTLEBLACK, brother to Ser Osmund and Ser Osney, a captain in the City Watch,
  —NOHO DIMITTIS, envoy from the Iron Bank of Braavos,
  —{SER GREGOR CLEGANE}, called THE MOUNTAIN THAT RIDES, dead of a poisoned wound,
  —RENNIFER LONGWATERS, chief undergaoler of the Red Keep's dungeons,

—Queen Margaery's alleged lovers:
  —WAT, a singer styling himself THE BLUE BARD, a captive driven mad by torment,
  —{HAMISH THE HARPER}, an aged singer, died a captive,
  —SER MARK MULLENDORE, who lost a monkey and half an arm in the Battle of the Blackwater,
  —SER TALLAD called THE TALL, SER LAMBERT TURNBERRY, SER BAYARD NORCROSS, SER HUGH CLIFTON,
  —JALABHAR XHO, Prince of the Red Flower Vale, an exile from the Summer Isles,
  —SER HORAS REDWYNE, found innocent and freed,
  —SER HOBBER REDWYNE, found innocent and freed,

—Queen Cersei's chief accuser,
  —SER OSNEY KETTLEBLACK, brother to Ser Osmund and Ser Osfryd, held captive by the Faith,

—the people of the Faith:
  —THE HIGH SEPTON, Father of the Faithful, Voice of the Seven
    on Earth, an old man and frail,
      —SEPTA UNELLA, SEPTA MOELLE, SEPTA SCOLERA, the
        queen's gaolers,
      —SEPTON TORBERT, SEPTON RAYNARD, SEPTON
        LUCEON, SEPTON OLLIDOR, of the Most Devout,
      —SEPTA AGLANTINE, SEPTA MELICENT, serving the
        Seven at the Great Sept of Baelor,
      —SER THEODAN WELLS, called THEODAN THE TRUE,
        pious commander of the Warrior's Sons,
      —the "sparrows," the humblest of men, fierce in their piety,

—people of King's Landing:
  —CHATAYA, proprietor of an expensive brothel,
    —ALAYAYA, her daughter,
    —DANCY, MAREI, two of Chataya's girls,
  —TOBHO MOTT, a master armorer,

—lords of the crownlands, sworn to the Iron Throne:
  —RENFRED RYKKER, Lord of Duskendale,
    —SER RUFUS LEEK, a one-legged knight in his service, castel-
      lan of the Dun Fort at Duskendale,
  —{TANDA STOKEWORTH}, Lady of Stokeworth, died of a
    broken hip,
      —her eldest daughter, {FALYSE}, died screaming in the black
        cells,
        —{SER BALMAN BYRCH}, Lady Falyse's husband, killed in
          a joust,
      —her younger daughter, LOLLYS, weak of wit, Lady of Stoke-
        worth,
        —her newborn son, TYRION TANNER, of the hundred
          fathers,
        —her husband, SER BRONN OF THE BLACKWATER,
          sellsword turned knight,
      —MAESTER FRENKEN, in service at Stokeworth,

King Tommen's banner shows the crowned stag of Baratheon, black on gold,
and the lion of Lannister, gold on crimson, combatant.

THE KING AT THE WALL

STANNIS BARATHEON, the First of His Name, second son of Lord Steffon Baratheon and Lady Cassana of House Estermont, Lord of Dragonstone, styling himself King of Westeros,

—with King Stannis at Castle Black:
  —LADY MELISANDRE OF ASSHAI, called THE RED WOMAN, a priestess of R'hllor, the Lord of Light,
  —his knights and sworn swords:
    —SER RICHARD HORPE, his second-in-command,
    —SER GODRY FARRING, called GIANTSLAYER,
    —SER JUSTIN MASSEY,
    —LORD ROBIN PEASEBURY,
    —LORD HARWOOD FELL,
    —SER CLAYTON SUGGS, SER CORLISS PENNY, queen's men and fervent followers of the Lord of Light,
    —SER WILLAM FOXGLOVE, SER HUMFREY CLIFTON, SER ORMUND WYLDE, SER HARYS COBB, knights
  —his squires, DEVAN SEAWORTH and BRYEN FARRING
  —his captive, MANCE RAYDER, King-Beyond-the-Wall,
    —Rayder's infant son, "the wildling prince,"
      —the boy's wet nurse, GILLY, a wildling girl,
        —Gilly's infant son, "the abomination," fathered by her father {CRASTER},

—at Eastwatch-by-the-Sea:
  —QUEEN SELYSE of House Florent, his wife,
    —PRINCESS SHIREEN, their daughter, a girl of eleven,
      —PATCHFACE, Shireen's tattooed fool,
    —her uncle, SER AXELL FLORENT, foremost of the queen's men, styling himself the Queen's Hand,
    —her knights and sworn swords, SER NARBERT GRANDISON, SER BENETHON SCALES, SER PATREK OF KING'S MOUNTAIN, SER DORDEN THE DOUR, SER MALE-GORN OF REDPOOL, SER LAMBERT WHITEWATER, SER PERKIN FOLLARD, SER BRUS BUCKLER
  —SER DAVOS SEAWORTH, Lord of the Rainwood, Admiral of the Narrow Sea, and Hand of the King, called THE ONION KNIGHT,
  —SALLADHAR SAAN of Lys, a pirate and sellsail, master of the *Valyrian* and a fleet of galleys,
  —TYCHO NESTORIS, emissary from the Iron Bank of Braavos.

Stannis has taken for his banner the fiery heart of the Lord of Light—a red heart surrounded by orange flames upon a yellow field. Within the heart is the crowned stag of House Baratheon, in black.

KING OF THE ISLES AND THE NORTH

The Greyjoys of Pyke claim descent from the Grey King of the Age of Heroes. Legend says the Grey King ruled the sea itself and took a mermaid to wife. Aegon the Dragon ended the line of the last King of the Iron Islands, but allowed the ironborn to revive their ancient custom and choose who should have primacy among them. They chose Lord Vickon Greyjoy of Pyke. The Greyjoy sigil is a golden kraken upon a black field. Their words are *We Do Not Sow*.

EURON GREYJOY, the Third of His Name Since the Grey King, King of the Iron Islands and the North, King of Salt and Rock, Son of the Sea Wind, and Lord Reaper of Pyke, captain of the *Silence*, called CROW'S EYE,
—his elder brother, {BALON}, King of the Iron Islands and the North, the Ninth of His Name Since the Grey King, killed in a fall,
  —LADY ALANNYS, of House Harlaw, Balon's widow,
  —their children:
    —{RODRIK}, slain during Balon's first rebellion,
    —{MARON}, slain during Balon's first rebellion,
    —ASHA, captain of the *Black Wind* and conqueror of Deep-wood Motte, m. Erik Ironmaker,
    —THEON, called by northmen THEON TURNCLOAK, a captive at the Dreadfort,
—his younger brother, VICTARION, Lord Captain of the Iron Fleet, master of the *Iron Victory*,
—his youngest brother, AERON, called DAMPHAIR, a priest of the Drowned God,

—his captains and sworn swords:

- —TORWOLD BROWNTOOTH, PINCHFACE JON MYRE, RODRIK FREEBORN, THE RED OARSMAN, LEFT-HAND LUCAS CODD, QUELLON HUMBLE, HARREN HALF-HOARE, KEMMETT PYKE THE BASTARD, QARL THE THRALL, STONEHAND, RALF THE SHEPHERD, RALF OF LORDSPORT

—his crewmen:

- —{CRAGORN}, who blew the hellhorn and died,

—his lords bannermen:

- —ERIK IRONMAKER, called ERIK ANVIL-BREAKER and ERIK THE JUST, Lord Steward of the Iron Islands, castellan of Pyke, an old man once renowned, m. Asha Greyjoy,
- —lords of Pyke:
  - —GERMUND BOTLEY, Lord of Lordsport,
  - —WALDON WYNCH, Lord of Iron Holt,
- —lords of Old Wyk:
  - —DUNSTAN DRUMM, The Drumm, Lord of Old Wyk,
  - —NORNE GOODBROTHER, of Shatterstone,
  - —THE STONEHOUSE,
- —lords of Great Wyk:
  - —GOROLD GOODBROTHER, Lord of the Hammerhorn,
  - —TRISTON FARWYND, Lord of Sealskin Point,
  - —THE SPARR,
  - —MELDRED MERLYN, Lord of Pebbleton,
- —lords of Orkmont:
  - —ALYN ORKWOOD, called ORKWOOD OF ORKMONT,
  - —LORD BALON TAWNEY,
- —lords of Saltcliffe:
  - —LORD DONNOR SALTCLIFFE,
  - —LORD SUNDERLY,
- —lords of Harlaw:
  - —RODRIK HARLAW, called THE READER, Lord of Harlaw, Lord of Ten Towers, Harlaw of Harlaw,
  - —SIGFRYD HARLAW, called SIGFRYD SILVERHAIR, his great uncle, master of Harlaw Hall,
  - —HOTHO HARLAW, called HOTHO HUMPBACK, of the Tower of Glimmering, a cousin,
  - —BOREMUND HARLAW, called BOREMUND THE BLUE, master of Harridan Hill, a cousin,
- —lords of the lesser isles and rocks:
  - —GYLBERT FARWYND, Lord of the Lonely Light,

—the ironborn conquerors:

—on the Shield Islands

—ANDRIK THE UNSMILING, Lord of Southshield,

—NUTE THE BARBER, Lord of Oakenshield,

—MARON VOLMARK, Lord of Greenshield,

—SER HARRAS HARLAW, Lord of Greyshield, the Knight of Grey Gardens,

—at Moat Cailin

—RALF KENNING, castellan and commander,

—ADRACK HUMBLE, short half an arm,

—DAGON CODD, who yields to no man,

—at Torrhen's Square

—DAGMER, called CLEFTJAW, captain of *Foamdrinker*,

—at Deepwood Motte

—ASHA GREYJOY, the kraken's daughter, captain of the *Black Wind*,

—her lover, QARL THE MAID, a swordsman,

—her former lover, TRISTIFER BOTLEY, heir to Lordsport, dispossessed of his lands,

—her crewmen, ROGGON RUSTBEARD, GRIMTONGUE, ROLFE THE DWARF, LORREN LONGAXE, ROOK, FINGERS, SIX-TOED HARL, DROOPEYE DALE, EARL HARLAW, CROMM, HAGEN THE HORN and his beautiful red-haired daughter,

—her cousin, QUENTON GREYJOY,

—her cousin, DAGON GREYJOY, called DAGON THE DRUNKARD.

OTHER HOUSES
GREAT AND SMALL

HOUSE ARRYN

The Arryns are descended from the Kings of Mountain and Vale. Their sigil is a white moon-and-falcon upon a sky blue field. House Arryn has taken no part in the War of the Five Kings.

ROBERT ARRYN, Lord of the Eyrie, Defender of the Vale, a sickly boy of eight years, called SWEETROBIN,
—his mother, {LADY LYSA of House Tully}, widow of Lord Jon Arryn, pushed from the Moon Door to her death,
—his guardian, PETYR BAELISH, called LITTLEFINGER, Lord of Harrenhal, Lord Paramount of the Trident, and Lord Protector of the Vale,
—ALAYNE STONE, Lord Petyr's natural daughter, a maid of three-and-ten, actually Sansa Stark,
—SER LOTHOR BRUNE, a sellsword in Lord Petyr's service, captain of guards at the Eyrie,
—OSWELL, a grizzled man-at-arms in Lord Petyr's service, sometimes called KETTLEBLACK,
—SER SHADRICK OF THE SHADY GLEN, called THE MAD MOUSE, a hedge knight in Lord Petyr's service,
—SER BYRON THE BEAUTIFUL, SER MORGARTH THE MERRY, hedge knights in Lord Petyr's service,
—his household and retainers:
—MAESTER COLEMON, counselor, healer, and tutor,
—MORD, a brutal gaoler with teeth of gold,
—GRETCHEL, MADDY, and MELA, servingwomen,

—his bannermen, the Lords of Mountain and Vale:
  —YOHN ROYCE, called BRONZE YOHN, Lord of Runestone,
    —his son, SER ANDAR, heir to Runestone,
—LORD NESTOR ROYCE, High Steward of the Vale and castel-
  lan of the Gates of the Moon,
    —his son and heir, SER ALBAR,
    —his daughter, MYRANDA, called RANDA, a widow, but scarce
      used,
    —MYA STONE, bastard daughter of King Robert,
—LYONEL CORBRAY, Lord of Heart's Home,
    —SER LYN CORBRAY, his brother, who wields the famed blade
      Lady Forlorn,
    —SER LUCAS CORBRAY, his younger brother,
—TRISTON SUNDERLAND, Lord of the Three Sisters,
  —GODRIC BORRELL, Lord of Sweetsister,
  —ROLLAND LONGTHORPE, Lord of Longsister,
  —ALESANDOR TORRENT, Lord of Littlesister,
—ANYA WAYNWOOD, Lady of Ironoaks Castle,
  —SER MORTON, her eldest son and heir,
  —SER DONNEL, the Knight of the Bloody Gate,
  —WALLACE, her youngest son,
  —HARROLD HARDYNG, her ward, a squire oft called HARRY
    THE HEIR,
—SER SYMOND TEMPLETON, the Knight of Ninestars,
—JON LYNDERLY, Lord of the Snakewood,
—EDMUND WAXLEY, the Knight of Wickenden,
—GEROLD GRAFTON, the Lord of Gulltown,
—{EON HUNTER}, Lord of Longbow Hall, recently deceased,
  —SER GILWOOD, Lord Eon's eldest son and heir, now called
    YOUNG LORD HUNTER,
  —SER EUSTACE, Lord Eon's second son,
  —SER HARLAN, Lord Eon's youngest son,
  —Young Lord Hunter's household:
    —MAESTER WILLAMEN, counselor, healer, tutor,
—HORTON REDFORT, Lord of Redfort, thrice wed,
  —SER JASPER, SER CREIGHTON, SER JON, his sons,
  —SER MYCHEL, his youngest son, a new-made knight, m. Ysilla
    Royce of Runestone,
—BENEDAR BELMORE, Lord of Strongsong,

—clan chiefs from the Mountains of the Moon,
  —SHAGGA SON OF DOLF, OF THE STONE CROWS, presently leading a band in the kingswood,
    —TIMETT SON OF TIMETT, OF THE BURNED MEN,
    —CHELLA DAUGHTER OF CHEYK, OF THE BLACK EARS,
    —CRAWN SON OF CALOR, OF THE MOON BROTHERS.

The Arryn words are *As High as Honor.*

HOUSE BARATHEON

The youngest of the Great Houses, House Baratheon was born during the Wars of Conquest when Orys Baratheon, rumored to be a bastard brother of Aegon the Conqueror, defeated and slew Argilac the Arrogant, the last Storm King. Aegon rewarded him with Argilac's castle, lands, and daughter. Orys took the girl to bride and adopted the banner, honors, and words of her line.

In the 283rd year after Aegon's Conquest, Robert of House Baratheon, Lord of Storm's End, overthrew the Mad King, Aenys II Targaryen, to win the Iron Throne. His claim to the crown derived from his grandmother, a daughter of King Aegon V Targaryen, though Robert preferred to say his warhammer was his claim.

{ROBERT BARATHEON}, the First of His Name, King of the Andals, the Rhoynar, and the First Men, Lord of the Seven Kingdoms and Protector of the Realm, killed by a boar,
— his wife, QUEEN CERSEI of House Lannister,
— their children:
—— {KING JOFFREY BARATHEON}, the First of His Name, murdered at his wedding feast,
—— PRINCESS MYRCELLA, a ward in Sunspear, betrothed to Prince Trystane Martell,
—— KING TOMMEN BARATHEON, the First of His Name,
— his brothers:
—— STANNIS BARATHEON, rebel Lord of Dragonstone and pretender to the Iron Throne,
——— his daughter, SHIREEN, a girl of eleven,
—— {RENLY BARATHEON}, rebel Lord of Storm's End and pre-

tender to the Iron Throne, murdered at Storm's End in the midst of his army,

— his bastard children:
— MYA STONE, a maid of nineteen, in the service of Lord Nestor Royce, of the Gates of the Moon,
— GENDRY, an outlaw in the riverlands, ignorant of his heritage,
— EDRIC STORM, his acknowledged bastard son by Lady Delena of House Florent, hiding in Lys,
— SER ANDREW ESTERMONT, his cousin and guardian,
— his guards and protectors:
— SER GERALD GOWER, LEWYS called THE FISH-WIFE, SER TRISTON OF TALLY HILL, OMER BLACKBERRY,
— {BARRA}, his bastard daughter by a whore of King's Landing, killed by the command of his widow,
— his other kin:
— his great-uncle, SER ELDON ESTERMONT, Lord of Greenstone,
— his cousin, SER AEMON ESTERMONT, Eldon's son,
— his cousin, SER ALYN ESTERMONT, Aemon's son,
— his cousin, SER LOMAS ESTERMONT, Eldon's son,
— his cousin, SER ANDREW ESTERMONT, Lomas's son,

— bannermen sworn to Storm's End, the storm lords:
— DAVOS SEAWORTH, Lord of the Rainwood, Admiral of the Narrow Sea, and Hand of the King,
— his wife, MARYA, a carpenter's daughter,
— their sons, {DALE, ALLARD, MATTHOS, MARIC}, killed in the Battle of the Blackwater,
— their son DEVAN, squire to King Stannis,
— their sons, STANNIS and STEFFON,
— SER GILBERT FARRING, castellan of Storm's End,
— his son, BRYEN, squire to King Stannis,
— his cousin, SER GODRY FARRING, called GIANTSLAYER,
— ELWOOD MEADOWS, Lord of Grassfield Keep, seneschal at Storm's End,
— SELWYN TARTH, called THE EVENSTAR, Lord of Tarth,
— his daughter, BRIENNE, THE MAID OF TARTH, also called BRIENNE THE BEAUTY,
— her squire, PODRICK PAYNE, a boy of ten,
— SER RONNET CONNINGTON, called RED RONNET, the Knight of Griffin's Roost,

—his younger siblings, RAYMUND and ALYNNE,

—his bastard son, RONALD STORM,

—his cousin, JON CONNINGTON, once Lord of Storm's End and Hand of the King, exiled by Aerys II Targaryen, believed dead of drink,

—LESTER MORRIGEN, Lord of Crows Nest,

　—his brother and heir, SER RICHARD MORRIGEN,

　—his brother, {SER GUYARD MORRIGEN, called GUYARD THE GREEN}, slain in the Battle of the Blackwater,

—ARSTAN SELMY, Lord of Harvest Hall,

　—his great-uncle, SER BARRISTAN SELMY,

—CASPER WYLDE, Lord of the Rain House,

　—his uncle, SER ORMUND WYLDE, an aged knight,

—HARWOOD FELL, Lord of Felwood,

—HUGH GRANDISON, called GREYBEARD, Lord of Grandview,

—SEBASTION ERROL, Lord of Haystack Hall,

—CLIFFORD SWANN, Lord of Stonehelm

—BERIC DONDARRION, Lord of Blackwater, called THE LIGHTNING LORD, an outlaw in the riverlands, oft slain and now thought dead,

—{BRYCE CARON}, Lord of Nightsong, slain by Ser Philip Foote on the Blackwater,

　—his slayer, SER PHILIP FOOTE, a one-eyed knight, Lord of Nightsong,

　—his baseborn half-brother, SER ROLLAND STORM, called THE BASTARD OF NIGHTSONG, pretender Lord of Nightsong,

—ROBIN PEASEBURY, Lord of Poddingfield,

—MARY MERTYNS, Lady of Mistwood,

—RALPH BUCKLER, Lord of Bronzegate,

　—his cousin, SER BRUS BUCKLER.

The Baratheon sigil is a crowned stag, black, on a golden field. Their words are *Ours Is the Fury*.

HOUSE FREY

The Freys are bannermen to House Tully, but have not always been diligent in their duty. At the outset of the War of the Five Kings, Robb Stark won Lord Walder's allegiance by pledging to marry one of his daughters or granddaughters. When he wed Lady Jeyne Westerling instead, the Freys conspired with Roose Bolton and murdered the Young Wolf and his followers at what became known as the Red Wedding.

WALDER FREY, Lord of the Crossing,
— by his first wife, {LADY PERRA, of House Royce}:
— {SER STEVRON FREY}, died after the Battle of Oxcross,
— SER EMMON FREY, his second son,
— SER AENYS FREY, leading the Frey forces in the north,
— Aenys's son, AEGON BLOODBORN, an outlaw,
— Aenys's son, RHAEGAR, an envoy to White Harbor,
— PERRIANE, his eldest daughter, m. Ser Leslyn Haigh,
— by his second wife, {LADY CYRENNA, of House Swann}:
— SER JARED FREY, an envoy to White Harbor,
— SEPTON LUCEON, his fifth son,
— by his third wife, {LADY AMAREI of House Crakehall}:
— SER HOSTEEN FREY, a knight of great repute,
— LYENTHE, his second daughter, m. Lord Lucias Vypren,
— SYMOND FREY, his seventh son, a counter of coins, an envoy to White Harbor,
— SER DANWELL FREY, his eighth son,
— {MERRETT FREY}, his ninth son, hanged at Oldstones,
— Merrett's daughter, WALDA, called FAT WALDA, m. Roose Bolton, Lord of the Dreadfort,

    —Merrett's son, WALDER, called LITTLE WALDER, eight, a squire in service to Ramsay Bolton,

—{SER GEREMY FREY}, his tenth son, drowned,

—SER RAYMUND FREY, his eleventh son,

—by his fourth wife, {LADY ALYSSA, of House Blackwood}:

    —LOTHAR FREY, his twelfth son, called LAME LOTHAR,

    —SER JAMMOS FREY, his thirteenth son,

        —Jammos's son, WALDER, called BIG WALDER, eight, a squire in service to Ramsey Bolton,

    —SER WHALEN FREY, his fourteenth son,

    —MORYA, his third daughter, m. Ser Flement Brax,

    —TYTA, his fourth daughter, called TYTA THE MAID,

—by his fifth wife, {LADY SARYA of House Whent}:

    —no progeny,

—by his sixth wife, {LADY BETHANY of House Rosby}:

    —SER PERWYN FREY, his Walder's fifteenth son,

    —{SER BENFREY FREY}, his Walder's sixteenth son, died of a wound received at the Red Wedding,

    —MAESTER WILLAMEN, his seventeenth son, in service at Longbow Hall,

    —OLYVAR FREY, his eighteenth son, once a squire to Robb Stark,

    —ROSLIN, his fifth daughter, m. Lord Edmure Tully at the Red Wedding, pregnant with his child,

—by his seventh wife, {LADY ANNARA of House Farring}:

    —ARWYN, his sixth daughter, a maid of fourteen,

    —WENDEL, his nineteenth son, a page at Seagard,

    —COLMAR, his twentieth son, eleven and promised to the Faith,

    —WALTYR, called TYR, his twenty-first son, ten,

    —ELMAR, his twenty-second and lastborn son, a boy of nine briefly betrothed to Arya Stark,

    —SHIREI, his seventh daughter and youngest child, a girl of seven,

—his eighth wife, LADY JOYEUSE of House Erenford,

    —presently with child,

—Lord Walder's natural children, by sundry mothers,

    —WALDER RIVERS, called BASTARD WALDER,

    —MAESTER MELWYS, in service at Rosby,

    —JEYNE RIVERS, MARTYN RIVERS, RYGER RIVERS, RONEL RIVERS, MELLARA RIVERS, others

HOUSE LANNISTER

The Lannisters of Casterly Rock remain the principal support of King Tommen's claim to the Iron Throne. They boast of descent from Lann the Clever, the legendary trickster of the Age of Heroes. The gold of Casterly Rock and the Golden Tooth has made them the wealthiest of the Great Houses. The Lannister sigil is a golden lion upon a crimson field. Their words are *Hear Me Roar!*

{TYWIN LANNISTER}, Lord of Casterly Rock, Shield of Lannisport, Warden of the West, and Hand of the King, murdered by his dwarf son in his privy,
  —Lord Tywin's children:
    —CERSEI, twin to Jaime, widow of King Robert I Baratheon, a prisoner at the Great Sept of Baelor,
    —SER JAIME, twin to Cersei, called THE KINGSLAYER, Lord Commander of the Kingsguard,
      —his squires, JOSMYN PECKLEDON, GARRETT PAEGE, LEW PIPER,
      —SER ILYN PAYNE, a tongueless knight, lately the King's Justice and headsman,
      —SER RONNET CONNINGTON, called RED RONNET, the Knight of Griffin's Roost, sent to Maidenpool with a prisoner,
      —SER ADDAM MARBRAND, SER FLEMENT BRAX, SER ALYN STACKSPEAR, SER STEFFON SWYFT, SER HUMFREY SWYFT, SER LYLE CRAKEHALL called STRONGBOAR, SER JON BETTLEY called BEARD-

LESS JON, knights serving with Ser Jaime's host at Riverrun,
—TYRION, called THE IMP, dwarf and kinslayer, a fugitive in
exile across the narrow sea,

—the household at Casterly Rock:
—MAESTER CREYLEN, healer, tutor, and counselor,
—VYLARR, captain of guards,
—SER BENEDICT BROOM, master-at-arms,
—WHITESMILE WAT, a singer,

—Lord Tywin's siblings and their offspring:
—SER KEVAN LANNISTER, m. Dorna of House Swyft,
—LADY GENNA, m. Ser Emmon Frey, now Lord of Riverrun,
—Genna's eldest son, {SER CLEOS FREY}, m. Jeyne of
House Darry, killed by outlaws,
—Cleos's eldest son, SER TYWIN FREY, called TY, now
heir to Riverrun,
—Cleos's second son, WILLEM FREY, a squire,
—Genna's younger sons, SER LYONEL FREY, {TION
FREY}, WALDER FREY called RED WALDER,
—{SER TYGETT LANNISTER}, died of a pox,
—TYREK, Tygett's son, missing and feared dead,
—LADY ERMESANDE HAYFORD, Tyrek's child wife,
—{GERION LANNISTER}, lost at sea,
—JOY HILL, Gerion's bastard daughter, eleven,

—Lord Tywin's other close kin:
—{SER STAFFORD LANNISTER}, a cousin and brother to
Lord Tywin's wife, slain in battle at Oxcross,
—CERENNA and MYRIELLE, Stafford's daughters,
—SER DAVEN LANNISTER, Stafford's son,
—SER DAMION LANNISTER, a cousin, m. Lady Shiera Crake-
hall,
—their son, SER LUCION,
—their daughter, LANNA, m. Lord Antario Jast,
—LADY MARGOT, a cousin, m. Lord Titus Peake,

—bannermen and sworn swords, Lords of the West:
—DAMON MARBRAND, Lord of Ashemark,
—ROLAND CRAKEHALL, Lord of Crakehall,
—SEBASTON FARMAN, Lord of Fair Isle,

—TYTOS BRAX, Lord of Hornvale,
—QUENTEN BANEFORT, Lord of Banefort,
—SER HARYS SWYFT, goodfather to Ser Kevan Lannister,
—REGENARD ESTREN, Lord of Wyndhall,
—GAWEN WESTERLING, Lord of the Crag,
—LORD SELMOND STACKSPEAR,
—TERRENCE KENNING, Lord of Kayce,
—LORD ANTARIO JAST,
—LORD ROBIN MORELAND,
—LADY ALYSANNE LEFFORD,
—LEWYS LYDDEN, Lord of the Deep Den,
—LORD PHILIP PLUMM,
—LORD GARRISON PRESTER,
—SER LORENT LORCH, a landed knight,
—SER GARTH GREENFIELD, a landed knight,
—SER LYMOND VIKARY, a landed knight,
—SER RAYNARD RUTTIGER, a landed knight
—SER MANFRYD YEW, a landed knight,
—SER TYBOLT HETHERSPOON, a landed knight.

HOUSE MARTELL

Dorne was the last of the Seven Kingdoms to swear fealty to the Iron Throne. Blood, custom, geography, and history all helped to set the Dornishmen apart from the other kingdoms. At the outbreak of the War of the Five Kings Dorne took no part, but when Myrcella Baratheon was betrothed to Prince Trystane, Sunspear declared its support for King Joffrey. The Martell banner is a red sun pierced by a golden spear. Their words are *Unbowed, Unbent, Unbroken.*

DORAN NYMEROS MARTELL, Lord of Sunspear, Prince of Dorne,
—his wife, MELLARIO, of the Free City of Norvos,
—their children:
——PRINCESS ARIANNE, heir to Sunspear,
——PRINCE QUENTYN, a new-made knight, fostered at Yronwood,
——PRINCE TRYSTANE, betrothed to Myrcella Baratheon,
———SER GASCOYNE OF THE GREENBLOOD, his sworn shield,
—his siblings:
——{PRINCESS ELIA}, raped and murdered during the Sack of King's Landing,
———her daughter {RHAENYS TARGARYEN}, murdered during the Sack of King's Landing,
———her son, {AEGON TARGARYEN}, a babe at the breast, murdered during the Sack of King's Landing,
——{PRINCE OBERYN, called THE RED VIPER}, slain by Ser Gregor Clegane during a trial by combat,

—his paramour, ELLARIA SAND, natural daughter of Lord Harmen Uller,

—his bastard daughters, THE SAND SNAKES:
  —OBARA, his daughter by an Oldtown whore,
  —NYMERIA, called LADY NYM, his daughter by a noble-woman of Old Volantis,
  —TYENE, his daughter by a septa,
  —SARELLA, his daughter by a trader captain from the Summer Isles,
  —ELIA, his daughter by Ellaria Sand,
  —OBELLA, his daughter by Ellaria Sand,
  —DOREA, his daughter by Ellaria Sand,
  —LOREZA, his daughter by Ellaria Sand,

—Prince Doran's court
  —at the Water Gardens:
    —AREO HOTAH, of Norvos, captain of guards,
    —MAESTER CALEOTTE, counselor, healer, and tutor,
  —at Sunspear:
    —MAESTER MYLES, counselor, healer, and tutor,
    —RICASSO, seneschal, old and blind,
    —SER MANFREY MARTELL, castellan at Sunspear
    —LADY ALYSE LADYBRIGHT, lord treasurer,

—his ward, PRINCESS MYRCELLA BARATHEON, betrothed to Prince Trystane,
  —her sworn shield, {SER ARYS OAKHEART}, slain by Areo Hotah,
  —her bedmaid and companion, ROSAMUND LANNISTER, a distant cousin,

—his bannermen, the Lords of Dorne:
  —ANDERS YRONWOOD, Lord of Yronwood, Warden of the Stone Way, the Bloodroyal,
    —YNYS, his eldest daughter, m. Ryon Allyrion,
    —SER CLETUS, his son and heir,
    —GWYNETH, his youngest daughter, a girl of twelve,
  —HARMEN ULLER, Lord of Hellholt,
  —DELONNE ALLYRION, Lady of Godsgrace,
    —RYON ALLYRION, her son and heir,
  —DAGOS MANWOODY, Lord of Kingsgrave,
  —LARRA BLACKMONT, Lady of Blackmont,

—NYMELLA TOLAND, Lady of Ghost Hill,
—QUENTYN QORGYLE, Lord of Sandstone,
—SER DEZIEL DALT, the Knight of Lemonwood,
—FRANKLYN FOWLER, Lord of Skyreach, called THE OLD HAWK, the Warden of the Prince's Pass,
—SER SYMON SANTAGAR, the Knight of Spottswood,
—EDRIC DAYNE, Lord of Starfall, a squire,
—TREBOR JORDAYNE, Lord of the Tor,
—TREMOND GARGALEN, Lord of Salt Shore,
—DAERON VAITH, Lord of the Red Dunes.

HOUSE STARK

The Starks trace their descent from Brandon the Builder and the Kings of Winter. For thousands of years, they ruled from Winterfell as Kings in the North, until Torrhen Stark, the King Who Knelt, chose to swear fealty to Aegon the Dragon rather than give battle. When Lord Eddard Stark of Winterfell was executed by King Joffrey, the northmen foreswore their loyalty to the Iron Throne and proclaimed Lord Eddard's son Robb as King in the North. During the War of the Five Kings, he won every battle, but was betrayed and murdered by the Freys and Boltons at the Twins during his uncle's wedding.

{ROBB STARK}, King in the North, King of the Trident, Lord of Winterfell, called THE YOUNG WOLF, murdered at the Red Wedding,
—{GREY WIND}, his direwolf, killed at the Red Wedding,
—his trueborn siblings:
  —SANSA, his sister, m. Tyrion of House Lannister,
    —{LADY}, her direwolf, killed at Castle Darry,
  —ARYA, a girl of eleven, missing and thought dead,
    —NYMERIA, her direwolf, prowling the riverlands,
  —BRANDON, called BRAN, a crippled boy of nine, heir to Winterfell, believed dead,
    —SUMMER, his direwolf,
  —RICKON, a boy of four, believed dead,
    —SHAGGYDOG, his direwolf, black and savage,
    —OSHA, a wildling woman once captive at Winterfell,

—his bastard half-brother, JON SNOW, of the Night's Watch,
—GHOST, Jon's direwolf, white and silent,
—his other kin:
  —his uncle, BENJEN STARK, First Ranger of the Night's Watch, lost beyond the Wall, presumed dead,
  —his aunt, {LYSA ARRYN}, Lady of the Eyrie,
    —her son, ROBERT ARRYN, Lord of the Eyrie and Defender of the Vale, a sickly boy,
  —his uncle, EDMURE TULLY, Lord of Riverrun, taken captive at the Red Wedding,
    —LADY ROSLIN, of House Frey, Edmure's bride, great with child,
  —his great-uncle, SER BRYNDEN TULLY, called THE BLACK-FISH, lately castellan of Riverrun, now a hunted man,

—bannermen of Winterfell, the Lords of the North:
  —JON UMBER, called THE GREATJON, Lord of the Last Hearth, a captive at the Twins,
    —{JON, called THE SMALLJON}, the Greatjon's eldest son and heir, slain at the Red Wedding,
    —MORS called CROWFOOD, uncle to the Greatjon, castellan at the Last Hearth,
    —HOTHER called WHORESBANE, uncle to the Greatjon, likewise castellan at the Last Hearth,
  —{CLEY CERWYN}, Lord of Cerwyn, killed at Winterfell,
    —JONELLE, his sister, a maid of two-and-thirty,
  —ROOSE BOLTON, Lord of the Dreadfort,
    —{DOMERIC}, his heir, died of a bad belly,
    —WALTON called STEELSHANKS, his captain,
    —RAMSAY BOLTON, his natural son, called THE BAS-TARD OF BOLTON, Lord of the Hornwood,
      —WALDER FREY and WALDER FREY, called BIG WALDER and LITTLE WALDER, Ramsay's squires,
      —BEN BONES, kennelmaster at the Dreadfort,
      —{REEK}, a man-at-arms infamous for his stench, slain while posing as Ramsay,
      —the Bastard's Boys, Ramsay's men-at-arms:
        —YELLOW DICK, DAMON DANCE-FOR-ME, LUTON, SOUR ALYN, SKINNER, GRUNT,

—{RICKARD KARSTARK}, Lord of Karhold, beheaded by the
   Young Wolf for murdering prisoners,
   —{EDDARD}, his son, slain in the Whispering Wood,
   —{TORRHEN}, his son, slain in the Whispering Wood,
   —HARRION, his son, a captive at Maidenpool,
   —ALYS, his daughter, a maid of fifteen,
   —his uncle ARNOLF, castellan of Karhold,
        —CREGAN, Arnolf's elder son,
        —ARTHOR, Arnolf's younger son,
—WYMAN MANDERLY, Lord of White Harbor, vastly fat,
   —SER WYLIS MANDERLY, his eldest son and heir, very fat,
      a captive at Harrenhal,
        —Wylis's wife, LEONA of House Woolfield,
            —WYNAFRYD, their eldest daughter,
            —WYLLA, their younger daughter,
   —{SER WENDEL MANDERLY}, his second son, slain at the
      Red Wedding,
   —SER MARLON MANDERLY, his cousin, commander of
      the garrison at White Harbor,
   —MAESTER THEOMORE, counselor, tutor, healer,
   —WEX, a boy of twelve, once squire to Theon Greyjoy, mute,
   —SER BARTIMUS, an old knight, one-legged, one-eyed, and
      oft drunk, castellan of the Wolf's Den,
        —GARTH, a gaoler and headsman,
            —his axe, LADY LU,
        —THERRY, a young turnkey,
—MAEGE MORMONT, Lady of Bear Island, the She-Bear,
   —{DACEY}, her eldest daughter, slain at the Red Wedding,
   —ALYSANE, her daughter, the young She-Bear
   —LYRA, JORELLE, LYANNA, her younger daughters,
   —{JEOR MORMONT}, her brother, Lord Commander of
      the Night's Watch, slain by own men,
        —SER JORAH MORMONT, his son, an exile,
—HOWLAND REED, Lord of Greywater Watch, a crannogman,
   —his wife, JYANA, of the crannogmen,
   —their children:
        —MEERA, a young huntress,
        —JOJEN, a boy blessed with green sight,
—GALBART GLOVER, Master of Deepwood Motte, unwed,
   —ROBETT GLOVER, his brother and heir,
        —Robett's wife, SYBELLE of House Locke,

—BENJICOT BRANCH, NOSELESS NED WOODS, men of the wolfswood sworn to Deepwood Motte,

—{SER HELMAN TALLHART}, Master of Torrhen's Square, slain at Duskendale,

    —{BENFRED}, his son and heir, slain by ironmen on the Stony Shore,

    —EDDARA, his daughter, captive at Torrhen's Square,

    —{LEOBALD}, his brother, killed at Winterfell,

        —Leobald's wife, BERENA of House Hornwood, captive at Torrhen's Square,

        —their sons, BRANDON and BEREN, likewise captives at Torrhen's Square,

—RODRIK RYSWELL, Lord of the Rills,

    —BARBREY DUSTIN, his daughter, Lady of Barrowton, widow of Lord Willam Dustin,

        —HARWOOD STOUT, her liege man, a petty lord at Barrowton,

    —{BETHANY BOLTON}, his daughter, second wife of Lord Roose Bolton, died of a fever,

    —ROGER RYSWELL, RICKARD RYSWELL, ROOSE RYSWELL, his quarrelsome cousins and bannermen,

—LYESSA FLINT, Lady of Widow's Watch,

—ONDREW LOCKE, Lord of Oldcastle, an old man,

—the chiefs of the mountain clans:

    —HUGO WULL, called BIG BUCKET, or THE WULL,

    —BRANDON NORREY, called THE NORREY,

        —BRANDON NORREY, the Younger, his son,

    —TORREN LIDDLE, called THE LIDDLE,

        —DUNCAN LIDDLE, his eldest son, called BIG LIDDLE, a man of the Night's Watch,

        —MORGAN LIDDLE, his second son, called MIDDLE LIDDLE,

        —RICKARD LIDDLE, his third son, called LITTLE LIDDLE,

    —TORGHEN FLINT, of the First Flints, called THE FLINT, or OLD FLINT,

        —BLACK DONNEL FLINT, his son and heir,

        —ARTOS FLINT, his second son, half-brother to Black Donnel.

The Stark arms show a grey direwolf racing across an ice-white field. The Stark words are *Winter Is Coming*.

HOUSE TULLY

Lord Edmyn Tully of Riverrun was one of the first of the river lords to swear fealty to Aegon the Conqueror. King Aegon rewarded him by raising House Tully to dominion over all the lands of the Trident. The Tully sigil is a leaping trout, silver, on a field of rippling blue and red. The Tully words are *Family, Duty, Honor.*

EDMURE TULLY, Lord of Riverrun, taken captive at his wedding and held prisoner by the Freys,
—his bride, LADY ROSLIN of House Frey, now with child,
—his sister, {LADY CATELYN STARK}, widow of Lord Eddard Stark of Winterfell, slain at the Red Wedding,
—his sister, {LADY LYSA ARRYN}, widow of Lord Jon Arryn of the Vale, pushed to her death from the Eyrie,
—his uncle, SER BRYNDEN TULLY, called THE BLACKFISH, lately castellan of Riverrun, now an outlaw
—his household at Riverrun:
  —MAESTER VYMAN, counselor, healer, and tutor,
  —SER DESMOND GRELL, master-at-arms,
  —SER ROBIN RYGER, captain of the guard,
    —LONG LEW, ELWOOD, DELP, guardsmen,
  —UTHERYDES WAYN, steward of Riverrun,

—his bannermen, the Lords of the Trident:
  —TYTOS BLACKWOOD, Lord of Raventree Hall,
    —BRYNDEN, his eldest son and heir,
    —{LUCAS}, his second son, slain at the Red Wedding,

— HOSTER, his third son, a bookish boy,

— EDMUND and ALYN, his younger sons,

— BETHANY, his daughter, a girl of eight,

— {ROBERT}, his youngest son, died of loose bowels,

— JONOS BRACKEN, Lord of the Stone Hedge,

  — BARBARA, JAYNE, CATELYN, BESS, ALYSANNE, his five daughters,

  — HILDY, a camp follower,

— JASON MALLISTER, Lord of Seagard, a prisoner in his own castle,

  — PATREK, his son, imprisoned with his father,

  — SER DENYS MALLISTER, Lord Jason's uncle, a man of the Night's Watch,

— CLEMENT PIPER, Lord of Pinkmaiden Castle,

  — his son and heir, SER MARQ PIPER, taken captive at the Red Wedding,

— KARYL VANCE, Lord of Wayfarer's Rest,

— NORBERT VANCE, the blind Lord of Atranta,

— THEOMAR SMALLWOOD, Lord of Acorn Hall,

— WILLIAM MOOTON, Lord of Maidenpool,

  — ELEANOR, his daughter and heir, thirteen, m. Dickon Tarly of Horn Hill,

— SHELLA WHENT, dispossessed Lady of Harrenhal,

— SER HALMON PAEGE,

— LORD LYMOND GOODBROOK.

HOUSE TYRELL

The Tyrells rose to power as stewards to the Kings of the Reach, though they claim descent from Garth Greenhand, gardener king of the First Men. When the last king of House Gardener was slain on the Field of Fire, his steward, Harlen Tyrell, surrendered Highgarden to Aegon the Conqueror. Aegon granted him the castle and dominion over the Reach. Mace Tyrell declared his support for Renly Baratheon at the onset of the War of the Five Kings, and gave him the hand of his daughter Margaery. Upon Renly's death, Highgarden made alliance with House Lannister, and Margaery was betrothed to King Joffrey.

MACE TYRELL, Lord of Highgarden, Warden of the South, Defender of the Marches, and High Marshal of the Reach,
—his wife, LADY ALERIE, of House Hightower of Oldtown,
—their children:
  —WILLAS, their eldest son, heir to Highgarden,
  —SER GARLAN, called THE GALLANT, their second son, newly raised to Lord of Brightwater,
    —Garlan's wife, LADY LEONETTE of House Fossoway,
  —SER LORAS, the Knight of Flowers, their youngest son, a Sworn Brother of the Kingsguard, wounded on Dragonstone
  —MARGAERY, their daughter, twice wed and twice widowed,
    —Margaery's companions and ladies-in-waiting:
    —her cousins, MEGGA, ALLA, and ELINOR TYRELL,
      —Elinor's betrothed, ALYN AMBROSE, squire,
  —LADY ALYSANNE BULWER, LADY ALYCE GRACEFORD, LADY TAENA MERRYWEATHER, MEREDYTH

CRANE called MERRY, SEPTA NYSTERICA, her companions,

—his widowed mother, LADY OLENNA of House Redwyne, called THE QUEEN OF THORNS,

—his sisters:
  —LADY MINA, m. Paxter Redwyne, Lord of the Arbor,
    —her son, SER HORAS REDWYNE, called HORROR,
    —her son, SER HOBBER REDWYNE, called SLOBBER,
    —her daughter, DESMERA REDWYNE, sixteen,
  —LADY JANNA, wed to Ser Jon Fossoway,

—his uncles:
  —his uncle, GARTH TYRELL, called THE GROSS, Lord Seneschal of Highgarden,
    —Garth's bastard sons, GARSE and GARRETT FLOWERS,
  —his uncle, SER MORYN TYRELL, Lord Commander of the City Watch of Oldtown,
  —his uncle, MAESTER GORMON, serving at the Citadel,

—Mace's household at Highgarden:
  —MAESTER LOMYS, counselor, healer, and tutor,
  —IGON VYRWEL, captain of the guard,
  —SER VORTIMER CRANE, master-at-arms,
  —BUTTERBUMPS, fool and jester, hugely fat,

—his bannermen, the Lords of the Reach:
  —RANDYLL TARLY, Lord of Horn Hill, commanding King Tommen's army on the Trident,
  —PAXTER REDWYNE, Lord of the Arbor,
    —SER HORAS and SER HOBBER, his twin sons,
    —Lord Paxter's healer, MAESTER BALLABAR,
  —ARWYN OAKHEART, Lady of Old Oak,
  —MATHIS ROWAN, Lord of Goldengrove
  —LEYTON HIGHTOWER, Voice of Oldtown, Lord of the Port,
  —HUMFREY HEWETT, Lord of Oakenshield,
    —FALIA FLOWERS, his bastard daughter,
  —OSBERT SERRY, Lord of Southshield,
  —GUTHOR GRIMM, Lord of Greyshield,
  —MORIBALD CHESTER, Lord of Greenshield,
  —ORTON MERRYWEATHER, Lord of Longtable,
    —LADY TAENA, his wife, a woman of Myr,
      —RUSSELL, her son, a boy of six,

—LORD ARTHUR AMBROSE,
—LORENT CASWELL, Lord of Bitterbridge,

—his knights and sworn swords:
    —SER JON FOSSOWAY, of the green-apple Fossoways,
    —SER TANTON FOSSOWAY, of the red-apple Fossoways.

The Tyrell sigil is a golden rose on a grass-green field. Their words are *Growing Strong*.

THE SWORN BROTHERS OF
THE NIGHT'S WATCH

JON SNOW, the Bastard of Winterfell, nine-hundred-and-ninety-eighth Lord Commander of the Night's Watch,
—GHOST, his white direwolf,
—his steward, EDDISON TOLLETT, called DOLOROUS EDD,

—at Castle Black
  —MAESTER AEMON (TARGARYEN), healer and counselor, a blind man, one hundred and two years old,
    —Aemon's steward, CLYDAS,
    —Aemon's steward, SAMWELL TARLY, fat and bookish,
  —BOWEN MARSH, Lord Steward,
    —THREE-FINGER HOBB, steward and chief cook,
    —{DONAL NOYE}, one-armed armorer and smith, slain at the gate by Mag the Mighty
    —OWEN called THE OAF, TIM TANGLETONGUE, MULLY, CUGEN, DONNEL HILL called SWEET DONNEL, LEFT HAND LEW, JEREN, TY, DANNEL, WICK WHITTLESTICK, stewards,
  —OTHELL YARWYCK, First Builder,
    —SPARE BOOT, HALDER, ALBETT, KEGS, ALF OF RUNNYMUDD, builders,
  —SEPTON CELLADOR, a drunken devout,
  —BLACK JACK BULWER, First Ranger,
    —DYWEN, KEDGE WHITEYE, BEDWYCK called GIANT, MATTHAR, GARTH GREYFEATHER, ULMER OF

THE KINGSWOOD, ELRON, GARRETT GREEN-
SPEAR, FULK THE FLEA, PYPAR called PYP, GRENN
called AUROCHS, BERNARR called BLACK BERNARR,
TIM STONE, RORY, BEARDED BEN, TOM BARLEY-
CORN, GOADY BIG LIDDLE, LUKE OF LONGTOWN,
HAIRY HAL, rangers
—LEATHERS, a wildling turned crow,
—SER ALLISER THORNE, former master-at-arms,
—LORD JANOS SLYNT, former commander of the City Watch
of King's Landing, briefly Lord of Harrenhal,
—IRON EMMETT, formerly of Eastwatch, master-at-arms,
  —HARETH called HORSE, the twins ARRON and EM-
  RICK, SATIN, HOP-ROBIN, recruits in training,

—at the Shadow Tower
  —SER DENYS MALLISTER, commander,
    —his steward and squire, WALLACE MASSEY,
    —MAESTER MULLIN, healer and counselor,
    —{QHORIN HALFHAND, SQUIRE DALBRIDGE,
    EGGEN}, rangers, slain beyond the Wall,
    —STONESNAKE, a ranger, lost afoot in Skirling Pass,

—at Eastwatch-by-the-Sea
  —COTTER PYKE, a bastard of the Iron Islands, commander,
    —MAESTER HARMUNE, healer and counselor,
    —OLD TATTERSALT, captain of the *Blackbird*,
    —SER GLENDON HEWETT, master-at-arms,
    —SER MAYNARD HOLT, captain of the *Talon*,
    —RUSS BARLEYCORN, captain of the *Storm Crow*.

the WILDLINGS, or THE FREE FOLK

MANCE RAYDER, King-Beyond-the-Wall, a captive at Castle Black,
—his wife, {DALLA}, died in childbirth,
—their newborn son, born in battle, as yet unnamed,
    —VAL, Dalla's younger sister, "the wildling princess," a captive at
    Castle Black,
        —{JARL}, Val's lover, killed in a fall,
—his captains, chiefs, and raiders:
    —THE LORD OF BONES, mocked as RATTLESHIRT, a
    raider and leader of a war band, captive at Castle Black,
        —{YGRITTE}, a young spearwife, Jon Snow's lover, killed
        during the attack on Castle Black,
        —RYK, called LONGSPEAR, a member of his band,
        —RAGWYLE, LENYL, members of his band,
    —TORMUND, Mead-King of Ruddy Hall, called GIANTS-
    BANE, TALL-TALKER, HORN-BLOWER, and BREAKER
    OF ICE, also THUNDERFIST, HUSBAND TO BEARS,
    SPEAKER TO GODS, and FATHER OF HOSTS,
        —Tormund's sons, TOREGG THE TALL, TORWYRD THE
        TAME, DORMUND, and DRYN, his daughter MUNDA,
    —THE WEEPER, called THE WEEPING MAN, a notorious
    raider and leader of a war band,
    —{HARMA, called DOGSHEAD}, slain beneath the Wall,
        —HALLECK, her brother,
    —{STYR}, Magnar of Thenn, slain attacking Castle Black,
        —SIGORN, Styr's son, new Magnar of Thenn,

—VARAMYR called SIXSKINS, a skinchanger and warg, called
  LUMP as a boy,
    —ONE EYE, SLY, STALKER, his wolves,
    —his brother, {BUMP}, killed by a dog,
    —his foster father, {HAGGON}, a warg and hunter,
—THISTLE, a spearwife, hard and homely,
—{BRIAR, GRISELLA}. skinchangers, long dead,
—BORROQ, called THE BOAR, a skinchanger, much feared,
—GERRICK KINGSBLOOD, of the blood of Raymun Red-
  beard,
    —his three daughters,
—SOREN SHIELDBREAKER, a famed warrior,
—MORNA WHITE MASK, the warrior witch, a raider,
—YGON OLDFATHER, a clan chief with eighteen wives,
—THE GREAT WALRUS, leader on the Frozen Shore,
—MOTHER MOLE, a woods witch, given to prophecy,
—BROGG, GAVIN THE TRADER, HARLE THE HUNTS-
  MAN, HARLE THE HANDSOME, HOWD WANDERER,
  BLIND DOSS, KYLEG OF THE WOODEN EAR, DEVYN
  SEALSKINNER, chiefs and leaders amongst the free folk,
—{ORELL, called ORELL THE EAGLE}, a skinchanger slain
  by Jon Snow in the Skirling Pass,
—{MAG MAR TUN DOH WEG, called MAG THE MIGHTY},
  a giant, slain by Donal Noye at the gate of Castle Black,
—WUN WEG WUN DAR WUN, called WUN WUN, a giant,
—ROWAN, HOLLY, SQUIRREL, WILLOW WITCH-EYE,
  FRENYA, MYRTLE, spearwives, captive at the Wall.

BEYOND THE WALL

—in the Haunted Forest
  —BRANDON STARK, called BRAN, Prince of Winterfell and heir
    to the North, a crippled boy of nine,
      —his companions and protectors:
        —MEERA REED, a maid of sixteen, daughter of Lord How-
          land Reed of Greywater Watch,
        —JOJEN REED, her brother, thirteen, cursed with greensight,
        —HODOR, a simple lad, seven feet tall,
      —his guide, COLDHANDS, clad in black, once perhaps a man
        of the Night's Watch, now a mystery,

—at Craster's Keep
  —the betrayers, once men of the Night's Watch:
    —DIRK, who murdered Craster,
    —OLLO LOPHAND, who slew the Old Bear, Jeor Mormont,
    —GARTH OF GREENAWAY, MAWNEY, GRUBBS, ALAN
      OF ROSBY, former rangers
    —CLUBFOOT KARL, ORPHAN OSS, MUTTERING BILL,
      former stewards,

—in the caverns beneath a hollow hill
  —THE THREE-EYED CROW, also called THE LAST GREEN-
    SEER, sorcerer and dreamwalker, once a man of the Night's
    Watch named BRYNDEN, now more tree than man,
  —the children of the forest, those who sing the song of earth, last
    of their dying race:
    —LEAF, ASH, SCALES, BLACK KNIFE, SNOWYLOCKS,
      COALS.

ESSOS
BEYOND THE NARROW SEA

IN BRAAVOS

FERREGO ANTARYON, Sealord of Braavos, sickly and failing,
—QARRO VOLENTIN, First Sword of Braavos, his protector,
—BELLEGERE OTHERYS called THE BLACK PEARL, a courtesan descended from the pirate queen of the same name,
—THE VEILED LADY, THE MERLING QUEEN, THE MOONSHADOW, THE DAUGHTER OF THE DUSK, THE NIGHTINGALE, THE POETESS, famous courtesans,
—THE KINDLY MAN and THE WAIF, servants of the Many-Faced God at the House of Black and White,
   —UMMA, the temple cook,
   —THE HANDSOME MAN, THE FAT FELLOW, THE LORDLING, THE STERN FACE, THE SQUINTER, and THE STARVED MAN, secret servants of Him of Many Faces,
—ARYA of House Stark, a novice in service at the House of Black and White, also known as ARRY, NAN, WEASEL, SQUAB, SALTY, and CAT OF THE CANALS,
—BRUSCO, a fishmonger,
   —his daughters, TALEA and BREA,
—MERALYN, called MERRY, proprietor of the Happy Port, a brothel near the Ragman's Harbor,
   —THE SAILOR'S WIFE, a whore at the Happy Port,
     —LANNA, her daughter, a young whore,
    —RED ROGGO, GYLORO DOTHARE, GYLENO DOTHARE, a scribbler called QUILL, COSSOMO THE CONJURER, patrons of the Happy Port,

—TAGGANARO, a dockside cutpurse and thief,
    —CASSO, KING OF THE SEALS, his trained seal,
—S'VRONE, a dockside whore of a murderous bent,
—THE DRUNKEN DAUGHTER, a whore of uncertain temper.

IN OLD VOLANTIS

the reigning triarchs:
  —MALAQUO MAEGYR, Triarch of Volantis, a tiger,
  —DONIPHOS PAENYMION, Triarch of Volantis, an elephant,
  —NYESSOS VHASSAR, Triarch of Volantis, an elephant,

people of Volantis:
  —BENERRO, High Priest of R'hllor, the Lord of Light,
    —his right hand, MOQORRO, a priest of R'hllor,
  —THE WIDOW OF THE WATERFRONT, a wealthy freed-
    woman of the city, also called VOGARRO'S WHORE,
    —her fierce protectors, THE WIDOW'S SONS,
  —PENNY, a dwarf girl and mummer,
    —her pig, PRETTY PIG,
    —her dog, CRUNCH,
  —{GROAT}, brother to Penny, a dwarf mummer, murdered and
    beheaded,
  —ALIOS QHAEDAR, a candidate for triarch,
  —PARQUELLO VAELAROS, a candidate for triarch,
  —BELICHO STAEGONE, a candidate for triarch,
  —GRAZDAN MO ERAZ, an envoy from Yunkai.

ON SLAVER'S BAY

—in Yunkai, the Yellow City:
    —YURKHAZ ZO YUNZAK, Supreme Commander of the Armies and Allies of Yunkai, a slaver and aged noble of impeccable birth,
    —YEZZAN ZO QAGGAZ, mocked as the YELLOW WHALE, monstrously obese, sickly, hugely rich,
        —NURSE, his slave overseer,
        —SWEETS, a hermaphrodite slave, his treasure,
        —SCAR, a serjeant and slave soldier,
        —MORGO, a slave soldier,
    —MORGHAZ ZO ZHERZYN, a nobleman oft in his cups, mocked as THE DRUNKEN CONQUEROR,
    —GORZHAK ZO ERAZ, a nobleman and slaver, mocked as PUDDING FACE,
    —FAEZHAR ZO FAEZ, a nobleman and slaver, known as THE RABBIT,
    —GHAZDOR ZO AHLAQ, a nobleman and slaver, mocked as LORD WOBBLECHEEKS,
    —PAEZHAR ZO MYRAQ, a nobleman of small stature, mocked as THE LITTLE PIGEON,
    —CHEZDHAR ZO RHAEZN, MAEZON ZO RHAEZN, GRAZDHAN ZO RHAEZN, noblemen and brothers, mocked as THE CLANKER LORDS,
    —THE CHARIOTEER, THE BEASTMASTER, THE PERFUMED HERO, noblemen and slavers,

—in Astapor, the Red City:
  —CLEON THE GREAT, called THE BUTCHER KING,
  —CLEON II, his successor, king for eight days,
  —KING CUTTHROAT, a barber, slit the throat of Cleon II to steal his crown,
  —QUEEN WHORE, concubine to King Cleon II, claimed the throne after his murder.

THE QUEEN ACROSS THE WATER

DAENERYS TARGARYEN, the First of Her Name, Queen of Meereen, Queen of the Andals and the Rhoynar and the First Men, Lord of the Seven Kingdoms, Protector of the Realm, *Khaleesi* of the Great Grass Sea, called DAENERYS STORMBORN, the UNBURNT, MOTHER OF DRAGONS,
—her dragons, DROGON, VISERION, RHAEGAL,
—her brother, {RHAEGAR}, Prince of Dragonstone, slain by Robert Baratheon on the Trident,
  —Rhaegar's daughter, {RHAENYS}, murdered during the Sack of King's Landing,
  —Rhaegar's son, {AEGON}, a babe in arms, murdered during the Sack of King's Landing,
—her brother {VISERYS}, the Third of His Name, called THE BEGGAR KING, crowned with molten gold,
—her lord husband, {DROGO}, a *khal* of the Dothraki, died of a wound gone bad,
  —her stillborn son by Drogo, {RHAEGO}, slain in the womb by the *maegi* Mirri Maz Duur,

—her protectors:
—SER BARRISTAN SELMY, called BARRISTAN THE BOLD, Lord Commander of the Queensguard,
  —his lads, squires training for knighthood:
    —TUMCO LHO, of the Basilisk Isles,
    —LARRAQ, called THE LASH, of Meereen,
    —THE RED LAMB, a Lhazarene freedman,
    —the BOYS, three Ghiscari brothers,

—STRONG BELWAS, eunuch and former fighting slave,
—her Dothraki bloodriders:
  —JHOGO, the whip, blood of her blood,
  —AGGO, the bow, blood of her blood,
  —RAKHARO, the *arakh*, blood of her blood,

—her captains and commanders:
  —DAARIO NAHARIS, a flamboyant Tyroshi sellsword, captain
  of the Stormcrows, a free company,
  —BEN PLUMM, called BROWN BEN, a mongrel sellsword,
  captain of the Second Sons, a free company.
  —GREY WORM, a eunuch, commander of the Unsullied, a
  company of eunuch infantry,
    —HERO, an Unsullied captain, second-in-command,
    —STALWART SHIELD, an Unsullied spearman,
  —MOLLONO YOS DOB, commander of the Stalwart Shields,
  a company of freedmen,
  —SYMON STRIPEBACK, commander of FREE BROTHERS,
  a company of freedmen,
  —MARSELEN, commander of the MOTHER'S MEN, a com-
  pany of freedman, a eunuch, brother to Missandei,
  —GROLEO of Pentos, formerly captain of the great cog *Sad-
  uleon*, now an admiral without a fleet,
  —ROMMO, a *jaqqa rhan* of the Dothraki,

—her Meereenese court:
  —REZNAK MO REZNAK, her seneschal, bald and unctuous,
  —SKAHAZ MO KANDAQ, called THE SHAVEPATE, shaven-
  headed commander of the Brazen Beasts, her city watch,

—her handmaids and servants:
  —IRRI and JHIQUI, young women of the Dothraki,
  —MISSANDEI, a Naathi scribe and translator,
  —GRAZDAR, QEZZA, MEZZARA, KEZMYA, AZZAK,
  BHAKAZ, MIKLAZ, DHAZZAR, DRAQAZ, JHEZANE, chil-
  dren of the pyramids of Meereen, her cupbearers and pages,

—people of Meereen, highborn and common:
—GALAZZA GALARE, the Green Grace, high priestess at the
Temple of the Graces,
  —GRAZDAM ZO GALARE, her cousin, a nobleman,

—HIZDAHR ZO LORAQ, a wealthy Meereenese nobleman, of ancient lineage,
  —MARGHAZ ZO LORAQ, his cousin,
—RYLONA RHEE, freedwoman and harpist,
—{HAZZEA}, a farmer's daughter, four years of age,
—GOGHOR THE GIANT, KHRAZZ, BELAQUO BONE-BREAKER, CAMARRON OF THE COUNT, FEARLESS ITHOKE, THE SPOTTED CAT, BARSENA BLACKHAIR, STEELSKIN, pit fighters and freed slaves,

—her uncertain allies, false friends, and known enemies:
  —SER JORAH MORMONT, formerly Lord of Bear Island,
  —{MIRRI MAZ DUUR}, godswife and *maegi*, a servant of the Great Shepherd of Lhazar,
  —XARO XHOAN DAXOS, a merchant prince of Qarth,
  —QUAITHE, a masked shadowbinder from Asshai,
  —ILLYRIO MOPATIS, a magister of the Free City of Pentos, who brokered her marriage to Khal Drogo,
  —CLEON THE GREAT, butcher king of Astapor.

—the Queen's Suitors
  —on Slaver's Bay:
    —DAARIO NAHARIS, late of Tyrosh, a sellsword and captain of the Stormcrows,
    —HIZDAHR ZO LORAQ, a wealthy Meereenese nobleman,
    —SKAHAZ MO KANDAQ, called THE SHAVEPATE, a lesser nobleman of Meereen,
    —CLEON THE GREAT, Butcher King of Astapor,

  —in Volantis:
    —PRINCE QUENTYN MARTELL, eldest son of Doran Martell, Lord of Sunspear and Prince of Dorne,
      —his sworn shields and companions:
        —{SER CLETUS YRONWOOD}, heir to Yronwood, slain by corsairs,
        —SER ARCHIBALD YRONWOOD, cousin to Cletus, called THE BIG MAN,
        —SER GERRIS DRINKWATER,
        —{SER WILLAM WELLS}, slain by corsairs
        —{MAESTER KEDRY}, slain by corsairs,

—on the Rhoyne:
  —YOUNG GRIFF, a blue-haired lad of eighteen years,
    —his foster father, GRIFF, a sellsword late of the Golden Company,
    —his companion, teachers, and protectors:
      —SER ROLLY DUCKFIELD, called DUCK, a knight,
      —SEPTA LEMORE, a woman of the Faith,
      —HALDON, called THE HALFMAESTER, his tutor,
      —YANDRY, master and captain of the *Shy Maid*,
        —YSILLA, his wife,

—at sea:
  —VICTARION GREYJOY, Lord Captain of the Iron Fleet, called THE IRON CAPTAIN,
    —his bedwarmer, a dusky woman without a tongue, a gift from Euron Crow's Eye,
    —his healer, MAESTER KERWIN, late of Greenshield, a gift from Euron Crow's Eye,
    —his crew on the *Iron Victory*:
      —WULFE ONE-EAR, RAGNOR PYKE, LONGWATER PYKE, TOM TIDEWOOD, BURTON HUMBLE, QUELLON HUMBLE, STEFFAR STAMMERER
  —his captains:
    —RODRIK SPARR, called THE VOLE, captain of *Grief*,
    —RED RALF STONEHOUSE, captain of *Red Jester*,
    —MANFRYD MERLYN, captain of *Kite*,
    —RALF THE LIMPER, captain of *Lord Quellon*,
    —TOM CODD, called BLOODLESS TOM, captain of the *Lamentation*,
    —DAEGON SHEPHERD, called THE BLACK SHEPHERD, captain of the *Dagger*.

The Targaryens are the blood of the dragon, descended from the high lords of the ancient Freehold of Valyria, their heritage marked by lilac, indigo, and violet eyes and hair of silver-gold. To preserve their blood and keep it pure, House Targaryen has oft wed brother to sister, cousin to cousin, uncle to niece. The founder of the dynasty, Aegon the Conqueror, took both his sisters to wife and fathered sons on each. The Targaryen banner is a three-headed dragon, red on black, the three heads representing Aegon and his sisters. The Targaryen words are *Fire and Blood*.

THE SELLSWORDS
MEN AND WOMEN OF
THE FREE COMPANIES

THE GOLDEN COMPANY, ten thousand strong, of uncertain loyalty:
- HOMELESS HARRY STRICKLAND, captain-general,
  - WATKYN, his squire and cupbearer,
- {SER MYLES TOYNE, called BLACKHEART}, four years dead, the previous captain-general,
- BLACK BALAQ, a white-haired Summer Islander, commander of the company archers,
- LYSONO MAAR, a sellsword late of the Free City of Lys, company spymaster,
- GORYS EDORYEN, a sellsword late of the Free City of Volantis, company paymaster,
- SER FRANKLYN FLOWERS, the Bastard of Cider Hall, a sellsword from the Reach,
- SER MARQ MANDRAKE, an exile escaped from slavery, scarred by pox,
- SER LASWELL PEAKE, an exile lord,
  - his brothers, TORMAN and PYKEWOOD,
- SER TRISTAN RIVERS, bastard, outlaw, exile,
- CASPOR HILL, HUMFREY STONE, MALO JAYN, DICK COLE, WILL COLE, LORIMAS MUDD, JON LOTHSTON, LYMOND PEASE, SER BRENDEL BYRNE, DUNCAN STRONG, DENYS STRONG, CHAINS, YOUNG JOHN MUDD, serjeants of the company,

—{SER AEGOR RIVERS, called BITTERSTEEL}, a bastard son of King Aegon IV Targaryen, founder of the company},

—{MAELYS I BLACKFYRE, called MAELYS THE MONSTROUS}, captain-general of the company, pretender to the Iron Throne of Westeros, member of the Band of Nine, slain during the War of the Ninepenny Kings,

THE WINDBLOWN, two thousand horse and foot, sworn to Yunkai,
—THE TATTERED PRINCE, a former nobleman of the Free City of Pentos, captain and founder,
    —CAGGO, called CORPSEKILLER, his right hand,
    —DENZO D'HAN, the warrior bard, his left hand,
    —HUGH HUNGERFORD, serjeant, former company paymaster, fined three fingers for stealing,
    —SER ORSON STONE, SER LUCIFER LONG, WILL OF THE WOODS, DICK STRAW, GINJER JACK, Westerosi sellswords,
    —PRETTY MERIS, the company torturer,
    —BOOKS, a Volantene swordsman and notorious reader,
    —BEANS, a crossbowman, late of Myr,
    —OLD BILL BONE, a weathered Summer Islander,
    —MYRIO MYRAKIS, a sellsword late of Pentos,

THE COMPANY OF THE CAT, three thousand strong, sworn to Yunkai,
—BLOODBEARD, captain and commander,

THE LONG LANCES, eight hundred horse-riders, sworn to Yunkai,
—GYLO RHEGAN, captain and commander,

THE SECOND SONS, five hundred horse-riders, sworn to Queen Daenerys,
—BROWN BEN PLUMM, captain and commander,
—KASPORIO, called KASPORIO THE CUNNING, a bravo, second-in-command,
—TYBERO ISTARION, called INKPOTS, company paymaster,
—HAMMER, a drunken blacksmith and armorer,
    —his apprentice, called NAIL,
—SNATCH, a serjeant, one-handed,
—KEM, a young sellsword, from Flea Bottom,
—BOKKOKO, an axeman of formidable repute,
—UHLAN, a serjeant of the company,

THE STORMCROWS, five hundred horse-riders, sworn to Queen Daenerys,
—DAAERIO NAHARIS, captain and commander,
　—THE WIDOWER, his second-in-command,
　—JOKIN, commander of the company archers.

ACKNOWLEDGMENTS

The last one was a bitch. This one was three bitches and a bastard. Once again, my thanks to my long-suffering editors and publishers: to Jane Johnson and Joy Chamberlain at Voyager, and Scott Shannon, Nita Taublib, and Anne Groell from Bantam. Their understanding, good humor, and sage advice helped through the tough bits, and I will never cease to be grateful for their patience.

Thanks as well to my equally patient and endlessly supportive agents, Chris Lotts, Vince Gerardis, the fabulous Kay McCauley, and the late Ralph Vicinanza. Ralph, I wish you were here to share this day.

And thanks to Stephen Boucher, the wandering Aussie who helps keep my computer greased and humming whenever he drops by Santa Fe for a breakfast burrito (Xmas) and a side of jalapeño bacon.

Back here on the home front, thanks are also due to my dear friends Melinda Snodgrass and Daniel Abraham for their encouragement and support, to my webmaster Pati Nagle for maintaining my corner of the Internet, and to the amazing Raya Golden for the meals, the art, the unfailing good cheer that helped to brighten even the darkest days around Terrapin Station. Even if she did try to steal my cat.

As long as it has taken me to dance this dance, it would surely have taken twice as long without the assistance of my faithful (and acerbic) minion and sometime traveling companion Ty Franck, who tends to my computer when Stephen's not around, keeps the ravening virtual mobs from my virtual doorstep, runs my errands, does my filing, makes the coffee, walks the walk, and charges ten thousand dollars to change a light bulb—all while writing his own kick-ass books on Wednesdays.

Last, but far from my least, all my love and gratitude to my wife, Parris, who has danced every step of this beside me. Love ya, Phipps.

George R. R. Martin
May 13, 2011

About the Author

George R. R. Martin is the #1 *New York Times* bestselling author of many novels, including those of the acclaimed series A Song of Ice and Fire—*A Game of Thrones, A Clash of Kings, A Storm of Swords, A Feast for Crows,* and *A Dance with Dragons*—as well as *Tuf Voyaging, Fevre Dream, Armageddon Rag, Dying of the Light, Windhaven* (with Lisa Tuttle) and *Dreamsongs Volumes I* and *II*. He is also the creator of *The Lands of Ice and Fire*, a collection of maps featuring original artwork from illustrator and cartographer Jonathan Roberts, and *The World of Ice & Fire* (with Elio M. García, Jr., and Linda Antonsson). As a writer-producer, he has worked on *The Twilight Zone, Beauty and the Beast,* and various feature films and pilots that were never made. He lives with the lovely Parris in Santa Fe, New Mexico.

georgerrmartin.com

Facebook.com/GRRMartinofficial

Twitter: @GRRMspeaking

ABOUT THE TYPE

This book was set in Electra, a typeface designed for Linotype by W. A. Dwiggins, the renowned type designer (1880–1956). Electra is a fluid typeface, avoiding the contrasts of thick and thin strokes that are prevalent in most modern typefaces.

Can't wait to know what happens next
in Westeros and beyond?
Neither can we!
But we are delighted to present you with
this special preview from

THE WINDS

OF

WINTER

————

Book Six of
A Song of Ice and Fire

BY GEORGE R. R. MARTIN

We don't know when for certain,
but Winter *is* coming!
So for now . . . enjoy!

SER BARRISTAN

Through the gloom of night the dead men flew, raining down upon the city streets. The riper corpses would fall to pieces in the air, and burst when they came smashing down onto the bricks, scattering worms and maggots and worse things. Others would bounce against the sides of pyramids and towers, leaving smears of blood and gore to mark the places where they'd struck.

Huge as they were, the Yunkish trebuchets did not have the range to throw their grisly burdens deep into the city. Most of the dead were landing just inside the walls, or slamming off barbicans, parapets, and defensive towers. With the six sisters arrayed in a rough crescent around Meereen, every part of the city was being struck, save only the river districts to the north. No trebuchet could throw across the width of the Skahazadhan.

A *small mercy, that,* thought Barristan Selmy, as he rode into the market square inside Meereen's great western gate. When Daenerys had taken the city, they had broken through that same gate with the huge battering ram called Joso's Cock, made from the mast of a ship. The Great Masters and their slave soldiers had met the attackers here, and the fighting had raged through the surrounding streets for hours. By the time the city finally fell, hundreds of dead and dying had littered the square.

Now once again the market was a scene of carnage, though these dead came riding the pale mare. By day Meereen's brick streets showed half a hundred hues, but night turned them into patchworks of black and white and grey. Torchlight shimmered in the puddles left by the recent rains, and painted lines of fire on the helms and greaves and breastplates of the men.

Ser Barristan Selmy rode past them slowly. The old knight wore the armor his queen had given him — a suit of white enameled steel, inlaid and chased with gold. The cloak that streamed from his shoulders was as white as winter snow, as was the shield slung from his saddle. Beneath him was the queen's own mount, the silver mare Khal Drogo had given her upon their wedding day. That was presumptuous, he knew, but if Daenerys herself could not be with them in their hour of peril, Ser Barristan hoped the sight of her silver in the fray might give heart to her warriors, reminding them of who and what they fought for. Besides, the silver had been years in the company of the queen's dragons, and had grown accustomed to the sight and scent of them. That was not something that could be said for the horses of their foes.

With him rode three of his lads. Tumco Lho carried the three-headed dragon banner of House Targaryen, red on black. Larraq the Lash bore the white forked standard of the Kingsguard: seven silver swords encircling a golden crown. To the Red Lamb Selmy had given a great silver-banded warhorn, to sound commands across the battlefield. His other boys remained at the Great Pyramid. They would fight another day, or not at all. Not every squire was meant to be a knight. It was the hour of the wolf. The longest, darkest hour of the night. For many of the men who had assembled in the market square, it would be the last night of their lives.

Beneath the towering brick facade of Meereen's ancient Slave Exchange, five thousand Unsullied were drawn up in ten long lines. They stood as still as if they had been carved of stone, each with his three spears, short sword, and shield. Torchlight winked off the spikes of their bronze helmets, and bathed the smooth-cheeked faces beneath. When a body came spinning down amongst them, the eunuchs simply stepped aside, taking just as many steps as were required, then closing ranks again. They were all afoot, even their officers: Grey Worm first and foremost, marked by the three spikes on his helm.

The Stormcrows had assembled beneath the merchant's arcade fronting on the southern side of the square, where the arches gave them some protection from the dead men. Jokin's archers were fitting strings to their bows as Ser Barristan rode by. The Widower sat grim-faced astride a gaunt grey horse, with his shield upon his arm and his spiked battle-axe in hand. A fan of black feathers sprouted from one temple of his iron halfhelm. The boy beside him was clutching the company's banner: a dozen ragged black streamers on a tall staff, topped by a carved wooden crow.

The horselords had come as well. Aggo and Rakharo had taken most of the queen's small *khalasar* across the Skahazadhan, but the old half-crippled *jaqqa rhan* Rommo had scraped together twenty riders from those left behind. Some were as old as he was, many marked by some old wound or deformity. The rest were beardless boys, striplings seeking their first bell and the right to braid their hair. They milled about near the weathered bronze statue of the Chainmaker, anxious to be off, dancing their horses aside whenever a corpse came spinning down from above.

Not far from them, about the ghastly monument the Great Masters called the Spire of Skulls, several hundred pit fighters had gathered. Selmy saw the Spotted Cat amongst them. Beside him stood Fearless Ithoke, and elsewhere Senerra She-Snake, Camarron of the Count, the Brindled Butcher, Togosh, Marrigo, Orlos the Catamite. Even Goghor the Giant was there, towering above the others like a man amongst boys. *Freedom means something to them after all, it would seem.* The pit fighters had more love for Hizdahr than they had ever shown Daenerys, but Selmy was glad to have them all the same. *Some are even wearing armor,* he observed. Perhaps his defeat of Khrazz had taught them something.

Above, the gatehouse battlements were crowded with men in patch-work cloaks and brazen masks: the Shavepate had sent his Brazen

Beasts onto the city walls, to free up the Unsullied to take the field. Should the battle be lost, it would be up to Skahaz and his men to hold Meereen against the Yunkai'i . . . until such time as Queen Daenerys could return.

If indeed she ever does.

Across the city at other gates others forces had assembled. Tal Toraq and his Stalwart Shields had gathered by the eastern gate, sometimes called the hill gate or the Khyzai gate, since travelers bound for Lhazar via the Khyzai Pass always left that way. Marselen and the Mother's Men had massed beside the south gate, the Yellow Gate. The Free Brothers and Symon Stripeback had drawn the north gate, fronting on the river. They would have the easiest egress, with no foe before them but a few ships. The Yunkishmen had placed two Ghiscari legions to the north, but they were camped across the Skahazadhan, with the whole width of the river between them and the walls of Meereen.

The main Yunkish camp lay to the west, between the walls of Meereen and the warm green waters of Slaver's Bay. Two of the trebuchets had risen there, one beside the river, the second opposite Meereen's main gates, defended by two dozen of Yunkai's Wise Masters, each with his own slave soldiers. Between the great siege engines were the fortified encampments of two Ghiscari legions. The Company of the Cat had its camp between the city and the sea. The foe had Tolosi slingers too, and somewhere out in the night were three hundred Elyrian crossbowmen.

Too many foes, Ser Barristan brooded. *Their numbers must surely tell against us.* This attack went against all of the old knight's instincts. Meereen's walls were thick and strong. Inside those walls, the defenders enjoyed every advantage. Yet he had no choice but to lead his men into the teeth of the Yunkish siege lines, against foes of vastly greater strength.

The White Bull would have called it folly. He would have warned Barristan against trusting sellswords too. *This is what it has come to, my queen,* Ser Barristan thought. *Our fates hinge upon a sellsword's greed.*

Your city, your people, our lives . . . the Tattered Prince holds us all in his
bloodstained hands.

Even if their best hope proved to be forlorn hope, Selmy knew that
he had no other choice. He might have held Meereen for years against
the Yunkai'i, but he could not hold it for even a moon's turn with the
pale mare galloping through its streets.

A hush fell across the market square as the old knight and his banner
bearers rode toward the gatehouse. Selmy could hear the murmur of
countless voices, the sound of horses blowing, whickering, and scraping iron-shod hooves over crumbling brick, the faint clatter of sword
and shield. All of it seemed muffled and far away. It was not a silence,
just a quiet, the indrawn breath that comes before the shout. Torches
smoked and crackled, filling the darkness with shifting orange light.

Thousands turned as one to watch as the old knight wheeled his
horse around in the shadow of the great iron-banded gates. Barristan
Selmy could feel their eyes upon him. The captains and commanders
advanced to meet him. Jokin and the Widower for the Stormcrows,
ringmail clinking under faded cloaks; Grey Worm, Sure Spear, and
Dogkiller for the Unsullied, in spiked bronze caps and quilted armor;
Rommo for the Dothraki; Camarron, Goghor, and the Spotted Cat for
the pit fighters.

"You know our plan of attack," the white knight said, when the captains were gathered around him. "We will hit them first with our horse,
as soon as the gate is opened. Ride hard and fast, straight at the slave
soldiers. When the legions form up, sweep around them. Take them
from behind or from the flank, but do not try their spears. Remember
your objectives."

"The trebuchet," said the Widower. "The one the Yunkai'i call Harridan. Take it, topple it, or burn it."

Jokin nodded. "Feather as many of their nobles as we can. And burn
their tents, the big ones, the pavilions."

"Kill many man," said Rommo. "Take no slaves."

Ser Barristan turned in the saddle. "Cat, Goghor, Camarron, your men will follow afoot. You are known as fearsome fighters. Frighten them. Scream and shout. By the time you reach the Yunkish lines, our horsemen should have broken through. Follow them into the breach, and do as much slaughter as you can. Where you can, spare the slaves and cut down their masters, the noblemen and officers. Fall back before you are surrounded."

Goghor smashed a fist against his chest. "Goghor not fall back. Never."

Then Goghor die, the old knight thought, *soon.* But this was not the time nor place for that argument. He let it pass, and said, "These attacks should distract the Yunkai'i long enough for Grey Worm to march the Unsullied out the gate and form up." That was where his plan would rise or fall, he knew. If the Yunkish commanders had any sense, they would send their horse thundering down on the eunuchs before they could form ranks, when they were most vulnerable. His own cavalry would have to prevent that long enough for the Unsullied to lock shields and raise their wall of spears. "At the sound of my horn, Grey Worm will advance in line and roll up the slavers and their soldiers. It may be that one or more Ghiscari legions will march out to meet them, shield to shield and spear to spear. That battle we shall surely win."

"This one hears," said Grey Worm. "It shall be as you say."

"Listen for my horn," Ser Barristan told them. "If you hear the retreat, *fall back.* Our walls stand behind us, packed with Brazen Beasts. Our foes dare not come too close, or they will find themselves in crossbow range. If you hear the horn sound advance, advance at once. Make for my standard or the queen's." He pointed at the banners in the hands of Tumco Lho and Larraq.

The Widower's horse sidled to his left. "And if your horn falls silent, ser knight? If you and these green boys of yours are cut down?"

It was a fair question. Ser Barristan meant to be the first through the Yunkish lines. He might well be the first to die. It often worked that way. "If I fall, command is yours. After you, Jokin. Then Grey Worm." *Should all of us be killed, the day is lost,* he might have added, but they all knew that, surely, and none of them would want to hear it said aloud. *Never speak of defeat before a battle*, Lord Commander Hightower had told him once, when the world was young, *for the gods may be listening.*

"And if we come upon the captain?" asked the Widower.

Daario Naharis. "Give him a sword and follow him." Though Barristan Selmy had little love and less trust for the queen's paramour, he did not doubt his courage, nor his skill at arms. *And if he should die heroically in battle, so much the better.* "If there are no further questions, go back to your men and say a prayer to whatever god you believe in. Dawn will be on us soon."

"A red dawn," said Jokin of the Stormcrows.

A dragon dawn, thought Ser Barristan.

He had done his own praying earlier, as his squires helped him don his armor. His gods were far away across the sea in Westeros, but if the septons told it true, the Seven watched over their children wherever they might wander. Ser Barristan had said a prayer to the Crone, beseeching her to grant him a little of her wisdom, so that he might lead his men to victory. To his old friend the Warrior he prayed for strength. He asked the Mother for her mercy, should he fall. The Father he entreated to watch over his lads, these half-trained squires who were the closest things to sons that he would ever know. Finally he had bowed his head to the Stranger. "You come for all men in the end," he had prayed, "but if it please you, spare me and mine today, and gather up the spirits of our foes instead."

Out beyond the city walls, the distant *thump* of a trebuchet releasing could be heard. Dead men and body parts came spinning down out of the night. One crashed amongst the pit fighters, showering them with bits of bone and brain and flesh. Another bounced off the Chainmaker's weathered bronze head and tumbled down his arm to land with a wet *splat* at his feet. A swollen leg splashed in a puddle not three yards from where Selmy sat waiting on his queen's horse.

"The pale mare," murmured Tumco Lho. His voice was thick, his dark eyes shiny in his black face. Then he said something in the tongue of the Basilisk Isles that might have been a prayer.

He fears the pale mare more than he fears our foes, Ser Barristan realized. His other lads were frightened too. Brave as they might be, not one was blooded yet.

He wheeled his silver mare about. "Gather round me, men." When they edged their horses closer, he said, "I know what you are feeling. I have felt the same myself, a hundred times. Your breath is coming faster than it should. In your belly a knot of fear coils like a cold black worm. You feel as though you need to empty your bladder, maybe move your bowels. Your mouth is dry as the sands of Dorne. What if you shame yourself out there, you wonder? What if you forget all your training? You yearn to be a hero, but deep down inside you fear you might be craven.

"Every boy feels the same way on the eve of battle. Aye, and grown men as well. Those Stormcrows over there are feeling the same thing. So are the Dothraki. There is no shame in fear, unless you let it master you. We all taste terror in our time."

"I am not afraid." The Red Lamb's voice was loud, almost to the point of shouting. "Should I die, I will go before the Great Shepherd of Lhazar, break his crook across my knee, and say to him, *'Why did you make your people lambs, when the world is full of wolves?'* Then I will spit into his eye."

Ser Barristan smiled. "Well said . . . but take care that you do not seek death out there, or you will surely find it. The Stranger comes for all of us, but we need not rush into his arms.

"Whatever might befall us on the battlefield, remember, it has happened before, and to better men than you. I am an old man, an old *knight,* and I have seen more battles than most of you have years. Nothing is more terrible upon this earth, nothing more glorious, nothing more absurd. You may retch. You will not be the first. You may drop your sword, your shield, your lance. Others have done the same. Pick it up and go on fighting. You may foul your breeches. I did, in my first battle. No one will care. All battlefields smell of shit. You may cry out for your mother, pray to gods you thought you had forgotten, howl obscenities that you never dreamed could pass your lips. All this has happened too.

"Some men die in every battle. More survive. East or west, in every inn and wine sink, you will find greybeards endlessly refighting the wars of their youth. They survived their battles. So may you. This you can be certain of: the foe you see before you is just another man, and like as not he is as frightened as you. Hate him if you must, love him if you can, but lift your sword and bring it down, then ride on. Above all else, *keep moving*. We are too few to win the battle. We ride to make chaos, to buy the Unsullied time enough to make their spear wall, we—"

"Ser?" Larraq pointed with the Kingsguard banner, even as a wordless murmur went up from a thousand pairs of lips.

Far across the city, where the shadowed steps of Meereen's Great Pyramid shouldered eight hundred feet into a starless sky, a fire had awoken where once the harpy stood. A yellow spark at the apex of the pyramid, it glimmered and was gone again, and for half a heartbeat Ser Barristan was afraid the wind had blown it out. Then it returned, brighter, fiercer, the flames swirling, now yellow, now red, now orange, reaching up, clawing at the dark.

Away to the east, dawn was breaking behind the hills.

Another thousand voices were exclaiming now. Another thousand men were looking, pointing, donning their helms, reaching for their swords and axes. Ser Barristan heard the rattle of chains. That was the portcullis coming up. Next would come the groan of the gate's huge iron hinges. It was time.

The Red Lamb handed him his winged helm. Barristan Selmy slipped it down over his head, fastened it to his gorget, pulled up his shield, slipped his arm inside the straps. The air tasted strangely sweet. There was nothing like the prospect of death to make a man feel alive. "May the Warrior protect us all," he told his lads. "Sound the attack."

AN **HBO** ORIGINAL SERIES

GAME OF THRONES

SEASONS 1-6 AVAILABLE ON BLU-RAY,™ DVD & DIGITAL HD

WITH HOURS OF BONUS CONTENT INCLUDING INTERACTIVE GUIDES, EXCLUSIVE HISTORIES, AUDIO COMMENTARIES & NEVER-BEFORE-SEEN FOOTAGE.